THROUGH
THE VALLEY
OF THE NEST OF
SPIDERS

Also by Samuel R. Delany

FICTION

The Jewels of Aptor
The Fall of the Towers:
Out of the Dead City
The Towers of Toron
City of a Thousand Suns
The Ballad of Beta-2
Babel-17
Empire Star
The Einstein Intersection
Nova
Driftglass (stories)
Dhalgren
Equinox
Hogg
Trouble on Triton
Stars in My Pocket Like Grains of
Sand
Distant Stars
Return to Nevèrÿon:
Tales of Nevèrÿon
Neveryóna
Flight from Nevèrÿon
Return to Nevèrÿon
They Fly at Çiron
Atlantis: Three Tales
The Mad Man
Aye, and Gomorrah, and Other
Stories
Hogg
Phallos
Dark Reflections

NONFICTION

The Jewel-Hinged Jaw
Starboard Wine
The American Shore
Heavenly Breakfast
The Motion of Light in Water
Wagner/Artaud
The Straits of Messina
Silent Interviews
Longer Views
Times Square Red/Times Square
Blue
Shorter Views
1984: Selected Letters
About Writing

GRAPHIC NOVELS

Empire (artist, Howard Chaykin)
Bread & Wine (artist, Mia Wolff)

THROUGH THE VALLEY OF THE NEST OF SPIDERS

Samuel R. Delany

Magnus Books
Cathedral Station
PO Box 1849
New York, NY 10025

Edited by: Donald Weise
Cover by: Linda Kosarin, The Art Department

ISBN: 978-1-936833-14-6

To Dennis Rickett
& for
Brian Evenson

A Note on Dialect

The southern contraction "yall"—plural of "you"—is most often written with an apostrophe. But I have dropped the apostrophe in this text for consistency. If we take "y'all" as a valid pronoun in its own right, it would be the only one that had one. As well, the multiple apostrophes it allows to worm their way into the possessive forms would be ludicrous. Thus I have omitted them.

"Except there's garbage, which is part of what we're trying to include in our work and our thought, which is to say, we are attentive still to what remains, what gets tossed away and off. We want to include the trash in many ways, thinking of this refuse according to all sorts of disposal systems."
—Avital Ronell, quoted in *Examined Life*

Horas non numero nisi serenas.
[I count no hours save the serene ones, *and* I tell time only when the sun's out, *as well as* At the time of my death, only the serene hours count.]
(Inscribed on a Venetian sundial by an anonymous monk)

"It's like appropriating, even though it's controversial on all sides of the barrier, the N word into your speech. Or saying, 'We're queer, we're here' and accepting and hi-jacking the very word—here's the trash can again, watch out—that is meant to insult and hurt and devastate. You take it on, you appropriate and use it, like a ballistic shield, a weapon."
—Avital Ronell, quoted in *Examined Life*

"Joy is power. Real power."
—Rane Arroyo

[G] THROUGH THE SECOND-FLOOR Atlanta apartment screen, out by the streetlight in the July evening, crickets scritched. Inside, his dad's floor lamp slid its gleam down along—and back along—the Bowflex bar's matte gray.

Then, at eight-forty, Eric finished his workout. "Okay—I'm done!" Sitting up in his green gym pants, the elastic loose in one frayed cuff and a soiled yellow stripe each side, he swung his bare foot over and off the bench. "It's all yours!" Standing, he stepped from the carpet swatch they'd used since the rubber mat split.

In scuffed work boots and baggy jeans, Mike walked in. "You wanna watch some TV in my room while I work out?" Shrugging his denim work shirt from a hard, dark shoulder, he turned to hang it by the collar over the head of a black and gold ceramic leopard crouched on a side shelf.

"Naw. I'm takin' a shower," Eric explained, "then I'm goin' to bed."

"You wanna use mine up here?"

The plaster on the walls and between the ceiling beams was painted ivory.

"That's all right." For ten months now, Mr. Condotti had let Eric have the room off the garage, with its phone booth of a shower and commode—a *big* improvement over Mike's living room foldout, though he missed the lamp's warm light. "I'll use the one down in my place." Eric had agreed to pay his dad half the twenty dollars more a month. Then the bike shop shut, where Eric had swept up and sometimes trued wheels. He'd given Mike eighty of the first year's one-twenty.

Even with forty owing, it was better not having Eric always upstairs under foot. "Well, remember, *take* one." A senior welder at work, recently Mike had gotten a raise; so he'd swallowed the rest—only somewhat grumpily. "Tomorrow's Saturday and I'm drivin' you down to your mama's in Diamond Harbor. You're gonna be seventeen in…what? Eight days, now?" Stepping around the coffee table corner, Mike grasped one handle of the exercise machine. "Barb'll wanna see how much you grew up. You get to Diamond Harbor smellin' like a goat, and she ain't gonna be happy."

"Don't *worry*! I told you, I'll take one."

"You're probably gonna miss your football buddies, huh?" Other than a pudgy Puerto Rican, Scotty, who, in his ancient Willy's, twice had picked Eric up for Saturday morning practice, Mike had met none of Eric's teammates outside a game.

Eric shrugged, took his T-shirt from the couch, and said, "Maybe. Yeah."

Mike thought: *What I should say is, You ain't at the bike place no more. Get a job.* Everyone said it's what good kids did. Well, that would be Barb's problem now. He glanced at the yellowish T-shirt Eric held. "You got another one, downstairs in your chest-of-drawers?"

"Yeah—probably."

"Then—*please*—leave that one here. I'm doin' a laundry tonight. I know you love it—you ain't had it off all week."

"I don't have a thing for this one especially." Eric tossed the shirt back on the couch. It slid to the floor. Mike let go of the bar and stepped toward it, but Eric said, "Naw. I dropped it. I'll get it." He swiped it up and returned it to the couch arm.

With his shaved head and brown leather wrist brace, lighter than his dark, dark skin, Mike Jeffers was an easy-going black man from East Texas. He'd been a welder eleven years.

Buzz cut for summer, Eric was blond, with steel-blue eyes, the issue of a two-week affair between his mother—Barbara was Dutch and Swedish— and a long-vanished Atlantic City blackjack grifter, a smiling, tow-headed twenty-six-year-old of Scots-Polish parentage, called Cash. Barbara had never known Cash's last name. Seventeen when Eric was born, at nineteen she'd become an exotic dancer in Baltimore, where she'd met Mike. He'd adopted two-year-old Eric a month after their marriage—but before jail. Afterward, it would have been harder.

Though Mike had made nothing of it since the decision two weeks ago (Barb had phoned to suggest it, out of the blue), Eric's coming move was convenient for two reasons.

First, it put off a confrontation Mike had let slide since school had ended. June was done. It was two days beyond the fireworks and rowdiness of the Fourth: What was Eric *doing* with himself? He'd read comics and history books in his garage room. He'd walked or biked around the city. For a while he'd been a bit of a couch potato. The only TV was in Mike's bedroom, with the computer. But now Eric did extra Bowflex workouts (two-and-a-half years ago, Mike had bought the machine off Jake at work for a hundred-twenty bucks) and—he said—didn't even turn the television on. Whatever occupied him involved no real friends Mike knew of. With small talk about the places he'd been exploring, Eric was always home for dinner. Three quarters of the time he cooked it—or at least heated it in the microwave. One or two afternoons each week he spent at a gaming store on lower Peachtree, where...well, loser-dudes is what they were, played Magic and Risk and sometimes D&D. And the police hadn't brought him home *yet*, the way, regularly, back in East Texas during the early eighties, they'd brought home Mike's older brother, Omar, for petty vandalism and siphoning gas—and, a few times, Mike.

Eric asked, "You really want me to have the machine?"

"Soon as I finish tonight, while the laundry's workin', I'm takin' it apart and puttin' it in the box—" Mike's walk-in bedroom closet held more computer cartons and Game-Boy boxes and Styrofoam packing forms than clothes—"so I can stick it in the trunk tomorrow. It'll give you somethin' to do down there. If I really want to keep it up, I can get another one. Or some weights. When you get downstairs, put as much of your stuff together as you can, now. We wanna be outta here tomorrow by eight or eight-thirty."

The second convenience involved two women, only one of whom Eric knew about. Mike was considering moving in Doneesha, a black nursing student, once Eric had been gone two weeks and Mike was sure Barb wouldn't phone hysterically to take him back. (Mike was certain that, for the first few days, Barb would be ridiculously strict. Then, after the fifth or sixth blow-up, she would give in and let him run wild. Not that he'd do anything terrible. Eric *was* a good kid—and had a brain.) Eric had liked Doneesha, the time Mike had taken them all for dinner at Applebee's. Till then Mike could have some fun here with the other, Kelly-Ann, Jake's new office intern. (Kelly-Ann was a chestnut-haired, green-eyed Dominican.) Even Jake didn't know they'd made it—in the Chevy, pulled off among the trees behind a derelict window frame factory, the second time Mike had driven Kelly-Ann out to her aunt's.

"I already started packin'—I told you when we were eatin'."

Mike liked his kid. He'd miss Eric.

Mounting the bench, leaning back on the object somewhere between a time machine and a bicycle, Mike gripped the bar and smiled. "I don't know why I keep rememberin' this."

At the change in his father's voice, Eric looked over.

"One time or another, I've thought about this every day for the three years you been here. Maybe I'm tellin' you now 'cause you're goin' off."

Eric had the indulgent look of someone pretty sure what Mike was going to say. Actually Mike came out with the story regularly.

"When I got home on the bus—that time I come back from the pokey, when we was in Hugantown—the door was open, so I set my suitcase on the porch and walked in. I wasn't even sure I had the right house. But you was standin' in the hall, and you seen me. And your eyes got so *big*—I thought at first you was scared. But then you opened your arms and got this...*smile!* And I realized you recognized me. So I grabbed you up and hugged you, and you laughed, and laughed. You was *so* happy!" Eric had been five when Mike had spent fourteen months in jail—his third arrest, his single conviction (coke). Inside, Mike had done a fair amount of lifting. He'd told lots of people since, jail had knocked some sense into him. That had been when he and Barb had been in West Virginia, before he'd got to Georgia. "I started callin' out for Barb. She was in the back and come in. I'd been afraid you wasn't gonna know who I was. You hadn't seen me in more'n a year. Then we're sittin' in the kitchen, all three of us, you on my lap. And you reached up and started pattin' my head—'cause, you remember, I didn't shave it back then. At first I didn't know what you was doin'. So I sat there—and so did Barb. You turned to your mama, and you said, 'Daddy's got puffy hair. Mama, I want puffy hair. Like Daddy's. I want puffy hair, mama. Why can't I have puffy hair?' And we started laughin', and I hugged you so hard." Both Mike and Eric had neat, small heads with neat, small ears, though Mike's features were broad, full, and black while Eric's were sculpted and Slavic, gilded by Georgia summer. Even so, because of their shared head shape, some people, who'd never known Barbara, assumed Mike was Eric's blood father despite the extremities in hair, in hue. It tickled Eric and—sometimes—annoyed Mike. "I mean, I'd always wondered how that was for you: a white kid with a black dad. But right then, I realized, you was *my* kid. I mean, completely and *absolutely* mine."

"I still think black hair is more sensible and better lookin'." Eric's indulgence became a grin. "But it's interestin' to know how long I felt that way." Three weeks ago, with the battery clippers, Mike had cut it for him again. "Nappy hair's a lot better than the straight white…*stuff* I got."

"Well, next time I see you, if you got some fool white boy dreadlocks or come in here all cornrowed or anything else stupid lookin', I'm gonna tell you straight out you look like an asshole." With a smile and mock gruffness, Mike returned the indulgence.

"Yeah, yeah. Don't worry." Eric reached up to rub his eighth of an inch of white-blond growback. "Hey, it's my head, ain't it?"

Mike grunted. Then they both laughed. A year ago, Mike thought, he'd have gotten mad at me for saying that, even as a joke. (Though he better *not* come back here with no dreads…) Yeah, he's growing up.

* * *

[F] THRESHOLD UNDER HIS instep, the ball of his foot pressed linoleum. His heel lifted from carpet.

In the kitchen, streaked with gray gravy, four foil trays from the Hearty-Beef Hungry-Man dinners they'd eaten earlier leaned in the sink—waiting to be rinsed before going into the trash. Beside the microwave at the counter's back, Eric pushed through the stairwell's blue door—his rear foot left smooth flooring. The forward one came down on cloth—while the repeating *squeee*-clink from what would be Mike's last session followed him down the shabby runner, irregularly tacked to the stairs.

By the mailboxes (MICHAEL MALCOLM JEFFERS/ERIC LINDEN JEFFERS, which Eric had lettered on an index card with blue, black, and red Sharpies, then taped to the steel face), he went into the dark garage, skirted Mike's Chevy—underfoot, the concrete was cool—pushed open the door, and loped up four wooden steps to his room—the boards were warm—digging a forefinger into his nose, scraping loose what crust his nail caught, then sucking it off his finger.

It was a habit he'd become addicted to in earliest childhood, which—at least for today—he was trying to do only when alone.

The thick-tired wheels from his mountain bike hung on the green planks. In the corner leaned the frame. Three cartons stood open around the floor in which he'd already put his Magic cards, his Phillip Pullman and horror novels, his Tuckman, his Scama, compilation volumes of *The Walking Dead* and the Hernandez Brothers—on top of Howard Cruse, Belasco, all the issues of *Meatmen* he'd been able to find with *any* drawings by "Mike," half a dozen Hun volumes, the two issues of *Porky*, and the single (so far) *Brother to Dragons*. With only the street light through the leaves outside the window, Eric pushed down his gym pants—he did *not* shower—and collapsed on the iron daybed's sheet and rumpled army blanket, already masturbating. Five minutes later, he gasped in a big breath, then licked the ham of his thumb and three of his fingers, his palm, his wrist. Taking another breath, he wiped the rest on his belly, and rolled to his side. The last time he'd talked to Barbara on the phone, she'd said something about a porch doing for his room in Diamond Harbor. It didn't sound too private. But she'd also said they were off in the woods, somewhere. (Barbara, he figured, was between boyfriends, which is probably why she wanted him now. With trepidation he wondered how long that would last.) Between the bed and the wall, a brown bench was his night table. When his breathing slowed to sleep's rhythm, his fists were between his thighs, his gym pants were on the floor, and the digital clock on the bench said nine-oh-four.

* * *

[E] WHEN IT SAID five-forty-two, Eric woke up, sat up, stood up—

Because of the street light outside, through the high window he could see none of the blue behind the leaves, nudging Atlanta toward its six-twenty sunrise. On the bench Eric moved the porn magazine, cover uppermost: CHICKS (in case Mike came in) WHO LOVE 'EM BIG & BLACK!

Picking up the KY tube under it, he went into the tiny bathroom, foreknuckled up the switch, then, beneath the unfrosted bulb dangling from the overhead plasterboard, sat on the wooden ring. (Sitting to urinate, he did only at home.) Below an unframed three-foot mirror, his knees brushed the board wall. While pissing, he didn't push—just relaxed, growled out lots of gas, and dropped a firm one. It splashed loudly.

The first turd always made you feel less groggy.

Pulling paper from the roll on the upright dowel he'd screwed—at Mike's suggestion—to the shelf, while his naked image turned away to do the same, Eric jackknifed his knee to get a bare foot on the ring, lifted his butt, reached under, and wiped.

Eric (and his image) sat up again and checked. The paper was clean. He glanced at the glass. With his knee still up, in the streaky reflection he could see the spaces among his broad toes—and yesterday's jam.

Behind a thick, heavy shoulder, with its clear cuts, over the paint-peeled wall a two-inch pipe rose to the overhead flushbox.

When he leaned to push the paper into the water, his knuckles got wet. He fingered clean one foot—but not the other.

Lifting the lubricant tube from the shelf, Eric flipped the KY's top back and, with one hand, squeezed a clear worm across three fingers, left to right and back, three, four, five times. Putting the tube down, again he stuck his hand under his buttocks. Taking a breath, he relaxed, as if for another big one—then, at once, slid three, then four fingers, as fast and as far as possible into his rectum. (In the spotty mirror, he watched his mouth open a little, his blue eyes widen.) Turning his hand left and right, while the sting subsided, he spread them, thumbing up into himself as much jelly as he could, tightening and expanding his butt muscles, pressing his fingers together, releasing them...

Since last summer, above and below his navel's sunken half-hooded knot, beside his shin and, behind it, his thigh, you could count Eric's abs, which was the Bowflex and something Mike said he should be proud of. From the team's horsing around in the school shower, Eric knew nine-tenths of the guys had no such definition, no matter how many squats, push-ups, or laps, at Mr. Doubrey's barked commands, they endured through Saturday or after-school practice. Nor such arms, upper or lower.

Eric's cock rose heavily, catching under the wooden ring.

I could stay here and do it. (A dozen times through the summer he had.) Because this was his last morning in Atlanta, though, after a minute he pulled his fingers free, lifted his hand, and looked at it.

His fingers glistened.

On more toilet paper, he wiped them till the shine was gone, then—the friendly smell of his own crap reassuring him as he raised them—he dug in his nose with a forefinger, hooking out as much as possible, while, in the mirror, his narrow nostril bulged and bent. He pulled loose, then, as he sucked the yellow-green crust from his forefinger, watched his cheeks cave. He did the same with his middle.

It *didn't* look funny or stupid.

(In Florida, with a coupling of excitement and discomfort, three or four times over his visit he'd watched a dog, after much sniffing and circling, eat its own shit from the grass behind Barbara's trailer. It hadn't hurt the dog... and, finally, made Eric feel more comfortable about a couple of things he'd recently been doing.)

It tasted salty and...good.

For the last two years, except in the boys' room, Eric had been trying not to do it in school or at home or where people knew him—and had mostly succeeded. But on his own, biking or walking around the city, he'd developed his strategies for doing it whether strangers were looking or not. Pick it out, keep it in your hand for a full thirty seconds, *then* eat it when new people were passing. Or transfer it surreptitiously to a finger on the other hand. You could put that one in your mouth and nobody would know what you were doing...In his bravest moments, he'd do it wherever he was (if he wasn't too close to home or school) and fuck 'em! So what if I gross out someone I'll never see again? Thinking that, though, was like running over lines from a school play. A couple of times, too, it had backfired—but *only* a couple.

Why did people get so twisted out of shape by it, anyway?

It was good that, during his childhood, before the divorce, his parents had moved around as much as they had. At nine, in West Virginia, news of his habit had gotten out at school and made life hell—for three months. Then they'd gone to another state, where he'd been more careful about hiding it.

On the wall, about a third over the mirror bottom and two thirds on the grayish paint below, a stain spread just larger than a dinner plate. Many of its older drops and splats had turned yellow-orange—with a sweetish smell Eric liked—from the one-out-of-three times he didn't eat the stuff after he shot. He was proud of the size and thought of it as something to be added to a couple of times a day. Mike had never mentioned it. Of course, the last time Mike had been in, it had been a lot smaller. Maybe he hadn't known what it was. In Eric's first couple of months in the room, Mr. Condotti had come in three or four times to check the place out. But he'd never gone into the pillbox john.

A six-to-nine-time-a-day shooter, for the last eight or ten months—it went along with his snot eating—Eric had been doing it as many places as he could. Somehow beating off there made the sun speckled bench at the back of the park, or the top-floor school john, where, on the inner door of the stall to the right, some other guy (or guys) was making his (or their) own cum medallion—he'd added his own layer a few times but had never met the initial architect—or the truck loading port or the alley or the back of the empty bus parked on the corner or the deserted pinball room at the bus station better to revisit, now they'd been marked as somehow his own by what fell on the tile or splashed the grass or drooled the maroon cushion, dark boards, or bricks.

Should he run the electric over his face? Maybe when he came back.

Eric stood, pulled the wooden handle at the end of the flat-linked chain, and went into his room. Behind him the toilet gurgled, roared, then hummed. Sitting on his bed he tugged on some jeans, toed the runners from under his bed (one was upside down), sat on the sagging rim, and pulled them on. Twisting around, he found a short-sleeved shirt wedged behind the bed frame.

At six-oh-one, Eric left the garage. The KY tube was in his hip pocket.

In the light beyond the board fence, from the porch next door, Eric could make out Mr. Condotti's lawn chairs in the dark turned up against the table for a rain that hadn't come in two weeks. Picking at his nose, he could still feel some good stuff up there. Eric crossed the concrete of the tenants' half of the yard to crunch along the driveway's gravel by the building.

Mr. Condotti's was a one-time private house—with eight bay windows—now divided into eight apartments, two on each floor and two in the basement.

Eric looked at Bill Bottom's black windows in the foundation, then down the cement steps at the maroon Dutch doors, brick walls either side. A year ago, after Eric's return from a three-week visit to Barbara's in the Florida trailer park where she'd been living, Bottom had bought a bunch of inch-high brass letters, and, though he was not Jewish, with brads of the sort you'd use for your house number, nailed up the Hebrew words (in English transliteration) *"emet yeshalom yasood ha'ollam"* across the upper door and the Latin *"in girum imus nocte et consumimur igni"* across the lower. Bill had explained to him that the Hebrew meant "peace and truth are the foundation of the world," and that they had something to do with seventeenth-century Amsterdam and a man named Spinoza—though Spinoza had written neither. By now Eric had forgotten what Bill had said the Latin meant, other than that it read the same backward and forward. Once, in his yellow Bermudas, white sunhat, and broad cataract glasses that did odd things to the sunlight, while Eric was in the yard, Mr. Condotti had told Bill, "No, I don't mind. But I must be sure it offends no one who speaks the language. That's all." The cracks across the maroon paint and the six little panes over the metal letters made the door look old, so that Eric was repeatedly surprised that, next to himself, Bill was the youngest tenant at Mr. Condotti's. At the beginning of summer, Eric had asked Bill to explain the Latin again. Bill laughed and told him to Google it. But Eric had never written it down to take up to the computer in Mike's bedroom, which, unlike the ones in school, was still dial-up—and *so* fuckin' slow.

In moonless black, on the second floor of the building's far side, were Mike's kitchen and two rooms. Eric glanced up, walking beside the zombie gray the neighborhood's nightlights had rendered Mr. Condotti's pale green aluminum siding. (Behind him the garage was dark olive.) He came out under the street's wide maples, its tall hickories.

Among telephone wires at the block's end, crows cawed.

Between the houses east, Eric saw faint orange, with violet above it and black above that. Half the houses on Montoya were green. The other half were gray or blue. In the west, beyond the trestle, three stars still tacked up the dark. Heading toward the next streetlight, as he'd done every second or third morning all summer (often five or six days in a row), Eric turned toward the Verizon sign, back under the highway, behind which various homeless guys camped out among the saplings.

As he neared the corner, a breeze moved over the trees, so that, under the corner lamp, a branch swung down and up, down and up, putting the street sign's white letters on the green panel in and out of the light: Montoya…Montoya…Montoya…

Eric started across to the elevated causeway.

You could pretend it was the middle of the night. The street was empty. (He dug. He sucked.) Christ, Eric thought, I hope I get something quick.

Helped with some spit, the KY in him would get Eric through three homeless hillbilly fucks (*Okay—I'm done. Now, get on, son*) if they were seven inches or under. Men with significant meat—eight, nine, ten—used the stuff up faster. The tube in his pocket was in case things got complicated.

Eric preferred it complicated.

For the last ten days, "complicated" had been two homeless black guys, one of whom, Big Frack, was well into his forties and had the largest cock Eric had ever seen or, until Frack had turned up sleeping on the old mattress back there, imagined. Scott had told him that super big men had trouble getting hard. Not Frack. Soft, it was clearly more than—and hard, it was easily four inches over—a foot! His own cock was pretty much all Frack talked about, to the point where, after four times with it, Eric had wondered if Frack's obsession with what this nigger bitch or that white cocksucker had done for him back in Frisco or down in Houston or up in Denver to get a hold of it hadn't *caused* his homelessness. After half an hour, as a topic of conversation (monologue…?), it was…well, boring. When Frack sat cross-legged on the mattress, shirt and pants gaping, jerking at it absently and rambling on, the hooded head before his sunken chest rose higher than his teats' black knobs—which, either side of his in-sloped breast bone, practically faced one another, like crossed eyes, or the decayed nodules on fruit.

Besides his cock, Frack had no other prepossessing features. He was not smart. With his caved-in chest, he was built like a six-foot-seven bowling pin, with no incisors, upper or lower, the teeth either side long, stained, and slanted inward. Fortunately those barrel thighs were hard. But that's not what you saw first: Frack shambled about like a towering black Shmoo. Still, it was fun to watch him play with himself inside his pocket—Frack had ripped out the bottom and could make it stick four inches from the frayed pocket rim; he would walk around like that because, he explained, with the skin forward, people didn't know what it was and thought it was a piece of black pipe; displaying it like that kept it hard—or rubbing on it through the outside of his threadbare jeans, which he did nonstop: *I'm 'bout half-hard all da time—an' I'm pretty much jerkin' off on it—at least half ways—all da time, too. An' you* love *to watch dis mule-dicked nigger play wid it, doncha, white boy? And so do da ol' fart.* The "ol' fart" was Joe. On the far side of fifty, Frack's partner Joe had a good seven incher—the same as Eric's— and was able to put up with Frack's phallocentric filibuster. The two took turns fucking Eric a couple of times in tandem, each morning he showed up, or letting Eric see how far he could take them down his throat.

Come on, Frack. Sometime there you gotta *let da cocksucker breathe!*

Eric was getting good at relaxing his neck muscles and killing his gag reflex.

Don't worry. I'll back off if I see 'im 'bout to pass out.

Joe would smile, having heard it before—Eric figured.

Frack had no trouble coming in Eric's mouth or ass, even when Eric only got in the first ten or so inches. Joe had to work up a sweat to get off in Eric's mouth. (In Eric's butt he did better.) And he always had a pocket full of condoms.

When Eric suggested Frack use one too, Frack chuckled. *Where? On mah li'l finger?* Frack's hands were big. *Don't worry—ain't nothin' been up mah hole this month 'ceptin' your mother fuckin' white boy tongue.*

Both men were really into "tongue-wrastlin' wid dis fine white bitch," which Eric had gotten used to and even liked, teeth or no teeth.

For Eric, the Fourth's real fireworks had come mostly before seven in the morning.

Over the last week-and-a-half a bow-legged black kid, twenty-two or twenty-three, kind of simple and good natured, called Pickle, who'd told them all how he'd started out in a Wyoming orphanage, would turn up every other day and hang around to watch, then get a blowjob from Eric when he'd finished with Joe and Frack.

When Pickle got excited about anything or even laughed hard, he peed his pants.

He didn't mind Eric feeling it, though, through the sopping denim. He was nice looking in a kind of goofy way. He'd got his name because someone had said he smelled like the inside of an old pickle barrel. Actually, the smell was old piss: he only changed his pants, he said, when someone, sorry for him, gave him new ones. At the beginning Eric had brought him a pair of his own and gotten a grateful grin, as Pickle put them on right there, then vigorously tore apart the discarded one's he'd been wearing and threw them out on the sidewalk; but when, two days later, Pickle was back and Eric smelled him, he realized replacing Pickle's jeans would be an endless job.

If Joe had a coffee, he'd let Eric—even Pickle—have a swallow or two, though Frack would say, *Don't let dem drink out dat cup, nigger! Day gonna give us some damned diseases or somethin'. If my ol' gift o' God start' dribblin' dat gonorrhea shit an' I gotta get my black ass stuck full o' needles again, or I come down wid dat HIV, I'm go'n' bus' some white an' black ass both wid sumpin' 'sides my dick!*

Joe would chuckle and say, *If de scumbags got diseases, Frack, we're a little late for dat now,* and pass Pickle or Eric the blue cardboard container, printed with white columns, which smelled so good and tasted so bitter under the sweetness—while Frack humphed.

Often Pickle would rub his groin—already soaked after only an hour— then suck his blunt, thick fingers. When Pickle saw Eric looking, he'd say, *The salt taste' good.*

Once, a hopeful Eric said: *Like eatin' your...* He dug a forefinger in one nostril, pulled it out, put it in his mouth. *Huh?*

Pickle frowned. *Why you doin' dat? Dat's nasty. Pee's better, ain't it?*

Which, as the other two bums there finally ambled off to panhandle outside the package store down by Ford's Little Five Points Market, is when Frack—ready to go again—bawled: *Hey! Get yo' scrawny white ass ova' heah, cocksucker!*

A train whistle ripped apart the morning.

Under the highway, Eric pushed into high grass and sumac to giant-step through, arms to the side, over crackling Styrofoam and mushy cardboard and Mylar condom wrappers, till, behind the Verizon sign's struts, the growth got shorter. On either side of the overhead roadway, the sky was now dark blue.

The men under the highway had changed all summer. Back in March during his spring break, one morning Eric had found a bearded German in a sleeping bag, who'd sat up naked in the grass, green canvas rucked down around a hirsute belly, pulled out a knife and, in a heavy accent, told Eric to get his faggot ass out of there. Eric had stayed away three days. When he chanced coming back, six hillbillies and a couple of niggers were lounging about or sleeping in the grass or sharing their Night Train, their Gypsy Rose. Finally two—a nigger and one of the hillbillies—took him behind the highway stanchion and let Eric blow them. Then the nigger brought him back to the others and announced *he* wanted to suck off all the guys there, and did—including Eric. It was one of the times when Eric was most surprised, because, complete to the gold wedding ring on his thick, cracked hand, the black guy was so muscular and masculine. What each of the others had to call him to get off was instructive:

Two called him a nigger cocksucker.

One called him a nigger bitch.

One of the black guys, without even closing his eyes, kept calling him his pretty blond baby.

Eric thought about all the cum in the black guy's mouth already, around his dick, which made him shoot his own load.

With all the various comments and jokes—Eric, the other black guy, and two of the white guys went twice—that March Friday had been the most fun Eric had had under there, if not the most sexually exciting.

In general, the guys who used the place were pretty friendly. By summer vacation, Eric had decided the friendly ones—which, because of Joe and his coffee, he stretched to include Frack—trumped the unfriendly ones.

And the knife puller.

The German notwithstanding, apparently among the homeless the place had a reputation.

As Eric looked up at the overhead highway, along chyme-smeared girders pigeons preened and strutted, nest to nest.

With a breeze, from one corner came the stench of shit and ammonia. Most of the time, that's where the guys relieved themselves.

He'd gotten used to that, too.

Eric walked back to the wall, then picked his way to the stanchion's end. Maybe he *should* have done it back home in the garage. If he waited, of course, someone might come. Time spent hanging out, or trying to cajole a fuck or a blowjob from whatever homeless guys were around, could take from five minutes to five hours. He did best, though, when they'd slept there and he got to them as they were waking.

Stepping over a smashed baby carriage—a month ago it had been in the street, where, for days, cars and trucks and SUVs had repeatedly run it over, till someone had thrown what was left up here—Eric reached the stanchion's far side. As he stepped from the shadow, through high weeds, at the world's rim, the sun ignited.

Eric closed his eyes, pulling back.

He walked around another five minutes. But, as happened once or twice a week, that morning *no* one was out…

No Joe, no Frack—or even Pickle.

And because Mike was taking him to Diamond Harbor, he didn't *have* hours.

Eric took a long breath, made the circuit *once* more (in case he'd missed someone, hugging himself down in the grass, beside the bridge support, maybe rolled up in a blanket, maybe not, off in a sleeping bag or passed out on his back in the weeds, an empty pint bottle inches from his head and mud under his hip, where he'd wet himself: that had been his first time sucking off hungover but affectionately grateful Pickle), then, with a resigned breath, started home from under the highway.

* * *

[D] A SLANT OF sun crossed Mr. Condotti's yard.

Beside the house, Eric stepped onto the loud gravel. Through a basement window he glimpsed TV flicker on a back wall. A pebbly step on and he saw, down the rock-walled stairwell, the upper Dutch door— open—at Bottom's.

The foundation of the world was in shadow.

As Eric passed, Bill moved into the frame, behind the lower door, and looked up. "Hey, Eric." Bottom wore a black leather jacket unzipped, with yellow metal teeth, and no shirt. Also he wore a full gorilla head mask. "Isn't it a little early for you to be out?" The stepwell hollowed his voice. He reached up and lifted the ape head away from an unshaven jaw and curly auburn.

Bottom was grinning.

Eric blinked.

"I thought during the summer all teenagers slept till noon." It sounded less hollow with the head off. Bottom had on tight jeans with frayed patches all over, where you could see through to his skin.

"I got up early," Eric said. "So I took a walk. What you watchin'? The news? I didn't think nothin' was on." It couldn't be much past six-thirty.

"DVD," Bill explained. "*King Kong*." He looked at the mask in his hands. "The uncut version that came out this past Christmas. That is an *awesome* fucking film. Did you see it?" Bill was a thirty-one-year-old accountant with a downtown Atlanta firm. He'd grown up in New York. "The new one, I mean. The three-disc version with deleted scenes." Turning, he tossed the gorilla head to a couch or table out of sight—or maybe back onto a bed.

"Yeah. I saw the regular movie last year, with Mike—at a mall, when we were driving back to Atlanta. Mike liked it a lot. I thought it was okay... *some* of it. But the end was stupid—I mean, when she falls in love. How's a woman gonna fall in love with a giant gorilla? She could *like* him, maybe. But not fall in love." Now that the mask was gone, Eric chanced, "Where'd you get the gorilla...thing?"

"My personal theory," Bill went on, not answering, "is that Peter Jackson was not really trying to remake the original. He knew it too well and loved it too much. What he was actually trying to do was remake the 1976 Dino De Laurentiis version, with Jessica Lange and Jeff Bridges— with homages to the original one all through it. *That's* the film he decided to remake the way it should have been made in the first place. And while he was at it, he worked a reconstruction of one of the scenes cut from the original back into it." Bill opened the bottom door and stepped forward to the crumbling stair. "I've watched that lost spider-pit sequence twenty-five times, both the one Jackson did in his own version and the black and white one he made to fit back into the original. Hey, you want to come in and see it? It's *totally* awesome. I was going to make some hot chocolate before I watched it again. The milk's already heating." He raised his brows expectantly. "If you'd like I can make some for us both."

"Naw, that's all right." Then Eric said, "Mike don't want me even goin' into your apartment." He remained up on the concrete. Suddenly, he said, "He's asleep now. So he wouldn't know." He wondered if the gorilla mask was worth examining. It had covered Bill's whole head. Was there fur on it? He'd seen it only seconds.

"It sounds like you're trying to convince yourself. But I have a better idea. I know Mike likes that sorta stuff, too. I'll lend you the DVD, and you can take it and watch it later with your dad. I'm going to bring up my little table and set it out. Then *I'm* going to bring up a chair—I only have one. But you go around and take one of Mr. Condotti's. He won't mind as long as we put it back when we're finished. Then I'm going to bring out two cups of hot chocolate. We can sit right here and enjoy a morning of each other's company—and Mike doesn't have to get his knickers in a twist. Want me to bring up the monkey mask?"

"Why? It's just a King Kong head."

"Oh, you kids are so cool today—you're gonna cool yourself out of everything interesting. How many people live two floors up from somebody who can say the magic word and change into a donkey, a phoenix, an ape, or a cockatrice? Hey, I like you guys—you and Mike. You're good neighbors. Go get that chair, now." Bill turned back through his sunken doorway.

Eric started toward the lawn table. And got in another finger-full. Lifting away one of Mr. Condotti's green enameled lawn chairs, he carried it back.

Bill was already at the head of the steps, positioning the three-legged table with its pebbled glass top in front of his own wire-backed seat.

As Bill moved it, the table's legs complained on the brick.

Speaking more softly, Eric said, "My dad don't want me to go inside your place 'cause you're gay." He put his own chair, clanking, down.

Bill let go the table, looking at it. "Now *how* in the *world*—" raising a hand to his jaw, with its two days, possibly three, of auburn stubble, he rubbed slowly—"did I figure *that* one out for myself? Hold on a second. I'll be back." He turned to hurry down his steps.

A minute later, he was up again with two black mugs. One had a white skull and bones on it, the other a red noose. He set them on the glass. Like heavily creamed coffee, slightly tanner but with a purplish cast, cocoa turned within the rims. "Sit, sit, sit, sit, sit, now." Sunlight on Bill's face made the unshaven hairs glitter. He pulled back his chair and dropped onto it, knees wide.

More slowly, Eric stepped around his and lowered himself, leaning his forearms on his jeans' thighs. He meshed his fingers.

A jay creaked among the sparrows that had replaced dawn's crows. "And while in no *way* am I suggesting that *you* bring the topic up with Mike, *should* your dad mention it again, you can tell him from me—*if* it occurs to you—I do *not* shit where I eat!"

Eric looked puzzled, unsure what Bill meant.

Bottom went on: "I *live* here, Eric. I would no more think of putting a hand on you than I would cut off one of my nuts with a spoon. A *dull* spoon. I am *not* a stupid man. And doing something like that would be *unbelievably* stupid—given how much of it's running around loose in Atlanta." Lifting the mug with the noose, he raised it toward Eric. "Cheers."

Eric said, "I bet Bottom's gotta be a rough name to have if you're gay. People are probably always making jokes about you and stuff."

Bill glanced at the clouds. "*Tell* me! But that's what you get if you're beloved of the fairies, the bottom of the dream of God, the great spool from which all tales are woven." Again he looked at Eric. "That's what a 'bottom' was, in Elizabethan English, by the way: a big spool at the bottom of a loom from which they took the thread for the brocades they were weaving." Over his mug, he blinked pale eyes. "The thing about the jokes is, everyone who makes one always thinks he's the first person to think it up—that's the part I never understood." A drop of chocolate rolled to the mug's lower rim, hung there, and shook. Across scuffed black, one of Bill's zipper pockets showed a red sliver. "You learn to ignore it." Between the jacket's zipper teeth, pumpkin colored hairs curved over his chest's freckles.

For a moment Eric held his breath. Then he blurted: "If I went inside with you, Mike wouldn't know—'cause he's asleep. It's my last mornin' in Atlanta. Soon as he gets up, we're gonna drive down to Diamond Harbor. My mom says she's got a new waitress job, and I'm gonna stay with her for the next six months, maybe a year. If we go in now, I'll suck your dick. You can fuck my ass—I got a third of a tube of KY up my butt already. You let me eat your ass out while you suck me off, and I'll shoot you a load that'll gag you. I don't got the biggest fuckin' dick in the world. But—" one of the things Eric had learned under the highway—"it ain't the smallest you ever seen, either—"

Bill came forward the same time his mug clacked the glass. "*Wooooah*, fella!" Sitting back, he frowned. "I thought your dad told me you were on your high school football team or something…?"

"Last term I played guard." In the white enameled seat, Eric sat back, too. "I'm the team cocksucker. Me and Scott. We do about a third of the guys. The rest don't even wanna *know* about no shit like that."

"You're a big, strong, *very* good looking boy, Eric. And butch as a beer keg. I admit it. I'm…surprised."

"Yeah. Everybody pretends it don't happen—at least with me."

"With that Young Superman physique of yours you've had for the past year or so, people are probably afraid you'll beat them up."

"I don't like fightin'."

"Well, probably *they* don't know that. I doubt it's that much different from the way it was back at my high school."

"I told my mom I was gay when I was twelve—when we was up in Hugantown—with *her* mom. She'd left the TV goin', on one of those HBO shows. The gay ones was all she watched. I jerked off three times that night, and the next day I told her. That's when her and Mike had broke up again. She said that was cool—me bein' gay, and how she would always love me whoever I wanted to go to bed with. But I should wait to tell Mike. So I did. I ain't told him nothin', yet."

"Dads being dads, probably she knew what she was talking about."

"I hope she remembers I told *her*—"

"When your kid says he's gay, Eric, that's *not* something you forget."

"I don't even *like* gay guys."

"Hey, now—*you're* gay…" Bill's puzzlement was disapproving. "How can you not like gay men—unless you don't like yourself? Let me add, *I* always thought you were likable."

"Sometimes—" Eric looked down at the vertical lines of sunlight on the nearer mug—"I don't think I'm *really* gay."

"Oh, come on. You just said you suck off half the football team—"

"A couple of the other line guys fuck me. I fuck Philly-Bob back. I hope he ain't got AIDS, 'cause he won't use no condom. He says that's for faggots—I don't know what he thinks *he* is. But I don't argue with him. Besides, I don't love those things, either—"

"And because *you* occasionally masturbate thinking of a threesome with a faceless young lady so that the quarterback of your dreams will be a little more turned on, you decide you're straight—"

"I *ain't* straight!"

"Okay, bisexual."

"That's not what I mean. I mean I ain't gay for the same reason I ain't straight."

Bill raised a reddish brow. Along the hedge, sedge and japonica bent and unbent.

"Like you said, gay guys are guys who…*what* was it? Won't eat their shit…" Eric shrugged, as if the connection were self-evident.

Bill said, "You're going to have to tell me more than that."

"Scott's gay—the other cocksucker on the football team. He actually *likes* those HBO shows. The one I watched didn't have *no* black guys on it. At all. And everybody's hookin' up and gettin' all upset if anybody screws anybody else who ain't him. Scott sucks Hoagy—one of the black guys on our team. But he says he'd 'rather not.' Damn, I told him I'd trade him Hoagy for any two of the white guys I do in a *minute*! Hoagy's a halfback. But 'cause Scott's Puerto Rican, he hogs all the niggers—I think he likes the white guys better—but they make him, anyway. And he's scared. You know, last term in school, Scott said we should spend some time hangin' out together—'cause we both…" Eric shrugged. "*You* know. He *really* wants people to call him Scott, but everybody calls him Scotty, anyway. I wished *I* had a nickname. I wouldn't even mind something crazy—like 'Cocksucker.' I mean, that's what I am, ain't I? And I do it good. But if he found out, probably it would mess up Mike's head. Our coach, Mr. Doubrey, he would think it was funny. He's gay too, but only me and Scott know—and Arnie Zawolsky. I mean, we're the only three Doubrey actually sucks off. And he says he'll kick us off the team if anybody finds out—not about us, about him. And *we're* all scared. Well, maybe not Arnie—he's too stupid to be scared; and big as he is he's got a tiny dick. Six-foot four, and he's like—" Eric held up his little finger, thumb covering the lowest joint—"*this*. But Doubrey says Arnie comes a lot. When I first got there, Arnie's name was 'Buckethead.' Now it's just 'Buck.' Buck Zawolsky ain't bad."

"You only *think* you'd like a funny nickname," Bottom said. "Believe me: funny names get old *very* fast. Take it from 'Bottom Boy' a.k.a. 'Bottom Feeder'—and I may kill you if you tell the wrong person. I've worked hard at being Just Plain Bill."

"Yeah?" Eric smiled. "Well, maybe…Anyway, I figured perhaps we should at least *try* to be friends—Scott and me. So one Sunday, he takes me to this place and we have a…fuckin' *brunch*! And he spends the whole time ogling these stuck-up gay high school kids and saying how he wants this one or that one, and how the person who loves him should never love nobody else. Then he reads me out this article in a gay paper that was in there about gay marriage and how important it is for gays to realize how necessary the right to be married is. And be sexually and psychologically responsible, because we'd been through AIDS already. And I'm sittin' there thinkin', I don't want one guy. I want maybe nine or ten. And I want each of them to bring home another nine or ten, and we'll all fuck: little guys, big guys, black guys, white guys, Chinese guys. In the library basement bathroom, a month ago, I had a feller what only had one leg. He was Filipino or somethin' and didn't speak *no* English. We practically tore down the stall. I thought they were gonna come in and catch us. I been lookin' for that motherfucker ever since. *I* ain't never known nobody with AIDS—"

"I have, mostly back when I was your age. But some things have changed. Though if you hang around with black folks—"

"Hey, I like old guys, fat guys, hairy guys, black guys, white guys—yeah, I wouldn't mind somebody like me, too. But Scott wants to be safe and happy and…monogamous. He doesn't even like the guys he sucks off on the team. But it's like there's a fuckin' rule—"

"Do *you*?"

"They're okay. Only most of 'em are straight. But that's the problem, see? Straight guys, gay guys, white guys, black guys, to me it's all the same fuckin' thing. Love me, and don't let me catch you lookin' at nobody else. Or if you suck off a bunch of 'em, none of 'em wanna talk to you afterwards unless they *have* to. *I* wanna hang out with somebody who wants to go to weird places and beat off together and suck each other off and watch each other do nasty shit with other people. Stand around with our flies open and our dicks hangin' out and see how long the two of you can do that before somebody says somethin'. Go to the movies and beat off in the back row and see how many people come sit there to watch. I did that by myself once and a woman came and sat a seat away. She was okay, man! She gave me some of her popcorn, and when I finished she said she hoped I had a good time. Hey, what's this guy—Scott's boyfriend—gonna *do* with himself? Change the curtains every week?"

"Probably the most important thing for Scotty will be that he pays his half of the rent. Which I suppose is in the same line, actually."

"But that's why I don't think I'm either one. I need me about a yard of dick every day," a line Eric had been impressed with from one of the hillbillies behind the Verizon sign, though he'd never said it before. "Know what I mean?"

"Actually," Bill said, "I *do*. Lord, the boy is *naturally* queer!" He shook his head, miming disbelief.

"But that's why I don't want nobody callin' me gay. I'd rather they called me a fuckin', cocksuckin', piss-drinkin', shit-eatin' scumbag…than fuckin' *gay*! At least that gets my dick hard. I don't wanna grow up like—" Eric looked at his joined fingers. Well, it *was* his last day—"like you. I mean, I don't wanna *sound* like you."

Lowering them, Bill bunched his brows. "My northern accent…?"

"Not *that*! I mean you and Scott. Like you're half a bitchy girl and half a man." In his chair, Eric blinked three times, then took a breath. "But I probably will, huh?" His hands came apart.

"Only if you start hanging out with a lot of *other* people who talk like…me. And Scott. And who you start to think are cool. Also, the girl— at least—has come along a *very* tough road." Again Bill's brows lowered. "Remember. She has reasons to be a bitch."

"I wanna sound like my dad…when he's all relaxed and stuff." Eric managed to drop his shoulders. "I wanna sound like the guys whose dicks I wanna suck and whose asses I wanna eat, and who I want to suck my dick and eat out my asshole."

"Dear God in heaven, he's *actually* a homosexual! He's interested in his *own* sex. You know, there're not a lot of you fellows left. Once more: Cheers." Bill settled back in the chair, and lifted his mug in both hands till it was just under his chin. "Aren't you going to drink your chocolate? It's Swiss."

"Oh." Eric leaned forward to take up his own mug with one. "I'm sorry." He glanced at his thick fingers. "Mike thinks I could be a welder, too. Like him." He sipped, then put the mug down. "But he always says I should do whatever I want—Hey, it's good."

"So much in life is, Eric." Bill sighed. "You don't *have* to drink it. I won't be offended. But I still don't see what this has to do with shitting where you eat. Or is that because you're horny and I'm not? I'm not, incidentally, because I had a *very* nice night three miles from here with some guys I hope will be my friends, though for job-related reasons they had to bring me home early. But if it doesn't work out…" Bill shrugged. "There's always King Kong to climb to the top of the Empire State Building with and gaze out on the city sunrise. Have you ever thought that maybe our big black homeboy was giving Christine Daaé—or whatever her name was—some really good head, off-screen, with his wide, wet, expert tongue? I mean, think of all those native virgins he'd been practicing on…? That's *really* why she loved him. One reason the first version is so good is because all the lovey-dovey stuff is left implied. Put it out there, and you *can't* keep people's minds off the sordid mechanics."

"Lickin' out her pussy?" Eric grinned—then remembered himself. His expression grew serious. "I could get behind that. Especially if some guy was fucking her at the same time. Hey…when's the last time *you* ate out a homeless nigger's ass who hadn't had no toilet paper for a week?" as, indeed, Frack had not, three days ago, when Eric had last messed with him. "I mean that nigger had a *big* ass, too, and his hole was so funky I didn't think I was gonna get to the other side of all the shit caked in there."

"Not," Bill said pensively, "so recently I can call it to mind."

"Well, I did, three *days* back."

"To be sure, the Road of Excess leads to the Palace of Wisdom, even when it takes you through the Valley of the Nest of Spiders. Just watch out for parasites. You really *wouldn't* suck off Peter Jackson's gorilla—wouldn't let it bone your butt? You don't want it to lick your balls, or stick your pecker up its ass and hump it till you shoot? Did you know, King Kong, out in the morning sun, is called Hanuman in India and Sun-We Kung in China, not to mention any other signifyin' silverback you can name? I bet you'd make him come all over himself. My, my, my…you *are* choosy about who you fuck!"

"And I *ate* shit—my own off guys' dicks. Lots of times. And…and drunk guys' piss, too." (More than a cup, in seven or eight dog-like spurts, all half dozen times he'd sucked off Pickle: *That just means it feels good. It happens when I beat off, too. Come on, you wanna do it with me and see…?*

(Can I drink the rest?)

(No! You can't*! Why you always want to do that nasty stuff?* Though his dark knuckles had already gone into his fly, Pickle looked uncomfortable. *If you get some pictures of naked girls, I'll pee on 'em with you.* So asking had been a bad thing. *You know, when I'm beatin' off and one of them surprise squirts sneaks up on me and jumps out, most of the time it hits my chin. Or my nose—that's if nobody's suckin' on it. The guys in the place where I come up always thought that was* real *funny. I'll let you see that, if you want.)* "So I…do eat shit or whatever the fuck you said. Right?" Eric was annoyed by the way Bottom turned aside all attempts to shock; at the same time, on some level, it reassured. "Anyway, that's another reason why I don't think I'm gay."

Holding up his mug, Bill looked at it, blew over the surface, then sipped. "Since I'm not going to take you inside and fuck you, I'll tell you a story—instead."

"About what? King Kong?"

"No. About me. Something you just reminded me of…that I did a long time ago. In New York, when I was in business school—at Fordham. I was nineteen—I think. You're what? Eighteen, now?"

"I'll be seventeen in eight days—no, a week."

"*Jesus!*" Bill glanced up at cloud wisps. "Well, possibly I was twenty. I wasn't as precocious as you. But it was about this time of the morning… probably earlier, because in summer the sun rises about an hour-and-a-half before it does down here. Anyway, I'd been up all night, walking around Central Park, trying to get laid in the *worst* way—and couldn't to save myself. Lots of homeless guys sleep there, and it was pretty warm that September. It was in the Rambles, and I was coming up to where some rocks made this wall.

"Beside it, a guy lay on some cardboard, asleep.

"He was curled up, back to the stones, facing forward, this middle-aged black man, maybe in his late thirties. *Mmmm*…at least he seemed middle-aged to me, back then. He didn't have any shoes or shirt—and no belt. Clearly he was homeless. He was real dark, a black guy, like I say—as dark as your dad. His pants were ripped completely apart in two places, waist to cuff, and his genitals were out, rough-skinned, uncut—and large. Not huge, mind you. Just large. They hung down over his thigh.

"I walked around him awhile, went away, came back, went away, and came back again. Finally I sat cross-legged on the edge of his cardboard.

"I could go on for an hour, telling you all the things speeding around in my brain over the next minute—would he wake up or not? Pull away or not, if he did? Hurt me or not? If he got mad, would it still be worth the pleasure and knowledge of the contact? Could I work up enough nerve to touch him? Then, somehow, I…I had him in my hand! (I *still* don't know how I did that.) I was *holding* him. He was thick, fleshy, heavy…I slid my other hand under his testicles. They were wonderfully warm. My body felt electrified—the only way to describe that tingle. It was cool out, and I was quiveringly sensitive to how much warmer his nuts were than the air. Their heat worked all into me. I wanted to suck him so badly the side of my neck cramped up while I was trying not to bend down. The guy was really out of it, and I was getting up my nerve, when he began to pee.

"This glimmering arc just…expanded, sparkling, one end fixed inside his foreskin's nozzle that was sticking out my fist.

"He wet one side of my shirt, the knee and thigh of my jeans, my cheek, my arm…

"I thought about letting him go, only I didn't—I *wouldn't!* It was so warm, and, because it was getting all over me anyway, I leaned down and drank. I bent way down, and put the first three, then four spurting inches in my mouth—about half of it. It tasted salty, his skin was rough, and his urine was bitter and hot. A lot ran over my hand. When it was running out, he moved a little and said, 'Da's nice…nice.' His hand came down to pat my head. I jumped a little. I'm surprised I didn't bite him. The guy said, 'Suck da nigga, white boy. Keep suckin' on it, real deep, now. Ah'm gonna come in yo' mouf. Jus' like you wan'.' I swear, that's the way he talked."

"Mike's got family who talk like that, in Texas—some of 'em. Like the niggers under the highway. We visited them—Mike's brother; that's my Uncle Omar. And Mike's cousins. They were nice. But they call each other 'nigger' more than the hip-hop kids."

"Now you know where it comes from: this *is* the South." Again Bill's voice dropped into black burlesque: "'So you keep suckin', now, ya' heah? Don' spiddit out. You swaller dis nigga's load, white boy. Just like you drunk dat piss.'"

Eric asked: "He said that?"

"*Um-hum.* 'You go'n' swaller it all down. Don' spill none, now…'

"I sucked.

"He hardened—and came.

"I swallowed.

"'Yeah, da's good. Make dis nigger feel *real* good, boy. Okay. Ah'm goin' back to sleep.' Really, it's what he sounded like. 'You go on to sleep, too, if'n you want.' Obviously he'd started out from somewhere around here. His hand was wood-rough and rubbed my face, and I stretched out, my cheek half on wet cardboard, half on the grass, that heavy penis still in my mouth, getting softer, shrinking.

"No one had come by, and we were kind of behind some bushes...

"Through my nose, I got in a breath, and hugged his thigh. He hugged my head back, I remember—with just one hand (but it was a hug. Not a press or a pat or a squeeze. It was a one-handed hug)—and, after maybe three breaths, clearly he'd gone back to sleep. So after eight, nine more—" Bill shrugged—"I did, too.

"Another half-an-hour or so and I woke. His cock wasn't in my mouth anymore. I thought he'd gone. So I looked up. *Somebody* was sitting next to me, hip right against my head. I raised up on an elbow.

"His back was to the stone. From somewhere, he'd gotten a cardboard container of coffee, though—unless it had been delivered by some meals-on-wheels charity group, rolling through the park while I was asleep—it was hard to imagine him, in those pants, leaving the place, making it barefoot to a coffee stand, and getting back. When I sat up, he was looking into his cup.

"I pushed up onto my knees, then I stood. With his kind of foggy eyes he blinked at me and held up the coffee. 'You wan' some?'

"The thing I remember, he was one of those guys whose hands—like your dad's—were completely black. I mean, his palms, the undersides of his fingers, his nails. To this day, I have no idea if that was weeks of dirt, or pigmentation, or if it was from being out in the sun for so long."

Eric said: "That's from his work."

"Oh," Bill said. "Well, I do know it was...incredibly beautiful.

"He said, 'I got some fren's. Dey gonna like you. Dey love to fuck a lil' redheaded white boy.' My hair *was* redder then. 'Dey love to have you suck on 'em. A couple of 'em is even white—like you. You get me some pants, an' I could really make same money offa you, boy. I give you some, too. No bitch o' mine ever complained I didn't treat her right. I ain't a rough daddy: I be a *good* daddy. I ain't got time to be mean and nasty. You gonna like hangin' out wid me—if you got some damned pants I can wear. An' maybe some shoes or sneakers. I'd be real good at sellin' yo' ass. I got a lotta experience at it, too. An' whenever you don't be workin' you can suck dis nigger till you can' suck no mo'. You can drink my piss. Eat my cum. An' I'll make love to you too, lil' boy. I like to lick my lil' fellas' noses out when I make love to 'em. You ever had anyone do dat to ya'?'" Bill chuckled.

"He said that?" Eric felt himself swelling to half-hard, let his legs fall wide, then brought them together.

"Um-hm," Bill said. "I mean I *have* seen you from time to time, out my window here, when you were walking to or from the garage and didn't think anyone was watching—"

"Oh..." Eric glanced down and rejoined his hands, tightening them with an embarrassment that had hounded him since a playschool teacher in Baltimore had noticed him at, and yelled at him about, his habit. "That sounds—" since Bill had noticed it, he was surprised that, till now, he hadn't mentioned it—"kinda complicated."

"But over the next five seconds, Eric, I went from thinking he was the most beautiful man I'd ever seen, with the most mouth-filling cock I'd ever sucked—and I'd sucked a pretty fair number, by then, too—to *totally* terrified. You have to understand, I had a walk-up fourth floor apartment on 112th Street and Frederick Douglass Boulevard. My lowest dresser drawer was full of old jeans, some of which, yes, had holes in the crotch, but even they were better than what he had to clutch together, just to walk around. And he's sitting there, saying, 'Come on, now. Sit down wid' me. Help me finish dis coffee.'

"When I didn't sit, he held it higher. 'Go on. Have some. It's good.'

"So I took the cup, and tasted it—*God*, it was sweet! It must have been a quarter sugar! I gave it to him, stepped back, and said, 'No. No, I'm sorry...!' Then I turned and...*ran* through the park, the bushes, the trees, the paths, everything!

"And, you know, Eric? I've often thought that was the stupidest thing I've ever done in my life—or *one* of the stupidest. I figured that out by eleven o'clock the same morning, once I'd had a few hours of real sleep. When I got up, I put some jeans I thought might fit him and some old runners into a brown paper Bloomie's bag and spent another fourteen hours walking in the park, looking for him. (Did I mention he was shorter than I was?) But New York is such a big city, people get lost from you—like *that*! Even in Atlanta, you have a better chance of finding somebody after you think you've misplaced them. I never saw him again. But regularly I think: Suppose I'd sat down with him and said, 'Okay,' and stayed.

"Even taken him to my place, to get some clothes—or just to finish sleeping.

"You know, I...might have been happy—for what? Half an hour? Ten hours? Until he brought the first guy to fuck me? Or the fifth? Or the fiftieth? Suppose I'd given him the pants that would have been nowhere near as difficult for me to get as it was for him to wander, half naked, to panhandle up some coffee and come back. Three days maybe? Or three weeks? Or even partnered around with him for a...couple of years? Dropped business school and done...a hundred and fifty—maybe a thousand of his 'friends'? Of course, I could have gotten my head bashed in. But with the few thousand I've done on my own since then—" Bill frowned—"I don't think so. Besides, that can happen in any situation. And like I ran away then, I could have run away in five hours, or five days, or five months. Or five years. But maybe that extra happiness—" and again he was smiling—"I might have had would have helped to make all the hours, when I was miserable over what, yes, this guy or that guy had done—like not even notice I was alive, mostly—a little more bearable. So, now we're prepared for the cold, naked moral that ends the tale. You ready?"

"Okay." Eric shrugged. "Sure."

"Good. Because I'm going to tell it to you.

"Eric, sometime in your life—it may be in twenty minutes, or two months, or six years, or twenty-five years—you are going to find yourself in a situation that, simply because of all the things you *have* done, you will realize holds the possibility of…happiness. Now it won't be like mine. But it *will* be something lots fewer people could understand than could have understood…well, what I just told you about. But when it happens, *don't* be like me, Eric. You say, 'Yes.' Because if you don't, it gets all bottled up, and you end up smashing your rifle butt into the bellies of pregnant women, or strafing perfectly nice gorillas off the Empire State Building or changing the curtains every week or jamming the handles of toilet plungers up the assholes of prisoners and attaching generators to their scrotums with alligator clips—straight or gay, because someone doesn't want you looking at anyone else; because you think, somehow, *that* will make you feel better; that will make you happy."

"*Wow*…!" Eric said. "You think it's like…? Man! You think *that's* how it works?"

"And remember. If it doesn't pan out, you can always change your mind. You can run away later. So when it happens, even though you're scared, say, 'Yes.' Okay?"

Eric frowned.

"I'm serious, Eric." Bill lifted his mug from the table and sipped.

"Yeah." Eric shrugged. "Maybe. Hey, I gotta catch a shower and get some breakfast. Look, don't tell Mike about none of this after I'm gone, okay?"

"Of course! Not only is the boy queer *and* a homosexual, but he's *totally* closeted—as who wouldn't have guessed. My lips, Eric, are sealed—"

"I ain't in no closet. At least not with Barbara—my mom, I mean."

Bill grinned. "You call your mom by her first name?" Quizzically he let his head fall to the side. "I knew some rich kids who used to do that in the private school I went to in New York."

Eric shrugged. "I started that when I was about seven, when me and

Mike spent about three months with his folks in Texas. Believe me, *they* weren't rich. They were about as poor as you can get. They didn't even have bathrooms. They still had out-houses. While we was there, we had to move from his brother's into his cousin's across the road, 'cause his brother's electricity got cut off. But Mike's mama and his stepdad and brothers and sisters liked Barbara a lot, 'cause whenever she'd visited them, she'd pitch in and really help out—cook, clean, wash windows, baby sit—like she was one of them, I guess. I think they liked her better than they liked Mike. And they really wanted them to get back together. When they talked about her, they all used to call her Barbara—or Barb, like Mike did. So I did, too. Then, once, when I went to Hugantown to stay with her, I called her that by accident—but she said she liked it, and I should keep it up. Later she said *she* knew some rich kids, too, who did that—when she was little. Maybe she thought it was elegant. Or somethin'. And I was only seven or eight. So I kept doin' it. Anyway, that's why I wanna get down to Diamond Harbor with her. 'Cause Barb knows I'm queer already."

"Eric?"

"Huh—?"

"A bit more advice from your gay Uncle Bill. Your mom—Barb—told you that you shouldn't tell your dad, right?"

"Yeah…?"

"You know he *has* to find out, someday…"

"I'm gonna tell him—someday."

"Good." Bill nodded. "I'm glad you know that. Well, for much the same reasons, Uncle Bill suggests that you *not* tell Barbara about the piss and shit and homeless niggers and…" He waved a hand back and forth. "And any other stuff that goes with them. Just go down to Diamond Harbor and be a nice gay son who helps his single mother and keeps the details to himself. *She's* not…black—like Mike? Is she?"

"Naw. She's my real mom…But that's pretty much how I figured to do it." Eric shrugged again. "I guess what *I* do ain't too elegant, huh?"

"Well, don't think for a minute you're alone." Again Bill nodded. "While, true, politically it's not very effective, still, the closet has its uses."

Standing up, Eric looked around the yard. The sun had widened over more than half of it. "Hey, my dad's gonna wake up around seven-thirty." The backs of his thighs tingled. As he stepped from in front of his chair, his shadow slid forward over Bill—who, in Eric's shadow, ceased to squint. "I should grab that shower and finish packin' my shit." Eric turned and, by the arms, picked up the lawn chair. "Lemme take this back. Then I'm gonna make some oatmeal upstairs—before we leave. Hey—*that's* pretty gay, huh?" Over one arm he grinned at Bill. "Makin' oatmeal for me and my dad…?" Then, holding the chair by its arms, he started for the table across the grass.

His mug again in both hands, eyes again narrowed, Bill called: "Have you ever seen the original *King Kong*? I mean the 1933 Merian C. Cooper version—with the uncredited Harry Redmond effects; and Fay Wray and Bruce Cabot? A Mrs. Fischer did the actual screaming for Wray."

Putting the chair down, Eric stopped to look back.

"They dubbed her in because Fay wasn't too good at it herself." Bill went on. "I'm not even sure Peter Jackson knows that. When my dad knew her in the fifties, Mrs. Fischer was a librarian in his elementary school up in New York City."

"I seen some of it—a few times, on TV." Eric lifted up the chair again. It wasn't that heavy, just clumsy. "The old one. I never watched the whole thing, though." He was still near enough to see that, through the basement window, no television flicker played on the wall. Bill must have turned it off when he'd gone in for their chocolate.

"That reconstructed spider-pit sequence—honestly, that's such a beautiful example of how you can have a childhood dream and, when you grow up—if you're lucky enough—make it real. Now, go on, put that back by Mr. Condotti's table."

* * *

[C] A CARDBOARD BOX in his arms, Eric was coming from the garage, when, in jacket, slacks, and loafers, Bill walked up.

"You're workin' on Saturday?" Eric asked.

"And without a jot of sleep, either. The tribulations of maturity." In shaving, Bill had left a goatee's shadow across his upper lip, around his mouth, and over his chin. "The trouble with having a gay uncle, Eric, is that once we start giving advice, we can't stop. Last year a friend told me—I just remembered it—he'd found a pretty active truck stop, maybe half a dozen miles north of Diamond Harbor. Said it was a lot of fun." Bill shrugged. "Since that's where you're goin', maybe you'll get a chance to try it."

"Yeah?"

"Um-hm." Bill nodded. "And having nothing to do with that, you can read this…when you reach your mom's." A July breeze moved through the leaves, as Bill held up a folded paper.

"Sure." Almost dropping his carton, reaching up with one hand, Eric got it. "Is this somethin' my dad—or Barbara—can see?" (Out at the curb, Mike was trying to refit duffle bag, boxes, mountain bike, and Bowflex into the Chevy's trunk and back seat.) Eric wondered how Bill's beard would look fully-grown.

Bill would look weird with a goatee…

Bottom smiled. "Of course they can. It's harmless—at least I *hope* so!" Then, laptop case hanging from the black, red, and green brocaded strap across his shoulder, Bill turned to crunch up the gravel. At the alley's end Eric saw him enter Montoya's sunlight. "Hey, Mr. Jeffers—Mike?" (The breeze ceased.) "Eric's got another carton coming. You guys have a good trip." Bill started toward Forty-Fourth Street for the Q-23 stop.

Coolness had slipped from the morning. Carton finally secure in one arm, Eric pushed the paper into his pocket beside his KY tube. He looked at the sun angling over Bill's crumbling steps. The cooler air had been pleasant an hour back. On its maroon ground, only half the brass foundation of the world was in shadow. In leaf-mottled sun, Eric read:… *et consumimur igni.*

It was just after eight.

* * *

[B] THE MOON'S CRESCENT hung high on the day. Below steel clouds and three-o'clock sun, the sea blazed. Along the ocean, the highway yielded up its baritone hum.

In the air-conditioned Chevy, Mike drove south. Eric sat beside him, looking out the car door's window—in order to dig out one nostril or the other. (Since he was facing away, Mike, from the driver's seat, couldn't see.) Finishing, Eric would again look through the windshield while the highway expanded toward them.

When Eric was younger, Mike had worried about his son's habit. But Omar's boy, Ralphy, did it, too—and when they'd stayed in Texas, Mike and Omar had talked about it a few times when the kids were in bed. *Man, you don' gotta worry about shit like dat. His fren's gonna shame 'im out of it—or he ain't gonna* have *no fren's.*

Yeah, but Ralphy's six, Mike explained. *Eric's eleven.*

I'll tell you. You catch 'im directly, go on—tell 'im right there, cut it out. Believe me, though, his fren's'll take care of it. Ralphies' done already started. So that's what Mike did; and wondered if that had anything to do with why Eric had as few friends as he did. And what about when you *didn't* catch him directly but he was looking away from you in the car; still, from his arm and shoulder movements, you knew.

Well, you had to let the kid live.

At *that* moment, actually, Mike was *not* thinking about Eric, but about how well Doneesha cooked—not that he was worried. And Kelly-Ann had a curious nature…and a movie-star *perfect* ass—as, something of a doofus, Jake had whispered to him more than a dozen times. Still, Doneesha's was fuller, firmer, and closer to Mike's own ideal. She was more relaxed about letting you do what you wanted with it, too. Yeah, after a couple of weeks with Kelly-Ann…

At *that* moment, actually, as he sat beside his step dad, again looking out the windshield, Eric was wondering what the coming months held for sex—not that he was worried. He'd tripped over it in Maryland and bedded down with it in East Texas: three houses away, Omar's sister (Mike's half sister) Lurlene, had a dark, all-but-silent, stunningly good-looking ten-year-old, Hareem. (Harry looked enough like Mike to make some folks in the neighborhood wonder.) Whenever eleven-year-old Eric stayed over, she'd put both boys in the bed in the back room with each other. They'd lain there three long minutes, till Harry had made the first move. His way of dealing with it socially, though, next morning (which, with intense whispers, Harry had made clear to his visiting white cousin), was that— during the day—You Didn't Talk About It *None*. Never. At *All*: Hareem would hardly speak to Eric during daylight, though that night they were all over each other the moment the door closed.

As for the nose picking, back then Eric had been trying harder to keep it private than he was now, so that, during their separate games on their separate sides of the sidewalkless East Texas road, Eric was—relatively— successful.

During the three months he'd stayed with Barbara at her own mother's in Hugantown once they gave up their own place, Eric (then twelve) had found another sexual outlet. Around the corner, at the back of an overgrown lot, through a crack in a bathroom window of an isolated cabin, he could peer in and jerk off while watching a twenty-seven-year-old Greek plumber's assistant, who was mostly doing the same. On the first day, where the frosted glass had pulled from maybe four inches along the frame, Eric had looked through into the shadowy john and seen that Costas—who, with his boss, Yoti, had once done a job for his grandmother, which is how Eric knew their names—had papered it all, even the ceiling, with pictures of nude or negligeed women cut or torn from porn magazines. The second time Eric had wandered back there, attracted by the grunts and whispers, he'd looked through and seen, in only a ripped T-shirt, black body hair pushing through the holes under the neck, with no shoes and gaping workpants, toes coming out the hole in one tube sock, Costas, leaning against the sink, pumping and muttering, *Mallakas…! Cock*-suckin' *bitch...! Mallakas...!* till he staggered forward to feed his semen onto one or another pair of bright lips yearning from the wall.

Outside, standing on leaves, pieces of a broken chair, old boards, Eric gripped the sill. Both breathing heavily, he watched Costas move back, sit on the commode's edge, and push his work pants down to strip out of them entirely, leaving them on the concrete floor.

Costas started in again.

Then he did it again.

Then again...

Sometimes, at his climax, gasping, quivering, Costas—naked, now, except for one sock—fell to his knees on the bathmat, near black with dirt, to spatter a cold, scarlet smile.

As low as Costas's scaly ankle and as high as his hairy ribs, the pictures on three walls and part of a fourth were as clotted and coated, much of it gone orange, as the dinner plate medallion in Mr. Condotti's garage, or inside the top-floor Atlanta school john door.

(There was *so* much, Eric had been looking almost an hour when it struck him what it was. Costas had lived there four years: that's how Eric recognized it two years later in the Atlanta high school boys' room.)

A creature of habit, Costas confined it to the bathroom—unless he slipped off to spill a few when he was out with cigar smoking Yoti at his job. Costas had a four- or five-load session in the hour-and-a-half before going into work, another couple right after coming home. Then he came in to drop a few more before turning in around ten. Staying up to watch those last got Eric yelled at by both his mother and his grandmother.

But the back wall of Costas' cabin, below the bathroom window, now carried Eric's own growing stain.

Saturdays and Sundays, Costas did it non-stop, leaving the john only to eat—or, more often, bringing in a sandwich wrapped with wax paper, a cardboard boat of French fries, and a king-sized Bud, which he parked on the tub's enameled edge, while, with stubble-blackened cheek and neck, tufted knuckles, sable chest hair, and hirsute arms bespattered, he labored to loose another load. Once fallen on thigh, belly, wrist, arm—or shiny photo—it stayed. As far as Eric could tell, three weeks without a shower and only a hand washing every couple of days was Costas' norm.

Till then Eric had thought he himself held the record.

But it was no contest.

That Memorial Day, in back of the creosoted wall, Eric got there before sunrise. He tried to keep up, but stopped after two hours—though he wouldn't leave except to return to his grandmother's for lunch and dinner. Between six in the morning and ten twenty-seven that night, Costas busted his nut twenty-two times that Eric counted, all over himself or his stained ladies. (Unlike Eric, Costas never ate his spunk, though he'd rub the remains around balls, belly, and gut.) Feeling a lot better about his—back then—five-to-six-times a day, Eric had left Hugantown to live with Mike.

If Costas was an indicator, half a dozen a day was nothing to worry about...

There would be something to do in Diamond Harbor.

To the highway's right a blue and white sign said TRUCK STOP ½ MILE. "We gotta pull in there."

"What in the world for?"

"'Cause I gotta shit—*that's* why."

"Oh...You know, Diamond Harbor's only a few more miles." Mike slowed the Chevy. "You'd think you could hold it fifteen minutes till we got to Barb's—"

"You wanna hold it for me?" Eric grinned. "Cup your hands. Look, I won't be long." (There couldn't be *two* truck stops so close...)

"I think you're more comfortable goin' in a public john than in your own home. Me, I can piss anywhere. But I *cannot* shit in no road-side can."

"Well," Eric said, "that don't bother *me*."

"You be happy you ain't got none of them hang-ups."

Like one of Mike's repeating stories, the exchange occurred on every drive of any length. Eric said, "I am."

Forty seconds later, they turned into Turpens Truck Stop. (A GEORGIA INSTITUTION SINCE 1937! in antique gold, green, and red on gray planks chained to a horizontal post.) Mike parked his car among some dozen pickups. Further down stood the big rigs.

To the right was the window for Turpens Parts & Notions, filled with boards of gaskets, towers of batteries, racks of calipers, rows of ratchets, wrenches, sparkplug testers, CBs, pressure gauges, and radar "cheaters," along with bandanas, coffee mugs, snap-button shirts, flags—American, Puerto Rican, Italian, Irish, Hells Angels, Mexican, Confederate, Union, Marine, Navy, one flag with horizontal white, brown, black, and tan stripes and a paw print in the upper left (Eric recognized it and Mike did not: in a gay bookstore window, derisively Scott had pointed one out to Eric that Saturday back in Atlanta: *That's for old, fat, hairy guys...Uhhh!* Eric had thought about saying, *So what's wrong with that?* But not to Scott), and one that said only Turpens—dashboard raccoons, fuzzy dice, and grass-skirted hula dolls, black, brown, and pink—and caps: "Turpens," with an eagle flying off above the visor. Left of the recessed entrance, another long window looked in on the blue booths, wooden walls, and slowly turning fan blades of Turpens Homestyle Eatery.

Around the car, mica glittered in concrete.

"Now don't get all caught up checkin' out junk in the store."

"Don't *worry!*" Eric spoke with the adolescent impatience Mike had learned to ignore—as Eric now ignored Mike's repetitions. "I'll be back in fifteen, maybe twenty minutes." Eric opened the car to climb out. As he turned, hot air exchanged with the air inside. "And I gotta go into the store when I'm finished. I need a cap." Holding the door's rim, he grinned at Mike, then slammed it.

Christ, Mike thought, looking at his bronzed step son in his blue tanktop, the wide body-builder shoulders and full, rounded arms, sheened already from seconds in the sun. That's one *good* lookin' kid. Remembering their Bowflex workouts, he thought: Yeah, he keeps me young.

Kelly-Ann (five months legal, as Mike thought of her) was only a year-and-a-half older.

* * *

[A] HEAT LIKE STONES on his shoulders, against his temples, Eric walked toward the double layer of glass doors across Turpens' entrance.

Between the pickups, wearing beige slacks and fingering a cell phone into a yellow shirt pocket, from which stuck a handkerchief's purple points, a thin man ambled over. To Eric, the handkerchief—and a slight sway, kind of like Bill's that morning—said "faggot."

At the same time, behind layered glass, Eric saw a second man walking forward, about to leave. This guy was a head-and-a-half taller than Eric (who was five-nine), stocky and in his late thirties. Six-five? Six-six…? Through the glare, Eric caught his dull blond hair, his orange cap, his brazen beard.

Well, if I follow the gay one, I'll find the right john fast. Eric paused, stood straighter, and rubbed his hands up his sweating face to let the slender man reach the doors, so that, once he was inside, Eric could follow, steps behind.

The gay guy pulled open the outer door and went in—which is when Eric saw that inside the bearded man had stopped.

Eric followed the thin guy through one glass door, through a second—

Turpens' lobby was frigid with air conditioning. In moments the cold was painful along the sweat trickling behind his ear, beneath his jaw. When Eric lifted a bare arm, someone slid a cold slab beneath it.

He did not look directly at the bearded man—though from the corner of Eric's eye, it seemed the guy wore a red plaid jacket. (In *this* heat…?) With darkly gleaming sleeves, it hung open. Under it—as with Bill earlier—he wore no shirt. Between the jacket's edges, over belly and chest, hempen hair swirled up to obliterate his navel's sink.

Then, because Eric was walking, the bearded man—standing still—was behind him.

On the wall to the right, another indoor plate glass window glared before automotive parts, case knives, more cowboy shirts, and oversized belt buckles with rhinestone letters: "World's Greatest Dad," "World's Greatest Lover," "World's Greatest Stud," "World's Greatest Trucker…" The inside door to Turpens Parts & Notions stood off to the left.

On the right, the indoor entrance to Turpens Eatery was beyond the motel-style counter. Keys with white tags hung before a rack of pigeonholes.

No one was behind the desk.

Eric watched the gay guy cross the lobby's plank flooring. In an alcove, silhouetted on the right was a small man and, on the left, a small woman. The gay guy—if he *was* gay—walked up and turned right.

Eric took two steps after him.

And slowed.

Then he turned—and risked looking at the bearded blond, full on.

The guy still stood, looking away from Eric. His cap said Turpens. The visor slanted down over the curly hair bunched above his left ear. Then he looked back—*maybe* at Eric…or the one who'd gone into the men's room.

Nor *was* he wearing a jacket:

A red-and-black plaid shirt hung, unbuttoned and wide, back from belly and chest. (His first glance, Eric had misread it…) The sleeves had been torn away—there were none at all. Thigh-thick arms—probably why Eric had thought they'd been enlarged by jacket sleeves—were gouged into muscle groups. Both bore full-sleeves of ink, shoulder to wrist. (Not many men that hairy had tattoos.) Thick as a D-cell, a thumb hooked his jeans pocket. On the back of that furry hand, in blue and green a serpent's head flicked a red tongue between yolk-yellow fangs. Green-scales coiled into heavier hair to drape the muscle. On his upper arm, barbed wire ran through the sockets of the skulls circling the biggest bulge. With blue fins, dolphins breached a blue-gray wave breaking along his lower. His triceps spilled stylized blood where a knife stabbed through. Spiraling his biceps, dragons dove from his shoulders among clouds and flashing zags and zigs. Even under the florescent lights hair hazed the smaller pictures. As were chest and gut, hands and arms were *so* furry that, despite the images, they looked like hempen bales.

As the tattooed and bearded man started, not toward the john but toward the hall running off beside Turpens Parts & Notions, Eric moved his glance away. . .

He let it return.

As the man was about to disappear, he looked at Eric—and smiled. Within his beard—shiny under the ceiling lights—his upper gum was all gap, teeth either side, like Frack's. The man reached down and gave his jeans not a scratch, but a...thick-fingered squeeze! Then, glancing down at himself, he lifted his crotch, pushing his hips forward.

Eric swallowed.

And started after him. His heart was beating hard enough to feel.

As Eric fell in beside him, big-armed, bare-bellied—no tattoos on stomach or chest—the man smiled again. "Where you runnin' off to, li'l feller?" In broad-toed work shoes, once orange, now scuffed to gray-brown, the man swaggered, thick, tall, and relaxed. "You're pretty pumped up there for a li'l guy." (Grinning, embarrassed, but pleased, Eric, though not six feet, didn't think of himself as short.) "Damn—" the bronze Goliath went on—"I gotta take me a wicked piss. It's backed up so far I can *taste* it." (But this guy was *tall*.) "See, the old head's in the rear." He nodded along the hall, the grip on his worn crotch become perfunctory scratching. "The one all the guys use who been comin' to Turpens since 'fore they built the single-room motel and peepshow stalls. Once this was the last place on the highway with dormitory-style sleepin'. Used to be down at the end, here. They closed that up twenty-five, thirty-five years ago, in seventy or eighty." He shook his head, chuckling. "It's still the last place you'll get a real key to your room, though, 'stead of them plastic rectangle do-hickeys. Guys used to bring me in here when I was a kid tom-cattin' around—a puppy like you—eighteen, nineteen." The smile widened into a grin. "Didn't have no front teeth then, neither. When I was twelve, eleven maybe, my Uncle Shad caught me suckin' off the neighbors' damned dog under my porch and punched the fuckers out on me—ol' bastard! Then he laughed and said since I was a cocksucker anyway, what the fuck did I need 'em for? Three years later, when I was fifteen and a head-and-half taller, I punched *his* lights out—at least I cracked his damned dentures. And told him I'd do a lot worse if I *ever* heard about him beatin' on no more kids—gay *or* straight!" He grunted. "Gay liberation, Georgia coastal style."

Eric's throat felt blocked. The man stopped walking—and Eric stepped nearer the colorful arm. With one hand he gripped between his own legs. They stood just beyond the inner door to Parts & Notions.

For the last five years such imitation was how Eric had learned pretty much everything he knew about sex.

No one else was in the hall.

"See—" the man glanced around—"I'm big enough now so that I can tell you anything I want about me—I'll fuck your face, lick out your asshole, or piss in your ear—and all you can do is say, 'Yes, sir,' or 'No, sir,' and hope I'm in a good mood. Suppose I told you, when I was a *real* little kid, what I liked to do more than anything was sit there in the school room, look out the window, and piss my jeans. First, it was all warm comin' out—then, in the summer there, it'd get nice and cool. And it always gimme a hard-on. By the time I was thirteen, that'd make me shoot my load without even touchin' myself. Course, half the time I smelled like a' ol' outhouse piss hole. When I was nine, they already done kicked me out three times—of school, I mean. Now, what you gonna do with that? Tell on me? Around here, anybody who could care already knows—and most of 'em don't. Care, that is. And if I ain't happy with the tone of voice you tellin' it in, I'll shove your head up your ass." Again, the man grinned. "Damn, boy." He glanced down. "Looks like your nuts is as itchy as mine."

Eric got his breath. "We can…*do* stuff in there?" though he wasn't sure where "there" was. "Somebody told me about this place."

Mockingly, the man blinked at Eric. "Yeah, we got a good reputation around here. Hey, they got a stainless steel pee trough where we can spring us a leak. Or, if you can find one that still flushes, you can climb up on the rim, squat on one of them shitters—none of 'em got doors no more—and drop a *big* ol' turd. That what you mean?" Between beard and hair, both curly, he winked an amber eye. "My partner's in there now. Probably that's what he's doin'…if he ain't suckin' off some nigger what come in to relieve hisself whatever way he can. My partner, he's a Mex—he don't talk. Spanish *or* English. He signs." The man made a gesture with his big hand: first a fist with the thumb on the side—which slid around to the front; then thumb and forefinger jutting. "ASL—good ol' 'Merican Sign Language; and from a natural-born wet-back, too. We been comin' down here together every couple a' weeks for…well, close to fifteen years. And me a lot longer. It's a nice place. We get a lot of black fellas, Injins, plain ol' redneck trash…like me. Truckers and boat fellas—me and Mex work the scow out to Gilead Island." With a thick forefinger, he reached up to dig deep in a nostril, scratching inside. "Everybody gets along, tries to be sociable. Understand what I'm sayin'?"

Eric asked, "Can I suck your…dick?" He blinked at the man's thick grubby hand. "I do it good."

"Damn…" Stepping closer, the boatman laughed. His hand fell from his face to Eric's far shoulder, over the tanktop's blue shoulder strap. Now he turned and began to walk the worn carpet again, squeezing Eric's shoulder repeatedly. His smell had old sweat in it, diesel fuel, and underarm funk. "You sound pretty hot to trot." Raising his foreknuckle against Eric's far jaw, he rubbed.

Surprising himself, Eric turned his head to take the broad, blunt forefinger in his mouth.

It was salty.

The boatman glanced at Eric—and raised a yellow eyebrow. Other than that, he gave no sign someone was sucking the finger with which he'd been picking his nose. "We can probably do sumpin' along them lines. But I got to warn you: ain't me *or* Mex got the time—or the inclination—to be what you call clean dudes. When's the last time you took you a shower?"

"Uh...this...mornin'." The man's hand muffled Eric's voice.

"Yeah? Well, with me—" he moved closer. Without getting stronger, the odor became disorienting, as though, at Eric's next breath, it penetrated another level—"it's more like a couple of weeks. And I wouldn't waste time speculatin' about Mex." Then he was closer, hip, thigh, flank pressed into, and moving against, Eric. "Though we got one planned for tonight—if we get back to Gilead in time. I'll wash him; he'll wash me; probably piss all *over* each other. He likes that, and—" he squinted, looking friendly—"I like it, too." As was the finger in his mouth, the palm on Eric's shoulder, either side Eric's blue tank top, was as hard as wood, as rough as rock. "You know, spics and Injins and redneck guys from around here, we ain't cut and skinned like you fellas up there in the city. We still got everything we come with, and inside that skin, boy, the fuckin' cheese builds up sumpin' terrible. Me, I don't *ever* hardly remember to run a finger around in there and scrape that stuff out. Most of the time, I don't have to, though, 'cause Mex'll do it *for* me...with his *tongue*." He made a face with a grin in it somewhere, behind bronze facial hair.

Eric came off the finger long enough to say, "I like cock cheese. A lot. Sure, with some guys who smoke, it tastes pretty foul—"

"Yeah? That, too, huh?" The man chuckled again. "Well, at six-fifty a pack, that's *one* thing with us you don't got to worry about. It makes you smell funnier than you already do, gives you cancer, *and* runs all the good cocksuckers off." The finger was up and waiting for Eric's mouth when he turned back for it. "Naw—that's one bad habit me an' ol' Mex ain't even thinkin' about." The man's hand slid further around Eric's face, pushing *two* fingers into Eric's mouth, moving them on Eric's tongue. "We got enough others already." He gave another grimace. "Hey, your fuck hole there feels pretty slick."

Still sucking for traces of salt, Eric looked over at the boatman. *Some* of it was probably sweat—

Out in front the man held his other hand down, smiling at it—the one with the green and blue snake's head, yellow fangs, red diamonds for eyes, and orange tongue. On bronzed skin, sun-bleached hair blurred the lines across his knuckles, clouded the serpent. Wide nubs bulged before the nails, outlined in black as with a ballpoint and gnawed well back of the quick. On the massive fingers, what was left of the nails were as wide as quarters (except the little, a nickel across) but, front to back, as narrow as half a dime. Thickened cuticle swallowed them. "Bitin' on 'em the way we do, Mex and me—the both of us—is bad enough." He turned his hand over, lifted his fist to his mouth, and began to chip at what remained on the broad flesh with his lower teeth. "That's why I first got to be friends with Dynamite—when we was kids. 'Cause he did it even worse than me. So does Shit—but then, the boy comes by it honestly."

Without taking his fingers from Eric's mouth, he turned, and together they walked again—while Eric felt some ineffable understanding of the hardness and history his tongue moved on.

Along both walls, within glass cases hung posters for a multiplex in some mall or a triple-X movie palace. ("The Opera House, Runcible's Oldest and Only 24-Hour Seven Days a Week Adult Theater!") Others displayed T-shirts, red, black, and blue, Turpens Truck Stop across the pockets. More and more cases were empty, though.

The long hall turned right.

The cases stopped.

Here the wall was weathered board, as though once the outside of an older building. "This used to be the dormitory. Now it's for storage. But they keep the old john open."

In a doorframe's upper corner, green joists had pulled apart an inch.

Saloon-style doors hung on cylindrical hinges, eighteen inches from lintel above and limen below. Under them, Eric could see, behind the entrance plank, patches of broken white-and-black tiles, surrounded by concrete, as though two layers of history contested for the men's room floor. Above the slatted doors, he saw an uneven green wall, run with pipes and cracks. Inside was a replastered patch, crossed with trowel lines and, still unpainted, white on industrial gray.

Finally, Eric pulled his mouth from the fingers.

The bearded man had dropped his other hand, opened his jeans' zipper, and tugged loose his genitals. His cock's base was thick. He arched forward, webbed with veins like wax cords a-wriggle on his skin. Bronze hair grew a third of the way along it. In front of his furry bag—one nut bigger than a fuckin' Spalding, the other as small as a goddam jack ball—his cuff shook each step. "Hey—ain't nothin' wrong with my nuts. They may look a little strange 'cause the one's so big. But they won't hurt you—you can't catch it. Sometimes guys worry about that, but most of 'em get into it. Doctors even got a fancy big word for it: orchitis. Fortunately, I got the kind that don't hurt. Itches sometimes, but that's all. I admit it: I lose a *few* guys right here—another reason I like to let you get a look before we go in. It feels a little funny if you decide to bolt once we get inside with the fellas. But that ol' ostrich egg has made more than one cocksucker fall down on his knees and shoot right there in his skivvies. Hey, you know, that's a genuine cocksuckers' dick you're lookin' at—'cause it curves down 'stead o' up. You get on your knees and that thing slides right down *into* your face. Dynamite's is longer, but him and that boy, Shit, both got the same cocksucker's curve. We're probably fourth or fifth cousins anyway. Down here, ever'body is—I never traced it through."

Eric asked, "Who's...Dynamite?" The big testicle oscillated in his mind between sexy and...well, weird. He asked, "You're goin' in there like... *that*?" But obviously he was. Eric grew even harder.

"This is one of them places where it's better to go on in with it all hangin' out. Besides, ain't you got someone waitin' in the car? I figured you didn't have all day. And you asked for it." Beside him, the big guy pushed the door with one hand and guided Eric in with the other. "Gotta get you a taste of Shit and Dynamite 'fore you leave. Come on, puppy. Learn a little of what's goin' on down here," as Eric pulled down his zipper—

* * *

[0] —AND LEVERED OUT his own cock (I hope it ain't too small for these guys...), full hard when Eric saw the men inside.

Some looked.

A couple of years older than Eric, one in a green workshirt with the sleeves torn off—like the boatman's plaid—grinned over the shoulder of a rangy older man—the boatman's age...?—whose pants were down around his hirsute thighs. (That's a nice cock, Eric thought.) The kid had close-set green eyes, a sparse beard you could see through to his face, broad bare feet, a tan mat of kinky hair, and a wide Negroid nose. He's black, Eric realized, though his skin was the same burned bronze as the boatman's, as Eric's. He shared a mouth with the older white guy. A smile deflected its line.

(Except for irregular patches of black and white tiling, cement had taken over the floor.)

Behind them were four others, three standing, one seated inside a doorless stall. All were looking at him.

In his dropped overalls, the older guy wore the same kind of shirt as the younger, its sleeves pushed up hard, heavy forearms, the front open over a black T-shirt.

The bearded boatman said: "That there is Shit—" the kid smiled— "and this here's Dynamite." The older man nodded.

The barefoot kid's nondescript pants were open, too—they weren't jeans—and, as he moved, his cock slipped from the older man's cheeks and, still hard, fell to a downward slant. Turning, the kid stepped over, reached out, caught Eric's cock in his fist, and—more surprisingly—wrapped his other arm around Eric's shoulders. "My hand's kinda rough," he said, with embarrassment. "I don't wanna hurt you."

"That's okay," Eric said. "So's my cock."

"No, it ain't." Looking down, the kid chuckled. "It's a nice one." With his other arm he hugged Eric—and (Eric was about to say, *It feels good...*) thrust his tongue as far down Eric's throat as he could!

Eric hugged him back—surprised. The kid's clothes were old, and he'd been wearing them a long time. Under their general funk was a smell like sweaty leather, which Eric realized was the kid himself.

The boatman had called him...Shit?

While their tongues rolled together and around one another's, Eric saw over the kid's shoulder that the doors on the three stalls were gone.

So were the seats on the commodes.

The partitions were enameled blue, grooved and gouged, inside and out. Even from within the embrace Eric could see, beyond Shit's bearded jaw, holes drilled through the stall walls, some half-an-inch, some two inches. Some were patched with tin squares; other holes had been drilled beside the patches. (Eric's tongue searched in Shit's mouth, and found no teeth at all—at least on the upper left. The surprise made Eric harder.) Among the eight men in the small room, Eric could see, a stocky Mexican sat on the last commode, barefoot like the kid with him now. (Eric pushed his tongue right. Gaps interrupted the teeth there, with—above and below—saddles of gum between.) The Mexican wore no shirt at all under a black denim jacket with frayed edges, open over belly and chest; nor any underpants: black jeans pushed to his ankles, he smiled with a wide, pockmarked face.

Eric thought: That's fuckin' sexy.

Along the trough urinal, a pipe began to hum till, from its perforations, like tongues of glass, with small floshes, flaps, flops, and fluffles, water flushed the steel backing, to rush along the bottom.

By the urinal's end Eric glimpsed a tall black man with a shaved head. (For an instant, he thought Mike was at the urinal. His heart gave a single astonished thump, before he recognized a different ear, a different head, a different shoulder, thinner arm, rounder back…! On the arm below the short sleeve were black tattoos he could not make out, since the man also shared Mike's coloring. In three beats, though, Eric's heart stilled.) Along with his stained dungarees he wore an orange and white road-worker's vest strapped over a gray T-shirt. He held his hands in front of himself, but was turned away so Eric couldn't see his cock.

Across the fifteen feet of cracked concrete by the Mexican's stall, two other black guys—one notably stockier than the other—were laughing over something. Their flies bowed open—which made Eric think one, the other, or both had been fooling with the Mexican. The bigger one had a fist inside his and, as Eric blinked over the kid's shoulder, pulled out a thick cock, not as long as the boatman's. Probably he'd put it away at the boatman's and Eric's entrance, and only now loosed it again.

The kid hugged Eric tighter, drew in his tongue, then rubbed Eric's neck with his face. His beard was softer than it looked.

Beyond the kid's smell was the odor of wet stone and moist cinderblock and what seeped through cracked cellar walls from the damp—a smell that, at sixteen, already Eric associated with a half hour here or an hour there, sitting in some basement john stall, at a library or in a truck garage or at a bus station, because some guy finishing at the urinal had flashed him, then hurried out, and he'd waited to see if anyone else would come—

Waiting for men…

Waiting for men like these…?

The kid was strong, as strong as Eric, and—both arms around Eric's chest—his grip was tight with bone and a desperation Eric recognized…

Eric slid one hand between the boy's and his own belly, to grip his cock, which had just been up the older guy's ass. It was about three-quarters of an inch longer than Eric's—a little thicker. Holding it, Eric realized, made his own feel bigger—as, between them, the boy squeezed Eric's with his rough hand. Eric thought: I wonder why he likes holding mine?

Beside them, the white guy bent to tug up his bib overalls. As he stood, on his once black T-shirt Eric saw a foreshortened dump truck, in gray, green, and more gray, before the denim rose over it. The john space was small enough for Eric to hear the suspender's wide wire snap catch a steel button.

Then the boatman raised his tattooed arm and put it around Eric's shoulder—a third arm around him. "'Scuse me, Shit. But this boy's gonna suck *my* dick now. You can have 'im soon as I'm finished." Taking a deep breath, Shit released Eric, stepping back, looking a little confused.

Disoriented, Eric looked left and right, still holding Shit's cock.

"Hey, Jay," Shit said. "I'm sorry. Sure." The boatman—Jay?—had *actually* called him 'Shit.' Till then, Eric had assumed it was a repeated miss-hearing, perhaps, of "Shim."

(In Florida, the security guard for Barb's trailer park had been called "Shim" and his mom had had a neighbor, Mr. Shippey, who Shim had always called "Ol' Ship"…)

"Now you—" which was Jay talking to Eric—"can hold onto *his* dick all you want, long as you're *suckin'* on mine."

Eric laughed. And the colorful, multi-headed arm lowered him to a squat.

Eric looked up at the boatman with his yellow beard and bare upper gum, grinning down. Above the boatman's jutting cock and bloated testicle, practically the size of a baseball really—the normal one a nodule at its side—from the john's uneven ceiling, the metal fixture around three incandescent bulbs suggested a glass globe had once softened their unfrosted glare.

Eric went forward, knees on the concrete.

With his callused hands, the boatman slid his wide hooded cockhead, with its full veins, its downward curve, into Eric's mouth. It was salty—and thick enough so that, when in, it filled Eric's mouth. Eric took it deep, then backed up and, tongue thrust under the meaty hood, troweled beneath the glans—God, there was a lot in there, faintly bitter, salted, mostly dry—till his tongue pushed the frenum, which stretched against it. The big-armed boatman gave a pleased grunt.

Maybe the Mexican's tongue *hadn't* gotten to it that morning… It felt good to get the guy's cock in his mouth.

Still gripping the other kid's dick—Shit's—in his hand (Was he three years older than Eric? Was he four?), Eric could feel Shit moving—an inch one way, half an inch the other—to position himself more conveniently. Eric came off Jay long enough to look up again. "You pack that stuff in there with a *spoon*?"

"Hell…" the big boatman drawled, "I thought you said you liked it."

Shit chuckled—and stepped nearer: Eric's arm bent.

"I *do*." Releasing Shit's cock, which bobbed up an inch, to hit Eric's ear—the head was wet—Eric brought that hand over to cup the boatman's immense testicle with the smaller, while four fingers of his other hand leaned like tent poles on a bit of cement. Again Eric swallowed dick, till the boatman's zipper cut at his lip.

Other guys laughed, watching, grinning. Eric grinned too—and in the dark space had a flash of spring clarity, the afternoon sun a-slant beneath the Atlanta highway—as Jay rubbed his head, the way the hillbillies sometimes had.

Eric thought: *Damn...*!

Someone said, "My kinda cocksucker, Jay," though Eric wasn't sure if the speaker was black or white.

Sucking again, Eric got to a rhythm, he could tell—from the way Jay pushed forward, his hand firm on Eric's head, the overhead grin—the boatman liked. For moments Eric wondered if he should not butt his chin into the enlarged scrotum. But after a few times—and he liked the feel of its hair against his lower face—Eric forgot it; or, rather, just enjoyed it; which the boatman seemed easy with.

Here is what, later, Eric thought: When you're sucking a good dick, you can get so involved with what's going on in your mouth—the way something as big as, or bigger than you, another tongue and of a different firmness, is sharing the space, the stretch of your cheeks, the way the palate sends one with that kind of curve down your throat—it *is* different from the ones that curve up, not that I'd send someone away because of it—and the rightness it transfers to you, each thrust; of the way the thicker part toward the back—at least with a cock like this—has all the hair and also most of the salt, like someone who's been working. Scott says he doesn't like hair on a dick. But Scott's fuckin' *nuts*—! *I* don't think Scott like *guys!* He'd be happier suckin' off chix-with-dix. (Imagine *two* nuts that big, in a real loose bag. I'm gonna jerk off over that...) You can live inside your own mouth, and all the world's in there with you. I guess you're aware of what's going on in the world, though it's not a third as important as what moves over your tongue, big tube with the little tube beneath, expanding in you, the quarter inch you keep between *your* teeth and *his* meat—

Behind Eric, hinges squeaked.

Everyone in the space moved—

At least a little—and Eric knew it and moved, too.

The boatman's hands firmed on either side of Eric's head, not to halt him but to slow him, so that the motion of Eric's mouth kept on: a way to let his cocksucker know (Eric thought right there) that whoever had entered was okay.

Or, maybe, Jay doesn't *give* a fuck...?

What *would* it be like to be *that* big...?

Could you learn such strength through knowledge alone...?

At the urinal, the black guy said, "Hey, there, fella. You come for a taste o' dis?" and—Eric could just see the man around Jay's hip, when he pulled back—turning from the urinal enough so that Eric saw what the shaved-headed black man in his safety vest held.

Jesus...! Eric thought—and got chills.

Who *is* that? Frack's *brother*...?

The newcomer moved into sight. Eric thought (though he couldn't be sure) it's the white guy Eric had followed into the place, who'd earlier gone into the front john, now here in the back. The man said: "Damn, Al, I hope you gonna shove that up my fuckin' hole. I thought you wasn't here—"

Eric reached up and got hold of Shit's dick again.

Laughing, bald Al said, "Soon as I get my motherfuckin' raincoat on." Digging in his pants, while, hooded in its crepe cuff, a foot-plus of charred hatchet handle, webbed in black cable and all that only half-hard, swung in front of him. Al pulled loose a square packet. Raising his hands (as though he might be nearsighted), he tore through brown plastic to pull loose an ivory condom that fell, unfolding, from his fingers. He shook it out.

"Goddamn, nigger!" one of the other black drivers said. "Dat ain't no raincoat! Al—da's a goddam *umbrella* cover—family size!"

"Yeah—well, I need me de big ones." (Someone else chuckled—probably the white guy Jay had called Dynamite.) With two thumbs in the latex collar, Al stretched it a couple of times. "Ted got such a sweet ass, I wait aroun' for this honkey motherfucker sometimes."

The white guy in the yellow shirt already had his slacks unbuttoned. His belt dangled open, and, held in one hand, his pants drooped down one leg. He grinned around the room.

Al grinned back. "Come on, you honkey fuck hole!" Al pulled the condom on. Stretching latex wrinkled first on one side, then pulled out smooth. "Back up on dis, Ted, and le's see you do what both the ol' ladies I'm livin' with is too scared to, 'cept in the damned dark."

His own stubby cock still in his fist, the black driver said, "Well, you can't fuckin' blame 'em. I'd be scared of dat thing too."

Leaning over, gripping the urinal's rolled edge, Ted moved toward Al's end, slacks slipping further down his legs.

"You ain't too scared to *suck* it." Al chuckled again. "At least de first seven or eight inches." While more guys laughed, he set cockhead in place, and, in his orange vest, embraced white Ted from behind. Unreadable in this ceiling light, black tattoos swarmed like bugs over Al's black arms. As Eric kneeled up, again Jay's scrotum pushed into his chin. In his pants, Eric's cock head dragged across a wet spot.

Sympathetic electricity made Eric's back tingle. (No, Al's was *not* as big as Frack's; still, it was in the same foot-plus ballpark.) He released the kid's cock he held—Shit's hand, covering Eric's, gave an acknowledging squeeze—and, while his other hand held the bearded boatman's hip, Eric slipped his fingers free and put them on the floor.

And something warm and rough covered them—Shit had moved his foot on top of Eric's hand. Eric rotated it beneath (the weight lightened in response), gripped the naked foot, and squeezed. Hard toes grasped the edge of Eric's palm. The foot seemed too wide for *any* shoe.

Eric pulled his hand loose—because, crouching low, he couldn't really get the base of Jay's cock in his mouth.

"You don't use no fuckin' spit?" asked a wondering driver.

Thrusting, retreating, thrusting, Al said, "He don't need no…fuckin' spit—he keep a…fuckin' tin o' lard…up there, anyway…Or sumpin' greasy—least when…he come lookin' for *me*, he do…Spit?" Al's voice had dropped almost an octave with disdain. "I'd spit in his goddam ear—or tear 'im de fuck open!"

"Ted, you musta been practicin' to take dat nigger," someone said.

"Come on, Al…!" Ted whispered. His arms and shoulders rocked above the urinal's rim he gripped, the pink gone from his knuckles to the skin between. "Shut up, and *fuck* my white ass, huh?"

"Oh, yeah! I remember what you like, motherfucker." Al was speeding up; his rhythm inflected his speech. "That's right—y'always wanna leave here…with your damn proof…o' purchase, doncha?…Okay. Here you go—" Al dropped his face onto Ted's neck, who put his head back and grunted:

"Oh, shit…*yeah!*"

The black man, Eric realized, had *bitten* him!

Helped on by Al and Ted (Eric suspected but was not sure), the boatman's big hands tightened: he shot in Eric's mouth.

Eric pressed his face into the rough denim, taking the cock as deep as he could get it—which was pretty fuckin' deep. God, it felt good, even if he couldn't see the two at the piss trough. For moments it was as if the orchitis was a pillow beneath Eric's jaw.

With one hand and the other, the boatman rubbed the back of Eric's head; and—slowly—pulled out.

The black driver with his fat cock had come forward to wait on Eric's other side from Shit. As the boatman's cock fell free to rest beside the enlarged testicle, Eric turned, expecting to see Al and the guy he was humping at the urinal. Instead he saw the cock in the driver's brown fist—and took it in his mouth, turning on his knees to face him.

"Sweet Jesus—" the driver breathed in sharply—"this boy got a' educated mouth." Though he was uncut and thick, he was…well, free of cheese and perspiration. And he only put one hand—too lightly for Eric—on Eric's shoulder.

Still, Eric was enjoying his enthusiasm. The driver came in under a minute. Eric took him deep and held him there, while he listened to the breathing above.

Finally, Eric slid off and grinned up. "You got an educated dick."

"I do?" The driver looked down, heavy brown face surprised. "Well, thank you, son. That's nice to hear. Real nice." His cock was softening. "Hey, Jay—he say I got a' educated dick. How you like that?"

As Eric kneeled back, the hood slipped forward.

"Well, I'm glad *sumpin'* about you's educated," Jay returned. "Somebody told me they seen you at Johnston's speakin' rally at the Interdenominational over at Hemmings. Don't tell me you gonna vote for a dumb white man like that? And vicious, besides. Nope!" Jay's forearm raised, his hand opened. "Nope. Nope! No politics in the damned john. I don't believe in it. And I ain't gonna start now."

The driver laughed, putting himself away.

A hand grasped Eric's other shoulder, slid under his arm, and pulled Eric up. He looked over and smiling at him was the tall unshaven white guy—Dynamite, yeah, that's right—in his overalls and work shoes. The bib hid most of the garbage truck. "Hey, there—we don't want your knees gettin' sore."

"Uh…thanks," Eric said.

Dynamite smiled: half *his* teeth were gone—and Eric thought, this forty-odd-year-old cracker, smiling at me, with his hazel eyes and brown hair—a head taller than both Eric and Shit—could have been cousin or brother to any hillbilly he'd ever had under the highway. Both Shit and the big boatman and the taller of the black drivers (in Eric's estimation) were better looking. Still, for pure raw sex appeal only the Mexican sitting on the shitter rivaled him.

With his thumb, Dynamite pointed over at Jay, lingering now by the Mexican's stall. "Jay MacAmon over there says you might be around awhile—you interested in a job?"

(So colorful before, across the john, the boatman's biceps—thick as tire tubes—were now wrapped in shadow.)

"Huh?" Eric blinked. "Jay…? Eh…yeah—maybe. What kind?"

"Over in Diamond Harbor. Haulin' garbage with me and Shit." The thumb went toward the light-skinned black kid, Shit. The very wide thumb (like Shit's) did not have a lot of nail left—nor, indeed, did any of his fingers.

(Why couldn't *I* have hair like Shit's…? Puffy hair—) To protect himself from the feeling of confusion, Eric was about to add, *Well, I dunno…*

—when, against the wall, watching the whole room and, clearly and equally, watching Dynamite talk to Eric, Shit raised an equally big and knuckly hand to his face, dug a broad forefinger into a broader nostril, pushed, twisted, pulled the finger free, and put it in his mouth, while he watched.

Chills engulfed Eric, not just on his back, but from foot soles—as if he no longer stood on the floor but rather atop six inches of raging electricity—to scalp. Suddenly everything sexual about the encounter so far, he realized, had been some version or another of the ordinary. Every sexual evaluation he had formed or forgotten over the six or seven minutes—really, it couldn't have been longer—since he'd entered the john revised itself into something extraordinary. If Eric had had any hair there to speak of, it would have danced on his scalp.

A collar of over-thick fingers, Shit's other fist hung on his dick, which, with the cuffed head protruding an inch, still looked hard. A droplet glimmered on the bottom of his foreskin.

(Eric thought about going over, squatting, licking it off...)

The urinal's timer turned over. (Since last time, it felt like five minutes—certainly no more than six.) Again water flushed the steel. (Fluffles, flaps, flops, floshes...)

With their unreadable black markings, Al's arms gripped Ted's yellow shirt. In his jeans, with his belt end swinging, Al's thrusting buttocks clocked the world.

Somewhere inside himself, Eric found the words, "Yeah. Sure, I..." obliterating his wariness. He hadn't intended to say them. But he had.

"You got somethin' I can write on?" Dynamite took three inches of pencil from his pocket, while Eric thrust his hand into his own pocket (I can't feel *anything*...! Glittering chills armored him...) and managed to get out the paper Bottom had given him that morning. He handed it to Dynamite.

"If you gonna be around a few months and serious about workin', show up at the Gilead dock come Wednesday mornin'—four-thirty, four-fifty. We get started by five." On the paper's back, with heavy, soiled fingers, Dynamite scribbled, then, keeping the pencil, returned the paper to Eric.

"Thank you—hey, thanks!" Eric found his voice. "Yeah—hey! Thank you! Sure." Taking back the paper, without looking at it, he returned it to his pocket. As if he were encased in electric armor, Eric reached between Dynamite's legs.

If Dynamite had knocked his hand away, he wouldn't have been surprised.

"Now what, son...?" Dynamite smiled. The skin on his neck and arms was sun-roughened and redder than Shit's. "You want some more of this Georgia cracker dick?" He pushed the pencil into a pocket on his bibs, moved...toward Eric, who still fingered the work-softened denim to grip the man's cock. Dynamite reached for his own chest, looked down, and unsnapped one strap, then the second.

As his pants dropped again, Dynamite's hands came out and took Eric by the shoulders. He bent his face down and opened his mouth.

Then, his hands like slabs supporting Eric's back, the back of Eric's head, Dynamite's tongue went in, thickening and thinning against Eric's. It tasted...God, *good*! The smell was like Jay's, with a different automotive overlay.

(Regular instead of diesel...?)

Shit had moved up, too, breathing hard, waiting his turn, finger still in his mouth.

Though he was no longer picking.

Through the long kiss, Eric thought: My goddam tongue is glittering—and finally dropped to his knees for Dynamite's cock—thick, big, uncut—that pushed against his upper lip, then went into his mouth.

In small, upward movements, surely timed to Dynamite's heart, it hardened.

It had salt and—Eric got his tongue under the skin and into the circular pocket around the head—cheese. This guy was *so* good—not, Eric thought, that Scott would agree. But Scott wasn't sucking the redneck sonofabitch. His mouth filled with that cock that was—again Eric took it to the root—bigger than Jay's, if not so thick as the black driver's, while, with another heartbeat, it expanded to the size of Shit's.

Fingers like bars, rough as rust, Dynamite held Eric's head, his cheeks. Denim bound Dynamite's thighs. Eric reached between them, under the long scrotum and moved his hand up warm buttocks, firm, flat, furry, to feel more testicles behind the garbage man, swinging into the back of his hand. Eric's fingers stubbed the firm stock moving there.

Shit had moved forward and was *again* fucking the guy!

Once Eric kneeled on a bib-denim strap across the tiles, as Dynamite tried to step with his big shoe and staggered. . . "Damn, boy—what you doin'? Tryin' to pull me over?"

"I'm tryin' to *see*," Shit rasped, softly, roughly, on Dynamite's back. "I wanna watch your fuckin' cock goin' in and out this white scumbag's mother-fuckin' suck hole!" Yeah, he *had* to be black...

Eric gripped one of Dynamite's hands—as big as Shit's—as he moved to the side.

"Hey, *yeah*..." Shit drawled from above in an uprush of pleasure. "I got it now. Good. I can see it. *Okay*!"

Eric heard shoes on the concrete behind him, then felt something press his back—a hand slid under his jeans.

"What you doin', Al—?"

And the other driver said, "Nigger, you gonna kill that boy—he can't take that thing like Ted!"

Al said, his voice like something way under the ground, "Why the fuck not...?"

Eric wondered if Ted had gone when his own attention had been elsewhere. (He hadn't heard the door springs.) How had he left such a small space without Eric hearing—even if Eric *was* sucking someone off?

Apparently, though, Ted had.

"Least I'm gonna try—" which was Al's voice lowering behind!

Reaching for his own waist with one hand, Eric thumbed his jeans' button out of its hole.

"See, dere—he don't min'. He wan' me to."

Someone—Al, on his knees behind him—tugged Eric's loosened pants back below his buttocks. Already Eric could smell him, adding to Jay's, the black driver's, Dynamite's automotive odors. It was not the smell of the black homeless men Eric had gotten used to in Atlanta. (The plastic road vest had its own odor.) It was the smell of a man who'd been working hard outdoors, like the smell of some odd wood, sawn fresh—cedar or sequoia—that Eric was not familiar with but wanted to smell again. He pushed as if he were taking a crap—the way, just two weeks ago (*De firs' time or so, da's de* only *way you gonna get it all in, bitch. So* push, *cocksucker!*) Frack had taught him. Al entered him. "Yeah—hey, da's goin' in jus' as easy...I *thought* it might..."

"*Goddam...!*" Shit whispered above them.

Al's arms gripped him—whatever wood it was ripsawed end-to-end, yielding its intense smell—and he no longer had to work at sucking Dynamite, because Al's rhythm moved Eric's head in and out. All he had to do was hold himself up.

"Jesus, boy—what, you come in here already greased, *too?* Da's fuckin' sociable!" Since Al was supporting his own weight, it felt pretty good. "I thought it was jus' niggers who was supposed to be so greasy. Not all you nasty white fucks." Eric heard Al's grin and—still sucking—grinned with him.

No, Al's cock was *not* as big as Frack's, but it would have poked from a ripped pocket by two or three inches. And did he care about the difference between fifteen and seventeen?

Three minutes later, Dynamite came.

Five seconds after that, Al grunted, "Oh. Shit...I *love* dese fuckin' nasty white holes." (Jesus, Eric felt really low and really good...) Then the warmth pulled from Eric's back.

He flinched, because, yes, KY or no, Al's pullout stung.

"Jesus, that looked fuckin' *great*..." someone said; it took a second for

Eric to realize that, over Dynamite's shoulder, it was Shit.

Dynamite had taken seconds to harden—and took seconds to soften. Eric sucked the firm cock as deep as he could and wallowed cum around it, even prizing his tongue beneath the foreskin to let some liquid in, till the man's hands halted his head.

The muscles at the back of Dynamite's cock tightened—familiar from Pickle—as a spurt of salt urine flushed Eric's mouth…surprising him (Pickle primed or not). Eric sucked deep again, swallowing. He kept at it, ten, fifteen, twenty seconds, hoping for more, even as he stilled his tongue. Finally, looking up, he saw the man grinning down. (Eric patted Dynamite's leg, squeezed it.) But that was all that happened. Dynamite's grip loosened around his head and he let Eric back away.

Sitting on his heels, Eric worked one foot and another under himself to lever upright, losing Al's hands from his flank. "Oh, fuck…!" He glanced back, to see Al, buttons opened around the latex sheath. "Hey, thanks," Eric said. He was breathing hard. As with Frack, he thought: *How did I get all that in…?* "That was…good!" *Maybe I'm learning…*

Or just stretching…

Al drawled, "I know damned well it was." Chuckling at Eric, he moved back toward the urinal. "I don't bother fuckin' *nobody* 'less I do it good."

Eric looked again at the garbage man—

"Ain't no point to it." Al bounced his sheathed cock on his palm.

Penis sagging, Dynamite stepped back; he grinned at Eric, too. Shaking his head, again he began to drag up his pants, then pushed himself into his overalls.

Eric managed to stand and, looking around, saw Shit coming back, over uneven concrete, edging between Jay and the driver Eric had sucked off, leading the other black driver, a solid, dark fellow in a blue T-shirt, in his late thirties or early forties.

Shit held the man's cock—pulling him by it, it looked like.

As he followed, the second driver smiled, looking somewhat embarrassed. (Dynamite had stepped over to Al. They were whispering about something.) Eric was slightly confused. But Shit reached out with his free hand and—now—took hold of Eric's cock. The driver Shit led stepped up to Eric and as Shit positioned himself before both of them, smiled at Eric, and put his arm around Eric's shoulder. His dark face was further shadowed by bushy brows.

Eric smiled back, curious.

Holding both penises, Shit dropped to a squat and, in his large, heavy hands, pulled Eric and the driver's penises together, both—one dark, thick-veined, and uncut, the other a heavy pink over an ivory skin, circumcised, and bullet-headed. The black one straight, Eric's slightly up-curved, both were erect.

Eric looked down at Shit's mustard nap. Already the rough hair had a thinning spot, though he'd have been surprised if the kid was twenty. Behind him, Eric could see his wide, bare feet, his cracked blackened soles, the toes of one propped up and turned under, the pads of the other stretched behind, dirt gone shiny from walking.

Shit put the black guy's cock in his mouth. Eric felt Shit's beard against his own dick. Then he came off and took Eric's cock in his warm, warm mouth.

Eric's smile became a grin.

Shit's thick-fingered hands—bitten nails and big knuckles, both lined with black—were grubby from his work. His mouth went back and forth. Looked at from above, his nose seemed particularly broad and Negroid, and—hell—sexy.

Now Shit glanced up. He chuckled. "I wish my dick was more like one of these or the other. But it's just in the fuckin' middle."

Eric was surprised—because Shit's generously uncut cock was between half and three-quarters of an inch longer than either. It had never occurred to Eric someone could want a cock smaller than his own.

Shit went back to sucking them both.

The black driver beside him smiled at Eric. As Eric looked at his face, the full mouth opened and came forward. The broad lips kissed Eric, who opened his mouth to receive the driver's tongue, which went no further in than Eric's lips. His unshaven face turned against Eric's.

The driver closed his eyes—then opened them; and pulled his mouth away.

Eric blinked.

The driver looked stern.

(Shit's mouth came back to Eric's cock. His hand moved around to Eric's leg, where, as his mouth went in and out, the fingers flexed on the denim.)

Softly, the driver said to Eric: "Did that man you was suckin' off before piss in your mouth, boy?" He nodded over toward Dynamite.

Momentarily, Eric was flustered: "Uh…Yeah. A little—I guess."

The driver's body stiffened. Without dropping, his arm loosened. He moved back a chilly inch. "Dat's the third time that cracker sonofabitch done that to some good lookin' fella what come in here in the last two months—it jus' messes it up for the rest of us. You'd think he was a damn tomcat, markin' his territory. And Jeb—my partner over there—*still* likes 'im." He nodded toward the taller, better-looking driver. "But then, Jeb is strange." Now he gave Eric's bare shoulder in its tank top strap a consoling pat, then dropped his hand. "Well, I guess it ain't your fault. I just gotta get to you guys a'fore he do." Shaking his head, he turned away, wiping his wrist across his mouth.

And Shit rose before Eric, a hand either side, his chest and then the waist of his pants dragging over Eric's cock. Shit's green eyes, his wonderfully broad nose, his mouth were against Eric's face. Eric's eyes were open to see both of Shit's, equally wide. Then Shit's tongue probed and rolled and wrestled around Eric's.

Seconds later, Shit pulled back to whisper: "I *like* how it tastes. It ain't bad—it's real nice. It's just regular redneck cracker piss. That nigger's *crazy!*"

Eric was glad of the reminder different people liked different things.

Shit's hard hand holding Eric's shoulder moved to Eric's back. At their groins, in an all-but-uncomfortable position, in which the pleasure of excitement turned into something interesting, their cocks crossed. Their scrotums hung against one another's.

With one hand, Eric held the back of Shit's neck and, with the other, the small of Shit's back. He could feel Shit's body, breathing, against his, even as he smelled him.

And breathed, thinking, for all the fucking around he'd done with guys he didn't usually get *this* close to them. This was really…nice.

Shit whispered, "You okay…?"

Eric whispered, "Yeah."

"Good." And Shit released him, and stepped back. "I hope he pisses in your mouth some more. Go on, try somebody else now."

Not sure he wanted to, Eric watched Shit back up against the wall, where, again (as though he had backed outside the circle of perception of all other eight men in the room, so that the aura of isolation made Shit even sexier), the kid dug his middle finger in one nostril, sucked it clean, dug in the other, sucked it, digging and sucking, digging and sucking—

Surprising himself, Eric stood, stepped up to him—Shit blinked his green eyes—and opened his mouth as if he was going to tongue wrestle Shit again; but Eric took in the forefinger, with its salted crust. Shit's hands were as big as Dynamite's, with the same teeth-tortured nails. Eric saw—and a moment later felt with his tongue—the gritty forefinger. Again the kid hugged Eric—with one arm, this time, and kissed him.

The finger was now back in Shit's mouth—

Till it reversed to push into Eric's—

Then back.

Then back and forth…

Finally, smiling, Shit whispered, "You taste good." Nodding toward Dynamite, he moved his face away, grinning. "It's nice lickin' piss outta somebody's mouth or asshole. You go kiss on Mex. He always drinkin' somebody's piss—Jay's or Jeb's or some other nigger's. Hey—I wanna shoot, now—I'm ready. You want it?" His jeans were up, but his cock—hard—and balls were still loose.

"Yeah…!" Eric dropped again to the tile. One of Shit's pants legs was torn, and his knee's smudged geometry showed through the rip. Since he'd have eaten out Dynamite's ass out in a minute, Eric was not going to die from sucking Dynamite's crap off Shit's dick.

He took Shit in his mouth.

Shit grunted, caught Eric's head, and, propping the toes of one foot on Eric's knee, began to pump. Eric hugged his legs. The cloth was some sort of brown corduroy, Eric saw—but it had been hard to recognize, because so much of the wale had worn away.

In forty seconds, Shit shot, too.

It was thick and nut like. Eric swallowed…a third of it.

Lingering, Eric sucked, hoping for piss from this one.

None came.

Then Dynamite was beside him, tugging him up to cover his mouth with his own—stubble ground on Eric's face—and plunged his own tongue as far in as he could.

Eric held to his hard shoulders, a head higher than Shit's, wondering at having so quickly gotten five loads.

When they broke for breath, Dynamite stepped back, breathed in deeply, one strap fastened, one hanging. "You know—" Dynamite grinned—"I was serious about what I was sayin' before." Their uncut cocks—Dynamite's and Shit's—were the same size, with the same down curve, same thickness. Eric held one in each hand. He rubbed the hooded heads together. "About that job—when Jay was introducin' us."

Both of them smiled, missing their different teeth.

Was Shit's a hair's breadth wider? Or maybe it only looked so because Shit was a hair's breadth shorter…

Reaching down, Dynamite gripped loosely and supportively the complex construction the two—then three, because Eric pushed forward with his own—cocks had become.

Eric was about to answer—

—when, with his blond beard and missing incisors, towering Jay (as tall as Al) stepped up beside him, a hand again on Eric's tank top shoulder, and pulled him away. "You know, you ain't come yet yourself, puppy. Get on over here. We gonna fuck Mex's face some—so you can get off and get outa here. Let's stick some dick into this spic cocksucker and finish you up."

"Huh? But I don't—" Eric gasped in a breath, looking for a sink or something to lean on, and settled one had on the urinal's rolled metal upper edge—"know if I really have to..." Protectively, Eric reached down with the other to hold himself. Probably it *was* time to put it away—

"Hey, don't worry." Jay rubbed his own tattooed arm. "I'll make you."

The heavy black trucker said, "Yeah—Jay's a good guy. He gets all concerned over that stuff."

Al was looking thoughtfully around the room and shucking on himself—still in his condom, its front inch full and sagging and ballooning another inch-and-a-half around the head, its liquid the color of pus.

...Flosh, flap, flop, fluffle—

—on its timer (another five minutes...?), water flushed the urinal's bright back.

Across his lighter palm, Al bounced his cock—or the half of it his hand held. On the urinal's back plate, distorted to unreadability, mangled and mingled reflections—of his black arms and their blacker marks—moved in the same rhythm.

"I guess Ted was in a rush—" Dynamite glanced at Eric—"but, then, he pretty much always is, ain't he? Hey, Al? How'd you know you wasn't gonna kill this boy here with that damned cattle prod? I mean, Ted's one of your regulars. But ain't that dangerous, stickin' so much into somebody you ain't gone into, a little more slow, before? I mean, careful, like?"

Chuckling, Al reached into his pocket and pulled out a familiar tube: KY Lubricant. "Well—" Al shrugged—"this done fell out his pocket when he reached in to get that paper you was writin' on." (Eric looked over, surprised...) "So I thought it was worth a try. It didn't feel like he was having a *whole* lotta trouble takin' my ol' phone pole, any more than he had suckin' on Dynamite's ol' pig fucker. Hey—" Al grinned at Eric; no, they weren't *all* there. But he had more teeth than either Dynamite or Shit—"you want this back, boy?"

"Oh...!" Reaching over, Eric took the tube. "Eh...Thank you!" No, feeling his pants he realized it *wasn't* in his pocket—!

Eric pushed it in.

"'Sides—you muscle boys is always *real* nasty. Least ways, the good ones I know what come in here is." Al grimaced. "Like Jay here." He nodded toward the boatman, with his brilliant arms, bulked like some wrestler's.

"Come on," Al said. "Gimme a hand with this."

Below Al's T-shirt sleeves, the black etchings caught the light with a different reflective index than the rest of his dark, dark skin...though still unreadable.

Again, Al bounced his own—yes—massive dick on his palm. (Two of those in one week, Eric thought. Is that luck, or…?) Eric stepped over to him; both looked down at what he held. "Ted run outta here 'fore I got a chance to shoot. Since I spilled this up yo' butt instead, dis heah is for you, now. Help me get dis fuckin' raincoat off…" Eric reached out and they slid the condom, yellow like dried airplane glue but wrinkly as Saran, from his penis.

With one hand, tall Al held the condom, bloated with what had to be four or five tablespoons full. The supersized rubber was almost a quarter full! With his other, Al knotted its upper end. "Now, see, you got somethin' to remember me by. A *big* ol' load o' prime nigger jizz—you carry it on home: dat can be yo' dessert tonight!"

"I swear," Jay said, "I seen horses what didn't come that much. Al's really half horse—everybody down here says that about 'im. Don't they? Hey, Al—you ain't gonna give that to Mex?" (Al shook his head.) "Fuck it, right *now* he's sittin' there grinnin' and tryin' to look big and brave for you guys in here, but unless I do sumpin' special for 'im, later he's gonna be cryin' in my arms." One hand on Eric's back, one on his arm, Jay moved Eric toward the stall.

Some of them laughed—including the broad faced Mexican on the commode. His cheeks and neck were like raddled leather, with pits and indentations from long-healed acne. A fold of flesh along one side of his jaw half hid a dozen craters, which Eric had an overwhelming desire to finger.

Knees wide apart, Mex sat on the stained, seatless enamel, cradling his own cock in a red-brown palm.

Mex's wide feet were as far apart on the floor as the black jeans around his ankles allowed. With thick fingers he lifted his cock now and again into sight.

Al said, "Maybe he can look up da kid in town at da Harbor dis evenin'. Dey can share it, 'fore you guys go on out to Gilead. Hell—dere's enough in dat thing for *three* cocksuckers! You always sayin' dat about my loads, Jay. I'm supposed to be a fuckin' horse, ain't I? Hey—" he gestured with the long latex tube to Eric—"slip dat horse rubber in your pocket, boy— and don' let it bust on ya'."

Eric took it. "Thanks—I…I guess." Surprised at how proud he suddenly felt he pushed it, flopping over the ham of his thumb, yielding under his poking fingers, into his pocket beside the returned KY tube. "Thank you, sir!"

Others laughed.

Flat on the tile, Mex's wide feet were as grubby as Shit's. They looked as rough and as hard. Inside the doorless stall, with one hand, Mex beckoned Eric—and opened his mouth…

Eric stepped forward.

Jay gripped him, pushed Eric within as Mex closed mouth and tongue around him, and moved his hand away.

His cock the center of it, heat engulfed him, rushed up Eric's belly, into his chest, down his thighs, pooling at the backs of his knees.

Down below a crease at Mex's navel, the stocky guy's amber ankles held apart the infinity sign his jeans made, without drawers. Broad nosed, wide-jawed, hair black and smooth, Eric's cock rounding his mouth, Mex grinned up with his pitted face. Forward of his foreskin, a ridge of whitish yellow encircled Mex's own cock head—which Eric could see down between the thick thighs below his chin each time the Mexican's mouth slid back. With the taste of Dynamite's cheese and urine and the memory of Jay's, Eric felt the simple sight of Mex's turning him on as much as the yearning in the man's raised eyes. Eric's cock slid in and out Mex's mouth. Left of them, the stall wall was thick with blue paint. In it were three ordinary sized glory holes. To the right, another Eric hadn't seen was wide enough for a whole head!

Beside Eric and, belly to belly with him, both of them turned only a little to the side, now bearded Jay slid his own cock into Mex's face alongside Eric's. Eric felt it rubbing, to the side and slightly below, his own.

As he often did, Eric thought: Why did I have to end up cut? It would be great to look like all these guys here; or Mike—

Wetness and heat increased around the flesh thrusting from Eric's groin.

"Hey, Mex. Here's that sumpin' special—"

Jay was *urinating*!

Eric could feel the Mexican swallowing around his cock, while he sucked them both.

And Dynamite had wedged up against Eric to hug him from behind. One of the drivers chuckled. "Dere go de white guys again, makin' some damned spic or a damned nigger do all the *real* work!" On one side, the boatman pressed against him, while, at his other, Shit slid in. (Eric thought: Well, Shit's a nigger. God, I wished to hell *I* was. Maybe they'd like me more…) Again Eric reached to grip barefoot Shit's thickly veined dick. His green shirt still hanging open, Shit put one arm tight around Eric's shoulder, staring down like an examining demigod. Looking with him, Eric saw that one of Shit's bare feet was over one of Mex's.

In the cave of Mex's mouth, boiling—it felt like—around Eric's cock, dripping from Eric's testicles, running down the barrel-solid Mexican's chin and chest between Mex's own black denims, dripping on Mex's own fist, running over Eric and Mex's cocks, the boatman's piss was…well, hot and incredible!

Between himself and Jay, beneath the hair, were crickets, fish, frogs, shells, shooting stars, scalloped leaves, waves spuming, clouds billowing, vine tendriling, atoms exploding, squid spewing.

Flames, red and yellow, flared over Jay's arm.

Eric came—

—and grabbed Mex's head, leaning forward. Like beads of buckshot, Mex's semen—warm—struck the bottom of Eric's (and probably the boatman's) testicles. Of course they didn't hurt—but they hit harder than Eric would have expected.

Jay pushed back, Dynamite loosened his grip, and Mex sat up, now, on the shitter's enamel rim…

Mex'd reached up and rubbed Jay's big ball.

Grinning, his cock a rod against his jeans, with his cream-and-coffee wool, Shit reached down where Mex's wet fist had returned to his dick. As Mex relaxed his grip, Shit pushed a thick forefinger under Mex's loose skin and, with the skin riding over the forejoint, circled the head. Mex made a sound like, "Urrgghh…!" opening his lips around the dicks in his mouth— piss and something thicker spilled his pitted chin—while Shit pulled his forefinger free with its flaky load, and, standing now, pushed it into Eric's mouth.

Eric sucked the stuff off, surprised—

—while the Mexican looked equally surprised…and pleased.

Shit stood, dug in his own nose with the same finger, sucked it, then pushed that into Eric's mouth, too. "I make even more of that stuff than *he* do." Shit nodded down at Mex with considered seriousness. "I mean, if you really like it. But mine all got rubbed off up *his* ass—" With his other wide, blunt thumb, he pointed at Dynamite (again fixing his bib)—"when you first come in. Otherwise, you coulda' had mine." His arm went on around Eric, and he hugged him again—and again thrust his tongue into Eric's face. While he was doing it, the boatman whispered something into Shit's ear.

Shit halted long enough to ask, "Huh?"

"Go on," the boatman said. "Do it again…go on, now. Like you did before. Do it."

"…Huh?" Shit repeated, frowning. Then he raised that same, heavy forefinger to prod once more in a nostril, turning it one way and the other. Eric has already seen that, where the nails were supposed to be, far back from his nubs, the flesh was gnawed into deep and broken pits. When the loaded forefinger came loose, again Eric opened his mouth.

Grinning, Shit pushed it inside.

"See..." The boatman smiled. "Sex is like cards, Shit, 'specially in this place. Remember. Lead from your strength."

Shit grinned at him—

"Yeah, you always tell me that."

—while on the expanded articulations of Jay's colorful arms, Eric saw:

A web beneath an elbow—violet along the strands' tops, dark red to black below—the darker flesh at the center gnarled as a walnut, threads decked with drops of dew: inked on each less-than-quarter-inch sphere, a curved reflection of a window that might have been in the parlor where the work had once been done but was not in Turpens' john. Seahorses, scorpions, moths, and spiders scurried under blond fur. Over a green and blue shrimp, with red highlights from a nearby fire, yellow hair swirled. Barbed wire made a doubled strand, the barbs themselves where one was twisted and cut before it sank through a skull's socket, emerged from the darkness on the other side of the bone's ragged nose hole. Through foam, cloud, and hair, a squid leapt from the sea with straining tentacles, two longer and broader than the rest, to challenge a dragon, diving from its cloud, astonishment on both non-human faces. In the same montage, giving the effect of something much, much closer—or much, much larger—a frog clung to a rock in the spume, inked with every bubble, splash, and splatter. It gazed up, where stars shot, yellow, green, and red, beyond curling cumulus, scalloped leaves, breaking waves, tendrils coiled below enfolded buds and bursting atoms. Toward his wide shoulders, red and yellow and orange fires entwined star-dusted galaxies and twisted vegetation, as though the world the boatman's biceps pictured was burning.

Shit's salty forefinger in Eric's mouth and the ruined nail's roughness in its callused bed prodded desire's central heat—

"Now, remember," Jay said. "You got your ride waitin' for you. You better get on."

"Yeah." Eric started to turn away, as from a moment of preternatural awareness. Dynamite nudged Shit's bare foot with his work shoe—Shit was prodding again in his nose with a thick middle finger. This time, though, Shit ate it himself, as unconcerned as Eric might have been, alone, exploring an empty Atlanta alley.

That unconcern, finally, was the most erotically loaded thing Eric had seen in the crowded john.

One of the drivers laughed, possibly at something else, while again more electricity pulsed through Eric. "Hey, thanks." That was to Mex, who smiled at him, nodded.

Would he see the black kid again?

Approvingly, Jay nodded. "Come on." The boatman's hand tightened on Eric's shoulder, then tugged. "You don't wanna get in no trouble—"

Wondering if he'd ever get closer to Al's black markings (and, he thought, I didn't get to tongue fuck yet with Mex…), Eric glanced at the tattooed boatman, to realize, as they pushed from the john door, now he could see all Jay's smaller pictures.

* * *

[1] EIGHTEEN MINUTES AND nine seconds after going in through the saloon-style doors, the hempen giant (with his arm fur, belly hair, and tattoos) came out, red shirt opened, jeans closed, his Turpens cap folded in his back pocket. Beside him, Eric tugged up his zipper.

In the hall, Jay chuckled.

When they reached the turn, ahead Eric could see the inside window—and the inside door—of Turpens Parts & Notions.

"Um…I gotta go." Eric didn't move but rocked a little, as if half paralyzed. "This was great. Really. I hope I…see you again—" Fascination held him.

"Awww—" At once the boatman's arm swung around Eric's shoulder for a surprising hug. He tugged. One of Eric's sneakers left the floor. "I'd count on it, if I was you. Diamond Harbor ain't that big, son. Mex ain't gonna believe this, but I wouldn't be surprised if maybe we got us another puppy."

Steadying himself, Eric found his hand plowing the hair on Jay's belly. Jesus, the guy was hard—and warm. "Hey…but, see, I need to get a cap. Real quick."

Jay released him. "Go on, then." Eric got his balance.

Eric grinned. "My name's Eric. Eric Jeffers. And you're…? I'm sorry—I forgot…"

"I'm still Jay MacAmon. Just like Dynamite told you. Like I say, Mex and me run the scow out to Gilead Island. Don't worry. We'll see you in the Harbor. Look for me or a barefoot spic. We're about as easy to find as fish scales on a fisherman's feet—though there ain't even too many of those 'round here no more. So are the garbage men—the one walkin' 'round with no shoes half the time is Shit." He winked an amber eye. "Morgan. That's his regular name. But I guess you know that."

He hadn't. "Yeah…" Eric said. "Okay. Sure. But I need that cap."

Jay nodded—and Eric turned, ran up the hall to the glass door, and pushed inside.

* * *

[2]   BRAVES, MARLINS, CARDINALS, Senators, Orioles, Rangers, Astros, Yankees, Pirates, Red Sox—ball caps hung on the backboard's hooks. (*I just got loads from five of them eight guys—some good cheesy ones, too. That ain't bad for fifteen minutes. And one's still in my pocket...*) Eric took down an orange one—Turpens, with its departing eagle—and walked toward the counter.

The unshaven counterman wore a cowboy shirt. His hair was salt and pepper gray. (*I even ate snot from that black kid...Wow!* That *was a first!* Shit's nose was even wider than Mike's. *I wonder if I'll ever get my tongue up that...*) Between his dark and light blue lapels, a rug of black covered his chest.

Eric passed a dummy in camouflage fatigues. "How much is this?"

"Baseball caps is nine fifty. That's just five. Not too many guys get the Turpens ones." Thrust from blue snap cuffs, on six inches of wrist, at the ends of long, long arms, a high-veined fist, with big knuckles, opened flat on the counter glass.

Eric reached in his pocket—and for a heart-thudding moment thought his wallet was gone. Then he felt his KY tube, below the folded paper Bottom had given him and Dynamite had written on. With a deeper prod, his fingers stubbed leather.

Someone said, "What took you so long?"

Eric turned sharply to see Mike. "Hey—I went as fast as I could."

"Actually," Mike said, "you did pretty well. You said twenty—and it's just that now. I came in to try the AC—'cause I don't like to leave it on in the car when I'm not drivin'. Uses up the battery."

"That's the God's honest truth," the counterman said. "You with the kid, here?"

Without looking at Mike, Eric said: "This is my dad."

"His step dad," Mike corrected. (Why did he *do* that? Eric wondered. He wished Mike would let *them* figure it out.) "I'm taking the boy to stay with his mama, at Diamond Harbor."

"Oh," the older man said. "Yeah. The Harbor's a nice place—now that it's summer. Nobody's around the rest of the time, though. Even *this* summer's pretty slow. Ain't hardly no fishin' boats at the marina. Runcible ain't doin' too well, either, with all them new tourist cabins they built goin' beggin'. Five dollars twenty-eight cents—with tax. That orange is a good color for you, son. Hell, 'cause you're gettin' a Turpens one, I'll forget the twenty-eight cents. Just gimme five."

He smiled at Mike, then at Eric.

By a corner, Eric pulled the bill with Lincoln's picture from his wallet. "Thanks."

Someone else said, "Hello, there, Abbott."

Eric looked over.

And started.

He looked at Mike, who'd begun paging through a catalog on the counter.

With his jaw clenched, Eric tried to make himself relax.

The guy in the yellow shirt—and the handkerchief—strolled up. On his neck was Al's purple hickey, like wrestling crayfish.

As Eric took the cap, the register man said, "Hi, Ted. What can I do for you?"

Eric felt as if he were plunging down some well with sparkling walls.

"Nothin'—I'm good. I came in to use the facilities and say hello, that's all. This is a scorcher, isn't it?"

"Sure is." Rangy Abbott looked at Eric. "You want that in a bag, son?"

"Thanks," Eric said. "No. That's okay." He opened his mouth, took a very slow, very long breath.

Ted said to Mike and Eric, "You guys picked a hot day to travel." He did *not* look at Eric, and Eric's heart got faster, then began to settle.

Mike said, "Mmm," pushed over a page of pictures, pushed over another, then turned away.

Jesus, Eric thought. He ain't gonna say nothin'. I gotta stop this…

Ted said, "'Bye."

But Eric's throat was so tight, the *Good-bye, sir,* he tried to get out would not sound.

Orange cap still in his hand—his thumb sweaty on its stiff material—Eric followed his dad.

(Maybe Ted had been so intent on Al's cock, he hadn't recognized…?)

With Mike slowing at piles of CB radios and racks of manuals and sparkplug boxes, they walked to the door.

As Eric pushed out behind his father into sweltering day, across the lot a blue pickup backed from its parking place. On the sagging tailgate, in silver gaffers' tape, someone had spelled out:

DYNAMITE

REFUSE

As it swung around, Eric made out where someone had filled in "Shit &," with a broad black Sharpie, probably like the ones in Eric's backpack behind the seat on the Chevy's floor mat.

"Shit &" slanted up over the "D" in DYNAMITE. ("Shit & Dynamite Refuse"—the truck read!) Eric breathed—and, because Mike wasn't looking, let himself grin.

The pickup rolled forward, but not toward the highway feed: it pulled to another exit in the diamond-wire fence and was gone on some local road.

"Hey! Eric—the car's over *here*!"

"Oh, yeah…" Mike hadn't noticed anything. Eric started walking again. But, then, often Mike didn't.

* * *

[3] GETTING INTO THE car was like climbing into hot oiled cotton. Mike turned the ignition. As they started forward, he switched on the Chevy's air conditioning. From under the dashboard cold air hit Eric's pants, flattening the faintly dirtied denim to Eric's shins.

"Hey…" Mike said. "That guy back there wasn't…botherin' you, was he?"

More sharply than he'd intended, Eric turned to his dad. "What?" He'd been wondering whether to brush at the cloth on his knees or to leave them so as not to attract Mike's attention.

"I mean in the restroom or anything. Lookin' at you funny, maybe."

Eric made himself relax. "What guy?"

By stubby white posts with white cable strung between, they rolled onto the highway's service road.

"The guy in the store. He had a birthmark or somethin' on his neck…"

It wasn't like falling into that well. "The guy behind the counter? He wasn't even *in* the restroom." But it was like leaning over its glittering edge.

"Not him. The *other* one—I saw him go into the place just ahead of you, the same time you went in. The one who stopped to talk to us at the counter when we were comin' out—?"

"*Him?*" Eric asked. "He *could* have been. I was in the stall…with the door closed. So I didn't see. Which probably means he didn't see *me*… unless he was lookin' funny at my…sneakers."

"Oh," Mike said. "Yeah. Okay."

Eric put his new cap on the dashboard, then lifted his butt to dig in his pocket. (A memory of when the KY cap had once come loose, lubricant messing his pants…) His middle fingers passed something splodgy: Al's knotted rubber. Glancing to make sure Mike was looking at the road, Eric pulled his hand free to touch his fingertips to his lips. They were dry: it hadn't ruptured. With the same hand, again Eric reached in his pocket to push the KY down. Again, it had almost slipped free—

Beside his wallet, he felt Bottom's paper.

Working it loose, he tugged the paper out and—with a deep breath—unfolded it. His rectum was vaguely sore, but with what, long ago, he'd learned to think of as a good soreness. And damp.

"What's that?" Mike asked.

"Something Bill said I should read when I got to Diamond Harbor."

"What's it say?"

Eric opened it again, to see Gothic letters—like the ones on the sign: *A Georgia Institution*…"He must have printed it out on his computer. This mornin'." Haltingly, Eric read it out loud:

"'He who makes a beast of himself gets rid of the pain of being a man—Dr. Samuel Johnson.'"

Mike said, "I heard that one before."

In ordinary type, Bill's message went on (and Eric read):

"'But note the good doctor said "beast," not "animal." For he who forgets the animal he is, has taken the first step toward becoming a beast.'" Eric looked up, frowning. The afternoon's image that briefly returned was Jay MacAmon's uncle, slamming his fist into the teeth of a tall twelve-year-old with wet jeans…

"That's some funny stuff." Mike moved the wheel. "But Bottom's a funny guy." Mike was thinking about Kelly-Ann, who, yeah, *could* be an animal…"He's okay, but he's…strange. You know, you should stay away from guys like that, Eric—Bill; or the one who was talkin' to us in the store, hear me? I met a couple of 'em in the pokey. Most guys don't even bother bein' polite to 'em. It just encourages 'em. And they're never gonna do you no good."

Eric nodded, turning the paper over. On the back, in big letters Dynamite had written:

SHIT & DYNAMITE
Show Up Gilead Boat Dock,
GARBAGE
4:45A.M. Sun.—Thurs.

So *that's* all it was.

Well, that's all Dynamite had said.

Refolding it, Eric pushed it back in his pocket past Al's pliant clam. "I think I'm gonna…try and get a job while I'm here. So I can give Barb a hand." *Had* he actually said *Yes* to Dynamite? Or had he only stood there grinning? He'd said *Hey—Thank you!* enthusiastically a few times. But either way he was going to find the Gilead boat dock.

"Now *that's* an idea," Mike said. "I'm glad to hear you talkin' that way."

At a turn, the orange Turpens cap slid forward off the dashboard's surface. Eric grabbed for it, missed—

But caught it with his forearm against his right knee. He smiled at Mike.

"You're probably gonna miss your football buddies." Looking out the windshield, driving, his father had not seen Eric's save. "Weren't there any guys on the team you really liked?"

"Maybe. I dunno." Taking the cap in his hands, Eric shrugged. "I wasn't really friends with none of 'em *too* much." (Maybe, besides running his boat with Mex, the bearded Jay worked at Turpens…?) "One guy, Hoagy—I wanted to get to know a little better." He glanced at his dad. "He was a black kid."

"Oh," Mike said. "I don't think I met him. Didn't some Spanish kid on the team—Scotty?—phone you a few times last term?"

Eric shrugged again. "That was for homework or somethin'. We wasn't really that close."

"Oh. Well, after you get to Barb's, see if you can hunt up some regular fellas to hang out with—guys who drink beer, shoot hoops, and talk about women. Know what I mean?"

"Jesus…" Eric looked back out the window. "*That* sounds like fun! Can I maybe hang out with some who do a little *more* than talk?"

Mike said nothing. But he smiled. In the car the cool air stabilized.

When they passed the green-and-white sign, "DIAMOND HARBOR, EXIT 3 MILES," the Turpens cap—orange visor pointed left—was on Eric's head.

Eric asked, "Dad, you remember that movie we saw a couple of years ago, when we were comin' back from Texas—in the mall we stopped at—just outside Atlanta?"

"Huh?"

"You know—where the gorilla and the dinosaurs were all fightin' over that girl—?"

"Yeah. That was a good one."

"*I* think it would be easier to fall in love with all the dinosaurs and things than…than with the gorilla. They were cool—even those giant bugs and stuff." Eric blinked at his father. "I liked them the best." He pushed back in the seat to sit up. "Anyway, that's what *I* think."

As he drove by the ocean, Mike's look grew puzzled. He frowned at his stepson.

* * *

[4] OFF THE HIGHWAY, Mike got turned around twice.

"You got your cell. You could call Barb—"

Mike took one hand off the wheel to touch the sagging pocket of his T-shirt where his cell phone hung. "I don't wanna give her the satisfaction of thinkin' the dumb-ass nigger she was stupid enough to marry once is a bigger fool than I actually am. Come on—we'll find it."

"You know," Eric said, "I wish I could say things like that, sometimes."

Mike raised an eyebrow. Then he chuckled and glanced at Eric. "You could—nobody's really gonna care. Least ways nobody who knows *I* brought you up." Then he added. "Course sometimes you gotta think twice about who you say it around." He shrugged. "It's just a kind of cussin', I guess."

And thirty-five minutes later they were on 31 East, where Barb had said they should be.

Mike muttered, "It's at the end of Front Street..." He looked under the sunshade.

"This *is* Front Street." Eric sat forward on the gray upholstery. "We just passed Front Street Drugs & Hardware."

"But it's closed up—"

"It's still Front Street," Eric insisted. "Hey, *there* it is!"

"This is the *end*...?" Mike slowed. "It ain't a whole block."

By the docks, blue siding framed a plate glass window with café curtains pushed back and blinds. On the pane, a gold and black decal of a lighthouse was fixed beside black letters—

LIGHTHOUSE
COFFEE,
EGG
& BACON

—to suggest an aquarium's interior, the window's floor, visible under the half-lowered slats, was covered with coral, green, and blue pebbles—though it was without fish, ceramic anchors, even a menu. Above, rust reddened the seams between the awning's pink and green panels.

Mike said, "I'm pullin' around with those cars near the water." The tires crunched into a small gravel lot, where three old pickups, two fairly new cars, and five old ones parked. Beyond, was the sea. "Yeah, that's your mama's Honda. She's *still* drivin' that thing—?"At the top of some steps of triple-width white cinderblocks stood a screen door. On one side ran a pipe railing, bright yellow. A plank ramp sloped from the other. It didn't look too steady.

Eric opened the car and again realized the discrepancy between the heat-drenched sunlight and the green tinted car window, which—with the air conditioning—had made the outside look ten degrees cooler than it was. As he stepped to the gravel and stood, he heard the *ga-lunk* of the door on Mike's side, opening.

Then the screen banged back on the wall and a woman in a blue waitress smock and no makeup came down one step, hesitating—as if she might rush back in.

Till age twenty-seven, Barbara had been stunningly attractive, if a little less sure of herself than she might have been. At thirty-four, from the self-assurance of having men so often want her, she was becoming both matronly and handsome. The woman on the steps—his mother, Eric realized after a breath, with surprise—was both excited and happy.

Eric called, "Hey, *Barb*…!" Behind him he pushed the car door closed. From the slam, he realized he had pushed it harder than he'd meant: some of the excitement was his. Over the Chevy's roof, Mike stood up.

"Oh, my God…" Barbara's smock had a white collar. Inside it, a gold chain crossed low on her throat. "Oh, my…oh, my *God*…you've gotten *so*…big! I mean, you're…" In wonder, she shook her head. Her blond hair was pinned up. "Your arms are…they're as big as your *dad's!*"

Eric walked toward his mother, thinking with the first step, her skin's a little looser beside her eyes, at her wrists: She's older…And, at his second: She's heavier. He said, "You look so…" and surprised himself— "wonderful…!" Which was not what he'd started to say—but she did.

"It's so good to see you!" Barbara turned her smile on her ex-husband: "And it's good to see you, Mike. It really is. It's good to see you…*both!* Come in." In blue flats, Barb stepped down a step. "Come in. Have a cup of coffee."

Mike said, "You want me to run Eric's stuff up to wherever it is you're—?"

Barb came down the last step—

—and Barbara and Eric hugged.

It was sudden—and surprised Eric.

"Oh, honey…it's so good—*so* good to see you!" By Eric's ear she sounded happy, and he was surprised to remember the deepening in her voice that signaled it. He hadn't thought of it in the year-and-a-half since he'd last seen her in Florida. Eric didn't particularly recognize her scent, but Barb had always liked different perfumes; and there wasn't a lot of it. Eric felt awkward and pleased and…happy, too.

Behind them, Mike laughed.

When Eric stepped back, so did Barb. "I wasn't expecting you to have… well, *grown* so. What were you doing this morning? Working on the car?"

Eric realized that must be some automotive odor held over from the men at Turpens—which, he realized now, even he could smell. He smiled, trying not to look proud. Barb looked at Mike and repeated: "How did he get so…?" But she kept an arm around Eric.

Mike was smiling, too.

She guided Eric up the steps and through the screen door. "Come in, you two. Meet Clem—and see where I work."

As they came in the side door, a country and western song Eric thought had been running through the back of his mind grew loud enough to recognize was coming from a booth CD player. The wood walled room had no air conditioning, but the tan blades of two ceiling fans turned above.

It was a *little* cooler.

In the room several men and a few women sat, most in booths along the side under the old faux-deco CD selectors, and three others at tables. Standing at the side counter, a heavy woman with orange hair, in another waitress smock, put down a coffee carafe on a tray covered with a checkered cloth, already stained with a spill.

"Clem—this is my son, Eric. I told you about him. This is Clem—Mrs. Englert. She runs the place. She's my boss."

"Clem Englert. Just call me Clem. Everybody here does."

Half the people in the room twisted in their seats.

"Clem, this is Eric's dad—Mike."

And Eric recognized the two fellows in the side booth: the tall unshaven one, who'd written where to show up for work on Bill's paper, and the light-skinned black kid across from him, with torn-off sleeves—in this light slightly darker than Eric but with kinky tan hair, the fuzz of a beard, and green eyes, near hazel, like the tall one's. Still bare, his feet were apart on the floor planks. It took seconds to recognize it was *really* them: Dynamite and Shit!

At the truck stop john their names had been…well, eccentricities.

In the seaside café they were absurdities.

Eric stopped breathing. He stopped thinking. His vision momentarily fogged—but he didn't stop walking. He blinked and looked away—only to realize then *they* had not looked at him any more than Ted had, back at the truck stop's Parts & Notions.

His arm stiffened, but Eric made himself relax it around his mother's back, hoping she would think it shyness before these strangers.

Last April, during spring vacation, the Sunday after the Saturday cocksucking marathon below the Atlanta highway, something had happened to Eric for the first time:

In the direction away from the overhead highway, two blocks beyond Mr. Condotti's, where Montoya crossed Rosemont, was Entin's Coffee Shop and Hamburgers, the Lamp Store and the Tobacco and Newspaper shop, the package store, and Ford's Little Five Points Market. Mike and Eric had been strolling down to Ford's to pick up salad makings—they'd done the staple shopping two days earlier—and were half a block away, when Eric recognized, standing before the iron gate over the package store window, the homeless black man, whom Eric had blown and who had blown Eric and all the other homeless guys the previous afternoon behind the Verizon sign. As Eric and Mike walked up, Eric's throat dried, his heart started to pound—and Eric thought: He's looking for me!

Eric did not glance at his dad, who was talking about last night's game: *The worst thing the Braves ever done was get rid of Ramirez. I mean, that was crazy! The* worst *thing they ever done! They gonna see. I'm not kiddin'*—

Eric's forehead had begun to sweat. Drops ran under the back of his T-shirt. His legs began to shake. We don't need to go to Ford's now. Let's go home. I'll get salad stuff later—but he couldn't speak.

Though Eric had been engaging in public sex all over Atlanta, it was the first time that he'd run into an adult with whom he'd had a sexual encounter when a parent was present. He opened his mouth and breathed, because breathing only through his nose seemed, now, suffocating. Suppose the guy said, "Hey, man, your son was suckin' my dick yesterday—and I was suckin' his, too! They're writin' an article about it for one of them gay papers!" just to fuck with Eric. "Your boy's a faggot. Not only that, he hangs out with me and I'm one, too. Someone was takin' pictures of us on my cell phone, while we were doin' it. Lemme show 'em to you. I got 'em right here—"

They got closer. Eric thought: Am I going to fall down on the sidewalk—? He felt as if he might.

The man turned and looked at them both—then extended his hand.

It was all Eric could do to keep from knocking it aside. On one dark finger the man's gold wedding band was as incongruous now as it had been the day before. His wife had found out and demanded he tell Mike…

Mike halted, dug into his pocket, pulled out some change, and funneled three quarters, a nickel, and some pennies (for seconds Eric was sure they were going to shake hands: this *had* to be some set up arranged weeks ago…) from his own black fingers into the man's brown palm. *There you go, brother. You catch the Braves last night?*

Naw. From under the broken bill of his crushed tweed cap, the man glanced at Eric.

And that was all.

If Eric could have torn loose what moneys were in his own pockets and pushed them on the fellow, dropping to his knees to beg his silence, he would have—but what he did was grunt, *Uh…*

Mike frowned over at Eric. *What'd you say?*

Eric tried to whisper, *Nothin'*, but, it was only a mouth movement. Because Mike went on walking, Eric walked too—and did not fall.

Then, somehow, the man was behind them.

They were in Ford's before Eric realized Mike's had been an absurd question. The guy was homeless! Had Mike thought he'd caught the game in some bar on TV—?

In Ford's they ambled by slopes of oranges and peaches piled as high as their heads, by tables of strawberries and raspberries in clear punnets, by two square yards of misted blue berries across a table, under plastic lids. They brought three cucumbers and four pounds of tomatoes—Mike put them in Eric's green basket with metal handles—three lemons, a head of romaine, a head of iceberg (they had celery and onions at home), some green and red peppers, and a bunch of radishes. (*Paper or plastic?* the Korean loader—she was a year ahead of Eric at the high school—asked, and Eric said, *Paper*, because he was conscientious.) Hugging the bag, Eric carried it out from the aisle, through the aluminum doors, and past the corner with Mike a step behind—the panhandler was now across the street, hand out over there. (As though, Eric realized, standing that close to the package store betrayed his goal too blatantly—which is when Eric realized the man had his own concerns, his own agenda…) Eric tried not to look and glanced anyway. Then he glanced again.

Mike was back on the absurdity of Jake's ideas on how to fix the Braves.

Minutes later, they turned down the driveway beside Condotti's. Having been rehearsing it for three blocks, Eric said, but at half the volume he'd intended, *I gotta go to the bathroom. You wanna take this up to the kitchen?*

Sure, Mike said, as Eric handed him the grocery sack. Where Eric had been clutching it, the paper was sweated through and rubbed into little rolls, around a hole as big as the ham of Eric's thumb. Mike frowned at it, then at Eric. *You feelin' okay?*

Yeah, I'm fine. He turned and hurried into the garage, not actually running—still afraid he might stumble.

In his garage room Eric sat on his bed and for three minutes, mouth wide, only breathed, feet and fingers numb.

And nothing had happened.

Ten minutes later, he was still sitting, still thinking: had the man been as uncomfortable seeing Eric as Eric had been seeing him? Whether it was Hareem in East Texas, or Mr. Doubrey after some maintenance storage room session when the rest of the team had gone home, wasn't it all about *Don't' say nothin', now,* and *If your parents find out, you'll be* really *sorry. And I don't mean just from me!* It had never occurred to Eric before that anyone who *could* spill the beans might not. He began to review the men he remembered. (God, there were a lot of them!) Maybe the knife wielding German, yeah…But the other homeless guys? *Hey, I've just been fuckin' your boy*…Wouldn't they get in as much or more trouble than Eric, if anyone found out? Sure, Mike would be furious. But whatever camaraderie and laughter was confined around the mattress behind the Verizon sign or in some men's room encounter, downtown in the park, *they* could end up in jail! They had as many or more reasons to keep the secret as Eric. Finally, sitting up, Eric thought: You have to make *sure* you don't, through your *own* fear, give things away. Sitting on his bed in the garage, it had taken Eric minutes to figure this out.

Despite Eric's having done a lot of growing up in the four months since, despite Eric's exhortation in Atlanta that morning to Bill Bottom about the life he wanted, despite Eric's exercises to make himself attractive to just these men, even with his considerable actions and experiences toward effecting it, and despite where his own not-particularly-unusual sexual desires and emotional needs regularly carried him in a world of licentious adults who desired him back, Eric was still a sixteen-year-old with the fears, repressions, and sensitivities that made such freedoms seem of worth.

Inside the Lighthouse door, with Barb beside him, Mike behind—and Shit and Dynamite in the booth at his vision's edge—Eric thought (not looking at them), okay, they're not going to do anything…now.

But how had they gotten here so quickly? Had that back road been a shortcut?

From in front of the counter, Clem released the carafe, turned, and said with surprise: "Good to meet you. Hello." And then: "His father…?"

"Hey, there, Clem. Good to meet you, too." Mike smiled. "I brung Eric down to stay awhile with Barb." Eric knew the plan was for him to live with Barbara six months or a year, but he also knew Mike was ready for it to go up in domestic chaos inside a month, if not a week.

"Well," Clem said, "I know she offered you a cup of coffee. The least we can do. Sit down. Enjoy it. You come down from the city?"

"Yes, ma'am," Mike said. "But the truth is, Barb, I need to get back up there as soon as I can. There's somebody expecting me."

"Oh," Barbara said, with a slightly raised head and knowing look. "Sure. Of course. But my shift here isn't over for another hour-and-a-half. I was hoping you could wait around till then. Oh, I suppose, you could unload Eric's stuff. I can take it up to the house when I get off—"

Eric drew in a breath. This was the first he'd heard of the later appointment. He was sure Mike had just invented it.

Mike flexed his shoulders in a kind of over-relaxed way he sometimes got. "Can't you tell me where it is? I don't mind running it up before I go—"

Eric felt his mother tensing again and dropped his arm from her waist. From the way he had stopped his sentence, probably Mike felt it too.

"Well, it's a little complicated. My place is back in the woods and the road doesn't go there straight—"

"Mrs. Jeffers?" From his booth, lanky Dynamite looked over. (Yes, they *were* the guys he'd sucked and tongue-fucked in Turpens. Till now Eric had been assuming—hoping—that a direct look would reveal them as guys who looked—and dressed—*like* the ones back in the truck stop john. But Dynamite had called his mother "Mrs. Jeffers…"!) Dynamite said: "Me an' Morgan's goin' that way now—*we* know where you live. We come there every mornin' for your garbage." (They were *Barbara's* garbage men…!) "It's on the way to the Dump." Now Dynamite nodded toward Mike. "Your feller there can follow me on up. We'll help 'im unload. Then he can drive down over the bridge and get on the highway—you know: at Exit Forty-Six. We'll bring the boy back here—this is our day off. We ain't got nothin' else to do."

Shit grinned at Eric—and from somewhere Eric found the presence to smile back. And was hit with a memory: only half the teeth were left in either Shit's or in Dynamite's mouth—something Eric's tongue knew, as it knew their foreskins' elasticity, the force of their erupting semen. (How *did* you look that good with half your teeth gone?) It was purely oral data, from purely oral pleasure…

"Oh, Dynamite—uh, Mr. Haskell." (And Barb knew *his* name…!) Barbara blinked. "Mike, can't you stay a *couple* of hours? Or for a while, anyway—Mr. Haskell, I can't ask you and your nephew to go out of your way like…"

For two-and-a-half years—three, actually—Eric's world had held lots of public sex. Often he'd spent hours a day at it. Whether at his grandmother's in Hugantown, at Mike's in Atlanta, or at Barb's in Florida, coming home and behaving as if those hours did not exist was adamantine habit. But under the ceiling fans in the Lighthouse Coffee, Egg & Bacon on the

Georgia shore, Eric intuited that his world had become much smaller.

Barb was saying: "Morgan, Mr. Haskell—that's *very* nice of you. Really. But, Mike, I was hoping we could make a day of it—"

"Come on, Barb." Mike sounded petulant and irritable, as he hadn't at any time on the drive down. "You didn't say nothin' to me before about stayin'. I bought Eric down—I got a car full of his stuff. You wanna let me leave it off here?" Mike looked around, the way (Eric thought) someone in a room with a known murderer might glance around for exits. "Or up at your place?" he repeated. "You got your car outside. If you want, I can repack his stuff now so you—"

From his booth Dynamite laughed. "Unless he brought just a knapsack or a duffel bag, I can tell you, it ain't gonna fit." With a foreknuckle, he pushed aside the spotted curtain at the booth's back beside the wall's CD player, leaned over, and glanced out. "All what you got piled up in the back seat of yours ain't gonna get in that thing Mrs. Jeffers got. And if you got more of his stuff in the trunk—Hey, we got the pickup. We'll put the tarp down. It won't get messed. I mean, Mrs. Jeffers has a pretty small car—"

Barbara was actually swaying, and rubbing her hands together, which nervousness, Eric knew, would make Mike that much more anxious to leave.

"Yeah, I know." Mike looked around. "Her Honda. That's why I said I'd take it *out* there." He looked up, blinking.

The way they could grate on each other was as familiar to Eric as Barbara's laughter, as Mike's repeated tags and tales. Because it was outside anyone's control, though, Eric felt upsurging frustration.

"Well, yes," Barbara said, "but I—"

Then, with surprise, Eric realized: frustration, yes. But he was not terrified by it, as, two, three, five years ago, he would have been. Only annoyed...

Standing up from the booth, Dynamite frowned at Morgan—

—who flapped both broad hands on the table edge to push himself up and step out, looking as happy as Barbara herself when she'd first seen Eric.

"All you got to do is follow behind us." Taller Dynamite looked back at Barbara, reached up and rubbed a thumb knuckle under his nose, while Eric thought: *These guys are* all *hands and feet!* "We promise not to lose him, ma'am. Come on. When we get there, Mrs. Jeffers, you want us to take it inside for you?"

"Well, if you put his things out on the porch..." Again Barbara looked around, as though hoping someone else would offer assistance. "That's going to be Eric's...room." (Clem had started putting juice glasses on a shelf and didn't seem about to suggest an hour off.) "I mean, the door's open…There's a bed out there. I put sheets on it already. But, really, I *can't* ask you to do—"

"You don't gotta ask, Mrs. Jeffers." Dynamite started across the floor among the tables. "We'd do it anyway. Come on. Once we get his stuff in there, your feller here can be on his way and *we'll* bring your boy back and have that sociable cup of coffee. At home I let Morgan do the coffee making—'cause he do it better than I ever learned. But the Lighthouse brew is pretty decent, I guess—enough to make *these* fellas come back and risk their kidneys on another cup." Three or four customers laughed. Dynamite chuckled at his own joke, nodded toward another coffee drinker—a black man, Eric noticed—then reached the door.

A little hysterically Eric thought, I was just suckin' off these guys in a fuckin' *men's* room, less than an hour ago…! Then, at once, the situation didn't seem dangerous or hysterical or menacing at all, but, well…funny! Looking after them, Eric laughed. "Come on, Dad," he said, only a little too loud. "They'll show us, Barb."

Shit walked past, giving Eric an even bigger grin. Then the two were out the screen, that chattered and banged closed, unslowed by the piston at the top, supposed to keep it from slamming. "We'll be back," Eric called.

Mike said, "So long, Barb. You and Eric'll have a good time, now. I know you'll have a good time together down here," and stepped toward the door. "I'm really sorry I can't hang around some." And Eric realized his father wouldn't see his mother again this visit—and had planned it that way.

Eric followed his dad to see Shit and Dynamite climbing into their pickup, cab forward in the corner. "Don't worry, now," Dynamite called, without looking. "You just follow us. We'll get you there."

As Eric stepped from the door, out on the water, beyond the postage-stamp lot, a wave broke to sputtering foam, aglitter across green sea beside them, advancing shoreward with the inexorability of distilled time itself. As Eric reached the bottom step, it vanished under the shoal, and, as he put runner to gravel, he heard it *roooosh* the shingle. (Thirty yards out, another wave gathered.) He thought:

I'm going to remember *that* wave the rest of my life!

He recalled it a dozen times that day—and half a dozen that night; and even a few the next day. But within the month its sound and look had melded with so many thousands he'd seen, both outside where Barb worked and from the Harbor's docks and marina and local beaches, from places among the trees that looked over the sea, some in leaden storms and some on glass clear mornings, neither that first nor any other could retain its specificity.

* * *

[5] IN THE CHEVY with Mike, they watched the pickup pull from the lot—it was painted two, possibly three, blues, with some orange on the front fender—with black marker (SHIT &) and silver gaffers' tape (DYNAMITE) across its tailgate (REFUSE), and all of it dusty. A chain rattled at the gate's side. Eric wondered if Mike had seen it back in the truck stop lot. But, as they followed onto a path that took them into coastal overgrowth, all Mike said was, "I can't *believe* your mama not only leaves her damned door unlocked down here but would *announce* it to everybody in a goddam public restaurant in town! But—hey, I dunno—maybe Diamond Harbor is that kinda of place."

Six yards ahead, country slow, Dynamite's pickup moved forward on the dirt path. The taped tail gate jounced and swayed.

"What you gotta go back to the city for?" Eric asked. "You gonna see Doneesha?"

Beside him, uneven ground joggled the wheel in Mike's dark hands. "Yep." (It was Kelly-Ann, actually. But Eric didn't need to know that.) "See, I told her I'd drop by when I got back. I'd really like to say hello—since it's the weekend."

"Oh." Both proud of his knowledge—incorrect as it was in detail—and at the same time uncomfortable with what felt like Mike's betrayal of Barb, Eric thought: yeah, sure you did. But he did not say it. Then—the thought came with his greater relaxation—wasn't Eric himself deceiving both his parents with the truck stop men?

Or was he?

Mike grunted. "Barb probably don't want me goin' up to her place 'cause she got some damned boyfriend at home and sittin' in her kitchen right now, who she don't want me to run into and cause no ruckus—"

"Oh, *Dad*—!"

"Not that I could *give* a fuck!" Mike looked over. "Hey, I'm sorry, son. I shouldn't be talkin' like that in front of you, I know…"

Since, whenever Mike and Barb had been together for the last half dozen years—or even talked on the phone—the moment they separated Mike *did* talk like that, Eric's protest and Mike's apology were more habit than true upset. But now Eric knew, for the first time—the knowledge was both new and surprising—Mike's motivation was guilt.

He hadn't a year ago—or even three weeks back!

Mike didn't put on the air conditioning. But, beside Eric, the window dropped into the door.

After two miles of turning paths, mostly unpaved, the house where the pickup slowed sat halfway up a thickly grown pine slope on a cinderblock foundation. Starting as a trailer, it had been enlarged with a fair-sized room built off the back. When they walked up to the porch—Eric's "room"—an outer door was hooked closed inside: they could see the latch through the screening. At the other end of the building, in the blistered siding, at the top of the built-out wooden stairs the kitchen door *was* unlocked.

Mike, Dynamite, Shit and Eric got everything except the Bowflex into the house and onto the porch in ten minutes. When he was walking out, Eric glanced into the living room, to see, on a shelf beside the sofa, three bottles of Heaven Hill near an oriental tin lamp (Eric recognized it from his Florida visit—another thing he hadn't thought about in a year).

One bottle was half empty.

Wondering how much Barbara was drinking, Eric returned to the kitchen, where, just stepping barefoot out the door, Shit glanced back.

"See." Outside, Mike rubbed his forehead with the heel of his hand and said, more or less to Eric: "That's why I spent so much time packin' the car this mornin'. It *unpacks* at lot faster that way."

"Now, there, Shit," Dynamite said to his nephew, who had ceased to be Morgan as soon as they'd gotten off from the Lighthouse—though the twice Dynamite had called his barefoot helper that, Mike hadn't seemed to be paying enough attention for it to register. "This man here knows somethin' you don't. About packin'. And he just learned it to you, too. Now *you* know it."

And Shit was grinning as much at Mike as he was at Eric. Shit's grin seemed so intensely sexual Eric had a brief panic—were they going to put the make on Mike, too? But that was crazy…

Then, one at either end, Dynamite and Eric carried the re-boxed Bowflex into the house, Eric going backwards, Dynamite going forward and giving grinning grunts: "Left—no, right!" (The first two confused Eric, since they were Dynamite's right and left, not his—but then he switched them in his mind.) Eric backed along the hall, and onto the porch. As Dynamite's side bumped a doorframe, and he moved over to get it past, with a smile on his unshaven face as though he were inquiring about the operation of an eccentric sex toy, he asked, head cocked and looking lackadaisically at Eric, "What the fuck is this goddam thing, anyway?"

"Um…" Eric got the cardboard more firmly in his right hand, which was beginning to sting. "It's just an exercise…thing."

"Oh." They set it down over by the wall in front of the screen. The rolled up carpet swatch was already there behind it. Dynamite shook his head a little, as if there was no understanding city folks. They walked out together.

After looking around the quiet trees, at the sparse clouds, or listening to the crickets, Mike-said, himself easy and smiling, "Hey, it's nice here. You guys is lucky to live someplace like this."

Dynamite took a long breath of the pine-rich air. "We think so."

Was it the landscape or just the minutes of labor that had relaxed Mike? Or even that Shit, however light-skinned, was black? (Somehow, that made Eric happy, too.) Turning now, Mike said: "You guys won't take no offence if I get on my way?" Or was it only getting away from Barb? "It don't sound too...friendly, I know. But I got to get goin'—there's some stuff I gotta do back in Atlanta."

"Course," Dynamite said. "You got your business to attend to."

By now Eric was positive Mike's city engagement was pure improvisation. A thought Eric had first had with glassy clarity at fifteen returned to him, equally clear now, days shy of his seventeenth birthday: Barb and Mike were *both* always inventing tiny deviations from the precise truth that had no other purpose than to upset the other.

"Not at all," Dynamite said. "Not at all. His stuff's inside—now that's Eric. Right?" (Eric thought: Teeth or no teeth, Christ, he looks good.) "We'll run him back to his mama at the Lighthouse." Shit—and Dynamite, too—smiled at them both.

"Good-bye, Dad," Eric said.

"Good-bye, boy"—then Eric found Mike hugging him. He hugged his father back, hard. A breeze rose among the pines, and Eric thought: It sounds like the...

"Down here by the sea, you're gonna enjoy it," Mike said, "and I'm gonna miss hell out of you." The hug tightened. "I really am."

Eric thought about saying, *Then why don't you stay?* But he was too curious—even eager—to know what would happen once Mike left.

And, among the trees, the sound of a wave stilled. But it was merely breeze.

Dynamite gave some instructions: "Follow this path dead on straight—it runs into a real road about hun'erd yards up—and take it on right down over a little trestle bridge onto the highway..." (Mike climbed into the Chevy.) "Take a right, and you'll be on your way to the city."

The window rolled down. "I think I got it." Mike called out. The motor started.

Dragging a cloak of reflected leaves across the door and fenders, the Chevy drove off into the trees.

When, between Dynamite (who drove) and Shit (who sat by the door),

Eric was in the pickup cab, hunting for something to say, suddenly he came out with: "All of you guys down here...*smell* so good! I mean at the truck stop—"

Smiling at the windshield as he drove, Dynamite said: "Well, thank you, son."

Something suddenly weighed on his foot. Eric glanced down.

His heart (and throat) thudded. Swallowing, Eric was actually dizzy.

Though he'd been too surprised by it to get an erection, Eric realized his response couldn't have been more sexual if Shit had reached over and grasped his crotch:

Shit had put his wide grubby foot on Eric's runner—Eric looked up at Shit, who smiled at him again over his missing teeth—as he had in Turpens restroom with barefoot Mex.

Eric glanced at Dynamite, who hadn't seemed to notice—any more than Mike would have if Eric had been staring out the side window, picking his nose.

Finally Eric got out, "You guys...ain't afraid of *anything* down here, are you?"

Shit actually laughed.

At the wheel, Dynamite said, "Well...we don't wanna rub nobody's nose in our business who ain't really interested. But mostly there ain't nothin' to be afraid of."

"Hell—" Shit spread his knees, one pressing the door, one pressing Eric's leg, while, with both hands, he gripped his groin—"soon as I go in there with this guy here, I pull his overalls down, let everybody see his furry ass, squat down and tongue out his shithole, stick a few fingers up there and wiggle 'em around. Then I dick the pig fucker. And while I'm dickin' 'im good, I make these good nasty noises—*Oh, shit! Oh, fuck...! He slippin' that wet hot shit all over my damned dick.* Actually, he's pretty clean— but they don't know that. And I don't give 'im time to get *too* dirty! But in that place, they like anything that's nasty. *Ooooh, that's one wet sloppy shit hole*—so everybody in there'll know how good it is. That gets everybody else turned on—you see, you need to do a little of that." (At the wheel, Dynamite was smiling.) "'Cause when you got five or six people in there who're on the shy side and don't know each other too well, you can stand around for half-an-hour, an hour-an'-a half, waitin' for someone to get up gumption enough to make the first move. So I throw myself right on in there—I don't give a fuck! Mex and Jay are pretty much the same way, ain't they?"

"Pretty much." Dynamite pulled on the wheel, then let it straighten.

"I'll go in there, squat down, and start suckin' the dick of the oldest fucker at the pee trough. That way everybody knows they can get started. I mean, who wants to hang around that place and waste half-a-day twiddlin' your curtains? Know what I mean?"

"Un-huh," Eric said, surprised he did—though he wouldn't have described it as his own way of entering a john. Still, he'd already begun to appreciate those who did.

"Ain't no reason for it. At least—" Shit closed his legs and moved a hand onto Eric's thigh, glancing at him—"if you live in the Dump."

Eric's response was not directly sexual. But chills rolled down behind his shoulders, his back. He looked at Shit, then Dynamite. "I still got that paper you gave me back at the truck stop."

"Good," Dynamite said. "Hope you use it. Shit'd like that. So would I. It'd be nice to have a big strong feller like you givin' us a hand. And it's money—not a lot. But it's better than nothin'. For the first three months, you get minimum. Not national minimum, either. Kyle Chamber of Commerce minimum: nine-fifty an hour. You keep it up for three months, and if it works out you'll be on permanent salary. Then you'll get the same as what Shit gets."

"Yeah," Shit said. "How much money am I makin' now?"

"Twenty-seven. That's assistant wages—but you stay on and you get cost-of-livin' raises every eighteen months."

"Hey," Eric said. "That's not bad."

Looking intently, Shit dug a middle finger in an equatorially wide nostril, twisted it out, glanced at it, then sucked it. "They take your taxes out and send 'em in for you, and you don't have to worry about none of that." Again, Shit grinned—sheepishly at his thumb knuckles. "You know, half of what I'm talking here is bullshit." Again looking at Eric, Shit lifted his butt a few inches—and farted, loudly. (Eric laughed. So did Dynamite.) "But the other half ain't."

At the brief smell, again Eric got an erection.

"Well, he won't have to worry about that for a while—three months, anyway." Dynamite said. "He may not like workin' with us."

"Oh." Shit sounded disappointed. "Yeah. But I hope you do. Hey." He glanced at Eric. "I pick out my boogers an' eat them suckers. You do it, too. Huh?"

Eric blinked, surprised—not at somebody doing it so much as talking about it. He swallowed.

"I wouldn't do it at the Lighthouse, though, where your mama works," Shit went on, "or nothin' like that."

"That's what I mean about rubbin' folks noses in it." Dynamite hauled on the wheel, while a sunlit patch moved over his thigh's greyed and stained denim.

"Oh," Eric said. He thought: I can't say it. Then, with that hysteria again, he thought: I can't *not* say it. "Yeah…Hey, I want…I always wanted a friend. I mean one who I…could do that with." Something had propelled him beyond a limit where logic no longer obtained.

Dynamite drove as if he wasn't listening—which, actually, imagining Mike, Eric found as hard to believe as he found the other.

Shit looked over, blinking his green eyes. "You do? Would you gimme some of yours? I'd suck your dick some more, like we was doin' in the john. I was gonna do it some more back then. But I didn't get a chance. You can eat mine, too, any time you wanna."

"Fact is," Dynamite added, "Shit talks about it, but he don't do a whole lot of dick suckin', either. He got to gee himself up for it."

"I suck dick, if it's somebody I like. You know that. I sucked on yours enough. I don't like gettin' teased about it afterward, that's all—like them fuckin' niggers in the Dump is always doin'."

Still lookin' ahead, Dynamite got a sly smile. "That must mean you don't like me no more—'cause you ain't sucked mine in a while."

"Sure, I like it," Shit said. "But you jus' like gettin' fucked so much. And I love fuckin' you. So we don't hardly get to the suckin' thing these days. That's the only reason." He looked at Eric. "But, yeah, for a hungry asshole like his, this pig fucker *loves* to get his dick sucked on, too. He fucks hisself with beer bottles, sometimes—you'll see 'im. I think he's happiest, though, when he's the baloney in a goddam suckin' and fuckin' sandwich—like we was doin' in the—"

"Come on, Shit," Dynamite said. "You don't gotta go into all our business with ever'body you meet. Let him find out sumpin' for hisself—" He glanced over at Eric. "It don't gotta be no beer bottle. You can use a couple of goddam fingers. That's good enough to get me off. You do *anything* with this boy, and he gotta tell everybody in the goddam Dump about it."

"Well, it's true." Shit's grin got bigger. "If you like suckin' *or* fuckin', though, we can make you *real* happy. And me, I'll fuck you any time you want. And you suck *real* good, there."

"Come on." But Dynamite was smiling. "You'll get this boy all excited again—and we done had our fun today." Without looking from the road, he laughed. "You two was already tradin' snot and cum, back at Turpens. Didn't that calm you down?"

"Oh," Eric said. "Yeah, I guess, well…a little."

Shit put his hand on Eric's tank top shoulder—and squeezed. (Again, Eric was surprised. It didn't feel like a calm-down squeeze.)

"Fuckin' kids!" Still chuckling, Dynamite shook his head. "What calms a regular person down, just gets 'em hotter. Well, come on. We need to get this feller back to the Lighthouse." Out the windshield, the sky burned gold behind lapped branches of darker and darker green.

"You're Dynamite's...nephew?" Barb had called Morgan his nephew.

Dynamite still looked out the windshield, as he drove. "Can you keep a secret, son?"

Eric nodded. "Uh-huh."

"He ain't." Dynamite chuckled. "Not really."

Eric looked back at Shit, who was grinning again. As they pulled around a turn, sun through the window moved over Dynamite's fists, high on the wheel. Shining behind Shit's beard, it made the tan momentarily look as blond as the boatman's from the afternoon.

"Oh," Eric said, confused. Then he said, "I ain't gonna tell my mom you give me that piece of paper about the job back at Turpens. I'm gonna say you told me I could work for you tonight, when we were drivin' back from the house—here."

"Usually I don't countenance kids lyin' to their parents." At the wheel Dynamite seemed to ponder. "But I don't think that one'll do no real harm." Now he grimaced. "I mean, Turpens Truck Stop...? You ever go to that place, Shit?"

Beside him, Shit said, "I been by it—maybe gone in there once or twice to use the bathroom, but I don't never *really* go in there."

"Me neither," Dynamite said. "I heard 'bout all *sorts* of nasty stuff goin' on in the men's rooms in that place—people wanna suck your pecker, stick their dick up your damned asshole—man, that's gotta hurt!"

"Yeah," Shit said. "Hurts so good I bet *you* can hardly stand it."

Eric flinched—and looked down.

Again Shit had dropped a hand between Eric's legs—and was rubbing.

Recovering from the surprise, Eric grinned; and, he realized, was *not* afraid of anything right now.

With only one hand, Shit got Eric's zipper down—once Eric reached down to help—and went in with heavy fingers to grip Eric's penis, again grown hard. Eric looked at him, to see him smiling toward the windshield.

Eric said, "I really like holdin' onto yours. I mean, 'cause it's so big. It makes mine feel like it's bigger. What you get outta holdin' onto mine, though?"

"I dunno." Shit shrugged. "'Cause it's a dick, I guess. Maybe it makes mine feel even bigger than it is."

"Oh...!" Eric was surprised.

With his other thumb, Shit pointed at Dynamite. "That's what he used to tell me, back before mine got big like his. He used to hold it—we used to hold onto each other's, I mean. You know, when we'd be in bed, goin' to sleep together. Or just drivin' around—like this."

Eric repeated, "Oh."

Then, shaking his head, Shit said, "God, Eric, you look so *good* suckin' dick—'cause you so strong!"

"Come on," Dynamite said. "I told you. Don't get this boy all worked up, now." The pickup shook on the pinewood's red-dirt road. With his darkly stubbled face full of gold light, Dynamite seemed to remember something. "Hey, you still got that load Al slipped you in that fuckin' scumbag of his?"

"Huh?" Eric saw the garbage man's knee flex. "Yeah."

Dynamite slowed the truck—

Shit asked, eagerly: "Was you gonna do anything with it?"

—to stop below over-arching trees.

Shadows ceased moving on their laps and chests and arms. Eric glanced at Shit, who was grinning. "I dunno."

"You could drink it down—rub it all over yourself. Use it to jerk off with. That's what Mex would've done with it, if Al done give it to him."

"Oh…"

Dynamite said: "If you don't got no ideas, though, you could give it to me." At the wheel, he shrugged. "I kinda like wearin' that nigger's rubbers, once he comes in 'em. Me and Shit only got eight-and-a-half—each. So neither one of us got no problem slippin' that elephant's raincoat on. You can slide it on me right now, it you want. That means I'll owe you—I'll have to do somethin' nice for you, the next time we fuck."

Eric said, "Okay…"

The evening's silence came through the halted pickup's windows.

Shit said, "Dynamite's crazier than I am. He likes watchin' people do nasty stuff—"

"And you *don't?*" Dynamite gave Shit a dry look. The truck stood by the immobile trees. "When I shoot in it, later, you know you gonna be wearin' it next, soon as I finish. Go on—get it out." He grinned at Eric. "If you still have it." Holding the wheel with one hand, Dynamite put his arm back across the back seat. "Go on—take my dick out. Untie Al's rubber—then slip it on me. Rub it around a little. When you're finished, put my dick away again."

"Okay." Eric went digging in his pocket. (Beside him, Shit chuckled. Again he was rubbing Eric's shoulder.) Eric found the quarter-full rubber, wrinkled but intact.

"Dr. Greene told me—" Dynamite swung his knees apart under the wheel—"that Al always comes so much 'cause he don't got good control of his bladder muscles. I mean, if you ever seen him come, it looks like snot shootin' out of a sneeze in November, but Dr. Greene says what comes out is a third cum, and the other two thirds is really piss. That's why there's so much. But, hell, that just makes it nastier."

Glancing at grinning Shit, Eric lay the thing, like a big slug, over Dynamite's frayed and oil-spotted leg and began to work the button at the top of Dynamite's fly. Then he tugged down the zipper. "You done this before…?" Reaching in (he'd already forgotten the man wore no underwear), he grasped the warm rope of Dynamite's cock—half hard—to pull it free.

"'Bout any time he gets a chance," Shit said.

"Aw, hell," Dynamite said. "Maybe three times in the last year. That ain't so much—"

Again Eric picked up the rubber.

"Like I said—" Shit turned to watch—"any time he can."

Opening Al's knot was harder than he'd thought. But Eric did it— Dynamite had pretty much gone down by then. But Eric lifted the cock and slid it into the loose and liquid filled tube.

"Go on, and rub that good stuff all around on it. Yeah, that feels nice." (Eric massaged, while Dynamite's cock hardened into the now familiar down-curved tower.) "How that look to you, Shit?"

Shit's hand on Eric's bare shoulder had stilled. He'd pushed his fingers under the tank top strap and was leaning over to see. "Looks good," Shit said, an inch away from Eric's ear.

"See, now—" Dynamite grinned at Eric—"Next time we fuck around, —I heard Jay say you like that dick cheese—so I think we're gonna keep 'em skinned forward for you till we see you again. Ain't we, Shit?" He looked back at Eric. "What you say to that?"

Eagerly Shit nodded beside Eric's cheek. Eric could tell by the way the beard moved against his face.

Eric said, "Wow…You don't mind doin'…stuff like that?"

"Hell, no…!" Shit said. "His middle name is 'nasty'." Then his inverted triangular face—the same shape as Dynamite's only the nose was three times as broad—came forward, and grinned as Eric looked over. "Dynamite Nasty Haskell. And both of mines is, too—first *and* last."

Beside Eric, Shit chuckled and squeezed his shoulder again.

"Go on, now," Dynamite said. "Put it away. So we can get goin'. I think I'll wear this thing for a while." He gave a grimace. "Thanks, son. That feels nice."

When Eric closed the zipper over it, Dynamite's cock made an odd looking tent in his lap. A bigger and a smaller spot darkened the denim where it had leaked from the rubber's collar. "Ain't people gonna think you got somethin' in there?" Eric asked.

"Naw," Dynamite said. "They're just gonna think I dripped a little, puttin' it away. I hope when we see you again, we can get some work done, too. I mean, you guys got to remember, we got some goddam garbage to haul—as well as all this fuckin' around. It ain't *just* about bein' nasty—though, yeah—" and he half-frowned, half-grinned at Eric—"that's a lot of it, too, I guess." Dynamite sat up and started the truck.

Shit's hand had dropped to Eric's groin, to rub. "Eric got a hard-on, too—like me."

"Yeah, well you always got a hard-on, nigger." (Eric felt his own cock stiffen more.) "Come on." Dynamite pulled around onto the roadside. "Don't worry. I'm gonna let you get your dick in this thing, once I shoot in it later. Leave the boy alone, now—so there's somethin' to do for next time. He gonna be here awhile."

*

When they walked into the Coffee & Egg, Barbara was taking a customer's order. Eric glanced down and to the side—you could see Dynamite's cock pushing denim forward. And the spots…

But they *were* half dry by now. And what *would* anyone say…?

Shit slid into a booth against the wall. Eric sat beside him on the outside. Across the table, as Dynamite sat, he pushed his rolled sleeves further up his hard arms, then folded his big hands on the tables planks. The neck of his T-shirt hung below the brown hair between his work shirt's open collar and above the denim bib.

On his shoe, again Eric felt Shit's foot.

Looking serious and unshaven, Dynamite said, "Don't let that thing Shit does there on the floor bother you. He do that with ever'body he likes—Mex, Mama Grace, Jay. Even me: he's got his other toes propped up on my shoe right now, under the damned table. It just means he's comfortable."

"Oh," Eric said. And smiled.

Shit leaned against Eric. "That's how our dog do—Uncle Tom. Back in the Dump. So I do it, too."

Dynamite looked up, as Barbara came over, two cups in one hand, one in the other. "Got his stuff all squared away, Mrs. Jeffers—right out there on your porch like you wanted. That's gonna be nice."

"Thank you, so much. Mike got off okay?" She set the cups down. "Anyone want a piece of pie? Morgan? Mr. Haskell? We got peach, cherry, and pecan." Barb's smile grew richer when she looked at her son. "Eric?

Really, that was awfully nice of you, Mr. Haskell." She nodded. And asked again: "Morgan?"

"Glad to do it, ma'am," Dynamite said. "Really glad to. Naw, the coffee's more than enough." He poured milk from the aluminum creamer, then passed it to Shit, who poured in maybe three times as much. Neither of them picked up the glass sugar container with the metal top. (So Eric didn't either.) "Your husband—the boy's dad, there—is on his way."

"Really," she repeated. "I can't thank you enough," dropping her own hand to Eric's shoulder. (Its softness felt odd, after Shit's rough grip.) "Sometimes I make him uncomfortable, I think—I mean Mike." She sighed—in the kitchen a bell rang. "I wish I didn't. There's Darrell's bearclaw." She stepped back. "He likes it heated—" and turned toward the counter with its window into the back.

"Hey." Once more Shit leaned over toward Eric, his foot's weight heavier, his whisper quieter: "I'm a bastard. What about you?"

"Huh?" Eric said. "Oh, uh…well." He dropped his own voice. "Yeah. I guess so. I mean, no, Barb—my mother—and my real dad wasn't—you know—married." He added, "She married Mike." Eric glanced across at Dynamite, but Shit was not trying to keep anything from him. So Eric didn't either. "They're divorced now." Though he'd told Mr. Doubrey in gym, he never said that to anyone else in school—not even Scott.

Shit was still leaning across the booth table.

Eric had forgotten his smell—kind of like leather and vinegar. Driving back, he'd thought it was the truck cab—but now it brought back Turpens' john. (The gasoline was Dynamite.) Well, whatever it was, he liked it.

"I figured you might be one, 'cause your dad there is one *real* fuckin' black nigger. I never knew her, but my mama was a nigger, too—weren't she?" Shit said *sotto voce* to Dynamite across the table.

"Your mama was a real nice colored lady," Dynamite said quietly. "I told you enough times."

"Yeah." Again Shit turned to Eric. "But I don't think she was quite as colored as *your* dad."

"Maybe," Dynamite said. "Not that it makes no never-mind."

Shit's foot grew even heavier on Eric's, as he leaned toward Dynamite and whispered: "Hey—how's Al's rubber feel on your dick?"

Softly, Dynamite whispered back, "Nasty as hell. Some of it's drippin' down my balls."

"Don't let it all run out," Shit said. "I wanna get my dick in that nigger's mess, too." He grinned at Eric. "Next time he gives you one, *you* can wear it around. It's fun. It keeps you harder than a damned cockring. We like to wear each other's. Maybe you and me could trade off one of these sometimes."

Over the next hour and a half, the conversation started, stopped, started again, with stretches where they only sat and sipped sugarless, milky coffee.

"You live near Barb—my mom?" Eric asked

"Naw," Shit told him. "We live about another mile-and-a-quarter southeast—in the Dump."

A few times both boys got to laughing and Dynamite leaned back and grinned. Eric tried to find out what there was to do in Diamond Harbor, only to realize soon, there wasn't much—or, anyway, not much Shit and Dynamite were going to talk about in a place where Eric's mother worked. Dynamite sat forward and again said under his breath, "You can wear each other's used scumbags. That's more fun than cow tippin'."

And Eric wondered what had happened to the two men he'd been terrified might say something in front of his parents…Runcible and Hemmings—outside the latter of which was a mall—were a little more lively. But not by much. "You read comics?" Eric asked, eventually.

"Dynamite reads them comics…sometimes, but me—I don't read *nothin'!*" Then Shit sat back with his hands, as thick as Eric's dad's, as thick as Dynamite's, on the table before him and said nothing, while Eric learned that, despite the occasional *X-Men* or *Spiderman* when he came across one, Dynamite did not know Moore, or Gaiman, or Wein, or Azzarello, or Ennis—which is also when Eric realized that, with Shit's silence, Shit's foot had moved away. So Eric went back to drawing Shit out, which he expected to be difficult: but with only a minute's more attention, Shit was grinning again and nodding, his foot again on Eric's.

After an hour, with lazy and lingering good-byes, when she came up, Dynamite turned to Barb. "I told your boy he could work with me and Morgan, if he wanted." And Eric realized Dynamite had saved him from the necessity of lying. "I wrote it down down on a paper there."

"Why, Mr. Haskell…that's really…that's really so *nice* of you!"

Eric was surprised. But it took some pressure off him.

Dynamite moved to leave the booth. "Course I don't know if you really *want* him workin' on the garbage run—"

"Barb, that would be great!" Eric started to stand too. "I really wanna do somethin'…you know, physical!"

"Well—" Haskell stood beside the table, taller than Barbara, Eric, and Shit—"slingin' garbage sacks is about a physical as you can get—next to diggin' ditches."

Looking a little confused, Barb reached over the table for the mostly empty cups. "If that's what you want to *do*—"

"He just gotta show up at the boat dock on Wednesday. That okay for you? It'll give you a couple of days to settle in—learn where everything is."

"*I* don't think the Harbor's big enough where he got to do *too* much learnin'—" Shit scratched his ear—"'less'n he go over to Runcible or Hemmings."

"I wrote it all out for him," Dynamite repeated. He and Shit both gave Eric a grin. "All he got to do is show up." He started out the diner.

Shit said, "So long. See you Wednesday," and followed Dynamite.

A broad black fellow picked up a leather cowboy hat from the table—the man who'd ordered the heated bear claw—and started out. Some others left too; some new folks came in.

While Barbara was hanging her smock on the wall hook at the side, from the counter edge Clem offered a sudden cascade of apologies: "I'm sorry, honey. You and your fella—back before—looked like you was about to have a disagreement. And that was a *big* man in here. Black or white, I don't like to get involved in them things in any way. I ain't like Dynamite. He ain't scared of black people—probably 'cause he lives with all of 'em, over in the Dump. He'll jump into anything—and thinks he's doin' good. Sometimes he even does it. But I've always kept my own council and let things run on without my interference. For me, that's the best way. I hope you understand."

"Oh, that's all right, Clem." Barbara looked over her shoulder—she'd changed into a short-sleeved white blouse, with lace at the arms and the collar, which made her look a lot more like Eric remembered her—then turned from the hooks. "It all worked out." She sighed. "I guess. And Eric's...here."

* * *

[6] TEN MINUTES AFTER that—

In her seven-year-old Honda, Barbara drove back through the woods with Eric. "Looks like you made some friends. That Morgan—Clem thinks he's slow...retarded. 'Cause he's illiterate. She says he can't even read his name."

"Oh..." Eric protested, as pine branches swept the window. "He's all right. He's...different. That's all. He's nice—they both are. Hey, tomorrow, when you go down to work, you wanna let me drive and you can navigate? I mean, I gotta learn where we are *some*time."

Barbara swung the car onto another turn off. "It *is* confusing the first couple of times, isn't it? That's why I didn't want Mike to do it alone."

"Yeah, he got lost comin' in..."

After a breath she said, "Maybe you'll meet my friend Ron."

Eric recognized that tone, too: so there *was* a boyfriend.

And chances were he was black. (Eric recalled Clem's surprise at Mike. Probably it was because both Mike *and* Ron—he was pretty sure—were colored.) Clearly Barbara had put off mentioning him until Mike was gone.

Ron *would* have upset Mike: Eric remembered the stonily grumpy evening with that black guy Barb had been seeing (whose name at this point Eric couldn't even remember) who had dropped by minutes after Mike had delivered Eric to Barbara's Florida trailer two summers before.

Eric took a breath—Barbara glanced at him—and thought: There's got to be another way to live…

Evening settled among the trees. Scrunching down, Eric squinted up through the window to see late sun flicking between leaves, and thought of sunlight in the froth of that wave…

Barbara asked, suddenly: "You have my cell phone number, honey?"

"Mike's got it," Eric said. "I don't."

"Well, let me give it to you."

"I don't have a cell phone."

"Oh…!" she said, glancing at him, surprised. "Well, you probably should get one. There's a couple of stores in Runcible—" from beside a meadow they again entered some woods—"and certainly in Hemmings, at the mall."

He noticed she hadn't offered to get it for him.

In the car, Eric pondered something he knew he was going to say, though at the realization his ears began to ring and his knuckles cramped in anticipation. Finally he decided to take three breaths and…do it.

He drew them in, trying to relax. Then he lifted his butt from the seat and went digging in his pocket, filled with his KY, his wallet—and the folded paper.

Pulling the paper out, he sat back, breathing heavier than he should be.

Barbara glanced over. "You okay?"

"Yeah." It sounded normal. Maybe he could make the rest of it sound that way, too. Maybe after another three—no, six breaths.

At the end of the fifth, Eric unfolded it. And the sixth: "Barb?"

"What?" She looked through passing trees.

"You don't mind me working with Dynamite and Shit on the garbage run while I'm down here? I thought that would be good, if I had some kinda job—"

Barbara laughed. "That would be *very* good," she said. Then she added, "But, honey, you really shouldn't call him that. His name is Morgan. I know practically everybody down here does—but he can't really like it very much. Would you?"

"I don't think it would bother me—I mean, if they weren't making fun of me when they did it."

Barbara drove a little longer. Then she said, "You know you really *have* grown up…" She glanced at him again. "They get started pretty early in the morning, don't they?"

"Yeah," Eric said. "Well, I get up early, too."

* * *

[7] "WHAT WERE YOU thinkin' about for dinner?" Eric pulled open the refrigerator's pink door.

"You like franks and beans," Barb said. "Or you used to. I've got both here."

"I still do," Eric said. "What were you gonna do with this chicken?"

In its Styrofoam tray, wrapped in plastic, it looked like a pale, chicken-colored hill. Between rubber-covered wires—along a few inches on two of the tines the white covering had torn away—down though the plastic roof of the vegetable drawer, Eric saw blurred tomatoes, the pale rectangle of a celery bunch, tan onions within red strings. (In Texas, Mike's relatives had smiled over Barbara's keeping onions in the refrigerator.) Up in the freezer, he already knew, cans of frozen juice and lemonade stood with collars of ice.

Behind him, Barbara said, "I thought we could have that—the chicken, I mean—tomorrow." (Outside he heard a car—one, he realized, he hadn't been in.) "I get off at four-thirty, and I could put it in the oven by five or five-twenty." (The car stopped.) "We could eat around seven—it would be nice if we could do it a little earlier, but that'll be all right…won't it? And could you close the door, honey? I don't want to let all the cold out," she said, as, in its base, the old pump began to hum.

Eric stood up and stepped back. "Oh, sure." He closed the refrigerator.

And outside, someone called, "Helloooo-*ooo*…?"

Barbara turned her head. "Oh, hi, honey."

"Can I come in?" It was throaty voice, a black voice. "I've got mac and cheese. I just wanted to leave you a dish. I'm not staying—" The screen door opened and a rather straight up and down black woman, not as old and not as attractive as Barbara, stepped in. She carried a casserole under one arm, the top covered with tin foil that looked as if it had been used and spread out and used again. "I thought I might be interrupting you and Ronny. But who is—oh, you're going to tell me this is Eric, now, ain't you?"

Barbara smiled. "It certainly is. Eric, this is Serena. She's been helping me keep body and soul together since I've been down here. Serena, this is my son, Eric."

Serena wore a colorful scarf around her head. Her features were broad and she looked like she laughed a lot. "Where in the *world*," she declared, "did you find a good looking boy like this? One this handsome? Naw, I don't think this is allowed, honey." She narrowed her eyes, like someone appraising. "Mmmm! She told me you was comin', so I brought a little somethin' over."

"Well, why don't you stay and have some with us? We were going to make some hot dogs—"

"No way, honey. Not on your first night. We both work at the Coffee and Egg. Different shifts, though. Clem used to let us run the place together, but I think she decided we was doin' more gossipin' than hash slingin', so now she keeps us apart. And the talk's got to be on our own time today. You can make me some decent coffee next Thursday mornin', and I'll drop by and you can tell me how it's goin'. Here, take this—" She thrust out the casserole.

Barbara took it and put it on the table. "Serena, that is so nice of you. Oh, it's still warm!"

Serena laughed. "I just wanted to be able to say I seen him. And now nobody in Diamond Harbor is gonna believe me when I describe him, unless they seen him for themselves!" (Such comments confused and embarrassed Eric—even as that is what he'd always hoped the Bowflex would give him.) "I'll catch you Thursday, honey." Again, Serena made the sound of someone savoring something delicious.

"Well," Barbara said, a minute later, after the screen door clacked closed—obviously happy: "I guess we have franks, beans, and macaroni," while outside, a little down the slope, the car motor started again.

*

On the darkening porch's bedstead, hands folded under his head, Eric lay on his back, smelling the new blanket, a strange pillow, the pines, the sea. From inside the porch, the Bowflex's spiring exercise rods put shadows down the night forest outside the screening—it had taken him an hour-and-a-half to assemble it, until finally he found one of the nuts he'd first thought missing in the corner of the box, so that, he'd decided (for the first time in months) to skip his workout—lightened somewhere by the last of the quarter-to-nine sunset on the other side of the house.

Mists lay above the trees, bringing…was it starlight? Flakes flicked across it, too small, dark, and angular for birds—

Bats, Eric realized. He'd see them above the evening trees in Hugantown, when he'd return from watching Costas. (He liked to imagine—and often had, since—that the plumber knew someone observed him and wanted it. A few times Costas had glanced at the window—once, as Eric shot. That time he'd bitten the inside his cheek and almost swallowed his tongue—a moment easy to remember.) More likely, though—at least Eric had liked to pretend—Costas didn't give a fuck, as long as whoever looked just spritzed the outside wall.

It's nice here, Eric thought.

Though it's kind of boring.

How could he get back to Turpens—which, not including Mike's getting lost, was six miles and seven minutes away? Pulling one hand from beneath his head, he reached down for his penis, which, already rolling up his thigh, flopped back toward his belly. He caught it—

—and began to pump.

Should he think about Shit and Dynamite?

No. Save them for later. What about Jay? No, Mex. He could wrestle the stocky little guy, kiss on him while Jay took a leak in his mouth, touch his face with its smile and its rough craters and suck the cheese out of his barrel thick, long-skinned dick. Was that the fantasy figure to break his new space in with—

As Eric had become more and more at ease in his garage room at Mr. Condotti's, more and more frequently for the last three months that fantasy figure had been Mike, maybe every other day, alternating with the most interesting fellows from under the highway. It's whom he settled with on the porch that evening—but was surprised how quickly (within a minute) it became Dynamite, with Dynamite's irregularly toothed smile, Dynamite's thick fingers like gray sandpaper, Dynamite's nails gnawed three-quarters away and his deep ridged knuckles shiny with cum that was two thirds nigger piss anyway. When Eric came he was leaning against Shit in the pickup, jerking off together, grinning at each other—because Shit had the same oversized hands, the same bitten nails ringed in black, the same knuckles, the same cock streaked with cum—it's overhang not pulled back a week now as Eric went down on it, digging inside with his tongue, while Shit dug a middle finger in a nostril, then let Eric suck it…

—he woke, on his side, night's crickets replaced by bird chirps and a breeze across his shoulder. Rolling to his back, he saw the screening crossed with sun. Outside, green boughs moved up and down. Eric stretched, feet taking away the blanket—to his hip, anyway.

From the kitchen, utensils clinked in a drawer—a pot top on a counter—and he remembered he wanted to catch his mother.

It could be as late as six-thirty, even seven!

Eric pushed up, then swung around to sit on the bed's edge, stood, and stepped through the duffle bags and cartons, around the knapsack on the floor, pushed out the door to duck across for the bathroom.

From the kitchen, Barb's voice came up the hall. "Sweetheart, put your *pants* on—*please*! There's two of us here now. Come *on*, honey…!"

And he'd had a piss-hard flapping.

Such things had never bothered Mike—who would even joke about them. (*What pretty lady* you *been messin' with this mornin'*?

(*That's for me to know and you to find out.* Eric tugged his T-shirt over his head.

(*Well, just make sure you clean 'er up.* Then Mike'd laugh and, naked, stride back into the bed room.) Living here, Eric realized, was going to be notably different.

(Did it mean anything that, last night, he'd abandoned Mike so quickly for Dynamite, for Shit…?)

Glancing down the hall, he saw, in her pinkish robe, Barb look up as she closed the refrigerator door. He thought about going in anyway—Jesus, he had to pee. Wondering if there was any chance, once he'd been working awhile, of getting his own place, he turned, went back onto the porch, slid into his jeans, looked around the boxes and bent to open the top. He tugged out a T-shirt, this one clean. (Bending over like that, you could pee all over yourself!) That's right. Mike had washed them all the previous night.

Shrugging into it, he went back to the john.

He stayed in there long enough to jerk off silently, eat it all, check to see that none had dropped. (Where might he start a medallion…? Probably not in here. Did Shit and Dynamite have one, perhaps?) Then he went back out.

He'd already noticed most of the trailer part of the house was plastic, pink or orange, soiled with time's gray. Basically the built-on porch and the built-on living room were wood and wicker—looking new and artificial, surfaces sunk below an eighth-of-an-inch of polyurethane.

Stepping into the kitchen he asked, "What time is it?"

"Ten to seven," Barb said. "You don't have to get up this early—"

"That's all right," he said. "If I'm gonna start on the garbage run on Wednesday, I gotta get up a lot earlier."

"The sea air down here does make you sleep." She moved from the counter, where a large yellow box stood with a picture of a heart-shaped bowl filled with cereal. "Clem Englert gave me some Honey Nut Cheerios from the Lighthouse. Those used to be your favorite…"

"I don't eat the sweet ones no more." Eric looked around. "But…well, since you got 'em, it's okay."

"Oh…" she said.

She was actually worried, Eric saw. "Really. It's fine." The trailer kitchen brought it back: when last he'd visited Barbara in Florida, he'd gotten really upset about some food he didn't like—which, if only because today he couldn't remember even what it had been, seemed silly.

That brought back something else he hadn't thought about since before they'd left the upstairs kitchen at Mr. Condotti's, yesterday morning. Eric went into his pocket—he'd put his lube in a box under his bed—and came out with his wallet. Sitting on a chair at the kitchen table, he unfolded it and fingered through. (He was glad the condom had gone off with Dynamite and Shit—one less thing not to have to worry about Barbara finding and his having to explain.) "I should've given you this last night. Dad told me to make sure you got it—it's his check for this month's money." Among green bills, he found the blue rectangle with HSBC across the front. Pulling it free, he held it out.

Barb stepped forward to take it. "Oh, honey—you could've lost that!"

Eric looked at her strangely. "No, I couldn't," he said—remembering when, in Turpens Notions, he'd thought his wallet gone. "It was in my wallet."

Barb took it, looked at it, sat down across from him. Then she looked up. "You know, you really *have* grown up so much. I've got to get used to you all over again." She smiled at the check. "Maybe Mike has, too."

Eric laughed. "You gonna let me drive you to work?"

"Sure—but you *can't* have the car all day. Sometimes things come up and—"

"That's okay," he said. "I was going to walk around anyway and explore."

When, in the gravel lot by the Lighthouse, they got out of Barb's Honda, with seven-twenty sun coming in across the waves instead of going out across them, the whole street seemed different from yesterday. By the yellow rail, Barbara walked up the cinder blocks, stopped to finger over her keys, found one, and pushed it in the lock.

Behind them, someone called, "Hey, there, li'l feller. Mornin', Mrs. Jeffers. Now this's gotta be Eric who you been talkin' about for the last three weeks."

With the door open an inch, Barbara—she was wearing pink jeans and white sandals (flats in her straw bag)—stopped and looked back.

A step below, so did Eric.

In the rough black denims he'd worn yesterday, open over his brown belly, with his broad rough feet, bare on the grass running between the narrow pavement and the street and his smiling blasted face, Mex walked a step ahead of bearded Jay, who towered behind him in a blue work shirt, his sleeves rolled up from colorful forearms. Under hay-hued fur, Eric saw an anchor he hadn't noticed yesterday—perhaps an older image, around which oranges, violets, and greens clustered and spiraled (probably it had been on the arm away from Eric when they were messing with Mex)—the denim buttoned up to three button holes below his beard, at the bottom of a pie slice wedge of chest hair. "How long you been here, son? A couple of days now? Or did you get in this mornin'? Yeah, your mama been going on and on about you for days. Probably I'd've recognized you anywhere…"

Was that, Eric wondered, Jay's coded way of saying that, at the truck stop yesterday, he *had*? (Maybe he'd already known Mike was black, and spotted him in the car through Turpens' glass doors…) Yet MacAmon's reticence said relax and be easy. So Eric relaxed.

"Good morning, Mr. MacAmon," Barbara said. "Yes, this is Eric. His dad brought him down from the city yesterday afternoon. I've talked to him on the phone, but it's been more than a year since we've seen each other. Hasn't it, honey?"

Eric smiled at them.

"Mornin', youngster. What's a matter? Cat gotcha tongue?" Jay gave him his grin without incisors. "Hey—don't you say good mornin' to folks?"

"G'mornin', sir!" Eric really *was* pleased to see them.

"Now, that's better—good to meet you." Jay reached out and shook Eric's hand, which momentarily vanished in Jay's, rough, hot, hirsute, and hard. "This here's my partner, Mex."

Eric shook again. He thought: I came in this guy's mouth yesterday, while Jay was pissin' all over my dick…Yes, though this meeting was all charade, it *was* easier. Mex smiled at him warmly.

"He's grown up so," Barbara said, "I don't quite know what to do with him yet." She laughed. "Eric's already got himself a job with Mr. Haskell."

"Dynamite?" Standing two steps up, Eric was as tall as MacAmon. "You sound like a busy young man. And responsible, too. Dynamite's a good feller—I don't think you could have yourself a better bossman. We used to work together, so I know."

"Well, that's nice to hear." Turning back, Barbara finished pushing the door open and went in. Mex and MacAmon followed behind Eric into the empty café.

"See—" MacAmon grinned at Eric—"your mom'll tell you: Mex and me almost always stop by and have a cup of coffee in the mornin' when she opens up the Lighthouse. We're pretty much always her first customers."

Beside Eric, Mex raised his fist and, in the sun and shadow around the curtains on the booth windows, made a rapid sequence of signs.

"Really—" Barbara walked to the counter's end and stepped behind to the urn, took a dinner plate sized paper filter, held it up in one hand, looked at it, put it down, and took two bags of coffee from the shelf with the other, tore them open, and poured both into the scalloped paper basket—"he's got so grown up. He's going to be tired of hearing me say it, pretty soon." She turned a spigot above the urn. Like a river in a cavern, water falling into metal rang through the room.

"Come on, let's sit down and have some coffee," Jay said, which may or may not have been translation of something Mex had just signed.

Swallowing, Eric thought: These guys have done something, been somewhere, seen something—and because Mex can't speak, the energy he carries with him is three times as intense as that of any ordinary person. Is *that* sexiness?

Or is that just to me…?

Eric followed, about to sit with them, but Jay leaned to the side and gripped a corner of one of the square tables and pulled it closer. "Come on—you sit there, Eric." Turning to Mex, Jay's great hand said something in silent signs.

Mex laughed—as silently—and signed something back.

"That's so you can see what we're sayin'."

Eric sat in the chair, looking at both men either side the table. "What… *are* you guys sayin' to each other?"

"I'm sayin'," Jay said, softly and pointedly, "I *don't* think it's a good idea for him to pull down his jeans, bend over the table, and let you fuck 'im right here with your mama standing at the—Hello, Mrs. Jeffers!" Jay sat up, smiling. "Yeah, we'll take that coffee, soon as it's ready." He turned back to Eric. "You gonna have some?"

Eric twisted around in his seat, to see Barb coming across the café, two cardboard containers in one hand, a cup—for Eric—in the other.

Mex sat back, hit the side of his hand under his nose twice, dropped his hands, made a double rub up his bald belly, then pointed with both hands.

"Mex is saying how that smells *real* good, Mrs. Jeffers," Jay announced, tall enough to look over the booth back with one arm across it.

"You're teaching Eric some of Mex's sign language?" Barbara asked. "Well, at least he'll learn *something* while he's here." She set the milky container before Mex, the black one before Jay, then put the third coffee—a regular white crock—on Eric's table. "I'm going in the back and scrape the griddle off—Coby leaves it in such a mess—then he complains all morning when he comes in. *Uggh!*" She turned back behind the counter.

"Thank you, ma'am," Jay called.

Mex signaled silently.

And Eric called, "Thanks, Barb."

Jay turned back to face the table.

"He can...hear," Eric said, "can't he? Mex, I mean."

"Yeah," Jay said. "Mex can hear just about as good you and me—if not better."

"Then why can't he talk?" Eric looked back and forth between Mex and Jay.

"'Cause some mean motherfuckers tried to cut his damned tongue out when he was a kid, and carved up his larynx with a knife while they was at it." Again, Jay's voice dropped. "It's a wonder he can still suck a fuckin' dick. Thank God he got across the border—and found *this* place."

Eric looked at Mex, who sipped his coffee, looking back with hard, dark eyes, then pointed up to the wall clock.

"Hey," Jay said. "We gotta get out of here and make another run. Or somebody might start complainin'." Jay hiked his elbow back and dug into a pocket to pull out a stuffed wallet that looked more like rag than leather. "I keep waitin' for this place to start chargin' sixty cents for a cup of coffee like all the places in Runcible. It ain't subsidized like the Dump or nothin'. Last place for a fifty-cent java. Throw a quarter on that, Mex, for Mrs. Jeffers."

So Mex went digging in his own jeans and tossed down a silver coin showing a horned bull's skull above the mountains—Big Sky Country. That was Montana. Earlier in the year, they'd seemed the only quarters you could find in Atlanta.

Jay slid from the booth. "We gotta go—"

"Can you show me the Gilead Boat Dock?" Eric asked. "That's where I gotta meet Dynamite on Wednesday."

Jay looked at him as if he thought perhaps he was kidding about not knowing where it was. "Come on. It's just down the street."

Mex got up.

So did Eric. "Barb...?" he called. His mother had finally gone into the kitchen. "I'll be right back."

Barb didn't answer.

He went outside with Mex and Jay.

They walked down pavement, grass, dirt.

"See—" Jay pointed across a lawn, where a cannon sat off center before a gray building with white trim—"that's the Post Office." He turned around. A wooden deck extended over the water. A wooden rail ran across it. To the left a boathouse was painted dark green.

"And this here's the Gilead Dock."

Beside it was a lamp post with, near its top, a gray metal shade hanging from a wooden arm. Beside the boards, a roughly painted barge-like boat—white—moved up and down on the water, roped to metal cleats fixed to the dock. "And that's the scow."

Mex took a peg out of the gate and lifted it. A series of rhomboidal forms changed their angles as it went up.

"Don't look like nobody's here. You still gotta make the trip if you don't have no passengers?"

Jay chuckled. "The Chamber of Commerce pays us to go back and forth—so if somebody *does* wanna get from here to there, there to here, there's a way to do it."

"Oh," Eric said. Three gray gulls—one, then two more—soared in, to land on the lamp spar. The sky was gray-blue. Dark green water was rolled and ribbed with waves.

"What are those docks over there?"

"That's what they call the marina," Jay explained. The several levels of wooden web wove over the water.

Eric could only see three boats.

"Captain Miller still keeps his fishin' craft tied up there. The other two are wrecks. I don't even know who belongs to that one. Hey." Jay crooked his forefinger and looked at it. "You seen your snot buddy again?"

"Huh? Shit? Oh…well, yeah. At the Lighthouse."

"I thought you two might get along, back when you was first suckin' on my finger before. Shit's been eatin that stuff all his life—first thing I thought of, soon as you started nursin' on mine. I guess nobody in the Dump ever told him to stop."

"When we was tongue fuckin'—before, back at the truck stop, me and…Shit. I…did it, with his finger, when he went into his nose like…well, what I did—with yours." Eric was embarrassed. "It just happened. I wasn't even thinking."

"Probably better you wasn't," Jay said. "It's okay during the winter. But sometimes Shit forgets and does it around the summer people—at least he used to."

"Do you do it…?"

"Nope." Jay said it flatly enough that Eric was startled. But then he chuckled. "It don't bother me, though. Fact is, I think it's kinda cute. That's always how I been with pretty much everything nasty." Suddenly he reached out and hooked his elbow around Mex's neck, and dragged him back against him, the way he'd hugged Eric in the hall outside the john the day before. "Like *this* piss-drinkin', shit-eatin', toe-suckin' motherfucker." Mex caught his balance against Jay, and grinned. "We love all that stuff, don't we, Mex?" Still gripping Mex in a headlock, Jay looked up at the clouds, the gulls. "So at least you got four people you don't got to worry about offendin'."

"Four—?"

"Mex, me, Dynamite, and Shit…" Jay chuckled—and released his partner, who pushed himself upright again, still looking pleased. "Shit got some devilment in him. He likes to have his fun. But he's a good kid."

Eric swallowed. "I…like him."

"Good," Jay said. "'Cause I got a feelin' he gonna be after you a lot. Dynamite seen how you and Shit was gettin' along; that's probably why he offered you the job. He looks out for that kid."

"But how did they know I was going to be staying in Diamond Harbor?"

"Same way I did. We *all* kinda figured yesterday you was probably Mrs. Jeffers' boy. I told you, Mex and me have a cup or two with her practically every blessed mornin'. She been talkin' 'bout how you was comin' for three weeks." He winked. "So then when you said you was…Eric—?"

"Yeah, I'd begun to figure you…knew me."

"Well." Jay laughed out full. "She ain't been talkin' about nothin' else. Hey—what's wrong? Don't worry. Nobody ain't gonna say nothin'. And Mex here can't. Why in the world would we wanna do that? *That'd* be pretty stupid, don't you think?"

"What about Shit's folks?" Eric asked. "Who's *his* father…?"

"I believe, if I remember right, you already sucked 'im off," Jay said, "back at Turpens."

"What do you mean?"

"Dynamite. Shit's Dynamite's boy."

"Huh? *Dynamite*—? But I thought you said he was…You mean he's *not* his nephew…? Dynamite, the guy whose ass Morgan—Shit—was fuckin' when we came in, is…his *dad*?"

"Yep." Bearded Jay nodded. "But you ain't supposed to talk about that. Though God knows people around here do." Frowning, he lowered his voice. "If anybody asks, you go on sayin' you think Dynamite's his uncle. Like everybody else. That's how we do it. A fair number of local folk know. But that just mixes it up a little. I don't know why, but people feel that's better—even those what suspect somethin' goin' on. Besides—" Jay stood up straighter, looking serious—"you don't know nothin' about them two foolin' around with each other, anyway, do you?"

"Huh? Oh…oh, I see. Like goin' to Turpens. Yeah…No. *No*, I don't know nothin' about that."

"Good."

"But—his own…dad? That's awesome…! I don't think I ever—What

about his mama?" Eric was thinking of Barbara. "I mean, I know Shit…
he's black. They said his mother was colored—like my dad—yesterday.
I mean…His eyes are green. And his skin's the same color as mine, just
about. I mean, his face looks like Dynamite's, except his nose…and his
hair—'cause it's yeller…or, I guess, brown. Tan—"

"Mildred—that was *her* name. I don't think either me *or* Dynamite
ever knew for sure what her last name was. She was about half or a quarter
black—so I guess Shit is, too. She run off six or seven months after Shit
was born. The three of us—her, Dynamite, and me—used to whore down
over in Turpens' back lot. She come to the Harbor for about a year, a
year-an'-a-half—she was twenty-five, maybe twenty-six. Me and Dynamite
was just twenty-one, maybe twenty-two. A little older than Shit, now. She
was around long enough for us both to fuck her a few times and decide
we didn't cotton to it. But we still kinda liked her, if you know what I
mean. Till he came out, it was a toss-up whether the bastard was gonna
be Dynamite's or mine, 'cause we usually fucked her at the same time. She
dropped Shit right there in spring—and took off with a Polack trucker
she met in the parkin' lot back out there on New Year's Eve. By the fifth
of January, she was *gone*—nobody done seen her since. Even while she was
here, Dynamite—well, Dynamite and me, with a *whole* lotta help from Mex,
once I hooked up with him—did more raisin' of that little bastard than she
did. I will say this, though—she breast fed him for four or five months, but
once she got tired of that, she'd leave 'im with me or Dynamite for three
or four days at a time. Takin' care of that kid was what got Dynamite out
of hustlin' at the truck stop. Kyle helped, too. She could always make more
than we could anyway, especially back when she was pregnant—for some
reasons, straight guys seemed to like that. They'd pay extra for it. Her and
Dynamite was never livin' together or nothing like that. But she'd drop
Morgan off and go to work. Only half the time she wouldn't bother to
pick 'im up. Hey, if I hadn't been his daddy's suck buddy since I was your
age—" again grinning, Jay pointed at the gap in his teeth with his sausage
of a thumb—"I might think Shit was a mite excessive in his beatin' off.
But he comes by it honestly. Dynamite was always a ten-time-a-day feller
hisself—"

"I do it *about* that much." Eric grinned. "Well, maybe…six or seven."

"Good." Jay snorted. "Then he won't worry about you, neither. Looks
like everybody wanted a taste of you—and everybody got one, too. They
know not to hog you on your first visit. Kinda pass you around—truck stop
manners."

Gulls mewed overhead, then circled down around the dock, the
lamppost, finally to fly off.

"Does your partner—Mex, really *like* that stuff? I mean you and guys... pissin' in his mouth and all?"

"Fuckin' loves it." Jay looked across the dock where Mex had wandered and called out: "Doncha, you piss guzzlin', asshole eatin' spic? *Get* back over here!" Jay winked at Eric. "When he gets real turned on, yeah, he'll eat my shit. Maybe we'll let you come watch some day."

Mex stood up, grinning, looked around the glittering waves, then turned to lumber, his thick legs slightly bowed, to where Jay stood at the dock head.

"I mean...how do you *know* he likes stuff like that?"

"'Cause we done slept rolled up in the same blankets for fifteen years now—" again Jay dropped his big arm around Mex's black jacketed shoulder—"my big smelly feet all up in his face and his big hard ones kickin' around my beard all night..." Again he chuckled. "He likes the salt, too: you learn that about your partner. Besides, he tells me. You know, every day about an hour 'fore I swing out of bed, Mex gets a lip-lock on my pecker—and I let 'er run. That's fuckin' heaven. And that spic don't spill a drop, neither. That's the only reason I don't stink like an ol' pee pot, today. This damned spic here wipes the fuckin' shit out my ass with his tongue and drinks my fuckin' piss. Doncha, boy?" Again Jay gave Mex a one-armed hug.

Fleetingly, Eric thought of Frack pulling wide his black buttocks. *Get yo' face on in dere, now*...cock beside his scrotum pendulating side to side like a trunk.

Grinning, Mex nodded.

"Hey—and I can call 'im any fuckin' names I want to, too—in front of anyone I want. Don't I, you shit-eatin', wetback fuck-face? But you—" Jay frowned at Eric—"say *one* bad word about 'im. Just one, I'm not kiddin', less'n I say you can, and I'll bust you in your fuckin' head. You hear me? *I* call him names, see, to let him know he's wanted—it makes 'im feel good. Let's 'im know he's got some *real* fuckin' respect. 'Cause if you can't let respect go sometimes, then it means you don't have it to let go of in the first place. And I respect this cut-down cheesy motherfucker more than anyone in the goddam world—you understand me?"

"Un...yeah." Eric nodded. "...I think so—"

"Good. So you respect 'im too. Look here—?" Again releasing Mex, Jay pulled out his denim shirt on one side and lifted it, to show a wedge of hair stuck flat over his lower belly above his broad belt—"That's where Mex cum all over me before we got up to walk down to the boathouse this mornin'." With one hand, he started unbuttoning the rest of it. "I ain't gonna wash that off at all. I'm gonna *wear* it off. That's what you call commitment. It's a…gay pride thing."

"Mmm…" Eric swallowed. Again, he'd begun to feel something in the conversation had moved over an edge that made him uncomfortable. Again, he tried to pull it back. "But you mean Shit and his…*uncle* really… really fuck around together in a public john? That's…so *awesome*! I mean, with his own father—"

"Uncle," Jay corrected.

"Yeah—I meant uncle."

Jay raised his palm to Mex's pitted face. "Hey. Try some of this." With Jay's forefinger closing one of Mex's nostril, then his thumb against the other, Mex snorted into Jay's hand.

"See, he knows what to do. We learned that with Shit." Jay grunted. "Here." And the hard palm was against Eric's mouth. Eric thrust out his tongue for the mucasoid and crusty slur. "That's right, puppy. Me, Mex, *and* his uncle all done that for Shit, at least since he was a little feller; we don't mind doin' it for you, too. But you start blabberin' to folks an' we ain't gonna give you no more." Jay with his gap, Mex with his yellow-white teeth, both grinned at Eric. "It's that salt thing, right? That's good, ain't it? That's what Shit and the three other snot jockeys I knowed *all* done told me." Suddenly the menace seemed gone. "Dynamite'll give you his, once he gets to know you—and he's sure you want it. Hey, you and Shit can trade that stuff back and forth all you like. I've tasted it, but I ain't into scarfin' it down like it was no major food group. But none of us don't mind obligin' you puppies."

Eric looked up from Jay's hard hand. "Jesus. I got a hard-on…again." Reaching down, he adjusted himself.

"Me too." Again the big man chuckled. "I don't have to ask about Mex." He took his other arm from around the shorter man's shoulder. "Probably so does Shit right now, wherever he is…by osmosis or somethin'." Jay wiped his palm on the thigh of his jeans. "You think you can handle two in your mouth at once, like Mex was doin' with us in the john? Or Shit?"

Eric nodded. "Sure." Another skill he'd learned under the Atlanta highway.

"Then you'll have some real fun with Shit and Dynamite. They'll throw you all the dick you can handle. Now, ain't him *or* Shit gonna force nothin' on you. That's Dynamite's gay pride thing. He gets that from bein' a dad. But they like to share—like me and Mex. Hey, you'll have some good fun with 'em."

Raising both hands, Mex signed something.

Jay glanced down.

Eric looked up at Jay.

Jay said, "He wants to know what you did with Al's fuckin' rubber full of nigger piss. You know—his jizz."

"Huh?"

"That load he slipped you in his damned rubber, back at Turpens."

"Um…Oh," Eric said. "Last night. I gave it to Dynamite—"

Mex exploded in grunting laughter, half of it sound and half of it just expelled breath. Pulling away from Jay, he stepped around the morning's wet dock boards, bending and recovering. Every three or four seconds, his hands moved into articulation, till he began to laugh and shake his head again.

Jay was grinning, too. "He says he knew that was gonna happen. He said he knew that fuckin' cum hound was gonna get that thing from you, one way or the other. I guess he was right, huh? Nigger cum ain't safe around that white boy. Dynamite been that way since he was younger than you."

Shaking their heads, both boatmen went over to untie the scow.

Then, moving onto the deck, Jay lowered his head under the chipped blue rim of the wheel shelter.

Eric watched from the dock as the motor began to froth at the stern.

"Hey," Eric called, "it was good to see you again."

One foot on the low rail, Mex leaned an elbow on a knee and waved his other hand.

"It was nice to see you, too, li'l feller," Jay called back, hands wide apart on the wheel. Open in the back and half the sides, the partial enclosure was not quite a wheelhouse.

"If you're around the Lighthouse, we'll be back in about two, two-and-a-quarter hours. That's about what it takes for a round trip run out there—" he nodded toward the horizon, where water and sky came together at the stone colored seam, like a scratch along a fifth of the horizon—"to Gilead and back." Jay was bending down to check stuff beside the wheel. Though the motor was going, the scow had not started moving. "Maybe you can take a trip out there with us soon, and see the island. The fare's three dollars—but seniors and Chamber of Commerce employees ride free. That's policy."

"Hey," Eric said. "That's…really awesome!"

A truck—a Nissan Cube painted brown—rolled by, turning up the drive beside the post office.

Standing again, Jay waved and called, "Hey, Wally—!"

From the truck window, a black man's naked arm came out and returned the hail.

Eric didn't see what Jay did, but the scow pulled from the planks and pilings. "So now you know where the Gilead Boat dock is—like you wanted," Jay called across the water, two thirds of his voice cut away by the motor and the roar and ruffle of froth. "Say so long to Mrs. Jeffers for us."

*

When Eric walked into the Lighthouse Coffee, Egg & Bacon, the blades on the ceiling fans were turning, and the cup was gone from the table where he had sat that morning. Two more couples sat at other booths. Five singles sat at center tables.

The wall clock said eight-ten.

In her smock and with her fluffy orange hair, Clem stood at the counter. "Good mornin', Eric. I just sent your mom out on an errand for me. She'll be back in twenty minutes. How'd you like your first night in Diamond Harbor?"

"Mornin', Ms. Englert," Eric said. "It was fine. The sea air is nice. It's okay if I sit down…?"

"I don't even want you to ask next time." Clem laughed. "Sure—you sit anywhere. Now, I call you Eric. You got to call me Clem. Go on, sit down now. I don't think we ever get *that* busy, at least not this year."

So Eric sat at a table across from the booths, wondering if he should ask for another cup of coffee—he didn't want one.

He'd been sitting two minutes, when Clem finished whatever she was doing with the big juice cans on the back shelf, and came around toward him. "Sometimes I think figuring how many breakfasts I'm actually gonna cook will run me nuts. I'm ready for six, and twenty-four people show up, every *one* of them wantin' sausage and eggs! I lay in for two dozen—and *maybe* the next morning I get three. And all *they* want is bacon and toast." She stopped by the table and frowned. "The next day everybody wants poached and toast—and the day after *that* nobody wants nothin' but a muffin! Tell me, honey—I was talkin' to your mama just a little while ago. Do you really wanna be a garbage man?"

Eric looked up. "Huh? What you mean?"

"I mean it seems a strange job for such a fine young follow to go into. It's so dirty, smelly—I was wonderin' why *you'd* even consider something like that. That's what you really want to do?"

Eric smiled, because he couldn't think of anything else to do. "I dunno. I guess so. Why…not?"

"Well, it's good honest work. I'm not sayin' it isn't. Still, it's not the most respectable job you could have. And Morgan and his uncle ain't the most respectable people in the Harbor. It seems to me—" Clem went through several expressions and settled on a smile that Eric wondered if it wasn't for some all-purpose explanation—"you'd want a job where some nice young ladies might look at you and say, well, what a fine young fellow he is. He'd make a real good provider—you know: someone with prospects. A good person to start a family with. I was only wonderin' why you'd wanna work with someone livin' over with all those…*strange* people—in the Dump. 'Course, with your dad, you could be used to it already. I don't know. Maybe it's different in Atlanta. But down here, you kinda get known by who you work with. I don't mean to say there's somethin' wrong with Dynamite—or Morgan for that matter, though I always thought he was a little odd—but there must be somethin' you could do that would…well, *look* a little better."

Eric said, "People need to get their garbage collected, don't they?"

"Yeah," Clem said. "But do *you* need to be the person who collects it?"

"Is the Dump all that bad?" Eric asked. "Is that the place they throw all the garbage?"

Clem laughed. "Naw—it used to be, maybe back in the forties and fifties. But see, it's like a welfare neighborhood—social assistance or somethin'. All the Chamber of Commerce people—at least a lot of them live there, thanks to the Kyle Foundation."

"Jay and Mex don't live there—do they?"

"Jay MacAmon? You met him today—?"

Eric actually started to say "Yesterday." But he caught himself and nodded.

"He got a place on the island—but it's the same difference. Almost." She seemed to sense his discomfort, though she was probably not sure of its cause. "I mean, how old are you?"

Eric said, "I'm sixteen. I'm gonna be seventeen on Saturday."

"You *are?*" Clem looked surprised. "Now, see—I thought you were already nineteen, like Morgan…even twenty-one or so. You're just sixteen? You looked like you were a bit…well, older."

"Naw," Eric said. "I ain't." Since he'd been progressing with the Bowflex workouts, Eric had grown used to people giving him between two and five extra years.

"So—maybe it *don't* make much difference. I mean, if it's just for a summer job…I was gonna say, you could even ask Barbara's friend, Ron, to see if he could get you a spot over in Runcible—you know, where you'd wear a clean shirt, a nice tie? And work in an office, like he does—with air conditioning." She nodded deeply. "Don't knock that air conditioning, son. Believe me that makes a *big* difference. I'd get it in here, if I could…"

*

When Barbara came back, with a brown paper sack of Granny Smiths for the afternoon's cobbler, Eric told her that he was going up to the house— "No, not in the car. Don't worry. I'm gonna walk—or jog some of it. At home, I'm gonna put my bike together and maybe ride down here again. Or—I dunno—around."

"You could put your stuff away, out on the porch," Barb said.

"Or do a workout. Or…yeah, put some stuff away." Though he wondered where he was supposed to put it.

"At least," Barb said, "move it out of the middle of the porch floor." Then she frowned. "Going up there, you won't get lost?"

Eric gave her a look, then laughed.

"All right," she said. "But try to be there when I get home—would you? I don't want to have to start worrying about you—not for the first few days, at least."

"Okay," he said. "That'll be my first job. Not to worry *you*."

* * *

[8] ON FRONT STREET, Eric started jogging, took the turnoff he thought would take him up to Barb's, got twenty yards along it and, beside a bank of quivering Queen Anne's lace, realized, in the passing breeze, it wasn't the right one: it was the road that had put Mike out on Front Street when they'd been briefly lost. So he went back—the one he wanted was the next double rutted path. He set himself a medium gait—but after ten minutes, had to stop.

It was all uphill.

Following car tracks over a meadow, he did fine. (Clem had said it was between two and three miles, and even though he'd walked more than half of it rather than run, soon he was at the pine-wood slope up to the house. It had taken maybe forty-five minutes.) Well, he thought, pushing into the kitchen, at least now he knew his way into town—and back.

He didn't put his bike together.

Eric lay down on his porch bed, jerked off, slept about forty minutes, woke logily, and decided, "Naw, this ain't no good," got up, moved some of the boxes up to the wall with the screen, then thought, "That's stupid. Suppose it rains," and moved them back against the other wall that was the house. He put the front wheel on the bike but not the back one, which was marginally more difficult because of the chain, set it in the corner, then did the last set-up needed for the Bowflex—and (finally) another workout.

It was hot, so he swabbed under his arms with yesterday's balled up tank top, wet a towel in the sink and wiped himself down, then started a laundry pile in the porch corner.

After that he felt better.

*

At five minutes after five when Barbara stepped in, she wrinkled her nose and said, "Honey, did you burn something on the stove?" and walked across to the small television at the back of the counter to flip it on.

Eric sat in the chair by the table. "Burn what? No."

"'Cause I smell something."

"I cooked the chicken."

"How?" she asked, surprised and automatically.

"I roasted it," Eric said. "In the oven."

Barb looked surprised.

Eric got up, went to the counter, where a tray was covered with a piece of wax paper. "I sliced up half of it—and made some tomato salad, too, like Grandma showed me, back in Hugantown. You remember. You always liked that. So did I." He opened the refrigerator, and took out the bowl. "You got mayonnaise and mustard and stuff. We can make sandwiches—if you want. That's what dad always liked, when I'd cook a chicken for him. Or we can have it plain, if you want."

"Um…" Then Barbara smiled. "It smells…good," she admitted. "I thought it was burnt 'cause I wasn't expecting it, I guess. That's all."

Eric grinned back. "You're forgiven." He put the tray on the table, where he'd laid out silverware and napkins. "You said you wanted to eat a little earlier. That's why I decided to try and have it ready when you got home."

Barb said, "You didn't set the table."

"Come on. Sit down." Eric said, "I was going to, when you walked in."

Barb came to the table and—almost cautiously—pulled out a chair. "What did you do all afternoon?" She moved away suddenly, went to the sink, and turned on the water—to wash her hands.

"I took a nap," Eric said, "actually. Then I did a workout, on the machine. You want some lemonade? I made a pitcher—it's in the refrigerator. Do you have glasses? I couldn't find 'em."

"Oh—I've only got those ugly plastic ones."

"Where?"

"You didn't see them? In the cabinet under the drawers—over there."

"That must be the one place I didn't look." Eric went to the refrigerator and took out the metal pitcher. Ice clinked against the sides as he brought it to the table. "You want to get them out?"

"Did you take a shower after your workout?"

"Um," Eric said, carefully. "No."

"You know you really have to start doing that."

"Why?" he asked. "I'll take one tonight, don't worry."

"Well, you'll smell, honey." She closed the tap on the back of the sink and turned around.

Eric stood there, smiling. He held his hands apart and open, questioningly. "Do I smell?"

She took in a deep breath that seemed more exasperation than an attempt to detect odor. "No..."

"Well, then?"

"But you *might* smell, sweetheart. And it would be a nice thing to do—especially when you're going to cook."

"I washed my hands," Eric said, not sure, actually, if he had or not.

Barbara stepped around him and turned to the table.

On the little TV screen under the upper cabinet, the Weather Channel showed a tornado's funnel, leaning, blurring, sending up a froth of dust and debris as it plowed along some horizon, beyond a truck with a dish antenna in the back, cameras, and—standing in the bed and staring toward the storm—young folks with binoculars, ponchos, rainhats, and knapsacks.

Barb hadn't gotten the glasses, so he went to the cabinet door beneath the drawers she had pointed to, squatted, and opened it. He took out a large, blue plastic tumbler. "These...?" he asked, holding it up for her to see.

"Yeah, I...guess so." (He came up with two.) "I wish I had some nicer ones. You know your father—Mike, I mean—used to have a very strong body odor, when he worked hard. Or even exercised. I mean, it could sneak up on you and surprise you. A couple of times, I remember, I was actually shocked—"

"But Dad didn't *do* a workout this afternoon," Eric said. "*I* did." He remembered his father's smell, acidic, and, yes, surprising in its intensity. When Eric had been seven and eight and they'd visited Uncle Omar in Texas, he'd loved the way Mike smelled when he got home from work at the filling station and would sit Eric on one knee and Harry on the other and read another chapter from Uncle Omar's old Tarzan books, *Tarzan and the Jewels of Opar*, or *Tarzan and the Golden Lion*, and how Mike would kind of snicker under his breath, as though it were a joke, whenever he read out a passage where the white men got mad and called the natives block-headed niggers, as though its humor went over the boys' heads: *Now, I don't wanna hear you fellas talkin' like that*, though Uncle Omar talked that way to and about everyone, including Ralphy and Hareem and Eric, not to mention Lurlene and Mike. Sometimes Eric felt everyone was in on it except himself…

Sometimes, especially when Uncle Omar was drunk and happy, and going on about this "nigger scumbag" and that stupid "nigger son of a bitch," and Lurlene was too busy for anybody to relax—except Omar himself—Eric would get an erection. He wondered if Hareem did, too.

"Really, I'm gonna take one later—"

"Eric—that's not the *point!*" she said it sharply and suddenly.

Eric started, feeling hurt and confused. Then he swallowed. "Hey, Barb—?"

She blinked at him.

"—are we having an argument about somethin'?"

She kept blinking.

So he asked, "You wanna drink?"

She took a big breath. Then she said, "Sweetheart, I want a drink so bad I don't know which way is up! I've been thinking about having one all the way home, and I'm standing here blaming it on you that I didn't walk right in and get one."

Eric said, "It's in the living room. You want me to get it for you? Or you want to get it yourself?"

Now she swept around the table in her pink jeans and strode toward the arch into the hall. "No, I've got it."

Moments later she was back with her own glass in one hand and, in the other, by the neck, the bottle of Heaven Hill. "Actually, I'm going to have it with some of your lemonade. And then we're going to sit down and have some of this very nice dinner that you were so sweet to fix. No, we are *not* arguing. At all." She sat. "I'm just a little jumpy—that's all. Hey—if you want a chicken sandwich, you go ahead. There's bread in the icebox—but I'm sure you know that. I'm just going to have a few slices on a plate. All right? You *really* remembered how grandma made her tomato salad…?"

As they ate—her glass tumbler half bourbon and—as she poured from the metal pitcher—half lemonade, Barb said, "You know we *can* turn the television off, but when you're by yourself, sometimes you like to have a little…I don't know: background noise."

"I don't mind it." Really, it was kind of annoying. "But no, we didn't watch too much TV at Dad's." Eric put a top slice of whole wheat bread on his chicken sandwich, then bit into it. "Mike likes video games." The only time Mike regularly turned on the TV in his bedroom was just before going to sleep. A third of the time, it would be on when he got up. He'd only flipped it off—sometimes—when he came from the bathroom after his first middle-of-the-night piss.

"Mmm." Barb took another sip from her bourbon and lemonade. "That's your dad—a big kid. Video games." Smiling, she shook her head, put the glass down, and looked at it. "You haven't gotten so big that I should be offering *you* one of these, now, have you…?" She nodded toward the glass.

"Nope," Eric said. "I haven't." He knew she thought of drink as something to fix the jumpiness, but he had learned—in Florida—it was something that, the next day, created it.

"Well—that's something." As there had been in Florida, Barbara kept a second TV in her bedroom, though not the living room. Was that, Eric wondered, a holdover from her marriage?

"You know, Barb, your boss is funny." Eric pushed the tray toward her. "Clem was sayin' before how she doesn't like to meddle in people's business. But she sure started meddling—I guess that's what you'd call it—in mine, telling me how she doesn't think I ought to work as a garbage man. I'm not gonna be a garbage man—just a helper."

"Oh, good God!" Barb laughed. "That's all Clem Englert *does* is meddle! Probably I should have warned you. She was going on to me about that, too—don't pay her any mind, honey. You listen, you smile, you even say thank you. Then you go on about your business. That's the only way you can survive down here—listen to your mother, believe me!" She laughed again.

And finally took up a piece of chicken.

Eric relaxed when she took a bite, then another.

"Why was she so bothered by it?"

"First, I think she thought you were a lot older. And second, all those black guys who live in the Dump—or work for the Chamber of Commerce, I guess—still kind of worry people down here a little. They shouldn't. They've been here long enough. You'd think they'd all have gotten used to it by now."

"Used to what?" Eric asked.

"Well," she said, "at least as I understand it, because…well, so many of them are gay, honey."

"They are?" Eric asked. "Since I am too—" there, he'd said it—"that shouldn't be any problem for me. Right?"

Barbara sat pensively and lifted a tomato wedge on her fork. "So you…" she began after a moment, "still think you're gay? I mean, you *feel* that you're…gay—still feel that way, I mean?"

Eric nodded. He'd wanted it to sound kind of light, kind of jokey: "Yeah." It had come out pretty serious.

"I thought, maybe, it was something you'd decide you'd…I dunno: grown out of." She ate the tomato. "You didn't put any dill in it."

"You didn't *have* any dill," Eric said. "We could get some."

"Down here?" She shook her head. "I don't think so."

"No," Eric said. "No—I haven't. Grown out of it, I mean. I don't think people do."

"Then it's probably good you're here," she said, sitting back. "I mean, I don't see how your being here can hurt."

Eric asked, "Does your friend, Ron…work for the Chamber of Commerce?"

"Oh, no," she said. "No. No, Ron is perfectly normal—I mean." She frowned. "No, I mean, he's got his own business over in Runcible. Computer programming. This has been such a depressed place for so long, they're trying to attract new business and things—make it more attractive. To people like Ron, and—I guess—the people in the Dump as well. You didn't go over there today, did you?"

"No."

"Well—you'll probably meet Ron in the next couple of days. Actually, he's away for a computer conference in Savannah. But he'll be back, I think, on Thursday. You'll see him then. He's *really* nice." How long ago, Eric wondered, had he learned that "*really* nice" was Barbara's code for black. But now he was sure. "I know you'll like him." Of course, he'd heard her say it to disbelieving and long-suffering Grandma, three different times back in Hugantown.

"You think I should ask him about a job in his office—too?"

"Honey—" and here Barb leaned forward. "I want you to do whatever it is you're happiest doing. Really. That's all. That's the only reason I wanted you to come down here." She sipped from her glass. "Honestly, sweetheart."

"You know, Barb," Eric said, "if I keep that job for three months, I can start makin' some real money. It's not as much as Mike makes—but it's more than twenty thousand a year. Twenty-seven, I think Dynamite said. That's pretty good for seventeen or eighteen."

Barbara looked at him, soberly. "You're going to be working with them *that* long—?"

* * *

[9] IN THE THREE days after Shit and Dynamite helped take Eric's stuff from the Lighthouse up to Barbara's, Eric ran into them twice—once on Front Street, going into the post office, and once up at the Citgo Station.

The first time, on the tree-shadowed concrete by the squat, square, black-and-aluminum pumps, Shit was still barefoot and in the same green shirt with the torn off sleeves; Dynamite was still in his work shoes, overalls, and garbage truck T-shirt—just what they'd worn at Turpens.

The second time, beside the large orange and brown roadside sign for Hurter's Seeds, Tools, and Lumber, both got out of the pickup to say hello. Eric looked down at the frayed cuffs of Shit's pants to realize Shit, though still sockless, now wore falling-apart basketball sneakers, from which his soiled toes showed through three rips in the rubber and the once black cloth. Some of the eyelets had pulled loose from the cloth and one sneaker was laced with brown twine.

Both times Eric assured them he'd be at the dock on Wednesday, four forty-five sharp. Both times, with Georgia seaside seriousness, Dynamite answered: "Sure. That'll be good. We'll see you," while Shit stood behind his "uncle's" shoulder, in the sun, looking so pleased Eric thought he might shout out in the street.

Over those same Harbor days, Eric learned Shit was called variously "Morgan" or "the Haskell boy" or "Haskell's nigger bastard" by most of the Harbor's permanent residents. From both black and white customers at Clem's by now, he'd heard all three. (Maybe he felt "Shit" was an improvement.) Apparently Shit was only six or seven weeks beyond his own nineteenth birthday, which Eric also knew—now—came at the start of the second week in May. Over the same time he learned that Jay MacAmon lived out on Gilead Island at the old Kyle place—with his uncle Shad and that dumb (as in mute) Mexican of his, and Kyle's cousin Hugh.

Both MacAmon and Haskell were nigger lovers—a term Eric already knew from East Texas and Georgia and West Virginia, all three, since it had been repeatedly applied to his mom. It had wounded him deeply till, in a kind of despair, he had adopted the strategy that a young, liberal, eighth grade teacher had told his class about—appropriating the enemy's term: like the Radical Faeries and the Wry Crips. And Eric decided (he was not quite brave enough to do it out loud, but it represented a major internal change), Okay, that's what I am! As well as a goddam cocksucker—and felt a little better.

And he'd started sucking a lot of cock—much of it black.

At five forty-five on Wednesday, four days before his own seventeenth birthday, after hiking down the dark path through the pine woods, over the meadow, and into town, Eric reached the surprising openness of Front

Street and its night lights and the Gilead Boat Dock, where he started
work for Dynamite Haskell.

*

In the pre-dawn dark before the sea, under the florescent ring in its tin
shield above the dock's slat gate, unshaven Dynamite waited, one big hand
splayed over the truck's forward fender's two-and-a-half colors. "Good to
see you, boy."

To the left a similar light lit the dimmer web of the marina's docks.

Now, looking again at the garbage vehicle, Eric saw that the orange
between the two grays—one of them blue in daylight—was rust, not paint.
"This is a good day to come—we can use you." The hand slid off into
shadow. Dynamite stepped forward.

Moths and things that looked like fleas flicked at the headlights, at the
overhead circular bulb, or *ting*ed its metal cone.

Grinning over his missing teeth, Shit reached out a hand as big his
dad's and grabbed Eric's, to help him into the cab.

"Hey," Eric said, as, on the other side, Dynamite opened the door and
pulled himself in. Dynamite slammed the driver's door. Eric said: "I...had
fun, you know, thinkin' about what you guys was doin' with...um." He
sounded awkward to himself. "Al's rubber—that I gave you."

Dynamite and Shit both looked over at him. Shit finger was just
coming down from his mouth. Eric wondered if he missed a dig and a
suck—probably. Both were grinning in the dashboard's lights.

"I mean, you know...jerkin' off over it." Eric wondered if he'd needed
to say that.

The pickup's motor turned over. "Well," Dynamite said, "good for you.
Then all *three* of us got somethin' out of it." The truck moved forward.
"Only now it's time to haul some fuckin' garbage."

"It's just pickin' up bags and throwin' 'em in the truck bed." Shit slid
over to make more room for Eric. "Foltz Truckin' handles the recycled
stuff—the tied-up paper and the plastic. They take that out the county.
We don't even see that shit. We just do the black-bag stuff. It ain't nothin',
really."

The dark seemed to blow through the cab window, even flicker above
green and red dashboard lights, as Eric took his first run along the garbage
route. "Right in there." Beyond the rubber-padded wheel and outside the
windshield—wipers had smeared it with arcs of bugs—Dynamite looked
at the tufted mound the headlights lit along the dirt road's center. "There's
our first stop." Between red parking reflectors, the truck lights washed

the corner of a cabin, laundry hanging across the porch, and three black garbage sacks beside the steps—the lowest of which had come loose on the left.

Dynamite parked. They all got out, while quietly, Shit said, "This is Miss Louise's place. She's sixty-four years old." Apparently, she was also already up.

As Eric lifted one bag against his belly, he saw her inside the screening, sitting at a kitchen table in something limp and green, thin hair undone, drinking a mug of coffee and smoking a cigarette above a broad flesh-colored ashtray where ceramic Disney figures of the seven dwarfs paraded after Snow White along the edge, in which were mountains of ash and butts.

Walking back from the next house over, lugging two trash sacks in each hand, Dynamite tossed them in and turned from the truck's rear. "Hey—put your dick back in your pants. And don't tell me it kinda 'accidentally' got loose."

"Well—" Shit grinned—"it did."

Eric looked over and down, saw—it made him start—where Shit hung, visible among his trouser folds, and found himself grinning.

"He's doin' that 'cause you're here." Dynamite looked sourly at Shit. "Keep that for when you go to the Opera." He looked over at Eric. "Someday he's gonna do that when she decides to step out and tell us somethin' about her fuckin' crap—she's gonna see his thing hanging there. And she's gonna—" in an abrupt crouch, Dynamite leaped with a growl (Eric flinched, then felt stupid at his own surprise)—"rip that sucker off!"

Inside, behind her translucent curtain, Miss Louise glanced at the window, then at her cup.

Shit pulled back, but only smiled, while his father stood up. The smile went to Eric.

And Eric realized (as he'd soon learn about all coastal jokes) it had been performed before.

But Shit pushed himself—leisurely—back in his corduroys.

As he walked to the cab, Dynamite chuckled. "Someday he's gonna hang himself with his goddamn pecker." At the fender, he turned to face them. Then, standing by the amber parking light, with work-gloved fingers, suddenly Dynamite yanked down his own fly, reached into his overalls, and tugged free his testicles. The heavy penis flopped forward over his glove's knitted wrist. In the yellow gleam, he swung them side-to-side, six, seven times. "Now you know *he* ain't the only one with enough to shake at you." He pushed them back in and, in his gloves, fingered for his zipper, got it, tugged it up. He reached to open the cab, turned, and climbed in.

Chuckling, Shit climbed in the other side. He wore those low-cut basketball shoes, coming apart at heel and sides—and *still* no socks. Eric climbed in after him, dazzled by two generations' display of such raunch.

Dynamite started the truck.

Eric looked up to see Shit still grinning at him. "You can toss them bags two at a time, if you want—even four. It goes faster."

"Yeah—okay." Did Shit *own* socks, Eric wondered.

"Give 'im them gloves we brung him." Dynamite switched gears.

Shit pulled them off the dash's counter to hand to Eric. "But you ain't gonna need 'em till we get to them stores in Runcible. Mostly around here it's just house garbage. But sometimes there're broken bottles and stuff…"

They drove through coastal dark. Across the seat, the three of them felt like twice as many people as had sat there before. Only now Shit's leg leaned easily against Eric; Dynamite's arm pressed his arm. No one scrunched over so as not to touch another in a space in which that would have been impossible, anyway. It was more comfortable and relaxed than the three individuals who had been there before. (Later, Eric decided, perhaps only he had done the scrunching; or maybe Shit, in response.)

When they weren't hauling green rubber trash barrels or black plastic sacks, but were driving, Shit pulled off his own gloves to lay them in the wedge with Eric's between their thighs—half-an-inch of thumb on one of Shit's had frayed away—then (once more) dropped his own thick-fingered hand around on Eric's far shoulder—

—and began, rhythmically, squeezing.

While he squeezed with one hand, Shit bit at the nails on his other, or prodded in a nostril wonderfully wider even than Mike's, then put it in his mouth. Yes, it got Eric hard. A few times Eric did some nose picking, too—then glanced at Shit to see him grinning over in a flicker of road light through the cab, chin tufted with a late teen's tan beard, his nostril rim or his eye-socket roof lit by the dashboard dials. Then he changed hands. Eric imagined offering him some, but finally ate it himself.

Lifting first one hand from the wheel, then the other, with committed intensity Dynamite gnawed at his own nails. Driving, he paid as little attention to the boys as Mike would have. Eric fingered and fed himself those saline crusts, those lengths of mucus—and caught Dynamite giving Shit a grin, which, because he was looking, now shifted to Eric, as one or the other of the boys sucked a finger clean, index, middle, or ring.

A few times, during that first morning's ride, in a headlight's gleam over the road from the other side of the trees, or from Shit's leg moving against Eric's on the seat cushion, Eric saw that, in Shit's baggy corduroys, the wale was worn flat on both thighs.

Shit's fly was *still* open.

From the crotch hair glimpsed in there, clearly Shit wore no underpants. Did he have any? (Back in Atlanta, Buckethead Zawolsky said his mom had simply never bought him none. And Scott used to joke that, for all Buck's six-four height, his dick was too small to raise sweat enough to need them.) *Goin' commando*, the guys on the team had called it, giggling.

Could it have been poverty?

How old *were* Shit's pants? Did he have others?

When Shit got down to haul garbage, Eric also saw that the wale on his butt was equally flat-worn.

At Barbara's, Eric had a carton full of socks: a third he'd brought with him from Atlanta; two-thirds Barbara already had with her. (She lived as if she always expected Eric to turn up, unannounced, and move in: but, till now, he hadn't.) Three times Eric had started to offer to bring Shit some of his. But now, Eric thought, as they bounced through the night's end: I'm thinking like a kid again. That's silly. I'm just scared—and you can't be too scared to help people. "Hey, Shit?" he said. "You guys brought me the work gloves. I'm gonna bring you some socks next time I come—tomorrow, I mean. That's gotta be more comfortable."

"You got some of them socks?" Shit turned with a wonder at their potential presence as great as Eric's had been at their absence. "Oh, wow! That'd be great. I bought some of them white ones, once, that come in a package—a dozen for six dollars? But you wear them things twice and wash 'em, and they come all to pieces. That's expensive. I didn't have enough to get no good ones what'll last. Oh, fuck, man—that would be *great*!"

With Shit's gratitude, Eric felt relief cascade through him, chest, back, and belly. "Sure. I'll bring 'em tomorrow. Hey—you don't use no work shoes, like..." He hesitated between "your uncle" and "Dynamite," then chose: "Like Mr. Haskell, there?"

"You mean this ol' pig fucker?" (Again, Eric was shocked, though Dynamite drove on.) "Yeah, I got 'em. But I don't wear 'em 'ceptin' on the days we take the stuff over to the Bottom to toss—and even then. I mean, at least, most of the time, I don't bother. But, man, if you can loan me some socks, I can wear 'em again."

"Loan 'em? I got enough to give you a bunch." Then he wondered if that meant the work gloves were only a loan. Still, the relief left him even more silent than he had been before, rather than more voluble.

The next ten minutes' driving seemed the longest in Eric's life. But what ended it? Did they reach their next job? Did Shit say something? Or did Dynamite? He remembered his glimpse of Miss Louise through her curtained screen or Dynamite swinging his nuts outside the truck, though he could recall no other detail from the dark hours of his first garbage run—except stopping just down the slope from Barbara's, tossing her sacks in the pickup, and driving on to the next house without comment.

For years, though, the rest of the day remained as clear as a film.

Behind clouds squashed on one another over the sea, the sun rose and, for four or five minutes, stained sky, sand, and water a scarlet as intense as a neon tube or an LED display.

"Now, that's a color you don't see around here so often," Dynamite muttered as they coursed beside the beach. The flesh on his own neck and face looked as if it had been burned a brick hue by the light through the window. "I mean, you get coppers, oranges, all sorts of golds. But not that red." Even as he spoke, the sun started paling to orange. They turned away, and the dawn was redder than the earth piled by the highway constructions they pulled past or what heaped in a new foundation's sloping pit, or—seconds later—where a cinderblock wall rose beside a leafy turnoff.

Then the clouds were gone. Blue reclaimed the sky.

They turned from a smaller road onto a larger. Over the trees the sun was full up and an unwatchable white. The dash's clock said six-twenty, though Eric seemed to remember that's what it had said when, in the dark, he'd first climbed into the truck. Maybe it was broke. Beyond a wooden rail lay a good-sized cornfield. Hundreds of tasseled ears moved together. Beside it stretched another, a foot shorter. On the far side, dark green and purple produce grew knee high. Dynamite turned the truck in by what looked like a two-story barn—or a barracks. Half the ground-floor wall was widely spaced slats. Spots of light in it suggested the back wall was the same, letting through sunlight from the field behind.

They pulled up, and Shit was out the door and down by an old fashioned hand-worked pump, painted orange and standing high as his shoulder. As Eric followed Shit from the truck, he saw the pump sat on a six-inch concrete base. Three pickups—only one less than three years old—and two cars were parked near.

"We gotta get the bags outta them cans." Shit nodded toward a row of ten oil drums along the barn/barrack's side wall, with—in most—black bags bulging from the top and dangling red ties down the sides from under metal lids that, in two cases, had slipped off, one flat on the ground, one to lean against the dented drum.

In a knitted cap and sleeveless thermal vest, a strong-looking black fellow ambled around the building corner:

"Hey, there, guys. I thought you'd be here half an hour ago."

"We got a new man with us today," Dynamite said, as though that explained it. "This here's Eric. He's gonna be helpin' me and Shit—" who had already gone to the first drum, tossed the cover against the building wall, and hauled up one, two, three sacks, then, with his other hand, reached in and hauled out two more.

Eric went over and did the same to the second drum—the thing must have held six. As they went back and forth to toss them into the truck bed—the last clattered, full of glass and cans—another black fellow came around, lugging a brown shopping bag in each hand. He was heavier and darker than the other. "Hey—Dynamite! I put some good stuff together for you. Some green peppers—and I know you like that corn. There's some eggplants, some onions, some potatoes…"

"I like the corn." Dynamite grinned. "But it's a little rough on the teeth—when you don't got so many."

"You don't have to eat it on the cob," the fellow said. "Boil it up, cut that stuff off, give it a few scrapes with the back of your knife to get the good shit out, then fry it up in some bacon grease with some cut-up onions and peppers—put some of them summer squash in there, salt and pepper, and you got your dinner. Do it with some *real* bacon—and it's a *good* dinner, too."

Dynamite said, "You gonna come over and cook it for us?"

"You guys don't want no fresh herbs, do you?"

Eric asked, suddenly: "You got dill? And maybe some basil?"

"Dill and basil, comin' up! I thought Ronny and his goddam cookin' class was the only ones interested in stuff like that." He wandered off.

In a minute, he was back with the herbs, one leafy, one stringy and feathery, both roots wrapped in squares of newsprint. "Here you go."

"Thanks." Eric took them and tossed them in through the truck's window.

"You know how to cook?"

Eric said, "A little."

"Wow…!" Shit said, full of wonder.

The man laughed, a high, black laugh that Eric associated with his Texas relatives. "Why don't you bring that cute nigger you done whelped over here more often—and, hell, this one, too—" he nodded toward Eric, as he turned back for the next can—"so we can feed sumpin' *real* good to both these boys."

Dynamite said, "I told you a long time ago, Horm." He started toward the cans now. "When Shit's gets twenty-one, he can come over any time he wants. And fuck anyone of your black asses he has a mind to." He flung off a lid, and grabbed up one, three, four bags in one hand and four in the other—as did Shit. Both Shit and Dynamite's all but nailless hands, during actual work, seemed big as steam shovels. Everyone was always saying how large Eric's own hands were, but he could just about hold two in each.

Had his inexperience really delayed them half an hour?

When he came back for the next can, he made himself carry three and three—and by the time, even in the gloves, he got to the truck bed (one sack nearly dropped)—the skin between thumb and forefinger on his left hand was a burning agony. The thumb on his right throbbed. But he went back for six more.

The fellow who had set down the shopping bags hooked his thumbs under the sides of his jeans, and pushed them down from the upper half of his copper buttocks and the crevice between. He turned away and backed up, displaying his bare bottom. "You mean you gonna let that pig fucker make you wait dat long to run yo' sweet dick up my easy-meat canyon—?"

Suddenly Shit dropped his sacks, snatched one of his gloves free, and swung his hand to smack Horm's butt. But Horm hooted and leaped aside, then doubled over laughing, thumbing his jeans back up. In a moment, Shit had the sacks again, carrying them to the truck.

First Dynamite, then Eric started laughing.

They climbed back into the cab. Shit and Eric's knees rattled the paper bags the fellow had sat on the truck-cab floor. In tan letters, a-slant the bags' brown side, it read: DUMP FARMS PRODUCE.

Eric picked the newspaper-wrapped herbs off the seat.

"Hell." Shit grinned at Eric, as they drove back. "I been fuckin' Horm's asshole in the Opera—and fuckin' around with the gay guys out here at the Produce—which is all of 'em—since I was twelve, thirteen, fourteen. He—" from the nod, he meant Dynamite—"knows that."

"Sure I know it," Dynamite said. "But you still gotta keep up appearances." Then he frowned. "I never snuck you into the Opera when you was no twelve-years-old."

"I know." Shit frowned. "But that didn't stop *me* from sneakin'."

"Oh…" Dynamite looked puzzled.

Shit chuckled. "They used to treat me pretty nice." (Out the window they passed a sign in red and gold letters on gray planks: DUMP FARMS PRODUCE, like the bags. On the side of the sign was a large picture of the orange water pump. Driving in, Eric had not seen it. Perhaps he'd been looking out the other window.) "That's 'cause they knew *he* was sittin' down in the front row, beatin' his meat. But they used to get back in some corner with me, and let me go to town on 'em. When I was a little guy, I loved to fuck more than just about anything. And all them fuckin' farm niggers knew it, too."

"Like you still don't," Dynamite said dryly.

"Sometimes if it was a few of 'em together, they'd wait in line for me to finish with one and go on to the next." Sunlit shadows rushed over their laps, their arms, and—down in the bags—the green husks, the yellow and black tassels, the peppers shiny green between their knees, with the dill and basil in their newsprint wrapping on top of the one between them.

Eric looked back up. "They give you food for takin' away their garbage?"

"Naw," Dynamite said. "Everybody gets vegetables and stuff from the Produce. That's Kyle's, too. He's my friend—me and Jay's—what started the Dump, where we live. They bring it down to the market at Dump Corners. But we get ours in the mornin', 'cause we're out here."

As, again, the truck neared the beach, half the sky was a silver too bright to gaze at. The sand was white-gold and stuck with umbrellas. Half with trunks to their knees, beachgoers wandered about, some with towels over their shoulders, some carrying beach chairs or baskets. Hours after, beyond wire-woven pickets, the sea's edge swarmed with swimmers. You had to squint. By ten to noon, the July Wednesday was over eighty-five.

Finally, they finished with the squalid houses along forty miles of forking back roads.

Four miles away in Runcible, they pulled up just beyond the Opera House and two doors down from a tattoo and body piercing emporium, Cave et Aude—in purple curlicue letters, with gold highlights.

They'd stopped at the clinic building.

On the broken pavement's corner were two four-foot posts topped with black tarnished horses' heads.

Dynamite took Eric in through the red-framed door. Colorful wall posters showed smiling black, white, and Latino young people, advertising HIV medications. Mr. Haskell told the heavy black woman with man-short hair at the desk that Eric wanted a test. "But I don't think he's too anxious his mama should know he's gettin' it."

"Of course." She smiled at Eric.

"Me or Jay'll come by and pick up his paper in a couple of days for him, if he can't get over here hisself. He works for me, now—like Shit."

The woman slid her hands out to the blue blotter's edge. "You know, Dynamite: the rules are that this has to be confidential. We'll give the results to the young man here. But he's the only one who can get 'em."

"I thought," Dynamite said, "yall could bend 'em a little: he lives in Diamond Harbor and don't got no car of his own. But we'll do it however we have to."

"Fine." She smiled at Eric again. "We have to get a little blood from you; that's all. You step into that room there—" it had a Dutch door, like Bill's in Mr. Condotti's basement; except it was all white—"and someone'll be with you in a minute."

While they waited, Dynamite talked with lazy openness about who he could fuck with in the Dump and who he might hold off on, none of whose names stuck in Eric's mind. In return, Eric told Dynamite about getting the test before in Atlanta, when Mr. Doubrey had sent him and Arnie to the free clinic there.

When they were again in the pickup, Dynamite slammed his door.

In the middle, Shit looked back and forth between them.

Dynamite said, "When they get it, she'll give it to Jay. She's Hugh's cousin: she knows we look out for the puppies comin' 'round this part of the coast. You don't have to tell your mama if you don't wanna. I mean, that's the damned law. Every nigger in the Dump got his. That's one of Kyle's rules for living there. We should all probably have 'em laminated and nailed up on our doors."

Eric grinned. "I guess it's like the foundation of the world." He wondered if either would say anything about that. But neither did.

Shit asked, "They stick that needle in you?" (Probably because he didn't understand it, he didn't ask about it.) "It don't really hurt. Hey, you want some boiled peanuts?" From somewhere, while they'd been inside, he'd gotten a bag. Probably it had been down in one of the Dump Produce sacks.

Outside, a white police car with two blue lines around it, separated by a thin red one—"Runcible Township & Highway Constabulary"—rolled by. "And that there's another," Shit said, though Eric wasn't quite clear what that meant. But neither Shit nor Dynamite explained.

"If you end up inside one of them cabins and you wanna mess with one of them black bastards—" back in the cab, Shit made fists near his shoulders and stretched—"don't be shy. Down here we figure any kind of suckin's okay; kissin', anything like that. But when it comes to fuckin', you need your paper—or a rubber." Yawning, he raised his elbows.

Dynamite positioned himself at the wheel. "Ask to see it and make sure it's less than four months old. It's free, and it don't cost 'em nothin' to come over here and get it. That's been keepin' the guys in the Dump pretty healthy since eighty-five, eighty-six now."

While Eric wondered if he should ask more about Kyle, Dynamite started driving.

At about two, they drove back to the Harbor, where they stopped to say hello to Barbara—she had another shift at the Lighthouse Coffee & Egg.

Jay and Mex were there. Eric grinned when he saw them. Dynamite hailed them—and they all squeezed into a booth together. It was as easy and anxiety free as that first day had been fraught. "You know, this guy here—" Jay grinned up as Dynamite sat beside him—"has been my best friend since I was a lot younger than you." Today Jay's arms were covered in a denim work shirt.

Two other black men came in—"Hey, Randal," Jay called.

Dynamite said, "Eric, this is Randal and Tod."

"See," Shit explained. "This here's our boss man, Randal. He tells us where to go every morning."

"It'd be fun to tell *you* where to go, if I thought for a minute you'd go there." Randal squeezed in next to Eric, and grinned at him. "How you like workin' with these clowns?"

Tod was thick and friendly looking and hovered about twenty-five—he sat across from Eric, next to Shit. Then got up and got a chair, put it at the tables end, and sat once more.

Randal's leg cleaved to Eric's, and for a moment Eric wondered if Randal was hitting on him—or if it was just some country way.

Pressed around a single booth table, four garbage men and two boatmen, Eric realized, *did* have a smell. It wasn't even unpleasant—but it was recognizable.

Shit said, "You got to get Jay to show you all them pictures on his arms. Tank and Cassandra did that, right over in Runcible. He got some good pictures on 'im."

Eric frowned a moment, then realized that—probably conscientiously, the whole Turpens experience had fallen out of their conversation, even as—for Eric—it made everything about it that much more vivid in memory.

"Yeah," Tod said, who was only a couple of years older than Shit. "Go on, show us, Mr. Boatman. If he shows them half a dozen more times, I may go get me some."

Barbara brought coffee for them all.

Jay sipped from his mug loudly and did not open his shirt.

In the corner, with his black denim jacket and (still) no shirt beneath, his pockmarked smile, and his big hands folded on the table, Mex was still the winner for sex appeal, at least for Eric. Finally, Dynamite (still close second) said, "I think we're gonna run Eric here out to the Dump to see how the other half lives. We'll get you back by the time your mom gets home."

"Good idea," Jay said. "Have fun."

"Dynamite'll bring 'im back to the house by dinner time, Mrs. Jeffers," Shit called—and sounded a little awkward, doing it. "Cross my heart."

Dynamite slid from the booth to stand and stretch.

As the crush at the booth table broke up, the chair at the end where Tod had been sitting scraped back. Guys stood, digging in their pockets for wallets or change. "So long, Mrs. Jeffers," they called.

Stepping away from Jay and Randal, Mex and Tod, Eric called, "So long, Barb."

Tod ambled over to joke with another customer about something, while the three of them went out to the truck to drive to Shit and Dynamite's cabin.

Easing around on the pickup's seat, Shit's hand went back on Eric's shoulder, again to squeeze. "Me and Dynamite, see, we live in the nigger part of Diamond Harbor—what they call the Dump; 'cause that's what it used to be. Randal should be over there, too. He's as gay as a plaid rabbit."

"Yeah," Eric said. "He was sittin' pretty close."

"Was he, now? Randal?" Shit asked. "Ol' Randal? Rubbin' his leg up against some good lookin' white boy he ain't never seen before? Naw, I don't *believe* it—I'm surprised he didn't have his hand under the table before we left, jerkin' you off!"

Dynamite and Shit both laughed.

"He lives over in Hemmings," Shit went on. "Now the whole thing is Mr. Kyle's. He lets all these gay niggers live over here. He got a' office in Hemmings, where they interview you and everything. You just gotta be gay and homeless and not smoke. And black, pretty much mostly. But he kinda liked Dynamite. If you're some serious alcoholic or drug addict, you gotta go into rehab for three months. They pay for that, too. It's Mr. Kyle's experiment. Besides, 'cause I'm a nigger—and my mama was a nigger whore who worked outta Turpens' back lot, hustlin' the truckers, that's why we can live there—and my daddy was Kyle's suck-buddy when they was kids, anyway. Dynamite, here, and Jay too, whored out there when they were my age; I done it a few times. I'll take you over and show you how, if you want. You can get yourself a little spendin' money that way—fifteen, twenty bucks. Last time I did it, a guy gave me fifty. Then I never did it again. I don't know why—Jesus, that was two years ago, at least. He said I was real nasty, and I don't think he meant it in a good way at all. He said the cheese in my cock was disgustin' and at the motel made me wash it out—but he sure liked my dick up his fuckin' butthole. I mean, he wasn't like you at all. Hey, I like livin' over there 'cause I get to fuck with *all* these niggers—the ugly ones, the cute ones. I bet you gonna like it better over there, too."

"Eric ain't interested in that shit," Dynamite said, not looking at them while he drove. "Hustlin' down at Turpens, I mean. Besides, his mama wouldn't like him doin' that. And I don't think *yours* would either…though I told you, since she done it, I done it, and Jay done it, too, I couldn't really tell you 'No' on that one. But if his mama learns you're takin' him over there, and pimpin' him out, she ain't gonna let 'im work with us no more.

The guys who use Turpens ain't like the niggers in the Dump, Shit. The ones who use the back john, like us, is okay. But the ones who cruise in the parkin' lot and wanna spend twenty bucks on some teenage crack head, that's every faggot up and down the coast. They don't know how to keep their own council. They're all blabber mouths—" he turned to Morgan "—like you."

Shit grinned. "See, Dynamite's always sayin' he knows everything about that stuff, 'cause after he done it for a few years with Kyle, he done it for a few years with Jay. But I'll still take you if you want." He stretched. "Though he's probably right about your mama, huh?"

Parking, Dynamite rolled the truck back and forth a few times. Then he pulled up the ratcheting brake. They had reached a slope, over whose edge you could see the sea, with a scattering of houses in a web of aimless roads.

Eric remembered looking out the truck window for the first time at the slope, at the ocean. About them stood various cabins, some closer together than others.

Shit was saying, "See, before—we didn't have no place to live for a while. I mean, he was too proud to ask Jay or Kyle for nothin', 'cept maybe a job—they didn't even know we was livin' outta the truck—"

"Well—" Dynamite interrupted, looking at Eric—"this is the Dump. Hey—you wanna come in? Maybe try out some of them truck stop moves you was gettin' us off with, back at Turpens…? You guys bring in them produce sacks."

* * *

[10] A WEEK BACK, the question would have set off a cascade of sexual anxiety. (With all the sex he'd had in parks and public rest rooms, Eric had never gone home with *anyone* before!) Eric asked Dynamite, "You were homeless?"

They still sat in the cab's crowded front seat.

Dynamite said, "Yeah, sort of. We was back and forth between the truck and the boathouse at the Harbor for six weeks, once. We'd sneak in there after dark and get out by the mornin'. Then Jay found out and made us stay with him and Mex out on the island for another six weeks—then told Kyle he'd *better* find a place in the Dump for us, or we was gonna be homeless again—whether we was white *or* black." Dynamite chuckled. "Jay always been my good buddy, ever since we was kids."

"That was about ten years ago," Shit said, "when I was nine." Then, from out of nowhere, he added: "Mr. Kyle owns Turpens."

"Hey—if you *don't* wanna hang around, I'll run you back to your house right now. You can come visit some other time. Or not at all, if you don't wanna," Dynamite said. "We don't mind—"

Surprised, Eric said: "Oh…! *No*, I thought…I mean I'd like to…come in. I thought you said you wanted me to…so I could—"

"O-*kay*, then!" Dynamite laughed.

"Course he wanna stay," Shit said. "If he's anything like me, that's all he been thinkin' about since he come down to the dock this mornin'."

"Kinda…" Eric admitted. "But I didn't know if you—"

"We just gotta get the work done," Shit said, "first."

"Yeah," Dynamite said. "He's like you? Well, I didn't see *his* dick comin' out his damned pants all mornin'—like yours."

"Oh…!" Eric said.

Shit shrugged. "Well, yeah—I figured it couldn't hurt to remind him, now and then, what was waitin' for 'im after the run. I didn't want the nasty part to slip his mind, see?"

Dynamite grinned. "Now, look—if you stay, you can't do no major penetration till you get your paper. But I'm a good suck—and Shit's imaginative. And if it comes to that, we got some rubbers around someplace. But he don't like 'em, and I don't, either. Hey. You can relax a little, hang out with us for an hour or so, take a shower with us—if you can wrassle him into the john. He gets into his own funk sometimes—hell, so do I. But at least once a month I make him take a good wash. Like that test, there, you probably shouldn't tell your mama about none of this—leastways for a while. But you can help us get cleaned up; maybe grab a nap with us, do a little huggin', a little tongue fuckin'; rub yourself off on my big ol' redneck dick—that is, if you want. I like little puppy dogs shootin' all over my belly—and I like shootin' all over theirs. Hey, I'll carry you on back this evening. You know what you *should* tell your mama is that she ain't oughta be in that trailer she got up in the woods. Two or three big storms come, and them five or six cinder blocks proppin' up that thing're gonna sink right down or wash away, and that whole place'll fall over or slip down the slope. Tell her to get a little place in Runcible—probably it'll end up cheaper, anyway."

"Damn." Shit opened his door. "So you comin' in with us?"

"Sure!" (Years later, Eric would say, "That was the fastest 'sure' what ever come out *my* mouth!") His heart had started to pound again.

"Hey," Dynamite said. "You gotta speak out and say what you want, boy. Nobody gonna read your mind."

"Yeah," Eric said. "I'm sorry. Sure. Yeah. Sure."

Shit pushed off the torn blue seat out onto the dirt, and, in his falling apart sneakers, with their frayed heels and toes, kind of danced around on the circle of his own shadow. (Eric thought: I gotta remember those socks.) Shit squinted expectantly back at Eric.

Pulling the DUMP PRODUCE FARMS shopping bags along with him, Eric jumped down. Despite the heat, Shit's arm fell heavily around Eric's shoulder.

"Mr. Kyle, he owns all this." Shit squinted around the slope, with cabin, and tufts and banks of weeds and lawns irregularly cut. "He's a real black feller, like your daddy. When they was kids, Jay, Kyle, and Dynamite couldn't get their damned dicks out of one another's assholes—or mouths—for more than five minutes. At least that's what they always told me. That was in the summer—in the winter, it was just Jay and my daddy. Kyle, see, even though he was a nigger, 'cause he was rich, he used to go to school in Europe and all sort of things—and then come back to the Harbor and they'd fuck some more. That's why he decided he was gonna build the Dump."

"Hey," Eric said, "has Dynamite still got Al's rubber?"

"Huh?" Shit asked. "Naw. Soon as we got home, I made him let me wear it. He helped me jerk off in it—it was kinda a mess. But it was the kind of mess I like. Then we took it across and gave it to Whiteboy, and let him chew on it awhile. Maybe we shoulda saved it and give it back to—"

"Naw," Eric said. "Naw. That's okay."

"Every once and a while, if a black guy comes along with a white boyfriend, Kyle'll let 'em stay here, if they want—like me and Dynamite, or Black Bull and Whiteboy. But basically, it's for black guys. Anyway, then we went home to bed." Eric glanced down to see Shit had pushed his free hand into his own fly. "You know I busted the zipper on my pants about two months back: see, I'm tryin' to find out how long it takes somebody besides fuckin' Dynamite to notice. It's like *my* experiment. But every once in a while my dick falls out. All by itself. Really." Then, deliberately, he pulled himself free—it was three-quarters hard and slanted forward. "Like that." He grinned. "But if *he* saw that, he'd think I did it on purpose." Turning his head, Shit brushed Eric's ear with his nose (only it was wet. Shit had *licked* him! Eric found himself with chills—and almost sneezed) to call back to Dynamite: "So what *you* wanna do with this guy?" He gave Eric another hug. Eric almost stumbled.

Catching up behind them in the hot sun, Dynamite said, "Come *on*, now, Shit! I told you. Put it away, till we get inside." He'd shrugged off his shirt, hooked the soiled collar on one finger, and carried it back over a hairy shoulder.

"Why?" Shit grinned. "Ain't nobody gonna see it but Black Bull—or Whiteboy." He grinned at Eric: "Black Bull used to suck my dick when I was a little baby. That was when he was baby-sittin' for me. 'Cause Dynamite tol' him that's how we did it—Mex an' him." He looked over at his dad. "That's how they could always get me to stop cryin' when I was a baby. Ain't that right?"

"Yep," Dynamite said. "It still makes him pretty happy."

With pines behind it and fern banks beside it, the cabin sat a few yards up the slope. A single story with a flat roof, it was the same dark creosote as the boards inside Eric's porch room at his mom's. The roof extended to the front and out on one side. Looking at the blocky solidity, Eric thought: It's like my porch room at Barb's, turned inside out and blown up even bigger—more than twice the size of his mother's entire trailer. Some chairs and cartons and—well—just junk stood on the roofed deck. A couple of windows and doors were on each wall.

They walked up the steps.

In the kitchen, Dynamite flung the empty peanut bag, which he'd carried crumpled in his fist, down in a full metal trash can just inside, its edges covered with a black plastic liner. (It was funny: so much stuff leaned against the walls and in the corners, inside it looked *smaller* than Barb's!) Dynamite lay his shirt over the cluttered kitchen table's edge, turned, fell into a chair, and leaned over to untie one work shoe, then the other. "You guys put that stuff in the vegetable bin in the bottom of the refrigerator. Don't leave the corn out. You can set the onions and the potatoes on the table—if you can find room." He glanced, frowned at the open toolbox and the stack of plates and the pile of wood. "Or on the floor right down there. Just don't forget 'em."

"Come on," Shit said, taking one of the shopping bags from Eric. He opened the refrigerator door.

Sitting up, with the toe of one shoe Dynamite pushed off his other. Then, with his sock toe, he pushed off the first—which fell over on its side. (Every window in the room had a lot of stuff in front of it.) Something like curtains hung in front of the blinds in three of them: red, green, yellow, orange, and blue towels, threaded onto curtain rods. Eric grinned—it was colorful...

Shit had just closed the refrigerator and stood up, his hip and arm pressing into Eric—there was hardly room for all three to stand—when a black dog rushed from around a carton on the floor and began to jump up on Shit, equally eager to nose between his hand and lap. Without releasing Eric, Shit said, "Hey there, Tom. Well, hello, there! Uncle Tom—this is our new friend." Bending over and pulling Eric with him, Shit rubbed the dog's head with one hand, gripped his lower jaw and shook, so that the ears flapped, then rubbed the black shoulders. "Hey—this here is Eric. That's a good dog—that's a *real* good dog. Yeah, Eric, this here is Uncle Tom. Tom, this is Eric...You wanna see this sonofabitch hump my leg?" Tom's tail beat one of the empty bags, knocking it over, where it roared under one of Shit's sneakers as he stepped around.

"Jesus, Shit...!" Eric laughed. "All you *like* is nasty stuff!"

Grinning, Shit licked Eric's nose, then ran his tongue up Eric's right nostril. Pulling his tongue back in his mouth, he leaned away. "Un-huh. Yeah. Damn—it tastes as good as mine. I was wonderin' about that all this morning." On the floor, the dog waited, eager, expectant. "Come on...let's go to bed." He nodded over to where his father had moved a piece of board with a metal housing for a motor bolted to one end from off the sink and was washing his hands.

Eric tightened his own grip around Shit's shoulder.

Two inches taller than Eric, Shit sort of shrugged, and a moment later, Eric realized, was squirming a little, as though in Eric's grasp he couldn't think that well. "Um...we wanted, you know, for you to be, *um*, so..." An unfocused smile filled Shit's face, that made Eric warmly happy and which, despite this bawdiness, after seconds he recognized as embarrassment! "We was real anxious for you to be—" Shit shrugged, but within the grip, not to get out of it. "You know, I mean—be okay, I guess...so, like..."

Standing up and moving to the sink, Dynamite glanced at Eric, then turned, shrugged, and made lean muscles, the thinner skin on the inner sides of his arms run with veins, faintly blue through his tan. He yawned and stretched. "We wanted you to like us." Dynamite spoke it with the emotional sureness Shit had lacked. "So you'd wanna come back. Like Shit told you, it's a real big bed and you guys can do what you want in it. It ain't gonna bother me." As they walked into the back room, Eric looked down at Dynamite's feet—he'd stripped his socks off. Between his broad big toe and the toe over was a line of black at least a quarter inch wide. Black lines ran between the others, too.

Amber flypaper strips spiraled down from three of the bedroom's corners. A large unmade bed, its covers pushed down to the foot, almost filled the room. Shit pointed to a smaller, made-up bed by the wall, covered with a green blanket. Boxes and what looked like a year's junk, including a broken oar and part of an outboard motor sat on it. "That's my bed," Shit said. "We can use it if you want, but we'd have to clean it off first. Most of the time, though, I bunk in with my dad, unless I'm sick or got a cold or something. His is bigger and more comfortable. And he's warm."

"Sure," Eric said. "That's fine."

"Come on." Holding Eric tighter, as if steadying himself, Shit said, "Take your clothes off and lie down with me. We can make out. He gonna be asleep in fifteen minutes, anyway: this is when he takes his nap. When he wakes up, he'll grab some nookie off you, though…in about an hour, an hour-and-a-half."

On striped sheets, to the right, maybe two feet end to end, an irregular blotch was stiff with—Eric realized what it was—*weeks* of spilled semen. When he looked up, Shit was grinning at him. "We keep most of that stuff on my side—'cause wet or dry, it don't bother me. In fact I *like* rollin' around in it…oh, hey! Look at you grinnin' there. What? You like that, too?"

Their medallion…?

Shirtless, with his back to the bed, Dynamite dropped his pants, then pushed down his gray briefs (a frayed hole showed one hairy cheek), particularly soiled along the seams, and eased onto the bed's left side. The mattress gave.

As Dynamite started to swing up his legs, Eric said, "Wow, you got some *dirty* feet. Why don't you let me clean that stuff off for you?"

Dynamite said, "Huh…?" and put his feet back down and sat up again. Shit laughed.

Eric pulled away from Shit, went around to the other side, and dropped to the floor, cross-legged, in front of Dynamite—who looked down at him curiously. "You sure you wanna do that?"

"Un-huh." One of Dynamite's big feet was under Eric's shin, and one was in front of him. "I did this a few times for some homeless guys I used to mess around with, in Atlanta." Well, three times, anyway. The fourth, actually, was why he'd stopped. "They liked it."

"You gonna scratch *mine* there, when you're finished?" Having dropped all his own clothes, Shit sat beside his father.

Eric lifted Dynamite's foot up onto the knee of his jeans. He pulled the big toe away from the toe next to it—

"Ow…!" Dynamite said.

Eric looked up. "You okay?"

"Yeah, sure. But that's like mud—it dries and holds the hair on ya' damned toe joints together."

Not just a line, the dirt was a black wedge (it might as *well* have been mud) a quarter of an inch wide—and a quarter of an inch thick. With his forefinger, Eric broke it off in three long pieces and two short ones, so that it fell, crumbling, on the gray, gritty rug.

Then he ran his finger down between two others.

"Like drillin' for oil," Dynamite said. "Ain't it?"

At which point Eric reached the space between the little toe and the toe over. There was almost as much dirt between those two as in the wedge beside the big one. The broad nails were bitten or picked back from the quick as badly as on Dynamite's hands.

"Feels good, you runnin' your finger down between them suckers," Dynamite said. "Go on, do it some more. Then do Shit's."

Shit poked at Eric's shin with his own toe. While his feet were pretty soiled, they weren't as bad as his dad's.

While he was fingering between Shit's toes, Dynamite left his foot on Eric's knee. "How you doin' with the smell? You wanna kiss 'em, or sniff 'em, or hug on 'em, that's all right with us. Suck 'em if you want. I promise." (Probably because he went barefoot half the time, between Shit's there wasn't actual mud.) Dynamite chuckled. "We won't tell."

"We ain't got nobody to tell," Shit said. "'Cept maybe Black Bull…and Whiteboy."

"We'll let 'em find out on their own," Dynamite said. He reached up and took Shit's shoulder.

"Naw." Eric looked up and grinned. "That's all right. That…*looks* a little better."

"Yeah," Dynamite said. "That feels better, too. That could be part of your job every afternoon—if you wanted to take it on."

"I mean," Shit added, "that's some garbage we *don't* need." Shit pushed the wide ball of the foot Eric had finished with into Eric's crotch. "I'm tryin' to feel if you done come in your pants, yet. One friend of mine over at the Opera shoots a load in his jeans every time he gets to playin' with them things."

"Hell," Dynamite said. "Who does? I'll have to go look 'im up."

"Fuck it," Shit said. "I don't remember his name." He pushed his foot harder into Eric's lap, scrunching his toes through Eric's pants. "Hey, he's got a hard-on, at least." Shit reached down, grabbed Eric's arm, and tugged him up. Dynamite's foot slipped free; his heel hit the rug. Some of the dirt jarred loose from Dynamite wide foot.

"Come on around here and get ya' jeans off," Shit said, while Dynamite swung up his feet and this time lay down on his back.

Eric pulled loose from Shit and walked around to the other side of the bed to look down again at the twenty-five inches of stiffened bedding. Shaking his head, he said: "That's fuckin' impressive. It's bigger than the one I used to keep on my wall in the john."

"Yeah, I figured you might like that." Shit went on, swinging himself around onto the side of the mattress. "You get proud of that thing. And we do it a lot. Hey—most of it's just jerkin' off, me in the mornin' and in the afternoon sometimes, and my dad—" with his chin, he indicated Dynamite—"at night."

Dynamite bounced over two or three times, to turn his naked butt toward them. And Shit pulled Eric forward on top of him. They stretched out beside Shit's father.

Twenty minutes later, naked Eric whispered into naked Shit's neck, "You make me real happy; I wish I could make everybody else feel the same way." The pillow's ticking stuck from the ends of the mismatched cases, which probably weren't the right sizes.

Shit said, "You don't gotta whisper. *He* can sleep through anything." Besides bigger, the bed was more comfortable than either Eric's, out on Barbara's trailer porch, or his army cot in the Atlanta garage. "He don't care—you can play with him now, if you want. See…?" Shit reached over his father's faintly freckled hip to lift Dynamite, as, furrowing the hair on his chest with one hand, Dynamite rolled to face them.

Eyes still closed, with one hand Dynamite reached, sleepily, to catch one or the other boy in a hug and muttered: "Yall sure make a racket when you shoot. Hey! Come *on*, Tom! Stop lickin' my damned nuts! You sonofabitch! You can't do that now! We got company! *Get* outta this goddam bed—!"

"No—Don't stop, just 'cause *he* say so!" Sitting up cross-legged on the bed, Shit laughed at his father. "Besides, that ain't Tom."

Reaching down, Dynamite opened his eyes. "Oh…! That's *you*?" Looking down over himself, his other hand came to grip Eric's head.

"He do that good, don't he?" Shit said. "He was doin' it to me, too. That's how he got *me* off…See? He can take it *all* in."

"Goddamn!" Dynamite began to move his hips. "You suck like a nigger, son."

Shit said, "Like a good nigger, too." He squinted at Dynamite. "So you got two niggers, now, you ol' pig fucker—that's what I call my dad 'cause he's white. Hey, pig fucker, and *one* of your niggers is a white boy, too!"

*

As Eric was getting ready to go, he said, "Hey—why don't you lemme wash your dishes before I leave?"

Standing in the archway to the bedroom, Shit asked, "What you wanna do that for?" He had not put on any clothing.

"So you'll have a clean sink." Eric and Dynamite had both put on theirs, though Eric's shirt was still unbuttoned. "That looks like about a week's worth."

"More like two," Shit said.

Dynamite smiled, the way you might at someone you'd just learned was a little simple. "I ain't gonna say 'no' if you got your heart set on it."

"That'll take you all afternoon," Shit speculated. "Usually we just wash what we need—"

"Fifteen minutes…?" Eric suggested. "You got a bottle of detergent in the corner there—and soap pads. And some sponges—" He turned on the water, which broke warmly over his wrist and chattered amicably over dishes, cups, and plates. He rubbed the soapy sponge on the inside of the sink and a peppery discoloration wiped free—as the water became too hot and he had to turn on some cold and squeezed an orange tear of detergent onto a sponge he was holding. Then he went into the sink with both hands. There were only two plates, two bowls, and two mugs, but the white enamel sink bottom, with black chips here and there, was covered with what looked every knife, fork, and spoon from three different and complete services for twelve. "I ain't dryin'," Eric said. "I'm just settin' 'em in the drain rack. If those pots are still here tomorrow, maybe I might do some more." Across one corner of the rack lay an upside down lid for a Dutch oven, open on the stove. The lid had something red stuck inside it, one circle in it charred black.

"I won't hold you to it. But you're gonna shame Shit into cleanin' up this place. The sink and stuff are supposed to be his job."

"No he ain't," Shit said. "I like watchin' 'im do it." He grinned at Eric. Eric grinned back. For the next ten minutes, while Eric worked through handfuls of soapy spoons and forks—now and again, water splattered his stomach, his jeans, his chest—and filled the silverware holder with clattering utensils. Falling water mumbled and argued and made jokes on the far side of comprehension.

He ended, flinging three fingers full of dirty-dish gunk, scraped off the drain guard, into the garbage. "Okay, come on."

*

It was maybe five-fifty when Eric got down from Dynamite's pickup and climbed the slope to Barb's. Barbara was sitting in the kitchen, with a cup of coffee—and a drink on the table beside her. "Hey, sweetheart—how was your first day?"

"It was…really great!"

"You know, it's funny," she said, pensively.

Eric pulled out a chair and sat down across the table.

"This afternoon—" outside a breeze's rush rose and fell among the pines—"when all the guys came into the Lighthouse Egg & Bacon, there, for coffee, and I was standing by the counter, watching…this whole bunch of working men, crowding there in the booth, laughing and joking and I realized you were there in the middle of them…my own boy. I felt like it happened a little fast for me. It wasn't supposed to be practically the day after you got here. I don't know. Maybe that's something you can't ever be ready for—not the first time. But I'm *glad* it happened—"

"I didn't leave any money for my coffee—"

"I would have gone into the back and cried, if you had. No, that was fine. I should have given everybody free coffee this afternoon, to celebrate. But I didn't think of that until later. Still it was…strange. I was very proud—in a whole new way. But it means—well—I don't have a little boy any more. And that's…good. That's a good thing. You know, they come in there all the time. They're nice young men. They joke and laugh and have a good time. Sometimes they make some rough jokes—but that's how working men are. Basically they're polite. They enjoy themselves. I know they work hard, too. But they're still good boys, and you don't ever hear about any of them getting in trouble."

"Probably that's because half of us are gay—" Leaning forward on the chair back, Eric pushed his chest against crossed forearms.

"Now I don't know anything about that," Barbara said, quickly. "But…" Again she slowed and took a sip from her cup. Ice had pretty much melted in her glass; only bits floated on the top. "I liked it, seeing them, and seeing you, in the middle of them. You looked like you were really happy." She looked up, where Eric was smiling. "I don't mean you were ever a mopey child—or an unhappy one. But I don't have a lot of memories of you really…happy. It was nice—it was wonderful to see, Eric. Today. It took me a few minutes to figure that out. But I did. I really liked seeing you there like that."

"And I like it that you liked it." Eric sat up. "Um…You got any thoughts about what to do for dinner?"

Barbara frowned. "Actually, I haven't. You know, your mother's not a big evening eater. I snack pretty much all day long, down at Clem's. But there's still some chicken left in the refrigerator, if you want to slice some onions, put some lettuce and tomato on if and have another chicken sandwich—"

"Sure." Eric stood up. "That's fine. Yeah. But I'm gonna grab a shower first."

* * *

[11] ON ERIC'S THIRD day at work, after a two-hour stopover in the Dump (the second day the pots had not been touched; but nobody mentioned them, including Eric. The third day they had all been cleaned and stacked on a shelf above the sink; and Eric wondered if he was a good influence—or a nuisance), again at five-thirty Dynamite drove him home.

When Eric came in and the truck was growling off outside, Barb said something to him he didn't hear. Still, he called out, "Yeah," and turned into the hall. The night before, she had taken the newspaper of dill from the refrigerator and left it on the counter, because she said the smell reminded her of her mother's house in Hugantown. Eric had missed it that morning, so it had remained out. A year ago, in Atlanta, when making tomato salad, he'd learned that fresh herbs lost their scent quickly. Bill Bottom, actually, had suggested Ziplock bags to him, but Barbara had none in the house.

The porch smelled of pine and creosote. Eric sat on the bed, lay down, and—

"Honey, wake up! I told you, *Ron* is coming by. He's taking us out to dinner—and you haven't even showered. And, yes, you do smell—this time. Come *on*, sweetheart!"

"Jesus…" Eric said. "I'm sorry. I forgot." In truth he had no memory of it. "Couldn't I just sleep—and meet him some other time?" Logily he sat up—

"*No!*" Barb's hair was wrapped in a blue towel. "Come on—jump in the shower, honey! I already turned the water on for you."

"Okay, okay, okay." He stood—and was actually dizzy.

"Why did you go to sleep in your clothes anyway?"

"'Cause I was *tired*—"

"Honey, don't be grumpy. I told you last night, Ron wants to take us over to Hemmings. For dinner. He's looking forward to meeting you."

"But it's my third day of work. I don't wanna be late on my fourth."

Barbara looked wounded—

"Okay. Really—" Eric said, "I'm sorry. I'm goin' in the shower—right now. Sorry, Barb. Really." He shook his head to clear it.

In the rain of warm water, heating his neck, the backs of his arms, he began to feel better—though not by much. Then the hot water went cold. "*Argggbb—!*"

"You okay?" Barb called from the living room.

At least it woke him. Again on the yellow mat, toweling at himself, he called through the inch open bathroom door. "Can I wear jeans?"

"If they're clean, sweetheart."

Back on his porch, he was tempted not to put on any underwear. (Like

Shit, if not, half the time, Dynamite…) He put on clean socks; then, sitting on his bed, he leaned down to tug down the Velcro fastenings on his runners. Eric found a brown short-sleeve shirt, still folded up, shook it out, and put it on. As he came into the hall, starting for the kitchen, a drop of water ran down the back of his neck—

Only he realized his mother and someone else were sitting in the living room when he walked by.

"Oh, hey—!" Eric stepped back.

"Hi, sweetheart. This is Ron—my friend, I told you about…?"

Eric smiled. "Hello." (Yeah, he was black…) He stepped in on the woven black and orange rug.

Barbara was sitting on the couch in a pale blue dress with a white jacket, something glittery up its edges. On the table beside her, she had a glass and had already offered Ron one, which he held in front of him in both hands.

A tall, solid man, the color of a dark tobacco leaf, Ron sat forward in the easy chair, his knees wide. Forty or so, he was more good-looking than not, with full, rounded features. "Hello! I was just sayin' to your mama—" He wore brown slacks, brown loafers, and a tan short-sleeve shirt, its color nearly that of Eric's—"I'm takin' you guys to a nice place tonight—I mean, it's really somethin'!" He nodded. "Everybody says it's as good as anything you could find up in the city. Understand, there ain't a *lot* of choice down here. But this place just opened up about two months ago—in Hemmings. They got a great cook—his name is Ron, too. Like mine. Now what you think about *that*? By the way, I'm Ron Bodin." He grinned over at Barb. "I don't know what Ronny-the-cook's last name is."

Since the man was smiling, Eric smiled back.

Ron sipped his drink. "So this is the young fellow who Clem was sayin' wants to get out of that funk and junk and stink and find a *good* job at a nice place with some air conditioning, and work with some nice people, where you don't have to get up at four in the goddam mornin'." Looking serious, he nodded at Eric. "Right?"

"I'm okay…"

"Aw, come on! You want nice things, don't you? To have a nice house? Nice clothes? Be friends with nice people? Go to nice places—well, that's a little hard to do if you're a…refuse maintenance engineer." He gave a loud laugh; then looked around again, as if for approval. "And in case you ain't sure, that's a fuckin' shit shoveler!"

Barbara said, "Oh, Ron…that isn't nice."

"He knows what I mean! And especially in the Dump."

Though he didn't say it, what jumped to Eric's mind was: *I work with two real nice guys…I fuck with 'em, too.*

But Barb looked serious and waited.

Eric asked: "Is that what Barb said—my mom?"

Ron ducked his head. "She didn't *have* to say it!" His voice seemed bigger—more enthusiastic about everything it turned to—than Ron was, himself. "You're a regular normal guy, ain't you? You don't wanna have to be no garbage man."

"Ron's been talking to Clem," Barb explained.

"Oh," Eric said. "Well…No—I like what I'm doin'…now: workin' outdoors."

Barbara said, "We probably should get going, honey. We've been waiting for you for ten minutes. Ron made a reservation—we don't want to be late."

"Hey, I'm sorry!" Eric felt certain he hadn't been *awake* ten minutes. He couldn't have been in the shower more than three. "Okay. Sure."

"Hey, it's great to meet you, son!" Standing up bruskly, Ron held out his right hand. Eric stepped forward to shake. Barb stood slowly.

Through the kitchen, they went outside, where Ron's four-door Lexus sat on the slope—Ron stopped to look at it, happily.

So they did too—though Ron said nothing (Eric wondered how many months old it was)—with streaks of early evening reflected on its blue hood. Finally, Ron said, "You wanna hold the door for your mama?" Then he went around to the driver's side.

When Barb was in the front, next to Ron, Eric got in the back. He'd thought the shower had woken him. On the gray upholstery, enveloped in the motor's hum, however, as they turned onto a still larger road, while Ron and Barb chatted and chuckled in the front, after minutes in the rear, Eric leaned back in the failing day, and closed his eyes.

And was somewhere between an intense memory and a vivid dream of riding through the night in Dynamite's pickup, with Shit beside him, holding Eric's hand in his work-roughened fingers—

—and woke, alone, slumped on blue plush. For a moment, staring at the window's blank blue, he couldn't tell if they were moving or not. Then, through the glass, black trees flicked by.

Eric sat up.

In the front, Ron and Barbara were talking too low to hear. On the highway, more trees were silhouetted against the evening. He could have been asleep two minutes or two hours.

They drove through a collection of small houses. Turning in the front seat, Barbara said, "This is Hemmings, honey." Holding back one side of her hair, his mother's comb glittered. She did look nice, Eric thought. But *why* did they have to be going out *this* evening?

Soon, they turned in at a driveway, by a two-story house with lights shining up from the lawn over the building's white facade. Ron announced, "And this is Shells," which was apparently the restaurant—the first Eric had heard its name clearly enough to repeat.

Hanging beside the front steps was a sign not very different—Eric thought—from the one on the road that had said Turpens Truck Stop. It read, SHELLS, and below that, "Established 2007." It *was* 2007, which seemed odd, unless it was the owners' way of announcing they intended to be around awhile. As he got out on the gravel beside the grass, Eric frowned at the sky, overcast and gray. "What time is it?" he said in his mother's direction.

Barb stood up beside the car. "Well, Ron had a reservation for seven thirty. I don't think we're more than ten minutes late—"

Ron said: "I guess it's about seven-thirty, maybe seven-forty…seven-forty CPT. Your mamma tells me your daddy—your legal daddy, I mean, is a black man. A hard workin' black man, like me. So I guess you know all about CPT: 'Colored People's Time.'"

"Oh," Eric said. "Yeah." Though the first he'd ever heard the phrase was from Scott, who had told him about "Puerto Rican Time." When he'd asked Mike about it, Mike had laughed and told him about what a bougie black girlfriend of his had told him about CPT, before he'd even met Barbara. "Mom!" Eric looked at his mother. "I'm supposed to be in bed and asleep by now." He tried not to sound querulous. "I have to be up at four—" And realized he'd failed.

"I know, sweetheart. But I thought you could have *one* late night. You don't have a lot of chances to go out somewhere really nice." She brushed her skirt forward. "And I don't either." Turning, she said to him, "Instead of hanging out at Dynamite's after you guys get off—" though it had only been three days since he'd started working for Haskell, she had taken to calling him Dynamite, the way Eric did—"tomorrow you can come right home and go to bed an hour earlier. That way you can catch up."

"I don't *wanna* go to bed an hour early." Eric knew he was irritable *because* he was tired. Still, it was all he could do *not* to say, I wanna stay in the Dump and fuck and suck myself silly! "I *don't* wanna go to bed three hours *late*!"

"Oh, try to have a nice time, sweetheart! Really, I'm sorry—"

"Are you two arguin'?" Ron stepped around the front of the car. "Come on—we can't have no arguin' tonight! This is gonna be too nice a dinner!"

Someone came out to move the car while they walked up to the porch under the portico and climbed the steps. Summer thunder rumbled.

It *was* a nice place.

After three awkward seconds within the ivory vestibule, a young Asian woman in a black high-collared dress hurried up. "I'm sorry. Yall want to follow me?" She led them through a lounge, where people sat on puffy ottomans and wall seats, waiting for others in their party. The place was as heavily air conditioned as Turpens. Through one arch Eric saw a dozen people eating at white-clothed tables. At a podium the hostess checked Ron's name. "Yes, Mr. Bodin. We have you upstairs—the way you asked. Is that all right?"

"That's fine, honeybunch. You can have us any way you want. I been tellin' them about this place all evening. See—" he turned to Barb and Eric—"this is about my fifth time here. But I ain't been here before with nobody as pretty as your mama."

The young woman said, "We're glad you like it, Mr. Bodin."

"And I'm glad yall like me. Come on, take us upstairs, now."

Bending behind the podium and standing with a sheaf of black-backed menus, the young woman started through the room. They followed, up a narrow stairway rising beside the wall.

"When this was a private house," Ron said, looking around, "it musta been quite a place!"

First Barbara, then Ron, then Eric went up the steps, holding the banister.

"See, the kitchen's upstairs," Ron announced. "We're closer to it, where we're gonna be sittin'. That's why I asked to be up there, when I made the reservation."

Over the rail, Eric saw three black couples among the whites, eating in the lower room.

Another couple—a big bearded white man in a denim shirt, orange work shoes and plaster-splotched jeans (he looked like a heavier relative of Jay MacAmon's) and a small, nervous woman in a polka-dotted, scoop-necked dress—were seated against the wall. Both looked out of place among the sports shirts, the slacks, the ties and jackets and jeans with creases, the pastel shirts, the dark dresses and pants suits—as if he had been a carpenter or a workman treated by the management to a meal. Looking up, the bearded man glanced at Ron—and Eric realized that, despite the black couples, Ron and Barbara were the only interracial pair.

On the second level—the walls were dark wood. Eric tried to hold in a yawn—and failed. Ron glanced at him, grinning.

"We have you right over here," the hostess said. "Marvin will be yalls server tonight. He'll be over for the drink order in a few moments. This is the spot you asked for…?" Under a creamily white cloth, the round-cornered table stood beside a floor to ceiling window, some sort of balcony beyond it. The panes were open. The hostess said, "If it turns chilly, we'll close it."

"You wanna sit inside, beautiful?" Ron asked Barbara, as the young woman moved the table to the side. "Or out?" With its orange bulb, the brass lamp in the middle softened the surrounding shadows. "Yeah, you get in. Me and sleepyhead here—" he grinned at Eric again—"will sit on the outside, so we can look at how pretty you are. You know, your mama is one pretty, pretty woman." Ron waited till Barbara got seated—although he didn't help her with the chair—before he sat. So Eric waited, too.

"Now—" Ron pushed out his arms as he sat, another way (Eric thought) to take up more space than seemed his due—"what are we all drinking? I'm gonna stick with your mama's good bourbon. I always liked a woman what could handle a man's drink. Come on—sit down. Sit down!" So Eric sat. "How old are you, anyway, son?"

Barb said, "Eric's going to be sixteen tomorrow—"

"Barb!" Eric said. "I'm gonna be *seventeen*!"

"I *meant* seventeen," she said. "Put your napkin in your lap, honey."

"Why?" Eric asked. "There's nothin' to eat, yet."

"Because we're in a restaurant. That's always the first thing you do—now put your napkin over your lap."

"See," Ron said. "That's the way to let the waiter know you're ready to tell him what you wanna drink. Or get started on stuff." (The definiteness with which he explained it convinced Eric that Ron was making that up.) "You're only seventeen—?"

"Tomorrow." Barb picked up her menu. "Saturday."

"Then I guess this is kind of a celebration." Looking very happy, Ron beamed over the top of his own.

Eric looked down at his. There were two *poulets*, three *poissons*, three *viands*, three *pastes*, and—at the bottom—a collection of *legumes*, which included a corn *soufflé*, an artichoke *mousse*, and bok choy in white sauce. Most of the menu was empty space.

"You ain't even drinking age," Ron said. "So, what was Clem so upset about? I thought you was twenty-one, twenty-two, boy. I was gonna tell you, if you wasn't twenty-one yet, as soon as you hit it, you run get you one of Johnston's Business Incentive Loans—you could figure out *somethin'* you wanted to do, and that way get the money to do it. That's what I done with my computer consulting business. See, Johnston, he wants to build this whole part of Georgia up. Bring in hotels, bed-and-breakfasts—more restaurants. Businesses. I know that's how the Demming brothers financed *this* place. That's what Clem ought to do—figure out what the Lighthouse really needs in order to thrive. Air conditioning. A new kitchen. Some ovens that can handle some *real* food—she could make that little place as popular as this one here." He looked around. "Almost, anyway. Then, soon as you got it planned out, go *do* it—that man is just *dying* to give away money. And people down here too scared—or too country dumb—to take it. Unless it comes along from some crazy no-account like Robert Kyle—"

In a black shirt and white tie a curly-haired waiter stepped up. "Good evenin'. My name is Marvin. I'm yalls server tonight. How yall doin'?"

"Fine, thank you. But we'll be doin' a lot better when you bring us two bourbon-and-branch." Ron looked at Eric. "What kinda pop you want?" Eric felt as if the three or four years Ron had learned separated him from a bank loan had also truncated most of his humanity.

"What kind they got?" Eric asked. "You got orange? That's my favorite."

"I'm sorry." The waiter smiled. "We have Pepsi—regular and diet. And we have Fresca."

Barb said, "Take the Pepsi—Eric. That's got some caffeine in it. It'll wake you up."

Eric didn't want to wake up. "I'll have some Fresca." He wanted to fold his arms on the tablecloth, put his head down, and sleep.

Ron looked at the menu, frowning. "Would you do me a favor, Marvin?"

"Certainly, Mr. Bodin."

Here Ron looked up, sudden pleasure on his face. "See, Marvin here knows my name. That's 'cause I been here before."

"You were here the second night we opened," Marvin said. (Clipped to his black pocket was a copper pin with "Marvin" in black letters.) "And you've been several times since."

"I certainly have," Ron said. "See, they remember me here. Hey—I want you to run back into the kitchen and see if Ron has got a minute to come out and meet these very nice people I'm here with tonight. I know he's busy—" He looked at Barb, at Eric—"but he'll come out if that boy says it's me...I told you, Ron is the cook here."

"Certainly," Marvin said. "I'll tell him Mr. Bodin would like to see him for a—"

"*No!*" Ron insisted. "Don't you go tellin' him no 'Mr. Bodin' wants to see nobody! You tell Ron that *Ron* wants to see him!" Ron's eyebrows rose mightily. "That's what you say. Okay? He'll know who I am."

"Certainly, sir."

"Is the chef part owner of the restaurant?" Barb asked, as Marvin turned and strode away toward what, as it swung in and out with its circular nautical port ringed with brass studs in the dark wood, was the kitchen door.

"Naw—Frank Demmings put up most of the money. Marvin's his cousin or nephew or something. Ron ain't the owner of nothin'." Ron frowned back at the menu. (Eric had figured out "legumes" meant vegetables, from a memory of some science teacher who had once told a class about leguminous plants.) "But that's a nigger—'scuse my French, there—a man what can cook up a storm. I mean, fancy stuff. Parisian dishes, and Aye-talian. See, I was born in nineteen seventy, in California. My mama was a big fan of Governor Reagan, 'cause he was always one of her favorite movie stars. So that's what she named me—Ronald Reagan Bodin. Then, in '80, when he got to be president, she figured that was a pretty good sign—she always told me that maybe I could be president, too. Now, of course, they got this other black feller, talkin' about runnin' him. I tell you, if my mama was alive today, she'd probably write the Democrats a letter sayin' to get him out of there and run Ronald Reagan Bodin, instead of that crazy African Arab or whatever he is, 'cause *I'd* have a damned chance." He laughed. "But that was my mama, God rest her soul. Course, that black feller ain't never gonna get in—white people in this country would shit a brick. If they really let 'im run, somebody's gonna shoot his head off anyway. And if he gets in, you know they ain't gonna let 'im do nothin'. And runnin' Mrs. Clinton against him *sure* ain't the answer. A woman and a black man? I'm afraid the Republican's gonna get this next one, 'cause the Democrats don't got sense enough to—" he chuckled—"run somebody like Ronald Reagan Bodin. Hey? The Republicans is better anyway, since at least they know *somethin'* about money. That's what my mama would tell you. You see anything you want for a starter? That's all the stuff down the side, there. Clams, snails, calamari—that's like octopus or something. They fry it up—real light, too. It's good."

Marvin returned with a tray on which was a glass of Fresca for Eric, two shot glasses of bourbon, a bowl of ice, two glasses of water...As he put them down in front of Barb and Bodin, he said, "I spoke to Ron. He said as soon as he gets a moment, he'll be out—" at which point a black man in a white short-sleeved jacket and a chef's cap stepped up behind the white waiter and smiled.

While Barbara spooned two cubes into her glass, Ron said, "Well, *here* he is now! Hey, there, Ronny! How's it all goin' this evenin'? Looks like yall got a good crowd at the place tonight."

Marvin looked up, and practically jumped back.

Whether because of heat or politeness, the chef removed his cap and held it before him. "We're doin' all right." Gaunt and with a shaved head, Chef Ron looked at them with what seemed to Eric friendly patience. "Not quite as many as last weekend, but that's probably 'cause of the weather we're havin'." In response, a splatter like buckshot tinkled the pane. Another thunderclap; the curtains billowed into the room. Then a gust slammed shut the window—the curtains fell. Marvin turned to grab and fasten the frame. In her chair, Barb started, and said, "Oh…!" and Chef Ron looked over, chuckling. "So how yall doin' tonight?" He smiled around the table, dark chin and cheekbones taking bronze highlights from the table lamp. "Yall havin' a good time?"

"Sure am," Ron said. "Hey, Ron, was you named after Ronald Reagan—like me?"

"Huh?" The cook smiled. "Naw—my aunt raised me in Tuscaloosa. I didn't even get a name from my parents, 'fore they got killed in a car wreck. If they named me, nobody knew what it was. So when my aunt took me in, they named me after my mama, Ronny Francis. They said Ronny could be a boy's or a girl's name."

"Oh," Ron said. "So you ain't Ronny Reagan. You Ronny Francis."

"No," the chef said. "I'm just Ron—or Ronny. *Two* girls' names was a little much for a boy to carry around, at least in Tuscaloosa."

"There you go. But we still got pretty much the same handle. You think you could tell us what's really tasty?" Bodin nodded to Barb. "I always like to get the word from the man who *knows*!" He looked at Barb and Eric. "And *that's* Ron here. He won't let us go wrong—will you, Ron?"

"Everything," Chef Ron said, thoughtfully (as Eric wondered where the introductions had gone, though he was glad to dispense with them), "that we got here is good—otherwise we wouldn't be servin' it at Shells. But maybe yall can tell me what you're in the mood for. Fish—we got bass, tilapia, bluefish. For fowl, we got some real nice game hens—and some duck. Or for meat, we got osso buco; that's a lamb shank braised for hours in a real tasty stock, tomato, and green pepper stew; we got center cut pork chops, stuffed with some prosciutto, or a very nice sirloin, with a red wine reduction. Do one thing sound more to your likin' than another?"

Barb decided on the fish—"I really think you'll like the tilapia, ma'am—" and Ron on the osso buco—"Now, that's a hearty dish. You get a lot of food with that. Be ready to take some home"—and Eric, who'd asked for chicken, got the game hen. "That's like a little tender chicken, but you get it all. It's very moist, and it comes on a bed of spicy risotto, with a little pot of tomatoes, onion, and garlic pureed up all together. Say—" here Chef Ron frowned at Eric—"ain't I seen you around the Dump, helping out Dynamite Haskell and…Morgan Haskell, the boy who works with him?"

"Huh?" Eric brightened. "Yeah," although he had no memory of the man.

"That's his summer job." Putting down his menu, Ron laughed. "Don't think that's his career or nothin'." (Eric saw Barbara smile.) "This is his mother, my friend Mrs. Barbara Jeffers."

"I *thought* that was you." Chef Ron nodded, still looking at Eric. "Nice to meet you, Mrs. Jeffers. And it's nice to see you—" he said to Eric, still smiling, still nodding—"at Shells. Good evening to yall. I'm afraid I got to get back to work, now." He stepped away.

"Hey—!" Ron called after him.

Chef Ron looked back, questioning.

"You think they gonna let that black man be president? They done had black mayors in New York and Washington and New Orleans—"

"Who?" he asked. "Obama?"

"Yeah," Ron said.

"With all these crazy white folks around in this country?" The chef turned back and walked away. "Not a *chance!*"

"What did I tell you?" Ron said, chuckling.

"You know," Barb said, "this place is *so* small down here." With the lights outside, rain made a sparkly backing behind the white curtains.

Marvin and Chef Ron retreated.

"He's already seen you, Eric," Barbara said. "Clem keeps tellin' me. But I guess it's true. Everybody around here *does* know everybody."

"That's why you gotta watch yourself, boy." Ron looked seriously at Eric. "You can't get away with nothin' down here like you can up in Atlanta. So don't you go trying no drugs or marijuana cigarettes or crack cocaine or nothin'." Again, lifting his bourbon, he smiled at the absurdity. "Now we're gonna really have us a good dinner—see, 'cause the chef knows who I am. Like I *guess* he already…knows you, too, Eric." He took a deep breath. "But I guess a chef has got to know who his garbage man is. Ain't I right?" He seemed to think this was very funny. "Ain't I right, now? Go on—*tell* me I ain't right!"

*

Marvin had already brought them dessert menus—cardboard cards with blue seashells across the top and bottom—then gone again into the kitchen. They looked down—both Eric and Barb had said they probably wouldn't have any, but Bodin had insisted—when again Marvin came out the swinging doors, carrying a small chocolate cake, a yellow candle burning in its center. Several waiters fell in line behind him, singing, "Happy Birthday to you…!" while Ron declared: "Why…? It *must* be somebody's birthday around *here*! Yeah, *somebody* or other must be havin' a birthday!"

"Oh, Ron," Barbara said. "You didn't have to go and do all this!"

Marvin put the cake on the table, in front of Eric.

"Well—" Ron put his hands on the cloth's edge and leaned back— "You said somebody just might be havin' a birthday around now." Ron's nails were notably cleaner than Eric, shower or no. "So, I figured a little birthday cake couldn't hurt nothin'—now, could it?"

"Oh, honey!" Barbara looked at Eric. "Say thank you to Mr. Bodin!"

Ron's hands dropped beneath the table edge and he sat forward. "Ron— Eric got to call me Ron, now."

"I was gonna say thank you." Eric sucked in his own breath to keep from adding, If you'd give me a chance—

A white haired couple at the table next to them smiled at them.

Barbara said, "Make a wish, honey."

Ron grinned. "I told you, you couldn't get away with *nothin'* down here. Imagine! Havin' a birthday and not tellin' everybody. Happy birthday, boy."

Eric looked around the table, said, "Oh, wow…Hey, Ron, thank you. This is…great," and thought: Please. I wish I would wake up in my own bed and have three more hours to sleep…He blew out the flame.

Using a knife with a fancy handle, Marvin cut into the chocolate buttercream. The slice came loose.

The cake was chocolate all through.

Eric took a big breath—and thought: I know. I'm not gonna get my wish. But I'm gonna smile through it, say thank you, go home, and go to bed. Then it'll be over. He glanced at Barb.

She was smiling.

Could this, he wondered, be what growing up was all about?

Eric was not exactly allergic to chocolate. But when he had been eleven, in Hugantown, one afternoon he'd eaten much too much of it, thrown up, and had diarrhea for three days—so that the flavor, ever since, had made him queasy.

*

All the way back from Hemmings, Eric slept in the back seat. The next morning, miraculously he overslept by only twelve minutes.

Stepping out the kitchen door, in his gray hoody, onto the wet wooden steps, he was about to take off into the blackness, when he grabbed the doorframe and swung around. Out loud, he said, "*Jesus—!*"

For the third day, he'd left without Shit's socks. Sprinting back through the house to his porch room, from his sock carton on the floor against the wall, he grabbed a handful, carried them into the kitchen, pulled out a plastic bag from where Barbara kept them folded behind some empty copper canisters marked rice, flower, and sugar on the counter. As he pulled the bag loose (the canisters clinked into each other), he managed to unfold it, and shoved the socks in. Behind him, he noticed a pair had fallen to the floor. He picked them up and got them in, too. There were only seven pairs: the things were bulkier than he'd figured. He'd wanted to make it a dozen. But that would do for now.

Then he took off, through the kitchen's screen door and into the dripping, pre-dawn dark.

Except for a road light here and there, the run down through the pines was black and wet, and the lower legs of his jeans were sopping by the time he got to the dock.

"We was about to take off and go without you," Shit said. "'Cause *you* was out partyin' last night—over at that fancy place, in Hemmings." He wore a gray, button-up sweater with a couple of large holes that looked like it had belonged to someone else—maybe Dynamite.

"He's lyin'," Dynamite said. "We wasn't gonna leave without you. What was you doin' over at Shells?"

Shit's sweater buttons were in the wrong holes, too; one side hung lower than the other by three inches. It looked like he had no shirt on under it, either.

"How'd you know I was there?" Eric asked. "Barbara's friend took us out last night—Jesus, I thought I was gonna go to sleep on the table, I was so tired."

"Well, now you know." Dynamite chuckled. "It's hard to work a job like this and party all night—though I know you're gonna try it a couple of times. Everybody does."

"When we was startin' out this morning," Shit said, opening up the cab door, "we seen Ron comin' home from work—he's the cook out there. He said he done seen you and said hello and all like that."

"Oh," Eric said. "Yeah, he said hello to me. I don't remember ever seein' *him* before, though."

"You know," Shit said, pausing at the pickup door, "right across the road where Bull lives…?"

"Un-huh," Eric said (who wasn't really sure who Shit meant), ready to climb up after him.

"Well, his is the house thirty or forty yards to the left, toward Dump Corners."

"Oh." The plastic bag in one hand, Eric pulled himself up and inside. Now he held it out. "Hey—I got a present for you."

Shit asked, "Huh?"

"Remember?" Eric grinned. "I told you I'd give you some socks."

"You got 'em…?" Shit looked bewildered. "I thought maybe they was too expensive after all, or something. Or your mama didn't want you to give 'em to me. I figured yesterday I wouldn't say nothin' and make you feel bad. But you *got* 'em!"

"Oh, fuck…" Eric said. "Now I *do* feel bad. Yesterday, I just forgot. That's all. Here. Put on a pair. Go on, I mean if you want…"

Shit took the bag and held it. "Ron said it was…*your* birthday last night. We should have a present for you."

"You did," Eric said. "Those gloves you're lettin' me wear, till I can get some of my own. You know. My hands? Your feet? Besides," he added, "givin' presents on your *own* birthday's fun."

Dynamite finished whatever he was doing outside the driver's open door—pissing on his fender, Eric realized from the sound—then opened it further, and, in his usual work shirt and T-shirt under his bib, climbed in.

"Hey," Shit said, as Dynamite slammed it after him. "Look what Eric gimme." Between Dynamite and Eric, in his baggy sweater Shit clutched the plastic bag in his lap—but didn't move to put them on, though. "Socks."

"You can really use them things." Dynamite grasped the keys swinging from the steering post and turned on the ignition. "That's good."

The side windows were droplet speckled. The truck started moving. Drops slipped down the windshield into the wipers' half circles.

Shit's sweater didn't look as if it would keep off much water. (Where the sweater had slid from Shit's shoulder, Eric saw, Shit did wear an old T-shirt—with more holes in it than the sweater.)

Eric was—surprisingly—*not* exhausted.

At first.

Still, in the wet morning, as he lugged dripping plastic sacks over lawns and driveways and porches and sidewalks, he felt as if his body's pieces were connected along edges and angles, rather than by rounded joints.

That afternoon, they drove back to the Dump, left the truck, and walked with long, tired strides to the steps and up onto Dynamite's porch—yes, that must be Chef Ron's, over there, left of Bull's—

With his unshaven smile, Dynamite asked, "So how you like this job *now*, after doin' it in the goddam fuckin' rain?"

Eric stepped in a puddle on the boards that rilled to the edge and spilled over. "I like it…"

"You—" Morgan Haskell said, gripping Eric's shoulder with a wide, wet hand—"are a lyin' sack of shit!" Though he was grinning.

Inside, they stripped naked and lay down in the big bed, Shit on his belly, Eric on his back, with Dynamite beside him. Then Shit practically leaped on Eric, who, surprised, grabbed his shoulders, while Shit's tongue went into Eric's mouth and his face twisted against Eric's. Their tongues went seeking gaps and crevices and wetnesses Eric had hardly realized were there. The garbage assistant's arms shook with the force of his grip— then the grip relaxed.

As Shit pulled away, Eric saw his eyes were closed. Shit's hand dragged over Eric's chest. Eric looked…to see the downward arc of Shit's engorged cock retreating, shrinking, softening.

Shit, he realized, was…asleep!

And in another minute-and-a-half, so was Eric

To the feel of a shaking mattress, Eric woke on his side to see Dynamite on his back, naked, beside him, vigorously pumping. The garbage man turned his head and, with his unshaven face, grinned at Eric, his fist slowing. "Well," he said, quietly, "since you two fuckers is too out of it to service a hardworkin' Georgia redneck, what the fuck *else* am I supposed to do?"

On his other side, eyes closed, Shit said: "He's just kiddin'—he likes to beat off by hisself from time to time, no matter how much nookie he gets offa me—or you. If he don't, he gets all evil."

Outside on the cabin deck, again Eric could hear the sound of rain—like insect wings beating the boards, the walls, the roof.

Dynamite's fist, and the bed's shaking, increased in speed. Then, from his fist, his cockhead erupted—

Four gouts, the second of which almost hit the green ceiling and the third of which shot up four or five feet.

They fell back over Dynamite's belly, flank, wrist. His heavy hand urged the skin up over his dickhead. His fingers closed over it, in the gleaming spillage, as he rolled toward Eric. "Here, you go…" Releasing himself, he pushed two drooling fingers into Eric's mouth—beneath the running mucus, his flesh as hard as wood. (Cold and kind of damp, Shit's butt pressed the small of Eric's back.) And Eric was again asleep before Dynamite pulled his fingers loose, as though texture, flavor, or both had put him out.

* * *

[12] SHIT'S GRATITUDE FOR the socks erupted into sex three times—once at Dynamite's the day of the giving (an hour later, Eric woke with Shit—cold feet against his ankles, face and belly warm—on top of him, his tongue lancing eyes, nose, mouth…), once behind the Citgo Station in the Harbor the next afternoon; and the following morning, to Eric's surprise, Shit was waiting in the dark, outside Barbara's trailer: "Hey… Eric! Come'ere…!"

"What you doin'…?" Eric had chills: for a moment he'd thought someone had been about to leap out and grab him.

"Come on—over here!"

Twenty yards down another path joined it, where a road light stood.

"I come up early, 'cause I wanted to see you. Come'ere and gimme a hug." When they'd been fucking around in the bushes ten minutes, a police car (of course) rolled by on the road, though they were sure they hadn't been seen.

Then Shit took Eric's hand and they walked down toward the Front Street dock. (Hadn't he been dreaming something like this…?) Eric remembered how baggy Shit had looked on his rainy birthday.

This morning, Shit wore no shirt at all. As they walked down to the Harbor through black morning and the occasional road light dragged its illumination around them, he looked to Eric like the god of sex himself. Shit said, "You never come that fast when I sucked your dick before, back at the cabin. I gotta do that more often. I like makin' you come. It's fun."

"Well, I was surprised…" Eric said, "I guess. I liked it—a lot."

"I know you liked it," Shit said, "the way you was huggin' on my damned head. I liked it, too."

"That's 'cause I was real sensitive. And if you moved too much, I was gonna have to shout out."

"You can do a little shoutin'," Shit said. "That ain't gonna hurt nobody." Both of them laughed. "Dynamite don't think you should do too much fuckin' before you go in to work. But that's my favorite time. And makin' guys I really like shoot off in my mouth where I can feel it and taste it is fun. You tasted good, too. I'm gonna have that taste in my mouth all mornin'. I may not even say nothin' no more—so I can just enjoy it while I'm slingin' shit. "

"Yeah…" Eric looked around the dark road. "It *was* fun. Should we be doin'…*this*, though?" Eric lifted their joined fists. "Suppose that police car comes back?"

"It won't," Shit said. "Besides. You can't get arrested just for this—I live in the Dump. So it don't matter," which didn't make a lot of sense. But Eric let it slide.

At the dock, Dynamite and the pickup waited.

"What the fuck you two been doin'?" Dynamite said. "It's time to take this stuff to the Bottom."

"Bottom?" Eric said. "That was the name of a friend of mine, back in Atlanta."

From the middle of the truck seat, Shit grinned. "Did you fuck 'im?" (In the bedroom talk flowering lazily among them in their previous afternoons at the cabin, Shit had bragged to Eric about his—if not Dynamite's— fooling around over the years with practically everyone who lived at *their* end of the Dump…)

"Naw. But I should have." Then Eric said, "He lived in our building. I was scared my dad would find out."

"Well, my dad's good about that. 'Cause he's a faggot, too—like me."

When they joined him under the dock light, Dynamite said, "Hey, I'm glad you two hooked up. I thought you might miss each other, when I run Shit up there near your place."

"I sucked his dick," Shit said. "I took 'im right off in the bushes beside the road, got down on my damned knees, and sucked him till he shot. He shoots almost as much as you do—not as much as Al. But I felt it. I ain't never took Eric's load *all* in my mouth at once, before, 'cause you always wanna see some of it and play in it. But it was nice."

"Um...yeah," Eric said, surprised.

"*He* really liked it, too. So don't talk about me not suckin' no dick. We seen a police car. But that wasn't nothin'. They didn't even stop."

At the wheel, Dynamite glanced over at him—and took the truck onto a narrow road. (Eric wondered if the glance was an accusation of cowardice or an offer of sympathy.) "See, I told 'im if he wanted to keep you around, he better catch a little more of what he pitches."

"It's nice suckin'," Shit declared. "'Cause I know you're feelin' what I'm feelin' when you doin' it to me. And there ain't no fuckin' thing that feels better."

Dynamite chuckled. The truck pulled forward.

*

Working with Eric that day, Shit and Dynamite finished the houses along the Runcible Road toward eleven. Dynamite said, "Now, like I told you, we gotta take all this over to the Bottom, see, and toss it."

"I can show off my new socks to Al, there. Hey, these are really great!"

"Honestly," Eric said, "it's nothin'. I'm glad you like 'em."

At the storage Dumpster beside an abandoned railroad car, they reloaded the truck.

Twenty minutes after that, when the sky had begun to lighten, Dynamite turned the truck down a path where the brush whispered on the sides, till they reached an eight-foot fence topped with helixes of razor wire. Dynamite climbed out to lift the horseshoe hasp from the vertical pole, then pushed the gate back. The bottom grated on a round of cement. In the truck again, they rolled through to pull up by a shack that looked as if, years ago, it had been painted gray. A black man stood to the side, in jeans and work boots. He wore a black knitted cap and a white and orange road vest, but, like Shit, no shirt. "Recognize 'im?" Shit asked Eric. "The nigger there's Al Havers. He fucked your white ass—in Turpens."

Eric recognized the black man with the shaved head.

Again in the truck, Dynamite had already started to back up and turn the truck around, to back further toward what looked like a cliff. For a second, Eric thought they were going over, and lurched forward to grab the cab window's edge. But Dynamite set the hand brake, then called out the window, "Hey, Al. This here's our new helper, Eric."

"You got another one now?" Al said, with not much enthusiasm.

Shit grinned. Then he called out, "Hey, Al. You gonna let me get out this time so I can show Eric here how to empty the truck? I gotta show you my new socks, too. They're green. You can see 'em right through the holes in my sneakers."

"Dynamite—" Al ambled over—"tell yo' nigger bastard I ain't lettin' him set foot on dis ground if he don't have some real work shoes. He know dat—you both do. He can't come around here barefoot. I done told you guys dat before. Dis ain't play, now."

"Oh, I see," Shit said. "Oh. So, you don't want me to get no splinters in my toes, here. Al's a *real* thoughtful feller. That horse dick he got swinging between his legs is just full of that there compassion."

Ignoring Shit, Dynamite was saying, "He ain't gettin' out the truck." He blinked at Eric. "Come on, son. Get y'ass out. I'll show you how we do it. Shit knows he got to stay inside."

Eric opened the door and jumped down. Junk strewed the dirt. Coils of cable lay about, metal wrapping loose here and there along it, points protruding. A pile of hubcaps leaned against the shack's wall. Eric started toward the cliff edge, curious to see what lay over it. Dozens and dozens of birds made their loud arcs on the sky.

"And you—?" Al said.

Eric looked back.

"You only got on a pair of runnin' shoes? Hey, I ain't gonna let *you* work here less'n I see work gloves and a good pair of shoes—or you stay in de damned truck with Shit. We don't got no insurance for dumb ass nigger kids *or* dumb ass white kids what cut deah feet all to hell an' come down with tet'nus or somethin'. I wouldn't let my kids come out here like dat—" His next look went to Dynamite. "I don't see why you brung *dis* one along if he ain't got no proper shoes." That nod went back to Shit, who grinned out the truck's side window.

At the mention of work gloves, Eric turned back from the cliff's edge to the truck.

Shit must have read his mind, because he reached in and handed out the striped gray canvas.

Dynamite said, "I was just wonderin', Al—" (beside him, Eric felt Dynamite nudge him with his elbow—) "if'n you wanted to take this boy here over to the cabin for a bit, while I'm tossin' sacks, maybe mess around a little with him. You two was getting' it on pretty well the last time I seen you together, and it's his birthday…"

"His birthday, huh?" Al took a leisurely step, then—slowly—frowned. "Oh…yeah. You's dat white kid Jay brung into that Turpens shithole wid us all, ain't you?" Al let his head fall to the side. "How'd you like dat load I sent you home wid in my used scumbag?"

Eric said, "It was…real nice!" He glanced at Dynamite, and grinned. "Yeah…" He looked at back at Al—

—who'd dropped one hand to the fork of his jeans. "You think you can wrestle another load of prime nigger cum out my mother-fuckin' black snake?" Dark fingers squeezed the once-black denim, mostly gray-brown now.

Eric swallowed. "Yeah." His heart had started to beat hard again. "Sure—"

"Then you go get yourself a decent pair of work shoes and come on back here with these low-down scumbag cocksuckers, and I may even let them stand around and watch us—and maybe let 'em lick up some of the leavin's." Standing up straight, Al dropped his hand from his pants. "But I *still* ain't lettin' you run around here with nothin' on you damned feet, I don't care *how* sweet your honkey butt-hole feels slidin' up and down my big, black dick." Al flung out a hand. "With them things on, you might as *well* be barefoot as dat damned nigger deah." He spat to the left. "Next time I see you, I'll take you in de shack. But after dat, we gonna wait till we run into each other at Turpens again. Or maybe at the Opera. Okay?"

Eric looked up at Dynamite—who grinned back at him.

"Yeah." Eric looked at the gatekeeper. "Sure. That's okay."

"'Cause this is work out here, cocksucker—at least most of it. It ain't no play." Then he grunted. "Motherfuckin' birthday, my left *nut*…!" But he was smiling. In the gray light, over Al's dark arms, though he looked for them, because of the clouded-over morning, Eric couldn't see Al's tattoos.

"Al here's a real busy man," Shit explained from the pickup window. "He got three wives and—what is it?—seven little Havers runnin' around Split Pine—and all his fans at Turpens and the Opera. And sometimes he has a little trouble arguin' them ladies into given' 'im some nookie. That's why he's always grabbin' a little man-tail on the side."

"Two wives," Al said, "and *five* kids. That's right now, anyway. Still, it's more'n you, scumsucker. And however much trouble I have wid 'em, they better than the bes' piece *you* ever had!"

"Aw, come on," Shit said. "You gotta have a few by some you ain't actually married to, yet."

"Well, yeah—" Havers' smile got broader—"but I lose track of those. Hey—I may have another of dem raincoats tied up around a little somethin' for you, from time to time. I like to give dem things to my faggot fren's—so dey don't forget what a straight guy can do for 'em. Now, you go on and dump them damned sacks today—but get yourself some motherfuckin' work shoes."

Leaning from the truck window, Shit called, "Hey, Al—somebody done told me you just fill them rubbers up with piss. That ain't no real cum."

Al looked up. "You don't think da's my real cum? You ever taste it?"

In the window, Shit made a big show of shrugging his shoulders. "Yeah. Maybe a...*little* of it."

"What it taste like?"

"Like horse jizz." And Shit and Dynamite both began to laugh.

Al reached between his legs and gripped his cock through the worn cloth. "Maybe I'll let you suck a full load outta it someday. Den you can tell me if it tastes more like horse or like nigger."

"Sure," Shit said. "And this nigger here—" he pointed at Eric— "would love to suck on it too; 'specially if you'll lemme watch you put it up his white boy asshole, after he got it all slicked up."

"Well, since it's his birthday, maybe we'll work somethin' out with him and *this* here pig fucker." He dropped his hand and looked disgusted. "Once yall get some motherfuckin' shoes, dat is."

*

When they were driving back, Eric asked, "Does the garbage just go down to the sea?"

"Naw," Shit said. "They wouldn't let that happen. From up there, it looks kinda like it does. But there's strip a land, maybe a hun'erd, a hun'erd-fifty feet wide, that closes it off from the water on the other side."

"Eventually they gonna bury it, like they did the Dump," Dynamite said. "It's gonna be more landfill."

Shit said, "You can walk all the way around it, if you want." Shit scowled. "I mean, on land. I don't like that place. It stinks—I mean *really* stinks." (Eric thought: it did.) "And it's too high, that cliff you got to throw the bags over."

Dynamite said, "Shit don't like *real* high places. He can go up any hill or bluff, but not if it's sharp and sudden. If it's like the Bottom—a cliff or somethin'—he gets that vertigo."

"Christ, it stinks," Shit reiterated. "I mean, *this* truck's bad enough. But they put *everything* in there. I seen a dead cow down there, once. And a pig. I swear they got human bodies in there, too, smellin' it up. People done disappeared outta Runcible and nobody never seen 'em again. I bet my black ass they're in half a dozen pieces in plastic sacks, rottin' down in the Bottom, underneath all that junk."

"Does Al live in the Dump?" Eric asked.

"Naw," Shit said. "He's straight. Him and some of his wives live in Split Pine, a little place up back of Hemmings—right across the street from each other. I don't even know how many he got. I hear a couple he divorced a few years ago came on back and moved into places just down the street from 'im, and he drops in to see 'em pretty regular. People say he's supposed to live a couple of days with one and a couple of days with the other. Probably them women run that nigger crazy. I don't think they'd let him do that if he was white."

"Well," Dynamite said, "he divorces 'em first, but they're always changin' their mind." The garbage man chuckled. "I just know he stops off at Turpens pretty regular—"

"—when he ain't at the Opera," Shit added.

Dynamite said, "You gonna get them shoes?"

"Yeah, I am." Eric wondered if fear of heights was the reason Shit was shy of work shoes.

"Good. Maybe your mom'll help you get 'em," Dynamite said. "They're a good investment if you gonna work 'round here. But they're expensive."

"See, if Al lived in the Dump," Shit said, "you could suck that mule-dicked nigger any time you wanted. Just walk down the road and knock on his door—and he'd probably grin at ya' and whip it right out while you fell on your knees. And I could walk on down there with you, and watch. He *likes* people to see 'im—like me. We almost got in trouble a couple of times, at the Opera House, takin' it outside in the street. But 'cause he's straight, you kinda got to work around it, there—grab it when you can. Damn, that nigger is *so* dick proud—"

"Yeah," Dynamite said. "And you ain't? Shit, you either gotta watch out for that or keep it in the Dump, one. You can't be doin' it all over the road and in the Harbor—even when it *ain't* light out."

Shit humphed a little. Then he grinned at Eric.

As they drove back by the beach, bird cries over the Bottom grew quieter behind them. "See," Dynamite said, "that's what the Dump *used* to look like. My daddy told me that—Shad remembers it." Now *he* humphed. "They *had* a couple of bodies in there, too. I know that nigger Shad shot went down in that—that's was an outright murder and shouldn't a been condoned. But then they filled it in, poured in a few tons of lime—bulldozed it all down. Even put some big ol' cement bracin' down in there. Now—" he shrugged—"it's where *we* live."

"At least all the faggots like us do," Shit said.

Dynamite said, "Shit, you ain't supposed to say that."

"Oh," Shit said. "I'm sorry. I meant all the nigger faggots like us. Hey, *you* want a birthday present?" Taking Eric's hand, Shit pulled it into his crotch. "You could suck on this…"

*

In the cab, between Dynamite and Shit, Eric sat thinking, as they drove. "You know—" they had finished the last houses; the sun was high—"it's funny down here. I mean, the first day after I was messin' with you guys in the truck stop—"

"Turpens—" Dynamite changed gears.

"Yeah—I'm sittin' in the Lighthouse, talkin' to Mex and Jay out on the dock, and all at once it hits me: I'm havin' what *sounds* like a sensible conversation with a pair of guys about how they eat each other's goddam shit! And I'm thinkin', where the fuck *am* I? Then, yeah, like back at the Bottom, sure, I'd like to bounce up and down on Al's fuckin' horse cock again—I mean, it was really good. But there you was, my boss, I mean, talkin' about givin' Al my ass as a *birthday* present, the first thing when we get in to work—"

"Hey," Dynamite said. "I was talkin' about him givin' *you* some dick—"

Though he wasn't laughing, clearly Shit thought it was funny. "You're the one who said you like givin' presents on your birthday."

"But Al ain't even gay—at least, *he* don't think he is. Or even…the two of you. What the hell did you say to your dad this mornin'? Hey, I wanna grab some nookie off Eric? And what did *he* say? Okay, I'll run you up near his house, so you can catch him comin' down. But don't take too long. We got to get to work. Or, maybe, let's get home in time so you can fuck my butthole before we go to sleep. Who the hell says things like that to his father? I mean, that's not jokin' around, like the guys out at the Farm. I don't know. It makes me feel…a little crazy, I guess."

"What's so crazy about us?" Shit asked from beside the window.

"Well, you're…related, for one thing. And pretty close related, too."

"Un-huh," Shit agreed. (Eric could hear his grin.) "I think that's fuckin' nasty, ain't it?"

"I guess—" Dynamite brought them around another curve, again into the sun—"all this is a little new for Eric. Maybe we got to remember that about him, Shit."

"Still, it's the *stuff* guys down here talk about, suckin' toes and fuckin' some black guy with an elephant cock at work, father-son...incest. I mean, that's what it *is*. And, like I say, eatin' shit—"

"You sucked his shit off my dick pretty much every afternoon since you been here—includin' at Turpens," Shit said. "I love that—so does he. Makes us both shoot some big ol' loads."

"Yeah, but I *know* you two—"

"You worried about it," Shit went on, "you go see Dr. Greene. He'll tell you—long as everybody eats plenty of fresh vegetables and don't pick up no parasites lickin' out the wrong fella's asshole, nothin's gonna happen. That's the only problem with the Opera. Once every year or two, they get a half-a-dozen cases of them things, if the wrong homeless guy starts hangin' around in there. But they got medicine for that, too. Him and me had that humera, once. *Yuchh!* That was a mess...But we don't now."

"Oh..." Eric said, surprised. "Well, it still...*sounds* crazy."

The road got straighter as it prepared to feed onto a larger highway they could see below the grade.

"I guess 'crazy,'" Shit said, "is just your word for 'nasty.'"

Which surprised Eric.

"See, Shit was brought up thinkin' 'nasty' was a *good* word." Dynamite was smiling.

"'Bout the best one in the language," Shit said, "I figured. But we can call it crazy, if you want."

"See, you just gotta decide," Dynamite said, "which is crazier: talkin' about it and doin' it—or *not* talkin' about it and doin' it. 'Cause one way or the other, the doin' part's gonna get done. I can promise you that."

* * *

[13] DAILY, DURING THE first hour-and-a-half or two hours of work it was still dark, ten and twelve days could go by without their seeing anybody before copper light filtered along the road's edge or through the banks of pine.

During that time, Dynamite was pretty loose about where he'd take a morning piss: off the Gilead Dock, against the pump at the Citgo Station, on the front fender of his truck, or all over the tailgate, before he'd go climb into the cab to pull away from the shoulder of a wooded path.

It wasn't till the third week that Eric noticed—the first couple of times he thought it was happenstance—Dynamite *always* took his testicles from his pants along with his cock, as his stream began to chatter on new leaves or hissed over the tarmac's rim.

A few times in the first weeks, Dynamite had looked over at Eric and asked, "What *you* starin' at? Ain't you ever seen a fella take a piss before? Son, this whole town's my personal urinal. Makes me feel like I own it, pissin' all over the fuckin' thing."

"I'm starin' at your nuts," Eric would answer.

Shit would chuckle.

"You like them things, doncha, boy? Back at the cabin, you always suckin' on one or the other of the damned things."

"You ain't never told me to leave off 'em, yet."

"And I probably never will. A little tuggin' on them suckers feels nice."

A mess of morning bugs swarmed the orange ends of the florescent tubes under the awning off the Citgo office, and Shit, who was pissing on the corner of the garage, cracked up, finding this hysterically funny.

"Well, see, now—" Shit shook himself off—"I guess that's somethin' people don't do up in the big city." He pushed himself inside, but his flies were broken so there was no pretense at closing them. "Up there, I guess, everybody just holds it in forever. You don't *ever* get to flush it out, huh?"

Dynamite raised his chin, and said, "Oh," as if that explained it. "Well, look all you want. You'll get a mouth full of 'em later, anyway."

Eric had decided Dynamite's urethra must be twice the width of most guys', since his urine stream seemed twice as thick. The garbage man slid his skin forward so that for seconds he splattered over his own dusty shoes and jean's cuffs, and even on Eric's. "Come on over here." He beckoned Shit with his chin. "Lemme mark you, boy. I wanna mark you two the way ol' Tom marks his trees and the porch steps and his rocks and things." That day Shit had showed up to work barefoot; now, Dynamite swung his stream around in the middle to pee on Shit's foot.

Under the florescence, the pavement darkened and a brown leaf rose beside Shit's instep, turned, and swept away on his father's urine.

Eric felt a thrill of envy, while Shit stood there and said, dryly, "I sure hope you're havin' fun."

His father grinned. "Yep—kinda. But you know me."

Back at Barbara's, out on his porch, while bats flicked through the twilight outside the screen, when Eric would have his before-sleep jerk off, he would imagine Dynamite smiling at him and saying, "Squat on down, son," and that racehorse waterfall splashing and splattering into his face. He would force himself to keep his mouth and his eyes open. He would

imagine the encounter occurring all over Diamond Harbor, in the cool
evening, in the warm morning, on the marina, on the back roads, beside
the post office, out on the dock, behind the Citgo while hot, salty urine fell.
The image could always make him come.

* * *

[14] ERIC WAS DISAPPOINTED when Shit said, "You go on to the mall
by yourself. I don't like that place. I go there an' people always lookin' at
me funny."

Dynamite chuckled, pulled the oil stick up from the engine, frowned
at it, black and bronze in the sun, then wiped it with the cloth balled in his
other hand that was half black and half brown and kind of yellow between.
He moved his head from under the hood. Shadow pulled away from his
long nose and oily fingers. His fingers were black. "If you put some damned
shoes on, wore a T-shirt instead of that old rag with no buttons half fallin'
off you, and stuck a belt in your pants so that people couldn't see the hair at
the top of your dick and three inches of your damn ass crack, they wouldn't
grin at you so much." He slipped the oil stick back in its collar and screwed
down the cap. "He likes to go and hang around the johns—he does pretty
well out there, don't you? That's when he wants a change of nookie—
which with Shit is pretty much all the time. Ain't it, boy?"

"Well," Shit said, "yeah. I don't mind the grinnin'—just that they keep
it up. I guess I used to—a few years ago, I mean. Go to the mall. You show
enough skin, you can get your dick sucked pretty much anywhere. But you
have to wait so long out there. I have more fun at Turpens."

Dynamite laughed again and stood up.

"But I don't like to go there to buy nothin'. You go on—you can get the
shuttle bus, if you want."

So, in the gray halls that ran from clothing store to Radio Shack to
Rite Aid to Atlas Power Tools, looking pretty much like the mall outside
Hugantown and the one outside Orlando and the one they went to near
Atlanta, Eric found the Verizon store. On the TV screen keyboard at the
front, he typed his name and watched it appear on the overhead screen at
the bottom of the list of four other customers.

Forty minutes later, he left the gray-carpeted interior with a new cell
phone that had some colored lights that blinked on the front around the
little window with the time on it. He dumped the considerable plastic and
cardboard packaging in a blue wire refuse basket. At first, he thought about
sitting at the food court, but it was awfully noisy. So he went to the rest

room that was at the end of a hall where someone had put three aluminum ladders, on their sides, down against the wall. Eric sat on one.

Then he punched Mike's number.

With the rectangular phone pressed onto his ear, after the repeated buzz, what sounded like an anonymous black voiced answered, "Yeah…?"

"Hi." Eric leaned over with an elbow on his knee. "How are you?"

"Huh…? Who's this?"

"Dad?"

"Eric…? Oh, hello…everything okay?"

"Yeah."

"Your mom ain't givin' you a hard time, is she?"

"Naw," he said. "No. Everything's fine. Barb's fine."

"Oh. Well, that's good."

"Yeah," Eric said. "I got a job, too. I mean, a good steady one. But I don't work today."

"Well, I do," Mike said.

"Oh, yeah. I'm sorry. Naw, I just wanted to let you know."

"Good. What you doin'?"

"Haulin' garbage. You remember the guys who helped us get the stuff to Barb's? I work with them, now."

"Oh," Mike said. "Well, that sounds okay. They seemed like good guys."

"Yeah, they're real nice. I like 'em…a lot."

"Well…that's good."

"It sure is better than goin' to school."

At the other end of the phone, there was silence.

Finally, Mike said, "I was just gonna ask you, if you was givin' any thought to your schoolin'."

"Just that I don't think I wanna go no more."

"You know Doneesha just got started in nursin' school a couple of days ago. She says she really likes it—and she's gonna be able to make a lot more money. And I had to go to the technical college for my weldin'."

"That'd be fine," Eric said, "if I was gonna be a nurse—or a welder. But there ain't no classes you gotta take, at least down here, to be a garbage man. And it's good work—it's hard. But it's fun."

"You told Barb, yet?"

"Naw. I ain't really talked about it."

"Don't be surprised if you have a' argument on your hands, when you get 'round to it."

"Yeah," Eric said. "Maybe."

"You really think droppin' out of school's okay?"

"It ain't like droppin' out in the middle. I just wouldn't start in September."

"Well, if it's what you really wanna do, I guess so."

"It sure would be nice. So far, I really like the job."

"How long you been workin' with 'em?"

"A week—ten days. Maybe nine…"

On the other end of the phone, Mike laughed. "Oh…!" He laughed again. "Well—all I can say is, see what it feels like after a month. Or three."

"Yeah, that would be kinda smart, wouldn't it?"

"Smarter than makin' up your mind right away. Hey, I got your number. In a few weeks I'll call you, maybe—or you can call me. We'll see what you're feelin' like, then. You got my number in your phone, don't you?"

"Um…well, I know it. But I'll put it in."

"Good. I gotta get back to work, though. Okay. It's nice to know you're doin' okay. Remember, workin' hard is always good. I love you, boy."

"Me, too," Eric said. He took the phone from his ear and closed it.

Next to the men's room door stood a man who looked to be about thirty-five or forty. He was leaning against the wall, and as Eric looked at him, he dropped his hand from his crotch and looked off down the hall.

Eric frowned. Was the guy cruising him? Two other guys came out of the men's room. Eric wondered what would happen if he sat there, but he also wanted to get home to help with dinner. And the guy was not as interesting looking as either Dynamite or Shit.

Suddenly the guy stood up, and left.

Probably Shit knew what he was talking about, having to wait a long time out here.

So Eric left, too.

Twenty yards along the mall corridor, Eric was trying to remember which direction to go for the shuttle back to the Harbor, when someone called, "Helloooo-*ooo!*"

He turned to see Serena, in a purple and orange headscarf, carrying three very large shopping bags, which bulged out the top with cushions and pillows.

"Oh," Eric called. "Hey…!"

She came up to him, looking proud. "The bed place was having a sale, and I've been wanting something to add some life to my little eagle's nest, up over the grocery in Runcible. That's where I live. I wish you and Barbara was over there—it's so lonely out where you guys are. Are you goin' back to the Harbor? Or are you gonna hang out here for a while?"

"Naw," Eric said. "I was gonna get the shuttle back."

"Oh, come on," Serena said. "You'll be waitin' for that thing half-an-hour, forty minutes. Lemme give you a ride. I'm finished here, anyway."

"Hey," Eric said, "thanks. You sure?"

"Sure I'm sure," Serena said. "Besides, I still have to steal a cup of that Dutch diesel fuel from your mama." She turned and looked at him under lowered brows. "You like that stuff your mama makes and calls coffee?"

"Naw," Eric said. "I don't see how she drinks it."

Serena grunted. "Oh, God—me neither. But there ain't nobody else around here I have more fun sitting with and tattlin' about folks—that's if she ain't too busy takin' care of Ronny Bodin. Hey, I'm parked in the back over by Penny's." They turned by a square glass column into which etched letters told where the movies and the perfume and the comics were. Down another hall, guys in jeans ambled with their wives and girlfriends among crowds of loud adolescents.

*

The next day, in the truck, Eric told Dynamite he had a cell phone now, as they jounced through the morning.

Dynamite said, "You know the best way to use that fuckin' thing, don't you?"

Wedged between Dynamite and Shit, Eric looked at the lighted numbers in the dark. "Huh? How?"

"You put my number in yours. I'll put yours in mine." A morning highway light swept through the cab. "Then we both forget we got 'em. And you just be where you're supposed to be—and I'll always come get you when I'm supposed to get you. That way, don't neither one of us have to ever use the motherfucker." Another light swept through.

Eric looked at Shit—

—who was smiling, with his missing teeth, sexy, and superior: "I don't use them damn things, 'cause I can't read the letters."

Eric wasn't sure if the annoyance in Shit's voice was at the phones or at himself.

* * *

[15] ERIC'S PRESENT, WHICH came home that Monday, three days late, from Barb—in a square, green and white Atlas carton—was a set of work shoes.

"I wanted to give them to you Saturday, on your birthday. I went to the mall outside Hemmings. But they'd run out of them," Barbara explained, "in your size."

"Thanks, Barb!" Surrounded in the box by green tissue, they had reinforced steel toes (like Dynamite's) it said so on the box top Eric held.

"Hey, I really…needed these."

"Sure," she said. "I'm glad I'm giving you something you can use." She had brought home ice cream, too—and a *vanilla* birthday cake, whose white box with green letters from the Hemmings Mall Bakery still sat on the table, not yet put away. "We can have your…*real* birthday now. I know you'll be in bed in an hour-and-a-half. Hey, I know I keep asking you the same question. But *is* it sixteen or seventeen, honey? I *can't* keep it straight. You're going to think your mother's retarded." Then she added, "Ron is coming by to take me out, later—but you're going to be asleep by then. That won't bother you, will it?"

"Naw," he said, wondering why she'd think it would.

* * *

[16] SHORTLY, SHIT GOT an open-topped wooden box from Black Bull across the road in which to keep the socks Eric had given him, under his own unused bed—at the end where, when they came out the drier, Shit's clothes lay in an unfolded heap. Eric's gifts Shit folded neatly, the unused pairs to one end, the ones he'd worn for two days of work folded and pushed to the other. At the end of two weeks, he safety pinned them together—Dynamite's suggestion—and put them in the wash, dried them, took the pins out, and folded the socks and pushed them to the unused side, while loose safety pins slid over the bottom.

Shit never actually said thank you for them.

But once Eric had given them, he'd smile at Eric off and on through the rest of the month with what looked to be a species of incommunicable joy. And whenever he folded them up, or put them in the machine, he always looked over at Eric with the same smile. Six months later, he was still taking them off, folding them up, and putting them away, every day after they finished their run.

And still smiling.

Once Dynamite said, a little grumpily, "He knows he can wear any clothes I got—socks, shirts, shoes. But Shit likes runin' around lookin' like a bumpkin."

"'Cause I get more nookie that way. Even Eric says he likes it. Hey— you wanna wear some of mine? I mean, the ones that Eric gave me? I like to wear Eric's 'cause he likes takin' 'em off me so much. If you don't wear some socks in your shoes, you don't hardly get no smell. That'd be okay…" Shit looked questioningly at Eric.

"Sure," Eric said. "You can both share 'em, if you want."

The next morning, Dynamite said, soberly, "Hand me a pair of them things out your box."

And, grinning, Shit did.

After work, cross-legged on the bedroom rug, beside the bed, Eric stripped off first Dynamite's (and gave his big foot a hug, then a sniff and another hug) and then Shit's.

Dynamite smiled quietly behind four days of unshaven moustache. Shit had his happiest, goofiest smile. And when Eric got tugged up onto the bed by both of them, in a complicated hug, everyone seemed pretty happy.

That smile and Shit's playful, plentiful sex were clearly Shit's way of saying thanks at an intensity that was as luminous as it had been on the first day. Sometimes, watching Shit sitting on the bed's edge, taking them out or putting them way, Eric felt he could *hear* Shit thinking: *I got socks to wear! I got socks!* Then he'd grin at Eric again as if he'd just received them.

* * *

[17] AUGUST'S LAST DAYS brought a steady breeze in from the water, which, on the twenty-third and again on the twenty-fifth and the twenty-seventh opened into full out rain. During let-ups, the truck window by which Eric regularly sat took on a cataract of mist, which, when he wiped it away with his hand's heel—so that for moments he could see a gray-green lawn, pine trees slipping beside the road, or an aluminum sided house with a window crossed by a branch shadow—grew back its fog in three breaths. Dynamite slowed before another driveway and, leaning forward between them, Shit whispered, "Come on. Let's work!"

The morning of the thirty-first was drizzly, though by noon clouds had unwrapped the sun.

That afternoon, Shit and Eric were walking—both barefoot that day—on the road's red mud, up from Dump Corners, where Dynamite had let them off, and were coming home with their eyes full of the light on cabin walls and sides of trees that seemed to have been gone for weeks.

They neared Chef Ron's, with the grove of pine beyond it…or *was* it Bull's: Black Bull was on the steps with a coil of rope over his big shoulder. Whiteboy squatted, scrawny and naked, at his feet.

But it *was* Chef's place. Bull turned to the newel under the porch roof and ran the rope through some kind of hook there—then gestured to Whiteboy, who stood up.

In his leather vest, Black Bull lifted Whiteboy's bony arm and tied the rope around it, up near the shoulder, then again down at his wrist.

Eric said, "What're they doin'?"

"I dunno," Shit said. "Probably deliverin' one of Bull's messages."

"Huh?"

Now Bull squatted and ran the rope around Whiteboy's lean thigh, then again around his ankle. He worked quickly with deliberate movements. Then he was over at the far post on the porch, and tugged the rope—which ran through some metal eyelets screwed into the lintel, across the top. Whiteboy's arm and his leg were tugged up and out, so that he stood on only one foot. His deep armpit looked as if it had been hollowed by a rotated fist. A tendon stood out taut from groin to leg.

Bull went back to the other side. The rope formed a web, Whiteboy at its center. Moments later, Bull looped another length around Whiteboy's scrawny ribs.

Shit stopped about fifteen feet away, so Eric stopped, too.

Bull said, "That tight enough for you, you stupid piece of shit?"

Whiteboy grunted, then looked over at Shit and Eric and grinned. "This nigger's tying me up real good. He knows how to do this stuff."

Lumbering in his big boots, footfalls oddly soft, Bull came around the front, looped the rope about Whiteboy's head, knotted it, then, after running it through two more eyelets set into the porch pole, grabbed Whiteboy's ankle and tied that. Whiteboy lost his balance and began to swing from the ropes. One arm hung free. Ankle high, his naked bony feet were stained with rusty mud. (Bull grunted, "Y'okay?" and went to the side, where he hauled on one of the ropes.) So were the edges of Bull's boots. The entire web, with Whiteboy in it, rose between the porch poles.

"Yeah," Whiteboy said. "That's good. Yeah, you really got me good now."

"I sure do, you honky piece of shit."

The door in the gray blue wall at the back of the porch opened. In a pair of jeans and an unbuttoned black shirt, Chef Ron first looked out, frowned, then stepped outside. "What the fuck are you—?"

Whiteboy looked back over his shoulder. All the ropes had tightened, and he wasn't swaying anywhere as much as he had been. Bull was tying up Whiteboy's other arm. Whiteboy's diminutive, uncut penis hung down one side of his high, tight nuts. "This nigger's tyin' me up real good, with no clothes on, right here on your goddam porch, so everybody who walks by gotta see me."

Chef Ron said, "So I gather…Bull, what are you—?"

From inside, someone called, "Ron, what's goin' on?"

Chef Ron called back over his shoulder, "I'll be honest, Joey. I don't know. But I sure don't—"

But now Bull vaulted over the porch railing and walked up to Ron. "Come on, see how I got him tied up there. I can show you just how I done it, too—"

Ron frowned. "Now why do I wanna know how you truss up a—" at which point a younger black man, by about half a dozen years, came out on the porch, and said:

"Jesus Christ—!"

"You Joey, huh? Good." In his big boots and his black vest, Bull said, "Hey—come on, both of you. Take a look how I done this, now."

"Come on, Bull," Ron said. "Why you wanna tie this poor sonofabitch up on my porch like this?"

"Why the hell not?" Bull said. "'Cause he likes it. That's why. It's humiliatin'."

Whiteboy said, over his shoulder. "Yeah, Bull knows how to tie up any motherfucker. I can't move at all. See, now he can whip me—stick stuff up my ass." In the web, naked Whiteboy shrugged. "He can suck on my dick, if he wants. Now everybody can see what a tiny dick I got. And I can't do shit about it."

Bull dropped a big hand on the younger Joey's arm—he was wearing what looked like an old high school jacket. "You want somebody doin' you like that?"

Joey chuckled. "Well, you know—maybe, sometimes. I guess I…"

"Then lemme show you both how I done it. That's what I was sent over here, for. One or the other of you been talkin' to Dr. Greene. See, the main part of it, you gotta use a double rope for the support, here, here, and across here."

Eric felt Shit's elbow against his side.

"You want me to tie you up like that?"

"Huh?" Eric whispered. "Naw—I don't think so. I mean…No. I don't."

Shit said, "'Cause Bull knows all these fancy rope tricks and things." Overhead birds—two, then a third—gave out rough calls.

Bull said, "It supports 'im in enough places where there ain't none of them gonna hurt 'im. Hey, fuckface—tell 'im about the safeword."

"Yeah," Whiteboy said. "I got a safeword, too. Somethin' I can say if somethin' goes wrong and I need to get down—but I ain't never used it, yet. Except when we givin' demonstrations, like this one. But I can say it any old time I want—and Bull gonna let me go, no matter what he's doin', see?"

Bull brought Joey, in his red and blue jacket, over to the web that held Whiteboy like an albino insect. Bull pointed. "You see this line up here? That's the one you tug on to raise and lower the whole thing."

Whiteboy looked forward, at Eric and Shit. "Bull does this stuff real good. See, we got messages to deliver—and this is how we do it. We show people how you get it done. We can come if the sun is out shinin' or even if there's rain'—"

Suddenly Bull moved across to the other side of dangling Whiteboy, grabbed a rope, pulled it—and Whiteboy flung up an arm and twisted in the air. The ropes all slid through their eyelets at once and Whiteboy dropped in a naked crouch on the porch's upper step. One of the ropes fell over his shoulder, the others lay around him on the boards. One was still loosely around his wrist:

"—see there?" Grinning, Whiteboy looked up.

"That's his safe word," Bull said. "'Rain.' The second he says that, no matter what, I stop what I'm doin', I don't care what it is, and pull the safety—and the whole thing comes loose at once."

"Now, you gotta learn how to fall in that thing," Whiteboy said, standing, rubbing at his groin. "Soon as you feel it go loose, you gotta throw your left arm up and over, so you turn proper. Couple of times, man, when I was first learnin' all this shit, I plumped down on my goddam bony whiteboy ass. Nigger like to busted his gut, laughin' at me—'cause I looked so stupid and surprised. But now, see, I know how to do it."

"So you wanna learn how this is done?" Bull asked.

Chef Ron was looking a little bewildered.

Joey laughed. "Come on, Ron. Let 'im show us."

Sort of resigned, Ron said, "Okay…"

Boots silent on the steps, Bull came down to turn before the house. "I can have anyone of you up there again in five minutes…or all three of you, if you want—"

"Come on," Eric said. "Let's go home. I wanna try tyin' you up in the bed sheets."

"Hey," Shit said, "I don't wanna get tied up."

"Good," Eric said. "'Cause I don't wanna get tied up, either." As they walked back, Eric said: "But I guess *they* like it." He looked at the road, with footprints on one side and the other of the central tuft down the middle. Dynamite's cabin was beyond the grass and up the slope. When they'd gone half the distance to Bull and Whiteboy's cabin, Eric stopped.

"What you lookin' at?" Shit said.

"The foot prints." Eric frowned. "There's Whiteboy's—and back there're ours." The prints were narrow and though this one or that one was smudged, all had the indentions of heel and bare toes. "But where's Bull's—I mean, there ain't none with boots."

Shit laughed, kind of falsetto. "You mean you ain't looked at the bottoms of Bull's boots when he's sittin' on his porch, one leg crossed over the other, readin' a paper or somethin'?"

Eric frowned harder.

"There." Shit pointed. "Them are his."

Indeed, they were the biggest, with heel and the raised curve of instep, fronted with the spatulate indentations of five, broad toes. Then Eric saw, around them, a line—clear here, faint there—circling the prints, left and right, in the shape of a shoe. "What's—?"

"Bull don't got no bottoms on his shoes—his boots, I mean. At least, mostly. Underneath them things, where you can't see, he's goin' barefoot all year."

"Huh?" Eric asked. "He does? How you mean?"

"When he gets a new pair, the first thing he does is cut the soles off so he can feel the earth with his naked feet. Even when it rains or snows or anything."

"Wow…"

"Yeah…"

"That's kinda strange." Eric turned and frowned back along the road, where, at Ron's, Bull had completed another web in the porch entrance—though, because of the trees and the angle, Eric could not make out who, if anyone, was in it.

They turned across the grass and started for Dynamite's. "Well," Shit said, "Black Bull's kind of a curious nigger. So's Whiteboy, I guess."

* * *

[18] ERIC'S FIRST TRIP to stay over with Jay and Mex on Gilead was somewhere in Eric's eighth or ninth week. Garbage collection happened only four days a week: it was his day off. That day's last trip out to Gilead was after a handful of lazy back and forth journeys, themselves after a morning sitting around at the Lighthouse Coffee & Egg.

As they stood in the shade to the side of the café's parking area, Jay told Eric, "You can come on out on the scow with us, if it's all right with your mama. If you wanna get rid of him for a night, Mrs. Jeffers, we can take him out and bring 'im back with us tomorrow morning on the first run, since Mondays he don't work. We got a bed for 'im—a whole room, in fact. We'll feed 'im good. And we won't let 'im fall in or nothin', I promise."

Leaning against the low board fence, Mex grinned, then said something in sign. Eric caught two words he'd recently learned: "inside" and "onions." It had to do with the bag of onions and the bag of potatoes Barbara was carrying from her Honda toward the Lighthouse steps.

"Sure," Jay said. "Go on and help her take that stuff in."

Mex stood up and reached to take them from her.

"Thanks, Mex." Still in her blue apron, Barbara stepped back. "But that's okay. I know where they have to go. I'll take 'em up."

"Oh," Jay said. "I guess you wanna be liberated."

Without a smile, Barbara said, "Yes. I want to be liberated."

"Well," Jay said, "truth is, we all do. We wanna be liberated, too. Still, we'd be real happy to take the boy out overnight."

Barbara said, "That's a lot of trouble."

"Ain't no trouble at all," Jay said. "It's nice out on Gilead. Next time you get a day off, we should take you both. Cook hamburgers and hotdogs on the back deck. Bring that boyfriend of yours, Mr. Bodin, out, if yall can stand us for an afternoon."

"Oh, Mom—come on! I wanna go out there. Today—*tonight!* Please?"

Jay said, "He ain't got to be back at work with Dynamite on the garbage run till Tuesday. We ain't gonna let him stay up all night, believe me. We're up and movin' by four thirty—we'll have him back here when you get in for your shift. And we'll give you a call."

Twenty feet away, below the shingle, the sea made the sound of something rushing off somewhere, even while late-summer waves moved in toward grass, sand, and rock. At the world's rim, an elongated gray-green scab crossed a fragment of the horizon, one end notably thicker than the other: Gilead Island.

Barbara started up the steps, a sack hanging from each hand by twine handles. She looked back. "All right. You can go. Thank you, Jay, Mex—really, that's nice of you two. I mean it's something for Eric to do besides sitting around at Dynamite's all afternoon."

"Oh, Mom—thanks!"

"You thank Mr. MacAmon—and Mex." She managed to open the door and went in.

"We'll phone you," Jay said. "We won't let him forget."

So, among anticipations of new orgies and excesses with the two boatmen, joking and relating his recent adventures on the garbage run with Dynamite and Shit, while Jay swaggered and laughed and fumed in mock disbelief, and, with his blasted face, barefoot Mex looked about the silent autumn, while western light gilded the glass and made white enameled window frames near platinum, on the evening street, Eric wandered down dusty Front Street to the wooden gate of the Gilead Boat Dock. Now and again Mex commented with big, quick fingers. A third of his signs Eric knew by now, though he still couldn't turn them into sentences. So he laughed and nodded when Jay did—and wondered if that was helping him learn.

On two previous passengerless trips, they'd gotten out on the island dock. But they'd gone no further inland.

No one was waiting at the dock to go out this time, either. Jay didn't even look around for anyone. He just unbound two of the ropes—Mex loosed the third—then went into the wheel shelter and dragged up the throttle. The motor thrummed.

*

When the scow pulled into the island, Eric said, "I gotta take a piss."

"Off the side," Jay said.

And while talkative Jay and mute Mex tied up in the island boathouse, Eric tugged his fly aside with a forefinger, looking down from the scow's edge at concentric rings expanding around his falling water, its sound drowned in the sea. He wondered if either man would come over and put his hand under his stream. But Jay stood with a work shoe up on the base of one of the cleats on the boathouse dock, swinging a rope around it.

Neither joined him.

In the two earlier trips, they'd never left the boat house itself, but now they walked up the wooden steps into Gilead's uneven greens, ferns, and rocks, jungle thick, left and right, while evening's mist dulled details.

If you'd asked Eric after that first visit he would have said Jay and Mex lived three-quarters of mile from the island dock. Actually it was slightly more than a mile-and-three-quarters up the six-and-a-half mile island. During that walk, night fell and filled sky-colored spaces between hemlock branches and scrub pines and the earth-hued interstices between the ferns and sumac. A couple of times, Eric asked, "What's that…?"

"That's water down there." Jay was just behind him. "We're pretty near the edge, here." Or he'd *thought* Jay was behind him—only, no, the voice was in front. So the wordless rustle behind was Mex.

"Oh…"

At other places, Eric wondered how the boatmen negotiated this journey through the night and—as he stumbled on root or rock—if coming here had really been a good idea. (They had a pickup on the island, they explained. But mostly they didn't use it.) Then Mex dropped a hand on Eric's arm, steadying him in the dark; and Jay said, "Watch out—it gets a little steep, goin' down." Or, "This part's easy now." Or, "You got about seven steps to climb. Yeah—hold this railing." Eric held—and climbed—but could see nothing.

Then they stopped.

Eric asked, "How much more...?"

"We're here, puppy." Jay chuckled. "Hold on a second."

Above was a dusting of stars. To the right, something large blocked many of them: a hulking rectangular shape, at one with the black ground. There and here he could see light around what must be closed shutters or heavy drapes, on the first floor.

He heard a soft snap.

Across the overgrown grass, flame-shaped lights rose at either edge of a door between wooden columns. On this side, in silhouette, Eric could see Jay, belly, shoulders, and broad belt tongue sticking forward, for all the night like a cock to match the bulge his enlarged testicle made, pushing forward his jeans. Jay stood before some sort of podium, which must have held switches on its shielded panel. Jay fingered at one: a voice crackled from a speaker: "Hi, there—you fellas home?"

"Hey, there, Hugh. Yeah. We brung the puppy—" (Eric heard the grin and felt Jay hand fall rough and warm for three, even four seconds on his nape.) "—we was tellin' you about."

"That's nice. Shad and me's waitin' up—like usual."

Mex gave his breathy laugh.

"Shit—and I was hopin' the old bastard done got tired and gone to bed. Well, we're comin' in."

Fifteen feet of stone flags cut through overlong lawn to the door. As he looked around the dim facade, Eric realized the house was three stories.

No, over there he could see: It was *four!*

"Come on," Jay said.

They started toward the building, while Eric tried to shake from his imaginings the house—*maybe* a little bigger than Dynamite's cluttered cabin—he'd been expecting.

Was this building twenty-five rooms? Was it *thirty*-five?

Here in the island woods, it was more than twice the size of Mr. Condotti's entire house!

On the porch, under the night-light, the paint was as blistered as that on Dynamite's—or Ms. Louise's—steps, even if these were three times as high and as wide; and roofed over, too.

At the top, Jay pushed in the door, and Mex guided Eric into and through a glassed-in vestibule, with mahogany walls and a checkered stone floor, black and green.

Jay pushed open a second door. A curtain quivered behind its glass. It put them in a hall where a stairway curved down to the wide, worn carpet. A dozen heavy newels supported the banister. Near the bottom, one had broken off.

From an arch that went halfway up the wall—the ceilings were at least twenty feet high, and there was even a balcony inside—a bald black man came in wearing a bathrobe and slippers.

"Hey, Hugh," Jay said. "This here's Eric. We got any dinner?"

"Hello, young fella," Hugh said warmly. "You got some okra, Jay. You got some lima beans. You got some stewed tomatoes with onions and peppers. And you got some chicken stew—with corn and mushrooms. Yall gonna come in and say good evenin' to Shad? He's in his chair, in the livin' room."

"Far as I recollect, there ain't no way to the kitchen *except* through that place, unless we go outside and come in the back. So I expect we don't got much choice." Jay walked into the room. "I don't mind bein' a little rude. But I ain't quite got to *that* point—yet." He glanced at Eric, then back at Hugh. "You said you was gonna get that room across from ours ready for Eric here?"

Hugh nodded. "I think you'll be comfortable." He smiled at Eric. "If there *is* something you need, you tell them or me."

"Yes, sir," Eric said, bewildered by the size—the scale—of things here.

"Thanks, Hugh," Jay said. "Thanks a heap." Jay turned around, looking about the high-ceilinged hall. "Maybe we could get a carpenter in here and have him tear out another couple of doorways so that we could get to the kitchen without ever seein' the old bastard. But, then, life ain't supposed to be *that* easy, now, is it? Let's go."

They followed Hugh under an archway, through two smaller rooms, in one of which no light burned at all. They emerged into a larger. A ratty rug covered the floor. Several holes in it were wide enough to see warped planks beneath. Above the fireplace, a stone eagle spread its wings, mantel end to mantel end.

Above it, on the wall, a stained rectangle on the wood paneling told of an absent painting.

Across the room, with wispy hair and rounded shoulders, sitting in a wheelchair with wooden wheels, an old man in a faded sweater faced slightly away.

"Hey, there, you mean ol' bastard." With a grin, Jay threw himself down in an armless leather chair. "How you doin' today? What you been up to?" He turned to Eric. "Go on. Sit down—on the couch there. With Mex."

They sat, and, because of the sofa's sag, Mex's leg slid against Eric's. Its warmth surprised him—and felt good.

"I said—" Jay's voice doubled in volume—"how you been? What you and Hugh been doin'?"

Colorless hair overlong, like the grass in the night outside, Shad's head turned toward Jay, but probably not enough for Shad to see him.

"This here is our friend, Eric. He come to stay over with us. His Mama's Mrs. Jeffers—works at the Lighthouse Coffee & Egg."

The old man coughed.

In a normal voice, Jay told Eric, "That's his way of sayin' 'good evenin'.' He don't look like he's gonna be too talkative tonight—which is a blessin'. Otherwise you'd have to listen to him go on about how you're goin to hell, like me and everybody I know. When I was a kid your age, his favorite thing to do was killin' my pets—he done poisoned three dogs and kilt four cats and busted the heads off more toads and chipmunks and rabbits than I can count. At least he *ate* the rabbits."

By the fireplace, Hugh stopped with his hands in his robe pockets. "That's 'cause he thought you was havin' unnatural relations with them animals, Jay. They had to be purified—the only way you can purify a beast is to kill it. That's what he believed. Lots of people around here used to think that way."

"I was," Jay said, "havin' unnatural relations with 'em. At least with the dogs. Other than Dynamite and your cousin Kyle, them dogs was the closest thing I had to a regular love life. Course the *dogs* all seemed to feel it was pretty natural. But how you gonna have unnatural relations with a cat?"

Hugh laughed and looked at Eric. "Jay's just sayin' that to shock you."

"And with a rabbit—? Them things'll bite you if you mess with 'em wrong. I liked 'em 'cause they was soft and fluffy—" Jay was going on—"but he kilt 'em on me anyway. Knowin' him turned me into a damned atheist. Otherwise I woulda put his ass out to live off the road. That's what Christians around here do to each other what don't measure up to their idea of what a Christian ought to be. At least the ones I knowed. Naw, God's too much about payback—killin' off this tribe 'cause of what it believed and destroyin' that city 'cause of what its sinners done. I'll tell you, bein' good to people because they're innocent, poor, and powerless is just as sick as bein' good to 'em 'cause they're selfish, schemin', and rich—which is what most people are into, anyway. Revenge? Reward? Cleanliness is next to godliness? So you send the clean people to heaven and let the dirty ones go to hell. Naw. You do good to folks 'cause it makes *you* feel better. Hey, when I realized all Shad's God bullshit was just that—payback; and, yeah, he had a shitty life, so he had a lot to pay back for—I realized you could be a good person not 'cause that was the way you wanted everybody to treat *you*, but because you thought it would make the whole world better, by doin' somethin' right. So I took him in—and I'm glad I done it. But I'm glad he can't hear no more, too. And *I* only have to listen to him tell me how evil and depraved and wicked I am two or three times a month, when he goes off on one of his anxiety toots."

Hugh said, "Jay, what you are is a contrarian. You just like to say things and do things that's gonna shock people."

Jay looked at Eric. "You shocked?"

"No," Eric said. "I don't…think so."

"See there?" Jay raised his bearded chin and looked at Hugh sideways. "You do as many nice things as you can, boy, for as many people as you can. Feed 'em. Give 'em a place to sleep. Hug 'em and keep 'em warm—'cause it's gonna keep you warm too and make you feel better, if you're down. You do good things for people for the same reason you beat off—it makes *you* feel good."

"See?" Hugh said. "I told you he just wants to shock you. Hey—you gonna show the youngster around the house?"

"I just want some goddam dinner. That's what I want." Jay rocked forward, stood, and walked to the old man. Bending, he put his arm around the hunched shoulder—and took a breath. "I sure don't love you. But maybe if I do enough good things for you, to you, with you, I may learn how. Right?" He hugged the old fellow. "I feel sorry for you, though—I hope that's a start." Standing up, he looked around. "Come on out to the kitchen."

Eric stood quickly, Mex slowly.

They followed Jay, till, at the door, he stopped. As Eric stepped up, Jay looked down at the molding on the wall's base. The rug's frayed edge came almost to it.

"You got to pardon me, this evening. But I'm hungry and I'm tired. And we gotta get up at four." (Only now did Eric realize Jay was talking again to him.) "I'll show you one thing, though. There—see that mark? The black one, right there?" Jay looked down. On the molding, a black dent darkened the varnish, as if hard rubber had struck it and left some of itself.

Eric looked puzzled.

"That's where the ol' bastard kicked my cat, Cindy, to death—when I first come out here to live—twenty, twenty-three years ago. I was stayin' here with Hugh and Kyle, and he come out to bring me home. 'This your cat, ain't it? I was *wonderin'* where she got off to. But you brought her with you, didn't you?' I swear, I can look at him today and see how he was smilin' when he said it. Only then he was a fifty-nine-year-old man standin' up, not a seventy-nine-year-old man sittin' in no wheelchair. And the next thing he done was hauled his boot back and kicked her all the way across the room, broke half her ribs, then come up and stomped on her head. Then he kicked her against the wall, again—hard, too, to make sure she was kilt. See, he probably didn't want her to suffer any more than she had to, since he was gonna stomp her goddam brains out.

"Which is what he did.

"Then he turned to me. 'Okay—you still wanna stay? You won't have Cindy no more to keep you company.' Then he laughed. But, see, he didn't think I should ever have no pets. Because of the dogs. At all. Yeah, he was drunk—but that's how he was. And I said, yeah, I'd still stay. Two weeks later, on the mainland, two days after his birthday, he had his accident. So, 'cause I was the only family he had, once they let him out the hospital, I took him in." Jay turned one way, then the other, as if, momentarily, he was unsure where to go. "Hey, why do I kid myself? I hate 'im as much today as I did back then. But I do try to be nice, even so. Some people said 'cause him and one of Johnston's men was both drivin on I-Twenty-two at nine o'clock at night, drunk as skunks in opposite directions, and whammed into each other and Shad caromed off into that ol' hemlock and broke his back, shattered his shoulder, smashed his hip and broke one leg in three places and the other in four, it was God's retribution on 'em both. Johnston's feller was dead and gone and I can't even remember his name, 'cept he was redheaded and only about nineteen. Farklin? Franklin? Somethin' like that. But I say it was luck bein' cruel to a couple of men who both drunk way too much. And down here, probably both had their reasons. Fact is, I'm surprised Shad hadn't kilt hisself already. I mean both his damned step daddies beat on him all the while he was growin' up, so he wouldn't be no sissy—like me. And two wives done already left him…I think he even loved one of 'em. But both just wanted to take him for all they could get—as if there was somethin' *else* you could do with a bastard like that." Jay's laugh was harsh.

Then, behind them, harsher: "You're *all* damned sinners—damned and goin' to *hell! That's* what I say!"

It was loud and surprising enough that Eric flinched.

"See?" Jay grinned. "There he goes."

Eric glanced back. But in his wheelchair and sweater, Shad hadn't seemed to have moved.

"That's Shad's 'good-night' to you. Right, Mex?" And Jay walked away through a dark hall, pushing aside a hanging drape and chuckling. "…Crazy coot." They followed, while, before them, Jay shook his head. "Next time we come out here, I'll take you around and show you a few other things. It's an interestin' old place. But, like I say, tonight I'm kinda beat."

As he walked, Mex smiled. In the shadow, it looked to Eric like general embarrassment.

They came into the long kitchen. On the ceiling, in rows of four, florescent lights were already on.

Fifteen feet down the space, barefooted Mex went to the refrigerator. Over the counter, sink, and stove, the windows were black.

Jay strolled to the range. "I'm turnin' on the big burner for you," he said in Mex's direction. Then he nodded to Eric. "Go on, sit down, there." A table was covered with red and white checked oilcloth. "We'll phone your ma, and you can let her know we ain't hog-tied you and violated your honor—yet."

When Jay let him speak to Barb, on the blocky red phone's receiver, the first thing Eric said was, "They live in a *real* big house out here!"

"Yes," Barb said. "That's what Clem told me."

The chicken stew Mex heated up was good.

Between spoonfuls, Eric asked, "This is…*your* house?"

"It's Hugh's, now." Outside, cicadas chirped. "It used to be Kyle's— Hugh is Kyle's cousin. I mean Kyle still owns it." Jay's spoon clinked the ceramic rim as he helped himself to more. Mex had also heated up a bowl of corn-off-the-cob with cut-up green and red peppers and onions and another bowl of okra. With their wrinkled edges blackened, the red peppers in the corn were hotter than Eric expected.

Noticing he hadn't taken any okra, Jay said, "You know how to eat that stuff, don't you?"

"Huh?" Eric asked.

"Put a piece in your mouth—" Jay forked up a vegetable tube like a two-inch length of green dowel—"then press it against the roof with your tongue—just once, now—for the flavor. Then you swallow it right down. Don't chew it—don't chew it at all—or it'll go to a goosh even a snot jockey like you would up-chuck over, once it goes to slime. Press and swaller. Press and swaller. Ain't that right, Mex?" Mex nodded, while Jay put the okra in his mouth—and (it looked like) pressed and swallowed. "Do it the right way, though, and it's damned good."

"Oh…" Eric said. He reached over to get the two-liter bottle of Pepsi Mex had set out and refilled his glass.

"Hugh's Kyle's cousin," Jay repeated. "He used to work for Kyle and his family. After Kyle left to look after his business in Columbus, he said Hugh could live here, if he wouldn't mind a friend of Kyle's occasionally stayin' with him. I knowed Kyle and Hugh long as I knowed Dynamite. We was all kids together—'asshole buddies' they called us. Which is another way of sayin' we was the elementary school faggot mafia. When Kyle said Mex and me could come out here and stay in a room or two, Hugh said he was happy for the company. Besides, I'm handy—more handy than Hugh, anyway. And I don't mind fixin' this and that—an old house like this needs a lotta that kinda work. Takin' care of Shad gives Hugh somethin' to do, he says. If I had to do it twenty-four/seven, I'd've killed him already, probably. Hugh and Mex get along—but Hugh's the kind of feller what gets along with ever'body. Four people in a place what used to hold a family of six with another ten servants—the older term, I believe, is 'house niggers'—slaves, to you—don't get in each other's way that much."

When they were finished, Jay carried the dishes to the sink and rinsed them. "Mex'll put 'em in the dishwasher. We go to bed pretty early, 'cause we get up before light. But on the garbage run, you're used to that. You're gonna have to get up, too, 'cause we promised to have you back with your mama by the time she opens the Lighthouse. So let's show you where you'll be sleepin'."

"That's all right," Eric said. Then, after a moment, he asked, "I ain't bunkin' in with…you guys?"

"Nope." Jay grinned at him. "Not tonight."

"Oh," Eric said. "Oh…Okay. It would bother Hugh…?"

Jay grinned. "Hugh don't give a fuck…" But he let it hang without elaboration. And Eric had no idea where to take it.

Somehow, first, they went out and across the hall into Mex and Jay's bedroom to get something—it was as cluttered as Dynamite's back in the Dump, which made Eric feel better. Or at least more comfortable. They showed him the bathroom at the end of the hall and gave him a towel. (There was another commode stall off the end of the kitchen.)

Then they took him down the hall to his room.

It was pretty bare. A day bed stood against one wall. A table and a chair with a lamp on it stood against another. "We'll come wake you when it's time to rise and shine."

Mex gave Eric's shoulder a squeeze. Eric wondered if he could at least ask for a goodnight hug, but, while he was debating how to put it, both Mex and Jay went out—and closed the door.

Eric took off his clothes, went out into the hall to the bathroom at the end, urinated, wondered if he should take a shower, but because there was no curtain around the tub, decided to give himself a washcloth wipe at the sink. He dried himself on the terrycloth, then went back down the hall, barefoot over the hallway's uncarpeted planks, hoping either Mex or Jay might come out of their room just then and catch him naked. It would be easier to start something that way. Legs, arms, and the small of Eric's back were cool with leftover damp.

In his room, Eric sat on his bed's edge for a couple of minutes. He ran his hands out over the spread, with its embroidered knoblets every inch-and-a-half, that rubbed on his palms, already roughened from the near two months of garbage hauling.

He turned his hands up, put them on his thighs, and looked at them.

I like having rough hands, he thought.

(He remembered the first few weeks when he'd been proud of the dirt that had worked all but permanently around his nails and into the lines deepening on his hands. Only now he'd stopped thinking about it at all, when he realized that wash as much as he might, it would be back again in a day.)

Maybe, he thought, the boatmen don't.

He got up, pulled back the covers' edge so he could get in, then walked over and turned off the lamp. Darkness filled the room and his eyes, like ink poured—fast—into a glass bowl. He walked back over the rug until the bed tapped him above the knees, turned, and sat, turning his head left and right in the pitchy black.

This is where Robert Kyle lived and grew up, he thought. This is where the Dump—or the idea for the Dump—probably began. If not in this room, then in a room near it. He worked himself further back on the bed. Maybe Robert Kyle sat here, twenty-five, thirty years ago, in the dark, like this, and thought about a stretch of land on the mainland, a scattering of houses and cabins, and how he'd tell his friends Dynamite and Jay...

Eric moved still further back.

Tugging at his penis, he leaned over, lifted his feet, and slid them under the sheet, while the pillow caught his head—

—and woke.

Eric lay a long time, wondering what the hour was. Suddenly, he pushed back the covers, stood up, and walked toward the wall he remembered held the door. If he turned on the lamp...but it was more fun—hell, more *interesting* in the dark.

Eric felt around the wall to the left, but encountered no jamb. So, fingering gritty wallpaper, he worked back the other way—till he felt the door molding.

In the hall, orange came from the nightlight behind the partially open bathroom door.

Adolescent devilment surged suddenly, and Eric thought: I'm gonna explore this whole place tonight, naked!

In the kitchen, the formerly black windows were filled with the moon's silver, lighting the sink, the counter, the stove, the floor's vinyl. A minute later, somehow back in the dark living room, he padded across the rug, notably warmer under the balls of his feet than the boards of the previous rooms. On his left, a walk-in fireplace was the ghost of an entrance to another world.

From somewhere he found himself wondering if time itself were not increasing its speed, even as—was it the chill on the nighttime house?—in the forward hall he swung around the newel post and, two at a time, sprinted up the stairway.

How big *was* this place? At this point, Eric was still uncertain how many floors the whole of it had.

When I get to the top, I'm going to find I've become some old man, fifty-five, sixty-five years old—with white hair and everything. I bet this house is a hundred years old—even two hundred. That's how it looked when I came in—like walking into someplace two hundred years ago. And now it's two hundred years *later*. And I'm a hundred, two hundred years older than when I came in...

Reaching the top step, Eric swung around to sprint down a wide corridor—books filled the shelves to the left. He glanced right, and realized he was on an internal balcony, looking down into the living room. He swung through another arched doorway and smashed into moonlight—

Which was empty, bright, and without resistance.

It came from a large window at the far end of the...upstairs hall he'd entered. Couches, arm chairs, more books on the walls...

Eric walked onto the carpet, gritty beneath his feet. He moved along behind a sofa, between tables and armchairs. He slowed to rub his genitals. Once he felt something like a piece of gravel under his instep. As he stepped further, it occurred to him that, under heel or ball, it would have hurt. He moved among dark furniture, ghostly ivory from the windows. To the left of the great room, the wall was covered with shelves. Left and right of them were dark arches, which, at first, he thought were more shelves.

He reached the farther of the two—doors or halls into other rooms? Eyes fixed within, he came within twelve, eight, five feet: a stairway's wraith rose behind the wall to the right, leading to a still higher floor.

From beside and behind him came a sound, like a squeaking wheel. Naked in the great room, Eric turned—

Crouching, he staggered back, six or seven inches. At the same time, chills enveloped him, so many and so thoroughly they did not feel like something within his body, but like waves and waves around him, rolling through him, across him, over him. He'd closed his eyes, tightly—

And opened them again.

What he'd seen was Shad, in his wheel chair, directly behind him. Only, with a blink, it was a *huge* Shad, a Shad three times as large as life! But that was impossible...Was it Hugh, in his dressing gown, sitting in some great chair—watching him?

The figure, in moonlight, was...Eric made himself stand up straight— twenty feet away, in the corner.

It was not directly behind him.

But it was big—and, he realized now, it wasn't a seated figure at all.

Again outside, a wind made the sash grate against its sill. A branch beyond the window moved before the moon, and smoky light drifted back and forth over the immense statue.

Eric stepped forward.

A very large bear...bull? Boar? Was it stuffed...? Real...?

He stepped closer.

Nor was it rearing on its hind legs, one claw high, one claw—no, not a claw, but a hand—out, as if to sweep in the world. It was a bull, only it squatted like a man. Or kneeled, anyway, one knee down. The other, up before it, was some immense bird's claw, big enough to grip his head. Those were wings, back in the shadows, but not bird wings. They looked like a bat's—only not like any bat Eric had ever seen. Somehow, because he hadn't been looking for it, he'd missed it in its dim corner. But, moving with the branch outside, moonlight kept making the forward of the two arms...move.

At last he was right in front it. It was...a minotaur? Or something like one, winged and kneeling on one leg in the corner. Between its thighs— the one it kneeled on seemed human enough, as was its great foot—he could see the huge lengths of its tail, like a serpent, thick as a thigh, rolling and coiling behind it. Knowing it was a statue, Eric reached out and up, expecting to feel the rough fur of ancient taxidermy on its forearm.

He touched the huge, extended hand.

It was metal—black with tarnish.

Eric's heart began to still. Its pedestal represented rock and branches, with a shell among them—and a starfish—as if it kneeled on a length of beach.

Bent before him, the feathered knee shone where the patina had worn away; as it had on the knuckles of the upturned fingers—a hand for which, easily, Jay's could have been the model—and the flattened snout, a pig's nose on a bull's horned head. He imagined generations of children, during holidays in this hall, at Christmas and high summer, Halloween and Easter, feeling the parts that extended, wearing the stain from its bronze, so that the yellow metal showed through, turned platinum by the moon.

Eric looked at the creature's groin. One side of its hanging penis, joined to the sack of its testicles, had also been rendered a white gold by how many surreptitious touches when no one else was there.

Eric backed away, breathing more easily. At last he turned, walked into the archway, and started up the stairs.

Then, with a hand on the heavy banister and the energy of the night's adventure, he began to run. Maybe I'll come out a *thousand* years from now—

And came out at the head of the broad railing, in a small room—small compared to the room below—which, as he turned to orient himself, he realized, was round. About the walls, crowded bookshelves alternated with shelf-to-roof windows. Two of the windows had shades pulled down—one only a few inches, one at least two-and-a-half feet.

Beneath them, under moonlight, through old panes, he could see the sea.

The smell was like old wood and—ancient?—varnish. Was *that* smell, he wondered suddenly, owls? (Where had he smelled owls before? In Texas…?) On a wide desk that fit as if it had been made for the room, against the curved wall, stood an orrery.

Eric knew neither the word nor what the object was.

It looked, however, like some complex oversized medieval gyroscope, sitting on a snake coiled over the back of the great cast tortoise, its base.

Supported over it were rings and spheres, clear and scrolled, with scales and rods projecting from the crystal at its center. Now, on those rods, he began to recognize moons and planets—that one, because of the rings, he realized, was Saturn. Certainly it had been constructed before the discovery of Uranus's rings—or before Uranus itself, not to mention the post-Plutonians. He reached for it, started to move one globe—and all the other rods and globes began to sweep at the same time, some faster, some slower.

He jerked his hand back, as if the material universe around him might topple and tumble from his disturbance.

The model stopped moving.

Turning away, Eric looked at the books on the shelves. (No, the room wasn't round: it was octagonal.) The ones that stood in moonlight, so that he could read the titles and authors embossed in dark leather, were three volumes of *François Villon*, by Typhony Thayer, *Travels in Arabia Desserta, Volumes One and Two*, by Charles M. Doughty, *Die Welt als Wille und Vorsstellen*, also in two volumes, by Arthur Schopenhauer, several unnumbered volumes by Benedict de Spinoza—*Ethica, Tractatus Theologico-Politicus, Principia Philosophiae Cartesianae, Tractatus de Intellectus*

Emendatione, Cogitata Metaphysica, Korte Verhandeling van God, de Mensch, en deszelfs Welstand—and still other books by Lessing, Herder, Goethe, and Novalis—

Shelf after shelf of books bore the same titles in worn gold letters: *Comedie Humaine*. Under it were two volumes of *Le Juif errant* and three of *Les Mystères des Paris*, and six, seven, eight of *Les Sept pêches capitaux*—

Momentarily the room flared silver, flickered—and thunder filled it up, then fumbled away. Eric looked out the window. He looked out one of the others...and was surprised to see drops on the glass.

A storm...starting?

On one shelf directly in front of him, he saw a framed picture—no, with the moonlight coming in behind, he realized it was a glassed-over newspaper photo. Across the top of the page with its feathered edge it said *The Hemmings Herald*. The headline read:

HEIRESSES MEET ON GILEAD

Indistinct with the early technology of another century, it showed three women sitting at a lawn table, in bizarrely outdated summer dresses, identified, beneath it, as:

Mabel Dodge, Nancy Cunard, and Doris Pitkin.

The date was 1923.

Beside it was another, larger picture, under glass—this one an actual photo, maybe eight by twelve, glossy, with a thin white border. Looking back and forth between them, Eric realized the women were the same—indeed they even wore the same clothing they'd worn in the newsprint picture. The table behind them was the same. So was the background vegetation. The two pictures might have been taken minutes apart, even less. (He imagined the photographer calling, "Now, just the ladies...") But in this picture, each woman stood with a man. The man beside Mabel was a solid looking fellow, in western clothing, who could easily have been an America Indian. Black braids hung at the side of his head. The man beside Nancy and the man beside Doris were both distinctly African American. Were they servants? Eric wondered—though the tall and heavily braceleted Nancy had her hand on the black man's arm, which made Eric doubt it.

Below was a line of names:

Mabel Dodge, Tony Lewan, Nancy Cunard, Harry Crowder, Doris Pitkin, Robert Kyle...

White light filled the windows both sides of the wall. As he looked, the photograph turned black. In the rectangle of glass over it, now Eric saw the reflected books and bookshelves on the wall behind. He stepped backward, then turned to look at the other bookshelves, as lightning lit them. Thunder filled up the room; the lightning faded. For moments Eric thought the tower was cracking and crumbling. And moments later, again he was looking at the three couples smiling under glass.

Though Eric had been a high school history buff, his expertise did not overlap enough of the history of the artistic production of the twenties, thirties, and forties to explain the gathering.

Standing in the middle of the floor for five, six, seven breaths, waiting for more thunder, he walked back to the stairhead and, holding the banister, started down. Only when he had gone some seven steps, did a flash behind startle him, so that for a moment his shadow folded before him, down the stairs' maroon carpet.

In the flare, after two more steps, thunder came again, more distant— as if the house were trying to absorb it.

At the bottom again, in the grand second floor sitting room, Eric walked from the arch; and again flinched, because—outside—the branch had moved, and, again, he had been sure the metal beast had swept its great arm and a great wing through the moonlight.

Catching his breath, and trying to suppress the tingling that tidaled his back and thighs, his belly and arms, Eric hurried away through the chairs and sofas and tables, trying to see the entrance to the stairs that would let him return to the ground floor.

"I'm not going to find it," he whispered, wondering if he would end up sleeping, naked, on one of these couches—when he stepped around the edge of a bookshelf and found himself at the descending steps.

Down in the corridor with the doors to Jay and Mex's room, the bathroom, and his own bedroom, finally Eric stopped. He walked toward his own—it was an inch ajar—then hesitated.

Because he heard something up the corridor.

Eric looked to see Jay's door pull in and a tousled Jay, naked as Eric himself, lumber into the hall. Only after three steps did Jay glance up and see him. "Hey, there, puppy. What's a matter? Can't sleep?"

"Naw," Eric said. "I'm okay. I was just…Hey, Jay?"

Lumbering by, Jay frowned. "What…?"

"Can I come and bunk in with you guys?"

"It's kinda late for that, puppy." Jay headed on toward the bathroom at the hall's end. Back over his heavy blond shoulder, he said, "We gotta be up before daybreak." Walking away, he rubbed his big, colorful arm with a blond hand. "You shoulda asked about that earlier, if that's what you was interested in."

"Oh," Eric said—he thought he had. Pushing into his own room, moving slowly lest he stub a toe or bark a shin, finally his thighs bumped the mattress…

—someone sitting on his bed's edge woke Eric. "Oh, Mex. Hey. I guess it's time to get up…?"

Mex had turned on the lamp.

As Eric pushed out from the cover, Mex—who had on his pants but no shirt—enfolded Eric in his arms. Eric hugged him back. Jesus, it felt good holding the thick, warm-chested fellow. Mex released him, put his thumb tip to his mouth, and tilted up fisted fingers, which Eric knew, by now, meant, *Want some coffee?* (or, when he did the same thing to Jay, with the fingers a little tighter, *Want a beer?*).

"Yeah," Eric said. "That's a good idea. Lemme get my pants on."

At the kitchen table, they drank from their mugs. The windows were as dark as they had been at dinner.

It made Eric feel strange.

The walk back through the woods reminded him of his four-thirty hikes through road and meadow to meet Shit and Dynamite.

When they entered the boat house, Mex flipped on the florescent lights: Eric saw Jay's Technicolor arms as the boatman stood with one work shoe on one of the metal cleats by the dock edge. He remembered Jay had left the house in only a thermal vest. As nonchalantly as he could, Eric said, "I thought maybe me and you and Mex were gonna…you know, fuck around out here. The way me and Dynamite and Shit do in the Dump." Even Eric could hear that he sounded petulant—the tone he'd wanted to avoid.

Stepping down onto the scow's deck under the light from the boat house ceiling, then looking back, Jay raised a hempen brow. "Yeah? You did? Now, what made you think that? Nobody said nothin' about fuckin'—*you* sure didn't." With one great hand (and his toothless grin), Jay gripped the rail.

Mex had wandered over to where the ropes were wrapped around a metal cleat on the scow's deck. Squatting, he began unwrapping the hawser.

"I don't know." Eric shrugged. "Maybe…because, well, how we done back at the truck stop." Without the pressure of desire, he might have been able to explain that his first afternoon with Shit and Dynamite had formed the expectations of his visit to Jay and Mex's. *Their* behavior, however, had been as unexpected as the house itself.

"Now, you ain't eighteen yet. You're still seventeen. What did you think? We was gonna jump on you, bring you down, and rape you in our own guest bed?"

"I don't know…" Eric swallowed, looking around for something to do. If he could help, he knew he'd feel better. "It was a little…funny." Eric didn't shrug. He didn't feel like shrugging.

"Well, yeah," Jay said. "A good fuck is nice sometimes—especially with your friends."

"I guess…maybe you don't think you should do nothin' with kids under eighteen…?" It was more than petulant. It was plaintive.

"I didn't say that. But I do think that if you're under eighteen, you got to be able to ask for it, clear and direct—especially if you want it from older guys. You know, this sex business ain't about mind readin'. It's about sayin' what you want, gettin' an answer—yes, no—and acceptin' it."

"How did I ask for it back at the truck stop?"

Stepping up on the damp dock matt, Jay crouched, leaned forward, and grabbed his crotch—with a sudden and surprising grin. (Eric remembered Dynamite, outside Miss Louise's in the parking lights.) "'Can we do stuff in there?' As I recall, puppy, them was the first words out your mouth I ever heard." Jay straightened up, his hirsute chest broadening between the padded vest's edges. "And the second was: 'Can I suck your dick? I do it good.' Sure, I like suckin' and fuckin' with puppies like you. But I figure if you ain't big enough to ask for it, then you ain't big enough to do it. That's all." Jay gave his crotch two, three rubs, then dropped his hand. "That's a nice thing about havin' a big ol' house. You can do pretty much anything you want in there, and nobody else really got to know about it. But you still got to know what you want and be ready to ask."

A hand fell on Eric's shoulder. He looked aside to see Mex—who was grinning. Then he looked down.

Mex's fly was open.

Mex's thick penis was in his other, wide, callused hand.

Eric closed his own hand on the Mexican's warm cock. "Oh, Jesus, Mex—thanks." (Mex…growled. Was that a laugh?) "Yeah, hey—I wanna do…*somethin'*, at least…" He took another breath, and chuckled, hearing his own nervousness. "For a minute, I thought you guys had given up on me. Can't we do…*somethin'* —?"

Jay moved toward them, and put his arms around them both.

"…before we get home?" Eric finished. From outside, a first sun sliver lay brightly along the dock matt. "Look," Eric said, "can I *please* suck some fuckin' dick?"

Jay stepped back. "Jesus, boy. I don't know—I mean, I didn't take no shower this mornin'—neither one of us had time." He nodded toward Mex. "And the truth is, this is one of them days Mex didn't even have time to get to it. I got so much fuckin' cheese under my fuckin' skin—I mean, all yesterday's and the day-before's—the damn thing feels twice as heavy as it usually do, with all the shit in there." The bottom of the vest's armholes were all frayed and stained with summer's perspiration. (In the scow cabin, Jay kept a denim work shirt hanging on the back door, like one of Mike's, which, as summer had progressed, he wore less and less.) He began to claw—slowly—at his jeans. "And I know this fuckin' spic got enough fuckin' dick scuz in 'im for a half a dozen fuckin' enchiladas. See, that stuff up in there makes me so fuckin' horny, I don't even know if I can wait long enough for you to get on your knees and tug it outa my damned pants. I may just shoot right in your eye—or your fuckin' ear. You ever had somebody so fuckin' hot that he shot it all in your hair while you was on your knees tryin' to put it in your mouth? I mean, I'll *try* to hold off. But—" Jay sucked his lower lip—"I don't know if I'll be able to—"

"Jesus, Jay!" Eric said. "You're gonna make me come in *my* jeans, talkin' like that—even if you're kiddin'!"

Beside them, his dick still in his fist, at Jay's performance Mex was rocking forward and back, laughing louder and louder.

"What the fuck makes you think I'm kiddin'? Will you—" in mock anger Jay yanked down his fly—"*please* hurry the fuck up?"

Later, when they were on the boat and Eric was standing under the wheel shelter on the scow with Jay, and Mex had come up to stand at the back of the space, one bare foot propped up on its toes, Eric said, "Hey— you know I really liked it, Jay, when you took a piss in my mouth. I mean a real one." Eric drew a breath. "I mean, Mex—" he glanced back—"I think I can understand what you're about with all that. I wish the fuck I could ask Dynamite to do it...maybe when we're joking around, I could get Shit to."

Jay looked out across the shattered flat of water, still dark under half light. "Whyn't you ask him? You didn't have no trouble askin' me."

"That's 'cause you and Mex already do that...stuff." Eric shrugged. "With Dynamite, I just...don't think I can. It's like I...want it too much, I'm afraid he'd say no—and I wouldn't know what to do. I mean, hell, I admit it. I'm scared."

"Maybe—" and Eric saw something that might have been a smile (or maybe a frown) in the curling gold that hid Jay's lower face—"you're just gonna have to learn to deal with that, scared or not. Anyway, right now we gotta get you back to your mama's." The three of them stood in the sea's whispering, as they pulled nearer and nearer the Harbor.

*

That night in the mainland woods, in bed on the porch back at Barbara's trailer, Eric dreamed about looking over a cliff into the Bottom, to see a city, flickering with green fire, along all its alleys and avenues, luminous and putrescent, with doorways and signboards and letters on them in languages he could not read—Japanese? Sanskrit? Russian? Hebrew? Greek?

Windows in its tenements were backed with sky—a city glowing, growing, shifting up from the Bottom, beside the ocean. Among great mansions and falling apart cabins, for a while in the dream he was in a bare room, without light on the ceiling or any lamp, looking out at gold and green flickers through and around a yellowish window curtain. Then he was walking through streets not yet finished, coursing with black water, dropping suddenly onto lower shelves, over whose edges he could look down and see urban offal, pulsing, weaving, changing, as if on a great machine. All of the refuse was churned and braided into walls and bridges and pipes and electric wires and antennas. Four and five feet above streaming liquid, huge gold fish floated between stone walls, coming from the mouth of subterranean tunnels, passing a silhouetted fountain, to be caught and lovingly reformed by a naked woman with red, living hair. Sometimes someone held his hand, but if it was Dynamite or Mike or Shit—or even Mex—he wasn't sure. Serpents flew and cockatrices preened on teal beams, gulls and eagles and dragons shrieked—in celebration or in warning? He wasn't sure, but he careened, further and further through cobbled alleys, into city lots, empty, where, through shadows from the wire gates, herds of scorpions, seahorses, and spiders crawled at angles to his headlong lope.

* * *

[19] A WEEK LATER, when, at Dynamite's, Shit and Dynamite lay down with Eric after work, the evening sun came in a gold spear through the Dump cabin window, bending at the wall corner. Eric got one rough, puffy tuft of Shit's beard in his mouth and sucked it and chewed on it, till all the salt was out and there was only its wiry texture in his mouth. Finally, he let go and asked, "You mind me doin' that?"

"Naw. Go on. It's in'erestin'." And a little later Shit said, "I wonder what'd happen if you sucked on my dick like that." Outside, sea birds kept up their mewing, as they did all through the Dump. "I mean for hours and hours and hours."

On the other side of the bed, Dynamite chuckled. "I guess everybody thinks about that at one time or other. It's one of them questions everybody eventually has." Moving closer, he rubbed his rough hand low over Eric's bare back. "You mind me doin' *that?*"

"No. Go on. It's nice."

Dynamite slid nearer. "When I wasn't that much older than you two, I set that up once, with a friend of mine. Kyle, actually. I'll tell you both, either the cocksucker gets tired—or you get bored. It don't take no hours and hours, neither."

"Naw." Shit looked up at the cabin's uneven ceiling. With one hand he nubbed the rough hair on his face. "I ain't gonna get bored, believe me." Shit's other hand moved under his father's on Eric's back, and Eric realized their fingers had meshed to slide down to Eric's naked rump. "I know *that* much already. "Hey—I don't mean workin' at it real hard. I mean just holdin' it in your mouth, lazin' your tongue around on it, so I could relax, drift off, maybe think about strange stuff." Shit glanced down. "You wanna try that someday?"

Eric looked up and said, "Sure." Then he added, "*I* always wondered what it would be like if somebody stuck his dick up my ass and left it there for a few hours. He could fuck me when he wanted to, but mostly he'd just keep it in there and hold on to me and leave it sit."

Turning now, Shit pulled Eric closer. "That sounds good, cocksucker. And after we do that, we can tell the ol' pig fucker here what he's missin'."

Dynamite grunted from his side of the bed. "I forgot to tell you—your mama called and left me a voicemail. She's goin' out with Ron tonight, and they may be out late. She said she wondered if you wanted to stay over here—and if I would mind keepin' you." He chuckled, not looking at them. "Tomorrow's a day off, too. Be nice to have you around—"

"Damn," Eric said. "Sure…"

Eventually, Eric realized that what happened later that night was only because the next day *was* a day off.

But with the yellowish light from the lamp beside the bed in his eyes, Eric woke to find naked Shit cross-legged on the mattress, while, with his rich doggie smell, panting Tom lay on his back, one leg up and kind of kicking. On his side, Dynamite watched, head propped on a fist, while Shit gripped Tom's bristly sheath, rubbing as the red, wet, white, and raw cockstock with its irregular point thrust free further and further.

Shit ginned at Eric. "Go on—suck this horny sonofabitch till he shoots in your mouth. My daddy likes to fuck that stuff when you got a load of it up in your face."

Dynamite grinned down at him, too.

Eric said, "Huh…?"

"Hey," Shit said. "I'll do it, if you *want*—"

"Naw," Eric said. "Naw, that's okay. The damned dog's got a dick." He moved himself further down in the bed—"I'll suck it—" then took the white and red stalk in his mouth. It was kind of slimy. And salty.

Under the Atlanta highway, there'd been no sex with animals, but the men there had described and joked and spoken endlessly about sucking and fucking cows, horses, sheep, dogs, and goats so that Eric felt as if he owned the experience already. His mouth against Shit's callused fist, he looked up to see Tom had put his head back and was vigorously tonguing with Dynamite who was licking back.

"Oh, yeah," Shit said. "I can feel it. This dog's about ready to shoot. That's why he was up here botherin' us."

Tom hunched, quivered, and stayed hunched—and Eric received the first, narrow, three or four second stream of dog cum, followed two seconds later, by another. And another—and another—and another.

"He gonna be doin' that for a whole minute," Shit explained. "Don't spill none, if you can help it."

Eric was surprised—and excited—by how different a dog's orgasm was from a human's. As well he marveled how quickly that led Dynamite, then Shit right after, to follow and fuck his face, while Eric gripped first Dynamite's buttock and worked a thumb up his ass, then held Shit by his lean, thrusting hips till he erupted after his dad. Among their sexual repertoire it was the only thing whose passion made Eric suspect it was beyond negotiation, though for all that, it felt wonderfully settling, wonderfully safe—and among his favorites. When they'd laid their two-in-the-morning loads on top of hefty Tom's—Eric came in Dynamite's hand, lubricated with a handful of spit—and all four, finally, lay, panting and nuzzling knees, toes, claws, hips, muzzle, or tongue, while Dynamite licked his fingers.

Shit reached over and turned out the lamp.

They dozed.

"G'night, puppies." In the dark, Dynamite rubbed the head of one or the other, dog or boy, with a callused thumb or forefinger behind the ear.

Shit was awake enough to laugh. ("He gets that from Jay.") And Eric enough to hear it.

* * *

[20] STILL ANOTHER DAY-off morning, when he woke in Dynamite's bed, with Shit's arm flung over him, from the empty sheet on his left, Eric realized Dynamite was already up. Turning his head, he saw, through the open porch door, sunlight fall over the cracked and blistered porch rail.

"Hey—!" Dynamite called from outside. "Get up and come on out here. Come on, now! Get on out—take a look at this!"

Stretched across the foot of the bed, Tom lifted his head, looked over one paw, then put his muzzle back down.

Sleepily, both boys untangled themselves and slid off the bed, naked, then walked out the side door onto the uneven boards. In the ratty undershirt he'd slept in that night, Dynamite was down among the tall growths beside the porch. He beckoned them. "Come on. I wanna show yall."

As they went down the steps on bare feet, Shit first, Eric following, Eric realized, without pants, Dynamite was himself naked from the waist down.

"Get on over here, now—and look." Dynamite dropped to a squat before the ferns.

Shit said, "What the fuck you goin' on about this early in the goddam mornin'?"

"Come on," his father said. "Hunker down here."

The sun had cleared the cabin's corner. Morning gold—it couldn't have been much after six-fifteen—burned through fronds bending about them.

It was cool, with direct sun making a warm spot on a shoulder, a hip.

Eric squatted. On tickling stems, dew wet his buttocks, his thighs.

Beside him, with a forward gesture of his big hand, Dynamite said, "Can you see her, there?"

Behind them, Shit, too, dropped to a squat, a hand supporting himself on Eric's shoulder, the other on his father's. "Damn," Shit said. "If you wasn't such a good fuck, I'd take Eric and go get my own cabin so at least for a couple of mornin's a week I could get some *real* sleep."

"No, you wouldn't," Dynamite said. "You get off on watchin' your brother here suck my dick too much."

"Oh, that 'brother' thing gets him all excited." Shit took two squatting steps forward. "Kinda turns me on, too." '

"I know." Dynamite glanced back. "That's how I can always getcha up to fuck me." Eric glanced down, where grinning Dynamite jogged his knee. "Why would he wanna give that up to be a hermit?"

Two tall fronds leaned widely apart. Between scalloped threads, a grand web rayed silvery lines from its center. Toward the middle, the dozen strands lost their precision. Hundreds of dewdrops caught along its lines, a third like diamonds in direct sun, another third in shadow became pearls, and still others, where reflected sunlight from the window behind them poured through its lattice, became prisms. Up on the left, in one patch, a marauding cricket had gotten snared, torn some lines, and been enveloped with white, while the net had been repaired around it. Yet most of the matrix was symmetrical perfection—or, better, symmetrical perfection adapted to its asymmetrical firmament. Eric shifted his weight—and dozens of dewdrops all over the morning web flickered and flashed. Prisms shook myriad colors.

Yellow and black stripes on her less-than dime-sized abdomen, the spider, having crawled halfway toward the center, paused to move a black leg, slowly, in a welcoming gesture, four, five, six times—for exercise, for relief, or some arachnoid dance—before crawling further on the bright lattice.

Eric glanced back at Shit. "You *see* that...!"

"Yeah..." Shit's voice was lower than Eric's.

Was that, Eric wondered, wonder?

"Back when I was seven or eight," Shit said, "you took me out to show me one of these, and I thought it was the most beautiful thing I'd ever fuckin' seen—and I still do."

"You remember that?" Dynamite asked.

Shit just grunted.

Eric said, "I never seen that before...I mean, up close, with dew on it."

In the chaos that overtook its center, in the irregular boundary, and in the rhythmic order between center and rim, each thread with a line of droplets, it was a glimmering polychrome glister.

Behind him, after a confirming squeeze of his shoulder, Eric felt Shit stand. His voice came from above: "I'm goin' inside an' make you fuckers some coffee. 'Cause *I* sure want a cup." He heard Shit move away, back to the steps.

Off in the brush, Eric heard Uncle Tom moving—whose interests were food, sex, rubs, and hugs, with all of which, Eric figured, they were pretty generous.

*

In front of the kitchen window, Shit was sliding the carafe from under the drip hopper by the handle, when, outside, something moved the long grasses, chain clinked, and boots thudded up the loose board.

Some ways outside the door, two large trees down the slope stood tall before the sun, so that the light was a white gold net among the lapping shards the leaves became, filling the doorway, when it pushed in.

Sitting on a carton and roughhousing with Tom, Eric looked up to see the stocky silhouette step across the lintel. "What yall doin'? If I'm interuptin' yalls Sunday mornin', I'll come back later."

Eric's ears said the man had walked up through the brush, but for all the world Eric's eyes said—at least momentarily—the stocky figure had swung down from the branches to land on the kitchen porch.

Something squatting behind the man's right leg lingered outside, while the fellow yanked the chain leash that ran up to one wrist. "Come on—

get in here, you two-bit piece of shit." His voice was deep and black and country.

As if recognizing it, Tom pulled up and out of Eric's grip, to hurry toward the door.

Naked (except for his T-shirt) in a kitchen chair, its front legs up off the floor, Dynamite rocked and said, "You ain't interuptin' nothin', Bull. Come on in. Shit just made some coffee. Pour Bull a mug—put lotsa sugar in it. And no milk—that's how the Bull likes it, right? Black and sweet. Come on in and drink it with us."

"Sure." The loose cuffs of Bull's once black jeans, now between brown and colorless, were pushed into the tops of his scuffed boots. Over a naked chest, he wore a black leather vest with no fastenings. His muscles rivaled Jay's out on the island. "How about it, now—I get a chance to drink coffee and watch you all scratchin' your balls!" Bull exploded with basso laughter, while Shit spooned two, three, four teaspoons from the wide-necked sugar jar into the just-filled mug, then handed it to Bull, who took it and lowered himself onto the seat that Shit had been sitting on.

Shit took his own mug and went to the table, turned, and pushed himself up on the edge. "Hey, Whiteboy? You want some coffee?" Shit looked over toward the door, down at the floor.

Bull looked over, too. "Don't give that retarded piece of mule shit no coffee. He already had too much this mornin'."

Scrawny Whiteboy squatted, naked, on the floor before the half-closed kitchen door. His black dog collar was attached to a swaying chain that ran to Bull's leather wrist brace. Tom had gone straight for him, and with grubby hands Whiteboy was playing with Tom's black and brown head while Tom licked at Whiteboy's mouth. "See, he wants to kiss me—that old hound really loves me, don't he? Well, come on—I don't care. You can kiss on me if you want. I'll kiss on you, too…" Suddenly, Tom dropped his head and, as the kid bent over him, went for the wrinkled belly and below. "Oh, fuck—!" The folded skin behind his knees and at the bend in his arms made Eric suspect that the grubby "kid" was in his thirties, rather than his teens or twenties, the first impression he always had. The "kid'—if that's what he was—fell over on his back. "Tom just nipped my goddamn balls!" His legs and soiled feet were in the air, and he was laughing.

"Yeah," Shit said from the table edge, "and now he's eatin' out your asshole, too," while Tom, head to the side, licked vigorously, his nose between grubby hairless buttocks.

Dynamite said, "Whyn't you make that boy put some clothes on, before you go visitin'?"

"Why? Your boys ain't wearin' none." Bull looked over, haughtily. "And

you just got on that ratty T-shirt. Besides, this is the fuckin' Dump. This is
work I'm doin'. I wear enough for everybody, especially you dumb fucks!"
Again Bull's manic basso exploded.

Eric grinned. (From earlier meetings he'd already learned that Black
Bull's concept of humor lay at right angles to anything Eric ever found
funny. But the limp and lame jokes Bull thought were riotous made Eric
laugh, if only for their eccentricity and lack of logic—something he'd failed
to explain to Shit, who responded, *Naw, the nigger don't know how to tell no
joke. That's all.*)

Falling, Whiteboy had jerked the chain, pulling Bull's heavy wrist.
"Jesus Christ…!" Coffee sloshed over the mug's rim. Bull swiveled on his
chair, sat the mug among the pans and dishes crowding the counter top,
stood up, and with his booted foot pushed the dog away.

He stepped astraddle Whiteboy.

At once, Bull hauled back his fist, so that the muscles beyond the vest's
arm hole were a clutch of perfect spheres, as black as gun metal in the
sunlight through the kitchen window. Then, grinning, he swung his fist
down, almost too fast to see, at Whiteboy's head—

Whiteboy gasped, grunted, and jerked away on the floor.

Eric almost fell off his box—even as, a beat later, he realized it had been
a feint and the black boulder of Bull's fist and Whiteboy's stubbly blond jaw
had not connected.

Grimacing, Whiteboy pushed upright.

The swing had carried Bull into a crouch. Shaking his head, he stood
again, looked for his coffee, found it, and sat again on his chair.

The leash between Bull's wristbrace and Whiteboy's collar swung.

From his seat on the table, Shit laughed (that, apparently, he found
funny)—and Eric looked bewildered.

Dynamite was still rocking in his chair, still scratching himself.

Tom had walked off some three steps to sit and watch.

Hands on the table edge, either side of his legs, Shit said, "See? That's
how Bull makes Whiteboy shoot his load—"

Whiteboy's cock thrust from its tow-haired tuft like a bone-straight
five-inch length up his heaving belly. Whiteboy panted. A colorless splash
glistened on the wrinkling and unwrinkling flesh. Moving back against the
wall, with one hand Whiteboy rubbed his stomach then raised his fingers
to suck them. Then, with the same hand, he rubbed his jaw where the blow
might, indeed, have connected. Looking around, he said, "Bull beats the
shit out of me, a lot. He knees me in my nuts. That hurts real good—or
punches me in my face. Yeah, it makes me shoot. But that's 'cause I don't

cum like most guys." He looked down at his belly and rubbed again. "I shot this 'cause I was scared. That's what makes me cum."

From the table Shit said, "But with you it lasts longer than with regular people. Ain't that right?"

Whiteboy nodded. "Un-huh."

"I mean, you're still cummin' now, ain't ya?"

"Un-huh." Again Whiteboy nodded. "When I have a' orgasm, like now, it goes on and on for, you know, four, five, six minutes. It feels real good. I'm still gettin' chills all up and down my legs and my back—and under my balls."

"Yeah," Shit said. "He's' more like a dog. You know when Tom comes, how long he goes on shootin'."

Whiteboy nodded. "Once I timed it with a clock—it went on for nine whole minutes. You can tell with me—I'll be cummin' till you see my dick go down." He grinned at himself again, and, with his thumb, pushed his cock forward. Still hard, it snapped back against his stomach. He looked around, grinning. "It feels real nice, now. I like it when Bull makes me come like that."

"It calms the scumbag down," Bull said to Eric. "That's all."

On his own chair, Dynamite nodded.

Kind of dreamily, Whiteboy said, "Most of the time, Bull just fakes it—like then. But it still scares me. That's 'cause every six, seven times, he *really* hits me. Hard, too. That way I don't never know if it's gonna connect or not. It's the bein' scared that makes me have a' orgasm. The ones where he really hits me, those is the best—the longest ones. Like that nine minute one. But Shit and Dynamite know all about that. Bull likes me to tell people what might not understand, like you. So they don't get upset."

"He knows you're all relaxed and calm, now," Bull said. "All right, Mr. Garbage Man—" Bull took a long swallow, then set his mug back on the counter—"I got a message for you."

Dynamite said, "Huh?"

"We oughta go on outside, though." Bull eased forward and stood. "Get off that box now." He gestured to Eric. "Yall come on with me."

Eric frowned at Bull. "Huh—?" echoing Dynamite.

"You, too. I ain't playin', cocksucker."

Bull gave the leash a tug. Still crouched, Whiteboy scurried toward him. Bull pushed out the screen door. Dynamite stepped after him. Eric and Shit followed. "Seems I gottta take me a goddam piss." Bull stepped forward. One boot landed half on a yellow-handled screwdriver that lay on the porch planks. Bull kicked it inside. It slid across the threshold, hit

Dynamite's foot—who put the toes of one foot on top of it, and with a push rolled it further back into the kitchen, till, through the screen, Eric saw it hit another carton.

Dynamite plodded over the porch.

"Get on down them steps!" Bull barked at Eric.

Whiteboy pushed out between Eric and Shit. The leash tugged around Eric's shoulder. "Bull pisses on me, all the fuckin' time—in my mouth an' everything. He makes me drink it." (The leash slipped up Eric's shoulder, to slide there.) "You like doin' that?"

Eric said, "Um…" Chills started somewhere behind his knees. Except for Dynamite's T-shirt, everone but Bull was naked; for a moment Eric wished they weren't. "I dunno. Maybe, I guess…"

Shit was watching, grinning, walking down.

"Bull," Dynamite asked, "what did Doctor Greene send you over here for?"

Bull took Dynamite's shoulder and stepped with him to the side. He called to the others, "Get on down there, turn around, and look up here!"

Still grinning, Shit said, "We better do what Bull says. Bull ain't used to havin' people question what he wants—" He had one hand on the back of Eric's shoulder, one hand on the back of Whiteboy's.

Up by the porch rail, Bull was saying: "It wasn't Dr. Greene—Dis one come from you frien' Jay, out on Gilead."

At the steps bottom, Eric, Shit and Whiteboy all looked up. The earth beneath Eric's naked feet was soft.

By the porch rail, Bull said, "Get that dog outta there. It's gonna be enough of a mess without 'im carryin' on and getting' in the way."

Again, the leash had stretched out straight.

Whiteboy reached down and grappled passing Tom to drag him up one, two, three stairs and sat. The leash sagged, and Whiteboy got panting Tom under one arm to sit with him.

Again, Bull turned to Dynamite, his hands at the waist of his beltless jeans. "You know, fella, that new son you got there is a prime guzzlin' piss pig—" Bull looked down at Eric. "That's a title you can be proud of, comin' from Jay."

Dynamite leaned forward, frowning. "What you mean? How's he gonna be a prime anything? He's a fuckin' kid…"

"I mean what you think I mean. Jay done told me—and if anyone should know around here, it's Jay. It ain't like you ain't never pleasured one before—you like it, too. I seen you at The Slide—"

Dynamite said, "I don't go there no more."

"Well, you *been* there. And you done spilled your ten or twelve pails of fun—if you ain't drunk up a few as well; even if it *ain't* been for a couple of years. Eric probably ain't like Whiteboy—yet. Still, you gonna have to do a little topppin' for 'im." He grinned at Eric. Somehow Bull had most of his teeth—at least the front ones. They were broad and ivory colored.

Eric felt prickles up the backs of his legs, along his neck.

Through the porch newels he saw Bull unsnap his steel waist button. A triangle of worn cloth fell from snarled pubic hair. Bull pulled up his thick penis. With two fingers, he slid back his black collar from the brown head. He looked down at Eric. "Open your mouth, son—"

Shit chuckled and stepped back. "Oh, fuck…!"

"—Hey…" Dynamite frowned.

Among Bull's fingers and within the thick hood, Eric saw the pee-hole that slit the head widen.

The width of a kitchen knife, a yellow blade leaped forward, fell from the porch, down, to break on Eric's chin. A quarter of a second before hot urine hit, Eric felt like somebody had given him an electric shock that rose up through his body, paralyzing it.

Shit whispered, "Open your *mouth*…!"

Eric opened it. What was happening to Eric had only registered as real with the splash's heat. He remembered when he'd first seen Shit eat snot in the men's room. . .

"Go *on*…"

Brine drowned his tongue, and he swallowed—and swallowed—keeping his mouth open and working his throat. That first heat had made him think the urine was actually hot. But it was just warm. Drops bounced out around his mouth's edges.

"You like that, cocksucker, don'tcha? I *bet* you do!"

"Oh, wow…Look at that! Oh, fuck—*look*…!"

From the corner of his eye, Eric saw Shit reach forward with one hand. Shit took hold of his chin, to position Eric's jaw. Then he slid one, then two fingers into Eric's flooded mouth, before taking them out, to suck them, then dropped his hand. "Oh, Jesus…!"

From the steps, Whiteboy said, "That turns Shit on. See how he's *really* jerkin' off, there?" (But because his head was up, it was outside Eric's line of sight.) "Naw, Tom. Stay on back here! With me."

Up on the porch, Bull glanced at Dynamite. "Look at that. Shit there's gonna blow a load all over your piss-guzzler's knee, pig fucker!"

"Hey!" Shit's fist sped up—at least Eric glimpsed the motion in his shoulder and upper arm increase. "Is it…all right if I…do that?" Eric could hear Shit was breathing hard.

"Go on…" Dynamite said, almost with wonder.

Bull said, "You can do anything to 'im you want, far as I'm concerned—if it's okay with your dad." Again Bull looked down at Eric.

"That feel good, boy?"

Eric nodded without spilling anything. Warm urine ran down his neck, his chest, his shoulder, electrically exciting. He swallowed again, again. Looking up at Dynamite, he hoped to see him smile. But the garbage man's unshaven face held the frown of a man taking a math test.

"Hey, Dynamite—" Bull laughed—"you piss in this boy's mouth, now."

Dynamite took his dick in his hand. (Had he solved the equation…?) He put his other hand on Bull's shoulder. "Goddam, boy—" which went down to Eric (and again made Eric's shoulder's tingle)—"I hope you're *really* ready."

From the porch, Dynamite's stream joined Bull's. (It *was* a wider stream than Bull's…) For three seconds the cave of Eric's mouth overflowed, to run like warm fingers rubbing the left of his jaw, his neck, his back—until Eric began to swallow twice as fast. Every third swallow, he managed another breath.

Above him, Bull's stream lightened. "Aw, see, now—" He chuckled—"I can't keep up with you."

Shit crouched further. "Oh, look—look at Eric drink that piss! Oh, *fuck*—!" Shit's fist sped to invisibility. "Wow!" Semen hit Eric's thigh, a hotter temperature as it struck, a thicker consistency as it rolled.

Bull's stream ran out. "Hey, next time, Shit, maybe I'll do some more beatin' on *your* black ass—" Bull shook his cock.

Eric glimpsed Shit give Bull a sour look, then turn away toward Eric, with his usual post-orgasmic smile.

Dynamite's stream ran thicker, wider, harder.

"Hey, *that* sure looks good!" Now Dynamite…laughed.

It went on a long time. Somewhere in it, Bull tromped down the steps. "Hey, Whiteboy—give 'em back their damned dog. Come on. We still got work to do."

"Un-huh," Whiteboy said. "Yeah, I'm with you, Bull—" Someone tromped down in the leaves; then a pause…

"Come on!" Probably the leash jerked. "Get on over here, now—you stupid scumbag."

"Un-huh…un-huh! Yeah, Bull—" with a tone Eric now heard as contentment.

When—at last—Dynamite's wide stream weakened, thinned, dripped, then halted, Shit had gone halfway up the stairs. Tom was on the porch again, head between the newels, now looking down, now looking out among the trees.

Eric swallowed and coughed. And gasped—and coughed again. "Oh, wow—!" He blinked at Dynamite, who stood watching him, bony hips and hairy legs below the T-shirt's raggedy hem.

Eric rubbed his face—and took a step back—then another, forward. He really didn't know what to do.

Dynamite said, "Come on up here, son."

Eric started up the steps, holding the rail, the paint rough and dry beneath his bare feet.

Dynamite reached down, caught Eric's arm and, as he tugged him up on the top step, moved with him back from the edge—

His arms went around Eric, who hardened in response.

Eric hugged Dynamite tightly back.

Dynamite flexed his hips against Eric. "How you feelin', now? Is that what you been wantin'?"

Because he was breathing so hard, Eric nodded. "Yeah…" Saying it, he still got chills.

Dynamite's voice was rough and low and—was it?—slightly confused. "How come Jay had to send Bull up here? Why didn't you *ask* me? It makes me feel like a dumb fuck I couldn't figure it out." (Eric felt the soft cloth of Dynamite's T-shirt wrinkled up under his arm.) "Besides, ain't I been givin' you a squirt now and then? If you want some more, all you got to do is *say* so."

Eric said, "I…I was scared. I was afraid…that you wouldn't do it. You was givin' me just enough to…make me kinda crazy."

"Aw, come on." Shit stepped forward on the porch. "You know how Jay is. He thinks sending that nigger to piss on a cocksucker outside your front door on a Sunday mornin' is funny." He chuckled. "Actually, 'cause it's Eric, it *is* kinda hysterical." (Tom's wet nose butted Eric's calf; the dog began to lick his leg.) "Besides—you're the one always sayin' Eric ain't growed up with us down here. He got to learn how we do things—"

"Yeah, I know." Dynamite's face moved against Eric's neck.

Eric was aware of the bone frame within the plates of muscle. Dynamite's penis slid around to lift, warm, hard, and low on Eric's belly.

Eric held onto Dynamite. In return Dynamite held Eric. Once, when Eric moved his left hand, he felt a spot of wet cloth. "I'm still drippin', where you guys wet me down," he said, into Dynamite's shoulder. "I think I got *you* wet, some."

"I pitched it—most of it," Dynamite said. "Catchin' a little ain't gonna kill me." He licked Eric's ear.

"Hey," Shit said. "Hey—look here."

Eric pulled back and looked over.

So did Dynamite. "What's a matter?"

"See?" Shit moved work-grayed fingers away from his cock, out over his thighs. His broad member jutted from his tan tuft, one color with his skin, to curve down toward the front. "You two huggin' up on each other like that done gimme a boner." He grinned over missing teeth.

Dynamite reached toward Shit and took his erect penis in his fist. "Come on here, and hug with us."

On his wide feet, Shit stepped up closer; Eric took his arm down to pull in Shit's shoulders, with his collar bone, his sun-darkened chest with its small, sparse curls as tight as those on Mike's...Eric said, "You gimme a hard-on, too..."

Shit hooked an arm around each one of their necks. Dynamite's nuzzled down between the boys' faces, while Shit's dick wedged between them. "You guys both got hard-ons," Shit said. "Course, I always give this pig fucker one, don't I? Given' you fellas fuckin' boners is my job in this fuckin' family."

Still nuzzling, Dynamite nodded.

Dynamite lifted his unshaven face and kissed his son. Shit closed his eyes. Eric could see Shit's jaw working and imagined Shit's vigorous tongue inside with Dynamite's, rolling and wrestling within.

Finally, Dynamite said, "Let's go into the bedroom."

Shit pulled loose, opened the screen door and stepped in, walked through the kitchen. As sunlight dragged across his shoulder, Shit said, "You know—" he followed Eric and Dynamite inside—"your web down there got all splattered up with pee—the drops is all gold now. I saw it when I looked over the rail. It's pretty. It didn't tear or nothing."

Dynamite smiled at Shit and sat on the bed.

Eric put his hands on Dynamite's T-shirt shoulders, one frayed, one torn, and pushed him back. "Lemme get on top of you and hump your big cracker dick!"

Dynamite slid down. "I still don't understand how you don't have no trouble askin' for that—and you can't ask me to piss in your fuckin' mouth? I *like* doin' that, Eric."

"Jesus," Eric said, "I don't know. You...do? Hey, I'm gonna get better at this stuff. You just gotta gimme a little time."

Dynamite raised his chin. "Where's Bull...?"

"Him and Whiteboy run off." Laughing, Shit bounced on the mattress on his belly. "This is their workin' day, in the Dump."

"Probably had more messages to deliver." Dynamite said. "Well, at least I ain't the only one. Getting them messages can be a little hard on a fellow sometimes."

"Yeah—if he thinks he a fuckin' stud like you what can do anything."
Shit turned over. "Aw, hell—he probably got to go up and let Whiteboy
show ol' Brick a better way of suckin' off that damned mule of his or a
better way to brace hisself when he takes it up his ass. Or bring some
nigger up on the bluff some better crab-lice medicine." He rolled back the
other way, laughing. "Damn, Eric! Whenever Jay ain't around, we been
pissin' in Mex's mouth all our lives, ain't we? Pissin' on a guy is fun. So's
watching a crazy nigger like Bull walk into your house, take Eric outside,
and piss in his face. How you want me to help you shoot?"

Eric said, "You already shot, Shit." His thigh was still wet. "You don't
have to do nothin', if you don't wanna—"

Shit said, "Hey—I can always make both you fellas cum. I *wanna* help
you. That's how *I* have fun."

Which is when Dynamite pulled Eric down on the rumpled sheet—
half off the mattress by now. Under him, Dynamite took a big breath.
"You know, I understand some of it. I do. A lot of times, you *can't* ask for
what you need. Sometimes you can ask for what you *want*. But if you was
comfortable askin' for it, you wouldn't *need* it. It's different with different
people. And you gotta wait around till somebody decides to give that one
to you. That's the only way you gonna get it."

"There he goes," Shit said. "My dad, Mr. Know It All." Suddenly, Shit
vaulted upright beside them, feet deep in the mattress. "Hey!" Squatting,
he got his hand in the small of Eric's back and started rubbing. "I remember
the first time Dynamite said that to me, back when I was ten, twelve years
old."

"And I remember," Dynamite said, "the first time Kyle said that to *me*.
That's where I learned it. Somebody had told him that, off in Europe, I
guess it was. And he told it to me, when he come back and we was hangin'
out together."

"Damn," Shit said, still rubbing. "Kyle said that to you? When?"

"Like you said, about twelve—no, wait. It couldn't have been then 'cause
that's how old we were when he had his Christmas party out on Gilead,
and we was already doin' it then. So we must have been ten or eleven. He
wanted to go to bed with me so bad, and there he is, this scrawny black
boy, scared to death to ask me. So one day, I just said to him, hey, let's go in
the old boathouse and lie down so we can fuck each other. I mean, I knew
all about that shit from my cousins. And I realized that's why he was so
nervous. But, see, he didn't have no cousins like I did, I guess. And when
we did it, he acted like he was so happy he was about to cry. Then he said,
'Some things you just want so much, you can't even ask for them. You can
only be given 'em.'" Underneath Eric, Dynamite adjusted himself. "Later,

he wrote that into the what-and-why he made for the Dump. You know, what he called his 'mission statement.' See, Eric, if you learn to ask for what you want in the right way, you got a lot better chance somebody's just gonna up and give you what you need—only I didn't learn that part till eight, nine years afterward."

"Damn!" Shit said, still rubbin'. "Now I didn't know that."

"Well, that was Robert Kyle," Dynamite said, "the Third."

"He really wanted you that much…?" Shit leaned into Eric's back, as he flexed his butt. Eric thought, he really *is* pushing me toward a goddamn orgasm…which he already knew would make Dynamite shoot within the next three minutes.

"That's right, son, take a ride on my fuckin' cracker dick. Go on, now, hump that hard old thing…"

"I'm already humpin' it," Eric said.

"Good," Dynamite said. "Hey, I'll piss in your mouth anytime you squat down and look like you're waitin' on it. Shit will, too—"

"Sure," Shit said. "*That* ain't hard! Hell, Dynamite used to be Mex's steady, before I was born. And I pissed in Mex's mouth all the time when I was a kid—he'd pretend he didn't like it. Then he'd laugh at me, and bet I wouldn't do it again. So I would."

Still excited, Shit lay down with them and began to rub against Dynamite along with Eric.

That morning, Shit, Eric, and Dynamite all came within the same six seconds—Shit for the second time.

"Where's Tom?" Dynamite asked, pushing himself upright. "I thought he'd wanna couple of licks of this."

"Naw," Shit said. "He run outta here after Black Bull and Whiteboy left."

Eric said, "Oh," and stopped looking around the bed.

"Damn." Shit peeled himself away from Dynamite. "*That* was a surprise. I don't think we should try doin' that too many times, though." Lazily, Eric and Dynamite were eating it off each other's hand.

"Why?" Dynamite asked, and sucked his own wide thumb—then sucked Eric's.

"'Cause I don't think we could ever do it again if we aimed for it."

Dynamite said, "Lemme run you back over to your ma's…" He stood up from the bed.

"I thought you said you wanted me to hang out with you guys today…?"

"I do," Dynamite said. "But if you don't spend *some* time with her, she ain't gonna be so happy about you comin' over here so much."

"Oh," Eric said. "Yeah…What'd Bull mean about beatin' your ass?"

Shit humphed. "Nothin'." So Eric decided not to push it.

Dynamite picked up his jeans—not overalls, today—and ran a leg into them, ran the other in, and with one hand shoveled balls and penis inside—

"He's just doin' that to turn you on again," Shit said from his side of the bed, his head propped on his hand.

"It's that or walk around all day with 'em hangin' out my fly." Dynamite zipped himself up. Without putting his socks on, he pushed one big foot, then the other, into his work shoes.

Eric—and Shit—grinned.

"You go see her, maybe go in with her to work. It ain't a garbage day— you can come on back, afterward." Dynamite nodded. "Besides, as good a suck as you are, every once in a while I like to be shut of you." He looked at his son. "Sometimes I wish the fuck I could be shut of you both."

Shit grinned—then so did Dynamite, while Eric began to hunt his clothes from the clutter.

Outside, when they were getting ready to get into the pickup, Eric stepped among the ferns, looking briefly for the great web. But he couldn't find it. Maybe Tom had decided to run through it.

Or licked it.

Or something…

* * *

[21] BEFORE SIX, AMONG the pines on the slope below Barbara's, Dynamite's pickup slowed. When Eric got out, the first thing he decided to do was change his underwear. Minutes later, in the bathroom of Barbara's trailer, bare toes over the edge of a broken away vinyl square, so that he could feel the plank floor beneath his toes, arm and hip pushing against the cartons stacked by the shower's plastic wall, he looked at the dark-and-light green razor handle in his hand—then at his reflection in the mirror over the sink.

He turned to the side so he could see his sideburn's platinum feathering his jaw, across his chin, over his upper lip. He pushed three fingers against his suntanned cheek and watched his reflection do the same.

As raucous here as at the Dump, broken music from the birds neared the bathroom window—he glanced at the pale orange blinds—and drifted away. Eric imagined them outside, nearing and retreating.

How long *would* it take him to grow a beard like Shit's? Of course it would never be like Shit's irregular tan tufts. But if I want a beard, I have to stop shaving.

That's all.

So I will.

Eric put the razor on the back of the sink, where, thinned by use, a bar of soap had dried to the enamel. He shouldered into the narrow hall. Large amounts of Febreze and Glade had never quite covered the musk of the cats who, for all practical purposes, had been the house's tenants before Barbara. Eric passed the porch—built out from the half wall removed from the trailer's back, with his bed in it—and into the kitchen area.

Out the kitchen, Barbara was just getting back. From Ron's, of course. Couldn't she hook up with some other nigger? Erik wondered. But then, she no longer complained at all about Dynamite and Shit and the garbage man job. If Ron was what she wanted…

Fortunately, the trailer had two bathrooms, one right off her bedroom.

At the table, under the fan, with its clutch of four glass light shades (one of which was broken), she sat down on an aluminum tube chair she'd told him had come with the place. The plastic seat and back were the same orange as the bathroom blinds.

She wore white Bermuda shorts and a blue sleeveless blouse. On the green Formica by her forearm was a mug of black coffee. With one hand she held a yogurt container with rounded corners to the table and, with the other, peeled back the plasticized foil. "Hello, sweetheart." She smiled up at him. "You want some? There're a few more pear and a couple of peach in the refrigerator. And at least one raspberry. Go get one—or a couple, if you want. Just leave me two in there for later." She licked the yogurt that adhered to the foil's underside.

"Naw," he said. "That's okay. You got a clean uniform today? I washed one in the laundry I did day before yesterday, but they're still out back drying."

"I got one hanging in the closet, down in the kitchen in the back at the Coffee and Egg. Hey, get yourself a cup of coffee, if you want." She put the foil on the table. It had rolled into a cylinder.

"Jesus, Barb." Eric flopped down in one of the chairs at the table. "*Your* coffee is like motor oil." Often she'd make a twelve-cup pot and reheat it four or five times over three days. "How do you drink that?"

She laughed again, picked up a spoon, and began mixing the yogurt. The foil on the table rocked and black coffee swayed in its mug, as yogurt-covered cubes of fruit rose around her spoon's turning handle. "I come from a family of strong coffee drinkers."

Across the table he could smell the yogurt's fruit.

"You remember how grandma's coffee was."

"Well, I wasn't drinking it, I guess, back then."

"Does that mean you don't want any?"

"Not right now," Eric said. "Maybe I'll get a cup down at the Lighthouse."

"Now, see," Barbara said, "to me that stuff Clem makes tastes like dishwater." She lifted the spoon, put it into her mouth, then pulled it out slowly. "Honey, can I talk to you about something serious?"

"Sure." Eric shrugged. "I guess so. What?"

"You've worked pretty much all summer. Serena says the high school over in Hemmings opens in two, three weeks—we can still drive there and register you. You only have another year. Then you'll have your diploma. I'd really like to see you do that, Eric."

Eric looked at the table and took three long breaths. "I don't wanna go to school no more." He closed his hands around the side of the chair seat. "I wanna work. I'm seventeen. If I really need one later, I can get a GED." It hit Eric that he had not called his father since that first time, the day he'd gotten his phone out at Hemmings. Somehow, Dynamite's injunction on using the things had carried over to everybody else. Occasionally Barbara phoned him, but that had been the only time it got used.

"Well," Barbara said, "you'd be able to work at a much better job, if you had one—a high school degree. You're...very smart. I bet you could even go to college."

"And get a job. In an office—with a suit and tie?"

"We talked about this before, I know. But do you really want to be a garbage man *all* your life?"

"Why not?" Eric pushed his hands in, on the chair's edges. "That's what Dynamite does. He didn't go to high school. Neither did Morgan. And I don't wanna have to get in no more fights, just 'cause I'm the new kid. I did that in Texas; I did it in Hugantown; I did it in Atlanta. Hey, you remember? I'm gay—okay? That's rough on a guy in a new school."

"Well, do you have to tell everyone?"

"Come on, Barb. People find out. You know how that works."

"What about Dynamite—and his nephew. You didn't tell them, did you?"

"Of *course* I did." He moved side-to-side, backing onto the chair. "Yeah."

After moments she said, "You didn't tell me you told them. And they're okay with it?"

"Un-huh."

"Looking at them, that's not the first thing I'd think."

"They joke about it sometimes—but...that's all. And that was only for the first couple of weeks. They think it's funny—and they're glad I like to cook." He wondered how much he would someday tell her...But no, not (he decided) about them both.

"Maybe, honey—" Barbara took another spoonful of yogurt—"they don't really know what gay means."

"Of course they know." Momentarily, Eric hesitated. Then he dared, "That's what they joke about. They live over in the Dump, where *everybody's* gay—a year and a half ago, even before you came here, they told me, they had another guy who used to help them out, from over there. He was gay, too. One of the black guys—so they're used to it." This was close to the truth. They'd stopped working with Hal, Dynamite had explained, because though he'd fallen in bed with them twice in the first three weeks, after that he'd stopped putting out at all. Nor—Shit said—did he work very hard.

(If he had, Dynamite had added, they would have kept him on, nookie or no; Shit had humphed. *But this way, with you,* Shit explained, *it sure is a lot better!*)

"Well, yes, Serena said something about that." Barbara frowned. Then she repeated, "Of course, Serena says a lot of funny things about —well, everybody. Unless you want to be a crazy person, though, in a town like this you've got to learn how to ignore four-fifths of what you hear. I don't pay it much mind. People have been saying funny things about me all my life, and—"

"Yeah," Eric said. "That's 'cause your boyfriends are always black guys."

"Not *all* of them," Barbara said. "But, yes—a lot of them. Most of them. So I *am* used to people talking." She took in a breath, then leaned forward. "Are you sure *you* know exactly what gay means, sweetheart—?"

"Of *course* I do," Eric said, "Come on, Barbara. Look—you know, I'm *not* a virgin." Barbara ate another spoonful of yogurt, staring at the container, and when she didn't say anything, Eric went on, "*You* stopped going to school when you were fourteen. I'm the same age now as you were when you had me. I'm not that different from you."

"That," Barbara said, "is a frightening thought. I remember how much I *didn't* know about sex—or anything else—when you came along."

"Look. I don't wanna get in no more fights in school. I don't like that, Barb. Hey, I really like Dynamite and Shit. They're fun to work with. And 'cause I didn't go to high school in Hemmings before, over there they'll probably make me go for two years, until I get out, anyway."

"Honey, it wouldn't be *that* bad—"

"Besides. I been down here four months, now. Right—? *Almost* five. How much money have you had to give me since I been living here? Yeah, you gave me my shoes. Which was great. But I haven't asked you for *anything,* have I? And every week—except that one time there—I bring a big bag of groceries from the Produce Farm for us."

"Yes, you certainly have. And you even asked me what we needed, before you did it." She sat back. "Now, you know *I* bought some things for you, even though you didn't ask. And God knows, I'm not holding them against you. I was very surprised—*and* very proud of you. But…well, it isn't the money—"

"The week I didn't was 'cause I wanted to buy some stuff for Dynamite—he been letting me eat over there with them so much."

"Yes, I know—"

"So I don't even know if we could afford for me to go to school. Hey, I really like taking care of myself. I really, really, really don't wanna go to school no more. I got a job. And I wanna keep it. You stopped going to school when you were fourteen. Mike stopped when he was thirteen. I went for two years longer than you and three years longer than him—"

"Honey, I know I stopped—and so did your dad. But that's why I know it wasn't such a good idea. And your dad went back to the trade college when he was a grown up, remember?"

"Well, I can, too, if I need to."

"Look, sweetheart. I don't want to have an argument—"

"Then let me do what I want. I'm not making problems for you. I'm trying to be a help—a real help."

"And you *are*—"

"Hey, it's not something crazy. Leavin' school, people do that. You and my dad did it. And it's what I want to do. If I keep the job for three months, and Dynamite says I'm really working hard, then the Chamber of Commerce'll put me on the payroll, like Shit. 'Cause Dynamite's supposed to have two helpers anyway—and it won't just be minimum wage. That's why he's giving me a chance. If I do go to school, we'll just be scufflin', you and me, and not able to do nothin' for the next two *years*. It'd be better for me—*and* it'd be better for you, too."

Barbara sucked her teeth, ate another spoonful of yogurt, and looked at the table. Finally, she said, "It's your day off. What are you going to do with it?"

"Just hang around. Go over to Dynamite's, maybe. He says I can practice drivin' the truck in the Dump. And I'm teaching Morgan to read the truck's GPS system. Soon, he'll be able to get his real driver's license. We'll hang out—and talk and stuff. You know, Morgan ain't stupid like people say he is. He just…can't read."

"Can Mr. Haskell?" Barbara asked warily.

"He reads, some—the newspaper. He reads my comics…"

Barbara shook her head. "I'd just like to see you do something more with your time off than sitting around over on the other side of town, watching television all day."

"They don't even *got* a television, Barb. I only watch that when I'm here—'cause you got yours on *all* the time." Confirming the observation, from the bed room a trumpet fanfare ended and the six-thirty morning anchor's voice began to review traffic conditions along the coast. "That's half the reason I go over there—to get away from it. I'll drive you down to the Harbor, leave you the car, then walk around, or come home, or…or somethin'."

"You're going over there today. And I know you'll be there tomorrow, too. Are you *sure* they want to see so much of you?"

"Yeah. He asked me to come. So I could help Shit…I mean Morgan."

The table legs were paired aluminum tubes, which, below the corners, separated into small forks. Two nights ago, Eric had pushed his socks into the fork by his own place.

"They get up at four. On their days off, like today, they're up by six."

"Well, then…" Barbara sighed. "But I keep expecting Mr. Haskell—Dynamite—to drop into the Coffee & Egg and tell me that 'cause you're hangin' around there all the time, you're being…well, a pain in the *ass!*"

Eric pulled the socks loose (one fell to the floor), lifted an ankle onto the thigh of his jeans and tugged the dark tube up over toe knuckles, ligaments, veins. "I don't think he's gonna say that. I try to be as helpful over there as I am here. And if he does, I promise, I'll stop going over there so much. I don't wanna fuck up my—"

"Eric—!"

"—mess up my job. I like it too much. If they didn't want me around, I'd figure it out." Eric's foot thudded to the floor. He leaned forward to swipe up the sock that had fallen. His other foot came up, and he tugged on the second.

"Sweetheart, those are your *socks*—!"

"Yeah…?" Eric moved both feet over the floor.

"Don't put those there, sweetheart. Keep them out on the porch with your other stuff."

"I thought it would be easier, 'cause my shoes—" Eric pointed at the high topped work shoes beside the door, standing below the jackets and coats hanging on the hooks—"are over there."

"But things have to have a place."

"I thought that *was* a good place. For socks, I mean. I'd only worn 'em twice." Pushing back his chair, he stood up, went to the refrigerator, opened the pale orange door, and got out a rumpled plastic wrapper in which was half a whole wheat loaf. He set it on the counter and looked at the toaster. Then he went back to the refrigerator and, from the side door, got the green plastic margarine dish. "You want a piece of toast, don't you?"

"Yes, sweetheart," Barbara said. "But I was going to have that down at work."

"I'll make it for you," Eric said. "One for me, too." He put two slices into the bright, stainless cube, then pushed the handle. The slices wobbled into the slots. As he looked down, horizontal threads and reflector plates inside turned orange, glowing against the bread.

Reaching up, Eric opened a cabinet door, took down two saucers, then opened a drawer, removed a kitchen knife from the wood-walled knife compartment, and put it up on the counter beside the margarine. He turned to lean back against the counter edge. "Barbara—you know what I wanna do, more than anything?" The counter's rim creased his butt. "I mean, what I wanna be?"

"What?" She smiled at him.

"I wanna be a good person."

"Honey, you *are* a good person."

"No, I mean a *really* good person, who helps other people. Like Jay and Dynamite and Serena and the guys in the Dump help me…even you and Mike—"

Barbara smiled began to question. "*Even* me and Mike…?"

"Well, *you* know—you guys are my parents. But I wanna be a person who does things to make other people feel better—have an easier time— like get their fuckin' garbage out of the way and off to the Bottom." For a moment, Eric frowned. "You know, every time I see Ron, I always come away feelin' really bad, 'cause he wants me to feel like a loser. I *ain't* a loser. I have a lot more fun workin' with Dynamite and Morgan, probably, than Ron does at his desk, workin' on his business. It's just a different *kind* of fun—that's all. But it's like he can't feel like a winner, unless he's got people he can look at and *think* they're losers. I don't wanna do that to anybody— to Shit, or to Dynamite, or to you, or even to Ron. Every time I finish collecting the day's garbage, I feel like I won—like everybody around here has won because of me and…Morgan and Dynamite. I like workin' the route. I like to do it, 'cause it's useful."

"Getting 'fuckin' garbage?'" Barbara asked. "You know you don't *have* to use language like—" But she smiled.

"Oh, come on. *You* know what I mean."

Barbara sighed. And smiled again. "Yes—I do. And it's true. It is useful. But you can take this 'being-good' thing a little *too* seriously. You don't have to go and give Morgan half your socks, for example."

"He didn't have any. Barb, he used to go to school over in Hemmings— not the high school. He never went to *high* school at all. Dynamite did. He said he went there for about a year, and they weren't too nice when he was there, either. But when Morgan was in the regular school, he told me, kids would beat him up there 'cause he couldn't read. They would tell him he was stupid—then they'd beat him up. Dynamite had to take him out—of school. You know, when he was tellin' me about that, I almost started cryin'. But I didn't—'cause I didn't want to look like a crybaby. If you want to help people, you have to be strong—strong enough to hear what happened to them."

"So you're going to grow up and be—" Barbara shrugged—"Spiderman or something—and save the world?"

"No!" (Behind Eric, the toaster's timer growled a moment before the spring snapped.) "I don't mean anything like *that!* I don't mean nothin' religious, either. I just wanna be a good person—do stuff that don't hurt anybody. Do stuff that helps them. Dynamite's a good person. That's why he takes care of Morgan—and why he collects the garbage. Why he...lets me work with 'em." Eric turned back to the counter, took out the toast, put both slices on one saucer, then cut off a pad of margarine from the stick in the dish and began spreading it on the toast. "Last week we were by Ron's house—in Runcible, I mean—gettin' his garbage. I looked up and seen him in his upstairs window, watchin' us. It was just getting' light. He was in his bathrobe, and was lookin' down. I waved, laughed—he didn't even smile. Just turned away. I didn't let it bother me, but it was weird." Beneath the knife, the margarine thinned, turned translucent, then liquid, to run into dells and indentations, even reflecting the trailer ceiling's florescent lights, still on, despite the outside sun. He cut them corner-to-corner, moved two wedges to the other saucer, and took both to the table.

Eric went to the door, stuck a foot in one work shoe, then a foot in the other, while Barbara said, "Thanks, sweetheart. I'm not used to this Queen-of-Sheba treatment." Eric returned to the table, laces flopping, their plastic ends clicking on the linoleum. Because she hadn't mentioned it, he knew she was probably bothered by his story about Ron. Odd to know things like that about people you knew well.

"You should be." Eric sat, picked up a triangle of toast, and took a bite that left crumbs on his both sides of his mouth. "I hope you are, someday." Then he added. "I really didn't let it bother me, about Ron. But it was a little funny."

Barbara sighed—"You know—" and picked up her own toast, bit it, then put it down—"I'm always saying it. But you really *have* grown up a lot. I don't think I was ready for it. I mean—" She reached over, and, with a foreknuckle wiped one corner of his mouth—he flinched a little, then realized what she was doing, so leaned forward again—and she brushed crumbs off the other corner—"you're always going to be my wonderful apple dumpling—"

"Barb, come *on*." He sat back and rubbed his mouth with the heel of his own hand. Then he picked up both pieces from his own saucer and bit them together. He'd washed his hands before, but they were still kind of gray—lined at the knuckles and the rims of his nails.

"My very strong and very handsome and very good and *very* helpful apple dumpling." Sitting back up, she reached down to lift her yellow pocketbook from where it had been sitting by her chair. Opening it, she took out her purse, removed her car keys, and slid them across the table toward Eric. "You're wonderful, Eric. I'm serious. I really think you are. And, yes, you can drive me down to work this morning."

He grinned. "Thanks."

Two minutes later, as Barbara started to reach for hers, Eric got up and swiped away the toast saucers. "I got 'em." He put them over in the sink and turned toward the door.

Barbara put the spoon, clinking, in after them, while Eric said, "Come on—let's go. Wait." Eric stopped, frowning. "Wait—what did I do with the car keys?"

Without looking, Barbara said, "Try your shirt pocket, honey."

Eric raised his hands from his hips to slap his chest. "Oh…yeah. I put 'em there so I wouldn't forget 'em."

"And as a personal favor to your mom, do you think you could wash your hands off between the time to put your socks on and the time you make the toast?" At the door, Barbara glanced back. "And tie your shoes."

"Yeah. Yeah, I'm gonna tie 'em." From where he'd dropped to one knee, Eric heard a breeze move through the pine branches.

*

Ahead of him, Barbara stepped outside. After he drove down to Front Street, for the rest of the day Eric walked around and looked around and waited at the dock for Jay and Mex to get in with the scow, then sat in the Lighthouse Coffee & Egg, then walked around the town some more. Finally, he went home, masturbated (that alone, Eric thought, is the only reason I can live in this place…), then made some potato salad from the second of two recipes on page forty-five of the first volume of that old two-volume paperback cookbook Barb had—and put some pork chops out to thaw on a plate on the counter for dinner.

He divided the potato salad in two, covered one bowl with foil and left it in the refrigerator, put the rest in a plastic container with a blue top, and carried it over to the Dump.

* * *

[22] SUN-BURNED FOREARMS crossed over his bib overalls, Dynamite leaned against the cabin corner. Gulls and blue spans among rumpled silver made the kind of day the summer people called perfect—though the three had knocked off work an hour early, and, Dynamite said, he dared any motherfucker to complain. Within smelling distance someone was barbecuing ribs.

It was a hot Indian summer.

Dynamite wore no shirt. His overalls' straps did not quite cover either of his day-old tit rings, gold on his sun-browned chest, in the chestnut hair.

"The ones Jay got was surgical steel." Dynamite scrunched his unshaven chin down into his neck to look. "But I like these more. That's the kind the niggers around here always get. Maybe that's 'cause I live over here with 'em in the Dump. It was funny, though—this woman, big as a house, stickin' a needle right through them things. It was Tank who done it. She surprised me, too. She had me sittin' on that old, enamel, like-a-dentist chair they got in the back, and told me to take a deep breath and count to three." It was perhaps his fifth time through the tale since he'd gotten them—with Jay—yesterday on his day off. "Only as soon as I breathed in, she goddam stuck me! By the time I got to two, she had that sucker in!" Possibly, Eric considered, it was Dynamite's sore chest that had made him quit work early. "Then she done the other one, before I'd even settled with the first. She give me this aerosol can, too—it ain't nothin' but seawater. Or just plain salt water, for all I know. I'm supposed to spray 'em a couple of times a day for a week. Hey, son—" which was to Eric— "you wanna spray your daddy's titties?" At the same time, he dropped his hand on Shit's naked shoulder; he stood shirtless and just behind Eric. "After a week, *you* can go back to suckin' on them things, like you like so much—if you want. Jay's talkin' about gettin' some more pictures, on both his legs—from his ankles all the way up to his pecker. Cassandra's busy drawin' him up some ideas for 'em. But tattoos is a little much for me."

"Them rings is gonna be interestin'." Shit frowned. "Maybe when I'm fuckin' your asshole, I'll reach around your chest and twiddle 'em for you." They all laughed. "Surgical steel, huh?" Shit went on: "Naw, I think I like the gold ones, too."

"When you gonna get some, boy?"

"Oh, I dunno." Shit rubbed his head, where perspiration glittered under the edge of his tan hair. "Maybe a couple months after Hell freezes over." Again they laughed.

In the cabin's kitchen, a pot of Eric's Brunswick stew from the weekend was reheating—chicken, sausage, corn, carrots, celery, onions, mushrooms, and, over the top, two-and-a-quarter-cups-Bisquick-and-two-thirds-of-a-cup-of-milk dumplings.

Shit had made a pail of lemonade. It sat—already half empty, along with some mismatched glasses—on the porch steps.

Inside, half a plastic bag of ice was still wedged in the refrigerator freezer.

"Hey," Shit said, "did you ever talk to Jay about how he sent Bull over here to show you what to do with Eric?"

"I talked to him and Mex both," Dynamite said. "Why wouldn't I? They know all about that stuff, 'cause they do it regular. Even though I liked it, see, I never had no kid around like Eric who really needed my piss before." He grinned over at Eric. "A few times, some cocksucker over in the truck stop. But that's all—and that, not for while."

"What'd you say?" Shit wanted to know.

"What you think I said?" Dynamite answered. "I said 'Thank you.' Jay and Mex both say it sounds like I'm doin' it right. I'm supposed to ask Eric here if he's happy with it." He gave a rough chuckle. "You happy, son? Is your daddy pissin' in your mouth enough?" The chuckle became a laugh. "Damn, it tickles me to talk nasty like that to you, boy!"

"Un-huh." Eric swallowed. "Yeah…"

"Just don't forget how to suck regular." Shit said. "I'd really miss that…"

"I don't think you got to worry," Eric said, "not with all the dick cheese you niggers make." (Father and son grinned at each other.) "Anybody hungry yet?"

"Yeah," Shit said. "Me."

Overhead, Gulls swooped in from the sea and curved out again.

* * *

[23] BARBARA BROUGHT UP his finishing high school two more times. "Naw. I ain't changed my mind. I still wanna keep my job."

During the final week of registration, though, she hadn't mentioned it at all.

Then the term was over—and he was still working with Dynamite and Shit.

"I guess she's gone along with you," Dynamite said. "Goin' to school woulda been good for you. I mean, you probably could do that stuff, the way you read and things. But I'm glad you're still with us."

Shit grinned, then asked, almost shyly (they were lying, naked, in bed, all three, after work), "Hey, li'l brother. You're such a cute blond-headed little nigger, can I fuck you?" He reached out and rubbed Eric's butt, sliding one, then two fingers deep into the crevice between.

"Sure." Eric grinned back.

"I'm gonna make you cum, too."

* * *

[24] ERIC WAS OVER at Dynamite's much of October. On the morning of November seventh, when they were lumbering out of bed, with only the bedside lamp on, and still horsing around before the pitch black windows—naked Dynamite stood beside the mattress. Shit was standing up on the bed, laughing; and, Dynamite's dick in his mouth, Eric sat on the bed's edge, also naked. Finished running his tongue under Dynamite's skin around the head, with the hard shaft in his fist, Eric took it out of his mouth to say, "Come on. Go ahead—do it. You ain't gone to the bathroom, yet."

"Naw," Dynamite said. "Then I'll have to smell that stink on your breath all mornin'."

Eric said, "You're supposed to like it."

Fisting his cock and practically straddling Eric's shoulder, Shit said, "Aw, you know damned well—he likes it as much as you like smellin' that good stinky dick cheese. It'll keep the pig fucker turned on, that's all, and he'll want you to suck him off half a dozen times over the rest of the day— 'stead of haulin' crap." He laughed. "That's what it do to me."

"Here—" Dynamite leaned back, taking his own cock in his rough fist, and, with the palm of his other hand, rubbed the head in its wrinkled overhang—"I'll get it goin' for you. Get ready…Okay, son, here it comes…" He dropped his hand from the half uncovered head, as it erupted.

Eric moved his face forward. Dynamite moved his big foot over Eric's on the gappy board floor. Standing on the bed, Shit put a foot on Eric's thigh.

"Oh, wow…look at it, there. Look at that yellow waterfall spillin' into his mouth. Go on, drink it all down, Eric. Bet you gonna spill some—"

"No he ain't," Dynamite said. "You don't know your brother."

Eric held Dynamite's bony hips.

Two hands rested on Eric's head. A third one, Shit's, joined to press Eric's face into Dynamite's chestnut fur, while Eric took great, rhythmic swallows. He could feel Dynamite's urine fill his belly.

"Damn, that feels nice, son. Jay says Mex does this for 'im every fuckin' mornin', then sucks him off besides. But I swear, I don't see how they get no work done. After I shoot, I get all lazy."

"Well, they don't have to drive around and pull up twenty and forty pounds sacks of garbage all day. They just go back and forth on the scow." Shit's pumping fist brushed and brushed Eric's shoulder. Shit's foot shifted on the mattress by Eric's hip. "You want Eric to stop when you run out?" His toes flexed on Eric's thigh. "Or you want him to finish you off?"

Dynamite slid his hands further around Eric's head. "Since he started, he might as well go on." The salt flush was hot and bitter and tonic. "Hey, you know I ain't gonna do this for you more than but once a week."

"Why not?" Shit asked, voicing what, swallowing rhythmically, Eric wondered.

"'Cause I got some pity on his goddam kidneys."

"Hell," Shit said. "Doc Greene said you could do what he's doin' four or five times a day and it wouldn't hurt 'im none. I'll piss in your mouth any time you want, Eric. Guys do that up at The Slide all the time. You see Mex—after he drinks enough out of enough guys, eventually it comes shootin' out his ass. Hey, you can have anything what comes outta *me* you want. It's all I got to give you, anyway. You can have my fuckin' puke if you want it. I told you about Frank, the guy from the factory? He was into that—what they call it? Projectile vomitin'—now that's a real fuckin' mess. But he would gimme these pills that made it easy to barf your cookies—"

"I didn't like 'im takin' that stuff," Dynamite said. "But he had to try out everything, you know…"

"I only did it two or three times. I didn't like it all that much, really." Shit moved himself around. "Oh, yeah—back up a little, and lemme watch it spurtin' in the white boy's motherfuckin' mouth. That's really good."

Dynamite said, "I'm spillin' on the bed, Shit—"

"So the fuck what? I seen you piss in the bed, jump up and go work, let it dry and we didn't changed them suckers for another two months—"

"Yeah, I know," Dynamite said (while Eric moved an inch to the side; warm urine rolled down one side of his chin), "but that was a long time ago, when you was really into all that nasty shit. And so was I—"

Its acidic force cleansed morning itself for Eric.

"Hey…" Then Dynamite chuckled. "What you tryin' to do, Shit. Shoot a load in Eric's goddam ear—?"

Under the lamp on the night table, Dynamite's cell phone chinked out *The Battle Hymn of the Republic.*

Eric jumped a little, aware that Dynamite had not moved at all.

Dynamite said, "Now who in hell is that supposed to be at this hour?" With a slight shift, his urine continued strong in Eric's mouth.

(Maybe once a month Randal would call with something about road conditions if there'd been a bad rain or, once, an accident…)

A hand left Eric's head. Without cutting his stream—it was so strong, Eric figured he couldn't—Dynamite bent to the side, picked up his cell, and stood again. Above, Eric heard him say, "Hello…Oh…yes, ma'am… yeah. He's here…Who? Obama?… He did?…You sure? I mean, it ain't a joke or somethin'…huh? Yeah, well…Okay, just a second. Sure. He's in the john. He'll be out in a minute."

Without losing Dynamite's cock, Eric tried to look up, over the ridges of the garbage man's belly.

"It's your ma," Dynamite called back over his shoulder, as if Eric was in the john. Finally, his water lessened. "Finish up, and come on out of the bathroom and take this."

Eric was surprised how unsurprised he was.

A couple of final squirts—Eric swallowed them, went forward, then pulled back.

Dynamite held the black and silver phone in a hand unwashed since yesterday. He rubbed Eric's cheek, once sliding his broad, salty thumb with its mere third of a nail into Eric's mouth.

Dynamite's cock still in one hand, Eric took the phone with the other, breathed in, sat back on the bed, and put his knee up. "Hey, Barb?"

"He won, sweetheart!" he heard his mother say. "Last night, at about eleven, I guess it was. McCain conceded. Barack Obama's the next President of the United States!"

"Naw…" Eric was disbelieving.

Still on the bed, Shit moved around in front of him, still pumping.

Eric let Dynamite go, reached down, squeezed one of Shit's feet, then looked up and pushed at him. "Come on, cut it out—!" He put the phone back against his ear. "Shit's horsin' around here. You sure it ain't some kind of hoax?"

"You sound like Ron." Barbara laughed. "But Serena called me five seconds after they announced it! No, it's for real. I knew you all would be asleep, and I didn't want to wake you. So I waited till now to call and tell you."

"There're gonna be a lotta surprised white folks wakin' up this mornin'," Eric said. "Why didn't you call on my phone?"

"Your phone isn't on, Mr. Not Available…"

"Oh—it must be still charging…" It had been charging, out in the kitchen, Eric only now remembered, for two days…He said: "I guess there are—at least down here. But probably they're going to be a lot of surprised black folks, too."

"Ron said he wouldn't believe it for certain till he got up and saw the headlines. But the TV news is already carrying in. He's president elect—I guess that means he's the next one."

"Yeah," Eric said. "If somebody don't shoot his black ass." He took a breath. "I hope they don't."

"Me too," Barbara said warily. "Anyway, I thought I ought to let you know."

"Yeah, well…Hey, thanks. Some people in the Dump gonna be pretty happy about it. But I don't know about outside." Though they had talked about it, the registration period at the Dump Social Service Office had passed and they had not voted.

"Well," Barbara said, "*I* think it's a good thing—though Ron and me were arguing for an hour last night, till I decided to let him have the last word. He's still asleep. For some reason he thinks Republicans are gods."

Eric chuckled. "They got the most money."

"Anyway, I wanted to catch you, before you guys took off on your route."

"Well…thanks."

"Probably you'll hear it a hundred times in the next few hours, anyway."

"Okay. Thanks for callin' and tellin' me." Eric thumbed "end," closed the phone, leaned over, and put it back on the table.

Dynamite had gone into the bathroom to wash his face, his hands, his crotch. Now he came out, bent, and swiped up his gray underpants and his bibs from the floor.

Still balancing on the bed, Shit said, "Come on. You wanted Eric to finish you up. Go on. Let him suck you off."

"He can do that in the fuckin' pickup once we get started."

Still standing on the bed, Shit bent. His hand fell on Eric shoulder and he ran his stone rough palm around the back of Eric's neck and tugged. "And you're gonna suck me off right after him, ain't you? While you still got a mouth full of his cum. That's *real* nasty, when you got a mouth full of somebody else's cum, and get to suckin' on me next." Grinning, he stopped pumping with his other hand long enough to reach up and dig in a nostril. "It's like your mouth's an old used scumbag. I'm gonna stick some snot under my skin for you. That sound good?"

"I told you," Eric said, "that's not quite the same thing for me—"

"But *I* like it. I like that a lot." Then, standing, Shit took a big jump off the bed—hanging a moment, naked and awkward in the ill-lit room, to land and, a second later, stagger into the Bowflex. It almost turned over. As it righted, the spiring exercise rods swayed.

"Hey, *watch* it—!" Eric stood up.

Coming out the bathroom door, Dynamite said, "Look out, boy!" He stepped toward Shit.

But Shit was laughing. And the machine still stood upright.

"Come on," Dynamite said. "It's cold out there, Shit. Put on a warm shirt now, at least. And sumpin' on top of it—you can take it off if you work up a sweat. I'm gonna sit there in the truck for the first hour, after I shoot in your scum suckin' face, nigger—" He grinned at Eric—"and let both of you do the fuckin' work for a change."

"Sure," Shit said. "We don't mind, do we?"

"That's fine," Eric said, and went into the john to begin the long piss that, as usual, by the end had Shit and Dynamite both laughing.

"Well, you're doin' that for the two of us, I guess," Dynamite said, when he came out. "Come on. Get your jeans on."

Minutes later, as they walked out onto the front porch, Eric said, "You know, this means, I guess—my dad, Mike, could even be president. Or you, Shit…"

"Me?" Shit said. "How'm I gonna be president?"

"I mean, nobody can stop you just 'cause you're black."

"Oh…" Shit said, frowning, puzzling. "I don't wanna be no president. I can't read or nothin'. How'm I gonna be president if I can't read?"

Dynamite said, "Well, I always thought—" all three in work shoes this morning, in the dark they clumped down the porch steps, to start toward the pickup, fifteen feet from the door—"the best person for President I could ever imagine was Robert Kyle, the Third. The only difference between him and that Obama nigger in Washington is that Kyle's two shades darker and as good a cocksucker as you are, son—and maybe a little smarter 'cause he was pretty much the smartest guy, black or white, *I* ever knowed."

Shit laughed—and so did Eric.

They'd climbed in and Dynamite keyed the ignition. "Hey." In the light from the dashboard Dynamite looked at Eric. "Since they *got* a nigger in there, I bet you're glad it ain't Ronald Reagan."

It took Eric a moment to get it.

"You know…" Dynamite said. "Ronald Reagan Bodin."

"Oh…Yeah—I guess I am," Eric said.

* * *

[25] WHEN, AROUND FOUR, Eric reached the cabin, the sun was bright against summer-baked siding. As he sauntered up, with dried grass sticking at his ankles under his jeans cuffs, next to Dynamite's pickup sat a green car—the same model Chevy as Mike's, he realized, though it was a lot dirtier and more beat up. Had Mike just driven down...?

Dynamite sat out on the porch, leaning forward with his elbows on his knees, looking at a magazine.

Three steps closer through the long grass, and Eric saw it was a comic. As grass gave way to gravel before the porch steps, he saw the comic Dynamite read was one Eric had bought and left at the cabin—the gay, dirty ones Fred Hurter sold down in the store down at Dump Corners.

Dynamite looked up and cocked his head to the left. "Hey, there, son. Good to see you. When you gonna bring us some more of that potato salad, like you brought last month? That stuff was good."

"I'll make you some over here." Eric climbed up the porch. "You got a big pot in there somewhere? That's all I really need, to boil up the potatoes."

"I might hold you to that." Dynamite looked back down at the folded back pages. "Shit's inside—he got somebody in there with him. Just so it don't surprise you or nothin'."

"Oh," Eric said. He *was* surprised. *Would* it be Mike inside...?

"You can go on in," Dynamite said. "You ain't gonna bother 'em."

From the porch, Eric went into the kitchen, walked to the bedroom door, and stepped in. Across the front wall lay a wedge of late afternoon sun. On the bed, under the green sheet, two figures slept on their stomachs— the sheet down around the waist of the lighter—Shit—and up near the shoulders of the dark brown one.

Eric hadn't realized they were in bed. He'd assumed Dynamite had meant in the kitchen, talking—

Eric frowned and whispered, "Um...oh," and felt confused. Then the darker one put an arm out, over Shit's shoulder. And Eric felt more... confused.

On the pillow, Shit turned his head, blinking his green eyes. "Oh..." Then, as if remembering something, he pushed up on one arm. "Oh, man, *you're* here!"

"Um..." Eric said, surprised how fast his heart was beating. "Oh...hey, I'll get out..." Turning, he saw that Dynamite had come in and now stood in the doorway, legs apart, a forearm high on either jamb.

The dark fellow rolled over, frowned at Eric, then at Shit. "Who's he?"

"Oh, man..." Shit repeated.

Eric looked back at the bed, where, first Shit, then the other guy were pushing themselves to sit.

Behind Eric, Dynamite said, grinning amiably, "Shit, what the fuck is the matter with you?"

Shit said, "Huh…?"

Dynamite said, "Come on. You remember how I done, that time you come home a day early and walked in on me with that big Spanish feller's dick up my goddam asshole? Don't you?"

"Huh…?" Shit repeated. "Oh, wow. Yeah. I'm sorry—"

Eric wasn't sure if that was to him or to the other man in bed—who looked maybe ten years older than Shit.

The man frowned again, pulled his feet up, and hung his arms over the tents in the blanket his knees made. With a cautiously inquisitive intonation, the man asked, "Hey, is my bein' here a little awkward? You said your uncle wouldn't mind—"

Behind him, Eric heard Dynamite shift position in the doorway. "Go on, Shit," he said with repressed impatience. "You know what to do. Unless that ain't the way you feel about Eric—"

"Of course that's the way I feel!" He actually sounded angry. "I'm just wakin' up. That's all."

"Then you better hurry up and let him know," Dynamite said. "Or he gonna walk outa here and go home."

"Uh, yeah…Uh, Eric, this is Bull…Bubba? Bob—?"

—who drew a breath. "Bones. Bones Lubba—I told you my name down at the store. Course, I ain't too sure what yours is, neither…Morton?"

"Morgan," Dynamite said from the doorway behind them.

"Yeah," Shit said. "Bones. Eric here is my main squeeze. My number one man. Here—" Shit took the sheet and swung it off the both of them— "let 'im see your dick. Hey—Would you mind if Eric climbed on it, so he could fool around with you, too?"

Bones—who was a pretty good-looking man, Eric thought, and cut (like Eric)—shrugged. "I dunno. I guess…if he wants." He took a breath. Then he smiled and shrugged again. "Sure. Come on in. That'd be fine."

Shit said, "Yeah, come on—that'd be fun. Bones is a nice feller—you'll like 'im. He does a lot of the stuff you like."

"Naw," Eric said. "Naw, that's okay. I don't think so. Not now…" Again he glanced back.

Dynamite had moved to lean on one of the jambs, filling the doorway, so that Eric could not leave—though he wanted to, desperately.

"Oh," Shit said. "Well, in that case…" He swung his legs out of the bed, stood up, naked beside it. "I'm sorry—but I guess I'm gonna have to ask you to go, then, Bones. See, my number one guy done come back…I didn't know what time he was gonna be here. That's all. Hope you don't mind."

Bones looked a little surprised. "No. Sure. Sure, that's fine. Besides, I wanted to be outta here by three or three-thirty, anyway. And it's what—" He glanced at the three-footed clock on the table by the bed. "Damn—it's already five-to-four." He added, a little lamely, looking at Eric. "We wasn't even doin' nothin'. We was just sleepin'."

"We was fuckin', when we first got in," Shit explained. "Bones got a good asshole, too. You gonna have to try him, someday." Smiling, Shit stepped up to Eric and put his arms around him. Shit's body projected warmth like an electric coil. His odor was at once fiercely familiar and strange. Eric tried to pull away, but Shit just pulled him back. He gave Eric a big, long hug, pressing his face into Eric's neck. "Hey, I'm glad you come here—we was wonderin' what happened to you."

Bones was getting up out the far side of the bed, bending down to pull up the jeans he'd left there, working a foot into a shoe, picking up a plaid shirt and pulling it on. "Oh…Well, hey. Yeah, okay, I understand." Glancing at Eric, he seemed uncertain whether he should say anything more.

Arms still around Eric, Shit said without looking at Bones, "Hey, it was fun. But, like I said, Eric here's my number one. Maybe we'll run into each other some other time. Okay?" He glanced back at his recent bed partner. "Maybe we can do a thing, then, the three of us—or all four. But when Eric's in the mood. I don't like to do nothin' if *he* don't wanna."

"Oh," Bones repeated. "Yeah," Again he glanced at Eric. "I'll see you around." He buttoned one and then a second shirt button. Leaving the rest open, he started around the foot of the bed. "Hey, did I have my…oh, no. That's in the car."

"It was nice to meet you," Shit said.

"Yeah…" Eric remembered to say.

Dynamite stepped aside in the doorway as Bones edged out. "So long, fellas."

Moments later, the car motor revved outside.

From what moved back and forth between their touching bodies, naked and clothed, Eric found his discomfort dissipating.

"Damn, Shit," Dynamite said. "*That* sure took you long enough to get started on. You got to do that right away. If your main guy comes in here, like Eric done when you're grabbin' some other motherfucker's tale, you can't loll around lookin' stupid and sayin' 'Duh…' You want Eric to stay, don't you? You gotta handle that the right way from the get-go. You don't get a lot of chances to fuck that up."

Shit's hands moved over Eric's shirt, over the butt of Eric's jeans, the back of his neck and head. "Yeah. Yeah, but, well…I was half asleep. That's all—so I wasn't thinkin'. Hey, I'm sorry, Eric. But you surprised me a little, that's all. I'm glad you're here. God, you feel so good."

"I told you before," Dynamite said, "if you gonna fuck around, you got to be *ready* to be surprised like that—and remember what to do!"

"Yeah," Shit said. "Sure…" Smiling now, he looked at Eric. "You okay now?"

Looking back and forth between grinning Dynamite and—yeah—grinning Shit, Eric said, unsteadily, "I guess…yeah. I think so."

"We could fool around some—you keep your clothes on and I'll make love to you all nekid. We done it the other way around. Now we could do it *this* way." Shit's hand slid down Eric's stomach and under his pants. "You want Dynamite to strip down and add a little more skin to it all, to make it familiar and…friendly?"

Beside them, Eric saw Dynamite raise an eyebrow. "Um…do you think, son, you would feel completely abandoned and rejected," Dynamite said, "if I sat this one out and went outside and finished readin' your story book?" He raised the comic, rolled up in his big hand: the third issue of *Porky*, which had finally come into Hurter's at Dump Corners. "'Cause I'm almost halfway through it, and it's pretty good."

"Sure," Eric said. "That's okay."

Now Dynamite stepped aside for him.

"Hey, don't worry," Shit called. "I ain't gonna forget you're number one. Ever. You—and whatever you want—come first. You and him is the only ones who's *really* important. Really. I *ain't* gonna forget that." He grinned at his father. "For one thing, he wouldn't let me. For another, you *are!* I hope you know that, now. The rest is just somthin' to do. Come on back here and get another hug—or I'm gonna come after you."

*

Three weeks later, when Eric was over at Barbara's for dinner for the first time in three days (frozen dinners, which Mike would put up with for as many as two and three days in a row, were a wipeout with Barb: the first time he tried them in the microwave, it was an evening of six or seven stiff drinks and no food for her at all—which wasn't good for anyone. Today, four green and orange boxes had become a block of bubbled ice in the back of the freezer), Barbara asked her son, "Honey, are you growing a beard?"

"Yeah…" Eric shrugged. "I guess so." With his thumbs, he pushed loose the top from the plastic icebox dish: a dull click. "You want some tomato salad? It's got dill in it—and onions *and* cucumbers. And celery."

"That would be nice. I'd love some." She frowned at him. "You're gonna look like Jay MacAmon, there—if you keep it up."

"That would be good. But I don't think my beard's gonna be full enough. Jay's has got some curl in it. You know, on the census, his family always put white. But he says he thinks he's got to be part black. He says everybody down here is. Not just Shit—even Dynamite."

Barbara laughed, then frowned. "Jay's a sweetheart. But that's a little *too* much of the grizzly he-man look for me. Sometimes I wonder where you get these ideas—no, that's not what I mean. I know where you *get* them. I just wonder what you're thinking when you try to follow them through. Still," and she shook her head, "it's your face."

* * *

[26] THE PICKUP STOPPED beside Eric, who backed a step into roadside brush. Above the hood and over the cab, branches broke up the sun.

Bare shoulder out the driver's window, forearm along the shadowed door, Dynamite wore no shirt under his bibs today, either. "Your mom's okay with you spendin' a couple of more days with us, ain't she?"

"Her and Ron gone to visit his daughter in Valdosta," Eric said. "They gonna be away till Tuesday. Whyn't you take me over to the Opera today?"

"I could," Dynamite said, thoughtfully. "One reason is you still ain't—quite—eighteen, though." He moved his tongue around under his bristly cheek. "That's where Shit is now—maybe that's his birthday present to himself." It was the second week of May. "I was thinkin' of goin' over there, later." He chuckled. "If I didn't run into you."

"Come on," Eric said. "I'll be eighteen in six weeks—"

"Then you don't have to wait all that long," Dynamite said.

"Aw," Eric said, "that's forever!"

Eric edged forward, cut in front of the truck, and loped to the other side. He pulled open the door—the handle was loose, and you had to hold it right to get in on the first try—and climbed in. "I could be *part* of Shit's birthday present." In the last months, a spring had come loose under the seat that made a lopsided hump Eric had grown used to sitting on.

"Well…" Dynamite leaned forward. "Hammond'd probably like it if you turned up, I mean a few weeks early…" The truck bounced a couple of times. Then leaf light slid up the windshield's dust, and over its lapped semi-circles smeared by the wipers. "The more young stuff's runnin' around in the theater, the better they do. I figure takin' you over there's part of my civic duty."

Eric said, "You took Shit there the first time when he was fifteen. Both

of you told me guys under eighteen are always hangin' around in there—
you said Hammond's okay with it, if they behave themselves."

"I took Shit there 'cause it was easier to keep an eye on 'im if he was
in the same place I was. And, yeah, I thought it was better for kids to be
lookin' at pitchurs of people fuckin' each other than it was to have 'em
watchin' pitchurs about people killin' each other. Everybody *says* that—but
not a lot actually have to do it. I mean, too, all he'd done was fuck with
other guys around the Dump—so I thought at least he ought to see *some*
men and women with each other, even if it was just in the dirty pitchur
show. Lotta good *that* did." Dynamite snorted. "He likes to watch pretty
much anybody fuckin' anybody. But doin' it he's still more comfortable
with guys, he says." Dynamite turned onto a larger road, and shrugged.
"Which goes to show you."

"How come he's already over there? I mean, why didn't he go with
you...?"

"Part of his present. One of the guys in his 'fan club'—Larry, I think it
was—called up yesterday and told 'im they was all comin' in this morning
after work. He wanted to go over there and meet them and say hello."

Shit had bragged to Eric about his 'fan club': half a dozen workers
on the graveyard shift at the twenty-four hour canning factory north of
Hemmings. When they got off at two-thirty A.M., now and then they'd all
drive over to Runcible for the Opera; Shit had been messing with them,
well...since before *he* was eighteen. Shit had even spent the occasional
weekend at a couple of their houses. But, he'd told Eric, he preferred
tricking with them in the theater. Besides (he said), three of 'em was neat
freaks, and he was always afraid he was going to break something.

"I run 'im over to the theater about three o'clock this mornin',"
Dynamite explained. (The Opera ran twenty-four/seven.) "Then I went
back to the Dump—figured I'd catch a couple of hours sleep and go over
again at a *decent* time. Only here you is, messin' things up." He grinned at
Eric, to let him know that was a joke—mostly.

"If you took me in there," Eric said, "even if Barb found out, I don't
think it would bother her."

Dynamite chuckled, "I could always tell her I was tryin' to turn you
straight—'cause they play the straight movies."

Eric laughed. "Ron would like that."

"But Ron done lived down here long enough to know what goes on
in the Opera House—no matter *how* straight the movies is." Dynamite
chuckled again. "I don't think he'd believe it."

"I already told Barb me and Shit was messin' around. About every two
weeks, she asks me, you know, in that special voice, how the two of us is

doin', me and Shit. I tell her we're doin' fine."

"Are you?" Dynamite's brows pulled together.

Eric nodded. "Yeah."

"Good." Dynamite turned onto a bigger road, this one paved. "She ever say anything about Shit and me—or me and you?"

Eric said, "I don't think she knows."

"She's the only person in Diamond Harbor what don't, then." Dynamite leaned down and looked up (to see under the glare) at some sign or other. "Or at least suspects." He sat back and speeded up some.

"I mean, probably she's heard," Eric said. "But she don't believe it, 'cause she likes you."

"Well," Dynamite said. "I guess that's somethin'."

"Look—you said you was goin' to the Opera. Come on. Get me in there. Today. I'll take responsibility for it. If Barb finds out, I'll say I got Shit to sneak me in. It'll all be on me—not you. In six weeks, I could go in anyway."

"The responsibility's mine, no matter what *you* say." Then, after silent seconds, Dynamite said, "But it's true. That's how I would've raised you if you'd been mine to raise. It's important. You gotta learn how to handle that stuff."

"You took me and Shit to Turpens," Eric pressed him, "half a dozen times in the last three or four months—"

"Hey, two of them times you went with Jay and Mex. Shit and me just run into you there and gave you a lift back home 'cause they wanted to go on to Hemmings—"

"The point is," Eric said, "I never got in no trouble for goin' *there*."

"Turpens?" Dynamite asked. "You go to Turpens? Hell, I never been in that place. I wouldn't think you'd been in there, either. I heard all sorts of nasty stories about what goes on in there. Naw, I wouldn't go in there. And neither would you—"

"Yeah, yeah," Eric said. "I know—I ain't ever been there either...I guess."

"But the *real* point is," Dynamite said, "Turpens has a fuckin' *public* john, and anyone can walk in and use it. Nobody's got to be sneakin' you in the back way, like at the Opera." Indeed, the Opera's seven-dollar admission was a hardship on many of its patrons, and Hammond and Dusty, who ran it, Eric knew, had a sliding scale—the only thing to call it—with many of their patrons, depending on their sexual generosity. They were pretty autocratic about it, actually, which kept arguments down.

"Come on," Eric said. "I'm askin' you, outright. Get me in there. I wanna fuck around with Shit…and you, too. And see what's goin' on—"

"Nigger," Dynamite said, "shut the fuck up. Let's just see what happens, okay?" He looked over at Eric, perfectly seriously. Taking one hand from the top of the wheel, he dropped it on Eric's leg and pushed it over into his crotch. "Callin' you a nigger—that still give you a hard-on, son?"

"Un-huh." Eric nodded.

"Good," Dynamite said.

Eric said, "You gonna get some beer and take it in with you?"

"You want me to?"

"Yup." Eric felt between Dynamite's legs. "'Cause you piss more."

"Okay. I'll pick up a six pack." Slanting along his thigh, Dynamite's cock was steel hard. "We'll make a day of it. You gonna come with me down to the front row, squat between my knees, sit on the floor there, while I open my pants up, push 'em down, and you can stick a few fingers as far as you can up my asshole. Then you gonna suck on your dad's dick for a *real* long time, while I drink my beer and watch the movie…?"

"Yeah," Eric said. "Sure, that's fine…Dad."

"You're a real nasty nigger, son. A Georgia white man like me would be proud to have a nasty nigger boy like you for a kid, suckin' on his fuckin' dick." He glanced at Eric, then looked back at the dusty glass. "You like that?"

Again, Eric nodded.

"Hey, you know, there's another nigger kid—a *good* friend of mine. Real good friend. I known him all his life. I think you've known 'im too for a year or so, now. I told you, he's already at the Opera, fuckin' his brains out with some friends. But he probably gonna come by and sit with us. That nigger's as nasty as you, son. He likes to play with my balls and watch stuff like that and jerk off while he's watchin' it. Maybe when he gets there, I'll stand up and take a piss in your mouth, while he's sittin' there and ticklin' my nuts. You gonna let me stand there and piss in your mouth like that, son? He really loves to watch that—he'll jerk off all over you if I do that. And it was *his* birthday already this month."

"Sure, Dad," Eric said. "I know. Yeah." Under his own hand, Eric could feel Dynamite's heart beating in his hard dick. Dynamite's leg moved on the clutch. "I'd really like it if Shit did that, too, Dad."

"Shit loves to see that." Dynamite nodded. "Well, son, I suppose I can understand it. We're just lucky I got a good friend like that goddam nasty nigger kid, Shit—right?"

"Un-huh," Eric said. "And I wouldn't be embarrassed, 'cause I like that stuff."

"I guess we all three do," Dynamite said. "Now, when he comes, he's probably gonna stick his dick up my butthole and look down at me pissin' in your mouth." Dynamite frowned. "But then, you already know how he likes to watch me do that to a little nigger like you. You ain't gonna take your fingers out my ass, just 'cause he sticks his dick up it, are you?"

"Un-un," Eric grinned. "Naw, Dad. I ain't. I like feelin' his dick up there, rubbing up against my fingers. And you got a big butthole. I like fuckin' it as much as he does, almost."

"I know you do." Dynamite laughed again. "The more stuff I got shoved up there, the easier it is for me to piss."

Nodding, Eric started to chuckle. "You know, Dad, you're gonna make yourself shoot in your pants—or me, one—before we even get there, you keep talkin' like this."

"So?" Dynamite shrugged. "If I do, you can nose on in there and lick it clean for me." He took a long, deep breath. "Then you'll just have to suck a little longer in the Opera, till I work up a second load. But right now, why don't you hold my dick—like you're doin'—and I'll hold yours—like I'm doin'…And *both* of us can shut the fuck up till we get in there and find Shit." Dynamite laughed and kept driving with his left hand on the wheel.

Soon they crossed the wooden bridge covering the rocky stream marking the edge of Runcible Township.

*

New Runcible was three stretches of tourist cabins with a canal through two of them, running in from the sea. Dynamite and Eric drove by some smaller houses through a city center. Many of the places had been servants' quarters or out buildings to bigger houses. They had survived Sherman's invasion, while other townships forty miles to the north had not—so went the lore—to become gift shops, clothing stores, eating places, and all of them far enough from the Hemmings Mall to keep the area from being as popular as half a dozen places north and south of it (Jay had once explained), at least in the summer (Mex had added, with his heavy, rough fingers). Some of the bigger houses had gone to ruin and fallen down or been pulled down. Four six-story office buildings had been built in the early-eighties, around a place called Johnston Square. Two were still half empty. Ron had his business in one of the full ones—and lived in the ground floor of a two-family house three streets away, downstairs from a Mrs. Emory, a black woman as old as Miss Louise, who survived frugally and whose source of income, above and beyond social security, was a mystery. (*Probably she's just another friend of Bob Kyle's*, Dynamite had speculated, when Eric asked him about it.) Apparently, Barbara made her uncomfortable.

(Well, Ron had said, *the old bat's just gonna have to get used to havin' a pretty woman livin' downstairs from her.* Barbara had not actually moved in. But she spent a lot of time there. *You're about as nice and helpful to her as you can be, honey. I don't know what else we could do.*

(Barbara, who wasn't happy not being liked, had sighed.)

Old Runcible was, on the other hand, practically a graveyard—a wide, abandoned Main Street and a derelict cross street (Clarringdon Road)—with a number of falling apart warehouses around its dock end. A resurgence of fishing in the nineteen seventies had not worked, though it had left a few bars, a few boarded-up buildings (a tackle shop, a boat shop, both with nothing behind their glass windows today), and, across from what had once been a fancy restaurant as late as 1971, the Hanging Gardens (also boarded up), and the Opera House.

Regularly hippies and Mexicans and coastal drifters squatted on this floor or that of one condemned loft building or another. Still functioning were:

Two head shops...

Tank and Cassandra's tattoo parlor, Cave et Aude...

(Beneath, in English, it said "Look Out and Listen Up!" which, only recently, Eric had learned was a translation.)

The clinic...

A coffee shop that, at least this month, was shut again, though, along with the rest, it had been generously subsidized by the Chamber of Commerce, intent on bringing *some* life to the moribund neighborhood.

Three blocks up from the water, stood a four-story rectangular wedding cake, with its molding, its corner statuary, and its ornate marquee: The Runcible Opera House.

A home to real operas both before and after the Civil War, then a vaudeville palace through the Great War, and eventually a film theater, in the seventies, it had actually made modest monies by showing film classics, which, because Georgia was a driving state, people would actually come a hundred, a hundred-fifty miles to see. When, in the seventies, the classics finally changed over into hardcore porn, first on the weekends, and by the end of the eighties, all through the week—it was still doing enough business to keep going.

In the mid-nineties, when the country took its radical swerve into sexual conservatism, under the excuse of the AIDS epidemic, some gay voices in the Kyle-dominated Chamber of Commerce declared the site historic, and drenched what southern gay press there was with articles on the sort of activities that went on there, claiming it was necessary to preserve them! Finally—after closing for (only!) eighteen months—it reopened as an historic site...still showing straight porn. Along with social experiments such as the Dump (and Turpens), running twenty-four hours a day, the Runcible Opera thrived.

As was chuckled over, inside and outside the Dump, it was astonishing what a few million dollars could do—six was the sum of Robert Kyle's investment in the area—fifty thousand there, a hundred-fifty thousand there—wrote one Chamber of Commerce Newsletter, reprinted in gay bar throw-aways all over Tennessee, Alabama, Mississippi, Florida and Georgia (with fuller articles in the gay press back when Eric was nine: so he'd never seen them)—in a county where no one was making enough money to care. Tourism—and Kyle's money, as well as educational programs—had undermined much of the religious fanaticism once endemic to the area.

*

Dynamite stopped the pickup beside the theater building's rear wall—red brick—with a black metal ladder slanting toward a covered metal porch—also painted black—jutting from the second floor.

"That's the back door—" a street level fire exit, pretty firmly closed— "You may have to wait five, ten minutes. Maybe fifteen. But it shouldn't be no longer. Someone'll let you in. If some other guys come by, just...well, wait around with 'em. They'll be good fellas. Probably. They're all here for the same thing." He pulled the paper sack with the beer closer to his hip. "Go on, now. If I'm not the one to open it, once you get in, like I said, you can find me in the front row in the orchestra—that's the ground floor, my regular stompin' grounds."

"Okay," Eric opened the cab and jumped down. In the last months they'd been over how this worked—how Dynamite had been getting Shit in the place before he was of age, for, well, sometimes it was six years and sometimes it was ten—so many times, Eric felt like he'd done it already.

The pavement was broken. Beyond the alley's end he could see the ocean behind some seaward shacks, some pilings.

Fifteen feet away, along the upper cornice of the deserted building letters spelled out "Western Union." It too was abandoned.

Dynamite's pickup growled backwards, pulled out of the alley, and disappeared.

Eric looked at the solid door—the theater's emergency exit. Five minutes later, he was remembering a story Shit had told about once having stood here for an hour and forty minutes, in a drizzle, because whoever had brought him over—Mex, Black Bull, Red, somebody when he was fifteen or sixteen—had gone inside, sat down, and gone to sleep without letting him in...

A thrash and clunk of metal bolts against metal came from inside.

Then one of the double portals swung in, and an older man with a fringe of hair around a bald head leaned out. He wore a short-sleeved shirt, glasses, and jeans. "Hello, young feller," he said. "So, you want to spend a day here at the Opera. That right?"

Eric nodded. "Yes, sir."

Pushing the door open further, the old fellow looked Eric up and down. "Okay."

As light fell into the dark space, Eric was glad to see, a step behind the man's shoulder, Dynamite, smiling.

"Yeah, you should be okay," the old man reiterated. "I guess your friend Dynamite has done told you here what you can expect—and what we expect of you."

"Yes, sir," Eric repeated.

"Now, we keep a friendly place. People are *real* friendly here—that's how we like it. I don't mean you got to say yes to everybody who grabs after your nuts." The man nodded down toward Eric's crotch. "But I don't wanna hear no reports that you're barkin' at our customers and tellin' them to get the get the fuck outta your face, either. Understand what I'm sayin'?"

"Yes, sir," Eric said for the third time.

"Good. You can always say no if you want to—but you say it polite. And since you ain't payin' to get in, I expect you to say 'Yes' a few more times than you might ordinarily—and to some guys you might not ordinarily say 'Yes' to. See, it ain't *all* about you—understand? It's about everybody havin' a little fun." (Now Dynamite moved up beside him.) "I'm Mr. Hammond. I run this place, and what I say goes. You got a problem, you come to me. Or Dusty. You'll see him around, sweepin' up. But just remember, if somebody has a problem with *you*, they're gonna come to *me*. And if I have to put you out, I'll do it in a minute." Now he looked back at Dynamite—and nodded. "He's a nice lookin' kid. Strong, too—I hope that's from workin' out—not fightin'."

"No, sir," Eric said, surprised.

"Good. I hope it goes okay. Hey—" Hammond frowned at Eric. "You got an eleven inch dick?"

Eric swallowed. "No, sir." He swallowed again.

"Well, remember," Mr. Hammond said, "we got some in here who do—but there ain't *nobody* who's got so much we won't kick 'em out if they make a nuisance of themselves, whether they got three or thirteen. Understand?"

Eric recovered. "I got seven—but I know what to do with it." It hung in the air like a punchline fallen at the wrong place, to the wrong joke.

Hammond took in a long breath—and Eric realized that Hammond had his speech and wasn't interested in comebacks, snappy or not. "I don't wanna hear about you askin' nobody for money, either. If somebody tells me that's what you're doin'—and they *will* tell me—I'm gonna ask *you* for some. I'm gonna get it, too, or get it outta your hide. Hear me?"

This time Eric only nodded.

"This is a place where people come to have fun. And you can have as much fun as you want—from the moment you come in here, you can whip that sucker out and beat on it till the damned thing falls off, for all I care. You can fuck, you can suck, anyway till Sunday. There's a basket of condoms down in the lounge, outside the men's room door—and upstairs in the back of Nigger Heaven—that's the top balcony. Now, we don't get a *lot* of ladies in here. But when we do, show a little respect in how you carry yourself. You can sit with a seat between you and them and jerk off all you want, especially if she's makin' out with a boyfriend—that's what usually happens. This *is* a public place. So as long as you got a seat between you, nobody can complain, unless you're makin' noise. But don't let me hear you been pawin' and pettin' at somebody who don't wanna be pawed and petted at, male *or* female. That's the rule. This is a big place. There're always plenty of seats. So if somebody moves away from you, say, three times, don't go runnin' after 'em for a fourth. And that's whether you start out with a seat between you or not. Got it?"

Dynamite said, "He understands all that, Hammond. We told him all about this place. He ain't stupid."

Hammond lingered at the door. "You know, me and Dusty had to kick a kid outta here a couple of days back." He was speaking to Dynamite. "Nice kid—white kid, too. Big strong, good lookin'—probably wasn't more than half a dozen years older'n this one here. Had a good eight-inch dick on him, too. Local boy—the kind I like to help out. Only I think he'd got in trouble in his family, and they didn't want him around no more. So we let 'im live here at the theater for three, three-and-a-half weeks, doin' his push ups and chin ups in the back balcony every mornin', sleepin' on some blankets down in the john. After the third day, I don't think he *had* a shirt no more. At least I never seen it on him in here. And everybody likes to see a strong young feller like that show a little skin. He had his dick outside his jeans more than in, and he wasn't too particular about who came up and gave it a tug or a suck—only for anything too much more complicated than that, truth was, he was only interested in the black guys. Now there ain't nothin' wrong with havin' a preference. Everybody does."

"Didn't you tell me once the ones you make sleep down in the john—" Eric could hear the smile in Dynamite's voice—"is the drunks what pee all over themselves every night?"

"I didn't say he *wasn't* a drunk. But if you told 'im somethin', he was always obligin' about it. Unless he was takin' a quick run down to the bathroom, though—or comin' down at night to catch a few winks—you didn't see him anywhere but the top two balconies." Hammond turned to Eric. "Probably Dynamite done told you, the higher up you go in the Opera, the blacker our clientele tends to be. So up there is where the kid stayed pretty much. And 'cause he was a good lookin' and friendly enough, he could always find somebody to go out and spring for some pizza or a hamburger or a sandwich to bring back into the theater for 'im. He was even kind of a health food nut, and had a couple of his regulars bringin' 'im apples and fruit and salads and things. At the same time, yeah, he was goin' through two, three, even four six-packs a day…which is why we put 'im down in the bathroom at night. The tile's easier to hose off. And with a lot of our guys, you know, that's par for the course. Danny Turpens—born and bred around here, so you could have even run into him."

"The *beer* sounds like it's par for a goddam Turpens." Dynamite grunted. "One of them Turpenses? Hammond, you know they're bad news. Why's it a surprise you had to get rid of him?"

"I don't know. But it was—a surprise, I mean. He was such a nice, strong, good lookin' friendly fella, polite and helpful, if you asked him to do somethin', or move his stuff. Yes, it surprised me—'course he *had* been in jail."

"You are a fuckin' romantic asshole, Hammond." Dynamite laughed. "A drunk Turpens jailbird—and *you're* surprised he was trouble?"

Eric said, "Turpens? Does that have anything to do with the truck stop?"

"Maybe fifty years ago it did," Dynamite said. "But all them Turpens fellas today is too drunk, or too retarded, or just too ornery and restless to hold onto a business and keep it goin'."

"Over the years," Hammond said, "we had three or four of his cousins— and maybe some Wilsons—in here who just wanted to hustle a ten or a twenty out of the older guys. And, yes, we had to eject 'em. But that didn't seem to be what he was into. At least nobody reported it."

Eric asked, "What did he do that you had to put him out?"

"Well, pretty soon, people started comin' to me with these funny stories. After his second king-sized six pack, up there in Nigger Heaven, he'd start rilin' up the black fellas, tellin' 'em since they were only animals anyway, why didn't they get together and do somethin' that'll…well, I don't know *what* he told 'em the reason was. But he wanted a gang of 'em to hang out and catch one of the white guys who comes in regular with a prostitute, grab her, and rape her ass right there in the theater. Or beat up this man or rob that one—this is the white people, see, he wants the black guys—along with him—to savage. Now you know, all our boys, black or white, are pretty laid back. That kind of thing don't go on here. This is a public place and a historic institution with a tradition to maintain. He wanted to catch one white boy and have all the niggers stand around and drown 'im in a washtub full of piss. You're sittin up in the balcony with a good-lookin' stud, jerkin' each other off, doin a little suckin' and asshole fingerin', and he starts tellin' you that you ain't really a human being, you're just some kind of animal, and so, 'cause you can't have no morals or ethics, you should fuck up somebody else with 'im or beat 'em up or rip 'em off and that's okay. Half of them I guess thought he was a crazy drunk and that it was just the beer talkin' funny. The other half told 'im to shut up and leave 'em alone. But he'd start in again, how, 'cause they just animals, it don't really matter what the fuck they do. Animals don't have no ethics or morals, and neither should they, 'cause they're niggers. The ones he's havin' sex with maybe took it in stride, most of 'em—laughed it off, I guess. People'll put up with a lot for some good nookie or some good dick, and I gather he was okay in both departments. But some of the others was getting' tired of it. He told one black feller up there that, though he would do it, he didn't really like to have sex with real human beings—other white guys. He only liked doin' it with sheep, goats, dogs, pigs, cows, and niggers."

"Actually, that don't sound too different from me when I was this one's age—till I started hangin' out with Jay as well as Kyle—and a Haskell ain't even close to a Turpens." Dynamite chuckled. "But I didn't go around gettin' in no fights over it."

"And he's tellin' 'em it don't matter, 'cause they ain't real human bein's anyway—well, some of our black customers didn't take to that. They told me about it, too. Well, after the fifth fight started up there in Nigger Heaven, with him in the middle of it, I was afraid somebody was gonna throw 'im over the damned balcony rail. Even Al—he gets a lot of that kinda stuff (he broke up three of the fights)—lost patience with 'im and said he didn't care what the fuck happened to him no more. So, mostly for his own sake, as well as some peace and quiet, Dusty hauled 'im front and center and I told him to take his damned eight inch pecker and get the fuck out." Hammond turned at a bend in the hall. "And he's still all smiles and 'Shucks…' and 'Oh, I'm sorry,' and grinning—still didn't have no shirt either, and his fly was gapin' (I think he musta busted it) and grinnin' at us like he's all embarrassed…and left. I think he really liked the place. Hell, I kinda liked *him*. But you can't have people startin' fights in a public place."

"Come on," Dynamite said. "You're good to be shut of 'im—a fuckin'

Turpens. Stop jawin', and let us in, now—"

"Yeah, well…" Hammond looked up. "I suppose so."

"I told you. Eric knows all about what goes on here."

Hammond stepped back into the doorway. "But it ain't gonna hurt him to hear it again, all at a shot. Now come on in, boy."

Eric stepped in, and Dynamite, smiling, fell in beside him.

Above them, small orange lights made a long row; Eric's eyes had only started adjusting—

Something brushed his pants, then settled between his legs—it made Eric jump a little, but he smiled, looking at Dynamite (one of whose hands was in his overall pocket, and one arm was hooked around the bag with his beer), then at Hammond.

Hammond had groped Eric—and now looked over at him. "There— that's *just* the smile I want on your face when anybody goes reachin' for your dick. That don't matter if they're seventeen years old or seventy- seven, black *or* white." The hand patted Eric's groin and moved away. "Like I said, I ain't tellin' you that you gotta say 'Yes' to everybody who comes on to you. But you do have to smile and say your 'No's' politely. And maybe even think twice before you say 'em, since you ain't payin' nothin' to be in here."

"Yes, sir," Eric said. "I understand."

*

That night, Eric had a late conversation in the bedroom of the cabin in the Dump. Outside the windows the sky held enough blue for it to be eight- thirty or nine. Dynamite snored. Eric asked, "Hey, Shit?"

Shit turned toward him and—almost automatically—put an arm around him. "What?"

"Suppose you're at the Opera, like I was today, and somebody real old, like fifty-five, sixty, comes onto you. How do…*you* tell 'em to go away?"

"Huh?" Shit pulled himself closer. (From earlier, a wet spot on the sheet cooled Eric's knee.) "What you wanna tell 'em to go away for? They got guys in there what're seventy, eighty—probably ninety, for all I know. I like the old fellows. They hardly got no teeth so they can really give you a *good* suck."

"You…do?"

"Yeah." (Eric realized Shit's dick was rising against his belly.) "Besides, they make me feel like a little kid again—like I'm nine or ten years old. I guess that's 'cause back then, *everybody* looked to me like they was a hun'erd years old. Even guys I know now was just thirty or thirty-five—I used to think suckin' dick was what old guys was for. When I go to the Opera, hell, I still do. And they're interestin' to talk to, sometimes." Shit pushed his face into Eric's neck. "But I still like a few young scumsuckers, like you. Hey—" and he pulled his face away—"before we get up tomorrow, suck off my dad. I bet he still got a can of that beer in 'im somewhere he needs to get rid of. I know I got some pop in here."

"What are you tryin' to do? Turn me into Mex?"

Holding Eric, Shit shrugged. "Sure—if that's who you wanna be."

From the other side of the bed, Dynamite stopped snoring enough to mumble, "That's too high for Shit. He don't go up in them balconies, especially the top one. He gets his vertigo and stays away from that. He's stays downstairs in the lounge restroom. Come on—shut up and go to sleep."

Within the blackness of his own closed eyes, Eric remembered how, as he'd adjusted to the Opera's obscurity, the theater's dark had begun to pull back...and back...and back...The space was...well, like a fuckin' cavern! He'd been standing in a side aisle. Acres of seats stretched away. You could look up and see the balcony rails, the first, the second, and the top one. And like a hundred feet off, on the screen, two naked women and a naked man were doin' their thing with each other. He hadn't really realized it would be straight porn. Though, it turned out to be a lot more interestin' than any gay stuff he'd seen. Soon they were showing the coverage of some porn convention that must have been in Europe, because everyone spoke Italian, and, in some huge hall, a man was fucking a woman on a desk in odd positions while about a hundred photographers, mostly men but some women, were crowded around, taking pictures, sometimes just inches away.

At first Eric hadn't thought there was any audience at all in the theater—then he'd realized he could see some heads...maybe twelve of them, scattered along that row, nine along another, six or seven guys sitting together...probably there were more than a hundred people! But the space—just the orchestra—was built to hold ten times that. And when he'd looked down at the seat beside him, he saw this stocky black guy right in the aisle seat, who looked up at him and said, *Hey...How you doin'? Remember me?* Then the guy had looked down into the darkness of his own lap. *Freddy—stop suckin' my peter long enough for me to introduce you to a friend.* It was the black driver Eric had sucked off back at Turpens, when he'd met Shit and Dynamite the day he'd first come to the Harbor. The guy said, *Hey—I was* wonderin' *if I was gonna run into you again!*

Then a head lifted from the darkness of the driver's lap—black haired, sharp featured, probably Latino. *Hello...!*

Yeah, the driver said. *This white kid here sucks almost as good as you do,*

Freddy. Grinning, he'd nodded. *This is my friend Freddy.*

Fred had reached up. Eric had reached down. They'd shaken hands in front of the guy. Eric said his name...

Fred said, *Yeah,* then dropped his face back into the driver's lap.

In the dark, Eric blinked. "Hey...?" he whispered. "Shit are you still awake? While I was at the theater, I saw that guy who we—"

"Goddam," Dynamite said, loudly, from his side of the bed. "Tell 'im in the fuckin' mornin', will you? Now, go to *sleep*...!"

Shit chuckled. And squeezed Eric.

And they slept.

* * *

[27] ERIC FIRST SAW
THE KYLE FOUNDATION
NEWSLETTER FOR
THE DUMP

topping a stack of papers fourteen inches thick, bound with brown twine that creased the F, went between the T and the E, lay to the right of the P, and continued across a lush photo of pine trees and the bluff slope below heaping cumulus. The stack sat askew on the grass slope next to the gravel road.

Eric and Shit were walking through the Dump.

Eric assumed the bound papers were for the Foltz Carting Company that picked up the recyclables—or perhaps had even been inadvertently left behind.

Still later, in Dump Corners, when they went into the lumber, magazines, and houseware section of Fred Hurter's Steel, Seed, and Lumber, beside the cash register was a stack of the things. Someone just ahead of them took one—apparently they were free. Eric thought about taking one and didn't. But a day later, when they were in the post office, among the fliers and adverts in Dynamite's box was a copy.

"Hey, lemme see that," Eric said.

Dynamite handed it to him, before dropping the rest in the square trash container beside the gray table with all the little shelves below it for custom forms and certification forms and express letter forms and the dozen others.

In the pickup, wedged between Shit and Dynamite, Eric paged through the magazine, to find himself in an article on the school system and class visits to emphysema wards and lung cancer wards to meet amputation victims—fingerless, toeless, legless, handless—with nicotine allergies only recently diagnosed, congestive heart failure wards, and how effective this had been in creating a generation all but non-smoking from the working class on up in Runcible County—

"What you readin' that for?" Shit asked, as Dynamite drove. "That ain't no comic."

So Eric closed it. "Shit, when you were in school, did you take class trips to the hospital?"

"Yeah. I didn't learn much in the classes. But I sure learned how them poisons like alcohol and nicotine could kill you—'cause we met a lot of people they was already killin'."

Dynamite chuckled. "Yeah, that was something Kyle was really interested in—makin' sure workin' people knew how rich people didn't give a shit about sellin' 'em stuff that was gonna wipe 'em out. I drink my six-pack over the weekend, then I stop. He sure got *me* convinced of it."

In the pickup, while sea breeze tumbled through the window, Dynamite said, "I don't know why you carryin' that one with you. You can find them things all over the Dump."

Eric held up the folded magazine. "Well, I got this one already…"

Dynamite chuckled and changed gear. "You keep readin' that thing, we'll have you goin' to town meetin's for us."

"Good," Shit said, looking out at the passing shore. "Maybe that means you can let up on my ass about goin'."

Later that afternoon, Eric settled on the steps to read more.

Eventually, Shit came out and asked, "Can I sit here beside you and put my arm around you while you read, and just like…sit up against you?"

Eric blinked up at him. "Sure."

So Shit did.

Like a web whose strands reached—glittering—over the landscape, the Robert Kyle Foundation held almost everything in the county together.

With the Foundation's support, the high schools taught evolution, women's studies, black studies, and courses in animal (and human) homosexuality.

The Robert Kyle Foundation, which had built the Dump and currently controlled the county Chamber of Commerce, with its credit union and its pension plan and its broad range of subsidized public services, was the most influential institution in the area and had been for more than a decade and a half.

Those who protested were told they could move. Many had, while a fair number of others, concerned with their children's health and education, whatever their feelings about the Dump, had moved to the area.

Eric had starting learning much of this from a photograph of a bronze plaque fixed on the red bricks of the Social Service Building at Dump Corners:

This is the original office of
The Robert Kyle Foundation
that first opened its doors on April 25, 1984,
the week of the announcement of the discovery of
the HTLV-III virus (HIV),
an institution dedicated to the betterment of the lives
of black gay men and of those of all races and creeds
connected to them by elective and non-elective affinities.

Eric had read the plaque out to Shit, and as they'd walked back home in the August sun, Shit had said, "Hey, I never knowed that. That's 'cause I can't read. But I remember them school trips, though."

"You want me to read this to you?" Eric asked.

"Naw," Shit said. "'Cause I'll just get bored. I don't know what them words mean—and I don't wanna know, either. It's better me sittin' here and maybe imaginin' what you're readin' about. That's more interestin'."

When Eric finished the article, he asked Shit, "So what you imaginin' about?"

Shit chuckled. "How my daddy and that rich nigger, Kyle, used to suck each other's dicks and fuck each other's assholes every chance they got—at least that's what he told me. He even lived with him for a while, out on Gilead, once Kyle's parents died. I mean where Jay lives now. That was before Jay went out there. But Kyle had to travel around a bit, and my daddy just wanted to stay down here and take care of me, I guess. So they finally split up. They're still friends, though—I think."

Eric looked down to see another article under the banner type:

BLACK STUDIES, WOMEN'S STUDIES, GAY STUDIES,
AND EVOLUTION TAUGHT IN THREE RUNCIBLE KYLE
FOUNDATION FUNDED HIGH SCHOOLS...

Eric read the classes over to Shit. Then he looked up.

A big green Foltz recycling truck rolled down on the road.

"Now, them classes actually sounds kinda interestin'. Maybe I should'a given a try to that high school thing..."

"Why?" Shit asked.

"I don't know. Just because..."

"Ain't that thing supposed to be so you can get a better job?"

"Well, yeah."

"So what kind of job you gonna do where you got to know about niggers and women and faggots—I mean what about 'em can't you learn from nosin' around on one most nights like you do me? Or walkin' around through the rigs in the evening out back of Turpens when the horny guys leave their doors open or hangin' out in the damned back lot? Besides, your mama's a woman, and you know pretty much all about her."

"Well, I—"

"I mean, is there some special job you gonna get 'cause you know all that shit? Somebody's gonna pay you more money—?"

"Well, you know, *maybe*," Eric said, "knowin' how other people got along in the past and what they were able to do might help you figure out how you wanna do things now. I mean, I bet Robert Kyle had to know a lot of that stuff, just to set up—"

A clatter of claws clicked on the steps.

They looked down as Uncle Tom bounded up, to flop a paw on the open newsletter and lick at Eric's mouth.

Shit released Eric's shoulder, reached around, grabbed the dog's head, and pulled him to the side. "Hey, come on, dog. Cut it out, Tom. You wanna kiss on somebody? Come over here and kiss on me. Eric's readin' now. He's learnin' stuff. He ain't a dumb dog like you and me."

Down on the road, two more of the recycling trucks grumbled by.

* * *

[28] THE VERY FIRST time Eric had asked Shit had been only weeks after they'd met. Shit's answer had been flat and sure—so flat and so sure, Eric wondered about it: "What do I think about little kids havin' sex with older guys? Hell, I been havin' sex with niggers and white men around here—and even some of the summer tourists—since *I* was a kid! I mean with grown-ups. I wasn't even interested in havin' sex with people *near* my own age until way later. Hell, my dad and a dozen damned niggers been suckin' my dick since I was a baby. It didn't do me no harm. None of 'em never hurt me nor did it when I didn't want 'em to. I liked it then; I like it now. You can suck it right here if you want. That always feels good to me."

When Eric had lived in the Harbor through his first tourist season (if you could call the week or two-week vacations of the sixty or seventy people who materialized over July and August a "season") even Eric had realized that, with his ruined nails bitten three quarters off his fingers and his missing teeth and his nose-picking and his on-going affair with his dad (with his nails in the same shape) and a third of the men in the Dump and out of it—not to mention his terror of heights—illiterate Shit was not most folks' ideal young man.

The summer people socialized only with each other, were polite enough to the "townies," but somehow assumed you were always free and willing to work for them.

Still, nobody knew the beaches and bluffs and backwoods, the escarpments, rocks, and gullies over Gilead and along the mainland coast better than Shit. Nobody was more generous in wanting to share all—from his body to his time to his knowledge—with Eric. And no one had ever shared Eric's own "perversion," much less shared it with such enthusiasm. No one had ever been so generous with urine and affection, semen and cheese, with or without sex. The result was that Eric had discovered a great craving for it, which, from Shit—and, soon, much the same, from Dynamite—he could fill.

Up the beach, a grotto of rock and old logs and long grasses gouged into the mainland's sloped flank. A rill of sea foamed in and out over its bottom. Shit and Eric often went there to talk, to masturbate themselves and each other from a frenzy into dozing (and Shit, sometimes, actually drooling: Eric was astonished) idiocy—Shit said the drooling had something to do with his teeth—to fuck, or even sometimes, singly, to be alone. Both enjoyed it because, often, when one had been there for ten or twenty minutes, the other might come, look in, and join.

Though Dynamite knew of it, it was not where he chose to be with them, unless he was looking for them because of some change Randal had decreed in the work schedule.

A number of conversations occurred there over the first winter, which began when Eric gave voice to something he's been pondering.

Eric started the first one. "Shit, do you really like your name?"

"Huh? Sure." Stretched on his back, one arm up under his head, Shit said, "I picked it myself—back when I was maybe nine, ten. When I stopped goin' to school, anyway—fuck, that school was *really* borin'. I didn't like nobody there and nobody liked me. It was more fun, playin' around the Dump—and workin' with my dad. 'Cause I like to bite my nails and pick my nose and eat it, like you—and beat off. Him and some of the niggers who lived near us was the only ones who didn't gimme grief about it—and him and Jay would even let me have some of theirs. I guess that's when it turned into sex. "

"But why did you *choose* that one? Shit...didn't people tease you?"

"Yeah, some of 'em. But it was like a test. People who could call me Shit, I figured, were okay—course, most of them were niggers I was fuckin' already. And the rest, I didn't care. My dad—Dynamite—he liked it, too.

Everybody used to call me a little shit, anyway. So that's why I did it. I wanted a special name, like his—only real different. So I got me one."

Eric grunted. Down between Shit's legs, he lay on his back, his head on the crotch of Shit's old work pants—Dynamite's, with three inches of cuff cut off.

Shit asked, "*You* like it?" He reached down to rub Eric's hair.

"Yeah. I do. Sometimes I wish I had one too, like 'Cocksucker,' or something."

"You want me to start callin' you that?"

"You already do—you and Dynamite both, when I'm suckin' your dicks and you're about to come. Jay calls me 'scumsucker'."

"I'll call you that all the time, if you want. And I know you like us both to call you a nigger. If I do, you can bet *all* the niggers in the Dump'll start callin' you that—or maybe 'Nig.'"

"Naw," Eric said. "That's okay. I like it the way it is."

"Okay. But I always figured, the people who like me, like my name. That's why I picked it."

"Dynamite don't really treat you and me the same, does he?"

"What you mean?"

"Well—" Eric felt Shit rubbing his head—"he treats you more like you're his...best friend, I guess. You both mostly call each other by your first names—the way I call Barb. You're always jokin' around together. A lot of the summer people don't even know he's your...uncle. Part of that's 'cause you're black. But part's the way you two act together. Then, half the time he calls *me* 'son'—and whenever we're foolin' around in the cabin just the three of us, he always calls himself my daddy."

"You mind that?"

"No!" Eric looked back. "No, I *like* it! Like Jay and Mex callin' me 'puppy.'"

"Me, too—him callin' you that."

"Why?"

"For one thing—" Shit sounded like he was yawning—"it makes 'im goddam easier to fuck!"

"Huh?" Eric turned his head to look up, puzzled. "How you mean?"

"See, I get off pretendin'—" Shit shifted a leg to rub a bare ankle up and back over the beltless waist of Eric's jeans—"Dynamite's this real sexy older fuck buddy of mine, who has a son—the nigger he fools around with, named Eric. That's *you*, in case you ain't fuckin' figured that one out. It turns me the fuck on the way he talks to you." Shit deepened his voice into a passable imitation of his father's: "'Hey, son, lay out here with me. If you get a hard-on, just climb on your daddy here and rub off on my belly. I'll hug you and tongue fuck you till you shoot all over me. You want, just stick it in your daddy's mouth and I'll suck you off.'"

Eric laughed. "I *still* can't figure out how kissin' on two guys what ain't got half their teeth gets me so hot—"

"Me neither," Shit said. "But I guess it works. I figured that out about you the first time we was kissin' on each other, back at Turpens—the way you was goin' after them holes between 'em. Anyway, I can pretend like I'm his friend what he'll let watch him, and even let me grab a piece off you both, whenever I want. Now—getting' involved with a daddy and his own kid—ain't *that* about the nastiest thing you can think of?"

Under the back of his neck, Eric felt Shit hardening in his canvas work pants. "I guess so. Yeah, that's pretty nasty…"

"You're fuckin' *right* it is!" On 'right' Shit gave Eric's head a push. "But see, now, if he came on that way to *me*, all the time—I couldn't tell you exactly why—but it would make it a little more hard for me to shove my big black dick up his Georgia cracker asshole in the mornin', and then let his nigger kid here—" he pushed Eric's head again—"suck it clean for me, after I was finished. 'Hey, son—'" once more Shit's voice became his father's—"'my damned dick's growed so much fuckin' cheese last night, you think you could tongue that out for me and maybe swallow a couple of piss squirts besides? Oh, and when you done, give a suck to our friend, Shit, here.'"

Eric laughed at the exactitude of the performance. "He says that stuff 'cause he knows I like it…But he likes it too."

"So do I." Shit laughed. "It's complicated, ain't it? Or the way sometime we pretend you're the nigger and I'm the white kid. That's fun. It changes things. But see, I don't *want* 'im sayin' stuff like that to me—'Come on, son. Fuck yo' pappy's ass—'"

"Come on." Eric laughed. "I *never* heard him say 'pappy.'"

"Well, when I was little, I knew some kids around here what did. Anyway, I was exaggeratin'. But I'd rather listen to him sayin' it to you than to me. That's what gets *me* off. And I'll fuck anybody if he's my friend—and he wants me, too. Dynamite said he learned that from Kyle."

"I like…watching you two the way you are," though Eric wondered if liking something sexually and liking something because it made you feel warm and wanted were the same. Or the opposite? Or…? "I guess the only time he really treats us the same—" Eric stretched—"is when he snots into his hand and says, 'You boys wants some lunch?'" at which Shit erupted into high laughter and a moment later they were tussling on the flanking beach grass—

"*Owww*…Hey, cut it *out*…come on…"

"*You* stop it…come on…Please, *please*…"

"No, *no*…move *off* me. Come on…"

"Lemme get on top. It's too sandy down there…*please*, now."

"You get anywhere you want! Just lemme *do* it, come on…"

—which, between them, became the rhythms of their non-penetrative frottage, while they held each other and eyes, noses, tongues and mouths received their lingual storm.

The second one—perhaps ten week's later—Shit began. "Hey, what do drinkin' me and my daddy's piss mean to you?" Shit lay on his back.

"Huh?" Eric lay between his legs with the side of his face on the lap of Shit's pants. "How you mean?"

"I mean, I been pissin' in guys mouths all my life—like Mex. Whenever I was off with Mex and Jay, they always told me, when I had to go, I should just go over, whip it out, and stick it in his face. And 'd I do it. Mex'd drink it down and Jay would laugh—he thought it was real funny—and they'd *all* laugh. Then, when I got older, and started fuckin' with guys for real, I learned lots of guys really dug it—like some of the guys I used to sneak out and fuck at the Dump Produce farm. But I never really thought on it, serious like, before. I mean, I never got no messages about it before. You got any idea why so many people like that so much?"

Eric frowned. He had one leg and one hand on Shit's hard thigh. "I don't really know—I mean, afterwards, I feel awful good. And before it, there's hardly nothin' you can imagine wantin' more. Maybe it it just reminds me how important you all are—you and Dynamite, I mean."

"Huh?" Shit moved his legs a little.

"You guys are the fuckin' garbage men, Shit. I mean, suppose lightening hit the mayor of the city. It wouldn't make no major difference how things went. Ever'body would dotter on, doin' more or less what they do anyway, till they got a new one. I can't even *remember* who's mayor! But suppose all the garbage men upped and disappeared—Randal and Tad and you and Aim and Dynamite and Al and me…you couldn't even have no city here. Pretty soon people wouldn't even be able to negotiate the place. The smell and the junk would take over everything, and everybody would have to move away! Inside of a couple of months, they'd have to close this whole place up and go look for a new spot. And in the mornin', when you and Dynamite are about to get out of bed, you two roll over and plug into me and let it run, it feels so good 'cause I'm lettin' you relax for another couple of minutes, and I can go dump it in the toilet for you—and we got something to laugh at and have a good time over. And it really makes me…feel like I'm doin' a little somethin' special that most people don't probably have anybody to do for 'em." Eric stretched in the fork of Shit's legs. "Course, even me just sayin' it, I guess, sounds a little silly. I don't know, Shit—maybe it's just sex. I mean, like suckin' dick or getting' fucked, or just rubbin' on each other—that feelin' that a dick is supposed to go in your mouth or up your ass. I mean, since Bull came by with his message, sometimes when we're really into it, Dynamite'll plug himself into my face and be holdin' onto my ears an humpin' in my mouth as hard as he can, and just start to run 'cause he can't help it. That's really exciting, at least for me. And when he does that, you get off on it, too—I seen you. I mean, drinkin' piss is more of a 'why not?' kinda thing than a 'why?' thing. The fact is, anything that comes out of a dick is good. And I guess if you're Jay or Mex, anything that comes out of your partner is good—I can sure understand that, even if I don't take it as far as they do. Cheese is important. Cum is good. And piss is great. That's…the way it is."

"Well, in your mouth or up your ass—anyplace warm and wet—that's where my dick feels like it's supposed to go." Reaching down, Shit slid his fingers under Eric's face. "And you ain't supposed to let your dick get too far away from me, either. Yeah, I think I'm beginnin' to see what you're talkin' about. Yeah, it's beginnin' to make a whole lot of sense. So why don't you go in my pants and suck on my big, important dick. 'Cause I got a lot of important stuff up under that thing—I checked before I come out here. And I can give you a damned quart of somethin' great. And if you wanna go on workin' at it, I'll give you somethin' good as well. Then I'm gonna lie around and *suck* on your dick, and eat out your asshole and fuck you butt till you're staggerin' around like a bow-legged hooker out in the lot back o' Turpens," which, over the next two and a half hours, they did—one of the advantages of the grotto in autumn.

Eric was still breathing hard when, finally, Shit pushed up on his hands. "Let's go swimmin'!"

"Huh?"

"Yeah! Come on!"

Eric rolled to his side. (As he pulled his pants off one leg, sand stuck to the sweat on the bottom of Shit's ropy forearm.) "You mean right here?"

"Yeah!" Shit sat up and slipped his pants from his other, tossed them to the grass, and pushed himself forward. "Come on—you can swim, can't you?" (This had been back in the early weeks…)

"Yeah—some." In Hugantown, at the civic center swimming pool, Eric had passed Red Cross Senior Lifesaving the summer he was fourteen—though he hadn't been in the water more than a year, and only once, in Florida, in the sea. "Don't we gotta have suits?"

"What the fuck for?" Naked Shit started running forward, while Eric grinned at Shit's ass—there was no sunburn line, like Dynamite had—and stood to run after.

Under Eric's feet, sand and water went from hot and dry to cool and wet. Then his feet were splattering water, between shells and ropes of weed. Water surged around his ankles—and fifteen feet ahead, the froth-laced sea was up to Shit's knees. Then Shit dove—and struck out. Eric ran another dozen steps and drove his flailing body into the soft and cold that was the September sea. When he stood on the ooze and sand, he lifted his arms from the water for balance, opened his mouth to laugh, and a drop rolled into his lips, giving him a taste of salt.

"Come on over here."

They swam together awhile, Eric tiring first. Somehow the water was up above their navels now. Standing before Eric, water diamonding his face, Shit put his hand on Eric's chest and slid it down his belly to his crotch, to hold his penis below the surface.

"What you doin'?" Eric asked.

"Holdin' your dick."

"You're gonna gimme a hard-on again."

"Good…!" Under the water, Shit began to rub and massage him. Over Shit's sun-browned shoulder was the wedge of Gilead Island, against the horizon, green and gray. "Oh, fuck, it's gettin' so goddam big! Oh, man, that feels good. Wow—that's feels *so* good. Damn, it's getting' *so* big, too." Shit moved closer, so that Eric could smell his breath through the ocean's tang. "Hey, you think you could jump up in the air and spin all the way around and maybe bust me in the nose with your pecker?"

"Huh?"

"I mean while it's all hard like that. Go on. Jump real high and spin yourself."

"I don't think I can get it as high as your shoulder—"

"Well, go on try it! I'll squat a little. 'Cause you're in the water, I bet you can get up higher—"

"Okay." Eric laughed. "If you want me to." He squatted in the sea, and felt himself slip from Shit's grip. He went down until his head was under the surface, then pushed up as strongly as he could, felt himself clear the surface—the tug of the water, pulling his hard cock down, was just this side of painful—and flung his arms and shoulders around.

His erect cock, free of the sea, only caught Shit's shoulder, but at the height of his leap and spin—he could feel the water, mid-thigh—he was facing the shore.

As, in the air, he hung in the instant, up on the roadway he saw three young women, looking at them from the shore road.

Surprised as he was—he realized Shit had engineered his exposure.

And he was naked and with an erection.

Involuntarily he wheeled his arms—but kept turning, though the women had started laughing. He came down in the water, almost facing Shit again—who was laughing, too. "Hey, they was *lookin'* at me—"

"Yeah, they got a *good* eyeful of your fuckin' pecker, didn't they?"

"Hey. Why'd you do—?" Then, laughing himself, he threw himself at Shit and the two were wrestling in the water. They tussled and pushed and tugged and grabbed. During the minutes of their horsing around, Eric thought, *How wonderful if this was the rest of my life...*

When, panting, they halted, Eric looked back at the road.

The young women—with their laughter—had walked off.

"Them was summer people," Shit said, taking big steps with widely swinging arms, in toward the beach, "what ain't gone home yet."

"Yeah," Eric said. "I'm gonna get you good for that."

Shit looked back grinning. "Good. I can't wait, hardly. Gonna make me suck your dick again? Or are you gonna suck mine?"

Back in the grotto, Eric slipped into his pants. Shit took his up and, swinging them in one hand and his shoes in the other, they walked back to the Dump, Eric in just his jeans, Shit naked. "'Cause it ain't far enough that you got to put you clothes on anyway," Shit explained. "At least this time of year."

*

What occurred at the grotto that actually worried Eric, however—not about Shit, but about the ideas he had accepted from Shit that ran so counter to the world's wisdom—happened in Eric's second Diamond Harbor summer, when briefly he'd forgotten the timing between deserted winter and the tourist months.

One June Saturday, Eric was sitting on a log in the grotto, beating off, when he looked up—

A child stood on a rock, maybe ten feet to the side and above, a fist pressed to a naked belly, the other hand up near the mouth. The dark hair was clipped short, so that you could see the skull through the remaining fuzz. The dark eyes were close together, and, as Eric looked, the child swallowed—then swallowed again. In sandals and metallic blue bathing briefs, he looked about eight.

(Half a dozen tourist cabins sat up across the beach road. But through the mild winter, none had been occupied.)

Eric slowed, smiled, stopped pumping. He said, "Hello..." After a long, long pause, he nodded down at himself. "You like that?"

The child did not speak...or move.

Eric tightened his fist, tugged at himself—three, five, seven times. "You know what I'm doin'? You're curious, ain't you?"

The child remained frozen.

Eric kept smiling. "You got a hard-on yourself, in there." He nodded. "I can see it from here." An innocent ridge slanted the blue briefs. "You wanna come over and look? I ain't gonna hurt you."

The child took two steps down the rock, then paused.

Eric said, "You wanna touch it? You don't have to. But it you wanna, nothin's gonna happen. Believe me—I promise."

The child took another step, then, in a hoarse voice that may have been fear or a speech defect, said, "You gonna hurt me if I don't?"

It took perhaps three seconds for the question to register. When it did, Eric was startled. Yes, in his aroused state, that evident and immature curiosity had attracted him...sexually. But he was also sure his primary urge, more than sexual, had been...instructive. The question had brought home—startlingly—that the field into which he had been about to pursue his lesson, however benign he'd assumed it to be, was neither empty nor innocent. That was what he had no control over. Eric pushed himself back into his jeans and stood up. "Hey—" still smiling, he tugged his T-shirt down—"probably this is a game you shouldn't be playin'. Nobody's gonna hurt you. Believe me, not me. But you can always learn about stuff like this later. I guess you can live without it now." Stepping forward, he climbed over a fallen branch, then pushed toward the place between the rocks by which he usually left. Once he looked back where...well, where the child had been.

The moment Eric had moved, the boy had turned and fled.

Eric told Shit about it, later that day, who said, practically enough, "Probably somebody been doin' stuff to him and hurtin' him. He thought you maybe was gonna do the same thing. But that ain't *your* fault." Eric's own mental explanations ranged from the possibility that the boy was an incipient masochist who'd wanted to be hurt to the possibility that he had already been deeply abused, or even that it might seem a natural question for someone that age, to a stranger, given what parents were always telling their kids these days.

Shit suggested they find him, take him off, and initiate him into sexual play so that he'd know they wouldn't hurt him. "Jesus," Eric said, "with two guys as big as *we* are? We'd scare him to death!" He went so far as *not* to point the child out to Shit when they passed him with his young parents on the Harbor's busy summer streets. Eric saw the child three more times in town—the second, it hit him that perhaps the "boy" was, indeed, a prepubescent girl. (The erection he'd thought he'd seen could have been a fold or light play in metallic blue? Occasionally girls under thirteen or twelve wore boys' briefs…) The mother's hair was as short as the child's. As she walked through the street, her husband's hand in one of hers, and her son or daughter's in the other, all three wore Bermuda shorts of different plaids. Then Eric's questions were elided, rather than solved: the family's two weeks Harbor vacation was over. The child had never looked directly at him again—for which Eric was grateful.

Assuming it was a girl (or, for that matter, a boy), Eric wondered if the encounter would evolve into some anecdote of violation and oppression, or if his benign intentions had somehow gotten through and the tale would join still others that, in maturity, would allow the young woman—or the young man—to recount how the incident had been part of an arrival at some healthy and open understanding of sex. That, anyway, was what Eric hoped. But he revealed neither that hope—nor its dark obverse—to Shit. There was always the possibility that, through repression, and because there was no one he felt comfortable sharing it with, it would become as small a part of the child's memory as it eventually became of his.

The next thing that troubled Eric's feelings about underage sex, in spite of Shit's claim to first-hand knowledge of its harmlessness, happened… well, still months later.

Jay MacAmon had pulled up to the Dump cabin in his own maroon pickup. (They kept one in the dockside lot.) He'd come to the mainland on his day off from the scow, only it was Dynamite's day off too. He'd run up to Hemmings for something at the mall. Only Shit and Eric were home.

"I wish you'd brought Mex," Shit said. "I'd sit him right down here and get myself a good blow job. Mex still sucks some good dick, Jay."

"I know he does," Jay said. "But he's doin' the run in the scow back and forth by hisself, so I could come over here and visit." He looked around at the junk that filled the kitchen. "Hey—" Jay sat on one of the chairs by the few inches of free kitchen wall—"I haven't thought about this for a coon's age." (A kettle of potatoes was bubbling on the stove. Eric was making potato salad that weekend.) "But I remember when you was a little thing, Shit, maybe one-and-a-half, two-and-a-half years old. Me and your dad and Mex was all out here at our old place in the Dump. You was runnin' around nekid, and Dynamite picked you up on his lap, and he laid you out there and dropped his face on your belly and goes…" Jay wagged his bearded head back and forth and made a blurred sound like *Mubblewubblegubble*… "You laughed and laughed…I think you was just startin' to talk. 'Cause I remember you shoutin' out, 'Do it again, Dynamite! More! More! Go on, do it again!' And Dynamite did. I remember sittin' there and laughin' too, and thinkin' all of a sudden, I'm glad Dynamite took you to raise. 'Cause I wouldn't have had the self-control to keep my hands off you and not try somethin' stupid that might've really messed you up there. I mean, you know there was a while when we was thinkin' about whether me and Mex should raise you out on Gilead or whether Dynamite should bring you up. But that's when I realized we'd made the right choice."

Shit said, "What you mean, Jay?"

"What you think I mean," Jay asked, from his chair, "out there on that island? With nobody but Mex, me, them Injuns, and that graveyard, as sure as you're born, I would have got you off somewhere and tried to stick my damned dick up your two or three year old asshole—*that's* what I mean!"

"Aw, fuck," Shit said. "You wouldn't have done that, would you?" Most of the time, Eric thought of Shit as indefinitely older than himself. But now Shit's twenty-one years seemed surprisingly young. "I mean, if I said no, I didn't want you to. I wasn't ever scared of you, Jay."

"Maybe you shoulda been. Maybe now I wouldn't. But back then, I don't know. Yeah, I probably would'a done it—at least once, out of curiosity... then tried to figure out some cockamamie reason why it was really all right, anyway, even if your ass *was* bleedin' like a knife-stuck pig's."

"But I stayed out there with you, lotsa times." Shit protested. "Just likes Eric does there, with you guys now."

"But you wasn't *livin'* out there with us—*all* the time. That's a different thing. And your dad *did* tell me, more than once—" he rocked on the back legs of his chair—"in a real fuckin' friendly way, now—that he would kill me if I ever did anything to hurt you."

"But when I'd come to visit out there with you—" Shit turned away from the cabin window—"we fooled around. A lot, I remember."

"Yeah, but we always let *you* start it." Jay grinned at Eric. "This kid couldn't keep his hands off of anything that was body temperature. I mean, we had a dog—big as Uncle Tom, there—" who raised his head off his forepaws, looked around, and again dropped his muzzle "—and I remember once comin' in and you was playin' with its...Oh, never mind."

Eric laughed. "He was probably doin' him just the way he does Tom today."

"Hey, you did it, too..."

Jay looked back at Shit. "But that was later."

"When I was twelve or thirteen."

"When you was *fourteen*. Not thirteen—or twelve. Besides suckin' your dick and beatin' off together ain't fuckin' your ass. And fourteen ain't twelve. Twelve is when Shad punched my teeth out. So I know what I'm talking about. And twelve *sure* ain't the same as three, five, seven...No, you got the best deal, Shit, along with the best daddy. Admit it."

"Well, I know I got a damned good one."

It didn't change Shit's ideas on the topic. Over time, when it came up, Eric saw Shit end a couple of arguments at one bar or another about underage sex, which got pretty heated, with his flat, "Hey—just look at *me!*" But Eric was never that sure. When he was worked up, he still found Shit's history a turn-on—especially the segments before he himself had come to the Harbor: Shit claimed to love it. And because Eric loved Shit, he loved whatever history had made Shit into Shit, as he'd loved Dynamite and Mex and Jay for being part of it, even if he was not sure what they did as a way of life was right for any but the four of them.

"And I tell yall this, too…yall know Jay MacAmon? Well, ain't nobody punched *my* damned teeth out when I was a kid." At the bar, Shit and Eric would drink more Coke. "Actually, most of them fuckers sorta fell out on their own…"

* * *

[29] DYNAMITE DID NOT take Eric to The Slide his first visit.

When Harlen couldn't go with Fred, and Fred asked Dynamite to come help him load some deliveries for the store, on a Monday afternoon at a little after two o'clock, Shit drove Eric over.

"That's about when they open up. Saul won't mind." Shit pulled up the gearshift on the pickup. "Ain't nobody gonna be in there yet, and he likes the company. Besides, Saul remembers when the drinking age used to be eighteen—'stead of twenty-one. He says if you can take a gun and go off in the army and kill people, and if you can go over to the public school and line up and go in that booth there and decide if you gonna have a nigger or white man for a president—and Saul'll tell you, right out, gettin' that nigger in the White House was the most sensible thing this country ever done; now all them big corporations and their representatives in Congress we call senators for some reason gotta let him do what he gotta do, but Saul don't think they will—somebody who can do all those things ought to be able to go in and get a beer—and all I want is a pop, anyway."

In a clearing among the pines, they stopped.

Out the window was an ordinary gray, two-story house, just off the road. A couple of cars sat near it—

There was room for more.

In the back, some kind of board construction, maybe twelve feet high, fenced in an area maybe thirty feet long all the way up to the building's rear. The only things that let you know it wasn't an ordinary house were that the windows were black and without curtains—and in two of them were neon beer signs: Coors in one, Molsons in the other.

"Used to be a sign what said 'The Slide' out front." Shit opened the door and got out. "But a couple of years back, somebody run it down, and they never put it back. I guess they don't really need it."

Not that it was far from the Harbor. You could have walked to it from Front Street or Dump Corners, either one, in an hour-and-a-quarter.

Eric followed Shit around the front, up the ramp that was closer to them than the steps, onto the porch, and through the door.

Inside stood a bouncer's stool, though no one sat on it.

Behind the long counter before them, a heavy black man, with short cut, ash-white hair and a sleeveless undershirt, plunged glasses into a rinsing sink, lifted them, and let them drip back into the water, then set them on a tray. He reached over to douse two more pint glasses.

Over the bar burned red, blue, orange, and yellow lights.

Toward the back, some overhead cleaning bulbs put the whole space in enough light to see.

Off to the side, in front of the bar, sweeping the floor with a wide push broom was a young black fellow in an upper body harness, leather pants, and boots.

"What can I do for you fellas?" the bartender asked, dunking two more glasses. He did not look up.

Just then, a door in the back wall opened, and a very muscular, very black man backed inside, carrying something. It was some kind of bench or table, and someone—an equally muscular white guy—came in frontward, carrying the other end.

Neither wore shirts.

Still without looking, the bartender called, "Hey—Jos? Dan? Put that back along the same wall it was at before you took it outside to fix it."

The bare-chested men carried the bench over to the wall and set it down. Their muscular arms rivaled Eric's. Standing up, they stepped back, and looked down at it.

Over the bar's black walls, sunlight poured in the open door, making Eric realize how bright the outside was.

One of the two men—Eric wasn't sure which—said, "I think it was over about a foot." So they picked it up, then moved it.

"Hey, Saul," Shit said. "I come to show Eric here the place. We been tellin' him all about the Slide, and I thought he should see it."

"Take a look," the bartender said.

Eric realized that, for some reason, he'd been expecting Saul to be white.

"You want somethin' to drink, Mr. Morgan Haskell?"

But Eric felt relieved he was black.

"What would you say," Shit asked, "if I ordered a triple whiskey with a pint of Guinness for a chaser?"

"I'd say fuck you and the horse you road in on—and wonder why you were pullin' at my leg like that."

"Saul knows I don't like to drink no hard liquor," Shit explained to Eric. Saul kept washing. (He hadn't looked away from his work once.) "That's one thing that you can say about kids who was raised in the Dump. They don't drink and they don't smoke. You can't smoke, if you're an adult. And them counselors are always taking groups to the hospital and lettin' 'em see what it does to people—kids and grownups, both. That works pretty good on the young ones." Saul snorted. "It's pretty effective on us older guys, too. It made *me* quit. You and your friend want a glass of pop?" Without looking up, he took a towel and began wiping down some surface too low for Eric to see.

"Sure," Shit said. "That'd be nice. Hey—" he was speaking to Eric— "Sometimes I'll have one drink—maybe a beer. But I don't see no reason to have much more than that. Besides, as soon as I start to feel it, I figure I've had too much anyway."

Saul put two glasses on the counter, pulled up a siphon. One after the other, he filled them with Coke. "Take those—" he still hadn't raised his eyes—"and look around all you want. They're on the house."

Shit stepped up, took a glass. "Go on. You take yours."

Eric stepped up, got his glass, and, following Shit, walked around the bar's oval end. Actually, the bar was half an oval. One end went up to the wall and stopped.

"Hey, Billy," Shit said.

"Hello, Shit," said the tall guy pushing his broom. "You say your friend wants to see things? Here, lemme turn on some lights." He took his broom over to the wall, and on a bank of switches, just above shoulder level, he reached up and flipped one, two, three switches. On the side of the oval away from the door, beneath some eighteen feet of counter, all the way to the wall, one after the other three sets of lights came on, the bulbs hidden up under the bar. They shone on the tile backing and down into the recessed trough that was sunk four inches into the floor. The space under the bar went almost two-and-a-half feet back.

Half a dozen stools stood in front of it.

Eric looked down. Every eighteen inches, drains were fixed along the trough's bottom. On the stone floor in front of the four-inch drop, presumably they caught any spillage. The smell of disinfectant was sharp on this side, though it had been undetectable at the entrance.

For some six feet, the front was open. Yes, you *could* squat down in that, even turn around and sit crossed-legged on the tiling under the bar counter. But the final dozen feet had widely spaced rods rising in front of it—bars, Eric realized, making the last fifteen feet a cage: a piss cage!

The whole thing was a big stand-up—or sit down—urinal.

The shirtless, muscular young men had wandered up.

For all his muscles, the black one was on the fleshy side. He wore jeans and—Eric glanced down—combat boots.

For a moment Eric thought that the white one was wearing black jeans and—for some reason—a pair of white (or gray) briefs pulled over them. He had on engineer's boots. Now Eric saw a few jailhouse tats, including two tears on his face, under the outer corner of one eye. He had a friendly, welcoming grin.

As he got closer, Eric saw now they *weren't* briefs. The whole groin area of his jeans had been cut away, so that they had been turned—more or less—into a pair of chaps, fastened to the sides of his wide leather belt. Holding his privates was a very worn, very gray (probably, Eric realized, very dirty) jockstrap. When he turned again to look at the bench they'd set against the wall, Eric saw the crevice between his butt cheeks, within the gray elastic bands that curved over his buttocks.

The black one—Jos—said, "Do your friend know what guys do in that thing? I mean, how we work it on piss nights?"

"I kinda told 'im about some of it," Shit said, gesturing with his Coke glass. "Go on. You explain it."

"Well—" Jos, then Dan, moved over to the counter, to sit on two of the stools before the urinal—"if you're a piss freak, you can come in here and take all your clothes off—or only some of 'em if you want—and get down in that thing, and go behind the bars there, and sit, or kneel down or squat—or lie down and stretch full out, if there ain't too many guys in there. Come on. Sit down with us."

Eric and Shit moved either side of them—Eric by Jos, Shit by Dan, on stools of their own. (On the counter, they had set their glasses.) "And the serious beer drinkers—"

"—like me," white Dan said, grinning to one side, then the other, like a happy farm boy.

"—stand there at the bar, drink their beer, and when it's time to take a leak, they whip it out and let it go." Black Jos took up the tale again. "The guy who had this place before Saul—the one who built it—told Saul he got the idea from a bar he saw in Australia, when he was there as a kid. Only it was just a workin' man's bar—it wasn't for no piss freaks. They had a urinal right under the counter, just like this one, so you never had to leave off drinkin'. While you were puttin' it down, you could flip it out and let her run right there."

"My kinda of bar," Dan said. "But I don't mind if there a few thirsty niggers under there while I'm spurtin'. It's fun."

"Don't even have to go to the john," Jos went on. "They can just whiz into the pisser—and on whoever's in it. If they want a blow job, they can stick their peckers through the bars, and one of the guys down there'll suck it."

On the far side of the bar well, Saul had turned around. "It's two-thirty. We're open now—you can have your first one." Walking across, he had gotten out two bottles of beer. He sat them on the counter, one in front of Jos, one in front of Dan. "Treat 'em kindly. After the first three, you only get one an hour." Again, he turned and walked back to the other side, where he'd be facing entering customers.

Dan looked around Jos at Eric, then over at Shit, then back, grinning. "Hell, I already killed a six pack 'fore I got here. I really like pissin' on the niggers. They're fuckin' animals, anyway. I don't usually like messin' with no white guys. It ain't nothin' personal, I mean. But I'll let niggers do pretty much anything to me—'cause it don't really matter. But pissin' on them's always fun—and those is the niggers we mostly get in here at The Slide."

"Is your name…" Eric started. "What was it…?" He tried to remember what Hammond had told Dynamite, months—or was it a year ago, now?—back. "Danny Turpens…?"

"Un-huh." Dan's smile became expectant of an explanation.

"Damn," Shit said, "I didn't know there *was* no Turpens faggots. You bisexual or something? My daddy ain't gonna believe this. Well, I guess things change in the world all the time."

"Yeah," Eric said, "somebody told me they met you…over at the Opera."

"Yeah?" Danny kept grinning. "But I don't go over there too much no more."

Jos picked up his bottle, took a swallow, and set it back on the wet ring it had left. "Dan's a good guy—he talks a little crazy—but he's okay."

Eric, though, was trying to recall the details of why Dan had been ejected from the theater.

"'Cause *you're* white—" again Dan smiled at Eric—"that's why you and me wouldn't get along."

"Hey…!" Shit leaned forward to talk past Jos. "Ain't I a nigger?"

"Huh?" Dan turned away from Eric to frown back at Shit. "Well, if you *told* me you was white, I wouldn't argue with you; I got too many cousins and uncles and aunts complected about like you, and they swear all up and down they're as white as you can get down here." He chuckled. "Fuckin' bullshit…But, sure, if I was just passin' you on the street, I'd probably think there was a touch of the tarbrush about your nose and your hair—and you don't got no half moons on your fingernails—at least what's left of 'em that I can see."

"Then what the fuck makes you think *this* boy's white—Eric there? His dad is blacker than Jos, here. I shook his damned hand, when he brought Eric down here to stay with his mama. So I know."

Now Jos frowned at Eric. "Is you the kid who's helpin Shit and his uncle on the garbage run in the mornin's?"

"Un-huh." Eric nodded and drank his Coke.

"Yeah," Shit said. "This nigger's Eric."

Jos frowned even more deeply at Shit. "Yeah, I remember somebody sayin' he was in the Lighthouse when your daddy brought you down here, last year—and that he was as black as the ace o' spades. At least that's what he said." Jos took another other swallow from his bottle.

"So that means Eric's gotta be at *least* as black as I am," Shit said, sitting back on the stool. "Or blacker if you seen his daddy."

Dan looked at Eric, and for a moment a frown ruptured his rural grin. "Well, *that's* okay, then. I mean, it's possible. I seen niggers before what was as light as you. Not many. But some. Yeah, then I wouldn't care if you done stuff to me, too."

Jos chuckled again. "Danny means it, too." Suddenly he turned to Dan, took Dan's bottle from the counter in front of him, and leaned back on his stool. "Watch this here."

Shit and Eric both leaned back.

"All right, you white racist scumbag." Jos brought the neck of the bottle sharply forward, between the straps of Dan's jockstrap, thrusting it hard in the crack between his butt cheeks.

On his stool, Dan straightened out his big shoulders and gave out an "*Ughhh…*"

"See. He'll let any black sonofabitch do shit like that to him. That's why he works here. He's a good bouncer, 'cause he don't really mind all that much getting hit, long as it's by a black fella. Funny, ain't it?" Meanwhile, Jos was twisting the bottle one way and the other. More and more of the neck disappeared between Dan's buttocks, till they spread apart for the thicker cylinder of brown glass.

Finally, Jos let go and sat up.

Lodged in Dan's butt, the bottle was firmly stuck.

Forearms on the counter, Dan leaned forward, grimacing.

"How's that feel, you white piece of shit?"

Dan grunted—and said through the face he was making, "Like a fuckin' nigger just shoved a beer bottle up my ass! But you guys can do that, 'cause you're just fuckin' animals—black animals. You don't got no ethical faculties at all, is what it is." Again he grunted.

"Well, yeah, he's right. I sort of lose 'em around him." Jos picked up his own bottle and took another swallow. "Funny. I ain't never been too much into no S-and-M before." He chuckled. "But somethin' about Danny here brings it out in me." Again he leaned back, reached down, and gripped the bottle bottom, lodged in Danny—and yanked.

"*Arhhhhh....!*" Dan's head went up and his back arched.

"It ain't as bad as it looks. He always keeps a pretty good supply of grease up his hole, in case somebody suddenly tries to fuck 'im." Jos came forward and slammed the bottle's bottom on the table in front of Dan. "A nigger, I mean. Now drink that, you racist scumbag!"

"Huh?" Shit said. "Eric do that too, sometimes, when he comes over and see us, don't you, brother?"

Eric couldn't tell whether that registered with either Danny or Jos.

Dan lifted one naked shoulder, lifted the other, arched his back again, and again grimaced.

Foam pushed from Dan's bottle neck to run down the label to the counter.

"Can I wipe it off first?"

"*No!*" Jos declared. "Drink it just like that, you white fuck!"

"Oh," Dan said. "Okay." He lifted the bottle, drank, and set it down. Wrinkling his nose—and the two tears under the corner of his eye—he said, "I can sure smell where the fuck it's been."

"Good," Jos said.

From across the bar, without turning, Saul said "You fellas wanna bring me up four buckets of ice?"

"All right," Dan said. "I guess we gotta get back to work." He lifted his bottle again—and probably finished it.

"Yeah," Jos said. "Come on." They got down from the stools and started out the open back door, through which sunlight still fell. A step outside, Eric saw Danny reach back and rub his butt, move his fingers over—he heard him grunt again—and scratch deep in his ass crack.

"Come on," Shit said. "Lemme show you the rest." He climbed from the stool, so Eric got down, too. They walked to the bar's end. "See where it goes up against the wall—under there, that's actually a little half-pint door that they leave open at night, and after you gotten yourself hosed down till you're happy, you can go right out there, and you're in the back.

There's a shower right where you come out. You can rinse yourself off—I mean, if that's what you wanna do. I seen Mex come here a couple of times and wear that stuff all fuckin' night—and not just Jay's piss, either. Come on." And, leaving the Coke glasses on the bar with the bottles, Shit led Eric out the sunny, full-sized door, still open.

They were in the wood-walled enclosure they'd seen from outside. Up against the house, three showerheads stuck from high metal pipes. A rubber base beneath had four drains. And on the wall beside it, near the water spigots, Eric could see a small door's outline, about as high as his belly button—the height of the bar counter within.

"The part that ain't a shower is like their outdoor grope room. This is where everybody really gets it on." Shit looked around the space, with the board walls. "There ain't nobody here now. So unless you just want me to fuck you out here so you can say you done something more on your first visit than watch a nigger shove a bottle up a white Turpens asshole—"

"No," Eric said. "No, that's okay. We might as well go back. At least I know what's out here, though."

Just then, on the other side of the clearing, from a trap door that Eric hadn't even seen, much less realized it was open, first Jos then Dan came up, lugging pails of ice in each hand.

"Okay," Shit said. "Let's go, then…"

They followed the two men back into the bar.

The cleaning lights were off now. Jos must have turned on another switch, because the red and blue and yellow lights were blinking all around the ceiling. Music was playing.

Without his broom, tall Billy said, "Close that, would you? We don't usually open it till after dark."

"Oh," Eric said. "Sure." He turned back and pulled the door to.

"Hey, Saul! Thanks for the Cokes," Shit called as he rounded the bar end.

"Yeah," Eric called, coming after him. "Thank you."

Saul didn't look and didn't speak.

Out on the porch, they walked down the steps this time, instead of the ramp, and went back to the pickup, as a car and another pickup, one behind the other, rolled into the parking area. "Guess some payin' customers are startin' to get in." Shit climbed in the passenger cab door.

"You sure Saul likes the company?" Eric asked, as they turned onto the tree-enclosed road.

"Yeah. He really does," Shit said. "He told me so once."

"You ever get in under there? I mean, in the trough in the back." He climbed up into the driver's side, then moved under the wheel.

"Yeah—a couple of times, with Mex, when I was a kid. We took all our clothes off. Then we climbed in under there. I sat in his lap, and he hugged me from behind, and guys pissed on us for two or three hours. All his gay deaf friends was there. And Jay. And Black Bull—all of them, and lots of guys I didn't even know. We're talkin' sign language, and guys is pissin' on us, all night. It was fun. Most of 'em probably thought I was a little deaf kid—which is why they let me in there. Like it was somethin' that deaf people did, so it was okay that I was doin' it. People are funny about things like that. There was a few other guys under there with us, too. We was all splashin' around. Mex had a hard-on the whole night—and drank half of it down what the guys was hosin' on us. Then he pissed it out—all over my butt, mostly. It was fun, but I didn't get no hard-on at all."

"What did it feel like?" Eric asked.

"Warm. And wet…And fun. I mean the warm and play-in-it and splash around and have fun part I can understand. But that's why, you know, I was askin' you before about the other part. The I-gotta-get-it-all-inside-me-as-much-as-I-can part. That's the part I don't quite follow." Shit shrugged. "But then, I don't have to. That's just somethin' you like. I got stuff that makes me special—and you got stuff that makes you special. That's all it is—at least I think so. And it don't hurt that what makes you special kinda turns me on. I just hope it works the other way around."

"You mean the part of you that's gotta stick his pecker in any fella that walks by? Yeah, I kinda like that part of you, Shit."

"Oh," Shit said, sounding surprised. "Well, good…"

After more bouncing along the unpaved road, Eric said, "That was kind of nice, what you did in there—about me bein' black. But I wasn't quite sure why you was doin' it."

Shit said, "Well, Danny sounded like the kinda guy you might like to get a lip lock on, one of these days. And I just thought it'd make it a little easier for you, if he thought you was a nigger. Jos is okay—but I don't see you wantin' no beer bottle shoved into you when you ain't expectin' it."

"Naw," Eric said. "I don't think I would."

"I mean—" Shit cackled—"I don't care *how* greased up you was!"

They pulled out onto a wider road.

"Hey, we still got the rest of the day. You wanna take us over to the Opera? We can get in there and fuck around with each other, or maybe find somebody we ain't had, yet—or had *too* many times. You could put a dick in one end of 'im. I could put mine in the other, and we could have some fun."

"That'd be somethin'…Sure—why not?" Eric reached over the top of the wheel to tug it around and take the sharp curve that brought them out from under sun-shot leaves. "If we're there more'n an hour, you can call the old pig fucker—unless you wanna run over and pick 'im up and bring 'im with us…?"

"Nope," Shit said. "Let's not."

"No…?" Surprised, Eric glanced over, where Shit stretched his knees wide and pushed an arm along the seat back, behind Eric's shoulder.

"No matter what happens in the Opera, you know damn well once you heat up them sausages and that spaghetti sauce you got in the refrigerator for dinner, you, me or both of us is gonna wanna a shoot a load up his butt. He'll be nice and happy about that. But if he gets all tired out at the movies, he'd gonna go to sleep before we get to it. He's always sayin' he can't keep up with us—and I don't think he can, no more."

"Well, yeah," Eric said. "That's true…"

"I'm just used to fuckin' him at least once before we go to sleep—and it looks like you about got used to it, too, by now—no matter how much nookie we all get durin' the day."

"I guess so." Eric drove another three minutes. "You know, it's funny, Shit. 'Fore I come down here, what I was lookin' for was all the goddam motherfuckin' sex I could find. I mean, I figured there'd be *somethin'* to do around here—somebody to fuck or suck with. But I didn't think I'd have *all* the goddam dick I could want, within a dozen miles one way or the other of Diamond Harbor."

"Oh, you mean," Shit said, is his mocking tone, "you get more sex down here in the country than you do up in the city, Mr. Big Ol' Sophisticated Atlanta City Slicker?"

"Well, I do," Eric said. "Between you, your dad, Turpen's johns, the Opera House, and the guys who hang around waitin' to pick you up for a fuck around Hurters, not to mention Uncle Tom, and now The Slide— yeah, I think I got all the sex I can fuckin' handle. And I don't have to spend six and seven hours a day runnin' after it, either. At the most, it's a mosey down the road—if it ain't already at the house. I was thinkin', you know, now I got it, I should do something with it."

"How you mean—do somethin'?"

"I mean, go on and do something else along with it, 'cause I'm really satisfied in that department. I told Barb, last year. You know what I'd like to do?"

"What?"

"I wanna try bein' a really good person—'cause I'm so happy and get to fuck and suck so much." He glanced over. "I didn't tell her about the sex part and what that had to do with it. But that seems like a good reason."

"Yeah?"

"Yes. So that's what I'm gonna start doin'."

"I think you're a pretty good fella already. You make our fuckin food damn near every night. How much better you got to be?"

"As good as I can. I mean, I'm gonna have to put a little thought into it. But I'll think of somethin'. You be as satisfied as I am, and it's just a shame to waste it all on yourself and get *too* lazy…"

"Well, that's gonna be interestin'. A really good person, huh? Am I supposed to give you a hand?"

"I'm serious, Shit."

"I'm serious, too, nigger. Hell, it's gonna be interestin' to see what one looks like."

As he drove, Eric felt Shit's hand fall over his thigh, then push on between his legs. "What you doin'?"

Shit shrugged. "Helpin', I guess. See, I'm gonna suck your dick on the way to the Opera, while you think about all the good things you wanna do. You sound all sexy when you talk crazy like that."

"I do?" Eric grinned. "Damn…!" Feeling his dick harden under Shit's hand, Eric slowed some. "Go on, then. Suck it."

Shit twisted in the seat. His other hand joined the first. "I figured that'd be some kind of help, no matter what you was doin'." He lowered his head. "Get you damn elbow up—so we can get ready for the movies…"

* * *

[30] NOT A FULL two months after Eric's eighteenth birthday, in September of oh-eight, Barbara gave up her house in the pines and moved in officially with Ron in Runcible; and Eric moved permanently to the Dump with Shit and Dynamite. Over that week, at the Lighthouse Coffee & Egg, Barbara had several conversations with the garbage man, who stopped in a couple of times without the boys right after work, where, sitting across a booth from her, he said, "Eric works hard, Mrs. Jeffers—and he don't get in no trouble. He's a good influence on my boy—tryin' to teach Morgan to read and stuff. I could never do it." (Eric had also managed to make Shit more circumspect about eating his snot in public, unless the two were trying to gross someone out in the Runcible bus station or in the Opera House, where, soon, Shit was the one who would let him in through the rear service door. But that remained unmentioned.) "Since you're movin' to Runcible with your friend, Mr. Bodin, if you don't mind Eric stayin' with us, ma'am, me and Shit…uh, Morgan—we'd both be obliged."

Shit was goofily happy at the prospect.

And, as Eric said, it was what *he* wanted, more than anything.

So, with only some misgivings, Barbara agreed. Her friends and regular morning coffee customers at the Lighthouse Coffee & Egg, Mex and Jay MacAmon, both clearly fond of Eric, said they thought it would be a good idea.

For a while now, Barbara had known that Eric and Morgan shared a bed in Dynamite's cabin. (No one had mentioned Dynamite slept in it, too.) And Ronald Reagan Bodin had said several times he was not that keen on living with an adolescent—especially no gay one.

Finally, Barbara had been impressed by how committed and consistent Eric was about his job. He had an account at the Dump Credit Union, where, these days, a check from the Chamber of Commerce was deposited for him every two weeks, the way it was for Shit and Dynamite.

After his three-month probation with the Chamber of Commerce had ended and he'd gone on salary, they sent Eric a plastic card in care of Dynamite's cabin, with the fliers and other junk the postman left in their mail tube on its stick by their steps, while they were all out hauling. The card had a colored picture of the orange water pump, the barn, and part of the cornfield and a kale field at Dump Produce.

Dynamite kept a card for Shit. "It's right here in the very back of my wallet, under all the others. Now, if anything ever happens to me, first thing you do is get that card out and take it. Long as you got money in your account, you can get it out of any bank in the country. You just gotta remember your number, like I told you when we got it."

"Yeah," Shit said. "It's my birthday."

"That's right. So don't forget it, Shit." In front of the forsythia bushes beside the Credit Union, Dynamite frowned. "But you ain't supposed to say that it front of nobody else."

"Why?" Shit asked. "It's just Eric." Shit always had a disbelieving look when, one out of five visits to the bank, Dynamite would tell him this. (It was like one of Mike's repeated tags.)

"Well, yeah. I guess that's okay." Dynamite pushed his wallet into the back pocket of his overalls. "I guess." They started walking toward the pickup.

As he'd done in Atlanta and at Barbara's out among the pines both, in the Dump Eric took over most of the cabin's cooking. It was nothing new, though doing it *all* the time for the first months was hard. (Half of one of the other rooms got cleaned out, a chair and a table put in it, and given to Eric—*I mean, if you ever wanted to sit and beat off by yourself.*

(*Oh*...Eric said. *Does my doin' it in the bedroom bother you?*

(*No more than mine bothers you*, Dynamite said. *Or in the kitchen or the bathroom—or out on the porch, for that matter.*

(*I like you doin' it. And...hell, when one of you walks in on me, and just sits down next to me and sticks a couple of fingers up my ass till I finish, it even helps, sometimes.*

(*See*—Shit grinned—*I told you.*

(*Yeah*, Dynamite said. *But havin' a little more space ain't gonna hurt none of us.*)

Father and son liked Eric's food; so they helped, cutting, frying, stewing. It wasn't boring.

Eric didn't complain.

Though a lot of times they had the same sausage and lentil stew or chicken and summer squash casserole and a lot of pork chops, greens, cabbage and cornbread three and four days in row.

Since it *was* an improvement, they didn't complain, either.

Thanks to Eric, Shit now knew what all the words on all the road signs said within thirty miles of Diamond Harbor—and could at least print his nickname (he'd grin and say, *I just wanted to learn it 'cause it was nasty*; the Sharpie letters on the pickup tailgate had been a failed attempt by Dynamite to teach the same thing); as well as Eric's; and Dynamite's.

"Which," Dynamite had said, grinning at the two with uncontainable pride, "I guess is enough for dumb fucks like us, right? Now Shit can get a real license." And this time, he did.

For three hours, a number of the Coffee & Egg customers noticed Barbara was more than a little thoughtful as she worked.

And when Jay and Mex came in the next day—since it was slow that morning—she actually sat down with the boatmen through a mug of coffee, all around. "I mean...really, what do you two think of him being over there, in the Dump, in all that mess they got stashed in that cabin? I mean, you know the kinds of things everybody's always saying go on over there...I don't pay that any mind, really. But still..."

"Well—" Jay leaned back holding his mug, while Mex leaned forward over his, as if waiting for a verdict—"Eric's seems happy out there. When I drop in, all I ever seen is three guys sittin around drinkin' coffee—'bout the same as they do here. And they like havin' 'im. How much *could* be going on?

"After all, their bed's in the same room Dynamite sleeps in, ain't it?"

* * *

[31] AS MUCH TIME as Eric had spent around the Dump, much of that had been in Shit and Dynamite's bed. Living with them, however, produced a few changes—in Eric's picture of the place and of their place in that picture.

In the first week after the official move, Shit and Eric were walking through the Dump's grassy hillocks, below the bluff. "What's nice about livin' here," Shit was saying, "is if you wanna fuck someone, all you gotta do is walk in through any front door and fuck 'em—if they ain't too busy or sumpin'." Shit had said it many times, only there'd never been any reason or opportunity for a test.

This time, however, Eric said, "You know, you been sayin' that since I got here. But I ain't never seen you do it. I mean, between me, your dad, Turpens, and the Opera, I know damned well you like fuckin' more'n just about anything. So how come you never...you know, take advantage of it?"

"How do you know I ain't?"

"Probably 'cause you're too busy fuckin' me and your dad."

Shit looked at Eric and stopped walking. "Hey—you don't believe me?" Shit put one hand between his legs and gripped himself, enough so his cock showed its shape through the worn cloth. They were a pair of his dad's old jeans that had replaced the corduroys that had practically fallen off him. Eric had sewn back the three belt loops that, at top or bottom, had broken. A length of clothesline they'd found beside the road held Shit's pants up.

"I didn't say I didn't *believe* you." Eric laughed. "I said I never *seen* you."

"I'll show you," Shit announced. "Pick a house—we'll pick a house. Then we'll walk in and fuck whatever nigger lives there—"

"—if they're not too busy," Eric said.

"Yeah." Then he frowned. "You makin' fun of me?"

"Naw!" Eric insisted. (For a moment he believed he wasn't.) "That's what you told me. What house you wanna pick?"

Shit looked around. "That one." He glanced at Eric. "What about that one?"

Eric looked across the rolling sand and grasses that were the Dump. "Okay." He shrugged. "Sure." He felt uncertain; if this *was* Shit's exaggeration, how it would fall apart? For one thing, he didn't want it to, and he suspected there was less chance of that if Shit made the selection.

"Come on." Shit strode forward up the dirt road.

The back right leg of his jeans had a nine-inch rip, so that each step Shit took, Eric could see the worn heel and the safety-pinned back of Shit's low-topped sneaker. That day, again Shit was sockless.

(Eric had learned that, while lack was a huge axis of poverty, habit played its part.)

Looking back over his shoulder, Shit called again, "Come on, now! You don't think I'm gonna do it?"

"Sure I do." Eric sprinted after Shit, who hadn't slowed. "I'm comin'. Wait, now—"

Up the slope, the porch had orange steps. The railing and the posts supporting it were brown. The front wall was yellow. Because they were approaching at an angle, they could see that the side wall, which was mostly what you saw further down the bluff, was gray-blue. From the porch roof hung wind chimes, a string of shells, some feathers on a braid of red and green twine. Beside the steps was a profusion of greenery, which Eric recognized as tomato vines—though they were yet without fruit.

Shit started up the steps. Eric took a breath and went up behind him. Above them, as if it was a doorbell, the wind chimes tinkled in the mild November. The plants were higher than the steps.

"Are you gonna knock?" Eric asked, as, after they crossed the porch, Shit reached for the doorknob.

"Naw." Shit closed his hand around it. "I'm gonna walk inside—and fuck." He twisted the knob and pushed in the door.

Eric peered forward over Shit's shoulder.

Shit stepped inside.

In the living room, a gray television screen—off—stood in the far corner. Drapes hung at the window—dark blue drapes, down to the lighter blue carpet. Behind them, translucent white curtains covered the glass. Sitting in a large armchair, someone looked up from a magazine—and smiled quizzically.

While Eric crowded in behind him, Shit hunched up his shoulders and began to shift from one sneaker to the other. "Um…Mama Grace, I was just walkin' by—with Eric, here, and, um…"

In the chair, in a flowered robe, the slender black man uncrossed his legs, looked up, smiled, waited.

"…well, you know, I couldn't help rememberin' that time I was so horny that I went into that ol' outhouse you got in the back and I sat down on the seat and got my pants down and started…you remember, pullin' on myself and—what'd you say, how when you got out in the yard, you heard me gruntin' and huffin', in there? So you opened the door to see who it was, and you was just as nice about it—"

"Morgan—!" the man said, in surprised protest.

Shit looked aside at Eric. "Yeah, Mama was *real* nice. He didn't get mad or nothin'. He reached down and felt around on my thing, and smiled and all, then got his jeans down around his knees, turned himself around, and sat right down *on* it."

"Now, *Morgan*—!"

"Yes, you *did*." Shit nodded. "He was all greased up, too—already. Go on—" He reached for Eric's hand—Eric started a little—and pulled it back to his groin. "Take my dick out and show it to Mama. Eric and me fuck around all the time. And 'cause I was so horny, I thought if we come on in here, you'd let me stick my dick up your asshole. 'Cause that would sure make me feel good, and I bet it would make you feel good, too—Mama."

"Morgan," Mama Grace said, "hold *on*, will you...?" Mama Grace breathed in. "That's...very sweet of you—I suppose. But ...well, I don't know if this is the most convenient *time*."

"It's convenient for me," Shit said questioningly. "It don't look like *you're* doin' much of anything right now, neither. It wouldn't take long. Fact, it looks to me like it's convenient as *hell!*"

"I mean," Mama said from his chair, "well...the truth is, I was... expectin' someone in...um, about...oh, it doesn't matter. Look. Actually, I'm *very* flattered. But—"

"Who you got comin'?"

Eric saw Mama Grace take another breath and waited for him to say it was none of their business.

Under Eric's hand, Shit's dick inside his jeans was hardening.

Gulls mewed and cawed outside the cabin.

"Well, in just about forty minutes I'm expecting Wally—a gentleman who drives a truck locally—to stop by and...have a cup of tea with me, probably, before we get on to other things—"

"Aw, fuck," Shit said. "I ain't gonna take no forty minutes. I *can* make it last fifteen or twenty, if you really *want*. But I can get outta here in ten, too. Come on, Eric, take my big ol' dick outta there so Mama can remember what a *real* nigger looks like. Wally—*shit!* He's probably some penny-peckered white boy, ain't he? I got a nice one—you *said* how nice it was, yourself, when I come in here the last time. Go on, Eric. I told you, Mama keeps hisself all greased up—"

"All right, then, Morgan." With what sounded like total frustration, Mama leaned forward, hands on his knees, then pushed himself upright. "Go on, fuck me—and get *out* of here! Jesus, you boys are so..." Turning, he pulled up the back of his flowered robe.

Shit grinned at Eric.

With one hand, Eric held the waist of Shit's jeans, knuckles against Shit's belly. With the other, he pulled at the tab on Shit's fly—it stuck at first, then—when he yanked it—came loose.

"Damn," Shit said, looking down. "It's all hard and big, ain't it?"

"Wally is actually a very respectable colored gentleman, on all fronts. And…" Suddenly Mama Grace let out a breath. "Oh, never mind!" Leaning forward to support himself with one hand on the chair's heavy arm, Mama glanced back over a shoulder. "Go on, Morgan—if you're gonna do it, do it. You have the strangest sense of timing. Come on. Get it in there."

Almost dragging Eric with him, Shit moved forward, grasped Mama's hips, as, in his fist, Eric tried to set the head of Shit's cock between Mama's brown buttocks. Shit made a sound something like, "*Ennnn*…!" and went forward.

"Morgan!" Mama said, "Oh, *Christ*…!"

Eric started to step back but, leaning forward, Shit encircled Mama's waist with one arm and hooked Eric's neck with the other, to pull him over. Already he'd begun bucking. Pulling Eric down further, he planted his mouth over Eric's and pushed out his tongue.

"*Jesus* Christ…" Mama said. "What, you want me to take on the *two* of you? Come on! You can't *both* do it at the same—" He drew in a breath at Shit's advance. "I don't think…"

Chuckling, Shit said, "Why not?" With one hand he had let go and with the other went back to feeling around Eric's groin.

Eric had grown hard—pretty much because of Shit. But hard was hard. Now he felt Mama's hand, bonier, longer, reaching back to grip him through denim. Mama began to push back to Shit's thrusting.

Over the next minute-and-a-half, with only Shit's "Oh, fuck… Oh, fuck…Oh, fuck…" a repeated whisper, Shit's tempo increased. His breathing became faster and shallower. Shit's rough hand was down there, too, feeling between Eric's legs. "Oh, here it come…" He gripped Eric's cock. "The nigger gonna shoot, now. The nigger gonna shoot. It's comin', now. It's comin'…" and he went in. And stayed. And went out. And went in again. And stayed again. "Oh…*fffffffffuck!*" He gasped, gasped again, staggered, then stood. "Okay, go on. *You* do it now. Put that hard dick of yours up his black ass—go on!"

"*Damn*…" Eric whispered.

Somehow he did, with Shit gripping and gasping and guiding.

Shit still had one arm around the wrinkled silk over Mama's shoulder. Eric had one arm along Shit's.

With his other hand, he held Shit's cock, still hard.

"No offense back there. But are you two getting' off on each other, or are you fuckin' me?"

Eric felt embarrassment surge, enough to make his cock retreat half an inch within Mama's rectum.

But Shit's drawl was all grin. "'Bout half an' half, seems to me. I mean, all three of us is friends, ain't we?"

"Fine," Mama Grace said. "That's fine. A lady has to take what he can get. I don't know your friend's *name*. But, if you say so, Morgan—"

"Nigger, shoot that big white load up this black bitch's hole. Go on, now." Easily, Shit started humping Eric's fist. "Don't all them little shit balls rubbin' up against your dick feel good? They sure felt good to me. I musta squirted so much cum all over that damned crap, it should be oozin' down your leg by now, Mama."

It did feel good.

Mama Grace said, "For a boy who don't read or write, Morgan is so verbal."

"And you love it, too, you fuckin' nigger slut." Shit chuckled and tightened his grip around both Eric and Mama.

Within a minute, Eric shot.

Shit still was wrapped around both of them.

"Man," Shit said. "That some sweet stuff, ain't it?"

Eric panted. "Un-huh…"

Shit bent down and kissed Mama's rouged cheek.

Mama said, "Now, will you two get on *out* of here?" Pushing back from the chair and standing, he seemed to shake them off. "This ain't the time to get all lovey-dovey now. Wally's gonna *be* here in a minute."

Shit stepped back three steps; Eric stepped back one.

Then, outside, a grumble swept by, cut by a horn's hoot.

"*Jesus Christ*…" Stepping to the side (suddenly chilly, Eric's cock sagged in air), Mama's flowered robe slid down over his buttocks. He circled the room, robe rippling its blooms behind Mama's dark legs—

—and for the first time Eric noticed the shelves around the upper walls, on which were ranged a dozen ceramic doves, taking off from ceramic branches, standing on the edge of ceramic nests, swooping, preening, wings spread or pulled in.

At the window beside the door, Mama Grace pushed back a curtain and peered. "I swear, if Wally comes in while you're here and even raises his *eyebrow* about our regular four o'clock appointment, I will personally pull both your peckers loose and tie them round your necks! Oh—" Mama Grace touched his throat, still looking after the retreating truck. "Thank God! Wally's truck is deep rose. That one's green, so it's not him…*yet!*" He glanced back from the window, then frowned. "*Will* you put your damned dicks away and get the hell out of here!"

"Hey, I thought that was pretty good."

"Actually—" Mama Grace looked back again, drew in a breath, and stood up straight. Then he smiled—"it was lovely. Just what a lady needs to start off what I hope will be a busy afternoon and evening. Jesus—" He set his rather sharp features into a quizzical expression, while he pulled his robe further around—"Don't you boys have any friends your own age?"

"Huh?" Shit said, the quizzical expression shifting to his own face. "Whiteboy, I guess."

"I mean," Mama Grace said, "someone who isn't retarded, deranged, *and* depraved. One or the other is all right. But the three together *aren't* a good combination."

"Most of the time," Eric said, "he's busy with Black Bull, anyway."

"Probably," Mama Grace said, "that's to your advantage," while Shit frowned at him, the joke having apparently not quite registered. "Have you boys met Lurrie? That's Ezra Potts' nephew, who's staying with him for a few months. He just got here two days ago. Now, other than that *very* odd hat he insists on wearing, *he* looks like a nice, normal, ordinary, young gay man. Whyn't you make friends with someone like him? He's down here for the winter."

"What kinda hat?" Shit asked.

Eric asked, "How old is he?"

"I think his uncle said he was seventeen."

"Oh…" Eric looked at Shit.

"I guess he's a little younger than you two. His parents wanted him to spend some time around normal, ordinary gay men. Where they think they're gonna find that in the Dump, I haven't really figured out yet—"

"We're normal," Shit said, "ain't we?"

"Well, I suppose…" From the place where he'd briefly glanced at the ceiling, Mama dropped his eyes.

Shit stopped, then looked back. "Um, this guy here—he's Eric."

"Did I say I was pleased to meet you, Eric? I mean, I've heard about you, of course. And I think Ron—you know, he cooks out at Shells; he said he met you, once—even pointed you out to me once. But…well, it *is* a pleasure to meet you. It really is. I expected I would eventually get to say 'hello.' But…well—I didn't expect I'd run into you…like *this!* And, actually—" He smiled. "Actually, Morgan, it was rather fun." Suddenly he drew in a breath. "But you *must* get out of here—now! Really, both of you. Please. Go on. Get, get, get…" He made shooing motions with one hand, nails aglimmer with clear polish. Then, again, he seemed to relent. Lowering his shoulders, Mama let his face relax into a smile. "Perhaps something like this may…who knows—even happen again. When I'm not expecting someone."

"Okay," Shit said. "We're goin'…" As Shit started for the door, Mama

Grace stepped aside. "But, Mama…?" Shit's tone was pensive.

"Yes?" So was Mama Grace's.

"Your name is Mr. Davis, right?"

"Yes, Morgan. It is."

"But you like people to call you 'Mama'."

"That's right, Morgan. That's been my nickname for a long time. I'm very comfortable with it."

"Well, sir—I mean, Mama, my name is Shit. That's what my daddy calls me—like everybody calls him Dynamite. That's what Eric calls me. That what everybody around the Dump calls me."

Mama Grace smiled. "Now, you must have told me that at least three times in the last four years—you're very patient with me. I always say I'm going to do it. But then I forget. I *will* try to do that from now on, Shit. I apologize. You tell me that's your name. So that's what I intend to call you."

"Thank you, sir…ma'am…Mama, I mean."

"Good. Since we're friends, I'm glad we've got that straightened out."

At the door, Shit turned and opened it.

Behind them, Mama said, with sudden insistence, "Would you *please* put your cocks inside your pants, now?" of the sort you'd use to talk to a very small child. Eric smiled—then glanced at Shit to see that he'd stepped out on the porch, with Eric beside him, his cock still in his hand. Eric heard the door's latch catch behind them.

On the porch, Shit grinned. "Hey—see? What did I tell you?" He pulled at himself absently.

"That you could just walk into anybody's house around here and… fuck with 'em." Eric was pushing his own cock back into his jeans—and wondering how fast he should do it. He wasn't getting any hint from Shit.

"You believe me now?"

"Yeah." Eric took his hand away and, exerting great effort, did *not* pull up his zipper. "I believe you." Because Shit hadn't. "Come on, let's go."

As they started down the steps, Shit's near hand fell on Eric's shoulder. "Hey—you wanna suck me off?"

"What—you gotta go *again?*"

"Well, the last one wasn't that good. 'Cause I was kinda rushed, you know?"

"You…*you* were nervous?"

Shit took a breath and looked around at clouds and high sea birds, rocking on the sky. "I wasn't nervous. I was just rushed." He leaned closer to Eric. "But we ain't bein' rushed out here." Eric glanced down to see Shit pulling his fist free of his cock, still half hard, then wiping his palm on the thigh of his pants. He gripped himself again and pulled his fist off it once more. This time he raised his hand and sniffed his fingers. "Man, my dick really stinks after stickin' it up that nigger bitch's asshole—"

—when a redish-brown Nissan Cube (...rose?) turned off the road, onto the offshoot that could take it only to Mama Grace's door.

Shit's hand fell.

Eric thrust both hands down to zip his fly—then glanced, to see that, yes, Shit was—finally—closing his pants.

Nearing, the truck bumped side to side.

They stepped to the shoulder. First through the windshield, then the side window, they could see the driver was a thin black fellow with glasses and a bald head. He glanced out at them then looked forward again. The truck thundered toward the house.

Beside him, Shit raised a hand and waved. "Hey, Wally—she waitin' for you. We got her *good* and primed, too!"

Eric started walking. Shit pranced after him. As they turned onto the road, both fell to laughing.

Eric found himself thinking it was both stupid and hysterical. They turned toward the Dump's center. Though he knew in no way could Wally have heard Shit's brag, what Eric *believed* was that three or four people might just let Shit walk in and fuck them, though because of the way Mama Grace had treated them, only the one—Mr. Davis—might tolerate it. If it was, Eric wouldn't have been surprised.

Ambling beside him, Shit said (as if reading Eric's mind), "We coulda gone over and fucked around with Black Bull and Whiteboy, I mean if they wasn't workin'—only thing is, whenever I do that, it always gets so fucked up and messy with them two." Shit sucked his teeth, frowning at the grass-tufted ridge along running between double dust ruts. "Hey, I'll mess with 'em. But I don' mess with 'em a *lot*. It's too complicated."

Forty yards later, tar and cinders covered the road.

Eric let Shit catch up with him and put his hand on Shit's shoulder. Shit was biting at his nails, and, a moment later, picking in his nose. Suddenly, he smiled at Eric. "You want some? Here."

When Shit pulled his finger from Eric's mouth, they walked along the warm dust between autumn grasses either side the road. Shit leaned closer. "Well, whatever we do, I wanna do *somethin'* nasty."

Eric grinned. "What else is new?"

"Whatcha mean?"

"Nevermind. I thought we *did* somethin' nasty, Shit." Eric's statement was half a question.

"Naw," Shit said. "I mean *real* fuckin' nasty." His hand grew heavy with "real" and began to rub on "nasty." "I think I'm gonna suck *your* fuckin' dick!"

"Well," Eric said, "I don't have a handkerchief, but maybe I can find *somethin'* to wipe it off—"

"What you gotta wipe it off for?"

"'Cause it's just been up somebody's asshole, and I think you said it: It *was* an asshole full of shit."

"Aw, hell," Shit said. "A little crap on that thing ain't gonna hurt nobody."

Eric made a face. "How do *you* know?"

Shit slid an arm around Eric's neck. "When I was a little kid, Dynamite used to suck my dick—but that's all he did. Sometimes he'd lick my butt out, but mainly he sucked me off. I used to love it, too. I couldn't hardly get enough. I started comin' in his mouth when I was nine, nine-and-a-half. By the time I was ten, ten-and-a-half, I got my first hair down there. And when I got to be twelve or thirteen, Dynamite decided I needed to learn how to fuck ass. So—" hooking Eric closer, Shit shrugged—"I started out on *him*. Well, when you ain't done nothing but come in guys' mouths—Mex's, my dad's, a couple of the summer folks who liked to oblige me—you got to *learn* how to come up an ass. I mean, I did it okay a few times; I was real proud of it, too. But sometimes, I couldn't get myself to shoot, no matter what I did. So I'd pull out and beg my dad to bring me off in his mouth. I'd wanna come so bad I could cry. And he'd do it." Shit gave a grimace. "*He* never wiped it off—and it didn't kill *him*."

"But that was mostly his own, wasn't it?"

"His, Mex's, and so many of the summer people's, I don't remember. Even Bull's, a couple of times—before he got Whiteboy. When I was a little shit, Bull didn't mind if I fucked *his* black ass. But afterward I'd have to nip across the road and let my daddy bring me off—and he didn't wipe *that* nigger's shit off my dick any more than he wiped off his own."

Eric started laughing. "The idea that *you* had to learn how to fuck an asshole—"

"How *else* you gonna do it? See—" once more Shit tugged him near— "I was an arrogant sonofabitch. I'd fuck these guys, and finally I'd *pretend* to shoot—"

"You was fakin' orgasms?"

"—then I'd pull out and get back here to the Dump—sometimes when I got here I couldn't hardly walk, my balls was so damned blue—and beg my dad to suck me till I came. He'd always stop what he was doin' to do it, too…at least for a while. Finally, though, he made up his mind and broke me of that."

"How?" Frowning, Eric pulled away. While he'd not been watching, the road had joined with another that was paved.

"He let me have his fuckin' ass whenever I wanted it—let me do it real easy. Take as long as I wanted—go all slow and fuck that thing inside out, bend him over the kitchen table, or outside on the porch rail, in bed in the mornin'—that was my favorite, even then—or on the floor, anywhere. Pretty soon, I got me some control so I could splash up in his—or anybody else's—damned shit shoot as easy as I could in his damned mouth. But he wasn't a dick wiper with none of it." He winked at Eric. "And *you* ain't, either—"

"Hey, that's just with you and Dynamite."

"—so," (Shit shrugged) "why do *I* have to be?"

"I guess...well, you don't. But—" Again, Eric pulled his head away. "Hey, Shit, are you kiddin' me?"

"Yep." Shit grinned again. "I'm kiddin'. I'm only tellin' you dirty stories about me and Dynamite to turn you on..." Again Shit brought his own head close to Eric's. "Most of the time, if I couldn't shoot, I'd just go somewhere and beat off. Still, that don't mean them stories ain't true—some of them— just 'cause they get your dick stiff."

"Hey." Eric sucked his teeth. "Where you wanna—?"

"There's a men's room behind the produce market."

Eric had never noticed. "There is?"

"Un-huh. I did some guys there when I was a kid. But the supermarket guards was always runnin' me out, 'cause I wasn't eighteen. It's supposed to be 'gay friendly' or somethin'. But they was never too friendly to *me*. Since I actually got to *be* eighteen, I don't even think I even gone into that place to piss."

They were in sight of Dump Corners.

Houses were closer together.

Several one-story offices included a Dump Housing Office (stand-out aluminum letters ran along the red-brick wall), with a deck in front on which four large plants stood in polished gray-stone pots. Dump Social Services Offices—with its bronze wall plaque on the red brick—had its name decaled across its long picture window, with long blinds, three-quarters down, behind tinted glass. Shit dropped his arm, as he and Eric wandered closer. Beneath the blinds, Eric could see, inside, a row of free standing monitors.

To the left and right of the Social Services Offices were shops. To left of the Housing Office were others.

Why Dump Corners was plural, Eric didn't know. It looked like a single corner to *him*. Twenty yards away, in front of the Army-Navy Surplus Outlet, was the Plexiglas bus stop shelter with an aluminum bench under the clear roof, where, twice a day the shuttle—two alternating, dark green SUVs—to Runcible, Hemmings, and the Hemmings Mall came through the Dump.

Beside the Army-Navy Outlet was another broad glass window, backed with blinds: The Credit Union, with three touch-screen ATM windows in its blue and green vestibule. Two was the most people Eric ever saw using them at one time. (Shit always waited outside and let Dynamite do his withdrawals for him.) The only time Eric really had had to go inside was to talk to an officer when he'd set his PIN. He'd used the vestibule money machines three or four times before he'd noticed there was no withdrawal fee—for anyone, with any kind of card. It was like the ATMs in the Union at the University in Atlanta that, for a while, in order to save the two dollars, he and some of the other high school kids had gone to.

Half a dozen people walked in the streets—all of them black, all of them male. Two, Eric was *sure* were gay: they looked the busiest. He watched someone turn into Fred Hurter's Lumber, Steel, & Seed—a hardware, air conditioner, and auto-parts store, with a decent wall of comics and some porn magazines.

They even sold gay comics—Class Comics—which Fred Hurter must have gotten as remainders; Eric had bought a couple back in Atlanta: nine bucks a piece, while Hurter's sold them for two-fifty.

Eric owned pretty much all the ones that turned him on—and wondered who in the world responded to the others.

While Eric was wondering if they should go in, Shit hurried on for the Produce Outlet—really, a small supermarket—its grocery carts nested in a row out front. "Come on." He looked back at Eric.

Eric sprinted after.

All the way behind the Produce Outlet—the paving gave out again— was a single-story red brick structure, with a sloping roof, in which Eric could see a skylight. The inset door was set back under a cement slab that said, MEN'S ROOM and under that it read "Gay Friendly." (By now Eric had noticed how his predawn work schedule interfered with his learning the specifics of the local landscape. He'd never come here before.) As they walked toward it, they saw a young black man—tall, rather gawky, and round-shouldered—with glasses and a white fisherman's sunhat whose brim covered the upper part of his face, walking toward the door.

The young man's green jeans were baggy and, like many of the summer peoples', stopped at his knees. He wore what could have been a large football jersey that hung midway down his thighs.

The red crepe paper flower was the size of a coffee saucer. It bobbed on a stem with several large leaves that looked like green plastic, rising from his hat brim. The fellow walked purposely toward the door and through— when he stepped into the shadow, the flower turned orange—perhaps six seconds before they reached it.

Was that, Eric wondered, *the* hat?

Eric stepped into the john's vestibule after Shit. To the wall was fixed a plaque, darkened with patina, where Eric read:

If Gay Activity Offends You, Please:
Take Your Business into a Stall,
Lock the Door—and
Don't Loiter.

Eric laughed. "I never seen a sign like *that* in a john before."

Shit was already ahead of him inside. Since Shit didn't read, Eric wondered if he even knew what it said.

Shit waited and, when Eric stepped beside him to look around, took hold of Eric's arm. "Come on, take your dick out your pants. I told you. I'm gonna suck it, right here."

"...maybe go into a stall or somethin'?" Eric realized he distrusted the invitation.

"What the fuck for? Come on."

Or was at least made uncomfortable by it.

Sun through the wired glass in the skylights lit a wall that ran down the room's middle. The floor was oversized maroon brick. From where Eric stood, he could see that down either side the central wall of yellow tile stood a row of old fashioned, floor-to-shoulder white porcelain urinals. In one of the walls opposite, windows of opaque glass let in light from outside. On the wall's other side, opposite the urinals, were a row of stalls with gray doors in gray frames, most closed—though a few stood open, an inch to three inches.

The young man had gone down on the side with the windows, to the last urinal. He stood there, very close to it, gazing down. Once he looked up, but dropped his eyes again. His flower swung.

At the wall's front hung a framed sign, containing two messages, one on the left, one on the right:

IF YOU DON'T WANT TO BE BOTHERED OR LOOKED AT, USE THIS SIDE. PEOPLE HERE JUST WANT TO URINATE.

PLEASE CONFINE TEAROOM CRUISING TO THIS SIDE. STALLS ARE FOR EVERYONE BUT BE CONSIDERATE.

An arrow under each pointed to the left (the side with windows) and the right (the side with the stalls).

Below, a smaller sign read:

Please Confine All Masturbation to Completion
To Commode Stalls.

And below that:

Remember,
You wouldn't want to have to mop it up either!

"Come on," Shit said, "whip it out, motherfucker. I'm hungry for some goddamn nigger dick." He stepped from sneaker to sneaker, as if the brick floor were hot as the sunny macadam outside and he stood on it, barefooted.

"You sure you want mine, then?"

"I know I want it hard," Shit said. "And I know callin' you that's the best way to get it that way, you black sonofabitch."

Eric took a deep breath, wondering why something said specifically to get him hard *got* him hard, as though the intent itself was sexy. (The kid with the flower wasn't looking.) He pulled his shoulders up and fingered for his zipper. A moment later, Shit grasped him in his hand, and led him by the cock down between the urinals and the windows.

"Hey," Eric said, softly, "don't you think we ought to go around the *other* side?"

Shit looked over at the kid, who was concertedly not looking at them. "We ain't gonna bother him—besides, I wanna see what the fuck I'm suckin'." He glanced at the wire-covered windows, their marbled glass backed with sunlight. "You got such a *nice* one! I like to see what I'm eatin'." Shit dropped to a squat, put his head to the side—and, when the wet heat enveloped him, Eric grasped Shit's head, which began to retreat and advance. A second later, Shit's fist left Eric's hardened cock to grip the hip of Eric's jeans.

Eric made a sound louder than he intended.

So did Shit—who moved off it long enough to say, "Now *that* tastes like the fuckin' cock from heaven." Then, mouth wide, he caught it again and moved in. And went in so that his face ground Eric's lap, as if he wanted to swallow not only Eric's dick, but balls, bladder, and prostate.

Eric whispered, "Aw, *Jesus,* Shit…!"

Going down on one knee, Shit kept sucking.

"…excuse me?"

Eric was not paying attention.

"…excuse me…? I'm sorry, but…"

While Shit's incredibly warm mouth slid in and out, Eric looked over, where the gawky black kid blinked at them behind his wire-framed glasses, with a distressed expression:

"...excuse me, please. But, see I..." He shook his head. His flower swung. "I can't pee if you guys are...you know, doin'...*that*." He looked away, his flower bobbing.

Shit must have heard him, because Eric's dick went cold. "Why the fuck *can't* you?"

"I don't know. It's just..." The tall kid's hands were clutched between his leg. "Maybe, you know, you could...go around the other side?"

Eric said, "See, I *told* you—"

"There're two of us and one of you." A knee on the floor, Shit's shoulder twisted back. "Why don't *you* go around the other side?"

"Oh, yeah...sure. I just meant because of the sign."

Eric's hands still caged Shit's head. "You know, really, he's right—"

Shit looked up, head rotating between Eric's fingers. "What you mean, he's right? You guys are fuckin' crazy—*I* wanna suck some goddam dick!" Shit turned back and his rough hair rubbed Eric's hands. His green eyes went up to Eric—and he grinned. "And you must wanna get sucked, 'cause you ain't lettin' my head go." Again his mouth closed on Eric's cock.

Through the returned warmth, Eric looked down at Shit's hair between his thumbs, its rough cotton a dirty tan over his bony skull, more rectangular than round. Already Shit had a tongue of flesh, one at each temple, as well as, in the exact center of his mustard matt, a thinner spot where you could see to the bony scalp. Shit's head moved out and back, taking Eric's hands, taking from those hands only the rhythm and speed, while gums and tongue slid hotly around him. In such a rush of pleasure— like Shit's cartilaginous ears on Eric's palms—all these fore-signs of age, as they were unusual on someone of Shit's years, were themselves the stuff of beauty.

As Shit sucked, eagerly and—hell!—expertly, the gawky youngster at the hall's end put himself away and moved forward, his back to the windows, watching and blinking behind his glasses. His lower legs looked scrawny. Whenever his flower moved into direct sunlight from the windows, again it turned bright scarlet. His face and arms were only slightly browner than Shit's hair. Near enough so that his whispery voice was a surprise, he said, "Excuse me...?" The kid was talking to Shit. "But, uh, maybe you want to...um, get him up against the wall. So when he comes, he won't fall down or nothin'." He coughed, one hand—a loose fist—rose before his mouth, then dropped back to his crotch. "That's I how I did it, the time I was in the train station in Washington...um," (and Eric frowned) "but he was a policeman." He stood again between windows.

Again his flower was orange.

Eric felt Shit's mouth slow.

Both his knees on the brick, Shit came off Eric, settled back on his haunches, and looked aside. "Now, why the fuck are you tellin' me *that*?"

Eric heard Shit take a breath. Looking down, he saw Shit's own cock slanted up, from his open fly, now outside his pants.

The kid's eyes moved between it and Eric's. "Um...I'm sorry...I mean, you know...maybe, I don't...but 'cause this is supposed to be—" He blinked. "...friendly?"

Shit drew another breath. "Get the fuck around the other side and finish your goddam piss. And lemme suck this goddam dick, will ya'?"

From the other side of the wall, someone called, leisurely, loud, and muffled within a stall. "Will you fellas shut the fuck up? I'm tryin' to take a shit!"

At the same time, the kid said, "Oh, yeah. Sure..." darted to the wall's end, and dashed around it—flower swinging, first scarlet, then orange behind.

"When you're finished," Shit called after him, "if you wanna come back here and watch—maybe jerk off or something—that's okay. I'm gonna take my time. It's really nice suckin' on this fucker, you know?"

Eric whispered, "Why'd you tell 'im that?"

Looking up, Shit shrugged. "I don't know." He raised up on his knees again. "*I'm* bein' friendly." Shit spoke as loudly as before.

From the wall's other side, the enclosed and echoing voice came over: "Come on, guys. This ain't no hog callin' contest. It's a fuckin' men's room. Shut *up*."

Now Eric called back, "Hey. It ain't a public library, either!" Looking down he saw Shit wince.

"What you tryin' to do, huh?" Shit whispered, from his knees. "Start a fight?"

"Come on," Eric said, voice as soft as Shit's. "Will you please suck my goddam dick? You started it, now—and you don't do *that* so often so as I wanna give up in the middle!"

"Damn, I'm spoilin' this nigger." Shit caught Eric in his mouth again, pushing himself forward at the same time.

Moments later, Eric staggered—and stepped back, as, kneeling and spilling from his fist, Shit spattered the brick between his knees. Eric's shoulder hit the wall and the back of his head hit the window frame's side—though not hard. Wired glass rattled behind him, and he started to protest. Then didn't...

His hands were back on Shit's head.

Moments before he came for the second time that afternoon, Eric looked up.

The tall kid with the red paper flower and the scrawny knees had come back. He had his hands between his legs, under his long shirt.

Eric shot. It was as if, outside, a cloud slipped from the sun and the windows along the wall, either side, filled with light. He closed his eyes, raised his head. And the growing light was inside, not out. Opening them again, again he began to breathe. (Shit's hand slid from Eric's hips to tighten around his butt. He ground his face against Eric's jeans.) "Come on…come on…not so…!" (Shit stilled.) Eric, sensitive and tender, pushed Shit's head away and grunted.

Shit released Eric, and, while Eric shoved himself back in his pants, Shit looked over at the kid. "What you doin' here again?"

"Oh, gee…no, I'm sorry—" the kid began.

Shit rocked back on his toes, and, in an awkward motion, stood.

"You told him to come." Eric zipped his jeans. "He's bein' friendly—" He looked at the lanky kid. "Ain't you?"

"Oh, no…yes, no, I didn't…I mean—"

"What…?" Shit looked the kid up and down. "You want yours sucked, too? I'm tired."

"You know," Eric said, "really, *we* should'a gone around the other side. He should'a stayed on this one. That's what the sign says."

Shit asked, "What sign?"

Eric grinned. "The one telling everybody where to go if they just wanna piss, or if they wanna fuck around. Or if they just wanna jerk off."

"Tellin' everybody where to go," Shit said. "That don't sound so friendly to me. Why can't you go wherever you want?"

"Sure," Eric said. "Maybe," as, slowly, Shit put himself away. "But we *should* have been around there on the other side."

Between the edges of his open shirt, Shit nubbed his hard, ridged belly. "But this is the nice side—it's got all the light. *This* side should be for the fellas who wanna suck and fuck and jerk off together—I mean, if it was *really* gay friendly."

"Maybe—" and the kid's red flower bobbed again—"they got it so that you can duck into one of the stalls if somebody comes in what you don't want…you know, to see. Around that side."

"Actually—" Eric grinned—"havin' a place like this where you got to run and hide ain't very friendly, either."

"Oh." The kid frowned. (By now he seemed much younger to Eric than he had. Fifteen or sixteen? Eric wondered if he *himself* could have seemed that young two years ago, when he'd arrived at Diamond Harbor.) "I hadn't…you know. Thought about that."

Shit pulled his shirt up on his shoulder, where, open and mostly buttonless, it had slid off. "The fuckin' john at the back of Turpens Truck Stop is more gay friendly than *this* place."

Someone said, "Hey…" from the end of the room toward the entrance. "You guy's here is all crazy, huh? I mean you're all gay…?"

All three looked.

Standing behind the wall's edge, wearing a plaid shirt and jeans, buttoned down over a full belly, stood a white guy in a blue cap, peak backwards, who looked between twenty-five and thirty-five. If he had turned out a cousin of Jay MacAmon's, Eric wouldn't have been surprised, except that he was half a head shorter than Eric, rather than two heads taller. A stocky man, he had no beard but was as unshaven as Dynamite usually was.

"That was really weird, what you guys was doin'—where everybody could see it, and stuff. Wow!" From his wide belt, a chain looped down over one thigh and back up to a ring with a bristling sphere of keys on his hip and two pocketknives hanging from it. Under the rolled-up short-sleeves, Eric just saw a tattoo of Porky Pig in a sailor's suit and a large-toothed groundhog, standing on its hind legs, conferring with each other. His jeans went down to frayed cuffs, lapped over once-orange work shoes as worn as Dynamite's—or Shit's, when he wore them. "Someone told me there was a—what did he call it?—a 'gay friendly' restroom around here. I'm just deliverin' bottled water to the market. But I figured I had to see this." (Only now, Eric realized from the voice, it was the man who'd shouted for quiet from the shit stall.) "I mean, I ain't gay—but I was curious. I never knowed any gay people. The ones outside, walkin' 'round, they look pretty ordinary—even if they all black. Till I learned about this place, I didn't even know black people *could* be gay. Kind of figure you black guys are too mean, huh?" He chuckled, looking from one of them to the other. "But I guess, yeah, you guys is *all* crazy, right…?"

The silence drew out. Since Eric wasn't sure what anyone was supposed to say, he said nothing.

After a while, the driver said, "So I guess you guys'll suck anybody's dick what comes in here, right? Well, yeah, *that's* kinda crazy. I mean, out where people can see. I guess it ain't bad if it's what you're into. But I ain't into it." Reaching up, he rubbed an ear.

Again the silence drew out.

"You know that place—Turpens—you was talkin' about? The truck stop out on the highway? Someone told me a *whole* lot of faggot fellas go in there. In that place, there ain't supposed to be nothin' else *but*, half the time. I done stopped in there, I mean occasional like—used the restroom, too. But I ain't never seen one. Fact is, I don't think I never seen a gay feller in my life, except you guys. Maybe sometimes you see a guy in the stall, lookin' over, but unless you lookin' back, you wouldn't even know. And I don't see how just lookin' gonna make you gay. I mean, everybody gotta be a little curious, know what I'm sayin'?" He stepped back toward the door. "Well, I gotta go and make my deliveries." Turning abruptly, he walked out the restroom door.

Now Shit asked, "Hey—are you that kid, Lurrie?"

Surprised, the gawky youngster turned. "Oh—yeah. I am. I'm Lurrie Stone. How'd you know?" The red flower was going up and down.

Shit said, "Ain't that many people around here I don't know." He ran his thumb under his jean's rope. "So if you hear about somebody you don't know and you see somebody you don't know both, chances are they're the same person."

"Oh," Lurrie said. "Yeah—I guess so. I'm down here for the winter with my uncle—Ezra Potts? You know him? He's gay, too—like me."

"Yeah," Shit said. "I seen him." He looked at Eric. "Dynamite sees him all the time at the Dump town meetin's."

"Yeah, my uncle goes to those. He was tellin' me all about 'em." Lurrie said. "My mama's his sister—she sent me down from Chicago to spend the winter with him." Lurrie looked uncomfortable. "Before I go to college. She wanted me to meet some nice, respectable gay people—you know? There're supposed to be a lot of really nice gay men livin' around here…? Black ones…?" The statement had ended in an inquiry that Eric felt Lurrie was waiting for them to confirm.

Shit had started looking at the opaque glass in the window frames along the wall. Suddenly, though, he put his fists up beside his neck, raised his elbows, and yawned—the one time when his missing teeth and the two or three rotted-out ones looked a little strange even to Eric. Shit's belly thrust forward between his shirt's green edges, his shoulders went back. A moment later, he rocked back and stood up. "I'm fuckin' tired. That's 'cause I been workin'—you know: workin' at havin' fun. That's what my daddy says."

"Oh, wow," the gawky kid said. "Are you…the garbage man's kid?"

"Hell," Shit said. "I'm Garbage Man number two. This here—" he dropped his fists and stood up again—"is Eric, Garbage Man number three. You can call me Shit, though, if you wanna call me at all." (Lurrie had gotten a big smile, which Eric could see he was trying to hold in.) "Hey." Shit shook his arms, and stepped around on the tile, moving closer. "Can I ask you a personal question? I mean, I don't wanna offend you or nothin'. But—"

Eric thought the question was going to be about the flower.

"—I was wondering why you wear them big ol' baggy pants you do, that look like they're fallin' off your ass—like I said, I don't mean to be rude. But you see kids in them things, all the time comin' down to the Harbor. I asked a couple of 'em, a couple of years ago. But they never seemed to know."

"No," Lurrie said. "Ain't no offence in that. It's the fashion."

"That's what the other ones said. But why?"

"What somebody told me," Lurrie said, "is that it started with the hip-hop kids, when they started hip-hop music."

"You mean that stuff when some nigger talks so fast you can't hear what he's sayin'?"

Apparently, Lurrie found that an amusing characterization. "You can hear it if you listen. But a lot of the first guys doin' that were goin' in and out of jail—you know, that's why they called it gangsta rap. And there were all these shootin's and things. And when you're in jail, you can't have no belts. 'Cause you could go and kill yourself or get yourself in a fight and use it to strangle somebody. So they started wearin' clothes that made 'em look the same way, when they came out."

"You hear how *he* talks, so fast like that? That's how all them people from up there talk. That's funny." Shit stopped to grin at Eric; then he looked back at Lurrie, who still hadn't seemed to take offence. "Why would somebody want to look like they been in jail?"

"I guess it was a kind of a rebellion," Eric said. "Like you callin' yourself Shit."

"Oh," Shit said, puzzling the two together. Then he kind of pulled the corners of his mouth back, so that his lips got even thinner than they were. "But what sort of a rebellion is it if *everybody's* doin' it?"

"Fashion," Lurrie said. "That's what it means, I guess. Could I ask you a question back?"

"Sure," Shit said. "What?"

"I don't wanna offend nobody down here, neither. But…well, you was suckin' on his dick, and you said I could come back and watch. Do you think…well, maybe…*um*, him…or you, even…I mean that it would be okay to even—"

"You want one of us to suck you off, too—?"

"*No!*" Lurrie exclaimed. "No—that's not what I wanted. I mean…un-un. No, I wondered if…well, maybe—"

Eric was frowning.

"—if you could…fuck me. I mean, if you wanted to. Either one of you—

or, both of you, if you wanted. I wouldn't mind. I mean…I was hopin', maybe, I was gonna find *someone*…you know, who could—"

Shit had started chuckling.

"I didn't mean to be insultin or nothin'—"

"I ain't insulted," Shit said. "I'm just tired. We started out pretty early this mornin'." They had begun the day, as they often did on their days off, with a session with Dynamite, before Shit and Eric had wandered off together—and dropped in on Mama Grace. "I'm afraid I'm about fucked out for the day. I'm really sorry. Maybe some other time."

"Hey." Eric fingered his fly again and pulled down his zipper. "You wanna hold my dick for a minute?"

"Huh?" Lurrie looked totally confused.

"His, too," Eric said. "He'll let you—won't you, Shit?"

"Huh?" Shit said. "Oh, yeah—sure. You wanna?" He looked almost as confused as Lurrie.

Once again Eric pulled out his penis. "Come on—take it out and let him play with it. Just so he can go home and at least say he had his hands on a couple besides his own, today."

"Oh, yeah," Shit said. "Sure. I know what *that's* about."

"Wow…It's all right?" Lurrie's narrow shoulders had gotten even narrower. "You ain't gonna do nothin' to me? I mean, you ain't makin' fun of me, are you?"

"Naw," Eric said. "I'm serious. Take hold of 'em—go on."

"If you don't wanna," Shit said, "you don't have to. Nobody gonna make you do it."

"I don't know if I should."

Eric said, "If it was all right for us to fuck you, it should be all right for you to hold 'em."

"Yeah, but I…done got fucked before."

"Come on," Eric said. "Grab hold—then you can let 'em go. That's all. And you got somethin' to take home with you and think about."

Lurrie breathed out. Reaching forward, he put one hand around Eric's, the other around Shit's. His fingers were thin. His oval nails were neatly cut. The expression on his face was that of someone doing something both delicate and difficult.

"See," Shit said, "they ain't gonna bite ya'."

"*Wow*…!" He looked up, smiling—and looked back down. "That's… awesome. They're…nice."

Eric found himself wanting to laugh, with his penis in Lurrie's grip.

Shit reached up and put his hand on Lurrie's shoulder—and, Eric saw, began to squeeze.

Remembering how that always relaxed him, watching made Eric relax.

"Do you know," Shit said, "even with all the fuckin' I been doin' today, you're actually givin' me a hard-on again?"

Lurrie said, "He's getting' one, too."

Shit said, "Bet *you* are, too. You gonna show us yours?"

"Aw, no..." Lurrie let go of both.

Shit looked over at Eric questioningly.

"No...I don't think I...I should do that."

"Why?" Shit asked. "We let you hold onto ours."

"I dunno," Lurrie said. "I guess, 'cause...well, if you saw it, you wouldn't like me."

"Why not?" Shit asked.

"I dunno..." Lurrie looked around as if he dropped something on the floor. "I guess 'cause it's...small."

"Hey," Eric said, "that's nothin' to worry about," though he sometimes wondered if it was.

"Look—" outside his pants, Shit dangled loose—"you guys is just kids. But I'm a goddam old fart. *I'm* getting' tired." (It was one of Dynamite's lines.) "How about we go on home, so I can catch a nap?"

"Yeah," Eric said. "We probably should." He pushed his own softening cock back in his jeans, and, with his thumb, tugged his underpants forward, so that it slipped within.

"Un-huh," Lurrie said. "That was really nice. I wished I'd...kissed 'em."

Now Shit got a kind of ironic look. He pulled his out again: "Go on and kiss the fucker, then lemme get outta here. Okay?"

"Jesus..." Lurrie whispered. He bent down, and the red flower caught against the waist of Shit's jeans, while again he took Shit's cock in his fist. After looking at it for five second, he let his face move forward, kissed it, and stood up. Alternately the red flower flopped left, then right. "Uh... thank you. Thank you." He looked—longingly, Eric realized—at Eric's crotch.

Lurrie blinked. "You're just so...beautiful!"

"Yeah," Shit said. "He is—ain't he?"

"No," Lurrie said. "I mean...*both* of you!"

"Huh?" Shit frowned now. "Hell—I ain't good lookin'. I'm just a dumb-shit half-breed nigger. But, yeah, *he's* fuckin' amazin'." With a foreknuckle he prodded his upper lip away from his gum. "See," he spoke with a distorted voice—"I don't even got none of my teeth no more, hardly. But *he* says he likes that."

"Yeah," Lurrie said. "I guess that makes it feel better when...you know, you're suckin'."

"Well...yeah." Eric said. "That, too..." Embarrassed, he'd been thinking about pulling himself out again—but Lurrie was already standing. "Hey," Eric said. "I like your hat—I mean that flower you got."

"You *do*—?" As he stood there, a smile spread over Lurrie's face. (Eric thought: The kid's *ears* are grinning!) "My girlfriend gave that to me. Marlene. She's my best friend in the whole world—in Chicago. She made it for me and gave it to me as a goin'-away present. Out of this special paper that changes colors. She said she thought it expressed my inner consciousness. It's just like one she sent me on Facebook. I think it's lovely—and it *does!*" Behind his glasses, Lurrie raised his eyes as if, despite the sunhat's down-turned brim, he might see it.

Eric found himself smiling.

"My uncle thinks I shouldn't wear it. But I wear it anyway. I think it's good to show your inner consciousness like that out where everybody can see what it is. Don't you?"

Clearly not sure what he should answer, Shit looked at Eric.

"Sure," Eric said. "Ain't no reason not to."

Lurrie said, "My uncle thinks it's gonna get me in a fight."

Shit said, "It could—yeah." Again he glanced at Eric. "But not over here—this is the Dump."

"I should go back and find my uncle." Lurrie suddenly made nervous fists, opened them again, and then—equally nervously—patted his stomach under his basketball shirt. "He's probably looking for me." Looking up again, he blinked back and forth between them. "You guys are awesome."

Eric smiled. In a year-and-a-half, the word had fallen out of his vocabulary, since he never heard it here.

Shit said, "Well, thank you. You down here for the winter; we'll see you again—probably."

Lurrie nodded, smiled, then turned toward the john's front. He walked out the door.

Shit said, "That was interesting," and turned after him, Eric at his side.

Across the empty lot, coming from the back door of the Produce Outlet, perhaps ten seconds later, they saw a man, cocoa-skinned and wearing jeans and a white short-sleeved shirt, maybe in his late forties or early fifties. He wore a green army cap, turned to the side. He had seen Lurrie and was hurrying toward him. "Lurrie, where in the world have you—?"

"Mr. Potts," Shit said softly, to Eric, as their own path carried them closer.

"I was in the bathroom..." Lurrie's explained in his whispery voice. "That's all—"

"Well, what were you doing in *that* place?"

"Huh?" Lurrie asked, beginning to sound bewildered. "I was goin' to the bathroom."

Shit chose then to call out, "Nice to meet you, Lurrie. We'll see you some other time."

Lurrie turned. "Oh, yeah—Good-bye!"

"And what in the world were you doing with *those* two?" Mr. Potts demanded, voice twice as loud.

"Nothin'." Lurrie's was twice as soft. His inner consciousness was permanently red in the sunlight.

"Don't you know that's Morgan Haskell. You are not to go into that place again, do you understand? That's not what your mother sent you down here for. And she did *not* send you here to associate with those two— or anybody like them. *You* are not the sort of person who has sex with strangers in men's rooms. Do you follow me?"

"Uh-huh."

"That place is an embarrassment—and thank God nobody ever goes in there." Now Potts turned directly to Eric and Shit. "And I do not want to see either of you with my nephew again—he's seventeen years old, for God's sake! I am trying to raise him to be a good, proper young man!"

Mr. Potts looked completely frustrated. He turned away and started across the bare dirt behind the row of stores.

Shit and Eric had both stopped walking.

Lurrie glanced at them, then hurried after his uncle.

Suddenly Shit called after them, "Hey!"

Mr. Potts and Lurrie walked on across the Dump's hot dirt behind the delivery entrances of the Dump's town stores. Lurrie glanced back at them. Mr. Potts did not.

"Hey, Lurrie! Did I look like the scuzziest, low-down motherfuckin' nigger in the Dump when I was suckin' *this* goddam motherfucker's great big black dick? I hope I did—that's what I was *tryin'* to do. 'Cause that's what makes me feel fuckin' sexy as hell!"

Stopping a second time, Lurrie glanced again, but Mr. Potts just strode purposely forward. Then Lurrie turned to catch up to his uncle.

"You know, this guy right here, he *looks* white—" Shit went on shouting, stepping back so that he was outside Eric's line of sight—"but he's really the blackest fuckin' nigger you ever met! He's more of a nigger than your goddam uncle. You don't believe me? You should see his daddy—next time he comes around. He's so much blacker than *your* fuckin' uncle, you'd fill up them fuckin' too-big pants with shit if you saw 'im—you better believe it! I mean, you lookin' for a nigger to suck, this—" from behind him, Shit's hands fell on the shoulders, left and right, of Eric's T-shirt, pushing forward, as he gazed across the space—"here's the nigger you wanna be suckin'!"

Eric laughed, but his nervousness was an electric tingling around his arms and chest and back. He whispered, "Come on, now! Cut it *out*, Shit—! You're gonna make things worse for the kid."

Shit stepped around beside him. "How they gonna get worse?" He raised one hand to his nose, closed off one nostril with a wide thumb, snorted, then closed the other nostril with a forefinger and its broad, ruined nail, and snorted again. Moving his cupped, glistening palm over before Eric's chin, he said in a whisper intense enough to shock Eric. "Okay, you *eat* that! *Now*—and I don't wanna even *see* you look around to check out if anybody's watchin' or not. You do, and I'll bust you in your rock-hard nigger head right here, white boy." Shit's other hand had risen in a knuckley fist: he hefted it like ball of bone and meat and callus.

It was all Eric could do to slay the habit of checking, but—because neither Lurrie nor Mr. Potts were looking, at any rate—he lowered his chin and licked awkwardly at Shit's palm. He hardly tasted it. But he saw Shit move his hand back before his own face to lick off the rest.

"Okay," Shit said, "*now* you can do all the Nervous Nelly lookin' around you want!" He took a breath and started walking. Eric walked after him, looking around as he caught up.

He expected to see no one.

But what Eric saw was the thick delivery driver, in his cap and with his keys at his waist, wheeling an empty hand truck from the rear entrance of one of the stores toward his truck. The driver was looking directly at Eric and Shit—and looking surprised, too.

Eric had gone through some barrier of embarrassment, and, on the other side, was now in some kind of neuter hyper-nervousness. "Shit...?" he whispered.

"What?" Shit seemed to have returned to some sort of normalcy—if that was the right term.

"You say you know everybody around here—you know him?"

"Who?"

"The other guy in the bathroom." He nodded toward the driver, who, with a rope through a bright brass grommet, briefly blazing in the sun, was now tying the corner of a blue tarp down over his delivery.

"Him?" Shit started walking, Eric with him. "What you mean? Yeah—I *seen* him before."

"Who is he?"

"Why?" As they came out in front of the Produce Outlet, and turned toward Hurter's Lumber, Steel, and Seed, Shit began to grin. "You wanna suck *his* dick?"

Eric felt a tingle. "Yeah, he *is* kinda cute. But I was wonderin'—that's all."

"You'll probably learn yourself," Shit said, "in not too long."

In front of the stores, they walked by the plastic-walled Shuttle Stop with its metal roof. The sunlight was distorted on the pavement beside it. The tingling nervousness had…stopped.

Eventually Eric said, "I like Lurrie. He's all shy. But he seems like an interesting kid. Sort of young, though. But he'd still be fun to know."

"I like him, too," Shit said. "Too bad he's got to deal with that asshole uncle—Potts!"

"Yeah." Eric sighed again.

"You know, Eric?" Shit said, after a moment. "You're a really good feller." They moved over the gravel, dirt, and dried tufts. "You're a lot gooder'n I am." Then, while Eric was wondering what to say, suddenly Shit asked, "Hey, what you think *my* inner consciousness is?"

Eric frowned a moment. "Well…You ever seen rabbits fuck? You know how the buck gets on the doe—bip, bip, bip, bip, then jumps off on to another one: bip, bip, bip, bip, bip? And then another one?" There had been rabbits in Texas…

"Yeah…?"

"Well, you could have a hat with a big ol' furry, friendly, horny rabbit on the top, hoppin' up and down. That could be *your* inner consciousness—"

"Oh, fuck *you*—!" But both were laughing. "What's that Facebook he was talking about?"

"I dunno. I think it has something to do with computers."

They turned onto the dust road—more dust it seemed, anyway, than dirt—toward the Dump's edge that took them back to Dynamite's. Shit grunted: "Oh. Probably it's somethin' you got to read."

Eric frowned. "Maybe not a lot…"

"Well, it's a book, ain't it?"

* * *

[32] OVER THE NEXT weeks, they met Lurrie—without his uncle Ezra—coming from the beach or sitting in the Coffee & Egg or walking down Front Street at the Harbor and at the comic store (not Hurters but the one in Runcible). Once they took him back and forth on the scow with

Jay and Mex, and Shit spent the afternoon showing them both things and places on the island (*Don't worry—I ain't gonna tell my uncle I was hangin' round with you,* and then to Eric, *You really black?*)

(Shit said, *Sure he is. Can't you tell?*

(*Oh, yeah—sort of, I guess,* and Lurrie frowned, bending his head to the side.

(*Naw, I ain't really.* Eric laughed. *I wish I was, sometimes. But he's right: my dad was. And when I pretend I am, it turns me on.*

(*You guys is really lucky. Hey, you know this feels good…*) that were new even to Eric.

On Christmas, Dynamite said he could take the pick-up, and Eric drove to Runcible to spend the day with Barbara and Ron. Eric felt funny that Dynamite and Shit hadn't been invited, which he was sure was Bodin, not his mother. There were some friends. Dinner was at three. At five, he said, really, he had get back to the Dump, basically because he felt uncomfortable. As he was leaving, Barbara thrust into his hand a shopping bag with half a turkey in it, half a Dutch pineapple Christmas cake, and plastic refrigerator dishes of greens and yams and walnut stuffing and a jar of eggnog and more icebox dishes of creamed onions and giblet gravy. "That way," a guilty Barbara declared, at the kitchen door, "you all can have some Christmas, too."

When he got back to the Dump, the last blue had been gone from the sky for minutes, though it was not yet six. No lights shone in the cabin windows. Because they worked the next day, Dynamite and Shit were already in bed. He got the food into the refrigerator. When Eric crawled between them, immediately both wound themselves around him.

Dynamite said, "You smell like whiskey, son."

"Eggnog." Eric yawned. "I put some in the ice box—" which is what both Dynamite and Shit called the refrigerator, so Eric had been calling it that too—"for you, with some turkey and stuff Barb sent over."

"Smells good," Shit mumbled.

Already Eric could feel Shit's hard-on against his thigh, though he was sure in moments it would go down.

"It's nice havin' a drunk nigger crawl in bed with you on Christmas." Shit pushed harder against Eric. "Makes me all horny."

(Or maybe it wouldn't.)

Shit squeezed him again, even as Dynamite relaxed and moved back an inch. "Chef Ron come over here on the way to work at Shells," Shit mumbled on, "with some goose and some chestnut and sausage mush-up what he said was stuffin' and let us have 'em. That part was pretty good. But the goose was a little funny—maybe that's 'cause I never had none before." He gave a contagious yawn, beard and mouth both against Eric's chest—and, yes, his hard-on *was* subsiding. "Uncle Tom got most of mine, though."

Three days after New Years, Dynamite drove Shit and Eric down to Turpens. "We're stayin' here for an hour—one hour, that's *all*. Then I'm goin' home. I wanna take me a goddam nap." They all split up to start out, at least, in different johns, though they'd come here enough times together to know they'd all end up in the active back one.

Eric was walking across the lobby when, from the archway with its silhouetted MAN and WOMAN, he saw the stocky white driver, in his cap and his chain swinging down from belt to his bristle of keys, come out and amble toward the door.

Eric wasn't planning to say anything—maybe just nod—when the fellow grinned at him. "Hey—how you doin'? You been…" He looked around, kind of shrugging—"hangin' out in that…what was it, 'Gay Friendly' place over in the Dump? I go in there, you know, but there ain't never nobody in it. You fellas was the first guys I seen there the last three times I went."

"Yeah, I don't think it's too popular." Eric laughed. "Naw—I ain't been back since we saw you there."

The man glanced around—but, besides them, the lobby was empty just then. "Hey, you was givin' that nigger on his knees back there in the Dump john a good time—you ever do any dick suckin' yourself?"

Eric laughed. "Truth is, I do more suckin' than gettin' sucked. Actually."

"A big guy like you—with all them muscles? They look pretty hard. But, then, that's why I asked, I guess. I'll tell you. I come in here, horny as a motherfucker—and if you wanted to—" Looking around again, the man grasped his crotch and squeezed—"do a little suckin' on…my dick, I wouldn't chase you off. I mean, 'cause it's New Years."

"Oh." Eric laughed. "Okay. Sure."

"Hey," and the man stepped closer, while Eric bent a little to hear him, as he began to whisper: "When you and your friend was comin' out that place and doin all that hollerin' at them two back there, I thought I seen you and him do something…fuckin' *nasty*. I mean…" He shook his head.

"What you mean?" Eric asked.

"Well, it was…" The man stood up. "Aw, it was probably just me thinkin' I saw it. You know, in the bright sunlight, sometimes it's as hard to see as when it's half dark. You can think you see somethin' that's just in your mind—"

"What was it?" Eric asked. He was trying to sound innocent.

"It wasn't nothin'. Somethin' I used to do, sometimes, when I was kid— and it kinda tickled me to see you doin' it with each other—especially after what you was doin' together in the john. But I probably was, you know, misperceivin' things." He shook his head. "But I had me a cousin who did it till he was eighteen, twenty-one years old—then he went to Mobile; and from then on I ain't really seen him at all. But, see, I stopped when I was a kid and people started getting' disgusted with *me*, you know? Hey—I'm gonna go in the john. You wait three minutes, then come on in. I'll be in the second to the last stall on the end—on the right. You come on inside, but if anybody's in there, you wait around for him to leave. *Then* you slip on in, and I'll let you have it." He joggled his crotch again.

"Okay," Eric said, resigned.

"Now, if somebody comes in there while we're doin' somethin', I'm gonna zip up and slip out. You can wait in there for me—and when it's safe, I'll come back, after whoever comes in takes off. All right?"

"I got a better idea," Eric said. "Why don't we go into the john in the back of this place? Everybody who knows about that one, knows what's goin' on in it and don't mind—"

"Aw, *no!*" Raising his unshaven chin, the man shook his head. "Too many people in there—I mean, they got all them gay guys in here. They don't like straights like me. And I don't wanna get in no fight or nothing with 'em. I mean, in the back, a whole bunch of 'em is always lookin' out for each other."

Eric said, "They'll look out for *us*—if somebody who really doesn't belong there comes in."

"Naw—come on, now. You do what I say. You don't wanna fool around with none of them gay guys. They're crazy. That's crazy."

"Okay…" Eric repeated.

With his keys and his chain swinging at his leg, the man walked into the front john.

A minute or two later, Eric followed.

But the third time he found himself sitting with the door closed, alone in the end commode stall, waiting for the trucker to return, his jeans around his knees, Eric thought: What the fuck am I puttin' myself through this for? Well, he does have nice cock—it had turned out both longer *and* thicker than Eric had expected (it was in the same realm as Shit's and Dynamite's, actually)—and, yes, it had kept him there that long.

"But," as, the three were finally walking across the mica-flecked Turpens lot toward the pickup, Eric explained to Shit and Dynamite, "nice as it was, it wasn't *that* nice. I mean, I wanted to suck him off and I did—got his load, too. As dicks go, it was all right. But the rest of the stuff around it—runnin' in and out and gettin' scared and startin' and stoppin'—I don't have time for that bullshit, not with the old john in the back, and me wastin' my hour

sittin' up front." Eric grimaced. "He was a smoker, too. You could tell from
the taste of his damned dick cheese."

At the pickup's blue cab—Dynamite had left it down beside the old
scales, the worn planks with their metal bands, today lopsided in their pits,
from when Turpens had had a working weigh station—they slowed to
stand a few moments. Beyond the wire gate, trees whispered.

You saw so much around here through diamond-linked steel, sometimes
Eric wondered if that wasn't why Diamond Harbor had its name, rather
than the sun on the summer or winter sea.

Shit grinned and opened the pickup door. "Told you you'd learn who
the fuck he was, 'fore long." He climbed in and Eric climbed in after. "You
know, I think Turpens is more gay friendly *and* more straight friendly than
that place in the Dump." It was about the tenth time he'd said it.

"Yup." On the other side of the truck, Dynamite climbed in, pulled the
door to, and started the ignition. "That's why we come here—and don't
bother goin' there. That gay friendly john's *one* of that nigger's ideas—
Kyle's, I mean—I don't think ever really worked. Though I still swear by
some of his others."

Dynamite drove from between the trucks and, after driving down
the long parking lot aisle, turned through the gate in the fence, out of
Turpens, under the trees, and onto the graveled back road that would take
them directly home. "Now if you still wanna suck some *good* Georgia dick—"
Dynamite dropped a hand between his legs, as dappled leaf light and
sunspots ran up his forearm, and over his dirt-grayed denim. He thumbed
apart one after another steel fly button (the pair he sometimes reserved for
Turpens)— "you don't gotta do too much more than climb over that boy's
legs there, sit in the middle, and get your head down here and stash this
nasty ol' thing inside your goddam face. I can promise you a *good* load, too,
'cause I didn't leave a thing back in the john—and you *probably* gonna get
one from him 'fore we get home. You know, you done got us both pretty
well trained by now to do all our fuckin' around in the old head there,
then wait till we meet up with you again for the big finish—know what I'm
sayin'?"

Eric laughed—Shit looked very serious—and levered himself up to
climb over. Shit gave him a hand and slid under Eric toward the door with
its open window. In two minutes, while Eric's face was in Dynamite's lap
(*Salty enough for you, son?* Eric nodded.

(And Shit chuckled. *That's* my *piss, all over his dick—too*), Shit had a
hand down the back of Eric's jeans and two fingers sunk two knuckles deep
in Eric's butt. Eric guessed that they were somewhere in town or near it,
when he heard Shit call out the window, "Hey, Lurrie—how you doin'?

Wan' us to give you a lift?"

Dynamite hit the brake a little too sharply. "Come on, Shit—you gonna make the cocksucker bite my damn dick off. Don't joke around like that!"

Eric raised his head.

"Lurrie ain't out there." Shit chuckled. "I'm just funnin' yall."

Though he got the promised load from Dynamite before they reached the Dump, Eric did not get his load from Shit in the pickup.

He got two from him, though—one in the cabin bed, one out on the cabin porch—in the hour after.

* * *

[33] AT THE OPERA, Shit and Eric met a black kid just between them in age, called Big Man. Slightly under four feet tall, Big Man lived down the coast with his dad—a contractor, Joe Markum, who, seventeen or eighteen years before, had built most of the seventy-five cabins in the Dump and who, though not gay himself, was almost as permissive with his son as Dynamite. Big Man had a withered leg, walked with a crutch, and wore a permanent urine bag. Shit had known him vaguely back in school. His quarter of the sea-side Victorian down in Pinewood (half the second floor, with rubber rimmed fire doors between his rooms and the rest of the house) smelled like Dynamite's deck the time Whiteboy had come over and they'd all had a piss fight out there and it hadn't rained for a week.

Shit had insisted it was Whiteboy's stink. But both Eric and Dynamite told him, no, that's what old pee smelled like—finally they got some disinfectant from Fred and sluiced it down.

It reminded Eric of a few spots he'd smelled on Gilead.

Big Man didn't have much dick, nor did it get hard, but he was a scrappy little guy, a cut-up who delighted in foul talk. From under his dark bony brow and black wooly hair a dwarf's wide-set eyes stared out, welcoming and enthusiastic. He loved to get fucked and had nothing resembling a gag reflex.

Over years Eric had suppressed his. Big Man didn't *have* one.

Shit and Eric had fooled around with him mostly in the alley *behind* the Opera, at Hammond and Dusty's insistence, or down in the Opera's tiled restroom; or, at his home, in the "piss pool"—Big Man's term for his rooms upstairs that his father had built him, with their rubber flooring, rubber mattress, rubber rimmed windows and doors, rubber sheets, and drains around the raised bed: when his connector hose to his urine bag worked loose from his cock in the midst of sex, he'd pee all over you.

(*Yeah,* Joe Markum said. *I want the damned kid to have some fun! That's what him and some of his friends call it…*)

The November day was warm enough for June. Barbara had wanted Eric to come help her with some flowered decals she'd decided to put up under the windows. Then Serena phoned to ask her over, so she changed her mind. They'd do it later. Eric had walked back to the Dump—but Big Man had already driven up in his Camaro with the special pedals, picked up Shit, and taken him down to his place.

Dynamite asked Eric to lend him a hand.

As they started back from Hurter's Lumber, Steel & Seed at Dump Corners to Dynamite's cabin, Dynamite picked up his tar can to lug it by the wooden grip on the curved wire handle. In a cloth Dump Produce bag, Eric carried trowels, a leveler, nails, and two dozen shingles.

In the long grass beside the dirt road or over the sparse growth beside the asphalt stretches, they passed the cabins—each on its acre and a half of land—that, years before, Big Man's father had built to Robert Kyle's architects' specifications.

Walking beside Dynamite, looking at their two o'clock shadows moving ahead over the dust, Eric wondered what Shit was up to with the ebullient dwarf. Now and again, he grinned at Dynamite, who smiled back, his jaw dark with chestnut stubble, and whose chest hair curled between the straps of his bib overalls, clawing over the frayed top. When he glanced to one side or the other, his rings flared white-gold—again, today, he wore no shirt.

Eric's mind had started to wander, when he felt the big hand on his shoulder. (Today it was Eric who was barefoot.) Beside Eric's footprints, Dynamite's work boots left broad, sliding ones. This near Dump Corners now and again a car or a pickup still rolled by.

"You know, we don't *got* to get right into roof patchin' soon as we hit home." Dynamite sounded thoughtful. "This *is* our day off, after all. I'll tell you what I'd really like: we go up on the back porch, put this stuff down, and maybe just do some sittin'."

Ahead, one after another, three crickets jumped off the asphalt edge into brush and goldenrod.

Dynamite squeezed and released Eric's arm, then slid his rough hand around Eric's neck to rest there, without rhythm.

It felt wonderfully affectionate.

Above the bluff, behind their own cabin, a bank of clouds had risen, so that the silver was gone, replaced by deep gray. The light around them had taken on a sourceless radiance, like that in an eclipse.

"Son—you wanna stick a finger in my fly and feel around on my dick?

Fact is, I got somethin' in there for you—had it on all mornin', since you got back from your mama's."

Eric frowned. With his free hand, he reached over for Dynamite's crotch.

"That's right. But get it inside. Two of the buttons done popped. You'll feel where they were—"

Eric pushed two fingers between the frayed cloth's edges, to touch something wet and smooth. "What happened—you come in your pants, you ol' pig fucker?" He laughed.

"Not exactly," Dynamite said. "But when you and Uncle Tom went over to your mama's earlier, Black Bull stopped by with Whiteboy in his pickup. He'd been out deliverin' some of his messages for Dr. Greene. A bunch of those young fellows on the other side of the Dump is goin' up to the city for a weekend, and he was there showin' 'em how to put on a rubber. I guess they were all helpin' each other out, and he got a little over excited and shot his load in his damned scumbag. He remembered I kinda liked them things, if they had a good load of nigger jizz in 'em. So he tied it off, stuck it in his vest pocket, drove by the cabin, and give it to me. I took my dick right out and slipped it on—that's what I call neighborly." Dynamite chuckled. "He even got Shit grinnin', before the half-pint come by and the two of them took off. I been wearin' that nasty thing all mornin' and feelin' kinda good about it." Dynamite set the can down on the road's edge, and slid his arm further around Eric's shoulder. Leaning close, he dropped his voice. "Shit put a load in it too, 'fore he left—"

"And you just didn't bother to tell me?"

"Well, I wasn't sure you'd be interested. And I was still thinkin' about the roof." His whisper was close enough to Eric's ear to sound like thunder. "Son, how'd you feel about openin' up my overalls when we get back home, slippin' a couple fingers up under my balls and inside my Georgia cracker asshole, to play around with the shit up there, and suckin' on this half-toothless cracker's big ol' dick at the same time? I tell you, I'm about to piss all over myself. I'd be right obliged to give it to you and you could suck that black bastard's thick ol' nigger slime off my thing. I'd really enjoy you swingin' on my meat when I let loose."

A hand around Dynamite's wide back, Eric pulled him closer. He let the sack clank to the macadam. "You been savin' up your cheese for me?"

"Heyyyyyyyy...!" Softly, Dynamite grunted in Eric's ear, to end by turning his tongue in the ridged trumpet. "I guess—" he pulled his tongue back in his mouth—"you ain't licked up under my skin in a few days. You know how much of that stuff me and Shit both put out."

Eric began laughing. The laugh bloomed into something manic, and he pulled from Dynamite and staggered from the road's rim, turned and almost bent double. Straightening, about ten feet from Dynamite, he watched the man's big, rough fingers thumb apart the metal fly buttons. "Yeah...okay. Jesus, Dynamite, you still the nastiest cracker son of a bitch I met down here! And you're as nasty today as you was on the day I come!" Eric's bending and standing was more like one of Shit's bursts of humor than his own. He pulled in a breath. "How come you were the first person I met when I got to Diamond Harbor—or almost the first person? And here I am almost half a dozen years later and we're still fuckin' around together?"

Dynamite shrugged. "You just lucky."

"Yeah, I'm gonna suck you off. But I'm gonna do it right here, outside, on the road. And if somebody comes by, we ain't stoppin'. I don't care who it is. It can be Ron and my mamma for all I care. And I ain't waitin' till we get home, either. Okay?"

Dynamite raised his eyebrows, then shrugged. "That's fine with me. Go on." He pulled his cock loose, three-quarters of it sheathed in ivory rubber, the forward half inch filled with something that hung straight down. With thumb and forefinger, he gripped it and hauled it loose. Lifting the condom, he frowned at it, tied it, then pushed it into a pocket on his bib.

Eric stepped forward and gripped Dynamite's down-curved cock. It was more sticky than wet. He squatted, one knee going down onto the dust beyond the shoulder, then the other grinding through denim onto macadam. "This is Bull's, right? And Shit's...?"

"Well, I been leakin' in it myself all mornin'."

Eric took it in his mouth—with its familiar size and shape and it's unfamiliar taste: it was *very* salty—which tasted good; more like sweat than cum. He slipped one hand into the fly and got his fingers under Dynamite's loose sack.

"Come on," Dynamite said. "Take your time, son. Take your time..."

Back under and behind Dynamite's testicles, Eric pushed one, then two fingers into Dynamite's hirsute crack, running his fingers up and down till he found the sphincter.

"Oh, *fuck*, boy...!"

It wasn't tight, and both went easily in.

Eric supported himself with his other hand against Dynamite's hip, till the lanky garbage man reached down and gripped Eric's with his hard fingers.

Almost at the same time, what Eric had thought was the rising sound of a breeze became a nearing motor!

Oh, Jesus, he thought. From behind him, somebody *was* driving by.

Why hadn't he at least looked around to see…?

Watch it be Chef Ron, Eric thought. Or Ezra Potts. Maybe Mama Grace—or some summer visitor, with no real knowledge of the Dump at all. Still, he continued moving his head in and out.

When the vehicle got in the way of the sun, the engine slowed. The shadow that had pulled over them stilled.

A voice very loud, very black, and very familiar said: "Hey, you ol' pig fucker, couldn't you wait till you got home…?" Followed by a great laugh too big for the day.

"Hey, Bull," Dynamite said. "How's it goin', Whiteboy? You guys just getting' back?"

But Bull said, "What's he doin', suckin' your dick out here?" He laughed again. "Well, I guess Whiteboy gets like that sometimes when we're just drivin' around. Fact is, sometimes so do I."

"Oh," Dynamite said. "'Cause I was afraid there for a minute you hadn't never seen nobody suck a dick before."

"I seen it!" Black Bull declared. "Yeah, I seen it! Sure I seen it this mornin'." He laughed again.

Whiteboy said, "Eric looks funny down there." (He must have been sitting beside Black Bull in the pickup cab.)

Eric thought about comin' off and giving Whiteboy both the finger and a grin. But he went on sucking.

"You'd look funny too, if you had a mouth full of my big black dick and was suckin' on it beside the damn road. Hey—Eric! Eric? Did this ol pig fucker tell you what we flavored that thing with this mornin'? Did he tell you how we got it tastin' so good for you?"

"Why you think the nigger couldn't wait till we got home?" Dynamite asked. "That's why he had to get started here."

Again Black Bull exploded with laughter. "Yeah—yeah! I just bet he couldn't. This one here's the same way. Ain't you, you two bit piece of hog crap?"

Eric heard Whiteboy grunt happily, "Un-huh."

Again the motor revved, then slowed: "You pissin' in that boy enough?"

"Huh?"

"I'll get out and give 'im some right now, if you dry—"

"I'm pissin' in 'im now," Dynamite said. Though he hadn't been, the cock head in Eric's throat erupted hot urine, as it pulled forward in Eric's mouth. It pushed forward again. Eric gulped.

On his third gulp, Eric thought: Jesus, why the fuck am I so happy doing this…?

Because, in every glittering extremity of Eric's body, he was.

"Well, that's what you supposed to be doin'," Bull said. "And that's what he's supposed to be doin'. Jus' make sure that other crazy nigger you got knows it too, if you all gonna stay together."

"Don't worry," Dynamite moved one foot so that it was against Eric's knee. "He does."

The engine got louder. The pickup pulled away; sunlight pushed off the shadow.

Eric squeezed Dynamite rough hand—and drank.

Dynamite squeezed back. "You okay…?" Eric coughed, and a dribble ran down and under his jaw.

Eric nodded. And went on drinking.

Dynamite called: "I know he'd stop and say thank you, if he wasn't a little concerned about spillin' some."

Bull called back (the truck must have stopped only ten or fifteen feet further away): "And I know you brought that piss pig up right. Both them is good boys, Mr. Garbage Man."

Eric squeezed Dynamite's hand—who squeezed it back.

Bull's oversized voice came again: "Seein' that nasty cracker doin' ol' Eric like that gone and got me all excited again. You wanna suck on dis here?…Damn, Whiteboy, at least lemme get my elbow out da way! Course I never knowed you when you *didn't* wanna suck my dick—yeah, there you go. Come on, we goin' home now." Once more the motor got louder. Tires rasped on the small stones, the fading sound coming back to where Eric knelt in the road dust.

It took a long time for Dynamite to run out. After a while, he moved his work shoe again and said, "Come on—get on up, now."

Eric backed away, and with a tug from Dynamite, pulled himself erect. He felt both unsteady and satisfied. He looked east, where, beyond Bull's cabin, the ledge dropped away to the lower beach, then west, where, beyond Dynamite's, the bluff rose toward blue and white and swollen silver cloud. Even the most familiar things—like Dynamite's cabin, just over there— looked, somehow, new and bright.

Now, down across the road in front of Black Bulls', the black pickup had pulled up. Either Bull and Whiteboy had already gone inside—or they hadn't gotten out.

Beside Eric, Dynamite sighed. "You know, son, I worry about Shit, sometimes—not things like him eatin' his snot. 'Cause then I'd worry about you, too. But I figure you both can decide if you wanna do it in front of other people or not. And since it don't bother me, what you do around other people ain't my affair." Dynamite looked after a flock of gulls.

Eric looked up, too. More gulls fell and pulled away at angles over the sky. "I wonder if anyone but me ever realizes how kind and helpful and funny and...well, carin' that boy is. Just how much of a good person."

Eric said, "I do."

Dynamite looked down, questioningly. "Yeah, you do—don't you. But what I mean, see, is I wonder about...well, the job I did bringin' 'im up. You got this kid all of a sudden—a man now really, the two of you—and you love 'im to death and think he's the greatest thing in God's world—and you know you're doin' things together that a lotta people wouldn't approve of. But he seems to like it as much as you do. Then, pretty soon, you realize he's got a couple of what folks would call...well, pretty bad habits." Dynamite dropped his hand from Eric's shoulder, and brought it out in front of him. He looked down at the back of his own heavily veined hand, then turned it over in a loose fist and lifted it to his mouth. With what were left of his lower teeth, he began to demolish even further the ruins that had retreated—like Shit's—more than half an inch back from the nubs. (Like Shit's, Eric had figured, most of Dynamite's nails, left alone, would have been big as quarters, or bigger, though, cuticle to nub, what remained were less than a dime's diameter.) Dynamite started walking again, still biting on his own.

Eric stepped up beside him.

Around his gnawing, Dynamite said, "I mean...this goddam nail bitin'—maybe I could have broken him of that one. Made him normal, like."

"Could you?" Eric asked. "I mean, since you do it so much yourself—ain't it kind of like hustlin' down at Turpens, when you was a kid?"

"Hell, I don't know. I just figured if I'd done give him a couple of whacks when he was real young, he might have stopped. But, you know, I never could hit a kid. And I seen too much of that when *I* was comin' up—too many kids around here who got beat on. It didn't help none of them. And since, like you say—" Dynamite moved to another finger—"I bite hell out of mine, it never really bothered *me*—except a few times when I ate 'em down to where they was bleedin' bad or the whole nail come off—so I just left 'im alone about it the way I wished folks had left me alone about it when I was comin' up. And you got to admit—" He glanced over at Eric; and winked—"if you gonna stick 'em up somebody's asshole, this is a lot better than the dirty ol' claws some other guys let 'emselves get."

Dynamite started walking again. Eric started, too. (For that reason, Eric kept his own short, though he rarely bit them.) Dynamite switched his tar can—and began biting on the fingers of his other hand. "You know Kyle really didn't *want* people to be afraid of what other folks thought," he said, suddenly and seemingly unconnected. "And he was willin' to spend money on it, to make it happen. Sometimes it's hard to know what you want, if somebody hasn't figured it out and just handed it to you. That's how all the best things come."

"You said that before—that Kyle said it."

"And I'm probably gonna say it again. I swear, I ain't never knowed a nigger with more crazy—but interstin'—ideas, about how things should be. I mean, here was this brainy black sonofabitch, who went away to school every winter and sounded more like a Yankee than he did like a local black boy, tellin' us all how sayin' 'ain't' and 'yall' *wasn't* mistakes and too country, like everybody around us was always tellin' us, but was real words what had developed to talk with, and how we should use 'em and be proud of 'em 'cause it was part of our dialect, and even how cussin' and swearin' and callin' each other names—what did he say, now?—'wove a community of culturally-invested language,' and that we should all do it, as long as *any* of us could use it. 'Culturally-invested language is for includin' people, not for excludin' them.' I remember him tellin' us that, too—and, the first time he said it, I thought that was the stupidest soundin' thing I ever heard, and only half because I didn't know what the fuck it meant."

Eric frowned. "'Invested language'...?"

"Swearin' and cussin' and callin' people dumb-ass fucks and crazy nigger bastards and cracker shitheads. He was the first person, black or white, who regularly called me a 'nigger.' The first few times, it made me feel about as funny as it probably makes most black folks feel when a real ignorant white guy does it. The first few times, I didn't know what it was supposed to mean, 'cause I'd been told that was the worst thing you could call a black person, even though *they* said it all the time and so did I and everybody else. But pretty soon, it was makin' me feel so damned proud as well, I practically busted my britches puffin' up with pride, there. I mean, half of Kyle's ideas *was* crazy—like that 'gay friendly' men's room of his in the back of the Dump. But he was also the first person, black or white, with enough money to make them ideas real and actually built the damn thing to try it out—and a few years later, when I had Morgan to take care of, and I thought he probably didn't even remember me no more, he went and made his teen-age white trash fuck buddy the damn garbage man for *all* the niggers around here."

"Did you love 'im?" Eric asked. "Kyle, I mean?"

"I liked him—I still do. A whole lot. But we was just good fuck buddies, for a few years there—him and me, me and Jay; him and Jay, too." Dynamite chuckled. "I love Shit. I love 'im so much I don't know what to do sometimes. And—yeah—I love you, too, Eric—I do. 'Cause Shit loves you the way he do—and that kind of love spreads around."

"Yeah. I...love you," Eric said. "And I love Shit. And I know he loves you. What...would you like from me, Dynamite? I mean, what could I do for you?"

"You really want to know?" Dynamite grinned at him.

"Un-huh."

"Well," Dynamite said, "what *I'd* kinda like is if maybe we just went on up to the cabin, and took our clothes off and lay down on the big bed inside while we waited for your brother to get back. I could climb on top of you and rub my ol pig fucker around on you till I shot a load on your gut. Or if you wanted to, you could shoot one all over mine. It's fun shootin' on a scrappy nigger like you."

"Sure." Eric bent to pick up the bag of tools, which clinked again inside. He hefted the sack. "Then we could lick it up afterward."

"Yeah." Dynamite grinned at him, then picked up the tar can. Again they walked. "Now who you callin' nasty, son? Still, sometimes, I wonder if all the stuff we done together was really good for...Shit. I never hurt Shit—I never done nothin' with him or to him I wasn't pretty sure he wanted. The only problem *I* ever really had with him was when I couldn't beat the little fucker off me. Especially when he was twelve, thirteen, fourteen...I had to work real hard to teach 'im sometimes that there was other things we could do beside fuck and suck. But still, somehow, in all that we got to be pretty close friends." Over a few more steps, new gulls soared up from the sea. "But a couple of times we went across the road to Bull's...you ever talk to Whiteboy—I mean about some of the stuff his *real* daddy done with him, before he come to the Dump? And stuff his mother just let his daddy do it, 'cause she had six other kids—four of what his dad was already fuckin' in the house?"

"A little," Eric said. "And Shit told me...some things."

"I mean, how many years was it, he told us once, he was chained up in that loft in the damned barn—we still ain't really sure what state it was in or what town it was near—if Whiteboy ever knew for sure. I mean, that's how little they taught him. If they could be sure it was in Georgia, believe me, Bull woulda gone lookin' for the guy—probably with a gun. But that's why Whiteboy still don't really talk right or move right, though he's a lot better at both than when he first got here when he was ten or eleven. Whored out for a sexual punchin' bag—for anybody what would pay five dollars for half an hour to beat on 'im. He told Bull himself, if it had been an hour 'stead of a half hour, he'd probably been dead a dozen times over. Then, see, you realize he got so much of that kinda treatment before he was even nine or ten, once he got away, he spent a year runnin' around the country tryin' to get guys to do 'im that way some more, along with stuff that was already crazier than his dad and his dad's friends—till Black Bull found him sleepin' in the rain under one of them derelict rigs they used to have in the back at Turpens by the old scales. Yeah, I guess it's better, if that's the way you are, if you got somebody doin' it who actually cares about you and wants good things for you. But the whole thing can make you stop and wonder, sometimes, what the fuck you're doin' yourself. Well, that's what I have—what *we* have—livin' across the road from us, now, for the last dozen years."

Eric said, "Maybe having Bull and Whiteboy there keeps you...I don't know, thinking about you and Shit, so you...don't take things for granted. And having you across the road from *him* helps Bull do his best for Whiteboy, even with all the weird stuff *they're* into."

"Maybe," Dynamite said. "At least I hope that's how it works. Come on. Let's go on up in the house and mess around."

"Yeah," Eric said. "I wanna do some of that. I wanna hold onto you awhile. Come on."

They turned up toward the cabin.

"Course, sometimes, yeah, thinkin' about that stuff with Whiteboy's family makes me wonder if me and Shit ain't gone a little *too* far. But then, when it does work, it's hard to imagine Shit bein' any happier. Not to mention you—" Dynamite grinned—"you nasty little piss hole."

When they reached the cabin steps, Dynamite took two steps up, then turned and waited for Eric. When he reached Dynamite, Eric asked, "Dynamite, did you ever play blackjack, I mean, professional blackjack... in Atlantic City?"

"Huh? Naw—I never played no cards hardly at all. Where's that Atlantic City anyway—is that like in Las Vegas? Why'd you wanna know?"

"'Cause, well...it's in New Jersey. But that's where my real dad was. When I was little, sometimes I'd think maybe Mike *was* my real dad, the guy Barbara met in Atlantic City, but because I come out so stupid blond and dumb-ass white lookin', they told me it was somebody else—Cash, she said his name was. But, well, sometimes I...I wish you *was* him, like you're really Shit's father." Eric looked at the ground. Then he looked up. "That would make it even better when we did stuff together...Huh?"

Dynamite smiled. "You're just saying that 'cause you know it turns *me* on, ain't you?"

"Well, yeah. Some. But also 'cause it's...true."

They walked up the last three steps together. "You happy, Eric?"

"Yeah, I'm happy," Eric said. "With Shit and you? I am."

Above the bluff, clouds rose higher and grayer and darker, indicating, Eric was sure, only the changes in light and beauty the landscape placed about them.

Together, they reached the deck.

Again he heard Dynamite set the tar can down—on boards this time, not earth. A second later, Dynamite stood up, reached around, and ran his hand down the back of Eric's jeans.

Eric dropped the canvas sack from his hand. It clanked the deck. One corner landed on his little toe but must have contained only some nails and, maybe, the trowel's wooden handle so—miraculously—didn't hurt. He pulled his foot sharply back anyway.

Eric felt his front button ease open and his pants slip down. With the same hand he grabbed the waist to hold them up.

Over the deck rail, out between the pines, across the Dump's grasses set with clumps of fern and stubby sumac groves, between the cabins and beyond the rise, Hurters and the Dump Produce Market, the shuttle stops and Dump Corners were out of sight.

The air moved his hair, now long enough to tickle his ears.

Beside him, Dynamite rubbed belly and chest against him. He ran a hand over Eric's shoulder, his arm. "Hey, strong fella, your muscles feel nice."

The wrist of Dynamites other arm tugged the back of Eric's jeans. "So does your hand." The front button of his pants was open. So was his fly, pulled out around his hips. "How many fingers you got up my asshole?"

"Three," Dynamite said.

Eric grinned. "I couldn't tell if it was two or four."

Dynamite's wandering hand came to Eric's chin, his mouth, his neck. "Come on, you little sonofabitch, let's go inside. We can put one of them pillows in the middle of the bed under your hips. You can stretch out on your belly over that thing, and I can stick my redneck dick up your goddam asshole."

Eric looked back over his shoulder. "Yeah—that's sounds good." He tried not to smile too much.

Dynamite pulled his hand loose.

They turned toward the door into the bedroom.

Inside, while Dynamite pulled away the covers and pushed a pillow into the middle of the mattress, Eric dropped his clothes and lay down over it. One of Dynamite's work shoes then the other thudded to the floor. With his hands folded under one cheek, Eric closed his eyes. He heard the rush of Dynamite's bibs dropping to his ankles—and the click of a metal snap against the side of the bed. The springs gave beside him as Dynamite's knee sank into the mattress.

When Dynamite knelt astraddle Eric's legs, he pushed one hand on the small of Eric's back. The other felt around, prodded the crevice of his butt, then retreated. A moment on, the head of his broad cock wedged into the crevice and pushed.

The condom was gone, doubtless stripped off and crumpled on the night table under the lamp.

Eric raised his head and looked back. "Hey, ain't no hole there! Down about an inch! You been fuckin' my ass since I was seventeen. Ain't you figured out where it is by now?"

Dynamite grinned down. "Well, turn your butt up a little!"

The pressure slid down—and eased in. Eric whispered, "Oh, shit… yeah!" Above him, as the garbage man came forward, Eric felt Dynamite's heat and breathed in his automotive smell, as the garbage man lay out his full weight on Eric's back.

From somewhere, Dynamite dragged over another pillow to support his own head. With one hand, he gripped one of Eric's muscular arms. With the other, he pushed beneath him to finger Eric's face. "Hey, it's good you got your lube in already."

"Well," Eric said from under Dynamite's chest, "I figured this is where we was headin' all along. It's feelin' pretty good, too."

"Come on," Dynamite said. "Lemme stick some fingers in your mouth, so I can play with that slick suckhole of you got. You know how that turns me on."

"Yeah…" Eric said. Three, then four fingers went in to hold—and move over—his tongue. Dynamite's hip pulled back and pushed forward, pulled back and pushed forward.

In reverse rhythm so did Eric's.

Between Eric's hips was a glassy pool of pleasure; the front two inches of Dynamite's cock dipped into it and disturbed it and stirred it about and made it ripple and flutter and splash.

With one hand, Eric gripped Dynamite's forearm. "Yeah, fuck me, big guy…!" Though Dynamite probably didn't understand him, since he spoke with a mouthful of Dynamite's fingers.

It was a leisurely fuck. At each plunge, the pool grew fuller, spilling through Eric's body. He didn't know if either of them was going to come— nor, right then, did he care. Eric closed his eyes.

Dynamite had been fucking him for twenty or twenty-five minutes— perspiration's salt had long gone from the rough fingers he'd been sucking—when Dynamite's hips halted, and he whispered through a big grin, "Hey, you stay there, boy. I'll be back in a second."

The weight and the heat on his back lifted. The hand pulled from his face. Eric was tempted to open his eyes as the garbage man left the bed. Within the second the bed sagged again—he was already returning.

Eric pulled in a deep breath, to ready himself, bent one leg, then straightened it. With an urgency that was foreign to the garbage man, once more Dynamite straddled him—

One hand grasped Eric's hip. With a sureness that was simply not Dynamite's, the cock pushed home.

Someone not Dynamite said, "Oh, fuck, man...I'm gonna dick this nigger and make him shoot. Gonna make you come, too, y'ol' pig fucker! You guys is just foolin' around!" A weight that was not Dynamite's at all fell on Eric, hips already bucking.

Eric said, "Shit...?"

It was Shit's hardness and Shit's musculature and Shit's smell with other smells mixed in. Eric opened his eyes, because one of Shit's shoulders, on top of his own, began shaking at a convulsive masturbatory rhythm.

Dynamite was laying across the bed again, this time on his side. (Eric hadn't even felt him.) Shit had reached up and grasped his father's cock and was vigorously jerking it. "Go on—yeah, go on. Stick it in the nigger's mouth. You like watchin' 'im suck your big cracker dick much as I do."

Trying not to loose Shit's pistoning cock in his butt, Eric strained—and Dynamite pushed forward, so that for five, ten, twenty seconds Eric sucked Dynamite's forward inches while the back of Shit's fist beat his mouth.

Then Dynamite laughed and pulled away.

Shit grunted and let go. "Go on, then—jerk yourself off." Gripping Eric's shoulder, his mouth just behind Eric's ear, he said, "You know he gets off watchin' you and me make it—don't you, y'ol' pig fucker?"

Beneath Shit's pulsing weight, Eric managed to ask, "What you doin' back here...?"

"Same thing I was doin down at Big Man's. Naw, see, I got home and come on inside and I seen you two at it. So I tossed my jeans into the corner and told him in Mex's sign language to get up off you so I could get in here and do what had to be done—the way you two were goin' at it, you'd'a been there all day! Besides, you know me—whenever I get home from fuckin' someone else, I'm always horny!" Shit laughed and pumped harder.

"Uh..." Eric grunted. "Yeah—!"

Shit's arms wrapped under Eric's chest. He rubbed his face hard on Eric's neck. Perspiration wet the flesh between Shit's chest and Eric's back. Shit held Eric with his arms and knees and pumped with twice Dynamite's speed.

The pool splashed and frothed and crashed against the insides of Eric's back and belly, trying to break what contained it.

Shit rasped, "We gonna do it now, yeah...yeah, we gonna do it...fuck...

fuck…fuck…fuck…fuck…!" Springs squeaked and clashed.

For moments Eric was sure his testicles were spinning in his scrotum, the friction heating them toward eruption. "I'm comin'…"

Shit said, "I know y'are…!"

And all the seas of the world whirlpooled over Eric's back. Shit still hugged and pumped, stirring a pleasure that spilled through Eric's knees and arms.

Eric blinked to see, a foot from his face, Dynamite's fist close over his cock's head. Knobby and heavy, the fist quivered. Then, between each joint and juncture, milky slip rolled out, over veins and joint hair. Dynamite whispered, "Oh, shit…!" and pushed forward again, his groin nearing Eric's face.

At the same time, Shit whispered, "Fuck…!"

Breathing deeply, Dynamite said, "Come on, son. Aw, Jesus, that was amazing'." His flexing fingers pulled away from his cock, semen gleaming all over its veined thickness.

Everything between Eric's chest and knees turned to light, growing and glowing—till, of a sudden, it collapsed between tingling flanks and thighs. Eric felt his own cock spurt all over the pillow under his hips.

Dynamite sat up, shifted his position, then his face was down with Eric's, his fist turning and drooling between them. "Come on, son. Help your old man clean this up nasty mess." Dynamite licked one knuckle, then another.

Shit's face hung three inches above Dynamite's and Eric's. "There's a big glob on the back of his thumb. You eat that off, Eric. And you got all that runnin' over your wrist—get that, Dynamite."

And they did.

Shit's speed increased to something beyond the parameters of velocity itself. Supporting himself on one forearm, he reached between them, and with blunt nubs dozed semen first into his father's mouth, then into Eric's. He let out all his air, went in, and did not retreat. His head collapsed between them.

Dynamite laughed. "Hey, don't pass *out*, Shit…!"

Shit managed to whisper, "If I do, it ain't gonna kill me…"

Deep in Eric's gut, he felt Shit spasm, again and again. For a moment, Shit's forearm hurt Eric's neck. Next to Eric's ear, Shit made great gasps like ripping cloth.

While Shit's breaths grew quieter and slower, Dynamite moved around so he was stretched out beside them. He put his arm over both of them. "What you wanna do now?"

Eric said, "I think he's asleep."

"Oh," Dynamite said, and, as if that gave him permission, yawned, then rubbed Eric and Shit's backs. "Okay…"

Suddenly Shit seemed to wake, reached down, and yanked the pillow from under Eric and balled it up again his cheek, turning his head—eyes still closed—back and forth.

Eric looked around, found another, and said, "Why don't you use this one here—it ain't got cum all over it." He pulled it nearer.

Eyes still closed, holding Eric with one arm and the pillow with the other, Shit grunted like a grumpy four-year-old. "Naw, naw—I want the wet one! I always sleep on the wet one. You know that." Then, more gently, he said, "Hey, you can put your head up here on this one with me, if you want." He stuck his tongue out to lick the pillow, without opening his eyes. "That's nice. That's how I do it."

Eric shook his head—but both Dynamite and Shit's eyes were closed. "You sure smell like you was messin' around with Big Man."

Eric put his head down and closed his own. And took his own very deep breath.

"Yeah, well that little guy can get up quite a stink when his pee hose pulls loose a couple of times—and it did. Hey. When we wake up," Shit said, sleepily, suddenly, "I'm gonna suck the rest of the cum and stuff off my dad's dick so he can't go around complainin' I don't never suck him no more. But I'm tired, now."

* * *

[34] "WHAT— " BARBARA PUSHED through her kitchen door with its tall glass windows— "in the *world* are you doing here and…what are you *doing*?"

On the stove, his mother's large kettle let loose steam from under the lid, first on one side, then on the other. In one hand, from the bag, Eric pulled out two ears with their lined husks and tow tassels, their ends touched with brown, then looked up.

"Um…" Stepping in, Barbara pulled the door closed. "What are you boiling?"

"Nothin', yet," Eric still wore his work shoes and workpants, but he had changed into a clean orange shirt. "I was just gettin' the water hot—for the corn. I thought I'd come over this evening and make you and Ron some dinner."

"Oh…" She frowned. "Well, that's very nice of you. Actually, though, Ron's gone up to a computer convention in Atlanta. He won't be back till tomorrow evening—"

"Yeah." Eric grinned. "I saw Serena this morning at the Lighthouse, and she told me he'd be gone tonight and you'd be on your own. So I thought this was a good time to come over and fix you somethin'."

Barbara laughed. "Not very subtle, are you?"

"Oh, come on, Barb. Ron doesn't like me, and I don't exactly love him launchin' into me every time I'm around for more than five minutes, about how I'm wastin' my life and how I don't have nothin' and ain't *never* gonna have nothin' and nobody'll wanna know me—like we didn't have no friends at all, over in the Dump."

"Oh, he doesn't dislike you, sweetheart. He just doesn't understand you. That's all." She came further across the white and yellow floor. "What are you making?"

"Well," Eric said, "it's a recipe Horm told me over at the Produce Farm on the first day I went out there with Dynamite and Shit. Every year since, soon as the sweet corn comes in, he tells me again. He told it to me this morning, too; I guess he tells everybody. So, I thought, hell, this time, why don't I go make some for Ron and Barb? If it tastes halfway decent, in a few days I'll make some up for Shit and Dynamite."

"What is it?"

"You'll see—and don't worry about Ron. I knew he wasn't gonna be here. But I'm makin' enough so there'll be some left for you and him tomorrow—probably for the next day, too."

"What're *your* men folk eatin' tonight, while you're over here treating me like the Queen of Sheba?"

"Well, it only took me three years, but I got Shit to where he ain't scared of takin' some microwave dishes out the refrigerator, loosenin' the tops, stickin' 'em in that thing, and pressin' some buttons. Since it rings when it's ready, he don't have to read nothin'. As long as they can eat it right out the bowls and don't have to turn it out on no plates, he'll do. So I divided it up for 'em. They got some chicken stew I left."

"You brought some of your stew over here a few months ago—it was tasty, too." Barb frowned. Behind her, on the door panes, long-stemmed flowers were etched into the glass. "So this is a recipe you been sitting on for…how many years, now? Eric Jeffers, that's so like something your daddy would do. I remember once out of a clear blue sky, Mike decided to make a sweet potato pie, crust and all—and I didn't even know he could turn on the stove. He used up every dish and bowl in the house to do it. But it came out looking fine and tasted good."

"I guess as far as cookin', then, I got the best of both sides."

"I guess you did." Barb looked over the table, spread edge to edge with vegetables. Overhead copper rimmed blades on the ivory-colored ceiling fan turned just quickly enough to blur. "Now...*what* exactly is it?" Back in the trailer, the fan had always seemed to cover the entire kitchen ceiling. But the Hemmings kitchen was more than twice as big. Barbara moved around the wooden table.

"Horm said to boil up some fresh corn, cut it off the cob, then cook it with some bacon and some cut up vegetables—garlic, onions, peppers, celery, mushrooms, jalapeños, fresh thyme, and oregano. And some zucchini. He said it'd be real good."

"I imagine it will be." Barbara took a large breath. "Can I make one... two...three...*four* suggestions? Then I'll go pour myself a drink, come back, sit in the corner, and leave you alone until you say it's ready."

"Sure." Eric turned from the table and went to a counter drawer to take out of knife. "Go on."

"First, mince your garlic and brown it four or five minutes in some butter. Don't let it burn. Then put it aside and mix it in when you're putting everything together toward the end. That's one."

"Okay—how much garlic should I use, anyway?"

"Two cloves for you, two cloves for me—and two for Ron. Second, slice those beautiful big white mushrooms you got there and sauté them in some olive oil—I have a bottle in the cabinet—then put them aside, too. They go in at the end. Too much stirring, and you'll break 'em all to pieces. They'll taste fine. But they won't look very good. Three, I have a vegetable chopper up on the shelf. It's not electric. You have to turn it by hand. But it'll still cut up your onions, peppers, and celery in one-tenth the time you could do it with a knife. I'd cook all of them about ten to fifteen minutes before I mixed them in with the corn—then let it all go another ten minutes. And four, don't forget to salt your corn water. You'll probably need to cool your ears before you go cutting. You can do that with cold water in the sink. Oh, and after you cut the kernels off, run the back of your knife up and down the cob to get out the seed roots. That's the sweetest part."

Eric said, "I knew about the mushrooms. But thanks for telling me about the chopper."

That evening, when, at the kitchen table, Eric dug the big aluminum spoon into the crock bowl of corn, red and green peppers, zucchini, onions, and brown bits of bacon, the handle clinked against the bowl's rim. He blinked at Barbara.

"Well," Barbara said, while Eric starting grinning. "It *smells* good. This would make a very nice side dish. But it's a great meal all by itself."

As they ate, Eric asked, "How much do you think I need for the three of us over at the Dump? Just with three ears for the two of us, I didn't realize it was gonna be *this* much."

"I think," Barbara said, "the whole purpose of this is for some kind of extender, when you've got a few ears of corn left over." She took another fork full. (Barb hadn't touched her second drink: Eric wondered if he'd discovered something useful for curbing his mother's drinking.) "Still, for a main dish, if this is all you're having, I'd say two ears apiece. For each person use one red pepper and one green one, one or two jalapeños, an onion, and three or four sticks of celery—and *that's* going to be a *big* kettle of food! And three slices of bacon per person. Your grandma used to do something like this when I was a little girl—of course she would have died before she put garlic in it."

"When I first started cookin' for 'em," Eric said, digging in, "Shit and Dynamite both did some frownin' at the garlic—but I was in the habit 'cause Mike used to like it in everything, when I cooked for him."

"Yes. I remember." Barbara smiled.

"I like it, too—and *I* was cookin'. Now, they just call 'em my 'Aye-talian' dishes, even if it's beef stew." He laughed with her.

From somewhere outside, a woman called: "Hello-*oooo*—anybody home? Anybody want some blueberry-peach pie? I even brought the Cool Whip—"

"Serena—?" Barbara sat up and looked over her shoulder.

Serena pushed through the door from the garage that was always open, a shopping bag hanging from one brown forearm, with a large red Hemmings Mall logo slanting around on three sides of the brown paper, and a green checked scarf around her head. She held a glass pie plate, through which, here and there, Eric could see the crust directly against the glass, a map of the generous amount of shortening used to make it. "Oh, now don't great minds run in a track, like they say? I figured your chief admirer, here, next to Ron, had taken you out to wine you and dine you at Shells—or maybe Chili's—and I'd just stick all this in the refrigerator and leave it for you. But since you're here—"

"Honey," Barbara said, "you wanna taste something good? Get yourself a plate and have some of this—you know where they are. Eric came over and made dinner. Then we'll all have some of your dessert. There's more than enough. And Eric can listen to *two* old ladies gossip for a bit. Look. You *have* to sit down and tell me about Ruth's daughter. Is that girl in the family way or not—?"

Serena looked at Eric with widening eyes. "You mean *you* cooked dinner for your mama?" She set the pie plate down on the green matt. Its lattice covering had been gilded with an egg white glaze that had gone gold in Serena's oven no more than twenty minutes ago. "I should have been so lucky as to have a son *or* a daughter who would come over and cook for me. What you got here—Lord, that smells good!"

Now Serena closed a cabinet door and, with a plate in hand, came back to the table, while Eric got up to get her some silverware.

*

Three evenings later, at the Dump, Eric asked Shit, "You wanna help me clear out this mess in the sink?"

"Nope," Shit said. "But I will. Come on. What we gotta do?"

"Well, you can start by moving all that stuff off the counter, so there'll be room to cut up those onions and peppers."

"Cuttin' all them things up—" Shit frowned—"ain't that gonna take a long time, like maybe forever?"

"See that shoppin' bag?" With the orange Hemmings Mall logo, it was the one Sarena had brought over to his mother's, which she'd left him so he'd have something in which to carry stuff back here. "That's got Barb's vegetable chopper in it. She let me borrow it. I gotta get one of those for us."

An hour-fifty minutes later, when they were sitting at the table eating—from plates—Dynamite said, "Damn, that's good! When I was a kid—" Dynamite and Shit both held their forks in their fists—"all I ever wanted was meat." A lot of the stuff had been stored under the table. Eric had his shoes on a carton that hadn't been there earlier. "But now, it seems like all I ever get a real cravin' for today is vegetables. I tell you, Eric—this Aye-talian corn and peppers hits the spot."

"You like them mushrooms?" Shit asked.

"Yeah," Eric said. "I do."

"They ain't bad," Dynamite said.

"I mean—" Shit shoveled in another mouthful—"I'm gonna eat 'em, 'cause they're food. And it's good. But to me, they don't taste like nothin'."

Dynamite grinned across the table at Eric. "You know, every time we sit down to eat, you gotta say somethin' about Eric's cookin'. It ain't like you're the one doin' it."

Under the table, Shit's big, bare feet joined Eric's work shoes on the carton, and he began to rub and grip and wiggle them on Eric's lower leg. "Hey, I didn't say I didn't like 'em, did I? And I'm eatin' 'em."

Eric said, "That's okay. I know what Shit means."

Shit said, "I like anybody what'll put good food in my mouth. And Eric's gonna let me put somethin' back in his that's gonna feel *real* good after dinner, ain't you?"

Eric grinned. "Didn't you do that when we got home?"

"Well, we'll just do it again. See, I got 'im thinkin' about suckin' on my big, nasty Georgia dick. You can tell, 'cause it embarrasses that boy. He looks cute, grinnin' like that. But that just makes me wanna get it in there even more." On Eric's ankles, Shit's feet rubbed harder.

"Gettin' your dick sucked," Dynamite said, "is what *you're* always thinkin' about! Me, though, I'm curious." He looked from Shit to Eric. "What's goin' through *your* mind?"

Eric took a fork full of his own. This batch *was* better than the one he had made and left half of in his mother's refrigerator for Ron's return. "Actually?" He swallowed. "What am I thinkin' about right now?"

Dynamite nodded. "Um-hm." Besides the washed-out bib straps, across his chest's chestnut hair, one ring flared like white gold in the low sun coming through the kitchen window in the five-o'clock blue. In shadow, the other was dark as iron.

"Actually," Eric said, "I was wonderin' just how many people there were who were like me."

"You mean," Shit said, still eating doggedly—"how many of 'em like mushrooms? And Aye-talian stuff? Which, by the way, I think is fuckin' good!"

"No…!" Eric was surprised. "Not *that*! I was actually wonderin' how many people…you know, like to drink piss. And, maybe, suck a dick as soon as it comes out their ass."

"Now, there…" Shit said. "That's a' interestin' question."

On the side of the table where nobody sat, a tool box stood next to a kid's pail full of nails and pieces of pipe, beside some wood Shit had pushed to the side when they'd sat down to eat. As usual in the house, Shit wore no shirt. Eric still had on his work clothes, though his shirt was unbuttoned.

"And maybe like to fuck as much as they like to get fucked?" Dynamite said. "Don't forget that."

"Yeah," Eric said. "All that stuff. But I guess that's more normal, isn't it?"

"There ain't no normal," Shit said. "That's what *he* always told me." With his scruffy beard, Shit pointed his chin toward Dynamite. "There's just comfortable and uncomfortable. And I like to be comfortable with pretty much everything."

Dynamite put his fork down, thumbed a piece of red pepper off his lower lip up into his mouth, took Eric's cell from his bib pocket—something had finally given out on Dynamite's, so Eric had let him have his—flipped it open, and pressed buttons with a forefinger that seemed three times too thick for just one. "Hello…? Is Dr. Greene in? Oh, this *is* you, sir…This is Dynamite Haskell. I was here with my boys, and one of 'em had a question…No, sir. It ain't medical—least not really. Naw, there ain't nothin' wrong with 'im. It's about sex." Dynamite listened a few seconds more, then said: "Okay." And extended the cell to Eric

—who said, "Huh?" and, "Hey, I don't need to ask him right *now*."

"Go on," Dynamite said. "He'll talk to you. That's what the Foundation pays 'im for."

Shit's feet stopped rubbing. A grin crossed his face.

Dynamite pushed the cell at Eric, who took it mostly to keep it from falling onto his plate. He held it up, looked at it, bewildered, then put it to his ear. "Hey, sir…? I don't have to ask you about nothin' right here. I mean…if you're eatin' dinner or something—"

The voice came over the earpiece: "Hey, Shit. How're you doin'? You wanna tell me what's on your mind? What you and your daddy are talkin' about, there?"

"Naw…" Eric said. "I mean, this ain't Shit. This is Eric."

"Eric Jeffers?"

"Yes, sir."

"Oh, well—now, this is the first time I must have talked to you like this. Shit used to phone me up with questions all the time back when he was thirteen or fourteen. But I haven't heard from him in a while. I guess I must've answered all of his. Probably if there was somethin' you wanted to know, you should ask him. But if it's something I know anything about, I'll tell you—or I'll look it up and get back to you."

Across the table, Shit took one more mouthful, watching. "Dr. Greene knows everything about gay guys. All about any medical things we got. That's his specialty. And anybody in the Dump can call him, any time, and ask him. That's what the Kyle Foundation hired him for, see?"

"Well," Eric said. "I was just wondering, I mean…Um…I…well, sometimes I like to drink…urine. Piss. A lot of it. And…I was just wondering…"

After a moment, the voice said, "…if it would hurt you? No—at least not if your kidneys are okay. You can put away pretty much all the piss you want. Lot's of guys do. The main thing to remember is: Don't try to save it. At least not if you intend to drink it later. After a couple of hours it starts to change into ammonia. That gets lethal pretty quick and can make you sick, if not kill you. But you can pretty well smell that. If it's even close to makin' your eyes water, throw it out. But long as you and your partner—or partners—are in good health, and you're getting it fresh out a dick—or a pussy—it's not gonna hurt any of you."

"That's how I always drink it—out their dicks, I mean."

"Well, Dynamite knows what he'd doin'. And after all this time, Shit ought to. Have you been to The Slide?"

"Yeah, Shit took me over there a couple of times. But we went in the afternoon." Eric looked around the table. Dynamite was eating. Shit was grinning. "We don't go out too late—'cause we gotta get up and get to work early."

"Well, The Slide doesn't really get active till nine, ten o'clock. Or later—That's a really good place for drinkin' lots of piss. 'Cause everybody who goes there's pretty obligin'. That's what it's set up for. And most of it ain't too strong—just beer piss."

"Ain't none of us here really bar-type drinkers. And I got about as much as I want right here at home."

"Well, if you went on the right Saturday night, you might see some guys put away some downright heroic amounts."

"Yeah, I heard about that—under the bar in the back. Till it comes shootin' out their butts. But, well…a year or so back Bull came over and—"

"Yeah, I know. I told 'im he might drop around to remind you folks there that you have a few special needs—that's after Jay called to tell him a little bit about you," Dr. Greene said, "and asked him pretty much the same. Now, look, you're gettin' enough from Shit and Dynamite?"

Eric looked across the table, where Dynamite and Shit were both smiling. "Yeah. Yes, sir. I am."

Dynamite gave a small nod, as if he could hear Dr. Greene's end of the conversation.

"Good. You make sure you drink lots of water, too. That's always a good idea. And get yourself a box of baking soda—to brush your teeth with and rinse your mouth out. That's to keep the acid down so you don't end up loosin' your teeth."

"Oh, yeah," Eric said. "I will. Sure—"

"Go on," Shit said from around the table's corner. "Ask him your question. You ain't asked him nothin' yet."

Eric took in another long breath. "Um…I was gonna ask you, see, how many there were—guys like that, I mean."

"Like you?" Eric could here him smiling. "Well, I don't have percentage figures on that to hand. In the Dump proper, there Fallow Jones, and his partner, Earl. I guess you already know about Jay MacAmon and Mex out on Gilead. I know yall're friends with them. Johnny Einman is pretty much into that—though he doesn't have a steady. But he's over to the Slide pretty regular, these days. And he has a regular thing with the Markum boy. You met him, yet? Of course, neither one of them live in the Dump. Still, that might be fun for you fellas. Then there's Sam Quasha and Abe. And I don't know whether I'm supposed to count Brick and that donkey of his—now that's a relationship that sometimes worries me, 'cause Brick is only five-and-a-half feet tall, and a four-footed animal can tear you up, if you let it get too deep inside you, much less him drainin' it dry like he tells me he does pretty much every other day. But he says he's been doin' it for years, so if there was any *real* worryin' to do, it should've come ten or twelve years ago when they got here. There's maybe another half dozen I could think of. So what's that, now? About twenty percent? And it's one of those things that changes. You do it a lot for a year or three—then somehow you get out of the habit and forget about it—then, five years later, you pick it up again."

The names were all known to Eric, though half of them he did not have faces for—but simply knew they were residents among the seventy-five dwellings making up the Dump.

"As long as you got someone you can count on to keep you from getting dehydrated, in all this heat, you should be okay." Dr. Green chuckled. "That's how Sam and Abe always put it to me, when I talk to them about it."

"Oh, yeah…" Eric said.

"Good."

"Um—Shit and Dynamite are both…pretty obligin'. I mean, since… Bull come by."

"Well, lucky you, son! You don't mind if I mention you to some of the fellows around here I told you about—they'd probably like to know you. And then you'll have somebody you can talk to who knows about that stuff first hand."

"Oh, yeah, I…guess that's okay."

"I mean, Bull told me he was gonna come over and deliver his message from Jay. So I assume that worked out okay…?"

"Yeah, it…it did."

"Good. Well, if you got any more questions, you give me a call. From five to seven is when I take calls. For medical problems, either make an appointment, or just walk in. I'm rarely that busy. Just drop into the office, from eight in the morning on."

"Oh, yeah. Sure…"

"And have a good evening. I've got another call, now."

The line clicked.

Eric took the phone from his ear and looked at it; that was the longest conversation he'd had on a cell since the day he'd bought it and talked to Mike about dropping school. "That's kind of strange stuff to be talkin' about at dinner." Frowning, Eric put down the phone. "But I guess that's better than not talkin' about it at all."

Shit said, "I bet he told you about Sam and Abe and Einman—and

Brick, drinkin' his damn donkey's piss whenever he can catch him spillin' it. I seen 'im do it out on the road a couple of times. He don't care who sees 'im, either. There wasn't nobody out but us when I caught 'im at it, squattin' down under that donkey's belly, holdin' its dick in his hand and hosin' it into his mouth. I took my dick out and jerked off while I watched him. When we finished, he got up and come over; we grinned at each other, and that ol' nigger bent down and fingered my cum up off my foot and ate it. Then we nodded—and went on. I mean it…was kind of friendly."

"He…did?" Eric asked.

Dynamite said, "You know that 'ol' nigger' ain't no older than I am."

"Oh, you know what I mean." Then Shit said, "Now, *I* would've asked Dr. Greene about *us*."

"What you mean?"

The weight that had been resting, motionless, on Eric's shins under the table suddenly vanished. Shit scraped his chair back and stood. Upright, he stuffed a last fork-full in his mouth. Then the fork clattered down on the table. Shit stepped around the table toward where Eric was still sitting. "You know…How many guys was like you and me. How many did what we like to do."

He leaned against Eric's shoulder, then pulled back to take his hand and cup it under his nose, and with a forefinger closed off a nostril and honked into his hand. Then with his thumb, he closed off the other hand and honked again. On his brown palm, among the dark lines of dirt that webbed the hard, heavy flesh, were three pieces of dried mucus. The biggest was green, and looked like cracked jade, irregular and faceted. On the ball of his thumb lay two smaller pieces, also irregular, one half green, half yellow, dry and flaky. The other was as delicate as a fragment of dried yellow leaf. "Go on—which ones you want? I'll eat whichever one you leave."

Eric looked up at Shit, then down at the excretion. Suddenly he dropped his head, and got two of them in his mouth. They were chewy. And salty.

"God damn!" Shit whispered. And raised his hand to mouth the remaining one. "Mother fucker—now *look* at that! Go on—look! See how you got me?" He pulled open the top button to his pants. The cloth fell loose, and Shit's cock pushed out. "Hard as a goddam rock, that's what I mean. Come on, nigger. Gimme a big kiss, and lemme feed you the one I'm chewin' on. You wouldn't have to suck it more'n three times before I filled up your goddam mouth with cum. I thought that's what you was gonna ask the doctor about. How many was there like *us*?"

Eric hugged Shit's hips and rubbed his face against Shit's groin. Shit bent over him and hugged his head.

Leaning backward in his chair, Dynamite rocked on his back chair legs. "Are we finished eatin' dinner yet?"

Shit said, "I don't know. Maybe." Then he said: "I know this ain't nobody's idea of the best dinner table conversation in the world. But about two weeks ago, after I talked to Bull and Dr. Greene, I went in right behind you when you'd left a big hunk floatin' in the commode, and I reached in and broke me off a piece. And the same day, later, I pulled a piece of Eric's out there, too—and I ate 'em down. Both of 'em. It was sort of like magic, I was tryin' to do, so you two wouldn't ever go away and leave me. I mean, I wanted to get bounded up with the two of you sons-of-bitches. Now, I could say, I'd been worried and wanted to ask Dr. Greene whether that would hurt me any—but the fact is, I know it won't. 'Cause I seen Tom eat enough of his own, not to mention him goin' in and chowin' down on what any of us leaves in the shitter. And it ain't never killed him."

"Now *that*," Dynamite said, thoughtfully, "don't sound like Dr. Greene *or* Bull. That sounds like *you!*"

"Well, the truth is I done asked 'em both after I done it, not before. So there wasn't nothin' nobody could about it." Shit leaned back.

"You know, it ain't just his name," Dynamite said. "This boy been crap-crazy since he was a little thing. When he was in Pampers, he used to love to play with his own. And if you happened to leave some in the commode, soon as he could toddle around, all he wanted to do is get in there and fuck with it. It mean he was a damn mess."

Shit laughed. "Well, my dick comes outta your ass today, and if it's got a few of them brown stripes runnin' up and down it, lookin' at 'em can get me up for a second round—even if it's soft; which it ain't usually."

Dynamite put his fork on his empty plate. "You actually done eat a piece of your daddy's crap, boy? I mean last *week?*"

"Yeah," Shit said. "It felt…kinda spiritual, actually. I hope it works."

Dynamite snorted. "You probably don't remember it 'cause I don't think you was more than two, two-and-a-half. But Jay and Mex stopped over here and I was tellin' 'em about it—and Mex said, well, let 'im go and do whatever the fuck he wants to do with it. Maybe that'll get it out 'is system. And, who knows, you might learn something about your boy. Then he went in to the back to drop a friend. When he come out in the kitchen, I told him I didn't hear 'im flush. And he said no, he hadn't closed the bathroom door after himself, neither. But by then, you were *gone* into the back—and somehow we got to talkin' and kind of forgot about you. And maybe twenty minutes later, you come out the bedroom, grinnin'—and *covered* in shit. I mean, from your ears to your toes. I couldn't tell you how much had gone into your mouth—but you also looked as happy as I think

I'd ever seen you! Jay looked up first and saw you, and begun laughin'. Then Mex started in after him. And when I realized what it was, I didn't know if I was mad or thought it was as funny as they did. But I told Mex, right, 'This was *your* idea, you crazy spic! You get 'im outside and hose 'im off! *You* can clean 'im up!' So Mex got up, took you by the hand, and went out in front of the house with you and uncoiled the green hose we used to have out there and washed you down. For all I know, he licked you clean. I wouldn't put it past him—and right then I didn't even wanna know about it! It only took about fifteen minutes. I made him clean up the bathroom, too. And I remember, years later, when you picked your name, I thought about all that stuff. And a dozen years after that, here it is, all comin' home to roost." Dynamite snorted. "Well, that ain't gonna be my problem." He lowered his brows at Eric. "It's yours, now, son."

Frowning, Eric looked up over Shit's all but bald chest, with its few tight curls, to his irregular beard.

"Damn," Dynamite said. "If anybody's interested, *I* got to take a wicked piss! Anyone who wants to watch or take part, come on in with me."

* * *

[35] COMING UP THE road, through sun speckles jumping around beneath the blowing pines, Shit was ginning like someone with news.

Eric was coming down from Mama Grace's. The Dump's back road smelled of dust, sun, and pine resin. This side section of the Dump, around the edge of the bluff, for two weeks had been like a new and once hidden world—but somehow, with Eric's fifth and sixth visit, it had become as familiar as the main road running between Bull and Dynamite's cabins, down past Chef Ron's and into Dump Corners.

Shit slowed down and said, "Hey—you know anything about a three-wire switch?"

"What you mean?" Eric asked.

"I mean do you know how to fix one if it gets broke."

"I don't know—you don't mean one of those things where you got a switch at the top of the stairs and another at the bottom and you can turn a light on and off from either one, do you?"

"Yeah—that kind."

"Sure. But I ain't done it in a while."

"How you learn?"

"We had a shop course in the ninth grade—I learned about dimmer switches and all that kind of stuff. And we had one of them that didn't work in the back stairs. So my dad and I together went and fixed it for Mr. Condotti—he was our landlord, back in Atlanta."

"I was askin'," Shit said, "'cause Fred Hurter said that Hoke just decided last week that he was gonna go off to Chicago. Some guy invited him up there to stay with him. So he's gonna go and see if he likes it."

Hoke was a local Dump fellow, in his late thirties, who did most of the handy work in the community. He was on salary from the Chamber of Commerce.

"Fred said if we wanted to do some of that, when we weren't working on the garbage routes, we could try our hand at it and, if it worked out, we could make a little extra."

"Sure," Eric said. "Why not? And I can put a washer on a leaky faucet."

"Come on—let's go over and see Fred."

"All right."

Shit turned, and they started back under the branches, heavy with needles in the warm October.

Up the slope, was a cabin built back into the hillside—it belonged to Sam and Abe, two of the men that Dr. Greene had mentioned to Eric on the phone. As they walked past, up the slope the door opened and Abe came out on the porch. (Two pickups—one brown, one green—were parked beside the porch's end.) A tall, gaunt black man, in his early forties, he was light enough to have freckles pretty much all over. You could see the spots, brown and reddish, all over his face on his chest and shoulders from here. He wore a set of loose jeans—no shirt—and a tweed cap. Walking to the rail, he looked out, then over, saw them, and waved.

Eric waved back and they walked on. "You know, the first time he did that, I got all scared we were gonna have to go up there and, you know, get to really know 'em and have to have some big meetin' together with all the piss drinkers in the Dump, where we all talked about drinkin' piss and how we got started at it and all that shit." The hello's and the nods and the smiles had started with the black men Shit had identified to Eric as Einman and Abe and—coming down through Dump Corners with his donkey and three wheeled cart—Brick, days after the call to Dr. Greene; who apparently had been as quick to call the Dump's other urolangliacs about Eric a day after he had told Eric about them. "But I don't think they want nothin' like that—I mean, some full-out support group or some consciousness-raisin' meetin'—any more than I do, like I seen on TV once for shoplifters." He pulled his breath in—and was surprised when Shit took his hand. "But you know—it's funny. It *is* nice to know they're there." He looked at Shit, who smiled. "And that they know we're here." Together, the two headed on down to Hurters to get their first handyman assignments.

* * *

[36] DRIVING SLOWLY BESIDE the sea, in the new garbage truck the Chamber of Commerce had delivered to Dynamite the previous day, with a new experimental low-emissions motor, the lanky garbage man said, "Now we gonna celebrate a little. It's the weekend. We got some beer and some Coca-Cola—and I don't expect to do nothing except lie around and do nasty stuff with the two of you till at least Tuesday mornin'. It drives nice—but it don't quite smell right. To me. Yet…"

"Sounds like that's gonna be some major cuddlin' time to me," Shit said. "Nobody gonna get riled if I do a little fuckin' while we're at it…?"

"Long as somebody wants to suck on my big Georgia dick, you can fuck me till the cows come home—and probably Eric, too, if I judge right." Dynamite put his big hand on Eric's shoulder and began to rub. "But I do not intend to go to into the bathroom from the time I get home to the time we next get up to go into work. So—" he looked at Eric—"son, you gonna have to do a little runnin' back and forth to get that stuff in there for me."

"Sure," Eric said.

"Long as I can watch." Shit's far arm hung out the window down beside the door, "—and do a little kissin'—it sounds good to me."

"Damn," Eric said. "Dynamite, you're the one who always says we shouldn't fool around at work. But—well, how long have we been together, now—and I still get a damned hard-on every time you put a hand on me."

"You mean like this?" Dynamite let his hand drop in down Eric's chest to land in his lap, where the big fingers curled around Eric's crotch.

"No," Eric said. "I mean anytime you touch me at all—even on my shoulder like you was doin'."

"Really?" Dynamite grinned out the windshield. "Maybe that means I still got a little energy there—you know. For gettin' it on."

Eric put one hand in Dynamite's lap—who was iron hard across his crotch, and one hand in Shit's—who, not surprisingly, was the same. (Sometimes Eric wondered if the two of them weren't connected by arcane telepathy.) Shit's hand came in from the window and dropped down on Eric's. "Well, I don't even need to go home. I mean drivin' along in a new truck while somebody's sittin' there playin' with your pecker's always kinda fun. Least ways, I always like it when he done it."

Woods on the left and sea on the right chattered at each other, while handfuls of birds mewed and called above.

* * *

[37] UP OR DOWN Gilead's six coastal miles facing the mainland, only Jay, Mex, Shad, Hugh, and the Holotas actually lived there. Last month, some Indian kids from out of state had gone camping on the island's far side, near the old Creek graveyard.

Standing on the Gilead dock, Jay explained, "Ruth Holota made up this Indian dish out of bolted cornmeal and took it out to 'em. Walter's a real Injun—he grew up around here. But his wife is a white woman, though you'd never know from the way she cooks. I mean she can do them *good* Injun dishes—roasted goat and stuff. You ever tasted that Aye-talian polenta? I mean that's what it was, really. When I was a little kid, half the fishermen around here who wasn't black was Aye-talian—I had it a bunch of times. I went out there with her, too—she gimme some. It was pretty good." He turned from Dynamite to Eric and back. "But they all gone back to school." He dropped his hand on Eric's shoulder. "So you comin' out there with us?" Late-day summer light glinted in his bronze beard.

"Yeah," Eric said. "That'd be fun."

(That September was even warmer than usual.)

"It's fine with me," Dynamite said, "long as you got 'im back here by Monday."

Sitting in the door of the pickup, barefooted, shirtless, Shit grinned. "What you guys gonna do? Give him a belated birthday present out there?"

Jay said, "Well, I wasn't thinkin' of that exactly. But, who knows, we may do a little of that. Now you sure you don't mind us borrowin' this little fuck-stick for a night?"

"Hell," Dynamite said. "When they're this age, they s'posed to be humpin' anything that moves. I'm just glad I'm still wigglin' enough to get mine."

From the pickup door, Shit said to Eric, "Don't worry. I'll take care of this one here while you're out doin' them two."

"Hey," Eric said. "I'll see you back here tomorrow." Then he waved and followed Mex onto the scow. "By the way, Mex, I got somethin' for you." He went digging in his jeans pocket. "Yesterday, after work, Dynamite took us over to the Opera—when I was up in Nigger Heaven, Al gimme somethin'—he said it was for my birthday, too—but I thought I'd pass it on." He pulled out the oversized quarter-filled rubber and held it up, as its viscid load collected in the bottom. "Dynamite let me keep it in the refrigerator last night."

Mex's large hand fell on Eric's shoulder. With a single hand, he signed:

Listen up, boy. Every time I see one of these things, it always surprises me all over again. I'm gonna drink this down right here—you can have some, if you want. As they stepped over the scow's edge, Mex took his hand down and with both said: *This here is gonna be my goddam lunch. That nigger's got enough to keep half the cocksuckers in the state happy. It's like I can never remember how big the damn things are till I actually see 'em again.*

"Me neither," Eric told him—as Mex took the bulbous tube and hefted it on his callused palm.

*

That night, all three slept in Jay's bed.

It was fun, too. With Mex and Jay, Eric had four orgasms inside an hour and fifteen minutes, for the first time in his life. (*That* was the kind of thing Shit prided himself in doing, usually! Not Eric. Maybe, though, it was rubbing off.) He felt drained and, at once, wholly refilled.

When he got up, Eric climbed over Mex and went out into the little john that looked like it wasn't finished. It still needed a patch of drywall over some recently replaced copper piping.

Naked after his crap, he wiped himself with paper from the wire roller, stood up from the commode, flushed, and padded into the hall and out to the long kitchen.

Though the screening, over blue sky and bluer water, sunrise's gold spilled in through oceanward screens, aslant the kitchen's wooden walls. Covered in yellow oilcloth printed with red and green flowers, the table was so bright he felt as if he'd never seen it before. Eric looked…not breathing, lest that luminosity—which seemed something added to the sunlight rather than something that came from it—vanished.

Sleepy and tousled, Mex walked in, with his pitted and indented cheeks, from the adolescent acne that had been so fierce. Eric still found that pockmarked face all-but-unbearably sexy, ever since he'd seen him sitting on the commode, barefoot and shirtless, in his denim pants and jacket, in Turpens. He remembered moments from the night, when the thirty-eight year old Mexican had chuckled voicelessly, while, in the dark, Eric had fingered the uneven skin of his cheeks and neck that bore craters as from buckshot. At the orange counter, naked Mex pulled over the black and silver drip pot from under the window. A few pits dented his buttocks and the sacral slope above.

It was all Eric could do not to go over, bend down, and lick them… some more, the way he had last night.

On the sill, against the screen, stood a cut glass vase, in which a twig leaned. Had that held a flower?

Unsteadily, stretching, yawning, Jay lumbered in. "...Jesus." With big bright arms bunched and raised, he looked like a bearded statue in a museum, flocked with blond fur. He lowered his muscular arms, pictured all over. His gut, flattened into his belly, lowered into place. "Will somebody scratch behind my balls for me—or do I gotta do it myself?"

At the counter, Mex put down the carafe, turned back, and signed to Eric: "*You do it. I'm making coffee.*"

"Oh," Eric said. "Sure. Yeah." Turning, he reached between the heavy, hirsute legs, to slide his hand into the warmth behind Jay's testicles. (Eric looked again at the orchitis. In three years Jay's other testicle had also started to swell: today it was as big as a medium-sized tomato, next to the one now half again as large as a softball—though Jay, at least, was not worried. Last night he'd said, *Actually, I like the idea of them fuckers matchin' a little more.*) On the right of his abdomen, Jay's appendectomy scar gouged through hair and flesh.

"Both of 'em," Jay said. "Yeah, like that—in the back, you little Aryan bastard scumsucker. That's good."

All three were naked.

"The doc—that's not Doc Greene, either. I got a special one, just for my nuts. The Foundation pays for it—always says there ain't really nothin' wrong with 'em except them extra fat deposits. But every two or three days—" while Eric scratched, Jay shook his shaggy head—"especially when I come more than once in a night, I wake up and the thing is fine. Only then, soon as I stand up and take two or three steps, it commences itchin' and ticklin' like a *mother*fucker!" A drop from the nozzle on Jay's flopping penis wet Eric's wrist, rolling over the back. "Oh, yeah—that's good." He smiled at Eric. Sunlight gave a gold backing to Jay's amber eyes.

Still rubbing, Eric grinned. "Hey, that's my pet nut—the *real* big one."

At the counter, Mex looked back, signed something quickly, then turned to pick up the black plastic scoop and measure out grounds from the red and yellow Bustello can.

"Huh? Jay—*what* did he say...? *'Yours...in Runcible'?*"

"He said, 'Yours and every other cocksucker's in Runcible County.'" Jay shifted his weight. "Them things is popular, boy."

Still scratching, Eric laughed.

"You know—" Jay grinned down at him—"that's why I like to get the nigger puppies in here—'cause they got that rough hair. Sometimes when it's really plaguin' me, I put a foot up on the chair and get one of them boys to squat down and put his head under them things and rub it around like you're doin' with your fingers. That hair us fuckin' white guys got is fuckin' *useless* for scratchin'." (Since he felt more or less the same, Eric grinned.) "Yeah, now *that* feels like fuckin' heaven, scumsucker! Not that what you're doin' ain't nice. But if your balls ever really start to itch you, get your brother there to get down and do that for you with his wool. That nigger's got the hair for it. Man, it's somethin'. Go, on—harder. You can really tear into 'em. I do the same thing for them boys with my beard… though it ain't quite identical. Still, it's better than white folks' hair. That ain't got no holdin' power at all. Yeah, *harder*—believe me, it don't hurt me none. Mex'll tell ya."

"His balls are very tough—very strong."

Though he got a word or two from context, Eric understood it all. (Today, largely because he could spell, Eric was more facile at sign language than Shit.) He scratched harder. "That's what you do with the black kids?"

"Ask your fuckin' brother when you get back to the Dump, if you don't believe me. They laugh at me sometimes, 'cause they think I'm funny. But they *do* it—Nigger Joe, Paten—they don't live around here no more—and the one I always called Dog Turd, 'cause that's the color he was. God, he was a good lookin' little black buck. What the hell was his real name?" Settling a hirsute arm around Eric's shoulder, multicolored in the window's sunlight, Jay gave Eric a squeeze, tight enough so his muscles actually shook. The last time Jay had hugged him like that—an hour back—he'd been sucking Eric's cock, his arms wrapped around Eric's butt while he'd shot—and seconds later Jay had shot his own load into one end of Mex or the other. Holding Jay's head, in the dark, with his eyes closed, Eric had not actually seen which…

From the counter, Mex turned back to sign, *"Ben. His name was Ben, you dirty racist fuck."* Grinning, Mex stepped over to fill the carafe at the sink.

"Yeah, well—Dog Turd's what the puppy wanted us to call 'im. Hey, that's good, y'Nazi shit stain. You can't say I don't spread it around. Keep that up for another minute or two."

Two more drops fell on Eric's forearm.

"And he wasn't no puppy. He come to the Harbor in the summer, with his parents."

"He was a puppy when he first come out here—with Shit. That's why he had to get himself a new name—Dog Turd. 'Cause Shit had his. And he was jealous—and he wanted one that was nastier. I had to think of one for him in about three seconds. That was the nastiest one I could come up with. But he couldn't tell his parents. Course, we didn't start no *real* puppy trainin' with him till a few years later, when he was seventeen, maybe eighteen. You remember, Mex. We used to keep that collar out here for him. Hey, Mex is gonna make his special chili, tonight—that was Dog

Turd's favorite. I tell you, that's a real popular dish around here. He used to eat it out a dog bowl, right down on the floor, there, while we sat up and ate ours at the table. That nigger was a *good* puppy. He'd do anything me or Mex'd tell 'im." Jay put his head to the side. "You think you'd be interested in somethin' like that? A dog collar, maybe? I don't mean right now. But sometime, if you find yourself takin' to the idea, lemme know."

"Maybe." Eric shrugged, scratching harder—enough to make Jay sway. "I don't know..."

"If it sounds interestin' to you, talk it over with your dad and your brother. We don't got to rush nothin'. The idea is to do what makes you feel good and comfortable, like you belong. It ain't about goin' to no extremes, just so you can say you done it. Okay, there, puppy—you can stop now."

Eric pulled his hand away.

"Did...Ben tell *his* parents what you were doin' out here—with him?"

"No!" Jay looked surprised. "If he had, his father would have been out here with a shotgun or an ax, tryin' to take some heads off. But, see, Dog Turd didn't have a daddy like you got, now. One he could talk about things like that with—get some advice." Turning, Jay walked bare-assed back to the table. "He was one sweet nigger puppy, though." He turned to sit. "Damn, that always happens, too, when you scratch that thing—look at that. It got me drippin' piss all over the damned floor. Hey, puppy dog, get down and lick that up."

Eric dropped to one knee, then lowered his face over the vinyl tiles, where Jay had left an irregular puddle half the size of Eric's palm. One of Jay's toes had smeared the edge. Smaller drops made an irregular trail to the chair. Because he'd done it for Jay before, licking up Jay's pee felt more comfortable than talking about eating from a dish. The collar sounded nice—like the goth kids used to wear in school. It *was* funny, sometimes, what could make you feel good.

From the floor, Jay's spilled urine tasted like...well, urine. It wasn't anything special. Still, he liked it, anticipating it, remembering it.

And Dynamite...

"Okay, puppy dog—" In the chair, Jay's knees were wide—"come on over here now. Let ol' Jay show you how much he likes you." Heading between Jay's legs, Eric paused to lick up another drop from the floor. Then Jay leaned forward, caught Eric's head, and began to rub and rough it. "There you go—good boy! Good boy! Good puppy! Come on, puppy. Come on—gimme a kiss. Come on and swap some spit with this nasty toothless Georgia racist—" Jay glanced at Mex—"redneck fuck." Eric turned up his face, still between Jay's thick, rough hands, and felt tongue and more tongue pour into him. Jay's face turned one way and another, as he rooted around in there. Eric moved one hand over Jay's foot, his other onto Jay's thigh. He wondered if he should growl—and growled.

Jay growled back, grinning.

After some thirty or forty seconds, Jay lifted his face. "Man, that tastes good. You'd think you'd been lickin' piss up off the floor, son." He let go of Eric's head with one hand, pushed a thick forefinger into one nostril, stretching it, twisting it. Pulling his finger free, he glanced at it, then pushed it in Eric's mouth—more salt. "That's for bein' such a good little puppy. Now get on over there and give my personal spic a suck." His callused forefinger dragged free of Eric's face, for a moment turning down Eric's under lip.

Swiveling on all fours, Eric had assumed Mex was still standing at the counter. But the Mexican had come to sit on one of the heavy chairs, which he'd moved forward of the table, his shoulders hunched down, his feet pulled back under, one hand in his lap, absently tugging himself.

As Eric's face moved between Mex's knees, Mex caught Eric's head, pulled him forward, and began to push himself repeatedly into Eric's mouth, hips lifting from the chair cushion. Soon Mex locked one leg behind Eric's. Grunting and moving his hands around over Eric's head, Mex guided Eric's rise and fall, first slowly, then faster—and faster. Through all that, Eric was aware Jay himself had gotten up and moved to a closer chair—presumably to watch. Mex's separate grunts became one growl—as had happened before when Eric had blown him. He wondered if the man would fall out of the chair (as had happened on a previous visit), when the tube along the underside of Mex's cock, while still moving in and out, thickened on Eric's tongue, retreated, and thickened again to flush Mex's semen into Eric. Mex's hands locked behind Eric's head. His abdomen heaved, hardened, softened again on Eric's forehead. When the meshed fingers loosened, Eric pulled back. For a moment Mex's cock head caught on Eric's chin. "Jesus, that was fuckin'...*real* good, Mex. Thanks."

Mex's eyes were still closed. The pockmarked face settled into a smile. Grinning down, with only his mouth, suddenly he blinked black eyes as bright as Jay's amber irises.

Jay stood beside his partner, bending over; Eric saw Jay had stuck his arm down and his hand under Mex's butt. "You see," Jay said to Eric's questioning look, "I gotta stick three fingers up this spic's asshole so he can come—or you'd been suckin' his dick all fuckin' day." He pulled his hand free and, standing, raised it to push his fingers against Mex's mouth, who took them in and began to tongue them. With his funny half-smile, Jay pulled his hand loose and lowered himself into a chair. "You see, Mex came with us last night. But he didn't shoot this mornin'. You gotta keep track of that sort of thing if you're gonna roll around in bed with a lotta people what ain't in your own immediate family. You got your truck-stop manners down pretty good, puppy. Only now you got to work on bein' polite with your general over-all everyday orgy carryings-on—it's just as important. Trust me."

"*Okay, now.*" In the air, Mex's big hands signed: "*Let up on the boy. He pulled out my load. He's a good puppy—you don't gotta be on his case all the time.*"

"You know as well as me," Jay said. "It's the same with boys and dogs. A well trained puppy is a happy puppy."

"*Besides.*" In his own chair, Mex still grinned. "*I don't got to come so much no more. I had a lot of fun. It's not important.*"

"Mex," Jay said, "is tryin' to be polite to *you*, there." Jay turned to Mex. "What you mean you don't need to come no more? You come when I *say* cum, you shit eatin' wetback bastard! Otherwise, I'm gonna stand up here and piss in your fuckin' mouth, make you roll around in it on the floor, and the *two* of you gonna lick it up! I'll make you fight over it, with a good tongue wrasslin' match. See—" Jay sat back, and pointed over to Mex with a wide thumb, not even looking—"he already got another hard-on."

Which, now, smiling sheepishly, Mex pulled one hand over to cover.

Eric had one, too.

"But what we're gonna do *now*—all three of us—is sit at the table and have us a cup of coffee and not say much and look out the window at the sun on the ocean there. It's a real pretty mornin'. You got to sit and look out at the mornin' a fair amount, if you wanna live a goddam civilized life."

Eric sat back, then put one hand up on the table, to lever himself from his knees. Already three mugs sat on the oilcloth. So did the carafe—on a green tile trivet, like a fragment of sea.

"Sit down, there, puppy. Will you two—" Jay looked back and forth between them—"stop pullin' on your dicks a minute? All we gonna do is look out the window and be quiet and enjoy some coffee—and the sun."

Backing up, Eric looked behind to determine where his own chair was—then sat on it.

"You got a hard-on," Eric said, nodding at Jay.

"I don't care. We done fucked away half the mornin' in bed already. It's gotta be at least six thirty. So—" Jay repeated—"we gonna sit here now and have some damned coffee. And look out to sea." Which is what they did.

What they'd done the rest of the day, Eric could not have reconstructed. Had they gone out exploring the all-but-empty island, stopping to talk to the elderly Mr. and Mrs. Holota, who, a half-mile away, were sitting out on their side deck, their backs to the road, also watching the water? Had they stayed in, played pinochle, or Chinese checkers? Had they relieved Hugh and taken grumpily silent Shad in his wheelchair for a roll outside? Had they fooled around in one of the grottos or just taken a nap together at the house—"'Cause," as Jay explained, "we done so much relaxin' already, we gotta take another fuckin' nap to get over it."

What Eric did remember was, late that afternoon, how he'd stood at the orange counter with Mex.

Along with the walk-in pantry at the end, the kitchen was the length of the entire house. Beams rose over the wooden walls, crossed the ceiling. The room's far end, where the freezer was and a couple of ancient stoves Jay said no longer worked, had become a storage area. Junk filled more than half the space. You could think that part was Dynamite's kitchen in the Dump. But this end was clear, with pots beside their red tops, hung from wall hooks beside different sized skillets over the dishwasher next to the modern electric burner a dozen feet down the counter from the stainless steel sink.

At the counter Mex cut up onions and green and red peppers, big and little ones, pale and dark ones, and, in a large clay bowl crushed tomatoes and tomatillos, with the bottom of a water glass. Following instructions, Eric scraped the spatula back and forth across the skillet, frying up chopped beef and ground veal and cut up sausages (already cooked in another pan), while, from his seat at the table, Jay explained how you had to have extra cumin to make chili with store bought chili powder have any taste at all. "And that stuff picks up mites faster than a big rig driver can pick up crabs from a twenty dollar hooker workin' Turpens back lot." Sometimes Mex leaned on Eric's shoulder, or now and again slid his hand down Eric's back and stuck a finger under the back of his jeans to trowel between Eric's buttocks and even push his fingertip into Eric's ass, a quarter of an inch, an inch. "Mex, *what* you doin'?" Eric grinned at him.

Mex took his hand out to sign: "*You liked it last night. You don't like it today?*"

Then Mex would go on to explain how at least he hadn't used the hand he'd held the hot peppers with when he'd cut them. "*A friend of mine he do that to me, one time. He think it's funny—fucking asshole!*" Eric asked Mex to slow down and repeat it for him. From the kitchen table where he was sitting, watching, his long sleeved denim shirt lopsided over the back of the big, solid chair, with his big solid arms, their colors hazed in gold, Jay started to translate.

"No—I'll figure it out," Eric said. "Jay, I'll get it by myself. Don't tell me. Once more, Mex…"

"*If I did that, your hole would hurt bad. It really stings. But I'm your friend. I don't make jokes like that with my friends.*" Then Mex took his hand away and sucked his finger that, moments back, had been, to the second knuckle, in Eric's butt.

Eric said, "I guess I'm pretty clean back there."

"No you ain't." Mex grinned. *"But you smell good. And taste good, too."*

Jay sat at the table chuckling. "The first time Mex was makin' that stuff, he had me cuttin' up them little green jalapeños—and like a damned fool I took a break and nipped into the john to piss, run my finger around under my skin to wipe the cheese out, and sucked that stuff off it, skinned it back to piss and shook it dry, and while I'm comin' out, my mouth *and* the head of my dick start feelin' like they're getting' roasted over red hot coals. I told Mex right there, cuttin' up them peppers is fuckin' spic work. The third time I accidentally done that, I decided a white man's too fuckin' stupid to slice them things up. A white feller's gonna forget, reach down, scratch himself—and burn his damned dick off, every time."

Again, Eric grinned at him—and shook his head. Mex could be *almost* as bad about excrement as Uncle Tom. (These days old Tom ate his own shit, every third time he crapped.) In his black denim jacket, no shirt or pants, and bare feet, the thick, bowlegged Mex was nearly as solid as bare-chested Jay, who sat, shirtless, with great arms like a hemp-paled Christmas trees, a muscular haystack with his full beard and his Turpens cap still on, grinning at Mex.

Yellow hair blurred the inks, knuckles to shoulders.

There were still no pictures on Jay's chest or back. But, in fur, his gray-red nipples were the size of acorns, enlarged (he'd explained) from three successive sets of tit rings, each of which he'd had to take out: the first ones, he'd told Eric, at Shad's insistence, to shut the old bastard up; he'd taken out the second pair for a cat scan over at the Runcible Memorial (which, of course, had turned up nothing), and the last for that emergency appendectomy four years ago—"Just about a year before you come here—" that had left its gouge on his right flank. "They always keep them electric heart-starter paddle things ready with any operation, no matter how damned simple—in case. They told me, if they used them when I had my rings in, they'd burn my tits off me. They don't even want you to have in no earring." With each, he'd waited too long to put them back in. The holes had closed—in less than two weeks. So, each time he'd had them re-pierced and new ones inserted. "And each time my damn titties would grow up twice as large as they was—well, it gives Mex somethin' to nurse on at night, when he gets tired of my toes. You was doin' pretty good on them things, yourself, puppy."

(Again Eric grinned.)

Sometime in the next week, Jay *and* Dynamite were planning to visit

Tank and Cassandra's in Runcible—Jay for a fourth set and Dynamite for a thicker gauge. "Your daddy won't get no tattoos. But he'll go have a number fourteen needle jabbed through his damned titties." Jay shrugged. "Well—that's your new daddy and my goddam best friend. I hope your old one—your real dad was a nigger, right?—had more sense. Your mama must really like them black guys." He was referring to Ron.

Eric said, "She does."

"Right now, your dad looks like your brother. Your real dad I mean." (Eric had once tried to untangle the complexities of his parentage, and Jay had responded: *I don't care if he's a nigger. He raised you, didn't he? Then he's your fuckin' dad—like Dynamite's your dad now.* And Eric had felt a wonderful relief, near to nepotistic love. *'Cause he's raisin' you now. That's how it works down here. You can count yourself lucky, 'cause you was raised by black and white— like Kyle.*)

"Naw," Eric said. "He probably looked more like…Dog Turd. My dad's *real* dark. He never had no collar. But he wore a brown leather wrist brace."

"Well, see," Jay said, "he probably didn't know it, but the nigger was gettin' you ready for *us*."

With a hairy hand, Jay massaged his forearm, over scorpions, starfish, seahorses, pressing down hairs like gold wires, which, when the cracked, soiled, and callused palm passed on, rose again.

Then Mex explained, "*Now, you have to jerk off and put it in the chili pot—*"

"What? *What* did you say…? Jay, what did he say, just now?"

So Mex repeated it.

"Aw, come on, Mex." Eric said, "You're kiddin', aren't you?"

"He ain't kiddin'." Jay's broad hand flattened on the yellow oilcloth beside the glimmering metallic yellow and green of his Coors can. "*That's* more important than the goddam chili powder *and* the cumin! If you don't add some flavor to that stuff, it don't taste like *nothin'!*"

"You *gotta* be jokin'," Eric said.

"Am I jokin' when I let you suck my dick? Go on, puppy, take your meat out and start tenderizin' it." Despite laughing and kidding, Eric realized they meant it. "Don't worry—" nodding seriously, Jay turned on his chair. Rearing back, he unzipped his own fly—"we gonna help you out…At least give you some encouragement. Come on. Let's see how long it takes."

So, beneath the single line of florescent bulbs along the ceiling, Eric stood in the middle of the floor, opened his pants, and let them fall midway down his thighs.

"Turn around, so Mex can see your butt cheeks clenchin' up. That's what *he* likes." With one heavy arm out, its images deep in fur, Jay gestured in a circle with a blunt forefinger. "Me, now—I wanna see you shoot." When Eric was nearing orgasm and making little gasps, Jay said, "Go on, catch it, there. Catch it—catch it in your other hand, puppy dog. Don't waste that stuff…"

Finally, Eric stood with the puddle in his palm, breathing hard. "Now… now what do…you want…want me to do…to do with it?"

"Pour it in the pot with the beans," Jay said. "And the meat. And the tomatoes."

"No. Come on, you don't really—"

"You ate enough of that stuff in your life before, you know it ain't gonna kill you."

"Yeah, but—"

"*Go on,*" Mex signed. "*Put it in.*"

So, shaking his head over the stove, Eric shook off his hand above tomatoes, meat, and beans. "You guys are crazy." Like smaller and larger meteors, semen droplets hit the wavering red, leaving momentary craters—and were gone. Eric turned back, licking the rest from his palm and the ham of his thumb—to show he was a good sport.

"Yeah," Jay said, nodding deeply. "Cum crazy, maybe…But you are, too, scumsucker."

Now Mex was on his knees in front of Jay, pulling at the laces of one of Jay's high-topped shoes.

"There we go." Jay reached down to rub Mex's head. "Now we're on our way to some *real* chili. You *gotta* have some wetback jizz in with what us white boys put in. Otherwise it ain't authentic."

"What's he doin'?" Eric asked.

"Pullin' off my shoe."

And, a minute later, when the half-collapsed work shoe slid from Jay's foot, a smell came out that Eric realized was, all over again, giving him an erection. Eric said, "Damn, Jay—that's some real foot stink. I can smell it over here."

"I know it is. Dynamite and me both always had powerful feet. But if it gives you a hard-on, it's doin' its job."

Eric rubbed between his legs. "Kinda, I guess…"

A minute later, Mex had tossed Jay's socks, knotted together, across the floor tiles and had Jay's big toes in his mouth, sucking at them, prodding between with his tongue. Mex's jacket was off on the floor—all he'd been wearing. Seconds later, Mex was on his side, holding Jay's bare foot.

Jay rolled Mex onto his back. The Mexican's cock flopped up against the gut hair, his wide cock head, dark pink as bologna, pushing from its brown hood. Two lapping cheese rings circled it. The foreskin had shoved out one, retreated, then shoved out another.

Eric said, "Can I suck Mex off...?" Because of his cheese and his thick foreskin, sucking Mex's barrel cock was really fun.

"No, you may not." Jay put a broad foot—paler than the rest of him—on Mex's groin. Blushing in spots from the pressure of his shoe, the foot looked too big even for a man that large. Jay rubbed and rolled Mex's cock back and forth, while Mex's brown hips hunched and lifted on the vinyl flooring. Mex held onto the foot's cracked edge with one hand, and Jay's frayed denim pants leg with the other. "Hey," Jay said, "I *think* this fuckin' spic is about to shoot, too. Ain't you, you shit eatin' scumbag? Hey, help him out and call this fuckin' low down cocksucker some nasty names with me. It ain't like the fucker's deaf, you know. You wanna take a piss in his face, puppy dog? Come here, we can both do it." Most of his weight on his remaining shoe, Jay stood. "'Cause this is his second time today, we gotta be a little creative. He ain't like your brother back in the Dump what can come any time he wants all day long." On a wall shelf a ceramic skeleton embraced a pot, the skull-face leering around the neck. Beside it stood a carefully painted figure of a black motorcyclist in black leather, mounted on a miniature Harley.

Pushing his cock down with all his fingers, where it jutted from his jeans, Jay aimed. "Come on. Mex here is gonna give us a *good* load."

Eric stepped over, unsure if any urine was in him.

"Open wide, you dumb-ass spic," Jay said. "We both gonna show you how much we like you, now."

Mex opened his mouth and waggled his tongue back and forth.

And Eric was hard again.

"Drink this," Jay said, and let loose.

Eric took a big breath, and after six or seven seconds, began to drip. The drip became a dribble—then a stream.

"Right in his fuckin' mouth—yeah, just like you doin'. Get the floor wet, and *you* gonna clean it up, puppy dog. With your tongue, too," Jay said. "That's right. Just like he was squattin' under the bar at The Slide and you was standing with me at the counter, havin' a pop and too lazy to go out back and do it in the outdoor john. Look at him swallow that puppy piss—as well as this big ol' dog's. Hey, I just felt him go off." Jay laughed. "All under my toes—see it there? I tell you, you treat this spic right and you can make him shoot a *big* load every time—almost as much as you, puppy."

With one hand on the table, Jay lifted his broad foot from a shiny splat, irregular and off center, over Mex's belly, with, below it, the wide triangle of curly black.

While Mex lay on his back, breathing hard, Jay turned his cracked sole up against his calf, reached down and dozed his forefinger over it, to scrape up a rill of mucus. Then he scooped the same finger's tip into the trough behind his toes. "Might as well get it all." Jay dropped his foot and walked—still in one shoe—to the stove, then flung his hand down over the kettle. Steam whipped from the edge. "There…!" Now he scraped his finger on the pot's edge. "You know, this is how religions start—with that communion stuff and all."

Eric wondered if it burned. Jay's fingers were so tough and callused, though, probably it didn't.

"But we don't need to take it that far." In front of the oven's green enamel door, Jay turned. "All right—which one of yall cocksuckers wanna bust *my* nut, now?" His cock still thrust in its downward curve from his jeans. "I done had all day to recuperate." Pushing from his fly, his larger testicle was fully visible along with half the smaller. Tall and thick as Jay was, his cock was not more than six-and-a-half inches, hard—an inch shorter than Eric's, soft. But Jay always brought so much attitude to his carryings on, by the time you were doing stuff with him, mostly you weren't paying attention to such things.

Eric wondered if he was expected to go over, squat down, and suck Jay off. He was feeling a little queasy.

Mex had rolled over, though, and, on his knees, smiled at Eric. "*You do that good, puppy.*" Mex moved his hands down. "*Real good. Thank you.*" Mex turned to the stove, crawled across the kitchen, then stopped to sign back, "*You take a good piss.*"

In sign language, Eric dropped his fingers from his mouth in a quick, *You're welcome.*

Eric watched Jay rub Mex's head, in that way that always felt so friendly, whenever you were sucking the big boatman—when they were alone on the scow and Jay was at the wheel or sometimes out here at the house. How many times, now in Turpens, sometimes with Shit, sometimes alone, something joining in, sometimes not, or down in the boat house, even out here, had Eric seen Jay and his partner have sex?

Only it hadn't been in their own kitchen, before, nor had it involved… well, what was supposed to be dinner.

"There…" Grunting, Jay wiped the back of his wrist on his beard. (Occasionally, before he came, like Shit, he drooled a little. Again, it was probably because of his teeth.) Reaching down, he helped stocky Mex to his feet. "Don't swallow that stuff, you cocksuckin' spic. That's *my* supper contribution." One hand on Jay's hip, then the other on Jay's upper arm, Mex rose. "Go on, Mex," Jay said. "Spit my fuckin' load right into that pot. I tell you, boy, if chili ain't *really* nasty, it ain't fit to eat."

Mex leaned over the green-enameled stove and made a hawking sound. His broad shoulders pushed forward.

Kind of quietly, Eric said, "I don't think I'm gonna want any of…"

As Mex's head pulled back, steam rose by his cheek.

Jay rubbed the back of Mex's neck. "See, now." Both of them turned from the green stove. Mex grinned. Jay hugged the naked Mexican into his hairy flank. Reaching around to thumb something off Mex's chin, he stuck it in his own mouth, "that's gonna be some *real* good chili. We all made our contribution—the three of us. From our own goddam nuts. Now it'll taste like chili's *supposed* to taste."

In the dowel-backed chair, Eric sat by the table, feeling strange. "You're…*really* gonna eat that?" He didn't think they'd heard him. Because it wasn't any of the things he was used to taking in—snot, shit, urine, or cum from a dick or hand, its contact with Jay's foot had, somehow, turned it into…well, ordinary dirt.

Without looking at him, Jay said, "Yup. You are, too, if you want dinner."

"What about Shad? And Hugh?"

Jay grinned. "We ain't gonna tell the mean-ass fuck about the secret ingredients. But that's his dinner, too." Four rooms on the other side of house were reserved for wheelchair bound Shad, apparently content not to be included in his nephew's socializing. "His loss. And what Hugh don't know won't hurt him."

Grinning, Mex signed, "*Hugh knows. He don't mind.*"

Sometimes at the house, sometimes at the Harbor, Eric would see Hugh or Jay—and, occasionally, Mex—rolling Shad in his chair one place or another. Eric always said 'Hello, sir,' as Jay had instructed. Sometimes Shad would nod his acknowledgment, sometimes not. "Probably that stuff's what's keepin' the bastard alive. 'Cause he's a straight sonofabitch, you gotta sneak it to 'im, the way you get a dog to take its pill—stuck in a piece of meat."

In the solid kitchen chair, Eric tried to cut himself loose from his sense of violation. It was Jay and Mex joking around—amiable craziness. It's what he came over here for, wasn't it? They weren't doing it to *make* him feel this way…

Only when Mex got up and, with the ladle, filled big soup plates with chili over rice, then put one in front of Jay—Jay had hung his Turpens cap over the ketchup bottle at the oilcloth's edge and taken the long-sleeved denim from the chair back and pushed his arms into it—did Mex put a plate at his own place. He slid another in front of Eric, who picked up his spoon, but only held it.

Jay hadn't buttoned his shirt. He and Mex were already digging in. The stuff *smelled* good…

Eric said, "I don't think I'm that hungry...right now."

Jay raised an eyebrow. "Suit yourself. That's the thing about chili. You can always eat it later."

Chewing a big mouthful, Mex put his spoon down, glanced inquisitively at Eric, then signed above his bowl toward Jay, "*What's wrong with him? He don't feel good?*" He turned to Eric. "*You don't feel good, my friend? Your stomach don't be good?*"

"Naw. I'm okay."

Jay dug up another spoonful and gulped it in. "Man, this is some good chili, Mex. Some of your best. Hey—ain't nothin' wrong with Eric." He gave a nod over the table. With a half-knowing smile, he chewed beans and meat and rice. "We just been playin' with the puppy a little rough. That's all. He needs a while to settle hisself."

Eric looked out on the night, along the opposite wall. Now the windows were black.

Mex put his spoon down and, with his big hands that seemed so clumsy but, Eric knew, could be wonderfully firm, wonderfully gentle, formed the words in the air: "*We not do nothing to him.*" (With the washed out denim tight over upper and lower arms and his forested chest between the unbuttoned fabric's edges, the serpent's head on his right hand thrust from under the cuff, Jay looked like...well, someone else.) Mex was still naked. (The night before, when he'd first come, it had been Eric who'd ended up bare-assed by the time they ate. That had been fun, sitting naked at the table, watching how the two men kept glancing at him, between their jokes, ribald and easy through the evening...) "*We didn't do nothing to him we didn't do with Whiteboy and Dog Turd and Shit and Nigger Joe when they was even younger. All them puppies was real good boys. He's crazy, maybe?*"

"He ain't crazy," Jay said. "He's just different from 'em, Mex. For one thing, he wasn't raised to it, like most of them. For another, until he come here, his daddy was a straight guy—like yours, like mine."

Eric said, "Hey—I really like bein' your...puppy, Jay—and yours, too, Mex. It's fun, with you two—I mean it. Last night, in bed, we had a *great* time. Really, I like—"

"Course you do," Jay said. "But nobody ever taught you *how*. You been havin' to learn it all by yourself. And sometimes you hit a stretch you don't know nothin' about, and it gets you a little confused. That's all. You got to learn how to act with other people—*and* you got to learn how to think and feel about yourself. Well, it takes time."

"*Yeah, my daddy, he was straight,*" Mex signed again. "*But I used to dream about the stuff we do, here—now. All the time, when I was a kid. I dream it. I pray for it to God, when I think there was a God. All the time. When I was thirteen,*" *fourteen, fifteen. That's why I love it so much, now. It's my dream—and real.*"

"Yeah." Jay lifted his can, to drink his Coors. "Sure—you used to *dream* about it, Mex." Where the oilcloth didn't cover the wood, the Coors can clicked the table corner. "But if, back then, you'd really stumbled onto any of it, you woulda turned around and skedaddled like a spooked rabbit, so fast you wouldn't even knowed what direction you—"

To which Mex cut him off with a dismissive downward wave, then upward extended middle finger: "*Yo*, fuck *you....!*"

Eric said, "I said I liked bein' your fellas' puppy. Hey, I *do*! Really. It... makes me feel...good. Most of the time...*real* good. Like you really like me. It's like some of the most...fun I ever had."

"We like you, too. And we know you do," Jay said. "That's one of the reasons we do it. Not the *only* one—but it's one."

Eric picked up his spoon again, touched the tip to the chili, then moved it from over the plate, gripping the handle. "Hey, Jay? Mex? It ain't the cum. I swallowed more jizz outta both you guys since I got here yesterday *mornin'* than you put in the pot. Back home I finger the dirt out from between Dynamite's toes a couple of times a week, when he don't get no shower. Shit's, too. It's like one of my jobs. And, yeah, a lot of times it makes me hard. We all laugh about it. Shit even rubbed me off once, with his foot—and broke Dynamite up, laughin'. It ain't the spit, either. Both of you had your tongues down my damned throat last night, so you know it can't be that. I *love* to tongue-fuck. You seen how it makes me shoot, last night. And most of the jizz in here is mine anyway. And I eat *my* own stuff all the time—you seen me do it."

"Like your daddy." Jay nodded. "Dynamite. It's a real turn on, too..."

Putting down his spoon, Mex asked, "*What is it?*" He looked seriously curious.

"It's..." Eric made a face, then looked at Mex. "It's the...his feet."

Mex asked, "*What you mean, his feet?*"

Eric grimaced again.

Mex said, "*You tell us, before, his feet make you get a big hard-on.*" Mex made "big" a big two-handed gesture.

"Yeah," Eric said. "I know. Dynamite's do, too. Yeah, and I...*like* the smell. Shit's don't smell much at all, really, 'cause he goes barefoot all the time—like you, Mex. But, see, likin' to smell 'em and clean 'em and hold 'em and sniff 'em ain't the same thing as...*suckin'* on 'em. Or fingerin' cum from out between your toes—and puttin' it in...*food*. That's all it is." Eric shrugged—and took a breath. He put his own spoon on the oilcloth.

Mex turned in his chair and looked intently at Eric.

Mex raised one hand—

Jay interrupted, "Hey, puppy dog, nothin's wrong with my feet—you know it, too. Like you said, they're like Dynamite's. That's good ol' 'Mur'c'n workin' man two-week-old sock-and-toe foot funk. That's all. Hey—that stuff turns *everybody* on, puppy—niggers and Polacks and bohunks and Greeks and spics and Ay-talian wops and even little bastard Nazi scumsucker puppies like you what don't know *what* the fuck they are."

"Yeah," Eric said, still uncomfortable. "I know, but—'

Again Mex began to sign, *"What you sayin'? What you sayin', my friend? Jay's feet is wonderful. They stink—yeah—they stink and they stink and they stink and that's how they make me shoot all over myself. Every night, I go to bed, with them up in my face. I love to suck them—suck them every night. I suck his toes, I lick his asshole, I love to eat his shit and drink his piss. You seen me do it, the time Shit brought you over here and you just watched us. Your brother jerked you off, while we did it. You loved it, you said. It really got you off. I suck Jay's toes, I suck out his ass, I suck his fingers, I suck his dick, but most of all I suck his toes, because they stink so wonderful, my friend."*

Eric said, "Uh…yeah."

Jay said, "You ever had a stoned toe-sucker, like Mex here, give you a real foot bath? It's right up there with havin' a nigger head-scratch your nuts. Man, there ain't nothin' more relaxin' than a tongue-bath on your toes—once you get over the tickle. You see if you can get Shit or Dynamite to do that for you, when you get home. See if one of them'll do that to you. Or, hell, Mex here'll do it, if I tell him to. I got to *tell* him, though, 'cause there's a couple of things he likes to be faithful about. But part of our agreement is he'll do anything I tell him to…" Jay scowled wickedly. "Long as it's *nasty*. Thing is, I don't know if your feet is powerful enough for Mex. Course you wear them basketball sneakers. A puppy dog can work up a pretty good stink in those things, if he don't change his socks *too* often. You know, Mex is kind of a romantic about that stuff." Jay reached over and rubbed Mex's head.

Mex looked up, grinning.

Eric picked up his spoon—and pushed it into his chili. "Jesus, with everything I had in my mouth—" he still felt embarrassed—"some cum off your damned foot, Jay, ain't gonna kill me." He dug in the beans and tomatoes, and lifted it to his mouth. "I'm just actin' like a fuckin' fool. Hey. I'm sorry." Probably, he thought, it was because he *was* so hungry.

He put the full spoon in his mouth…

Christ, it *was* good!

Jay took another spoonful from his own plate.

Mex's grin had gotten…huge!

Eric swallowed. "I don't think you can taste it at all. The cum, I mean.

It's just…" He took another spoonful. "It's just the *idea*…that's all. The heats gonna kill anything, anyway—even if it ain't *all* mine. It's just your fantasy—" Eric stopped and sat back. "Aw, *shit*…!" He put his spoon down again and looked up at the two men.

Jay, then Mex, frowned.

"I got a…hard-on." Bewildered, Eric looked back and forth between them. (Jay took another swallow from his beer.) "I thought I was gonna maybe…I mean, I was afraid I was gonna throw up or something—if I ate it. But I got a *hard-on*…instead!"

"You got a hard-on?" Jay demanded, mocking Eric's bewilderment. "You got a fuckin' *hard-on*—? Come on, lemme feel it." He put down the can, reached around under the oilcloth's edge, and dropped his hand between Eric's legs. He began to massage Eric's groin…more gently than Eric had anticipated from the energy behind the motion. "Well, damned if he don't, Mex. He's a freaky little puppy, now, ain't he? Getting' a hard-on from your chili, there. Move around here, Mex, and finger the puppy's asshole like he was likin' so much last night. Maybe he'll let you lick it out for him, again."

Eric began to laugh. Mex's chair legs scraped around on the floor as he slid closer. "Hey," Eric said. "You *knew* that was gonna happen, didn't you, Jay? As soon as I started *actually* eatin' it. You *knew* it would do that to me, huh?"

"No." Thoughtfully, Jay picked up his spoon again and fell back to eating his own, without taking his other hand from Eric's lap. "Actually, this is the first time I seen anybody get *that* excited…over chili—Mex's or anybody else's."

"Come on," Eric said. "What? It's the hormones, right? From the…the semen or somethin'? Hey, that feels nice." With one hand, he took Jay's wrist to hold the hand against him. With his other, he ate some more.

"Naw," Jay said. "I don't think so. We had a *few* people sit out on Mex's chili before—a couple of guys we brought back from Turpens we thought would like it—only once they seen what went into it…they kinda acted like you, there. So that wasn't *really* no surprise…"

"*It surprise me it be you,*" Mex signed.

"But if you got a hard-on, whatever made it pop up, believe me, puppy, that's in your *own* head. You can be damned sure about that."

Mex put his rough hand up to his face and snorted from his nose into his palm and passed his hand to Eric.

"See," Jay said. "That's a peace offerin'."

Then—once Eric had shot again, in Mex's and Jay's hands together—they finished dinner, then turned in early.

Eric began the night with his cock wedged into the crevice of Mex's buttocks, his arm around Mex's chest. "Just reach down with some spit and stick it in his spic ass anytime you want. He don't mind," Jay said. "He's one of those guys you can fuck 'im in his sleep, and he don't hardly notice. You ever done one of them before?"

"Un-huh," Eric said. "Under the highway, in Atlanta. Least I *seen* some old guy doin' it there—"

Both boatmen gave out grunts—Mex's longer than Jay's.

"Yeah, I forgot. The big city slicker here seen and done ever'thing." Jay said it with amused acceptance.

Mex signed something but, because he was facing away, Eric couldn't see. "What did he say?" Eric asked.

From the other side, Jay said, "He said you done everythin' before, except get a hard-on over a bowl of chili," then reached over on the table beside the bed and turned out the lamp.

In the dark, Eric drifted off, remembering what had happened that morning, the sunlight, the strong coffee. Eric gave Mex a squeeze. The mute Mexican reached up and patted Eric's hand.

The bed was more comfortable than Dynamite's.

Mex and Jay had to be up before sunrise to make the first trip back to the mainland.

Eric slept through the night.

Back at Dynamite's, when Eric had told Shit about the secret ingredients, and made up a pot, of course Shit insisted they both "contribute"—and not tell Dynamite. When they were eating, sitting around the kitchen table in the Dump, holding his bowl practically under his chin and shoveling it in, Dynamite said, "Damn, this is pretty good chili, son. It tastes like Mex's. But what you put in this stuff, anyway? Whatever it is, it's givin' me a hard-on."

"Hey, that's funny," Shit said. "Me, too…" Then both Shit and Dynamite started laughing.

Eric said, "Hey—Jay or Mex musta told you. That ain't fair. You knew. They told you about me. Or Shit told you…what we did. You knew—one of 'em went and told you what happened…"

"I don't know nothin'," Dynamite insisted. "But *somethin's* makin' my dick hard."

"Mine, too," Shit said.

"Hey," Dynamite said to his son, "everything gives *you* a hard-on, nigger!"

"Yeah—you too!"

"Hey—that ain't me," Dynamite said. "At least, not no more, son.

That's *you*!"

They all started laughing again, till Shit actually fell down from his chair and started rolling around between the junk over the cabin floor.

Sometimes Shit had to overdo things like that.

It was still pretty funny.

* * *

[38] WHEN SHIT TURNED twenty-four (Eric was still twenty-one for another six weeks), a free dental clinic took over an abandoned building in Runcible, around the dusty corner from the HIV clinic with the two horse-headed hitching posts (and a hole still in the pavement for a third). While the sunlight made ghosts in the dust of the plate glass window, Eric got all four wisdom teeth pulled, then badgered Shit into getting an upper plate and a partial lower. "Why don't you make my damned dad get one, 'stead of me? You like kissin' on him better 'cause he got more gum than me. When you're lickin' around in his suck hole, you think about that half-toothless motherfucker suckin' your dick and that's what makes you shoot—"

"Oh, Shit, it ain't like that—"

"That's sure the way it works for *me*. I mean, I don't *care* or anything—"

"Look. Once you have yours, we can *both* start in on him."

It was…*kind* of a success.

"It makes food taste a little funny, though. And you say it don't even make me sexier—you want me to take 'em out, before we start fuckin' around. I thought that was why I was goin' *through* all that shit!"

Still, the following Sunday, from the old dock down at the beach in the Dump, they took Dynamite's outboard in the dinghy to Gilead to show off Shit's new smile to Mex and Jay.

On the Kyle mansion's deck, outside the rollback windows on the back sitting room's wall, against tangled leaves and standing stones beyond the deck rail, for moments Jay's heavy arms looked like the greenery itself. Then, after Mex's shoulder lamb chops and greens in the kitchen, Shit and Eric walked back to the Gilead boathouse.

The evening was layers of light and green.

Under the roof, the dinghy rocked on glistening black, while the walls ran with silver from the low sun. Light wove and unwove on the gray planks, on the scow's white hull in the other slip, on the walls beyond the barrels and coiled ropes and cleats and empty three-foot spools.

Shit climbed down the wooden ladder to step, barefoot, into the outboard's sloshy bottom. One hand on a rung, he got over the middle bench and turned to sit on the front seat.

Eric started down after him. Reaching the boat, in quickly soaked runners he stepped to the back seat for the tiller.

While Eric sat, Shit leered the leer of someone who, till then, had often thought twice about smiling too broadly.

Eric pushed the starter. The propeller whirred below water. The boat's stern lifted, then settled.

Twisting, Shit loosed the rope and draped it through the lower ladder beside them.

Eric pushed down. The outboard got louder; the boat moved toward the opening, into the low sun.

* * *

[39] IT WASN'T TWO full weeks afterwards that Eric was walking back up toward the cabin on the crinkly grass, when he saw—at first he thought it was Dynamite—someone standing by the corner. He was holding something in his arms. Then—from the sneakers, actually—he saw it was Shit.

Shit cradled the dark thing—and Eric saw the forelegs thrust out together, claws in different directions.

As he walked up, Eric asked, "What happened?"

"Uncle Tom," Shit said, looking up. "He died." His voice was bleak and inflectionless.

Despite the afternoon's over ninety heat, cold spread through Eric, from his throat down his chest to his belly and his gut. "When?" It swirled away like the far sound of a March breeze.

"This mornin'." Shit looked up and blinked. "Maybe last night. I don't know."

"When you find him?" Because of the blank look that came through Shit's tufted beard, Eric stepped up and put his arm around Shit's shoulder.

Tom's eye was open enough to see a white sliver.

"Maybe ten minutes ago. I seen he hadn't eat no food what you left for him this mornin'. So I picked his pan up and banged it on the porch post. Usually, that'll bring him out from under the steps, you know?"

"Un-huh."

"But he didn't come out. So I looked in under there—and I seen him. And he wouldn't move when I called. Then I crawled in and pulled him out."

"Does Dynamite know?"

"Naw," Shit said. "He's down at the Seed and Steel. He was a real old dog. Sixteen, seventeen years. You know how he was real stiff...? Dynamite said he wasn't gonna last much longer. He was pretty weak. Remember how he wouldn't come up the steps no more, most of the time? Hey, I gotta put him in a sack, so we can bury 'im. I don't think he was too happy no more, anyway." He sucked in a big breath that sounded surprisingly wet. "Probably it's better."

"Un-huh..." Eric squeezed Shit, who laid his head on Eric's shoulder. And sniffed.

Shit said, "I played with his dick—to see if that would get him hard. But he ain't gonna get hard no more. He's dead."

"You better put him on them newspapers up on the porch." Eric looked around. "Then we can walk down to Hurter's and see if they got a sack—and tell your dad."

"I was gonna hug him a little. But I done that now. Dynamite's gonna be sad," Shit said. "I liked ol' Uncle Tom a lot. He was my dog, but my dad really liked him. And you fed 'im all the time..." Shit drew in a large breath. "You liked him?"

"Of course I did," Eric said. "I sucked his damned dick, didn't I? I liked him—a lot."

Tom's muzzle lay out along his forelegs, black lips back from his remaining teeth.

Shit pulled away and began to walk loudly up the steps.

When he came back down, lean arms swinging awkwardly like emptied tongues from his ragged armholes, Shit said, "We gotta get that sack so we can take 'im out to Gilead and bury that ol' boy in the graveyard." He looked up the steps, where Eric could make out the gray-black bulge through the porch newels. "That's where he goes. That's where all our people go." Turning back, he shrugged. "Uncle Tom was almost...a people."

"Yeah..." Eric said, because he couldn't think of anything else.

Shit walked on past him, so Eric turned and caught up, while Shit said, "My dad'll call up Jay and Mex and tell 'em we're comin."

The next morning, all three carried the sack down to the Dump docks. "You comin' with us?" Shit asked.

"Naw." Dynamite took a breath in the misty March morning.

Shit smiled. "I didn't think you was."

"You guys can go and plant 'im. You say hello to Mex and Jay for me, you hear?"

In the rear of the outboard, they took off into the foggy overcast, just as they had when they'd gone to show off Shit's teeth. After about ten minutes, Shit said, "It's funny. The last time we was comin' out here, two weeks back, it was to show 'em how I could smile, now. 'Cause I got my teeth. I sure as shit don't feel like smilin' now, though." The sack lay between them in the bottom of the dinghy. Shit gave a sour smile, anyway.

After they tied up at the boathouse on Gilead, they started up the wooded path. They took turns lugging the burlap with the tied corners. Eric would have sworn that Tom weighed two or three pounds less than he had the day before.

They hadn't been walking three minutes when Mex came down the path in the other direction. He was carrying a piece of wood.

"What's that?" Shit wanted to know.

Eric took the wood, which was stained and varnished. "It's a marker. See? It says 'Uncle Tom, Good Dog, of Morgan Haskell, Wendell Haskell, and—Eric…'" surprised he looked up—"'…Jeffers.'"

"Jay run that up on his power tools," Mex explained. *"He'll meet us at the house. He got some shovels for you. Some of it, he carved himself last night, by hand."*

"That's nice." Shit was looking over at its carved letters upside down. "I can't read it. But it looks nice."

Then Eric and Mex picked up the sack between them and started walking again. Shit carried the polyurethaned wooden marker.

* * *

[40] ERIC PARKED ON the sea-road. Indian summer moved through the pickup's windows. Three cars and two trucks were parked across in the pull-off, where Randal was climbing down the pole's staples. Five young people watched and joked—three black women, and a Latino guy whom he didn't recognize at all, with no shirt, a scattering of jailhouse tats, and kind of sexy because of it, and all within three or four years of Eric's age. Below the swoop of wires and the size of a small door, a solar panel tilted toward the clouds up near the sun. High on the pole hung some kind of transformer; and above that a light.

"Damn," one of the women said. "I think we got 'em all up. That didn't take long."

And one of the men: "That was a short three months. It seems like we put the first two up a couple of weeks back—but it was August, when all the summer people was gawkin' at us."

On every pole along three joining roads was a 300-watt generating panel. Eric had already grown used to them, twenty feet up the thirty-foot poles, leaning into the day.

Randal stepped back, looking up, then around. "Well, why don't you all go on to Fred's. I'll see you there." He turned and saw Eric in the truck. "You goin' toward the CC office? I still ain't quite figured out why the Foundation had to pay the company to let us install 'em. But we still saved a little money by it."

"Hey, I'll run you over."

"Good," Randal said. Then he called across his shoulder, "I'll see yall back at Fred's later." He strode across the rode, opened the passenger door, and pulled himself into the cab. "I'll see you over there, Ace."

The shirtless Latino raised a hand and smiled, as Randal climbed in with Eric and closed the door.

"He's pretty nice lookin'," Eric said. "You ready?"

"Sure—" Randal cleared his throat. "He's cute—but he's shy."

Eric started the truck.

"Talk about a fast three months—but you been here…how long now? Two years? Three…?"

"I got there in July oh-seven."

"That's just over three years." Randal shook his head. He was a stocky black man from Arizona. "I remember the first time Dynamite called me and said he wanted to start you on the Kyle plan—and I thought he had him a black kid. 'Cause I'd heard about your daddy—I guess everybody down here did. Then you and Shit walked in, and I was really surprised. But, like you say, it's worked out pretty good. I was just thirty-nine, back then. Here I am, forty-three. But I been kind of wonderin' how me and Ace are gonna do—with just the two of us."

Again, Eric was surprised. "You guys are…together?"

"Um-hm." Randal looked around. "At least I guess we are. We been sleepin' in the same bed, and I hardly wake up when he ain't down between my legs, tryin' to suck me off. I don't come that way a lot. But if *he* don't mind it, *I* sure don't: It feels good. I got him at Turpens—fished him out of this real orgy they were havin' in there in the back john. And he grinned and come on with me. But he was really enjoyin' all the guys at once—that's a taste, I know. The way you guys like doin' two at once; and he likes…" Randal shrugged. "Ten or so, I guess. Only we ain't been back there again. At least I ain't. I mean, a couple of times he got off by hisself for most of a day and I figured maybe somebody gave him a ride up there. That's fine with me. And he always come back wanderin' into my place, later. Makes me feel kinda young. Now, if I could manage to get an hour's more sleep at night, it'd be perfect." Randal chuckled.

"Well," Eric said, "that's sounds pretty good. How old is he?"

Randal shrugged. "Twenty-nine—thirty, thirty-one."

Eric made a considering sound. "Maybe he's getting' ready to settle down."

Randal made one back.

"Hey." Eric turned up the north road. "You two wanna come around next Sunday? I'm gonna be roastin' some ribs. I can always put another rack on the grill. We'll have some slaw and some corn-on-the-cob with butter. That'll give you both somethin' to do—not to mention some food that ain't your own cookin', or Clem's..."

"We been eatin' in the Lighthouse a lot."

"Yeah, I seen you in there a few times now."

"Well, hey—that's nice of you." Randal pulled his arm back through the window and joined his hands—the blue cuffs pushed up his dark forearms—in his lap. "You sure that'll be okay with Shit and Dynamite?"

"Sure it will," Eric said. "They're always curious about new guys like Ace."

That's when, up ahead, under the trees to the right, Eric saw Shit wandering in their direction.

"Well, there's Shit now—" Eric moved his foot from gas to break— "We can ask him." The pickup slowed.

Randal sat forward and, as Eric stopped the truck, opened the door.

Shit stuck his head in—"Well, this is a surprise—" then pulled himself up. "Hey, boss—what you doin' in the truck with Eric? Come on, move over. Move over, there—so I can get in." He squeezed in and—now—slammed the door. "Hey, Eric, what we gonna do with this fine lookin' ol' fella? We gonna take 'im out in the woods somewhere, lay 'im down on the leaves and trade off fuckin' 'im and suckin' 'im till he comes like a damned fourteen-year-old? You remember how I used to come with you when *I* was fourteen, I bet!"

"Actually, I do." Randal chuckled.

"I still do it that way, too." Shit grinned, and moved one leg—a square kneecap pushing through the hole in his jeans—over Randal's. "That's a real good thing I done inherited. And I don't think you ever even had this fella here, yet. Eric is some *good* nookie—*real* enthusiastic. A couple of times with him and he'll have you so he just gotta grin at you and you gonna stiffen right up. That's about how he's got me doin'. And don't even *talk* about Dynamite—"

"Actually," Eric said, "I just asked Randal and *his* young fella to drop over for ribs and corn next Sunday." The road got slightly smoother. "If you and Ace aim for one o'clock, that'll be about when the first rack comes off the grill."

"Oh, hey," Shit said. "That sounds real nice. We can have us some good food and a good orgy, too, all of us together. Eric cooks up a storm. We don't mind old farts like you and Dynamite—and it sounds like Ace don't, either."

Randal laughed out. "Shit, do you think you could hold off on the orgy part? Ace is a little on the shy side, and that might be a bit much for him on a first meetin'."

"Oh, don't worry about me." Shit slid his leg off of Randal's. (Somehow the knee on his jeans ripped further; Eric heard it.) "I'll break out my company manners if you really want me to."

Ahead on the left, behind a scrap of lawn, stood the rough-out timber planks of the Diamond Harbor CC office. Two women from the solar panel installation crew sat on the steps. "Hey," Randal said. "You can let me out here—my car's around the back. That's real nice of you guys. Ace is probably inside—he likes that air conditioning they got in there. Next Sunday—we'll come over around one."

"Good," Shit said.

As the truck stopped, Randal reached over for the door. Then, after climbing and laughing ("Oh, Randal—come on, stay on my lap awhile. Gimme one of them lap dances everybody tells me you do so good— *oooooh—wheeee!* That feels *nice!* When you come over, you gotta teach ol' Dynamite how to do this."

("Come on, now. Let go of my ass, Shit! Lemme out of here—") Randal was down on the side of the road. "See you this weekend." Laughing, Shit pulled the pickup door closed.

Again the truck began to move. Here the road was shadowed with pines.

"So he gonna bring that Spanish fella who been stayin' with him over?"

"Yeah," Eric said. "I think he's a little worried that Ace ain't enjoyin' hisself while he's around here as much as he might. So I just thought I'd be neighborly. He might have some fun—and get some good ribs."

"Enjoyin' hisself?" Both Shit's eyebrows rose. "Enjoyin' hisself is about all that scrawny jailbird spic do! You remember last day off, when I left you and Dynamite alone at the cabin to have some of that there quality father-son time the two of you like so much, and I went and hitched a ride to Turpens, where, as you know, I don't ever, *ever* go: I seen Ace over there, too. I had him three times, in the front john, in the side one, and then out just behind the rear one with four truckers, who I was showin' the way around the place, and how we do back there. You don't have to worry about me tryin' to start up nothin' raunchy with him out at the Dump come Sunday. I already had 'im three ways goin'. So I think I can restrict myself to ordinary social intercourse, 'cause I ain't got curiosity raggin' me on. I already know how good it is." Shit moved over the seat and dropped a hand on Eric's thigh. "He should be pretty happy with old Randal. The nigger ain't keepin' 'im on what you'd call a short leash, no more'n you or Dynamite does me."

"Now, why should I be even vaguely surprised—" Eric laughed—"you already had your dick in that feller, stirrin' it around and gettin' you a taste of it before all the rest of us?"

"Aw, come on. You know that's just who I am. That don't mean you ain't number one." Shit's rough hand moved further over between Eric's legs. "I'll bring you on down to the truck stop with me next time, so if he's there you can grab a taste, too—"

"Oh, that don't bother me, Shit. You know that." Eric hauled on the wheel. "I was just hopin' it don't bother Randal. He's a good boss-man feller."

* * *

[41] AT OCTOBER'S END, ESPECIALLY on Mondays and Tuesdays, many of Jay and Mex's autumn runs on the scow carried no passengers. (Ruth Holota came in to do her shopping at the supermarket in Runcible on the second or third Thursday of the month—these days about the closest thing they had to a regular customer.) Still, the Runcible (i.e., Kyle's) Chamber of Commerce paid Mex and him to go. When the heat returned, Jay would make the run on the *Gilead*—the motorized flat-bottomed scow—as barefoot as his partner. Since there was no garbage collection on Sundays and Mondays, often they still took Eric (and sometimes Eric and Shit) with them, for company.

On the *Gilead*'s deck, Eric would look at Jay's immense feet, coming out from his frayed jeans cuffs, and wonder how a man as big as Jay—or Dynamite and Shit, for that matter—could bite their toenails as bad as their fingernails.

It was pretty amazing.

Jay stood by the wheel, under the wooden half-shelter in the front, steering with one hand, when Eric finally broke down and asked.

When you asked Jay something that might embarrass another man, Jay would get this smile that, in the bright afternoon, you couldn't but half see behind the curl and fall of his beard's brass, bronze, and gold—a smile that said something like *Wouldn't* you *like to know*…Then he'd go on and tell you anyway, no matter *what* it was: "With our teeth, mostly—my side ones, I mean. Naw, I ain't *quite* as limber at it as I was when I was your age.

But I manage." When the wind was from the front, the *Gilead*'s blunt prow rose and smacked the water, so that they could feel it bumping. "Mex'll do 'em for me, sometimes, if I'm too lazy. But you gotta be pretty close with a cocksucker before you can let 'im bite 'em *for* you. You ever bite Shit's?"

"Naw. But Dynamite let me bite off a couple of pieces for him a few times."

"Well—" Jay squinted out the sea-streaked window above the wheel's spokes—"there you go."

"But you really *bite* 'em?"

"That's about the only way to get 'em right. Sometimes I pick 'em, with a needle—or a knife point." He patted his pocket where he kept the red-sided Swiss Army knife with its near-dozen blades, including the file, the spring locked scissors, and even a magnifying glass, which several times he'd shown Eric. "When we was kids, me and Dynamite used to have contests to see who could get them things back further. Dynamite always won. I did 'em good, but when they'd bleed too much, I'd stop. He'd attack them suckers, though, like he didn't care. A few times I seen him take a whole nail off his finger, so there weren't nothin' left but a big old bloody wound. Shit's the same way. Me and Mex is bad, but not so bad as them."

"Yeah." Eric rubbed one sneaker on top of the other, because his upper itched. "I know."

"It probably turns you on, don't it?"

Eric said, "It didn't used to. But since I been workin' with 'em—and we been fuckin' around—*everything* about 'em, just about, that's different from ordinary guys, can make me shoot my load, if I think about it right. I mean tongue fuckin' with them two 'fore they're even out of bed and got a chance to spit in the toilet—"

"Hey." Jay looked to both sides, then glanced down at Eric. "You wanna hear 'bout somethin' nasty?"

"Yeah." Eric grinned. "Sure—"

"Like I had to ask." Jay moved the wheel. "Back when Dynamite and me was real close jerk-off buddies, we both discovered, kinda by accident, that we liked it if, when one of us was suckin' the other one off, the other one would stick a finger up the asshole of the guy he was suckin'."

"Yeah," Eric said. "Dynamite still likes it when I do that."

"And I *don't*…no more. I think that's sumpin' to do with my balls blowin' up. But I used to. Or maybe I just grew out of it. If somebody do that to me today, I can't even get off. But the thing here I was sayin' about bitin' on our nails, Dynamite and me would go on real serious about how it was better that we bit 'em down, so we wouldn't tear up each other's assholes, stickin' our fingers up there. Now, I know that was an excuse.

We woulda bitten 'em all to hell, anyway. I mean, 'cause we still do. But you should have heard us goin' on, back then, to each other." Jay chuckled. "You know, I'm the guy what started callin' him 'Dynamite.'" he nodded toward the horizon. "Bet you never knowed that. He ever tell you why?"

"No," Eric said. "Why?"

"Well—" against the summer evening Gilead's dark coast was a quarter of a mile off—"he wouldn't. But in the winter, when Kyle would go away to school in Europe and fuck all them fancy white guys and crazy Africans he was into over there in Denmark, and nobody at all was really left in the Harbor, sometimes we'd go into the old boat house and lay back on them dock mats they used to pile in there and beat off together. See, when I'd shoot, my jizz'd jump up four, five feet in the air. And don't you know, it would fall *right* back down…guess where."

"I dunno," Eric said. "Where?"

"Right on my goddam face—*every* time! I mean, I'd try to aim it somewhere else, so that it would land on Wendell, maybe—that's Dynamite's real name, you know: Wendell Haskell—" various bits of mail at the Dump cabin from the Credit Union and the Chamber of Commerce had already told Eric that—"but in the last few seconds, when I'd be really gettin' into it, ready to pop my peter, it would always swing back to the same angle, I mean to a *tenth* of a degree. I swear—! There was no way I could help it— there it would go, right on up, and down—*splat*, on my cheek or my chin. Well, *he* thought that was the funniest thing in the world. Then, when he'd shoot, you know what would happen?"

"What?"

"*He'd* hit the boathouse ceiling—and a couple of seconds later, it'd gather itself together and some of it would drop off…and the first time, you know where it dropped?"

"Where…?"

"Right in my face *again!* I thought that boy was gonna have hisself an apoplexy, laughin' hisself to death. He was rollin' around the floor and still pantin' from comin' so hard, and clutchin' hisself, I thought he was gonna fall over the edge, into the water and drown. He'd break up, like Shit do today sometimes, when he pulls a joke on you. Really, it was one of them things that if you paid us to do it, we couldn't't'a' made it happen. But, anyway, *that's* why I started callin' him Dynamite. 'Cause he *always* hit the boat house roof—even if it *didn't* catch me comin' down. I told him one day he was gonna blast that ceiling right off the place, shootin' like that. Pretty soon, it's what everybody was callin' him, though half of 'em didn't know why…Maybe some of them figured it out. And he sort of preferred it to Wendell. I would have, too.

"You know, Kyle brought a lot of interestin' people back with 'im in the summer to the Harbor. And most of 'em wanted to suck your dick, at least—which was nice. So we was always friends with 'em. Them Africans was real funny—I mean they ain't like 'Mur'c'n niggers at all. They talk real funny, of course—and they got to be the *politest* people, this side of goddam chinks! He still works with some of 'em, too—the same ones he met overseas, when he was a kid. Anyway—I was tellin' you…

"Dynamite shot a whole lotta mess up on that boathouse ceiling. You could see it for the next ten, fifteen years. Whenever I'd go in, it would be on the edge of the beam or the boards just to the side, in the back, above where they put the mats, till Shit was maybe ten, eleven years old. Once Dynamite told me the little bastard had started beatin' off hisself—we used to call him Li'l Shit, till he told us we had to cut it down to 'Shit' or cut it out. I took the puppy in there and showed it to him—said that was his daddy's, only I wouldn't tell him what it was. I wonder if *he* figured it out. 'Cause it had been there so long, I thought it was gonna be there forever—even after we hadn't gone in there for a few years. I mean, just to jack off.

"Only that was when the boathouse roof started leakin', real bad.

"When it was rainin' hard, you could go in there and think you was still standin' out on the dock, so much water was coming down inside. One day, I was in there and I looked up: all that stuff had *finally* washed away. Between the warps and the mildew, you couldn't see *nothin'* no more. That's when Kyle had the Chamber of Commerce close it up, tore it down, and built the new one—that's the one there now—back when Kyle gimme the job runnin' the scow. In fact, that was about the first thing Kyle did when he took over: had 'em replace the old boathouse. God knows we needed it, but I was kinda sorry to see the old one go."

"I used to shoot mine on the wall in my bathroom, back in Atlanta," Eric said. "Shit and Dynamite just do theirs all over the bed sheet."

"Yeah, that was always Dynamite's style."

"But I seen him hit the ceilin' out in the Dump. Shit can, too. I'm more like you, though: I can do it from one side of the big bed to the other—"

"Yeah, we *know* you can. Damn—" Jay grunted—"it ain't fair…that a man his age can still shoot that far. Four, five feet? Today, I'm lucky if mine goes ten inches." At the wheel he shook his head. "Two big ol' Georgia boys, me with busted-out front teeth and always smellin' like old piss, and him real quiet and just as friendly and sweet, who'd do anything to help you out—a daddy at nineteen—and as goodhearted as anybody you'd hope to meet, and all we wanted was get off by ourselves and beat our meat together and stick our fingers up each others assholes and suck each other's dick. After all this time, he's still my best friend—even if him and his own nigger bastard been fuckin' each other like jack rabbits since Shit was a kid."

"I don't think Dynamite fucks Shit too much," Eric said. "Mostly it's the other way around. Both of them fuck me—Shit does it more. Like he does with his dad. I suck 'em both off, a lot—and then both love watchin' the other one get head. Dynamite can always pull a load outa Shit, just by pissin' in my mouth and lettin' him watch."

"Yeah? Well, that sounds…friendly." Jay grinned sideways. "Me and Mex got them boys trained for you, before you even done come down here." The half-hidden smile again. "I'm surprised Dynamite didn't end up with Mex instead of me—though they did their fuckin' around, too. I guess we all have. The Harbor's a little town." Jay dropped one hand to the crotch of his jeans, to rub. Maybe his enlarged ball was itching him. "What is it he says? 'Boys and dogs, boys and dogs—jerk 'em off, and they'll be your friends for life.' That was always Dynamite's philosophy. He ever told you that?" (Eric shook his head, no.) "Well, then that's somethin' you don't know. But he pretty much used to live by it. He got that from *his* dad. Old Haskell was pretty easy goin', and I was kind of fond of him, too. You know, one of Kyle's friends told me they got the same sayin' in some African village—the same village it takes to raise a child. Can you imagine that? Anyway, old Haskell was a damned sight better than Shad. I'm glad he did as much raisin' of me as he did. My mom was kind of a waste—Shad was her step brother, and she was just scared of 'im."

"I kind of like my own mom," Eric said.

"I like 'er, too. She's a good lady." Beard above the instruments, Jay looked through the front window. "You're lucky you got her. It's too bad Ol' Haskell's life didn't go on any longer than it did. He used to joke with both of us, tellin' us that all the damned jizz we used to spill in his hand there kept it soft for his wife—Dynamite's step mom. He was the first person who jerked us off together. And she was a hard-workin' woman who at least put up with us. These things are cultural, puppy. I'm talkin' tradition here. Dynamite's dad dropped dead of a heart attack when me and Dynamite was both about the age you was when you first come here—so we was pretty much on our own, both of us. My mama lives in Ohio now with another husband, whom I do not get along with. He's Shad all over again, 'cept'n he's runty. One is enough, I figure. I used to tell people that once me and Dynamite plugged our dicks into each other, we didn't take 'em out for a few years. But that's was just in the winter. In the summer, the truth was more like we both plugged 'em into Kyle."

Eric's own genitals had begun gathering his body's blood. "You want me to suck you off, 'fore we leave the boat?"

"Actually," Jay said, "what I want you to do is go back to the other side of the shelter in the stern, where Mex is sittin' cross-legged on the deck, splicin' them hawsers. And I want you to squat down and put your arm around 'im and give 'im a big old hug, then kiss on 'im and put your tongue as far down his throat as you can and wiggle it around there for at least a damned minute and let him play with your pecker in your jeans and you can rub on his—by that time, we gonna be in the dock, but don't worry. I'll get us tied up by myself. Then, when we're walkin' back to the house, I want you to hold his hand and grin at him a little. Once we get to the ridge, where the pine trees close over the road, I wanna see you pull his pants off him and lay him out on his back in the dust there—take a look, 'fore you do it and make sure they ain't no pebbles or no sharp rocks—and hook his knees with your elbows and pull his legs up, he can go almost double: I know 'cause I got him pretty limber over the years, and let him wrap his legs around your back and you sink all seven inches of your white boy dick as deep up his wetback asshole as you can—he always keeps hisself greased up, 'cause he never knows when me or some nigger around here is gonna want to rip us off a piece—then you fuck him till he shoots right between yall, and rub your belly all around in it.

"*Then* you can come up his ass."

Eric laughed—

"Now this is *important*, Eric. Mex likes you a lot. He thinks you're the best thing to hit this coast since Martha learned to slice bread. We both like you. But you can't spend all your time fuckin' around with me— Mex and me, we *share*. I told you that. So you got to share, too, when you live like we do. And you can start by fuckin' *him*. Right now, Mex thinks you're pretty wonderful. But if he starts gettin' unhappy about you, 'cause he ain't gettin' any and I'm gettin' it all, you ain't gonna be able to come see neither of us. I'd let you take a hammer to my nuts 'fore I'd do anything to make that man unhappy. He's done too much for me. He's the reason I'm alive today—besides the fact that I love 'im so much, if I think about it, I can't hardly breathe."

"Yeah, I feel that way about Shit...and Dynamite." Then Eric blurted, "I like Mex—I mean, sexually. I jerk off thinking about stuff with him more than I...do with you." Which was true. "But sometimes you're easier to get stuff started with."

"Yeah?" Jay pulled the wheel around sharply, looked out at the nearing island shore, changing its angle with the scow. "Well, you just work a little harder, startin' on Mex, then. That's what it's about."

"I'm...embarrassed a little, 'cause the stuff he does that really turns me on is so...fuckin' dirty. Like his tongue..."

"What about it?"

"You know how they cut off one side of it, and sliced it loose off the muscle at the bottom of his mouth, and messed up his voice box with the knife, when he was a kid…"

"Yeah…You say that turns you off?"

"No—no, it turns me *on!* If we're tongue wrestlin' together for more than a few seconds, I'm gonna shoot. I won't be able to hold my…you know, orgasm back, long enough to fuck him."

"Well, now, I'm not surprised. That's what turns everybody on about that nasty spic. That and his big feet. And, yeah, he's got a nice thick dick. But you're gonna have to exert a little self-control, take that embarrassment, and…put it away. Otherwise you're gonna embarrass yourself out of some fun with both of us. If you do what I say, you think that spic's gonna be anything but shit-faced happy? Now, get on back there, puppy, and do what you gotta do. Ol' Jay's serious now."

"Yeah." Eric ducked from under the opened back wheel shelter. "Okay." He sprinted around the passenger shelter in the scow's mid-deck.

Though that's how it started out, it didn't *exactly* follow Jay's plan.

Once they reached the island boathouse—by then it was three-quarters dark—Mex insisted on pausing to help Jay secure the boat—the only reason Eric *didn't* shoot his load in his jeans. As they were leaving, Eric was going to take Mex's hand, but there was still something that Jay had to do inside. Finally, Jay flipped off the fluorescent lights along the boathouse ceiling, and they stepped out on the big square dock.

In the ten minutes they'd been inside, the sky had gone pitchy—blacker than a school blackboard sponged free of chalk dust. The lights went out across the dock boards. Eric looked up.

And thousands of stars, handful after handful, prickled the black.

It's not that Eric *hadn't* seen the opening into the greater universe hanging over the sea—called night—when he wandered the mainland beaches, on the odd boat at night, or even on former trips to the island. But tonight it seemed vaster, clearer, bigger by an order of immensity. One after the other, two meteors etched white scratches across the part of the sky he stared at. "*Jesus*…" Eric whispered.

They walked across the dock. A hard hand grasped Eric's—for two steps, he thought it was Mex. But—he glanced to see the tall shadow blocking stars beside him—it was Jay. As they reached the dock's corner, the breeze stilled and Eric noted the sent of old urine. At the bench there, Jay released him to turn and sit. Eric sat, too—Mex was sitting on Jay's other side. "*Jesus—*" Eric repeated, leaning on his knees, looking up again—"this is fuckin' beautiful…"

Between them, Jay was leaning back, arms out along the rail behind them. Again, the breeze ceased. Eric laughed. "I guess somebody uses this here corner to take a regular piss in." He'd recognized the odor—like under the Atlanta causeway.

"Yeah," Jay said, pensively. "A couple of rains'll get rid of it, though."

As Eric stared at the night's immensity, Jay said, "Hey, puppy—Mex's is trying to get your attention."

"Huh?" Eric looked down.

Mex was leaning forward, looking around Jay. In starlight, he had one hand between Jay's legs. With the other hand, he was signing. But it was too dark, with Jay between them, to see exactly what.

"What's he saying?" Eric asked.

"He's telling you to put your hand on my big Georgia balls. What you *think* he's sayin'?"

"Oh…" Surprised, Eric reached over and felt the fork of Jay's jeans. Mex's hand moved enough to let Eric's settle, then settled over Eric's. At the same time, Eric realized the warm—no, the *hot* denim was…drenched!

"Hey…"

He could feel Jay, hard, under the soaked cloth.

"When I'm hard, like now," Jay said, "I do it like a dog—in spurts. That's how I like it. Now how many years you got to be friends with a guy before he'll let you know that about him?"

Eric could hear Jay's grin.

He started to say that that was the first thing he'd learned about vanished and homeless Pickle…Not sure what he was supposed to do, but, guided by Mex, Eric rubbed. And finally decided not to talk at all.

"You like that?" Jay asked.

Eric took a breath. "Yeah…kinda." Not that it was particularly sexual. But it was warm and…reassuring.

In the dark, as if in response to Eric's uncertainly about what more to say or do, Jay laughed…quietly. "Here I am, thirty-nine years old—and don't you know I'm still the same piss-in-his-jeans fuck I was when I was seven or eight? It's funny, how you learn what really makes you happy so goddam early. Then, 'cause you spend so much time looking for someone who can share it with you, you get discouraged and forget it. Then you learn it again. And forget it again. And learn it again…and maybe again."

For another minute, a minute-and-a-half, they sat.

Jay said, "Anybody wanna drink? I still got a few more squirts in me."

Wanting in the worst way to say, 'Yes,' it occurred to Eric that perhaps he should leave that for Mex. He squeezed the wet cloth, with its firm cock. Mex squeezed his hand around it.

Jay said, "Okay, come on, then. Let's get up to the house." He rocked forward and stood up between them. "And get these jeans into a washin' machine."

They left the deck and started up the trail, onto the bluff. When they reached the pine trees, remembering his instructions, Eric put his arm around Mex's shoulder. "Hey, Mex, I wanna fuck you right here in the damned road." (Mex's arm came up around Eric's back.) "What you say to that?"

From the way the solid little guy hugged him in return, it seemed he liked the notion.

But Jay said, "I got an even better idea. Let's take it on back to the house and do it inside, where I can shuck out these damned wet pants and join in."

"All right," Eric said, without dropping his arm from around Mex. (The smell of gasoline and body odor—and maybe garlic—was strong on the Mexican. Eric didn't want to let any of it get away from him.) "If that's how you want to do it. You're the boss, Jay."

So that's what they did.

That was the visit Eric learned that one of the Kyle mansion's cellar rooms was given over to a rack of barbells and weights and a workout bench and a set of rings hanging from ropes on the ceiling and mirrors on the walls. The weights surprised him. Till then, he'd always thought Jay—and Mex—had gotten their muscles from work. Under a five-foot wall poster of Jimmy Wang-Yang, "The Yellow Redneck!" (who Jay said was his favorite professional wrestler, 'cause he was a Georgia boy) stood a wicker hamper, which turned out three-quarters full of muscle building magazines, interspersed with old gay porn: *Bear, Mandate, Men's Health, Prime Beef, Daddy, Black Inches, Latin Inches, Machismo, Straight to Hell...* Today, however, Mex worked out more than Jay.

*

Three days later, on the mainland behind the Dump, Eric and Shit climbed the bluff, looking at the clouds, as if they mounted into a map of all tomorrow's silver.

With his rough hand, three steps from the slope's tufted top, Shit took Eric's hand. (Eric thought of Mex and smiled.) Eric looked over, to see him grinning at him—and grinned back. "You know, it's funny, Shit."

"What?"

"A couple of days back, when I was out going across with Jay and Mex, I was thinkin'—for pure physical sex appeal, in all the guys we fuck with,

Mex has got to be the sexiest."

"Yeah," Shit said. "He's cute. He's halfway between a little bull and a little bear. And when he does his nasty shit, I can watch him and beat off for days over it."

"And because I get turned on by him the most, he's still the one I have the hardest time comin' on to. Ain't that funny?"

"You do?" Shit looked surprised. "I don't. Any time he sees me beatin' off, he's right down and suckin' on that thing."

"That's 'cause you beat off and like to watch and hear dirty talk a lot, even more than me. But I mean, maybe that's just the way things are with people. Still, it's…odd."

Grinning, holding his hand tighter, Shit moved closer. He wore one of his torn shirts, and the breeze turned and brought Eric his easy, leather-like scent. "I hope it ain't hard for you to get turned on by me…"

"Nope," Eric said. "At least not when you smell like that, it ain't."

"I mean, after all this time and everything . . ."

Eric repeated, "Nope." He put his arm around Shit's shoulder.

"Good. Now, you open your mouth and lemme lick around in that suck hole—then I'm gonna stick my dick in it. Okay? But maybe before we do that, let's lay down here here, and you can tell me somethin' *real* nasty you did with Mex. Or Jay…" Shit's arms locked around Eric's chest and he slid to his knees. "Hey, I bet Mex was suckin' on *your* dick—and lickin' out your asshole, too. I may beat off…I mean, a *little*, first…" He nuzzled Eric's warn denim crotch. "That's before I lick your balls and fuck you—maybe piss in your eye some, like my daddy do when he aims for your mouth and misses…"

* * *

[42] ON SUNDAY MORNING, just after twelve-thirty, Eric finished grating the carrots into the stainless steel bowl he held slanted on a folded towel on the kitchen table, between the tool box and a pile of old magazines. Beside it, on the place he'd wiped pretty clean, a cabbage sat in two halves. Eric picked up one and began to draw it back and forth over the wire half of the vegetable grater, which snowed white cabbage over the orange pile. "Shit, you wanna get the mayonnaise out the ice box? That little bowl with the aluminum foil over it is some grated onion. You wanna bring that over here too, with it?"

"Sure," Shit said. "And you want that celery salt, too—don't you?"

"That's right."

Dynamite stepped into the side door and said, "Hey, I just slopped some of your vinegar and hot pepper sauce over them ribs outside on the grill. They're smellin' real good."

"Thanks," Eric said.

"I'll leave turnin' 'em to you, though," Dynamite said.

"Next time I touch 'em," Eric said. "They're comin' off. They're pretty much done."

Outside a car grunted and growled, nearing.

Shit said, "I think our company's here."

"Then let's go say hello." Eric pulled off the tin foil (and felt his eyes begin to water), dumped in the onions, and ran the wooden spoon back and forth over the bowl's bottom, then through the slaw. —Tapping it on the edge, he turned to follow Shit and Dynamite out onto the deck to stand beside the grill. Near them, against the wall, stood a bag of charcoal.

On the table next to it stood a coffee can of barbecue sauce in which leaned the handle of a brush. Over the table's boards, irregular splotches of sauce made a trail from the can toward the grill.

The car door of the dirty yellow Dodge opened, and Randal slid out. He had on a new plaid shirt—which made Eric aware that Dynamite was wearing a pretty spotty T-shirt under his bibs; though it had come out the dryer yesterday evening.

"Hey, there, Randal," Dynamite said. "Good to see you, boss."

"Hey, guys. I know I'm a few minutes early. But I was sittin' around by myself, feelin' antsy—till, finally, I decided, hell; I'd just come on over. If I'm in the way, tell me, and I'll drive around and come back. Maybe I can run over and pick up somethin' for you, if you need it—"

"Naw, naw," Eric said. "This is fine. The ribs are done. You couldn't've timed it better."

"You're always welcome, boss-man," Dynamite said. "You want a beer? You boys go on in there and bring some out—I know *you* ain't gonna have none. They got lemonade for them. Shit made it up this mornin', fresh. You can have some of that if you want."

"Maybe later," Randal said. "No, I'll take that beer."

Shit asked, "Where's Ace—he want one, too?"

"Naw." Randal pulled in a big, loud breath. "It's just gonna be…me, today."

"Awww," Dynamite said. "I was lookin' forward to meetin' 'im."

Eric took a step back toward the kitchen, but because Shit did not, he hesitated.

Dynamite said, "He comin' later? Sit down—sit down, boss-man. Right here." Dynamite dropped his hand on the back of the bench.

"No," Randal said. "He's gone. Ace left yesterday. I asked him if he didn't wanna stay another few days, just to come on by and try out your ribs, but he said, no, he wanted to get on. So I run him down to Turpens and I'm damned if he didn't pick up a ride in ten minutes, just walkin' around the back lot and askin' the Saturday rig guys if any of 'im would take 'im. I was gonna call you and tell you not to fix for him. But it was funny—once I got back home, I kept on thinkin', maybe he'd change his mind and come on back. It was like I was expectin' him to walk through the front door, sayin' he'd changed his mind." Randal shrugged. "But he didn't."

"Awww," Dynamite repeated, taking longer to say it. "Well, I guess that just means there's more for us."

Eric said, "I'm goin' in and get you that beer." He turned and walked over the deck.

"Come on up and have a seat."

"Them ribs do smell good," Randal said and started up the steps. "You do 'em with that vinegar sauce? That's the kind I really like—it's what I grew up on. The rest is all ketchup and sugar. I guess that's okay, but to me that ain't barbecue."

Eric stepped into the kitchen.

Out on the porch, Randal was saying, "So you guys have been together three years, huh? That's somethin'. Ace said since the solar panels were all up, he was gonna take off, get a ride to Florida, and spend the rest of the winter down there. I guess three months was all he could stand of my black ass. But I tell you, I'm gonna miss his little warm butt up against my belly every night." Eric went to the refrigerator—vaguely aware that Shit had stepped into the kitchen behind him. Eric felt a little odd that the guest of honor had not come. But since Randal was there, it would probably be okay.

Eric opened the refrigerator door and stood looking into the crowded shelves—

Something grappled him from behind and whispered against his ear, "Jesus…!"

A cage of bone constricted around him—that's what it felt like. Eric reached up and grasped Shit's forearms, locked high across his chest. Shit whispered, "Please, please, please, nigger—don't go. Don't decide you wanna go to Florida. Or…or Atlanta. Or anyplace like that!"

Eric tried to keep his balance—because Shit had raised one leg and wrapped it all around in front of him. "Hey…! Don't worry! I ain't!"

"You sure?"

"Yeah, I'm sure!"

"Really?"

"Yes, I am really, really sure. Would you get the plates and take 'em out there, with the beer—and gimme five minutes to finish up my damned cole slaw—*please*?"

"Sure. You know I'll do anything you want—anything you ever ask me."

"Well, take the beer to Dynamite and Randal—"

"—and lemonade for me and you?" Shit's grip loosened.

"Yeah. Take the glasses outside, and I'll be out with yall in five minutes."

"Hey, I wouldn't even know what to do if you left." Shit drew in a breath—like Randal's when he'd stepped from the Dodge. "I mean, what would happen...?"

"Well, for one thing, you wouldn't get no ribs. Come on, now. Go outside and take the plates and the beer and the lemonade."

"I'm gonna have to come back for that—"

"Then get goin'." Eric turned—to be surprised by Shit's wide green eyes, blinking rapidly, brightly.

So Eric hugged him—and again was surprised by the strength of the hug Shit returned.

*

Around five, when Randal had been gone over an hour, Dynamite forked up the last half dozen ribs still on a piece of bright, crushed foil, straightened out now on a platter. The largest pulled slowly free, to fall back onto the plate. "Someday you gonna have to tell me how you get these things so tender. And that boilin' you do at the beginnin' really gets out the grease. You actually been here three whole years, Eric? Well, that's gotta be the fastest damned three years in *my* life! It feels more like *maybe* six months. But time passes faster as you get on, I guess." On the table beside the ashy Foreman—extinguished since three—another foot of foil had been spread over another plate. On it a palm-sized pool of butter was broken by aluminum facets, the pale yellow swirled with black and red pepper.

Against the porch newels stood a Dump Produce shopping bag, its sides darkened in splotches with grease and over whose edge stuck cobs and bones, tassels and husks.

Overhead, indolent autumn sea birds played with the breeze.

Dynamite frowned into the gentle blue. From another cabin, you could just hear a western song playing. "So I guess we get back to work tomorrow."

* * *

[43] ERIC'S FIRST BIG coastal storm—September's Hurricane Edna—
was when *he* seriously got to fuck Shit's ass. Black Bull had come over and
told them a radio message had gone out to evacuate Gilead, and that Jay
had phoned to say they were bringing Hugh in who was going up to help
his people in Pinewood: Jay and Mex were coming to stay at Dynamite's
and were bringing Shad. The Dump was fairly elevated, considering—
more than forty feet above high tide level. "He say he givin' de old fella
one of his calm-down pills every four hours. Yeah, he know it's a lot. But
if he don't keep the motherfucker drugged up, Shad's just gonna worry us
all to death wid his complainin' about niggers and faggots and dat we all
gonna burn in hell 'ceptin' *his* nasty-mouthed Christian self." The wind
had started by the time they finished nailing plywood over the windows. To
the sound of hammers, Jay and Mex arrived and rolled a sedate Shad in his
gray sweater and old-fashioned wooden wheelchair into the kitchen, while
rain blew in through the door until they got it shut.

It was pretty crowded.

Jay stood over near the door, nubbing at the back of his head under
his orange cap. "Hey, I'm gonna take a walk around the Dump for a little
while—check in on a few of these cocksuckers and see how they doin'.
Give 'em a hand if they need help with the storm fixin's—'sides, I had this
fuck with me all afternoon." He nodded his beard toward sullen Shad. "I
need to get me some air."

Mex signed: *I look out for him.*

"Thanks, Mex." In his dark plaid, Jay turned and lumbered toward the
door. "I'll be back in an hour, hour-and-a-half."

Minutes later, Mama Grace came in with a big pasta casserole under his
yellow poncho. Black Bull had made up a kettle of chili. ("Dis is *yo'* damned
recipe, Mex. I don't know what we'd do without ya', ya' half-pint spic.
Whyn't you come over and mess wid us sometimes—if Jay'll let you loose?
I know some niggers what could really make you happy, boy.") They'd
pooled their lemonade, pop, and beer. And Chef Ron—who still worked
over at Shells in Hemmings—had cooked a whole mess of greens and ham
hocks, as well as boiled up two dozen ears of corn. With all the rest in
the back of his Dodge, he brought a dozen roasted game hens, which had
been supposed to go over to the restaurant that night, but the management
decided not to open because of the hurricane.

A couple of others came, too.

They ate off plastic plates and stood around—or sat on the floor, leaning back against the dingy hull that had been dragged inside or sitting on cushions—and all but tripped on one another, moving around the house and between the junk. Eric confirmed what he suspected from his single trip to Shells three years back: game hen was pretty damned good, Ron told him, spooning another half hen onto his plate. "Me, I always thought chicken and chili was one of the greatest taste combinations there is—only you got to be really hungry."

Then Shit put his plate down, stepped over, and squatted in front of Eric to say, "Hey, come on. Let's get outta here and watch the storm from up the bluff." The idea was that only the very top was likely to be hit by lightning—so they wouldn't go all the way.

Eric put on his orange Turpens cap with the visor to the side.

As they opened the door, a flash and crack made Eric think half the Georgia coast had broken off—to crumble into the ocean!

Outside, Shit seized Eric's arm and, in pelting rain, said, "We gonna go up there and fuck like crazy men. That okay with you?"

"What do you mean?" Eric asked. "Oh—Okay...Sure!"

Behind the cabin, Shit started pulling Eric up the grass and rocks, over the slope. "You gonna fuck my asshole, too, this time," which, in their years together, had not yet happened. Eric had been content that it was about the only thing they *hadn't* done.

Still, it startled him.

As the foliage beat at their chests and faces, they came up through falling water. Shit said, "You should be able to do that, can't you? You don't got no problem fuckin' my dad—or Mex." (That was the time both had gone out to stay on Gilead.) "I seen you pork 'em both. Shouldn't be no reason you can't fuck me, too."

"Sure..." Eric repeated, as lightning ripped apart the sky so that it bled, white light, bleaching the evening, like burning magnesium, making him turn away, squinting—again, then again; and again. With the rain heavier and—for a few minutes—colder, they climbed. He wondered if...if he *could* fuck in this meteorological chaos.

After fifteen minutes, Shit had to yell, "Come on! Right here!" Then they were naked in the hill grass, rolling into and out of embraces with as much laughter and water in them as wind and flesh. "Damn," Eric said. "This is like goin' swimmin' on top of a mountain."

"Yeah. It is." Shit grinned; they exchanged deep, rainy kisses, miming a desperation that rose higher and higher with its own performance.

Somehow, with lots of spit—and rain—Eric got himself lodged in Shit's ass...and started humping him. Belly down on the growth and little stones, now Shit growled: "Come on, you white sonofabitch, *fuck* my black ass—fuck it harder!"

"Hey…" Eric paused for a moment, to move his knee outside the fork of Shit's legs. "You okay—?" It was interesting—and sexy—to hear Shit talk to him like Shit himself talked, sometimes, to Dynamite.

"*Fuck* this nigger's asshole, till you fuckin' pass out, you mother fuckin' white cocksuckin' scumbag!" (Among overturning slabs of sea, beyond Gilead, spastic mantises of white fire strutted across black water, under black sky.) "*Fuck* my ass till it splits open, you piss-drinkin' asshole eatin' scumsucker!" (Eric thought: It's probably good you can replace "fuck" with "suck" in pretty much any sexual exhortation. If Shit had been egging Dynamite on, it *would* have been "suck.") "That's it. Yeah. You fuckin' it *good* and hard, now! But I *bet* you can fuck it *harder*—"

That's what Eric was doing when another crack and bolt—he felt Shit jerk beneath him—jarred and blinded him enough to make him lose half his hard-on. He hadn't pulled loose, though. With three more breaths and the sound of Shit under him, moaning, his face on its side in the dirt "—Aw, Eric, fuck this nigger…! Hey, go on. Fuck this nigger, white boy…! You do it so good. Yeah, fuck this goddam nigger…!"—it was back again. Near his shoulder, Shit gripped a fistful of gravel, grass, and sand, which spilled between his knuckles.

Eric's orgasm within Shit was the strongest feeling he'd ever had, till then, in his life. (Being white had never turned him on before, and it scared him that it did so much now.) Its force disoriented.

During his next five desperate breaths, he couldn't remember where he was, or why water rushed over him. Half the water on him was sweat; half was rain. He held onto Shit's hard shoulders so tightly his arms shook. His face dropped blindly into Shit's neck. He was afraid if he moved more, an electrified knife would slash his groin and gut him.

Up beneath his chest and over his opposite shoulder, one of Shit's hands now gripped one of Eric's, grit and grass between them.

"Jesus…" Eric said. "Stop movin' your butt, nigger—you gonna *kill* me! *Gimme* a minute." Finally, he asked, again, "You okay?"

Beneath him, Shit nodded. "What about you?" Rough hair rubbed Eric's cheek, all wet.

"Yeah. I'm good. Did you come?" Eric wanted to know.

Shit turned his head. "'Bout five or six times. It wasn't like regular comin'…but it was about as much as I could'a stood." Then he turned his body beneath Eric's—

In the wind, Eric screamed, "*Ahhhhhh!*" and Shit caught him and pulled him close. Their faces and groins and chests pressed one another's. The knife had slashed. Eric's body had been sundered through its core.

But he'd survived.

Shit said, "I spilled so much jizz in this grass just now, I expect the rocks around here is gonna birth my first six kids. I'll tell ya', it was fuckin' great." He kneaded Eric's shoulder. "They gonna put you in jail, nigger. 'Cause makin' another nigger feel that good has *gotta* be a crime!"

Eric grinned. "Yeah, I know what you mean…"

"Every once in a while—not a lot, now, 'cause you'd kill my nigger ass if you did—but you gonna have to do a little somethin' like that again. Maybe a couple or three times a year. It's like the time we all three come so hard together, after Bull came over and pissed on you—"

"Oh, yeah…" Eric said.

"I mean that was another one of those where I came so hard I thought it was gonna kill me. Hey—most of the time, though, can we do it like usual? Please…? That's better, day to day…All right?"

"Yeah…" Eric said, gratefully. "That's not gonna be no problem." He closed his eyes, thankful, under rain.

Shit squeezed him. "Thank you…I mean, it's great. But I don't think I could stand too much of that."

A little later, as lightning lit the insides of their closed lids orange, Eric asked, "Did Dynamite ever fuck you?"

He felt Shit shrug. "Yeah—a few times, back when I was a kid. But that was 'cause I asked him to. I wanted to see what he was feelin' when I cornholed *his* butt for him. He said he didn't think a father fuckin' his own son was all that good of a' idea. He said that was child abuse."

Eric rocked back with laughter. "He thought *that*—" He opened his eyes—"was child abuse—?" to see Shit's eyes and face go from gray-white back to green and bronze as lightning dimmed.

"Yeah. I had to beg him—then go get a beer bottle and stick it up my own ass. Like he was always doin'. So, finally, he said, cut it out, okay, he'd do it for me. Then he got some lard—and did it real nice, real greasy, and real slow. I liked it. But I figured since now I knew what it felt like, the next person who did it, he'd really have to lay me the fuck out. Yeah. And in case you're wonderin', that's *you*…But I figure now I don't have to do it *that* often, either."

Eric shook his head. "With all the suckin' and fuckin' and ass lickin' and pee fights and beatin' off together and jerkin' each other off all over each other and all the piss drinkin'—"

"Hey—now the piss drinkin' is what *you* like doin'. Me and Dynamite just like doin' it *to* you—"

"—*that's* what he calls child abuse?"

"—'cause *you* like it. Well, you see—" and, almost as if the storm itself wanted to hear, the rain stopped, and the sound around them dropped by half—"a lot of that other stuff started when I was a baby. Whenever Mex or Dynamite or Jay or even Black Bull was baby sittin' for me, they'd suck my dick to keep me from cryin'. It worked, too. Mex explained it all to Jay in sign language—how mamas in the villages near his home in Mexico used to do that to keep the boy babies happy."

"Well, *you* musta been a pretty happy kid."

"I *was*!" Shit grinned up at Eric. "Hell, I still am. But I guess they just kept on doin' it. And I kept on really likin' it. By the time I was eight or nine-and-a-half—I shot my first load, I'll never forget it, right in Mex's mouth. When I felt my pecker start to go off, I grabbed both his ears and held onto them things for dear life. I'm surprised I didn't rip 'em off. He had red blotches on 'em all afternoon. It's funny how something what feels so good can about scare you to death. I shot my second load in Dynamite's hand, when I come to him to find out what had happened the first time and he tried to show me—well, I tell you, soon you couldn't *get* Mex and me apart. Dynamite was thinkin' about making a deal with Jay to get Mex to stay with *us*, permanent, to do regular suck service for us both. Only then I discovered I could do it in my dad's butt hole and that was as good. Course, everything Dynamite did to me, I wanted to do to him. The first time I made that man come in my mouth, I was so proud I didn't know what to do. I had to run around and tell pretty much every nigger in the Dump— there's still a couple of 'em, down at the south end—Phillip and Everett— what don't really like to talk to us 'cause they think our relationship is unnatural, though they're as gay as Mama Grace. Black Bull was the only one what really stayed sociable—but I guess that's 'cause what he used to do to some of the guys he had was a lot worse...maybe. These niggers around here may be gay, but the truth is, they don't hardly approve of *nothin'*!" (To Eric it sounded like an exaggeration.) "Naw—that's the truth. It is. That's what people said." On his back, Shit shrugged. "The rest I guess kinda just followed."

On the slope, in the rainy grass, Eric nodded. "Mmmm." Finally he asked, "Shit, how come you wanna be a nigger so bad?"

Shit said, "Huh? What you mean? I *am* a nigger—'cause my mama was one." Then he laughed. "Naw—it's just something I get into when I'm doin sumpin' nasty, like with you or my dad. Why you wanna be white?"

"I *don't* wanna be white!" Eric raised up his head and looked down at grinning Shit.

"Well, neither do I." Grappling Eric, Shit pulled him back down on him. "Bein' white, like you and my dad, that's nasty—" Shit gave a grimacing smile—"ain't it?"

"Yeah...I guess so."

"Bein' white's about the *nastiest* thing I can think of." Then he growled. "That's why yall white guys turn me on so much," and he opened his mouth all over Eric's mouth and Eric's nose and Eric's cheek, and began pushing his tongue in Eric's nose and in his mouth and in his ear, till he pulled away to breathe. "Bet you think bein' a nigger's nasty, too." Shit narrowed his eyes for a wicked admission. "Besides...callin' me a nigger gives me a hard-on, especially when white guys do it who wanna suck my dick—like you and my dad." Then, immediately Shit thrust his tongue into Eric's mouth again before Eric could answer, turning his face, grown gigantic with its nearness, on Eric's.

Eric pulled his mouth from Shit's. "Yeah, me too, I guess—'specially when I'm doin' it with one of you. Or when you do something like that, to get me hot. But, then, I don't go around all the—"

In the grass a *pock*-pock-*pock-pock*-pock-pock had begun. Then first hail hit the back of Eric's head, his buttocks, his thigh, his cheek, his shoulder...

"But *I* do," Shit said—then his grin dropped away and he squinted up. "'Cause *I* wanna fuck *all* the time. Hey—we gotta get *outta* this...*Owww*, man! Oh, *shit*!" and they were up, grabbing jeans (Eric), cap, and sneakers (Eric) and jeans (Shit).

They hustled back down the slope, Eric's arms and back and hips stinging under ice pellets.

The long grass seemed to hold twice the number of twigs and small rocks and scallop shells as on the way up.

Jay was going in through the door when they got down past the path's last turn.

Six seconds behind him, bursting into the kitchen, dropping their clothes on the floor, hopping on one foot and brushing off the other, then switching, Shit asked if anybody minded, 'cause they were both in their birthday suits, while hailstones bulleted the roof. Eric had on his soaked cap, but that was all. Everybody laughed. Both boys were covered with leaves, grass blades, small scratches. Shit had a cut on his cheek, under his beard, and another on his shoulder from hailstones. Eric had scraped up one knee pretty bad—but there was no other blood.

Sitting cross-legged on the floor by the sink, Chef Ron was eating an ear of corn. "That'll teach you fools to go runnin' around in a hurricane with eighty-five-, a hundred-mile-an-hour winds, buck-ass naked!" On the roof the hail's rattle increased. Over his cob, he grinned. "Sure wish I'd been out there with you."

Eric said, "You really brought over some good food. That chicken was good—I was so tired, that night I had it at the restaurant, I don't think I got to taste it."

"Well," Ron said, "the rest wasn't bad either."

And Jay said, "You ought to done figured it out by now. *Anything* worth a tinker's damn down here always comes outta the Dump."

Shad had eaten a paper plate full of chili and was asleep in his wheelchair. A few beans over it, the plate balanced on his knees. Black Bull was trying to help Mex get spilled beans out Shad's beard with a piece of paper toweling.

"Looks like I shoulda been up there helpin' you fellas out," Jay said, taking off his soaked plaid and hanging it on the kitchen doorknob. Beneath, the bulk of his hairy arms displayed their undersea and surface colors. His big laugh filled the house. "Now *that* sounds like it mighta been some fun!"

A day later, on Gilead, half the trees had been torn out by the roots. Near the island boathouse, right behind the dock, a twelve-foot piece of cement had turned up to lean on its side against a bolder. "It looks more like a goddam earthquake—" Jay scratched his head—"than a hurricane." A part of the roof on a maintenance shed behind the Kyle mansion had blown loose. So they all went back and forth in the scow a couple of times to bring over supplies and help put on a new one—the new one was supposed to be hurricane proof—and had another potluck chili dinner in the long kitchen.

Dynamite and Black Bull kept trading these jokes about the chili that Shit kept laughing over, while Eric pursed his lips, or—sometimes—smiled.

* * *

[44] IN 2013, THREE days before Christmas, at seven twenty-five in the morning, gray-white sun seeped beneath the overcast to make a quarter of the winter sea dull steel. In the cab of the half-loaded truck, in his overall bib pocket, Dynamite's new cell-phone played the opening notes of "This Land Is Your Land"—which it had been programmed with when he got it. Dynamite had not known the song; though Eric had and told him about it. Now Dynamite fingered it free, looked to see who it was, then raised it to his ear. "Hey, Hugh. How you doin'?…Oh, yeah…Hmm?…Oh…! Jesus— well, how're you holdin' up?…Yeah…Yeah…Oh…Yeah, sure…But you're okay…Okay, I will." He dropped the phone toward his lap, blunt thumb seeming to press three buttons—though he was only pushing "end." (Eric wondered sometimes how he could do it.) He took a breath, then dropped the phone back in his pocket. One denim edge had come half loose and hung down.

Ten seconds more driving, and Dynamite said, "Shad died this mornin', out on Gilead. Hugh can't raise Jay on the scow. He wants me to go down, wait for 'em to get in at the dock, and tell 'em."

Between them, Shit looked first at his father, then at Eric, with the puzzled humor of a child facing the momentous. "Oh, fuck—*Wow!*" At twenty-five, faint wrinkles held Shit's green eyes. "Shad's dead…"

Already, Eric was wondering what the death would mean to Jay—or Mex. Or even Hugh.

Again Dynamite lifted the phone, thumbed it open, looked down to thumb up a contact, then raised it to where his brown hair, run with white, curled over his ear. "Hey…Tad?…Yeah, this is Dynamite. I'm gonna run back to the Harbor and wait for Jay and Mex to get in…Shad died this mornin', out on Gilead…Yeah, the old man, Jay's uncle…Nobody can get Jay on the scow…Un-huh…I gotta tell him. Can you phone Randal and let 'im know? Then, maybe, you could swing round and do the Runcible-Hemmings half of the run this mornin'. Yeah, it'd be a favor, and I'd appreciate it. Well, do what of it you can. I don't think nobody's gonna go crazy if we get back to it tomorrow…Yeah, I'll call you after I talk to Jay."

This time when he put the phone away, Dynamite slowed the truck, pulled off the road into Mrs. Morganhill's driveway, turned around, and started back to Diamond Harbor.

*

Yards before the dock, Shit said, "I think Jay's gonna be *glad* the ol' coot's gone."

Dynamite nodded. "He might be. But then, he might not. You know he been takin' care of that ol' fella a long time." The truck slowed. "You get used to things like that, Shit—even Shad. Sometimes it's hard to go on without it."

Beside the dock light on its post, Dynamite parked the garbage truck. As Eric glanced up and Dynamite pulled out the hand brake, Eric saw the florescent ring-bulb still burned. In the winter, its timer turned it off at seven-fifty.

They got out. Cool damp chilled Eric around the wrists and neck of his thrown back hoody. Under his bib, Dynamite wore a waffle-knit undershirt, neck opened, its frayed and buttonless collar dark gray, despite a trip through the washing machine last week.

Shit wore a gray-green flannel with no buttons at all. Not that it was really cold—it felt like the mid-forties—and hauling sacks could keep you fairly warm. Still, Eric wondered how much of Shit and Dynamite's insistent ignoring of the weather was metabolism and how much some sort of theater they indulged for one another.

By the time the scow pushed its hedge of foam and froth into shore, Eric glanced up to see the bulb was now gray—he'd missed its going out.

With a work shoe on the dock and one on the scow's rim—rising and falling above the winter waters—Mex gave them a grin and a wave, then bent to secure the scow's front to the dock cleat, while Jay came out from the shelter of the wheel housing to call, "Hey, there, guys. What yall doin' out here this late?" and went down to tie up the stern.

A dark young man in black denim jacket and jeans, a watch cap, and a white turtleneck showing above his collar, carried his green duffel sack toward the scow's edge. He was wearing a shirt that said:

IAIA

And below that:

Tie a feather on it.

—though Eric wasn't sure what that meant.

Black hair in a ponytail over one shoulder, he waited for Jay and Mex to finish. Roan Holota was returning to school at the Institute of American Indian Arts, in Santa Fe, after spending part of his holidays with his aunt and uncle, Walter and Ruth Holota, on Gilead, in their cabin up from the Kyle place.

Eric had seen him in town twice that week—and smiled at him now. By the scow's edge, Roan nodded, without smiling. The facts of his visit had come to Shit and Eric from overheard conversations at the Lighthouse, on a couple of drop-ins for coffee.

Jay finished tying up, stood, stepped to the dock, and, in his gray and blue jacket, strode over, grinning in preparation for another hello.

Roan stepped over, too, to walk only a little more slowly, looking around as if—Eric thought—he wanted to remember all this before he left.

Taking the spike at the gate's edge from the metal eyelets, Dynamite dropped it on its clinking chain and lifted the folding rhomboid of slats up against the light post. The spike swung down to *tink* the pole three times, each more quietly than the last. "Afraid I got some bad news."

Jay slowed (and so did Roan, though Eric suspected Roan was trying not to look too curious). Through his beard, Jay's smile faded. "What is it?"

Dynamite turned to him. "Hugh phoned me up when he couldn't get through to you. Your Uncle Shad passed, out at your place—about an hour, hour-and-a-half back."

Jay stopped. "He did?" He raised a hand and scratched his nose with his thumb. "Well." He looked down at his shoes, shifted his weight from one to the other, then looked up again. "That ain't no surprise. He had that sedentary pneumonia. Dr. Greene come out and looked at him, twice. Jesus—the last time was just yesterday mornin'. He wasn't eatin', he wasn't movin' much—wasn't talkin' none."

"He throwin' up?"

"Naw," Jay said. "It wasn't like your daddy's heart attack at all. It was just like, you know, he stopped talkin' and hollerin' and quit all his hell-fire preachin', and…gave out."

"Oh," Dynamite said. Then, from somewhere, he started to chuckle. "You had Dr. *Greene* out there—?" He tried to swallow his amusement.

Jay said, "He's the best doctor we got and he's on the Kyle Plan—"

"Hey," Dynamite said. "I ain't sayin' nothin' against 'im. He's the one Shit, me, and Eric go to—when we remember." He grinned over at the boys.

"Besides," Jay said, "he's the only one around here what'll come out and make a house call. All them white doctors'd just tell you bring 'em in and stick 'im in the hospital—and you know that would've been the end of Shad, right there."

"Yeah, I know," Dynamite said. "But Greene is as black as the Ace of Spades. *That's* probably what killed Shad—havin' a black doctor look at 'im. His heart couldn't take it. And a *gay* black doctor at that!"

"To me, it didn't even look like he noticed," Jay said. "Which was just as well."

"Hey, you know, I'm sorry, Jay. I didn't mean nothin'."

"I know you didn't. But I just…" Jay took a deep breath. "I don't know *what* I just was…feelin' there."

"Relief?" Dynamite asked.

"Naw. Not exactly." Jay turned around, and hollered across the dock. "Hey, Mex. That pneumonia done took Shad this mornin'. He's dead." (On the scow's edge, Mex stopped working, stood up, and waited.) "Hugh called and told Dynamite."

Pausing for seconds, Mex stepped down to the dock—he had on work shoes today—and started across the boards.

"Eighty-seven years that man spent, makin' as many people as he could manage to, miserable. Now we get to be miserable for *another* couple of days, till we can get him in the ground."

Mex stepped up beside Jay, and moved his hands. *"Hugh called and told you? We knew it was coming, right?"*

"Yeah, that's what happened." Jay nodded. "I was just sayin' here to Dynamite, it weren't no surprise."

"You remember," Dynamite said, "he wanted to be planted in the church yard, over in Hemmings—the place that's the Interdenominational now. That used to be Shad's church. You gonna carry 'im back over here and put him down there—?"

"*Hell*, no!" Jay said. "He's fuckin' dead—and he was a bastard *all* his life. I never knowed nobody what was *less* of a Christian than what he fuckin' was. I don't *feel* like draggin' his dead ass back across the water a last time. I'm gonna put him in Gilead Graveyard where he belongs, with our own people and yours—" He looked over at Roan—"and yours, boy. That's where he goes."

Roan volunteered, "I'm sorry about your loss, Mr. MacAmon. I couldn't help hearin'—" He seemed unsure if he should stay or go.

"Thank you, son. You remember three years ago, how me and Mex drove you all the way across to school—we had fun, didn't we? You know, I'm tempted to say fuck it, get in the truck and drive you there again. But…" Jay shook his head. "Well, I guess that ain't so realistic. Hey, you go on and catch your bus over at the Library, now. It should be there in a few minutes—you don't wanna miss it. Ain't another one till three thirty."

"Yes, sir." Roan hefted up his green bag, nodded toward Shit and Eric—who nodded back—and started for the street's grassy edge.

Mex put his arm around Jay and hugged him.

"Hold up, there," Jay said. "I got one more thing I gotta do—call the funeral place in Hemmings, so we can get the damned burial permit." He reached into his jacket pocket, took out a cell phone—and frowned at it. "Damned thing's turned off. No wonder Hugh couldn't get me." He opened it and pressed a button, which, Eric figured, with hands like Jay's, Shit's, and Dynamite's, was as much an achievement when Jay did it as when Dynamite or Shit did. "You'd'a thought I'd knowed it was comin' and didn't wanna be bothered. Well, maybe I didn't."

*

Then it rained.

With his shirt open and back from his chest, Shit ambled upright, ignoring it. Trying not to hunch against the sprinkle, Eric hurried out of Hurter's to the pickup. In a plastic sack, he'd bought two Sharpies, one red, one black—and, at the Produce Market, a large jar of Hellmann's mayonnaise. Shit unlocked the passenger door and tugged it open. Opening the driver's door, Eric pulled himself up and slid beneath the wheel. "Okay, come on. Let's get back before the water in those potatoes boils all away. I don't know why Dynamite can't boil a goddam pot of water without burnin' it." Eric started driving.

"You told 'im to watch 'em for you; he'll sit there and watch 'em burn all up, then wonder what he's supposed to do about it. Nigger, am I glad you know how to cook."

"I guess I am, too." Eric grinned. "'Culturally-invested language.'"

"I'm gonna culturally invest you up side your head," Shit told him. "Why you always sayin' that?"

"You know what it means. I told you a couple of years ago. So did Dynamite."

"I know. But that ain't no reason to say it every time I open my fuckin' mouth."

"Well, it's about the only kind of language what come out of it." Eric laughed. "Okay. I'll cut it out." He wondered if the death of the mean-spirited invalid didn't signal the proper time to retire certain jibes, be more mature, admit he'd grown older.

Back at the cabin, with the onions, celery, and peppers he'd already cut up in the big bowl, Eric finished making potato salad. He covered it with tin foil and put in the refrigerator. To the back of the stove was a pot of beans he'd been cooking all morning with onions, peppers, and a pork shoulder, till it was pretty much falling to pieces.

At the kitchen table he'd lettered on a piece of cardboard:

NO BOAT SERVICE TO
GILEAD ISLAND TODAY
ON ACCOUNT OF A DEATH
IN THE MacAMON FAMILY

Eric had put blue highlights on the left side of the letters.

"Damn," Shit said. "That looks real nice. What's it say?"

Eric read it to him. Then he said, "We'll string it up on Gilead Dock with some wire when we go out there tomorrow morning with Captain Miller," one of the remaining black fishermen at the Harbor. Miller had volunteered to go out for the burial anyway and was taking a boat load of people.

Someone knocked at the door.

Shit said, "You could be a' artist or somethin'—or a sign painter, I bet—I mean, if you wanted to."

Dynamite went to see who it was. Opening the door, he called back over his shoulder, "Hey, it's Chef Ron," who came in with a large crock of chicken salad.

In his yellow slicker, Ron explained, "Yall tell Jay and Mex I can't get away from the restaurant. But at least I thought I'd send them somethin' to nibble on."

"Well, I know they'll appreciate that." Then Dynamite frowned at the crock, which was eighteen inches across. "Hey—how much salad did you *make?*" He took the bowl from the shaved-headed black man. "This thing is heavy." It joined the pork and beans and potato salad on the table.

In his rain jacket, Ron grinned. "There ain't no rush for the bowl back—" it was a handsome, glazed ceramic—"but maybe, Eric, you could rinse it out and get it back to me in a couple of weeks...?"

"Sure," Eric said, walking over.

"Your beans smell right good." Chef Ron smiled. "You guys give my condolences to Hugh and Jay and Mex, all right?" As he went outside, Ron pulled his yellow hood up over his dark, gleaming head, and hurried down the puddled steps to his blue jeep—fenders, hood, and windshield flecked with drops.

*

They put the stuff in the pickup's bed with a tarp under it and another over it—the full-sized garbage truck they'd been using for the last two years stood beside it—then drove it down to the marina.

Walking up and around the maze of docks from the boat, holding a family-sized, black umbrella, came a heavy black man, with a dark suit, a rough white beard, a black denim shirt and a black tie that Eric only just noticed, and a white captain's cap.

In the rain the man was barefoot.

"Hello, Dynamite. Mornin' there Morgan, Eric—good to see you boys. Too bad it's such a sad occasion."

Shit said, "I don't know how sad Jay is actually gonna be, Cap'n Miller."

"Oh, you don't gotta say that." Under his umbrella—two circles of black cloth that let the wind escape between the bigger and the smaller—Captain Miller waved his hand dismissively. "Shad and I had some good laughs together, back when him and me was your age—or just about. Course, that was 'fore he found religion and the Aryan Brotherhood. He was ten years older than me. I got Eddie on the boat, 'cause it's my Saturday to baby-sit. But we're all gettin' on. I want him to see the Indian graveyard. If he stays around here, probably that's where he's gonna end up."

(Eric was saying, "Hey, Shit—hold the sign for me, so I can get it wired up. Yeah, that's right. No, over about three inches. Lemme put it around this one, now...")

("You think it's gonna run?")

("Well, them things is supposed to be waterproof." Eric stood up. "I hope it don't. That's about the best I can do for now.")

"Eddie's in his Sunday best—so am I." Captain Miller grinned down at himself. (Eddie was Captain Miller's "surprise" child, with Doris, his third wife, twenty-two years his junior. Arriving in the Captain's fifty-ninth year, Eddie had just turned seven.) "Only I don't got my shoes on yet. I'll stick my feet in 'em if we get there and it looks like anybody's gonna be offended."

Falling from the morning overcast, plumes of rain swept the multi-leveled marina. Boards and macadam streamed with what looked like molten glass. Bits of matting flicked and shook as wind dozed away the water.

A gray SUV pulled into the all-but-empty lot. The side door slid back, and a large person emerged in a glistening red rubber rain suit preserved from four or five wars ago. From the driver's door, a not very large umbrella with pale blue and pink blossoms all over it opened up, and a very large woman stepped out under it, in flapping pastels. The wind caught it up. The rain, Eric saw, soaked the dress in seconds. In her dripping pastels she walked around the headlights and started across the lot in what looked like bathroom thongs.

The one in red rubber leaned back into the car to lug out a wicker trunk.

Over the rain, Dynamite said, "We got some stuff to bring on board, too, Cap'n."

"Oh?" Captain Miller looked puzzled. He turned around, raised the umbrella high, cupped his hand beside his jaw and shouted, "Billy?—*Billy!* Get your lazy self on out here and help these boys carry on some of these collations."

In a dark green watch cap and a sweater with a few snags and holes, a young white man, maybe Shit's age, came hurrying up the dock, hunched over, through less and less falling water. Billy's black sweater must have been soaked. Like his captain, he, too, was shoeless, his feet wide, wet, and red-toed, with frayed denim strung around the heels.

Shit said, "Looks like everybody's goin' barefoot. I should take off these goddam clodhoppers and get myself fuckin' comfortable again."

"Go on and get your stuff," Captain Miller said. "Looks like you got five minutes of let up, before it starts to pour again. But watch the language there, Morgan. Eddie don't hear too much of that kinda talk."

"With this guy around?" Shit raised his eyebrows, and looked at Billy, who, starting to laugh, declared:

"I don't cuss none in front of the Cap'n's kid. Cap'n Miller'd skin me alive, if he caught me."

"Darn right I would." Captain Miller lowered his umbrella. "I'm tryin' to raise a good, well-behaved boy."

"Then I guess if I can't cuss, I'll keep my shoes on—to remind me."
Shit turned to the truck. "None of that invested cultural language, huh?"
Probably he didn't expect a response—and got none.

Looking over their heads, Captain Miller called, "Hey, honey-bunch!
How you doin', sweetheart? Good to see you ladies come to pay your
respects. Shad MacAmon was a good Christian, and it's nice to see good
people comin' out to respect a good Christian's departure to the better
place."

In the now-sopping, flowered dress that clung to her breasts, her hips—
easily she was three hundred pounds—a few steps ahead of red-suited
Tank, Cassandra walked up, looking around, bronze hair a wet helmet that
became a bronze veil over her freckled back and shoulders. "Christian!"
Two tears were tattooed on her face, beneath her left eye, from a juvenile
jail term. "That man a Christian?" She humphed. "I guess it was a day like
this one I last saw him alive—'bout a year-and-a-half ago. Jay and Mex was
rollin' Shad in his chair through Runcible, and it started to pour. Just like
now. So they brought him inside our shop, out of the wet—and suddenly
he went off. He called me and poor Tank here every sort of Salome and
Jezebel and whore of Babylon they got in the damned Bible and six or
seven others besides that they wouldn't let into no holy book."

Under her red rubber hood, Tank's sharply pulled-back hair was a thick
black outline around her Indian features, as she watched her partner.

"Daughters of Sodom and all the whores of Babylon and I don't know
what-all—and there we are, with five sorority girls from the college in
Valdosta who want to get some lady-like butterflies on their right butt
cheeks. Jay MacAmon is my good, good friend, and I know it wasn't his
fault. He was tryin' to shut 'im up. But it was all I could do to let 'im sit
there and embarrass them poor students and not throw that foul-mouthed
reprobate back out in the rain. He's just yellin' and screamin' every kind of
nastiness that you could think of at two women tryin' to do their day's work."
Cassandra shook her head. "He about scared them women to death—naw,
Jay is our friend. And we're goin' out there *because* he's our friend. But I
don't have nothin' good to say about Shad, other than that he's dead. And
Tank ain't seen the graveyard for a while—have you, sweetheart?"

Tank transferred the hamper from one hand to the other, but didn't say
anything.

Here, Cassandra put her heavy arm with its load of flesh around Eric's
shoulder. "Hey, honey—when you gonna come and let me put some
pretty pictures all over you? You always tellin' me how much you like the
ones I did for Jay. I know these two fellas—" she nodded toward Shit and

Dynamite—"is too chicken to let me go stickin' a needle in their cute butts. And Dynamite here is basically another hairball, like Jay—if he got 'em, you couldn't see no pictures on him for the fur. But—now, Eric—you got the right kinda skin for some real good needlework. You could be a prime sample. I can show you some things me and Tank been thinkin' about recently."

"Hey," Shit said. "That sounds nice. Can I come and watch?"

"Sure, you can, honey," Cassandra said, while silent Tank smiled.

Billy called, "Hey, come on, get your stuff. Let's get it on the boat, before we get soaked again. Okay? Come on now—"

Then they were at the back of the truck with Shit handing down the bowls and crocks and pots. In single file, they started out to Captain Miller's *Doris*, lugging pots and bowls against their bellies.

One by one, forty feet along the walkway, they climbed on the twelve-meter New England lobster boat that, locally, had been converted into a tourist fishing vessel. It rose and fell beside the boards. Tad—still the youngest of the black garbage drivers—was already on deck, to help carry things into the galley. "Set 'em on the floor by the wall. Or you can put some of them on the counter there—'cause it's got an edge."

In an incongruous blue suit, tie, and brown leather loafers, a slim black child looked around: Captain Miller's son, Eddie.

"Ain't he a big boy? He just had his seventh birthday two weeks back," Billy said and laughed. "He's almost growed up." When Billy set his pots down, he looked out the galley's screen door. In the sky were a few clear patches. "Come on," he said to Eddie. "Lemme show you what I was about to do when your dad called me."

Eric stepped out behind them.

On the deck by the galley door stood a number ten tin can with no top. "See, you want me to take a big handful of them wriggly-squiggly nightcrawlers and eat them suckers right now?"

Eddie looked a little horrified. "*Nooo....!* What you guys always wanna do that for? That's disgustin'!"

"Oh, you *wanna* see me do it, then. Well, that's good. 'Cause I'm gonna show you," Billy said. "Like this." He plunged a large, nail-bitten hand into the can and pulled up the churning and twisting worms, with their red, segmented bodies and feathery gills, green-black, along their sides. Between his fingers, bits of dirt and seaweed mulch fell back into the rim or on the rain-slick deck.

At the sight, Eddie, in his tie and white shirt, grew mute, if not paralyzed.

"That's what they use for bait," Shit said to Eric. "That's probably left over from the fishin' party he had out yesterday."

"Yeah," Eric said. "I know."

"They real good," Billy said. "I eat these things for breakfast *all* the time." With its wriggling and unwriggling load, Billy raised his fist, opened his mouth, and strung half a dozen of the very live creatures over teeth and tongue, closed his mouth, and, with his lips sealed over them, began to make exaggerated chewing motions with his jaws, while the hanging worms curled and uncurled over the Billy's blond stubble: "*Mmmmmm, mmmm, mmmm.*" Again he raised his hand, covered his mouth, spit the worms out into his palm, so that they dangled and twisted from both sides. "Wow, them things is *real* good. They're salty." Tad, Shit, Dynamite—and Eric—were laughing now. "Them suckers make a real good breakfast." Billy held out his fist to Eddie. "Don't even need no salt and pepper. You want some?"

"Noooo…" Eddie got out. "That's *awful!*"

Dynamite said, "I don't think you better let Cap'n Miller see you doin' that stuff."

"Hell—he was the first one who did it to me, back when I was this one's age." Billy nodded at Eddie.

Shit leaned toward Eric. "They been scarin' kids who come on the boats for a hundred years with them nasty wigglies. They don't hurt you."

"They used to have a wrestler called the Boogie Man who did that," Eric said. "But he used regular worms, I think."

"They did?" Shit asked. "Well, how about that!"

Then Eddie blurted, "My daddy would *never* put nothin' like that in his mouth!" And the men—who, Eric figured, had seen different in their own childhoods—laughed.

More people were coming down the dock—all Harbor working men, and three Eric knew from the Dump—with pies and custards and cake boxes.

*

When the *Doris* docked at Gilead, Jay was waiting beside the boathouse.

"Let's do everybody a favor and put the food in the back of my truck out here. And let's use *my* tarp—" he grinned at Dynamite—"not the one you brought over."

With his easy smile, Dynamite said, "Hey, you know this *ain't* the tarp we use for the fuckin' garbage. This one is clean. I know enough not to mix the two of them up, especially around nobody's food."

"I know that," Jay said. "And I know *you* know that. But this way, nobody else out here got to wonder about it. It'll just look a little better."

"Suit yourself." Dynamite smiled. "And I ain't taken no offense, neither." So they loaded the pots and cake platters and crocks across the deck beside the Gilead Island boathouse and into Mr. Holota's pickup, on the blue plastic tarp—which Eric had to admit to himself, looked notably cleaner than the black-stained green one they'd brought from Dynamite's truck. Fourteen people were there—

*

The Holotas had volunteered both a car and their own pickup and were waiting at the Gilead boathouse. In two relays, Mex and Ruth Holota drove people up to the Kyle place.

Hugh had moved two tables into the living room. "My God," Eric said, looking over the platters spread across them, with the oval hard-boiled egg halves, topped with paprika stars, "how many deviled eggs did you guys *make*?"

Tank pushed her hood back, opened her red rain jacket, and shrugged out of it. She was wearing a dark blue, brocaded shirt under it. "I didn't know how many people were gonna be here." She frowned. A black braid hung down her shoulder. (He remembered Roan.) "I could put two of these trays in the refrigerator, maybe—and take 'em out later if we need 'em."

"Yeah," Eric said. "That'd be a good idea. Here, I'll carry one of them. We only got about sixteen, seventeen people. The kitchen's this way."

"Yeah," she said. "I know."

In the kitchen, they left two trays on the oilcloth covered table to move food around in the refrigerator. Eddie, who followed, said, "You know where my daddy is?"

Tank said, "Cap'n may have gone back down to the boathouse to make another run."

"Oh...!" Eddie looked distressed.

"Don't worry," Eric said. "He'll be back in ten minutes. He ain't gonna leave you behind."

Hugh came in. "Look. You all can go out to the graveyard—I'm going to stay here and take care of the food."

"Well, what's gotta be taken care of?" Eric asked.

"I'm gonna put some fire under your pork and beans, for one thing."

"You're not goin' out for the burial?"

Hugh smiled. "Nope. I'm not."

"Well, all right," Eric said.

Hugh explained, "We figured all this out last night. Don't worry."

"You know where my daddy is?"

"Hey, there, boy," Hugh said. "Come on with me, Eddie. I think I seen him come in just a second ago."

*

In an odd happening of the sort that sometimes occurs at funerals, the rain ceased as they stepped from the mansion. Strips of cloud peeled from the sky, and sunlight fell through wet trees and across droplet-speckled underbrush, as twelve men and three women gathered in front of the Kyle mansion to walk along the wet path, further up the island, to the graveyard.

Maybe a hundred-fifty yards beyond the Holotas' cabin, the Indian cemetery was not a clearly defined space. Rather it was an area of the woods where burials had taken place for six hundred years, sometimes more of them, sometimes less. At one point, when the Kyles had begun to bury their own people here, Orbison Pitkin built a stone wall around the part where a number of the white people were interred. No more than two-and-a-half feet high, a stone hedge ran some thirty feet off to the left, which halted, then after a twenty foot gap, ran another fifteen feet along the back at an odd angle. At that time, so the story went, the Creek families still on the island at the time objected that even so small a wall as this would halt the passage of the souls of the dead to whatever hunting ground they were destined for. So it was discontinued—and some of it torn down.

While waiting for stragglers, Eric walked off to look at a stand of trees from which hung rags of moss, like ghosts—or, more, like sheer things ghosts might have discarded. Something moved in it, he realized. A step closer over the rocks, and Eric saw dozens of small spiders scurrying and stopping, scurrying and stopping, basically downward. It made him feel a little itchy. Somewhere above, a nest must have just hatched. He saw no webs.

When he walked back to the others, Shit was asking Jay quietly, "Who done the diggin'?"

"The Hemmings people came by with their boat yesterday afternoon and dug out the grave for us—like that, by seven o'clock. Gilead's the largest island out here—but it ain't the only one, you know."

"Oh," Shit said. "Yeah."

Jay added, to Eric, "A lot more people used to live away from the mainland, than do today."

A mound of dirt lay on a green cloth, with three shovels sticking in it and two more shovels on the ground. The casket sat beside the rectangular hole.

"It's a lot prettier here than in that pipsqueak cemetery behind the

Hemmings Interdenominational," Cassandra said quietly to Tank. "I think Jay's doin' him a favor, putting him here."

"It's funny," Tank said. "But if somebody's buried out here, you can't think but so badly of 'em."

Jay asked Billy and Tad and Mex to help him lower the coffin.

Then the men eased back, looking up and blinking in the sunlight still low for morning.

"Hey." Jay stood up and let his canvas strap drop to the ground. "I'm gonna say somethin'. Yall listenin'? First—" He stood straighter, one work shoe in the loose loam that would go back in—"I wanna thank yall for comin' out here to be with me, for this. And for bringin' all that good food back at the house we gonna be eatin' in a few minutes. The fact is, at least years ago, before his stomach went, Shad liked his food. He really did. So that's somethin' good about 'im—a pleasure he could enjoy. All that warms me. Part of me, I'll tell you the truth, wanted to get 'im planted and covered up and have done with it. Yall know I think he was a mean, ignorant, small-spirited man—and I can measure my whole life out watchin' him, in my mind's eye, do one awful, cruel, horrible, horrible thing after another—to me and everybody else around him. And then he'd go try to call it godly and good. Knockin' my damned teeth out when I was a kid was the least of 'em. I know of three people he killed, two of 'em black men that never lifted a finger against 'im. I admit it, that's the part that sickens me most. Then there was the time him and them boys tried to burn down The Slide, where they coulda killed me and a couple of dozen others, if Kyle's men hadn't'a stopped 'em. I ain't gonna stand here and make a list of his sins—though you don't know how tempted I am to do *just* that. 'Cause I think it would be really awful if we forgot that that's how some people have acted in this amazin' world we live in, that, yes, has as much good and beautiful in it as it does." He sighed. "Yeah, I wished I was different or more forgiving or…more *somethin'* than I am. I do. But I couldn't lie, though, and say most of what he done was anything but self-righteous and arrogant cruelty." Jay sucked in a breath. "I know you're only supposed to speak good of the dead. But we'd have a completely silent burial here, if we held to that." No one laughed, though a breeze came up, and a thousand droplets fell suddenly from the leaves around, many sparkling. "Now, you also know this isn't where Shad wanted to be. But I'm doin' this for—I admit it— really selfish reasons. *I* think it's beautiful here."

In his denim work jacket, plaid shirt, and green tie, white-haired Walter Holota nodded. Ruth Holota stood just before him, her sweater buttoned up to her neck, her own work shoes half sunk in leafy earth.

"The fact is, I can't imagine nobody in this place—in a place as beautiful as this—what didn't have *somethin'* good about 'em, even if *I'll* never know what it was."

Captain Miller said, "Shad wasn't all bad, son. He had a sense of humor—yeah, sometimes it could get kinda vicious, especially if he thought the people he was playin' his jokes on was no accounts. I know about them black people. But I'm black, too—and I can remember some good things about him. Not a lot. But some. And eventually, I suppose, Shad was the kind of person what thought everybody was a no-account *except* him. But his humor was there, and it made me laugh…a few times—at least when I was a kid." The Captain pulled one large, bare, black foot from the soft dirt. (A tired Eddie was back at the house with Hugh.) Captain Miller set his foot down again—water eased up around his foot's cracked edges.

Jay smiled, and Eric looked at the gap along his upper gum. "Well, that's nice to know, Cap'n Miller." Jay looked around. "It really is. Thanks for sayin' it. But maybe that's why I need to know he's out *here*, where I'm gonna be some day, and maybe some of the rest of you are, too." Again he looked around. "Anybody wanna help me fill this thing in?" He reached over where the three shovels stuck from the mound.

Eric felt a hand push at his shoulder.

Dynamite said, softly, "Go on, you two…" So Eric and Shit moved over to the pile and took up the other shovels—with Billy and Tad (who already had one)—and began to shovel dirt down on the glimmering blonde wood.

(Eric liked watching black and white folks labor together. For him it braided with what gave meaning to his labor—and his love—for Shit.)

"Move over," Tank said—again in her red rain jacket—and, picking up a shovel from the ground, she began to scoop and toss, twice as fast as the others. "You gonna fill this thing up, you gotta *fill* it!"

It went quickly. (Eric smiled even more broadly.) A quarter of the dirt was left over, even with a three inch meniscus bulging from the grave. Then everyone—Captain Miller, Dynamite, and Tank in the lead, Billy, Jay, and Cassandra at the rear—walked back to the house.

*

During the last minute of the walk back, it rained again.

Eric came in through the vestibule, turned by the foot of the steps, and went into the living room. Tables and piles of plates and silverware and linen had already been set out. Five—no, six—people were already eating. In the middle of the sagging couch, Captain Miller was sitting, knees wide, his shins crossed in his black jeans. Gray dirt was drying on the cuffs. Mud was drying—gray, red, and brown in streaks—along the Captain's feet.

Hugh said, "Get yourself a plate—those beans and pork are good, Eric. There's whiskey on the sideboard, if you want a drink."

Jay laughed. "Dynamite's boys ain't drinkin' boys—you know that Hugh."

"I don't need no whiskey." Shit laughed. "I'm already crazy enough." He walked to the table, lifted a deviled egg—

"Put that on a napkin, at least, Shit," Eric said.

"Okay, okay . . ." Shit took one of the small plates though. "Hey, these are good. What they got in 'em? Mustard?"

"And celery salt," Tank said, from where she sat in the corner, eating pork and beans and chicken salad. "That's all."

"Naw, I don't need to get no crazier," Shit repeated, then raised his plate to Hugh, walked to an empty chair, and sat.

It was a relaxed hour-and-a-quarter of eating and talk.

Eric said, "I wouldn't be surprised if it started *really* comin' down again." He glanced at the room's high ceiling, edged with floral molding.

Cassandra sat in a large armchair. She had a glass of something. "You ain't gonna mind driving us back down to Captain Miller's boat, are you?" There were still rain droplets on her full fleshy face, which sat near the two, blue inked ones.

Walter Holota said, "I drove you up here, honey. I'll drive you back down. It's good to see you two again. I know a while there, about ten years back, you was havin some trouble with Tank's mama."

"Mr. Holota?"

With his flat, red-brown face, Walter Holota looked over at Eric.

"I was just wonderin'—your nephew, Roan, he had somethin' on his shirt, about…I think it said, 'Tie a feather to it.' What was that supposed to mean?"

Mr. Holota's face erupted in a laugh. "Oh, that. Well, the boy's an artist—over at the Indian arts college, in New Mexico. He makes jewelry—like they sell in some of the stores in Runcible and Hemmings. See, the kids in the jewelry classes wanna make modern jewelry, like all the other modern jewelers do. But people who come to the college and the shops around there, want the stuff that looks Indian—I mean, authentic work. Hell—" He looked down where his own silver buckle had a stylized eagle with blue stones for the feathers—"I like that kind of stuff, too. I admit it. But the kids don't wanna do that no more. They're tired of it. Problem is, that's the only kind they can sell. Then awhile ago, someone figured out you could make pretty much any old piece of silver or copper you wanted, and if you soldered a silver or a copper feather onto it, like as not it was gonna sell. 'Cause now it *looked* Indian." He chuckled. "I admit, I don't understand half the things he makes. But, like he says, tie a feather on it, and he can keep 'em movin' in the shops."

"Oh," Eric said. "Yeah…"

"Yes, but that's long over with," Tank was saying to Ruth, a few feet away. "Cave et Aude's doin' nicely. It ain't makin' us rich, but we're eatin'."

Cassandra let a loud sigh. "This is so nice out here," she said. "Even in the rain."

Eric frowned, wondering what it would be like to have a problem like Roan's. Maybe, when Roan came back, Eric would ask to see some of his work…

Over a plate carrying only potato salad, Ruth Holota was saying to Jay, "You know, I'm a big believer in tradition—and this was not what I'd call a traditional funeral, by anybody's lights. Still, I wanted to tell you, Jay, I appreciated what you had to say out there about Shad. I really did. But that's because I love that place, out there. I do. I know your uncle was a hard man. I mean, you knowed him all *your* life—and I knowed him fifteen years longer than you did. We had our own grievances against him, though all that's forgotten now and in the ground out there with him."

Eric had refilled his plate with pork and beans. It *was* tasty—surprisingly so, even though he'd cooked it himself. And there'd be enough left over, he'd begun to figure, for a week—

The sound—to Eric—was like an animal's distant slaughter. Logic told him it was outside the house, but at once, everyone in the room turned to look toward the hall into the kitchen.

Shuffling from the dark archway, hands over his face, bleating miserably, Eddie came forward. "I'm scared…" he got out through his sobs. "I'm scared…where's my daddy?" His tie was gone, his collar open, though he still wore his dark blue suit jacket.

Billy and Cassandra looked questioningly at one another.

So did Tad and Mex.

Captain Miller put his plate on the sofa cushion beside his hip. "What's a matter, boy?"

"He was tired," Hugh said, with a deeply questioning frown. "So after you went out to the graveyard, I let him lay down in the room inside, down from Jay and Mex's."

"I'm scared…I'm scared…" Sobbing Eddie moved forward, blindly toward his father. "I wanna go home…I'm scared." Eddie came around the end of the sofa. Under his jacket his shirt was rumpled and half out at the waist. "I wanna go *home*…"

"Hey, there, big boy." Captain Miller opened his arms. "What scared you, now? You want somethin' to eat? They got chicken salad—you like that."

"I don't *like* no salad...I wanna go home..." Eddie repeated, rubbing his eyes, his face.

"Well—" Captain Miller held the boy at a distance, but Eddie broke away and pushed up against him—"if the truth be known, maybe it *is* time we all thought about gettin' back to the mainland." He embraced his son. "This was a real nice spread. Jay, I think you done fine by Shad. Given some of the stuff that man pulled on you in his time, I know a lot of people wouldn't have done this much."

Through the room people grunted assent.

Tad said, "You know we *should* be thinking about gettin' back. I'm supposed to be in bed in about an hour, and tomorrow's a workin' day." He stood up from the chair he was sitting in and put his plate on the sideboard's white doily.

"Come on, Ruth," Mr. Holota said. "Let's run these people back down to the boathouse. You wanna drive the other car?"

"Certainly. Hugh, Jay, Mex—it was nice to see yall." Her plate clinked on the pile. "This was very nice. You know if there's anything we can do, we're just up the road."

"I wanna go *home*..." Eddie wailed.

"Come on, now," Captain Miller said. "We're *goin'* home. But we gotta get to the boat first. Be a little quiet now..."

Billy said, "It was probably wakin' up in this big old house all alone that scared him. I bet he ain't never even been in a place this big before. Hey, Eddie, you have a bad dream while you was nappin'?"

Eddie turned his face away from barefoot Billy, against his barefoot father's chest. "I dunno. I wanna go *home*..."

"Well, we're *goin'*," Captain Miller said. "Now, you gotta hush up, and let us get you there. I guess your mama was right—I shouldn't've brought you out to this thing."

"I'm *scared*," Eddie repeated.

"You done told me that," Captain Miller said, with his hand on Eddie's back. "But there ain't nothin' to be scared of now. I'm here. Come on—you wanna go to the bathroom?"

"Naw," Eddie said. "I wanna go..."

"Well, I do," Captain Miller said.

"It's right through there—down the long hall," Jay said, "on your left."

"Come on with me, then." And Captain Miller with his arm around Eddie, started across the floor out through the back arch. "Maybe when you get there you'll change your mind."

The minute they'd gone, Dynamite frowned. "Did somethin' happen to that boy?"

"Naw," Jay said. "Naw, he just woke up all by himself and got spooked. That's all."

Then Mex stepped in front of Eric. With his hands, he signed, *"Jay wants you guys to stay here—we can put you up. We'll get you back to the mainland early tomorrow."*

Eric said, "Sure, Mex."

"I asked Dynamite and your brother—they said yes, too."

"Oh…Okay."

"It's a shame he's so scared." Cassandra's filmy flowered dress was all but dry. "This is such an interestin' old place."

Although it took three times as long as Eric would have figured, complete with an argument about whether they could all fit comfortably on Captain Miller's boat or whether Jay should make a special run with the scow (to which Captain Miller made hand-waving protests: "That ain't necessary. That just ain't necessary"), eventually everyone was out and—in two trips—back down to the boathouse.

They filed onto the *Doris*, which, however crowded, was returning with three fewer people than it had come with. People at the rail waved. The boat pulled from the island dock.

*

"What you gonna do with all this food?" Dynamite asked. "If them things could still hatch, you'd have enough deviled eggs left to start a chicken ranch."

Standing beside the sideboard, Hugh scratched his head. "I guess we'll eat 'em." He took another from the tray and bit into it. "They're good."

"Yeah," Shit said, "they are."

Eric asked, *"You* think somethin' happened to him?"

"He was asleep an awfully long time," Hugh said. Then he shook his head. "No—he just woke up and didn't remember where he was. Probably he was afraid to get up and find us, and just lay there gettin' scareder and scareder. When he came out, I was actually thinking I should go in and check on him. I remember the first few times I visited here when I was a kid. This place can be pretty overwhelmin'."

"Hey—" Dynamite sat down at the side of the sofa—"I think the rain put a little damp in here. You got some wood around somewhere? Why don't we make up a fire to take the chill off?"

Jay grinned. "If you wanna burn the whole place down and kill us all with smoke poisoning while you're at it, we could."

Laughing, Hugh leaned back against the sideboard, eating his deviled egg. "Wendell, there ain't been a fire in that thing in ten, fifteen years. They'd have to sweep out the chimney real good before we could have it working. Right now, it's blocked up about full."

"Oh…" Dynamite said. "That's too bad. I remember some nice fires in here, back when you first came out to stay, Jay."

"Maybe you remember them back from when Kyle and his folks lived here," Jay said. "When we were kids, I mean."

"It could be," Dynamite said. "'Cept for the storm, I ain't been in here myself for seven or eight years. But I would've sworn I'd seen you use that thing since Kyle went to Columbus."

Jay pushed up from his own chair to stand before the empty fireplace. "Hey—I got something I want to show these fellows. Mex, where did I put that thing?"

"You know right where it is," Mex signed. *"It's back in the bedroom, lyin' out on the bed where you put it this mornin'. Showin' these boys that nasty thing is all you been talkin' about for two days."*

"That's right," Jay said. "It is, ain't it?" He grinned. "I come across it upstairs and brung it down to our closet six months ago, so when they came out here next, I could break it out and show it to 'em." He turned and left the room through the arch the led to the kitchen and the bedrooms, where, on his first visit, Eric—and that afternoon Eddie—had slept.

From his seat on the couch, Dynamite asked. "What the hell is this all about?"

Finished with the egg, Hugh folded his hands in front of him. "It's just Jay's craziness."

"About what?" Dynamite asked.

From his own chair, Shit leaned forward on his knees, looking eager. Eric was smiling, even as he felt wary of the extremity that sometimes dogged Jay's humor. He wondered if it was anything like the late Shad's…

Jay returned, holding a twenty-four inch by eighteen inch framed picture. The back was covered with brown paper—all that showed. A wire cable crossed it—for hanging. "I been wanting to show you guys this for years—me, I think it's great. It was one of Kyle's favorite pictures. I thought it was pretty cool, too. It's *one* reason I first wanted to be your daddy's jerk-off buddy—and why I always figured there was hope for at least *some* of the Turpens. I was thinkin' after all this time, maybe I should give it to you."

Dynamite asked, "What the fuck you got there, Jay?"

Jay walked over to the empty fireplace. "You ever wonder, Eric, why some people call your old man a pig fucker?"

Eric laughed. "Mostly, that's just what Shit calls him."

"I used to hear the guys at the Produce Farm call him that." Shit shrugged. "So I picked it up. I never thought it *meant*...nothin'."

Jay lifted the picture, turned it around, and—

. Hugh said, "Jay, you gonna be sorry about this," while, grinning, Mex moved behind Shit to put his hand on Shit's shoulder.

—leaned the framed color photograph back on the mantel.

Behind the glass, two inches of matting surrounded the twelve-by-sixteen inch color enlargement: some trees, a cabin's edge at the side: in the middle stood an orange hand-worked water pump on a concrete pedestal. On the pedestal stood a large pig, it's head up. Behind the pig, leaning over him—definitely the pig was male—holding it by a leather collar, stood a barefoot, lean-muscled young man with no shirt, his jeans pushed to his knees.

Looking out at the room, he had a pleased smile. His naked feet were in the grass with denim bunched around them. His knees were slightly bent.

Watching, eight or nine more men stood around. A few were white; most were black. One of the white guys was a chunky fellow with glasses—and no clothes on at all. He stood with his erect penis in his fist.

The young man gripping the pig collar was also engorged, most of him, however, sunk in the pig's fundament.

Shit began to laugh. "Who the fuck is *that?*"

One of the black men also had his pants open, his cock out, and was masturbating. Two others were feeling their crotches.

"The one naked as a jaybird—" Jay explained, stepping back to get a better view—"is Miles Turpens. He's waitin' his turn. I think when it come to pigs, that boy had a thing for sloppy seconds. That's out at Miles's farm. He had a whole circle of friends who...what can I say, kinda liked that pig."

"Jesus Christ," Dynamite demanded. "Where'd you get this picture, Jay?"

"I *took* the damned thing." Jay looked back over his shoulder, his toothless grin splitting his beard. "You don't remember? The black guy beatin' off is our crazy friend, Robert Kyle, the Third," Jay said to Shit and Eric. "He was never one to let a white feller get the better of 'im in straight out nastiness—especially your dad. I give Kyle that picture, and he made the enlargement."

"He never showed it to me," Dynamite said, "when we was fuckin' around."

Hugh stood smiling by the sideboard. "That's 'cause my cousin was more civilized than *this* barbaric contrarian." He chuckled.

"Probably it was all that fancy schoolin' overseas that done it—Kyle's nastiness, I mean." Jay laughed. "That's the only explanation I could offer for it. I guess he figured that picture was for him. The black guy with 'em is one of Kyle's African friends he'd brought here that summer. I remember, that black boy said he was real impressed with the level of pig fuckin' we had goin' on around here." Jay shook his head. "I wouldn't'a' thought they had pig fuckin' in Africa. I figured that was a Georgia specialty—like boiled peanuts or peach pie—but apparently, in some parts, they do."

Somehow, gazin' at the grinning Georgia boy above the mantel, who looked out at them from nearly thirty years before, Eric began to make out a likeness. "That's...you—!" He looked back and forth between the photograph and Dynamite.

Dynamite said, "Jay, now *why* you wanna go show 'em *that* for?"

Still grinning, Shit declared, "I think it's *great!*"

Eric asked, "How old were you when you guys took that?"

"Seventeen," Dynamite said. "Maybe eighteen. Kyle still had to be in boardin' school—then he went to college, I remember, a year ahead of the usual age. He was *so* fuckin' smart."

"Hey—" Shit settled back in his chair—"you gotta tell me what fuckin' one of them things feels like."

"It feels like fuckin' a *pig*—is what it feels like," Dynamite said.

"Why didn't you guys use a sow?" Shit asked. "Wouldn't that've been easier?"

"Naw," Dynamite said. "Ol' Stove Pipe there was raised to it, see—from the first. He wanted it. You'd walk around on Miles's little piss-anty farm, and that old pig'd run up to you and back up against you and rub his nuts all over your knees. Miles Turpens had about four or five niggers workin' for 'im, and about half their job was keepin' that pig satisfied. I'd just come by to get mine. He was gonna gimme a job out there, too, but we never got around to it. Mostly I was just a drop-in."

"It's the truth," Jay said. "There ain't nothin' like a lecherous pig to turn a farm like that into an equal opportunity employer. You gotta take who you can get—probably it sounds prejudiced, but you can start out as white as Miles Turpens there, and if pig fuckin is the skill you need to have around, you probably gonna end up with more black fellas workin' for you than white ones. I seen it happen more'n once. Probably don't mean nothin'. If he was here, Kyle would explain how there was other social forces involved. But that's *still* the way it works."

Dynamite mused. "There was another black feller workin there for Miles—big feller, too, named Tooker—who was tryin' like hell to break in another of Miles's hogs. But he couldn't do it. He wanted me to help, but after a couple of times, I told him, 'No. If a pig don't wanna get fucked, you don't fuck it.' Tooker ain't in the picture. Must have been *his* day off, or somethin'. But—damn!—the squealin' and cussin' that used to come out that barn when the two of 'em was in there! He musta got himself pig-bit fifteen or twenty times. I'm surprised that nigger still had a dick. I think once he told me *he* bit the damn pig back, he was so mad! But he still couldn't make it happen. Stove Pipe didn't give you those problems."

"Maybe gettin' bit was what Tooker was into," Shit suggested.

"Could be," Dynamite said. "But he could also've been a big dumb nigger who didn't know no better. Tooker took his turns with Stove Pipe, like the rest of us, though. But he wanted to break one in all for hisself."

"That pump looks like the one they got on the Dump Produce Farm today," Shit said.

"That *is* the pump they got at Dump Produce today," Dynamite said. "The one whose picture's on your credit union card. Look at that buck naked little cocksucker—Miles, I mean. Sometimes I fucked him, and sometimes I fucked his pig. It was the same with the niggers who worked there, too. Miles's butt went with the job. He had the land, but it was just a little shit-ass farm, with six pigs, three cows, and a chicken coop out behind his cabin. And one of the pigs was Stove Pipe."

"Kyle brought that place from him 'bout three or four months after we was out there takin' those pictures," Jay said, thoughtfully, "and started turnin' it into a real farm. Only thing wrong with it was Dynamite didn't get no more pork butt."

Hugh humphed and stood up from the sideboard against which he'd been leaning.

"Now see, Hugh?" Jay said. "They ain't upset—are yall?"

"I ain't," Shit declared.

"I don't think so," Eric said. "I'm fine with it," though he didn't know how he'd feel about it had Dynamite and Shit felt differently.

In his visits to the Kyle mansion, because of Shad most of Eric's explorations had been confined to the part he had seen on that first night. Once Hugh had sent him to get something, and he'd walked down halls he had not yet explored and realized that there were rooms—many rooms—in the building he was not privy to. But tonight Jay said that, if it didn't bother them, they'd sleep in Shad's old bedroom.

'Cause it was already made up.

"It don't bother *me*," Dynamite said.

*

Eric went to look at the room in which he'd first stayed at the mansion. On the bed by the back wall, the spread was rumpled—probably from when Eddie had been napping. Eric left, walked down the dark green hall—near the ceiling there was water damage—and into the bathroom. Gray-green paint had been put over the wall where the pipes had been replaced. It still looked new, which gave him a sense of how long the rest must have gone without painting.

By now he knew there was a back stair, which he found. It was paneled, waist high, with dark wood and narrow. A hand on either wall, he walked up and came out in an alcove on the second floor. Stepping out, he stood in the great upstairs sitting room, with its orange and brown sofas and mustard armchairs.

In the corner, by the window, Dynamite was standing in front of the statue, whose head was half-again higher than his. Horned, tusked, and winged, the black creature kneeled on its immense bronze knee. Evening light through the undraped panes turned parts of the hulking sculpture a gray-violet that seemed sourceless.

As Eric walked between the chairs, Dynamite glanced at him and smiled.

Eric got nearer; Dynamite said, "Kyle's grandmamma made this thing—I only met her the once—first time I was here, when I was twelve. She was a real old lady then. That was Christmas, too. I guess by the second time I came back, she'd passed. You know, she's buried out there, probably not that far from Shad. They used to have a lot of her things around, but they give 'em all away. I think this one was just too big. You ever really look at it before?"

"First time I was over here—" as he neared, Eric slowed—"I was walkin' around up here, at night, in the dark—I almost bumped into it. Damn, it scared me."

Dynamite chuckled.

Eric said, "I was wonderin' if that's what scared Eddie."

"Could be—but he probably would'a said something." Dynamite rocked on to his other hip. "But maybe not—if he thought he wasn't supposed to be up here, anyway." He chuckled again.

"Hey—" Eric looked back into the arch with the stairway mounting to the next floor—"you know what that room is, up there?"

"Sure," Dynamite said.

"What is it?" Eric asked.

"Come on. I'll show you." Dynamite turned on his worn-down work shoes and started, with his listing gait, back to the stairs' foot.

Eric followed.

They started up the carpeted steps, Dynamite ahead. "This tower room, here, used to be Kyle's—the first time I come over here, it was kind of like his old nursery room. A playroom, with all his toys. That was when *we* was twelve. He brought me up to see it—at that first Christmas party he had, with all the kids from around here—black and white, rich and poor. And I was about the poorest. Then, later, when he was older, it was his study—his library, he used to call it."

Dynamite, then Eric, came out at the head, into the octagonal space, with its bookshelves between the windows.

Eric walked forward—and after a few steps, glanced back. The lanky, unshaven man in his big collapsing work shoes, jeans bunched under his belt at the waist, and the ropey arms coming from the green short sleeved work shirt, looked like someone he had never seen before, as though the unfamiliar setting drained him of all familiarity. A bit wildly, Eric thought: But this is the man Robert Kyle the Third loved…and probably belongs here more than Hugh and Mex and Jay and me and Shit. Dynamite frowned. "What…?"

"Nothin'. I was thinkin'. That's all."

Dove gray walls rose to an intricately vaulted ceiling, crossed with beams that Eric had no memory of at all. Perhaps he'd never looked up…

"Yeah, I was rememberin'…something." Dynamite looked around at them—"that I swear, I ain't thought about it in a million years."

"What…?" Eric asked.

"Well, you know, I told you Kyle and me used to fool around when we was kids—in the boathouse and behind the fillin' station and out in the woods on the mainland and the island woods."

"Yeah…?"

"So when he invited me out here with all those other kids around here to his Christmas party, I figured we was probably gonna do *somethin'*—only I wasn't sure what. So I was just kickin' back and lettin' him show me around and stuff—and when he suddenly took me away from where everybody was, downstairs, I figured something was up. I was just a kid what till that day had lived in a two-room cabin and hadn't never *been* in more than a four-room one—I mean, the biggest house I'd ever been in, where anybody lived; I don't mean no office nor a store—was half the size of what we live in today in the Dump. So this was all pretty impressive."

Eric nodded.

"Anyway, Kyle got me up these stairs here, and as soon as he got to the top, right where you're standin', he turned around and reached between my legs—he used to have all these toys in here. Puppets and science sets and blocks and trains and books and *stuff*—and damned if the nigger don't take my dick out and hunkers down, right and front of me—and I'm lookin' around at all his fuckin' stuff! He squats right in front of me and sucked me off. After I shot, he grinned like he did, and I asked, 'Can we play with some of this stuff, now?'

"And he said, 'Are you all relaxed?'

"I said, 'Huh? Yeah.'

"So he stood up and said, 'Then come on around here—and lean over the rail.'

"I knew what he was gonna do. So I said, 'Okay.' And I stepped around there—" Dynamite moved behind the railing along the stairwell's edge and leaned over it—"and I didn't close my pants. He got behind me, and I leaned on that thing and he put his arms around me and his face next to mine. And with a handful of spit he stuck his dick right on up my ass. And I remember, he asks me, 'How come after you shoot, it's so easy to stick a dick in your asshole?' and I said, 'I dunno,' which wasn't exactly true— 'cause I had three married cousins, Mikey, Red, and Bulldog, what been fuckin' my butt a couple of times a day, one, the other or all three, since I was four years old—not to mention my daddy; who got on me about once a month." Again Dynamite chuckled. "It just meant I always been able to take it pretty easy. And ol' Mikey had some real meat on 'im, too. But I didn't want nobody to know—so I hardly never told nobody, until later, when me and Jay got to be fuck buddies. *That* was when I was fifteen or sixteen. And we bought Kyle on in with us." Dynamite took a big breath and pushed out his shoulders. "After Kyle fucked me, I asked him, 'Can we play, now?'

"And he said, 'Sure.'" Dynamite shook his head. "And I remember, I thought, Damn, that was worth it. His daddy came up later and found us lyin' out on the floor, both of us asleep. When I woke up, with him standin' over us, I thought he was gonna think we'd been doin' somethin' bad, 'cause my pants was still unbuttoned—Kyle had closed up his. But mine were gapin'. Only he just run us downstairs to the others and some dinner. I don't think we got to do much playin', though. It's funny—I think about Kyle and Jay and all the shit we got into together, like Myles's goddam Stove Pipe and them pig-fuckin' niggers—but I hardly never remember the first time out here, with Kyle." Dynamite stepped around the newel and started down. "Back then, that first time I come up here, this room had a big blue rug in it, with little gold stars all over. But I just remember all them toys."

Eric looked around at the dark red carpet, then followed Dynamite down. And realized he hadn't remembered to look for the photographs…

"It's funny—" Dynamite paused to let Eric catch up and raised his hand to his mouth to gnaw the nails on his spatulate fingers—"how you remember some things and don't hardly never think about the others. I never liked Mikey too much—he always used to slap me around, while he was fuckin' me. But Red and Bulldog was nice. So was my daddy, and they'd keep Mikey from messin' me up too much. When they'd get drunk, they'd all fuck each other's wives, too—except my daddy. Mama maybe suspected, but she didn't really know nothin' about how them boys used to do me." They started down again. "And I learned to keep my mouth shut—and pretty much how to take anybody. After a few years of Mikey and Bulldog, didn't nothin' really bother me goin' in back there. I can get comfortable under anybody."

Eric grinned. "That's why you're always ready for Shit and me to jump on you?"

"Probably. By the time I was messin' with Jay, them boys had all left Diamond Harbor, anyway. None of 'em got to eighteen without bein' married at least once. And besides his wife, Mikey always had at least two girls on the side he'd take down and sell on Friday nights in Turpens' back lot—that retarded one, Betsy-Ann. She had red hair, and the truckers in Turpens' all thought he was pimpin' out Red's simple-minded sister and would really get into that; Red'd go right along with it and they'd always pay a little more—like they'd do with a knocked-up whore." Dynamite was silent, three, four breaths. Eric watched—and thought about Shit's mother. "Finally, Betsy-Ann's aunt took her to Valdosta, and later I heard she died there. Then there was Merilee—she was real pretty. But she run off with some driver she met in the lot. Mikey was real mad about that for three goddam weeks. Somebody told me once they thought they seen her working in a flower shop, but I don't even remember where. I figured eventually Bulldog, Red, and Mikey would all go away together, but they didn't. They went to different places—different times, too. Maybe they'd got tired of each other, after all that. But my daddy stayed here. And had his heart attack…"

From the bottom of the tower steps, they walked back out into the sitting room.

Halfway across, Eric realized that, coming down, he hadn't even noticed the creature. He glanced back at the big metal shape. (Dynamite paused to put his hand on Eric's shoulder—and began to bite at the nails on his other hand.) Outside it was getting dimmer. Eric had been imagining Dynamite's story and his cousins and his dad and what it was like to be a twelve-year-old guest at this labyrinthine palace.

"Are your people out in the Indian graveyard?" Eric asked, as they walked between the couches and the armchairs.

"My daddy is." Dynamite rubbed the back of his neck.

For a moment, Eric thought that sunlight was falling through the roof. He looked up. One wall of the great room was notably higher than the other. The ceiling went halfway across the room, then slanted sharply up. Along the taller wall, between molding shaped like white amphoras with white bunting draped between them, rectangular windows in ornate frames with shells at the corners let in slabs of sunlight that fell into the room, cutting it into slices—the first time he'd ever seen that effect. "Not your mama...?" Eric squinted.

"Naw." Dynamite turned away from the falls of sunlight that cut up the great room. "After my daddy died, she went back to her own people in Tennessee. She's buried over there somewhere."

Looking at the floor, Eric could see what was probably years of dust on the carpet. Dynamite's shoes looked all spread out and flattened, like a few toes were ready to bust free, there or here.

"My granddaddy's here, too. He was a half-breed Injun and pretty much a drunk—least that's what my daddy tol' me."

Eric looked up at him. "You mean you're a quarter...no, I mean an eighth Injun?"

"Yep. That'd be enough to make me a full-out nigger, if he'd been a mullotter. But then every body in this neck of Georgia is got some Injun in 'em from someplace." He chuckled. "And the tar brush been splashin' around these parts pretty liberally, too, since I don't know what-all. You can't get away from it—unless you're Aye-talian or Portugee." Dynamite grinned. "Probably that's why I'm so good-lookin'."

They had stopped walking now—Dynamite in shadow, Eric in sun. "Did you see their graves," Eric asked, "when you were out there today in the graveyard?"

"Naw," Dynamite said. "I saw 'em once when I was a kid. But I come back a couple of years later, with Kyle, and we couldn't find none of 'em, 'cause the markers were all gone or washed away or somepin'. Not to his people or mine. Besides, just knowin' they're out there, not too far way— that's enough. And Kyle says, if I want, I can be buried there too—though, to be honest, I don't really give two shits. Though, I guess it's kinda nice to be with your friends." Dynamite snorted out a laugh. "In a way, it's too bad about Shad. I think he really thought they was gonna put 'im over in the Hemmings Interdenominational plot, what used to be the hardcore Baptist graveyard, where he would be shut of all these nigger lovers and sinners and perverts. But I'm kinda with Kyle on that one—once you go, I just don't think it matters no more." He stepped forward into the band of light. "Come on, son—let's go downstairs." With Eric, he moved around another sofa, and they started down the steps to the ground floor.

*

In the large room, with four windows on one wall and a worn carpet over the floor, Jay, Mex, Hugh, and Shit turned over the mattress on the sprawling, oversized four-poster—larger than a king.

"You ever been in here before?" Eric asked, when Hugh was out getting sheets.

"Sure," Dynamite said. "This used to be Kyle's daddy's bedroom. After *he* died, Kyle slept in here. So I slept in here with him. Hugh has the one next door, where Kyle's mama slept, when she was alive. I got some good memories of this place," and Eric thought: this was many houses to the many people who'd spent time there.

Dynamite's voice grew thoughtful. "But I'm *sure* I remember when Kyle used to make a fire in the fireplace…"

Holding sheets, Hugh came in. "Now it don't bother yall sleepin' in a dead man's room…? Yall ain't afraid of spooks or nothin'." He looked playful.

Shit said, "Nope."

"What?" Hugh said. "You don't believe in no spooks?"

"Naw," Shit said. "I believe in 'em—but all the spooks and me is friends, see? They protect me, run interference, make sure nothin' gonna happen to me. I never wished Shad no harm. I know he shot a couple of niggers just for the fun of it—which probably means he would'a shot you and me, if he had a chance. But he didn't. So I figure if his spook is still hangin' around, it's gonna be friendly like all the others."

"Well, that's a good attitude." Hugh unfolded the sheet, then unfolded it again—then again, as the edge swept the floor. "So you don't mind his chair, sittin' there in the corner?" It was the old wooden wheelchair. (Shit had already dropped his jeans over the arm and was walking around bare-assed in just his shirt.) "If you want, I can take it into another room."

"Well, don't do it on my account," Shit said.

Eric was thinking of the moment, on his first visit, when he'd thought he'd seen giant Shad in a giant chair, in the corner of the upstairs hall…but he was still wondering how it had been so easily and silently decided that the three of them would sleep in one bed.

Dark wooden steps led up to it.

They spread the sheets over the mattress, tucked in the bottom one— Eric skinned his knuckles on the wooden rim around the side, tugging down the upper. Over it all they unfolded a worn but warm-looking quilt.

Hugh left. Outside, rain hissed on the windows behind the long curtains, once white, now gray and yellow with time.

Dynamite said, "You gonna let me sleep on the outside? I'm the one who's gonna have to get up in the middle of the night to take a piss."

"No you won't," Eric said. "You can sleep in the middle. I wanna cuddle up to you and play with that big ol' pig fucker of yours. I look at you now and think about that pig, and I get all...you know. Excited. Christ, that's thing's amazin'!"

Shit laughed. "Hey, ol' Dynamite here wasn't gonna let none of them niggers out-do the white boy in prime nasty."

Dynamite chuckled too. "Yeah...somethin' like that."

Forty minutes later, when the lamp was out, and they all lay together, Eric said, "What you thinkin' about?"

"Kyle, I guess." Dynamite folded his hands under the back of his head. "I remember how he told me once, right here in this bed, one night, if he didn't happen to have a thing for bony red-necked white boys with bad teeth, everything about his life, includin' the Dump, would've been a lot simpler." Dynamite chuckled.

"How you mean?" Shit asked.

"Well," Dynamite said, "he wouldn't'av ever got involved with me, for one thing. You know, it's funny, just last week, Fred Hurter was sayin' since Joe and Ron went up to New Jersey, got married there, and come back, somethin' like thirty-one percent of the guys in the Dump are either married to each other or got some kind of official domestic partnership relation. You see, that's what the Dump *would've* been—just black guys with other black guys. But 'cause Kyle liked fellas like me, along with the seventy-two black guys livin there now, they got fifteen white fellas, too— includin' you, Whiteboy, and red-neck pig-fuckin' me. But you figure, if Kyle hadn't been like he was, Shit and me wouldn't've been there. That probably means you wouldn't've ended up there, neither. You know, after talkin' with Fred, I was wonderin' if maybe it wouldn't be a good idea for Shit and me to go somewhere where *we* could get married. Course, that would be incest." (Behind Eric, Shit grunted.) "And I suppose if I tried to marry the both of you, that would be bigamy."

"*And* incest, too." Eric closed his fingers around Dynamite's flaccid penis, hefting it under the covers. "All I know is that what you were doin' in that picture was a fuckin' turn-on."

Across the room, in the three-quarters dark, they could see its top over the foot of the bed. The glassed frame stood on the floor, propped against water-stained wallpaper.

"Yeah, Kyle thought so, too. That's one of the things he liked about his local white fellas—that we fucked cows and niggers and horses and pigs and goats and dogs."

"How many of you *were* there?" Eric asked.

"More than one of us," Dynamite said, "fuckin' 'im—probably in this

same bed here—that was the only way he got Miles to sell 'im his farm."
(Behind Eric, his arms around Eric's chest and his bearded chin nuzzling
Eric's neck, Shit chuckled.) "But I always figured—" Dynamite put his
arms around both boys and hugged—"I was the one he liked best—but he
had black fuck buddies, too. And a couple of Chinese ones. I mean, that's
how *I* learned they was *all* good."

"He's right about that picture," Shit said. "When I was down suckin' on
your dick, I swear, I could taste the barbecue sauce left on that damned pig
prod, after all these years, too—"

"Oh, shut up, Shit!" Dynamite gave his son a push.

"Unless that was just some old cheese you left in there for Eric." Shit
crawled over to the other side, laughing. "It's funny; I fucked a lotta people
I didn't know too well in our own bed. But this is the first time I fucked
both my favorite people who I know the best in the world in a strange
one. Hey, how come you ain't never taught me to fuck no pig? I fucked
a goddam cow a bunch a times—that's fun, but it's a mess. You gotta pull
back the tail and stick your damn hand up her ass past your goddam elbow
and pull out a handful of cow shit every ten seconds or so, or they'll crap all
over your belly—I mean, right while you're fuckin' 'em. They really like
it when you hand fuck 'em in the ass, too." He raised his fist to make rapid
punching motions. "Like that. Even so, they always gonna move around.
Then you rub up their pussies with your knuckles for a few minutes. And
they leak all that cow pussy juice over your belly and your balls, while
you're humpin' 'em. Mostly that's what turns you on, anyway—at least it
did me, so that half the time I'd end up jerkin' off all over their damn ass
with a shitty hand. So did Big John."

Dynamite frowned. "I never showed you how to fuck no cow—" he
over looked at Shit questioningly—"either. Where'd you learn?"

"Yeah, 'cause you was white, I had to show all those niggers out at the
Produce Farm I could be as nasty as they was." Shit grinned. "Otherwise
they wouldn't believe I was black. Or they pretended they didn't. Hank was
the one who would let us in and then sit on the rail and watch. He sucked
dick pretty good, too—me, John, and a couple of the horses. Stickin' my
dick in his hairy face when he'd just took a mouthful of stallion cum and his
beard was soaked with it could always get either one of us off. You have to
jerk a horse off with both hands about a foot apart, and getting the head in
your mouth is like swallowin' a goddam toilet plunger, 'cause them things
flare out at the head. Still, I seen half a dozen guys who could do it."

"Me, too," Dynamite said. "You just gotta pull it flat and force it all in.
I showed Kyle once how I could get one of them things in my mouth—
'cause he didn't believe anyone could. It turned him on for a couple of

damned days, just watchin' me." Dynamite chuckled. "He was one turned-on nigger—and the horse was happy, too."

"Damn," Shit said. "That's somethin' I ain't ever done. I'm gonna hafta try that."

Dynamite said, "Don't go and kill yourself—"

"I just mean—" Shit took his hands from under the covers—"every time we go someplace or do somethin' different, I end up learnin' somethin' about you I never knowed. Like my daddy could suck off a horse."

"I only got it to come in my mouth two or three times—" Dynamite coughed—as if remembering. "Them things'd put out enough to choke you, if you weren't ready for it. But Kyle could go crazy over them livestock—and them white boys what was into that."

"It turns me on, too," Eric said.

"That's 'cause you're half nigger," Dynamite said. "Like Shit—'cept I guess with you it's the *other* half."

Again, Shit grinned. His hand went under the quilt to join his father's around Eric's balls and cock. "At the Produce Farm, it was mostly niggers doin' all the animal fuckin'."

"How come you never told me you was into that?" Dynamite asked.

"Well, I knew you was okay about niggers. I just didn't know how you felt about no livestock."

"Oh…" Dynamite chuckled. "You know, you're more like I am than I realized, Shit."

"Hey, Eric's hard," Shit said. "I guess this stuff turns 'im on."

"Yeah…" Dynamite rolled to the side; against Eric's hip, Dynamite's own cock had hardened.

"Then, come on." Dynamite's hands moved over Eric's chest and under Eric's shoulder. "Bring yourself on over here…"

Eric breathed in deeply.

Still later, Dynamite lay on his back, arms folded on the pillow under his head. "Hugh was wonderin' about Jay showin' yall that thing, but I think Jay just put another couple of years extension on my love life. How'd a fuckin' picture like that get you two so excited?"

"I dunno," Shit said. "Probably it's just the bed—"

"Like hell it is. You two ain't been that turned on by this old man since Eric first got down here—" Dynamite stretched—"Course, I always *did* have a good time comin' out here around Christmas."

"Thinkin' about the same dick I got in my hand now—" (Dynamite's shoulder was warm under Eric's head; he held the firming cock)—"up some goddamn pig's ass, it just got me all excited. I couldn't help it."

"Well, you just cuddle up here, and keep this old pig fucker warm."

And later Eric whispered, "Shit's asleep…"

Dynamite looked down. "He is? How you know?"

"'Cause his dick's up my ass—and it's soft." (Dynamite gave a sort of soundless laugh.) Then Eric said, "I know Shit don't think fuckin' with grown ups ever bothered him. What about you? Do you think it did you any hurt? I mean when you were a kid?"

Eric felt Dynamite tense beside him; Dynamite's fingers tightened on Eric's shoulder. "Well, I had my daddy, Red, and Bulldog to pull 'im off me if he got too rough. Which he did regularly. But I sure could'a done without goddam Mikey beatin' on me every time he a stuck his goddam dick in me." He humphed. "And he did, a lot."

"Oh…" Eric said. Because of the anger in Dynamite's voice, he was surprised to see the smile on his face:

"You know, you make a pretty good pig yourself, son."

"Well." Eric shrugged. "I figure, there ain't no use to doin' nothin' if you don't *really* do it."

"Yeah, that's sounds right. You know, I always did have a good time sleepin' in this room." Dynamite yawned. "Probably it was wasted on Shad."

* * *

[45] ERIC HAD SEEN the posters around Runcible and even one on the blackboard in the Diamond Harbor Post Office, across from the wanted fliers: Father Goldridge Hanover's New Order of Holy Luminescence Rally at St. Martins in Hemmings, the Baptist Interdenominational. Under a picture of a white-haired man wearing a black coat and a white clerical collar, gazing benevolently upward, against a deep blue background over which floated heavenly clouds, red letters quivered:

ABORTION!

PERVERSION!

AIDS! SIN!

SCIENCE!

LIBERAL LIES!

DINNER WITH

$35.00 JESUS $35.00

When Eric read it out, Shit looked puzzled and asked, "Are they for 'em, or again' 'em? I like that perversion. We got a lot of that down here—but we could always use some more."

"Yeah, well…" Eric said, "The Dump's pretty good about keepin' out the AIDS. 'Course sometimes I'd feel more comfortable if I could hear a few more liberal lies—just to balance off the conservative ones. Not to mention the science."

*

Back at the cabin, Dynamite put his cell phone away in the leg pouch of his overalls. Streaked with sunset, the window above the sink looked out on cabins further west.

"Tad can't work tomorrow, and tonight's the rally at the Interdenominational in Hemmings. The Chamber of Commerce wants us to make a special run to pick up the refuse from the church tomorrow mornin'. Gonna be a lot of it—'cause they're havin' their Holy Luminescence Dinner with Jesus in the basement."

"They gonna talk about science stuff? That's too complicated," Shit said. "It just makes me feel stupid. That's why I don't like it."

"Probably," Eric said, "that's gonna be the point of the sermon. That's how they work, Shit. They tell you anything that's different from what you been hearin' all your life or makes you feel uncomfortable 'cause you don't know it already, has gotta be bad for you and you should stay away from it and vote against it." From time to time one or another religious talk show played over the Lighthouse radio, and Eric had found himself listening to them over coffee with bemused fascination. (*Well, since I don't never vote anyway, that shouldn't make no nevermind,* Shit had said.) Sometimes it even made a kind of odd sense, till they'd get on homosexuals and Eric would remember they were talking about him and Dynamite and Shit and Chef Ron and Lurrie and Mr. Potts and the guys at the Produce Farm and Mama Grace...

And Jay and Mex.

"You better be glad for that science stuff," Dynamite said. "It makes your lights go on when you flip the switch, and your cell phone connect up when I press the buttons, and your teeth fit in your head so your smile can look pretty—not to mention makes the aspirin take your headache away when you swallow a couple of them things with a glass a water."

"Well, when people talk about it, it makes *me* feel stupid," Shit said, punching his fists in the bottom of his pockets and leaning back on the cluttered table's edge.

At the sink, Dynamite turned on the water, bent down, and splashed his face. He stood up, rubbing the side of his hand across his mouth. "You sound like them people what get all upset when they hear we all come down from them hominids. When we was kids, Kyle showed it to me in a big book he had, out in his library on Gilead—you'd'a liked it, too, 'cause you didn't have to read nothin'. It was all pictures of fossils and how they all related to each other, in like a big, big tree, that went on for seven or eight pages. You used to like pictures of animals. He showed me how to follow right along with that thing. I wonder if Jay and Mex and Hugh still have that book—Kyle had books about pretty much everything. And could get 'em about anything he wanted. But all of 'em wasn't pictures like that. It would be nice if they still had it. I wouldn't mind takin' a look at it again."

"I don't like books," Shit said. "'Cause most of 'em is readin'."

"Well, not this one," Dynamite said. "There was *some* words in it—but Kyle just let us look at it and see."

"I think most of the people who don't want to be related to monkeys," Shit said, "just don't want to be related to each other. That's what it's really about."

"The point is," Eric said, "everybody's related to everybody and everything—even trees and mosquitoes and minnows flickin' around in Runcible Creek. That's kinda reassurin', I think."

Shit asked, "I wonder if Jay felt that way about bein' related to Shad?" which got them laughing, as Eric went to the refrigerator and took out the roasted pork loin he'd cooked over the weekend.

*

The motor that had more hum to it than a regular internal combustion engine revved down. Eric got out the truck, while Shit dropped to the night grass behind him.

In the three-quarter dark, black plastic sacks went more than halfway up the church's side wall—they weren't that far from Shells, where some lights still shone from the back windows, though it was past three. Because of the Rally refuse, they'd started an hour early.

A story-and-a-half high, the pile ran the length of the church.

"Damn," Shit said. "How many people come to one of these things?"

"Randal said they get as many as five or six thousand drivin' in from everywhere all over the south. But they only do the dinner for about two or three hundred, in two shifts, in the basement. The mall does great on these weekend rallies." Dynamite wandered forward, looking around. "They put speakers all over the commons out there, so people can hear the sermon. They do the dinner for the ones who'll pay out thirty-five dollars for a plate of potato salad with no celery or onions or hard-boiled egg in it, a couple o' pieces of dried out chicken, and a biscuit. But you figure, three hundred times thirty-five, for what can't cost more than a couple of bucks a piece—that Dinner with Jesus brings in some money. And they're sellin' Jesus flags and Jesus dolls and Jesus CDs and Jesus fishin' poles and pretty much Jesus everything. They do all right."

"Seems to me," Eric said, "they should feed the couple of hundred poorest folk who come to this thing, not the hundred with money—"

"Well—" Dynamite (he'd already pulled on his canvas gloves) rubbed his fists on his overall sides—"people get them ideas turned around all crazy backwards real easy." Stepping forward, he gripped three bags with one hand, then three with the other, pulled them loose—above, two sacks slipped down four and ten feet—and carried them back to toss into the truck hopper, while, lugging four more apiece, Shit, then Eric, followed.

It took twenty minutes to load up the big truck, and forty to drive to the Bottom, dump them, come back for a second load, and fill the truck again. Two trips and they'd taken maybe half the stuff.

The big truck, as Dynamite never got tired of saying, could hold some damned garbage.

Then they started in on the third. In the middle of it, when Shit had just thrown in some bags and was passing Eric on his way back to the church wall, he swung his arm around, bent over, and swiped up something from the grass. "What the fuck is this...?" He looked at what he held.

Eric stepped into the headlight.

In blue and gray, between Shit's gloved fingers, the tube was about two inches long and half an inch across. Foil gleamed at both ends.

"It looks like..." Frowning, Eric moved back so that the light fell again on Shit's grimy glove—"breath mints."

"But why's it got that picture on it?" Shit asked.

Eric pulled off one of his own gloves to lift it from Shit's hand.

"'Jesus is Coming Breath Mints,'" he read, from beside the picture of the holy face, with its downcast eyes, its beard—which a teacher had once told his class couldn't be what Jesus looked like because he was a native of the middle east and probably was more like a particularly dark Arab. "It says 'Breathe Easy'."

"Damn," Shit said. "I seen about half a dozen of these, lyin' all over." He took the mints back and pushed them at the pocket of his shirt, which was somehow still intact.

"Probably they were givin' 'em away at the rally." Eric glanced up. "Or sellin' 'em for three dollars a pack."

They went back over where, in the truck light, Dynamite was tugging loose black gleaming sacks.

When they came back to start loading for the fourth trip, all but one of the lights was out at Shells.

Eric picked up two sacks that had rolled away from the wall, tossed them, and instead of going back—it looked like Shit and Dynamite both had gotten most of them—walked around the church corner.

Yellow light slid from the crevice between the high front doors, to slant down the stone steps.

Did the same urge that had, how many years back, propelled him through Jay's home on Gilead, make Eric climb the porch, grasp the metal ring, and tug?

The door swung out, heavily but with no resistance, and not far. Wondering if its being left open was an oversight, Eric pushed sideways through. The parallel backs of blond-wood pews scored the great space, suggesting the seats in the Opera's orchestra.

Eric remembered the retreat of the dark the first time he had entered the Opera House. But here, as he looked up and around, everything seemed the Opera House's opposite. The three internal stories—a balcony was, yes, more or less flush with the gray wall—were beige, gray, and natural wood, as if it was some immense office, instead of the Opera's *faux* castle or ballroom, ornate with murals and molding. Yet, in the last century's sixties or seventies, the architect who'd designed it clearly had a sense of how beautiful the functionality of an office might be, and had cleared it of all excess to create a holy space, a modern bourse, with the austere effect of a Japanese temple or sand garden. Devoid of distracting symmetries, left and right or back and front, what held the rising space stable, with cathedral clarity, were three tall triangular windows on one wall and four on the other, each a different height. All leaned their apexes toward a spot, even higher, above the altar, where a glittering metal star (of Bethlehem...?) hung, abstract and sparkling with rays and points. Several feet below it, the simplest cross hung above the altar, even as a smaller cross of silver stood at one end—a silver chalice at the other—on the altar table's white cloth, declaring Christ's certitude.

Black tessellations told that the windows were stained glass.

For the night, though, the color was black—

—save low on two at the east wall, where a flush of gold, orange, green, and scarlet betrayed sunrise. On the wall, up near the balcony, hung six metal boxes with double cleaning lights—the same as in the Opera. Their beams fanned down the pigeon-colored plaster.

Three hefty candles flickered at different heights in tall glass tubes, inches around, in a floor-standing holder beside the organ console's ivory bulk. A white bench stood before it. The keyboard was covered.

Eric walked down the side aisle over polyurethaned wood. On the other side, at the front, he could see the pulpit, tall and unornamented. Behind it, three rows of high-backed chairs with wooden canopies awaited a choir.

As he slowed in the internal tower, Eric heard Shit call from the doors, "Hey…Eric?"

Eric looked back, to see Shit half in and half out of the door.

"*Wow*…!" Shit came all the way in, without letting the door go, eyes raised to the vaulted roof. His gloves hung from his hip pocket. His work shoes echoed. "This is…*pretty*!" Suddenly Shit leaned back out, and—his voice quieted by braced wood—Eric heard him. "Hey, dad? Dynamite—come on. Come on in and see this—"

As Shit let go of the door and stepped forward, Dynamite slipped in behind him, following him down the side, toward Eric.

Shit said, "Hey, I don't think I ever was inside one of these." He looked back at Dynamite. "Was you?"

"Not one like this." Dynamite looked up into the rising wood, the curved beige.

"What do…they do in here?" Eric asked.

"Get married," Dynamite said. "Mostly—I think. Or come around on Sundays to hear some preacher talk a whole lotta nonsense. Like all them people last night. I know they got a big kitchen and a big meetin' room in the basement what holds as many people as this does up here. Or more. That's where they had the dinner—probably."

"They sure put out a lotta garbage." Then Shit asked, "What they wanna get married for?"

"Well," Dynamite said (he didn't sound sure), "when people love each other, and have—you know—a special relationship, sometimes they want to make that…I guess, official—"

"—in a beautiful place," Eric added. "Like this. With all their friends together, I guess. That's how I figure."

The three moved a step, a step and a half closer.

Dynamite looked around.

Shit said, "We got a special relationship, too, don't we?"

"Sure," Eric said.

"Um-hm." Dynamite nodded.

Eric was not surprised when, from behind, he felt Shit's hands on his shoulders (Shit had taken off his gloves), but when they slid forward, one on each, over his chest and Shit's chest and belly moved up against his back, and Shit's arms enclosed him, more and more firmly, and he felt Shit pressing himself against his butt, now again and again—

"What the *fuck* you doin'?" Dynamite asked, though Eric was surprised he was less than half as far away as he'd been moments back.

Shit's cheek was against Eric's, and his face lowered into Eric's neck.

Shit whispered, "I thought it would be nice to have our…you know, special relationship *here*. In a real nice place."

"Come *on*," Eric said. "Cut it out, Shit. I ain't gonna let you fuck me— here! I don't got no lube in me. I left it back at home."

"Hell, I could use spit." One of his hands reached down as far as Eric's groin. "Ain't nobody here but us. Lemme pull your jeans down your butt. I'll lick out ya' asshole now and get it all nice and—"

"*No!*" Eric said. "Not…" He could feel Shit was hard and was hardening himself in response.

"What about—" Shit released him, stepped in front of him, and was up the three altar steps, to turn himself, put his hands behind his hips on the altar's cloth. He jumped up to sit back on the table, taking some cloth to the side, so that it wrinkled under his thigh—"you suck on my big black nigger dick, then? Okay…?" Shit leered around the space, eyes returning to Eric with his biggest smile. "Come *on!*" It was mostly gum. "Suck me off." (Neither father nor son had brought their teeth that morning.) Leaning forward in his sleeveless shirt, Shit pulled one hand back between his knees to rub his crotch. "Come on. You *wanna* do it. I can tell. You was hard there just a second ago—I felt you. I wanna do it, too—*now!*"

Dynamite turned and walked to the front pew, sat down, and stuck both feet out to rest his work shoes on their heels. He stretched his wiry arms along the pew's back. "I think yall *both* fuckin' crazy." Sighing, he dropped one hand, which found its way between his legs. "But I'll sit here and watch."

"Come on! Look, Shit…" though Eric was starting to smile.

"See, *he* don't mind." Shit raised his shoulders enough to get both hands between his legs, pulled down his zipper, pushed a hand inside, and levered out his cock. He began to run his left fist up and down it, at increasing speed. "We ain't hurtin' nothin'. Come on—it's real *pretty* here. *Suck* my goddam dick!"

"Okay, all right…" Eric said. "All right, I'll—" He walked up the steps in front of Shit, who was grinning even harder. As Shit took his fist away, Eric bent down and mouthed the forward curve.

"Oh, *fuck*…" Shit grunted. "Oh, yeah, that's feels *so* fuckin' good! Yeah, *suck* that big ol' thing. Ain't it feel good in your mouth? I like that, that's so nice—my fuckin' cocksucker loves me and my dick *so* goddam much, I can tell from the way he's suckin'. That's fuckin' beautiful, nigger—" One, then the other of Shit's hands curved and caged Eric's head. "Yeah, that's right, get my balls out and lick them suckers—yeah, that's good. Oh, man, this nigger cocksucker *always* knows how I like it…" Eric moved his head up and down.

Arms over Shit's thighs, while Eric sucked, his face was warm in Shit's lap and smell and the cave his belly and chest made.

Then the table moved…in a jerk.

And something pushed against Eric's arm. Raising his head, Eric saw Dynamite had left the pew, to sprint onto the dais. He too had turned and jumped back on the altar table, to sit thigh to thigh with Shit.

Dynamite hunched over, fly already wide, balls out and his own cock in his pistoning fist, his mouth half open, eyes fixed on Shit's dick which Eric took into his mouth again, prising under the skin and troweling beneath the rim, for the night's discharges.

"Oh, fuck—that's *so* good, cocksucker! Hey, my daddy's up here too, now. Yeah, go on and suck him—lemme watch you work on his dick. You look so fine suckin' his fuckin' dick. Go on. His is just as fuckin' nasty as mine—you know that. Keep suckin' that big white cracker dick, and I betcha he gonna take a piss in your mouth."

Dynamite's voice was lower, more urgent, more strained. "Go on, son—go on, suck it! Go on—yeah…" while Eric moved around their knees (Shit had put his leg over his father's), "and take my motherfuckin' dick in your motherfuckin' face, now." (Eric took Dynamite's, surprised only at how much cooler it was.) "Yeah, I'll piss in your mouth. I know you like that, son." (Eric backed off to lick and suck first one, then the other of Dynamite testicles, then went back to the cock that Dynamite had started pumping again.) "Oh, yeah, suck my Georgia redneck dick. Suck it, you goddam nigger cocksucker…"

Dynamite's whisper was low enough that Eric could imagine his not wanting someone to hear it.

Beating again, and leaning close to watch, Shit chuckled. "Hey—*I'm* the nigger here—not him. That's a goddam *white* cocksucker, Dynamite! Ain't he?" Shit's voice filled the space with its easy, loud obscenity.

"You both fuckin' niggers tonight," Dynamite said hoarsely. "Now *suck* my big white dick!"

"Oh, yeah—I see it now. Yeah, I see." Shit's voice hung between parody and ribaldry. "Yeah. *Suck* that fuckin' white dick, nigger—"

And while Eric held Dynamite's legs, Dynamite suddenly took a breath, and pushed himself off the table. "Gonna piss now. Get on down—get on down on the floor, nigger." It was eager and urging. "Gonna piss in your mouth—"

Shit was down too, holding Eric by the shoulder, as he dropped, cross-legged, on the upper step. Dynamite put his work shoes apart, pushed his skin forward with his fist. Piss shot down, in a full, spattering stream, into Eric's mouth, salty, harsh, to back up his nose with his first too-eager swallow—though he didn't choke on any.

Somewhere in there, Eric came—an orgasm muted with the strangeness of it.

Forty seconds later, as Dynamite ran out of urine, Shit said "*God* damn…!" and pumped out a load all over the side of Eric's face—two of the five spurts went in Eric's mouth.

Eric got his knees under him to kneel up, while Dynamite leaned back on the altar's edge—and, holding onto one of Dynamite's hands and one of his pockets, Eric finished him, while now and then Dynamite reached down with his free hand to rub away some of Shit's semen from Eric cheek, and suck it off his own fingers…fueling his own orgasm—

—which, as Dynamite grunted above, filled Eric's mouth. Again, Eric swallowed. He went forward, sucking deep, while Dynamite's hard, hard cock slowly, slowly softened.

Still kneeling, Eric moved back.

Dynamite's cock pulled loose, the collared head dragging Eric's cheek, leaving liquid. "That…" Eric caught his breath—"was fuckin'…intense!" Dynamite's work shoe under his knee, Eric started to stand.

"Oh, wow…!" Shit helped him, then hugged him, then stuck his tongue deep into Eric's mouth.

Dynamite moved forward from the table edge, blinking at them, breathing hard. After a moment, the lean garbage man put his arm around both boys. He pushed his face between to kiss them, first Eric, then—longer—his son, as all three held onto each other. Finally, he let them go… and went down the steps.

"Damn." Shit's arm loosened around Eric. "That's almost as good as at home. Only thing I didn't do was fuck your damn assholes—both of you. We gonna do that later?"

Eric said, "Probably—if you want."

Dynamite glanced back.

As they walked up the aisle, Shit took Eric's hand. Eric looked over to see that Shit—and his father—were both biting on their nails, vigorously, committedly. Was it nervousness…? Eric felt some himself. Only then Shit paused to say, "I feel real good now. Real good. This really is a…*real* beautiful place!"

Dynamite pulled open the door and they went through.

Outside, Eric moved off to the bushes beside the steps to tug his dick from his semen-sopped jeans—and take a piss.

Dynamite stepped up, dropped his bony fist from his mouth. "You didn't spill no piss, did you? In the church, I mean?"

"Nope," Eric said. "I didn't spill none at all."

Dynamite reached over, put two fingers in Eric's stream, then raised his hand, sucked them, and grinned. "Well, at least we got you trained so—" and went back to gnawing, as, beside them, the door closed to a sliver and the light swept from Dynamite's face and fingers—"you don't make too much of a mess." The smile had been audible.

Eric shook and put himself away.

As they walked back to the truck, Eric swiped up a last sack that had fallen beside the back wheel and hurled it into the hopper. His cock stuck to the inside of his jeans, where the load he'd spilled was already getting gluey. He scratched himself. It was also getting cool. "That place looks so much like the social service office, in the Dump—it's the same colors and everything—I wonder if it ain't Ron's. I mean, the one he should be goin' to, if he don't already."

"Hey, now," Shit said. "It do, don't it? That's *just* what it looks like…a real beautiful office. I probably wouldn't mind workin' in it—if I didn't have to read none."

Shit, then Eric, got in the cab.

Stopping outside, Dynamite called up: "Hey. You drive."

"Me?" Shit looked over, grinning. "You want me to? Yeah. Sure. Why?" Sitting up, he slid further over under the wheel.

"'Cause I feel good—and I wanna sit by the window and look out." Dynamite climbed up beside Eric. "And let everybody else do some goddam work for a change. I'm tired. And I wanna relax and get my breath."

"Sure," Shit said. He looked at Eric. "*You* feel good?"

"Yeah…" Eric admitted, as, after a proud look at the dashboard, Shit started the ignition. Eric said, "You guys made me come in my pants—again."

One hand on the wheel, with his other Shit fingered his pocket. "You wanna breath mint?"

"Naw," Dynamite said. "Them things taste funny. It's all I could do gettin' myself used to what you two taste like."

"Oh." Shit stopped fingering and took his hand down. "Yeah, I guess so." With gray, grubby fingers, again he hooked the wheel's lower rim. "Hell, I didn't feel like suckin' on Jesus anyway."

Deep blue and light blue, gold, copper, and teal, behind strips of morning cloud, the first of the day spilled between trees and houses and electric poles as they made the last trip to the Bottom—Shit had gone from gnawing to nose picking.

When Shit's wide finger—something slimy on one side, something dry hanging from it—pressed his lip, Eric started as if he had never considered the act it represented, much less indulged it. He thought he was going to jerk back: his body refused to pull way. Nor would his mouth stay closed. His head would not turn away—as if a dozen self-preservational reflexes (as had his gag reflex even before he'd come to Diamond Harbor) had deserted his body.

Shit's finger pushed in.

After prodding in his own nostril, Eric gave Shit some, who, while he drove, gripped Eric's finger between his gums (Eric was glad Shit and Dynamite both had left their teeth home that morning) holding it within his mouth, licking at the nub, releasing it only after more than a minute

Then Shit laughed and, with one hand, let go of the wheel to reach over and feel between Eric's legs. "Yeah—you come in your fuckin' pants all right. Or you busted a fuckin' egg in your pocket." He laughed even more loudly, at the joke Eric had heard eight, twelve, fifteen times in those last years.

"Hey," Dynamite said. "We ain't stopping in the middle of no more jobs to fuck around, now. Okay? You hear me?" Looking out the side window, he took a long breath. "I'm too old for it. Save that for home."

"Goddam," Shit said. "We ain't done that in a long time—had sex out on the garbage run—more'n a year. It was nice."

"Yeah," Dynamic said. "We *still* ain't doin' it no more."

For moments, the morning road got rougher.

Shit looked at Eric; Eric looked at Shit—first one, then the other chuckled.

Under them, it smoothed again.

* * *

[46] SINCE ERIC'S FIRST year at the Dump, pretty much every three weeks, sometimes every two, Dynamite had driven the boys to Turpens (where of course they absolutely *never* went) for a few hours in the johns there. Of the five bathrooms around the truck stop, two were built by Robert Kyle back when he purchased the place. The two johns in the front were mostly a waste, though most guys would at least glance in.

Making the rounds between them, you could have a fair amount of fun. A population of twenty-five or thirty people Eric had gotten to know pretty well—and an itinerant group of drive-through visitors, stopping off anywhere from five minutes to a few hours—kept you busy most days and into the evenings.

On alternate weekends, they'd spend at least one day at the Opera. Once, when Eric was twenty-four, after letting them in, Dynamite went to sit in the orchestra's front row, as usual, settle back in one of the seats near the side, open up his pants, and wait for one of a dozen regulars to come on by and service him, while Shit and Eric went off and explored various corners on their own. The first few times, it had been together, but soon pretty regularly they went off by themselves, since Shit confined himself to the orchestra and the downstairs men's room, while Eric explored the balconies, which is where most of the black guys in the theater hung out anyway. Usually in Nigger Heaven, from age eighteen to seventy-five, twenty-five or thirty black fellows usually lay back in their chairs, eyes closed—quite ready for Eric or any other halfway descent cocksucker to ease in beside them, open up their pants, and go down on them; though it took Eric three visits to learn that *all* of them were. Frank, Roggy, and Calvin would open their eyes and, if they really weren't too tired, go over the recent weather with you, comment on a basketball or football game, or recount the doings of this or that eccentric relative (often one they weren't speaking to)—while the others, whose names he didn't know, pretended to sleep through the whole thing. Other than Mac, who took forever to come, you could get a baker's dozen loads—or more—in a couple of hours.

Working his way through, Eric had already done Calvin, then Roggy, sucked on Mac for ten minutes (then left him with his dick hanging out his jeans for someone with more staying power), and was finishing another "sleeper" (Did they *tell* each other how to do it, before they started coming? Or did they just look around and imitate one another? Probably both) when, with one hand on the chair back in front of him and one on the wooden seat beside him, he pushed himself up to stand. Reaching down, Eric patted the bony shoulder in the worn plaid shirt. Without opening his eyes—or ceasing to snore—Lucius reached up and patted Eric's hand in turn. "Thanks," he said, eyes still closed. "You was good." The snore took up again. Looking around, Eric noticed a white guy in a denim jacket a dozen seats away. He stepped from the row, in the guy's direction—though not very purposefully.

Since the guy was neither sleeping nor pretending to sleep, Eric was curious. Denim jackets often meant tourists, who assumed that's what a gay country dude would wear and wanted to blend. Probably he was a visitor who had decided to check out the uppermost level.

Eric was curious whether the guy was masturbating or not—since he was sitting on his own. Sometimes that was a reason to come up here and distance oneself from the lower floors, where a lot more obvious action was going on, and guys walked up and down the aisles.

Eric went down a couple of steps and looked at the man, then away. Suddenly, he turned back and walked up again. In the flicker from the far screen, the man's hair was dark red and curly around the retreating space of a bald spot. He looked over at Eric.

Where the notion came from, he wasn't sure. But Eric began to frown.

The man frowned back. Sitting three seats in from the aisle, he seemed to be in his late-thirties.

Eric stopped walking. A row in front of him, he turned back and asked, "Eh...hey? Is your name Bill?"

The man's frown got deeper. "Yes...?"

Eric asked, "Bill...Bottom?"

With inquisitive surprise, the man said, "Yes...?" Mixing in with the frown was a puzzled smile.

"*Emet yashalom yasood ha'ollam,*" Eric said. "You had that on your door. And somethin' else in Latin. I'm Eric—you remember me?"

In the three-quarters dark, the smile and the frown that asked for more information mingled like miscible oils. "You remember *that?*"

"Yeah, but I don't remember the other one. I'm Mike Jeffers' boy."

"Of course...Eric!" Recognition illuminated the face. "*In girum imus nocte et consumimur igni.* Hello! How *are* you?" Bill Bottom leaned forward and pushed out a hand.

"*In girum...?*" Hesitating, Eric grasped it and shook. "I could never remember the other one. I don't even remember what it means. Hey—how you been? What you doin' here?"

"Just...trying to have some fun. What about you? It meant, by the way, 'We spin through the night, and are consumed by fire.' It's a palindrome."

"The same backwards and forwards—yeah, I remembered *that*. But I didn't remember the words."

"I'm here with...some friends." (Bottom kept pumping Eric's hand.) "We were driving through Runcible, on the way to Jacksonville. We'd read about this place, and we thought we'd come in. One of my friends is even a straight guy." Bottom laughed. The hand shaking stopped. "He was curious to see it. Right now it doesn't look like a lot's going on, though. I can't believe you remembered those lines—I'd almost forgotten them. For a while I thought they were really profound."

As Eric let it go, Bottom's hand seemed incredibly soft. He wondered if the more than half-a-dozen years of labor separating them had left his own hand as surprising.

"I have some friends downstairs, too." (Didn't Bill have some sort of beard the last Eric had seen him?) "But *I'm* up here suckin' my goddam brains out!"

"Yeah? I'd heard this wasn't a bad place for that. But I'd just about decided it was little over-rated—"

"You like suckin' niggers," Eric said. "I remember you tellin' me you did. You should be in hog heaven."

Bill gave a grin and a small snort. "Everybody looks like they're asleep."

"Naw—they ain't, really. Just pick out one you like, go on in the row, drop down on your knees, and open up his pants. Some of 'em are a little salty—you know, from the sweat."

"Salt I can deal with. Actually, though, I was looking for something a bit more…mutual."

"Oh," Eric said. "Well, for that, probably you do need to go downstairs—on the first floor. On the left. Don't bother any of the guys on the right. That's for the ones who wanna beat off and be left alone. I hope that's where your straight friend ended up."

"Sounds like you got a system going here." Bill grinned.

"We do." Eric chuckled. "More or less."

"This place *is* kinda famous," Bill said. "I read a couple of articles about it in some gay newspapers I was looking through last year. Isn't there someplace called…the Dump not too far from here?"

"Yeah. That's where I live," Eric said. "My friends and me. It's nice. They wrote an article? Hey, what'd it say?"

"It said some black gay philanthropist started a living development for black gay men."

"Yeah. Robert Kyle."

"Thanks to your dad, you're kinda passin', huh?"

"I dunno." Eric shrugged. "Maybe—I guess so. I'm not sure." Halfway through the sentence, he realized Bill must mean Mike, not Dynamite. "A lot of the black guys in here really like white guys—and a whole lot of others are *only* interested in other black fellows."

"That can be confusing."

"Keeps it interesting. And most of 'em don't really care one way or the other." Turning now, Eric sat down in the end seat. "Hey, you know?" He put his arm over the back of the empty seat between himself and Bill. "That was some pretty good advice you gave me."

"What advice?"

"Don't you remember—the mornin' Mike and me took off for the Harbor, here? You told me I should be ready to try anything that was gonna make me happy. And I should be ready to say yes to it."

"I did? Well, that *is* my general philosophy of life. But I said it to *you*?"

"You don't remember?"

"Not very clearly—"

"Just before you was goin' into work. You made some hot chocolate for us, and we sat out and you told me all about some nigger—a black guy in the park in New York, who took a piss in your mouth, and then wanted you to stick around so he could pimp you out—"

"I remember…the chocolate. But I told…*you* about that?"

"Yeah. A nigger pissed in *my* mouth about an hour ago—but that was downstairs. It was nice, too. He's real friendly. One of my…friends likes to watch him do it."

"I remember the man—certainly," Bill said, frowning. "I just don't remember *telling* you about it."

Eric frowned. "Damn…" He looked at the screen, then back at Bottom. "You don't remember? After you told me, you wrote out something else for me and made me put it in my pocket and only read it when I got down here…"

"I did?" Bill smiled. "I don't remember that, either."

"You don't?" Eric was surprised.

Bill shook his head.

"Well, that was some good advice, too—I mean, it took me a while to figure out what you were saying. But…"

"What was it?"

"Hey, if *you* don't remember—" Eric laughed—"I ain't gonna tell you."

"Oh, come on. I told you what the palindrome was. You got my curiosity up. I was always comin' up with funny little things for people. Who knows—I may even have a second installment for you."

"Nope." Eric laughed. "If you don't remember, it couldn't have been that important…to you. I'll keep it for myself."

Bill smiled and gave a laugh with little sound. "Okay, then." He sucked his teeth. "I won't bug you about it. Although I want you to know, this isn't easy."

"You still in the basement at Condotti's? Over by the highway?"

Bill frowned—then shook his head again, this time clearly meaning 'No.' "Oh—uh-un. I haven't been there for years. Things have really changed in Little Five Points. You wouldn't recognize Montoya Street. It's like a different neighborhood now—since they tore down the causeway and put it underground. That was almost two years of digging. You read about that, didn't you?"

"Oh, yeah—was that *our* highway they turned into a tunnel?"

"Sure was. Anyway, after your dad left, actually I had another place in the same building for a while. In fact, I moved into *you* guys' old place, on the second floor—"

"You *did*?" Eric grinned. "Wow!"

"But that was three, four years back…Then, for a year, I was working up in Chicago, before I got lonesome for the south again, spread my wide mysterious wings, and flew back to Atlanta. I don't even know if the building is still there—they built apartment towers all around there. You knew Condotti died, didn't you?"

"No…" Eric said. "I didn't. Naw, Mike never told me that. Maybe he didn't know…Hey, downstairs—" Eric lifted one foot up to the wooden seat (the chairs in Nigger Heaven were wood, without cushions)—"there's a guy who's probably just what you're looking for…in the balcony under this one—off on the right. Nice lookin' black fella—about your age, I guess."

"Really…?" Bill asked, with falling inflection.

Turning, Eric pointed at an exit above them to the back and left. "Go down them stairs, up there. You'll see 'im. As soon as you come out, you gonna see him sittin' right there. Least, that's where he usually parks himself—hey, don't fool around checkin' him out. Just go and sit next to him, get in there between his legs and take it out—he don't got no zipper on his fly, anyway—and start suckin'. He won't be asleep, neither. But that's what he likes—a white guy like you who knows what he wants. He don't take a long time, neither. And if you want his piss, after he shoots, tell him. He'll give it to you—but you'll probably smell it on 'im, anyway. He leaks like a motherfucker."

Bottom laughed. "Be still my heart." He looked around, then stood up. "I'm going to check *that* one out right now!"

"See," Eric said, "most of the guys in here ain't into courtin'—they're into corkin' any hungry cocksucker what comes around."

"A good description of yours truly—well, that's what it said in the article I read. Still, I was a little wary of…well, plunging in."

"Plunge, motherfucker. Plunge." Laughing, Eric got up and stepped out into the aisle, so that Bill could get by him. "A lot of these guys practically live in here. They can sleep when they want. Guys bring in food—Dusty and Hammond let them in and out for free, if they'll put out for the payin' customers that come around from—well, from all *over* Georgia, I guess. Like you. People come down from Atlanta, even over from Tallahassee."

"I'm in Alabama now," Bottom said, "actually. But, like I told you, I'm on my way to Florida for a while." Stepping around Eric, he glanced back. "Hey—come on. Tell me what it was I told you that you still remember."

Eric just laughed. "You better get on downstairs, before Coal Car decides to go and sit somewhere else. It don't get *real* busy till after four-thirty or five—so you'll get 'im. If it's his first one of the day, it's gonna be a big load, too."

"Coal Car? Oh, come on—be still my racist heart! My mind is not racist, but God knows—and you *are* talking to an atheist here—my dick is, I'm afraid."

"Well, so's his, white boy."

"Hey, Eric—I'm gone!" Bill chuckled. "I hope I run into you again, soon."

"If you come around here on weekends, you got a good chance of it."

Eric watched Bill hurry up the aisle toward the entrance he'd pointed to. Then, shaking his head, he turned back and sat down on the aisle seat. He wanted to rest awhile—since he'd gotten his dozen. He thought: *In girum*...But again the rest of the Latin had fled his memory. "We spin through the fire and are consumed by night..."? No, it was the other way around. So he said out loud, "Peace and truth are the foundation of the world..."

The older black fellow he'd sucked off earlier, Rudy, who sat three rows down from him, dozing, lifted his head, turned, and frowned back at Eric. Eric nodded to him, smiling. Rudy put his head back down and closed his eyes. The light from the screen played over the bald spot in the horseshoe of crinkly gray.

*

Later, when, down in the front of the orchestra, he reconnoitered with Shit and Dynamite, Eric said, "Hey, I ran into a guy I knew up in Nigger Heaven—from Atlanta. I mean, he's in Alabama now. But he used to live in Atlanta."

"Who?" Shit asked. "The nigger with the two foot long dick? Or was it the Greek fella who used to jerk off thirty-five times a day?"

Eric laughed. "It wasn't neither of them—he was just a friend of mine. Somebody I knew." A phoenix, an ape, a cockatrice...

...with wide mysterious wings.

As they walked into the sunny lobby, Dynamite fastened his coveralls. Through the glass doors, sunlight put back the lines and angles into Shit's and Dynamite's faces, marking their shared heredity. Shit took a breath. "Nigger, you talk more bullshit than any white fella I ever knowed." Absently, he reached between Eric's legs—Eric flinched a little. "Look. He got a hard-on—'cause I called him a nigger."

Eric didn't—but began to get one now. But he said, "Naw. That's 'cause before I come down, and was gonna look for my friend again, I ran into Al. He was just finishin'up and gimme his full-up raincoat. I got it on now."

"Oh, goddam—" and Shit began to grin. "We gonna have some fun tonight, ain't we? I get it next? Or are you gonna give it to the pig fucker, here?"

Not looking, Dynamite pushed open the theater door and glanced at Eric. "Sure, he gonna give it to me. Eric's a good boy—he knows his ol' man needs a little latex to keep his pecker warm, and some of that nigger lubrication to go along with it."

"But he wants to see me jerk off in it first, don't you?" Shit put his arm around Eric's shoulder. "That way, you got something to suck, ain't that right—while he's getting' it on."

"Oh, you two are crazy," Eric said. "Come on, now—"

Shit kept on grinning as they headed toward the pickup. "Well, you're the one wearin' that big nigger's scumbag—"

"I know," Eric said. "I just gotta see who treats me the nicest, when we get back to the cabin, 'fore I make up my mind."

Behind them, the theater door swung closed.

"Oh, you gonna give it to me." Shit slid his arm further around Eric's neck to hook him closer.

"Hey, watch it—"

But Shit got Eric in a headlock, while three people came down the street, passed them, to stop at the Opera's ticket booth—while a grinning Dynamite opened the truck's left hand door.

***

[47] SHORTLY BEFORE HIS twenty-fifth birthday, during Mike's fifth visit to Diamond Harbor since he'd brought Eric to the town eight years ago (none had lasted more than a couple of hours), Eric told his dad.

Later, he tried to figure out why he'd chosen then to do it. But it seemed, if anything, his stepfather might soon be too old to understand.

Recently Mike had been paroled after another year-and-a-half in jail. (More coke.) Arrested along with him, Doneesha had lost her nursing job over that. They were no longer together.

In the shadowy cabin at the Dump's edge with no light in the front room and a screen but no glass in one window, junk piled all through (the Bowflex was in there, somewhere, unused for the last years and buried under cushions and folded canvas tarpaulins and lawnmower parts and behind half a fiberglass rowboat and cases of tools and cartons of outdated carburetor components), Mike said, "How you mean you been together with this barefoot retard since you was sixteen? I didn't bring you *down* here till you was seventeen."

Eric looked serious and didn't correct him.

Mike said, "I think you're crazy. I think you're an asshole—but, then, it's your ass. Yeah, I got my dick sucked a couple a times when I was in the pokey—my first stretch." (That surprised Eric.) "Not this last one, though. But *you*, well, I guess they ain't put *you* in jail…yet." At which point Dog-Dog, the year-old half-Rottweiler, half-mutt and the scrappiest boy-pup in the litter Sam Quasha's bitch had thrown a couple of years back (Shit was standing, in the corner, shirtless, quiet, and curious, digging a thick forefinger in a broad nostril), chose then to hoist his hind leg beside the right ankle of Mike's slacks. "Aw, *fuck*…! You guys is *nuts*!" Looking down—"*Aw*, Jesus…!" —Mike stepped about unhappily, tracking the puddle over the cabin's sand-colored floorboards. (Shit used the distraction to eat his pickings, which Eric saw but Mike didn't—or, anyway, gave no more response to it than when he used to catch Eric at it.) "And *you* don't got nothin' to say about any of this—sleepin' in the same room with 'em?"

Standing by the always wide-open door (mostly for light), Dynamite said, "Dog-Dog's a good li'l sonofabitch, only he ain't a real house dog yet."

Shit said, "I almost got him trained where he'll do like my old dog Tom used to do—drop a turd right on my bare foot, outside in the grass, turn around, and lick it right up off my toes. Mex'll do that, too, sometimes. He's Jay's—"

"Come *on*, now," Eric said, softly and firmly; so, blinking around, Shit shut up and began to gnaw at the stub of the nail on his thumb.

Mike said, "I don't mean *that!*" He was responding to Dynamite's achieved apology, not Shit's broached enormity—which hadn't registered, since Mike had never met Mex *or* Jay. "Jesus—you and these guys and the fuckin' dog is *all* takin' your turns with each other? God *damn*, Eric…!"

Standing by the opened back-kitchen door, in his overalls and buttonless shirt, biting at the wreck of his own thumbnail, Dynamite repeated over a callused knuckle what, seven years back, he'd said to Barbara: "They're good boys. They work hard—and they don't get in no trouble."

Shaking his head, Mike stepped out of the garbage men's cabin, onto the sagging porch boards under evening's pale, pale gold. Above, gulls floated on long arcs. Their whines came up the slope, over the day. "Hey—I'm runnin' up to Runcible to see Barbara and Ron, anyway." The permanence of Barb and Ron's relation had eventually let Mike, in his intermittent visits, enjoy them socially—at least for a brief hour or two; though this would be his first without Doneesha. Going to see them now, Eric realized, Mike felt vaguely unprotected: where, Eric wondered, had *he* learned that? Mike turned back to call in through the door: "And I ain't saying *nothin'* about none of this to your mama. *You* can do that when you're ready. Jesus *Christ*…!" Frowning down, again Mike shook his pants cuff.

"I already told her." Eric's voice came out after him. "She knows." Inside, someone was blowing his nose, either out on the floor or into his hand.

(Whether it was Dynamite, Shit, or Eric, Mike couldn't tell.)

Starting back for the pickup in which he'd driven down, Mike shook his head. Borrowed for the visit, it had no AC. By now, both of Dynamite's trucks, the ethyl alcohol pickup and the full solar powered ten-wheeler, did. Last Spring the Chamber of Commerce had given Dynamite a grant toward four-fifths of the big truck's (used) price.

On the slope behind the cabin, grasses and squat bushes passed their wutherings up the Dump's bluff.

* * *

[48] A CHRISTMAS OR so following, Big Man Markum had them down to his dad's place for a party with some friends from the Opera and The Slide. Before going off to a visit with an ex-wife, Joe Markum had turned the house over to his son with a exhortation not make too much of a mess.

When they came in the front door, Shit said, "Hey, Big Man. How you doin'? You're lookin' good."

Eric and Dynamite came in behind him.

Big Man wore a maroon denim suit, one leg pinned up and sewed closed, and a white shirt of some shiny cloth under a deep red sports jacket. "Hey, Shit," Big Man returned, looking up with his wide-spaced eyes and broadly spaced teeth. "Eric—Mr. Haskell. Good yall got here. Come on in."

Shit stepped inside. "Can I carry you around a little?"

Eric said: "I can carry him, some, if you want—"

Beyond the arch into the living room, they could see half a dozen men stood or sat. Two were in wheelchairs.

"I'll do it first," Shit said. "If I get tired, you can have 'im."

"Just for a few minutes." Balancing on his one foot—the smaller otiose leg hung inside his pants—Big Man held up both his arms, his single crutch in one hand. "But I'm gonna walk mostly tonight. Don't worry. I got lots of places to sit."

"I know." Shit, who was in his usual worn short-sleeve shirt, ragged work pants, and falling apart sneakers, bent down and lifted him in both arms. "But we just like carryin' you."

"And I *like* 'em carryin' me." Big Man said to Dynamite. In a practiced move, the forty-eight pound dwarf turned himself so that his butt was back on Shit's strong forearm. "But sometimes you kinda forget I get around okay by myself. You're gonna have to put me down, real soon." He spoke to Shit. "We got people here, and I have to be sociable. Come on—watch out for my pee sack. It'll be a mess if it comes loose."

"Don't I know it?" Shit laughed.

So did Eric.

The polyethylene bag was strapped to the outside of Big Man's working hip. Though often, when he went out, he wore it inside his pants, he'd explained it was more comfortable outside. The tube snaked in through an opening beside his fly.

As they went through the arch, several of the men—all black, Eric saw—said hello. Others of them smiled. Big Man said, "That's Pike. And that's Kelly—you probably know him already." That was a guy in a motorized wheelchair. "He lives up there with you guys in the Dump. Hey, what you wigglin' you hand back there for, Shit? This is a goddam dinner party—not a fuck fest." He grinned.

"I know, I know," Shit said. "It's a Christmas party."

"It ain't no Christmas party," Big Man said. "That's one of the things me and my dad differ on. I told you on the phone when I invited yall, this is a celebration of the fact that on January second, they gonna officially restart the space program. That's what it is. It ain't got nothin' to do with *nothin'* Christian. I don't think them religion things is no good for nobody—none of 'em. Especially me."

A few men laughed.

There was a Christmas tree, however, though its decorations were stars and ringed planets and spaceships—at least half a dozen various-sized versions of the Millennium Falcon, the Enterprise, the Roq, and Avatar dragons—along with comets and meteors, and even plastic rayguns. (Those were Big Man's, who was a committed science fiction fan.) Probably because it was Mr. Markum's floor of the house, though, red ropes of Christmas cards—oversized colorful ones from his construction clients—hung under the mantel and on the upper edges of the glassed-in china cases around the living room walls, behind overstuffed chairs.

"Hey—" Big Man said. "I'm serious now." (Perhaps Shit's fingers had started "wiggling" again.) "Don't try to carry me off and fuck me in some other room—much as I would enjoy it. I wanna stay in here and talk with people."

"What about Eric?" Shit grinned at the fellow in his arms. "He could probably take you off on the back porch or somethin' and bone you even quicker than I could. He'll have you back here in five minutes. Neither one of us takes long when we gotta hurry."

Dynamite grinned—but Pike, about twenty (who wore orange, black, and green plaid slacks), Eric saw, looked surprised, if not appalled, by the banter.

"Come on. I'm serious, now. Between Danny outside and you two in here, I don't want this to turn into no fuckin' animal house."

Dynamite chuckled. "You know, my boys here can be a little crude. Come on, Shit—keep it in your pants."

"Hey," Big man said, "time to put me down, now. I wanna walk."

At which point, a heavy man—the only one Eric had seen in a sport coat besides Big Man—came through a swinging door from the pantry or the kitchen, carrying a frosted bowl. "Anyone want some eggnog? It's ready." He lugged it over to a sideboard that looked a little too big for the living room and set it on a silver tray, circled with glass cups. "We couldn't find no ladle." The man stood up and turned.

"Just use a cup there for a dipper. Come *on*, Shit! Don't fuck around. Put me down." And Shit set Big Man on the green rug, while the dwarf got his rubber crutch tip planted, to pull the bar back under his arm. "You want a cup, Mr. Haskell?"

"Sure," Dynamite said.

(With one hand Shit held up his waist and with the other reached down inside his jeans. Carrying Big Man had apparently given Shit a boner.)

"Jimmy—dip out a cup for Dynamite here. He's an old friend of my daddy's. Everybody go on and get some." Big Man turned back to Dynamite. "Too bad he ain't still here to say hello to you, sir."

"Oh, I see him now and then when him and his guys come up to the Dump to do some repair work. Oh—" and Dynamite turned to take a cup of eggnog. "Thank you, Kelly. Good to see you."

A few minutes later, leaning on his crutch, Big Man called to everybody. "Hey, come on out and meet Buddy and Danny." The black dwarf led them over the green carpet, through the swinging door, into the kitchen, where, at sink and stove and counter, four of Big Man's friends—three black fellows in jeans and one in a very frilly apron—were cooking. One of the black guys, Larson (a clothing salesman at the Hemmings Mall), seemed in charge.

That night it was a roast beef dinner, Big Man explained.

Greased muffin trays of greenish metal—they looked as if they'd been used many times before—stood along the counter. "After Thanksgiving, I'm so tired of turkey—" Big Man laughed—"I don't know what to do. Larson says I should leave it all to him. He says he's gonna make Yorkshire puddin' with it."

"That's *just* what I say." Larson wore a bright red shirt.

Big Man pushed open the kitchen door, and they followed his short, swaying figure outside onto the boards. "Hey—and out here's is where I keep my friend, Danny."

Larson stepped out behind them. "Danny, do you or Buddy want some water?"

Eric looked back and saw Larson was holding a metal dish. He put the dish down by the side of the door on the porch's green boards.

Big Man laughed. "What Danny wants is a *beer!*"

"Actually—" Larson snorted—"I was thinking more of Buddy."

In the steel gray afternoon, his back to them, on the top step sat what looked like a hulking, blond farm boy—near Eric's age, maybe twenty-seven or twenty-eight. Now he looked over his shoulder, smiled, then stood. Chains dragged (Eric heard them before he saw them), as he turned to grin. Danny was still thickly muscular, with bright blue eyes and all smile. As he stood, swaying a little, Eric saw that—again—he wore no shirt, but a black leather upper body harness over his muscular chest and full shoulders. His stomach was ridged as deeply as Eric's.

Nor, again, was there a crotch in his jeans.

This time he wore no jockstrap, either.

The denim had been cut away, and the edges reinforced with brown leather. Below his belt buckle—and further below a red-brown tuft of pubic hair—heavy genitals hung loose and low. In scuffed black engineer's boots, Danny put one foot up on the top step. On his arms and pectorals were the old tats—jailhouse work, rather than Cassandra's elegant decorations: a lopsided swastika; a childish skull; a World-War II fighter swooped over his forearm; the word "FUCK" and a capital "U" were inked above one pec—and, Eric saw, the tear, under the outer corner of one friendly blue eye—like Cassandra's two.

(Eric tried to remember if they'd all been there at The Slide that first afternoon. Was it five years back…? Or seven…?)

"Hello…" Danny raised his hand. "Yall here for Christmas? That's real nice. Me, too."

Just behind Eric, Shit said, "Hey, ain't you the bouncer what used to work up at the Slide?"

A black mongrel looking dog walked up the steps. It could have been from the same litter as Uncle Tom. It took a few steps over the porch, stopped, and looked around with lolling tongue.

Danny nodded. "Naw—I ain't been there in a few years. Saul didn't want me around no more. Said I got on his nerves." He looked very happy. "I been workin' a real job for a while, though. At the factory over at Hemmings. I gotta work with fuckin' white guys. But they leave me alone, pretty much. And I don't mess with 'em. Big Man said me and Buddy could come down here and have ourselves some Christmas with yall." He bent down and roughed the dog's head, then went back to looking around at them. "I'll have a lot more fun here."

On his crutch, Big Man hobbled forward. "Now most of my friends, I guess it's no surprise—" He reached down and lifted his translucent urine bag, a third full—"are pretty much into piss, *one* way or the other." Some laughed. "I guess they gotta be to stay friends with me. But this ain't no orgy—piss or any other kind."

Kelly said, "Hey, don't go makin' judgments about *all* your friends, now, Little Man—some of us, you know, just *like* you."

Three of the other called out, "*Big* Man...It's Big Man, Kelly! *Big* Man..."

Kelly said, "I'm sorry. I *meant* Big Man. I used to have another little person for a friend. See. We called him Little Man. That's all."

"Yeah, yeah," Big Man said. "I know, all us little people look alike."

The others laughed again.

Big Man went on, "Naw, it's a party. This ain't no fuck fest—unusual as that is for me. Remember that. Still, if you want somethin' special, don't come botherin' me for it. Bring your glass out here, or you can get it right from the source—" Reaching over, he lifted Danny's cock in his thick, stubby hand. "If you know Danny, you know he ain't gonna mind. He got his case of beer right here for the night." The carton sat to the side of the upper step. Three king-sized Coors cans already stood beside it on the porch's green boards.

Some of the guys laughed.

In another yard, lights went on in two windows with wreaths in them, scored by the slats of Venetian blinds. It was overcast enough so—though it was not yet three o'clock (the hour set for dinner)—it wasn't surprising.

Though he wasn't Al, Danny was pretty well hung. He smiled down, where Big Man held his penis.

"There ain't a better Piss Master on the goddam Georgia coast than Danny Turpens."

Danny said, "Yeah, I can be a Piss Master, but—" actually he sounded sheepish—"really, I'm a fuckin' slave. It's nice of you guys to let me and Buddy come here, and it's real nice of Big Man to chain me up back here so me and Buddy can have some Christmas, too."

Kelly said, "You ain't comin' in with *us*...?"

"Naw." Danny practically beamed. "Big Man ain't gonna let me in there with you black fellas."

Big Man drew himself up on his crutch and barked like Marine Sergeant Ermey, "*Tell me why, you white piece of crap!*"

Eric, who had been to bed with Big Man half a dozen times, with and without Shit, was surprised that that much sound could come from him.

With his farm boy grin cast down at the porch Danny moved the toe of his boot back and forth. "'Cause I'm too low down and even nastier than *you* are." He glanced up at the guys. "So he gonna keep me chained up back here—with my dog, Buddy."

Eric noted no chain held the dog.

One black guy who'd come out with them asked someone beside him in a kind of nervous way, "That's what he *wants*...?"

"Naw," Danny said, "he ain't gonna let me inside. I gotta stay out here, in the back."

Big Man let Danny go. Danny's eight-inch cock flopped down over his testicles.

Leaning on his crutch, with his broad dwarf's head and his maroon suit, the little fellow lumbered around on the porch. "That there is gonna be Danny's Christmas dinner." He pointed to a metal bowl beside where Larson had set the water dish. "That is to say, Danny and Buddy's Space Program Recommencement dinner," he corrected himself. "Right? So when yall finished eatin', you come on out and scrape your plates into that bowl, there. Then you can leave the plates up on the table over there. Okay? You got to do that, otherwise they ain't gonna get nothin' to eat. Understand?"

"Big Man gonna keep me chained up out here, while you guys have fun inside. I'll be here if you need anything off me. But that's how me and Buddy gonna have our Christmas." Danny nodded. "Me and Buddy *always* eat out the same dish—we share our food."

Behind the bowl stood three glass Mason jars. One already had three inches of clear yellow liquid in it.

(It was maybe forty-five degrees out, but Danny didn't seem to mind.)

Walking over—the links clinked—to stand behind it, Danny scratched his pubis in his cutaway jeans, then took his penis in his own hand, and pointed it down. A stream of urine fell into the jar's rim. "I don't lie about it. I'm a fuckin' beer drunk—but I really have to cut it out." As his water roared into the Mason jar, through the glass Eric could see the surface become froth. "When you fellas wandered out here, I was about to take a leak anyway." He looked around with his farm boy grin, while his water chattered down. "Anybody want some? Come on and get it, if you want. I don't care. If I'm pissin', anybody can bend down and take a drink." Nobody said anything. Eric looked around to see some of the black fellows were grinning, though. "Well," Danny said, seconds later, when he was running out, "maybe after a while, then, when things are gettin' on. Doc says if I drink too much more beer, it's gonna kill me. But I been drinkin' pretty steady, since I was a kid—'cept for when they put me in the jail. The

Doc says that year off from the suds is the only reason I'm alive—I couldn't drink for a year, 'cause I was locked up. Well, maybe someday I'll be able to quit. But not for a while, I don't think."

Danny shook himself, then ran his thumb over his cock head, then underneath and around what Eric had only recently heard someone in the Dump call a "Georgia sun hat." Letting himself go, he put his thumb in his mouth to suck away the urine. "That stuff is good…" He grinned at them. "But you—" he pointed to one of the older black men watching—"already know that, don't you. Yeah, I remember you. You musta drunk a couple of gallons of it back behind The Slide. Right?"

Over by some shovels and rakes in a corner, someone else chuckled.

"Okay, now," Big Man said. "Come on. Let's go back in and have us some good times and some good dinner, and leave Danny and Buddy to their thing out here—" he reached over and rubbed the dog's head, who got up and began first to lick his hand, then turned and started nuzzling and licking the urine bag—"Hey…!" Big Man stepped back. "Cut it out, dog! You bite a hole in this thing and *I'll* bite your fuckin' nuts off!"

"He likes it 'cause it probably got some salt," Danny said. "From the piss."

"Oh, yeah?" Big Man said. He stepped back again. "Well, fuck *him!*"

The guys laughed again.

As Danny turned, Eric saw now that his crotchless jeans were completely split up the back, so that moments of pale skin flicked between the edge, as he went back down a couple of steps.

Shit must have seen it the same time. "Hey—"

Danny looked back. "Huh?"

"You ain't got no ass in your pants," Shit said. "Can we fuck you?"

Dynamite said, "Come on, Shit. Big Man already told us, this ain't a fuckin' party. It's just for eatin' and talkin'."

"Well, I mean," Shit said, "I wouldn't take him inside. I'm cool with that. But since it was out here, I thought maybe—"

Danny reached up to grip the chain attached to his leather collar. "Naw—the Big Man ain't gonna let me come in there with you guys. I gonna stay outside with Buddy."

"You wavin' your dick around," Shit said, "and anybody who wants can get a drink or a suck, I just thought, since your asshole was flickin' in the wind, maybe you wouldn't mind a dick or so up that thing."

Danny said, "You niggers can do whatever the fuck you want with me—long as it's okay with Big Man, here. That nigger's the boss tonight, ain't he?"

"Come on." Big Man started back across the porch. "Whatever you do out here's fine, long as nobody starts screamin' bloody murder. You know, we got people livin' next door." (As if in response, two more windows in another house lit up.) "Let's go inside. I'm gettin' hungry."

Danny laughed. "And I'm gettin' fuckin' thirsty." Stepping from the jars to the carton—the Coors—he bent. (The flaps of his jeans slipped open over a slice of white buttocks, split by the crevice between.) Pulling loose another king-sized can, he stood, popped the top, and upended it over his mouth, while, with his other hand, he moiled his genitals.

As they started back in—ahead, the wheels on Pike's chair bumped over the sill—Shit said to Eric, "Hey, that's neat. Havin' your own slave outside—like Bull and Whiteboy." Beside them, Eric saw, Buddy sat, then stretched out on the porch, muzzle along the boards.

Shit said softly, "You remember Danny?"

"Sure, back when you first took me over to Saul's."

In the efficient looking kitchen, Larson had half removed the roasting pan from the upper oven and was ladling hot grease from it into one of the muffin tins, while Earnest, with a bowl of batter, beside him, spooned it into the tin. Immediately it bubbled and hissed, as—spoon after spoon—he filled one cup after another.

A dubious Shit whispered in Eric's ear, "What's that...?"

"I don't know," Eric said, "but Chef Ron ought to be here. That's somethin', huh?"

"Maybe," Shit said. "I guess so. It smells a little funny—but it looks interestin'."

"That's the puddin'," Earnest said, glancing at them. "The Yorkshire puddin'. Now, come on, get outta here—or it won't be no surprise."

Moments later, as they were leaving to go back into the living room, roast and muffin pan both went back into the upper oven.

Still later, when they were eating, Shit said, "It's fried bread—that's all it is!" (Shit's judgment.) "I guess it's...okay," while others were more praiseful.

There was a fair amount of joking, and Kelly and Pike got into an argument about gay spirituality and black spirituality and whether there were similarities—Pike was the one who had sounded uncomfortable about leaving Danny out back.

That's when Eric looked up to see that Shit was gone. Minutes later, while the lazy conversation moved to laughter and back, among the men sitting around, some with beer cans on their own, some with glasses of red wine, Shit came back in, looking very pleased. Every once in a while, Shit adjusted or rubbed at his crotch.

Waking up in the big wing chair, Dynamite asked, "What'd you do with your plate?"

"I scraped it into the dog bowl and left it outside on the table like I was supposed to," Shit said jocularly. He shook his head, then said, "*He* don't never think I can do *anything* right."

One of the other guests—Larson—looked over; and Eric realized that he probably hadn't realized Shit and Dynamite were father and son; or nephew and uncle; or lover and lover; or whatever...

One of the others—who apparently did—laughed.

Jesus, Eric thought. I bet he was out there and fucked that goddam drunk! Next he thought, I could use a glass of beer piss myself. Dad's and Shit's is always so strong. And I'm pretty full—maybe, just so I can tell Shit I did it. And also to see if the guy can still walk. Eric carried his plate through the kitchen, clinked all his silver but his knife into the sink, where it was piled for rinsing, then went outside.

Beside the mason jars, the dog dish was half full of scraps, beef and vegetables...and a couple of Yorkshire puddings (probably from guests who'd felt about them like Shit had). The first Mason jar was filled with gold urine, greenish in the evening overcast. The other two were about a quarter full each.

Two cardboard flaps had been ripped from the beer case. Half a dozen cans stood next to it—empties, Eric assumed.

Danny sat a step down, leaning over, doing something. Over his sculpted shoulder, a black strap loosened and tightened on its steel ring, as he moved his muscular arm.

Eric stopped to scrape his own leavings into the dog bowl—using the knife—then stacked the plate on top of the others on the table corner.

Inside the conversation had been interesting enough so that he hadn't noticed when men had left it or returned. He stepped over to see what Danny was doing.

Buddy was on the step below the big country boy. The dog lay on his back, head up and panting. On the step above, knees jackknifed and leaning wide apart, Danny had reached down with one hand to hold the dog's penis in his labor hardened fist, massaging it. Three inches of red and white streaked inner cock thrust from its sheath as Danny rubbed. Now and again, Buddy leaned forward and licked at himself. Danny looked up, with the same grin he'd had before—and kept rubbing. From his unfocused smile, Eric realized he was more drunk than before.

"Hi—Danny Turpens." Danny reintroduced himself, then raised his other hand and thrust it toward Eric; clearly he had no particular memory of Eric among the others.

Eric took it and shook; his grip was firm, dry, and rough.

"Eric Jeffers," Eric said.

The grip between them held long enough for Danny to start smiling even more. "I'm just makin' sure ol' Buddy here gets some Christmas, too." The chain from Danny's neck draped over one knee. "He really likes it when I jerk him off. You ever suck a dog?"

"A few times," Eric said. "We got one, back in the Dump. We just about got 'im so he'll climbs into bed with us, and Shit likes to watch me do that. So does my dad—Dynamite. It gives 'im somethin' to beat off over."

"It does? Lucky you." Danny chuckled. "My daddy caught me doin' that once and like to fuckin' kill me. But that was before I went to jail. He's the one whose cockamamie scheme got me in there in the first place. He's still *in* the fuckin' hoosegow—'cause the drunken ol' fool accidentally kilt a damned guard trying to rip off that old warehouse."

"How did he…accidentally kill 'im?"

"Hit a guard in the head with a length of pipe—an' the dumb bastard had a heart attack and died. Ain't that a bitch? Hit somebody in the head, and because he got a weak heart, it stops. You know, when I was in jail, they kept on tellin' me that niggers wasn't really human. They was all really animals—and I used to pray that they was right. I can't even hardly go to bed with most white guys, unless I pretend they're at least *half* some kind of animal. You know what I mean? Course, if you're at this party, I guess you gotta be part animal yourself. Right? So I could probably fuck with you—if you wanted to." He frowned at Eric, as though the ghost of a memory remained. "Big Man is fun—he's easy to fuck with. He's like fuckin' with a monkey or a raccoon—some animal that's always pissin' all over you." Danny shook his head. "Since my daddy's been away, I can live by myself, and I can do whatever the fuck I want. I been suckin' off this hound every day since I goddam got the sonofabitch. He loves it, too. He come right in my mouth. You got to hold it real firm, though—otherwise he gonna pull loose. See, they can lick themselves, but they can't make themselves shoot. They need a person for that. That's why man is dog's best friend. Or somethin'. You wanna suck 'im? I mean, you know how to do it so the sonofabitch'll come? That's what I was gonna do—"

"Naw," Eric said. "Naw, that's all right."

"So, what can I do for you?" Danny looked quizzical.

"I want some goddam piss." Eric grinned. "That's what I want."

Danny reached down to lift his genitals from where they splayed on green painted wood. "Well, you come to the right boy. Actually I was tryin' to make up my mind whether I was gonna take me another leak or suck off my damned dog again. You want it right out the spigot, or—if you like—I'll do it in an empty can, and you can take it inside with you and nurse it awhile."

"I might do both," Eric said.

"That's fine too." Danny leaned forward, stood up, turned and climbed back up to the top step. "Come on—get down on your knees. I can't hold her back too much longer."

Eric went forward and down—and got a splash on his cheek, before he got it in his mouth. One of the things Eric had learned at the Slide was that, with most pissers, you had to keep your tongue away from the head. Usually, any touch would stop the flow.

Not Danny.

Eric's tongue was all over his cockhead, and deep into the piss slit as well, his tongue only pushed out by the stream's force. After he ran out, Eric sucked for another minute, before Danny asked, "You okay?"

Eric pulled off. "Yeah, I'm fine. That was nice."

Released from his grip and flopping down, Danny's cock began to drip on the boards. "Three of them cans next to the case is already full—but if you don't mind waitin' a few minutes, I'll have to go again in ten minutes. I'll fill up one with some hot stuff, and you can take it inside." Danny stepped over, pulled another king-sized Coors from the case, popped it, upended it, then picked up another can already sitting out, shook it to make sure nothing was in it, and brought both back to the steps. "Come on and sit down with me—we can jaw a spell and swap lies." He lowered himself. "Or you can just sit and watch me suck off Buddy. You wanna jerk off while I do it, I don't care. You say your kinfolk like doin' that anyway…"

Eric laughed, then went to sit next to Danny on the steps, who held both the cans down between his knees, now. "It's funny, every time my daddy ever remembered I was a goddam faggot, he'd try to fuckin' kill me. But I think, sometimes, bein' a goddam faggot—especially the kind of faggot I am—was the luckiest thing what ever happened to me. I mean, I met so many interestin' people—and interestin' *kinds* of people. Like Big Man—I never would of knowed him if I wasn't. I wouldn't be out here, haven't this nice talk on Christmas Day with you—or all these guys. You know, where I live, I don't sleep inside no more, I sleep out on the ground, most nights, on some old blankets, with Buddy. I drink my case of beer, pass out, and hug on that hound, and pretty much every night I piss all over the two of us. Sometimes I wake up, and he's up and lickin' my nuts, or eatin' out my ass. It's nice. I got a couple niggers—they're the same way, just *like* Buddy—only they bring the beer. That's how I met Big Man. They come on out to my place, we drink beer together till I pass out on them blankets under the stars, and I hug on 'em all night long, and pee all over 'em. I don't know why, but they really like when I do it in my sleep. After a while, I wake up and they're suckin' my dick, or lickin' out my hole—like

Buddy. I'll fart in their face or somethin'. Niggers like that. Probably 'cause I'm white. Only Buddy likes it, too, and I don't think he really knows. Like I say, I don't like real people too much, but niggers and other animals is okay. I guess that's why I like you. 'Cause you're a nigger—I can tell."

Eric chuckled. "Hey. You ever run into somebody named Jay MacAmon?"

"Huh?" Danny hefted the two cans. Raising one, he drank. "I heard the name—MacAmon. I mean, I'm a Turpens, so we all know that name. But I ain't actually met too many of 'em."

"That's the name of the truck stop," Eric said.

"Yeah," Danny said. "Turpens used to be in my family. Before that crazy nigger Robert Kyle bought the damned thing from my great uncle, Joe Turpens—back at the beginning of the 'eighties."

"'A Georgia institution since nineteen thirty-six,'" Eric quoted.

"A Georgia institution for a lot longer than that!" Danny looked at Eric. "That's just when it used to be a real weigh station and everything. That place goes back before World War I. Probably back to the Civil War. We just didn't want our name on it till after prohibition was over. 'Cause it was always for guys pullin' illegal loads and gin runners and crap like that—plus, it was the same kind of faggot hangout even back then, like it is today." He laughed again. "But then that crazy faggot nigger, Robert Kyle, decided, I guess, he was gonna make it a *famous* faggot hangout, back in the eighties or something—and bought it off of Uncle Joe, 'cause he still had the papers on it. By that time there wasn't too much left of the Turpens family. We's all pretty much what we are now—drunken thugs, doin' crazy shit all up and down the coast, with all of us in and out of jail every other year—*that's* if we're lucky." Again, Danny shook his head. "Jay MacAmon—I think an uncle or somethin' of his kilt a cousin of mine, once, in a car wreck or somethin', on I-22. I was just a baby when it happened, but I heard about it a lot growin' up. That's right, Franklin Turpens. MacAmon's uncle was…Shad MacAmon…? I remember they said *he* got messed up real bad. But Franklin was fuckin' *dead!* We all thought it shoulda been the other way around."

Eric frowned. "That's right…Your cousin worked for Mr. Johnston back then, didn't he?"

"Hell, all us Turpens work for Johnston one time or another—except me. That damned Johnston asshole is the worst thing that ever happened to us Turpens, if you bother to ask Danny Turpens, here. He comes up with some fool scheme and goes out and gets a bunch of Turpens—and maybe a few Wilsons and a couple of Ricketts—gets 'em drunk first; then tells 'em to do it for 'im. Only we're the ones what get caught and end up goin' to jail. And 'cause we used to be a little higher and mightier than we are, we're fools enough to keep on doin' it, like somehow it's gonna get us somethin'…Fuckin' asshole!" Again, Danny looked down at the two cans. "I mean, my daddy would wanna smack me in the head with a two-by-four if he heard me sayin' it, but sometimes I think Kyle had the right ideas, about helpin' faggots to get organized and get somethin' for themselves. I mean, I was a goddam bouncer in The Slide—best fuckin' time I ever had. The Slide's just as much Kyle's as goddam Turpens is today." He shook his head. "The best time—'cept when I'm sleepin' out on my blankets, with Buddy. Or with one of my niggers." Again he looked up, with his drunken grin. "You ever go to bed with Big Man?"

"Sure," Eric said. "Me and Shit both fucked around with him."

"That black cut-down half-pint is a fuckin' mess, ain't he?" Danny grinned. "I mean, you been up in his part of the house. Upstairs—through the fire door his dad put in for the smell."

"Sure."

"That place stinks like my goddam yard and my goddam blankets when it ain't rained for a fuckin' month. With that fuckin' piss bag of his, when he takes his hose loose off his pecker—man, that's pretty foul. I love it, though. He's gonna keep me chained up here in the back till after you all go. Then he's gonna let me in and maybe help him clean up a little. I love takin' orders from that little guy—I mean, if I can still stand up and ain't passed out, yet. Then we're gonna go up to his part of the house and mess around. I mean, get the two of us wrastlin' around together and we're a fuckin' mess, man. Oh, here we come—here it comes. I'm gettin' ready." Danny slid forward so that his genitals slipped off the step's edge—

"Hey, don't get no splinters—!"

"Don't worry. I been sittin' here all day, and I ain't gotten none yet." Danny moved one of the cans under his long-collared cock head. "Grab my cock there and point it in there for me, so I don't piss all over the stairs, okay? We'll get you a nice hot can." He raised the other can and drank.

Eric reached over, put one hand on his thigh, and held Danny's thick cock—which began to squirt. Drunk or not, apparently he'd had some practice, and his water chattered into the hole in the can top.

Then Buddy was up, pushing his head over Danny's far leg, to lick, spilling urine over Danny's rough thumb.

"*Get* the fuck off, dog!" Danny barked. "You can have some later. This is for the damned nigger here."

Buddy yanked back and looked up at his master, then at the can.

"You don't mind a little dog spit in with your piss, do you?" Danny asked. "Most niggers don't. Buddy and me kiss on each other all the time, and I ain't never come down with nothin'."

"Naw," Eric said, chuckling. "I guess not."

Danny drank from his beer some more—and pissed some more in the empty hanging in his fingers, between his shins.

Finished drinking, Danny wiped his mouth with his wrist, then set the new empty on the step beside him. The urine still flowed, though, and the sound from within the can grew higher and higher.

Again, Buddy started forward.

"*Get* back there, you sonofabitch!" (Buddy jerked back.) "You'll get yours. You know I don't forget you." Grabbing Buddy's collar with his free hand, he held him away.

When his urine ran out, his cock dripped on his thumb. Danny raised the can, sucked his knuckle, then offered the can to Eric. Suddenly he brought it back, took a drink, then offered it again. "Yeah, that's real hot—good beer piss. I was checkin' it for you, you fuckin' nigger scumbag. Hope it's to your taste." He grinned at Eric.

Eric laughed again. "Thanks." He took the can, took a long drink, then nodded. "Yeah. That's nice."

"Wow," Danny said. "This has been such a fuckin' great Christmas, with all you niggers. Really. The way Big Man got me all chained up back here and won't let a piece of fuckin' white trash shit like me into his house—with all you niggers. That's so great. Hey. You know what the last guy who came out did?'

"What?" Eric drank more.

"It was fuckin' amazin'," Danny said. "He come out here, made me lean over the rail, and fucked my goddam ass—'cause I'm so drunk, he didn't even use no spit. Then, you know what?"

"What?" Eric asked again.

"*He* pissed in our food bowl. Then he made me eat it—Buddy ate some too. At home, me and Buddy always eat out the same bowl." Danny, Eric realized, was repeating himself. "I mean, that's real nice when people do that who wanna do it 'cause they know you like it. It makes you feel good. In jail guys'd gang up on me, once they found out I'd do that kinda stuff—and they'd make me do it. And laugh at me—and beat me up, sometimes. And, you know, *sometimes* I could even pretend that they was really bein' nice. But it ain't the same."

Eric said. "That was my brother—Shit."

"Your brother?" Danny looked surprised. "The *other* nigger?"

"Yeah—he's a nice guy like that."

"Oh…*Wow*! Yeah, it's better when they're doin' it 'cause they like you."

"I gotta go inside now." Eric stood up. (Buddy got loose and began to lick Danny's cheek.) "You're a real good Piss Master, Danny—and a real good slave."

"Thank you," Danny said, unsteadily. "Hey, you niggers are really lucky. And I'm pretty lucky to know you."

Eric went back through the kitchen and took his beer can into the living room to sit down and rejoin the conversation that had moved onto the media's suppression of gay news.

Soon, outside, headlights swept across the living room window curtains, and Eric heard a car pull up. Suddenly, Big Man was standing, saying jocularly but quickly, "I think it's time to break the party up and send you fellas back home now. I hope you had a good time." They'd come in about one. Dinner had been at three thirty, so that to Eric, used to going to bed in sunlight, it didn't seem so early.

From his chair, Pike said, "That roast beef was out of this world, man."

"Thank Larson, Bill, Sammy, and Leonard, for that," Big Man said, swaying on his crutch.

In the vestibule, a key turned.

"My dad's back, and I told him I was gonna have yall out of here by the time he come home."

"Oh," Pike said. "Yeah, sure. Where did you put the jackets...?"

"In there," Big Man said.

Then the door swung open. A broad black fellow in slacks and work shoes came into the room. "Hello, guys. Yall still here havin' fun?"

"They was on their way, Dad," Big Man said. "I thought you said you was comin' back at seven or seven-thirty. It's ain't six forty-five."

"Yeah, I'm sorry. I'm a little early. Hey, yall don't have to run outa here like that."

"No," Kelly said, returning with his overcoat. "No. We were just gettin' ready to go, anyway, Mr. Markum. Besides, we ate up all your food."

"No. No..." Mr. Markum said. "No. Really, I come home a little earlier than I said I was. I know that...

Big Man said, "They ain't ate it *all*. There's still enough for you to have a plate full. And one tomorrow. And one the next day. And one the day after that, too—probably."

Markum looked around. "Hey—Dynamite Haskell? What are you doin' here with all these crazy fellas?"

"I was here with my boys." Smiling Dynamite, a head taller than Markum, stood up out of the chair. "Your son put out a real nice Christmas spread for us, Joe."

Big Man just smiled—and did not chose then to correct him on the occasion's celebratory nature.

"Hey," Markum said. "I knowed this fellow for years. He was Robert Kyle's friend, back when I was first building all them houses for 'im, over in the Dump. And—what, now you're livin' in one of them, I hear."

"That's right." Dynamite looked around. "You know my boy—Morgan."

"This is...Morgan?" Markum sounded astonished. "My God, son— last time I seen you, you was—what? Ten years old? Eleven? I seen him come in here a couple of times with Big Man. But I didn't realize you was Dynamite Haskell's boy. Probably I should'a figured it out. "

Behind him, one and another of the men were pumping Big Man's hand and slipping out. Pike called, "Merry Christmas, everybody!"

"And Happy Space Program," Big Man said, as Pike's wheels thumped. "And this here is Eric—who works with us on the garbage run."

"Yeah, I seen him come here, too. But now it's good to know who you are, son. Eric, huh? You wanna sit a spell, maybe have another drink?"

"Naw," Dynamite said. "We got to get up and go to work tomorrow, anyway."

"I think," Shit said, "I better be the...what do they call it? Designated driver? I had *one* cup of eggnog, when I come in. That was gonna be your job, Eric, but I seen you slip out and come back four or five times in the last couple of hours, stealin' poor Danny's Christmas beers." Shit made a mock disgusted sound, then grinned at Eric. "So I guess I'm the one, huh?"

Markum frowned. "Is *he* here...?"

"Yeah," Big Man said. "Danny's out on the kitchen porch."

Markum shook his head. "Am I supposed to go out there and say hello to 'im and Merry Christmas? I mean, if he's got on them crazy pants with nothin' over his privates, I...well, I admit it. I try to be open-minded, but I just don't feel comfortable walkin' up to a man dressed that way and shakin' his hand. I keep thinkin' he expects me to shake somethin' else. And that just ain't the way I'm built."

Big Man stepped back around to say, "Dad, it's just Danny. You don't got to do *nothin'* with him, if you don't want. Leave 'im out there. I'll take 'im up to my place by the back way. If you're still hungry, like I say, there's some good roast beef in the refrigerator. Whack yourself off a couple of slices. And there's some slaw out there that won't quit. And half a pot of greens. There's still some yams. You can make you a nice plate of leftovers. And we'll get out of your hair."

"Well, yeah, that right considerate of you." Joe Markum looked around, and seeing that it was down to Eric, Shit, and Dynamite, he seemed to relax. "The truth is, I *am* pretty tired. I went over to Jordan's—that's my second ex-wife—she invites me every year, and every year I say I ain't goin' again. Then I do—and after three hours there, I'm so uncomfortable I wanna scream sometimes. That's why I come home so early. I'm really sorry, son—especially if I broke up your party."

"Naw," Big Man said. "Maybe if it was the first time you done it, but the truth is I was kinda ready for it. Hey, thank yall for comin'. Maybe we'll see each other at the Opera or somethin' like that. I gotta get that drunken skunk up to my place before he makes a *real* mess. I really like him—he can be lots of fun." Leaving Mr. Markum at the door to the kitchen, Big Man walked across the living room to the front door with Shit and Eric, Dynamite ambling behind him. "Hey, you know what that crazy drunk told me the other day?" Big Man asked, under his breath, grinning now at one, now at the other. "He told me there ain't really no black folk in the world at all, there're nothin' but niggers. And he said that's was 'cause niggers was a lot more powerful. Call somebody a nigger," he said, "and you make 'em angry, or you make 'em laugh, or sometimes you can even make 'em cry—and sometimes you can even give 'em a woodie. But when you call somebody black, he said, it don't do *nothin'*!" He laughed. "Danny really tickles me sometimes. He got a real interestin' way of lookin' at things. But he can be more of a slob than I am. And that's sayin' somethin'. Good-night, Shit, Eric—Mr. Haskell."

*

In the pickup, Shit drove them back up toward Diamond Harbor. Dynamite sat in the middle.

"You have a good time?" Eric asked.

"Huh?" Dynamite said. "Yeah. Sure. Them yams were good. So were them greens. The slaw was nice, but your potato salad's better."

"Thanks," Eric said. "You just didn't say very much."

"Well," Dynamite said. "I like listenin'."

"He slept for half the party." Shit looked alertly over the wheel, out the windshield onto the dark road.

Dynamite laughed. "I don't know. I guess I'm kinda like Danny."

"What you mean?" Eric asked.

"Danny really likes bein' out there in the back," Shit explained, "when there's party goin' on. He likes listenin' to it, and that makes him feel good. But he don't really wanna be inside with the people. Havin' to talk, and what all, that's worrisome to him. I think Dynamite's like that." Looking out at the oncoming lights, he made a face. "White guys."

"Yeah." Dynamite laughed. "I guess that's kinda the way it was."

"He just wants to be there and get drunk and play with his dog." Shit looked across his father at Eric. "By the way, I knew damned well that wasn't beer in them beer cans you was drinkin'. I just was lookin' for an excuse to drive. I thought that was a pretty good one."

Eric laughed.

Dynamite said, "I knew it wasn't no beer, neither. Whyn't you ask me to come out there with you—I was gettin' a little jealous of that boy, son. Once when you was out there with 'im, Big Man told us he was a Turpens, you know. I don't know about *that* one—but you seen all the jailhouse work all over 'im. Most of them fellas ain't very nice people."

Maybe Dynamite didn't remember Danny from Hammond's tale, Eric thought, all those years back.

After a moment, Shit leered across at Eric. "You fuck 'im?"

"Once," Eric admitted.

"I boned his butt out there on the back porch *three* goddam fuckin' times. Left a load in 'im, with every one, too!" Shit laughed, and hauled on the wheel. "You know, seein' that wasn't no orgy or no fuck fest, but just a regular...Space Program dinner, I think I had me a pretty good time, even with all the bullshit they was talkin' in there."

The pickup pulled through the darkness, sea visible, when outside Eric's window, trees lowered to the right.

After a while, Dynamite said, "Hey, let's go home, get in bed, hold onto each other real tight, and get some sleep—so we can do some fuckin' work tomorrow."

*

After New Years, winter lingered even past Shit's birthday into the months usually marked as spring. On a late May night, Eric lifted up the quilt to slide under, as Shit rolled against him, heating him with shoulder pushing shoulder, toes gripping ankle. Eric grunted, "Don't knock me out the fuckin' bed—!"

"I ain't. I'm just tryin' to get you warm. What happened tonight?"

"The debate was kinda in'erestin'. Kyle—on that computer screen they had in there—said what Kyle says—and Johnston said his usual thing—about how, because of the depression, we have to knuckle under to outside economic forces. He called it adjustin'. I'm glad Kyle's the one with more money."

Shit chuckled. "You sound like Dynamite," who snored over on his side.

"Mr. Potts was there—I said hello to him, too."

"Good," Shit grunted. "He say anything back?"

"Nodded—kinda grunted. Lurrie was down—he said to tell you hello."

"Yeah?"

"You know that boy's twenty-four years old now? He's wants us to come over to his new place, he says, and look at his yard—maybe do some levelin'."

"We could do that. Did he have his...what did he used to call it, his inner consciousness out there, floppin' around?"

"Naw." Eric chuckled. "Naw, but he had his cute Haitian boyfriend with him."

"The one I fucked down at Turpens last month?" The cabin bedroom at night was a geometry of shadow.

"Probably." Eric moved his elbow up under him. "You know, it occurred to me, listenin' to them talking in the Social Services Meetin' Room tonight, how Johnston ain't nothin' but another rich white boy who didn't want niggers to have *nothin'*. And he ain't even interested in white folks havin' too much either, unless they already got a whole lot of money and want to give *him* some. And that's gay *or* straight."

"Yeah, that's what Dynamite always says." Shit put his hand, rough as stone, on the side of Eric's face.

"And what'd Dynamite used to say about Kyle?"

Shit laughed. "That he was a crazy nigger whose parents had more money than God. His great-grandmamma—Mr. Kyle's that is—was some kind of artist—a white woman. She inherited all these millions of dollars—back when a million dollars meant somethin', I guess. She was kinda like your mama. I mean, she really liked black men. When she was twenty-nine, she married one of 'em, even though it was against the law. I mean, she'd been livin' with 'im for six years, already. The story everybody used to tell was that he couldn't read or write when she met him—like me—but five or six years later, he become this lawyer; and four years after that, he was a millionaire on his own. He was one of the guys who made them little radios—that went from tubes to those little things..."

"Chips?" Eric said. "Now, I didn't know *that* before. Or do you mean transistors—?"

"Yeah. I think the second one you said. And you know those doors that open when you walk up to them, like in the supermarket or the bus depot, in Runcible? He invented those, too, or backed 'em, or manufactured 'em— or, anyway, made a *whole* lot of money off 'em. Course Kyle used to tell my daddy that people sayin' Mr. Kyle, her nigger husband, couldn't read and write when she married him was crazy. She used to tell her grandkids that it was a lot closer to the truth that *he* taught *her!* Eventually, when Kyle was eighteen, nineteen, all that money went to him—for a while he was the richest nigger in Georgia. Maybe in the country. And he got the idea that he wanted to put a lot of that money back into the community—the black gay community—so he put about ten million dollars into the Dump, at the end of the seventies. I mean, that's all. It wasn't even that much—just a pip on his fortune. But 'cause he was a black faggot, it was the black faggot part he put his money in. He put Jay in charge—he was gonna make Dynamite in charge of part of it, too, but Dynamite said that wasn't what he was good at, and he didn't wanna do it. Besides, they figured Jay was already one too many white men in the organization. And Jay said he'd only do it if he could do it while he ran the scow back and forth."

"If he wanted a black guy, why didn't he get his cousin Hugh to do it?"

"'Cause Hugh don't got the personality for it. Hugh helps Jay do all the paperwork—that's his part. And he took care of Shad. Anyway, when we fell on hard times and was livin' between the truck, the boathouse, and Jay's, Kyle asked my daddy what he wanted to do. He said he'd be the garbage man, if he could have a place to live. So..." Shit shrugged. "Kyle said sure." Eric felt and heard, rather than saw, Shit grin. "My daddy said as long as there was niggers around who wanted to fuck and suck with him, and nigger garbage to haul away, he'd be happy."

The snoring had stopped some seconds ago. From the bed's edge, Dynamite said, "Shit...will you shut the fuck up? You gonna have this white boy thinkin' I'm more of a redneck racist than I am. You got to remember, Eric was raised mostly black—that stuff's important to him. Like it *should* be to you!"

"It's important to me," Shit said. "The niggers around here won't let it *not* be important to me. And *you* drum more of that stuff into my head than most of *them* do. You been boned by so much damned nigger dick, it's got you blacker than me."

"Good." The spring groaned as Dynamite turned.

"Hey," Eric said, "I don't think you're no redneck racist!"

"Well, I am." He could hear Dynamite's smile.

"Why?" Eric asked. "You raised Shit and—"

"'Cause I was born down here and grew up down here and the richest nigger in Georgia was me and Jay's best friend and fuck buddy from the time we was eleven years old till we was almost twenty. No—Kyle showed me that."

"How?" Eric put his arm over Dynamite's shoulder, at the same time Shit's arm fell over his, and he felt the older boy pull himself closer.

"By givin' me all the niggers I could want to suck my dick, to fuck my ass, and all the nigger garbage on this part of the coast to haul off to the Bottom." He chuckled—and Eric realized, though Dynamite's arm had fallen over Eric, his hand was back further, holding his son. "He did it by makin' me fuckin' happy. That's how." And as Eric's naked belly and front pushed against Dynamite's, Shit's pushed against Eric's back.

Wedged between them, Eric said, "Shit, you *should* come to the town meetin's. You live here. We vote on things that affect all of us. That's how they keep the Dump a good place to live, where you, me, *and* people like Potts can all get along."

"Naw." Shit's voice was soft and rough over his own shoulder. "I ain't goin'. Stop it, now. I been to 'em—"

Dynamite said, "When you was a kid—"

"Look. I can't read." (He knew Shit was pressing the side of his face ever more firmly into the pillow.) "And I can't understand that stuff. Tryin' to makes me feel fuckin' awful. You goin' for me—you know that! I get in some place like that where people gonna expect me to understand somethin' that I can't, and it makes feel like I'm on the top of a big tall cliff and there ain't go rail and I'm gonna fall off and—"

"Yeah, I know. Come here, now. I know." Between them Eric twisted himself over, onto his back. Both their arms moved around him, their cocks bars on either hip. Dynamite's sleepy tasting mouth found his, to pour his tongue into him—until Shit's face displaced his father's. Shit's tongue pushed aside Dynamite's, falling and troweling around Eric's.

How, Eric wondered, would you describe the difference in tastes? Or was it more a difference in energies?

While Dynamite rubbed his engorged groin regularly, lazily on Eric's hip, Shit took a deep breath and said, "Look. We get into this argument almost once every three months—in one way or another. And it makes me feel like hell for the next three days. Could we...just not *do* it no more?"

Actually surprised, Eric said, "Sure...!" Although he hadn't realized he'd been arguing. And then, "I won't."

"Okay," Shit said. "*Now* let's get warm!"

"Hey..." Dynamite said. "Thanks for goin' to that thing for me. You can tell me about it tomorrow..." and, as Eric turned toward him now, so that the curve of Dynamite's body grew more protective, and probably, again, the lanky man slept, while Shit began to push harder, rhythmically, finally to reach down and position his cockhead in Eric's butthole.

* * *

[49] YEARS LATER, BECAUSE Shad's death and Big Man's Space Program celebration were both within days of Christmas, memory squeezed out the years between. Several times Eric talked of the Christmas when Shad had died *and* Big Man had given his Space Program Celebration Party, where they'd run into Danny Turpens doing his slave bit on the back porch, while memories were displaced before or after this—now—singularized point...

But, thus, the middle years of many not committed to chronicling their own lives' folds and foreshortenings produce the effect by which the recent past rushes by far faster than the past of our childhoods.

Over time, Shit and Eric were no more exempt from this than anyone else.

Eric kept the garbage collecting job—and enjoyed it; and enjoyed living in Dynamite's cluttered cabin with him and Shit, while, day following day, year following year, his heart sped up on entering the acceptance within it and, finally, stilled so that he could participate in it comfortably and enjoy it as much as Shit did, as he enjoyed the time around it with its labor and its looseness—for twenty-one fairly complicated years.

* * *

[50] ONE AUTUMN AFTERNOON, Shit and Eric dropped into the Harbor and wandered into the Lighthouse. They slid into a side booth—and Eric felt Shit's foot settle over his, under the table beside the wall.

(Barbara had not worked there for more than six years...)

Two tables away sat Darrell, a retired black state trooper with a wide brown leather belt and a cowboy-style leather hat, who had been married and had five adult children, and who, a year after his wife died of diverticular complications, had announced he was gay and moved into the Dump—with a black, unmarried carpenter, Renfrew, a year his senior. Wife or no wife, both men claimed they'd had a twenty-nine year relationship, though Darrell still preferred Diamond Harbor proper to the Dump for socializing; his friends were here.

He had been in the Lighthouse the afternoon Eric had arrived at the Harbor with Mike.

There today, Darrell was explaining something to a white lady who worked in the Post Office, and whose name, Emma Cready, Eric had only known for three years, though he had seen her forever. Two days before, five women, between twenty-one and thirty-two, among the last of the summer folk, who—with a number of others—had been using the old South End of Diamond Harbor Beach for nude swimming and sun bathing, and had, after being out on the sand, walked through town—topless—to come into the Lighthouse, sit down, and ask for coffee, "Just like in one of them big cities what you see on television, where the women go swimming and walking around the boardwalks like that *all* the time! To be honest, I thought it was nice, for once, to see us lookin' like we wasn't the armpit of the universe, twenty years behind everybody else, gettin' all upset and askin' 'em to leave and stuff. And Jane, who is a perfectly modern and intelligent woman, went right over, took their order and smiled—then brought them their pastry and coffee. The only thing about it all was when one of them dropped a piece of pecan pie off her fork, right down between her, you…know what I'm talkin' about. She had to wipe herself—the sides of her titties, there—with a napkin. But I guess she was as nervous as they were makin' everybody else in here, at least at first. I wanted to kinda laugh. But I was laughin' *with* 'em. Not at 'em."

To Darrell's tale, Emma said repeatedly, "Well, I don't know…I just don't know…I mean, that's certainly not the way we do things here…So I really don't know."

And Darrell said, "Well, maybe we got to *start* doin' things differently. Look at the Dump. I bet *you* remember when people used to talk about Kyle like he was the Creature from the Black Lagoon or somethin', settin' up a Temple to the Antichrist hisself—when all he was, was a man puttin' up some houses where people like me and Renfew could live a comfortable life."

And Emma—who, yes, drank tea with lemon—sipped and said, "Well, I just don't know."

In their side booth, Eric leaned across the table said quietly, "You interested in seein' that?"

"Seein' what?" Shit answered. "They been swimmin' around here nekid since I was a kid—at the South End, I mean. Topless, bottomless, any other kind of 'less.' People who wanted to do that, that's' why they come to the Harbor, instead of goin' over to Runcible and Hemmings and them beaches there. Naw—I already seen it. A bunch a topless women sittin' here in the Lighthouse drinkin' coffee? That ain't gonna look too different from a bunch of topless women sittin' on towels and beach chairs drinkin' pop out the cooler. It's the same thing like in the Opera, ain't it? I mean in them movies." Topless beach scenes were a staple of the pornographic features at the Opera House—often in the sunset settings before the obligatory lesbian love scene.

"Yeah," Eric said. "Well, I guess so."

"On the way home," Shit asked, "you wanna stop by and sneak a peek through the bushes? Kids used to do that on the way home from school, when I was comin' up. You can still do it—it's easy. If they're any of them out there, you'll see 'em."

"I already done that," Eric said—some half a dozen times in his early years.

Another day, they came in and caught Izaak, the current owner—he was leaving later that afternoon—saying, "But I don't interfere. The TV says that's what they're doin' all over these days. Though, I swear, it was all I could do, the first time, not to go up to those women, and tell them, 'That's just *not* the way we do it here.' But, I guess now we…do. It was comical. I mean, I walked up to that table, all big and brave, ready to make my announcement. Then, when I got there, all I could say was, 'Would you ladies like some more coffee?' Probably that's because Jane had been servin' 'em for a week already. I mean, it would look too funny, after all this time, makin' a big thing out of it *now*. Jane had already made it clear she didn't mind. And she's the one whose got to serve 'em. But, before, they always came in when I was in the back or out."

Ten minutes later, outside, several walked past the Lighthouse Coffee & Egg. Half a dozen customers got up and went to the window to watch them go by. Eric had asked Shit, "Does that turn you on?"

Shit had stayed at the table.

"Your fuckin' *dick* turns me on!" Shit's foot—today, he was wearing work shoes, a pair Barbara had given him the year before last—pushed down on Eric's, almost hard enough to make Eric cry out. (But he grinned.) "Naw," Shit repeated. "It's just like the movies at the Opera—that's all."

A few times, apparently, Dynamite told them, when, sitting on the cabin steps, they were eating Eric's shepherd's pie, within the month *he'd* snuck out to the beach to look through the grass and see. "I guess I shouldn't'a been sneakin'. But they're nice to look at." Both boys had teased their dad about turning straight.

While gulls creaked above the Dump, Dynamite said to Shit, "Ain't *you* glad I'm straight as I am—or your black ass wouldn't *be* here, nigger!"

Saturday, *The Hemmings Herald*, August 12, 2021, printed a photograph of six topless women (with two male friends) sitting on the beach, under a headline, "Yankee Ways Hit South Beach"—calling the South End after the famous Miami strip had been a running joke in Diamond Harbor for thirty years—and the subhead: "And *Almost* Knock Us Out of the Water!"

The article detailed how a state trooper had started to ask them to leave, then changed his mind.

* * *

[51] THOSE WITH A penchant for history are often fascinated by the logic of "Wonder Decades": the eighteen nineties, the nineteen twenties, the eighteen thirties…

The first such decade which the twenty-first century presented the world was, of course, the thirties—if we can look ahead a moment.

As commentators of any sophistication have realized, however, such decades are always something of an illusion. During their passage, often they are only recognized as wondrous by a few particularly vocal folk. Half their aura may, indeed, be the present excitement, which a few artists, a few cultural philosophers sense. Finally, they are incomprehensible if one does not pay serious attention to the decade before.

In the eighteen-seventies, Walter Pater called their iconic figures, new and common, "diaphanous," that is to say, transparent to the forces of history. But the other half is a hindsight that grows from an awareness of the greatness of the change, the break, the rupture with what came before—and with what is to come.

Their spectacular moments speak of years of development and preparation, which only historians truly appreciate, while in later decades people look at these images and assume they represent sudden and marvelous—or catastrophic, it barely matters—transitions.

Take an arbitrary image defining the nineteen-sixties: The photograph from the August 28, 1963, March on Washington for Jobs and Freedom, when 187,000 blacks and 63,000 whites rode on more than two thousand busses into the nation's capital. (The night before in Ghana, at age ninety-five, Dr. W. E. B. Du Bois had died.) So many of us know that image of Dr. Martin Luther King, Jr., on the steps of the Lincoln Memorial, hand high, head up, greeting with his dream the heads stretching into the distance— thousands and thousands—around the mall pool's reflecting rectangle, to the spire of the Washington Monument and beyond. What a spontaneous outpouring of revolutionary zeal!

Certainly that *is* America's nineteen sixties.

But both students and working folk from the nineteen-seventies, eighties, nineties, and the century beyond—unless they have studied the matter—are probably unaware, however, that, during the fifties, and even the forties and thirties, hundreds and hundreds of marches on the capitol took place, when loads of citizens left by bus from New Jersey and Kentucky and Kansas and Maryland and West Virginia and Florida and Tennessee and Ohio and Pennsylvania and New England and New York to convene before the Capitol Building. Some, yes, were as small as thirty or forty marchers. Some had only a hundred or so. Others had a thousand, or three thousand, or five. At least one had more than sixty thousand. Not ten, not twenty-five, not forty, but hundreds of such marches—and the connections and networking and organization and planning that grew up to facilitate these fifties "freedom marches," and before—for soon that is what they were called—made possible the great March of August '63.

It's hard to imagine an American who has not seen the picture of the outpouring of afternoon amblers in New York City's Columbus Circle on that uncharacteristically warm April 26, 2032, men and women, many holding hands, many laughing, almost everyone smiling, most wearing open jackets, so brightly colored, black folk and white, Asian and Latino, the women topless, the young men shirtless, middle aged, and older. (Could such a gathering have taken place had not iPhones and iPads given way to airPhones and airPads—a techno-social shift completed in the first third of the twenties, another change transforming the look of cities…wholly bypassing Shit, Eric, and Diamond Harbor?) That image represents the thirties for many. As recently as three years before, it would have been impossible to find a public street in a major city, a third of the people airBorn, save in a few Bohemian enclaves (and even there the feel would have been very different), with such a look.

For many in the country—in the world—that picture *is* the American twenty-thirties.

Neither Shit nor Eric saw that particular photograph until well into the forties, however—in a montage displayed in a retro-thirties-clothing store window on Gilead Island. And certainly neither one particularly noted it, when he did, though both had long ago grown accustomed to the cultural situation it pictured. Both were enough outside the culture's mainstream that they were among the least aware of how ubiquitous that spectacularly joyous image had become.

(*Dreyfus, qui ca…?*)

In twenty years, it had been reproduced half again as many times as the picture of sailors and their girlfriends in Times Square on D-Day. Again, however, only an historian would realize that, all through the twenties—and, indeed, well before—as if in cultural preparation for that ebullient afternoon of sartorial freedom, hundreds of local newspapers around the country, not on page one, but on page three, and page five, and page twelve, had featured pictures such as we have cited from the Saturday, August 12, 2021 *Hemmings Herald*, which would ready the nation for the change that would be culturally acceptable ten years later.

For all of Eric's adolescent interest in history (and life had worn much of it away), that is not where history had taken him. Ten, fourteen, eighteen years after that picture, neither Eric nor Shit was particularly aware, at least at the time, that a wonder decade was occurring—and Shit would not have believed it had he been told.

* * *

[52] WHENEVER HE USED to see Miss Louise in town, regularly Eric said hello—to her and fifteen others. Then, somehow, she was dead (three days; four months;…)—and Ran's Grocery stood where they'd bulldozed away her house. Then, six years on, Ran had given up the store and the place was another boarded-up wreck—though the road was paved now. It hadn't been, that first night, how many years ago back in 'oh-seven.

The fact is, Eric didn't retain that much from his early days in Diamond Harbor, though he felt he remembered *most* of what had happened; still, it was simpler not to argue with Shit, especially if the argument had no consequences—and usually it didn't. More times they ended up laughing than not.

Odd, Eric thought, how time's machinery moved moments out of initial wonder into the everyday to the blurred recall of the blurred—

Walking on the beach, Eric would think through the details he'd preserved: What happens to a late-middle-aged man, shirtless, six-four, with pumped, tattooed arms, on a house deck in front of massed greenery, with his mute, stocky partner…?—no, *was* that Miss Louise? A woman, at a table, smoking and drinking coffee at four in the morning? (*Naw*, Shit said. *I don't remember who it was, but I don't think it was her*…) Or a crude father (almost as tall as Jay), out beside a garbage pickup before dawn, joking more suggestively with his illegitimate son than Eric had ever imagined, in a way that had both terrified and thrilled?

Or that same man easing more and more into calling you "son" and his son referring to you more and more as his "brother," whom you slept with—both of them—daily?

Dynamite's blocky hand, dry and pumping one moment, the next webbed with a flush of mucus, from knuckle to knuckle, puddling over the crevices in his palm as his hand peeled gluily from his thick-veined cock. Cum pearled the hair on wrist and abdomen as he raised his palm to spill into his gap-toothed mouth, before he sucked these two, then those two fingers, licked the back, the front, the sides—(*Yeah. I eat mine too. Like you. Always have; always will. But Shit don't. That's 'cause it ain't snot, though Dr. Greene says it might as well be. Maybe you want some…?* Dynamite had said on the third time he'd jerked off in the truck cab with the boys and offered his wet, knuckley hand for Eric to share, which today Eric remembered each time he did it, in bed or on the porch, as if it were the refrain of a country-and-western song) an almost daily happening, for a while, that mesmerized Shit and could always pull from him a second—or a third—orgasm, no matter how recent the one before. More than blow jobs or fucking or even nose pickings shared with Eric—a lazy, even a gentle perversion, after all— *that* was the habit Eric shared with Dynamite that bound Shit to Eric, as

Eric was bound to Shit's dad.

One night, thunder's grumble had risen over the hiss of rain, till it crackled apart.

From the lamp on the night table, under the vellum shade, gold light came on to fall across the bed. Naked, Shit stood beside it, hard flanks glistening, hair and tufted beard droplet speckled. "Hey…! You gonna get up and come with me? It's a good one!"

"Wha'…?" Eric blinked and got his elbows under him. "What is…?"

"Come on!" Shit reached out a hard, wet hand. "Bull let a bunch of people out his cellar to show 'em the storm. You wanna watch, too?"

Naked on his back, Dynamite flung a forearm over his face and grunted. "Seen it…"

"Come *on*, Eric!" Shit's voice was rough and low, as if he didn't want to wake his dad completely.

Groggily, Eric sat. Reaching over, he ran a hand under Dynamite's testicles, leaned down, and nuzzled the warm flesh moving over moving fingers. "Love you, you big-balled bastard."

Dynamite's other hand dropped to rub Eric's head.

Pulling away, Eric slid over the semen-roughened stretch of sheet he and Shit slept on toward the bed's edge.

Half crouched, Shit whispered, "Come *on*…!"

Eric stood up on the rug; Shit grinned at him. "I love it when you do like that, nuzzle on his nuts and stuff." On Shit's face frown and smile, wonder and certainty mixed. "You love that man, don't you?"

Eric chuckled. He bent, reached under the lampshade, and pulled the chain. The room filled with chatter of falling rain and rain-filtered moonlight and thunder. "You like watchin' that?" Standing, Eric put a hand on Shit's wet shoulder. "How come?"

"It makes it easier to remember how much *I* love 'im." They stepped through the doorway, with its tattered curtain, onto the wet deck. As they tromped down the sopping steps, for the first thirty seconds the rain—on Eric's shoulders, nape, the backs of his hands, his butt—was cold. Then, as they pushed through slopping ferns, the peppering—as August rains did—became a neutral surround.

The third time Eric stumbled on something and almost fell to one knee, Shit seized up his hand. "Hold onto me—you still half asleep!"

"It's two in the *mornin'*! What the fuck you expect?"

They came from prickly brush onto the road that was two inches of mud; it swallowed Eric's feet and held him by the ankles.

Eric looked at the wild clouds wriggling down the night over the bluff.

As they passed Bull's porch, the front door stood wide. The flame and bronze and leather interior flickered, as if with firelight. Turning at the muddy road's corner, they went toward the cliffs.

The ten-foot doors to Bull's basement dungeon were open, out and back. Thunder's grumble, which had accompanied them, rose again, so that Eric had the impression of great doings in the darkness, though logic said their neighbor's cellar dungeon was empty. He found it as hard to walk as it was sometimes in a dream— wondering for a moment if he *was* awake.

"Hey—what you two doin' out? I ain't never seen you at one of these before?" It was Chef Ron. Beside him was Joe—in a leather body harness. Both wore baggy shorts. Both smiled in the intermittent moonlight—they, too, were holding hands.

"Most of the time we're workin'," Shit said. "But tomorrow we got a day off. So this is probably Eric's first one. You know, you gotta get a storm and Bull and the week's calendar all comin' together. And usually it don't work that way—"

Joe said, "The last time Bull done it, it was back in March—or maybe even February. That's a little cold for me—"

"What about your uncle?" Ron asked.

Shit laughed. "He's seen it before—he's sleepin'."

Joe and Ron looked at each other and laughed. Joe said, "That's what Ron wanted to do." He sucked in the night. "Maybe we see you later…"

They moved into shadow.

"Hey," Eric said. "Should we be wearin' clothes or somethin'?"

Shit said, "What the fuck for?" He tightened his grip on Eric's upper arm. "Come on—this way."

The cliffs were not sudden—otherwise vertigo would have defeated Shit. Combed over with wooden steps and decks, rocks and sections of stone and stubby vegetation pushed through, and the wooden stairway angled across to take them down another level. And another. Here and there, on one level or another, benches stood in the rain, in intermittent moonlight.

At the upper rail stood a donkey.

"I guess Brick come out to watch the show," Shit said.

The animal munched in a scuffed leather feed bag. He swayed from side to side. Inches behind the seam along the canvas and leather sack, a wet eye glimmered. Eric's hip brushed the dripping hide. The animal stepped about in the night grass.

Starting down the first set of steps, Shit paused and nodded to the left. "Nigger over there don't got no clothes on, either," Shit said softly.

Eric frowned. "Who is…?"

The head was shaved and he was tall, angular, sitting on one of the benches. The man was doing something in his lap with his fist—and Eric recognized Al. "Jesus…!"

Shit chuckled. "What's that supposed to mean…?"

Sitting naked on the bench, one ankle crossed over his leg, Al ran his fist absently up and down his towering member.

"'Cause he looks twice as big as he do normally in the Turpens john or Nigger Heaven at the Opera…What's *he* doin' in the Dump?"

"I guess he's here for Brick."

"The old donkey's owner? Brick really drink the donkey's piss and let him fuck his ass—?"

"They're sort of friends—him and Al."

Eric said, "Well, I'm *sort* of Al's friend…"

"Yeah," Shit said. "But you gotta do a *little* foreplay to accommodate each other. Brick don't gotta do nothin' but come around, pull open the rip in the back of his jeans—if he's wearin' any—and sit on it. That's the kinda ass Brick got."

"I guess you fucked it a few times, so you'd know…"

"Well…Yeah. I have."

"Al *would* like that—well, they can take care of each other. Man, that's a fuckin' scary dick—at least in *this* light!"

"You had it in you on your first day here—"

"I know. I know…" Eric hunched his shoulders. "Come on—let's go. No. I don't want Al to see me and get no ideas. He can wait for Brick. We can go on this way…"

Half the sky was layered in cloud fragments, which broke up the moon's light and flung silver about the stairs, down to where the sand made the beach a ribbon around the ridged and rippling sea. Rain across the surface made it rough as silver sandpaper. Waves broke on a stand of rocks, rushing into shore.

"Down there. Who's that…?"

"Bull. Those are all the folks he got with 'em."

"They look like they're all tied together—"

"They are. See, that's Whiteboy. He got one end. So they don't get away. Not that they'd wanna…" Perhaps fifteen were on the two lowest levels. More stood down on the sand. Bull strode back and forth, before them.

"What's he doin'?"

"Preachin's his crazy shit—about what a big black powerful nigger he is."

Night fissured on platinum cracks. Then thunder rolled up. Some down on the sand had flashlights. Circles of light slid over the beach, throwing shadows from tufts of sea grass.

Above, cloud wedges broke away to let through the glitter of—through this sliver and that rent—stars.

Shit said, "Let's just sit and watch." So, on the top step of the next level, they sat, feet splayed over the wet wood three steps below.

"I can't hear 'im—"

"You ain't missin' nothin'," Shit said. "He's just a crazy nigger all full up with 'isself; and all them niggers—who about as crazy—kinda believe it, at least while the lightning's flashin' and the thunder's comin' on." He chuckled beside Eric—and slid his foot on top of his partner's. Wet grass that grew up through the backs of the steps tickled the rear of Eric's calves. "I used to like to listen to it—but it's just stupid shit. That's all—"

Then—

Like a serpent of light, zig-zag lighting broke apart the sky to crack free half the universe. Light spread, and spread, and spread over the water and sand and rock and ocean, so that the mound of Gilead itself out at the horizon, which, moments before, he'd been unable to see, was stark and luminous. Eric could see trees on it, and—he was sure—their *leaves!*

And rocks along its edge.

He almost pushed himself erect, thinking, suddenly—*I've seen how large the world is!*

Because he had never seen anything so huge before as the miles and miles that had been lit, and at the same moment, in the chasms between heartbeats, he knew the world was bigger even than that—

When the thunder cracked, deafening him, it was as if he had been snatched up from the space he sat on and hurled into the sky.

It wasn't that he'd actually seen the world. But he'd seen the part of it he knew in enough light to suggest how large—or indeed, how little—a part of the world it was, so that, from it, he could seriously tell the size of the earth that held it…

And—yes—moments later he was back, sitting on the steps, holding the post beside him, his thumb over the cross grain of an inch-by-inch wooden peg, cut flush with one of the beans, one of the hundreds helping hold the structure together. Eric heard his own voice: "Jesus Christ, what the fuck was…?"

Shit whispered, "God *damn*…!"

Eric began to laugh. "Wow…!" Because both sounded so tiny.

"What *was* that…?"

Shit reached to grip Eric's leg.

Thunder still faded—there were three, four, six after-flickers.

"Anybody ever get hit by lightnin' out here?" Deep in his chest Eric's heart was a loud as the thunder. "It was like I could see how big everything in the..." and stopped, because his own voice still sounded so puny, so distant—

"Not down here," Shit said. He breathed heavily. "Maybe up on the bluff, sometimes. Even then, if it happened, I ain't heard about it."

Rain gusted up the steps. Lightning flashed close enough so that thunder came with it—again Eric was startled back.

Two stairways over, people came hurrying up. Like a flickering phantom Whiteboy moved, naked, among the dark men, older, younger, naked. Bull was close enough for Eric to hear: "Get on, now—get on *up* them steps, you damned fools! *Get* on, goddamit!"

Silently, as if both had agreed it was time to go, Shit and Eric stood and stepped up. Moments later, they walked along one of the runways. Bull's group had already disappeared over the cliff's upper rim.

—I've seen how large the world is!

Something warm hit Eric's cheek. He stopped and looked up.

In the slant moonlight, from the rail above two black faces looked down. The upper one was Al's. The lower was rough, broad nosed, hairy and pugged like a bulldog's. Between the rails, Eric could see the broad belly, the wide apart knees. A head above him, black toes clutched the wooden edge. Under the stomach, his fist gripped his stubby cock and hung.

"Damn, Brick," Eric said. "Why you go spit on me...?"

"Weren't no spit." Rick's voice was sullen, deep, sure. "Al got 'is dick up my damn shit chute and pumped me till I come. What—I hit you? Di'n' mean to. Couldn't do it again if you paid me."

Shit laughed. "I bet it was that last big flash, nigger, that loosed your juice!"

Brick chuckled.

"Hey, I bet it *was*..."

"Well," Eric said, "watch out. Wish I'd been up there to get it all."

"Yeah," Brick said. "Too bad you wasn't."

At the next steps, Eric and Shit started up.

Al and Brick lingered at the rail. As Shit and Eric reached the top step, Al, who was behind the naked squat carter stepped back.

Eric saw Al fall free. (Like a piece of firewood, Eric thought...)

"Damn...!" Shit said.

Grunting, the little bow-legged fellow moved to the side. He pulled himself to stand fully upright, as Al stepped away. Brick grinned over at Shit and Eric, leaned forward, big hands on his knees, and—from his flat buttocks, streaked with rain and moonlight—Eric saw the black eruption jump about six inches out, then splat down on the planks behind his heels.

"Jesus," Shit said, "why you gonna crap all over the steps, Brick? People gotta walk here."

Brick still grinned at them. More shit came out his ass—and flopped on the runway. "Da's jus' natural. Da's how Donkey do it. It gonna rain again 'fore mornin'. That'll take most of it away." He stood up, his full five feet—and without holding himself, began to urinate over the edge to the boards below, where Eric and Shit had been walking.

Eric wiped his cheek.

Brick turned and—still urinating; his stream swinging left and right—walked directly through the mess he'd left on the boards. "Gotta go get Donkey and see what he needs, now I got mine for the night." He turned to call. "Hey, thanks—Al."

Al said nothing but wandered away.

"See, he won't speak to me, long as any of these Dump niggers are around—'cause he's straight and I'm jus' a donkey fuckin' faggot. But he sure come over here, sniffin' out my goddamn ass, 'cause it's big and hot and wet, jus' like he like it. If a man tell you he wan' a tight asshole, that jus' means he don't got no meat of his own. That's all. And that ain't Al Haver's problem. Un-un." Again he laughed.

"I'm sure that last one was what made him shoot," Shit reiterated.

Eric's ears still rang. "And I thought the mud was bad 'cause of the rain." Shaking his head, Eric started along. "Damn—" Then he began to chuckle. "Did Jay ever tell you why he started callin' your daddy 'Dynamite'?"

"Sure, he did," Shit said. Then he shook his head. "Damn—I thought maybe I was gonna get me a helpin' of sloppy seconds off that bowlegged little nigger."

"Yeah, well…"

When they reached the top, Donkey was gone.

Back at Bull's, two people with flashlights stood at the head of the open basement. Three ambled down the steps. Most wore leather of some sort or another—vests, harnesses, masks. Two sat on the top step. Most (Eric knew) would be strangers to the Dump. The rain began again, and some stood up and hurried down.

It had been so great, so bright, so searing…

*

The source of the lightning had moved east, looking and sounding as if confined to a distant sky cave.

Together they walked through wet, silver ferns, elbows high—till Shit grasped Eric's hand again. "Storms like that always make me wanna fuck."

"For God's sake, Shit—everything makes you wanna fuck!" Joined fists swung through wet fronds. They started up the cabin steps.

"Yeah—but this time we're gonna do it different. Usually I just jump 'im 'cause he's all greased up from earlier." (Shit was talking now about his father...) "And you'd get around in front of 'im and suck his dick till he shot that big ol' cracker load right in your mouth. But this time, you're gonna fuck 'is ass, and I'm gonna get around and suck his dick till you help 'im come in my mouth. Okay?"

Eric said, "Sure." Stepping up on the deck, behind Shit, still holding his hand. "But don't you think it'd be a good idea to ask Dynamite if that's okay with *him*?"

"Why?" Shit glanced back. "What the fuck for? We got a day off tomorrow. And he says he likes it, when we surprise 'im with shit like that."

"Okay..." Eric's tone said, *This is your idea...*He was still thinking, *I've seen how big the world is...*

They stepped into the bedroom.

Shit pulled Eric to the bed's edge, released his hand, then vaulted. The mattress—and Dynamite—moved up and down. There was enough light to see that Dynamite lay on his side, back to them. Eric climbed on the rough sheet, and ahead of him, Shit got one leg over his father, and seemed to squat on his hip. With one hand he got hold of Dynamite's cock.

"Damn, boy...!" Dynamite grunted. "You gonna pull my dick off."

"Naw, I ain't," Shit said. "You got a treat comin'. I'm gonna *suck* you off."

"Well, you know where it is, son." Dynamite actually chuckled—

—while Eric got himself behind the lanky garbage man. He pressed the side of his face against Dynamite's hairy shoulder.

A muffled Shit asked, "Where's Eric...?"

"Right behind me."

Eric felt (and heard the bed shift) Dynamite's upper leg move. Then Shit's hand came through, reached forward, and grasped Eric's cock. From in front of Dynamite, he tugged Eric forward.

Eric felt a rhythm start somewhere in Dynamite's body. Shit was jerking off his father.

"Damn," Dynamite said, as he did frequently. "You got your grandaddy's touch, Shit. It's downright uncanny. If I closed my eyes, I could think it was *my* daddy, come into the back room and stickin' his hand under the covers to beat my damned meat when I was a kid."

Now Eric grinned. "Did you like it when your dad did that?"

Eric heard Dynamite grin. "Well, yeah, I was kind of fortunate, there. He'd do it to any boy who'd hang around with 'im. So I saw a lot of it. Besides, nobody ever told me I wasn't supposed to like it. They didn't start sayin' that till ten or fifteen years later. So, yeah, I did. Come on, Shit. It's funny how when you're just jerkin' it, it's like suddenly my daddy is alive and well. Hey, Move Eric's dick down 'bout an inch…"

Shit positioned the head of Eric's cock in Dynamite's crevice. Eric slid forward into the lubricant already there. He pushed within Dynamite's anal sphincter. The muscles slid around his cock shaft.

"Uhhh…" Dynamite grunted.

"That okay?" Eric asked.

"Hell," Dynamite said. "That's *real* okay, son!" Shit's hand withdrew, then came around Dynamite's upper hip to reach over and grasp behind Eric's upper buttock, pulling him forward.

"Come on—pump that big o' fucker up your daddy's shit chute. Yeah, son. That feels pretty nice—that is to say, it feels like it's damned well supposed to. I'll tell you if we need more of that pig-fuckin' lube."

From down around Dynamite's belly, Shit asked, "How's this feel…?"

"Oh, son—*Jesus*, Shit, that's fuckin amazin'!" Dynamite's hips moved forward and back. His hands were down gripping the sides of Shit's head—while Eric held his shoulder with one hand, his flank with the other. And pumped. Dynamite's ass seemed to suck at his cock. "Come on, little boy. *Suck* daddy's big ol' cracker dick! Now that's somethin' my daddy did not do, at least not a whole lot. Oh, yeah! And you pump out that asshole, and help me get out my load, right in his mouth—like he wants it!"

At one point, when Dynamite ground his hips forward, Eric said, "Hey, don't *choke* 'im…!"

Shit came off Dynamite's cock long enough to say, "Hey, I'll tell you, since we all gotta go sometimes, right now this don't seem like a bad way to do it."

"Come *on*, Shit. Get it back in there. I'm about to unload!"

Shit came all over Eric's foot. Moving his toes in its familiar viscosity, Eric came up Dynamite's ass, squeezed him, then rolled back, panting, one hand still under Dynamite's shoulder.

—*I've seen how large the world is!*

Eric closed his eyes and may have slept or not—

Someone—he was *pretty* sure it was Dynamite—was licking the cum off his foot. Before he could be sure, though, he was asleep.

*

One morning in '24 or '25, at five-forty, Eric stepped out on the porch of his mother's Runcible house. Barbara stepped out behind him, and, as he turned, gave him a hug, urging him, as usual, to bring his partner, Morgan, around more often ("And Dynamite, too—we'll have you all for dinner." Eric hoped it wouldn't happen—or at least wouldn't happen till Ron was at some conference or other), apologizing for the uncomfortable couch he'd slept on.

Bending, he hugged her back. "Hey, Barb—I slept fine. Really."

Today, Barbara was a thick and handsome woman. Smoothly her hair had gone from silver blond to silver white. She still wore it pinned up. As he released her and stepped away, Eric thought she looked flushed. A pink glow helmeted her head. Eric squinted, as her hand slid down the arm of his dark hoody—which, for some reason, looked...faintly brown. That's when he realized that the pale pink nail polish his mother had worn as far back as he could remember was intended to look as if it were completely clear. Somehow *everything* had shifted to the red. Glancing up, he saw sky and clouds were both deep rose.

Again, Eric kissed her cheek. "We'll come see you—and Ron." He turned and stepped down onto the flagstones taking him across the lawn to the sidewalk. As he loped toward the stop for the six A.M. shuttle back along the shore to Diamond Harbor to meet Shit, he looked over between the houses to see, on the other side of the parking lot among the cars and pickups, the beach and bottom third of the sky was the same red he'd seen during the Harbor sunrise on his first garbage run in Dynamite's long-gone truck—a vivid scarlet—*how* many years ago now?

It was only the second time he'd seen it that color.

Salmons, lavenders, pinks, oranges, and all shades of coppers, grays, and golds were common—even ten morning minutes of emerald ocean, before the sea went silver-blue.

But bright red beaches at dawn were—really—rare.

* * *

[53] ONE EVENING—IT was October—Eric took a walk down to Dump Corners, went into Hurter's, with its skylights and the naked I-beams intersecting under the upper part of the ceiling, to the back wall to look at the comics.

This particular afternoon, somebody was over in the corner, in front of the porn magazines, a heavyset fellow, in shorts and sneakers. Though Eric only saw him from the back, the keys on his left hip and his general build at first made Eric think of the trucker he'd met a decade (or more) ago in the Gay Friendly restroom, then again at Turpens, though he hadn't seen him now for...well, years.

Down through the girders, the ceiling's sourceless light skewed all values and colors, but—Eric realized—the guy was doing something with one hand before himself that...made his shoulder shake! From his back, he looked like he had a magazine in one hand, one of the nude gay ones Fred kept up there. When it struck Eric what the man *was* doing, he began to grin. Yeah, so much for being straight.

Suddenly, the guy stood up in his white T-shirt, breathing heavily.

Eric frowned. This guy's hair was dead black. Also, he was much too dark for the white trucker.

Also—the last to hit Eric—he was ten years too young!

The guy closed the magazine, put it back on the shelf, among the Technicolor array of naked men, and turned.

Either Mexican or Indian, the young fellow was someone Eric didn't know. One hand was still under the waist of his olive drab shorts, on the lap of which, off to the left, was a wet blotch, darker than the cloth around.

Sharply, the kid pulled his hand from his under his waist and blinked.

Wondering if he should say something, Eric smiled—

But the Indian youngster dropped his head and started walking forward, and moments on was gone from the whole magazine area.

Jesus! He hadn't even taken his dick out to do it.

Well, when I was that age, a fair number of times (Eric thought) I didn't even get to.

Eric went toward the corner, trying to spot which of the magazines the kid had been looking at. But the whole range of flesh and muscle, genitals veiled by swimsuits and boxers, gym pants or spandex, at least on the covers, for all its diversity—white, black, Asian, and Latino—had grown anonymous and swallowed their histories, even histories only a minute old.

A memory—a desire of Eric's—welled; and Eric decided on an experiment—

The next day, when they finished hauling sacks and drove back from the Bottom—it had been a dumping day—it looked about to rain. "Now, this is a *good* day for a nap," Dynamite said, frowning up at the all but featureless cloud.

"You mind running me down to the Corners?" Eric asked. "I wanna see somethin' in Hurter's."

"Sure." Dynamite shrugged. "You ain't comin' in and nappin'?"

"I'll be back in about an hour," Eric said, "an hour-and-a-half."

"Okay." Dynamite shrugged.

"Can I go with you?" Shit asked, more bewildered than not, but also intrigued at the change in their usual pattern.

"Come on," Eric said.

So Dynamite had continued on to the Dump's center, dropped them off, then swung the truck around to drive home alone.

Shit and Eric walked into the familiar hangar-like store. Eric made his way to the back, while Shit followed, stopping to look at the five and six year out of date electronic equipment. When he reached the back wall, Eric went to the general magazines instead of the porn, but—with the faintest tingling—stopped, pulled down his zipper, and pulled out his dick.

He took a breath.

Three or four other people stood around, but Eric was trying not to look at them.

Shit stepped up beside him. "What you lookin' at?"

Eric shrugged. "Just stuff."

"Oh," Shit said. "Like usual, huh?" He grinned at Eric—then his eyes dropped. He glanced up again with blank surprise.

His voice was much lower. "What—you gonna jerk off? You know, this ain't Turpens. In fact it ain't a john at all—it's a public store."

Eric put the magazine back. "I wasn't actually gonna jerk it—just be ready, in case I wanted to eventually, 'cause somethin' turned me on."

Shit began to smile. "You're fuckin' crazy," he said. Then he looked around.

"Naw—it's just an experiment."

"Oh." Looking back at Eric, Shit frowned. Suddenly he reached down, unzipped his own pants, took out his cock—*and* his testicles (probably to go Eric one better). Putting his hands on his thighs, he looked down at himself Then he looked at Eric, as if to say: *Okay, what next?*

Eric said, "Yeah, that's probably better." He reached in his jeans and pulled out his own nuts. He *did* look around, because he couldn't help it. He thought he saw somebody look away. "Let's go look at the dirty magazines, now. Maybe somethin'll inspire us."

Shit grunted, but he turned to walk over, ahead of Eric, to the corner. Like he's decided to run interference for me, Eric thought, and grinned.

Basically Eric was curious who would be the first person to say something—that was all. Visual porn had never particularly turned him on, so, as he paged through this magazine and that, while he admired the naked photographs (in the past few years, all the American ones seemed to have vanished and been replaced by German, Dutch, Brazilian, and Danish), nothing seemed particularly arousing.

Over the same fifteen minutes, Shit, however, as a non-reader, paging through one and another, twice got a full-out hard-on (with its slight downward curve), then lost it, though he hadn't touched himself. Probably he was responding to Eric.

Three different older black guys looked at them unabashedly—two of them, who were with one another, laughed. (Summer visitors—lingering into autumn.) Two different men about their own ages just stared. Eric found their interest made his dick drift from one side of his scrotum to the other, but that's all.

He started reading a letters to the editor column that appeared in German with an awkward English translation beside it, when someone said, "Hey...?"

Eric looked up—

—and repressed a flinch.

A heavy man in a green sunshade—superfluous with the overcast sky outside—and shirtsleeves stood to the side. "Oh. It's you two." He smiled, nodding at Eric, as Shit stepped over. With a gesture of his fist, he said, "What's this, now? Since half the women are runnin' around Diamond Harbor with their tits hangin' out, you think *you* gotta make a fashion statement in here? Jesus, Shit," Fred said, "I used to catch you in here, doin' this kinda stuff when you were twelve or thirteen. What—you're gettin' your second childhood early?"

"Yeah," Shit said. "And you used to run me out of here, when you caught me, too."

Eric was surprised.

Fred said, "Were you aware back then, Shit, that I'd *always* wait till you was finished—before I'd come up and made you skedaddle?" He looked like a heavier cousin of Jay's, though closer cropped, with clean hands, and who had not destroyed his nails with gnawing.

"You did?" Shit looked surprised, now.

"Un-huh." Fred shook his head, still smiling. "Anyway, someone stopped me up front to make a comment."

Shit said, "Was they complainin'?"

"Not what I'd call complainin'," Fred said. He chuckled. "They thought yall was cute, actually. But...well, they *did* mention it. So I thought I'd come back here and check it out myself."

"Oh," Eric said. "You want us to put it away—"

"That's entirely up to you. Anyway—" Fred put a thumb under his belt—"since it looks like you're takin' up old habits, I just wanted to say the same thing to yall I said to Shit here when he was a kid: don't get no mess on the damned magazines. Or on the floor, if you can help it. Bring a handkerchief with you and do it in there. I got to sell these things—and nobody wants 'em if the pages is pre-stuck, 'fore they get a chance to look at 'em. Okay?"

"*Um*," Eric said. "Yeah..."

"But you guys standin' around in here, stickin' straight out like that's good adverisin' for them magazines. That just lets the other customers know they do what they're supposed to do." Fred reached out, bypassed Eric's proffered hand—lifted Eric's cock, and shook it. "Nice to see you again, I guess."

Eric swallowed—and almost, but did not quite, step back.

Fred laughed out full. "See, that's how I shook with him, the first time I had to talk some sense into his crazy head—you remember that? When you was twelve?" He looked over at Shit. Fred released Eric's penis, reached over, and shook Shit's—which immediately got hard.

Shit said, "Sounds reasonable."

"And that's just what yours done when I shook it in here when you was a kid."

Shit put one hand over himself now—and, in his loose grip, while his skin slipped forward, his penis retreated within his wide fist.

"You guys do what you gonna do." (Shit dropped his fist, to reveal his dick at half-mast.) "But like I say, just don't mess nothin' up, now. If you do, I'm gonna make you buy it. That's all."

Fred smiled, then turned and walked toward the front.

Somehow, the experiment seemed finished.

Eric zipped his jeans.

Then, buttoning the waist button on their denims, they looked at one another—Shit shrugged—and walked back to the front of the store after Fred, passing spools of electrical cable, stacks of seed bags, aluminum sheets, brooms and hoes and shovels, cases of nails, the key copying machine, nodded to Fred in the pen beside the register, who nodded back and smiled.

"Okay," Shit said dryly. "Now that was just the most fun I done had me in a dog's age—and *you're* a fuckin' nut! What you wanna do, now?"

Eric shrugged. "I don't know. Maybe go on home. Roll up against Dynamite and grab a nap."

"Good," Shit said. "'Cause *I* wanna take that nap so bad I may just bring you down on the side of the road and make you do me right there before we *get* home."

When they stepped outside, it had begun to sprinkle.

*

No, this was still 2025, not '35, nor was Eric any sort of sexually-rebelling university student with patches of transparent vinyl in his pants and shirt, intent on challenging the status quo, as it might have been framed in the newly-remerging "alternative plasma media" (as plasma inductance screens became more common than regular "hard" computers, as they were briefly known: neither Shit nor Eric ever owned one) when, ten years later, such incidents became commonplace.

In '27, '28, '29, and even '30 itself, various articles appeared in various magazines, on and off line, looking forward to the "Sexually Uncomfortable Thirties." After '31, however, such articles stopped, because people under thirty-five, then under forty, couldn't understand them.

Eric read half of one such, which came into Diamond Harbor in a northern print magazine, brought by a tourist—an Atlanta academic—and left on a table in a local eatery called Reba's Place.

He didn't finish it—because he didn't understand it, either.

* * *

[54] SOMETIMES SHIT AND Eric would argue whether this took place in '27, '28, or '29. Doctor Greene had ordered Dynamite to take six weeks off from the garbage run—and had filled out papers for him to get compensation from the Chamber of Commerce. They'd all gone over to the Opera, and Dynamite had gone down to the front row, put his beer under the seat, pulled out his dick, and gone to sleep that way for about three hours. Certainly that was the afternoon that Dusty asked the boys if they wanted to spend a few days working in the theater, sweeping up and bolting down some loose chairs. Hammond had gone to spend *his* three-week vacation that autumn in Key West and had phoned to say he was taking another week off. Dusty had showed them the little apartment up over the projection room. There were no sheets on the bed, Eric remembered, but there were blankets—and they slept like that the whole time. It was only later when he mentioned it to Barb that she made him take some an extra pair of hers...

They'd been staying at the Opera, helping Dusty at least a week.

Then Shit had gone back to the cabin to spend a day and night with his dad, when Eric got an urge to see them.

In the projection booth, he told Myron to tell Dusty he'd be gone for a day, maybe two. Myron, who wore thick glasses and was bald, nodded. Generally at the beginning-of-the-week, business trickled irregularly into the three-balconied theater's twenty-two hours of darkness.

(And two hours from four to six with the work lights on...)

Eric hadn't planned for it, but, when, back down in the lobby, he glanced outside, a November moon hung, full, high, and small as a quarter, among the clouds striping the night. A couple of hours later, at eleven-thirty or a little after, he left the theater—'27's had been a warm November (if it wasn't '28's)—to walk down to the service road's shoulder and turn along the sea.

Fifteen feet ahead, as it pulled over, he recognized Abbot's Jeep. (Abbot *still* worked behind the notions counter at Turpens.) After ten seconds, the passenger window jerked irregularly into the door and, in his denim jacket, Abbot leaned out: "Hey, I *thought* that might be you. Can I give you a lift?" Beside the steel buttons, the breeze shook his white chest hair.

"Thanks, Abbot—naw. I'm walkin'. It's nice out."

"It's a little cool." Abbot leaned further. "Where you walkin' to?"

"I'm goin' to the Dump, over at the Harbor."

Abott frowned. "That's a-ways, son." He hadn't shaved that day. "And it's cool out," he repeated. "I don't mind dropping you off—"

"Got my hoody on. I'm good."

"Okay, then." Abbot eased back. "Suit yourself. Hell—" Abbot's chuckle drifted from the car window—"I thought maybe I was gonna get myself a blowjob tonight. But you ain't in'erested in no geriatric case like me, now, are you?"

"I don't know." Eric shrugged. "Maybe I'd like that—if I hadn't made up my mind to take a walk and a good look at the water. You're on for next time, though."

"You are *such* a liar." Laughter followed the chuckle. "Truth is, though, you don't gotta gimme none. Someone like you just got to promise me some—and I'm happy." Rising, the window glass halted, two black inches from the top. "I know you're thirty somethin' or close to it. But when I first seen you walkin', I coulda *sworn* you was some seventeen-year-old I hadn't even *met* yet. You know you *still* look like a kid?"

"Yeah, you love that jailbait, don't you?" Eric was thirty-seven (or thirty-eight) but a thirty-seven year old who'd worked hard. "That's why you stopped—right?"

Laughing again, Abbot's ghost disappeared from behind the glass to slide back across and under the wheel. The Jeep rolled forward.

"Hey," Eric shouted. "I ain't kiddin' you. At least I'm too old for *that*. You come around the Opera—I'll show you what I can do…" and realized, from trying to talk over it, how loud the sea was.

Because he felt good, Eric passed up three more rides—from Arlene and her aunt, both of whom worked at the Stop & Shop, then from Franklin and Mark, and finally from an old and new guy together in a farm pickup from Dump Produce, neither of whose names he remembered, though he knew the older by sight.

Eric walked the six miles from Runcible to the Harbor.

The smell of halides and ozone blew in from moon shot waves.

He thought about Ms. Louise.

He thought about Dynamite, in what must have been the middle of the night, with a work gloved hand reaching into his pants, pulling loose his nuts, and waggling them by his pickup's amber parking light. Eric had been too surprised to laugh.

He laughed now, though—which meant he'd changed.

He wondered if some moment from this walk would join the frequently remembered—perhaps the teal around the full moon and across a fifth of the sky, as if the orb had dispersed half the night.

Would he think of it again and, if so, how often?

As he reached the Harbor's ancient docks, where moonlight made the life preservers roped to the boathouse wall look like carved chalk, Eric thought: I've been through a wondrous experience, walking back over the Dump's bluff in the moonlight, with ice chip stars, here and there, balanced on slack cloud ribbons across the sky, uneven land under shoe, and trees and brush coming up now, on one side, then the other, falling away—only it isn't the words I use to remind myself of it, but the *nowness* of it, moments, minutes, half an hour ago, that pulls the memories up:

—that leafless branch *really* was a foot to the side of my face.

—that rock, for two steps, *actually* was under my foot, before the ground again grew loose and squishy.

—that breeze tugged my hood from my right cheek, so that I stopped and pulled it over. When had I turned it up...?

(Did I eat any pickings along the crossing? Can't even remember, which is as close as I'll get to bein' normal; forget I'm different—that *we're* different. And forgetting we're different is certainly easier.)

Above him, the sky was doing something like the eye itself: by revealing only half the night, it suggested a night so *much* bigger...

Eric turned to hike the last three-quarters of a mile to the Dump. I've finished doing something nobody has ever done exactly with the same steps and the same breezes and the same stubbly grass and the same slog up and the same lope down, though a million, or a million-million folks through three centuries (or forty centuries if you count the Indians) have done something near it, Indians, blacks, whites, so that they'd recognize that wondrous thing from their own memories.

That's astonishing.

And it makes me—or, anyway, makes my life—astonishing

Fifteen minutes later, Eric circled the railway car, with its glassless windows and no seats, on twenty yards of unattached rail, from how many years back when real operas were sung at the Opera House.

While grass shivered between the rocks in the breeze and the silver light, he tramped the bluff. He was tired. The moon had gone from an ivory coin above him to an orange drumhead low between the hills.

Ten minutes more and Eric could see Dynamite's cabin along the slope. No lights were on.

The walk had taken three-and-a-half, maybe four hours. Reaching the cabin path, Eric looked back to see, across the road, light from Black Bull's window edges.

He turned away to climb Dynamite's cabin steps, pushed in the door, didn't turn on the light, but worked off one shoe, then the other. (This place smells like home, he thought.) His feet stung. Sweaty and slightly sore, they felt as if they were expanding on the kitchen's gritty boards. Here and there, he made out vinyl patches.

Years ago, Dynamite had turned Shit and Eric loose for a weekend with trowels and screwdrivers to pry up the remaining stuff. But because they'd failed, three years later the new floor covering still hadn't gone down.

It was in incredibly dusty boxes under the sink.

Threading his way around the junk, Eric stepped through the archway into the bedroom.

Again, he was surprised by the new, blue, crinkly quilt pushed down at the foot of the bed. (He'd gone with Shit to buy it at the mall, to replace the ragged maroon one with the stuffing coming out on three sides, when, at Dr. Greene's diagnosis of retained liquid and the threat of congestive heart failure, Shit had gotten it in his head that Dynamite needed something warm to sleep under, though most of the time, in the mild winter, it rarely got pulled up.) Eric looked at the two men, naked, asleep—to realize a third lay with them. Taking a breath, he shook his head and grinned.

A moonlit trapezoid slanted across Shit's still-boyish butt; part of the light caught Dynamite's hairy lower legs and turned-in feet. The stranger lay on Shit's right, the upper part of his back crossed with the blind slats' shadows. On Dynamite's right, the top of Shit's head was pressed into his father's armpit.

At various times, years ago, when Eric had gotten up in the night to go to the bathroom, he'd realized Shit tended to sleep with his head under his dad's arm. (Usually Dynamite slept on his back, one arm up over his head. Tonight he was on his belly.) Eric had figured it out: when they went to bed, Shit immediately wedged the back of his head there. Six to ten minutes later, while he slept, he'd turn around to face his father, nose and mouth in that pungent cavity, a little too strong for him when he was awake, but irresistible when he slept, an arm across his father's hirsute chest.

At the Opera House, in bed in the little upstairs apartment they'd been staying in, Eric had tried (with considerable curiosity) sleeping on his back, stomach up. And, yes, within seconds the back of Shit's head was under Eric's own raised arm. Minutes later, in actual sleep, a hundred-eighty-degree roll put Shit's face there, while his arm slid across Eric's chest.

Despite Shit and Dynamite's lackadaisical approach to hygiene, Eric himself showered every second or third day. Now he'd dropped regularly and rigorously down to once a week—on Mondays: like Dynamite. At the Opera, work grew sweaty, and as he'd push between the rows of seats with the broad broom, smelling of booze or worse, some homeless fellow might comment, "You're gettin' a little strong, there, Mr. Jeffers."

"Well, Rudy, only one person's *gotta* like it. And that ain't you." Eric chuckled, raising a seat with the toe of his work shoe to get the broom under. "And *he* ain't complainin'—yet." Fact was, Shit not only didn't complain, he was generous, even profligate, with grins and big inhalings and underarm nuzzlings and *"Ahhhh....!"'s* and *"Christ*, you smell *real* good..."s. Also, *more* than one person liked it—Abbot for instance, as well as a black professor who'd drive over from Montgomery College, and a rather heavy black insurance actuary, who stuttered a lot and three or four times had asked Eric to come back home with him. Eric had explained, "Naw—if we're gonna do sumpin', let's do it here. I'm workin'." Though there wasn't enough skin on Eric's dick to justify a seat in Gorgonzola Alley, except as an admirer, Eric had his fans.

In the cabin bedroom's clutter, Eric dropped his clothes, climbed up on the bed's foot—the largest space was between Shit's back and the stranger's front. The stranger, he realized now, was a tall Asian. Eric put his head down, when the Asian flinched: *"What* the...*fuck—*?"

Shit turned to face the Asian and whispered, "Hey...that's just Eric. He's okay. Everything all right at the Opera?"

"Um-hm." Eric felt Shit's arm slip around him, as he put his own arm around the Asian, who, yes, smelled a little strange—like deodorant or toilet water or something...

"Oh," the Asian said. "This is all right, then?"

"Yeah," Eric said. "This is all right."

From the other side of the bed, Dynamite muttered, "Jesus H. *Christ—* can't a man have one night alone with his own goddam boy? I gotta keep all *three* of you happy now?"

"I was gettin' lonely over at the Opera," Eric whispered. "So I took a wander this way. Myron says he'll keep the place goin' through tomorrow. Hey, I'm sorry—" God, he thought, the Asian is a little much. But *they* both smelled good...

"Funny thing was," Dynamite whispered back, "we was gettin' a little lonely, too. We was just sayin' that, 'fore we went to bed. Wasn't we, Shit?"

"Un-huh," Shit said sleepily. "Open ya' damn mouth and lemme get my tongue in'ere 'fore he tries to slip his dick in it."

"You talkin' to me or your daddy?" Eric asked. "Or your new friend, here?" He gave the Asian a little shake, just to be friendly. The Asian patted his forearm back.

Which made Dynamite mutter again. "Sometimes that boy knows how I operate *too* damned well. You two go on, then. Hell, I'm tired, anyway."

Thirty-five minutes and four orgasms later (two of them Shit's), all four slept, and since Dynamite wasn't working right then—which, after all, was why Eric and Shit had taken over for Hammond and Dusty, on their two month vacation from the garbage run (another nicety of Kyle's Chamber of Commerce organization)—it was a lazy, vigorous morning.

* * *

[55] SHIT WAS UP to make coffee for all four. "Least I can do," he said, a little under his breath to Eric, though Philip (the Asian) could have heard if he was listening, "since I guess I brought a surprise to bed for you." Apparently, they'd picked up Philip last night when he'd needed a lift into Hemmings, and ended up here. (He'd come down to visit for a long weekend with some vacationing friends.) "Hey, Philip...this is Eric. I told you about him. You remember from last night."

"Gee, I hope I didn't...I mean, sorry if I—"

"Naw." Shit got the blue coffee tin from the freezer and scooped four, five, six scoops into the hopper, then turned to the sink. "Eric knows he's my number one fellow." He gave Eric a hug—who, though he ignored it, was happy for it. "He keeps me on a loose leash. That ain't no problem."

Swaying in junk and sunlight, sleepy Philip rubbed his forehead, his black spiky hair, fingered his ear, then, smiling shyly, looked around for his glasses, his T-shirt. "Hi..."

In only his ragged T-shirt, one fist gripping his dick, Shit tugged the glass carafe from under the hopper to pour half a mug for himself. A drop fell, to hiss and bubble on the circular plate, around whose rim a few metallic spots had worn through the black, before he slid the carafe back into place. In the glass, bubbles rocked on the liquid's rim.

"Hi." Eric nodded to where the dark denim legs of some new-looking jeans hung over a chair back. "This what you're lookin' for?"

"Oh. Yeah." Philip stepped towards them, but took his cue from Shit and did not slip them on. "Thanks."

When they were sitting on the porch, halfway through coffee, Jay drove up to call out the pickup window, "Hey, guys? Since you're not haulin' garbage, whyn't you go over to the Opera to give Hammond and Dusty a hand sweepin' out that place."

Shit called back, "You're a little late, motherfucker. We're already been over there all month," and it was a big joke. Shit rubbed at his floppy crotch, grinning.

"Well, if you are, then at least I can start makin' sure you get paid." Getting out of the pickup, Jay clumped up the porch steps. "Actually, Dusty done told me. You been doin' it just to be nice. Might as well let the Chamber of Commerce give you somethin' for it. It won't be much— but it'll be somethin'. Hey, Dynamite—these boys takin' care of you?" He nodded to the Asian and grinned—"Good mornin'. Well, you look like *you* done been takin' care of." Slowing as he got to the top, Jay stepped in front of the porch rail and leaned back against it.

In his chair, Philip sat with one hand over his groin, as though he hadn't been quite ready for company. Clearly, though, it didn't bother Jay.

Sitting on the bench, still in just his T-shirt, looking over his coffee cup, Shit said: "I been doin' it so I can fuck some ass down in the bathroom—to be nice, *too*, I guess." Then he drank loudly from his mug. (Shit still eats and drinks like a fuckin' slob—and after all this time I still think it's fuckin' sexy. Eric smiled. I wonder if this guy thinks the same thing?)

"Yeah," Jay said. "Tell me somethin' I don't know. Well, I guess I'm on my way." Standing, he turned back to the steps, and started down.

Philip looked around. "I hope I get a chance to come back here. This was...yeah, fun." Getting up, finally he put on his jeans, as though Jay's going had freed him to slip his long, bony legs into them. "Your friend's pretty nice, too," he said—and took some more sugar. "Yeah. You guys are fun."

"So are you," Dynamite said—while Jay's pickup started grumbling, then eased forward.

"Come on," Shit said. "Pull your pecker loose from your jeans again. You Chinese fellas is hot. I wanna watch Eric suck your dick some more 'fore you go, so I can come on it later when he's suckin' on mine. You don't even have to shoot, if you don't wanna. I got that safe in my head from last night when you blasted all over my dad's face."

Smiling sheepishly, looking around, Philip pulled out his (hard) penis.

* * *

[56] IT WAS IN one of those three years that they officially took over the Opera, during Hammond and Dusty's three-week vacation down in the Keys. They would open the window in the musty apartment upstairs over the projection room. (Hammond and Dusty had their own place, two blocks away from the theater.) Barbara even gave them two more sets of sheets, which, between the first year and the second year, they actually left there. Next year, they were unmoved, rumpled over the double bed. Sometimes on his own visits, Dynamite would go up and nap there himself, cap on the chair beside the bed, his jeans unbuttoned and pants unzipped. (Once Eric came in to find Shit sitting on the bed, with faintly snoring Dynamite facing forward on his side. *Whacha doin'?*

(Shit shrugged. His hand was in his father's open pants. He smiled, sheepishly. *Holdin' on to my daddy's dick*, he said, quietly, *while he's sleepin'.*

(Eric asked, Huh?

(*Yeah,* Shit whispered. *It makes me feel like I was a little kid again. I used to do this sometimes, back when I was still too little to a raise a hard-on.*

(On the bed, Dynamite shifted.

(Grinning, Eric shook his head. A minute later, Shit came up behind him and encircled him in his arms. *I wanna hold yours now.*)

*

Leaves swatted the van's roof; branches crackled under the tires. Eric in the back seat, Shit in the front, they bumped along. Out the window a sapling swung away and flopped back through the foliage, rustling and roaring.

In his iridescent blue, green, and purple headscarf, Mamma Grace drove.

"Jesus...!" Shit held to the roof handle over the door. "Mama, this is a car-and-a-*half!* You're usually such...well—" the car lurched—"kind of a delicate...person. I'm surprised you can handle a big ol' four-wheel drive like this."

"Honey—" Mama swung the wheel to avoid a fallen tree trunk— "when Mama's comin' through, Mama's comin' through." Mama had on his false eyelashes and a lot of rings. At the top of the wheel's arc on his dark fingers, stones glittered, red, purple, green. "You got to be able to get around, I don't care *how* much of a lady a feller is."

Pine branches struck the windshield and pulled around the side, dragging shadows through the van. Eric leaned forward, looking over Shit's shoulder.

A big bump—Eric's head touched the roof: but it was a tap, not a bang.

Mama Grace stopped the car. "Okay—we done got here." He took a breath and sat back.

Outside, beyond green saplings, stood a wall.

Green siding covered part of it. Creosoted slats had fallen loose from cinder blocks. In it were a window's vertical edge and bottom sill, in blistered white wood.

Mama Grace opened his door, turned, and slid out the side. Shit opened his door and got out. He had on jeans, even shoes today, and a washed-out blue and black flannel—though he hadn't buttoned it.

Eric slid to the back door, opened it, and stepped into the tall growth. In his work shoes, he walked to where Shit had wandered forward of the front fender.

"What's that?" Shit turned back. His shirt had slipped down over a red-brown shoulder. Without a belt, his jeans were already down on the left below the blade of his hip. In the front you could see the top of his pubic hair. (How many years we been together, Eric wondered. It's good to be able to walk around with somebody who looks like that without even thinking—and knowing you can have him pretty much when you want.) But, then, whatever clothes Shit wore always seemed to be falling off him. Most of them were *still* Dynamite's, with cuffs or legs cut down (or ripped away), a habit neither father nor son seemed about to break.

With his thumb, Eric pulled his own jeans up. "I think that's…probably The Slide. Or what's left of it."

"Damn," Shit said. "They really done tore that thing down, huh? From what Dynamite said, I just thought they'd closed it up or somethin'. Has this all grown up here since then?"

"No," Mama Grace said, fist on the hip of his fatigues. "They were in here with bulldozers. It's a shame. It was really an interesting building."

"Yeah," Eric said. "I mean, the piss bar and…everything."

"Yes, even that." Mama Grace walked forward. Along with a pair of designer jeans that had sequins up the sides, he wore work shoes, too—like Shit and Eric.

They went around in front of the headlights, which were blinking—even though it was daylight. Mama Grace had turned them on for the trip through the woods.

"Which wall *is* that, anyway?" Eric asked. "Was that the window to Saul's office in the back?"

"Jesus," Shit said. "As many times as I been in that place, I don't think I ever came around *this* side. So the road we *used* to drive up was…over there, right?"

"No." Mama Grace pointed as if over invisible obstacles. "It was there."

"I'm lost," Shit said.

"I ain't," Eric said. "I know right where I am. As much piss as I drunk in this place, I ought to know where I—"

Shit laughed. "As much of Dynamite's beer and my Coca-Cola as you put down—" He stepped to the low wall's edge and over. "Oh, *fuck*—!"

"What?" Eric said. He hurried up after Shit.

Mama Grace laughed. "You better watch out, boy, or you gonna break a leg—or an arm. Or both."

"What is it?" Eric said again. He put one shoe on the lowest part of the wall.

"Come on," Shit said, frowning. "Lemme get back over there. This is too high for me." He vaulted back over. "I didn't know there was gonna be places like that." He moved behind Eric. "You shoulda told me, Mama."

Eric looked out over littered flooring. In it, darknesses gaped. One lay a foot-and-a-half before him—which, as he looked into it, he realized went straight through into a cellar.

Mama walked along the edge, till he reached a place where twenty or thirty feet of flooring was torn away. "What I have to find," Mama said, "is where Saul put those drapes I gave him twenty years back. He always said he was gonna hang 'em up down there. I know people been lootin' this place for a month." He moved further along. "I'm just hoping not too many people been goin' downstairs." With his hands out, as though walking some balance beam, Mama Grace turned the corner and continued along the far side of the building. "Oh—there it is. I see it now." He turned and stepped out on the boards.

Even though heights did not particularly bother Eric, the thought of walking on that rickety flooring, a third of which, here and there, had already been pulled up made him swallow hard.

A cloud slid from the sun. Over the foliage droplets began to glitter—from the shower that had ended only twenty minutes before. Eric looked over the edge…and was staring into a basement:

Down in the dark, chains hung from brick walls.

From a beam that had once held up the flooring hung three rubber (or fabric) slings. The end of one had broken, so that its chain lapped down on the floor to curl over the brick near a drain. Not far away stood a white enameled operating or examination table, with metal stirrups and all sorts of brown and black stains at one end—all of it fifteen or eighteen feet below them.

Along the wall, a horizontal beam crossed the stone, where a dozen thick candles, black and red and two more that were the yellow-gray of cut pear were, each of them, stuck in its mound of wax. Each had run over the edge to drip on the floor.

"Besides their piss bar," Eric said, "they had a regular dungeon down in the basement. I never knew *that*—"

Shit settled one hand on Eric's shoulder. "I don't like this place." His other hand, dry and leathery, joined with Eric's, who gave it a squeeze. Shit was actually shaking a little.

"Do those kinds of things upset you?" Mama Grace asked. "Looking at them, I mean?" Standing about twelve feet out on the floor, he held one arm across the chest of his green army jacket. "Things like that always bring to mind the scourging of our Lord—a holdover from the time I was in the seminary." Mama Grace spread his legs, dropped a hand, bent over, caught a metal ring, and tugged.

A trap door that Eric hadn't even seen opened upward, with a swirl of dust in the new sunlight.

"Hell," Shit said, still looking straight down, "the chains and stuff don't bother me. That's just like Bull's basement. But it's too fuckin' *high*!"

Eric glanced aside. "Oh…" He stepped back from the edge, taking Shit with him, whose steely grip relaxed, now that they were out of sight of the cellar's edge.

"I'll take any goddam nigger who wants down in there and fuck *and* whip his black ass till he can't walk no more. I don't mind that. But I do *not* like no sharp drops or things. Hey, Eddie—" And Shit let go of Eric entirely.

Eric looked to the side.

Through the underbrush, which he only realized now was just a slight wall between the building and a clearing, twenty-year-old Ed Miller pushed through with big steps. In one arm, he held his five-year-old half-brother, Hannibal, up on his shoulder.

Once Captain Miller had died, Doris had sold the boat named after her. She'd remarried six years ago. Hannibal was Motley Anderson's boy—Motley was no spring chicken, either. The half-brothers were very close.

Eric said, "What you doin' out here?"

Ed stopped and his other arm came around to the support the child.

Out of what embarrassment he was unsure, Eric offered, "We come with Mama Grace to see if he could find some stuff he gave to Saul. Maybe twenty years ago—before *I* even got here. He phoned up, too, and Saul said if nobody else had run off with it, it was still in the closet in the basement where he'd first put it."

Shit grinned. "Hey, Hannibal. How you doin'? You come out with your big brother, Eddie, to look around?"

Blinking, Hannibal pulled back against his half-brother's shoulder.

"Hey, there." Shit grinned. "You know who I am?"

Ed said, "That's Mr. Haskell. And that's his friend, Mr. Jeffers."

Eric smiled at the quick answer Ed had given to avoid Shit's nickname. (How many years ago was it, Eric had asked Jay, *He your new puppy?*

(Pausing with the rope he was unwrapping from the dock cleat, Jay glanced up scornfully. *Nope. That kid is a straight as an arrow. Naw—what's that guy with the one-to-five scale? Kinsey or somebody? No, he's the wrong place on the chart. Doin' anything with him is an idea Mex and me retired a long time ago.*)

Shit smiled, too. He said, though, "Mr. Haskell, sure—and Mr. Jeffers. We're the garbage men, Hannibal, for Diamond Harbor and Runcible. And Hemmings."

"But right now," Ed said, "they're managin' the big old movie theater in Runcible, while the regular managers is on vacation."

Hannibal pulled back even further.

Shit said, "Why you so shy, Hannibal? We ain't gonna eat you up."

Holding on to his brother's shoulder, Hannibal didn't say anything. Ed said, "He scared 'cause you guys are white."

Shit turned sharply. "Did you go tell this boy we was white? Hell, I ain't white. I'm as much a nigger as either of you!"

"Aw, come on," said very dark Ed. "You know what I mean."

"Goddam," Shit said. "The niggers down here don't know nothin'—less they live in the Dump."

From somewhere, Hannibal located a stash of moral bravado. "They don't show nice pitchers in that theater."

Eric, Shit, and Ed all laughed.

"That's right," Shit said. "They don't. But you'd be surprised how many people from all over the place, up and down this coast, come there to Runcible to see 'em anyway."

Ed was grinning. Above Ed's shoulder, Hannibal looked serious.

"Hey, Hannibal," Shit said, "you ever stuck your finger up your nose, then put it in your mouth?"

"Yeah," Hannibal said. "But I ain't supposed to."

"See, there?" Shit turned to Eric. "He says he does I, too."

"I *hope* he don't do that!" Ed hefted his younger brother higher on his shoulder. "That's disgusting—why you wanna ask him if he do stuff like that?"

There was a noise behind them, and Eric glanced back. Mama Grace was finally coming up the steps, with a great pile of something in his arms. About a meter square, it was wrapped in brown paper with a few rips.

Eric turned back to see Shit, looking all excited and grinning back and forth between him and Hannibal. "If your big brother thinks *that's* disgustin', I'm gonna show you guys somethin' that'll *really* gross you out. Now, see—Eric here is my partner. That's why we can do somethin' like this, an' it's okay. And by the way, I don't think he'd do this with no white feller. I sure wouldn't. Come on, we gonna show Hannibal what we can do."

Knowing where it was going, doubtfully Eric said, "Okay—go on."

Shit reached over and pushed his forefinger into Eric's nearer nostril. When Shit did it straight out like that, because his fingers were so thick, it stretched enough to hurt. But Eric let him.

Ed asked, "What the *fuck* you doin'—?"

"Now, watch it here, Hannibal. Watch it, now. Come on, Eric. Snort somethin' out—gimme a nice big crusty piece. Eric, see, is like *my* little brother."

Eric gave a sharp snort to loosen anything further up, while Shit turned his finger one way, then the other. Eric felt the wreckage of Shit's fore nail against the inner flesh.

Ed said, "What the…?"

"Okay, now let's see what I got." Faintly hooking his finger, Shit pulled his hand down and free. Something dry peeled loose inside Eric's nose and dragged something softer after it.

"Now, *look* at that!" Shit said. "Ain't that a *real* nice piece? All crusty and yeller and got a *big* blob of wet stuff hanging off it—"

Ed breathed, "Goddam…" through a scowl.

"Hey—! That's the nicest piece I seen in a *real* long time." Then Shit put his ladened forefinger in his mouth—and pulled it out…clean. After making exaggerated chewing motions with his jaw, he swallowed and said, "See, now—all gone. Wow, that was a good one! Real tasty."

"Jesus!" Ed stepped back. "Why you gonna show 'im somethin' like that for? Yall are crazy."

But it was Eric who laughed. "Hey, it don't mean nothin'. You know how the boat guys is always doin' that stuff with the night crawlers, hangin' 'em out their mouths? Pretending to eat 'em up?"

"Or that wrestler they used to have on television a hundred years ago," Shit added, "who ate the worms. I don't think he's been on for a while now."

"Yeah. But Billy—" whose own boat went out pretty infrequently these days to take the parties of summer people—"didn't actually *eat* the fuckin' things!"

"Huh?" Shit asked. "Come on, Eddie. You don't think I actually *ate* a finger full of Eric's goddam motherfuckin' snot, do you? Hey—it's a *trick*!"

Frowning, Ed asked back, "Huh?"

"It's a trick, I said." Shit grinned.

Ed asked, "How's it a trick...?"

Shit said, "I can't tell you *that*. Then it wouldn't be a trick no more."

"But you gotta have two people in on it," Eric said. "Just one can't do it by himself."

"Come on," Shit said. "Don't go tellin' him how we do it. Shut up, now. But it's a good one, ain't it? Betcha Hannibal ain't never seen one like that before."

Ed said, "Well, I know people always talked about how, when *you* was a kid, sometimes they'd catch you eatin' your own."

In delayed response, Hannibal scowled. "*Oooooh*—that's *dirty!*"

"Yeah, just like Hannibal, here." Shit grinned at the kid, who did not grin back. "But, see, that's why I went and learned how to *do* the trick," Shit said, stepping to the side. "So I could gross people out who'd think I was *really* doing it."

"Oh..." Ed did not sound convinced. "Yeah..."

Then, from behind them, Mama Grace called, "Success!"

Eric and Shit turned to see where Mama had come up, stepping carefully over the ragged flooring, holding the great package of folded cloth. "Now Scarlet will be able to have her very own ball gown. You know I gave these to Saul to put up, twenty years ago. They were my aunt's drapes, and Saul was going to decorate the whole downstairs. A dungeon—with drapes? I think that's *so* cunning. Only he never got to it. These things have been sitting there in that closet, right where we put them, all this time. Well, I am going to eventually take them with me to Savannah, when I get around to movin'." Then he frowned back and forth. "What yall standing around lookin' so funny about?" (Mama Grace's potential move had been talked and anticipated and prepared for more than a year.)

Ed said, "Shit here—um, Mr. Haskell just ate a finger-full of Mr. Jeffers' boogers to show Hannibal. He said it was a trick."

There was something about Ed's seriousness that started Shit laughing; then Eric started, too, because it really *was* funny—to see the bemusement on Ed's dark face.

Mama Grace said, "Really, Morgan..." and shook his head. "You know, I think the time you two very nice young fellows have spent over in that movie house has...well, coarsened you. I'm not saying anything against it. I've been known to drop in there myself, and occasionally have a very pleasant time. But that is, well...still a little crude."

"Yeah, why don't you come over there and say hello? You know we'll always let *you* in for nothin'—"

"Oh, I don't mind payin' my own way," Mama Grace said over the package's top.

"You, too, Eddie. You can't bring the little guy in." Shit reached over and pushed Hannibal's chin with his foreknuckle. "It ain't like it's gay stuff. The movies is all straight—except when we run them 'queer classics,' like *Kansas City Trucking*, or *Boys in the Sand*, or *L. A. Tool and Dye*. But we always put up an announcement outside for *them*, so folks don't wander in by mistake 'cause they're expectin' women with big titties gettin' their cunts all fucked."

Hannibal looked over at his brother: "You gonna go see them pitchurs?"

Ed just set his jaw and stepped back again. "Come on—don't talk like that."

Mama Grace said, "Ed, you want us to run you into town? There's room."

"We walked out here," Ed said. "We can walk back. Thank you, though, I guess."

"Suit yourself." Mama Grace blinked his artificial lashes. "Morgan, you look like you're about to fall down and roll around on the ground there. Ain't nothin' *that* funny. Come on, now. Get yourself together, and take these back to the car…"

But Shit was laughing so hard Eric took the package from Mama Grace instead.

*

In the van, when they were driving back, Shit pulled his work shoe up on the seat and started to unlace it. At the wheel, Mama Grace said, "Morgan Haskell, if you take that shoe off in here, I will stop this car and put you out in the woods, and you can *walk* back to the Dump. I am *not* kidding! A couple of times I walked in on your father at your place when he'd just taken his off—I know yours can't be much better, and I do *not* want that smell in here!"

"Okay, Mama." Shit's voice held as much humor as resignation. He slid his shoe to the floor.

"I wanna get back and make sure Dynamite gets somethin' to eat," Eric said. "There's a whole refrigerator full of food I run up for 'im—stuff he likes, too—but he'll get up and walk all the way down to Hurter's and get a candy bar or a stick of jerky 'stead of takin' food out the refrigerator and heatin' it up."

Shit grunted.

"And you ain't too much better," Eric said, over the seat back. "Hey, Mama?"

Mama Grace pushed the gearshift and they swung to the left. "What…?"

"You really think we're coarse?"

"As a persimmon against its growth, a week before it's ripe."

"And you think that's from workin' over at the Opera?"

They bounced through the woods a few seconds more. "Now, that's an interestin' question." Mama sounded thoughtful.

Eric bounced along in the back seat, waiting.

"You know pleasure is a funny thing. It always comes on the other side of some barrier or other. I mean, sometimes it's just payin' a man at the ticket booth, so you can get in to see the picture show. Sometimes, it's havin' to climb up a hill, so you can see the view—or even turn around and stand there long enough to look out at something that you enjoy. Some of them barriers are a lot stronger than others. But even the most ordinary little boy and little girl that go slippin' off and start kissin' and makin' out, if their mama or their daddy catches them, then it's, 'Get outa there and stop that! Get on back to your house, now.' That's the one *they* gotta get through. It may not be a big one. But if it's two little boys, say, and they catch 'em carryin' on like that, instead of just tellin' 'em to get on home, they might go in, beat on 'em, maybe break their arms—that's what happened to some kids I heard about back where I was brung up. And if it was your older brother and his friends what caught you, sometimes they'd take you in the barn and brand you on your ass or your belly, like a damned cow. But to find that pleasure, you got to remember that barrier you had to get through, whatever it was."

"That's what folks like Shad wanted to do," Shit said. "But he can't do that no more—'cause he's fuckin' dead. Besides, Jay and Mex wouldn't let him. That's why Mr. Kyle set up the Dump."

"Oh, but there are still barriers. Even around here—with Jay lookin' out for us and Mr. Kyle puttin' some of his considerable moneys into Dump Produce Farms, and the Dump bein' a haven for people who, most of 'em, have had some bad times, and wanna be left alone to do like they want, now."

"What's that got to do with bein' crude?"

"Well, I was thinking, right when you were askin', that you two had a different set of barriers to cross to find your pleasure—to find each other, maybe. See, you learned to get through yours—or *over* yours, or *around* yours—up there in the city. Your father's disapproval, if not your mama's. And you, Shit, learned to get over yours down here—"

"Hey, I didn't have no barriers to *nothin'*," Shit said.

"Oh, yes, you did." Mama Grace nodded. "They were easier than Eric's. That's all." Mama Grace pulled around on the wheel. "I think learnin' how to get over the barriers that Eric done got over—'cause those were closer to the kind that I had to get over, too—gives you a certain sort of…well, moral strength. But, by the same token, living pretty much your whole life with that pleasure, like you done, because the barriers were so easy to cross that you didn't even think of them as barriers, *that* teaches you somethin', too—somethin' else, though. A kind of fineness of perception, a delicacy and an ability to know the details."

"But that's the opposite of coarseness—of crudeness," Eric said.

"Yes," Mama Grace said. "It is. But, you see, each of you knows something the other doesn't—and I wouldn't be surprised if it takes you both a whole lifetime to teach it to the other, if you ever do. If you're coarse, you're each coarse only relative to the other. That's all."

"Hey, Mama," Shit said—they were still not out of the woods—"you was gonna be some kind of priest, once—wasn't you?"

"A minister, dear. I was at the Baptist Theological Seminary, in New Orleans. A very serious seminary student I was, too."

"That would have been interesting—I don't think there are a lot of priests…ministers who look like you."

"Why didn't you keep on?" Eric asked from the back seat. "What happened?"

"Well, one day I was reading Spinoza—working my way carefully through the *Ethics*, perfectly charmed by the broad and generous vision of a universe constituted entirely of and by its god that underlay that intricate imbrication of definitions and axioms and theorems and scolia and demonstrations, when suddenly it hit me: there could *be* no God. Spinoza says as much: God cannot be a being apart from the rest of the universe who looks in on it and thinks about it and wishes it to be one way rather than the other. If God *wanted* anything, then he would be lacking something and thus could not be all-powerful and perfect—and therefore would not be God. It struck me with the force that the insight behind the second definition in chapter one must have at one time struck Spinoza himself—that mind could not effect matter directly, without the intervention of a living organic body—"

From the back seat, Eric said, "*Emet yeshalom yasoud ha'ollam…*"

Mama Grace glanced back. "What did you say?"

"*Emet yeshalom. . .*" Eric repeated, then shrugged. "I don't know, really…"

Mama Grace stopped the car, then turned in the seat, frowning. "I never knew you were Jewish, honey…"

Eric said, "I ain't."

"Well, then how come you can speak Hebrew?"

"I can't," Eric said. "That's all I remember. This guy had it on his door.

I remember he said it had something to do with Spinoza."

"What's this Spinoza?" Shit asked.

"He was a seventeenth century Dutch philosopher, my dear—his parents had come from Portugal, and he lived in Amsterdam, right around the corner from the painter Rembrandt," Mama Grace said. "At least when he was a boy. Eventually, he moved to a suburb, called the Hague. Do you know what it means—what you just said?"

"You said Hebrew," Shit said. "That's—Jew talk, huh?"

Eric said, "Something about Peace and Truth—"

"—form the Foundation of the World," Mama Grace concluded. "Oh, yes, I had to study Hebrew at the school..."

"What's that supposed to mean?" Shit asked.

"A...friend of mine had it on his door," Eric said. "I guess I learned it—you know how you remember things from when you were a kid?"

Mama Grace said, "It was written over another doorway, too, of a house that Spinoza's father would take his son to visit often, when he was a young boy in Amsterdam. And he saw it again and again—and read it over and over. Scholars have speculated that it influenced him, in his own pursuit of pleasure and knowledge."

"Now, see," Eric said, "I never knew that. What were his own ideas all about?"

"I think I actually have an old copy of the *Ethics*—that's his major work—somewhere on a bookshelf. That'll be my going away present to you, if you'll promise me you'll actually read it."

"Sure," Eric said. "I'll give it a try." He wondered if he'd seen the title somewhere before, and if so, where...

"Ah," Mama Grace said, turning back to the wheel and slipping the clutch into gear. "But will you give it *ten* tries—cover to cover? Or even three? It's not a very long book. But I'll warn you, it's *not* easy." The roomy van lurched forward. "Spinoza could believe in his universal godhead because he knew nothing of Daltonian chemistry—not to mention the organic chemistry that actually solves the intermediary problems in some ways we are still not sure of. Consciousness, at least as we know it, *has* to be a molecular phenomenon—not atomic, not mechanical—and is certainly restricted to the heat window in which proteins can survive. If its components had any existence at a greater or lesser granularity, consciousness would not be what its components form, any more than a bar of calcium, a gallon or so of water, and a bag of various minerals constitute a human or even an animal body." (Shit was looking out the window.) "And at the same moment—indeed, for me it was part of the same revelation—I realized that I did *not* have to take off my Maroon Passion nail polish every Sunday night with cotton balls and nail polish remover so that I could to go to class on Monday morning and not scandalize my fellow seminary students and teachers. What's more, I was free to do anything that did not hurt others that strengthened me and helped me in the one thing that we are all put on this earth to do: *help one another*—because it is the only thing that, in the long run, gives us pleasure, as receiving love and friendship and affection is the only thing that gives us joy and ameliorates the dread of our inevitable extinction." At the wheel, Mama Grace took in a long breath. "That very same summer, I came down here to Diamond Harbor for the first time. (You were about eleven years old and a perfect terror, Morgan—I'm sorry, I mean Shit—as I recall. My heart really went out to your father.) Six months later, they discontinued Maroon Passion—the cosmetics industry is fickle, fickle, fickle! With my complexion, I always thought that color did so much for me. It was elegant, understated, and hot as hell. There're colors that I make due with today, but—" he sighed—"they are *not* Maroon Passion."

"You know," Shit said, back over his shoulder to Eric, "I fucked Mama here the *first* time when I was twelve." He looked back. "Remember you had that outhouse behind your place? You didn't have no indoor plumbin' back then. I went and sat in that thing, all mornin', beatin' off, waitin' for you to come in there. And when you opened the door and looked down and seen me, you was so surprised...I *still* remember it." He laughed.

"And *that*," Mama Grace said, "is what I mean by crude."

The car bounced through the underbrush.

"I wonder if Ed was over there to see the murals," Mama Grace mused. They had hit a small macadam road, and down a slope they could now see the water.

Eric said, "What murals?"

Shit said, "What's a mural?"

"A mural is a big painting on a wall. When Saul first opened that place, he had really big plans for it."

"There ain't any walls left in it," Shit said, "and I sure didn't see no paintin's on the ones left."

"Downstairs," Mama Grace said. "In the cellar. You should have come on down with me and looked around. On the walls, there. Those are some of the wildest imaginings I've ever seen."

"You mean with all them whips and chains and slings and stuff?" Shit sounded interested.

"Yes—with *all* of them! But finally, it was easier to keep the top part of the bar opened and close off the cellar. Whenever I talked to him, Saul was always sayin' how in a year or two, he was gonna open the cellar back up and once people knew he had a real dungeon goin'. He was always talkin' about gettin' Bull to run a regular session down there. People would start comin' from *all* over.

"And then he'd put up my drapes.

"But he could never get it together enough to do either one—or open up the underground rooms. I hope somebody took a camera down there and least took pictures of the damned things—and truly damned, some of them were, I'll tell you. Though they ranged from visions of hell to paradise."

*

Later that evening, in their own pickup, driving back to the Opera, while the sky darkened to deep teal and clouds lost detail, sheeting above the sea, Eric said, "You remember a year or two back, when I sucked you and Dynamite off out in the Hemmings Interdenominational Baptist?"

"Yeah," Shit said. "It was beautiful in there." Tonight was beautiful, too.

"I was just wonderin' whether we should'a done that."

"Why? We didn't bother nobody. We didn't hurt nothin'."

"I was thinkin' that maybe it was—you know, a little…crude."

"*Fuck* you…!" Shit said. He looked disgusted.

Eric laughed. "Is that a promise?"

"You know," Shit said, "you are *real* funny, sometimes," with no smile at all. "Hey, I get all my crude real honest like, right from my daddy. Don't forget, that man was a first grade pig fucker 'fore he even got to work on you and me."

"Hey, I don't never suck his dick without thinkin' about that one."

"Oh, so that's why you're leakin' all in my hand when I play with your pecker while you're blowin' 'im."

"Probably," Eric said. "So you don't have to blame it on the movies. Hey, come on." He turned off toward the water front. "I'm just funnin' you."

"Oh," Shit said. "*That's* what you call it!"

* * *

[57] FALLEN DOWN ON the right front corner, propped up with cinder blocks, fallen again, then propped again by the owner, Johnston Realty, with squat pneumatic tubes, the trailer where he and his mother had once lived still stood on the slope among the scrub pines. (Today the screening was gone from the porch; so was the iron bed frame.) For some four years,

Billy had lived there, with his five dogs and his sometimes girlfriend, Matty, who'd worked for Serena during the three years she'd owned the Lighthouse. Eric wasn't even sure where Billy and Matty—if they were still together—were living. To his clients, Billy had styled himself "Cap'n Billy," though no one but the occasional summer visitors had ever called him that. His name—William Cox—was not even on Randal's garbage route roster.

Today, though, the house was padlocked and unrented.

Alone, Eric sat on the needles among the trees. He had started out on a log, but after ten uncomfortable minutes, he'd moved over to some cardboard lying on the ground.

The paperback was open on his knees. (Mama Grace had given him three books, actually, all by Spinoza, but had told him to start with this one.) For the thirtieth or fortieth time he closed it, to look at the worn corners—they had not been worn a week ago—at the unevenness in the spine, at the curve in it from twice making the mistake of folding it to carry it in his back pocket. Still, it wasn't a thick book. The Renaissance painting on its cover had flaked. Here and there among its margins were Mama's pale notes, in a handwriting that, for all its neatness, Eric found illegible.

In a week of trying, he hadn't read any of it.

Well, that wasn't *exactly* true…

Yes, he'd promised to read it through *three* times, in fact. He'd read the first few pages a *hundred* times. No, he thought. Not a hundred—eight, nine maybe; *maybe* twelve. He hadn't understood a word. Only that wasn't true, either. He'd understood lots of words—"the," "and," "of," "God" (he was pretty sure he understood what people meant by God, however uninteresting he'd always found the notion, too small beneath the blue and silver immensity whenever he walked out of the long grass onto the rocks beside the sea), "cause," "itself," "understand," even "existing."

He understood the words as much as he did *not* understand the sentence: "By cause of itself I understand that whose essence involves existence, *or* that whose nature cannot be conceived except as existing." Now when he read it, he found himself mumbling at the page, "Well, that's what *you* may understand, but *I* sure the fuck don't!" But that didn't count, because, for one thing, Mama had *told* him he wouldn't understand much of it. He should be ready for that. And he was supposed to read the whole thing before he started over.

But maybe you *couldn't* do that—

Which was when he took a deep breath and decided he was going to do it anyway.

The day he'd got it, he'd asked Mama Grace, "Is that supposed to be a painting by Rembrandt or someone…?" He meant the cover.

"Actually," Mama Grace had told him, looking over his shoulder, "that's a painting by somebody who very much *wanted* to paint like Rembrandt. For many years, Rembrandt lived in the same neighborhood as Spinoza—right down the street from him, in fact. Though nobody knows if they actually knew each other. They could have met, however—and probably did know each other, at least by sight."

Bats flicked through the upper branches. Eric had made a try at the "Introduction," but given up after three pages, because it all seemed to be about other philosophers whom he didn't know anything about and wasn't interested in. And Mama Grace had said that he should read the introduction only *after* he finished the text proper, anyway.

As far as Eric could tell from that initial encounter, Mama had known what he was talking about.

Eric, who had read one Shakespeare play in high school back in Atlanta (*Macbeth*), turned over pages till, once more, he reached the first of the text:

The Ethics
DEMONSTRATED IN GEOMETRIC ORDER
AND DIVIDED INTO FIVE PARTS,
WHICH TREAT

I.	Of God
II.	Of the Nature and Origin of the Mind
III.	Of the Origin and Nature of the Affects…

First off, he wasn't sure what "treat" meant. (And he was sure "affects" weren't the same as "effects.") You gave somebody a treat, or kids went trick or treatin' on Halloween. Or a doctor treated a disease—cured it with medicine. But that didn't seem to be it. Probably he would need a dictionary for this thing. He had a paperback one, which he'd brought from Atlanta, among his boxes when he'd first come down, but it was in the box with his other books he hadn't cracked since he'd been in the Harbor, stored somewhere with Barb—if she still had it. Maybe he'd have to go get it, soon. But couldn't he make *some* progress without it…?

He skipped a few lines and started at the top of the text itself, reading the words and frowning, more and more. (*Deffinitions*, D.1…D. 2…D. 3…) On the second page, he got halfway down and—at *Axioms*—looked up. The frown had become a look of pain; more, an actual pain across his forehead.

Eric took a breath; the pain lessened…some. He turned back to the first page but hesitated before beginning again. He'd begun the thing with the expectation of not understanding it the first time through. Only he hadn't realized his "not understanding" would be so total, so absolute, the way you might not understand something written in a foreign tongue.

"Cause," "essence," "substance," "finite," "infinite"…those were words he understood, or, at any rate, *thought* he'd understood. Well, I *said* I was going to read it three times.

So I am.

That's all.

He began again, making himself move his eyes across words that were meaningful, but had fallen into phrases, sentences, paragraphs that were not, on and on, and on…

After what seemed a very long time, Eric stopped—and glanced at the page's upper corner. It was page seven. Whatever he was getting out of it, it wasn't worth it. That—he was convinced—was certain. But what about keeping his promise to Mama Grace? Maybe, he thought, easing back on the steps, he could pretend that was the beginning of his first reading. And just go on. No. He had to read it *through*. (That was a gift to him from Diamond Harbor's boredom.) Go back, start your *first* reading now, and make sure you keep going.

Wouldn't it be interesting, he thought, if he could understand finite causes and infinite essences? As he looked through the leaves at the sky, clouds moved with stunning slowness across it. A black check mark suspended in air, a bird soared—which suddenly broke, flapping, and turned. *Were* there such causes, such essences out in the world? Right now, he doubted it.

Yes, on the second time through, the first six pages were easier to—well, not *read*, because there was still no comprehension. But the words were easier to get through, because, surprisingly, he remembered lots of them from the first meaningless encounter.

This time he made it through to page nineteen.

Then started again—but stopped after three pages.

It's *going* to be meaningless, this first reading.

You *know* that!

Mama Grace had already told him that.

Get that through your head and stop hoping for something else. Just *do* the first reading. He realized he was almost in tears. No, he mustn't tell Shit or Barbara or Dynamite or Jay about this, he realized. They ain't *never* gonna understand this thing I'm doing.

He wasn't sure he understood it himself.

One part of why Eric was doing this, of course, was that he'd promised Mama Grace. But—Eric realized vaguely—an even larger part of that was because he was in Diamond Harbor. (Had he still been in Atlanta, promise or no promise, he'd have given up the entire project after half an hour.) Winters in the Harbor were dull. When all the garbage work or theater sweeping with Shit was done, when you'd gotten all the affection and pleasure you wanted from the two of them and given them all you could, if you didn't get off and do *something* by yourself about which you were obsessive, the boredom could be nightmarish. (Shit regularly disappeared to study the minutia of the shore, the streams, the rocks.) So, again—Eric turned back to the first page of the text—he took a breath and decided that, now, he would begin his actual *first* reading of the whole text, whether he understood it or not—

He looked up, then back down at the page.

It had become too dark to read.

* * *

[58] ANOTHER THING THAT made the time confusing was that Shit remembered —and Eric didn't—when Dynamite had driven them over but didn't go into the Opera. "I'm goin' back home. I just wanna take it easy and sit on the porch and look at some of Eric's comic books this afternoon. Somebody'll give you a ride home."

When Jay explained that, since the doctor had again told Dynamite to take some time off—and had (again) wrangled to get him medical compensation pay from the CC—they could get on salary at the theater, if they wanted to make some extra for themselves sweeping up. And Dusty said they could use the apartment over the projection room again this year, till Dynamite felt better and they could go on back to the garbage run. "You mind us stayin' upstairs over here—to help out Hammond and Dusty?" Shit said into Hammond's cell phone after Eric punched the numbers and handed it to him.

"No—go on. It'll be a blessin' to have the bed to myself. Be that much nicer to see you, when you get back. The refrigerator's full of food."

"Well," Eric said, moving his head next to Shit's, "if you'll *eat* some of it..."

What Eric remembered and Shit didn't, however, was late on one of those nights, when they were still sleeping just on the ticking, and, in the dark, Eric reached over to jog Shit's shoulder.

"Wha..."

"Hey, Shit...!"

"What? I'm sleepin'." Shit's long, hard arms took Eric in and pulled him over as if to warm and calm and mollify him in a gesture. "I gotcha here. You're all safe. Go on back to sleep." It was Shit's regular response to any nighttime waking that wasn't a sexual advance.

Often it made Eric wonder what terrors the coastal calm had held for Shit in his own childhood. Shit's automatic sharing of the safety that—certainly—his father had first imparted to him, was something Eric loved. But this time he said, "Shit—Did we go down in the basement of that place?"

"What place...?" Outside the window, moonlight was absolute and silver. But not much of it made it in through the window screening.

"I don't remember. I think I was...dreamin' maybe? No, we went down in the basement, didn't we—with a flashlight, looking at these paintings on the walls...they were really amazing."

"Shhhhhh...no. It was too high for me. Now go back to sleep."

"Oh...yeah. But I thought there, for a minute, that we..."

Shit's body began to squeeze against Eric's and relax and squeeze again. And relax...and squeeze. "Come on, stick your fuckin' tongue in my mouth and lemme suck on it..." Shit's hand cupped the back of Eric's head. Eric held him around his hard, flaring flanks. But after three, four, five more hunches, Shit's hardened genitals softened, his breathing slowed. Their mouths pulled apart and Shit's head fell back in the moonlight—eyes closed, mouth half opened, lower lip wet—and Eric turned his face down against the rough hair over Shit's jaw, their ankles, toes, arms, and knees enmeshed.

On the windowsill sat the three books that Mama Grace had dug out of a carton and given Eric three weeks ago.

* * *

[59] BEFORE SUNRISE, RAIN wrapped the Harbor's Front Street, its one and two story buildings, with dark foil. At midday, sunlight blanched the blues, pinks, greens and even black tar paper to the rattiest ghosts of themselves, which you could not look at directly without squinting. (Ghosts, risen in light...) Nets and ropes wound through chalk-white lifesavers in store windows. Oars leaned against the buildings' water-ward walls. Beyond all, the sea flamed.

* * *

[60] BECAUSE IT REPRESENTED such a change, Eric could never fill in with certainty all the things that had happened in the six months before the evening he and Shit got back from Runcible together to find Dynamite, sprawled on the cabin kitchen's floor, mute, blind, and paralyzed—and, twenty minutes later, in the truck on the way to Runcible Memorial— where he sat between them, Dynamite's head sagged forward. Overlong brown hair blew about his forehead—

Simultaneously they realized he was dead.

"It's a stroke. He's caught a stroke…"

"Shut the fuck up!" Eric heart pounded as he drove. "You done told me that, ten *times* now…!"

Then they turned around and drove his body back in the dark to the cabin, since they knew he'd wanted to be buried out on the island—and both of them knew enough local lore to understand that, if Runcible Memorial took him, almost certainly that would not happen.

Through the night, it was Eric now, who did the long holding and reassuring. With Shit, that meant several bouts of sex during the morning hours. "You really want to?"

"*Yeah*, I want to. Will you stop jawin' and lemme get off?"

"Hey, it's okay. That's fine. Lemme get on down there and you grab a-hold my head, the way you like."

Later, Eric woke to a haze of purple light, flooding from the open door to the side porch and through the windows open toward the sea.

Naked, Shit stood by the bed, as if unsure whether or not to climb in. Behind him the sheet lightning flickered, faded, flared again, and was gone.

Shit held something—small—in both hands up near his chest.

Eric pushed up from the pillow on an elbow. "Hey, what is it?"

"I got…my money card." Shit sounded wholly lost. "I just remembered… that I should probably have it."

"What you mean…?"

"You know. That he keeps for me. When he gets my money…at the Union. How he said I should have it…"

Twisting up his face, Eric realized Shit meant his ATM card that Dynamite had kept in his own wallet. "Oh, yeah…that's good. Did you get his?" He took it from Shit's fingers. It bore the picture of the orange water pump before the Dump Produce fields that had once been Miles Turpens's.

On the bedroom wall, four feet from the door, hung Jay's framed enlargement of the same pump, smiling Dynamite, ol' Stove Pipe, and trees instead of fields that Dynamite had hung there at Shit's urging.

"You should take his whole wallet. That stuff is yours now."

"That's stealin'…"

"No, it ain't, Shit," Eric said. "At least I don't think so. Go on. Bring the whole wallet in. We'll put it in the drawer by the bed here—probably we're gonna need that stuff later. You know—his cards and things."

"The money and everything?"

"Yeah. Really. It's yours now."

"I just thought I'd take the card, and you could hold it for me—like, you know, he did."

"Sure," Eric said. "I'll do that. But we gonna need his other stuff, too…"

Shit turned and went outside—and Eric thought, *I should have gone and got that for him! What am I makin' him do that for? I ain't thinkin' clear!* On the porch, the tarp rustled and crackled. Again, summer lightning bleached the sky pale purple.

Shit walked back in, slowly. "He's really dead. I thought before, maybe I'd go out there and he'd be breathin' again. But he ain't. Damn, takin' his wallet like that—that felt funny." He thrust it forward over the bed. "Here—you put it away, now. It got sixty-two dollars in it."

"You counted it already…?"

"Yeah…before. The first time. When I got my card. I thought somebody might wanna know. So I could tell 'em how much was there. And that… nobody had taken none."

Eric sat up and took the dark leather rectangle with its rounded corners and its curve from Dynamite's hip. Against it was Shit's ATM card. He put them on the table.

"You gonna leave 'em there?"

"Just till we get up tomorrow.

"Oh…"

Eric could not imagine Shit sounding more desolate. "You know your card number?" Or…any younger.

"It's got it, right there—across the plastic."

"No," Eric said. "I mean your…code number—your PIN number, that you have to enter to get your cash."

"Oh, yeah." Turning, Shit sat on the bed, one knee up on the mattress. "It's my birthday. I remember when we was gettin' 'em, they told us we shouldn't use no birthdays, 'cause that was too easy for people to figure out. Or your license plate or stuff like that. So *he* decided since nobody would be usin' that, 'cause they'd told 'em not to, I'd use that for mine anyway—that way I could remember it. And nobody would figure on it, 'cause they already said we shouldn't. The ninth of May, nineteen eighty-eight."

"Oh, yeah…" Eric took in a breath. "Sure. Come over here with me, now." Shit turned and pushed over the bed toward him. For moments Eric thought, with hands and feet and knees and chin all together, Shit was trying to climb into him or through him. He was making whimpering noises, not quite crying, even as his dick hardened against Eric's belly.

"God, I wanna fuck him. I wanna fuck 'im again. At least once more. I wanna fuck him—so *bad*..." He hugged Eric tight enough to hurt Eric's neck. Then he whispered, "When I was goin' into his pants, for the wallet...I got a hard-on. You think I could go out there and just stick it in him, somewhere? Up his asshole or something—"

"*No!*" Eric said, and held him back. "No, you *can't!* I don't think that's healthy, Shit. Besides, he's probably too stiff—you know, with rigor mortis."

"Maybe it might wake 'im up. Or jar his heart, or somethin'."

Lightning again washed the sky with purple. The expression on Shit's face hung—surprising Eric—between frustration and terror.

"No, Shit. He's really dead. *I* wish he wasn't, too..."

"Then I'm gonna fuck *you!*"

"Fine! Go on..."

In a light drizzle, Dynamite lay on the porch outside. Newspaper under him, the tarpaulin above him, through the night he stiffened. Bone and muscle wrapped Eric's chest. Shit's hips hammered Eric's buttocks—as he felt tears slide between Shit's jaw and across the back of his own shoulder.

Closer to morning, when the rain became heavy, and their feet tangled in the blue quilt at the big bed's bottom, Eric sat up, leaned to the side, and pulled the lamp chain so that the light came on through the reddish-yellow shade. The wallet and the Credit Union ATM card lay beside him. Shit was already sitting up, hugging his knees, while the pock-pock-pock of big drops on the roof beckoned Eric toward sleep. He glanced to see Shit looking at him with an intensity that, for moments, along with the exhaustion, made Eric feel he didn't recognize the bearded face of the coffee-skinned black man in bed with him. As Eric leaned forward to tug the sheet loose from the quilt, Shit hooked an arm around Eric and pulled him back against him with a firmness that convinced Eric that Shit had been searching Eric's body—Eric's mouth, his rectum, under his arms, his body's entire surface—with his tongue, his penis, his rough thumbs and fingers, for something sex simply would not yield.

Sitting up once more, Eric managed to pull the lamp cord again, and, in the dark, turn and return Shit's embrace, astounded and excited enough to overcome his exhaustion, in the grip of Shit's toes, his fingers, his knees. In the cabin, natural and adopted sons, the two grasped each other, while outside, above the Dump, purple lightning shocked the summer sea—

Did Shit think sex would release him from mourning?

But that's how Shit was made. Though Eric wondered about it, it didn't actually *bother* him…

The Asian—Philip—had been in winter. The summer lightning the night of Dynamite's death meant…well, Dynamite had died in summer. Yet the fact that Dynamite's comment, from that night with the three of them, "…Hell, I'm so tired, anyway," came back to Eric, as he lay with Shit, made it seem it was only a few weeks, even days before. And that, *both* knew, was impossible.

* * *

[61] AT THE OPERA, Myron—the projectionist—came through, though. "I know Mr. Haskell is real upset about his daddy. Don't blame 'im. Them two was close. Real close. Dynamite did ever'thin' for that boy—probably gonna take him a while to settle into the idea he's gone." Flatly, Myron refused to call either of his erstwhile bosses other than "mister," though both were his junior by more than a decade. "I could say somethin' about that's what happens if you get too close with your own kin. But I don't need to. That ain't no part of my business."

Eric sighed. "Yeah, Shit's pretty upset." He tugged his hands from his jeans pockets. "It's like he's really depressed. I'm sorry this has all happened right now, Myron." He wasn't sure he wanted to talk about his and Shit's sex life. Still, he said, "I guess everybody around here knows about Shit and Dynamite, huh?"

Myron took off his glasses. "Your mama don't." He pulled his handkerchief from the watch pocket in his vest to polish the lenses. "And it sure ain't *my* place to tell her." Despite the black rims, his lenses were the kind that darkened in the sun. Myron was proud of them. Shit and Eric had chuckled about them together, since Myron spent days at a time in the theater without going out into the light.

"I wish I *could* tell Barbara—she really likes Shit. I know she'd want to help him. But you're right, she don't know about that—about what he's really grievin' over."

Myron blinked at Eric, and Eric wondered: Is he thinkin' about me…?

Myron said, "Your mama's a good lady. If she sees Mr. Haskell, she'll know he's hurtin'. She'll do the right thing by him. You gotta trust that one."

"Yeah," Eric said. "Maybe." Though he wasn't sure.

"My second cousin, Obeline," Myron said, "was that way about her brother—and I tell you, nobody in my family had a decent word to say to either of 'em, 'cause Hector was a nasty drunk and beat Obeline and wouldn't work, and all he wanted to do was lay up with her and live that nasty life they had, in that old fallin' down trailer of theirs. But you couldn't say a word against him to her, or she'd take a skillet to your head.

"'Nobody understands me like Hector.' That's all she had to say.

"Then he died. Drunk himself to death—probably out of guilt for gettin' five kids off his own blood kin—the two boys that lived, anyway.

"It took Obeline three years 'afore she could talk civil to people who were only trying to pass the time o' day with her and be respectful of her loss. I felt sorry for her—mean ol' bitch. The kids run off and don't nobody know where they are, ceptin' they run in opposite directions. People go the way they go; and grieve the way they grieve."

"Yeah. I guess so." In the darkness of the upper balcony aisle, beside the projection room door, the theater had a smell that Eric had wondered about recently. "You don't think Shit's gonna take three *years* to get it back together, do you? Or maybe ever…I mean, losin' a parent should be natural—" What interrupted him were some thoughts about why losing a parent like Dynamite might not be.

"You was pretty close to that man, too…"

A wave of sadness welled in Eric and made him sway, with burning eyes. "Yeah…I guess I was."

Myron put on his glasses, looked up, and blinked at the ceiling—only ten inches overhead here—with its pastel gods and chariots and swans and giant butterflies, far enough away to be invisible from the orchestra (unless the cleaning lights were on), but so low that, here behind the waist-high wall along the back of Nigger Heaven—Eric was gripping it now—with many of its original hardwood seats down toward the top balcony rail, some two dozen black men and that big retarded homeless white guy from Tennessee, Haystack, sitting or sleeping among them. When he came to the Opera, Al Havers couldn't even walk upright here.

In the three-quarter dark, you could raise your hand and touch the dim paint.

"Far as I'm concerned," Myron said, "this here is an act of God. Take a couple more days—a week if you want. I'll get Josh to come in and lend a hand with the cleanin'. When you come on by, give me a twenty for 'im and I'll slip it to him. But I don't want 'im to have no fifties—not enough for a full bottle of the hard stuff. You do that, and he gonna get hisself sick."

"Sure." Though Eric was not enthusiastic about giving Josh the run of the Opera, Hammond and Dusty still had a week before they were expected back, and stuff remained to do at the Dump—cleaning out the cabin, going through bags of bedding and clothing that never *had* made it into the wash, getting ready for the burial, over on Gilead, which—somehow—Jay had arranged.

Eric had already been back and forth twice that day.

* * *

[62] WHEN, FOR THE third time, Eric got back to the Dump in the pickup, Bull was there, pulling together a load of junk from in and around the cabin. Out on the deck, Eric asked Shit quietly, "Did he *ask* if he could have that stuff?"

"I told him he could take anything he wanted—long as it wasn't yours. I don't wanna see *none* of it no more," while, in his great boots and no shirt, the waist of his pants halfway down the crack between buttocks black as two cannon balls and, when he turned, his snarled pubic hair above the sagging steel button on his jeans, Black Bull tramped in and out, choosing this piece of an outboard and that wheelless barrow and fifty other things— rusted tools, an old amp meter, a box of screws, a roll of electrical tape.

"Where's Whiteboy?" Eric asked. "Ain't he gonna give you a hand with this stuff?" Sometimes Eric felt odd referring to the scrawny man, now in his middle or late-forties, who moved so awkwardly and smelled bad, as a boy. But that's how it had settled.

"He's kinda busy." Bull frowned at a length of chain he'd picked up. "Don't worry. He'll be dere for de funeral, tomorrow."

Eric looked at Bull's pile and wondered if this wasn't how junk circulated eternally through the Dump. Askew on it was an open shoe carton— probably it had been sitting on some shelf—full of old-fashioned ovoid incandescent bulbs—that, vaguely, he remembered Dynamite replacing, years ago, with the spiral, low-wattage florescent ones you saw everywhere now, even in the back john at Turpens, so that you no longer noticed them. In the box, the round milky ones—each with a cap of dust—though, today two decades old, looked ancient.

Mama Grace brought over a casserole—which they heated in the oven and generally picked at—and hauled junk in the garbage truck off from the cabin to the dumpster.

Shit himself hadn't done much—and only what Eric had asked of him —to hold a box, to move some stuff from the porch.

Eric, Jay, and Mex did most of it. (They'd come by, half an hour after Bull.) Basically Shit sat and stared over the deck rail and rocked on the back legs of his chair.

Jay had gotten the internment sanctioned with the help of a funeral home in Hemmings.

"'Cause I know neither of you know how to get a man buried around here—these people helped me with Shad." The previous morning, they had taken the body away so quickly, Eric had begun to wonder if he'd ever see it again. "They're pretty oblign'."

Apparently, Jay—or the Chamber of Commerce by way of Jay—was paying for that, too.

"Oh, wow!" Eric stood in front of the cabin with Jay and Mex and the dark-suited funeral manager. (Up on the porch, Shit looked as if his grayed jeans were going to fall off him any moment, while he stood watching.) "*Thank* you! I don't…don't know what to say."

Eric looked up at Shit again, who was clenching his jaw. Two tears crawled from Shit's right eye. So Mex turned, went up to the cabin, then hugged Shit, who clumsily hugged him back and made a sound, deep in his throat, as though he were the one who couldn't speak.

"Or at least," Jay said, "I got Kyle wrangling with the Chamber of Commerce from Columbus to make them foot some of the bills for a goddam public servant of thirty-seven years. At least I *think* it's been that long—he was the Dump's garbage man since he was nineteen. For a couple of years on and off, I remember, he was ol' Hank's assistant, before Hank retired and went to live with his mother-in-law in Tallahassee. Hey, Shit? That goes for you, too, son." He nodded at Eric. "Kyle, he really thought your dad was somethin' special." Jay sighed. "Hell, so did I."

Shit just looked bewildered.

Eric had never heard of Hank before—but assumed he was someone who had hauled garbage for the county. It was interesting to think of the two or three years of Dynamite's life as a garbage man, even before Shit became his helper, that he'd never mentioned.

For Eric the afternoon was a bunch of strangely disparate details. The man from Hemmings said that, as next of kin, Shit had to sign some papers.

Shit looked toward Eric and said, "*He* do that."

In his glasses and dark suit, the Hemmings man looked confused. But Jay nodded at him to go ahead, so the man handed the paper and a red ballpoint pen to Eric, who, using the cabin rail for backing, wrote down "Eric Linden Jeffers for Morgan Haskell," and Shit put an "X" beside it.

As easy as it was for Eric to say, well, Shit's father, workmate, and major sex partner since his, well…infancy, had just died, along with the disorientation from having the major adult in Shit's life vanish, Shit's lassitude worried—no, scared Eric. Was it the same disorientation Eric himself felt, only at a greater intensity? And, if so, how much greater? Shit had two ways of describing his feelings: he felt fine—or he felt poorly. Nuances of poorly—or nuances of fine, for that matter—were not easy for Eric to get, apart from what Eric could figure for himself from the situation. In the three days since Dynamite's death, Eric's quiet inquiries, "How you feelin'?" had all gotten curt "poorlys."

Remembering the marathon sex from the night of Dynamite's death, that evening Eric tried to involve Shit in sex again: Shit had done it—but about as half-heartedly as Eric could imagine someone doing it who actually dropped a load.

*

At the Lighthouse Coffee & Egg, five-thirty the next morning, Barbara arrived two minutes after Shit and Eric and Mama Grace, to let them in. (Izaak had loaned her a key.) She wore a white dress, black and white shoes, and, as far as Eric could tell, no more lipstick than the one-time-seminarian. Looking out as the car turned away, Eric asked her, "Ron ain't comin'?"

"No, honey. He's gonna come back up here later and get me, when the burial's over."

"Oh."

Then Black Bull and Whiteboy's pickup coughed outside. Both climbed out and, seconds later, shouldered into the place, in black jeans and black denim jackets (now, at least, Bull wore a belt) buttoned up to the collar, and their scuffed engineers boots. Black Bull looked massive and uncomfortable and sat down in the corner, crossing an ankle over his thigh.

Eric glanced over.

No sole covered Bull's cracked and blackened foot bottom. Within the oval, cut (or worn) away in the leather, from the immense pads of his toes to the broad heel, the rough, broken skin was dead black and bare. Bony, gawky, Whiteboy stood behind him, smiling, grubby, and nervous. Under his jacket Whiteboy's dog collar sat below a ring of grime around his neck. Above it was a lighter streak where it seemed to have rubbed away *some* dirt.

Eventually, Bull switched ankles:

The other boot sole too was gone. Did anyone else see—or know, Eric wondered—or remember?

The ceiling fans were gone. Three years back Izaak had put in air conditioning.

Al Havers and Eddie Miller and Tad showed up in work clothes, as had Eric—and Shit, who kind of wandered between the Lighthouse chairs and tables without really focusing on anything. Ed's hands and green T-shirt were clean—and he wore new black and white basketball sneakers. The others looked as if they were getting off work, not starting in. Having gone on at four, though, probably the garbage drivers *were* getting some of the day off for the burial.

Mama Grace entered in drab fatigues, with a black scarf around his neck and his hair pulled back in a rough ponytail. Though they'd never met till now, Barbara and Mama Grace fell to discussing how nice mornings were this time of year. Then Jay and Mex came in—Mex in work shoes *and* socks—with the man from the Hemmings funeral parlor.

Jay told Eric he'd already asked the garbage drivers if they would dig.

Two minutes later, outside Eric heard a car. Through the scallops of the Lighthouse Coffee & Egg's café curtains, Eric saw the top of a gray vehicle slow, then stop. He wasn't really paying attention to it—or he would have realized who it was. To the extent he was thinking about it, he thought it was an early customer who expected them to be open. Or maybe it was Izaak, who'd stopped by to see how things were going but wasn't going to the island.

Seconds later, someone knocked—an odd way to come into a coffee shop. Though, of course, it was still before seven.

Because he was standing near it, Shit turned to pull back the door.

Standing with a hand on the jamb was a broad black man, balding, in black jeans, a black denim jacket and a blue denim shirt beneath, like a neater version of Whiteboy or Bull.

It made Eric aware of how worn, frayed, and ragged Bull and his partner were.

The top three jacket buttons were open; so were the top two shirt buttons. A gold chain hugged his dark neck. "Hey, Shit—me and Big Man came up 'cause—you know—we wanted to pay our respects. To your dad…? And to you and…" Joe Markum nodded over Shit's shoulder— "well, Eric, here."

That's when Eric realized that Shit blocked his view of a second person in the doorway. Eric stepped to the side to see the small fellow, with his broad, high forehead down at his dad's waist, his wide shoulders in an oversized tweed jacket, supporting himself on *two* half-sized crutches today, his crooked half-length leg between in a cut down trouser leg. He smiled up at Shit.

"Hey," Eric said, for the other people in the room, "it's Big Man, and his dad, Mr. Markum." And maybe for Shit, too, who looked as if he hadn't recognized them. "Hello, Sir. Hey, Big Man."

"I mean," Joe Markum said, "I hope it's okay we come—that we come by, I mean. If we ain't in the way—"

Then Shit did something kind of…strange. He squatted down, and, in his short-sleeve green shirt—there was a rip, Eric saw, for the first time, under one arm—flung his arms around the little guy and buried his sparse beard in Big Man's neck. One of Big Man's crutches got knocked from under his arm, to clatter across the sill.

Big Man laughed. "Hey—wait up, there! Come on, Shit—don't knock me *over!*"

Even with Shit in a squat, Big Man had to strain upward on his single leg to get his chin over Shit's shoulder.

"Come on, now, I said. Don't hug me so tight. You gonna bus' loose my hose pipe and wet us both down!" Big Man's thick, short fingers barely got around Shit's green shoulders.

The shirt wasn't tucked in and Shit's beltless jeans pulled three inches down his butt crack. (As usual, he wore no underpants.)

Finally, Big Man moved one hand up around the back of Shit's head, to pat him there. And grunted.

From the way Shit's back was shaking, for moments Eric thought he was laughing. Big Man must have realized, first, though, that it wasn't laughter.

"Hey, come on now—it's gonna be all right. It's okay. It's okay, now. Don't worry, it's gonna be okay. Believe me, it'll be fine." Big Man's wide stubby hand patted Shit neck. "You ain't feelin' too hot, now. But you'll be okay."

The shaking continued. At the same time, Shit's body began to contract and relax against the little fellow.

"Hey, come on, now. Come on—you relax, now."

It was neither surprise nor disbelief—more ironic recognition: Aw, *Jesus*, Eric thought. He's gonna try and fuck the little guy right *here…?*

"Come on," Big Man repeated and, with his arm on Shit's shoulder, began to push him away.

Finally, Shit raised his head to rasp in a breath. "I'm sorry…" His voice sounded like any lost alcoholic's among the homeless crashing at the Opera. "It just feels better when I…hold somebody."

"Sure," Big Man said. "Sure. I know."

Eric stepped over, put one hand on Shit's shoulder, then bent to lift the fallen crutch and handed it to the black dwarf, who pulled it under his arm and hopped a step back, while Shit pushed upright, his face smeared with tears.

"See," Joe Markum said, "we just wanted to come by, 'cause we wanted you to know we was feelin' for you."

"Un-huh," Shit managed to say. "Thank you. Yeah, thank you."

"I mean, if we won't be in the way."

Eric felt a sudden weight against his shoulder, a hard arm around him. Something blocked his vision—and almost pulled him down.

Shit was hugging *him*.

So Eric held Shit awkwardly, rubbing his back, while Shit cried against his neck. "There, you're gonna be fine. You go on and cry," Eric said. "Nothin's wrong with that."

Over Shit's shoulder, Eric watched Big Man get his balance on his crutches and smile again, though his expression was uncertain.

So was Joe Markum's.

*

At the Gilead dock, they got the plain pine coffin from the hearse and slanted it over a two-wheel hand wagon. Shit kept saying, "Hey—I got it. I got it. Lemme have it—" so they stepped back for him. With great care, looking over this way, looking over the other, he wheeled his father's coffin up the plank Jay had thought to bring, and onto the scow.

Or, maybe, he always kept it in there.

* * *

[63] ON GILEAD, BESIDE the boathouse dock, Jay had parked his pickup. Taciturn Al climbed into the truck bed and said nothing. They made two trips, with the guys—including Shit and Eric—in the back, sitting on the casket's edge.

Eddie stood, leaning his butt against the pickup's cab to ride, standing, because (he said) sitting on a casket made him feel funny: twice he nearly fell out the truck.

Tad said, "You better sit down, fool—I don't wanna be the one to have to scrape you up off the goddam road." Ed grinned but still stood.

Eric watched him, smiled, and thought: Jesus, he's probably half a dozen years *older* than I was when I fell into bed with Dynamite, Mex, and Jay the first time—not to mention Shit. Yeah, I'd been working out six times a week on that damned machine, trying to keep up with my dad, trying to make sure nobody would mistake me for the scrawny little kid I knew I really was, trying to make myself look like a grown-up muscle man. *Could* I have been that naïve? But I'm alive. Does that mean those men were simply very, very good people? Some—like Mex—are here, helpin' us, today. I don't know. If you needed a reason why someone that age—

much less six years younger—shouldn't get sexually involved with grown-ups, who might accidentally expect them to know something, Ed's your example walkin' around on two legs.

(But then, Jay and Mex *never* done nothin' with Ed. He guessed the others knew it, too...)

Were we just different kinds of kids...?

Eric kept wanting to say to Shit, Ain't it odd, how the last time we come out to a burial, Ruth and Walter Holota were here. But now *they're* gone... But there didn't seem any easy way to interject it.

They left Barbara and Mama Grace at the Kyle place with Hugh. Big Man in Eric's lap and Mr. Markum's black jeans and jacket already blotched with dust, everyone else rode on to the graveyard.

Only three dug at any one time...

Every twenty minutes, Jay made them spell each other digging, so that nobody got too tired.

"You didn't come to dig none," Jay told Mr. Markum, when Big Man's dad picked up a shovel. "That ain't what you come here to do."

"No," Mr. Markum said. "That's okay. Diggin' out is my damned business. Come on. I'm gonna dig."

"I guess you gonna dig, too, huh?" Jay grinned down at Big Man.

"Hey," Shit said, sharply. "Don't make no fun of him."

Big Man said, "You wanna hold one of these for me? I damned well *will* dig for you." Turning on one crutch, he waved a stubby hand at Morgan. "Come on, now, Shit. He ain't makin' no fun. That's just his idea of a joke. See, I pulled loose my pee tube and squirted it in his damned face at the Opera enough times. After somebody do that to you, you *can't* make fun of 'im!"

Jay actually glanced over at Joe Markum, who didn't seem to be really listening—for which Jay actually looked grateful.

The eleven men took two-and-a-half hours to dig a hole that went down five feet.

"It should be six, but *I* ain't gonna say nothing," the man from Hemmings said, a hand on the side of his black suit jacket.

While Tad and Al were in the midst of digging, a few feet away among the wooden grave markers, Ed—who'd finished his turn fifteen minutes ago—was rubbing at the ground with his sneaker toe, when he started laughing. "It says 'Poppinjay' here—on this plaque! Jay—that ain't the bird—that parrot—yall used to have, is it?"

"Yep." Jay looked over. "It was Hugh's—been there longer than I was."

"You got that *bird* buried in here?" Ed looked like it was going to break him up.

"Sure—lived in his room for about forty years."

"Aw, come on, Jay. You can't have a bird buried in a people graveyard! Can you?"

"Why the fuck not? When he passed, Mex and me made up a box for him. That bird acted like more like a part of my family than—say—Shad ever done."

Ed began laughing—and suddenly coughing—as if he were gonna be sick on himself; still, it looked as if it was the funniest thing he'd ever heard.

Then, as they were finishing, Hugh, Barbara, and Mama Grace walked up among the trees and graves. ("He got a *bird* buried in here—in its own grave!" Ed was saying. "Hey. A parrot? You guys around here is *all* crazy." Ed's rough hair was a little long and kind of uneven. Eric was used to it on Shit, but on Ed it looked strange.) In the dappled forest light, under the funeral manager's direction, Jay and Al got the coffin positioned in the hole.

By now, it was minutes past ten. Through the humid morning, birds chirped, lazily, insistently.

As he was standing by Mama Grace, Eric looked down where Mama had his hand in the pocket of his jacket. Something gleamed, and Mama looked over to see Eric frowning.

Eric looked around for Uncle Tom's marker, but they didn't seem to be in that part of the graveyard.

Mama took out a stubby steel cylinder. "Oh, this…?" He reached around with his other hand and pulled a small tab, and a length of metal ribbon, bright yellow and scored with black measuring lines, extended three, six, eight inches. "Long time ago, I learned if you gonna go to a country funeral, it ain't never a bad idea to bring your own tape measurer, for when they start diggin'." He pressed a button. With a quick *whirrrr* the measuring ribbon rewound.

"Oh," Eric said. "Yeah…sure."

"I just mean," Mama Grace said, "if anybody wants to check for certain. I'm sure they don't need it, but I been to at least two where they didn't have one and could'a used it. You just never know."

Unsure what he was supposed to do, Eric wandered a few steps away. Once he asked Ed, "How's your little brother?"

Drawing himself up, Ed looked surprised. "Hey, I wouldn't never bring *him* out here," he said—though Eric wasn't sure *what* Ed thought he'd asked him.

Underarms and the small of his back still damp from his own twenty minutes with the shovel, Eric moved over to stand beside Whiteboy, who looked around and whispered, "This is *so* fuckin' pretty out here…!" His turn at digging had exacerbated Whiteboy's body odor. In the cup of his ear, Eric saw a crust, the color—and nearly the size of—a penny. Blackheads scattered the cartilage's curves and ridges.

In the leafy breeze, Eric thought, I know I smell strong, but…while Whiteboy reached down to maul his crotch with a knuckly gray fist. Eric said, "Yeah, it *is* nice." Whiteboy's smell was not the odor of someone who had worked a week without washing, but of someone who had slept in shit—old shit and old piss, repeatedly…old enough so that it no longer smelled like either excrement or even ammonia. The way our bodies' smells bind us, Shit's and mine, Eric wondered, *could* that odor have bound that man to Bull…?

Whiteboy glanced over with eyes as blue as Eric's and a questioning look. Then he ducked behind to step forward up on the other side. "Wha'dya say? Huh? That's my dead ear. I don't hear *nothin'* outta that one."

Eric grinned. "I said, 'Yeah. It's nice.'"

"Oh," Whiteboy said. "Un-huh. It is."

For the last five seconds, Eric had let Shit drift from his thoughts. Looking around now, Eric saw Shit, standing about ten feet away, absently hitting at one leg of his jeans with a piece of branch and frowning. He'd been thinking a lot about Shit all morning…

Leaning on his crutches beside his dad, Big Man stood across the grave.

The man from Hemmings said, "Would anyone like to say something over the deceased? I understand this is a nonsectarian funeral."

Jay pulled off his orange cap and took a lumbering step across the dirt.

Beside the mound sat—in the hole, off center—the pine box, with six, seven, eight brass wing nuts around the edge. "Yeah…I wanna say, um… Dynamite Haskell…um, Wendell Haskell was my best friend, pretty much my whole fuckin'…I mean, you know, all my whole life. I'm gonna miss 'im. Mex gonna miss 'im, too." Mex looked up, raised his hands, and said something hurriedly in sign language, which Eric was at the wrong angle to follow. He looked for Shit, and realized he probably couldn't see it, either—though Shit wasn't even looking at the stocky, pockmarked Mexican.

A mumble of assent moved through the garbage drivers. Jay looked around, swallowed, then stepped back from the grave.

Eric found himself thinking that, with the exception of Tad, Barbara, and twenty-four-year-old Ed, this could be a gathering in Turpens' rear john.

Jay looked over at Shit. "Hey, Morgan. What about you? You wanna say somethin' about Dynamite? Maybe it'll make you feel better."

"Un-huh…" Shit glanced up, with the look that, since Dynamite's death, kept making his features seem as if they didn't all belong to one face. "Yeah, he was…he was my frien', too." Shit nodded and stepped forward. Then he seemed to think better and stepped back again. "My dad…you know—" he looked from side to side—"Dynamite…"

Eric would not have been surprised if Shit dropped to his knees and howled. But Shit just stepped back.

"Does anybody else want to speak?" The man in the black suit looked around. Was it because of the digging—and the dirt that had been in the air—that his hair seemed colorless? Before, on the scow, Eric remembered it as light brown. A scatter of dust occluded half of one lens in his glasses. "If that's all, could you men, who have been so generous with your help so far—"

Joe Markum said, "He was a good fren' to me and my boy, here, too. We gonna miss him at Christmas." He looked from Shit to Eric. "I hope you boys still keep comin' out to see us. You always welcome—and pretty much any other time, too. But you know that."

"Thank you," Eric said. "Sure. Yeah."

Bull's voice was too loud, hoarse, and clumsy. "He was *my* frien', too—all the time I been at the motherfuckin' Dump!"

"—give us just a little more of your—yes…?" Quizzically, the man from Hemmings looked up. "Oh. Yes, you wanted to talk—?"

Bull went on. "Yeah. That Haskell was my *real* good frien', a frien' to me *an'* this dumb shit Whiteboy, too. Weren't he?"

"Yeah." Whiteboy nodded. "Un-huh…Bull'd let ol' Dynamite mess wi' me—" He was grinning at Shit, who still wasn't paying anyone much attention. "Yeah, he'd let 'im yank my pants—"

Eric started to frown.

Bull interrupted his partner, "*Shut* de fuck up—*fool*! Don't talk about dat heah. Dis a funeral!"

It didn't stop Whiteboy's grin, but Whiteboy ceased speaking.

"Of course," the man from Hemmings said. "Mr. Haskell was a *good* friend—to many people here. To many of us. Yes. Thank you." He looked around again, to make sure of no more interruptions. "But we'll need some more help to fill this in…I mean, anyone who wants can return to the house, but…" He looked as if he wasn't sure that was the right suggestion.

Shit said, "I'm gonna stay. I'm gonna bury him."

Stepping forward, Eric said, "Me, too…"

Jay said, "Aw, come on. You guys done enough. You already dug half the grave. That was the work. We'll take care of the rest."

"Yeah," Ed cajoled; to Eric, Eddie seemed a boy trying to sound like a man.

Jay said, "Go on back and have some coffee—Hugh made cookies. We'll take care of it. Coverin' 'im up don't take half as long as diggin' out the hole."

"Naw," Shit said, looking around for a shovel. "Naw. I'm fillin' it in."

"All right, then." (Eric could see Jay was figuring.)

Basically, Eric realized, Jay had decided to let Shit—and Eric, too, probably—do whatever they wanted.

"Well, then. Good. Let's get to work."

Eric turned to look for Barbara. Stepping nearer to her, he said, "We'll be back at Jay's soon," and she turned to him, face sliding from beneath the hat brim's shadow.

Putting her hand on her son's hard forearm, from which his shirt sleeve, missing its buttons, was rolled up, Barbara said, "Sure, sweetheart. And you bring Morgan—when he's ready. I know how he feels. He wants to say his good byes to his uncle. I can understand that. Mr. Markum?" She looked diagonally across the grave's corner. "You're comin' back to the house with us, with your son, for some coffee?"

"Yes, ma'am. That'd be nice." Mr. Markum looked down at broad headed Big Man. "Come on, fella."

Somehow Eric was the last to go, along with Bull and Whiteboy. The others moved ahead, and since Bull and Whiteboy were almost uncomfortably silent, Eric decided to leave them and move on up toward the others.

He had wandered a few steps ahead. So he heard the blow—though he didn't see it.

Eric turned back to see Whiteboy rubbing his jaw. He had staggered a few steps ahead of Bull, who had stopped, his fist out from his side. "That's what I think of you, you piece of fuckin' rat shit...!" Then Bull strode forward, on past Eric.

Whiteboy moved unsteadily on.

Eric frowned at the grubby man. "You okay...?" he asked.

"Uh-huh," Whiteboy said thickly. He rubbed his jaw some more. Finally he straightened up. "See, I didn't wear my leash today. 'Cause it was a funeral. Besides, at a funeral he can't go callin' me names like he do, regularly—I mean in front of other people. But when he don't do enough of that, it's like I stop believin' 'im, and I start feelin' like he don't care about me no more. But neither of us thought it was right. For the occasion, I mean. But, see, I wasn't feelin' as safe as I usually do."

"Oh," Eric said. "But you're...okay now?"

"Yeah," Whiteboy said. "Now I'm feelin' real good. 'Cause he really hit me." The two of them went on through the sunny green growth. "He thinks

I'm a piece of rat shit now—so I'm okay." Whiteboy smiled uncertainly. A red welt crossed his jaw. "I'm gettin' those chills and everything. I'll be okay."

*

At the Kyle place, pecan cookies and a peach upside-down cake stood on the sideboard. There was a coffee urn—but no full meal. Still, it was nice. "You know," Eric said to Jay, "I was wonderin' if Robert Kyle was gonna show up—I mean, him and Dynamite was so close and everything...there for a while."

Jay smiled.

And Mex signed, *No, I don't think he like to come out here no more. Dynamite would understand that.*

"What you mean?" Eric asked. They stood before the dark fireplace.

"See," Jay said, "this used to be a pretty grand house. Once it was really beautiful. And it's where Kyle was born and grew up." He looked around, at the warped floor, the sagging furniture, the chairs with the leather broken away at the corners and the stuffing, gray and yellow, pushing through. "Now it's a wreck. Kyle don't mind us stayin' here—but comin' out here himself makes 'im feel...pretty...poorly, I guess."

"Oh..." Eric looked around. He had been surprised that as few people had turned up as they did. But then, Jay and Mex were older than the last time there'd been a funeral here. It would have probably been a lot harder for them. "Oh, yeah. Maybe it would...I can see that."

*

When the scow reached the mainland, in his baggy gray suit Ron was waiting to pick Barbara up. Barbara stopped, nevertheless, to give Eric, then Morgan, a hug. While she embraced him, dirt that remained on Shit's hands from the cemetery made smudges on the shoulders of her white dress,

"Thank you—for lettin' us be there with you, and lettin' us help you some with the digging." Joe Markum stood by the door of his car. "I'm glad we could do that for you."

"You gonna feel better. It's gonna be okay." Big Man reached away from his crutch to tug at Shit's wrist. "It will. Believe me." Shit looked down at him, as though surprised—again—he was still there.

"Yeah," Shit said. "Yeah. Thanks. For lettin' me hug on you some."

"Aw, that weren't nothin'," Big Man said. "Glad to do it."

"We'll see you soon," Eric said.

Big Man looked pleased with both of them.

Shit said, "Probably we'll catch you at the Opera—before we come down for Christmas—for the Space Program celebration I mean."

Eric wondered if Mama Grace was going to say anything to him about the book. But the former seminarian only smiled at him, above the loose knot of his scarf, then gave Barb a friendly hug and said how nice it had been to meet her finally. It ended with how fond he had always been of Eric—and Morgan, both. They were very helpful boys. "I guess I should say 'young men.' Sometimes I forget how long I've known them."

"Yes," Barbara said. "They are."

A bit dusty, Ron's red Camry sat outside the Lighthouse as Barbara climbed in.

Then, in Dynamite's pickup, Eric drove Shit to the Dump.

Eric had relaxed some—though Shit was not really more talkative than before.

Unthinking, Eric still expected the cabin's familiar clutter. When they stepped in, the bareness surprised him. He'd forgotten they'd cleaned out so much of the bedroom.

The big bed had its head to one wall. Shit's smaller bed stood by the other (still unslept in). A couple of boxes, and, between them, its half dozen exercise rods, like spiring antennae (one badly bent—by Hannibal a few years back when he'd come by and Eric had let him fool around with it, then left him with it and gone outside...), free of surrounding junk, the giant mantis of Eric's Bowflex held the room's center, waiting for someone to decide whether to keep it or throw it out...

That night, Eric wandered out the door to the deck, clear for the first time since he'd been there, where Shit was sitting, looking in the direction of Bull's cabin.

Black Bull's truck stood beside it.

The sky was deep, deep blue.

Shit said, "It was nice of Bull to come to the funeral."

Though his flat tone made Shit's comment seem oddly empty, Eric said, "Yeah. It was..."

Shit added, "An' Whiteboy."

Though Eric had not been expecting any particular turnout from the Dump, now he wondered whether its lack—no Mr. Potts, no Llewelyn and Fred, no Chef Ron—had meant anything. But then, all the guys they'd worked with on the old garbage run had come out, except Randal, who was on duty—and who had called the day before, with his apologies.

Headlights from someone's van pulled into Bull's yard to sweep over the junk on Bull's porch before turning off. At the sides of the curtains and the shades, orange light flickered behind and around the lowered shades in the two front windows.

"They got a fire goin' in there," Shit said moodily, "tonight."

"Guess so," Eric said. "It ain't really cold enough for one, though."

Then, six or seven minutes later, Shit got up, walked across the deck, and started down the steps.

"Where you goin'…?" Eric called.

"I dunno," Shit answered in that vague voice that was one with his irresolvable mourning. He walked straight, though, toward Bull's cabin. Only at the front door, did Eric see him turn aside and start around it.

Eric frowned.

Within moments—not minutes—the sky went from darkest blue to black. Eric looked up. It had become night, and a starless one.

Eric was exhausted. Getting up from the bench at the edge of the porch deck, freed of junk for the first time in so long, Eric moved to the chair. The seat was still warm from Shit.

How long, he wondered, *should* he wait?

A sensation of loss startled him, pushing him toward tears. Shit's so alone. And I can't help him none. Sitting on the deck, that night he thought some melancholy things, starting with all he'd kept from Barbara, which made it impossible for her to be his confidante. She knows I sleep with Shit. She thinks its okay. Probably she *suspects* I'd fooled around with his "uncle," but left that for us to deal with.

Eric felt powerless, small, and on the verge of being crazy, because he was thirty-eight and for more than a dozen years he'd been partnered with someone, now forty, who was probably psychotic, anyway, and who—till three days ago—had been fucking his own father for more three decades—

But, then, they both had.

And that father had died.

Suppose Shit had died and left Eric with Dynamite?

However it went, Shit and me'll probably both end up in the blackest cell in the lightless basement of some asylum. Well, as long as I'm with Shit, he thought bravely, I don't give a fuck. Yeah, that's brave, he thought. Brave *and* stupid. What reason, it occurred to him, would anyone have for keeping us together? They'd want us as far apart as possible, in different buildings, different hospitals, different states—

Which is when Eric woke.

(In his dream, some man, who looked like the Hemmings mortician, had been driving him in a pitch black armored car to a different state…)

Half a dozen lights in half a dozen houses, mostly to the right, had gone out.

(Before he'd been shut into the car, he'd been in a black cell in the basement of an asylum, and that had been...he shivered.)

He'd never had a dream like that before—one that went on and on, without any light. In the front room of Black Bull's, orange light flickered beside Bull's lowered shades.

Had he drifted off for twenty minutes...? For two hours...?

How late *was* it?

Eric stood, went to the cabin's side door, and looked in. He didn't have to turn on the light—though he did anyway—to make sure Shit wasn't in bed. He pulled in a long breath, turned the light out again, and walked back onto the deck, moving across the uneven boards. He got the rail in his hand and stepped down.

It was chilly—and, in the dark, he walked over ferns and grass.

(He thought suddenly, even hysterically, who will point out, now, those jeweled webs across morning...?)

Night was a cool hollow with an uneven floor.

Walking over the road's dust, he stepped onto the grass before Bull's porch. When he stepped onto the boards, at first he thought to go around the side to see what was in the back, the way Shit had done. But the light edging the shades was too dim to see anything.

Finally, in front of the door, Eric knocked. First, he did it quietly, thinking: If they're asleep, I don't want to disturb them...Perhaps Shit had continued walking across Bull's yard, then for the cliffs, to wander down to the beach...But, then, maybe he hadn't—

And I want to find out what's happened to him.

Eric knocked harder, standing upright.

After seconds, he was about to knock again, when the latch turned over. The door pulled back.

Someone stood there, firelight behind—a big black man? *Was* it Bull...? The man was naked. Warm air from the fire surged out the door, against Eric's knees, his face, his hands...

Eric strained to make out the alien features and suddenly realized...

A grill crossed the mouth. Other grills covered the ears. Lenses before the eyes were black circles. The head was encased in full leather.

From the flicker behind him, Eric could see the man's shoulders, flanks, arms, and—Eric looked down—lower legs ran with perspiration. Down black, blocky calves that practically filled them, sweat rolled under the tops of his boots.

Beside him, naked and barefoot, Whiteboy crouched.

"Whatchu wan'?" It was Bull's rough, outsized voice.

Eric looked up at the silhouetted head—

Eric said, "I'm sorry, Bull—if you're busy…?"

Bull dropped his head to the side. "What the fuck you want?" Then he gave the leash in his hand a yank. "Heel, you motherfuckin piece o' crap! *Heel!*"

On the ground, on all fours, Whiteboy sagged to the side. One end bunched in Bull's fist, the leash was attached to Whiteboy's collar. Grinning up at Eric, Whiteboy moved, like a spider monkey, nearer Bull's heavy leg.

"Is Shit over here? I wanna know if he's…okay. That's…" Eric swallowed—"all."

"So you wanna know how your partner is—how your motherfuckin' brother is holdin' up in my goddamn cellar room? How your fuckin' piece of nigger shit scumbag partner is trying to keep it together, mewlin' an' pukin' and peein' all over hisself, an sayin' 'I'm sorry, Bull! I'm sorry! I didn't mean it! I'll be good! I swear it—' just like he was *this*—" again he tugged the leash—"worthless piece dried-up dog puke—this lace-curtains piece of Mick garbage nobody ever even bothered to teach how to skin back his own fuckin' dick to keep it *clean*." On *clean* again Bull yanked the leash.

Eric looked down as Whiteboy sagged against Bull's leg. Whiteboy dropped his buttocks to the floor, looking back and forth between them with the manic grin Eric remembered from the Gilead cemetery. One hand back between his legs, slowly Whiteboy pulled at his cock—not large, but oddly shaped. As it slipped from the knuckles, Eric saw a bulge toward the back and a bend to one side. Off the end, three-quarters of an inch of skin made a scrawny spigot.

"So you want me to tell you how the little fucker's doin', huh? What, you think I'm some motherfuckin' magic Negro, what knows all the answers to your dumb shit-ass white boy questions?"

"Huh…?" Emerging from the simple surprise of the two of them, joined by the leash, Eric had all-but-decided that Bull—if not Bull and Whiteboy both—were stoned. "What you mean? What kind of…magic…?"

Eric thought it was going to be a drug.

Bull chuckled. "Da's a wise ol' Uncle Tom you think you can come up to, who knows everything you wanna find out in the wide world, the whole of it, who's ready to sit down wid ya', and spew you out all the good advice you can drink down your ignorant white boy gullet. Yeah, you wanna spend de night drinkin' down my fuckin' nigger puke. Well, too bad for you, boy, unh-unh—that ain't Bull. No, sir. That ain't your motherfuckin' Bull tonight. Not for you *or* ya' damn nigger twin brother." He lowered his masked face toward Eric's.

Eric swallowed. It was all he could do not to step back.

Pulling himself up again, Bull seemed taller than he'd been. "WHY DE FUCK IS YOU STANDIN' IN FRONT OF ME LIKE DAT FOR? *DROP* yo' fuckin' nuts down to de groun', dere! Go on! *Get* down, or I'm gonna *KNOCK* you down, nigger! An' make my motherfuckin Whiteboy scumbag gnaw yo' motherfuckin' balls off while I'm knockin' ya! Go on, I said! Get on yo' motherfuckin' knees, when you talk to me! YOU HEAH WHAT AH'M SAYIN' TO YA'? I GOT A MESSAGE FOR BOTH OF YOU!"

Chills cascaded the backs of Eric's shoulders, as he dropped. Bull *wasn't* completely naked, Eric saw, as his knees and knuckles hit the porch boards, and the bloom of pain stung under all four. Besides the mask and boots, Bull wore a black jock. Possibly from the firelight within, reflected off his own face, Eric saw its cup proper was linked chain. Bull's thighs, calves, and arms glistened with black sweat, droplets still or moving, turned orange and—some on the side—scarlet. The cup was not mail, but—now that Eric's face was in front of it—vertical chain lengths held together with horizontal links.

Scrotal flesh pushed some of the chains apart, like black bark, raddled and folded. At one place, smoother, part of his heavily curved penis, pushed between. "AND YOU GOT TO HEAR IT, TOO!"

Eric looked up.

In the same way that, before, Bull seemed to have grown taller, now he seemed taller still. Bull thundered. "YALL THINK, JUS' 'CAUSE YALL IS *WHITE*, YOU CAN STAN' UP TO A NIGGER POWERFUL AS ME? YOU THINK DAT, DON'T YOU? NAW, NAW—YOU GET DOWN ON YO' MOTHERFUCKIN' KNEES. *DA'S* HOW YOU WHITE SCUMBAGS GOT TO ACT AROUND ME—" Again, he gave Whiteboy's chain a yank. "Yall white scumsuckers ain't nothin' but left over nigger turds what nobody wants, anyway, till they done dried up and ain't got no color at *all!*"

Eric's head was on the same level as Whiteboy's, who, still grinning, pulled at himself. The skin on his shoulders, his calves, his forearms, his neck—thin and unevenly pale—held the faintest web of underlying wrinkles, as though he might have been fifty or more years older…

"That nigger talk to me like that *all* the time—" Whiteboy whispered. "It make me feel *real* good. Real nice—so I can get all relaxed. And all safe with him, 'cause that nigger is so powerful. He won' let nothin' hurt this po' piece of white shit." Whiteboy nodded in Eric's face. His hair tickled Eric's forehead. "'Cause that's what I am. Did Dynamite ever talk to you like that?"

"Huh…?" Eric asked, bewildered. "Naw—naw, he didn't…"

"'Afore you come down here, once when Shit was off explorin' around, Dynamite come over and Bull here made him talk to me like that for thirty, forty minutes 'for he turned ol' Dynamite loose and they'd fucked me good. Both of 'em. Together. Man, that was almost good as Bull doin' it by hisself. You know Danny Turpens? He comes around here and plays with us, sometimes. But 'cause he's a drunk, he pees all over *everythin'*..."

Bull roared, "PUT YO' HAN' ON DE FLOOR!"

Flinching, squinting, on his knees, Eric looked up.

"*Put* you han' ON THE FLOOR when I tell you!"

Eric looked down at Whiteboy for some explanation. There was only the manic smile. Eric put his hand in front of the hand Whiteboy was leaning on, over the cabin's threshold.

"Not THAT one, you ignorant scumstain! The *OTHER* one!"

Eric jerked his hand back and put the other on the far side of Bull's boot.

"He gonna step on yo' hand now. You gonna lift him up in the night on yo' own hand, and he gonna take off from it and fly around the whole motherfuckin' world! He gonna fly around and see the chinks in China and the niggers in Africa—and the Eskimos! All them Eskimos and all them penguins...Buck naked like he is, the ice ain't gonna hurt him, and he gonna walk through the volcanoes' fire and that fire ain't gonna hurt him one bit, either, 'cause he gonna drink that white hot lava, right down, runnin' over his fingers like the coolest water. You know, it's gonna burn his skin all black—blacker'n Bull already is, like it always do. That's how that nigger stay so motherfuckin' black, 'cause he goes into them roarin' volcanoes with all that heat and fire and lava and it chars up his skin. Like fuckin' coal. Like fuckin' oil. But it don't hurt *him* none. Black Bull ain't like us poor, stupid piece-o'-shit ignorant white boys. This nigger is the most powerful animal in the world. That's what Danny says. But you know that—'cause you live right across the road. See, this nigger is too—" Whiteboy whispered as if the word itself held immense magic—"*powerful* for nothin' to hurt 'im—"

Above Bull thundered, "PALM UP. You don't know *nothin'*, you ignorant rat turd! You ain't worth a drop of bloody pus out a busted pimple up this heah monkey's syphilitic ass." He jerked the leash again. Again, Whiteboy swayed.

Eric reversed his hand, so that, across the threshold, his knuckles were on the gritty carpet and his palm was up. Bull's leather boot rose from the floor and came down, the first third of it, on his upturned fingers.

Eric had been thinking nothing was *really* frightening in what Bull was saying, save what the transgression suggested might happen minutes ahead—or had already happened in another room. But it had put Eric in some strained place, so that his heart pounded and—despite his mind—his body responded with all the physicality of fear—

Bull's boot pressed Eric's palm—and for two, three, four seconds Eric *was* terrified something awful had fixed itself to the boot's soles.

Whatever it was, lived and wriggled and gripped him with warm flesh, moving over Eric's hand, over his skin. Eric tried to pull back, but Bull leaned into him, heavily enough to pin his hand. His knuckles stung—

Then he remembered Bull's boots *had* no soles.

Bull's toes were flexing. Callused flesh gripped Eric's hand. Bull's leathery toes—his whole foot—moved, pulsed. Did it breathe? Above him, Bull intoned: "The bottoms of my boots are ALIVE! They step over all of white mankind, while I walk through the stars, straddle the clouds, cram the moon in my mouth—"

While Eric tried to get his breath back, Whiteboy grabbed his other wrist. "Hey—can I pee in his hand? Come on, feel my cock and my nuts while I pee in your hand."

Again, Bull laughed. "YOU HAVE NO WINGS LEFT TO FLY. WHEN YOU SPLATTED OUT LIKE A ROTTEN FRUIT FROM A GARBAGE TRUCK RATTLIN' DOWN DA ROAD, DEY SAW HOW WHITE AND SICKLY AND PUNY YOU WERE! DEY PULLED YOUR WINGS OFF YOUR SHOULDERS THE SAME TIME DEY RIPPED THE SKIN OFF YOUR MEASELY WHITEBOY PECKER, AND FLUNG IT TO THE DUNG BEETLES AND THE SLUGS TO EAT—BUT THERE ARE STILL NIGGERS DAT CAN FLY." The pressure on his hand lightened —and Eric did *not* pull his fingers away. "You white boys can piss on the scumbag all you want. I don't give a fuck…"

Then Bull…*growled!*

Whiteboy pulled Eric's other hand back under him, and the spigot off his dangling cock brushed Eric's palm.

It was wet.

With one hand, Whiteboy held Eric's arm and, with the other, pressed Eric's hand to his groin. Whiteboy's pubic hair was silkier than Eric's. Eric looked over, to realize Whiteboy's grin was inches from his face. "You guys used to had a *real* nice dog, didn't ya'? You remember? That ol' black sonofabitch—Uncle Tom?" (In the doorway, Bull stood like a statue of black iron.) "You would go outta here on the garbage run, and he'd come right on over to see us—I used to suck that motherfuckin' dog's dick *all* the time. Me and Danny. We'd get 'im in the house—Bull *loved* to watch us suck off that big motherfucker. Dog used to love it, too. Or I'd get down like this and he'd climb on around me and Bull used to help 'im fuck my ass—you know, when a dog fucks on another dog, sometimes they get hung up in each other. You seen that, right?" (Crouching in the doorway, suddenly Eric found himself convinced that the iron was heating. And heating more. And more…) "That's 'cause there's a knot back there that gets stuck. But that's why it's better if he fucks a white boy like me… or some nigger like you—" inside the living room's door sill warm liquid ran over Eric's knuckles, dripped from them to the rug—"'cause you know how he got that big knot what swells up in the middle of his dick and don't let him get loose from another dog unless he shoots. But I can get *anything* up *my* fuckin' hole—or out of it. 'Cause Bull done been trainin' me for years—he stick anything up my ass. Bottles and tool handles. Even his fuckin' fist—and he don't use nothin' but nigger spit and nigger shit. And you seen the hands on that black bastard, ain't ya? So it don't matter whether that hound can come or not. He can still pull loose. In another dog, there's a bone there that keeps that thing from comin' out. That's why they get all hung up. I liked to kiss on Uncle Tom, too. And he really liked to kiss on me—you ever see that old dog eat his own shit? And after he'd do that, I'd kiss on him—Bull just loved to watch us doin' that nasty stuff. He'd kick us around, and laugh—and laugh. Hey, open your mouth."

Again Eric was bewildered. "Huh…?"

"Come on, *open* your mouth!"

Even as he started to protest, the upper end of the leash hit Eric's cheek. And from above: "OPEN YOUR FUCKIN' MOUTH, SCUMBAG. DO WHAT HE *SAY*, YOU HEAH ME…?"

Opening his mouth, Eric pulled back.

But he took Whiteboy with him, who, still gripping Eric's forearm, chuckled and let out more urine. "This is how that ol' shit-eatin' hound'd do me when I'd take a break from suckin' on his big red pecker, when it was sticking out his skin, and I had it shucked back over his knot." Whiteboy pushed his face around Eric's. His tongue began flicking in and out of Eric's mouth, licking the insides of his cheek and his tongue. Eric had forgotten how rancid Whiteboy's breath was. But on one layer, he recognized in the odor, because, when Uncle Tom had been alive, feeding the old dog had fallen to Eric: the smell of canned dog food. As though in mind-reading explanation, Whiteboy confirmed: "Das what Bull make me eat today— dog food…He don't even gimme a dish. He throw it down on the fuckin' floor!"

"Hey, Bull—" someone called from back in the room. There was the sound of a very big, very heavy door closing, like metal, perhaps even a vault door—"what you up to out there?"

Above him, Bull turned back: "Hey, Kyle—come on over and see what I got here."

Whiteboy pulled his mouth away, long enough to whisper, "That's Mr. Kyle—he's a real big nigger 'round here. He owns Turpens and all that property out on Gilead, where we was this mornin'. He's a real good friend of Bull's—like Dynamite and Jay..."

Eric looked up again. A tall man had stepped up behind Bull's shoulder. He wore a leather jacket, a white shirt beneath it. And—Eric saw, looking down—leather pants.

Bull said, "Dis heah's de other one I told you about. I tol' the first one he could come over any time he wanted. So I figured this one'd be over, too, pretty soon."

The black man looked maybe a little older than Jay, with rough, short hair.

Kyle chuckled. "You gonna take this one in the back, too?"

"Naw, I don't think he needs nothin' like that—DO YOU, YOU *FUCKIN'* SCUMBAG?"

Eric flinched again at Bull's volume.

Mr. Kyle actually drew back. "Damn, Bull—you're gonna scare the shit out of me, too, there." He chuckled. "Too bad that Turpens kid isn't here tonight."

But Whiteboy had leaned closer. "See," he was whispering, "we got five *big* ol' washtubs in the cellar with chains all around the edge and down inside—and people come here, and they pay Bull to chain 'em up in those things, sometimes a few hours, sometimes all day, and sometimes even a few days—and me sometimes for a week. But that's when we don't got any payin' customers—and Bull puts me in one, 'cause it makes me feel good, and I can show the others along with me that it ain't gonna kill 'em, and how to sit and sleep in those things, and we got to do our business in there, and piss in that tub, and he throws our food in there, and we got to fish it out and eat it. And he'll come by, and shit in ya' hand, or throw his shit right at you, right in your fuckin' face—then piss in there all over you, too." (Eric could not even see the mouth moving behind the leather mask.) "Then, afterwards, he'll take you out in the back, and hose you off, and tell you to get the fuck out of there. But sometimes, if he thinks I need some more, he'll chain me back up in my tub. When he takes me in the Opera, I gotta go around, and when somebody starts talkin' to me, I gotta tell 'em all the stuff that nigger can do, 'cause he's so powerful. You know, when I'd be chained up in there, sometimes I could look out the bars on the front of the cellar window from under the porch, and I'd see you guys comin' out your cabin. You and Shit is brothers or cousins or something—ain't you? You know how I can tell? Every since he was a kid, I'd seen Shit comin' out, and he wouldn't think nobody'd be watchin' him, and he'd be pickin' in his nose and eatin' his damned snot off his fingers, and I'd be chained up in my tub full of piss and Bull's turds floatin' in that thing and I'd think, wow, that's so astonishin'! Then, when you come, I'd be there and seen you come out and do it, too! I realized you guys had to be brothers or cousins or *somethin'*. Ain't that right? When y'all come out together, sometimes, I seen y'all laughin' together and twice now I seen y'all be eatin' each *other's*—that's fuckin' amazin'! I mean, *that's* pretty powerful, too. Hey—" Here, with a gesture of his head, Whiteboy indicated Bull above them— "he gonna piss in yo' face now. You better open yo' fuckin' mouth—"

Eric looked up to hear Bull's laughter again. Bull was fingering the chains that made up his jockstrap cup. "Your heard 'im, you white scumbag, OPEN your *mouth*!" Bull fingered aside some of the chains and released himself from between. Salt liquid fell first against Eric's cheek, then moved the inch over into his mouth.

Eric shook—he'd expected the piss to be scalding. This is crazy, he thought. I've got to get this together…

Right hand pinned under Bull's foot, and Whiteboy still gripping his left arm, Eric had no leverage with either. Whiteboy's hips hunched and hunched over his hand like a dog's, while Eric's knuckles continued to drip.

Above, Mr. Kyle said, "You know, I wasn't ready for Wendell Haskell to be dead. When we were kids, I loved that sweet, crazy, ganglin' cracker more than I loved bein' alive. There was nothin' you could keep in a barn that was safe from that boy—includin' the farmhands. Especially if they were black. And the fact that he didn't mind throwin' a bit of that my way, 'cause I was too, was fine by me." Above, Kyle shook his head. "I came back from school in Denmark, all fired up about making the Dump for black gay men—and Jay MacAmon had to sit me down and explain the real reason I was doin' it was because I was crazy about a nigger-lovin' white one." He took a long breath. "That's irony for you. You know I really wanted to go out there this mornin'. But I couldn't do it. I used to tell Jay, if Wendell had wanted a million dollars, I would have written out the check and signed it over to him like *that!* Which shows you what love—or infatuation, if you want to call it that—will do. But all he ever wanted was a decent job, and to have a fair number of black men around who liked to fuck, and be left alone to live his own life." Mr. Kyle sighed. "And now he doesn't even need that anymore."

From within his mask, Bull said, "Well, that's why these boys need it, as much as any of these other niggers do."

"Yes," Kyle sighed again. "I guess so…"

"You want me to take this one in back with the other…?"

"Naw." Mr. Kyle drifted a step into the fire-lit room.

The masked head turned enough to say, "Then shut the fuck up, nigger! You can't have no niggers if you don't have white folks. Just like you can't have white folks if you don't have niggers. Then it's just talk—"

From the black fist, moving among the jock chains, urine flooded Eric's face, splattered up his nose. Eric swallowed, then opened his mouth again. (Thank God, he thought, Bull had taught him—and Dynamite had trained him—how to do this. Otherwise this nigger'd *drown* me!) Still, he was coughing when Bull's water finally ran out.

"Bull…?" Eric managed to get out. "Mr. Kyle…? Look—I just…please, I wanna know if Shit's all right. Come on—that's *all*."

Bull shook his cock. Droplets splattered Eric—and probably Whiteboy.

The jockstrap chains clinked on one another, slipping back into place. "Look, you little turd! We'll send 'im back when he's ready. Don't expect him before." Bull moved his boot—his foot—from Eric's hand. From under the man's warm sole, cold filled Eric's curling fingers. "Want me to take you 'round to the side and hose you off? Or you just wan' me to send you the fuck home? So you can sleep in all this shit…"

"I wanna…I wanna go home. But I wanna make sure…you, know, about Shit—"

"Well, you don't always get what you want. See? Da's what you white boys gotta learn." Above, Bull yanked the leash again.

Eric's arm pulled sideways too, as Whiteboy staggered on his knees.

"Hey, you idiot motherfucker, stop humpin' the fella's hand like that. CUT IT OUT! What you think, you some kinda damn dog?"

"Yeah," Whiteboy was still grinnin'. "I'm your motherfuckin' dog, ain't I, Bull? Like Tom—like Dog-Dog. Like Buddy? Naw—I ain't a dog. You said I was a fuckin' dog *turd*. Ain't I a motherfuckin' dog turd, what you stepped in, once, and can't get rid of me, no how…Couldn't get me from between your toes?" But he'd released Eric. "Even though you had your fuckin' boots on. Even when you made me lick 'em for you. That's what you said I was, didn't you—?"

"SHUT DA FUCK UP, SCUMBAG! YOU DA MOST IMPORTANT PERSON IN DA WHOLE WIDE MOTHERFUCKIN' WORLD AND AT DA SAME TIME YOU AIN'T SHIT. YOU ARE DA WONDER OF DA ABILITY TO PERCEIVE WONDER. AT DA SAME TIME YOU ARE CAPABLE OF EVERY ERROR HUMAN KIND EVER MADE IN ITS BLIND STAGGER AFTER TRUTH. YOU ARE UNIQUE AND IRREPLACABLE—AND THERE IS NINE BILLION MORE OF US, EXACTLY THE SAME!"

Eric pulled his wet hand over the sill from the dirty rug to the dirty porch boards. His wrist was sore.

Above, Bull looked back at Kyle, shook his masked head, and said, "I swear! These motherfuckin' white sonsofbitches can run a nigger crazy..."

Kyle laughed. "That's the truth. Why don't they want something simple, like a good S&M session? That's something people could understand." He started to close the door. "But, no, Wendell wanted to fuck with his own kid—"

"Like his daddy done with him," Bull said. "Like mine done with me."

Whiteboy scurried backward. "Yeah, so did mine..."

Kyle looked down at the bony creature on Bull's leash. "So that means—what? *I'm* the only person around here who had a normal upbringing?" He chuckled.

Eric still squatted, breathing hard.

Bull raised his hand, unlatched the mouth grill, drew it aside. His head went back, then forward, and through the half opened doorway—from the hawking sound, Eric knew—he spat.

Saliva hit the corner of Eric's mouth, and *because* he was breathing hard, some of it went in. Automatically he swallowed. Some of it ran down the side of Eric's chin.

"Now get the fuck *outta* heah!" Stepping back into the sweltering room, Bull closed the door. The heat ceased to pour out. Coolness touched at his face, his arms, his neck. Eric heard the lock close.

Behind the door Bull said: "LICK DAT PISS UP FROM THE GODDAM FLOOR, WHITEBOY! Dis is my motherfuckin' *living* room where you be peein' all over on that scumbag—"

Eric wiped his face on the back of his wrist. Kneeling among the loud crickets, he went on breathing hard for almost a minute. He thought about circling the house, to see if he could get in from another entrance. Finally, he stood, unsteadily. He started along the porch, but there was a lot of junk on it and it was dark. After he had hit his shin on something, then bumped into two other things he couldn't identify, he turned, stepped off, and walked back across the road to Dynamite's.

He sucked two of his fingers on his right hand—Whiteboy's urine was strong. He breathed deeply. Why couldn't it have been some antiquated beer drunk from the old Slide, he thought.

But they'd torn The Slide down.

Jesus, he thought. I feel like a kid...

I feel, somehow, like I was...just born.

In the cabin bathroom, Eric dropped his clothes, got into the shower—but stayed in it not three minutes. Naked, he walked outside, stood on the deck awhile, in the cool summer darkness, sat in Dynamite's old chair awhile longer, drying in the night. Then he went in and lay on the big bed. On the slope beyond the porch, night hummed, buzzed, and chittered.

***

[64] THE MATTRESS MOVED. Eric woke. And Shit stretched out on his stomach, his arm falling on Eric's back.

Eric started to roll over, so Shit could get his head in place.

But the arm stiffened. "Naw—stay there."

"You okay."

"Yeah, I'm fine."

"You sure?"

"Pretty much."

Eric turned over on his side anyway and put his own arm around Shit's back. Shit turned to face him and grabbed him and pressed his face in Eric's neck and held him so hard Eric couldn't breathe. Shit quivered.

Pressing as firmly as he could, Eric moved his hand up, then down Shit's back. When he reached Shit's buttocks, Shit gasped, "*Owwww…!*" and relaxed his own grip.

"Jesus." Eric pulled his hand away. "What did they *do?*"

He felt Shit shrug. "You know…"

Outside, cicadas chattered.

"Did he get you in his…torture room?"

"Un-huh."

"Did they fuck you?"

"That's what I thought he was gonna do…" He twisted a little. "Naw. They didn't."

"What *did* he do?"

"He whipped my black ass till I thought I was gonna pass out." Shit's face moved from Eric's neck.

"Oh," Eric said. "Did you…did you want him to do it?"

"Naw. When he first come out and grabbed hold of me in his yard, there, I told him to get the fuck off me…but you know Bull. He had Mr. Kyle there, helpin', too. They grabbed me and wrestled me in there, chained me up, and did it anyway."

"Why didn't you yell…?"

"I wouldn't give him the satisfaction. 'Sides, if you heard me yellin', you'd of come runnin' or something. I didn't wanna get you all involved. I wanted—" Shit pushed himself up on one arm, in the dark—"Bull to do *somethin'*. That's why I went over there. I just didn't know what it *was*. I thought maybe he'd make me suck his dick again. But I guess he only does that to kids. After they kept beatin' my butt, till it was all red and probably bleedin'—I wouldn't even look at it, when he tried to show it to me in a mirror—he made Whiteboy piss on my ass. You know, the salt in that is wicked. They might as well'a rubbed some damned jalapeños on it."

"Oh, Jesus—"

Shit lifted Eric's wrist and rubbed his face under Eric's arm. "God, man. That's good. It's good bein' back here—I mean, I wasn't that far away. But—did Bull ever take you into his dungeon—I mean, where he does his work?"

"No," Eric said.

"He showed it to me once, years ago. But Dynamite didn't like me goin' into that place. It's pretty fierce. He got two human heads in there—two white guys. He said he cut 'em off 'em hisself. He keeps 'em stuck on sticks, either side the door. One's a real old guy, with thin, stringy hair, and his teeth is all out. The other ain't that old. A guy maybe fifty, fifty-five. Like the same age as Dynamite was—but lookin' at 'im, while I was chained to that table, after about an hour, I couldn't help thinkin', how it looked like it *was* my dad—and I started thinkin', maybe him and Whiteboy had went back to Gilead and dug him up—and Shad, too—and cut the heads off 'em and brought 'em back and stuck 'em on them poles inside the dungeon door, 'cause he figured out I was gonna be comin' over there—they don't got no eyes in 'em. But them holes can look at you and it feels like they lookin' through you, even more so then a rotted out eyeball would. The skin's all dried out—he says he cured 'em in salt and stuff. Here and there, the skin done tore on the bone under it. I tell you, them things must've smelled pretty rough, back when the brains was rottin' out—"

Outside, half the cicadas went silent.

Eric said, "You don't think he *did* go there and—" That much quiet felt heavy.

Five, six, seven seconds later, the other half quieted.

Probably it was past midnight.

The silence rang, like the highest dog whistle you could imagine.

"Naw," Shit said. "Naw, he couldn't. I mean, them heads've been in that place since the first time he took me in there, when I was twelve or thirteen, and Dynamite told me I had to keep out of there." (With the insect noise gone, Eric realized how loud the bedsprings' movements were.) "They was there, then. When I was a kid, I thought they was funny. But, then, I wasn't all chained up on a damned torture rack, either. It was just somethin' that got in my mind, when the things was lookin' at me out them eyeholes—and I couldn't get loose."

"Yeah, I can imagine—"

"But I swear—now, not the one with the stringy, white hair, but the other one—the longer I lay there and the more they whipped me, the more he got to lookin' like Dynamite..." Suddenly, putting his face down, he searched for Eric's mouth with his own. After a long, long kiss, he pulled away. "What you doin'? Drinkin' your own piss now? That's what you taste like. You still upset about Dynamite?"

"Naw," Eric said. "That ain't mine." He sucked his teeth. "It's Bull's— or Whiteboy's. I went over there, knockin' on his door, lookin' for ya'. But you know how he does."

"Oh," Shit said. "That must've been you, when all three of 'em went upstairs. I thought it was one of Bull's payin' jobs, what he was gonna put on hold 'cause I was there." They lay quietly, till Eric began to drift off. Then Shit said, "My daddy used to love to piss in your mouth, huh?"

"Uh-huh." Eric blinked himself awake.

"And I used to love to watch 'im do it. And kiss on you after you done it. That stuff *always* got me off. You used to love to drink it, too."

A strong urine flavor *was* in Eric's mouth. He wondered if death and his neighbor could banish the perversion. "Yeah, I did." Banish it at least awhile...

Shit said, "When he took me outside to clean me off and was hosin' me down, Bull told me *I* got to piss in your mouth now."

"He did?" Now Eric raised his head. Turning, he pulled a pillow under it.

"He said since I ain't gonna feel like doin' too much fuckin' for the next couple of days, I gotta give you every drop, don't matter where we are—here or at the Opera."

"You comin' back there?"

"Yeah, tomorrow. We'll both go over, finish up there, then come back here. We gonna have to do the garbage run by ourselves now."

"Yeah," Eric said. "It's gonna be funny doin' that without your dad, though." But he was relieved to hear Shit finally mention work.

"You know how to talk to people and ask 'em how they want us to do their garbage, and remember all that shit—like Dynamite did. Can't you?"

"Sure," Eric said.

Shit snorted—and Eric felt him relax. "Bull said if we was in the damned street and I had to go, I got to whip it out and do it right there. I asked him could we at least find a doorway or an alley or somethin'. He said that was okay. But if you ain't around, I got to hold it the rest of the day till you show up."

"I'll try not to get too far off from you then." Eric was more confused than enlightened. "Why does he want you to do that?"

"He says it'll make you happy. If I do something that'll make *you* happy for three whole days, *I'll* feel better."

"That's...interesting," Eric said. "It probably would. Make me happy, I mean. You wanna try it?"

"Yeah, sure. I gotta do *something* for somebody else. I can't spend the whole rest of my life mopin' and feelin' sorry for myself. But Bull said you gotta drink it whether you want to or not, though. He says you're gonna try to get out of it a few times, 'cause you think it'll be easier on me. So I gotta *make* you drink it. No matter what. Even if we gotta get in a tussle over it."

"Okay. Okay. I'll take it all. You wanna tussle me, you tussle me."

"He said *that's* what'll make you happy."

Eric frowned. "Oh...well. Maybe."

For seconds both were silent. Then, wanting to move the conversation to anything that wasn't Whiteboy and Bull, Eric said, "You're really fond of the little guy, ain't you?"

"Huh?"

"Big Man, I mean. You were really touched when he come up with his dad to the funeral this mornin'."

"Oh." Shit reached up and rubbed his nose, which ended in some picking and sucking, three times in one nostril, once in the other (while Eric felt himself harden). Shit settled to gnawing. Between and around that, he said, "Naw. It wasn't that. It's was funny, though—like, as soon as I saw him, the first thing I thought was how much the little bastard loves his own daddy—you know how he always talkin' about Mr. Markum? How big and strong he is? And all the stuff he gets for Big Man? And I thought, unless they both die together in some fool car wreck, one of them's gotta go before the other, and if it's Joe Markum, that's gonna kill Big Man—or come close to it. And I realized someday he wasn't gonna have *his* daddy." Shit's next breath had tears in it. "I couldn't stop crying for that. I wanted to hug him and hold him, 'cause thinkin' about him bein' without his dad tore me up so much."

"Aw," Eric said. He gave Shit a squeeze, even while part of him wanted to laugh. "Still, the way you was huggin' on him and half humpin' him, you looked like you was gonna screw the little sonofbitch right in the doorway, all over Joe Markum's shoes."

"Well, you know—" and now there was a grin in with Shit's words— "he feels so good when you hug him. He's all hard and strong on the top— like you—only down at the bottom he's all soft and squishy; and between the two of 'em, whenever I hold on to him, my dick goes right up."

"*You* hold onto a fuckin' mush melon and your dick goes up," Eric said.

"Yeah, I guess so." Shit began biting at his fingers again. "But not for a little while, yet, I don't think. At least I got it straight in my head now, that my daddy's dyin' ain't my fault."

"Huh?" Eric pulled back. "What the fuck you mean...?"

"Yeah," Shit said. "I know that now."

"Why in the world would you think it was *your* fault?"

"Don't everybody, when their dad dies?"

"I don't know..."

"Well, *I* did. But I don't now...not after that session with goddam Bull! Hey, lemme lift my hip here—and you get your face on down under there and put my dick in your mouth."

"Sure," Eric said, moving down the mattress. His feet went off the end.

"I'm gonna take a wicked piss—then I'm gonna fuck your face till I shoot like there's no tomorrow. 'Cause right now I don't believe there is. You can come any way you want, long as it don't involve nothin' with my asshole except lickin' out the sucker. That's about all it can take, right through here."

"Okay. But you sure you wanna be doin' that, with your back all sore and beat up?"

Shit rolled slightly to the side, grimacing. "Yeah, Bull said I probably wasn't gonna feel like doin' nothin' for a couple of days. But you know me. I gotta get off now, or I don't know what's gonna happen—"

On his back, Eric pushed his face under Shit's groin, and Shit's thick cock found his mouth and pushed in.

"Oh, fuck yeah..." Shit began to rock back and forth. "That's nice— hey, try not to grip my butt. Just the sides."

It *was* nice.

"Nigger, I'm gonna piss like a goddam oil well goin' off, 'fore I get around to shootin'."

And later, when Eric went in the bathroom to urinate, he stood in front of the commode—with its wooden ring, like he had back in the garage at Condotti's—and smiled at the rings from his falling water in the yellowing pool. I'm dumping Shit's goddamn piss for him. Yeah, like I used to do for his daddy. Why, he wondered, does that always make me feel *so fuckin'* important...?

But it did.

*

The next morning, in the truck, with Shit driving, they returned to the Opera House, where Shit cussed Josh out till Eric told him to cut it out. "Come on, Shit! Josh did the best he *could*—"

"Josh didn't do *nothin'!*" Shit turned again to the heavy old black man, who, if he didn't enjoy it as much as Whiteboy, at least looked as if was used to being yelled at.

"I'm just lettin' up on you," Shit said, "'cause *he* told me to!" He thumbed toward Eric. Then, picking up pail and mop, he went down into the basement lounge and got to work like a crazy man.

Josh said, "Mr. Jeffers, since you ain't gonna be needin' me no more, you think you could send me off with a hundred? Like severance pay or somethin'."

Myron started to say something, but Eric butted in. "You get a twenty, like before."

"That'll be fine, sir," Josh said.

Shaking his head, Myron said, "Mr. Jeffers is a nice feller. That's why you're gettin' anything." He started for the stairway up to the balcony.

Three minutes later, Shit came stomping back up the steps. "Come on. *Get* on over here. I was so mad at that damned alkey I almost forgot. I gotta piss like a motherfucker!"

Two of the homeless fellows were lurking in the aisle, waiting to ask about something.

Shit glanced at them. "I guess it ain't gonna hurt them to watch."

At the beginning, Eric—and, probably, Shit, too—felt a little embarrassed. But when Eric finished, stood up, and wiped his mouth on the back of his wrist, while Shit pushed himself back in his jeans, Eric felt... well, as if he were six inches taller. He turned to the waiting men. "Okay... now what the fuck you fellas want?" while Shit squeezed Eric's shoulder, then left for the downstairs lounge.

*

Later, in the top balcony Eric was walking by the projection room, when he stopped to wrinkle his nose. After a moment, he stepped over and tapped on the projection room door. "Myron! Hey, Myron...?"

Myron opened it and looked out. "Mr. Jeffers? What is it?"

"Myron, step out here a minute."

Myron came out, then closed the door so that the light did not fall over the chairs in the back.

"You know Black Bull's partner, Whiteboy?"

"I wouldn't say I *knew* him. I *seen* him—I know who he *is*." Myron's inflection ended with a kind of interrogation, as if to say, Why do you ask?

"Has he been comin' up here and hangin' out a lot? I mean, in Nigger Heaven? Bull brings him to the Opera from time to time, I know, but I usually see them in the orchestra—that's where they do their thing, when they do it."

"I don't think I've ever seen him up here—or Black Bull, either. Why you askin'?"

"Take a sniff."

Myron breathed in.

"That smells just *like* Whiteboy," Eric said. "Like really ol' dried-up… waste."

Two hours later, going through the door to the back stairwell that was supposed to be kept locked, but which you could open by joggling the knob the right way, Eric discovered Haystack, Dr. Greene, and the Breakfast Club having an afternoon meeting with some new, nice looking Latino kid named Carlos, who, predictably for the Breakfast Club, was fairly sloshed and finding it all great fun.

When he told Shit, Eric's second surprise was that Shit had known about them. "Yeah, I told 'em they could do it up there—if they kept the door to the back stairwell closed. I go up there with 'em once in a while. They're good boys—and that stuff gets me off."

"It *does*?"

"Yeah." Shit looked at the lobby's marble floor, about as close as he could come to getting embarrassed with Eric. "Haystack ain't the brightest bulb in the chandelier, but we get along."

"You go all the way up *there*—?"

"Well," Shit said, "when you got somethin' that'll get you off, it's kind of surprisin' what you'll put up with that you wouldn't be that interested in, ordinarily. Besides, it ain't out on no balcony. It's inside on a stair."

Eric said, "…Oh."

And Bull's strategy for getting Shit back on track—it didn't take years, months, or even weeks—and making Eric feel happy worked about as well you'd expect.

It took ten days.

* * *

[65] SHORTLY, THE RUNCIBLE Chamber of Commerce put them permanently in charge of the Opera House—because Dusty announced he was retiring in six weeks. (*Naw*, Shit said. *It was just a few days.*

(*Oh, come on, Shit. It couldn't a' been a few days. The Chamber of Commerce took six weeks to do* anything—*it always did. You know that.*

(That time, they argued over it for a while.

(*Damn, Shit*, Eric finally said. *How'm I supposed to figure out when we actually took over the Opera. You never tell me the same thing twice.*

(Well, I know it was after my daddy died.

(Now, was that before or after Mama Grace went and give me his Spinoza? You know, when we come back from The Slide...?

(Shit frowned. Before...?

(Well, that's what I mean, Shit. I ain't never gonna be able to get it straight, 'cause you got it different each time you go over it.

(But it ain't all that important, now, is it...?

(Yeah, but I'd just like to get a handle on the history of it, see?)

"Hey," Dusty told them. "I'll take you guys on a tour of the whole place—the basements and the back halls and everything—so nothin' jumps out and surprises you."

Shit said, "I don't need no damn tour. We been runnin' this place, downstairs and upstairs, in the basements and the back stairs and the halls, for the last three years, and I been comin' here since I was twelve."

And later, when Hammond, who walked with a limp in his apricot jumpsuit, took off with Eric, he opined: "Mr. Haskell's just feelin' a little contrary, 'cause he's still upset over his daddy. That's probably all it is."

As they made their way along one of the basement corridors, Eric asked, "What about these doors here?"

"I don't think nobody got the keys to these things no more," Dusty said. "Somebody told me they were storage rooms for old scenery and shit back when this was a theater. In the bottom drawer of his desk up in the projection room, Myron's got a ring with about two hundred and fifty keys on it that's supposed to be for all the locks in the building—and for basement rooms in some of the buildings around here, too. But it would take all day—hell, all week—to go through 'em."

In the green wall, the door looked solid, immobile, and oaken.

"The day you really wanna get in there, you probably gonna have to take up a damned ax."

As they wandered along the concrete corridor, with its drains in the middle of the floor, Dusty pointed up ahead. "That comes out right on the street."

The next day, Hammond announced they were retiring that week.

*

Since the maintenance job at the Opera House didn't *officially* start for two more weeks, and they couldn't yet take over the upper apartment *and* the Chamber of Commerce contract for them both was up on Friday, Eric talked over Randal's new suggestion with Shit: work for two weeks out at the Bottom, since Al Havers was ready to retire himself.

While rain runneled the windows and pocked the puddles on the deck, Eric could see through the open back door of the cabin and out onto the Dump's dirt road (red mud now), Shit said, "I don't like that place. I thought we was through with it."

Eric said, "I know you don't. But I don't mind goin' over to the Bottom for a couple of weeks, until they can get somebody officially to take Al's place."

"You know everything he knows?" Shit stretched one forearm out on the table.

Eric laughed. "Now, how many years we been goin' over there once every two weeks to toss the damned garbage down the cliff? If I don't know how to tell a driver to back up to the edge or shout out to hit the brakes before he goes off the cliff, I don't know my own name. It's a lot easier than doin' the damned routes."

Shit said, "I don't see why they don't let us start in on the Opera House right away."

"Well, Myron wants a vacation, too. They want to use the time to dig out that sewer outside in the back, there. And that's how long they said they needed somebody to take over for Al, since he's gonna retire when he gets out the hospital. Hey, at least we'd have somethin' comin' in. And you can stay at the theater and take care of the orchestra and the downstairs john."

Friday morning at six, Eric drove out to the Bottom.

Along the gate—the coiled razor wire had been gone from the top for years—he stopped the truck, hit the button on the dashboard, and listened to screaming birds. Outside, the lock clunked. Under the two camera posts, the entrance gate swung in. Eric drove the truck through and turned toward the shack, covered with fiberglass siding about three years ago.

It still looked pretty scruffy.

The stuff they'd started putting in the Bottom, maybe six years back, with the garbage to kill some of the smell had actually worked for a while. Then it began to add its own sickly stench, and the rotten odor came back with it. Shit always said he liked it better when it had smelled like really intense garbage. (*And I didn't like it back then.*)

Eric actually began to back the truck up to the cliff's edge, when he realized he wasn't there to toss sacks that morning. Jesus, he thought, as he drove the truck back to the cabin in first. I *must* be gettin' old. He took a breath and pushed the hand brake. It went easily and silently in. Shaking his head, Eric opened the door (the birds got louder) and jumped down.

The ground was junkier than usual—probably because there had been a few days' dumping, at least, when Al hadn't been there at all to make sure the drivers cleaned up after themselves. Or, maybe it *was* messier.

Eric glanced at the sky.

He wandered to the cliff and looked over. Some twenty feet down the sharply sloped white and yellow earth, garbage bags spread, thousands of them—black and crinkly, like the wrinkled carapaces of beetles, a hundred yards toward the sea's smoky green, a saddle a quarter of a mile from edge to edge, a black wave rolling up from the ocean to lap over the Bottom and cling, unretreating.

Gulls and kestrels cawed and mewed, soaring in flocks or peeling in separate flight. Something hypnotic about it all fixed Eric to the rim. Hadn't he dreamed of this—recently, maybe? Two weeks ago, three weeks? Or had there been several dreams? To the left, a third of a football field away, along the edge stretched a twenty or twenty-five yard ribbon, down to the water, of dirty white, from the years they'd dumped the garbage in white and transparent sacks at the end there.

Black sacks covered the rest.

Eric remembered. In the dream, it hadn't really been a cliff. It was only a slope, though composed not of the land's customary rust-red earth, but of this same yellowish-white, crumbly, sandy. He'd made his way down (… in the dream), under shrieking kestrels and kingfishers. Instead of lying in a mass, however, bags were scattered, black, white, or transparent. He'd crab-walked his way between. In the dream, the transparent ones sometimes held body parts, heads, arms, and shoulders, hips and legs in foggy plastic. As he glanced around, sometimes a mouth, a nose, a woman's breast or a man's open eye flattened against the inside. It never surprised him, as he walked, nor had it frightened him, though he'd wondered why or how they'd gotten in there. What must it feel like to be cut in pieces and bagged like that? A few still seemed…alive. Now and again, he was sure he saw a foot or a jaw or a buttock move. Once, he recalled how he'd watched a hard black penis pressed sideways against vinyl begin to soften and shrink. In another version, he'd walked the same bag-scattered slope, except it was night, under a bright moon. Spaces between the bags had become paths through walls of high-piled plastic. Sometimes the paths became descending steps. Green and luminous, water ran the stairs. Sometimes the liquid burned with lime-green fire. The bags made raddled plastic walls, canyon high. He'd looked up the black sides in the uneven green light, to realize the bags had closed overhead. He wandered in an underground maze, as if through the connected basements of a plastic city.

Was it *only* two weeks ago…?

No, more like two *years*…!

Eric had dreamed that, when he'd started to get anxious that he'd never get out, the tunnel had decanted him into a clearing. (Today he was the longest working garbage man on the coast. This was the city in which he was King...) He was outside, in the space, fifteen or twenty feet across, with board walls around it, behind the old Slide—or a place very like it: The Slide's enclosed outdoor john. In moonlight trees were visible above the board walls. Only, after moments, he realized it wasn't *quite* The Slide's john. For one thing, though trees rose around it, no commode sat on its raised stand in the corner. No aluminum trough was bolted to the wall. Men stood around, most naked, most black, at least one on his knees before another—but Eric recognized none.

In summer at The Slide, more than half would have been familiar.

In winter, all.

Also, one of the walls, he realized now, was not board—he walked over to make sure: It was firmly packed black garbage sacks. Eric prodded the plastic with a forefinger, then with three fingers, and realized, inside, was the articulated joints of a limp hand. He turned sharply to look across the enclosure—and saw that, again unlike the Slide, across from him was no wall at all, only moonlit tree trunks.

When he'd first come into the place, Eric had been relieved. He'd thought he'd known where he was. But if this wasn't the outdoor john in back of The Slide, where in hell *was* it...?

Eric blinked.

Looking across the Bottom to the sea, he turned from the cliff to start back for the truck—he should get his gloves and toss over some of the junk lying around, those cartons there, that bed spring propped against them...

But as he turned, he was assailed by...

A vision...?

A memory...?

Or was it just some cataclysm of the imagination...?

He was sure that, behind him, across the Bottom, stone towers had just risen up, some half fallen, some with glassed-in balconies. Bridges connected some. Down between them ran cobbled streets. Arched entrances opened on subterranean alleys. In a square (behind him, invisible...) stood a fountain that had once worked but was now dry. Through back streets and avenues, rushing in from a smoky ocean, green fire bathed the city's foundations. At some point—in what dream or dreams—he had stood in that place and looked out over the Bottom, its fuming ruin, its glimmering air of potential.

Eric turned back...

He was standing on a cliff, looking down at a quarter of a mile of black plastic garbage sacks, sloping to a far hill, fading to gray. (Does everyone, he wondered, have not only the individual and eccentric dreams we sometimes remember, but an entire alternative dream *world*, as filled with frustration and threat as the real one with its ability to isolate, to menace?) If he squinted, the plastic stretching below began to move, to pulse, as though about to swirl.

Odd, Eric thought. When he'd first started staying with Shit and Dynamite, he used to dream about the two of them all the time. When he'd fuck around with them after work, laying in Dynamite's big bed with them, he'd drift off to dream he was...in bed with them. Only he'd wake to realize they, also asleep, faced in different directions from the direction they'd faced in his dream. Or he'd dream one had a hand on his arm or his shoulder, only to find, awake, Dynamite had gotten up and was in the bathroom, taking a piss, or Shit's arms were curled tightly around himself and an inch of heated air separated Shit's butt and Eric's belly—

Because of the birds, Eric didn't hear the truck motor, but the clunk of the gate's release made him turn. Morning light wiped glare over the entering truck's windshield. Blue striations across the top for the solar strips, whose edges Eric could see as the truck rocked side to side, marked it as a carrier of one of the new hydrogen-ion engines. The truck halted, the door opened, and Tad swung down to jump from the step. "Hey, there... You sittin' in for Al?"

"I guess so." Since Dynamite's death, Eric was the only white driver left. (And once they moved to the Opera...)

The other door opened, and another fellow jumped out—"Owww! *Damn*, man!" A younger fellow, he began to hop on one foot, looking down. "Jesus—oh, *shit!* Somethin' almost went through my shoe—just about!"

"You cut yourself?" Eric stepped closer.

The kid put his foot down, tried his weight on it, then lifted it up and looked at the bottom. "Almost!" he repeated. "This is some dangerous junk out here." The young man—who, Eric saw, was perhaps twenty, heavy, and Asian—wore low-topped sneakers.

Eric said, "You're new, huh?"

"Yeah," Tad said. "Aim here's the son of a friend of mine. He's helpin' me out for a few days."

"Well," Eric said, "you gotta get yourself some real shoes. Otherwise, I can't let you out the damned truck. You could cut your feet up *all* to hell— it'll rip right through a pair of sneakers like that. Tad, *don't* let him come out here no more unless he got work shoes."

Tad said, "You know, Aim, he's right."

"Yeah..." The Asian kid stepped gingerly about, looking at the ground, where the slats of a crate and a couple of tin boxes lay—the corner of one of which he'd stepped on. "Yeah, I'll get some."

Eric said, "Hey, take your truck down about twenty yards there before you start tossin', okay? And—Tad, I'm serious—don't let that kid run around in no damned sneakers. Son, you could'a hurt yourself real bad. Okay?" He thought: Too bad Shit wasn't here. He liked Asians—he'd think the kid was cute. (And he was.) But that's how things happened…

"Yeah," Tad said. "He's right. Come on, Aim. Get back in, and watch yourself."

Asian Aim and black Tad looked at each other—then the Asian glanced around uncomfortably, and climbed back up in the gray cab, trying not to favor the foot he'd hurt.

* * *

[66] MAMA GRACE'S VOICE: "It's awfully nice of you boys to help me out like this. Really, I'll never be able to thank you." Somewhere, a convoy of what sounded like four, five, six Foltz recycling trucks they couldn't see rumbled toward Dump Corners.

"You know," Eric said, "I used to think because we picked up the bagged garbage and got it to the Bottom, we was the most important niggers in the Dump. Only one day I was walkin' up the road by the sea, and eight of them recyclin' trucks, half of 'em all packed with bound paper and the other half bulgin' out with bagged plastic, went on by me, one after the other, off to the recyclin' plant, and suddenly I realized, hell, as far as garbage collecting was concerned, we didn't do *shit*—"

"Now, that's not the right attitude." (They still couldn't see Mama, down amidst the plants.) "We all do our part, whether it's a small one or a large one—"

"Yeah," Eric said. "But, even so, that can make you feel…well—" The trucks were gone.

A breeze rustled tall grass.

Shit just grunted.

From the greenery beside the porch stairs, Mama's head—in his white sunhat, wearing purple sunglasses, fuchsia scarf, and white canvas jacket draped on his shoulders—rose, finally, above the leaves. Mama lifted his hands. In one, he held three yellow tomatoes, in the other, two. Looking down, he stepped forward, then to the side, on whatever path took him between the trellises holding up the vines. Coming from the tomato plants, he walked toward the house steps.

"It took you long enough finally to decide to do it. But we gonna miss you here, Mama." Shit laughed. "It was fun havin' you around for a quick fuck. In fact, I wonder if that wasn't why you kept puttin' in off—"

"Oh, shut your mouth!" Wind chimes and braided feathers were gone. "And I'm gonna miss you, too." Porch chairs had been packed in the U-Haul. "No—it wasn't you. Wally was just a little undecided there, when he thought he might take that other job they kept on dangling in his face in Valdosta. But it's awfully nice of yall to give up your weekend to help me out like this."

Eric reflected. They hadn't done that in more than three—if not six—years. Shit was still grinning. Suddenly Eric wondered if Shit had slipped in a few with Mama on his days off, when he'd come back to the Dump and left Eric at the theater, the way Eric sometimes did with aging Abbot. Maybe he'd ask him later.

If he remembered...

Without drapes or curtains behind them, the panes were the color of pencil lead. Fifteen feet off, the U-Haul stood on the rough dirt between the grasses, the back door finally down and lever locked.

A wicker basket of yellow tomatoes sat on the lowest step. Mama put his five tomatoes on top, stood up. "And thank you for taking some of these. So many people grow their own down here, Dump Produce can't hardly give tomatoes away during the season."

"We'll think of something to do with 'em, Mama." Eric grinned, now. "Probably we should get started."

"I suppose we should." Mama picked up the basket, and they climbed into the cab, Mama in the middle, the basket on his lap. "You got anything else you wanna be takin'?" Shit asked.

"Naw, I got it all." Mama's lean brown fingers—nails with Clear Rose polish—were together at the top of the basket handle. "Or if I forgot it, I don't need it."

*

Eric drove, braking in front of Dynamite's old cabin.

Shit picked the basket up from Mama's lap, pushed open the door, jumped down, and left it up on the porch beside the rail. "I don't gotta put 'em inside," he said, climbing back in. "Nobody's gonna walk off with them things. There're too many around for the takin'."

When they were driving Mama's U-Haul over to his new place in Savannah—they'd packed every inch with furniture, furniture pads, cartons and shopping bags; Eric was trying to ignore a slight pain from something pulled in his lower left flank—Eric said: "Mama, you ain't asked me nothin' about how I was comin' with the book in more than a year."

"I told you, honey," Mama Grace said. "It's *your* book, now. You'll look at it when you want to, when you need to. That's how those things work. Besides, I said all I could say about it already."

"Why you so anxious to leave us?" Shit asked.

"Like I told you, the Dump's been a wonderful experience. But it's time for a change. A lady gets antsy if she don't have some variety in her life. Besides—" squinting, Mama Grace looked around—"only about half the people live here as used to—and with the ones who do, it's too much like a hot house for me. *You* boys don't even live here no more."

"Well, that's just 'cause we stay at the Opera now."

"Well, if you were still in your old place there, you'd know what I mean. And Wally wants me to be closer to where he is—this way I will be."

In the last months, Mama had been to Savannah several times, so, with Mama navigating, they had no trouble finding the rundown black neighborhood and the shaky-looking two-story house where Mama was moving. They got out and looked at the gray boards—so different from Mama's colorful cottage in the Dump.

"I guess you gonna paint it…" Shit said, hands in his back pockets.

"Well, I guess I am," Mama Grace said, "when I can get to it." He didn't sound eager.

They carried the stuff inside—got the bed, the chest, and the end tables upstairs. They set down the sofa and the TV in the big room downstairs. "No," Mama said, hip against the sofa's flowered arm. "Don't unpack those boxes. I have to think about where I want all that stuff over the next few days, anyway."

Back in the Dump, the furniture had filled Mama's house. Here, spread out among two stories on the strange city's outskirts, it looked lost.

"Well, it's certainly more…roomy." Standing in the living room, Mama muttered, "It's amazin' what a lady will do for love."

With Mama, they turned in the U-Haul trailer at the renting office. It was just after three-thirty. Then they drove him back to the house, where Mama's four-wheel drive was already in the garage. "You boys get on back to the Harbor, now. Wally's gonna come by about six-thirty, and we gonna go over to his house and eat. But I wanna astound him first with how nice I have this place lookin' in just a couple of hours." After hugs and Say hello to this one and to that one and vigorous waves and Good luck's, and I'm really gonna miss you's that took three times as long as Eric would have guessed—mostly it was Shit and Mama—they climbed into the pickup and, with Mama waving his fuchsia scarf from the doorway, they started back, again Eric driving.

"You think," Shit asked, thoughtfully, "he was expecting us to give him some kind of a good-bye fuck or somethin'?"

"Actually," Eric said, "I don't think he was, Shit. Really. That wasn't the feelin' I was gettin'. Believe it or not, I think he just wanted us to help get his furniture into his new place."

"Oh." Elbow out the pickup's open window, Shit sat by the door, digging in his nose with a forefinger, sucking it, then gnawing some, collar and open shirt whipping about his neck and chest.

Every twenty or thirty yards, the stretch they drove had a McDonalds or a tuxedo rental store, or a Chili's, or a Radio Shack, when Shit looked over. "Hey—can you get me some money?"

Eric asked, "Huh...?"

"You got my bank card with you, don't you?"

"Yeah," Eric said. "But I got cash, too. You hungry or somethin'? We can stop an'—"

"Naw, I just wanna get some money. Not a lot. Five dollars—that's all."

"With the bank card, Shit, it's gotta be in twenties. Or fifties, now, I think—at least most places."

"Okay," Shit said, eagerly. "Fifty. That's okay."

"Sure. But what you want it for?"

"Well...my daddy, back when we first got them cards, he told me that once we had them things, as long as we had money at the Credit Union, we could get money anywhere we was—I mean, anywhere in the country. Atlanta, or New York, or Texas, or Washington. I wanna see if it really works."

Eric laughed. "Believe me, Shit—it works."

"But I wanna *see*," Shit insisted. "I don't wanna lot. I just wanna see if I can get it."

"Okay," Eric said. "Okay. Lemme find a bank—but you know it's gonna cost you five bucks to see it. They charge you five or so against your account, every time you make a withdrawal—unless you're at the Credit Union. It used to be just one or two."

"Well, just to see—'cause we're real far from the Dump and Diamond Harbor and Runcible and all them places. I mean, this is...Savannah! I wanna see if it'll really gimme some money over here, too."

"Okay." Grinning, Eric looked around. "Hey—there we go. That's a Sovereign."

"What's that?"

"It's a bank—the Sovereign Bank."

"And that card's gonna work there?"

"It's supposed to."

"Okay. Come on—let's go!"

Eric turned the pickup into the lot. Like an auxiliary building to a modern church, the structure of beige cement and glass stood near a low metal fence, cables between the stanchions and grass behind it, the back of some store beyond it.

Two women in jeans were coming from the glass vestibule.

Eric stopped the pickup.

"You *really* think it's gonna gimme some money?" Shit asked.

"Of course it is, Shit. If you wanna spend up five dollars to find out, that's how they work. Come on." Gold and black, the foiled lettering said "Nine A.M. to Five P.M." over the glass. Eric pulled back the door. "Come on in."

"You don't have to put the card in the slot to open the door?"

"It's still bankin' hours," Eric explained.

"Oh…" Shit stood there, looking uncomfortable.

"Come on inside—we can get your money."

"Naw—you do it. Like my daddy use to."

Eric frowned, and started to say, You know, Shit, you're gonna hafta start doin'—

Then he didn't. "Okay. You said your number was your birthday."

"That's right. Ninth of May, nineteen eighty-eight. You know that—"

"Okay." Eric stepped in and slowly the glass swung closed between him and Shit. On his fingers, Eric was counting through January, February, March, April, May to figure out which one May was—the fifth. Often Shit had gone into the Credit Union with Dynamite and watched him get money from his own account—and a couple of times deposit checks in Shit's. (Their salaries were automatically deposited, though summer and winter bonuses came to the cabin in the mail.) He had no memory of the exact numbers, but he had a bodily memory of Dynamite's pressing six numbers on the key pad below the screen: *dum-dum, dum-dum, dum-dum.* His own PIN was six figures, too.

Getting out his wallet, Eric fingered Shit's card from among the sheaf of cards, including his driver's license and the Dump Produce card—which he had never been quite sure what he was supposed to do with, though Dynamite had said he should keep it on him. Maybe it was for some sort of identification, but nobody had ever asked to see it.

Eric slid Shit's card in and out of the jutting card reader. While the screen flipped through three advertisements before getting to the next message, he slipped the card back in his wallet. The instructions—"What Language Would You Like to Speak?"—popped up in dark letters on the light green screen. He pressed *English* and it responded by telling him to enter his PIN. So he pressed 05 09 88.

Three humming seconds later, the screen announced:

YOU HAVE ENTERED AN INVALID PIN

Eric drew in a breath, got out his wallet again, and took out Shit's card once more. Again, he slid it in. Again, he pressed *English* and then 05 09 88. Only this time he kept the card in his hand.

YOU HAVE ENTERED AN INVALID PIN

He got the message four more times.

The air conditioning wasn't particularly good in the vestibule. The back of Eric's neck and the back of his hands were sweating.

He glanced out at Shit, who was looked quizzically in through the glass. Eric grinned, then turned back to the machine.

YOU HAVE ENTERED AN INVALID PIN

Again, he grew a long breath, stood up, and went to the door—as two more customers came in. Eric caught the door closing against his hand and leaned out into the heat.

Shit said, "It don't work, do it? I didn't think it was gonna." His face was blank—which was one way Shit masked disappointment.

"Shit, are you sure the number is your birthday—or that you got it right?"

"Hey," Shit said, "I don't know a whole fuckin' lot. But I know my goddam motherfuckin' birthday—Dynamite said we was gonna use that, so I wouldn't forget it."

"Well, it's not workin' for some reason. This is *your* card—it ain't Dynamite's. His got a different picture on it." Eric stepped from the door. "Yours and mine is the same."

Shit stood there, his sleeveless shirt open, his beltless jeans sagging low enough to see the tan fuzz above his groin. His big hands and his big work shoes looking as if they belonged more to his dad than to Shit.

"Only mine has a one-one-three at the end," Eric went on. "You got a one-zero-one, 'cause you got yours before I got mine."

Shit began to shake his head. "I knew it wasn't gonna work—that's 'cause we ain't where I was born and everything—nobody knows me around here. So nobody ain't gonna give me no money."

"But that's not the way it works, Shit."

"Does *yours* work?"

"I didn't try mine."

"Well, maybe they'd give you some—'cause you from up in Atlanta, in the big city. But I'm just Shit, the garbage guy's nigger bastard what helps with the junk. Hell, I wouldn't give me no money down here, neither."

"But Shit, they've got to give you your cash, wherever you are. That's the law."

"How can there be a fuckin' law that you got to give money to some dumb fuck you don't know and never seen before? That's crazy—come on. Let's go."

"Lemme try mine first. Maybe the machine's broken…"

"I don't know why you gonna bother with—"

But Eric was back in the vestibule. Again at the screen, he fed in his own card, punched his own number…

With its internal hums and ruffles and clicks, the ATM machine slid a fifty-dollar bill from the slot into Eric's hand. And while he thought, Damn, I should've gotten more; it's gonna cost me the same five damned dollars, no matter how much I take out, he turned.

The glass and its glare—not even locked by a time lock—seemed to put Shit not a few feet away but miles and years beyond all but the slenderest contact with the world.

Eric turned from the screen and walked to the door, opening it. "Naw, it ain't broken. See, it gave me what I asked for." He held up the fifty.

"Well," Shit said. "That's 'cause it's *you*. I *knew* it wouldn't work for me. Come on, let's get the fuck back home, huh? I don't like comin' around here, no way."

They walked back to the truck.

After twenty minutes of silent driving, they were going through another small town, when Eric swerved the pickup into another lot.

"What you doin'?"

"I had an idea," Eric told him. "I wanna see somethin'."

It was another bank—HSBC—one of three connected buildings. Eric parked, opened the door, jumped down and started over the tarmac.

This time, he had to insert the card in the door slot, since the bank was closed.

Following behind him, Shit said, "What's this? Another one of them banks?"

"Right." The door came open. "Now, your birthday is the ninth of May, eighty-eight."

"Come on, nigger—it ain't gonna work!"

"Probably," Eric said. He went inside.

At the screen (which showed an illuminated map of the country), Eric looked back at Shit, who mouthed on the far side of the glass, "It ain't gonna work, fool—!"

Eric got Shit's card out, put it in the slot—this one didn't give him a language choice—and said under his breath, "Oh-five, oh-nine, eighty-eight…" Only he pressed "oh-nine" first, then "oh-five," then the "eight-eight."

...PLEASE MAKE YOUR REQUEST IN MULTIPLES OF FIFTY

On the three-by-three button pad, Eric punched in "50." Behind the metal panel machinery hummed.

Below the screen, a fifty-dollar bill slid—horizontally—from the slot.

Eric took it, grinned, turned, and held it up—he went to the door. Stepping out, he laughed. "Well, it cost you five dollars and me five dollars, but at least you know the damned card works."

"What'd you do?" Shit said. "Get fifty with your own card and you're gonna give it to me, now, so I don't feel bad or somethin'?"

"*Naw*, Shit! This is your own fifty from you own account at the goddam Credit Union back in the Dump. I got you the money with your card right here in...whatever the name of this little do-hicky pipsqueak town is— right outside Savannah."

"It still didn't work," Shit said. "I mean, before."

"It was just *me*, Shit," Eric said. "I punched in the wrong number."

"You didn't punch in my birthday? But I told you—"

"They're two ways to write a birthday, Shit. Today, people put the month first, then the day, and then the year. But the old fashioned way—I remember somebody tellin' me, in fact it was my grandmother, back in Hugantown—that people used to put the day first. And I figured, maybe that's how Dynamite had done it when he first got your card. A lot of things are a little old-fashioned, sometimes, down here."

"Well, they're both my fuckin' birthday. Don't you think the damned machine ought to know that, at least?"

"The machines don't really know nothing, Shit. But the point is, you got your money when you wanted it."

"The point is," Shit said, "the fuckin' thing didn't *work!*"

Eric had long ago learned that Shit's arguments were not so much attempts to determine what was true as they were demonstrations of foregone conclusions. If the results were in any way ambiguous, it made no difference. "Take your money, will you?"

"You keep it," Shit said.

Shaking his head a little, Eric took out his wallet again and slipped the fifty inside.

But that's why he didn't take the argument further.

Back in the pickup, Eric started again. After about three minutes, Shit said, "You know I'm gonna fuck the shit outta you when we get home, nigger—I'm gonna stick my dick in every hole you fuckin' got. You think you're somethin', but you're just a fuckin' nasty nigger shit hole. I'm gonna shoot so much cum into you, you gonna hear it slosh around when you get up to go to the bathroom. You gonna like that, too, you nasty nigger fuck—"

"All right." Eric grinned.

"You fuckin' piss drinkin' nigger sonofabitch—" Shit reached over and rubbed Eric's crotch roughly—"you got a fuckin' boner already. God, you're a low-down nasty black bastard." Shit's hand went back to rub his own crotch. "I should make you stop this truck, pull over, and blow me right here."

"Sure," Eric said. "Come on—"

"Naw," Shit said. "Get us home first. I wanna do it where we can really get into it and get comfortable."

"Okay," Eric said. "You're on. Let's go."

Sometimes, when Eric was mad at Shit about something, he'd give him a hug—a real hard one—on the verge of *too* hard; it was a way of releasing anger through affection. Then he'd learned Shit had his own version of the same thing—that involved his violent invitations to sex.

Once they got home to the upstairs apartment over the theater, they had a pretty intense and good evening. After midnight, they drove back to the Dump, got the tomato basket from the porch—halfway back, driving now, Shit, stopped the pickup and demanded, "Get down and suck my dick so I can piss in your mouth, nigger"—then drove back to the theater and, in the bed upstairs, rolled up into one another for another couple of hours.

It was odd, Eric thought, the way sex confirmed their bodily closeness even as it signed a mutual acknowledgment of temperamental difference— an agreement that they would *not* argue about bank cards and the like any more, though, he knew, neither one had changed his mind about them.

*

One Thursday afternoon, Eric took a couple of hours off from the Opera. Finally, on the top steps of the porch of what used to be Dynamite's cabin, where a padlock hung on the side door now, he settled himself. (Fred Hurter kept the key in his office desk up at the Lumber, Seed, and Steel.) Today a third of the cabins in the Dump were unoccupied.

Mama Grace's defection had only been one of many.

From the back pocket of his jeans, Eric tugged loose the paperback and looked at the cover. He'd promised Mama Grace he'd give this thing a try—at *real* try. *Three* real tries, in fact.

Not just the lackadaisical, half-hearted attempts he'd been giving it till now.

Remember. He shouldn't expect to understand any of it on the first go through, none of it. At all. Which was funny, 'cause it was written in English.

(Originally it had been written in Latin, but somebody named Curley had translated it, Mama Grace had explained.)

The time before, up in the apartment over the Opera's projection room, eventually Eric had made his eyes move over all the words in the first thirty-one pages. Not a sentence had made sense—which wasn't *quite* true, either. But no more than a dozen had. And three days later, he couldn't recall a one of those…which also wasn't quite true. The last had kind of stayed—but that, really, was only part of a sentence, embedded in another: "But to those who ask, 'why God did not create all men so that they would be governed by the command of reason,' I answer only 'because he did not lack material to create all things, from the highest degree of perfection to the lowest'; or, to speak more properly, 'because the laws of his nature have been so ample that they sufficed for producing all things which can be conceived by an infinite intellect' (as I have demonstrated in p16)." He'd even gone back to check out "p16," which was *no* fuckin' help!

But at least the question made sense: "Why did God not create all men so that they would be governed by the command of reason?" even if the "why" behind the purposed answer was beyond him…even, Eric thought, if you weren't too hot on the notion of God in the first place.

But God or whatever…

What *was* "perfect?"

The pattern one picked up from a spider web between the ferns…

What one could see of the stars webbing the night…

Eric opened the book again, paged to thirty-one—where the first section ended. And thought: No, actually I read a page *more*—or, well, didn't *read* it, but looked at all the words. Somehow without really realizing it, he'd started the second part…

Again, he reran his eyes down page thirty-two.

One sentence that had made a kind of sense was toward the place he'd actually stopped. (Funny how everything you did you always did a little more or a little less than you intended…) "By reality and perfection I understand the same thing."

It kind of undercut whatever was half sensible in that non-sensible answer to the one question he remembered. He flipped the page back over to reread it.

Eric had no way to know that he shared a certain intellectual masochism with many great scholars throughout history—and, though he would never be a scholar himself, even a self-taught one, he shared their isolation—and intellectual boredom. (A number of scholars would have enjoyed him as a conversational friend, if he'd had the fortune to meet them…) Above that, however paradoxically, between Shit and the visitors and regulars at the Opera, he had as much sex as he wanted, which, in league with the boredom, had kept him at it.

Still later that day, back at the Opera, again at work, he wondered: was all this bodily pleasure at the Opera some reward? (Since returning an hour ago, he'd fucked around with two guys already—and on the second one Shit had joined in. And Eric had gotten loads from all three, which was pleasant enough to note.) Or a distraction? Or a way to ameliorate his frustration with page after page of the incomprehensible? Or all of those? Or entirely other? Anyway, he thought, as he pushed the broom up the second balcony's side aisle, wondering if it would be worth going after that big fellow over on the other side, once he was finished: soon he would take his book back to where Barbara and he had once lived and seriously return to his endlessly postponed *first* reading.

The one that would take him all the way through…

* * *

[67] THEIR SECOND SEPTEMBER at the Opera was a month of tarnished rains, of autumnal storms where platinum lightning electrified this or that half of the sky's dark pewter, of literal ambles on leafy sand in hours off, with the stench of halides and wet wood, of ozone sharp under the nasal cavity's roof…

Their first order for closing the Opera was a phone call from Jay—it was just for a few days. The municipal plumbers again had to get back into the water main to and from the theater—it was more than a hundred years old.

Besides, they wanted to see them on Gilead.

Robert Kyle wanted to talk to them.

"Mr. Kyle?" Shit said. "What's he want?"

"I don't know," Eric said. The night of Dynamite's funeral rushed up, surrounded him, and swept off under the sun like a wave near the grotto.

Later, when Eric was coming down the stairs, into the lobby, Rudy—who was already standing there—asked, "What are we supposed to do, Mr. Jeffers, while the movie's closed?"

"Well, you'll have to figure out something, Rudy. There won't be no water, so you won't be able to use the john. And the electricity's gonna be off as well."

Eric heard something behind him. Reaching the bottom, he looked back up the curving steps with their ornate gilded banister. Al was coming down, buttoning up a faded blue shirt with a rip in one of the forearms. (Eric noticed that his fly was open.) The towering black man sauntered easily behind him, in big old work shoes. "Well, if you gonna shut this mother fuckin' place up for a while, maybe it's time for me to get back out to Split Pine and see if Nancy gonna take me in for a little while. If she don't, maybe Lungey'll let me stay with her." Three weeks ago, Al had come into the theater, walked heavily up the stairs to Nigger Heaven, and, save for rare trips to the bathroom, had not come down since. His head was no longer smoothly shaved, and he was bald in front.

Eric said, "We're talkin' a couple of days here. Maybe three—MacAmon says it shouldn't be no more than four." Once Eric had gone up specifically to see how he was doing. Al had sat with his shirt off—it was balled up in a paper bag under his seat—and his pants gaping, eating a slice from the pizza Dr. Greene had just brought in. Eric and Al had talked together about fifteen minutes, mostly about this or that regular who was or was no longer coming to the theater, by the end of which Eric decided not to inquire about his domestic situation.

It didn't feel right.

"Mr. Jeffers," Rudy said. "A couple of times, when Mr. Hammond and Dusty had to close the place up, they let us leave our stuff in here. And if it's gonna be open again in few days…?"

"Fine with me," Eric said. "But I ain't gonna be responsible for nothin' that happens to it while we're gone."

When they'd explained things to Myron and pulled the gates down over the theater front, in the pickup an hour later, driving along the coast to the Harbor, Shit said, "Lucius and Micky asked me to leave the back door in the alley unlocked, so they could get in and out. Dusty used to do that, when they had to close up for a while. They said they'd look out for the place, and wouldn't even use it when the plumbers were workin' there. That okay with you?"

Surprised, Eric glanced at Shit. "Are we gonna lose our job over this?"

"Nope," Shit said. "'Cause Jay would have to fire us, and he wants them boys to have a roof over their head as much as you and me do. Nobody's even gonna know—except them. They'll only go in real late at night, or real early in the morning. They won't even go into the theater part. They'll just sit around in the hall—"

"—and drink?"

"Probably," Shit said. "It'll be okay, though."

Eric sighed. "Maybe it'll be better havin' somebody in the place in case anything really goes wrong."

"What the fuck you think Kyle wants to talk to *us* about?"

"I don't know." Eric shrugged. "You ready to see 'im again?"

"Sure," Shit said. "Why not?"

*

They parked the pickup in the Gilead Dock parking lot. Three dozen people had gathered near the water, which would have been a crowd in May or June—much less September.

"Damn…" Shit whispered. "Is all them people goin' out to see Kyle?"

"Maybe," Eric said.

Most of them were women, too, many younger, but a few of them older than Shit and Eric. Some they knew by sight—a few went back to their years of garbage running.

Behind them someone said, "Hey, Shit. Hi, Eric."

Eric turned.

A thickset woman wore a brocaded turquoise poncho, with dim yellow birds and diamond shapes around the edge. The black hair that surrounded her brown, oval face hung in a thick braid over one shoulder. One heavy earring was silver and turquoise—a skull with more blue-green stones inset in the eyes, nose, and mouth.

"Tank…!" It was the first time Eric had seen her in anything but an orange canvas jumpsuit or one of blue denim. "How you doin'?" And never any jewelry before.

"I'm good," Tank said. "Hey, I found the snake for you."

"Huh?"

"Last time I saw you outside the shop, you asked me if we still had the template for that snake we put on Jay MacAmon. I told you I'd take a look for it. Well, a couple of days back I was diggin' in one of the drawers where we store some old flash—and there it was, at the bottom. In six pieces. The way Cassandra originally designed it, see, it was supposed to start on the back of his right hand, wrap around his arm a couple of times, then run across behind his shoulders, below his neck, and make a knot. Then it was gonna wind down the other arm with the tail around his wrist. Then we'd've fit in all the other pictures around it. But Jay decided he didn't want nothin' on his back or his chest. So we just left the knot out. Now it just stops under some storm clouds we put on one of his shoulders and takes up again, out from under some more on the other. It still looks good."

Surprised, Shit said, "You gonna break down and get yourself some pictures on your arms?"

"I was thinkin' about it," Eric said; "I ain't sure yet. But maybe I'll let you do the part across my back too."

"If you want it all," Tank said, with the patience of someone in a profession in which client indecision was rampant, "we got it all."

"How's Cassandra?"

"She's workin' at the store today—so I'm the one who gets to go to the fancy meetin' out on the island."

At a familiar motor, they all looked out over the water where the Gilead's flat prow dozed toppling froth toward the dock.

At the prow, Ed (in two throws), and in the stern, Mex (with one) lassoed the cleats. Standing up, Ed called, "Come on. Come on, get back now. Stand back."

The sky was overcast. Fog twisted and untwisted beside the boat. Fixed to the wheel shelter's edge, a white spotlight put a bright triangle down the wall and over part of the deck. The motor stilled. Froth fell back into the black-green sea, spreading, dispersing.

In his thermal vest, Jay stepped from under the wheel shelter, and ambled over along the rail, so that for two, three, five seconds the light fell directly on him. These days, his hair was half gray. But the wedge of illumination made the colors on his arms flare and even pulse with blues, purples, reds and violets Eric had forgotten.

Yeah, he thought, I *would* like my arms to look like his. Don't know why I didn't do it years ago.

Then people started getting on the boat. Three of the younger women just wore open jackets with no shirts under them. Half a dozen younger black guys—and a few women—Eric recognized had come in from Dump Produce. Half of the men were among the newer residents in the Dump itself. (For half a dozen years, Dump Farm Produce had become a favored summer job for the women at a sorority over at the university in Valdosta, rumored to get more than its share of dykes.)

"Come on, now. Take your damned shirt off," Shit whispered. "I wanna watch everybody droolin' over you, when you walk around showin' your muscles."

"Aw, come on," Eric whispered back. "It's chilly."

"You want me to grab it and *pull* it off you?"

"Okay, okay…" Grinning, embarrassed, Eric unbuttoned his shirt. A moment later, he tied the sleeves around his waist.

"You know," Shit grumbled at him, "we gonna be old men before you know it? While we still got it, we better flaunt it." When Eric looked up, Shit's shirt was gone, too.

A few times, they went over and asked Jay what all this was about. He told them, "You gotta wait till we get out to Gilead. Kyle's gonna be there."

Which was interesting enough to think about.

Once Eric saw Shit wander over to ask Mex something. The mute signed: "*You wait for another hour—you'll find out.*"

"Hey, Tank," Eric asked, when he found himself standing beside her.

She turned, and he thought she looked surprised that he'd dropped his shirt.

"Did Jay call you about goin' out to meet with Kyle?"

"Yep."

Then, he said, trying not to sound embarrassed, "Shit said I had to take my shirt off."

"Good." She nodded. "That snake'll look nice on you. It looks damned good on Jay. And he's got all that body hair—on you, folks are gonna be able to *see* it!"

And when the island was moving—it seemed—toward them, Eric asked Ed, "Hey, you know why they want us all to come out here—I mean, besides meetin' Kyle?"

With a rope in his hand, Ed said, "Look. I'm just the straight guy. Them faggots don't tell me *nothin'*." Smiling, he shook his head and continued up the deck between the women. "Nothin' personal, I mean," he said loudly back over his shoulder, "But this is all about you funny fellas—and funny gals."

Moments later, Shit was back with him, frowning across the water at the island's approaching shore. "Hey—what'd they do?"

The last time Eric had been there, trees and shrubs had come all the way up to the dock and the boathouse, on both sides. Now, the growth had been cleared about ten yards to the left of the boathouse and maybe fifteen next to the dock's far side. As well, the path of roots and rocks that had led up and away into the trees and forest growth had been replaced by wooden steps, up the slope. They had a wooden rail, too, and perhaps eight feet of cleared earth either side.

It didn't seem a huge undertaking.

Still, Eric wondered who had done it and how, in the three months, since he'd last been to Gilead.

Tank stepped up beside them to the scow's edge. "Well, all that sure wasn't here the last time I seen it."

Mex and Ed roped the cleats, then Jay stepped out of the wheel shelter, to call, "Just go on up the stairs. Right on to the top. We'll be there in a few minutes."

Shoes scuffled and thumped on the board steps. Eric kept one hand on the rail. It seemed to Eric, as they climbed, he'd come to a different island.

Climbing beside him, Shit asked, "What they built this thing for?"

Eric had thought they might be going out to the Kyle mansion.

At the top, however, a clearing was now strewn with rock and low bushes, striped here and there with tractor tire prints, though no vehicles were visible. Clumps of ferns remained, along with various tree stumps. A few big trees had been spared.

Someone had put up a yellow and green striped tent, as in a fair pavilion. When the breeze pushed back one of the flaps, inside they could see white benches. Eric turned around: though only fifteen or eighteen yards wide, the clearing went into the distance, pine trees either side.

"I don't think I ever even *seen* this part of the island before," Shit said. "It was too grown up. Why they done cut all this down?"

Near the pavilion, four framing walls stood around pale floorboards. All of one wall and half of another were covered with board. Someone was building a...building. Beside it were three big rolls of Tyvek Insulating pad—though no one was at work on it.

"Yall wanna go into the tent there and grab a seat on one of them benches?" Jay called out, reaching the top of the stairs behind them. "Reba Taylor's got some coffee for yall and some sweet rolls."

Eric caught the striped canvas and pushed it back again to follow some women into the tent space. With grass and gravel visible under the back edges, just behind him, Shit said, "You know, when I was a kid, I used to love that man suckin' on my dick, and I could look at all them pictures on his arms, while he did it. Sometimes, there, he'd lemme hold on to his shoulder and hump on his muscles, like a dog on your leg—and I'd come all over 'em and rub myself on them things. He'd tell me rubbin' my jizz around on 'em with my dick made the colors brighter. And for a couple of years, I actually believed him. But I'm damned if it don't look like he ain't managed to trick me into comin' to *another* motherfuckin' town meetin'!"

"Well, your daddy would've been pleased." Eric grinned.

"Yeah—I guess so. Hey, I'm glad you finally gonna get some pictures on you. Them things is fuckin' sexy."

"And I'm glad you like the idea. I may even get me a set of them tit rings, like your daddy had."

"Oh, fuck," Shit said. "I'm gonna be able to hump your arm like Uncle Tom used to do on my leg—or I used to do with Jay when I was a kid, Hell, I'm just a fuckin' old dog anyway."

"You always sayin' I'm the one who talks bullshit—" Eric leaned his shoulder into Shit's—"but you know damned well that ain't nothin' but a load of crap."

"Well, I may try it, anyway."

"And if you do, I guess I ain't gonna try an' stop you. Hey, when are *you* gonna break down and get you some, Shit?"

Shit shrugged his shoulders together and kept them that way. "Like I told you before, maybe a couple years after Hell done froze over."

"Oh." Eric laughed. "So I guess nothin' done really changed."

"Right," Shit said. "Do it ever?"

"Hey—" Eric glanced at his partner—"if you want, you can go on outside and walk around and go explorin'. I'll stay here and tell you anything that's important."

"Naw," Shit said. "I come this far. Besides, I wanna sit down and drink my coffee."

Again, the canvas rose and dropped behind him; another woman caught it up and pushed it back again, to come in after them. (Following Shit and Eric's lead, some of the women had dropped their own shirts. Somehow, Eric realized, that made him feel more comfortable.) One table stood to the side, covered with white paper. Four coffee urns sat on it with two trays piled with muffins and sweet rolls and pastries. Stacks of cups stood between aluminum and black carafes for milk.

Eric followed Shit to the table, watched him load up his Styrofoam container of black coffee with sugar; Eric filled his own with milk.

They found a spot on the benches.

Sitting beside Eric, Shit moved his foot on top of Eric's work shoe.

Toward the tent's front was another table. It held some equipment. Two women and a man were plugging in jacks and setting dials. Behind it stood a big screen on a stand. Adjusting it, another woman turned, noticed the people sitting down on the benches, and smiled. "We won't be usin' this, don't worry. It's just a backup."

Some of the people sitting laughed.

A firm and familiar voice said, "Looks like you got some people there. Yall about ready?"

Eric tried to tell who had spoken, but couldn't.

Someone at the table answered, "Just a minute or so, sir."

Seconds later, someone at the table asked, "Ready, Mr. Kyle?"

The voice said, "Been ready for twenty minutes."

At the table, a woman with more tattoos than Jay adjusted a knob on the equipment. "All right."

And a shadow—life size—before the table solidified: a tall gray-haired black man in a dark suit sat on a stool. "Hello. Thank yall for coming here this afternoon." Neither he nor the stool on which he sat had been there seconds before. "As you probably know, my name is Robert Kyle. Sitting here and looking around at those of you who have agreed to come see me today—" (The large screen behind him, Eric saw now, reflected a tent full of people on benches—and the table to one side with its urns. On the screen, he could see Jay sitting on the back corner of the table, one leg up, one on the floor. Eric glanced behind him. In the back of the tent, yes, Jay had come in to sit on the table corner. Surely that was what

Kyle was seeing.) "—there on Gilead Island, where I was born and grew up, and spent so much of my childhood and young manhood. It makes me remember another meeting that we had, years ago—almost forty now, on the mainland in Diamond Harbor, when I first talked about starting a community for the benefit of black gay men, like myself. Jay, you were at that meeting, too—though I don't think you were twenty years old yet. *I* was nineteen. It was a different world—it was a different century. Here in Philadelphia, where I'm talking to you from, I've been thinking how to address the issues that I want to speak about today. A lot has changed in that time. Georgia made gay marriages legal twelve years ago, and the governor is a partnered black gay woman—my old friend, Marianne Hendricks—who is *not* married to her life partner, and while even fifteen years ago that would have seemed pretty odd to most people, however much we may have wanted it, today it's just a part of all our lives so that many of you probably hardly think about it now—though it would have been headline news back then."

Shit leaned toward Eric to whisper, "Is Governor Henricks gay? I didn't know that. Maybe I shoulda voted. But then, she didn't need mine, anyway…"

"The forces that were pressing on us to create a safe haven for black gay men, such as the Dump, while they have not vanished by any means, are not so cataclysmic as they once were. Georgia, Tennessee, and South Carolina are generally thought of as one of the most gay-friendly areas of the country. That's one reason—and, sadly, only one—that I have let myself cut down on the money I have been spending on the Dump. As a lot of you know, the Dump has lost almost a third of its residents in the last six years. So I have decided to let it become general public housing, within some fairly rigorous income restrictions. Yes, Jay—?"

On the screen, Eric could see that, from his seat on the table corner in the back, Jay had his hand up.

"What you gonna do with Turpens—and the Opera? Not to mention Dump Produce?"

"All three of them are much too productive to shut down. Of the three of them, the Opera House brings in the least money—and is still the most famous and widely known." Kyle chuckled on his seat. (Eric thought: I used to see this man at Dump town meetings. I saw him the night of Dynamite's burial. And now, here he is again. But each time he looks like a different black man.) "Next to the Dump itself, it's our major gay tourist attraction. No, I want them to go on just like they've been going on. As much advancement as gay men and women have made in this country, we still haven't shaken off the notion of 'gay pollution' yet—so I'm pretty sure that when we open up rentals in the Dump, we'll get a fair number of gay folks—men and women both, we hope—who'll want to live there. What the Robert Kyle Foundation is planning to do, however, is to set up another subsidized, gay male community in Oklahoma, where I also have some land—right now it's called the Fields—to which anyone currently living in the Dump may move at the Foundation's expense. Meanwhile, I am opening up a third of the land at this end of Gilead Island for development into a township, in which gay women—lesbians—will have first rights of purchase and can apply for subsidies. The settlement here will try very hard to maintain itself as a safe and protective space for women here on the coast…" Some nine hands shot up.

The next fifty minutes was heated discussion, even with a few raised voices, about the preservation of the island's ecology and wild areas, to its Indian history, and how areas to be built up would be decided on. By the twelfth time—pretty mildly, Eric thought—Kyle said, "Now these are *all* things that will have to be legislated by the women who choose to live here. I can only lay out the most general outline," Shit leaned over to Eric and whispered:

"Come on, let's go. We ain't gonna be livin' here, anyway."

So they eased from the row and walked toward the back. Putting their empty cups into the cubical smelter standing on the table (which, in its clear hopper, had already stacked up a dozen new cups from the old melted plastic, with its faintly ammoniac tell-tale odor)—Jay nodded and smiled at them—and they pushed outside.

Shit looked around the clearing, with the single building, half finished ten yards away from the tent. "So they gonna build houses and things all around here. Well, there used to be a few of 'em. But that was when I was a kid."

They walked over toward the head of the stairway.

"Damn," Shit said, halting. "That's kinda high. It didn't bother me comin' up…"

"You wanna try and go around through the woods?"

"Naw. I might as well see what I can do. But if I grab your shoulder, steady me, will you?"

"Sure."

Shit took a deep breath, gripped the rail. They started down toward the dock.

* * *

[68] HALF A DOZEN women and two more men from Dump Produce were already down in the boathouse, waiting to return to the Harbor. Eric and Shit hadn't been the first to leave. Minutes later, Mex and Ed brought in the scow, with Mex at the wheel.

"Damn," Shit said for the third or fourth time, as they rode back across the harbor. "Them women sure can run on, can't they?"

Eric shrugged. "Well, it's what I'd wanna know about if I was movin' out there."

"Hey, how'd they do that thing where he just appeared like that, sittin' on his stool?"

Eric asked, "You ain't seen that before?"

"Naw," Shit said. "Have *you*?"

"Well…naw," Eric said. "Not really. Seen it, I mean. But I read about it. It's some kind of virtual projection. Big executives use it so they can meet with people in two or three cities at once—or with people who ain't where *they* are."

"Oh," Shit said. "It looked kinda weird. But I guess that's Kyle. He's a weird nigger."

At the Harbor dock, they walked across to the marina parking lot, got in their pickup and drove to Dump Corners. In his desk drawer, in his office at Hurter's Seed, Lumber & Steel, Fred found the key to their old cabin and gave it to them, along with the loan of a sleeping bag that had a double air mattress and pump built in.

For two nights, with the bag spread out on the floor, they stayed in the Dump, going into the Harbor for breakfast. Then they drove to Runcible.

In the alley beside the theater, saw horses had been set up around a fresh patch of pavement. The back door was, yes, open.

Inside the hall door, Shit tried the third switch: along the hall ceiling, the line of orange bulbs came on.

The electricity was on again.

If guys had hung out in the hall, they'd been pretty neat about it.

Up in their apartment, they ate some cold chicken Eric had left in the refrigerator—it was a little dry—and went to bed.

The next morning they hauled up the gates. Then Shit went down to turn on the boiler and Eric went over to the Runcible waterfront, where he found Mike and Lucius and Red and a dozen more, singly and in groups, and told them they could go back into the theater. Coming back himself, he ran into Doc Greene, who was returning with Al.

"You get over to Pinewood?"

"Naw," Al said. "I hung out with the fellas last night at the docks. It wasn't too bad."

It's funny, Eric thought, pushing sixty, if not sixty-five, the towering black man—a little stooped—probably wasn't doin' so well, if he really had no place to stay (he had never been a resident of the Dump), no matter how big his dick was.

At Cave et Aude, just down the street, Eric left them and went into the shop. Cassandra was at the front, on her chair, behind the counter. "Hey, Tank said you found Jay's old snake. What'll it cost me to start with that one?"

When, two hours later, he came back, his bronzed arms glistening with lotion and the black outline, shiny under it, of the newly-inked flash standing out on his skin, even before the scales were colored in, on the broken tile flooring of the theater lobby Shit asked him, "How come you never got that done when my daddy was still alive?"

"I don't know," Eric said. "I thought about it. But I don't think he really would've liked 'em."

"Yeah, well…" Shit said. "It do make you look a little older."

Eric grinned. "He liked thinkin' of me as a kid, I guess. And, hell, I kinda liked him thinkin' of me that way." Then he narrowed his eyes. "What you think of 'em?"

"Aw, fuck," Shit whispered, "I think that's so fuckin' sexy I could jump on you right here, bring you down in the corner, and do you right here on the floor! You gonna get your whole arms done, like Jay?"

"Yeah."

"Good," and over the three weeks it took to finish the full inking, when Eric would return from Tank and Cassandra's shop with a new color filled in, Shit would say, "Hey, why you wanna do that to me? Can I lick it?"

"Tomorrow," Eric would say. "It's gotta heal for twenty-four hours. You know that. You can pee on it, if you want. That's sterile."

"I'm gonna do both." Shit grinned as broadly as his dad. "That's your way of makin' sure I never leave you, huh? Damn, them things is sexy."

"Then why don't you get some?"

"Hey—not me." Shit chuckled. "But I sure like to look at 'em—rub my dick on 'em. And nose around on 'em. I keep thinkin' they should smell like somethin'."

* * *

[69] IN THE APARTMENT above the Opera, Eric finished his first reading of the *Ethica* in which he went back and followed *every* reference to every other part, definition, demonstration, axiom, explanation, proposition, scholium, and corollary. There were thousands of them—well, not thousands. In the first section alone there were seventy-two, including one unfollowable one because, nestled in parentheses, it referred to something from Descartes and he didn't *have* any Descartes to check against. He'd done that for brief sections before but never for the whole thing. Actually it could make short parts somewhat clearer. With all the flipping back and forth it forced on longer sections, going through the whole thing that way still tended to gray out on him—even parts he'd thought he was beginning to get a handle on. Well, he'd just have to go through it that way a few more times.

Eric turned out the light, got up, walked into the other room, and, lifting the covers, slid in beside Shit, who rolled over to face him, hugged him, kissed him like a diver going after pearls with his tongue, then rolled onto his back, while Eric burrowed under his arm. "Hey, scoot down and park my dick in your armpit."

"What? ...okay."

The next day, they left the place to Myron and went for a drive.

First they'd gone to the Dump and checked out the old cabin. Then they'd left the pickup there and wandered up Dump Bluff.

Beyond the slope's height, they sat on the grass, the ocean and Gilead behind them, while autumn took the edge from the heat and a breeze snapped the long blades side to side. Eric held his knees with both arms; Shit held his with one, his other hand wedged down between his legs, absently squeezing himself in a way he'd repeatedly said, "don't mean nothin'," but that Eric had long ago figured meant they were between ten and fifteen minutes away from sex.

Eric had come out in his old jeans, sneakers, and work shoes.

That morning, Shit had walked out of the old cabin naked.

"Don't you think you should give it another week till the last of the tourists get home before you start goin' around like that?"

"Nope. Besides, we ain't goin' into town. We won't meet nobody, except maybe some Dump niggers I already fucked."

Eric wondered about that. Although that would have been fine ten years ago, today people actually lived in the Dump whom Eric didn't know and hadn't met—even some with children.

Down across the rough scrub, like patchwork below, spread the several fields of Dump Produce Farms. How near it was—how near *everything* was to everything else around here—could still surprise Eric. Few places they might want to go were more than a mile-and-a-half from the sea.

They sat, shoulder against shoulder.

"I thought you said you always wanted somebody to do crazy stuff like this with, anyway—walk around with no clothes on, sit down on the curb and beat off whenever we felt like it. Well, now you got the nigger and the town—at least the neighborhood—to do that stuff."

"I *do* want it."

Grinning, Shit turned to face him. "Then suck my dick, you fuckin' nigger-lovin' cocksucker!"

Eric put his arm around Shit's shoulder. "Someday you gotta tell me how come a sun-burned, brick-red nigger with no teeth can grin at me and tell me to suck his dick, and I get hard."

Shit glanced down to the left, then the right. "Probably it's the freckles on my shoulders. Mama Grace used to say them freckles were some powerful stuff, when I used to fuck him, way back when—when I thought it was more masculine or somethin' fuckin' a real lady-like faggot, like Mama. Really, though, it's 'cause he was fun and 'cause he was smart." Shit worked his arm loose from between them. "Hey, you don't gotta suck my dick *right* now." He put it over Eric's shoulder. "Let's just sit here…" while Eric whispered, "Jesus…!"

"What?"

"That's okay. Nothin'." But it was the smell loosed from Shit's underarm, like the vinegar on the fish-and-chips at the Coffee & Egg. He knew now what was making him erect.

Shit took a deep breath. "Jesus, I miss my daddy sometimes. Hey, reach between my legs and hold my balls."

Eric reached. The warmth of Shit's thigh moved up his arm. Eric's fingers moved between grass and scrotal flesh. The flesh of Shit's thick penis was soft against Eric's wrist. Damn, Eric thought. I'm sittin' here hard as a rock in my jeans, and he's sittin' here buck-naked with his balls in my hand and don't even got a boner.

They both looked down the sloping grass, out over the lake's edge beside the farm's fields that disappeared between the hills—like a black steel shield or a hole in the landscape.

When the silence began to stretch out, Eric asked, "You think a lot about Dynamite?"

"Huh?" Shit glanced over. "Naw. Not a lot. Why should I?"

"'Cause you said you missed him. I thought maybe you was thinking about him when we were out to the island at that meetin'. I mean 'cause he's buried back there."

"Naw," Shit repeated. "I wasn't thinkin' about him, really. But I do miss 'im, sometimes." The silence stretched out further, and, within it, Eric found himself relaxed and comfortable.

Then Shit said, "Hey, Eric. I'm…sorry."

Eric frowned. "What you mean—sorry about what?"

Shit shrugged. "You know…when Dynamite died. I was so busy grievin' and feelin' sorry for myself, an actin' like a damn fool, I didn't give you a chance to be sad and do your own grievin' at all. You had to spend all your time worryin' about me." He looked down between his knees.

"Aw, Shit—you don't gotta tell me that."

"Naw—I was just actin' like a big baby. Yeah, my daddy died. But, hell, he was as much your daddy, at least by the end, there, as he was mine."

"Shit—that's just who you are. That's all. I understand that. Damn, that's one of the reasons I love you—"

"I shouldn't've been so selfish like that. And I'm sorry for it." After moments, Shit looked over. "See, now you're cryin', there. I guess this is the first time I give you space to do it in. You cryin' for Dynamite?"

Eric could feel the tear running down his left cheek. But he was even more aware of the smile that had seized up the muscles of his face. "I guess I'm cryin' for you and me…and Dynamite too, and all of us."

"Come on here and lemme hold you." Shit reached for him and pulled Eric to him. Eric put his arms around him and held him in return. "And I ain't gonna start fuckin' on you—at least for a while."

They held each other. Eric was actually surprised that it didn't move toward sex. He wouldn't have minded, if it had.

Finally Eric said, "Hey, Shit…?"

"What?"

"Do you *want* anything?"

"Huh?"

"Is there something that you really want to *have*—eventually, I mean? A big house, maybe—like Jay and Mex got Kyle's? Or even a new one— that ain't a' old wreck on top of a theater almost over a hundred-fifty, two hundred years old? Or even a lot of money? Or maybe you wanna take a trip somewhere, on a *big* boat?"

"Hell, no," Shit said. "I don't wanna go no place. I'm like Dynamite. I like it here. I got pretty much everything I want. I like workin'—sometimes cleanin' up the theater is borin', but it's fun, too, jokin' with the customers— *and* fuckin' 'em. Hey, I bet, when we was garbage men, there was people we knew more about than anyone else in Runcible County, just 'cause we threw out their crap"—something Dynamite had said regularly, which Shit had taken to repeating. "And hell, at the Opera I get to fuck pretty much anybody I want—*and* you, too."

"You probably miss workin' outside, though. I know you don't like cleanin' the balconies, cause they're so high."

"Yeah, well…" Shit said. "The only problem is so many of the good fucks always go up to Nigger Heaven, where I don't like to go."

"Hey—any time I see somebody up there who's kinda your style, I tell 'im he's gotta go downstairs and sit in the orchestra. We're closin' the top for cleanin'."

"Yeah, after *you* sucked on his dick for a while up there." Shit grinned at Eric. They released each other. "But that works out pretty good. Ain't nothin' wrong with workin' at the Opera House—you can fuck five, ten times a day, if you want." Shit worked a little away. "Can you think of a better job?"

"Naw. But...sometimes I wish we *had* one, though."

"Hey, I got you, don't I—and for guys who like to fuck as much as we do, right now *I* don't think there could be a job no better. Man, I *like* to fuck. And I like watchin' you fuck, and you like watchin' me. Between Turpens and the Opera, there're probably more niggers to fuck than I can handle. And when I get too tired of all that, I got you."

"Is that a compliment?"

"Sure it is! 'Cause I got so many choices, the one I keep comin' back to—like three times a week—had *better* be somethin' special. It sure turns me on, when I catch you tomcattin' around, off on your side of the orchestra. Or down in the john."

Eric smiled at his knees, as Shit's shoulder began to push oddly against Eric's own. He glanced to see that Shit had dragged his foot back into his lap, lifted up, hunched over it, and was gnawing on a toenail.

"Jesus, nigger," Eric said. "You must got the biggest feet I ever seen. You gonna dislocate your ankle—or your jaw—or somethin' with it all bent over like that."

"It ain't dislocated *yet*." Shit looked up and spit a fragment. "Hey, you know my dick's pretty big, too. You go on, take your shoes off, now."

"What for?" Eric asked.

"You know what for. Soon as I finish with mine, I wanna nose yours."

"Shit, you could be workin' on them things for hours." But he reached around to undo the laces from the hooks at the top of his work shoes. "I seen you *and* your dad sittin' on the porch and chewin' on them things all day long."

"I'm just tryin' to get a couple of 'em right. Then I wanna bind with you." The word—bond—had come from Jay, though Shit could never quite say it right. He was as liable to say 'bounded' or 'binded.' "Damn... there." He moved to another toe.

"Shit?"

Shit grunted something that could have been *What?*

"You ever scratch under Jay's nuts with your hair?"

"How do you mean?"

"You know—put your head under there and rub your hair on his balls? 'Cause you got that really good black-style hair, with that good texture— even if it *is* brown, or tan, or whatever. When they was itchin' 'im, I mean."

"How you gonna do that?" Shit asked. "Show me what you mean."

Eric took in a breath. "Okay…like—this, I guess."

Because of the way he was leaning, while he worked on his toenails, one of Shit's buttocks was pulled up.

Eric put his head down to push it under, where Shit's long scrotum dangled, heavy with his testicles and darker than his pubic hair. The side of Eric's face flattened grass.

"Oh, *now* I see what you mean…" Shit sounded like he was still gnawing. "Yeah, that's real nice. Keep that up. I see what you mean now—like this." Gas growled from between Shit's buttocks. "Like that, you mean?"

Despite the stench, Eric did not pull his head away. "Come *on*, now!"

"Aw, you must wanna nose another one—and do some bindin', too, huh?" He loosed another, louder, longer fart.

"Shit, cut it *out*—I'm bonded with you so goddam tight already I sleep with my nose in your fuckin' armpit every night—"

"Yeah, when I ain't sleepin' with mine in yours."

Shit released his foot.

"*Owww!*" Eric pulled back. "Don't sit on my *head*."

Shit turned to take Eric's shoulders in his hands. "I want you to sit on my fuckin' *dick*, scumsucker! Hey, did Jay ever fart in your face when he had you out with him and Mex, treatin' you like a dog when you was lickin' out his asshole?"

"Naw," Eric admitted.

"Well, see, now—then you ain't done *everything*, jus' 'cause you a big-city scumbucket. I done a few things that you ain't done yet. I'm gonna eat out your fuckin' asshole till it's so sloppy you won't know what's goin' into it or comin' out of it. Then I'm gonna stick my dick in it and fuck you till you don't know which end is up. Jay and Mex trained me pretty damned good, I mean, a lot better than—well, better than *you!* When they finished with me, fartin' in *my* face didn't mean nothin' to me. But first I'm gonna sniff your feet and bound—"

"Bind, yeah," Eric said. "I mean bond. Okay—"

Shit released his shoulders and moments later had both of Eric's feet in his rough hands, pressing them to his face. "Oh, man…" he took a long, long breath—"you ain't gonna go and leave, now—is you?"

"Huh? What you mean?" Eric asked. "Why would I leave?" He looked at the cleft in Shit's buttocks, darker than his own.

"'Cause this is a little fuckin' harbor county where nobody fishes for a livin' anymore and there ain't nothin' to do except fight and fuck—and 'cause you wanna get back to the big city where all them interestin' friends are and where you could see people and stuff and do things that was fun, other than hang out with a stupid nigger who don't know shit about nothin' and can't do nothin' but fuck 'cause he's too scared to fight."

"Jesus, Shit," Eric said, "you know that bondin' thing works two ways."

"Yeah, maybe. But Dynamite ain't here no more. You sure the reason you wasn't hangin' around is because *he* was so good to you?"

"Shit…I wanna be with *you*. Yeah, I loved Dynamite, too. But that's because he was *your* dad."

"But you see, I got to know what it is *you* want." Shit's face was, now, somehow against Eric's neck. His rough fingers hooked Eric's shoulders. "You wanna go back to Atlanta? You wanna get a good job there, where you ain't just sloppin' ammonia round in the basement piss troughs 'cause another drunk nigger couldn't aim straight when some damned Polack state trooper down there finally convinced 'im he was serious about wantin' 'im to piss all over 'im—?"

"Shit, that was probably *me*," Eric said. "Don't blame it on the niggers."

"Yeah, I know. But you wanna go off and meet all different kinds of people—who I don't even know. Even maybe get married and have kids and stuff. With a woman, maybe. Or adopt 'em if it's a man. And maybe come down to someplace like this for just two weeks in the summer, and when you see me, not even nod, 'cause you ain't even sure you know me no more, 'cause the guy you done married wouldn't like somebody like me, anyway. 'Cause I'm too fuckin' dirty and stupid and nasty—"

"Oh, come on, Shit—*stop* it, now!"

"Don't go—cocksucker." Shit's arms had gone around him. Shit was talking into his neck. "I'm gonna rub all over you, and then come and piss at the same time, and rub it all in with my belly, and we ain't never gonna wash it off."

"Hey, I'll give it three days. But after that—"

"Don't go, you piss drinkin' snot eatin' nasty fuck. Don't go. I'll fuck your ass. I'll piss in your fuckin' face, over at work in the Opera House or out in the street in the Dump or up here on the bluff. Don't go. You can have anything that comes out of my damned nigger dick, my nigger nose, my nigger mouth, my nigger ass—but don't go! I'll lick out every hole you got for half an hour every day—then push my dick in there and leave it in for a *long*, long time—"

"Shit, I know how large the world is. I don't got no reason to wanna leave…"

Shit blinked at him, with something close to wonder.

"I mean, why in the world would you think I would wanna leave—?"

"'Cause I'm a half-toothless, green-eyed nigger what can't read or write and ain't got the patience to sit through a whole town meetin', where people are talkin' about important shit, and I don't even understand it and nobody wants to be around me 'cause I ain't got no nails left and I'm forty-four years old and I still I eat my own goddam snot and they think I'm some kind of fuckin' creep unless somebody told 'em how big my dick was and they wanna get fucked, and even then it ain't like I'm no super-buck like Al or that nigger you always talkin' 'bout knowin' when you was a kid back in Atlanta…while *you* look like some goddam gold-headed movie-star out of a fuckin' magazine—"

That's when Eric grabbed Shit and pulled him to the grass, tonguing eyes and nose and mouth. They gripped each other's backs and the backs of each other's heads.

Later, when Shit lay there, and they'd held each other with their tongues deep—and slowly moving—in each other's mouths awhile, Eric pulled his head back and said, "You're forty-four. I just turned forty-two this July. You think other guys our age who been together as long as we have still carry on like this?"

"You mean bindin'?"

"Well, that an' everything else," Eric said.

"If they don't, they don't know what they're missin'."

"Why do you think we do it?"

"Huh? 'Cause we're always fuckin' so many other people." Shit nodded in the grass. "It's 'cause we're always gettin' back together again—I mean at least every couple of weeks. Hell, sometimes we get back together two or three times a day. That's *always* good…!"

Eric laughed. "You think *that's* what it is?"

"I guess so. At least part of it," Shit said. "That's how I figured it. Besides, you *smell* good. I ain't never been able to get enough of it. It's strongest when you drink my piss—which reminds me, I gotta take a leak. Hey, when you go down on me, hug my butt real tight, so I can rub on your head and you won't come loose."

"Aw, you'll just get all excited and halfway through, you'll get all hard and won't be able to finish."

"That's what you think," Shit said. "Naw. That was me five years ago. But…um, you'll see." And when Eric came up, Shit gave him a long, long, tongue-searching kiss that ended with a relaxed sigh from Shit, as if, finally, something had been completed.

Eric propped his head up on one hand. "You know, you got a lot more reasons to leave me than I got to leave you."

On his back, Shit looked over. "How you mean?"

"Between the Dump and the Opera and guys in Turpens from all up and down the coast, you gotta have fifty people who're just waitin' for you to fuck 'em. I bet anyone of 'em would move you in with 'em in a New York minute if you was lookin' for a place to stay. And me...? Now where the fuck would I go? Back with my mama? That would mean puttin' up with all Ron's bullshit. So I don't think you got to worry about *me* runnin' off nowhere."

"Oh..." Shit said, thoughtfully. "But see, there was only ever *two* guys I wanted to fuck who I wanted to fuck me, too...now and then, that is. One of 'em was my dad. And he's dead. And I guess you know the other one."

Eric put his arm around Shit's chest and squeezed him.

And a little later, Shit said, "I'll tell you one thing that would be nice."

"What?"

"A little place out on Gilead—somewhere near Jay. And I could go to the graveyard and be with Dynamite whenever I wanted."

"You really *do* miss him, don't you?"

"Not that much—but when I do, I do. A couple of nights back, around three in the mornin', if we'd been out there, I would've gotten up and walked over there and hung out with him awhile." He snorted. "And when I got back, I'd of probably fucked hell outta *you*."

"You *did*," Eric said, "I think. You know, if we *were* out there, you wouldn't have as many people to fuck as you do now."

Shit took a big breath and rolled to his back. "Well, I'll tell you. *That* might even be interestin', too."

October's breeze whispered in the nearer, then the further grasses.

* * *

[70] CLOUDS AND CLEAR blue unfurled over cornfields and kalefields and fields of summer squash. Eric moved the truck up, turned off the ignition, reached down, and tugged on the hand brake.

Today there were two barns. While the orange hand-pump was still pictured on the plastic ATM cards for the Credit Union and loomed to the left of the big DUMP PRODUCE highway sign down at the junction with I-22, four years ago the clanking thing had been dug up, the concrete base smashed (Shit's dry comment: "*Now* where they gonna park the pigs when they go to fuck 'em?" which Eric never came by without recalling), and the whole area planted over with grass.

In the green siding of the New Barn, built three years ago, the roll-up door began to rise. (Today the refuse cans stood along the building's back. Although Eric had never had to collect the refuse there, he was sure it would be a nuisance because of the slope.) Opening the cab door, he twisted in the seat and, one foot on the step, swung out, holding the overhead handle.

It was warm and breezy.

Inside the lifting door, Horm walked forward from the shadows. He wore a sleeveless V-neck red shirt and baggy work pants with vents cut up the sides. These days, he lumbered. The shopping bag, with corn tassels and the green and purple curves of peppers and eggplants over the top, banged his calf.

As Eric swung out from the truck, Horm stepped into the sunlight and squinted. "Got your usuals here. You want some fresh dill for your mama?"

"Naw," Eric said. "She don't do much cookin' no more," which was what he'd said pretty much every two weeks now for two years.

"You know what to do with them artichokes?" Horm handed up the shopping bag.

Eric took the reinforced paper handles. "I sure do." He swung the sack up into the truck seat,

Horm said, "When you gonna bring that horny partner of yours around and let 'im fuck my black ass? Pretty soon, I'm gonna forget what hole that damned thing goes into."

"You know where to find 'im." Eric turned and climbed back up into the cab. "He'll be waitin' for you. He's always sayin' he likes 'em with experience."

At the same time, at the edge of the barn doorway, the scrawny kid everyone called Grubby looked out. He wore sandals and had a shaggy mop of bronze hair. Edging up beside him, was his black partner, Shooter, a devilishly good looking, coal-black Caribbean, in work boots. Both kids wore denim shirts that hung wide open over muscle-banded bellies. (Eric thought of them as "kids," though both were almost thirty.) Itinerant laborers, traveling the country, about four months ago both had gotten jobs at Dump Produce. Both spent their days off at the Opera, where they had latched onto Shit and Eric, which, so far, was working out.

"Hey," Horm said. "You heard about the Markum fella, didn't you? The little guy?"

"Big Man—you mean the dwarf? Joe Markum's son?"

"Yeah. The one-legged one."

"Naw. I didn't hear nothin'." Eric hesitated with his hand on the cab's open door. "What about 'im?"

"He died—" had a child been playing in a bowl of ice cubes and, with wet cold hands, turned and grasped Eric's lower intestine, it might have felt the same. It wasn't fear. But it shocked him—"yesterday. Yesterday afternoon. Down in Hemmings. He said he wasn't feelin' too well, lay down—and forty minutes later he was dead."

"Wow…" Eric said quietly.

"A lot of them little guys go early like that," Horm said. "A cerebral hemorrhage—that's what Dr. Greene said, when he told me about it last evenin'. He come by for his corn, celery, and tomatoes. I swear that's all the man eats. Corn, celery, and tomatoes. I don't know why he gets 'em here. He could grow 'em hisself. I guess you can make a salad with just tomatoes and celery. Dr. Greene said them little guys is prone to them things."

"Um…" Eric's heart was beating harder than it had been, but now it quieted. "I don't see why not?"

"It don't sound to me like it would taste like much. They're gonna have some kind of memorial for 'im tomorrow. With his family, I guess. At four. Down in Hemmings. You guys were pretty friendly with him, weren't you?"

"We used to go down there on holidays," Eric said. "Save a couple of times when he come up to the Opera and I got to nod hello, I ain't seen 'im for almost—well—six, seven months, now." Eric shook his head. "Shit's gonna be surprised."

Horm nodded. "A couple of years ago, I remember Shit drove by with him to pick up your vegetables, and I gave him a whole bag of stuff to take to his daddy—he was just as appreciative as he could be. He was a real nice little guy. It's funny, knowin' I ain't never gonna see 'im again. I'm kind of sorry I didn't run into him more recently than I did." Horm straightened, as though recovering from lugging out the sack. "He always had somethin' to laugh about. Well, you give my best to Shit."

"Sure," Eric said. "I'll tell him you sent your regards."

Giving a mock salute—"See you in a couple of weeks—" Horm turned and lumbered back onto the hay-strewn planks of the New Barn's floor. Ahead of him were stalls and a ladder, up to the loft.

Fifteen yards away, the Old Barn had just been painted blue and looked kind of odd, sitting there in front of the corn and kale.

At the edge of the New Barn's door, Shooter and Grubby still pressed together, watching Eric.

Eric grinned at them. Turning to face them, he took a hold of the crotch of his own baggy work pants and joggled himself.

Eric saw both of them laugh.

Then, closer to the wall, Shooter pulled down his zipper, tugged out his genitals, and Grubby—noticing—reached over and began to shuck on his partner's cock. Oblivious, Horm continued on into the barn's shadow.

Eric laughed, too, figuring it was their way of saying they'd be at the Opera in a few days, and swung the cab door closed. As he started the truck, the combination of sexual anticipation coupled with the shock of his friend's extinction, made his stomach queasy. He drove out beside the two parked tractors and the row of tool shacks—all relatively new—and out the gate.

It would be nice, Eric thought, to go down with Shit to Hemmings tomorrow for the memorial. Myron could sit in the booth for a couple of hours. It would be nice to listen to the family reminisce about the little fellow. As a little kid, Eric knew, Big Man had had a whole bunch of operations and Mr. Markum was always going on about how brave he'd been through them all. He wondered would they see Danny, if not Buddy. It would be good to say hello to Mr. Markum. He wondered if the conveying of his condolences would help heal the absoluteness of the shock.

Through the window, the March air was pleasantly cool.

*

Under the chipped and ornate arches and the mirrors marred with black stains and cracks, Shit stood with his mop in the ringer of the yellow plastic pail. "Naw," he said, "I don't wanna go."

Eric was as surprised as he had been at hearing of Big Man's death. "Huh? Why not?"

"I don't know. I just—" he shrugged—"don't feel like it."

"But, damn, Shit. Big Man and Mr. Markum both came to Dynamite's funeral—and helped us dig his grave."

"Yeah, I know."

"But…can't you tell me why?"

Shit turned back to the pail, took out the mop, and slopped it down on the red tile of the basement lounge area. "It's just…well—" he shrugged—"his daddy makes me feel funny, sometimes."

"When we go down there for Christmas," Eric said, "we ran into his dad a few times. He was all right—and he was always nice to us and Dynamite, both. And you're the one who told me how much you thought they needed each other."

"Yeah, but I don't know if they always *got* each other. Sometimes when I went down there with Big Man by hisself, and we was goin' up to Big

Man's part of the house, Joe Markum didn't have nothin' to say to me—not even 'Hello, dog.' You would'a thought I was goddam Danny Turpens."

"Huh?" Eric frowned. "Well, that's…"

From the arch into the dark part of the rest room, where the urinals were, someone's voice echoed within. "Oh…oh, oh, fuck me! Fuck me, man! Yeah, that's right! Fuck me—yeah! Harder!"

Shit leaned into the mop and moved across the floor. "You go on down there, if you want. You see Mr. Markum, you tell 'im hello and how sorry we are and all that stuff. If you wanna go, I don't care."

"Well, I'm gonna feel a little odd without you…" Eric already felt strange. "But I guess…" He breathed out—and didn't say anything more.

From one of the other arches, he could hear a quiet grunting. Only from its sudden quickening, did he realize someone had simply gone into the alcove to beat off. On the table against a red stone column, a cardboard box was less than half full of brown and blue plastic packaged condoms. I should go upstairs, Eric thought, and get some more from the carton under the cash register in the booth, and fill that thing up.

"Well, look—okay. I'll go. But, damn, I wish you was goin' with me. I'd feel a lot better."

"I wish I felt like I could," Shit said.

*

Six-thirty the next evening, Eric got back. Shit was coming across the lobby. "How was it? You have a good time?"

"Yeah," Eric said. "Actually, it was kinda nice. Pike and Larson and the guys we always see down there on Christmas—I mean, Space Program Day—" Eric chuckled, and Shit smiled—"was all there. They asked after you. I told 'em you was up mindin' the place here." Then Eric made an odd face. "It was a little funny, though."

"What you mean?"

"When I got there, the first thing I done is go to the house. But there was a piece of paper taped to the door with gaffers tape that said the Big Man Memorial was over at the Hemmings Community Center, so I drove over there. They were havin' the thing down in the basement. I guess Larson was in charge of settin' it up. About thirty people done come. I recognized about half of 'em. They had a table with some pictures of Big Man and some flowers and a couple of his toy rocket ships. And we sat down—in a circle, 'cause Larson said that's how Big Man always had meetin's—and Larson called on folks and they stood up to tell stories about him, and how much he liked them science fiction movies—"

"Anybody tell about tryin' to fuck that little guy when his pee hose busted loose and wet us all the fuck down, up there in his rubber bed with the rubber floor—?"

"Naw." Eric chuckled. "That's the kind *you'd* tell—."

Shit said, "You was there too, that night—with your damned dick seven inches down his throat while he was buckin' and bouncin' on me. *You* could'a told 'em about that!"

"Well, probably half the guys there could have told about somethin' close to it—but it didn't seem like the time."

"I bet they were probably waitin' on Danny to tell 'em about that kinda shit. That's the kinda thing they'd expect from a damn drunk Turpens."

Eric frowned. "Danny wasn't there. I thought maybe he'd show up, but he didn't." Eric put his hands in his pockets.

"They were all waitin' for the drunk white guy to tell the stories about the crazy little nigger. Otherwise, I guess they was gonna do without."

"You think that's what it was?"

"Yeah," Shit said. "Probably—hey, I don't know."

"Mr. Markum wasn't there either."

"Well," Shit said. "I ain't surprised about that."

"In fact, it didn't look like nobody from his family was there."

"Oh," Shit said. "Well…that's kinda what I meant. I figured somethin' like that would happen, and I just didn't wanna be there to see it."

Most of the lights in the lobby ceiling were out, so that the entrance to the theater was an indistinct hall of rococo half dark. "You know, his dad built him all that special stuff, that rubber bed with the rubber mattress and the rubber sheets, and the floor with the drains in it, with the hoses there so him and his friends could hose down the walls and stuff—like we used to do in there with him, after we'd fucked around; and the special rubber sealin' around the doors and windows so the stench couldn't get out—then he put in that fire door, closed it up, and probably never went in there again, I bet." As happened regularly, Shit's insights into what was actually going on among the long-time citizens of Runcible Country had surprised Eric. When Shit was right, Eric could feel lost in the confused margins of the social world.

And as Shit still did, often, when Eric felt that way, Shit stepped forward and put his arms around Eric, and hugged his face into Eric's neck, with his complex of smells from gasoline and sweat to Lysol. "Hey." Shit's voice was soft and rough in Eric's ear. "You know who's inside waitin' for you?"

"What? …Who?" Eric asked.

"The two little pigs," Shit said. "You know who I mean. Grubby and Shooter."

"They are?" Eric rubbed Shit's hard back. "What do they want?

Dinner?" For the last three visits, when the two farm workers had come to the Opera on their day off, during the later afternoon when Myron took over the ticket selling for a couple of hours, they'd actually invited the two men to come up to the small apartment and sit at the kitchen table and eat whatever Eric was warming up that night—pork chops, chicken stew, once Horm's corn, peppers, and bacon.

"They want your fuckin' *dick*!" Shit's arms tightened. "They already had mine. I fucked 'em both twice, already. "

"You took 'em downstairs?"

"I did it right in the aisle, soon as they come in—first Grubby, then Shooter. Man, that nigger takes my dick with no spit or nothin'. By the time we finished, about ten guys was standin' around, watchin' and playin' with themselves."

"Are you goin' through some kinda exhibitionist change of life or somethin'?" Eric felt good, standing there, holding his partner and being held. He liked the quarter-lit world where sex and affection both were accepted. There were a dozen guys at least who moved around the theater without ever putting their dicks in their pants. (Pretty much all the time that was Shooter; and half the time, Grubby.)

When he spoke, Shit didn't even move his face away:

"Maybe…a little. I like showin' some of these cocksuckers what I can do. When I finished, they went and sat in Gorgonzola Alley for a while—earned their keep, I guess. Then I went over there, called 'em out, and fucked 'em again. After that, they said they were gonna sit down in the first row and rest a while and wait for you to get back."

"They're hungry…?" Eric said again.

"What they're waitin' for," Shit said, "is to fuck around with *you* and piss all over themselves when they're doin' it, 'cause they know you like to drink it."

"Oh," Eric said. "Yeah, well—that, too, I guess."

"After that, come on and find me…and we can go upstairs and eat."

Neither one moved to release the other. "You know," Eric said, "I had a thought. Both Grubby and Shooter are *little* fuckers. But they're both big-handed guys, too. And both of 'em bite their damned nails bad as you and your daddy. I was thinkin' about how the last few times, after we ate upstairs, we sat around and wasn't talkin' about much and the three of you was goin' after them things, chippin' and chompin' like there was no tomorrow. And I was sort of sittin' there, relaxin' and watchin yall—and feelin' all relaxed myself. And it occurred to me, this is just like we was back at the Dump, after dinner, with Dynamite. And I thought, maybe that's why you liked it so much, 'cause it was homey in a nice and familiar way."

"Now, that's interestin'," Shit said. "But the truth is, nice as it was, I don't think that thought ever passed through my head. You know what I really like about them two?"

Eric moved his beard against Shit's. "Naw—what?"

Shit moved his head back—so Eric did the same—and looked at Eric with the wrinkles around his green, green eyes, and emphasized the next thing he said with nodding: "The fuckin' stink on 'em!"

"Huh?" Eric asked.

"I can sit around them two and just...*breathe*, and be happy." (Eric felt the shake of a muffled laugh in Shit's body.) "You didn't know that?"

"Well," Eric said, "I kinda suspected it. I mean, it don't exactly bother me. It's just old piss. But it don't actually get me off."

"It don't get me off, either. But it makes me think about gettin' off. Come on." Finally Shit released Eric. "Go on in, mess around with them for a while, then hunt me up and we'll go upstairs and eat."

Together, they crossed the lobby to the doors into the theater space. As they went in, Shit's arm fell and he turned to go up to the back of the theater. Looking around, his eyes not yet adjusted, Eric started down the side aisle to the front.

As he reached the first row, in the end seat someone said, "Hey, Mr. Jeffers—I was wonderin' when you was gonna get here. I gotta piss like a motherfucker."

"Hey, Shooter," Eric said. "Can I set down there beside you...?"

"Move my boots—you can put 'em on the floor. Grubby's down there playin' with my feet," Shooter said. "He likes the way they get to smellin' in them boots of mine..." (Somebody sitting on the floor moved.) "He was talkin' about wantin' to pee on you in the worst way..."

"Goddamn, this nigger smells good—I like to sleep with these things right up in my face." Down on the floor, Grubby laughed. "I been a sucker for niggers' feet since I was a kid. I bet you ain't never knowed no perverts like us before!"

"Oh," Eric said, "I've run into a couple. They're pretty nice fellas, too— like you guys." And because it was dark and—probably—they couldn't see, Eric thrust a forefinger up his right nostril, twisted free a pretty big crust, pulled it loose, and ate it.

*

Three months later, for two weeks in row, Grubby and Shooter didn't come to the theater. The third week, when they didn't show up, Eric said, "Hey, I'm gonna run over to Dump Produce and pick up our vegetables."

As they stepped out of the theater, it was an overcast steel colored sky. "Just to make sure them boys are okay."

"Yeah," Shit said, "I'll go with you. You wanna wake up Myron and tell him to take the booth?"

"Nope," Eric said. "In the next hour-and-a-half, two hours, the only person what's gonna come by is one or two of the homeless fellas who were out last night—" Eric squinted up. A fine mist was settling from the air—"and they'll know enough just to walk on in, find a chair somewhere, and go to sleep."

Shit sighed. "Yeah—probably."

At the Dump Produce fields, Horm and two other men were up already, moving crates around outside. "You guys are here early—hey, Shit! How you doin', good lookin'? I was thinkin' you done forgot all about the old man, here. My butt was getting' a little itchy—know what I mean?"

"I can't imagine what you're talkin' about," Shit said. "With all these young studs runnin' around, I don't see why you'd be thinkin' about me at all."

One of the other men laughed and went back into the New Barn.

Eric said, "Hey, Horm—you see them two kids who was workin' here? Grubby and Shooter?"

"What about 'em?"

"Well, they ain't been over at the Opera for a couple of weeks now. We was just wonderin' if they was okay."

"To be honest, I don't rightly know. They left here about two, three weeks back. You know how that type is. They blow on in, work a while, then blow on out with the wind. Naw, they been gone from here a while now."

"Oh…" Shit looked puzzled.

Eric felt disappointed. "We was—" glancing over, behind Shit's steady expression, he saw a stillness that spoke of the same feeling—"you know, just checking."

They got their shopping bag of corn, melons, greens, onions, and potatoes. When they started back, the truck windshield was covered in drops.

As Eric was driving, he grinned at Shit and switched on the wipers, which cleared away their half circles. "You know, Shit—" Eric turned onto the highway, across from the white rimmed sign with the orange hand pump in the corner and the single barn in the background against the cornfields under a sunny sky with faint cloud streaks—"I think both of us just went and fell a little in love, it looks like."

"With them two idiots? Come on," Shit said. "How we gonna be in love? We're forty-four, forty-six. They ain't even thirty yet, either one of 'em. I hope we got a little more sense than that." But he put his arm up, took Eric's shoulder, and squeezed.

Eric turned back to the road. With the highway's curve, the sign pulled beyond the edge of the rear view.

That evening Eric made French fries, corn on the cob, and hamburgers. When dinner was over and they were sitting at the table, beyond the window now and again lightning burst silent between the rumblings before and after out in the dark, while Shit worked on his wide nubs. Finally he paused. "You know—it's *was* nice havin' somebody to sit around with again and bite on these damned things, getting' 'em into some kinda shape." He looked over at the stove. "I was even thinking about gettin' Shooter—I mean, *he* was black after all—to apply for a cabin in the Dump. Since he was with the nigger, Grubby wouldn't'a been no problem. They wasn't addicted to nothin', cept each other's feet—and their own stink, like you and me. They'd'a let 'em in there in a minute. And we kinda like theirs and they kinda liked ours. Ain't that a good start for some good Dump citizens? Hey, you made enough for four of us anyway. You wanna take those extra burgers and corn down to Nigger Heaven and see if anybody there wants a change from pizza?"

"Yeah, I'll do that." While Shit got up, picked up Eric's plate and his own, and took them to the sink.

* * *

[71] IN THEIR FIFTH year at the Opera, Eric stepped out of the ticket booth to stand beside it. Across the gray street, empty gray houses and abandoned gray offices filled this end of town. Gold, gray, and ivory clouds moved down the sky. The street was windy. His shirt was sleeveless and unbuttoned. The breeze tugged it back one way, then turned and tugged it the other. Eric liked showing off his brightly inked arms (sometimes), the spiders and birds and dolphins and octopi that crowded the serpent and skulls circling them. (*The day you came back here with that snake all coiled and colored in and twistin' around your arm like it had crawled off Jay's and onto yours, I stuck my hand in my pocket through the hole there and started pullin' on my pecker till I came in my jeans, like I was a fuckin' kid again. I did it three times that afternoon, just sneakin' stares at you.*"

(Eric laughed. *Yeah, I seen you, too. And you remember how the last time, you came halfway up the stairs and let me lick it off your hand, like your dad used to do with his?*

(Oh, yeah…Hey, that's right. I done forgot about that part…

(How come whenever you do something like your dad, you never remember it?)
He leaned against the wooden edge of the shelf, into whose indentation, from inside, during that last morning hour, he'd pushed out only three yellow tickets with change (and taken four payments by debit). As usual, the street was deserted. Thinking about going back in, Eric dug in his nose with a forefinger, then put it in his mouth for salt—

When, from up the street, somebody said, "Jesus, that's fuckin' *disgusting*, fellow!"

Eric flinched, chagrin tingling his face, his shoulders. He turned.

Ten feet off stood a young man in a half-length leather coat. His hair was black and wet looking. He seemed too pale to have spent the summer around Runcible. In blood-colored slacks and oxblood loafers, he looked up at the Opera marquee, then over the theater's entire facade. Five years ago, primary colors had become a fashion choice for men, and while locals narrowed their eyes, they were even appearing on the Georgia coast.

Since it was the only reason anyone ever stopped, Eric bit back his embarrassment and asked, "You want a ticket?"

"What the fuck would I wanna go into a place like that for?" The narrow faced man blinked, shaking his head. "You don't work here, do you?"

"I'm the manager," Eric said. "One of the managers,"

"Aw, Jesus," the man said. "Well…" He walked to a glass case between curved pilasters to examine the poster inside (one of the old plot-driven heterosexual porn films from the nineteen eighties, piped in electronically, that made up their main fare. This one was *Barbara Broadcast*), shook his head again, then wandered down the street.

Eric watched for three more breaths—then turned back, opened the rounded door, mounted the steps, and climbed up on the gray stool with its spring back. First leaning over to pull the booth door closed, he reached up to turn on the fan above the glass's upper rim. He took the long-sleeved shirt off the chair back and shrugged into it. There were still people who could get upset over extensive ink—or, at any rate, had to start asking all sorts of questions and proffering all sort of speculations as soon as they saw it. And Eric still was not *that* much of an extrovert.

If it hadn't been so embarrassing, he would have gone into the theater to tell Shit about the passing man.

Dr. Greene was the only customer who came by during the next forty minutes. The black doctor bought his twenty-dollar ticket (the one dollar bill had been discontinued back in '26, and the five dollar bill in '29, though a few places down here still accepted the latter), said something like, "I'm just goin' in for a while," smiled, turned, and walked over and through the lobby's glass doors. Ten minutes later a purple Mercedes pulled up across the street. Eric's stool was high enough so that he could see the crows' tracks the nearer wheel left on the street.

The car's rear door opened, and two men got out. The first wore dark green slacks and another black leather coat. For a moment, Eric thought the next man was his mother's partner, Ron. About Ron's size, he wore a similarly baggy suit. But, Eric saw then, he was white.

The front door on the far side of the car opened, too, and another man got out—the black hair, the leather coat.

Eric stiffened.

It was the one who'd walked by earlier.

The man came around in front of the headlights—in his red slacks—to join the other two. The headlights were on, the way people drove in the rain. (Clearly, the baggy older one spent less time in air conditioning than the younger two. His suit and socks were bright yellow.) They walked toward the booth, the baggy-suited one in the middle.

As they neared, the man in the yellow suit called, "Hey, in there! Can you hear me…?"

Eric leaned over, unlatched the door, slid off the school, and stepped down. "What can I do for you?" He'd thought about staying inside. The curved glass had made the yellow-suited man look fatter than he was—and the others stronger. But you *couldn't* hear too well from inside, and he suspected this would be more complicated than a ticket.

"By midnight tomorrow," the man in the suit said, "yall gonna close this place up. Pull down the gates. Put a 'CLOSED' sign in the ticket window. Yall live upstairs, right? In the apartment over the theater?"

"Yes, sir," Eric said. Then he frowned. "Hey—are you Mr. Johnston?"

The man frowned back. "I ain't met you—I don't think."

"I saw you back at a town meetin', 'bout fifteen or twenty years ago, in the Dump. You was havin' a debate with Robert Kyle."

"Oh," the man said. "Oh, yeah—starry-eyed coon with way, way too much money, who thinks there ain't nothin' more important than the lives of some crazy black faggots." He grunted.

Though he was surprised, Eric laughed. "If you *are* one—a black faggot, I mean—that can seem pretty important to you, actually."

Then, the glass theater doors swung out and, a hand each, momentarily, on door and jamb, Shit stepped onto the sidewalk. "Hey." Both hands dropped to his sides; the glass closed behind him. "Rudy said you got some people out here stopped by to talk to you. What's goin' on—?"

Eric said, "Mr. Johnston here says he wants us to close the Opera House again."

"I ain't sayin' I want yall to close it. Yall *gonna* close it—by tomorrow midnight—that's Sunday. And it's not openin' Monday. Who're you?" Then the man in the suit frowned. "Hey. You Haskell's...kid?"

Shit grinned and put his thumbs under his jeans' loose waist. "Yeah, I'm Haskell's nigger bastard."

And Eric realized those were the words that the man's pause after "Haskell" had probably held.

"But you can call me Shit—if you don't know that already. Now who're you, again...?"

"I'm Johnston."

"Damn...!" Shit stood still straighter, grinned more broadly, and pushed his jeans far enough down it was a wonder they didn't drop to the sidewalk. "Oh, my God! Hey, Eric—yeah, this here is Mr. Johnston! Well, ain't that somethin'? And he come all the way over here to the Opera to see us? He's on the Chamber of Commerce, he is! I ain't seen you since I was a boy with my daddy, Mr. Johnston." He chuckled. "You remember Dynamite Haskell? Johnston here was *actually* our boss—yours and mine, Eric—for all the time we was doin' the garbage runs. 'Cause he was Randal's boss. Hey—did I fuck your asshole when I was a little kid? I mean, I fucked so many of you big guys, I can't even remember. Or maybe my daddy stuck his dick up your butthole." Shit grinned. "He got to a lot of you motherfuckers, even before I did."

Now Shit hiked up his waist, reached up, and rubbed his thumb knuckle under his nose. Then he turned his hand over, snorted something out into his palm, dropped his hand an inch, looked at it, then took a big lick. "Damn, I *love* eatin' that fuckin' stuff." Through a grimace, Shit grinned. (Eric could see Shit's tongue moving in his mouth.) "But that's 'cause I never got me all civilized, like you, sir. But you know all that about me already—right?"

The man in the suit leaned back a little—but didn't step away, as the other two had.

The leather-coated one in the red slacks said, "Jesus Fuckin' Christ! There're *two* of 'em!"

The suited man said, "You can eat my fuckin' shit, if you wanna fish it up out the commode. But you gonna close the damned Opera House—yall understand? Tonight at midnight. And I'm sendin' some people round to make *sure* it's closed, too. Come on." Looking between the other two, he made a disgusted sound, then turned sharply and walked away, with one of his...guards?

The other leather-coated one took a few frowning steps backwards, as if unable to look away before he turned. Then he swung around and hurried toward the car.

The one in the suit called back without looking, "MacAmon says you two can stay in your apartment upstairs, over the theater—though I sure don't know what the fuck for. But anybody else—the projectionist, anyone who you got in here—has gotta go. We're not kiddin'."

Eric frowned after them. As they got back into their car, he asked Shit, "You *know* them guys?"

"Johnston's just a fuckin' hot air balloon who thinks he's a heavy turd. Now, why's he wanna go mess things up for the guys who stay here…?"

Half an hour later, Tank came over from Cave et Aude: Cassandra had said Jay was on the phone from Gilead and wanted to talk with one of them, Eric or Shit. So all three walked from under the Opera House marquee, crossed the street's pinkish dust, and sauntered up fifteen yards by the corner hitching posts to the tattoo and piercing emporium's blue-framed plate glass window. Outside, shirt unbuttoned, in his old sneakers with his toes coming through the outside of the left one and no socks, Shit stood, hands hooked by broad thumbs on his jeans' frayed waist.

Inside, the phone lay on a glass case above a tray of various-sized rings with their ball closings—for ears, nipples, eyebrows, navels, lips. Eric picked it up. "Hello…?"

"Hey, will one of you please turn on your damned phones."

"Oh, I'm sorry, Jay…" With his free hand, Eric reached around to pat his hip pocket—but it wasn't there. Oh, that's right. It was upstairs, on the table beside the bed.

With Shit's.

"You crazy Luddites wanna come out here and do a few honest days work?"

"Huh—?"

"Yeah. Don't worry. Yall gonna be opened up and runnin' again in two weeks. But some new people on the Chamber of Commerce Board don't quite understand how we do things down here. Kyle gotta break out the Historic Landmark file again and convince them that another parkin' lot down there is not goin' to bring boomin' business, wealth, and prosperity to that end of town."

"Two weeks?" Eric asked. "Wow. I figured closin' down wasn't your idea. But this don't sound like the Chamber of Commerce doin' no plumbin' work. "

"Actually, it ain't much different. It's a zonin' thing—that's the barrel they got me over. And it's gonna take two weeks instead of a couple of days to get up off it."

"But where all the guys gonna sleep if we shut the place up?"

"Don't worry," Jay said. "That's what you always ask. They gonna sleep the same places they slept before they come to the Opera. It's good weather—half of them would be slippin' off to catch their shut-eye out under the stars, anyway."

Eric frowned. The weather hadn't been *that* good. "But some of our guys have been livin' in there half a dozen or more years, now—since before we took over. Suppose there's a storm—?"

"Get a TV—or at least watch the Weather Channel on somebody else's. Ain't gonna be no storms this week and probably not next. Look. You two come on out here. Stay with Mex and me for a while. I figure that's how long it'll take to open it up again. You can work on one of the construction crews—you'll make more money in *three* days out here than you do in a month in the Opera. We don't mind puttin' you up, Hugh, Mex, and me—we get lonesome for some company, anyway. I ain't even gonna try an' fuck ya'—you *or* your ol' man."

"Well, if you ain't gonna at least *try*, why we comin' out, then?" Which was something dumb to laugh over. "But I guess we'll be there."

Then Eric hung up, said thanks to Cassandra, who sat behind the counter in a voluminous blue muumuu, with her pastels, her oil crayons, drafting new flash: an elaborately scrolled planetary orrery among swooping comets and glittering stars, for someone's back, which Eric stopped to look at for a whole minute. "Hey, I really like that one…"

(Tank was in the back of the store with a customer, half visible behind a blue and red curtain, her needle humming.)

Cassandra called, "Thanks, sweetheart."

Then Eric went outside. In the doorway a drop from overhead hit his shoulder. He reached up to rub it away but didn't even look up. "Jay wants us to come out and stay with him and Mex while the Opera's closed up. He says it's for two weeks."

"Probably he's waitin for Mr. Kyle to get back from somewhere or other."

Surprised that Shit didn't seem more perturbed, Eric shrugged his assent. "Jay says we can do some construction work on the new houses out there. Make us a little money while the fuck films is shut down and we ain't got nothin' comin' in."

"Well, that's okay with me." Shit shifted his weight to the other leg. "If we have to close, we have to close. I guess doin' some carpentry'll be okay, long as they don't put me up no high ladders."

"Jay knows that," Eric said.

"*Jay* knows it," Shit said. "I just hope them construction fellas we gonna be workin' with knows it."

After seconds on the silent street, Eric asked, "Shit, how come you can do that stuff—like with that handful of boogers there; and I can never get it together to think up something like that?"

"What you mean?"

"Before—I was standin' by the booth there, and nobody was on the street, so I'm pickin' my nose like I do—like we done since we was kids. Nobody was around. But one of Johnston's bodyguards or whatever the fuck he was come by and caught me eatin' it—and said somethin', about how disgustin' it was. Now *you* woulda turned around and done somethin' right away that'd *really* gross him out—like you did with Johnston. But after all that, all I could do is was get chills down my shoulders and feel like two cents."

"You mean *I* grossed out that fat fuck?" Shit laughed on the empty sidewalk. "I guess I did, didn't I? But, hell—I been plannin' to do that for thirty-five goddam years. What happened to you today happened to me with Johnston the first time, when I was about ten years old, with my daddy." Shit chuckled again. "Dynamite had to go to Johnston's office—he was in the Hemmings City Hall, back then—oh, about somethin', and he took me along. The blinds was all half-closed at the windows and Dynamite's standin' in front of Johnston's desk, talkin' to him about somethin', and I'm standin' a little back and kind of beside him, just listenin' and watchin' and not thinkin', and doin' the same thing you was. Suddenly from behind his desk, Johnston yelled at me to cut it the fuck out! My ears got so fuckin' hot, I 'bout pissed my pants. When we was outside, I thought Dynamite was gonna be mad, but he just grinned and gimme a hug. Soon as we got in the truck, he laughed and told me I just had to be careful and choose who I did my nose pickin' around—that it was okay with Mex and Jay and people who liked me and didn't care. That's when I decided someday I was gonna *really* gross out that motherfucker Johnston! And here, thirty-five years later, I got my chance—that's all." Shit chuckled again. "See, that's the difference between a big city and a little town like Hemmings, Runcible, or Diamond Harbor, where you know everybody all your life—even if you don't see 'em for ten, twenty years or so."

"Oh…" Eric frowned—wondering if that was, indeed, the difference.

"Funny, though." As they returned to the Opera, Shit put his hands in his torn back pockets and looked at the ground. "Now, what *I* was thinkin', about the time you asked me, is that it didn't probably mean nothin' to the mean-ass motherfucker *after* all. He was just the kind of guy who liked to yell at a damned kid. Maybe he still does. Probably he thought that's how you were *supposed* to treat 'im." Shit sucked his teeth. "And after what I just done, I'm sure he don't think no *better* of me than he did—*that's* for certain. Still, I'm glad I did it."

Eric said, "Me too..." Though he wondered why.

Back at the Opera, they told laconic Myron that, starting at midnight, he had (at least) the week off—if not more.

With light out the side of the projector flickering on his vest and on his black glasses frames, Myron asked, "Am I out of a job?"

"I don't know," Eric said. "Jay says he's gonna try and have it open in two weeks."

Myron said, "It was closed for two months just before you guys took it over. Maybe he can get Kyle to help him. When the two of them work together, they can keep Johnston on his fuckin' leash. But Jay can't do that stuff hisself."

Before they helped Myron shut down the projectors, Shit went through the orchestra and Eric prowled the first and second balconies to tell the regulars the place would be closed for a while and they had to get out.

("Sure. That's okay." Shit told Jeremy and Owen, who were brothers. "If you got stuff stashed in here we don't know about, and you ain't gonna need it in the next couple o' weeks, leave it. It'll be here when you get back." But Eric felt uncomfortable. Suppose they *didn't* open the place up again...?

(Or there *was* a storm.

(Or at least a rain.

(There'd been enough of it already that month.)

Then Eric put their work shoes, work gloves, some socks and underwear, their electric toothbrush, and Shit's big bar of oatmeal soap ("See, that's how you know I'm a faggot. 'Cause I use a special soap. It ain't *just* 'cause I eat my snot—and yours"), and Eric's Spinoza, all into the green knapsack.

Next morning, while a dozen guys wandered out from under the Opera House marquee, three to amble up the street, five to wander down, and four to stand around watching, including the nineteen-year-old farm-boy, Pete, with his blond ponytail and no shirt and the short heavy black girl with the wild head of hair, Penny, in bathroom thongs and short shorts, whom he'd picked up when she'd hidden from someone who'd brought her to Turpens' rear parking lot. Generally, Pete moved around the back rows of the Opera with pudgy Penny tucked under his arm. Eric had explained to them: "Takin' a little money—fifty, a hundred, a hundred-fifty—is fine, long as nobody starts complainin'. Do what you do." Eric still thought of it as five, ten, fifteen..."Just remember, this here is for *public* sex—not private. If either one of you gets upset by people sittin' around and watchin, pullin' on their dicks, even coppin' a feel now and then, that just means yall in the wrong place—understand?" To which Penny said, "Hey, don' worry about me—I got this place *down*. Half the time I'm pimpin' *him* out." And Pete looked sheepish.

Eric and Shit pulled the metal gates down over the front and padlocked the place up about as tight as it could be.

Will—the freckled black guy who wore some kind of S&M leather harness instead of a shirt and wandered around the theater barefoot and wore a pair of ancient black jeans that were so raggedy Eric was pretty sure that, outside, a grumpy policeman might decide to pick him up within hours because you could always see most of his dick through the rips—strolled up and asked, "Hey, you want some help pullin' down the gate there?" Will had come to Diamond Harbor about ten years after Eric, and had started off with the cabin in the Dump. But one day he'd wandered out of it and never come back, living homeless around the Runcible docks for the next decade—which basically meant in the Opera House. (Will had a condition once called hebephrenia—too lazy or confused to wash or keep clean in any way—though the medication Dr. Greene brought him for it every week improved it greatly.)

"Naw," Eric said. "It's okay." That morning, Will smelled strongly of old urine—though somehow, he had his fans in the theater. Still, Eric wondered, where is a guy like that going to go?

With Shit carrying the knapsack by one strap over his arm, they caught the six-thirty bus up to the Harbor and waited for the scow at the Gilead Boat Dock.

Because it was Friday, Ed and eleven-year-old Hannibal were doing a stint for Jay and Mex that weekend (as they did now, time to time) on the *Gilead II*. In his sleeveless army shirt, Hannibal darted around the boat like a dragonfly, stacking luggage, tying and untying ropes, answering questions while Ed stood in the wheelhouse. Sure, Hannibal was kind of off limits; but, with his jeans rolled up his brown calves, his bare feet and his shoulders struck with droplets from a wave that had just splatted the boat's front, Hannibal was as cute as a button.

"Damn." Shit nudged Eric with his elbow. "I'm glad I ain't no goddam pedophile. I'd wanna fuck that kid like there was no tomorrow. What we gonna do when him and his friends come down tryin' to sneak into the Opera?"

"Same thing we do when any other kids comes in there," Eric said. "We gonna give 'em a free condom and a nice seat down in the front on Easy Street—" which was the regulars' nickname for the area to the side of the sprawling orchestra for those men who didn't particularly want to be bothered by sexual advances from anyone (on the opposite side to the area in the back, nicknamed Gorgonzola Alley, where they tried to herd together Ruddy, Will, Pete, and Al—when he chose to sit downstairs—

with most of the other uncut fellows; and where, yes, more than half of the action went on)—"and leave 'em alone. That's if his big brother, Cap'n Ed, don't figure out he's snuck in there, come in, and drag his ass on home. Then, if they wanna come back, we tell em like we do anybody else what looks even halfway decent: they got to be ready to put out or pay for their tickets, one. Then we keep tabs on 'em. And get ours when they ain't busy. That's all."

"Oh, you're so damned practical!" Shit grinned. "You know—" he turned to lean on the rail, squinting across froth and wavelets, their southwest slopes—a thousand-thousand, appearing and disappearing, across the sea—violet in nets of green—"we didn't really *have* to come out to Gilead. We could'a just shut up the place and gone upstairs in the apartment and taken ourselves a nice week-long vacation. Henry'd give us credit at the supermarket, if we asked. You know that. It could've been interestin', climbin' into bed together and holdin' each other and tongue-fuckin' you till my goddam jawbone was sore. I wouldn't 'a' gotten up for a week, not even to take a piss. I'd'a given it all to you and let you carry it into the john to get rid of it for us both. Oh, I might'a gotten up to take a shit, now and then—"

"—and, yeah, I could make you soup and fry you up chopped meat, and make you some tomato salad."

Shit grinned back, narrowing his eyes. "I'd make the coffee."

"Oh. Well, then—I guess *that* would be all right, then." Eric looked at his tattooed forearms on the rail, fists meshed above the foam. Cassandra *had* done as nice a job on him as she'd done on Jay. White planks at the boat's side sloped into the sea. (The *Gilead II* was an actual ferry that could carry four pickups, though there was only one on it today.) "You know I *like* makin' you breakfast in bed—or bringin' you a Coca-Cola and all that."

"I know you do. I like you likin' it, too." Shit slid nearer. "'Cause it makes you horny. When you do it, I can count on layin' back and gettin' a *real* good suck in five minutes. I mean, nice and slow, and no hurry, the kind my daddy used to like you to give 'im and I used to like watchin'. The idea that somebody likes takin' care of me, and wants me to lay out, and take it easy—"

"Well, that's 'cause you work so goddam hard all the time. 'Cause you don't like to do them top two balconies, in the rest of the place you work like a motherfucker—"

"Father-fucker, please…"

"You work like a nigger down in the orchestra and in the downstairs lounge and everything. You get me feelin' all guilty."

"Well, das' 'cause I's a nigger, Mr. Whitefeller." Shit snorted, dug in his nose. "Man, you *know* your nigger, too. If I'm gonna work at all, I like to work hard. That's just me." He took his finger out, looked at it, then offered his hand to Eric.

Eric sucked the hard nub free of its salt load and concertedly did *not* look around to see if anybody watched. "Yeah—you're *my* nigger." Jesus, he thought. And it still gives me a hard-on—and still surprises me, when it does. "And don't you forget it. Hey—all *I* got to do is vacuum between the seats, mop up every three days, and screw in some light bulbs. I even had Manny and Little Joe up there, keepin' an eye out so nobody steals 'em no more."

"Which one's Manny?"

"Well, you don't see him that much, 'cause he don't come down from Nigger Heaven all that often."

"He ain't one of the Breakfast Club, is he?"

"Sometimes—at least I think so. When he can swig a whole pint of vodka down to get himself up for it."

"Oh. Well, if he does his job, he can wolf down as much as Haystack, for all I care. I don't give a fuck. Send him downstairs for lunch, and I'll shit in his fuckin' face myself, if he wants." Shit took a long breath and watched the waves, moving, breaking, slipping past. The island's mist neared. Digging in a nostril, again Shit offered it to Eric, then returned his finger to his own mouth to gnaw the broken nub. "You know, when we get out there, we could just lie around at Jay's and do the same damned thing. I mean, with each other." The air tugged and flapped the collar of Shit's sleeveless shirt back from the tendons in his neck. "They got enough room. I wonder what it would *be* like to have sex with the same person three or four times in a row—even if it *was* you." He gave Eric a wicked look.

Raising his eyebrows, Eric looked back at his partner, as Shit pulled his finger—finally—free. Above the water, the moon, near full and visibly spherical, was an ivory ball on the afternoon's blue. Hadn't the moon been up the first time—how many years ago now?—Eric and his dad had driven down to the Harbor from Atlanta?

"Eric?" Shit began to frown at the water. "Do you mind when I tell you to fuck off, I mean, sexually. I don't ever really say 'no' to you, do I?"

"No," Eric said, thoughtfully. "You say, 'Fuck off, man. I'll hold your balls while you beat off,' and hold 'em about thirty seconds till you start snoring again. Or you say, 'Aw, man, I'm too tired to fuck you. Climb on my belly, stick your tongue up my nose, and glue the two of us together with a nice load on my gut,' then you go to sleep by the time I've hunched my third hunch—"

"—but I been keepin' my arms around you, ain't I?"

"That's right—when you're awake. Or you roll over on your stomach, tell me to get on top and rub off in the crack of your cute half-breed redneck ass, but I shouldn't put it in. And then...go to sleep." Eric humphed. "Again."

"Was that the time I got kinda squeezed out from under you, off the edge of the bed and fell on the floor?"

"Yeah. That's happened about *three* times, now."

"Hell—and I only remember the once."

"Well, you *were* asleep. But it's true, you *don't* never say flat out 'No.'"

Shit chuckled. "Well, one thing: you sure know how to keep this nigger laughin'. You're the funniest white man I know. And I *wanna* try screwing you three or four times in a row. Workin' with all that loose meat flappin' around there in the Opera has got me kinda crazy. Jay won't mind if we just took off and did that for one of the weeks we was out there."

"Shit—we're supposed to be *workin'!*"

"Well, then—let's just work *and* fuck. You and me. That's what ordinary people do, ain't it?"

"Okay. I'd like to try that." Eric grinned.

"Then let's do it. But don't forget—or get all distracted with your goddam book."

At the dock, Mex was waiting.

Among a dozen women, Mex, Shit and Eric, were the only men there that morning. (Several had come to meet visiting friends. Four together had come to meet a fifth, with much embracing and laughter. Another had come to wait for someone, who apparently had not shown up.) They walked up the steps from the dock, where, at the top of the hill, Settlement Road bloomed around them.

"Damn," Shit said. "The last time I was out here, it wasn't built up *this* much..."

Mex paused to look around. "*There's more*," he signed, "*on Rockside—the street over. That's gonna be for shops and stuff.*"

"*Two* streets?" Shit said. "This place got *two* streets now? What, they're trying to make it bigger than the Harbor? Hey, what'd you say the other one's name was?...Rockwall?" Shit translated Mex's signs.

"Spell it out, Mex," Eric said.

So Mex did.

"Rockside," Eric told Shit. "It's called Rockside."

"Damn." Shit squinted around in lingering amazement. "This place really *has* changed, ain't it? Hey, it's been so long since I seen you, I forgot half my sign language," though, of course, he'd never had the spelling part at all.

At Reba's—on Rockside—they met Jay to get some breakfast. He was waiting for them in a booth.

"Damn," Shit repeated. "This is as big as the Lighthouse Coffee & Egg—where your mom used to work. The last time I was out, there wasn't nothin' here at *all*."

"Hello, there." Jay turned around in his booth seat. "Hey, Reba, you wanna bring these boys some breakfast? When you guys was out here for the meetin', this was the only buildin' they'd gotten started on—'cause Reba said right away she was all for it."

Behind the counter, a very black woman in a white smock, who was straight up and down without a waist and had her head shaved, said, "That's what I'm here for—to keep the girls and boys from goin' hungry." She came out. "What you gonna have with your coffee, now? We got pretty much everything—bacon, ham, scrapple, seitan, eggs, muffins—grits, hash browns, home fries. Toast or English. Orange, cranberry, grapefruit, apple, tomato—and startin' Monday we're gonna be squeezing our own orange juice. When you're this close to Florida, you got to take advantage of it. Right now, though, it's still out the carton."

Probably, Eric thought, he'd seen her at the meeting, though he didn't recognize her. He remembered the single half-built building, but he would not have been able to identify where they were now from memory.

Through the plate glass window, over the curtains, on the other side of the street, was a…dress shop window (the sign above it said NIGHTWOOD) in which everything was black or silver, plastic or leather. Lots of things had metal studs on them. After the tourist blues, pinks, and oranges that dominated the bathing suits and summer ware up and down Runcible's mainland streets, they looked…weird.

While Mex was drinking his second glass of juice, Shit explained to Jay: "Now, I hope you told 'em, I don't read or write. And don't put me on no ladders higher than the second floor. You told 'em that, now—didn't you, Jay? I just don't want no confusion. Long as you told 'em that, I'll work my black ass off."

"Don't worry," Jay said. He was wearing a long-sleeve plaid shirt, so that, thrust from beneath his cuff, the snake's head alone showed on the back of one big, blondly furred hand. "I told 'em."

Others came in, mostly women, most wearing elastic orange, green, or brown halters.

The same serpent bared its gold fangs under the near-platinum fuzz on the back of Eric's.

Pausing over a fork—held in his fist—of eggs and grits, Shit asked softly, "How come they all wearin' *them* things? Half the women on the mainland go around with theirs titties all bare—I'd thought out here they *all* did."

"Probably," Jay said, "'cause most of the women who come in here are all gonna be doin' some work. Physical work, I mean. It's more comfortable, when you're gonna be bustin' your hump, if you got some support."

Right then, three people darkened the doorway behind the curtains. Then they were ambling leisurely in. The middle one was a bigger (and maybe a decade older) version of Reba. Under a desert army jacket, hanging open, she wore a halter. The much younger woman on her left was bare chested—and had nothing really to restrain. The one on her right was black, somewhat older—and also bare-topped.

They came between the tables. Jay swiveled at the end of the booth bench. "Hey, Darlin', how you doin'? These are the boys I told you about."

At Darlin's side, with no halter and breasts only a suggestion bigger than a boy's, the younger girl looked about eighteen. Her face suggested both Asian and Latino ancestors. "Hey," she said, suddenly. "You both got a lot of the same tattoos." Her smile swung from Eric to Jay and back. "Does that mean something?"

They all laughed.

"You guys worked with nanobolts before?" Darlin' asked.

"Huh?" Shit asked. "Naw."

"I didn't think so," Darlin' said. "But I can show you. Come on. Let's get out to the site."

*

Tearing off gray plastic from the piles of prefab wall units, windows of several sizes, flooring panels and framing pieces, on site, Eric and Shit had been working for half an hour, when Eric realized neither of them had answered her.

"Okay, now pay attention to this. It's real easy, so I won't have to explain more than a couple of times." Darlin' propped a piece of sheet board with braces backing it on top of a cinderblock that lay on the dozed slope.

"I gather ain't none of you 'cept Ruth—" who was a taciturn black woman on the crew—"used this stuff before. So I'll go over it with you as many times as you need me to. Get over here, Gus," who was the Asian-Latina. "It's like weldin', only with wood—or stone. Or metal. Or wood to metal or stone *to* wood. It's real simple. But like anything else, it helps if you know what you're doin'."

Shit said, "His daddy is a welder in Atlanta. His daddy's a nigger, too— like us. A real black one—like us. But Eric's just another nigger."

Eric had heard Shit say that too many times, starting at the old Slide, for the combination of sexual varismo and embarrassment to bother him any more. But he was curious—even a little anxious—about the women's response.

Darlin' frowned, dropped her head to the side, then lifted it upright—and chuckled. "Son, has anyone ever told you ain't supposed to be sayin' that word—specially to strange black ladies you ain't known for more than ten minutes."

"Hell," Shit said, "people been tellin' me everything what come out of my mouth I ain't supposed to say—since I been born. Not to mention what goes into it. I can't even tell most people my damned name, 'cause it's too nasty."

Darlin's smile filled out into a grin. "Well, you got a point there. So maybe that just means you should keep that mouth shut and pay attention to what I'm sayin'."

"Yes'm." Shit grinned back. Though Eric was not exactly sure what Darlin's grin meant—where on the scale from eccentric to lunatic to retarded she placed him (from the anxiety of meeting someone new, Shit's desire to impress could sometimes get out of kilter)—at least Eric knew that Shit's grin meant things were fine on his side.

"What're them little pieces of pipe stickin' out here and there all over things?" Eric asked.

"Nothin' you need to worry about. You can put in water works—sinks and bathrooms—in any room you want. Basic pipin' for hot and cold water is already in all the components. But that ain't your concern today."

Darlin' went on to explain how you put two pieces of wood or stone or metal together that had this gray plastic stuff painted along one side, then just touched it with the barrel of the sealing gun and pulled the trigger—a green light would come on and shine on the seam—and within three-quarters of a second, they sealed themselves together all along their length.

The prefab parts had single, double, and triple registration marks that you lined up. "But you don't even have to get 'em exact, as long as they're within an inch of one another. The bolting—that's the gray stuff—will pull 'em into line. Now, it ain't gonna pull 'em *more* than an inch. So you try to get 'em as close as you can. And if one piece is backwards or somethin', it ain't gonna turn it around for you. But it *will* line 'em up if they're half an inch, a quarter of an inch, an eighth of an inch off. Now, if you *do* have the wrong piece in place, or have it backwards, the sealing gun reads that and this yellow light comes on the first three times you pull the trigger. So if it turns yellow instead of green, you stop and figure out what you done wrong. 'Cause on the fourth try, it'll seal 'em up anyway—and you're more or less stuck with it. That's nanotechnology." She looked at the piece of braced board she was showing them. "Now don't be tryin' to line single registration marks up with double marks. Or double marks up with triple ones. I had a young feller workin' with me about three months ago, and she couldn't get that notion through her head any old way. Just remember: one goes with one. Two goes with two. And three goes with three. And if it's really off by eight, nine, ten inches—or two or three feet, you just got the wrong damned piece. Un'erstand? Also: I shouldn't even be tellin' you this until the very end—'cause it's a waste of time and just leads to confusion. But if you *do* make a mistake, you got exactly six hours to correct it. Turn this knob on the sealin' gun to red, pull the trigger again—and they'll come right apart. And you can fix up your glitch. After six hours, though, it's there permanent-like. But I warn you, it's a whole *lot* easier if you don't make no mistakes the first time."

Then she showed them how to put a two-by-four with that gray stuff on one end up against a cinderblock with the same gray stuff on it, click the sealer gun four times, and have a bond where the wood or the block would break first before the joint separated.

The girl said, "It's like that old Elmer's Glue-All—or Super Glue."

"Yeah," Darlin' said. "I been on crews where the girls *called* that stuff Super Glue. But it ain't glue. One person told me it was glue what been to university. The sealer gun sends out a message and the stuff works all into the wood or the metal, in little spikes, where the ordinary plastic turns into this special polymer that's harder than titanium steel. And—" she held up the gun again—"remember, you got six hours to fix any mistakes. Green light—it seals up. Red light, and it comes loose again." She twisted the little dial from one setting to the next, and back. "Yellow means you're a damned fool—and that's the one, at least at the beginning, you're gonna be seein' a lot."

Around them, floors and walls and staircases and windows began to rise without nails or screws. Gray plastic bags and red plastic ribbons in which the building parts had come made big piles. The wind pushed at them, between the sites, flattening the crackling plastic to the angular shapes within.

When they'd been working awhile, from behind the wall next to them, Eric yelled, "Oh, *fuck*...!"

"Wha'sa matter?" Shit called and ran over. Gus hurried behind him.

Darlin' had decided they were coming along real well and was on the other side of the road, helping some women in the trucks unload another delivery of great, gray plastic-bagged parts.

In the roofless house, the Asian girl stood there, looking confused.

Shit asked, "You hurt yourself?"

No. Eric had put up a whole stairway—a relatively complicated process—without putting in the braces along the side wall. "Jesus, I am a fuckin' idiot!" He set his teeth, looking at the lines of gray down the inner wall where no planks were, then—across the floor—at the bracing beams still bound in strips of red plastic. Quickly, it was clear that you couldn't slip them in, now that the steps had been set. "It's all got to come apart…!" The space smelled of cut wood.

"So—" Gus said—"let's just do it." The black bandana binding her head was printed with red-eyed skulls.

"Oh, fuck, man…" Eric reached up to rub his forehead.

"Don't worry about it," Shit said. "Just put on the red light."

"We better work together on this one," Gus said. "Somebody's gonna have to hold 'em, 'cause when they come loose otherwise, they're gonna fall."

"Yeah," Shit said. "I was thinkin' the same thing. Hey, you know I'm pretty glad it was you what fucked up, 'cause I was sure as my name's Shit it was gonna be me, see, 'cause I can't read and write. This way, *I* don't have to feel like I'm the fool."

"You can't?" Gus looked surprised.

"Nope."

"Come on," Eric said. He still sounded disgusted with himself. "Let's see if we can fix it."

So they did.

When they got back to the building they'd been working on, Eric asked, "You want me to go up and do the second-story work?"

"Naw," Shit said. "I'm okay. Long as you got the floor down and at least one wall up there, I'm okay—basically."

"Fine," Eric said. "But if you feel a little queasy, you call me. I'm on it."

Just then, the door in the half wall opened, and Darlin' walked in. "Hey, I seen you runnin' around up there." She was talking to Shit. "You work real hard, boy—harder than your friend here, and he ain't no slacker, either." With a thumb, she adjusted her orange halter over a breast.

"Yeah," Shit said. "That's 'cause I work like a nigger."

Darlin' looked at Eric. "He sure knows how to put his foot in his mouth, too, don't he?"

"Better than anyone I know," Eric said. "It's one of the reasons I love 'im."

"*Mmm*," Darlin' said. "Well, there's no accountin' for taste." She turned, went back across the floor, and this time stepped off where there was no wall, and—as she wandered back by a building they'd completed about an hour before—stopped to check a window that had been sealed into place, then a doorway, and finally bent to examine the set of steps leading up to it, none of which had been there three hours back.

She looked over at them and grinned. "You boys fucked up on this one and had to do it over again, didn't you?"

Eric sighed. "Yeah…kinda."

Shaking her head, but smiling, Darlin' went down the steps.

Gus came in from another room. "You guys are funny."

Shit said, "Hey—someday I may just show you how funny I really am. You know, when it's hard, my dick curves down, 'stead of up. Tell 'er, Eric."

She smiled. "Don't push it."

Then Shit hurried up the steps and they were back to work.

Eric had forgotten about the unanswered question about his snake, till they were all strolling along the path. It was almost four-thirty. Looking at the buildings coming into being at either side of the road, four of which had not been there that morning, Gus said, "You got some really nice ink. I'd like to get a snake like you got."

Shit said, "Get yourself over to Runcible. Eric got all those at Cave et Aude. That's Tank and Cassandra's. Or, if you wait a few months, they're gonna open up a place out here—you can get it then. Tank's got that thing wrapped around both of his arms—it goes across his back, there, and down to his hands."

"I'd like to," Gus said. "But I don't know whether I *really* want to—or if that's just when I see somebody else with something interesting."

Then Gus and the black woman—Ruth—turned off the path.

Shit and Eric both had been *really* impressed with the nanobolts.

Eric was silently awed. Shit ran on and on about them till Eric wanted him to shut up; sometimes Shit's enthusiasm could get on your nerves.

Shit walked along with his hand on Eric's shoulder. "You know, them nanobolts is so neat." Shit's palm had the texture of a slab of cement. And that, Eric thought, was exactly what a man's hand ought to feel like. They ambled on together. "And I can do it and pretty much understand it." (Eric ran his thumb over his own palm. It wasn't much different.) "I like that—and you get a whole lot done. And you're the one who messed up—not me. That's funny, huh?"

"Hey," Eric said. "Look, I ain't forgot any of the stuff we was sayin' before. And I know *you* ain't either. Let's go back to Jay and Mex's—we can lay around and hug on one another and do all sorts of nasty shit—"

"I got an even better idea," Shit said.

"You do?"

"I wanna go and look around at some of this new stuff out here. Just for an hour or so—and you wanna go sit down at Reba's, where we was for breakfast, have a cup of coffee, and read your book. Come on—lie to me and tell me you don't."

"Well, that actually would be nice. But the book's back at Jay and Mex's—"

"I bet she got some readers in there, like they do at the Lighthouse. She'd probably let you use one for a hour or so."

Eric frowned. "Well, yeah—probably." He was always a little surprised how much Shit actually knew about reading culture, for all his protests against it.

"Go 'head," Shit said. "I'll be waitin' for you." He stopped. "I'm goin' back this way. Hey, we got two weeks out here to be together."

"All right." Eric paused for a second, then sighed. "I won't be but an hour, an hour-and-a-half. Then I'll come back to Jay's."

"Yeah." Shit grinned, turned, and started at a trot down the road in the low gold light between the lowering trees.

Grinning quickly, Eric turned back to go toward the road into the new town.

He walked on dust mottled with late afternoon light and shadows, wondering when he'd first look aside and see water. It was after five. At the brown corner walls of the third building he passed, in a wedge of sun, ferns had already tangled as high as his shoulder, so that their fronds were as luminous as any green he'd ever seen.

Was this how wilderness transformed itself into town?

Eric turned and walked the four-foot width between the buildings—to notice a Styrofoam cup, already on the ground and stepped on.

If we come out here, he thought, we could be garbage men again...

Around the edges of the eves above him were the grooves every three inches that spoke of the solar panels on the roofs themselves. Eric reached the cleared part of the Settlement. A big (four story) glass-walled building stood up on the cliff. Eric wandered below it. On either side, he counted two, four, six, eight—then four more people, three women and a man— walking down the street: one of the men and one of the women he'd recently met in Ron's office when he'd dropped in to see Barb, back in Runcible. They smiled, nodded. Eric called, "Hi..." and walked on. The old stairs from the Gilead boat dock came right on up to Settlement Road, the ones you used to walk up to the rise, through the trees, out to Jay's.

After the—he counted—tenth, eleventh, twelfth house, the bulldozer had put an angle in the road. He looked at the blade's edging, still clear in the dirt. This would be a street soon.

Three months ago, when he'd last been out, only a little clearing had been done.

That, he thought, is fuckin' amazing!

The path on which he had walked to Jay's dozens of times had curved.

Now earthmovers and architects had reduced it to two straight lines at an angle.

A set of steps rose off the old stairs up from the boathouse—made of clean, white wood—to join up with Rockside.

Is this what a city looks like when it's born? Had Atlanta ever been like this? Or Diamond Harbor itself? Or the Dump?

Not only were Shit and he observers, they were abettors, constructors, enmeshed in the process…and, with nanobolts (he laughed aloud), they were doing it five or six times as fast as it might have been done a decade or two back.

As he reached the alley's end between the buildings, across the unpaved street, he could see NIGHTWOOD's window. Turning onto the sidewalk, he realized he had been walking beside Reba's—though from the back he hadn't recognized it. Swinging about, he went into Reba's front door and looked around the space, at the framed samplers on the walls, at the ceiling fans.

Four people sat at separate tables. Three were women. Eric slid into a booth, sat for a moment, then slid out again and walked to the counter. On the end, on a tray in a pile, were half a dozen readers. (He imagined the physical book, still in his knapsack, back at Jay's.) Their frames looked like damascened metal, but—when he lifted one—from its weight he realized it was plastic. "Can I use one of these…?"

"That's what I got 'em there for, honey." Reba paused, moving cups from one tray to another. She smiled and, he realized, recognized him from the morning. "You want some coffee?"

"Sure," he said. "You guys on a library program?"

"Sure thing," she said. "L-7, like usual. Though you're the first person to want it. Most people just want P-2…e-mails, bloglogs, and magazines."

"Oh." Somewhat embarrassed, Eric grinned.

He took the reader back to the same booth where he'd sat with Mex and Jay that morning and started playing with it, while Reba brought over a coffee cup. Since he'd never owned one, he always had to do everything four or five times to call up his book, which was stupid, since it was always the same one.

Then, out the window, something moved…

In the NIGHTWOOD window display, a huge TV screen had come on, draped around its edges with black and silver Mylar, at least six feet high and almost ten feet wide. Behind the flat face, a dark tree rose to spread its branches across the store's window's array of leather pants and black plastic jackets, strung with fishnet, a web above a glimmering reproduction of the sea. At either side of the display, giant mâché lobsters, each at least twelve feet from head to tail, painted in shades of kelly, olive, even metallic green, rose from molded waves to balance on their tails, claws poised. On the eyestalks of one (complete with brown pupils and long curling lashes) hung a sign that said "Keith." On the eyes of the other a sign read "Esmeralda." On the TV screen between them, the picture had just come on: the inside of a large theater, that could easily have been his and Shit's own Opera House, restored. The picture swept around the audience. On the screen, a woman in a black coat was looking at a microphone.

Later, he could not remember what prompted his curiosity. But Eric stood, leaving the reader on the booth table beside his cup. He hurried toward the door and pushed out to lope across the dirt and gravel between. What he had not seen before, but expected to find because he'd seen something like it in a few other shops in Runcible: on crinkly black cords three sets of earphones dangled before the window glass.

Eric lifted one set, slipped them over his head—and, because of the high electronic wail in his right ear, pulled it off, dropped it, and picked up another. When he slipped those on (there was no static here), he heard the woman say:

"...my good friend, Laurel Owen."

Applause grew. Now, also in black, with feathery blond hair, another woman walked out from the backstage confusion. Applauding, the audience began to stand.

As the two women hugged, one or the other said, "You're wonderful, honey. What a honor."

The audience quieted.

Holding hands, both walked forward. To the orchestra's quiet introduction, with her long bronze hair, the taller woman began to sing, quietly, pensively:

"The dawning sky is blue and gray,

"and blue and gray mists veil the hours—"

Here she looked down:

"annul the waters, hide the towers," She looked up, and added, *"erase the spires that crown the bay...*

"Ininity is blue and gray," Tossing back her straight hair, she sang on:

"The undefined and incomplete

"moment where sky and water meet,

"before the day is ripped by gray

"blades of gleaming metal gray.

"Swimming gull-forms melt and float

"in liquid air around the boat—"

The other joined her—*"that moans in blind flight on the bay,"* and the music's energy increased enough to make Eric step back, as the two turned at sing to one another:

"*Hold me, love. I quake with day,*

"*Blind beneath the staring hours.*

"*See the cracked reflected towers*

"*Burning crimson on the bay,*" and the taller tossed her mike from one hand to the other, turning to the audience, in some sort of totally naked confession, "*The dawning sky is blue and gray—*"

Again they were singing together, the words the same but not the music, notes stretched into a rich *retardondo*:

"*and blue and gray mist veil the hours,*

"*annul the waters—*" and on "*waters,*" they turned to high-five each other—"*hide the towers,*

"*erase the spires that crown the bay—*

The first syllable held for two seconds and the second for four, carrying both voices in a rising glissade that turned their bodies to one another and returned their voices to the tones they had begun with.

"*Hold me love,*" sang the shorter one, quietly again, which made Eric astonishingly, even uncomfortably, aware—because his body was tingling—of how intense the music had grown during the last chorus: "*I quake with day.*

"*Blind beneath the starting hours,*

"*See the cracked reflected towers*

"*Burning on the bay—*" and here both threw back their heads and sang out again:

"*See the cracked reflected towers*

"*burning crimson on the bay—!*"

Which is when Eric realized what the two women—blatantly, blankly, inarguably—articulated, though not in the words, but in the rising and tumbling shape of the melody itself and the harmony supporting it, that strove for a seventh and, not achieving it, tore down through it, covering a range that felt as immense as the theater on the screen, as the Opera he came down into, to work everyday with Shit, a theater whose edges he could not see. It hit him with an energy whose "why" till now he had never been sure of. That the audience felt, at least, its power and had risen throughout the theater was secondary. Again the women sang ("*See the cracked reflected towers. . .*"), with even more intensity, each with a fist clenched, each with her body spasming rather than shaking to the rhythm—and Eric realized he wanted to see Shit.

He wanted to tell him...

He wanted to tell him that they were making a world, a county, a city together, and that it was wonderful. Shit was the reason he slept through the night, that he woke and slipped from the covers—Eric began to grin. He thought: I'm grinning at myself, standing here, grinning—at what had been spoken, or sung, or celebrated, thanks to some song I don't remember ever hearing before, probably twenty-five or thirty-five or forty-five years old.

"...*The dawning sky is blue and gray,*" the taller sang—finally. Then they hugged.

And kissed deeply on the mouth.

The audience screamed.

Eric thought, Jesus Christ...at its electric sensuality. That's not even two men, he thought. Or a man and a woman. It's two women—and it's the most amazing thing *I've* ever seen!

He thought it nakedly, numbly, even reverently.

He felt air rush in, under and over his front teeth, expand his chest. And that's...

Raising his hands, he pulled the earphones from his ears. He had to find Shit—and find him soon. (The shorter woman looked dazed, while the camera followed her off stage...)

Eric turned from in front of the window and started along Rockside, in the direction of Jay and Mex's. Soon he was half running. As he glanced down, pebbles and rocks and sticks on the path flickered under his eyes; when he looked up branches and bits of sun flashed by. What am I going to say when I see him? I was just watching some old song on a TV in a store window, and suddenly I...fell in love with you, all over again! So I come runnin'—!

—sprinting, Eric felt as if he were watching himself run rather than running. I like feeling like this—

—he felt his foot twist. He flailed out an arm, expecting to fall. And didn't. His other foot came down—and he expected it to hurt, from the twist. He looked at the half hidden root in the road that had all-but-thrown him. It didn't hurt, actually—though he decided he'd better slow. And did, grateful not to have injured himself in this passion. It would be just like him to twist an ankle now.

Shaking his hands, looking around—Eric stood a moment, breathing—then again started walking. In the breezy woods, he tried to sing, "See the cracked, reflected...!" and laughed at his own voice, so rough, so wildly off-key.

No, Shit wouldn't understand if I did *that*...

But how the hell *do* you tell somebody...that? Was it something you could only do through the intensity of music? Or making music? Or making a town? Or making love? That's what Shit had wanted to do with his days on the island. And isn't that, he thought, amazing in itself…?

His feelings still a-broil inside, Eric tried to walk more carefully over the rest of the roadway, toward Jay's. It was like tiny lights, swarming up, down, around inside his chest, cool, comfortable fireflies, small but blinding whenever he tried to look at them directly, inchoate and precious.

To his left, trees fell back. Eric reached the first of the stony outcrops that made up this end of the island. For twenty feet he could see the seaward horizon's knife-edge above feathering shrubs. On his first trip to Jay's, in the midst of a moonless approach, he remembered how he'd missed it, and how surprised he had been at his first morning trip back, in the bird-lanced sunlight, along the path to the boathouse. At any rate, it meant he was about fifty yards around the bend from Jay's.

Wind rose, branches moved—and something way along his path on his left moved behind them. Momentarily, he thought it was Jay's pick-up, coming forward (and so rarely used on the island—but, since the construction had begun, certainly used more frequently, Jay had said only that morning at breakfast).

But it was Hugh—on foot. A faint fuzz of hair blurred Hugh's braided, salt and pepper cornrows, their ends twisted over his green shirt collar, opened over a sleeveless undershirt. With his walking stick, Hugh ambled up.

Eric said, "Hey—Hugh? Did Shit get back to the house yet? I was lookin' for him—I gotta find him! I wanna tell him somethin'."

"He came by." Hugh smiled benignly. "But he kept on goin' along the road. Looked like he was gonna take a walk maybe—probably went out toward the Holota place…unless he kept on to the cemetery. There ain't no place else to go out this way."

"Oh," Eric said. "Sure. Thanks." He hurried forward—and somehow didn't remember passing Jay's—

When he saw the squat Holota cabin with its flattened A-roof and its deck off to the front, the first thing he thought was that they'd done some clearing around it, too. Then, with another four or five steps along the road, he saw, beyond the building's corner, someone standing toward the deck's back, looking in the sea's direction. (*Had* you been able to see water from the road, before…? He didn't think so.) Shit? A wave inside him, both grateful and greedy, rose up. (What wave was it? It was—or was like—a very specific wave, once seen, and now returned, and—now—forgotten once more…) He started over the shrubs, reached the steps, hurried up onto the porch, and turned right along the boards, under the deck's roof. "Hey…" Eric stepped around the corner, hearing as much as feeling his own grin.

Shit turned from the back rail. His green eyes were incredibly bright—and the first thing Eric thought, was: of course, *he's* as excited as I am…

The features, blurred within Shit's beard, moved toward…no, it wasn't a smile—

Eric repeated, this time with curiosity, "Hey…?"

Shit said, "They're tearin' it all up." Then he blinked—and, for a moment, looked like someone Eric had never seen.

A tear moved in an angular line down Shit's cheek toward the fuzz, and Eric thought: Has he got somethin' in his eye…? Other tears stood on his tan cheeks.

Or, maybe, he *had* seen the expression. What returned, with ghoulish precision, was the night Dynamite died, when, with the rain and the corpse outside, for a few seconds they'd turned on the light…

"They're tearin' up the whole island. And we're helpin' 'em. It ain't theirs…" Out from his sides, Shit's big hands, not opened, not closed, moved a little this way, a little the other. He looked lost.

Eric said, "Huh—?"

"They're tearin' it all up." Shit shook his head, quick, like an animal dislodging an insect. "They shouldn't be doin' that."

Eric frowned, and felt his own joy of a moment back become battered, beaten, betrayed with unspecific brutality. "What do you…?" He closed his mouth, realizing the person betrayed, in some way he could not know, was Morgan, because he could not see through to its center, that betrayal wholly dependant on all of Shit's immaturity and ignorance, his cussed childishness. The words, hesitant, got out in spite of it. "Shit, they're buildin' a…"

"Look," Shit said. "Look—they're pushin' all the big rocks back into the ocean—with bulldozers. There used to be them big boulders back there. And I'd come out here when I was a kid and climb up on them things and sit and look over the saplin's—and they're gone. All the trees and stuff. They made it all flat, now—it's all dirt back down there to the sand. Like they're gonna make it into a lawn or somethin'. And we was out there, where they're getting all them little houses out of bags and boxes and stuff, half of 'em all the same. I went out to the graveyard—where we put Dynamite and Shad. And Uncle Tom—my dog, Tom. You know, they run the road right half way *through* that thing! You can't even see what graves was under there—"

That hit Eric hard enough to make him exhale. "Is…Dynamite's grave all right? And Tom's…?"

"Yeah." Shit pulled his slumping shoulders up. "But a lot of the old ones are gone—the old Indian ones. You know, the *important* ones. The ones Mr.

Holota told me about, when I used to go out there with 'im when I was a kid. All his people. And the other people, who're dead. That's *awful*…"

"Oh, Shit…" Eric stepped forward. He put a hand on Shit's shoulder, feeling the collarbone before the hard slope of the shoulder muscle under worn fabric. He slid his arm over Shit's shoulder, while his other arm pulled the man forward. For a moment, he hesitated. He knew he must hug him. Shit wasn't the sort who "needed his space" at such moments. He needed holding. If I've learned anything, Eric thought, I've learned *that*. Still, I always *start* to treat him as if he were me. Eric said, "That's awful." And gripped him—tight. Shit's arms whipped around behind him, to hold him back. (Then I realize he *ain't* me.) "That's awful, Shit—I'm so sorry."

Shit held him so hard, he shook. And after a moment, he whispered, "Come on. Let's lie down, here. We gotta do it."

"—here?"

"Yeah. We gotta do it now."

"Okay. But you gonna get splinters in your ass. 'Cause I'm gonna stay on top."

"I don't give a fuck."

They did lay down. Eric felt the curve of the boards under his arm, his hip. His face was over Shit, so that he looked across Shit's shoulder at the woods and forests, out through the rail post, the blue paint deeply faded but still visible. A few seconds later, from under his ear, Shit said, "There's a blanket inside."

"Then let's get it," Eric said. "Now that's bein' sensible." And suddenly he was hit was a wave of warmth for Shit that was as powerful as music, as the sea.

"Okay. But just don't let go of me."

"Don't worry. I ain't lettin' you get off from me." Perhaps twenty minutes later, as they lay on a double thickness of blanket over the deck's warped porch, while Shit panted in post orgasmic release, Eric said, "You feel a little better now?"

"Yeah. But we gotta do it again. And you gotta come, too, this time."

Eric grinned. "I *knew* you was gonna say that—that's why I held off before. Okay. You want it all over your crotch and your nuts?"

"Yeah. *All* over."

"Then lie there, hold on, and let me get up your nose."

"Come on. Just do it. I'll take care of *me*." And still later, when they slid lazily on the film their hugging and rubbing had left between them, Shit said, "That one felt real good. It *still* feels good…"

"Did you come again?" Eric asked. "You acted like it, but I wasn't sure."

"Yeah," Shit said. "I did." His arms tightened around Eric. "You know, it's gonna be nice gettin' back to the Opera, once they open it up again."

"Oh, yeah. Now that you used me an' abused me and finished talkin' all sweet about fuckin' together all week, you wanna get back where you can spread it around to some other people—what happened to wantin' to fuck three times in a row?"

"Well, we just did it twice—or I did. I gotta do it one more time, before we get back. I mean, right now. I think there's a pretty good chance of that, don't you? The thing about the Opera," Shit said, "is that the idea of you suckin' off somebody else or fuckin' somebody else or gettin' fucked—'specially by some big black hunky motherfucker; or even gettin' your dick sucked by some old toothless hobo hitch-hiker who's been thumbin' around and ends up there for the weekend—turns me on so much, I can't hardly keep my dick in my pants two minutes, if I start thinkin' about it. That's all I *ever* jerk off to. I think about a lot of other guys—but I always think about 'em with you."

"Well—" Eric grinned—"I guess that's *some* kinda faithful."

"I was the same way with my dad. And I guess, because of that, whenever you start tellin' me about how you're payin' a little more attention to one of 'em than you usually do, I'm always makin' up stories for myself about how it's okay, 'cause now I got somethin' new to jerk off over. You remember when you went off with that big heavy Asian feller for three days? That's why I was so easy over it. Or when you were you disappeared for a whole weekend in the motel room at Turpens with them Spanish fellers? You know, don't you? I stood outside yalls door and left at least three loads of cum on the damned doorknob, imaginin' what yall was doin' in there. But, see, I know, someday, I'm gonna be sorry, 'cause you're gonna come out and tell me you finally met somebody else you wanna hang out with a little more than you wanna hang out with me—and we're over with. And I'm gonna realize I'm the biggest fool along the whole Georgia coast—"

"Shit—" and the breeze rose outside the glassless window—"that's *not* gonna happen. That's kind of what I was tryin' to say before. You're too much of what I want—and what I always wanted. You look too much like I want a feller I live with to look like. You act too much like that feller. Your farts and your burps and your B.O. and your asshole when you ain't wiped yourself too good, and—hell, your damned snot—taste and smell too much like what I wanted it to taste and smell like. So do your damned feet—when you wear shoes long enough to work up a stink. And you treat me too much like I want to be treated. Your piss and your tonsils and your asshole all taste too much like his were supposed to taste like. That's 'cause you *are*...him. You, I mean. That's all. You're stuck with me, Shit. Like when you'd be walkin' outside the cabin barefoot and step on some turd Dog-

Dog left out by the deck in the Dump." (When they'd gone to the Opera, Dog-Dog had returned to Sam Quasha and immediately impregnated all his female relatives.) "You know how you can't get that stuff off your foot for so goddamn long? Well, *I'm* the piece of dog shit you stepped in."

Suddenly, Shit rolled back over to face him, grabbed him, and hissed against Eric neck, his rough beard grinding Eric's cheek, "Oh, you are one fuckin' *nasty* white feller!"

And after a while, Eric said, "Hey—hey...hey, wake up, nigger."

"Wha...?"

"Wake up. I wanna ask you somethin'."

"What—?"

"I wanna know how you can go to sleep with somebody lyin' full out on top of you, fuckin' on you, back or belly, for dear life!"

Blinking, Shit began to grin. "It's easy." He reached up and closed his arms around Eric. "It relaxes me. I love it—a whole lot. It makes me think of my daddy fuckin' on me when I was a kid. Maybe it's the rockin'. It puts me to sleep. *That's* how." With his grin relaxing, Shit closed his eyes again. "'Specially if it's you."

One way or the other, I guess we gonna be in bed with that man for the rest of our lives, Eric thought. But he didn't say it.

*

Back at Jay's and Mex's that evening, Shit—of course—told Jay and Mex, loudly in the kitchen, the details of everything they'd done, including fucking all over the Holotas cabin's porch. Hugh had started off in the room, but in the middle he'd smiled, got up, and excused himself.

Finally, Jay said, "Hey, you really like that place—that cabin out there?" At the table, Jay moved his hand on the yellow oilcloth, as if considering whether to pick up his Coors. "You guys want it? You can have it. Johnston says even if it ain't him what gives us a hard time, the Opera can only stay open a few years, at best. Why don't you come on out here on your time off and fix it up. Then you'll have someplace to move to when you have to leave Runcible."

"What about the rent?"

"If you take care of the place, Hugh ain't gonna charge you no rent."

"Then don't let him tear it up around there no more," Shit said. "That gets me all upset."

Jay said, "I'd rather have you as my neighbors, a hundred yards through the woods, than anybody else. Hugh feels the same way. So does Kyle—I called him up and asked him. What you say?"

Eric and Shit looked at each other—while Mex brought over the skillet of pork chops and onions and red and green peppers from the stove. And Eric thought: He *is* the reason I sleep through the night, get up every day, in this energetic, beautiful, nascent city that has already started to kill him...

"Jay, you wouldn't really mind—" Eric took up his knife and fork, as Mex passed on around the oilcloth covered table—"if Shit and me didn't go and work on them new houses tomorrow, would ya'?"

Jay started to say something, but Shit interrupted. "Naw. Naw—I'll go. I said I was gonna do it. So I'll do it. I don't care. And that Gus, she's fun. Besides, that stuff is in'erestin'. We just gotta work on it together, you and me—in case there's somethin' somebody gotta read, or they wanna send me up real high or somethin'."

"Sure," Eric said. "You know you can trust me on that."

*

The second night when they came in, Mex had finished up a skillet of sautéed chicken—it was on a platter in the middle of the yellow and white checked tablecloth—and, at the stove, was ladling out a bowl of peppers, leeks, and celery.

Shit grabbed a leg up from the platter, threw himself onto one of the chairs, and began to eat, chicken grease running down his fingers, then his forearms.

"Damn," Jay said. "I'm glad I known you since you was a baby. Otherwise, boy, I'd tell you to get the fuck up and go wash your damned hands."

"Man," Shit said. "I'm fuckin' hungry, and I'm fuckin' tired. That's all." Jay grunted.

Eric grinned—took two plates off the pile, slid one in front of Shit (in time to catch the chicken thigh that dropped off the leg Shit was biting into). Then he put a piece on the second plate and reached out with the big spoon to dig into the bowl of vegetables that Mex brought to the table.

"Hey, I'm gonna go to bed right after this," Shit said. "It ain't rude. It's just tired. That's all."

"Fine by me," Jay said, pulling the platter over in his own direction. "We still turn in pretty early, too. Hey, Mex, break out that orange juice and ginger ale we got for these guys, since they ain't gonna have no beer."

After eating, Shit went into the bathroom and washed his hands—and his face. When he came out, his beard and eyebrows were still wet.

That night, again they were in Shad's old room. Light still came in through the tall windows, but Shit dropped his shirt, then his jeans in front of the high-backed wooden wheelchair in its corner.

Eric asked, "Hey, would you mind if I sat at the table here and read a for a little while in my book? I'll be in bed soon."

"Don't mind a bit." Shit walked around the bed's foot to the steps beside it. It was still unmade since that morning. (Tomorrow, Eric thought, I could at least spread it up, before we get out of here.) "But I'm gonna jerk off, while you're readin'."

"Uh...yeah," Eric said, going through the knapsack leaning against the table leg. "Sure..."

The light that came through the long curtains was sepia and gold. In the chair, he sat down and opened the book in front of him—

> Desire is the very essence of man...that is...a striving by which man strives to persevere in his being. So a desire which arises from joy is aided or increased by the affect of joy itself...whereas one which arises from sadness is diminished or restrained by the affect of sadness.

—a rhythmic squeaking came from some slight looseness in the high bed behind him.

Frowning, Eric looked up. "Is that your way of tellin' me that, really, you'd like to have sex?"

From the bed, Shit said, "Nope." The squeaking continued. "It might have been, fifteen or so years back. Now it's just my way of tellin' you I'm beatin' off."

"Oh..." Eric looked back down at the book and read three more sentences. Then he read them again. Then he started them a third time; because they made about as much sense as if it were his very first minutes with the text. He looked up again. "*Um*...Hey, Shit? Would you *mind*—" Eric let the book close on the dark stained wood—"if I came up there and joined you?"

"Hey, that'd be pretty fuckin' good," Shit said. The squeaking went on.

Eric stood up. Chair legs scraped the floor. He stood for the count of three, four, five . . .

"If you're comin'," Shit said, "get the fuck on up here, please, and stick some fingers up my ass, and suck my goddam balls. Come on and bring them snakes and spiders and frogs and seahorses and creepy-crawly lizards and dragons you got all over you up here with me so I can kiss on 'em"— the squeaking got faster—"and roll around in 'em and get happy all over

them dolphins and squids and skulls and barbed wire and leaves and twigs
and seashells and galaxies and crap—"

Eric shrugged out of his shirt. Stepping over, as he put one hand up on
the bed, he saw the red and orange and green and violet move as his triceps
moved under them. "Yeah...!" Eric climbed, then vaulted.

Pumping, grinning, Shit caught him in one arm, and pulled him down.
Both of them started laughing.

*

And the third night when they came in...

***

[72] WONDER DECADES HAVE their dark undersides—by now we're
in one, if you hadn't noticed. Neither Eric nor Shit did. How often does
the acknowledged arbiter of the spectacular Jazz Age, F. Scott Fitzgerald,
begin his accounts of the twenties with the "horrific" events of 1919, when
New York City's mounted police trampled into the crowds of recently
demobilized farm boys, gathered to hear the Madison Square orators?

As much as the nineteen sixties is love-ins and be-ins and rock-'n'- roll
at the Fillmore, East and West, free music concerts and Woodstock and
astronauts dancing on the moon, it is also a string of appalling political
assassinations—Medgar Evers, President Kennedy, his brother Robert
Kennedy, Martin Luther King, Jr., Malcolm X, the Kent State massacre
of students by the National Guard, southern sit-ins and the three days of
the Stonewall Riots through Greenwich Village. But whether Icarus soars
in the sun or plummets into the sea, always some, in the words of the
poet, were eating or opening a window or walking dully along—who didn't
particularly want it to happen.

The thirties is, of course, the decade that saw liberal women presidents
in both the United States and the Federation of African Republics. It saw
the World Passport become a common form of identification. (Holdouts
in the US refused to acknowledge it for Americans, though if they wanted
any international tourist business at all, they were pretty much forced to
accept it.) It saw Europe, Africa, and most of Western Asia adopt a single
currency. It was the decade in which the Rhyman Hypothesis became the
Rhyman Theorem—proved by a collaboration of Polish and Japanese
mathematicians, which earned them that year's Field Medal.

Incidents that produced six-day media coverage, with profusions of coffee-table photographic volumes and visual documentaries in later years, included the birth of Tommy and Tong, the first human twins on the burgeoning international station on Mars, with its population of 31 then 33. Also came the devastation of the North East Flood, which began with an unprecedented earthquake throughout New Hampshire, Massachusetts, and parts of Connecticut during flood rains, and a rising tide line that for three days precipitated a near-Katrina like situation in several coastal cities, including Baltimore and New York. As well, they included the glorious coverage of the passing of Pemptus, the fifth and most sizable asteroid in a three-year period to come within two-hundred thousand miles of the moon—the closest—which was observed and photographed by an international team of astronauts in a dozen rocketships launched for the purpose, who, supported by a consortium of seven countries, soared near and circled and swooped between it and the moon and the sun, taking those extraordinary photographs shown again and again all over the world—and which came close, at one of the fly-bys, to an actual landing and a walk on its iron and rubble pitted surface, though at the last minute it was canceled because of technical problems. The consortium was the beginning of the Yang-Kopffus Doppler project.

During the height of their command of world attention, for Eric and Shit and many residents of Diamond Harbor, as well as residents of similar little towns across the country, who'd never had their Robert Kyle (and a few others who did), none of these was more than a flicker on a widescreen television behind a bar where they had dropped in for a glass of club soda and lime with beer-drinking friends, a headline, a full-page color photo on a newspaper left on a café counter by one of the summer people—or even an overheard conversation among their visiting customers at the Opera. All of these iconic moments bypassed the center of Shit and Eric's attention on that stretch of Georgia coast, until five, eight, twelve years later something that everyone else in the world seemed to know about made it—briefly—into their field of vision, like the left-over tar ball eighteen inches across that floated up on the beach in September of 2010 from the BP Gulf Coast oil "spill," that had begun a few months before, and now sat on a pedestal in the shadowed corner of a bar in Hemmings, with an explanatory plaque beneath it.

But we reiterate: Wonder Decades have their glories—and they have their dark moments.

The one that everyone knows from the thirties, of course, pierced even Shit and Eric's attention.

Three days after they came to Gilead Island to labor at construction work during the temporary closing of the Runcible Opera House, at four-forty on October 7, 2033—Shit was forty-five and Eric was forty-three—the largest single hour of man-made slaughter in human history occurred.

We mean, of course, the Three Bombs.

Their third evening on Gilead Island, Shit and Eric ambled into the dilapidated Kyle mansion living room. Both were looking puzzled. "Hugh," Shit asked, "did you hear sumpin' about somebody droppin' a bomb on California? That's what somebody called to tell Darlin', out at the site earlier."

Hugh said, "Well, somethin's wrong with the television. You can't get no news at all. They're just playin' old programs, again and again. The computers are frozen up—course, mine's about five years old. So maybe it's just bein' ornery."

"A bomb?" Jay said. "I don't think so. Maybe that earthquake came that they all been talkin' about forever and ever."

The news ban was lifted at nine o'clock that evening. What they were calling a "small nuclear device" had gone off in the middle of Los Angeles, still a media capital for the country. So had another in the middle of central India's Mumbai, the hub of that nation's Bollywood film industry, with its then eighteen-million inhabitants and still the world's most populous city.

Rumors of a nuclear explosion—fortunately false—had even trickled out of Nigeria's Nollywood.

The third "device" had, mercifully, been found and defused in Brazil's São Paulo—which gave it a good run for its money as far as population, if not film production. But the initial report was that a third device had gone off there as well: the name "Three Bombs" was forever attached to the incident. (Briefly it was written "3D," which soon became "3B.") The US death toll alone was estimated conservatively at twelve million in the minutes after detonation, with another fifteen million dead over the next six weeks. A mass exodus of survivors, if that is the proper name for those scarred and ragged men and women and children who—most on foot—poured from a huge strip of landscape rendered unlivable by panic and human barbarism on a scale inconceivable by any not there. For the next fifty, seventy-five years, an entire genre of novels, films, stories, and plays about survivors and people in Nevada and Oregon and New Mexico arming to protect their homes from the herds of the starving, the terrified, the wounded and the ill covered the country.

The death toll was forty percent higher in India, though the violence there was claimed to be less.

In Brazil, people rioted and stampedes of poor folk from the *favillas* swarmed across the city so that for years some were sure a bomb *had* gone off there, anyway. Scholars have put the international total for the first month's devastation at a figure higher than World War II's estimated fifty-to-eighty million deaths—though others put it just under.

The next morning, though Shit and Eric reported to the building site, only a third of the workers showed up. It's often claimed that more than three-quarters of a paralyzed country—indeed, the paralysis was world wide—stayed home (schools were closed, factories shut) to watch and ponder and make sense of the horror and destruction revealed over the next days in California and adjoining states, like nothing ever seen in this nation—or any other—ever before.

Since nobody was getting anything done on the site, Eric and Shit left to return to Jay's at three.

Hugh had moved his TV screen from his room into the living room, where it was playing two different online coverages, one on the left side, one on the right. Fourteen workers, ten of them women and four men, sat and watched the dual coverage, some on the couch, some cross-legged on the floor. Jay had gone out, rounded them up, invited them back to the Kyle mansion, and asked if they wanted to come watch, since, by now, it was drizzling outside anyway. Darlin' wasn't there—she'd gone back to the mainland to try and learn, fruitlessly, about her family. But, with her scarf around her head and her all-but-boyish breasts, Gus sat in what Eric years ago had come to think of as Shad's corner. She looked over blankly, then seemed to remember she knew them and smiled.

Eric smiled and Shit nodded back.

Two people were crying—one young man and a middle-aged woman—who had come from, respectively, San Jose and San Diego, which the rioting had already mostly destroyed—

A mad man from a small East Asian country had decided that he wanted to destroy the world's entertainment industry and replace films and DVDs with tracts of religious instruction. Neither Muslim, Christian, Jewish, nor Buddhist, he was apprehended two days after the explosion—and probably torn to pieces during a transfer from one armored truck to another between jails. Nothing of him—or the truck in which he'd been confined—was ever found for certain.

The Wonder Decade of the thirties also produced single inoculation birth control for both men and women, which was temporarily reversible with a pill, which both partners had to take, and which, by the 'forties end, brought the world population back down to twelve billion, then lowered it by a further thirty percent by the end of the fifties.

(Though many, many young people who came along later assumed otherwise, deaths from the Three Bombs formed less than one hundredth of one percent of the world population regression brought about by the birth control method, which simply demanded that pregnancy be by conscientious mutual consent of both parties.)

At that Wonder Decade's end, in the U.S., many drugs—especially recreational—were now legal. Possibly that was because half a dozen miracle drugs were common by then, among them Fillonin, which made severe alcoholism—as well as many other chemical dependencies—a thing of the past (*God*, Barbara told Eric one afternoon, sitting on her back porch, looking toward the Runcible inlet, *you remember how I used to drink, don't you? And you never saw the worst of it. At least I hope you didn't. Fillonin is the only reason I have a life today with Ron.*), though it might have eventually contributed to her death. A side effect, especially in the first few years, was a near three percent rise in the chance of renal cancer—one of the few cancers that still had less than an eighty-five percent remission rate.

Some readers will feel that my account hopelessly slights this one incident that, with the rest of the world, Shit and Eric paid serious attention to—the Three Bombs.

But the bombs are a historical atrocity that cannot be described.

However directly or indirectly they affected your life, many of you lived through them.

You know what that day was like—and what the days just after them were like; and the months. And the years...

Despite the many thousands on thousands of lives blighted by 3B, whether those lives went on for only hours, for days, for months, or for year after year, while the world sat and gasped and shuddered and wept, even the Three Bombs had already begun to become the past.

* * *

[73] THREE WEEKS LATER on the mainland, at the Opera—reopened now for two days—Eric vacuumed the upper balconies, while Shit swept the orchestra's aisles. Then Eric took another walk down by the docks, looking for any regulars who had not yet returned.

On the glistening boards—it had recently rained—Joady sat on an overturned barrel, leaning on his knees, looking at the sea.

"Hey."

Slowly, Joady looked up.

"You can come on back, if you want. I'm gettin' some pizzas in."

"Them Bombs were somethin', weren't they?"

Eric pulled himself up with a big breath. "Come on Joady—not you, too. Them things is all I've heard anybody talkin' about all month now. They're makin' me a little crazy."

"Did you see some of the pictures—that shit *is* crazy! Can you imagine—?"

Two weeks later, again finished with the upper two balconies, Eric carried the paint-speckled ladder down to the orchestra and parked it under the back stairwell that was supposed to be closed—a black chain hung across the steps—though three sleeping bags and a blanket roll were pushed around under the stairs.

Within three weeks, because of the Three Bombs, guys from California had started showing up...

Not that they were a real problem, but they seemed depressed, and you felt bad about pushing them to work—though the ones who found their way to the Opera House generally seemed to know what the place was about already.

Eric ambled down the side, and, six rows from the back, moved into a seat two in from the aisle. Five minutes on, coming from behind, Shit dropped down in the seat beside Eric and leaned toward him. "Hey, now— gimme some fuckin' snot, nigger." He twisted toward Eric, a rough hand gripping the back of Eric's neck, the other cupped under Eric's nose. "Block up a nostril and snort out a big one. I'm feelin' *real* nasty."

Eric chuckled. "Too late. I got all the good stuff."

"Fuck you, then. Well, at least lemme have some salt." He pushed Eric's hand away, then slid a heavy middle finger into Eric's nose. "Come on." The finger twisted.

"Hey, man!" Eric tried to pull away. "Come on, now. I always give it to you when I got it."

"I know you do. But *next* time, I ain't stopping with the salty stuff. I'm gonna make you shit in my hand and feed it to me."

Eric shook his head. "You're really gettin' into that, aren't you?"

Shit sucked at his middle finger. The hand that had been behind Eric's neck came forward and settled between Eric's legs, to start rubbing. "Well, I'm gonna suck your dick at least—I ain't done that in a while."

"Is this your fuckin' change of life?" Eric asked.

"Ain't you glad I'm goin' though it *with* you?" Shit squeezed Eric's groin, which had hardened with kneading.

Walking up the aisle, with his sports jacket and with his white fringe of hair, Dr. Greene saw them and slowed. Behind heavy glasses, he smiled. "I see you two are bolstering each other's immune systems. That's good—yes, that's good."

One of the homeless black guys—it was Rube—was two steps behind. "Hey, Doc—why you always sayin' that when you see them carryin' on with their nasty stuff—huh?"

The doctor looked over his shoulder. "'Cause that's what yall doin'. Eatin' dried mucus—even what *you're* doin'. The dead viruses and bacteria make you make antibodies. And nothin' lives too long in that stuff, anyway. Myself, I suspect it's either a slowly dying or a fast emerging evolutionary survival trait. Which reminds me. Speaking of survival—Rube, take this damned humera medicine, will you, while I remember I got it for you."

"What's that for?" Rube's hair was thinning around his bald spot and his shirt was torn in three places.

"Humera," Dr. Greene said. "Humera's what it's for. Because of our damned breakfast club and our damned new friends, half the guys in here got it—well, six or seven of 'em."

"What is it?" Rube took the small brown plastic bottle and held it up in the screen's light.

"Intestinal parasites. See, you pick up that stuff as soon as we let you fellas out of here, where we can't keep an eye on you. Thank god nobody picked up any amoebas or jardinière. At least I didn't find any in Shit or Haystack's crap samples—the two I ran tests for." Again, the doctor reached into his pocket to take out another bottle. "This belongs to you two."

"Why do I need this?" Eric made a face. "I don't mess around with you guys and that stuff."

"But you're very close with someone who does." Dr. Greene pulled his eyebrows together. "Close with several people who do, actually."

Shit chuckled.

"Oh," Eric said—as Shit took the bottle. As far as hair, Eric thought, Shit and Rube looked kind of the same. It was interesting that he still found Shit's really sexy and Rube's more or less indifferent.

Dr. Greene walked on toward the theater's back—presumably to distribute more pills.

At this hour of the evening, probably drunk—his wine bottle's copper cap stuck from his baggy hip pocket—Rube swayed in the light from the DVD on the screen. "Why can't you two do ordinary stuff, like suck each other's dicks or bang each other's buttholes? I can get into all of that—if I have a little wine. If you did that, I could get to like you guys."

Shit said, "Oh, you'll get to like us if you hang around here long enough."

"You want some of mine?" Rube asked. He shook the pill bottle, which chuckled dryly back. Then he put it in his pocket. "Snot I mean."

"Naw." Eric shook head. "I think we'll pass."

"Why not?" Rube frowned. "You suck my dick."

"'Cause your goddamn nails are so long, I'd poison myself with all the dirt you got under 'em."

"Mmm." Rube nodded toward Shit. "I guess *he* don't got that problem."

Shit chuckled again. "Go on take your medicine, Rube—so I can eat out your butthole again in a couple of days. And you don't infect no more of the regulars than you already have."

"Oh..." In the quarter-light, Rube looked a little bewildered. "Yeah, okay." Then he asked. "Who pays for the pills?"

"They're from the clinic," Eric said.

"Is that like the Chamber of Commerce?"

"It's the Kyle Institute," Shit said. "Far as *you're* concerned, that's the same difference."

"Yeah," Eric said.

"It's part of the arrangement for keepin' the place open. We have to distribute free STD medication. And the clinic across the street can run tests. Or Dr. Greene can take swabs and stuff in here—for chlamydia and clap and stuff like that, which we are pretty fortunate not to have had no cases of since *we* done been here—and get back to us about 'em..."

Rube, though, who had a pretty short attention span at the best of times, was wandering toward a seat in the front row.

*

On the sides of shuttle busses and on wall placards in the Hemmings Mall and on cardboard signs inside busses above the windows and on the middle pages of the *Hemmings Herald,* for the next few years Eric and Shit would see the cool green with thick red letters sloping down to the left:

REMEMBER CALIFORNIA

For years, probably, that was the most recognizable icon in the country— even in Diamond Harbor. Two months after the theater reopened, three black women and two young white men came by the Opera and asked Shit if they could put up a poster in one of the empty frames halfway up the steps from the lobby to the first balcony.

Shit told them, "Sure. Put the thing on up there."

Downstairs, Eric stood with his arms crossed, watching them slip the yard-and-a-half rectangle of green oak tag with its blocky red letters into the frame.

*

After three weeks, in his hurried trips up and down the stairs, Eric ceased to see the thick, red reminder of the national—the worldwide—catastrophe. Possibly that's why, on his way down one Thursday, for the first time he noticed, running along the bottom, in small letters, an internet address: NewOrderofHolyLuminecence.

At the bottom of the steps Eric continued across the lobby and out the glass doors. He paused at the ticket booth, a hand against the curved wall, and called in through the grill to Shit: "Hey, I'm gonna run over and see Cassandra and Tank for a minute. I'll be right back."

Up the street at Cave et Aude, Eric stepped over the puddle on the pavement from the lopsided air conditioner in the transom and pushed through the door. Cassandra was sitting at the glass counter in the front with an open sketchbook. On the wall across from the counter were reproductions of dozens of tattoos. She looked up. "Hey, there—you want to get another picture?"

"Hi, Cassandra," Eric said. "You guys got a computer in here, don't you? You think you could let me Google something?"

Cassandra put her head to the side. "Google…?" she asked. Then she frowned. "When's the last time you *used* one?"

Eric frowned back. "I don't know. Seven, eight years ago."

"More like ten or twenty," Cassandra said. "You're like Tank's cousin, Pete. He won't come near them things."

From the back, over her needle's buzz, Tank called, "Hey, Eric. Good to see you." She was with a customer.

"Hey, Tank—"

"But that's all right," Cassandra went on. "You two don't believe in none of this modern technology, do you?"

Eric chuckled. "It's not we don't believe in it. We just never got around to learnin' it. You know Shit don't have no readin' or writin'."

"What you wanna look up?" Cassandra asked.

"The New Order of Holy Luminescence," Eric said. "And what it's got to do with the 'Remember California' charities."

Cassandra reached up to run a heavy forefinger under the collar of her dress. "You gonna go to one of them rallies they're always havin'?"

"Naw," Eric said, "I just wanna find out what they got to do with those REMEMBER CALIFORNIA signs you see all over."

"Oh," she said. "Turn around. It's right behind you."

"Huh?" Surprised, Eric turned.

Where the wall of designs had been, a glowing picture of a church with a light behind it's steeple filled the wall—which Eric only realized now was a screen of some sort. Hundreds of people stood before the church.

Superimposed on the tableau were the familiar red letters:

REMEMBER CALIFORNIA

Behind him, Cassandra said, "You wanna hear what they got to say for themselves?"

Eric glanced back at her. "Yeah..."

—and a woman's gentle voice declared, "This is a message for all good, American Christians." (Though what Cassandra had done to turn it on, Eric had missed.) "Please, make your donations for the recovery of the great state of California through the New Order of Holy Luminescence, founded by Father Goldridge Hanover. That is the only way you can assure that eighty percent of your donation will be used to establish Christ's Mission in the Garden of Eden State of California. We know that you are dutiful, Christ-fearing Americans, all of you, and that you, no more than I, want selfish godless Jewish influences, Muslim evil, Buddhist devil worship, and Catholic paganism to reach its dangerous tentacles into that broken and wounded land that cannot fight back with the word of Christ, unless you are very careful about how you spend your money. So, once again—"

From the back, the tattoo needle ceased buzzing. Tank called forward: "What you turn on that bullshit for—?"

"It's somethin' Eric wanted to hear," Cassandra said loudly.

Tank grunted. Again, the needle began its buzz.

"That's okay," Eric said. "I heard all I wanted, anyway. Thanks Cassandra."

Eric had no idea what she did, if indeed Cassandra did anything, but the wall sized screen returned to the display of eagles, dragons, dolphins, flowers, lotuses, vines, butterflies, stars, birds, beetles, clouds, skulls, and flames.

"Any time, honey. When next you come, maybe we can do a little more work on you—make you even prettier for that sexy boyfriend of yours."

Eric laughed—and left the store.

By that evening, at the turn in the stair, someone had drawn a skull-and-cross-bones on the "C" in CALIFORNIA, and over the next month, in ballpoints and in felt tips, airplanes and swastikas and the schematic genitals of both genders began to cover green and red.

Two years later, in Chicago, a high-fashion house caused a scandal by using the same coloring and lettering for its advertisement of a line of cameras, computers, briefcases, and (the ones that twisted everyone out of shape) one-piece topless bathing suits for women and women's open evening jackets. Outcries of tastelessness hogged the front pages of two or three papers for two or three weeks. (*Remember California…?* The implication—wholly erroneous—was that the style had started there prior to the Bombs.) Six months after that, though, a few people grumbled, nobody seemed to object when a line of camping gear appropriated the logo—and began to run advertisements of people tramping through the recognizable ruins of the western countryside, with signs saying REMEMBER CALIFORNIA in the background.

Neither Eric nor Shit ever knew about those particular turns in the history of advertising imagery nor in the debates about them. By that time, though, since the defaced poster in its frame halfway up the theater steps had gotten ripped almost in half, Eric had pulled it out, thrown it away—and, basically, felt better now that it was gone.

* * *

[74] SHIT CAME OUT the lobby door, to where Eric was leaning beside the booth, because it was a little early for the after-work crowd to be buying tickets. "Hey—come on. I gotta show you somethin'."

"What?" Eric asked.

"I gotta show you. I ain't gonna talk about this one."

"But I should be in the booth, sellin'—"

"Come on! It'll just take a couple of minutes!"

Standing up, with Shit's rough hand on his shoulder, they went back through the lobby. To Eric's surprise, Shit turned aside for the steps up to the first balcony and began to take them two at a time. "Come on up here." Eric followed.

When they entered the back of the balcony, Shit turned aside. "This is too high for you," Eric whispered. "You don't like comin' up here."

But Shit led him around the back of the waist-high wall, before which the seats, mostly empty, rolled down beneath the slope of the balcony above, with its supporting beams, to the rail. "Right. I don't. But I gotta show you this. You'll like it, too." They walked down through the arch into one of the lower boxes. "Come on," Shit whispered. "Hunker down." Dropping to a squat, Shit held out his arms and duck-walked forward toward the box's molded railing.

Eric started after him. "I ain't afraid of fallin'," he said quietly, to explain why he was still upright.

Shit looked back up at him. "It ain't about fallin'. It's about someone *seein'* ya. Get *down!*"

"Oh…" Eric dropped to squat-walk after Shit, who had reached the curved wall surrounding the box. (Today, no chairs stood in any of the boxes—though one of the regulars had left his sleeping bag wadded against the wall. It smelled musty.) Shit put his hands on the inner wall, pushed himself up till his chin was over the edge, leaned his head forward and whispered: "Look on down over that—you'll see 'im."

Joining Shit at the rail, Eric did the same. "Why are we doin' this—sneakin' around like a pair of kids in our own goddam movie theater? Shit, this nigger better have a dick bigger than goddam Haystack." He pushed himself up further.

"It ain't no nigger," Shit whispered. "He's a white guy—".

"I meant 'nigger' in a manner of speakin'. Like you and me."

"Well, *I* didn't. Look on down—he's practically right under us. In the orchestra, about three seats to the left. He ain't too far from the wall light. You can see him real clear. But be fuckin' *quiet*, huh?"

Eric pushed up and looked at the empty orchestra seats below. A youngish, muscular fellow, with a mop of curly hair—blond, it looked like—slouched back in his seat almost directly below. He'd slipped his shoes off. One socked foot was propped up on his toes on the seat back in front of him. The other foot was over the back, hanging down into the chair in front. Eric saw that his jeans were opened and rucked six inches down his thighs. He wore no underpants. Respectably hung, he slanted up and to the side. His hands were joined under his chin—Eric could just figure that one out from the high vantage. As Eric watched, his cock levered up and flopped over to his other thigh. Then, seconds later, it raised again, by itself, and flopped back.

"You ain't gonna tell me now you got me up here to watch some cracker flop his dick left and right—Shit…? Like I ain't seen *that* maybe fifty times before in the last six months…?" Looking aside, he saw sweat beading Shit's forehead where, between his knuckles on the rails, his mouth was slightly parted, as his face leaned over the rococo gilt.

Beside him Eric heard Shit's rough breath.

Eric frowned. "Shit, you're scared to death! Come on, let's go back down. You don't have to be up this high. You're gonna get that vertigo—"

"*Shhhush*…!" Shit whispered. "It's probably gonna take him a few minutes to do it again."

Again, Eric looked forward and down.

The fellow had taken hold of himself with one fist and was pulling it slowly, overhand.

"He gonna do it soon, now. I seen him do it four or five times already." (So it wasn't shootin', Eric figured. Or *was* it…?) "That's why I run out after the last one to get you—"

Eric took a long breath; then, with the hand nearest Shit, he reached over to massage Shit's shoulder. "Relax, there—you ain't gonna fall. I ain't gonna let you fall. Really, this ain't so high up. It ain't no more'n twenty feet. Hey, if you *did* fall, you'd just crack a leg or an arm—"

"*Shhh*," Shit whispered again. "I know I ain't. But my body don't know it. Just watch."

"Okay, I'm watchin." Two-and-a-half, three minutes dragged, and Eric's attention shifted to the images intertwining on the screen…

Then Shit whispered, "There he goes."

Eric looked down. The young guy raised his head a little and, with a thick middle finger, closed off his left nostril and snorted into his palm.

It was loud enough to hear up here.

He moved his hand over, so that his thumb closed off the other side of his nose. Again he snorted into his palm. Now he held his hand out before him—he was sitting close enough to one of the sidelights so that you could see something glistening in a labor-hardened palm. Below Eric, the young man looked around, first left, then right. But no one was closer than ten or fifteen seats away. He dropped his face and gave a big lick across his hand, first one way, then the other; then he must have scraped it with his bottom teeth. Then he ran one and another finger into his mouth.

Shit turned his head toward Eric's arm. "Oh, *fuck*…!" Eric felt Shit's wet forehead press his bare shoulder. (That day he'd worn a shirt with the sleeves torn off.) A moment later, Shit's arm gripped Eric's back. "Oh, Jesus, that is so fuckin' *hot*…"

"Damn," Eric said. "Yeah, that's pretty good. It's got me hard. But *you're* carryin' on like some straight guy sneakin' his first a peek at a woman pushin' her titties into her bra, Shit!"

His forehead still against Eric's arm, slippery with perspiration, Shit whispered, "I seen him do that five times now. He must got a cold or somethin', 'cause that boy's snottin' up a storm. You know—" Shit chuckled—"the *first* time I seen him do that, I was comin' up from cleanin' the bathroom in the downstairs lounge, just walkin' up the orchestra aisle, when I looked over and caught him at it. I came in my damned jeans. I'm not kiddin'. I swear it. I had to sit down in one of the seats, there—so I could stop quiverin' and get to breathin' again."

"Did you see how old he was?"

"I don't know," Shit whispered. "Twenty? Twenty-one? He got sumpin' wrong with his face, so it's hard to tell."

"Yeah…" Eric chuckled. "But that means you could be his daddy."

"*Awww*—" Shit grimaced—"please don't say that!"

"Now don't tell me *that* bothers *you*…?"

"It don't bother me." Again, Shit grimaced. "But I figure it might bother *him*."

"Come on." Eric pushed back from the box wall. "Shit, ain't nothin' so hot you got to scare yourself crazy, hangin' over the edge of this damn box. Let's go down, where you can be comfortable."

"Okay." Shit backed from the wall on his knees, then turned. "But I'm comin' back here to watch him do it again in ten or fifteen minutes. So I can beat off." Now he took Eric's hand and pushed it down between his legs, where a bar ran diagonally under the lap of his work-softened jeans.

Eric squeezed him, then stood. Shit leaned back and stood up. too. They started up the balcony's side aisle, by ancient arches, some of which were nailed over with plywood. Finally they reached the entrance to the stairway. "Did you say anything to him, yet?" Eric asked.

"The second time I saw him do it, I went and sat about three seats away from him."

"What happened?"

"He's funny. He don't care if somebody sees him jerkin' off, but he don't want *nobody* to catch him at the real hot stuff. I was about to say somethin' friendly, and thought I'd dig out a finger full of my own and eat it for him, so he'd know I was...you know, like him. Only soon as he saw me do it, he got up, stuck his feet in his shoes, and moved off to the other side of the theater." Shit chuckled again, then glanced back at Eric. "He got some kinda harelip, what they sewed back together. That's why I wasn't sure how old he was. One of his eyes goes off a little. Actually, he's pretty good lookin'. He *could* be thirty, even thirty-five...And the lip thing makes him sorta cute." Shoulder to shoulder, they came down the curving stair. (Eric realized he hadn't seen the man's face at all.) "It's funny. You see somebody who does something that *really* turns you on, and the next thing you know, everything about 'em looks good. Once he moved, I figured he was kinda skittish, so I got up—and three minutes later, he was back. He really likes that seat. I mean, it's clear he's lookin' for a blowjob, wavin' his dick around like that. Hey, whyn't you go and over and suck him off? Then, when you got him busy, I'll come by...and just watch and maybe say somethin' friendly. Tell him we could be snot buddies, if he wants. That way, maybe he'll let me have some of his—or have some of mine—while you're...what'd Dynamite used to call it, when he'd suck on us while we was sittin' in the bed, eatin' each others'...? 'Encouragin" 'im. That would be *real* nice. I know it's a little late, and the regulars gonna start comin' in just a bit, so you're gonna be busy in five minutes. I should've got you before. But you don't even have to do it today—"

"Suppose he leaves?" They walked out into the lobby.

"Naw, he's permanent. I been seein' him in here for three days now. He's been there for two nights. So he's gotta be homeless—or *real* horny. He ain't no local guy. I'd've recognized him if he was from around here. The first night when I went out to bring back a pizza for the guys upstairs, I mean, before I realized he was anything special, I stopped and give him a slice. And Dr. Greene done brought him a sandwich yesterday. I hope he's one of the California fellas."

"Why?"

"'Cause they're so much more grateful when you help 'em out. It's easier to get nookie off 'em. You know that."

"Come on, Shit. Don't you think it's unfair takin' sexual advantage of somethin' like that?"

"Nope," Shit said. "You just get to know 'em a little faster. That's all." He snuffled, dug a forefinger in his nose, pulled it out, looked at what it carried, started to eat it, then offered it to Eric. As he pulled his finger from Eric's mouth, Eric found himself thinking it *would* be nice to try the new guy.

"So *you* already been feedin' him. Funny," Eric said. "And I didn't even notice he was here. Probably 'cause he was white—" Halfway across the dingy marble, Eric stopped. Shit stopped, too, with a questioning look. Then, frowning, Eric said, "You know, Shit? I just figured somethin' out about you."

"Huh?" Shit said. "Figured what out?"

"You're a damned snow queen!"

"What?"

"At least about snot eatin'."

"You mean, somebody who only likes white guys? Me? Hey, you know that ain't me. I fuck every damned nigger in this place. I got my eye peeled for 'em when they come in. And I mean nigger as in black—like me. The reason I like this place so much is 'cause we got so many black guys in here, three-to-one over the crackers. More than half the white guys I end up leavin' alone, anyway, unless they come after me. Sure, I wanna be friendly—maybe eat that kid's boogers with him. See if he wants to eat some of mine—or yours. But it ain't like I wanna move him in with us. When Dr. Greene was in here suckin' his dick yesterday—now *there's* your snow queen; he *always* goes for the white ones in here first—I overheard them together talkin' afterwards—and the harelip's a damned motor mouth. I mean, he's as bad as Big Man used to be and ain't as smart. He didn't *never* shut up! Not once. I know *that* much about him already. Hey, now what I *would* like is for us to get ourselves our own nigger. A nice young'n. A chunky one, I mean—*and* brainy. Like you, there. That way I could listen to the two of you talk back and forth and learn stuff. So even if I *am* a snow queen—which I think is a *real* laugh—you don't gotta worry about it none."

"Shit, I *know* you love fuckin' black ass—and you'll suck on anything if you think it'll make the asshole attached to it loosen up a little, black *or* white. You'd suck off a motorcycle tailpipe if you thought it would make it easier to stick your dick in the gas tank. But we been takin' care of this place here almost five, goin' on six years. Durin' that time, three booger-eatin' black fellows, at least that I seen, have come in here. Remember, one of them was that older guy—two of them was here for a few months each, and one of them just in and out? And I seen all three of them doin' their nose pickin' and finger suckin', and I had a nice, casual thing with all three of them. I told you about all of 'em, too. And what did you say? It was, 'Oh, yeah, that's interestin'.' Maybe you went to look. Or done it once or twice with em."

"What do you mean? I fucked 'em all—ten or twelve times, at least one of 'em there. He was *real* good, too."

"Only then some poor harelipped white 3B refugee comes in here, chowin' down on what's supposed to be goin' into his snot rag, you're ready to throw yourself at 'im over the damned balcony!"

Shit had his superior look. "Well, if I'm a damned snow queen—which I am *not*—maybe you so busy wantin' to be a nigger you done forgot you *are* a snowball, after all, Blondie. Hey? Ain't you figured it out, yet? All I am is a *you* queen. Or anything that's halfway like you."

"Well, I *know* that…"

"You sure?" Shit's disgust fell away to reveal the mocking smile beneath: he slid an arm around Eric shoulder. "You *really* sure?"

"Yeah, I—"

"So suppose your nigger dirt ball gets a little hungry? What you gonna feed 'im? You gonna feed him a finger full of that good white boy snot, or is you gonna let him eat his own or run around after what he can get in a damn place like this…?"

"Oh, come *on*, Shit—"

"Hey."

They reached the lobby.

"You got five people out there, by your booth, waitin' to get tickets." Shit nodded toward the glass doors. "You better get your black ass on back to work." Shit halted and scratched his crotch. "Hey, that motherfucker got me all horny. Hold up a minute. I wanna piss in your mouth. Go on squat down in front of me."

"Here in the lobby? Where the guys lined for tickets outside can see—"

Eric took a breath but moved around in front of Shit.

"Well, that's kinda the idea. Just a little advertising for the pleasures this place has to offer." Shit grinned as Eric dropped to a squat and went in to the front of Shit's loose jeans to pull out his cock. Shit moved from leg to leg, which he did when he was about piss. "Open your mouth, nigger…" His hard, thick fingers moved on Eric's scalp. Warm yellow spurted from the collared head and Eric, mouth wide, caught it, feeling himself thrill to the familiar and reassuring taste and pressure and heat. He began swallowing.

There was a faint fire in Eric's own cock that was not enough to more than half harden it, even though it was a definite sign of pleasure. Which was pretty much how Shit described the pleasure he took of urinating in Eric's suck hole.

(And how the fire was always greater if somebody saw them.)

Finally Eric mouthed Shit's half hard member as its urine slowed and stopped. He swallowed again, coughed, and stood. And Shit's arms went around him and his tongue invaded Eric's mouth. Shit was holding him hard; Eric held him hard in return.

Finally Eric mumbled over Shit's busy tongue. "Yeah…anybody out there see us?"

"Ugh…!" Grunting, Shit relaxed his arms. "Nobody even glanced in—I could've pulled your pants down and fucked you right here in the theater lobby if I'd wanted." He thumbed with one hand out the door toward the customer line—now seven long—beyond the glass door and in front of the booth. Then Shit dropped both hands to refasten his jeans.

Eric let a couple of syllables of laughter. Pulling from Shit, he started out, between the scrolled jambs, under the rococo lintels, carved with flowers and doves, the gilt on the molding worn away. "But you have to admit—" he called back over his shoulder and wiped his mouth with the back of his wrist—"the way you like them white boy snot jockeys explains a *little* of what goes on in my life—in *your* life…in *our* lives, I mean." He'd have the familiar, bitter salts of Shit's piss in his mouth for the next ten or fifteen minutes—a pleasure to contemplate across the boring ticket sales. It was astonishing what some of these cocksuckers just never saw…

"*I* don't have to admit nothin'," Shit said. "But *you* gotta sell some tickets. Maybe later, you can come in and encourage that white kid for me, so we can *all* get to know each other. And when the rush lets up, come on back in and hunt me up out of the shitter downstairs and we can sit down somewhere and watch the movie and you put your head in my lap and my dick in your mouth and hold it there for about a half an hour. I'll finger fuck your ass. You don't even half to suck me off—though if you wanna get a load or two, I ain't gonna argue with you…!"

* * *

[75] IN THE APARTMENT above the Opera's projection room, a conversation took place six or seven times. (Eric would have said it happened at least a dozen. Shit would have sworn it only happened twice. But the last time was the one both remembered.) Sitting on the edge of the couch, in minor frustration, Eric told Shit, who was standing by the window with its frayed yellow curtains, half looking out, "I know *you* can come standin' on your damned head with six jackhammers goin' at a construction site in the middle of a blizzard. But it's *hard* for me to get off, if you got your hands folded back under your neck when I'm humpin' you. At least you gotta put your arms around me and hold on."

To which Shit responded, "Oh. Okay. I don't mind that."

"Damn, Shit! Why can't you—"

"Hey, look. Have I *ever* not done somethin' sexual that you told me to do?"

"What I don't understand is why somebody who claims to be such a sexual stud like you has gotta be *told* everything!"

"Well, I can't read your mind!"

"Why the fuck not? I spend enough time tryin' to read *yours*! After all this time we been together, don't you think you could do a *little* mind readin'? I always want the same thing, anyway—"

Shit turned around, leaned his butt on the wall and pushed his hands into his pockets. There was always a hole in the bottom of the left one, that, whenever Eric got him new ones, he'd cut open for him—Shit was left handed—and, as usual (Eric could see the movement of his fingers and fist under the cloth), Shit would push through to hold his genitals, for security, or, sometimes, when he'd just take it out and work on it, standing in the back of the orchestra aisle, while five or six older guys sat around watching his, covert or not so covert, masturbation.

Now, though, Shit said something different from the last time they'd had this talk: "Hey—I really *like* it when you tell me what to do. I mean—" he looked at the warped board floor they'd polyurethaned in their first week there—"once you tell me and I do it, it makes me feel all good and safe and...*right*—and I can't make no mistake, 'cause I'm doin' what I was told." He swallowed, still looking at the ground. His voice got softer and... well, rougher. "Like I was...doin' it...with my dad, I mean, back...when I was a little kid."

(Why, Eric wondered, do I still find the idea of a forty-six year-old man playing pocket pool a turn-on?)

Eric looked at Shit then let his own head drop to the side. "Oh..." He took a breath. "Hey, you know...look, it ain't *really* broken, so there ain't no real reason to fix it. I mean, whenever I fuck around with Joady, downstairs—you seen him, the guy who sits on the side in the first balcony?—he does so much huggin' and holdin', it kind of drives me nuts. So, it's not like I don't get any at all."

"Joady?" Shit looked up. "*That* ol' guy? You mean the one who always calls me Mr. Haskell when he comes in? Hey—would you please tell him my goddam name is Shit and that's what he's supposed to call me...at least if he wants to keep comin' in the Opera for free."

"Well." Eric chuckled. "He calls *me* Mr. Jeffers—he's just tryin' to be polite."

"Polite's callin' people how they wanna be called." Without taking his hands loose, Shit pushed forward, then leaned back again. "We let 'im in for nothin'. He could at least say our names right." Again he looked at the floor. "It's a fuckin' fuck-film theater, for God's sake!"

"Oh, he earns his entrance fee. For the people who like the older guys, he's the most popular stud up there. I tried to send him downstairs to Gorgonzola Alley—that's where he should be. You seen the skin he got hangin' off 'im? But he says he don't like the competition with the youngsters—and he's kinda set in his ways, anyway. He calls everybody 'Mister'—except Doc Greene. He calls him 'Doctor.'"

"Well, good for him." Again Shit looked up, frowning. "But you can *really* come easier with him than you can with me?"

"He just knows when to hold onto somebody—when he feels they're gettin' ready. Naw, I don't have any problems there. With him, it's gettin' away later. *He* wants to hold on and cuddle with you the rest of the damned day."

"What you see in an ol' white guy like that, anyway? I thought you was into the blacks, mostly. I had him the first time he come in here—he didn't seem like nothin' special...his dick is smaller'n mine."

"'Mostly' ain't 'completely.' Like I say, he's a hugger and a cuddler. And sometimes, that's...nice."

"And you don't have to tell him when to do it?"

"It's more like I have to tell him when to let go. Besides, every once in a while, he makes me think back and remember Dynamite."

"He do? He sure don't look like my daddy to me!" Shit snorted. "He looks like every other fifty-year-old, snaggle-toothed cracker up and down the damned coast."

"Would you haul off and hit me if I said that wasn't really so far from what your daddy was, anyway—I mean, you know I loved him as much as you and thought he was the best man in the world—"

But Shit stepped from the wall, pulled his hands from his pocket, and strode across the room.

Eric stiffened, wondering if he was going to get at least a push.

"Hey, that's wigglin' out of it, cocksucker! That's fuckin' cold, man." Shit reached the couch, dropped down beside Eric, drew up a knee, and swung around to face Eric, one hand catching the back of Eric's neck. "By the time you'd been with us a year, that man loved you as much as he loved me. He was the most special man in the world. And the most special daddy. He thought you was the greatest thing in the world and pretty special too, and don't you forget it." Shit grabbed Eric roughly, one hand in front on his chest and one hand behind him. Eric twisted, to accept the clumsy and intense hug. "Hey, scumbucket, how many of them other snaggle-toothed crackers up and down the coast would let you lie around in the same bed with 'em, grinnin' at you suckin' off their own son, and then ask you, 'Hey, you wanna work on mine awhile?' and love you like you was a gift right outta that nature-or-God you're always talkin' about from that book of yours?"

"Not a whole lot of 'em." Eric pulled in a breath. "I know that, Shit."

"Not a whole lot, huh? Maybe only one—at least that you ever knowed. And maybe the world would be better if there *was* a few more of 'em, and not guys punchin' kids' fuckin' teeth out for suckin' dogs, like Shad done with Jay."

"Yeah, Shit. I *do* know that."

"Well, don't fuckin' *forget!*"

"Hey—I never forgot it. And I'm never gonna forget it—" He felt Shit breathing against him; he smelled the acidity of Shit's hard, unwashed body.

Like cables freezing into bars, Shit's fingers stiffened on the side of Eric's face. (Eric got his near arm free to hug Shit—as hard—back.) "Good." The hug was awkward. But neither of them stopped it. Finally Shit said, softly, "Course, I'd be a lyin' sack of shit if I said I didn't know what you meant." Shit took another big breath.

Then he said:

"I'm huggin' you so hard, 'cause I..."

Eric heard him sniff, and realized there was a near sob in his voice.

"...don't wanna hit ya'."

"Me too..."

"Yeah?" Now Eric heard Shit chuckle. "Come on, then, nigger. Let's fuck."

"You got it." There was a quick release, a quick half pulling free of

Shit's shirt, one leg of Shit's pants, Eric's pants, and the unbuttoning of his shirt—but he didn't get it off before Shit fingered loose his upper plate, put it on the table at the couch's end, and turned back to grapple him.

Later, on top of Eric, Shit pushed himself up on his elbow. "I know you said it ain't broken, but it ain't gonna hurt me none to fix it a *little* bit, now."

"You did." And thought: why does the grin he has on his face now, completely toothless, knock me out?

"After all, ain't I supposed to be this super stud who knows how to make all his little fuckers happy—like you, there?"

"Hey," Eric said. "You make me happy. I wanna do the same for you—and the fact is, the rest of it can take a flyin' fuck outta the window."

"No, it can't," Shit said. "'Cause that wouldn't make *me* happy." Then, later, when they had finished, Shit said, "Okay, now, I'm gonna put my ass in your lap, and you can hug me from the back, like Dynamite used to do. But that means you can't fuck me—just rub, if you're still horny. And you are."

"Sure, come on—that's okay. You know, sometimes I think that man's gonna be in bed with us for the rest of our lives...?"

Shit chuckled. "Well...you gotta admit, it could be somebody a lot worse. You mind?"

"No!" Eric protested. "It's kinda nice, actually. But it's...different."

A little later, when Eric had decided that Shit was asleep and was drifting off himself, suddenly Shit asked, "You wasn't tryin' to make me jealous, talkin' about ol' Joady, there—was you?"

"A stud like you—gettin' jealous? Naw. I don't think so."

"A couple of times—I mean, years ago—I tried to make *you* jealous, by talkin' about somebody I was screwin'. Just to see what would happen."

"You did?"

"Only it didn't work. It just got you horny. I guess it's good it gets me horny, too..." Outside the window, the sky's blue deepened toward night.

* * *

[76] IN THE OPERA'S broad basement corridor, at the bottom of the ramp, while Eric went through one key after another on Myron's great ring of...a hundred-fifty? Two hundred-fifty keys, Myron said, "They ain't gonna work. That's what they told me, twenty-five years ago, when I first come. They don't got the keys to these rooms down here no more. This is where they made the scenery, when they did the real operas and plays and stuff, back a hundred years ago. But nobody done had keys to these things in fifty, sixty years now."

On the hundred thirty-sixth or hundred thirty-seventh key, however, when Eric twisted, the brass barrel in the gray-brown wooden door turned.

Eric pushed down the handle. The door squeaked forward, grinding over the grit scattering the inner floor's cement. "Rip off a piece of that green tape," Eric said to Shit.

"Here you go," Shit said, who was clearly impressed. Again, he squeezed his big hand through the roll of green gaffers tape.

"Well, I'll be goddamned," Myron said. "They told me you couldn't open these doors no way at all no more."

Once they stepped into the spacious room, all they smelled was century-old dust. Save three saw horses, a chair and two ladders against the wall—across the ceiling, half a dozen pulleys, ropes looped between, and a catwalk for hanging backdrops—it was a large, empty room.

Someone had left a very old screwdriver on the chair.

"We're gonna put it together in here." Eric pressed the small piece of green tape on the key's head and rubbed it with his thumb. "Now don't let this come loose. I don't wanna have to go through all these damn keys every time I come in here."

"Why we gonna make it in here?" Shit wanted to know.

"'Cause the hallway's wide enough to get it out—once we're finished. And because of the ramp, we can get it up easier."

"Is that what that thing's for?"

"I don't know if that's what it's for. But that's what we're gonna use it for."

"God damn." Bald Myron wore a kind of baggy white shirt under his vest. "They told me—years 'fore you guys ever come and took over the place—there was no way you could get in these rooms. They told me they was haunted. I didn't believe that—'cause I don't believe in no spirits. But I still figured these places were locked for good."

From the ceiling came a grumbling—all three looked up, where a grate was inserted between two of the beams across the yellow-white plaster.

"Oh, shit—" Myron said. "That must go right up to the orchestra—backstage, there. I always thought that was for heatin'. They're grumblin' up there 'cause the movie just run out, and they don't know what to do with their damned dicks."

"Ain't very imaginative, huh?" Shit said.

Myron said, "I gotta run. Just bring them keys back up to the projection room when you're done with 'em."

"Okay," Eric said. "We will."

"You know—" Shit looked around, rubbing the back of his head, stepping from one sneaker to the other—"since nobody been in here in fifty, a hundred years, don't you think, we should probably break this place in. What do you say?"

"What you mean—? Oh...Yeah. Maybe we should."

"We could even bring a mattress down here—and if we found somebody nice, we could use it like a fuck room. I mean, just for us."

"I knew you was gonna say that." Eric laughed. "How do I know you so well?"

"I don't know. What you mean?"

"I mean, if I suck you off a few times here—like startin' right now, and help you get a mattress in here in the next week—you are gonna work your fuckin' ass off to help me get this business done. And if I don't, you're gonna lose interest and start driftin' off an always bein' somewhere else when I need you—"

"I am?"

"Yes, you are."

"Damn," Shit said. "Well, in that case, I think you better start suckin' my damned dick, nigger. I mean, like right now." He shook the crotch of his jeans.

"Come on, white boy." Eric pushed the screwdriver off the chair. It clattered on the floor. He turned and sat on the chair. "Bring that meat over here and let this nigger show you how it's done."

"Oh, man." Shit grinned. "I'm gonna be a white boy today!"

One chair leg actually cracked after about five minutes—it must have been a prop and not very well made. But Eric just went forward, on his knees to the floor, gripping Shit's hips; while, in return, Shit gripped Eric's head.

* * *

[77] THE COOKER ITSELF...?

Its structure was very much from all of Eric's—and Shit's—life. The burner units of the fundamentally portable stove came from a demolished diner (whose history Shit rambled on about for fifteen minutes—he'd gone there a couple of times during his school years; Eric had never seen it before) they'd glimpsed through some pines when driving along the old garbage run, one day for old times' sake, up near Hemmings.

For the rollaway frame, Eric had called on the half dozen teen-aged lessons Mike had given him in welding, back in Atlanta—he was surprised how much he remembered. And even though he'd used a little portable welding torch, damned if the thing didn't hold together, all hundred and thirty pounds of it—at least when the propane tanks were empty. When the two of them were full, it was heavier. Across the back of a flame-proof masonite board, calling on his time as a comics reader and an aspiring (well, amateur) artist, who'd filled a few secret notebooks back in Hugantown with drawings for a gay super-hero (one-third adventure, two-thirds clumsy pornography), called, not very creatively, *The Cocksucker*, a half dozen colored magic markers came out and with much guidance from Cassandra, Eric lettered above the three burners at the preparation-counter's back:

THE DYNAMITE MEMORIAL
FREE FEED-ALL

Throughout, Shit was as quietly helpful as an assistant to an interesting madman might be. The blower was bolted in place, overhead. Because he had a computer, Jay had ordered them some red and green striped, fireproof cloth (and refused to let Eric pay for it) for the awning. Because Mex had a sewing machine, Mex ran up it up for them.

They rolled it up the ramp, out into the Opera House lobby, and fitted the awning over the frame they'd put on the thing. All around, it was about three inches too big.

That's when Barbara dropped by to say hello. "Goodness gracious. You're gonna start selling hotdogs or popcorn in here now? Well, that's an idea." When they explained the problem, she stepped back in her white sandals and her pale green dress, and declared, "Haven't you boys ever heard of safety pins?" She had a dozen in the bottom of her woven straw handbag. In twenty minutes, up on the ladders, they got it folded, tucked, and fastened. It was a little bunchy at one end. "But it's supposed to be a stove," Eric said, "not a' artwork in a museum. It's okay. Hey, Barb—really, thanks. That's good."

Lurking around and not looking in too good shape that day, Joady said, "Mrs. Jeffers, you sure you wanna be hangin' around a place like this—with them movies they got playin' in there?" He gestured to one of the posters behind glass that was not, actually, for any of the DVDs on screen.

Barbara laughed. "Honey, I used to dance in a place that had movies like that and probably worse, playin' right up behind me on the screen." She shook her head. "I'm a little too heavy to do that kinda dancing now—but I could probably still surprise you—"

"Barbara...!" Eric said.

"Oh, let an old lady have a joke!" Barbara pulled her white wicker bag around in front. "The reason I stopped by—" she reached in and moved various things with one hand, then switched and reached in with the other, and pulled out two wide silver plastic bags—"was to give you two these things. I was out at the mall, and I saw them, and I thought maybe you could use them. You both wear your clothes till they're just about fallin' off you. So I thought, if you got these, maybe you'd use them."

"Thanks." Frowning, Eric took one. Across the front of the silver bag, bright letters declared: *A Permaclean Shirt! It's new! It's nanotech! And it's eighty-five percent natural!*

Barbara held the other silver bag out toward Shit, who pushed both fists down in his pockets and grinned. "Oh. Well, thank you, ma'am," but made no gesture to take it.

Barbara explained: "Now don't go and throw the bag away. You just hang the whole thing up in your closet. You take out the shirt, wear it, and when you take it off, put it back in the bag and close it up. Three hours later, it's completely cleaned, and every six months or so, you take the strip out the bottom and throw it in the washing machine to get out all the salt and stuff that collected in it. Then you put it back in the bag, and you can wear it every day, if you want, for another six months."

"Oh..." Shit said, sounding honestly surprised.

And Eric took the bag from his mother, because Shit didn't seem to be about to take it himself.

Though Shit did say, "Uh...thank you, ma'am."

That night they'd rolled the same stove outside and, in the street, tried it for the first time. Hamburgers. And sautéed onions. "Hey," Shit said, "these are pretty good. But try not to burn the buns up, next time."

"There's a kitchen knife there," Eric said. "You wanna scrape off the burnt part, go ahead. Hey—damn...!" Because just then, the kettle of water he'd put on the back burner, to see if it would get hot enough to boil, began to bubble and splutter. Eric reached over and turned the burner down—wedges of blue pulled from the kettle's bottom—leaving scorched black around the sides—to shiver beneath it. In three minutes, though, the water was still simmering. "Well—" Eric rubbed his red and gray apron—"if we can get it to do that when it's full of crushed tomatoes, we can cook some chili."

Around toward the back, Shit was frowning at the sign. Now he looked up. "You think my daddy would've really liked somethin' like this? I mean havin' it named after him." It was not accusatory. But it was dubious.

With the spatula, Eric pried loose a burger, which left a scab of gray chopped meat on the skillet bottom. "He liked comin' here to the Opera House." Over the theater's ornate cornice, the sky was darkening blue. Bats flitted over the street. "He brought you and me here enough times."

"Yeah." Shit grinned at Eric. "You remember how he'd always go sit in the front row and tell and me and you to run off and have fun? You'd go upstairs—and I go down. When I'd come back from fuckin' myself silly with them niggers who used to hang out downstairs in the men's room, you'd always be there, sittin' next to him with your face in his damned lap, and he'd be starin' at the screen, holdin' your head, and humpin' for all he was worth."

Eric chuckled. "Hey, I never made no secret of it. Next to you, I thought your daddy was the sexiest cracker in Georgia."

"Aww, you was just bounded to him, that's all."

"Yeah, maybe. But I still never taste your fuckin' dick cheese, today, where I don't remember his, back then. I mean, the two of you were so much the same, down there. But you're right. Everybody's tastes a little different," a point Shit made regularly, which he used to justify his unquenchable sexual inquisitiveness. "They're all different…"

"Yeah," Shit agreed. "That's what I told you. You know, it's only when you start talkin' like that, that I wish sometimes you wasn't cut. That way I could see what yours tasted like—your cheese, I mean. I fingered out enough of my own and ate it, damnit."

Eric looked at him.

"And so did he." Shit looked at Eric, waiting.

Finally, Eric said, "Shit, you remember that big storm we had, years back—Hurricane Edna? In oh-nine, I think it was. Remember how we took in Jay and Mex, when they had to leave Gilead? And how Dynamite and everybody workin' together to feed pretty much everybody at our end of the Dump?"

"Yeah," Shit said. "That's right, we did, didn't we?"

"Well, that's kinda where I learned to do somethin' like this. And that's why I thought I'd call it after your daddy—after Dynamite."

"Oh," Shit said. "Yeah…I see. I see what you mean. Now I see it. I thought before it was somethin' you maybe got outta readin' Mama Grace's book."

"Well," Eric said, "that too—a little."

Suddenly Shit grinned. "Only in that storm there, while you was learnin' that, I was learnin' something else." After a moment, he said, "*Damn*…!"

Eric narrowed his eyes. "Yeah, I guess you was. Hey, go on inside and tell the guys down in the orchestra that we got some hamburgers out here for 'em, if they want. They don't have to worry about gettin' back in the theater." By the handle, he centered the twenty-six inch skillet better on the burner. "I'm gonna put on another dozen. And Mex brought by that urn of lemonade. We got plastic cups. I don't think it'll go to waste."

Shit started back under the Opera's marquee. "I don't think it will, either."

Within minutes, two, then five, then nine men walked slowly from the lobby—some black, some white—in jeans, in T-shirts, a couple in tanks, a couple in work shoes, some barefoot, blinking in the seaside sun.

That's how the Dynamite Memorial Feed-Alls began.

* * *

[78] UPSTAIRS THE NEXT evening, Eric picked up the two silver bags from where they'd been lying on the table, carried them to the closet, and hung them by a hanger on the pole across the back. He started to close the door, then opened it again and pulled the zipper strip back on the first Permaclean bag to see the shirt inside was a red plaid.

He zipped it up, then unzipped the other: a green plaid. Eric grinned. "I guess that's yours—matches your eyes." He laughed.

Shit stood in the middle of the floor, fists in his pockets. "I'll probably give that to one of the guys downstairs. Maybe they can use it."

"Why you wanna give it away? It's a nice shirt."

"Well," Shit said, "it's that science stuff. I can't read the instructions, and I don't got the patience for you to teach me. If you tried, we'd just get in some kinda argument. Besides, that stuff always makes me uncomfortable, and you know it never works—at least for me."

"Oh, come on." Eric turned from the closet. "All you gotta do is wear it. Ain't nothin' more to it than that."

Shit shrugged.

"It's the same technology as them nanobolts, Shit, what we used to make the houses with, out on Gilead. You didn't have no trouble with that—You did it better than I did."

"How's cleanin' a shirt gonna be the same as that Superglue stuff?"

"They're both nanotechnology," Eric said. "The cleaning bag you keep the shirt in got these little tracks that run down on the inside. When you fold your shirt up, put it in there, and close it, these thousands and thousands of little molecule-sized machines get turned loose, and they work all through the fabric and take out the salt from your sweat and the dirt stains and the gunk that gets on it and carry it back to the bag wall, and then they move down those tracks to the pump in that strip the bottom, and then go back to their position and wait for the shirt to come back in there, dirty again. And you take out that strip on the bottom where they put the dirt and wash that out twice a year and your shirt's all clean and ready to wear again, every day—"

"Who told you that?"

"Nobody told me, Shit. I read it on the back of the bag, before I hung 'em up."

"Oh," Shit said. "Oh, I see. You *read* it. Get out of my face with all that reading nonsense, you fuckin' piss-drinkin' nigger cocksucker. That science and readin' stuff always makes me feel funny. Sometimes I think you fellas can't read no more'n I can. You just make it all up so I'll feel like a fool—"

"Okay, okay—forget it. I ain't gonna push it on you."

But the next day, Eric started wearing his red plaid; and wore it every day for three months, too. After two weeks, though, when he was down in the orchestra, he was surprised to see Shit coming upstairs from the lounge in the green shirt. The sleeves were gone.

Grinning, Eric asked him, "What'd you do? Tear the sleeves off?" That would be like Shit.

Shit looked down at one shoulder, then at the other. "Naw. They come off by themselves—I mean you can *take* 'em off, if you want. You remember that Velcro? It's kinda like that—only stronger. I can put 'em back on, any time I want. You remember that stuff...?"

"Hey," Eric said. "You get somebody to read you the instructions?"

"Naw," Shit said. "One of the California guys told me about it—and I tried it, like he said—you can't just rip it. You gotta pull it opposite to the way it looks put together, and then it comes right apart. I left the sleeves upstairs, inside the bag."

"Oh," Eric said. "Well...it looks good on you."

"Yeah, your mama got some good taste. Now why don't you take the fuckin' sleeves off *yours* and give us all a treat—you paid enough to get them goddam pictures you put all over your arms. Why don't you let us see 'em?"

"Okay," Eric said. "I will." Though, the next morning, after Shit had already gone down, when he tried to release the sleeves, he couldn't get them to work. Back at the closet, he took the cleaning bag out, sat at the table where he read his Spinoza, and went carefully through the instructions printed on the silver plastic—and, yes, the final paragraph of small type was a description of how to hold and tug to release the sleeves and put them back on—which didn't seem to work on his. For some reason, though, the last thing in the world he wanted to do was ask Shit to show him.

Later that day, in the theater, he even asked a couple of the regulars among the California guys if they knew. It would have been nice if harelipped, snot-devouring Loop—whom they *had* befriended for a while, before he'd moved on—had been there. But he'd been gone three months now. And Dr. Greene said he'd seen some people in them four or five years before when they'd been really popular, but not since. "Why don't you ask Shit...?"

"Naw—Naw, that's all right. Don't bother 'im about it."

"Okay..." Dr. Greene smiled, as though he understood something that was escaping Eric.

But nobody that he inquired from seemed even to know what he was talking about.

Fucking modern technology...

Then Eric thought—probably this is how Shit feels, much of the time. Suddenly not being able to follow the instructions became something precious. He'd been planning to get the bag for Shit's shirt and read that one, to see if there was a difference. But now he went over and carefully hung his own bag back in the closet.

Birds sang outside on the theater roof.

In his long-sleeved red plaid, Eric went into the stairwell and walked down the dark steps into the balcony.

* * *

[79] STANDING ON THE sunny sidewalk, half a dozen of the men—bored by the film inside, which they'd sat through dozens of times since it had been changed three days ago—had come out to see, while, for twenty minutes, Eric used the broad spatula to push onions back and forth over the skillet's bottom, then lifted the cast iron to scrape them into a kettle of crushed tomatoes. As he pushed them over the pan's rim, a shadow crossed him. When he could put the skillet down, he looked up. "Hey, Al—how you doin'?"

"This is a real nice day for your chili bash, boy." The big man looked immensely pleased. "Got somethin' for you. I assume you're doin' things according to Mex's special recipe...?" He nodded off down the stove, where Mex poured rice, like chittering cicadas, into a stainless steel steamer Barbara had once borrowed from Serena at the Coffee & Egg and forgotten to return a hundred years ago.

"Basically," Eric said.

"That's what I figured. When I was a lot younger, you know I used to go out and hang around on Gilead with them two—Jay and Mex." He nodded to the mute Mexican, quartering peppers and putting them into the plastic hopper, who grinned at Al. "Jay used to call me one of his puppies—I been at their house a lot of times, when they was making up that chili like they do. Slept over with 'em—ate with 'em. Just like you done." (Long ago he had learned—then recovered from the surprise of learning—that Al was less than ten years his senior. Today Eric felt more like Al's contemporary than the kid to Al's fixed adult he'd assumed himself on that first day back at Turpens.) Al reached into his shirt pocket and pulled something long and latex, up and out. "Believe me, them motherfuckers didn't do nothin' with you they ain't done with me. Maybe a little more, too. It wouldn't surprise me, 'cause I was one curious black sonofabitch. Anyway, I thought you might want some of this for it."

Swinging from his dark fingers was a translucent latex tube, a third full of pearly liquid. Because it was so large, it took Eric seconds to realize what it was—and remember when he'd last seen one. "Christ, Al—"

"I figured—" Al held it up to let it sway in front of Eric's face—"you just might wanna dump that in the pot. You know…the secret ingredient that makes it taste right." He lowered it a little, frowning. "Course they was younger, so maybe they weren't doin' that special stuff when *you* went out there with 'em…"

Shaking his head, Eric chuckled. "Hey, Al, thanks—yeah, I know what you're talking about. No. They were doin' it when I was there. But we ain't makin' it *that* special…at least not this time."

"You sure?" Al lowered the condom completely, now. "See, I just shot that inside, when I was up in the balcony. I figured I'd bring it on down and at least make the offer."

Salt-and-pepper haired Joady had ambled up beside them. He had a broad bald spot and wore a filthy white dress shirt. Under the frayed cuffs of his jeans, he was barefoot. "I tol' Al you wouldn't want that stuff. This ain't that kind of party. When Mr. Jeffers wants that stuff, he likes to get it straight out your dead black hosepipe right into his belly. See, Mr. Jeffers here is an equal opportunity cocksucker."

A red-headed fellow with sunburned skin and big ears asked, "Why you gonna talk about Mr. Jeffers like that, Joady—I mean, outside where everybody can hear?"

"I ain't sayin' nothin' about Mr. Jeffers I don't wish he was standin' there, stirrin', and sayin' about me. I'm grateful for the time and the tongue work he puts into gettin' a load outta me. Now in the piss drinking department, he's a bit more choosey. I feel free to comment there 'cause this old goat does have a thirst for the first full flush of dog, horse, or man. I've drained 'em all many times, black, white, brown, or the inscrutable Chinee. I give 'em all a head to hold and a handle to make love to. But if you're feelin' around in there, lookin' for a seat in the darkness, and off in the corner you hear the fall of fresh waters, the hot flood that slops and flushes down, that's gonna be Mr. Jeffers in a squat and Mr. Haskell standin' over him, looking fondly down on the fjords of his face, pouring his soul out into Mr. Jeffers' maw. Or, if not Mr. Haskell, someone Mr. Haskell has corralled in the urinal and before he's had a chance to run free, brought up to the back of the theater to watch—Haystack, Gorilla Man, Pope, or harelipped Loop when he was still a fixture in our artificial night, or Sloppy Joe—only three hours ago I heard him, like an old time Tin Lizzy, fartin' his way up the aisle—to service his lover like his daddy used to do. Hey, now Mr. Jeffers didn't get his recipe from them island guys. He got it from that book he's always in there readin', I bet. Ain't that right, Mr. Jeffers?"

"I guess you could say that." The chopper's buzz stopped. Mex twisted the top open, and Eric—who had really not been paying much attention to Joady's encolmium—poured the aluminum pot full of cut-up and sautéed peppers into the chili, then gave it three, four, five big stirs.

"So hey, now—how 'bout you give that to me, nigger?" Joady said. "I done had me a thirst for one of your loads for the longest time—months, fella. I seen you shoot enough of that damn stuff. I wanna find me out what it tastes like."

"If the boy don't want it, Joady—" Al still called Eric a boy, though Eric was well into his forties—"ain't no point in savin' it. If you want, it's yours."

Joady reached up and took the condom in a grubby, knuckely fist. "Damn, nigger—that's the biggest rubber I think I've ever seed. That looks like about six loads in it. At least."

"Nope. It's just one—my first one today, too. I thought if it was gonna go in the chili, I could spare it for the bash. But that's all it is."

Taking it now in two hands, Joady stretched the knotted end out, bit at it, pulling it out with his teeth, till at once the stretched latex tore. Now he up ended it and squeezed. Viscid and yellowish, it rolled from the condom into Joady's stubble-ringed mouth.

Two other guys had wandered over. One of them said, "Jesus—is that yours, Al? You give it to that old cocksucker?"

With gruff friendliness, Al grunted. "What the fuck you care?"

Pressed tight, Joady's fingers descended the length a second time. More welled from the tear. Finally, moving his tongue around inside his cheeks, Joady looked down and frowned. "Damn—that don't taste like nothin' from no human bein', Al." He put his head to the side, looking up. "I mean, black or white—even a damned Chinee. That's gotta be from a fuckin' horse!" He threw out a knuckley fist with an extended forefinger toward Al. "Yeah, I knew I recognized it! That tastes *just* like horse cum! It was too much for a man to shoot, anyway, I don't care how big your dick is. You went and put a load of fuckin' horse cum in that rubber—didn't you?"

"You one dumb white cocksucker," Al said. "I did not. Why'm I gonna ruin the man's cookout with a load from a horse? Besides, where am I gonna find a damn horse in the Opera House? "

"Joady, how you know what horse cum tastes like—anyway?"

"'Cause I used to work on a breedin' farm up in Tennessee, years back. The grooms and the jockeys all knew I was a damned cocksucker: they'd get together and pay me a hun'erd bucks to watch me drink that stuff down—"

"You sucked off horses…?"

"There was a couple of them stallions I had trained what would let me suck their dicks—it's like tryin' to get a damned toilet plunger in your mouth. Them things flare. Takin' 'em up your ass, you can get yourself killed that way. And if you actually manage to get the head in your face, and suck and rub on it, the sonofabitch can drown you, if you ain't ready when he goes off. But there're always a few guys who gonna work themselves up to it. It's always the little butch fellas, too."

"Then I guess you wasn't one of 'em," the redhead said.

But Joady was going on with his narration. "The easiest way, if you want horse cum—well, you seen them big long artificial leather horse pussies they got, that they grease up and slip over the horse's damn dick. He comes in that thing, and it all runs down into a jar they screw onto the end." Joady held up his hand, indicating the jar's size—about three or four inches high. "Them stallions fill that thing two-thirds, three-quarters of the way up. Some of it they use right away for breeding, and some they refrigerate. Well, I'd unscrew the cap off a damned fresh jar and drink it right down in front of all of them boys, and they'd just laugh and slap their knees and about fall out on the ground, they thought it was so funny. I liked it, too. Gettin' it straight from the horse's cock is good—but you can't always count on it. Either the fucker's gonna drown you to death or decide he wants to kick your head in. Like I say, you gotta work with 'em and get 'em trained. Mostly I'd take a bottle with me and use some of it to jerk off with later. But once you get it in your damned mouth, you can't confuse it with no nigger's—or no white man's, either. I've filled my belly up with enough of both to know. And I'd swear on my mama's grave, either that stuff I just drunk was fuckin' horse jizz…or *you*—" he turned to frown up at Al—"ain't a damned human bein'!"

Several guys laughed—including Al. "Can't you guys come up with somethin' else to say about me? I'm gettin' tired o' yall always talkin' like dat."

"Naw. You're a damned horse. You tired of it, you go live somewhere else and don't let no cocksucker with no horse sense get after ya' dick. Probably your daddy was a horse got after yo' mama in the field—"

"Don't go playin' that," the redhead said. "You don't got to be sayin' nothin' about the nigger's mama."

"Why not? That's the only thing that would explain it. I mean, I just drunk the fuckin' stuff, didn't I? And I know what the fuck I put in my own damned belly." Shaking his head, he fingered the torn condom down into his shirt pocket, where it wet through the cloth.

Not more than twenty, and with his black hair in a ponytail, Pope, who'd had been coming to the Opera pretty much every day for the last three months, suddenly said, "Hey—you know you old guys are really fuckin' disgustin'? You know that? You really are!"

"No, we ain't," Joady looked back. "We just got the balls to do what you kids wanna do but are too damn scared to."

"Whacha mean?" Pope asked. He wore a belt around his jeans that was set with myriad square studs.

"I mean, who gets to drink a load of the nigger's goddam cum, right out his own scumbag? You or me?"

"Well, why the fuck—" Pope emphasized it with a dropped chin— "would I wanna do somethin' like that?"

Joady grinned at him. "Don't worry, son. If you don't want it now, you will. Then you'll wish you had the horse sense to do it when you had the chance." He turned away to pad off, bow-legged, through the crowd, a tear across the seat of his jeans displaying his butt crack.

Al was still standing there, towering above the others. The sunlight on his black arms here and there caught his tattoos' darker markings.

"Hey, Al." Eric called. "Come over here a minute."

Al eased a few steps over.

"There's somethin' I been meanin' to ask you—for years, actually."

"What?" Al said. "You wanna know, too, whether it was my mama or my daddy what was the fuckin' horse—?"

"Come on," Eric said. "No. Not that stupid stuff. What's it say on your arms, there? It's hard to read—'cause it's black on black."

Al raised his right biceps, turned it, and looked at it. "Aw, that's just some stupid shit I had Tank and Cassandra put there when I was a kid and didn't know no better."

"What does it say?" Eric stopped stirring the pot.

Al moved closer to the cooker and raised his arm, protruding from his torn-off T-shirt sleeve, for Eric to see.

Looking closely, on the dark, dark skin, which seemed suffused with micro-diamonds of perspiration, Eric read from the ornate Gothic print: "'This...dick...fucks...everything...including...your...ass...Bend... over...bitch...I...love...you!" Eric laughed, stood up, and stirred again.

"It's all shit like dat." Al turned to the other side, to show his other arm. "I was an asshole when I was a kid. I thought that was real smart." He chuckled. "Since you was a kid, you done wrestled wid my fuckin' dick a lot. You always treated it with respect, too."

"Well, as dicks go, Al, yours is...pretty respectable. And most of my wrestlin' with it was in the theater, where it was dark." Again, Eric read from the tall man's proffered arm: "'It...takes...a dick...like...this...to... run...the...motherfucking...world!'"

"The ink's moved around so much on them things, you can't hardly read it no more. Tank drew up a whole alphabet for me, what they used to write this stuff out on my motherfuckin' skin." Ten or fifteen feet away, the two heavy tattoo artists—Tank in denim, Cassandra in pastels—milled among the others waiting for the food. "I wouldn't be surprised if I was their very first customer, too—or one of their first. I 'member me and Jay was both in there at once, a couple of times."

Again Eric read out: "'There...is...the...Eiffel...Tower...There... is...Cleopatra's...Needle...And...there's...MY...FUCKING...DICK!... Get...on...your...knees...and...I...may...let...you...suck...it...But... this...nigger's...dick...needs...some...shit...lubrication...at...least... three...times...a...day!'"

"Come on!" Al grinned. "Don't read that stuff out. Tha's embrassin'. I mean, you don't need to hear stuff like that. You always knew how to treat my dick, just natural-like. When's the last time you sat on that thing—I mean, up in the Opera?"

"I dunno..." Eric said. "What—six, seven months ago? Yeah, it was up in the balcony. Nobody had been botherin' you for a while, so I thought I'd come over and throw my ass in you face. Have myself some fun."

"Yeah, you always been a good boy, what knew how to do right by that thing. You get all down on the floor between my knees, take it out, and suck on it and make love to that ol' thing, and when it's hard, you stand up and sit on that fucker and I grab hold of you, and we *have* some fun, too—don't we?"

"Yeah. I guess we do."

"I was even thinkin', I ought to ask you to live with me for a while, six months, a couple of years even. See, when I was a kid, I'd never do nothin' like dat wid no men. Live with 'em, I mean. For more than a couple of days—like a weekend. I'd do it with women. I had about six women, there, once, all on the same street, what I was fuckin'. It was good, too. I didn't want nobody callin' me a faggot. But I didn't want nobody to think I was even friends with any of the men I fucked. The fact is, though, I'm older now—and I don't give a fuck what nobody calls me today. I can deal with anyone who respects my fuckin' dick and treats that nigger right. Man or woman, it just don't bother me no more. Some of them houses in Split Pine is goin' empty. So I thought, maybe, it wouldn't hurt to ask some guy with a nice ass to shack up for a bit." Al grinned. "'Specially if he could make chili."

"That's…nice to hear, Al. But the fact is, I'm kinda taken care of in that department."

"Yeah, you *think* you taken care of. But if I told you I wanted you and took my fuckin' dick out, and waved it in your face, you'd come a-runnin'. I seen it too many times—like I say, men or women. It don't matter. Yeah, you'd come if I asked you. Truth is, up there in Split Pine, I don't got *no* women right now—I mean, permanent. That's why I spend so much time down at dis place. So I'm thinkin' I should try changin' my luck a little. So you keep me in mind. I'll keep you in mind. And when I want you, you be ready to come. Hey—and give a shout out when this chili's ready. You know, some of my kids are runnin' around here today. I brought 'em over here. You make sure you give 'em some of that chili." Chuckling Al turned and walked away through the crowd.

"Will do." Shaking his head, Eric went back to the stirring—something was sticking to the pot bottom. He scraped at it, stirred harder, and turned down the flame.

Ten minutes later, in her voluminous flowered pastel, Cassandra came over to the cooker, laughing. "Hey, there! I was just talkin' to Jay." She nodded where, through the crowd, the tall, white-haired man with the beard was walking with his salt-and-pepper haired partner. "Seems like the only times we done seen him in the last few years is when him and Mex come out for your chili bash. They don't get past the Lighthouse these days when they come in on their runs—if that far."

"Well," Eric said. "They're gettin' on—we all are. They gotta be sixty now."

Cassandra looked at him sideways. "Closer to seventy, I bet."

"Really? Well, maybe so. Hey, Al was just lettin' me read over some of your early handiwork."

"That crazy stuff?" The two tears beneath Cassandra's left eye were faded enough to think, if you looked quickly, they were a natural discoloration. "You know, when he came to us, we had to have a whole evening's conference about him, Tank and me—Lord, he couldn't of been more than nineteen back then. And Tank was even younger—I was twenty-one and both of us was very idealistic. You would think we was havin' a political summit—all the talkin' we did."

"About what?" Eric asked.

"Well, we was startin' a tattoo and piercing business, and we had principles: no profanity—no bad language at all. Nothin' on the hands, below the wrists. Nothin' on the face. Genital piercings, but no pictures—on 'em or of 'em. And no swastikas—only, of course, the first ten people who walked through our front door, damned if that wasn't what nine of them asked us for. We thought we was gonna be like the big city places and hadn't realized yet that's why most of them was comin' out to the country. Jay with his damned snake on his hand—like the one you went and got." She nodded to where Eric was still stirring, the back of his hand heavy with veins and supporting its serpent head. "Then that dick proud nigger, Al, with 'nigger this' and 'nigger that' all over him. That wasn't what we'd set up, plannin' to do." Tank shook her head. She had a lot of earrings in one ear.

"So you changed your policy?"

"We had to make a damned livin'," Tank explained, stepping up. "You know what that boy had me tattoo on his goddam pecker—it was my first pecker job, too; though, God knows, it sure was *not* my last!"

Cassandra shook her blond head, chuckling.

"Jesus," Eric said. "He's got something written on his dick?"

Tank raised a heavy hand to move it over the sky, as if outlining a banner against the clouds: "'I…Am…the…Lord…Thy…God…!' It's black on black, like the rest of it. And he got it twice—up one side and down the other, comin' and goin'! No kiddin': you probably got to shine a flashlight on it to make it out today, but I bet you can still read it, twenty-five years on—or however long it's been. Frankly, I don't even wanna know—"

"I guess I never got that close," Eric said.

"The hell you didn't," Tank said. "You had it up your butthole—on the first day you come to the Harbor, too. That's what *I* heard."

"From who?" Eric let go the ladle. Slowly it leaned over against the pot edge.

"From Al and Jay and Abott and Mex and Shit and Dynamite and Tad and Abott and—" Cassandra began.

"You said Abott twice, so I suspect he's your real source, huh?" Eric laughed. "I think this goddam chili has gotta be ready!" Eric took up a padded mitten and turned to lift the cover from a second, simmering kettle. The smell rose with the steam. "Come on. Gimme a break…!"

"Now you know—" Cassandra put a surprisingly light hand on Eric's forearm, over her vivid needled hues— "that's why he wears a condom when he fucks."

"What you mean?"

"I mean, you didn't think it had anything to do with AIDS anymore, now, did you?"

"I thought he was just bein' careful."

"Naw, he don't want people to see what he got written on hisself. So he covers it up with a rubber. Every few years—" she nodded through the crowd, where tall Al had stopped to laugh and joke with another set of men (once more about his probable equine parentage, Eric figured)—"Al goes and gets religion for a while. He feels a little funny about advertisin' himself as the Lord God in Heaven."

"Well, I guess for a believer that *is* a little coarse."

"Coarse?" Stepping up beside her partner, Tank broke out laughing. "He's afraid he's goin' to Hell! (Hey, you got that chili smellin' *real* good!) But then another of his 'wives' decides she's had enough of his bullshit and decides to go back to school or gets a job in some other city that ain't Split Pine or even go out and be part of the life on Gilead, and there goes his faith, off comes the rubber—or at least he ain't quite so regular about hidin' his…aspirations there."

Eric laughed—while he tried, and failed completely, to remember if his own last encounter with Al in the balcony had been sheathed or unsheathed. "He said he was thinkin' of asking me to move out there with 'em. I could see it for a weekend. But that's about all I think I'm ready for."

Cassandra laughed. "Wonder what Shit's gonna say about *that*."

"Oh, he'd just tell me to give it a try for a couple of weeks, till I got tired of it, then get on home where the gettin's good—you know, cuddle up with him an' tell 'im all about it so he can get off over it."

"Now that's a wise man." Tank shook her head. "Watch your pot, there—"

"But I been gettin' a shot at it three or four times a year since I come to this place, anyway. Hell, Al ain't really into guys. But I guess I'm supposed to feel honored that he even brought it up." Eric gripped the ladle handle, stirred in one pot, lifted it out, then stirred the other.

"It ain't that," Tank said. "Like everybody else around here, he's got a feelin' you and Shit have somethin' goin' for you. He just don't want you to say no to 'im and realize he's wrong—that he ain't got the Lord God himself swingin' between his legs after all. He's just a good horse in the pasture—like my brother used to say."

"Was he gay?" Eric asked. "Your brother?"

"As you are," Tank said, patted his shoulder, and looked his arms up and down. (Today Eric wore one of Shit's old shirts with no sleeves.) "Yeah, that ink looks fine. I wonder why…? You know, people used to think there wasn't no queer Indians." Laughing again, she turned and walked away through the crowd.

A bearded black man moved up beside Eric. "Um…" he said.

Eric said, "Hey, Sandy." And swallowed.

"I was wonderin', sir—is this just for us black fellers in the place? I thought maybe…well, 'cause it was free, it was just for us."

"No. Yall can eat."

"Or maybe," Sandy continued, doggedly, "just for the gay guys. I thought maybe that's how you worked it."

"Weren't you here for the last couple of these cookouts?" Eric turned the long ladle through the red-brown mix. "No, I told you. You can have some, too. This pot's ready. If you're hungry, get yourself a plate—on the other side of the smelter there, from the cups. Shit'll be here in a second to dish you up some rice."

"So you mean the straight guys who just go in to watch the porn can have some? You don't have to be one of the ones you let in for free, 'cause they let the faggots suck their dicks…?"

"Like I said," Eric repeated, still stirring, "it's for everybody. And I don't ever remember askin' you to buy no ticket. Suck studs, cocksuckers—and even you regular jerk-off artists."

"Oh, hey, man. I don't mind a good blowjob, now and then. Even if it's a faggot—"

"Now, how did I manage to figure that one out already, Sandy?" Eric raised the chili ladle to scratch in front of his ear with his thumb.

"'Cause you love suckin' on this big black dick yourself—you just thought I was asleep—"

"Sandy—" Eric went back to stirring—"I'll let you in on a secret: not for one damned second!"

"But, see, I was wonderin'—" Sandy gestured over to the side— "what about them women there?"

Up the street, ten or a dozen women had gathered to stand and talk outside Cassandra's place, occasionally pointing down the street—some were laughing.

"It's for the women." Eric stirred. "It's for the men; it's for the guys who pay for their tickets; it's for the guys we let in free 'cause they're willing to work it off in trade." Eric said. "It's for gay men and lesbians—it's for straight men and straight women, too. It's for people who happen to be standin' around on the street. It's for anybody who's hungry. Even fellers from California." (Eric's was not a joke that more politically sensitive people were likely to make. Even before the catastrophe, Southern Californians had had a reputation for weirdness. Since the Three Bombs, that reputation had only grown.) "And it's for anybody who just wants to try some. Okay, now?"

Others were already edging around Sandy, plates ready.

In her Army jacket and her tent-sized fatigues, three hundred-pound Tank had gotten hold of a paper plate. "In other words," she declared in her hoarse voice, over the roar, "like the man says, this is for everybody."

"Well—" Eric grinned at her—"I wouldn't say that *exactly*. If it was for everybody—I mean *really* everybody—there wouldn't be enough. But let's say it's for everybody who happens to be around *here*. 'Cause that's how we figure on the proportions. Okay? But that's why some of you other people, who can afford it, might think of doing somethin' like this, too. For the ones who need it who can't get here today!" Eric turned, to shout the last part over the gathered heads. "It's for you and you and you and you and you…!"

A bunch of people, men and women, applauded, while others ran up.

"…Come on! Get a plate and get some rice!" Waving a long slotted spoon over his head, Shit was making his way forward, a large pot of rice that had been steamed upstairs on the stove there held against his hip. "I got the rice here!"

*

For eight years, Eric—with Shit and others pitching in—ran his Dynamite Memorial Free Feed-Alls, pretty much four times a year, mid-summer, mid-winter, fall and spring. That year *The Hemmings Herald* even published a profile on them.

"That's my crazy ol' man," Shit would say, sitting out on a stumped piling on the Diamond Harbor dock, beside Tony's Coffee, Egg & Bacon (which a few older folks *still* called the Lighthouse Coffee & Egg), watching the water's inward roll or standing in the back of the Opera or sometimes leaning against the wall with his dick dangling from his jeans, rarely for more than an hour without somebody coming by, squatting down, and sucking on it for a least a while, nor was he above snagging one of half a dozen regulars, including Eric, simply mumbling to himself; or while he walked in the overcast street in which it had started to sprinkle and it seemed too stupid to hurry up, 'cause either you were gonna get wet or you weren't. (For the first year or so people thought he was talking on one of the new invisible phones—but Shit didn't own one.) Or sometimes when, in the Opera's scenery storage room alone, he just stood, frowning at where the cooker sat, up against the wall, three empty propane tanks with green painted nozzles propped beside it, which they had to take back to the company, if they wanted to get their rebate. "He likes doin' that kinda stuff for people. And, yeah, I like helpin' 'im."

***

[80] SURELY A SIGNIFICANT number of readers have entertained the thought that Eric's four-time-a-year Free Feeds were in the spirit of the generous and large-hearted decade in which they occurred. (Writing her profile for the *Hemmings Herald*, June 22, 2034, nineteen-year-old reporter Mary Jane Jenkins, working for her uncle on the paper that summer, used the phrase "the spirit of the thirties" toward the end of her piece and felt it marked her as sensitive and prescient to the forces so many had been manifesting around the country for half a dozen years and so few were actually synthesizing in any systematically analytic way—though, four-and-a-half years later, the same phrase had become such an overwhelming cliché that, in rereading her article before she left school to move in with two of her friends on Gilead Island, it would redden her ears and make her delete all her early published local journalism, from both her personal files and from her back-ups. What she wanted to write, anyway, was poetry.) To many, it's clear today, that—at least for a while—those words seemed to characterize more and more activity in the country until repetition emptied them of all meaning, especially for the writers who had used them first.

At least one other incident of international importance that year impinged on Shit and Eric's lives—one that figures in the lists of the decade's many, many positive accomplishments.

Interruptions in the running of the Opera House they were used to. More than once, when the theater was shut down, at a request from Randal at the Chamber of Commerce Office Eric and Shit found themselves with three days or three week's work, back on the garbage run, to spell this or that driver who needed time off. Half the time they were allowed to go on living in the upstairs apartment in the temporarily empty theater, where, from the days when Eric took time off from cooking, pizza boxes and Styrofoam chicken containers and empty plastic soda bottles accumulated, until once a month, they packed them down into the Folz Recycling Bundler out in the alley, one of the dozen now standing here and there around the county and the most outré piece of nanotechnology Eric had yet seen.

That November, when the theater shut once again, Jay phoned to ask if they wanted to come out to Gilead.

They took knapsacks and rode the shuttle up to Diamond Harbor.

Ed was running the scow. A dozen young women were on their way to the island that afternoon—they were having some sort of shindig out there that night.

"What's goin' on?" Shit wanted to know, looking around the boat.

With a coil of rope over his shoulder, Ed told them, "It's that thing on the moon they been talkin' about for the last week."

"What's that?" Eric wanted to know.

"Those people up there." Now it was Ed who was barefoot. He nodded and wandered back toward the stern, where luggage made a pile that a tarp had been roped over. The prow smacked the water, which sheeted up on the sides of the *Gilead*.

Lights stood on stands around the settlement. At the top of the new wooden steps up to the new clearing were loudspeakers and a platform, above which hung a large TV screen. Tables had been set out in front of it. Music played, and many women—most looked like laborers who'd worked on the new houses—were milling around and talking together. "Hey," Shit said. "This is kind of fun, ain't it?" He was eating some sort of fried cake and stopped to look down at it. "It's kinda greasy—but it's tasty." Many of the dishes were Latino—as were many of the women, Eric noted.

It *had* been fun having all that going on the day they'd checked their Gilead place.

Then some musicians on the platform began to play. In succession, three women made speeches.

And Eric learned that this was all because tonight the first group was landing on the moon. Originally, they had planned it to consist of three couples, two with men and women, and one pair of gay men. Only lots of women—dykes, who, apparently the vast majority of the women around them were tonight—had started writing into the government, saying that was silly. They should make it even. It made more sense that way. Women had written them from Provincetown, and North Hampton, and Bolinas, and Bolder.

And a group letter had gone out from eighty-two of the women working on Gilead that Margaret Arnold had organized and taken around personally and gotten as many signatures as possible before she sent it.

*

The next day, when Eric had taken one of the trucks over to the Bottom and climbed out, he was explaining to Tad, while Shit leaned out the cab window, listening.

Finally, Tad said, "Yeah. Well, dykes would, wouldn't they?"

"The government knuckled under and said that was probably better. One of the women who made a speech last night said they was always leavin' out the lesbians and forgettin' about 'em, unless they made a stink. So they'd made one." Eric laughed.

Over Eric's head, Shit said, "I guess as stinks go, it must have been bad as the Bottom here."

Standing before the new, aluminum-sided shack, Tad said, "So you saw all that business on the moon last night?"

"Yeah," Eric said. "On that big television they had out there."

Shit said, "They said they brought a lot of that stuff in by helicopter. We didn't see that. But we saw it on the screen."

Tad said, "You really think they're gonna stay up there for three months? You know that thing was on all day."

"We just saw the end, when we was out there. We don't got no television. But we're gonna get a place out there—they're gonna let us have one of the old Indian cabins that's still in pretty good shape. The old Holota place."

Overhead, from the open cab window, Shit said, "They were havin' a *big* party in the Settlement all about it. They were makin' speeches and havin' free food. Probably got that from us—over at the Opera. And music—and that big old public TV screen, where you could see it. It was one of them 3-D things, where you don't even need no glasses."

"Yeah—I seen one of them at a bar in Manchester. But why was they havin' a party?"

"'Cause of the women," Eric said. 'Cause they're puttin' four couples up there for three months, instead of three. And one of them is women."

"Yeah," Shit reiterated. "Two regular couples, one a pair of guys, and one a pair of women."

"Oh," Tad said. "But why they havin' a party about that? In the show *I* was watchin' on it, they didn't hardly say nothin' about any of the gay ones at all. I don't even understand why they're doin' it that way."

"To see what they gonna do, each different kind, livin' all together on the moon for three months. Isn't that what they said?"

"They didn't talk a whole lot about that on the show I watched." Tad sounded uneasy. "They just talked about eight people bein' up there, half of 'em women, half of 'em men. Out on the island, they don't got nothin' *but* women out there, right? Dykes—lesbians, I mean. I guess *they* really liked that—"

From the truck, Shit chuckled.

"They got some men there," Eric said. "They got me and Shit. Like I say, we gonna be livin there. You know Jay MacAmon? Him and Mex are out there in the old Kyle place."

"Oh, yeah. That's right…" Tad reached up and scratched his head. "I forgot about them ol' boys."

*

Later on, when they were driving back to Runcible in their own pickup, Eric said, "You know who woulda really liked that party out there last night? I mean, he woulda really gotten into it—if he was alive."

"Who—what you mean?" Shit's gray hoody hung down his back.

"Big Man Markum. Remember how he thought the space program, once they started it up again, was the most wonderful thing in the world? You know how he was always celebratin' that instead of Christmas." Over the highway edge, Eric glanced out on the winter sea.

"Hey," Shit said. "You know, you're right."

* * *

[81] OUTSIDE REBA'S GLASS window, the sky's upper half was deep blue, while the lower half was streaked with violets and salmons, pale grays and breaths of green, and robin's egg blown across it.

Eric slipped into the booth across from Jay, while Shit hung back a little, listening.

Across Rockside, Nightwood's window—in the Gilead dress shop—was dark and empty. The huge, hi-def TV screen that had broadcast its advertising was gone, as was the woman who'd run it. Maybe eighteen months ago she'd shut the place up and left. Someone had said that soon it might become a medical clinic. Well, the Settlement could use a clinic of its own.

"So when's Johnston gonna shut down the Opera for good—this time?"

"That's why I asked you to come on out here to the island and talk." Jay shifted on the booth's wooden seat and said, "He ain't."

Shit said, "He ain't? What happened to all that stuff about buildin' the world's biggest coastal hotel up in Runcible?"

"Well, actually…he ain't interested in this whole section of the Georgia coast no more. And we done convinced people—again—the Opera's a historical institution they gotta preserve."

Eric looked at Shit, who was frowning something fierce. Then he looked back at Jay.

"Besides," Jay said, "he's pulled up and taken himself off to California."

"California?" Eric said. "What's he wanna go out there for?"

"Cheap land—at least he thinks he can get some of it cheap—cheaper even than around here."

Eric frowned too. "'Cause of 3-B stuff?"

"I guess, indirectly. But that was a while ago."

"Oh…" Eric said softly.

"And it's got Johnston and his like out of our hair down here—for a while. What do they say—it's an ill wind that don't blow nobody some good. I guess it blew us a little."

"It's gettin' time to do another Free Feed," Eric said. "They're gonna keep us on, aren't they? And they gonna keep runnin' things like they were?"

Jay nodded. "That's what it looks like."

"So our homeless guys still got a place to live?"

"They do. Come on out to the house and have some cod stew—that's what Mex's makin' for dinner. Ed'll run you back on the scow."

"Good," Eric said. "'Cause there'll be somethin' nice to celebrate."

"Come on," Jay said, "Tell me about it."

Shit said, "I think you're crazy, nigger."

Jay said, "I'll run it past Kyle."

Later, Mex and Jay went down to join Ed for a late night run through the moonlight, back to Diamond Harbor. While the sea rushed and slapped around them, Jay stood at the wheel and said, "Kyle said he'll even throw in a few bucks for you, on your pension." Eric was surprised the call had already taken place—though Shit, who'd lived there all his life, didn't seem to be.

"What you mean, pension?"

"Well, I assume you want to retire pretty soon."

Milky froth rushed under the night.

* * *

[82] RUSHING BELOW THE rail, night's end joined the whispering water, different textures though all but one color.

On the boat, shoulder-to-shoulder, they leaned together. Somewhere at the indistinguishable horizon, in minutes the sun was due to seep across the sea. "Come on," Shit said. "Take your shirt off. I done took off mine. See, it's tied right here." Ahead in the dark was Diamond Harbor's mainland.

"Why?" Eric couldn't see. "It's cold."

"No, it ain't. Come on, nigger. Please?" Shit slid his hand around Eric's neck. He rubbed.

"Why you callin' me nigger?" In the dark, Eric grinned. "You gonna fuck me? You know there're people still sittin' around, back there, on the deck."

"Maybe I will." Shit moved his arm up around Eric. "I wanna see them pitchurs you got all over you, when the sun comes up."

"Huh…?"

"Yeah. Come on. 'Fore it starts to get light, now."

Eric sighed. "All right." He began unbuttoning his cuff. The summer morning was…well, not warm. But an indifferent coolness moved up his forearm, down his neck

Shit's hand was warm and big and rough behind Eric's shoulder, on Eric's back. "Yeah, like that." Eric shrugged out his shirt, cloth tugging from between his back and Shit's hand, so the hand was suddenly both rougher and warmer. "See, now I can get behind you and hug on you and rub my hands all up and down your arms over them colors and wedge my dick in your ass crack. And by the time we get home, you gonna be beggin' me to go out to the end of the docks where you can get down on your knees and I can whip it out and piss right in your mouth there and you gonna be lookin' up at me, almost as happy as you were last week when I brung Haystack up from the john to pee in your face—"

"Happy as I was," Eric said, "actually I will be even happier."

"Oh, shit," Shit said. "You really will be, won't you? Come on, let's tongue fuck on each other for a few minutes before this old thing pulls in…"

"Just a second…lemme get the sleeve around the rail first." Eric assumed that was what Shit had done with his. "Like yours, there." Reaching though to grab the cloth, pull it back, and knot it, his wrist's knob hit a pipe. Eric grunted—

Shit asked, "What happened? You okay?"

"Wasn't nothin'." Eric tugged tight the double knot he'd made: his wrist throbbed. "You know, it's funny. I was thinking about the old Slide— before they tore it down."

"We had a lotta fun at that place." Shit said. His hand moved over Eric's shoulder, down Eric's bare back. "Yeah, Kyle shouldn't a sold it. For a while, everyone was sayin' how he was gonna build another one, with an even bigger piss trough in it."

"You know why that was, don't you?"

"What you mean?"

"Why it had to go. A couple of months after they pulled it down, I read an article about it in the *Foundation Newsletter*. That's was the year they passed the laws all over the country that gay marriages were okay. So suddenly all over the south, they began diggin' up these old hygiene standards for gay bars and places like that—and there wasn't no way to get The Slide past about half of 'em. Remember, that's what they shut down the Opera over the first time. It was all around the same time."

"It was?" Shit's fingers made scratching motions with their blunt, hard nubs on his back. That, he had often thought, is almost better than full-out sex.

"And you don't remember, do you? Well, they decided they'd just save themselves a headache and tear the whole thing down."

"Was people gettin' sick there, or somethin'? I never heard of nothin' like that."

"Naw—but the laws was about excrement and human waste. It didn't say nothin' about whether it was infected or not. You remember how Dr. Greene was always tellin' us there was nothin' wrong with waste as long as it didn't have no germs in it or nothin'."

"Yeah," Shit said. "I remember." He hooked his hand over Eric's shoulder. "But we did have an awful lot of good times there."

"And it's funny." Eric sighed. "I can't remember none of 'em."

"I remember," Shit said, after seconds, his hand flattening and moving further over Eric's back. "I remember one night when you and me and Bull and Dynamite all went there—to The Slide. And Bull kept tellin' you to get the fuck down in the pee trough, 'cause he had to take a piss, and he was already leakin' in his jeans. I felt him—and he was. Whiteboy was out on loan to some black friend of Bull's that night and came in later. But I remember the three of us standin' in a row along the back bar, Bull drinkin' his club soda, me suckin' on my Coke, and Dynamite with his beer—Bull on one side of me and Dynamite on the other. Bull didn't got no shirt on, and he keeps sayin' to me, 'Go on, Shit—piss in your brother's face, now. Go on—I just done it'—and I'll be damned if I didn't feel him grab my goddam dick up underneath there, and as soon as I let go, you started drinkin' it right down."

"I guess I would."

"Dynamite let go too, and all three of us started tellin' each other the dirtiest things we could think of or make up, probably, and, you know, when Bull got to talkin' about how he shoved his hand up this guys asshole and how he fucked some guy with diarrhea, who shit all over him like some goddamn cow in a barn; and once, down there, you sucked off me and Dynamite both together, with both our dicks in your mouth at once, while we was both pissin'—it got all over you. Then Bull grabbed my hand, under the bar and tells me, 'Hey, I'm gonna piss in *your* hand, boy—and your brother down there's gonna drink it when it goes rollin' off the other side. And, holdin' my hand up under his big ol' balls, that's what he done, and I could feel you holdin' the back of my wrist and your mouth on the side of my palm, drinkin', while it ran across, and suddenly, well, I…"

Eric said, "What?"

"Suddenly I…I don't know."

Eric frowned. "What you mean?"

"I mean, *you* remember any of that?"

"Um…I don't know. Kind of…maybe. That's the sorta thing we was always doin' there, wasn't it?"

"Yeah." Shit nodded.

"But…no, I don't remember that one specific time."

"But I do," Shit said. "Cause, all of a sudden, I fell in love with you."

"Huh?" Eric said. He repeated: "What you mean?"

"I fell in love with you—again, I guess. I always loved you, from the first time at Turpens I put my arms around you and stuck my goddam tongue down your throat. Back then I was thinkin' I better not hold onto you as much as I wanted to 'cause I had to give everybody else a chance. But when you was under the bar, there, at The Slide, and I couldn't even see you, and you was holdin' my hand and drinkin' that sweaty nigger's piss out my palm, I realized you was the most important thing in the motherfuckin' world." Shit stepped around, away from Eric, then moved forward. "You know how I like to fuck everybody. And how I really like it when people fuck with you and other guys so's I can watch—but I wasn't watchin'. I watched Bull jerk that thick black dick he had right off in your face. Damn, that looked so good. I was just…*thinkin'* about it. And all of a sudden it was like it all went up another floor. I reached down and pulled you out from under there, and you came on up, staggerin' into me, and piss all in your hair and runnin' down your belly, and cum all in your ear and your eye, and I put my arms around you and hugged you so tight. I hugged you so tight…so tight! And you was wet from head to toe. And you smelled so good. And you was all salty. And you hugged me back. And Bull started laughin'—at the same time, my daddy said, 'Hey, what's a matter? What you doin'?' And since my dick was out my pants, I said, "I'm peein' all over this cocksucker. What you think?' And then I did it. Holdin' you there and pissin' on you. And the music is goin', and people are walkin' around and some of them are cuttin' up and dancin' and laughin'. And Dynamite is just grinnin' at us—and so is Bull. You remember that—me holdin' you there at the bar? You got one foot in the trough and one on the floor, and I'm huggin' you so…damned tight."

In the darkness, Eric frowned. "I don't, Shit. I mean…well, you was always grabbin' me and huggin' me. And holdin' on to me. And I always, hell, knew, I guess, it meant you was…feelin' somethin' strong. Yeah, and I loved it. But I don't remember any…*one* particular time. At least, not at The Slide."

"Damn…" Shit said.

Beside Shit's shoulder the faintest orange lit the world's rim—out on the water—for what seemed only inches of the horizon's slash.

Shit's face was a carbon silhouette against it. He put his hand on Eric's chest, moved it to Eric's shoulder. When Eric looked down at Shit's hand, he could see a coppery light on Shit's knuckles…and the imbricated darknesses of Cassandra's greens and blues, her squid's arms and her dragon's wings, above and below the skulls circling his own upper arm muscle.

A voice—Shit's voice, so wonderfully familiar—came from the black face with words Eric had never heard him say; or, anyway, had never heard him say together in just that order. "God, I love you so much. And I don't think you ever knowed it." The voice, out of the featureless shape of his face, sounded distressed and confused. "Probably 'cause…you was so busy lovin' me. You know, I could always tell my daddy how much I loved you—and he was just as glad, because he knew we loved him back. That's the main thing I miss most about him. Bein' able to tell him about how much I loved you. But I didn't know lovin' someone was gonna be so…goddam lonely. 'Cause you don't remember it, none."

Shit's hand had gone to Eric's far shoulder. Eric put his hand up and squeezed. "Shit, that's just because we're two different people. That's all. Hey, I remember the first day you took me over there—to The Slide. And how we met Danny Turpens, the one who took up with Big Man. And Jos—the other one who worked there—"

"Was that his name?"

"Un-huh. And even how Dusty had told Dynamite about Danny the first time I went to the Opera. 'Cause I know, by the time we started goin' there with Bull and Mex and Whiteboy and Red and Jay, Jos wasn't there no more. And even Danny didn't stay that long. I remember that—"

"Me, too." And enough sunlight had come through so Eric could see generic features, if not expressions on Shit silhouetted face. "So you *do* remember that."

"Well, that's the thing," Eric said. "I remember it like somethin' somebody told me about us doin', rather than somethin' I actually did myself—" Eric turned to grip the rail with both hands. He rocked with the boat. "I remember how, after we would come in, if we wasn't draggin' somebody else with us, you and me would fuck till the sun came up." As he looked down, stained pale salmon now, froth billowed beside the boat. "I remember suckin' your dick till I thought the damn thing was gonna come off in my mouth."

"Well," Shit said, "yeah. I remember that, too. That's when it would *really* get good. I guess that's somethin'."

Ahead, the mainland boat dock seemed to come loose from the gray black into blue-gray, growing visible.

"And, of course, I remember after they tore The Slide up. And we went with Mama Grace to get his curtains—his drapes—before he gave me my book and we took him to Savannah. But I...swear, I don't remember a single time between 'em, where we went into the place and just stood around and enjoyed it."

Wonderingly, Shit said, "You really don't...?"

"I know I was there—what, a hundred times?" Eric asked. "Three hundred times? But I can't remember nothin' specific."

"You know what it could be." Shit turned to look out at the water. "Maybe, when you're gettin' a whole lot of what you love a lot, it's hard to hold on to." He glanced at Eric. "It could be like Bull told me, back when my daddy died. I just needed to piss on you more."

"Well, that could be." Eric was surprised—and found himself thrilling at the thought. "Maybe...I guess."

A gull mewed and, overhead, turned toward the coast.

* * *

[83] AND WONDER DECADES—even ones some fail to notice at the time—also join the past. Indeed, we've already slipped a year or so into another not quite so wondrous.

* * *

[84] ERIC DROVE ALONG the nighttime highway, through the half-dark. It was a July night, so it couldn't have been too long after his birthday, but ten years later, though the night itself stayed with him, to save himself he couldn't remember which birthday it had been. He was driving back to Diamond Harbor from one of the little towns around. Probably he was driving the car for one of the women on Gilead, but which one, he couldn't recall either...

Shit hadn't come—prying him out of the area, even for a few miles, a few hours, was a major undertaking and long ago Eric had given up on it. Truth was, Eric didn't relish such journeys, either. They got Shit too upset—then Eric would get upset. The easy way to avoid both was not to go. But, this time, he'd gone.

Out the windshield, the sky was deep blue and streaked with wriggles of white, suggesting an overcast early evening in imitation of the end of day. He'd been thinking about the touch screen at the Credit Union—which he used for a decade. Then they'd switched to a point screen—one that rose anywhere on the counter you stopped and looked at. And you didn't need an ID number. It would read your eye, and you could ask it for what you wanted it to do—and you needed very little money anyway because your ID card held all that information. So they'd used that for the last ten years. But, as he'd been saying to Shit that morning, their ten years at the Opera seemed three times as long as their recent decade on the island—which felt like a mere six months.

This time-flying business was kind of weird, when you stopped and really thought about it. How did you judge the duration of anything—at least if it lasted for months or years? The fact is if something was going to happen, say, two years from now—that just wasn't a lot of time anymore. Hell, the fact was, neither was five or ten.

Eric looked out the side window, where, between the dark banks of brush and vegetation in silhouette against the water, was a lake. It was a lucid blue, like a broad mirror at night. Across the water, he saw four, five broad stone stanchions, rising twelve, fifteen feet above the surface. As he pulled away, he realized it must have at one time supported some kind of bridge, long fallen down.

It was quite beautiful, he thought, as droplets began to spatter the glass outside. And now the reflected lights from the other side of the highway filled up the great insect eye the pane of glass had become in the sprinkle, with lights from the restaurants and moving billboard images and window displays along the wetter and wetter highway.

This is a beautiful night, Eric thought. And Shit is cursed—or is it blessed—with the detailed beauty within the circle of Diamond Harbor and environs and no more of the great world than that. And, Lord, that *is* beautiful. But every once and a while, I am allowed to see just a bit more of what glimmers and casts its reflections and images beyond it.

He took in a deep breath.

But I know how large the world is…

Or maybe I don't know anything.

Yes, I'm speeding along down the highway, racing through time, he thought, like that boy racing up the stairs in an old mansion that, for practical purposes, no longer exists…

* * *

[85] FROM THE MARQUEE'S lowest rim—painted with ivory and gold enamel—water fell to the bricks paving the area before the pilasters and plaster curlicues and faces and flutes and flowers that fixed the Opera House's façade to another century, an art and artifice entirely other.

Across the broken pavement, under the porticoes of the derelict Seaside Gardens building, from ages twenty to fifty or sixty, a dozen or so black men stood together, talking. Some were shirtless. Some were barefoot—though not necessarily the same ones. The rain had ended. It was a sunny ten-minutes to ten on a muggy July morning.

From down the street, someone else was coming up—another black fellow in sneakers and jeans, and with a blue T-shirt that had been ripped at the neck, all the way down the front, so that it hung open like a very loose vest. He hurried up by the ply-wooded up display window of the Seaside Gardens to talk briefly with them. Then he took off quickly across the street. As he reached the Opera House ticket booth, he slowed. "Mr. Haskell…?"

No one answered.

He called again, "Mr. Haskell?"

The curved glass of the ticket booth gleamed with the morning's reflection. You walk up to the place, buy a ticket, and go in—and because of the glare, still not be sure who was inside the thing. "Mr. Haskell, we been figurin' because of the rain this mornin', Mr. Jeffers maybe wasn't gonna do his Spring Feed-All." Under the ragged shirt, fastened over his bare chest, he wore a single strap with its heavy wire catch fixed to his ancient bib coveralls. Down the side was a rip, held provisionally shut by two safety pins, between which the material flapped enough to show the dark skin along hip and the top of his thigh.

The glare-distorted figure moved, becoming no clearer. "Rube, how many years you been comin' to the Opera here so you could sit in the first row on the left and pull on your pecker?"

"Huh?" The smile was both bewildered and embarrassed. "I dunno…"

"Well, it ought to be enough years to know by now it takes more than a little rain to keep Mr. Jeffers from making his chili. Besides, it's supposed to be clear for the rest of the day. He's just gonna get started a little late, once Mex gets here to give him a hand."

"Oh," Rube said. "What's he doin' now?"

"What you think he's doin'?"

"He's inside…readin' his book?"

"Hey. Now—that sounds like the Rube I know. See, that's the Rube who sits at the end of the first row in the orchestra and shoots his load all over the bottom of the screen, fifteen, twenty feet away."

"Hey, Mr. Haskell, I don't do that stuff no more—"

"I know you don't. Now-a-days you always got yourself stashed down back of Larry or Dr. Greene's tonsils, where that fuckin' blunderbuss you got belongs."

"Yeah." Rube grinned. "Somethin' like that. You know, Mr. Jeffers does it good, too."

"Yeah, I know *just* how good he does it. He likes to take care of some of you on your wake up call."

Rube nodded. "It's nice you let us sleep here, too. If you want, I can get up there with a pail and steel wool and wash that off the damned screen. After all, I put most of it up there—me and Al, anyway."

"Naw." Behind glare and glass, the figure shifted. "That's okay. It's off to the side. With these kinds o' movies, it don't get in nobody's way. Besides, I kinda like havin' it up there. It gives the older guys somethin' to reminisce about, when some of them could hit that thing, too. The kids who come sneakin' in through the back door on Saturday, it gives 'em something to aim for—in a manner of speakin'; see if they can at least get close."

"That sounds like something Mr. Jeffers would say." Rube grinned.

From behind the booth's curved glass, Shit said, "It *is* something Mr. Jeffers said."

Inside there was a clanking and grumbling. "Aw, man," Rube said. "Here it comes. Maybe I should go in and lend a hand…?"

"Don't worry," Shit said—and he moved behind the glare. The door in the booth's side opened. Shit stepped out. "They got it under control." He closed it behind him, took out some keys and locked it, then went inside. And, as if timed, Jay's pickup rolled up, and Mex got out. He walked to the back, reached over, and lifted out an orange burlap sack of Spanish onions, set it down near the back wheel, stood up again, and reached over for a brown paper bag full of mostly green peppers.

As Eric followed the stove from out of the lobby, pushing it laboriously forward by the handle, Mex stood up: *"I brought the electric chopper, like you wanted. We got most of the fixing, here. Jay, say to wish you the best—He wasn't quite up to coming, this year."*

"Oh," Eric said. "Well, I hope he feels better. Thanks, Mex."

* * *

[86] LITTLE CAN BE said about the transition between the end of Eric and Shit's baker's dozen years managing the Opera House as a porn theater in Runcible and their permanent move—in '41—to the Holota cabin Hugh had been holding for them, without much comment, half a dozen years now, on Gilead.

It came with still another threat to close down the Opera—this time, no kidding, for good—which threats they'd grown used to, and which, though they thought of it as an inconvenience and a major annoyance to them and the men who, now and again, made it a home, they'd learned not to take seriously.

Once it had been cleared out, the movies no longer running on the tan screen with its stains at the side, and the cleaning lights on under the boxes, Eric walked down the left aisle from beneath the first balcony, and, for three minutes, stood on the gray-black runner—last replaced sometime during the (first) Iraqi war with some industrial carpeting, back in another century, and which he'd shampooed with the big machine only last month—looked around at the peeling gilt, at the broken plaster molding over the cavernous ceiling, the mural, around at the orchestra seat backs—among which a dozen were missing, like broken cells speckling a honey comb—and up at the edge of the two rococo balconies, with their iron supports from when they'd held old iron spotlights from which the bulbs had all been removed decades ago. He thought the things you might think he thought, and because he was more imaginative than Shit, even wondered would he see the inside of the place again.

The theatrical space was large enough so that when it held fifty people, as it did most days and nights, it looked no fuller than it did now that it was empty. On weekday evenings, often it held two hundred and fifty—and looked not much fuller. The five or six hundred who gathered from up and down the coast on Friday and Saturday nights between five in the evening and one or two in the morning at least looked like *some* audience.

For the first months in which he'd been here, the daily take had always surprised him—even with the twenty-five to forty-five free tickets that went out to the working men. The first year he'd started coming here with Dynamite, tickets had been five dollars. The first year he'd started working there, on odd weekends with Shit, they'd gone up to ten. Now, after the devaluation, they were seventy-five—which was actually less than five, Dr. Greene had explained to him, at 2010 prices.

There'd always been handyman work to do out on Gilead—on a dozen weekends already they'd gone out there to visit Jay and Mex and found themselves with jobs. Moving out there permanently, especially since their Foundation pension kicked in next month, it'd be fine.

The dozen-plus years they had been at the Opera had encompassed Dynamite's death, Eric's own four-times a year Free Feeds, his first real encounter with Mama Grace's book—that is to say, a real encounter, where, after spending how-long-was-it learning how to read the damned thing, he'd gone through it and really thought about what he was reading.

(*Shit*—he had gone down into the basement lounge among its broken tiles and cracked and missing mirrors—*you know this thing here is really interesting...?* But for the first time, he'd said it with true wonder.

(*Well*—from the bucket Shit looked up and paused, his yellow rubber gloves gripping the mop handle—*considerin' how much time you done spent with it since you got it, I figured it* must *be*, and Eric realized Shit had no idea the level of interest to which his reading had suddenly moved. But that was Shit; it was okay.)

The day they were leaving, Shit didn't even go inside to say good-bye to the place.

He waited for Eric out by the ticket booth—where they had already brought most of the stuff down from the apartment, including Dynamite's four-poster bed frame, already disassembled, loaded it into their pickup to take it out to Gilead.

In later times, on several evenings, sitting in the hardback chairs, on the deck of the Holota cabin, they'd try to fix what year they'd made the actual move and finally gave up.

The fact is, though Eric had gone into the cavernous theater to assemble his thoughts on leaving, he returned to those thoughts—possibly because he had been successful and they *were* now assembled—no more frequently than he returned to his thoughts of his first, forgotten Diamond Harbor wave.

* * *

[87] ALONG WITH A maintenance shack and an open porch on the front, the Holota cabin stood a mile, then half a mile, then only a quarter of a mile outside the Settlement. It was still a fifteen-minute walk from their place to the old Indian graveyard, where Dynamite, Walter and Ruth Holota, and Jay's Uncle Shad were buried.

Yes, Uncle Tom had his grave there—next to Popinjay's (called "Pop"), the parrot Hugh had owned for years.

Mex had been buried there for two years, after the boating accident in which he'd drowned.

It was 2047.

Shit and Eric had been living there for six years, when the highway accident occurred on the mainland—Dr. Elliot had told Jay he'd lost too much peripheral vision to drive. (Probably because he wasn't Dr. Greene, Jay hadn't paid him much mind.) For the last few years Jay, ran the gossip, had gotten almost as pig-headed about such things as Shad had once been—only Jay hadn't been lucky enough to get himself crippled.

At seventy-eight, on one of his rare trips to the mainland, Jay had got himself killed instead. Ironically, he'd run his car into a Johnston Construction earthmover, whose driver turned out to have been drunk and already had four DWI's on his license. People had already started to wonder, given Jay's history with Johnston, if it really was an accident—or even a suicidal gesture.

In the wreck, Jay was the only fatality.

Through the plastic screen door, Ed left Shit and Eric looking at each other, not sad so much as surprised. Then Shit said, with wonder: "We ain't seen him in so long…"

"Not since Mex died, last year—no, that's *two* years, now!"

"Jay's just down the road," Shit said. "How come we ain't seen him in so long?"

"You know," Eric said, "we ain't seen a whole lot of people recently…"

Jay's death had been hours ago, sometime that morning—the funeral and burial were to be the day after tomorrow. Eric expected Ed to come—and he did. Jay had worked hard to make sure that boy got to take over the Gilead boat. Two days later, Eric and Shit went, of course. But—Eric's first surprise—practically every nigger left in the Dump had come out to the island, as well as fifty or more people from the Settlement.

"That's Mr. Kyle," Shit whispered quietly, nodding toward a tall black man in a dark suit, who stood with the black-denimed Bull, over at the side—and said nothing through the entire service.

"Yeah," Eric whispered back. "I *thought* I recognized him…"

Many people had stories to recount over the grave—how Jay had done this or that for 'em, saved this one's life, paid that one's mortgage, helped with that one's younger sister's schooling (who hadn't even lived here), brought heating oil for half the Dump the weird winter it hadn't gone above thirty-five for three whole weeks and had, for two and three days at a time, lingered below freezing. (With his face stinging, Eric had come into the cabin and Shit had grabbed him, and hugged him, and wrestled him around, saying, *Gotta get you warm! Gotta get you warm! Gotta get you warm*…till finally they'd ended on the bed under the blankets.) Tank had cried openly—while Cassandra, with two vague dots of blue under the outside corner of her eye, told how not only had Jay been their best tattoo customer, but after Shad had died and Jay inherited a third of Gilead island, he'd given her the land to move their home and business here. "If somebody wanted to name this place MacAmonville, I sure wouldn't object. Probably Jay would, though—because it was Shad's name, too. Come on here, honey," and she dropped a fleshy arm around Tank's wide shoulders. (Standing at the cemetery edge, under the trees, people chuckled.)

"Or maybe—" Tank paused to blow her nose in a blue bandana— "Jay'd think that was poetic justice—naming a colony of dykes after his…" she looked around, blinking her Native American eyes. "…homophobic uncle." Laughter rose and fell around the grave. Tank smiled, her face still tear speckled.

Eric's next real surprise was the last person who spoke. A good looking, very black man in his late-fifties wore jeans and a sports jacket and a pale blue dress shirt under it, which made him notably better dressed than almost anyone else there. He introduced himself as Ben Forman, and explained he was one of the summer people, who used to come out to the Harbor with his parents, years before, in the first decade of the century. Over a few summers, as a teenager, he had met Jay and Mex and spent some time hanging out with them. "Even after I stopped spending my vacations here, I used to phone Jay up, three or four times a year, and talk with him. Actually, I spoke with him three weeks ago," which was a lot more recently than had either Eric or Shit. "When I heard he was dead, from Hugh Kyle, I flew out here because I wanted to pay my respects and because I wanted to be here for Mex Jalisco. I didn't know Mex had already died two years back in a boat wreck." (The barrel-solid mute's drowning had decided Jay finally and officially to give over the scow to Ed.) "Jay never told me that, when we talked." (The fact was, Jay hadn't told anyone till a month later—even though Mex was buried right here. That had been strange…But it made Eric, at least, realize how far they'd drifted apart.) The man sighed. "He knew I would've come. But I don't think he liked to think about that too much." Among the group there had been random nods, more assenting *mmmmms*. "Maybe it made it too real. Yall know how close they were." Taking a deep breath, Forman looked at the dug up dirt. "Anyway—Jay MacAmon was certainly the most generous man I've ever known. I'm a biochemistry professor now, at Florida State. During the third time I went back to graduate school to get my Ph. D., things weren't going too well—that must have been in thirteen, fourteen, when the Recession was pretty bad. Once I was telling Jay about it on the phone, and how, because my parents had died, I didn't think I was going to be able to afford to keep up school in Massachusetts, where I was. He was so concerned and thoughtful—and made me feel so much better about myself, that I really believed I could withdraw once more, work for a while, then go back again. Only three days later, in the mail, I got a check for fifteen thousand dollars. From Jay. This was more than six years before the first devaluation, I mean, when a graduate student could actually live for six months on fifteen thousand dollars. I called him right away—I didn't know what else to do. I thought maybe it had come from Mr. Kyle. But he said, no, it was a present from Shad. I asked him what he meant. And he told me..." Ben took another breath and looked around at the crowd. "I stayed in Diamond Harbor enough so that I know there's probably nothing yall don't know about each other. So I doubt I'm telling any...secrets. And I'm both surprised and, I guess, not surprised that I know a good number of you, from when I used to come here, all those years back. You guys remember the old Slide—the black gay bar that used to be between Runcible and the Dump? Jay told me that once, back in the eighties of the last century, Shad and some of his cronies had decided they just didn't want a black gay bar around here. So one night, Shad and some boys went over there and tried to torch the place—and the white boys he was with caught some guys coming out and beat up a couple of them pretty bad." Some people made surprised sounds; from others came the assenting mumble of communal memory. "Jay learned they were about to do it, and he phoned the police and the fire department and told them he'd come bust heads if they didn't get over there right away. Well, they did. And they saved The Slide—nobody got killed. Jay was a pretty big fella, and you didn't want him bustin' your head—even if he was gay." Around the grave, people laughed. "They never arrested Shad or anything—he was a local, and that's not how they handled things like that back then. But yall know, later, when Shad had his accident and couldn't walk, Jay took him in and took care of him the rest of his life—he used to say he couldn't kill him because he was his own blood. But the family had some money—not a lot, but I guess it was a lot around here. Jay was the conservator. So Jay said as far as he was concerned, Shad owed a major debt to every black gay man in Georgia—not to mention Diamond Harbor—who hadn't gotten a shotgun and blown Shad's head off when Jay or Mex would come rolling him, in his wheelchair, into town." Forman laughed uncomfortably. "Because yall knew Jay, you know he didn't call us 'black gay men' anymore than he called himself a 'white gay man.'"

Among the chuckles, Black Bull's voice, still impressively deep at eighty-two, came clear and sharp: "He called hisself a nigger-lovin' redneck faggot cocksucker—'cause that's what he fuckin' *was!*" For some reason, at that, no one laughed.

Ben Foreman looked down. He said in a voice that kind of swallowed itself, "Well, somethin' like that. Anyway—because of the Dump, there were a fair amount of us in the Harbor." Across the crowd more folks chuckled. "Permanent and visiting. The day I got my first paycheck as a tenured professor, I phoned Jay and told him I was going to pay him back—at least the principal. Once I got that out the way, we could figure out the interest. Maybe you remember, inflation had become so runaway back then, that sort of thing had become real important to people. And, of course, he told me what I'd known all along. It wasn't a loan. It was a gift. He said if I couldn't *stand* havin' the money in my account, I could pass it along to any other black gay men I thought could put it to good use. I should treat it like it was a stipend directly from the Dump." Forman shrugged. "So that's what I did—I broke it in two and gave it to two young scholars in need. I told them it was grant from the MacAmon Fund." A few people applauded. "Anyway, my point: Shad—or Jay—is pretty much responsible for my being here now, or even more, for my having a job in the Biochemistry Department of Florida State and a really wonderful partner, who I only wish had been able to come with me, and whom I'm going home to when I leave here. Hey, thank yall for letting me tell this about Jay. He was a wonderful man—but yall know he wasn't much for tootin' his own horn; so I wanted to toot it a little for him." He smiled again. "With the rest of us." Then, suddenly looking uncomfortable, he stepped back among the others.

A few people dropped flowers into the grave, open beneath the May afternoon. (It was two days beyond Shit's birthday.) A line filed past, most picking up a handful of crumbly dirt from the mound beside the grave and scattering it like rust on the casket top—dark polished wood, not the simple pine that (Eric remembered suddenly) had been Dynamite's—showing between the white and pink blossoms. Eric said softly to Shit, "Did you know about Shad and The Slide?"

"Yeah," Shit said. "But if you were Jay's friend, you didn't talk about that."

As people were leaving, Eric went over to Forman and said, "Excuse me. My name's Eric Jeffers. That warmed me, what you said about Jay. He was a good friend to us, too. Eh…This is my partner here," because Shit had tagged behind him, "Morgan Haskell." (Listening, Forman smiled, with faint interrogation.) "We live together, right over on the other side of the Bluff. He knew Jay even longer than—"

Only now, Forman's face got an astonished look. Raising both his hands as if he didn't know what to do with them, he exclaimed, "Shit Haskell…!" He shook his head in bewilderment. "Jesus God in heaven! You still here—in Diamond Harbor? Oh, man!"

Shit grinned and said, kind of quiet, kind of smiling, "Hey, Dog Turd. I sure didn't expect you to come out here for this. It's good to see you again, boy."

"I didn't expect to see you, either. Oh, this is...well, amazing—!" Forman seized the shoulders of Shit's faded shirt. "Wow!" He looked at Eric. "Shit was my good buddy, back when I first used to come out to the Harbor—back when we were twelve, thirteen. In fact I think Morgan, you were the one who took me out here to meet Jay and Mex for the first time. They'd just started running the scow."

"So you're a professor, now—and I'm still 'Shit,'" Shit said, in the same low, easy voice, then looked at Eric. "You know, this here nigger was a sweet fuck, too, when he was a kid."

"Oh, now you're gonna tell on me to your partner—?"

Half embarrassed and half infected by the friendship's eruption, Eric said, "Hey, that's okay—"

"Jesus..." Forman repeated. "How many puppies from Jay's kennel are still running around this place?"

"Fair number." Shit glanced at Eric. "Us two was his favorite nigger puppies, back then."

"God, that man could keep us laughin—"

"Among other things..." Shit said.

Only more people had come up to talk; so finally Shit walked with Eric back over the rise. Kyle, Eric noted, with Bull and Whiteboy, had disappeared.

After maybe a dozen steps, Shit took Eric's hand. "That's so you don't have to worry about gettin' jealous or anything. He was a sweet fuck—but he was a little snot, too. At least when he was a kid. If anything, he looks like he's nicer now. I hope Jay taught him some manners."

"If he did," Eric said, "that would be Jay,"

"Could be."

After a moment, Shit asked, "What you thinkin' about?"

Eric laughed. "Dog Turd scratchin' Jay's balls."

Now Shit laughed back. "How's that make you feel?"

"Jealous," Eric said.

Shit's laugh quieted to a chuckle. "That's what I figured."

"But then, you guys got the hair for it." Eric glanced at Shit's head, a third of the scalp bare now. "Or you used to."

"Well, you can scratch mine when you get home. But, yeah, I know; it wouldn't be the same thing..."

That evening, Eric learned that not everybody had approved of Ben's revelations at the funeral. Standing on the deck of the *Gilead II*, talking with Ed, he asked: "But what didn't you like about it?"

The heavy-set black man tugged at the bill of his captain's cap. "I didn't think it was appropriate to be bringin' all that stuff up at a man's funeral."

"I thought it was pretty movin'."

"Yeah," Ed said. "Well, you would." Leaving a surprised—and uncomfortable—Eric, he moved off to help Hannibal, who was working on the boat that summer, to get the ropes tied.

Of all the deaths commemorated in that graveyard, Jay's was the one that had made Eric cry.

The night after the burial, Shit held him pretty much till morning, saying quietly, over and over, "Shhhhh—it's gonna be okay, now. Shhhh, now. You gonna be okay once it gets light."

"But it's so dark in there, underground," which wasn't really what Eric meant. "And he's so alone."

"Naw, he ain't. He got Mex now and all his old friends in there with 'im—like my dad," which was exactly what Shit meant. "And Tom. He'll be all okay."

At daybreak, Eric woke, moved over the four-poster to smell his partner's sleeping breath and body's scent. Shit's arm lifted and slid over Eric's back. Without opening his eyes, Shit smiled—then, after another three breaths, the smile relaxed and Eric knew Shit was asleep again. Eric watched him—the lips barely apart, a sliver of green between the lashes of the weaker eye (the left), and thought, Damn! How did I get lucky enough to be where I can reach out and touch his hip, his shoulder, his feet, his genitals, his jaw?

That was what being alive was...

From under the window shade, copper light fell, banding Shit's cheek, to tangle in his beard's tan wool. The flesh on Shit's head was two-thirds clear of hair, in two tongues back beside the sparse knap down the middle. (What world do I live in that has already given me more than three decades of this to manure life's roots so richly?) A vein scribbled the taut skin of Shit's temple. Shit's face was a third sunk in pillow. (Eventually, we gotta break down and wash these damned sheets and cases—under Eric's hip, the cloth had stiffened from their joint spillage of the last months.) Save for the slight concavity in his cheek where a couple more teeth had gone, when he was like this (and even then...), sleeping, Shit looked to Eric like a drop-dead handsome Georgia redneck, with a touch of the tarbrush about him and not a day over thirty—maybe forty...

Which, save that Shit was actually fifty-nine, is what he was.

After another minute's enjoyment of the proximity, Eric slid his shoulder off of Shit's hand, got up, went into the bathroom, then stepped outside.

Naked, he walked down through brush and long grasses. You would have thought (Eric recalled his upset from the night) that's how I should have felt about Dynamite's stroke.

He glanced back at the bed. He's the exact same age his daddy was when he died.

A momentary eruption of memories assailed Eric: quiet Dynamite and loud Shit, thirty years ago. Shit saying, *Come on over here, you ol' honkey cracker. You threw yourself a nigger bastard and now he's gonna fuck your goddam cracker ass,* then, walking in a few minutes later, Eric would see Shit's butt, bucking over his dad's on the same bed they slept in now, and Dynamite, grinning out from around Shit's elbow, in a way that said, Hey, don't be scared you got a hard-on, it's okay, and with Shit's panting and friendly: *Come on…Join the party…less'n you just wanna…watch and jerk off…*—still made Eric smile.

An arc of sky.

Son, suck your daddy's Georgia cracker dick—

An arc of water.

Nigger, fuck my cracker ass—

(Exhortations Eric had *first* heard and even grown familiar with, under the Atlanta highway, as much as two years before he'd come to Diamond Harbor, but which had moved so easily into what had become his own home, as he'd grown easy with Dynamite and Shit.)

*

The water was flat. The sky ballooned up and so appeared two, five, ten times as large. The seam was the edge of everything and, below and above, both were fabulous with milky colors—the dawn water with wavelets a dozen grays, more blues and greens, microplanes of salmons and silvers, gold and platinum reflections of the creamy glaciers of pastel mist, sweeping out, in filmy cloud, not quite to the horizon. (Most guys getting fucked look blank—he'd watched enough of 'em under the highway or at the Opera or out behind The Slide beneath the moon—with a smile or a grimace reserved for afterward. Getting fucked, Mex and Jay looked about like anyone else. Not Shit and Dynamite, though. Whether someone was fuckin' him or suckin' him, Dynamite had always looked actively happy—as did Shit: a legacy worth leaving a kid.) The actual sunrise was hidden by meridian-high cumulus. From behind, marking the rims with ivory and gold, it hurled rays around a third of the morning. (Dynamite never got no tattoos—even if he always said he liked Jay's…He'd kept them gold tit rings till he died. He'd been buried in them.) Eric imagined, in the hours since Jay's burial, Jay's inks running over Cassandra's outlines, seeping through rock and sand, to the sea, to return Tank's colors to the day, to the ocean, to the air.

(What would them things have been like on Mike...?)

Eric looked over the illustrations on his own arms, first the left, then the right: the Gilead scow, Pop, the serpent borrowed from Jay (Damn, Eric's arm had grown sore under the needle's battering point), Tom...

He'd loved Dynamite, almost as intensely as he loved Shit.

(What amazing luck that he'd gotten to make love with both and—so often—at the same time.)

But he'd wanted to *be* Jay.

Shit was the more emotional man, however, so that—two years before Jay's—when they'd heard about Mex's death, Shit had gone to bed for three days, leaping on Eric every time he'd joined him but otherwise taciturn, till finally he'd broken down and cried for two-and-a-half hours.

Then he got up, more or less all right—just tired. Or, however many years before that, when they'd still lived on the mainland, and Shit had found Uncle Tom rigid under the back steps, or even the afternoon Barbara drove by to tell Eric that Mike's brother Omar had phoned to say that Mike had passed after the last of three heart attacks over two weeks down in Pensacola (*Come on, Shit,* he'd cajoled, once she'd driven off. *There's nothin' for you to cry about. He was my dad—not yours.*

(*Yeah, but I always liked to pretend he was mine—there, when he'd come by to see you. 'Cause he was a nigger, like me*) or the night Dynamite caught his stroke and, in the truck, barely alive, propped between Shit and Eric, died on the way to Runcible Memorial and the marathon night of sex that had followed it...

...*Hell, I'm tired,* Eric kept remembering. But that had been Dynamite, not Shit.

And years ago.

The morning after Jay's burial, when Eric had stood by the water some ten minutes, Shit came down, equally naked, and took Eric's hand. "You okay, huh?"

"Yeah. I guess so."

Shit squeezed and did not let go. "I knew you'd be fine." On three sides the rush and thrash of the ocean rolled into the grass and rock. Yes, Eric was all right—again. Then Shit stepped around in front of him and gave him a long, long hug and whispered, "Come on, let's tongue-fuck a little..."—and got a hard-on, of course (as he would have even if they'd been clothed, Eric thought), that, as it lifted, lifted Eric's penis across it, hardening.

Then they went back up to the house.

"You did pretty good, there," Eric told him. They reached the bellied out screen door; Shit pulled it open. "You didn't try to fuck me but once, all night."

"Yeah, well…" Shit didn't look back. "I didn't mean to bother you none—after you said no the first time. But I thought maybe…" He shrugged…"it would make you feel better. It always does me."

Eric said, "Yeah." He smiled. "I know it does." A naked Eric followed his naked partner through the kitchen.

"While you was asleep, I beat off a couple a times. I put up a pot of coffee before I came down to see how you was doin'. Want some?"

"Yeah," and realized he could half-remember, cradled in Shit's one-armed embrace, lying all but asleep in the rocking bed with the rocking body against him—but not the familiar warm splash and splatter over hip and belly that he would turn to press again Shit's side, Shit's tight-haired crotch, Shit's flexing hand. (*Now don't go washin' that off tomorrow…*"

(*Don't worry. I won't.*) He'd drifted off before Shit's finish…

Like Jay, no, Eric wouldn't wash that stuff off. He liked being marked, like a dog. (Probably it was left over from when he used to fool around with Mex and Jay at their place on the island.) And anyone who said they could smell it, unless they put their nose right down on it, was a liar…

The one-armed embrace had metamorphosed into Shit's upturned hand under Eric's shoulder.

Then like Christmas, like the birth of a child, like a birthday, like the Three Bombs, like Jay's life and Jay's death—and the food and the drink and the reminiscing out on the deck down at Tank and Cassandra's (it had been generally agreed they couldn't put all that work on Hugh)—those events were a day, three days, six days in the past…

* * *

[88] THE CABIN HAD a small back room with a washing machine and a dryer stacked on top, which still—amazingly—worked. Even if Eric and Shit weren't sticklers about softeners and bleaches and separating whites and colors, both were pretty good at throwing their clothes in the machine. Once a ballpoint of Eric's, still in a shirt pocket, made it into the dryer—and melted—so that when Eric pulled the clothes out, the enameled insides were swirled with blue-black. A few stains marred the clothes themselves, but not—at Eric's falling "Aw, fuck!" Shit stepped up, lifted a shirt from those Eric hugged, and frowned at it—so as you couldn't wear them.

Just not for company.

They didn't have much company, anyway.

Once Eric got in there and tried to steel wool the ink swirls off. But after three or four more loads, it was baked on.

They did use those little tissues that were supposed to make your wash softer and smell better, then got all over the floor when you took the clothes out the dryer—Barb had given them three big orange and yellow boxes, and once they'd started using them, they kept it up. It was the morning of Eric's fifty-ninth birthday when he'd gone in to get the clothes out that he realized he was tramping all over the damned things—like skeletal specters of butterflies. He bent down and swiped some up, wrinkled and raddled, white and translucent, dry, soft, and scentless.

Finally stepping away from the unpainted wooden walls of the walk-in closet that was their laundry room, each fist crammed with sixty or seventy of the things, Eric went to shove them in the trash under the sink. "Hey, Shit? You think when you take stuff out the dryer, you could start pickin' up the softeners that fall on the floor? I mean, I ain't been doin' it, neither. But we could both start."

From where he was sitting in the sun on the doorstep in the open door, Shit looked over. "Nope."

"Huh?" Eric stood up and raised an eyebrow. "What you mean?"

"I said, 'Nope.' I can't do that. My hip pains me too bad. I can't bend down and pick up stuff like I could—even last year. It's just arthritis, that's all. But it hurts like hell when I bend."

"Christ!" Eric said. "Why didn't you tell me?"

"'Cause you didn't ask. And I didn't wanna bother you. But anything that gets on the floor, if you leave it to me, it's gonna stay there. That can be your job, if you want. Otherwise, leave it. I ain't gonna complain. But all I'm good for below waist level is fuckin' your goddam cracker asshole—which, as you know, to make happen all you gotta do is fart in my direction." He grinned waggishly. "This nigger's on it like flies on shit."

Even as he worried, Eric grinned back. But two days later, Eric made Shit go see Dr. Elliot (whom they started going to on Dr. Greene's retirement), who prescribed him some pretty powerful painkillers.

* * *

[89] BACK ON THE mainland, when her kidney cancer was found to have spread to liver, spine, and brain, Barbara transferred from Runcible Memorial into the Women's Wellness Hostel outside the city for what her

doctors were sure would be her last three to five weeks. There was a room in which Ron could stay.

For a few days, Eric and Shit visited, too.

The first day she came, Barbara went right to her room. Possibly it was the effectiveness of the painkillers they gave her. When Eric came in to sit with her, Ron got up slowly. He was a hundred pounds heavier than he'd been when Eric had first met him. These days, his suit looked permanently rumpled. But the fact was it was too warm for a suit of any kind, though he always wore one.

Barbara sat in a green leather chair near the window, with a bank of drips and tubes draped down around her, and three different monitor screens with their traveling green and yellow lights on a stand behind.

"Hey," Eric said, smiling. "You feeling a little better?"

She smiled back. "Not really."

He'd been planning to say something to Ron, but the heavy man had lumbered, slowly and silently, out.

"Oh...Do you want to...talk?"

She nodded. "Yes. I'm glad you came in." She spoke slowly. Her collarbones were gaunt between her pajama lapels. Her robe was loose—sizes too big—telling of the more than fifty pounds she'd recently lost, as Ron had gotten more and more shapeless, heavier and heavier. "There a couple of things I wanted to...I guess talk to you about." She coughed, a weak sound that could clear no phlegm. "Oh, you have to go over there and see that postcard Serena sent me. From the moon—sweetheart. Her daughter is a doctor on the moon. She sent it to her mother, in Ghana. And Serena sent it on to me. Really—it's so cute."

Eric turned and went to the desk against the wall. Among several pieces of paper, he saw the card with a picture on it. As he lifted it up, the image—five or six young men and women, most of them looking like high school students, of the sort he was used to seeing on the streets of Diamond Harbor in the summer months—began to wave and laugh and call out, "Hello! Hello—we love you. And we want you to get well." Brown and Asian, they leaned forward and waved. "Mama says you're not feeling so hot—" one of the young men said—"but you'll get better. We know it."

The inside of the lemon yellow room in which they sat was bare of decoration, save a few shelves with some pamphlets on them.

"Isn't that the cutest thing? You'd have to think of Serena, forwarding me something like that. It's funny—"

Eric turned away and stepped back toward the chair in which his mother sat, wedged in with pillows with pale blue covers.

"But I'm pretty sure I could run the business without Ron, if I had to.

I wonder, though, if he'll be able to run it without me."

Eric was surprised. "Well, didn't he start it…?"

"Yes," she said. "But things have changed so much. He's not happy. I wish I could see him happy. I love to see him happy—I think that's my favorite thing in the world. But I guess it's the one thing that's a little too big to ask right now. You know, practically everything we do today involves jack-work matrix schedules. We have clients all over the world. And those partial, double, and unmetered schedules take a sort of…well, maybe it's talent. Or maybe it's just being able to keep details and client needs in order. When Ron was looking at that postcard, it made him laugh. Then he started talking about getting some clients on the moon. I don't know whether we'll ever do that or not. And, one way or the other, I won't be here to see it. Anyway, I've always had a feel for it. Ron just finds that kind of thing a nuisance." Over the years at Bodin Systems, Barbara had taken various courses, quietly and at home, and had become more and more integral to the company—not that you'd ever know it from talking with Ron. Possibly because Eric was partnered with Shit, a near-Luddite, the occasional hint that Barbara and Ron—especially Barbara—were making extraordinary progress in computer matrix schedule provisions always seemed to be an exaggeration, or just more of Ron's self-aggrandizing. Did people really progress—and did they really progress down *here?* "When we started, it was like something I did on the side. But now when you look at our year-end spreadsheets, you can see it's practically taken over. But I haven't been able to do…anything for three months! And I just…well, worry about what's going to happen."

Eric wasn't sure what to say. "Do you do…any work for folks jacking out of Gilead?"

"About sixty of our biggest clients are out there."

Eric was surprised. "I didn't realize…"

"Or they used to be." Barbara sighed. "I don't know where they are now. I hope he hasn't just let them slip away—that he's going to be all right. I know you've always had your problems with Ron. But, really, he's such a sweet guy…This has been so hard on him."

Eric wanted to say, Hard on *him?* What about you…! But he didn't want to argue with her. "Ron'll be all right," he said. "He's pretty good at taking care of himself."

"But so much of it's been having to take care of me, while I just…lie here and let it happen."

Eric smiled. "I guess that's one way to look at it."

Then Shit stepped in. "Hey, Mrs. Jeffers—how you feelin', there?"

"Good as can be expected, I guess." But she smiled.

"Them folks that said we could ride back to the Harbor with 'em are about to go. I thought I ought to let you know."

"Oh," Eric said. "Well, so long Barb." He got up, went over, gave her a kiss. "We'll be back in a few days—and we'll call regular."

"I know," she said, still smiling, though not looking at them.

They went into the hall and, outside the cafeteria, said good-bye to Ron—who was staying with her.

They came back in six days—not a full week. They both were astonished at how much thinner she'd gotten even in that time. After they spent an hour with her together, they both sat for a while in the wooden chair on the deck and talked quietly about how it was really happening, that neither one of them had quite realized before that, yes, she was really dying.

Finally, Eric said, "I'm goin' back in and sit with her for a while."

"Okay," Shit said. "I'll be in the cafeteria—with Ron. That's gonna be *my* good deed for the day. That man better be glad I live with you—and you done set a good example to me for bein' nice to people."

There were no deathbed revelations, not that Eric had hoped for any— except perhaps the last name of his real father. But, with Barb's white hair frizzed against the pillow, behind half a dozen hanging drip tubes, while a blue monitor showing heartbeat and other vital signs chirped in the corner, Barbara smiled and shook her head. "Sweetheart, I never knew it. Really. I didn't. I wished I had—for your sake. I was with him in that little beach shack in Atlantic City for two weeks. Then he was gone—and six weeks later, when I was back with grandma in Hugantown, I realized I was gonna have you. I've told you before. Cash was a sweet guy…in his way. But I don't think you missed out on much by not knowing him. I sure don't feel like *I* did."

Again, Eric didn't argue that that wasn't the point.

Once, when Ron stepped out from among the pale orange walls— there were more tubes than the week before—from the chair where he was sitting Eric said, "You know, Barb, I learned a lot from you."

"Oh, come on," she said. "What'd you ever learn from me?"

"No, I'm serious." He uncrossed his leg and leaned forward. "You're the one who taught me how to go on and live my own life, go after what I wanted, and the hell with what other people said or thought."

"You didn't get that from Dynamite?" She shook her head. "I heard people in town sayin' some pretty awful things about that man—some of them even thought they had to say 'em to me, too—"

"But you didn't pay 'em no mind, did you?"

"Well, I knew you were as happy as a…well, a pig in shit, living over there in all that mess." She chuckled. "God only knows why. But since you were, that was fine with me. I knew if they were doing anything to hurt you, you wouldn't stand for it. And that you would have had sense enough to get out of it. You're a very good person, Eric. And I could tell you were happy. I'm very proud of you."

"Well, maybe it was both of you, then. But I know the kinds of things people used to say about you and Ron—'cause he was black. And because of Mike, too—back in Hugantown. I mean, if I did miss any of the nasty gossip, Grandma would always sit me down and tell me about it. And I knew what some people thought about Dynamite." For a moment Barb looked uncomfortable. "I don't see how, down here, you could have avoided it. I just hope I didn't make things too hard on you. But more than once, I thought, I damned if he doesn't have two of us to deal with now—'cause me and Dynamite were both gossip magnets."

"I kind of wondered," and realized he was about to let the conversation swerve into what he'd really wanted to ask her, now that Ron was out of the room, "since you'd already met Ron and were…well, friendly with him, why'd you want me down here with you, anyway? Why did you make Mike bring me here, since you were already with him—with Ron, I mean?"

Barb smiled. "Well, I knew you loved your dad. But you'd told me you were gay—remember, sweetheart? I figured…" She took a few breaths. "—you'd have…an easier time, with me." From the expression on her face, he realized she was working to remember. "'Cause you were getting older… You know, I met Ron…I mean, more than just to say hello—really met him, the first time, the day after I called up and told you and Mike I wanted you to come and stay for a while. Can you believe that for timing?" (Actually, she'd told Eric that as often as Mike, had he been alive, might have told one of his tales. Was he hoping the answer might finally be different…?) "I thought about changing my mind—I've told you that. But I'm glad I didn't." Her eyes closed and stayed closed eight, nine, ten seconds. They opened. "After all, if you hadn't come, you wouldn't have ever met…" Again, her eyes closed. She made a sound: "Shhhh…"

She had fallen asleep.

In her throat, Barb made a "…tttt…" (*Shhhttt*, she'd said; Eric smiled) before her breath went on.

Sometimes, in sleep, her exhaling seemed to go on nearly a minute.

There'd be a second's inhale—or only half a second's—before the air started out again.

Sometimes Eric thought she was emptying herself. Five times as much always seemed to go out as get in.

Had she started to say "Shit"?

Barb had always called him "Morgan."

Eric sat. His hands felt as if he looked down at them, he'd see them glitter with sparks against his denim thighs. His feet tingled in his work shoes.

Standing up, Eric stepped from around the chair and left the room, turning down the hall to the cafeteria.

The hall walls were pale green.

Just then, in his frayed jeans and bare feet, Shit came out and turned toward him. He grinned at Eric. "How she doin'?"

"Real tired. Did Ron come in there with you?" Eric sighed. "She's asleep again."

"Naw." Shit turned to walk with Eric back through the glass doors of the dining area. "Well, that's what they told you to expect." Then he said. "This is kind of hard on you, ain't it?"

"Naw. It really isn't. At least I don't think so. Yet."

"Well," Shit said. "It'd be fuckin' hard on me, I know."

"Hey." Eric smiled. "She called you by your right name, just now."

"Huh?" Shit asked. "What you mean?"

"Before she drifted off. We'd been talkin' about what would'a happened if I'd never come down to Diamond Harbor, and how I wouldn't have met you and Dynamite. And she called you 'Shit'." He shook his head, grinning at the floor's black and yellow tiles. "It must be the only time I remember her doin' that."

"Really?" Shit put his own head to the side. "Aww, well, that's nice. With her, though, I'd just about gotten used to Morgan. But I'm glad she did it."

"I mean—" already Eric was feeling guilty about what he realized was probably a lie—"she *only* said it once."

"Well," Shit said, "it was still nice. I understand—there's some people that sorta thing just makes 'em uncomfortable. But remember when they had that little piece about the new people movin' to Gilead in the paper last spring, and how I'd lived here all my life? They called me 'Shit Haskell' in the paper and nobody said nothin'. You read it out to me."

"Yeah." That had surprised even Eric.

The next morning, while the boys were sleeping and Ron was in the room with her, Barbara died.

Since they tended to get up before five, after he'd sat with her body for about twenty minutes, Ron came into their room to tell them. They went in—or rather Eric did, and Shit waited in the hall. The night aids came while they were in with her.

Some hours later they said good-bye to Ron, and he turned to shamble off across the parking lot to his Tata. Then Eric and Shit drove back from the Hostel to the Harbor. They left the pickup in the Harbor lot.

That afternoon, at the Gilead dock, they waited for Ed Miller's boat, under the light in its white enameled cone. Though not yet turned on, it made a perch for gulls, who stood on it, stepped around on the yard-long rod, glanced down, or flew off.

At four that afternoon, pushing an overturning hedge of froth and foam, *Gilead II* hove in, half again the size of Jay's old scow. (Eric never saw it without remembering the retired motorized barge.) With the other passengers, Shit and Eric wandered on across the parking lot.

While Eric waved to busy Ed, Shit said, "You know, your mama was the nicest white woman I ever knowed. She said a lot of funny things. But she was still the only woman who really liked me 'cause I was a nigger, 'stead of always being half scared."

"Yeah, well," Eric said, "you know, she liked her black men."

They rode across the water at the rail, quiet, together. Looking out on small waves, Eric remembered the chili in the refrigerator for dinner—he'd made it three days ago, from Mex's old recipe. At the recollection, he grinned. When Jay and Mex were still alive...the morning and its evening he'd learned to make it returned to him for seconds, at the rail of Ed's boat, Shit's elbow was against Eric's forearm, a coin-sized warmth in the afternoon cool. Shit set his bare foot over the front of Eric's work shoe. They looked at the sea.

(That previous morning, starting out for the Hostel, they'd had one of their non-arguments: *It's cold, Shit. It's forty-five degrees. Put some shoes on.*

(*Nope.*

(*Okay. Look. I don't care. They're your feet.*

(*Then don't say nothin'. Nobody there said nothin' the last time about me comin' in like that.*

(Years ago, Eric had given up arguing there had to be something sexual in Shit's always liking to stand in that position, when they were next to each other at the bar or on the boat or looking at a sunset or sunrise over the water. But Shit said, no, it just made him comfortable. *Uncle Tom always use'ta sit down by me and put his front foot on mine, the same way,* and while Eric wondered if that was leftover from some visit Shit had paid to Jay and Mex, for Shit that seemed all the explanation needed for the habit.)

Out at the Gilead cabin, back from the Wellness Hostel, Eric took the chili from the refrigerator (the last time they'd put any "special contributions" in it was long before Dynamite's death) and heated it on the stove.

Once they'd eaten, they walked out on Gilead Bluff, Shit still barefoot, Eric in his work shoes, both men, this time, shirtless.

The way people can, who've known each other very long and very well, without saying that's what he was doing, Shit returned to the conversation begun earlier that day on the far side of the waters. "You know, at first, she made me feel funny that way. But kinda like with you, I got to likin' it." (For moments it seemed as if they'd been talking of Barbara and her death a long, long time ago.) "Course—sure—I coulda done without Ron there…"

Looking across the lead-colored water at the clouded-over mainland, Eric pushed his own work-thickened hands into his jeans' pockets. "Me too…"

Next day Eric went back across and picked up the truck from the lot and drove to Runcible.

His copy of Spinoza was beside him on the seat.

He left it there, when he went in.

In the house where his mother had lived, Ron stood uncomfortably in the pale green living room on the dark green rug, while Eric asked him about a funeral. Eric said he hoped it wouldn't be expensive. But he didn't mind splitting the cost…

In his khaki slacks and jacket, heavy Ron walked to the aluminum legged desk, lifted a mottled black canister, and brought it over. "Her ashes, boy. She told me she didn't want no funeral. She don't got no people, at least around here, except you and me. I know neither of us is too much into funerals. So here you go." Holding it with both hands, he pushed it toward Eric. "You can do what you want with 'em."

Confused, Eric stood there. "Huh…? Why you go and do *that* for?" Hearing himself speak, he realized he was angry. "Why'd you go and…you know, cremate her?"

"That's what she wanted. They have the place right behind the Hostel."

"I know. But she didn't tell me," Eric said. "You didn't tell me, either."

"Well, she told *me*. She said she wanted to be burned up as soon as she went, once they got her eye things off—her corneas—like she wanted, in case somebody needed 'em. Your mama was a generous woman. That's probably where you get it from." He gave a small snort that could have been disapproval. "You can have the ashes, do what you want with 'em. I don't want 'em around. They make me feel funny. I told her I'd give 'em to you. She said fine—she wanted you to have 'em. You know you gonna get a little money, too—from what your grandma left her. She would never touch that. She said that was yours."

"Oh…" Eric said.

"It ain't much—only about a quarter-of-a-million dollars." Ron shook his head. "You know, I can remember, before the second devaluation, when a million dollars was some kind of money. Today, a hundred dollars'll buy about what a ten would when I was a kid. A quarter of a million—hell, you can't get a decent used car for that—you can't get a good car anymore, anyway, with all these damned gasless engines. You guys got a checkin' account? I'll send it out to you." He stood there, shaking his head. "Well, I guess you just decided to throw your whole life away, didn't you? Just couldn't do it, could you? Didn't have the backbone, I guess. That's such a shame—'cause you coulda done so much. Coulda made somethin' outta your life. Coulda had people lookin' up to you, knowin' who you were. Your mama always thought you could."

It was a pretty frequently repeated litany of Ron's, but this time it caught Eric off guard.

"Not that I did so much with my own. But at least I tried, son—I had me a business. I had me a nice house—liked to live a nice life and do nice things for your mama. She was the kinda woman you wanted to do nice things for. And now…" He breathed in. "I'm gonna go spend six months, maybe a few years, with my daughter in Valdosta. That's where my other family is. We'll see how that's works out. We never got along that well but maybe now, 'cause we're both older…You know, the very same week, four years back, that your mama first came down with her cancer, that's when Shells closed down. It sure wasn't what it used to be, back when it first opened—even then. But it was still a nice place. We'd still go over there, maybe once a month, once every couple of months. But when that place shut—I don't even like to drive by it anymore—I never felt like this was the same kinda place again, with real potential and a sense of itself no more. All that artsy-fartsy stuff out on the island, that ain't nothin' with real backbone to it. It's just a place where a bunch of pretentious losers throw away their lives. That's all. Well, at least you was never pretentious about it. You was just a loser, right?" He grinned at Eric.

"Ron," Eric said, "does sayin' stuff like that about me make you feel better about you?"

"No," Ron said, giving an expression of consideration, giving his head a shake. "Naw, but it makes me feel good to know I don't have to be a hypocrite and act phony with folks and can say what's right and true to them to their face."

"Well," Eric said, "if it does make you feel good, you go ahead and say it. Hey, you was gonna gimme that. Right?"

"Oh. Yeah…sure. Here."

Eric took the container. Once the canister was in his fingers, he realized it was some kind of plastic, supposed to look like stone. "I just wished you'd told me, Ron." He took a breath. "Before you went and burned her up. So as people could…you know. Say good-bye."

"I'm sorry." Reaching up with a brown finger, Ron rubbed behind a fleshy ear. "I should have, maybe. Hey, I don't mind payin' for it if you do everything else. But it was like I didn't figure it was really gonna happen. I mean, not so soon—not this mornin'. But that's how it is."

It had been yesterday morning, actually. Or even the day before. For Eric it seemed so long; for Ron it was still present. Eric thought over how the slim black programmer he'd met years before had become a fat black man, usually short of breath, his self-importance, his oddly-fitting suits rarely pressed, which made them look even more like tents than they would have. Barbara had put on weight herself…before the cancer had leeched it away.

Eric took another breath. "I'm gonna bury this in the graveyard, out on the island. It's pretty there. She liked Gilead." He looked around. And took another breath. "Um…you wanna come?"

"Nope," Ron said. Then he said, "Yeah, it is pretty out there. That's good—that's the thing to do. She really liked you boys. Both'a yall. She'd like visitin' out there with you."

"I hope things work out with your daughter." Eric had only vaguely known of Ron's former family.

"Well…" Ron sounded faintly lost. "That's nice of you to say it."

Driving back to the Harbor in the pickup, the canister beside him, standing on the book with its torn cover, it struck Eric, probably Ron's comment about Barb liking them was his way of saying Ron didn't, really—like him or Shit. Eric grunted. I should have brought him a pot of chili. After all, Ron was alone now. Eric grunted again, smiling: Maybe Shit and me could'a spiced it up special for him before I brought it. Or maybe taken it around and let all the niggers in the Dump add their contributions, the ones he could still ask for something like that. Naw, it would've been wasted on that nigger.

Back at the five-room Gilead cabin, Shit said, "So—he just went and had her burnt up and didn't say fuckin' 'boo' to you? Well, that's fuckin' Ronny Bodin, all the goddam way. I hope now your mama's gone, you don't intend to bother with that nigger no more. If he wants to pretend ain't nobody else in the world besides him, leave him alone and let him."

Uncomfortably, Eric said, "I'm gonna take these out to the graveyard."

Shit reared back in the kitchen chair, the front two legs off the floor, arms crossed over his bare chest. Dark beams crossed the white, low ceiling. "You gonna scatter her or you gonna plant 'er?"

Eric was surprised that Shit was even aware of the difference. In that canister, now on the table corner, *was* Barbara—he realized—not just something that had belonged to her. "I'm gonna make a hole and put 'em down in there—near Jay." His mama and Jay had been pretty good friends back during the years she'd waitressed at the Coffee & Egg (not that he'd ever told her what went on at Jay's house on the island, when every so often he'd visited for a day or two). "I'll get a shovel—ain't nobody gonna be out there now to see, anyway. You don't have to come."

"Like hell I don't." Shit's chair legs hit the woven rug that had ended up on the kitchen planks, under the table's slanted legs. Lankily, he stood. "That's your mama, Eric," he said, as though confirming Eric's insight. "I'm goin' with you. I never had a real one. But I sure had my daddy—he kinda did double duty, I guess. You go do what you gotta do. But once you do it, I'm gonna give you a hug and not let you go for a *real* long time."

In the kitchen corner, Eric started looking for a shovel. Rakes, spades, pick axes, long and short handled hoes leaning there clanked on one other, till he pulled one loose.

*

At the cemetery, with its grove of pines to the side, above which the sky was half gold and half gray, the road ran the whole mile up from the Settlement—and halfway through the graves. Above, leaves gnawed away the blue edging. Since he used to come out here back when they were building, he never looked at the thing without thinking of the graves under that tarmac—graves paved over how many years now. Hadn't even moved them when they put the road down. Eric still felt odd that he couldn't remember any of the names—not one—on the markers that once stood where the road ran.

Lots had been Indian, though.

(Had there been some Mikkos? Some Jumpers? Those were Creek names old timers occasionally mentioned, on the mainland…)

Somebody—probably a particularly militant lesbian from the Settlement—had put up a sign toward the cemetery's edge, on a piece of plywood of the sort they used to board over windows in wind storms. A post at either side, it was painted white. Inside red quotation marks, black letters read:

REMEMBER, THE DEAD DON'T CARE IF YOU'RE GAY.

Shit asked, "What's that say? I know it says 'don't' sumpin'"—the only word you might find on a road sign, the only words he could read.

Having found the two slanted boards that were the grave markers for, respectively, Jay and Mex, lopsided and already hard to read, Eric sank his shovel in the ground and tossed dirt to the side. Now looking over, he read the sign out loud, "Remember, the dead don't care if you're gay." Chuckling, again he pushed the blade into the gray and sandy earth, with its sparse grass, to pry up a second spadefull.

"What's that supposed to mean?" Shit wanted to know.

"It's kind of a joke, I guess." Eric dug some more.

"I don't get it," Shit said.

"Well…" Eric paused. "You know how Jay's Uncle Shad was always goin' on about how guys fuckin' around with each other was unnatural and how black and white folks together was evil in the eyes of the Lord and how we would all go to hell and everything?"

"Yeah. That's 'cause he was crazy."

"But you see—" Eric nodded across the mounds. Four graves over was the one in which Dynamite was buried, six feet down by the retractable steel measuring tape Mama Grace had brought with him that day—"*now* Shad don't care."

Three graves further on was Shad's.

"How's he gonna care?" Shit asked. "He's dead."

"Well, that's the *point*, Shit!"

"But it don't make no sense."

"Yes, it does." Eric was not planning to go down any six feet. For a plastic can of ash, two or three was enough. This time, one shoe on the shovel's edge, again he pushed the blade in—and felt it hit some piece of wood. When he worked it loose, roots and rocks fell from it back into the hole: six inches of broken plank. From a coffin…? Though never populous, the graveyard did go back to Indian times. "Some people get so upset about it when they're alive, like Shad—especially people who think they're goin' to heaven and you're goin' to hell—they get everybody around 'em all worried about all the bad things they're gonna be thinkin' about 'em through all eternity. Then somebody comes along with a sign like that and it reminds everybody that it really don't make no difference."

"But it *don't* make no difference," Shit said, "dead or alive. So why's it funny?"

Whether newspaper cartoons or jokes on the TV at the bar, this sort of thing was a monthly argument with Shit. Eric took a breath. "It ain't that important, Shit." Eric turned back to dig.

"Yeah, like your damned Spinoza book. I think a lot of people is stupid and say stupid stuff like that, 'cause it's *supposed* to be funny." He grunted. "Or philosophical."

"Well…that's what a joke is, Shit. Somethin' stupid that's funny."

"But it *ain't* funny. It just don't make no sense." Shit grunted again. "They gonna hafta put a fence around this whole place soon, to keep people from doin' what we doin' now."

"If they do, how are you and me gonna get each other buried?"

"We'll just walk in," Shit said. "Like we did with Tom. I dug that one—"

"Uncle Tom? That wasn't sneakin'. There just wasn't nobody here, except Mex and Jay." Today there was a gravedigger, Cora, in the Settlement, who used an electric backhoe—and who, everybody said, was never around when you wanted her. "But you know, they don't really let you bury pets and people in the same graveyard."

"Well, that's stupid. Hey, I'll dig the rest, if you want. But maybe you wanna do it 'cause it's your mama—"

"Naw, that's okay. I'm more than half done, anyway." After a few more shovels full, Eric asked, "You ever think about *your* mama, Shit?"

"Yeah," Shit said. "All the time, when yours was dyin'." Then he looked down from pewter clouds. "But mostly I don't."

Eric took the canister from Shit, stooped down, and put it in. While he was tamping it, suddenly Shit called, "Hey, Frankie. You can come out…"

Eric looked. Back among the trees they heard leaves brushing leaves. Eric frowned—but saw nothing.

Shit called. "Come on. I'll give you ten dollars, if you come out."

Eric thought: What's that, not quite what twenty-five cents used to be when I first got here? A lot of people even let you use the old quarters for a current ten spot, if you wanted. He looked at Shit, who waited like a dog at point. "Did you see her?"

Shit relaxed and shook his head. "Poor kid. I wish she wasn't so damned scared. We ain't gonna hurt her." He looked back at Eric. "Course, when I was her age, I was scared of ever'body, too."

Eric pounded the ground again. "Unless you was fuckin' 'em."

"Well, yeah…" Shit chuckled. "I guess so."

Eric stood up again. "Poor kid." With the back of the shovel, he bumped the earth some more, while Shit went back to humphing about how only lesbians would put a joke sign up in a graveyard, anyway, funny or not. Then practical Shit got a branch and raked around over the earth, so that you really couldn't tell how long ago it had been dug. "Since we don't got a permit," he explained. "We might as well be on the safe side." Then they walked up the trail to their cabin, the trees closing out the sky. Halfway, Eric realized Shit's preoccupation with the joke had put the long hug out of mind. He sighed. "I'm gonna leave a covered dish of chili out back for Frankie, when we get home."

"If it's gone in the mornin', it's just gonna be some damned raccoons what got it."

"Well," Eric said, "'coons gotta eat, too…Maybe she'll get it."

Once more in the kitchen, when they were sitting at the table, Shit suddenly stood up from his coffee mug, came over to Eric, and put his arms down to hug him. Eric's face pressed against Shit's warm, flat belly, chin against the ridge of Shit's jeans. (Well, he had remembered.) The muscles were still hard, but the skin over them was looser now. Under his cheek Shit's belly was warm; the denim under Eric's chin was cool. Behind Shit's back, Eric grabbed his own wrist and hugged. One of Shit's hard hands was on the back of Eric's head. He remembered how Jay would rub his or Mex's—or really, anyone's—head, when you were sucking him. Yeah, he'd been thinking about Jay. He thought now: And I ain't a puppy no more. I'm an old dog. Shit's other hand splayed over Eric's shoulder. Eric's arms were around Shit's waist. "What you thinkin' about?" Shit asked.

"Frankie, my mama, her mama—I mean, she musta had one—your mama…" Breaks caught on Eric's voice. "Just stuff…"

Shit said, "You wanna cry some?"

Against Shit's belly, Eric nodded.

"Go on—it's okay."

"I wanna," Eric said. "But I can't."

* * *

[90] IT WAS SPRING when they made friends with Anne Frazier. Like them, a recent island resident, her hair was short and brown; her skin was lightly tanned. Forty-six or forty-seven, out on Settlement Road, she had a kiln in a shack behind her house. Across the water in the Harbor and in Runcible, she rented shelves in three ceramic shops. Probably she had money of her own—that was Eric's notion. Although her large copper, bronze, and glass-green pots were expensive, he couldn't imagine she sold enough to support herself: her house was twice the size of their own cabin—a prefab but a good quality one. It had three rooms on the second floor, four on the first. Her kitchen had a skylight, and a recent wind had blown a couple of those things loose in other houses on the island's far side.

At Thursday's outdoor market, they were standing before the sign beside the awning over the boxes that still said DUMP & SETTLEMENT PRODUCE. (Back on the mainland, the eastern edge of the Dump had been bulldozed flat for beach parking a year ago, someone had told him. But who…?) On the commons, the Settlement Market is where, roaming among craft tables and food kiosks, they'd run into Anne, carrying her blue canvas bag. Over his shoulder, Eric had his orange one. Between stalls of green and fuchsia rhubarb, red and yellow tomatoes, green and red apples, and wooden trays of shaved ice spread with mackerel, cod, and shellfish, she told them how worried she was that hers would blow off too, and Eric told her they'd put up a wind trap around it for her.

People milled before the display tables.

"See—" Shit stood beside his bicycle (he rode their heavier purchases to the cabin; and, since he'd fallen and twisted his knee—badly enough for Eric no longer to trust himself on his bike—Eric carried the lighter ones), explaining—"if you get a real hurricane, like Edna, back in 'oh-nine, there ain't nothin' gonna keep that thing on. Don't be surprised if you lose your whole damn roof. But it'll do for most. Those prefabs like you got are solid. When they first started puttin' 'em up, I thought they'd come apart like matchwood. But they surprised me. For somethin' that goes up in ten hours, they hold together pretty well."

The next day, they arrived at three o'clock.

On Anne's sloping shingles, the trap was an eight-inch chimney of metal-braced planks around the skylight's lower half. With wind from the east, it served as a break and counteracted the Bernoulli effect that tried to lift the whole thing off and fling it twenty feet or more across the road in any wind over sixty-miles-an-hour. When wind came from the west, the trap caught the air and built up pressure to cut the natural lift that a full chimney all around would have created.

Inside, over the kitchen's black floor, flowered with images of foot-wide crimson and purple blossoms, Eric—on the upper steps of the aluminum ladder—reached through the six-inch opening with his cordless and buzzed the last screw into the brace that held the chimney wall vertical. Pulling his hand in, he scraped his knuckles on the edge, muttered, "Fuck…!" and came down the ladder again, as Shit walked in from outside.

"Well, if that don't do it, nothin' will." Shit grinned.

In bronze earrings and a bronze neck chain (and, like Shit, barefoot), Anne said, "Hey, I can't thank yall enough. I hope I'm not being forward. But I've got a tub of ribs in my refrigerator. My family was supposed to come out from Manchester this weekend. All yesterday and the day before I was making ribs and potato salad—not to mention three strawberry rhubarb pies. But my brother called this morning and canceled. Last night he broke his ankle at some political demonstration." Roughened from clay, she clasped her knuckley hands before her drab military slacks. "Would yall do a kindness to an Alabama gal on her own in Georgia and have supper with me? Ain't nothin' fancy."

Eric laughed. "Well, that's nice, ma'am." He pointed a thumb at Shit. "You know, I love 'im to death, but he ain't never learned no table manners."

"Huh?" Shit said. "Hey, I can eat polite. When I have to."

"Don't be silly." Anne made a dismissive gesture and turned. "I'm from forty miles southwest of Mobile—I had four brothers and six uncles, about as country as you can get. Really, I'd appreciate the company. Come on—we'll eat ribs, drink beer, watch television, and swap lies. How's that sound?"

"Well," Eric said. "That's nice, but—" about to decline.

But Shit said, "Okay. Yeah. That sounds good. We ain't beer drinkers. But maybe you got some pop—"

So that's what they did.

There was potato salad and slaw—

Red and black and running with sauce, the ribs came out of the kitchen's convection oven in a big aluminum bowl.

There were whipped turnips—

"I never had 'em before," Shit said. "You wouldn't be offended if I passed on those?"

"Oh, for God's sakes." Anne came in with a dishtowel over one sunburned and freckled shoulder. "Eat what you want and forget the rest."

—and green beans.

"Hey." Shit already had sauce in his beard. "These ribs are tender, ma'am. They're almost as good as yours, Eric—"

"I'm gonna take that as a compliment."

"Yes'm," Shit said. "If I didn't have my store-boughts in, I could still gum the meat off these things."

Eric said, "Do you think you could hold off and wait for the rest of us before you got started? Grab a napkin and wipe the stuff off your fur. We're company, now."

Shit blinked, surprised. "Oh, I'm sorry."

But Anne had gone out and came in now with Coca-cola. "Go on. It's there to eat. Someone down in town told me yall been together since yall were children—that yall go back to the twentieth century."

Following Anne, they sat around the coffee table.

"Naw—we got together in July oh-seven." Eric chuckled. "We're old, but we ain't *that* old."

Shit said, "We was *born* in the twentieth century—him in ninety, me in eighty-eight."

"That's wonderful." Turning to Shit, she picked up a beer bottle. "Can I open one of these for you? Maybe you'd like a glass…"

"Don't waste a glass on 'im, ma'am," Eric said. "He wouldn't know what to do with it."

"Course I do. Balance it on my head, toss up boiled peanuts, and catch 'em in it." Shit grinned over the white wall of his teeth. "Yeah—we ain't never been drinkers. Though my daddy would have a bottle or a can now and then."

She laughed, coming back with a large bottle of orange pop.

"Oh, you musta known he was comin'," Shit said. "That's his favorite." A moment later, the bottle cap fell on the coffee table's olive colored surface. "Here you are." With a questioning glance at Eric and a nod back from him, she set down a blue ceramic plate, which clinked the stone. After a serving spoon of turnips, a spoon of beans, and one of potato salad, she picked up the plate and passed it over. "Take as many ribs as you want. Use your fingers—I'm gonna."

Eric, too, was wary of the turnips. But he tasted a forkful. "These are… good."

"Mash 'em with vinegar, butter, lemon juice," Anne said. "There's nothing better. You sure you don't want a taste, Mr. Haskell?"

Shit said, "Well, maybe…"

"That's just polite," Eric explained to Shit. "See, ma'am, he was raised by his daddy—and like you said, his daddy was about as country as you could get. Dynamite was the best man in the world…once I was sixteen and come down here, he raised me, too. But there was never no mama in that house at all."

"See, Eric here," Shit said, "was my mama and my daddy and my first main fuck—excuse me, there—once my daddy died. Eric here's a pretty damn wonderful feller. I was nineteen—we met there in Turpens Truck Stop, right in the back john."

"Oh, yes," Anne said. "I've heard about that place."

"It's still there—too. It was kinda wild—sometimes it still is."

"Didn't they used to have a ladies night or something? Somebody was telling me about that."

"Yeah," Shit said. "Saul and Abott was real proud of those."

"But that was later—in the thirties. And it wasn't just a night, either. It was a whole weekend—last weekend in the month, all during the winter. They'd close the place down for men, and women would come from all over—and cruise the halls just like guys. A lot of 'em were truck drivers, too. That's when we were in Runcible, managing the Opera House. Turpens' dyke night's one of the things that started bringing all the women in for the Settlement, here."

Anne chuckled. "You know, I think we've lost a lot of ground since the thirties. That was a decade where there was real hope for people, not just gays and lesbians—for everybody."

"Yeah, well," Shit said. "But Eric and me got together a long time before that, and…in about two seconds, too. My daddy was right there with me, and as soon as we went out, I asked him if he thought there was any chance of me gettin' to this little guy again who'd come in there said he was movin' to the Harbor. And he just drove me over to the Lighthouse where his mama was workin' to wait for 'em. 'Course we couldn't say anything 'cause we done met him in a truck stop john, there, and it was his mama."

"But I didn't know that—" Eric laughed—"and as soon as I saw 'em, I thought they'd come to blab about everything to my mama, to my dad. I was a real dumb little shit…excuse me. But you know what I mean."

Smiling, Anne nodded, as if to encourage the tale.

"I was pretty scared, too—that he wasn't gonna wanna even talk to me no more. But my daddy said, 'Why don't you wait and see when he shows up?'" Shit breathed out, slowly, as if, for a moment, the anxiety was still with him. "Hell, I don't know what I woulda done without Eric. Best partner you could have. He can read. And write. That's real important, 'cause I can't. It's a lot better when at least one of you can do that. Hey—" Shit had just tried the turnips—"you know, these ain't bad? Easy on the store-bought, too."

"Mmm—" Anne forked up some potato salad—"I had a partner up until two months ago. Her name was Deborah. But she was young…we were together for seven years." She looked down, then up. "When you're nineteen—that's how old she was when I met her, a student in my pottery class in Charlotte—someone thirty-five or thirty-six seems worldly and knowing and romantic all at once. Then, you reach twenty-six, and the person who was thirty-five-year-old is suddenly on the other side of forty; we start to look like one-time interesting has-beens. That's what I turned into for her."

Shit asked, "You here waitin' for her to come back?"

Anne shook her head. "No—she's not coming back." She took in a long breath. "She wants to…to have fun, have a good time. And, well, she should have one. I want her to."

"Can't you just let her run around," Eric asked, "and have some hot soup waitin' when she gets home—or a good pot of coffee? That's what I used to do whenever he'd get randy and run off."

"Yeah." Shit dug into more potato salad. "He makes some good soup, too."

Eric said, "And he makes good coffee."

"The coffee was for when *he* was cattin' around." Shit took another big bite.

"I suppose," Anne said, "men can do that—some of them. Gay men, I mean. Some women can, too. But I turn into a crazed, jealous harridan, and when she'd come back I couldn't understand how she could do that to someone she loved."

"Sometimes—" Shit pulled more pink up from the rib bone—"it's pretty easy. And with him," he glanced at Eric, "he says he likes it—'cause I always come back horny as a motherfucker—excuse my French. He sure did. You know, it ain't somethin' she's doin' to you. She's doin' it to someone else."

"Well," Anne said, "that's the problem. And it makes me act like somebody I don't like very much."

"Now, you remember," Eric said, "a long time ago? I did tell you once, Shit, I didn't care about what you did with other people. But sometimes, it could make you act pretty funny around me when you got back. That would get me a little crazy sometimes."

"Yeah, I do remember that. I thought about that one a long time. I changed the way I acted, too, didn't I?"

"Yeah. You did."

"See—" Shit finished his cola and set the bottle down—"that's why we don't got no television, him and me. It's always telling folks how they should expect the people they love to give it all up for them, and how the person they love owes them that. And if they don't get it, they feel insulted and disrespected and got the right to act crazy-angry and bust the person's head open or kick 'em out. That ain't right. You love somebody, sure, you try to make 'em happy. But nobody owes you their whole life when you ain't there. That's nuts."

"Well, I guess I'm nuts, then." Something tightened in her voice. "Because that's what I want. Believe me, to me it don't sound so unusual."

"It ain't," Shit said. "That's what's wrong with it."

Eric wondered if Shit had gone too far. Shit had his opinions, and once he started he could run on.

But Anne retreated into explanation. "Oh, of course, I don't want the person's whole life—though Deborah used to say I did. I just wanted the security of knowing that the intimate part of our relationship was...only for us. And, yes, I do feel demeaned when I find out she's...Oh, you know what I'm talking about. I'm willing to give that up with other people. Why can't she?"

"Maybe," Shit said, "'cause she's twenty-six. And maybe nobody's tempted you, yet. Aw, hell—it used to make me angry, seein' people, gay ones, straight ones, gettin' all twisted out of shape 'cause they think the world owes them that. Now it just makes me sad—'cause so many really nice people, like you, are all walkin' around unhappy, thinkin' they ought to have had somethin' that, because they can't get it, everybody else thinks they're fools or stupid for doin' without."

"Well, I don't think I'm a fool for wantin' it."

"But you think you're a fool for puttin' up with not havin' it—'cause the television says you're *supposed* to have it."

"You mean you think—" Anne managed a smile, but Eric thought she had to work at it—"I am a fool for wanting it?"

"I didn't say it," Shit said. "But him and me—" he glanced at Eric— "done okay without it."

"You're lucky."

"Naw," Shit said, "we just stay away from the TV."

"You know, for all his talk," Eric said, "we don't do too much tom cattin' around no more—neither one of us." He chuckled. "It's easy for him to talk, now we're gettin' old—"

"—and ugly, too." Shit laughed. "It was one thing when we used to manage the dirty movie house over in Runcible. It was all just downstairs. We never even had to leave the building to get anything we wanted— either of us. And I mean *anything!* I thought I'd done everything when we started at that place. But we hadn't tried nothin' yet."

Nodding, Eric chuckled.

"But right now, we're probably the only ones who can stand each other in the sack, anyway—"

Anne looked up and, smiling, shook her head at the notion's outrageousness.

But Eric noticed she did not contradict Shit.

"It's funny." Anne sighed. "As nice as Gilead is, and as much fun as it is living in the Settlement, sometimes I think you can find a version of what I just told you in one-out-of-three houses all along Settlement Road. Really, they ought to call it Heartbreak Highway. Anyway—" She sat back and looked around her living room—"you can't want to spend the evenin' hearing about another old dyke's depressing love life."

"Damn," Shit said. "You ain't old. I bet you ain't forty."

Anne looked at him sideways. "Shit, you are a liar headed for hell."

(Eric had noted she did not use his partner's name often, but when she did, he liked her decisiveness.) "I'm nearer fifty. You're trying to be polite—"

Below palm fronds, on the electronic equipment by the wall a light changed from red to green. Simultaneously, a bell sounded three times.

"Oh." Anne looked over at it. "I'd said something about watching television. There *is* a program I'd wanted to see…But if it's not something that interests you, I'm recording it anyway. I can watch it later. You said you two weren't really—"

"No, ma'am," Shit said. "No. Let's watch your show."

"With all his talk about TV," Eric said, "as long as it's at somebody else's house, there ain't nothin' he likes more than watchin' television."

"He's right," Shit said. "Don't mind my runnin' on…"

"Oh," Anne said. "I see. Well, this one shouldn't bother you too much. It's a science program." Anne turned in her chair, waved one hand.

The wall opened.

Each a meter high and a meter-and-a-half side to side, three screens slipped forward and joined along their edges, to make a single, curved, near fifteen-foot screen, end to end. The blues and reds of the title and opening scenes slid across, gaining a third dimension. Bits of light, gleaming letters, and numbers shot into the room, then retreated deep within. Opening drumbeats sounded.

The show—the announcer, an authoritative woman with a European accent, explained—concerned the Universe, nothing less. Largely, it would survey radio pictures from the Yang-Kopffus Doppler Array, a collection of some twelve hundred radio dishes that had taken seven countries twelve years to send up, arranged in a pattern between the orbit of Saturn and the orbit of Jupiter, each just under six-hundred kilometers from the next, so that they were able to "duplicate" the image received on "an eye with a retina half again the area of the planet Earth, stretched out flat." Guided by initial pictures from the old Webb Telescope, that had replaced the ancient Hubble, still orbiting after thirty years, when its images were gathered and properly enhanced, the Yang-Kopffus could observe the red dwarfs and their planets—even continental forms on them—within a hundred-fifty light years; more, it observed the ribbons formed by the millions of galaxies weaving through a universe three times the size it had been assumed to be as late as 2002. As well, it could make out, among those ribbons, the faint emissions of many millions of what were called, somewhat inappropriately, "dead galaxies," alternate ribbons of galaxies older than the bright ones people had grown used to, made up of billions of small, dim stars, most all but extinguished, which comprised as much as a third of the matter in the greater multiverse—not the fabled and still mysterious "dark matter," but something like it. The announcer talked of "weird galaxies" swept clean of all black holes and the great rent in the web—"the Axis of Evil, as its discoverers at Imperial College, London, Kate Land and João Magueijo, named it back in 2005—and the compensatory bright spot among them," two- or three-hundred-thousand light years away. She went on to talk of the recent success of certain theories of asymptotic freedom and the subversion of the Higgs sensate…

"That Axis of Evil," Eric said. "That's like the Dump. And the bright spot is like the Settlement out here…" He looked at the TV flicker on Anne and Shit's concentrated faces. Neither had said anything.

Over an image of headlights streaming through the night along intertwined highway underpasses and overpasses, intersecting and interweaving roadways near some city, the announcer intoned, "Consider each headlight here a collection of many galaxies, each galaxy made up of two to six billion stars, rotating around a central black hole, moving along through infinite night. Now assume we can see much better than we ordinarily do, and…watch…" The scene switched to the green fire of nighttime cameras and, between the streaming highways, they made out sheets of marshy water, and, here and there, stretching through them, strips of dark land. "Think of the streams of cars with headlights as ribbons of visible galaxies. The water that we can see on either side of the highway is the empty space between those galactic ribbons. The struts of land, here and there between the roadways through the water, are like the ordinarily invisible ribbons of 'dead galaxies,' which weave beside and between them…"

"I never seen nothing like that on no highway—"

"Yes, we have, Shit—when we went with Mama Grace to take his furniture up to Savannah…"

After an hour and a half of galactic and stellar images, it was over.

"Now, see—" Anne waved the show off. The screens split and backed into the walls—"if my brother had come up, we'd have had to watch the next program. That's a show about how the world is only six thousand years old and all the species were put here ready made. And all variations from that original pattern are evil—" she laughed—"like us. They say homosexuality began not more than fifty years ago, when the Arabs blew up the towers in New York. The planes that ran into them released a special gas that started turning Americans gay."

"I know it's a long time," Shit said. "But I remember when them things come down. I been queer all my life—a long time before that. And so was my daddy."

Anne laughed. "Now, don't overdo it, Mr. Haskell. How could your father have been gay?"

"Well, he was."

"And what about all those famous people who were supposed to have been gay—Shakespeare and Sappho and that Woolf woman and Plato and Alexander the Great?" Several restaurants and even clothing stores by now in the Settlement displayed posters of famous lesbians and gay men. Eric had pointed them out to Shit.

"That's supposed to be part of the plot to fool people into thinking gay people have been here longer than we have—and besides, they weren't Americans."

"Baldwin…?"

"He was African American." Anne laughed. "Apparently, they don't count either."

Shit grunted. "They don't count me, 'cause I'm black—?"

Eric said, "That Axis of Evil was enough to make you think *that* was the religious program."

Anne laughed. "Sometimes that's what it looks like. Well, whatever—the point is," she went on, "that's called a science program, too. And people believe it. I don't see how folks can watch both of them and not realize one of them is taking them for a ride. Of course—" she eased forward in her chair—"most people don't watch both. And I know a whole lot of people who won't watch either one, 'cause they think it's…kind of dirty. But I always loved that stuff. Science, I mean. That's my own real perversion."

"Probably that's why I don't watch it—'cause I don't wanna argue with people like that," Eric said. Then he added, "Thank you for dinner, Ms. Frazier. That was good. And that show was interestin'. But we gotta get home. Usually, we ain't out this late."

"That's a *big* television," Shit said. "Your eyes could get tired watchin' that thing."

"You don't have a television at all? Even a little one?" She walked behind them to the door. Finally, though, she said, "I'd hate to think all the pain I've suffered is just because I'm a dupe to social conventions."

"Well," Shit said, "most of the pain most people suffer is because 'what should' is so far away from 'what is,' I mean, unless it's a physical pain—and even then."

"Last time I was over in Montgomery, I saw a tree nursery that had some willows they said they could ship right out here to the island for me. I was thinking about getting a couple for the back."

"You gotta watch out for them willows," Eric said. "The roots can do in your foundation. And run havoc on your water supply while they're doin' it, too."

"*Pshaw!*" Stopping at the doorway, Anne laughed. "They're pretty! Now, here's your money for the wind trap. It's all there, like we agreed."

"Ma'am, after that dinner—" Shit shook his head—"I don't know if we can charge you for—"

"Course you can! Go on take this, now. I don't want to hear that. Yall did your work. Yall take your money."

"Well, thank you." Eric took the sheaf of hundreds, folded them, and put them in the pocket of his shirt with the torn-off sleeves. "Good night, ma'am."

Shit said, "Good night, ma'am."

"Good night, Mr. Haskell," she said. "Mr. Jeffers. And thank yall for keeping an old lady company." Behind them, the door closed. When they'd stepped out, the front light had come on.

They started down the lawn path to the dirt road. Once they were beyond the motion detector's range, the light went out again. Between the trees, as their eyes adjusted, stars broke through the moonless dark. "I like 'er," Shit said. "She's like your mama used to be—'cept your mama was a northerner and talked faster."

Eric grunted. "I hope she thinks twice about them willows."

"Long as she puts 'em a good ways off from the house…" Shit said. It was dark. They knew each other well enough for him not to need to complete the sentence.

When they turned onto the path toward their own cabin, Shit asked, "Did that stuff on the TV, there, make sense to you?"

"Some of it," Eric said. "Yeah. I guess so."

As they walked, they looked up.

"I don't see no ribbons or webs of stars—or galaxies. They're just… stars all over the place, like always. I mean…the Milky Way over there. Maybe that's what they were talkin' about?"

"Naw," Eric said. "That's just our own galaxy, from where we're at inside it. We're lookin' at it on edge. That's why it looks like that."

"What's a galaxy, anyway? Just a whole lotta stars?"

"Yeah," Eric said. "Basically. They swirl around together, a lot of times in a spiral. You seen, they had pictures of 'em on the show."

"Yeah…" Shit said, pondering. "I don't know why people got to watch that kinda stuff. It's as bad as that damned philosophy. That's probably why they put it on a special channel—or only show it late at night."

Eric smiled—he hoped not enough for Shit to see.

On either side the road, crickets scritched through the night.

Usually, Eric did not think too much of Shit as a social philosopher, though he kept his council. But now he said, "Hey—I liked what you were sayin' in there to her—before the show."

"Mmmm," Shit said, as if considering. "But I could tell she was still hurtin' over that Deborah. That's why I backed off."

"Yeah, I know you did," Eric said. "I liked that, too."

Then Shit said: "I bet she asked us to eat over 'cause you was showin' off your tattoos. You think she wanted to fuck us?"

"What?" Eric said. "Huh? Why you sayin' that, Shit?"

"'Cause she was sittin' around with us, all night, with no top on and her tits hangin' out."

"Well, you don't have no shirt on either—and yours are startin' to hang a little, too, there, son."

"Yeah. But she's a woman."

"Come on, Shit. She's a lesbian. That's the way most women walk around today—at least out here in the Settlement. You tryin' to pretend that for the last twenty-five or thirty years, you ain't never seen women goin' around Runcible and the Harbor topless before? Even in the show tonight—"

"Yeah," Shit said. "But that's in public. This was in private—alone with two old men she don't hardly know."

"Yeah—two gay old men, remember—nearly sixty years old? Hey," Eric said, "if you're really interested, you can always go back, ring the bell, and ask if she wants you to spend the night. I ain't gonna stop you."

"Naw," Shit said. "I ain't *that* interested. I was wonderin', that's all."

"Well, I wasn't."

A minute later, Shit put his hand on Eric's shoulder and leaned in as they walked. "You know we could both go back and see if she wants to take on the two of us…"

"*I* ain't that interested," Eric said. "You're a mess, Shit."

"Then—" Shit stood up straight again, though he left his hand on Eric's shoulder—"I guess I'll just have to get you home in bed and rub all over you and pretend like she did, there, so I can come all over your belly."

Eric said, "If you can stay awake that long and don't fall asleep in the middle."

"Oh, you're always tryin' to be so funny there."

"You know, we *are* gettin' on. I can remember when you'd actually've left me here and gone back and done somethin' like that."

"Huh? Not with a woman—"

"No, with a guy, I meant."

"Oh…well." Shit frowned. "You would've, too…wouldn't you?"

Eric laughed—which ended in a yawn. "You know, we're both pretty tired. But we could do it in the mornin'. Have sex, I mean. That's always your favorite time anyway."

Shit grunted. "Aw, come on. When I get up tomorrow, you're gonna be sittin' out on the steps, readin' your damned book, waitin' for me to get up and make you some coffee."

Eric chuckled. "Yeah, probably." He looked off the edges of the dark road. "Actually, I gotta fill out that government stuff tomorrow. And I do have to get back to my book again. I almost got it, this time."

"You say that every time you read it. You only promised Mama Grace you'd read it three times through. You finished that a long time back—"

"But every time I read it, I get some more out of it. That's why I keep goin' through it again. I wonder how Mama Grace is doin', anyway?"

"Probably he's dead an' buried."

"That'd be a shame." Eric signed. "I hope not. But…you may be right." They wandered on over the rise. In the dark, a sea breeze touched their faces as they started down their side of the hill.

"Hey." Shit's hand fell from Eric's shoulder. "You liked them turnips?"

"Yeah," Eric said. "They were good. I could'a done without that tomato sauce all over them ribs. Made 'em taste like ketchup and candy. "

"Yeah," Shit said. "It was still nice of her to feed us—" they veered at the bend—"but they was easy to eat."

*

The next morning, Eric went out to sit on the cabin's kitchen steps. With a sheaf of government forms, a ballpoint pen that worked, a rock—and eighteen inches of pine planking—slowly he sat on the middle stair. Then he pulled the plank over the frayed knees of his jeans, and, on the step beside him, used the rock as a paperweight to hold the forms down. One at a time he began to fill them out.

When he'd been working twenty minutes, Shit stepped around him, barefooted. "Here's some coffee." He passed the mug down. Eric had a yellow one that said SHIT. Shit had a brown one that said PISS. Shit had brought them both in Turpens Parts and Notions for a joke—long enough ago so that neither thought much today about what they said. "You fillin' out them government papers you got in the mail?"

"Yep." Eric raised his reading glasses up to his forehead. "Thanks." He took the mug and sipped. "That's good."

Down the grass slope, water glittered beyond low rocks, becoming the blue-green of a Chamber of Commerce desk blotter, stretched to the earth's edge. It was a September morning, neither overly brilliant nor particularly gray; neither darkly overcast nor crystallinely clear.

Standing, Shit squinted at the sea. "Wished I knew why we had to fill out so many forms just to get old." Mug in both hands, he drank some coffee.

Eric pulled down his glasses:

…last name, first name, name of domestic partner, date of birth. He wrote them in. "Well, ain't you glad we got me to do it for you?" He grinned at Shit, then blinked at the ocean, which for so long had been his image for the repository of all past time—his own, history's, anyone's—though, from last night, he remembered today how much bigger and older the universe was than the sea.

Intermingled webs of blue and silver, the water ended at the horizon, which, this morning, Eric realized was the base of a robin's eggshell to cut him—and all humanity—off from any further glimpse of things; things further than the sun, dimmer than the moon.

* * *

[91] IN THE FIRST decade after Eric and Shit moved permanently to the Gilead cabin, Eric started attending town meetings in the Settlement as he'd attended them in the Dump. As he approached sixty, his energy was less. Things that occupied the meetings' hour and a half—first at the old Meeting Hall down at the ferry dock and then, once they renovated the old Kyle Mansion, in the Library Commons Room on the second floor—were harder for him to stay interested in.

Far more of the population in the Settlement than in the Dump made money from the production of one sort or another of art—as much as twenty-three percent. As well, more than sixty percent of the residents—overlapping with a significant number of the artists—did one form or another of "jack work," where, through computers, they plugged into light office or heavy industrial machines, all around the country, all around the world—often one on one day, one on another. (Several times there were mentions of Bodin Systems, but usually in the context of its no longer providing this service, or its no longer doing that. Then it wasn't mentioned at all.) That created whole ranges of political and economic problems in the growing town unknown in the Dump, with its local workers in local jobs, who'd never traveled more than half an hour or forty minutes to work. A jack job ten kilometers away or a job ten thousand kilometers away took the same three-quarters of a second to "turn on," but conflicting tax scales and out-sourcing fees for this group or that guild took up more and more of the meeting's discussion time. Eric had a harder and harder time understanding either the problems or the proposed solutions, so that by the end of the decade he was attending maybe two meetings a year and regularly abstaining from votes. The confusion and incomprehension he experienced often found him, the next morning, sitting in the kitchen across the table from Shit, fingers locked around his mug, while dawn light came in a bright line under the shade pulled down over the window behind the sink, gazing at Shit, who hadn't put his shirt on yet. The tight tufts of hair on his chest were completely white now. Sometimes his beard stayed mussed pretty much all day.

"What you lookin' at me for? Is somethin' wrong? What is it?" Shit would ask, curious.

"It's nothin'. I'm just thinkin' about the meetin' last night," but what he was thinking about even more was Shit's refusal, years before, to attend any of meetings back in the Dump, because they'd made him so uncomfortable. Through skipped meetings and their practically Luddite approach to computers and newspapers, they missed by a week the news of Robert Kyle's retirement—out in one of his homes on the Oregon coast. He'd "jack run" most of the business in his Hemmings offices from there and from Columbus. "You know," Eric said, thoughtfully, "I actually heard that man debate—in person. Back when he argued with Johnston, in the Dump."

But two weeks later they got the newsletter explaining that the Chamber of Commerce had dissolved and reconstituted itself as the Robert Kyle Foundation. It was no longer the Kyle Foundation, and the change was apparently significant, though how Eric wasn't so sure. From now on, that would be the name on their pension checks and their insurance correspondence.

"Yeah," Shit said. "And my daddy sucked that nigger's dick, too—when the nigger wasn't suckin' his." He laughed and poured the old coffee into the stainless steel sink, then ran water into the ancient carafe. Pulling loose a paper towel, he thrust in his fist that still had to squeeze to get through the carafe's opening and wiped around the inside.

"You think too much is gonna change, now that he don't got his finger in things personally?"

"You mean, more than it has already?" Pulling out the towel, Shit set the rinsed carafe on the drain board and looked superior.

* * *

[92] SOMETIMES WHEN HE was by himself, just walking down through the woods or along the beach—two nice ones had recently been cleared on the island's south shore—Eric would try to remember specific incidents of sex, purely between him and Shit. (You could train yourself to remember up to them, or the falling away, moments after, which is what made them good or not so good. You could even remember what you said about 'em. Orgasms themselves, though, were all-but-impossible to remember.) He could remember things that had happened between them hundreds of times—walking up behind Shit and hugging him, and Shit pressing Eric's hands against his belly with his own, slowly turning in Eric's tight arms—as Eric himself turned—till Shit was behind Eric, and soon had him down on bed or couch or rug and, wetting himself with a fistful of spit, he'd fuck

him; or, in the morning, now at Dynamite's old cabin, now in the bed in the apartment above the Opera House, now in Dynamite's old bed in its new home in the Gilead cabin, finishing up between Shit's legs and rolling over Shit's thigh, knee, and foot, from between, while Shit reached down blindly to pull him up and back against his belly, finally to pack his own still half-hard cock in the crevice of Eric's ass, and moments later, begin breathing quietly in sleep against Eric's shoulder, in a grip Eric had to break in order to wake him, or, yes, Shit taking Eric's face in his hands and with a violent kiss rooting within Eric's mouth with his tongue, his whole body quivering, till finally Shit cock's was lodged, at last, in one end or the other, and they could go on. When he tried to remember specific instances of sexual release, generally he could only recall two: once when Shit had sucked him off in the "Gay Friendly" Men's Room at Dump Corners, or—the other time—up on the Bluff in the storm, when he'd first fucked Shit's ass, which was odd because for every time he'd blown Eric, Eric had blown Shit twenty-five times, and for every time Eric had fucked his partner, his partner had fucked him close to fifty. But maybe because those two were so different—and had happened so long ago—they clung tenaciously to memory.

(It was like being able to remember hundreds and hundreds of times looking at the sea, or, with his elbows up and swinging, walking out into it, or swimming through it, or trudging in the grass and rocks beside it, looking down on it, but not being able to remember single and singular waves...)

There'd been a dozen years when Eric would say, repeatedly to their gay male friends, "For a natural top, that boy is as oral as any goddam mutt—you know, the friendly kind that wants to lick out your butthole and your mouth, an' ain't about to brush its teeth between," till he noticed that most of their friends were now women, some of whom looked a little... uncomprehending at the refrain. (Not as to what it meant but as to why he would say it.) Did this, he wondered, have anything to do with Mike's tendency to repeat so many things back when he'd been alive?

* * *

[93] HOLLY HAD TOLD Ed, "We can get Jeffers and Haskell to go over to the Library with the kids and oversee the moving."

The "kids" were six fairly "male-identified" young women in their mid-twenties to early-thirties. Three years ago, two had come to the Settlement homeless and camped out on the commons for more than a week. But now all were in a dyke commune (Shit: *It smells like a damned flophouse when you go in there. And forget it, if Laura got home really sick-drunk the night before—*

(Eric: *Shit, when have you ever been in a flophouse?*) with some dozen other residents, among them, Frankie, who had a speech defect and seemed to have been here since the Settlement began. Shit and Eric both could remember her as a fourteen-year-old panhandler when this was all trees and ferns, and she was a grubby, pathologically shy kid, living rough in the woods. Among the "kids" there were arguments. There were unbreakable friendships that, several times, had broken up. There'd even been some relationships with the more stable Settlements residents, which, more than not, hadn't worked out. In general, the best they seemed to manage was affairs with the more adventurous of the island's summer residents.

So they'd gone over to Jay's place, which was now the Settlement Library—in the truck, even though it was only a hundred yards.

As they got out under the trees, Shit asked, "So this is where you go for the town meetin's, now?"

Nodding, Eric looked around the familiar façade. The kids had gone around the back to get the winch. Today, lawn lay in front. No podium with switches and intercoms stood there, as there'd been when Eric had first visited.

"Now, don't you get started about how I ought to come to one of 'em. You know I don't—"

"Shit, I haven't said anything like that to you in fifteen years—"

"I know," Shit said, "but you had that look on your face like you was about to."

Eric laughed and sucked his teeth in exasperation. "Hey, come on inside. I wanna show you somethin'."

"What?"

"Come on. You'll see."

"What is it?" Shit had on a cap, which he moved around on his head a little to get comfortable. "I always feel funny when I go in there. It ain't like it's Jay's house at all no more."

"I don't wanna tell you. I wanna show you."

"Okay..." Shit said, warily. He followed Eric between the columns, up the steps, and through the front door. In the renovations, they'd torn out the first floor kitchen—and the living room off to the right had been broken up into offices.

They started up the stairs—which were completely new with a new banister, whose railing was black stone, which you could think the house had been built with, if you didn't know otherwise. The vestibule library at the head of the steps remained, though the space behind it was now a public room for meetings and events. On the back wall the windows' green electronic shades had been darkened to different opacities. Chairs had been set up in rows over a maroon rug for some up-coming evening gathering. The ceiling was a foot lower—which still left it higher than most—and speckled with hundreds, thousands of sound-absorbing holes. Eric led Shit to the side, beside the bookshelves and, among the desks with a few General Screens, glimmering, raised from them, and walked to one dark wood wall, hung with photographs in black frames. "Take a look at that one there." Eric pointed.

"What is it…?" Shit frowned.

"Look," Eric said. "Go on."

"What's it say?" Shit asked.

Eric leaned in a little closer, squinted, then leaned back again. Since he knew what it said, he didn't have to break out his reading glasses. He read/recited:

October, 17, 2012: Members attend a Town Meeting at the Dump, the Black Gay Utopian Community established on the Diamond Harbor Mainland by Robert Kyle, former owner of the Gilead Settlement Library Building.

"What's a 'Utopian Community'…?" Shit laid a spatulate forefinger against the glass, all but nailless. Enlarged scar tissue knotted before the quick: he still chewed at them.

"I think it's just a nice place to live."

"The Dump…?" Shit glanced at Eric, incredulously. "Well, I guess it wasn't *too* bad…" In their jeans and work shirts, half in peaked caps (completely unlike the one Shit now wore) and four or five with 'do-rags around their heads, clearly these men had been photographed forty or fifty years ago. Eric looked at the black men standing around, shoulder to shoulder, smiling out into the midst of the twenty-first century. Then Shit exclaimed, "That's *you* in there!" He turned to frown at Eric.

"Yeah, it is. Somebody must have taken that after one of the meetings in the old Social Services building. You see the window there—outside it, I mean. That's the old Hemmings shuttle goin' by."

"Yeah," Shit said. "It is—but that's *you!*" Looking at the photograph wonderingly, he seemed to relax, slowly and completely. "That's your old Turpens cap! Jesus—you were one fine lookin' feller. What were you then? Sixteen, seventeen—?"

"In '12?" Eric said. "I got here in oh-seven, about a week before I turned seventeen. So I was…twenty-two, I guess."

"Jesus, you was like a fuckin' movie star!" He grinned at Eric. (It was something he'd often said before.) "You had that cap forever. I remember—too—you had all your damned teeth. I wasn't used to that, I mean with local workin' guys. I didn't think you was gonna like me 'cause I'd dropped so many of mine." He laughed. "You know, Jay had to take me aside there, sit me down, and explain about how you was actually gettin' off on things like that about me and my dad, like the nose pickin'—only I wouldn't believe it at first. I mean, you used to live with your goddam tongue in my mouth. Finally, I figured back then, I'd let you live anyway you wanted to. Only then, I *wanted* to believe it so much I guess I started to—and by the time you told me he was right, I did." That was something Shit had said before, too; but not for a while.

Eric laughed. "Well, it still works." Reflected on one wedge of the glass were the shelves and books on the room's far wall behind them. The laugh became a chuckle. "You know, I *wasn't* that bad lookin', back when I was a kid." He glanced aside to see Shit staring at him with his green eyes over his beard and under his high forehead with the wriggle of a vein on his right temple.

Shit said, "*Wasn't*'...?"

Eric said, "Well, I sure don't look like nothin' today. I'm sixty years old and twenty pounds overweight—" He patted his belly—"You know, this stuff ain't muscle no more. I'm a fat ol' man now, Shit. But I sure didn't realize how good lookin' I was."

"Oh, yeah. Yeah, you're *all* beat up and rickety and fallin' to pieces. Nobody could ever look at you twice today. And you better go on believin' that about yourself, 'cause that's the only way I'm ever gonna get to keep you for the rest of *my* goddam life!" Shit drew in a sharp breath. "Don't you realize you're still the best lookin' thing up and down the whole damned Georgia coast?"

"Aw, be serious," Eric said. "That's just you. You been tellin' me that since I got here, Shit. I ain't nothin' special—"

"Yeah? Well, you just said yourself how good lookin' you was as a kid—"

"Okay. I was a little better lookin' than I thought I was. But probably everybody feels that way. I mean, when I look around today, sometimes I think there ain't *no* really bad lookin' kids. The ones with no chins, the big ears, the funny noses—that's all just cute. Or gives 'em some character. Or somethin'. It's a shame they don't know it, too—" Eric stopped. "What's a matter, Shit?"

Shit stood very still. Then he swallowed.

Eric frowned. "You're cryin', Shit…What is it?"

"Nothin'." Shit pulled in another breath. "I'm cryin' 'cause every once and a while it hits me how fuckin' amazin' it is that I got you. I mean, you're all I ever wanted—and when I'm messin' around with someone else, it's like you're always tellin me, from that book of yours, that I'm fuckin' with another part of you or the world or the universe and—I guess—God. 'Cause everything's a part of everything else, and that's why I always get home extra horny. And I always got you there to hump and hang onto your dick and nuzzle on your nuts and stick my fingers up your asshole and smell your farts under the covers and take a leak in your mouth and hug onto you and breathe in how your breath smells in the mornin' before you wake up and lick inside your nose and rub my dick all over your butt and gettin' it in and hangin' onto you. Or just suck your damned dick. And it's mine to hold onto pretty much whenever I want." Another breath, "Wow..."

Eric hugged him, feeling Shit's shirt bunch in front of his collarbone and Shit's buckle corner poking at his belly.

"I mean, it was like a goddam movie star had come on down here and met me in the back john at Turpens and decided he wanted to do everything nasty I'd ever thought about doin' and a couple of more I hadn't even tried."

"Movie star? Hell—I look like some dumb, big-muscled farm boy that ain't got a brain in his hard, dumb head." Eric laughed again and let go. "I wish they had a picture of you—or your daddy. Dynamite used to come to some of those meetin's. But I guess he wasn't there that night."

"Jesus, I know all these guys..." Again, Shit looked at the photograph again. "There's Fred, and Mama Grace, and...wow!" He took a breath, standing up. "I'm glad I ain't in it. If I was, somebody might expect me to do somethin' or be somethin'—like you."

"Ain't nothin' special about goin' to a town meetin', Shit—"

"You gonna get started again, ain't you?"

"No! I'm not startin' nothin'!"

"Hey, lemme tell you." Shit turned from the photograph. "Yeah, the truth is, I guess that could be a picture of a pretty ordinary lookin' white boy—at least in some places." Shit turned and stepped away. (Eric was surprised—and disappointed—Shit had not lingered with the picture more. But Eric followed his partner, who went on. The first time *he'd* seen the picture, he'd looked at it ten minutes, thinking over the things the passage of time between now and then had meant.) "You do look kinda like a deviled egg tossed into a pail of plums. But the fact is, that ain't no white boy in that pitchur. That's a town meetin' of a *black* community—you told me it says so, right under it, inside the frame. You read it out to me. A black, gay 'U—...' whatever it was."

"Utopian—"

"Yeah, like you read it. So maybe you are a pretty ordinary lookin' white boy. But you're a real interestin' lookin' nigger. And I know you is one, 'cause I met your damned daddy, and he was as black as the Ace of Spades. I bet you somethin' else, too. Half the people who stop there and looked at that picture and read out what it's a picture of, they're gonna be lookin' at you in particular and they're gonna think the same damned thing." He grinned again. "That is one interestin' looking nigger. Now—you got a hard-on yet?"

Eric looked around the meeting room, with its empty chairs, its vacant podium on the other side. No one was in it but them. Looking back, he took hold of Shit's hand and dragged it against his crotch.

Matter-of-factly, Shit said, "I guess you do," and squeezed gently and rubbed a few times. He looked around. "I can't even believe I had sex in this place here maybe a dozen times, even before you come down to the Harbor—and how many times afterwards, with you...? I mean when Jay and Mex lived here with Hugh. Wasn't Shad a mean sonofabitch?"

Eric looked up. One wall was notably higher than the others.

"I remember once I was suckin' off some Injun kid in here, when we come in here to fuck around, and Shad rolled on in with his wheelchair—and seen us and went off like a stick of damned dynamite. I thought he was gonna explode and have a heart attack—and I don't even remember the Indian kid's name, 'cause I never saw him again." The ceiling bent up sharply to join it. High up, six rectangular windows let in sunlight in veritable slabs that fell through the room, slicing the great space into light and shadow, glinting on the metal chair backs, striping the carpet. A memory struck Eric: molding, white plaster urns, drapery in relief across gray-violet plaster... Only today the second floor space had been redone in the insistently bland style of a century before—like (Eric found himself thinking) the flat, functional interior of the Hemmings Interdenominational, before they'd torn it down. "You know," he said to Shit, "a whole lot of your people are out here—in the Indian Graveyard: your daddy, his daddy, your great granddaddy—he was half Injun. Dynamite told me that."

Shit frowned. "Yeah...? Your mama's there, too. And I guess we'll be—if they remember to stick us in and don't go to burnin' us up in some crematorium. Hey, why you thinkin' about stuff like that?"

"I dunno. It's just...well, it hit me. This is the same place it aways was. This building, I mean...Kyle's old mansion. It looks a little different, and they keep giving it a new paint job or face-lift or whatever they do in here, to keep it from fallin' apart. But it's the same place."

"Yeah," Shit said, looking around, as though he were not so sure. "I *guess* it is..."

Chuckling, Eric walked with Shit back along the maroon rug, down the steps, to the ground floor.

*

With the help of the half a dozen "kids," who'd finally got the winch and chains and green quilted pads all arranged (Shit hadn't realized the statue was hollow at first, though it was still nearly eight hundred pounds: solid, as Eric had pointed out, it would have been more like a few tons), and they managed to get the great bronze—now in a back room of the library's ground floor—outside and onto the truck bed to drive it back, and finally move it to Holly's new stone base, which had stood vacant three months at that point.

The day they were doing it, while the sun blazed in the September heat, Ed wandered by, looked at the statue, and frowned. Shaking his head, he grunted like a brown bear. "I don't like that thing," he said. "I never have—from the first time I saw it, back when I was a kid. Why they got to put that thing out there—it's kind of obscene, actually. Somethin' to scare children with."

To Eric, in the sunlight the blackened bronze looked pristinely harmless, sitting on its plinth on Settlement Commons, as if the day had wrapped it in some protective shield that held in all its resonances and suggestions. "What you mean, Ed?"

"I don't know. The first time I saw that thing, I must have been three, four...maybe five—I know it was before Hannibal was born. My daddy brought me on his fishing boat with a whole lot of other people out here to Gilead, and we stayed in that old house there, when it was just a big old shell. It was stormin' and rainin'—I had no idea what they all wanted. Somebody had died, I guess, and they were doin' some kind of crazy religious ceremony or somethin'—that's all I can think it could have been. It was all creepy and weird out there. They went into the house there, and I guess some of them had sense enough to leave me behind and let me take a nap, and so I went to sleep in this room right near the kitchen—that I remember. Then I woke up. I was still kind of scared and didn't know where I was, really. So I got up and started sneakin' around. I found the back steps, I guess, so I went up there, and I come out in this big old room—I still remember it—with big old chairs and couches sittin' all around it. I think it's the one they use for meetin's and things today. I'm walkin' around, and suddenly the storm breaks, and it's rainin' against the windows, and I turn around...and there it was, in the corner. I'm surprised I didn't pee my pants.

"I tell you, I couldn't move.

"I was sure I'd stumbled onto what they were all prayin' to and all that Indian mumbo jumbo that they was tryin' not to let me see."

"Ed—" Eric began.

"I managed to find the steps I'd come up and scurried down those things, scared to death. I started callin' for my daddy and I was cryin' and he just wouldn't come. I don't know if he heard me or not. Then, finally, I found where they was all sittin' around, eatin' after it was all over, I guess—" Ed caught his breath, as though some bit of terror had leapt from the past to fix the present on its barb. "I told 'im I wanted to go home. He wanted me to eat somethin', but I swear, by that time, I figured everything you could have put in your mouth in that place had to be poisoned or somethin'." Ed shivered, as if wet breath had blown across the years. "But they finally got together and drove back down to where his boat was, and we come back to the mainland."

Smiling, Eric said, "You know, Ed—if that's the thing that I think it really has to be, I was there. So was Shit."

"No, you wasn't." Ed frowned. "I know Billy was—my dad's first mate."

"That's right." Eric nodded. "'Cause he'd done that nasty thing all them shore fishermen used to do with the night crawlers."

"But you wasn't there. I'd remember you—"

"Yes I was." Eric nodded. "So was Shit's dad, Dynamite—Mr. Haskell."

"Then what the hell were you all doin' out there, anyway—besides scarin' a three-year-old out of two years of his growth."

Benignly, the winged chimera's brazen hand reached through the sun— to placate both men with an offering of what the years between might have taught.

"And you wasn't no three-year-old. Or five, for that matter. You was at least eight or nine."

"Oh, no," Ed said. "I had to be a lot younger than that."

"I don't think so."

"And that thing was the idol presiding over all that mumbo jumbo they was doin' out there."

"There wasn't no mumbo jumbo, Ed."

"Sure there was. I remember there was all these eggs—they called 'em devils. Each one of them had a red star on top of it. There was a whole tray of 'em—and another one in the refrigerator. I looked in an' saw it. That had to be something to do with the some ritual."

"There wasn't no ritual, Ed. Them was Cassandra's deviled eggs. She just brought too many."

"Then what was the star for?"

"Decoration," Eric said. "That's all. You take a piece of paper, fold it up, then cut it right, unfold it, and you got a hole in the paper like a little star. You put that over the half an egg, sprinkle some paprika on it, and you get a nice red star there."

"Why was there so many of them? It wasn't supposed to be for some magic or something—like that nigger over in the Dump, Black Bull used to do?"

"No, Ed. It wasn't. Black Bull was somethin' else entirely—that was just some gay S&M that a few folks was interested in. So they'd pay him to do it. Really, Cassandra just made too many deviled eggs for lunch. That's all—"

"And that thing wasn't presidin' over no ritual?" Again Ed nodded toward the statue.

"There wasn't any ritual, Ed. Jay MacAmon's uncle Shad had died, and we all come out there to pay our respects and get him buried decent."

"There wasn't no preacher or no minister or nothin'. How could it have been a decent burial?"

"Jay didn't believe in no religion. You worked with Jay and Mex on the boat—for how many years? Didn't you ever ask him about that?"

"No…"

"Why not? He was your good friend."

"I was scared to. My daddy told me I wasn't supposed to go off with them by themselves too much or anything. You knew they was homosexuals."

"Course I did. So was everybody who was in the Dump—includin' us."

"Yeah, well I know about you." Captain Miller had died in his middle seventies, when Ed was…fifteen? Sixteen?

"I thought Jay was kinda like a dad to you."

"He was."

"He never touched you or did nothin' to you, did he?"

"Naw. But I always figured he must have had a special secret religion that he practiced on his own—I mean, back when everybody except my dad used to talk about him funny and say all that stuff about him. Like what it says about you gay fellas in the *Holy Luminescence Newsletter*. If you was there—which I still sort of doubt, or I'd remember you—I figure there's one of three explanations. You was there, and they kept it from you—"

"Which would have been pretty hard," Eric said, "'cause after you and your daddy left, we stayed over that night, me, Shit, and Dynamite—Mr. Haskell. Maybe 'cause we wasn't on the boat goin' back, that's why you don't remember us."

"Or you're confusin' something else with what I'm talkin' about."

"Well, I suppose that could be it."

"Or I'm confusin' a couple of times out there. I remember, though, once when I was tryin' to find out where I was, I went in to one of their rooms, and their was this nasty picture, lyin' katty-corner on a bed, of a man having congress with a pig. Now, you gonna say that ain't part of no satanic rituals? I seen that, and I turned around and ran—got up them stairs and seen this evil thing. No, that thing ain't no artwork. It's some kind of evil symbol for something deep and dark and terrible."

Eric frowned.

"Oh…" Ed drew in his breath. "But Holly thinks that statue is somethin' worth perservin'. I know it's a lot of nonsense. But I could have the thing burned up and melted down in a minute, and I wouldn't miss it a bit."

Later that afternoon, Shit and Eric bolted the creature down—though the Settlement Museum, the statue's new custodians, had still not officially opened. When Eric recounted this to him, Shit's responded: "Well, whatever he says, you know he wasn't no three or four years old. What three- or four- year-old could even recognize what a man 'havin' congress with a pig' in a situation like that looked like? Especially a three- or four-year-old like Eddie was."

Eric said, "Thanks, Shit. Sometimes you can be a good reality check, know what I mean?"

* * *

[94] OVER THE SETTLEMENT ferry rail, a floodlight clamped to the shelter roof put their shadows on the water, two decks below, a shaking gray on a secanted circle of smoky green, rushing across the night. "I will never understand why they named this thing *The Johnston*." Shit leaned and looked. "It should've been *The MacAmon*—or *The Jay MacAmon*, or *The Jay and Mex*. Or even the *Gilead III*. But *The Johnston*…?"

"You've said that to me every time we done rode on this thing since they started running it, five years ago." Eric leaned on his hands.

"It still sticks in my craw. *The Johnston*. I can't say it without my dinner wantin' to come up." Shit leaned down on crossed forearms.

"Well, the Chamber of Commerce agreed to name it after him to get 'im off our backs on the island. He wanted to go to California—so he gave 'em a nice chunk of change if they'd set up somethin' to remember him by."

"With all Kyle's money, what they need Johnston's for?" (Eric had his suspicions, from a couple comments he'd heard from Molly—the new young artist who'd bought Willi's old place—about the Settlement's own finances, but the inexhaustibility of Kyle's millions was one of the things you didn't argue about with Shit.) "Hell, he'd'a' gone to California, anyway—greedy sonofabitch. Tryin' to make money offa all them poor folk what still struggling out there."

"Yeah. But the Settlement wouldn't a' got the money—or gotten left alone to spend it."

"It still ought to be *The MacAmon*—you know: somebody you want to remember. Or the *Gilead III*."

"Yeah." Eric sighed. "You're right. It should be." He glanced at his partner in the dark blue thermal vest and no shirt under it. "Ain't you cold?"

In the upper deck's floodlight, the vest looked almost black. Standing up, Shit unfolded his ropy arms. They were still strong, yes. And he's still good-lookin', too. But his arms ain't never had no real bulk. "You been askin' me if I'm cold for thirty years now—if not forty. And I always tell you the same thing. No!" Shit looked over at Eric, who wore a buttoned-up sweater that had some snags and some outright holes. "You ought to be wearin' this. You got your pitchurs all up and down your arms. But three-quarters of the time, you cover 'em up, so nobody can see 'em, 'cept the snake head on your hand. What you get them things for if you didn't want nobody to see 'em?"

"And you been sayin' that to me for the same thirty—or…twenty, anyway." Eric's own arms still looked good, but—he knew—they were softening.

"Well, them tattoos still look fine," Shit said, echoing Eric's own thoughts, as he so often did.

Or was he the source of those thoughts?

Bending his elbow sharply, Shit thrust a thumb under his vest's armhole to push it out from his chest. "I'll swap with you right now. That way you'll know I'm warm, and you can stop pesterin' me—and I get to look at Cassandra's pitchurs. You know how much I like them things. I think you cover 'em up just to spite me."

"Naw," Eric said. "That's all right…"

Both had turned from the water to look at each other.

Across the deck, in her captain's hat, Lucille stepped from the wheelhouse and looked around. It was the final eleven-thirty run on Friday night. (There were crossings this late on Fridays and Saturdays; other nights, during winter, the last trip was at nine-thirty.) Among the dozen-and-a-half women on board—and the five men—someone stepped up to ask Lucille something. She answered, "'Bout six or seven minutes, I'd say." You could always hear her rough voice clearer than most.

Shit said, "I guess that means Ed must be thinkin' about retirin'."

Shit had said that, too, six times in the last three months. Still, Eric was surprised that he could follow the logic. The last years Jay and Mex had worked the old scow—*Gilead II*—between Harbor and island, more and more they'd left holiday runs, weekends, or especially early or late night trips to their nominal assistant, Ed—till Ed took over after Mex's death and Jay's official retirement. Now—though it didn't feel like that many years later (but it probably was), Ed was turning the things over more and more trips to his own assistant of the last decade, Lucille.

"I thought for sure," Shit said, "Hannibal was gonna take over the boat from Ed. When he was a kid, he sure loved runnin' *Gilead II*. I can see him now, waitin' at the wheel for Ed to give him a chance to pilot the thing—eager as a damned puppy at the door 'fore 'er walk. But I guess that boy's too smart for a crap job like this."

"It ain't no crap job." Eric looked around at the upper deck. On either side, webbed metal stairways went down to the car deck. "But since they got a real ferry now, they need a real captain. So that's gotta be..." He shrugged. "Lucille, I guess...or Ed."

Blurred off in a dark November fog you could feel on your neck and wrists, if not see, fuzzed pearls—two together, one apart, the last lights from Settlement Village—hung in the night. Make the trip two hours earlier—at eight-thirty or nine—and the whole north end of the island would have been a-glitter from lighted houses, lighted lawns, lighted street posts. Then, over the next two hours, the little city would sink into black, to become an image of the darkness that was its past.

Eric had told Shit about Ed's revelation. Now Shit asked, "You think Ed would have liked that talk? I mean, maybe he would'a learned somethin' from it—I mean, more'n me."

"I don't know," Eric said. "Maybe he would have—maybe he wouldn't."

The boat crawled over the night. Then, when they were thirty yards out, someone turned on the shore lights so you could see the truck tires fixed around the dock's concavity. Thirty seconds later, they thumped against them, moved to the other side to thump again. Everyone standing around swayed twice, then continued walking toward the boat's front.

With the other passengers, Shit and Eric climbed the concrete steps that connected with Settlement Road.

At the top stood the unfinished station for the free tram that ran for four miles along the Settlement's west edge—all the way out to the new Brown-Folz filtration system, which turned the island's septic sludge into algae that was released into the sea. Arlene—who'd once worked at some mainland supermarket—was the tram's terminal manager and, when she saw either Eric or Shit during the day, always hailed them to take the next car that came by, since it let them off thirty yards from their cabin.

Taking it as infrequently as they did, both Shit and Eric were proud of the thing—possibly because Arlene was someone they had known when they were on the mainland and she had been a produce stocker at the Stop and Shop, and sometimes because it was what, for six months now, everyone in the Settlement had been talking about. An old-fashioned mini-maglev, initially it had been built for a mountain town in the Apennines—destroyed by an earthquake in thirty-nine, before they could lay down the single buttressed rail. Because of the recession at the start of the forties, it had been stored in a Milan warehouse for a decade and a half. Then someone remembered it and shipped it here to Georgia. The Settlement had gotten it for shipping costs with the new international tariff abolitions. Above the tram-car doors, embossed metal letters read USCITA and INGRESSO, which in its six weeks of operation had already sedimented some myths about the Settlement's non-existent Italian-American origins, helped by the fact that the current mayor, Suzanna Faluddi-Cocio, was a first generation Settlement dweller, raised by a pair of Italian-American lesbians who had moved there back in thirty-four. Born in the Settlement, adopted by the Faluddi-Cocios, and raised there, Suzanna was the first man (and a straight man, too) to be elected mayor in the town's history.

Eric and Shit knew Suzanna by sight, but neither had ever done more than nod to him in the market and been nodded to and smiled at in return—they spent more time with the art people than the political folk—though at some function back in forty-six they'd been introduced to him in the basement of the same mainland church at which the lecture had been held that night. Back then Eric assumed he was a teenager.

On the ferry over, people had talked of Suzanna's turning up, perhaps, though no one had glimpsed him, either on the boat or at the church.

Sometimes if it was raining or looked as if it might rain—this had been a wet spring—they took it, with Shit going on from the time they got on to the time they passed the Settlement Library, which was their signal to get up to get off, about how weird the notion of public transportation on a place like Gilead was. Tonight, however, the tram station was closed up. The unfinished shelter was just a couple of plywood walls with aluminum-framed windows in one of them and lumber stacked near the foundation.

From across the lot, by her car door Phyllis called, "Mr. Jeffers? Mr. Haskell? They had the ferry going, but the tram's not running this late. We've got room for you. Let us give you a lift out toward your place." She held the evening's program in the hand hanging over top the car door.

"Thank you, ma'am." Shit waved. "But we gonna walk. We can use the air and the exercise." Which, even if the tram had been operating, is what they would have done in this weather.

"Well, of course." Phyllis laughed. "After the movie, it was a little on the stuffy side. But we've got room for you young fellers. You sure you won't ride?" (Phyllis was in her forties and thought calling sixty and seventy-year-old men and women "young fellows" was good fun.)

"It was a real nice event," Shit said. "But we like to walk in the fog."

"Well, all right, then." Dropping down and backing onto the driver's seat, she pulled the door to.

The car moved off, from one lighted area through another, as did three others, then two more, following their headlights into the fog and out of the glow that now lit only the tarmac, some board railing, and, behind it, trees.

Eric and Shit walked up through the quiet town.

"That first man who was doin' all that talking there about Mr. Kyle's grandmamma, where she went to art school and who she studied with and everything, did run on, though. The second one was better—at least he made some jokes. That stuff about how they wouldn't call her Mrs. Kyle in the newspaper down here 'cause her husband was a nigger—now that was interestin'. I never knowed that, and I was born here."

"Well, black people and white people couldn't even get married back then. It was against the law. But I guess she had enough money so she could pretty much do what she wanted."

Shit looked at Eric wickedly. "But I could marry you today, if I wanted to marry a dumb ol' white fuck—"

"—or I wanted to marry a damned nigger who didn't have enough sense to lay out and be lazy like a nigger's supposed to be and let his dumb ol' white fuck take care of 'im."

Shit humphed. "Anyway, the first one 'bout put me to sleep, so I couldn't hardly pay no attention to the second."

Eric grunted. He'd enjoyed them both, in different ways. But there was no reason to argue with Shit. Though it had been his "yes" grunt, he was sure Shit knew what he meant.

"You know, that's only the third time I been to a real church before—in Runcible. I mean, not when there was people in it. But Dynamite wasn't a church-goin' man."

"We was there, before," Eric said. "Don't you remember, when they had that dinner there and we met the mayor 'cause we were some of the oldest citizens in the Settlement?"

"Now, that's right. I forgot. That was the same place. They gotta start havin' the Settlement stuff out here in the Settlement."

"And when they do, you're gonna start grumpin' about how come they don't have them affairs on the mainland, like they used to."

Shit chuckled. "Probably. Hey—I remember when how you, me, and my daddy all fucked in there that mornin' we come by for the garbage. But now that you're all civilized and interested in art and shit, you probably forgotten that."

"I remember it," Eric said.

Shit started to laugh, quietly.

Then Eric started laughing, too.

In near dark, relieved now by a light from an antique-store window, now by the flickering LEDs—green, red, and blue—of a beer sign inside a closed bar, they reached the commons, where, only six weeks ago, the Thursday, Friday, and Saturday Outdoor Market had become the Wednesday, Thursday, Friday, Saturday, and Sunday Outdoor Market.

Right then, moving northeast, the fog bank cleared Gilead's end—dim and halfway up the night, the blurred moon that had given so little light they'd paid it minimal notice out on the water, became luminous, bright, gibbous, lighting the grassy commons with silver, the few permanent kiosks at the side, the blond-wood picnic tables here and there, which, during the day, were covered with craftwork or produce, fish or fruit, along West Rockside.

Thirty feet away, on its black stone pedestal, which Holly had worked so hard to raise the money for, two sides polished and two rough and purposely unfinished, the statue knelt on one knee.

Both stopped.

"Come on," and again Eric started toward it.

"Why?" Shit said. "You know what it looks like." But he walked after Eric.

It had been six weeks since they had helped bring the statue over from the library. For their efforts, along with the hourly pay they'd netted, Shit and Eric had received tickets to the mainland ceremony, documentary, and commemorative lectures and dinner in honor of the artist—Mr. Kyle's grandmother—in the church parish hall. So had all the kids who assisted, but only three of them—Laura, Billie, and Rhino—had actually gone. And they'd left early to explore a recently opened mainland women's bar once the film was finished.

(Shit: *I don't see why we gotta stay. I can't make no sense of all that talk about history and stuff.*

(Eric: *I'm kinda enjoying it, Shit. Come on, listenin' to it for an evening ain't gonna kill you. Besides, they're gonna give us dinner afterwards. That should be fun.*

(Shit: *Well, I don't really mind taggin' along. It's just sittin'—and I can look at the people. If you wanna, we'll stay. But don't ask me no questions about it*

afterwards—what I thought about this part, or what I felt about that one.
(*Don't worry. I won't.*)

Shit and Eric had remained for it all. Two days before Lucille had agreed to do a late run back out to the island for the residents who had to get back—about half the number they'd first figured on. None of the "kids" were on the return boat, though. Maybe they changed their mind about the bar and returned early. Or they were staying over on the mainland.

It had been interesting enough, watching the documentary, listening to the two lecturers, and attending the dinner honoring the late Doris Pitkin Kyle.

"Eighteen-ninety two," Eric read out loud, bending to see the inscription hammered into the base, "to nineteen seventy-eight." He stood up, stepped back, and squinted up at the bronze beast. "I saw this ol' feller back at Jay and Mex's the first time I went out there. I remember wonderin' if Jay had posed for him. But I don't think Jay could have even been born when she done this." Eric stepped back, then stepped back further. "Besides, the man at the church said it was probably Kyle's granddaddy—he was the model."

"Dynamite or Jay never said that," Shit said. "But the lecturer said it was in her journal. Maybe Kyle just didn't know."

Three times the size of a man, its brazen wings, like a bat's or a demon's, spread wide and gigantic under the moon. On massive shoulders, its bull's head suggested a flying minotaur. Only above its forward-curving tusks, its snout—indeed, the whole of its fore-muzzle—was that of a boar. Its arms were huge, the left pulled back against its chest, thick with muscle and ending in a demon's foot-long talons. The right arm reached down and forward, with a hand that, because of the artist's rough rendering, still reminded Eric of Shit's—or Dynamite's—and which now held out thick curved fingers full of moonlight. It kneeled on its human knee, its human foot back by the coils and piles of a circling and recircling anaconda-like tail. Before it, its other leg was a huge bird's claw, quite big enough to grasp your head and tear it loose. Feathers rose over its knee, its haunch, back to its hip. Around and under its claw, tail, and foot, for the bronze base, Doris had sculpted branches, a starfish, leaves strewn on sand, shells...

The creature had landed on, or was about to take off from, a place where the woods came down to the water.

"Naw." Shit spoke behind Eric. "That couldn't be Jay. You ever look in under it there, at its nuts? You can see 'em in there. Besides, its dick's too big—and both its balls is the same size."

Eric laughed. The more personable of the church event's two speakers had made some quietly risqué jokes about Doris's refusal to put fig leaves on her hyper-masculine nudes—which had gotten her in trouble in the early-twentieth century with several of her public commissions, as one small town after another had refused to display the finished work. Eric stepped forward again. "The first time I saw this, upstairs at Jay's, I almost bumped into it in the dark. It about scared me to death. But I told you that—back when we were haulin' it over here."

"First time I saw it, or saw it by myself when there wasn't nobody around to tell me to leave it alone, I was about five or six—maybe four or five, even. First thing I did was reach in under there and feel its balls and cock. They surprised me, too, 'cause they was all hard and cold. They wasn't soft and warm like my dad's."

Eric frowned over. "Now you didn't tell me that..."

"We had the kids with us. And some of them still ain't gotten comfortable with what they're always callin' my damned abused childhood. Or theirs, maybe. I figure there wasn't no need to go upsettin' 'em even more."

"Well, I'm glad you—"

"I still remember thinking that, though—'cause, yeah, I done played enough with Dynamite's by then." Shit frowned at Eric. "I told you how he'd sit me on his lap and put his arm around me and let me watch him beat off." The frown became a chuckle. "Then we'd play in the stuff that shot out. That was a mess—and I used to love it. So did he—lickin' it off my nose and my ear and laughin'. Anyway...when I climbed down off it, that first time at Jay's, I scraped my knee on the metal there—I mean, the first time I fooled around with it, I left my blood on that thing! Downstairs, Hugh put a Band-Aid on the cut for me. A few years later, though, I got to thinkin' that thing was like my guardian angel or somethin'—I mean, not with those words. But I used to pretend it was followin' me around, just outta sight, but protectin' me, 'cause it was hard and cold and big and nothin' could hurt it. Hey, come on over here." Shit moved around the base's corner. "Did Mex or Jay ever show you this?"

"What...?"

"Come on around here." For a moment, Shit squinted up at the onyx and ivory clouds, their blackest streaks darker than the night. "The moon's behind it, so I don't know if you can see it all that good. And when it was upstairs, this part used to be back by the wall, so you had to know where to look for it."

Beside the huge foot, propped on it toes, the coiled masses of its tail, loop upon loop atop one another, a bronze branch angled from under, to fork beside the carved scales, the thousands on thousands of them that Doris Kyle had etched over the nightmare's prehensile caudal appendage—seventeen feet long, if uncoiled, the second lecturer had told them, earlier that night.

"Go on. Look down there. Can you make it out? It's pretty small, so maybe you'll need your readin' glasses—"

"Naw—that's okay…" Everything before Eric was dark gray against darker gray. But he made out the filigree—

When he reached to touch it with a forefinger, the wires from which the web between the forking branches had been constructed gave slightly. Crawling down its rayed and circling strands, the body big as Eric's thumbnail, was a metal spider…a spider of blackened bronze.

"Mex pointed that out to me one afternoon." Shit stood at Eric's shoulder. "I'm glad I was as little as I was, or probably I'd'a' tried to climb in there and pull the damned thing off to play with, soon as I got by myself with it. That's why I didn't say anything about it when we was movin' the thing. Now them lecturers didn't say nothin' about that."

Eric glanced back. "I hope somebody else don't get the same idea, now it's out here."

"Later," Shit said, "again, when I was I thinking about it, I decided that the big guy, with his claws and wings and his big black nuts, was protectin' the little guy, the spider there—with her web and everything."

"Naw." Eric let out his breath. "Naw. They never showed me that. I never saw it before—as many times as I looked at this thing. I should come back here in the sunlight tomorrow and take a look." Then he said, "*The Spider's Guardian.*"

"Huh?"

"Nothin'," Eric said.

"Well, I hope some kid around don't try to crawl in there and steal that little bitty spider off it—or break the web, the way I would've, if I could have."

Eric moved around to the front, stopping to look at the huge hand reaching out under the moon. "I do remember lookin' at it when it was at Jay's and thinkin' its real hand there reminded me of yours—and Dynamite's."

"What you mean?"

"Look. Don't you see the way she done the nails on it?"

"Aw, hell." Shit laughed. "That's maybe Jay's—or Mex's. But if me—or my daddy—had that much nails left, we'd'a' been ready for an all-day sit-down dinner." The laugh became a chuckle. "If I had as much as he got left, it'd take me a week's work to get them damn things right—I mean, down to where they ought to be."

Eric laughed. "Well, yeah. Maybe so—"

Behind them someone said, "Mr. Jeffers—sir?"

Shit and Eric turned from the glowering nameless god—as the first lecturer had explained it, when its picture had filled the church's wall-sized computer screen.

"Oh, hey, there," Eric said, "Hannibal."

Six young people had walked out on the night grass.

"Mr. Haskell…?" Hannibal said; more quietly, the others murmured greetings. Two young women, one black, one white, and both topless, had their arms around each other's shoulders. It was nowhere as cool as it had been on the water.

Under the moon, Ed's kid brother's own dark skin was the hue of the bronze's near-black patina. "Did you guys go over to Runcible for the honoring?"

Eric nodded. "Was you guys there?" He's still one cute kid, Eric thought. It's kinda of a shame he only snuck into the Opera two or three times. "We didn't see you."

"No," Hannibal said. "No. We didn't go." He glanced at the statue, then at Eric. "Mr. Jeffers, you know my brother…"

"Ed? Sure." Eric thought: Even if I'd just gotten to do him once, at least it would have been fun remembering. "What do you mean, 'Do I 'know' 'im?' I've known Ed all your life and most of his, too."

"Well, we were talkin' about you two—not me and Ed. Just us here." Nodding, Hannibal gestured at the friends with him, another young man and five young women. "Then we seen you, so we thought we'd come over and ask you. Years ago, when I was a kid, seven, eight, maybe nine, perhaps you remember: we ran into you guys and Mr. Grace Davis, out in the woods on the mainland, Ed and me. And you showed us a trick. It was that trick, you know, where you…pick a…well, a piece of…stuff out your nose, and you…um…you showed us this trick you did with it, the both of you."

Shit said, "If it's the time I'm thinkin' about, you had to be a lot younger than nine—'cause Ed was carryin' you in his arms. You was more like three—maybe four or five."

"Yeah," Hannibal said. "I could've been…maybe." He looked around at his friends. "But after that, Ed talked about that trick you done for the next five or six years. Sometimes it seemed that was all he talked about—like he was scared of you fellers. He thought maybe you was gonna come and do somethin' horrible to him in the middle of the night. I mean, I know now you're his friends. But for half a dozen years, before he married Holly, he thought you guys were the devil incarnate—back while you was managin' the movie house in Runcible. Anyway, I was wondering if you could do that trick for us again, so they—" he looked left and right—"could see it. Do you remember? It's kind of a gross-out thing, like I told you," he explained to them. "Like the fishin' guys on the mainland, who rent their boats out to the tourists and take a handful of night crawlers and put 'em in their mouth and let 'em hang out and twist around all over their chins and crawl up over their lips and stuff to scare the kids." He looked back at Shit and Eric. "It's the same kinda thing, ain't it?"

"Yeah." Eric said. "Sort of." He shifted his weight and slid his hands into his hip pockets. "But, see, 'cause you're twenty-two, twenty-three now, if we showed it to you again, you'd see right away how we did it."

Among the loose group on the moonlit grass, the younger ones began to smile. Hannibal laughed. "Mr. Jeffers, I ain't been twenty-three for a long time. I'm thirty-six."

One of the girls said, "You just *wish* you were twenty-three! Well, I guess sometimes I do, too."

Eric was actually astonished. "Well...but..." He hesitated. "That's what I mean, though. You'd see right away how it was done. Then it wouldn't be a trick no more—for you."

Again, Hannibal laughed. (They still looked like teenagers—all of 'em.) "See, I wanted to see if they could figure it out." He nodded to the people with him. "Believe me, if I was twenty, I'd'a' been scared to death to even ask about anything like that."

Shit had begun to grin. "Hey. Come on." He turned to Eric. "Let's show 'em."

Shaking his head and sucking his teeth, Eric said, "Okay...all right." He lifted one hand, bent his head, put his thumb against one nostril, and snorted. Then, frowning, he looked at Hannibal.

Eric bent his head again, closed his other nostril off with a forefinger, and snorted out once more. When he looked up, though, he shrugged, and turned up both hands. "I'm afraid I don't got nothin' up there. Sorry—but there ain't nothin' in there to do it with." He shrugged again. "So—we can't do it tonight, Hannibal. I'm sorry."

"Oh..." Hannibal looked disappointed. "Well, maybe if you...um, another...time. I mean, we didn't wanna bother you, now."

"It ain't no bother," Eric said. "But two codgers like us, we ain't used to bein' up this late no more, anyway. We got to go home and get to bed. We're gonna go home now."

"Oh, yeah—sure."

Eric smiled, hoping it registered in the half-dark. Shit smiled, too. They turned to start across the commons for the road leading to their cabin on part of the shore still heavy with scrub pines and ferns.

Then, Hannibal called, "Mr. Jeffers—?"

Eric stopped—as did Shit—and looked back.

"When I used to help Ed out on the boat—the old one, I mean, not

the ferry—I remember one mornin', you guys were goin' to the mainland
with us. I saw you together at the back rail, and...probably you didn't
think nobody was lookin', but y'all were...I guess, practicin' your trick. It
looked—really...interestin'. But that's why I wanted to see you do it again.
Up close."

Shit laughed now. "Hannibal?"

"Yes, sir?" In the moon, even at this distance, you could see the boy...
the man blink. Waiting through the encounter, his friends, who had been
moving apart, drew together to recommence their walk.

"That wasn't no practice, Hannibal." Shit sounded tired; and friendly;
and content. (Eric wondered what in the world Hannibal made of it.)
Taking Eric's shoulder, Shit turned. Eric turned with him. They walked
between the darkened kiosks toward the road.

Behind them, at the common's north end, winged, clawed, and tusked,
ahead of its asymmetrical shadows, squatting, the chimera gazed over the
grass, the youngsters, the oldsters, the island, and the island's ages.

Going along the road, at last Shit said, "Back there with Hannibal, it
sounded to me like you had a good one up there."

"I did," Eric said. "I do—but I didn't feel like bein' part of no side show
tonight. Why? You want it?"

"Don't worry." Shit still sounded tired and content. "I'll get it in a bit.
But I know what you mean about that side show thing."

Then Eric asked, "How did that boy get to be thirty-six years old? It
can't be more than six or seven years since he was workin' with Ed on the
Gilead—the *Gilead II.*"

"I think that's more like sixteen or seventeen...years." Shit's laugh rose
over the crickets', then dropped level with it.

"That's a damned fast sixteen years," Eric said. "Or seventeen."

"Well." Above them, familiar trees closed out the moon. "They do get
to goin' by pretty quick."

Together they walked through autumn dark.

* * *

[95] TWENTY-ONE YEARS after Shit and Eric had moved to the island,
Gilead's own year-round population had passed two thousand. When
he felt grumpy, Shit called Gilead Settlement "the Curse" and said he
missed the time when it weren't but a graveyard, Jay and Mex, and two
or three other people on the whole island—four if the Holotas' nephew
Roan was visiting them. As Eric pointed out, though, it provided the two

bearded men—Eric's, smooth and silvery; Shit's, still tan and tufty—now (Shit) a gaunt year and a half older than, and (Eric) less than a year shy of, seventy-three, with as much handyman work as they wanted, a few friends among the older women artists, for whom they'd fixed leaky toilet valves and hooked up new light switches and unclogged septic tanks and changed washers in dripping faucets. As well, they had some friends, some regular invitations to holiday meals—Anne Frazier wouldn't let them miss either of her Solstice suppers, or her Equinox parties, even the year it was photographed by the profilers—throughout the island's violet winters, its misty silver springs.

* * *

[96]   THEY WERE ROWING along Gilead's shore, pulling, lifting, and leaning, pulling, lifting, and leaning. The island and its reflection was a frayed ribbon taping sea to sky. "Next time—" Shit leaned, pulled, lifted, pushed, leaned, pulled, lifted—"we gonna bring the damned outboard. That's fun but this…is stupid."

"Come on, Shit," Eric said. "We said we were gonna get some exercise, now. This is good for our hearts."

"I suppose with gasoline a hundred-sixty dollars a gallon, you could have a damned heart attack thinkin' about usin' a combustion motor…"

Eric grinned. "I'll spell you again in five minutes."

"You know what's good for our hearts is you climbin' on top of me or me gettin' all over you the way we do at three o'clock in the damned mornin'. Rubbin' ourselves off on each other…" He tugged, he bent forward; the oars dropped into the water behind; he pulled, and gray wood pushed the water, which rilled like a bolster of thick fabric. "You think you could maybe hold off till four? That way, afterward, we could get up at a reasonable time in the mornin'—together. I ain't seen your white ass flickin' through the kitchen in so long—I mean in the mornin' when I'm up—I forgot what the damned thing looks like. I know it used to be cute…" Then, before Eric could answer, Shit asked, "Scumsucker, you know what was the only thing I didn't like about fuckin' my daddy?"

"Huh…? What?"

"He never called me 'nigger.' I mean, when we'd get into it." Shit pulled, lifted, leaned. Leaden water wrinkled and smoothed. "It's like when we was in bed, he'd forget I was black." A drizzle had started and stopped twice since they'd started out. "I mean, you know that always gives me a hard-on—when someone does it who I know likes me, like you, or Jay or any of them niggers I used to fuck with in the Dump."

"Yeah," Eric said. "I always knew that."

"Well, how come you knew it and he didn't?" Lift, lean, pull, lift, lean…

"'Cause it always gave me a hard-on, too, when somebody called *me* one. But, thank God, *you* know that—"

Shit exploded with laughter. "Well, I guess I *do* know it!" Sun-darkened skin around his green eyes wrinkled. "I guess I do!" He pulled up the oars and shipped them. "Hey, nigger, take these damned things and row for a while."

Eric said, "Sure…" But before he changed places with Shit, he reached into his open fly and levered free his cock. "See, that nigger thing still works."

"Yeah…" Shit reached down, grasped Eric, and rubbed his cheek against Eric's cheek.

Then, with minimal rocking, Eric moved onto Shit's bench, and Shit moved around to Eric's.

"Okay…?"

"Got 'em." Eric had not put himself away.

"There…you go."

As Eric unshipped the oars and dropped their edges into the sea, Shit explained:

"When I was a kid, he only called me a nigger when he was tellin' me how great I was. He made me think I was real special—that he'd done somethin' to make me real special, by havin' me with a real special woman—a nigger woman down at Turpens. How he brought that one off, I ain't too sure. But he used to tell me right out, nigger women were better'n any other kind. I didn't learn till Jay told me, a couple a' weeks after his funeral, that she was the only woman he ever fucked—and then he was drunk."

"Yeah, I was there when Jay told you, remember—?"

"Course, even when I was a kid, I learned it was a bad word and you wasn't supposed to say it at all. So we didn't for a couple of years—only then I realized everybody else did. Especially niggers. And that it got me hot."

Eric pulled, leaned, lifted; pulled, leaned, lifted…"You know, Shit, actually Dynamite used to call you nigger…all the time. That's how I learned I could do it, and it didn't bother you—that you liked it."

"He did? Well, sometimes when we were just jokin' around. But not in bed…That's when I wanted him to."

"Sure, he did. Really. All the time."

"Naw…"

"Yeah. He *did!* But you was so busy fuckin' him, you didn't hear how he was talkin' to you." Eric pulled them along through the water. "'Fuck me, you nigger sonofabitch…Fuck my cracker ass, nigger!' Hell, he said it just like I do. I remember it would get you so goofy happy, after you'd come you'd wanna jump up and run out and show how your fuckin' dick was still hard to everybody up and down the whole damned Dump."

"I did do that once, didn't I—?"

"You did it about *six* times," Eric said, "that *I* remember! I remember you running into Lurrie once and him screamin' and coverin' his eyes." Eric began to chuckle.

"Naw…I *did?* Damn…" Shit put his heavy hands on either gunwale. "Well, they'd all seen it before, anyway. That was 'cause I was so happy you was with us. I was really just showin' off for you. You was always good about callin' me names when we was fuckin'. Unless you was nervous about somethin'. But I sure don't remember him doin' it." Quizzically, Shit put his head to the side. "And what you anglin' for with your dick all hangin' out like that, now? I ain't gonna suck you off, at least till we get home. So put it away."

"Yes, you are," Eric said.

"I *am*…?"

"You're damned right you are. You gonna suck my dick right here, you black bastard—you nigger scumbag, you low-down shit eatin' coon, you gonna suck this nasty white motherfucker's dick."

"Oh, all right. But they should put you in jail for murder, makin' me do this with my damned arthritis—"

"Come on. You took a pain pill before we started. I saw you."

"Well, that was just so I could row." Shit looked up at Eric, frowning. "Now, I ain't gettin' down there for no forty minutes till you manage to shoot. I'm just givin' you a taste, till we get back in."

On one side, then the other, Eric shipped his oars. "You mean, I'm givin' *you* a taste, you fuckin' nigger cocksucker. Get on over here, now!"

"Hold on a second." Shit stuck thumb and forefinger into his mouth and with that wrench that always looked as brutal as some sort of torture, tugged loose his uppers, to slip them into the breast pocket of his open brown and tan plaid. Then he was back to work loose his lowers and sliding them into the same pocket. "Okay. Here I go." He pushed himself forward, off the bench, to go down on his knees. Shit's mouth seemed as though it had shrunk to half its size. Under the boat's wooden floor grill, water sloshed up between the slats. Shit crawled forward on his knees, his jeans from the knees down sopping in seconds. His hands—one, then the other—left the gunwales, to grip Eric's thigh as he went forward. His hands, Eric thought, with their big fingers and knuckles, the ruins of his nails bitten back till they were more pitted scar than chitin, look so much like Shit's father's, sometimes the nigger was really like his daddy's ghost.

Shit took Eric in his mouth—

God, it was warm!

His hands moved up under Eric's open shirt to embrace him around his back.

"Jesus," Eric said. "That feels good…" Eric took his right hand from the boat's edge to rub Shit's skull. "Oh, that's so fine, nigger." The back of Shit's shirt was not tucked into his jeans—which had pulled down from his flat butt, another thing, along with his nail biting, Shit had gotten ·from Dynamite.

The two tongues of tight brown flesh that lapped away the hair at Shit's temples and behind them had joined years ago to make a wide bald stretch in the tan-gray wool. (Three or so times a year, one would take the electric clippers and shear the other.) Moving his knuckles on the rough hair matting Shit's cheek and jaw, Eric (whose own baldness was still limited to a spot on the very top of his head no more than the diameter of a coffee cup) thought: And I'd still trade his for mine in a minute. It just…is better; looks better, feels better, *is* better to take care of.

Over his right thigh, Eric could feel the weight of Shit's teeth hanging in his pocket, down between Eric's legs.

Shit's moving head stilled, and he released Eric from his mouth. "You know, I'm about ready to get me a T-shirt that says 'Toothless.' After all, I finally *am* fuckin' toothless. Since I got it, I might as well advertise. Maybe some good lookin' forty-year-old is gonna come up to me and ask me what I can do for 'im."

"Yeah—but I wanna get to lick around on your goddam gums 'fore you put your teeth back in."

Shit chuckled. "You can do this nigger anyway you like, white boy. It ain't like you don't know that already." Again, he took Eric in his mouth.

A couple of minutes later, Shit turned his face to the side in Eric's lap and again let him slip free. "It's funny. I was just thinkin' down here—"

"You ain't supposed to think," Eric said. "You supposed to suck."

"Well, I was thinkin', anyway. Sometimes, I guess, you want somethin' so fuckin' bad that when it does happen, it don't even stay with you…You know, sometimes I think I must be pretty fuckin' lucky—especially when I look at all the people around me, straight ones, gay ones: I lived most of my whole life with somebody I loved—you, I mean—and with somebody I never once wanted to murder. That's you, too. In case you didn't know. Oh, a few times, there, I done got annoyed with you. But I never thought about killin' you."

Eric was surprised. "Did you ever want to kill anybody?"

"Yeah—my daddy, once or twice."

The surprise grew. "Why?"

"For not havin' sex with me a couple of times when I was a little kid and really wanted it—and he didn't think it would be good for me. He was probably just tired." Shit laughed. (Eric rowed.) "But see, I didn't know no better, back then."

Eric looked down. "I guess all that 'nigger' stuff still works with you, too, huh?"

From his lap, Shit said, "Yeah. A little bit—some."

"What you mean, 'some'?"

"Well, it ain't as much as when I was kid. But 'cause it works for you, it lets me know how much you want it to work for me. And that's about the best thing there is—knowin' how much you really want me to…I don't know: want you. 'Cause you're still the fuckin' sexiest thing I know runnin' around the coast."

"Oh…" Eric said, actually surprised. "Hey, you want me to give you a hand up?"

"Nope. I'm stayin' down here and lettin' you row me home. Next time we do this, it better be in a damned bed—or, I swear, I'll gum your damned dick off!"

The boat moved on the sea's whisper and flap.

* * *

[97] WHAT HAPPENED WHEN they picked up a black twenty-seven-year-old—Caleb—on a visit to Turpens is a tale. Caleb had hitch-hiked over from Kentucky and had been living in Turpens' halls and johns and rooms for three days, with their loose doors that you could pry open with a credit card, when they ran into him. He had a low, broad forehead, low broad shoulders, and all his teeth. He wore black jeans and large engineers boots—and moved in with them at the Gilead cabin during Shit and Eric's joint seventy-fourth and seventy-sixth birthday blowout.

(*We're gonna have a party, this evening. Some friends are helpin' us with it. So we come over there for a couple of hours of pre-party celebratin'. You say you really like old guys—and I don't think a nigger's dick could lie that much. Why don't you come on over with us?*

(*Sure, why don't you come along? You might have fun.*)

Caleb hung around to help clean up the soda bottles and long looped balloons and pick up the plates with half eaten cake slices and chocolate ice cream pools—and stayed…three-and-a-half years. By his fourth day, like Shit, he was going barefoot most of the time, though he always carried an e-reader in his back pocket, with a narrow black and silver frame. "You know," Eric said as they lay in the big bed, listening to crickets and the ocean, "I still get a hard-on every time I see that man diggin' in his nose and eatin' the stuff or blowin' it into his hand and lickin' it off or bitin' on his nails. You believe we still trade with each other?"

"Yeah," Caleb said, "I get a hard-on, too, when I see either of you guys doin' that." (And again Eric was surprised someone had noticed what he still imagined private.) "Shit told me he's the same way about you. And I didn't think I was ever gonna meet nobody like me that got turned on by that stuff. Then, I meet two of you at the same time…I mean, fuck, man! And what's more, you're *old* guys—" Caleb took a breath that sounded as surprised as Eric had felt a moment before, in the dark—"like I always fantasized about. Hell, the only thing yall don't do that I used to dream about is eat each other's shit."

"Funny, I never got into that—I mean, more than what you ordinarily got to get down if you like fuckin' and suckin'—in that order. Which I do. Course, after a couple of years with Shit and Dynamite, I'd turned into a stoned piss freak." Moving his head on the pillow, Eric chuckled. "So I was pretty sure I'd eventually take up the other, too. Only I never did. Shit surprised me, though. I mean, he'll eat his own—and yours too, if you want, or anybody else's he really likes." A decade back, the Settlement Association had put up a road light some twenty yards down the new paved-over road, with the old macadam sticking from under its edges, outside their bedroom window. Its light came in around the shade's edges, pretty much all night. Shit had complained about it heatedly the first six weeks—though it didn't seem to keep him from falling asleep by more than a minute. Eric looked over at the window's edge. "Shit started that back at the Opera House in Runcible. A bunch of guys used to do it up on the landin' to the top balcony. Had 'emselves what we used to call a regular Breakfast Club up behind Nigger Heaven—what they used to call the place they put all the black people, back when it was a real theater. I mean, in the twenties and thirties—of the last century. Yeah, we called 'em the Breakfast Club. Anyway. I nosed 'em for two weeks before I found where they was doin' it—Stash and his buddy Polack Ron and a fella from Tennessee they called Haystack. He was a big, blond, hairy guy with the biggest dick I think I ever seen—I mean, *ever*, too. He beat out any nigger I knew. And there was some hung bucks who came in there pretty regular, 'cause they could always make a few dollars—or a few hundred, after the devaluation. Not just Al. And that ain't even takin' into account the three inches of cheesy skin he had hangin' off it. But...maybe there was somethin' wrong with it—like Jay's big nuts. You never knew Jay, but his nuts had kept on growin', first one, then the other. By the time he died, you know, one was bigger than a damned grapefruit. And the other one had started swellin' up too—like a big old navel orange, or something. Anyway, Haystack looked like one of Jay's relations—his *big* relations. People was always tryin' to get close to him, so they could suck it or sit on it—and he'd let 'em do it, too, to be obligin'. See, he was nice fella. A drunk—not real bright. And full-out died-in-the-wool alcoholics were gettin' rarer and rarer by then. But he was still a nice fella. He'd piss in my mouth pretty much any time I wanted. All *he* really wanted to do was eat nigger shit, get drunk, and tell stupid jokes that didn't make much sense. And would, too, when he got drunk enough—all of 'em was regulars. Finally, I had to make 'em take it out in the back alley and do it—prop the emergency door open with a cinder block, so they could get back in."

"That must have been in the thirties, huh? Everybody's got such great stories to tell from back then. Sometimes I think that's when I ought to have been around."

"Well, them Three Bombs were pretty bad. That's what I think about, when I think about the thirties. I don't even like to remember that stuff."

"I was born in Tallahassee—a couple of years after them things exploded. So I can't remember nothin' about 'em, other than what we saw in school. Other than all those little cars from India that were still all over the roads, I don't hardly remember the thirties at all." Caleb stretched. Then he said, "Yeah, Shit's done it for me a few times. I mean, he took a few bites off something I laid out for him—God, I never come so hard in my life! And I was just watchin'."

"Yeah...?" Eric was surprised again. He hadn't known. "Damn—I wish he'd tell me when he does somethin' like that. Well, it ain't all that important."

"Last time, I told him he had to hold out on doin' it anymore. It liked to kill me. I mean, I couldn't take it—I been beatin' off thinkin' about stuff like that all my life. I always have, since I was a kid. But sometimes when you find the real thing, it's...too powerful, almost. You know what I mean?"

"Sure," Eric said. "There're always things like that."

"Shit said he had this dog that used to drop a turd then turn around and eat it. And watchin' always turned him on. So when he met these other guys in the theater, he just started doin' it, too—"

"Uncle Tom." Eric smiled. "Oh, yeah. And Mex, too. He wasn't a dog. But he probably wanted to be." The smile became a chuckle. "So did I, back then. I guess that was how it started. I'd go out there sometimes and watch 'em all. I did it a couple of times to be sociable. But I could always pass it up…Shit, though? Once we got to the Opera House, there wasn't nothin' nasty Shit could leave alone. There used to be a bar on the mainland called The Slide—they actually had contests in the place. Who could drink the most piss or eat the most…well, you know. A few times somebody brought Haystack over from the Opera House, though—and that was the end of *that!*"

On the other side of the bed, Shit rolled on his back, and, without opening his eyes, said, "The thing about eatin' shit is, it's a group thing. You gotta get a bunch of guys together, see. And most of it's gonna be all nasty talk, gettin' up to it—a couple of yall lay some nice big ones there in the middle for everybody, and you can go around and around them things for forty minutes, pickin' up and passin' around and sniffin' at it, and puttin' down again. But by the end, two or three of yall got to get in there an' eat some of it for real. But with us, one of the two or three was always Haystack. Especially if that stuff had come out some nigger's ass—like mine. It always really tickled me when somebody wanted to get in there and kiss on 'im, when he had a mouthful of that stuff. I'll admit it, that's what I liked to do most, I think."

Eric said, "That's his standard speech about coprophagy."

"It ain't about eatin' no cops," Shit said, opening his eyes and glancing over. "It's about eatin' *shit!*" He closed them again.

"You know," Eric said, "you got to watch out for worms and parasites, if you really get into that. There used to be a doctor who was a regular, who used to be a Breakfast Club member in good standin'—Dr. Greene. He'd write out prescriptions for the fellas, and they'd get'em at the clinic. It was right up the street."

"See, if he was really into it the way I was, he wouldn't be tellin' you about no parasites. He'd just be talkin' all nasty to you and tryin' to get you to drop a nice big one right here."

"I'm tellin' him about parasites 'cause you done give 'em to me so many goddam times! At least back then. I don't mean I didn't pick up a few of 'em on my own. But you gotta keep them things under control. Hey, Shit, I didn't know you was eatin' this boy's turds—?"

Still on his back, Shit grunted, "Yep. Don't worry, though, I'll get to yours. Jesus, it makes the nigger go crazy. You should see 'im. Okay. Now me an' my hard-on both is gonna go back to sleep…don't mind me. You go on talkin'. It ain't gonna bother me."

"You know," Eric said. "Once I was talkin' to Haystack about it—and, yeah, fuckin' around with him, off on the side—and he told me it was like a Christ thing for 'im. He liked eatin' shit for all the guys who got off on it.

That's what really turned him on about it. Like I said, he was pretty thick. But sometimes ol' Haystack would surprise you."

Without turning over, Shit said, "You should tell 'em that the 'Jesus Christ' part was your addition. Haystack eats shit for ours sins—that's like somethin' old Shad would'a said. He just said he got off on other people gettin' off on him. That's all. Ain't nothin' weird about that. But, see, Eric got to find somethin' smart in everybody. That's just 'cause he's really smart hisself. But even ol' Whiteboy, there, toward the end—I mean, we even used to fuck with 'im. But finally, when they had to take Bull away, he got to be such a nuisance that I'd see 'im and try to slip off so I wouldn't even have to say 'Hello, how are ya'?' I mean, if *I* was treatin' 'im like that, you *know* how nasty he'd gotten. But Eric here'd talk to him, nasty or no. You even took him in the back and hosed him down, with soap and everything, a few times. Then he'd come back and tell you two or three things Whiteboy said that were really smart—that he thought was interestin'." Shit humphed. "'Interestin'"!"

"Yeah—Bull used to do that hosin' thing for 'im, every week or two. But once they took Bull off, Whiteboy wasn't together enough to keep himself clean. It's what they used to call 'hebephrenia'—where you were supposed to get so lazy and laid back you forgot to wash yourself, wipe your ass, take your dick out your pants to pee. Wipe food—or shit—off your face when you was eatin' it. A few times when we was livin' at the Opera House, I'd go back there and run into Whiteboy, take 'im upstairs and wash him down. I did his clothes for him three or four times. And I guess a couple of other people did it, too—though we probably should have been doin' it more. Because it was the Dump, though, nobody—or most people—would get too twisted out of shape if this scrawny white feller was walking around, starkers, or sitting in the road, nekid, beatin' off."

"Wow…!" Caleb said. "That place must've been weird."

"Well," Eric said, "sometimes it was."

And Shit had started to snore.

Later, Caleb asked with the brashness of the young, "I mean, you two are so…well, close. What's gonna happen when one of you dies?"

"If he goes first—" and Eric thought, nobody, not even me, says 'if' anymore; it's 'when'—"I'll get over it. Or over the part of it you *can* get over, anyway—after a good night's cry. If I go first, it'll take him about three to…um, ten days. Then he'll be okay," and thought about how he'd learned that.

On his own side of the bed, Shit went on snoring.

"I mean," Caleb said, "is it all right if I love the two of you old fuckers?" His hand was on Eric's face, against his beard—which so frequently he forgot he had, unless Shit's face was pressed against it.

"Maybe," Eric said, "we'll find out."

"Man," Caleb said. "Gerontophilia is a funny perversion."

"Is that what they call it?" Eric grinned. "I guess they got a name for everything. I used to try and find out the fancy names for all the ones I was really into myself—there was so many of them. I had some old guys—and some young ones. But that one was never anything really—I mean, special for me."

"Well," Caleb said, turning back to face him. "It sure is for me." He put his face up against Eric's side. "Old guys just…smell different." He breathed in. "And smell *good*…"

* * *

[98] THAT APRIL, BEHIND the steel and wooden counter, Molly was working there again. Eric looked around at the plank walls, at the glass panels letting in misty sunlight between tan-roofed buildings in front of the water. "Well, lemme pay my taxes and go home." He fingered down in the orange canvas. He'd put the papers in the envelope in that thing, hadn't he…?

Molly laughed. "They're paid, Mr. Jeffers."

On the wall hung a glassed in photograph of some Indians, squaws and braves, and some white and black men who looked like they belonged around a western campfire. "Now that—" Molly saw him looking—"we really ought to take down. Mr. Jenkins at the *Herald* brought that over to us three years ago." Eric had never really looked at it before. "At first, he told us that it was a picture from 1878, which is about when this building dates from." On the matt, below the picture proper, in gold foil letters, it read: *Gilead Island, 1878.* "One building in the background might even have been this place—at least that's what Mr. Jenkins thought, when he gave it to us.

"But then Mr. Jenkins' niece was digging in the files in the basement. Apparently the picture was taken in nineteen *sixty*-eight." Molly laughed.

Eric said, "Well, that's still pretty old. It's before I was born."

"The young fellow there in that gorgeous Indian costume is someone who lived out here—Walter Holota. That child strapped onto the woman's back board—?"

"His son?"

"No, his nephew. They took that in Hemmings at the old Baptist Community Church, just before they pulled it down to build the new one—that is, the one there now. It was a local celebration; when Indians were still out here—they broke out their ceremonial dress and came in for it."

People got older, sure. But it was hard to imagine that red, rough old man, kind as he was, who lived in the cabin before him with Ruth, ever looking like that. Maybe…what was his nephews name? Raven? Rome? Roan…? But not him.

"What fooled Mr. Jenkins is apparently some men used to wear their hair long, back then, too. But that's not nineteenth century wildness—just some late sixties' longhairs. We should take it down, but some of them *did* live on the island here—and people like it."

"Or at least—" Eric frowned—"put the date right."

Outside, Eric walked down the street. A short-haired woman with only one arm was putting up cardboard signs, with a brush and a bucket of adhesive, for a mainland fair. As he walked by, pictures of colorful rides—the Wonder Wheel, the Tilt-a-Whirl—turned and swung over the laminated surface; behind the bars of its wagon a leopard paced. The movement made you all but expect the figures to make noise. On the mainland, a few of the signs actually did. But out here the audio ones, with their babbling crowds and calliope music, had been banned as a nuisance.

At the clear-walled boathouse, on the metal dock, it's what Eddie said. Eric smiled, shrugged, and thought *I don't know. To me it sounds nuts,* and turned back to the elevator…"No—that's what they tell me." Eddie's brown sleeves were pushed up his heavy forearms. Today, he had a belly. "The old Tax and Record Office up there really is the oldest building on the island."

"But it don't make sense," Eric said. "I used to come out here—I mean, when you was runnin' around in diapers, Ed. There wasn't no buildin' there at all. I remember when they first started clearin' this end of the island. It was just trees. They had their first meetin' out here in a damned tent—"

"You wanna work tomorrow," Ed said, "you guys can come down to the Boathouse and fix the wires to them three switches in the back."

"Sure," Eric said.

"And if you get a chance, it wouldn't be a bad idea to fix the light in Hugh's kitchen. I was there last week, and it wasn't workin'. He probably don't care about it enough to mention, but I bet it would make things easier on him if you fixed it for him."

"Oh, sure."

The grass around Hugh's cabin was overlong, and you'd think it looked like something back on the mainland in the Dump. Eric walked up the steps. Hugh's cabin smelled really musty, and Hugh—who was ninety-seven and occasionally said he was a hundred—was sitting in a chair around on the side deck, in his sweater. After hellos and well, now, it's nice of you come and see me here, it really is, Eric said, "Come on, Hugh. You and me are old timers—since before Three-B. How can the tax office down there be the oldest building in the Settlement? That's just some nonsense for the tourists, ain't it?"

"Old-timer?" Hugh said. "You aren't no old-timer—you didn't come down to this place till you were sixteen, seventeen years old. I remember when Jay first brought you out to the Kyle place."

"So do I—"

"But I was born here. I spent my third birthday in the Kyle mansion, when they used to have the big Christmas party, and they invited everybody from *alllllll* over the state to come out." Vines twisted around the newels. Birds chirped. "People would come from Tennessee and Alabama and... they had Chinese people comin' and people from Europe comin'...."

"Yeah, I know. And they had black and white people, too, and they were proud of it."

"They sure were. And they'd bring out them little cracker boys like Jay and Wendell and Tennyson and the Johnston kids, too, from the mainland and local black fellas like me—even though Kyle was my name, too—to play and be together and see how everybody got along with each other. That was Robert Kyle's grandmother's idea, you know. She started that when she was a little girl, years before *I* was born—"

"Yeah, Hugh. I know about that. But I'm talking about the Tax Office—down town in the Settlement. You seen it. How can they say that's the oldest buildin' on the island? I remember when they started clearing back the forest—me and Shit came out here for that meeting. There wasn't no building there at *all*." Eric leaned back on the rail, looking around for another chair. "They were building Ms. Reba's place—and they had a tent up, where Kyle spoke that afternoon. Hell, *I* built half the buildings in this Settlement—me and Shit. The Holota cabin where we live now is older than *that* thing. Anybody can look at it and tell you, that's a new...you know...structure...new house, there."

Hugh sat and went on chuckling. "You know I don't put another chair out here, so that visitors won't stay too long. I like to sit here by myself and just look at things—"

"Don't worry, Hugh. I ain't gonna take up your morning. But I was trying to understand—"

"When they cleared it back—" Hugh seemed satisfied that Eric would go soon—"they did find that one house. But it wasn't exactly a house. It was a foundation. That's all that was left. And Ms. Reba said they might as well use it for her place. Only when they started, they realized it was an old, old building from years before—when there used to be an actual little township at that end of Gilead, from before the Kyle mansion even got built. So they asked Ms. Reba if she would take another plot, closer to the water, with a better view, and then they kept that old foundation and built it up. And since it used to be an official building for the Indian Records, they decided to use it for a record storin' place and tax place in the Settlement. You see how it don't sit even with the rest of the street? But they used the old foundation, just like it was. It's not the oldest building. But it's the oldest foundation. Now, they don't make a big thing about how it's all new, floor to ceilin'. They make like it's a real old place—and they done a good job of makin' it look kinda old—and just the clear wall, there, so you can look out and see the sky and water and the people passin' by, that they say is the new part." Hugh leaned forward and chuckled. "And half these fool women around here believe 'em."

"But I been livin' in these parts fifty years—and been out here on Gilead, comin' to pay my damned taxes there every year for fifteen years—or more—and I didn't know *any* of this stuff about it till now."

"The only ones who did were Jay and Mex and some of the old Holotas—and they wasn't really interested in it from a historical perspective. They had to hunt it up in old newspapers from the eighteen-nineties—the nineteen twenties. And, of course, they got some of it wrong, like that picture I give 'em, what Mr. Jenkins give to me. He didn't know when it come from—that date was just a guess—till his niece found the rest of the actual paper in the basement. That's all from these new ladies, who're always trying to hunt things up in the old papers they got in some of the offices on the mainland—and in the basement of the *Herald*."

"Hugh—what's history supposed to mean if you don't know it while you're livin' right when it's rubbin' up against you?"

"Not much of anythin', probably. You goin' home, soon?"

Eric sucked his teeth. "All these women around here goin' on about the place like it was the most important thing out here. Yeah, I'm leavin', Hugh. Oh—" He reached down into his orange shopping bag. "I brought some oatmeal raisin cookies for you. I know you like them."

"Oh!" Hugh sat back, smiling, surprised. "Now that's nice of you. You put 'em right over there, before you leave—"

On his way home, Eric thought, Damn, I forgot to ask him about the light. Well, maybe tomorrow when we get finished at the Boathouse. Yes, the Tax Office *was* an odd looking little building, out of alignment with the houses left and right of it. But he'd seen it all these years and thought it was either somebody's surveying mistake or just an anomaly—certainly little places like this could have them. As a breeze fingered under his shirt shoulders, it actually looked as if it might be part of a past township pattern somehow breaking out into the present.

These days the Kyle mansion was hidden under webs of scaffolding— had been for more than a year. (More renovations—renovations on the renovations, Eric guessed.) Trees flung shadows over it. Forty yards beyond it, Eric turned off and started through the woods. He walked till the ground began to slope and you could see out toward the water. Once he'd come there during a storm—and sworn he'd never do *that* again. It had been loud and he'd seen a tree blown up and watched it sweep around toward him and barely miss knocking him down—

Eric reached the stone bench—something that had been brought there, by the Kyles, for some sort of garden. Seventy-five years ago? Eighty-five years? More than a hundred?

Askew on the dirt, the stanchion and one end were half-buried, but you could sit on it. So he sat. He put down his orange bag between his old, scuffed work shoes. Going down into it with his right hand, he came out with his book. Eventually, he'd taped the whole cover over—back and front. The sea stretched toward a horizon that was identical to the one they saw out their own kitchen door, though the rocks and the whispering growth were completely different.

It smelled like dust and the sea.

Eric opened the book and started with the *Preface* to Part III, "Of the Origin and Nature of the Affects."

>...they seem to conceive man in Nature as a dominion within a dominion. For they believe that man disturbs, rather than follows the order of Nature, that he has absolute power over his actions, and that he is determined only by himself. And if they attribute the cause of human impotence and inconstancy, not to the common power of Nature, but to I know not what vice of human nature, which they therefore bewail, or disdain, or (as usually happens) cure. And he who knows how to censure more eloquently and cunningly the weakness of the human mind is held to be godly...

He thought, I can remember when that made no more sense to me than if I was reading it ass backwards. And now it seems lucid.

He read to the preface's end and decided: I think I'll skim the body of the argument this time; I remember pretty clearly what it is. I'd rather read the last two parts, "Of Human Bondage" and "Of Human Freedom." Long ago, he had realized the two were a single singing paean.

He turned over "Definitions" and "Postulates" and "Demonstrations" and "Propositions" and "Scholia." ("…No one knows how the mind moves the body…") He remembered the years when he used to read these pages, simply replacing the word "God" with the word "Nature," since, over and over, Spinoza had hammered in how they meant the same thing—were, indeed, two words for the same thing, but both had to be expanded and recomplicated just a bit from the way most people thought of them in order to reach that self-evident identity. But now he simply read what was there, and it seemed to offer no barrier, as he had by the same process— equally long ago—grown comfortable with a godless world, or rather with a world in which the gods had grown comfortable with his metaphorizing of them.

(It was wonderfully pleasurable to find a man who wrote four hundred years ago writing of "building and painting" in a landscape in which, only a few hundred yards away, Eric had built and had painted…)

Things strived to remain themselves—that striving was their *canatus*— and yet so many of them, it would seem if you looked at the histories people kept building around themselves, did nothing but fail in that endeavor.

Bondage, when all was said, seemed to be how we were subservient to a Nature that had been detailed in the book's first three parts—sometimes in sadness, sometimes in joy, and fell out from the perfect world of nature: That perfection existed in its variety because it could, not because of any human lack—a wanting—in Nature or God. Eric read on, happily bound by habit and familiarity…

"Hey—"

Eric looked up, "Oh, hi—!"

"No, don't stop," Shit said. "Go on readin'. I'm just gonna lie down on the bench here and put my head in your lap. You can rest your book on my forehead and use it for a readin' stand."

Shit lowered himself to the stone, his right leg out—the one where the arthritis was worse than in the other—and swung his big feet up to balance callused heels on the concrete.

Eric raised his elbow. Shit put his head down and turned on his side, nuzzling the bony back of his head against Eric's belly. Eric's elbows fell on Shit's shoulder. Shit brought up his upper hand between Eric's legs. "I ain't gonna give you no hard-on or nothin' if I play with your pecker through your pants, while I'm lyin' here, am I…?"

"Probably—" Eric said, turning a page—"not." Then he looked down. "But don't tickle."

"All right."

After another minute, Eric turned his open book down and put it over

Shit's ear, so that it covered his face. "Oh, that's nice," Shit said. "The light off the water was kinda gettin' to my eyes. Now that's usin' that thing for somethin' useful—like a sunshade. Now you can't really *do* that with one of them readers—"

"Shit…?"

"What?"

"I was just thinkin'."

"Thinkin' what?"

"We was at the Opera for eleven years—almost twelve. And this mornin'. I just went in and paid our taxes out here for what? The twenty-third or the twenty-fourth time out here? But I swear it feels like we was at the Opera a lot longer than we been out here."

"Yeah," Shit said. "You know, it really do." He moved his head. "That's probably cause out here I don't fuck even half the number of people I did when I was at the Opera, when I could could rip me off some nookie a couple of times a day, if I wanted—though, even by the end there, it was more like once every couple of weeks. If I could get up for it."

"But you'd think," Eric said, "with all the sex we had back then, the time at the Opera woulda gone faster, now. You know, times flies when you're havin' fun—and we had a *lotta* fun at that old place!"

"We sure as fuck did. But you're right—it does seem like we was there pretty much forever. 'Course we was on the garbage run even longer."

"Not much," Eric said, "when you actually count the years. I think it's just time goin' faster, when you get older."

"Well, like you say, God—or Nature—knows it does. Why you been thinkin' about that?"

"I stopped by to see Hugh—at his cabin."

Chucking, Shit turned his face up. "Did he tell you to get outta his face?"

"In a polite enough way." Eric took a deep breath, and starched. "Hey, you got to remember two things for me."

"What?" Shit asked.

"We got a job at the Boathouse tomorrow—and then we gotta fix the kitchen light at Hugh's. Ed told me about it—and when I was over there, I completely forgot to tell him we'd be comin' by."

Shit sat up. "I'll tell you to write 'em down as soon as we get home."

"That's all I want you to do. If I jot 'em down, I won't forget."

"Hey, they brought your boxes of food by today. Come on home and cook dinner for me."

"Sure," Eric said. "I am. Don't I always? What time is it?"

The sun was a white-hot spark in the trees, somewhere behind. Gold and mustard clouds under the faintest salmon and violet drifted over the sea. Eric looked around, and Shit said, "It's somewhere after four. Maybe even five…"

"Aww," Eric said. "It can't be *that* late. I just sat down here. It wasn't even noon…"

Shit said, "When you're out here readin' your book, nigger, you don't know *how* fast time passes…"

But Eric had already closed it and dropped it into the orange canvas sack. "Come on—come on, now. Get up, Shit. Let's get on home. So I can feed you."

* * *

[99] IN THE THREE years Caleb was there, odd things began coming into the house: an ancient DVD player, a wall computer monitor, and then Caleb asked them if he could put a General Screen on the back edge of the table. "I'll just install the pro-unit here, under the edge. I won't even pull it up unless you want to watch some news or—"

"You can do what you want," Shit said, "just as long as you don't expect me to do nothin' with it."

"Hey—" Caleb raised his palm, and the glimmering light screen lifted from the edge of the table's planks—"I could teach you how to use this thing in ten, fifteen minutes, Mr. Haskell—*half* an hour!"

"No, you can't. 'Cause I can't read no writin'. I told you that before!"

"You don't have to read anything," Caleb explained. "They got tutorials on this thing that are all pictures, like them cartoons you were laughin' over so much last Saturday.

"What's that?" Shit pointed to the screen.

"Where—what do you mean?"

"What's that? Right here."

"Huh?" Caleb said. "That's just the name of the Line Server."

"And that's writin', ain't it?"

"Yes, but—"

"And I told you, I can't read it. So I can't learn that stuff."

Caleb looked at Eric, who shook his head with half a smile. "Try him again in a week, when it's been here a while and he ain't feelin' so ornery. Show him some good porn—he'll like that."

Shit said, "If you wanna go on suckin' my damned dick and lickin' out my damned asshole, you'll keep that writin' stuff out my face, is what you'll do! I can get behind yours, yeah, from time to time—your shit, I mean. But I ain't interested in *that!*"

Clearly chagrined, Caleb dropped his hand, and the plane of light collapsed into the table under his fingers.

Over the next days, Eric found himself using it, however. A number of the market vendors were connected online, and he could get them to deliver most of his purchases—or put them aside for him, so they'd be waiting for him. Then, through some list Caleb had put his name on, someone started sending them flyers for a films series at the old Opera House—it hadn't been an adult film palace since Eric and Shit had given it up, all those years ago in Runcible.

In nothing but a baggy T-shirt, pouring coffee from the glass carafe at the counter, Shit explained, "Yeah, believe it or not, we used to take care of that place—for more'n ten years." With a cup in each hand, he turned and set them on the table in front of Caleb and Eric. "After we gave up the garbage route. It was a fuck film palace then—where niggers like you would suck each other off in the top balcony or jerk off down in the orchestra. You could always find some white guys in there, too."

"I used to have a good time in that place." Eric moved his hands around the warm mug. (While Caleb was here, Eric wondered if they should pick up some chocolate…) "Yeah, we each had a few regulars. Pretty much one or two of 'em, every day. Want a Danish?"

Caleb, who was kind of stocky, took one from the chipped plate. "Wished I'd been here for that. Sounds like fun." Then, holding up the pastry, he said, "Why am I the only one here who ever eats a whole one of these things?"

Still later, looking at the paper on the kitchen table, Eric saw there was a week-long retrospective of the films of Peter Jackson: *Lost Silver*, *Heavenly Creatures*, *The Hobbit, Part One* and *Part Two*, *Lord of the Rings* (all three films playing three times over two days), *The Frighteners* and *King Kong* ("With Deleted Scenes Completed and Restored"), *The Lovely Bones*. Hadn't he'd gotten into some argument about *King Kong* once—with his dad? But exactly over what, he wasn't sure. With a tattooed forearm, Eric pushed the flyer to the table back: the colors within his skin had migrated, blurred, faded. The yellow and white highlights that had made Cassandra's pictures special were gone. (Why hadn't they gone to her funeral…? Oh, yeah: because at the last minute her family had her shipped to Oklahoma. That's when Tank had sold both places, here and in Runcible.) The blue lines had thickened around her delicate vegetation, losing the precision that, once, decades back, so many had praised.

Caleb came into the kitchen, looked over his shoulder, and dropped one hand on Eric's back.

Eric said, "That's gonna be interesting. There're probably kids around here—I mean your age, under thirty—what never seen a real movie in a movie theater. There used to be an old thirty-five millimeter projector up in the projection room. Shit always wanted us to throw that thing out—but Myron, our projectionist, would never let him. That's probably the one they're using for this 'festival' thing right now."

Caleb's hand fell away. "I think I'm gonna go to Runcible and see some of those." From the dish in the middle of the table, he'd picked up a pastry. "I never saw *King Kong*. I mean on TV."

A few days later, sitting outside on the steps, for the first time in more than twenty years Eric retold—for the last time—the story Bill Bottom had told him, forty-five years before—with moral. As he told it, he thought: I'm almost old now. And to this boy, I ain't *almost*: I *am*. He wondered at the velocity with which age had careered into him. "Hey—just a minute." Eric stood and pushed back his chair. "You was in that Graduate School there, up in New England, and you was takin' philosophy, you said. You know anything about...here, lemme go get it for you." Eric went into the bedroom, and, from the bookshelf at the back of his dresser, he took out a brittle paperback with a cover under clear tape showing a man in a renaissance ruff and fancy hat. He brought them back into the kitchen.

Caleb took the books and frowned at them. "Spinoza...?" He looked up. "What're you doin' with these?"

"Readin' 'em," Eric said. "You know anything about 'im?"

"I know that's some pretty difficult stuff. How long you been readin' this?"

"I dunno." Eric said. "'Bout thirty years. Thirty-five, maybe."

"Yeah, well." Caleb turned the copy of *Ethica* over. "I guess that is the way you read Spinoza. If that print's too small for you, you can use my screen—" he reached for his back pocket—"and call up a larger—"

"Naw, that's okay. I'm used to these. One of 'em's a book about Spinoza—about his ideas and stuff. Otherwise I couldn't understand none of it. You ever read 'im?"

"A little bit," Caleb said. "In a course on Descartes and Liebnitz and a few of them other seventeenth century fellows—and Spinoza. He was the hardest. My teacher said Spinoza was his favorite, though—but we didn't read this one. I looked at it once, but it was beyond me. It's more like a book on geometry."

"Yeah," Eric said. "It's that 'Geometric Method' he uses."

"I remember," Caleb said, "that he figured everything in the universe was a part of God, because it was only the whole entire Universe itself, all together, that could do all the things that all the various people thought God was able to do. So that if there was a God, the totality of the universe itself had to be it."

"That's right," Eric said. "I remember that—that's what some of it's tryin' to say. I think. But there's stuff that's 'mind' and then there's stuff that ain't 'mind'—that's material…extension, he calls it—and they can't move each other directly. Only, somehow, in a living body, they're two sides of the same thing—the same thing looked at in a different way—"

Back against the white painted jamb, Shit sat on the threshold, the neck of his orange T-shirt sagging below one prominent collar bone, one wide, foot—bare—in the sunny trapezoid inside the kitchen door, the other down on a step outside. "That philosophy stuff is bullshit—right?" His eyes were closed. Along dark lids, silver lashes actually glittered. "Bullshit…yeah." His beard was a gray-white brush standing out in tufts below brown cheekbones. Shadows filled folds down his cheeks, grayed his beard. "Go on. Tell 'im like you told me, about how that's why you left that dumb university."

At the table, Caleb sat back to smile at the old man in the sunny door. Through the window screening on the wall beside him, sun fell over the knots of Caleb's dark fists on the table planks. "Now that's not exactly what I said, Mr. Haskell." Caleb was a meaty young man. He wore a black T-shirt with a white band around the neck, the arms, and the bottom, which (unlike Shit's) he didn't tuck in. On one side was a red circle with half a dozen white spots—a sign connected with a phenomenally popular TV series current years before. Even though its colophon had been absorbed by the greater culture, Eric had never seen it because they'd never had a TV.

Shit said, "That's what you said to me."

"I said—" Caleb let one arm bend—"that's what it made me *feel* like… sometimes."

"Ain't that the same thing?'

Eric chuckled.

Shit pulled his hands into his lap. "You can't understand it. It don't make no sense. So it's bullshit. That's just sensible."

"Sometimes," Caleb said, "it means you just have to work a little harder at it. Don't it, Mr. Jeffers?"

"Don't look at me," Eric said. "Talk to him."

"Oh, you're just tryin' to weasel out of it, now. Well, that's all right. You go on and weasel all you want." Shit opened his eyes and looked over toward the two men at the table. "He used to try and explain it to me sometimes. But he wouldn't admit that it didn't make no sense. And he wouldn't see that meant it was crazy bullshit. I swear, sometimes it would get me so mad, there, I'd wanna cry. Like all that business about baskets bein' in apples instead of apples bein' in baskets."

"Jesus." At the table Eric turned around. "Are you still worryin' over that one? That was fifteen, twenty years ago, Shit."

"Well, you just be glad I decided to laugh at your dumb white ass— 'cause if I hadn't, I woulda knocked your damned head in with a shovel!"

"And it wasn't baskets." Eric sat up at the table. "It was apples in piles; or apples in groups."

"See." Shit turned his face back to the sun. "There he goes again. He's tryin' to get me started."

"Oh, yeah—you mean the Spinozan 'in.'" Caleb looked over at Eric. "I remember that one now. We talked about it in class. But a lotta people have a tough time getting their minds wrapped around that. It is difficult, sir."

"There was nothin' to get your mind wrapped around," Shit said. "It's just wrong."

Caleb turned back to Shit, considering a moment. "It's not really that hard…sir. Try this, now. You and me, when we say 'in,' we mean something like: people are in groups. They're members of the group. Or an apple is in a pile—the apple is part of the pile. But when Spinoza wrote 'in,' he meant something else. He meant you couldn't have a group of people unless you had the individuals first. So the origin of the group, the potentiality for the group, is in the individuals. The potentiality for the pile is in the apples. The potentiality for the bunch is in the grapes. The potentiality for the sea is in the drops of water from the rain and streams and rivers that go into making it up. That's all he was saying. So when he says all things are 'in' Nature, he means 'in' in that sense: birds and fish and clouds and flowers, but also dinosaurs from a hundred million years ago as well as any species that might evolve ten million years from now—in the sense of their potentiality."

"Well, if that's what he meant, why didn't he say so?" Shit humphed, opened his eyes a second time, then shut them again. "Besides, fish and animals and birds are in nature. But piles *ain't* in apples."

"He did say it," Caleb said, "more or less."

"I mean *him*." Eyes still closed, Shit jabbed a thumb at Eric more than half again as wide as either of theirs.

"I tried to," Eric said. "But you were so busy tellin' me how stupid I was and it was, and what a dumb-ass I was, you wouldn't follow it."

"You didn't say nothin' about no 'potential,'" Shit said. "Least ways that I remember—besides, I ain't even sure if I know what 'potential' means."

Caleb laughed. "You and a lot of other people. But that's what everybody's arguin' about in philosophy departments, now; like 'difference,' about forty or fifty years ago."

"Well." Shit lifted his butt, then settled it again. "All it looks like to me is a lot of people usin' words they don't half understand to make everybody feel stupid and scared."

Caleb turned on his chair. The rungs creaked. "Well, sometimes, sir, feelin' stupid and scared is simply the human condition—especially when you got your thoughts up against some big philosophical problem—birth, death, difference, infinity, potentiality. Stuff like that—"

"Well," Shit repeated. "I gave up on that a long time back…feelin' stupid and scared, I mean. Weren't no gain from it. If I went with that, I'd be livin' three hun'er'd miles away from everybody, on another island all by myself. Hey, come on over here, boy."

"Sir?" Caleb pulled his hands back to the table edge and sat up straighter. "What you want?"

"I want you to unzip your jeans and get your black ass over here, so I can suck on your dick some. Then I'm gonna turn you around, stick my nose between your butt cheeks, and blow some air up your asshole so you can fart in my face. You got to smell a man's insides every once in a while. It's part of bindin'. Then, after we done that, I'm gonna get up from here and make another pot of coffee."

"Oh…!" Caleb stood, sharply, fingering the waist button on his jeans. "Yes, sir!" As he rose, he glanced back at Eric. "You sure, sir…I mean, Eric—" both of them had almost stopped arguing with him about calling them "sir" and "mister"—"you don't wanna use my reader? You can probably call up all them books you got and a lot more besides."

At the table, Eric opened the paperback Spinoza to the last part (Part V. "Of Human Freedom"), shaking his head, smiling some.

* * *

[100] THIS ACTUALLY MADE it into memory to pulse there over the years:

You'd have thought it was something tenacious and obsessive that had happened in childhood, though it occurred when Eric was seventy-six. He'd gone out for an hour and a half with the kid—well, Caleb *was* twenty-nine now—in the row boat, when, over three minutes, a surprise October fog had obliterated all sight of land. "That was awful nice of your friend, Anne, to have me over there at her big dinner again. I mean, she didn't know me at all, hardly."

"Well," Eric said, "you're a friend of ours—she's a friend of ours." Eric was a little worried, though he tried not to show it.

But leaning into the oars, Caleb began to row. "You know, out here like this, I can understand what Thales was all about."

"Huh?" Eric asked, one hand on the gunwale. "Who was Thales?" He wondered if he'd lost some thread of the conversation to some passing reverie of his own.

But Caleb leaned and pulled, leaned and pulled. "You know—that Greek philosopher—the first one. He thought everything in the universe was made of water."

"Naw." Eric smiled. "I never heard of 'im." He looked around the mist-diminished sea, which, without horizon, in that state, could look even larger than usual.

But not now.

Four o'clock sun was a faint pearl to the sky's left, dim enough to look at directly for five, six, seven seconds.

Caleb went on rowing—and laughed. "How can you know all about Spinoza, Mr. Jeffers, but...not know about *Thales*?"

"Don't ask me." Looking back down at cross-hatching on the boat's bottom, Eric laughed back. "But I sure don't." No, there was nothing to worry about. That was the sun, so the island was over there.

Then, as if to remind them they were moving with Caleb's labors, both in space and in time, surging through moist gray, Gilead gathered itself into visibility, right where it should have been, as the Earth might once have gathered itself according to nature's order, from the sea. (Looking at the sea too long always made Eric feel that there was something he should have remembered, something insignificant and particularly specific that had slipped his mind, that for some reason he could not bring back...) With its foliage, and buildings, and dock, the island loomed above the waves.

* * *

[101] ERIC PUSHED HIS rough forefinger into one nostril, turned it one way, then the other—and suddenly smiled. *I'm a seventy-seven-year-old man. And I'm still comfortin' myself by pickin' my damned nose and eatin' my own damned snot—same as when I was six or seven.*

The image that came to him now was not Shit, about whom, at seventy-nine, you could say the same thing, but—rather—sitting in the corner of the old island docking platform, before Anne or Hanna or Ed or Reba's Place or Nightwood or the Settlement itself—sitting beside Jay, with

Mex, under glittering night. Was anyone alive except him and Shit who remembered that old boathouse and the dock beside it, from before they had pulled it down to replace it with concrete steps?

Was there anyone who knew how much urine had once spilled in that corner, drenching those boards in starlight?

Or even smelled them the next day and wondered?

Other than him and Shit.

Eric pulled his finger free to suck.

Damn! It really was good. Why couldn't people accept it? Dr. Greene used to tell them it helped their immune system and probably accounted for why Shit and he never had colds.

Caleb had said watching old guys do any sort of nastiness got him off. Eric grinned. Now that was luck.

But good for you or not, why couldn't they let little girls—on the beach only that summer, behind a boulder at the wood's edge pushed out onto the sand, he'd seen a little girl doing it, and smiled at her, but, entirely in her own world, she hadn't noticed—and little boys who did it alone?

* * *

[102] ERIC WAS COOKING burgers on the side-porch grill, with gulls and the sea the only noise. (He had an orange stool he rested on when he was wasn't actually turning them with his spatula or checking them with the spatula's corner for doneness.) Sitting around waiting for them, Caleb and Shit started talking: "Did you get in a lot of trouble when you was a kid?"

"Me?" Shit asked. "When I was comin' up around here, there wasn't enough people out here to get in no trouble *with*. Besides, all I was interested in when I was a kid was bitin' my nails and findin' a place where I could get off and pull my dick—which wasn't too difficult around here, back then. 'Specially in the winter. I did the nail bitin' with my dad—he was into that, too. And some dick pullin' with 'im, too, actually. You live out here, and there's so few people—or at least there used to be—you kinda got used to doin' it when you wanted. And as long as it was somebody from the Dump came by, you didn't even mind that. At least that's what it was like in the Dump—the place we used to live. 'Cause all the niggers there was faggots, too. Then, when Eric hooked up with us, I had me a white boy I could always run off with and we could jerk off together as much as we wanted to. Or suck or fuck or eat each other's assholes out. I mean I was a fifteen-time-a-day fella—Dynamite, my dad, used to say I didn't have no time to get in trouble. I was too busy beatin' off."

Caleb laughed.

"Fifteen times a *day*? Come on. Don't exaggerate, Shit." Eric moved the three toasted buns to the aluminum foil spread over the table beside the grill. "You're worse than I am."

"Well, I could do it fifteen times in a day, when I wanted."

"Yeah—but you didn't," Eric said, lifting another burger with the spatula. "I mean not *every* day. Hell—that's nothin', anyway."

"Here he goes now," Shit said. "Here he goes. Go on, just watch 'im—"

Eric turned over two of the patties at the grill's back. "Well, I told you before. When I was in Hugantown, I knew this Greek guy who did it twenty-two times over one day. I counted, once—lookin' at him through a crack in his bathroom window."

"See, there?" Shit pulled a can of pop from the cooler's chuckling ice. "He always been like that—Mr. Eric Jeffers, big city slicker. You show him a nigger with a thirteen-inch dick, and he gonna tell you about one he knew with fifteen. I swear I wouldn't put up with him if he wasn't such a good cocksucker—and a decent cook."

"I *knew* one with fifteen inches," Eric said, while sun reflecting off the window behind him put a net of light through Shits beard against the dark siding. "I was fuckin' around with him, too, just a few days before I came out here to the Harbor for the first time. I went lookin' for him that mornin'." He shrugged and turned over a burger. "But I couldn't find 'im. So I made do with this nigger here, when I got to Turpens."

"There he goes," Shit said. "See what I told you…? Bullshit. That's all his talk is—bullshit, more than half the time."

"We could tell 'im about Haystack. We both knew *him*—"

"Oh, *shit*—" Shit said. "I forgot about *that* boy—he had enough to make you *wanna* lie about 'im—either add a couple of inches so that folks what thought *you* must be lyin' would just stop arguin' with you, or cut off a few inches 'cause there ain't no man what's *supposed* to have what that boy had swingin' down between his legs—"

"Between his knees, you mean." Eric turned over another meat patty.

"I just know he was white, about seven and a half feet tall, and his cock was bigger than a goddam can of Foster's beer—which they don't make no more—and that ain't countin' three more inches of the cheesiest skin you ever sucked on like a spigot hangin' off the end. And all you had to do was smile at 'im and he'd pee in your mouth, so when you look at our friend there flippin' burgers today, remember he done spent a few years in paradise around that boy. More, Haystack didn't care how close you wanted to get up and watch 'im do whatever he was doin', suckin' 'im, or fuckin' 'im, or lettin' him fuck you—he'd let me joggle on his nuts (with my hands *or* with my toes), or scratch his hairy back (he said that was *almost* better than sex)—so I got a kick out of him too with Eric. And all you had to do is snap your fingers and he'd shit right in your hand—if that was what you wanted. And there were times I did. It can't mean nothin' to you, I know, but every so often for the three years he was in Opera, you'd hear somebody gasp or grunt, 'Oh, Jesus!' or 'Oh, my Lord!' and you knew some newcomer had collided with Haystack's meat for the first time—as dumb as a brick and as friendly as a puppy, too. Back then he was about your age, maybe twenty-five years old—or even twenty-six or twenty-seven. But if you didn't know what you was getting' into, the first time that boy grinned and pulled aside the eighteen inch rip in his jeans, you could have an apoplexy!"

Eric took a great breath. "'Peace and truth are the foundation of the world.'" He turned back to the grill. "Even when you're arguin' about big dicks."

At the table, Caleb looked up, smiling. "But that ain't Spinoza. That was…carved on the stone lintel over a doorway in a merchant's house Spinoza used to visit with his father, when he was a kid. At least I remember that. He'd see it every time he went there. Probably it had an effect on him. I remember that from some book or other I read."

"Oh," Eric said. "Now I can't remember if I knew that or not." He spatulaed the last burgers onto a platter at the table, then stretched. "You know, not only am I a good cocksucker; I'm a good fuck, too. At least you always said I was."

Shit said, "I think the only reason Haystack stayed out of trouble was 'cause he was always too busy jerkin' off. Like me. And he was a hit at the Opera 'cause he loved guys to play with 'im—just like a little kid. Especially if it involved his dick."

Eric said, "Back when he was still alive, our dad—Shit's dad, anyway—used to say, 'Show me a kid who beats off more than ten times a day, and I'll show you somebody who's too *busy* to get in trouble—long as the wrong people don't catch him at it.'"

"I guess I probably shoulda done more jerkin' off, then—that way I wouldn't have been such a hellion when I was a pipsqueak." Caleb laughed. "I was in court three times before I was sixteen. I don't know why I never ended up in jail."

"Hey," Shit asked, "we got time to jerk off, once, before you finish them things up? I bet I could get this nigger here all excited, just talkin' nasty to 'im. Like I used to do with you. That'd really tickle me. You know how it feels so nice, boy, before the sun gets up, when you slide down in the bed between us and start suckin' on my dick—"

"No," Eric said. "You do *not* have time. Caleb could probably do it." He nodded toward the young man. "But it would take you at least half an hour—if not forty minutes. And they're done—now!"

Once more Caleb laughed. "You ol' guys are a hoot!"

*

Eventually, Caleb convinced Shit and Eric to go see the first of Jackson's three Ring films at the Opera House. (Eric had never seen any of them; Shit didn't remember ever having heard of them.) So they went. The showing ran over two days: the first was *The Fellowship of the Ring*, with the first half of *The Two Towers*. The second day they'd come back and start with the second half of *The Two Towers* and go on through *The Return of the King*. Eric told them, "If you never seen it, it probably helps if you know a little bit about it first. You see, some ancient magicians made these twelve rings, and one of them—"

After a few minutes on the boat deck, standing at the rail, Shit asked, "If you never seen 'em, how come you know so much about 'em?"

"'Cause everybody in two different schools I went to had seen 'em about three dozen times a piece. Besides, I read the books."

"You actually remember all that from a book you read all those years ago, from before you got here?" Shit wanted to know.

"Three books," Eric said, "actually."

"Well, damn…" Shit said. "That's probably even harder, ain't it? You know every time I decide this scumsuckin' motherfucker is just full of bullshit with all his readin' and crap, it turns out he actually knows somethin'." Shit shook his head—and Caleb laughed.

On the boat over, mostly they talked of showing Caleb their old quarters upstairs above the Opera House's projection room.

"The theater's got an old lounge, downstairs, and a big old tile and mirrored rest room—they closed up the women's room, but it was even grander—"

"That makes me remember the first time I ever seen Haystack. I'd just come in there, about five or six in the mornin', to mop the floors, and there he was, squattin' on one of the commodes—seven and a half feet tall, almost three hundred and fifty pounds, his big, dirty bare feet practically wrapped around the circular seat on the top and hands on 'im like backhoe shovels over his knees. I told him, 'Hey, son. You don't need to squat on that thing. We keep 'em pretty clean around here.'

"And the first thing he said to me was, 'It ain't the dirt. But if I sit right down, my pecker hangs about three or four inches into the water—and it's cold.' Then he puts one foot down on the tile, leans forward, and stands up and puts the other one down—and I damned near swallowed my tongue, 'cause I seen he wasn't lyin'!" Shit shook his head. He looked around at sky, as if the ferry sailed through the pearl time. "I'd already noticed he was one of those guys who chewed on his toenails and his fingernails both, pretty much like I do and my daddy did, and I confess it made me kinda cotton to 'im."

"Me too, when I met him a little later." Eric grinned. "Anyway, the place has got an orchestra and two balconies. They still called the back of the top balcony 'Nigger Heaven,' 'cause that's where all the black people—like you two—had to sit, back when there was segregation. They had regular fold up wooden chairs, up there—not them real comfortable padded theater seats, either. I used to clean up in the upper part of the theater, and Shit used to keep the basement and the orchestra clean. Sometimes we'd switch off there. But he didn't like workin' in the upper part of the theater."

"Because of that 'Nigger Heaven' place?" Caleb asked. "That would'a made me uncomfortable, too, I think."

"Naw," Shit said. "It wasn't that. I just don't like high places." He frowned at the approaching shore. "Sometimes I wonder what happened to Haystack…"

"But you said you lived up there—"

"Yeah, but that was in an apartment. With walls and everything— closed in. You got to it with a stairwell, with walls on both sides. It wasn't open—so you could run down the aisle and dive over the rail. *That's* the kinda place I like to stay away from—"

"Unless—" Eric laughed—"somethin' really interestin' was goin' on up there. Like the Breakfast Club."

Shit gave him a sour look.

"That Nigger Heaven thing used to bother me." Eric changed his position. "Well, not bother me. 'Cause it wasn't workin' no more—I mean the way it used to, historically. Though a lotta time there was more black guys up there than downstairs."

"See," Shit said, "that's where they went when they got tired of the white guys down from Atlanta who wanted to suck on some black meat. The white guys who didn't wanna be bothered, never figured out that they could escape a lotta bother just by goin' up there. They just got grumpy. They wasn't too bright—like I done told you: Haystack. But we had guys comin' in, especially at the end when they started writin' newspaper articles about the place, drivin' five and six hours in a day just to hang out there—"

"But sometimes—when we first started—" Eric changed his position against the rail again—"I would stand up there and look around at it—Nigger Heaven—and try to imagine slaves comin' there with their masters and goin' upstairs to watch while their masters sat downstairs in the comfortable seats—or, later, just regular black folk who wanted to hear the opera or see the show or the movie…I mean, before they had the fuck films goin' in that place." Gulls swooped above the boat. Behind them water rushed away. "Finally, though, I'd go and clean it up, mop the cum off the floor—sometimes, if it was a nice big puddle, I'd wonder which one of them black sonofabitches left it. And wonder if I could get to 'im next time, 'fore he finished up. I mean, it wasn't like they didn't wanna be bothered at all. They just didn't wanna be bothered a *lot*. Besides, most of 'em knew me and what I could do. Probably that made it easier—on us both."

The three of them grinned.

"After thirteen years," Eric said, "you get used to almost anything—I guess."

When they climbed from the bus in front of the Runcible theater, the first Eric saw was that the marquee had been torn away. Above the steel fire doors that had replaced the glass and molded ones, sawed-off stubs from the beams once holding it up thrust from the crumbling façade.

"You sure this is the right building…?" Shit wanted to know.

Before the theater, laughing and chatting about other films in the series, the audience milled. The ticket booth was gone, but you could see a rusted discoloration where it had stood on the broken pavement.

More than a dozen young men had come with transparent pastel crotch panels—the first time Eric had seen anyone wear them other than on the beach. "Damn," Shit whispered, "they're all so small."

"I think," Eric said, "that's the fashion. Only guys who don't really got no meat at all wear 'em. It's kind of a…I don't know: a rebellion. Like 'Fuck you! This is what I got! Live with it!'"

Shit frowned. "Well, I guess I ain't got no choice…"

Caleb chuckled.

Shit rubbed the back of his neck. "You remember when ladies first started goin' around everywhere with no tops on?" A group of seven or eight topless teenage girls were all laughing together near the wall, where Eric recognized a piece of scrolled stonework. Most of it had been taken down.

"Sure." Eric nodded. "That took me a little while to get used to."

Caleb looked up at the broken second-floor windows, backed with blue plastic. "I don't. That's been all my life."

Suddenly Eric frowned. "Hold on a minute…?"

"Where you goin'?" Shit asked.

"No place…" He started up the block through the crowded.

At the corner, yes, was where Cave et Aude had once stood. And right where that lot now collected chicken-wire, broken brick, plaster lumps, glass, and rubble, that's where the clinic had been where he'd had his wisdom teeth out. Him and Shit both—and Dynamite…

He looked down at the corner pavement. Two posts—two hitching posts. Yes, they'd been there when he'd gotten there and, as far as he remembered, when they'd left.

Nothing stood there now.

Then, as he looked down the sidewalk pavement, he saw three circles filled with cement. Eric began to smile. Okay, they weren't standing any longer. But certainly that's where they'd stood…? Yes, and there'd been two, with horse heads, tarnished black, and a space for a third.

Eric turned and started back down the street, among the gathered folks, till he saw Shit and Caleb. Caleb was the one who asked, "What were you lookin' for?"

Eric shook his head. "Nothin'."

"You try and figure it out," Shit said, "you'll be here all day. And don't ask him to explain, neither. That way we'll never get inside and see the damned movie…"

The crowd had begun to push through the opened-back doors, into bare lobby, and on into the theater space—

Every third or fifth chair was broken or missing and the floor was scattered with filth and old plaster. Someone had cleaned out half the orchestra, though. Every working seat was taken.

Shit was so upset at the theater's state—"Now, this place was okay for a hundred years! Can you imagine if we done let it get like this? Jesus Christ! But…what? Only twenty, thirty years more, and it's like…this?"—Eric was sure he wouldn't be paying much attention to the movie. "Hell, that ain't no time at all!"

At least, Eric thought, he'd found a *trace* of something familiar…

The audience was mostly young people, under fifty or outright kids, who, once the film started, loved it, applauding, laughing, cheering all through. For the beginning of the film, somehow they'd gotten hold of an ancient filmed announcement, which showed a quivering line across the screen, and to the sound of, first, a crying baby, then laughter, then talking, came the announcement in a northern accent: "Don't spoil the movie by creating your own soundtrack!" Here and there, people who remembered when cell phones didn't simply buzz in your ear but sounded out of whatever pocket the clumsy contraptions hung in, laughed.

In the first intermission, Shit had gone down to the restroom and when he came up, Eric realized he was stonily silent—though likely Caleb didn't notice.

Once, after the second intermission, when the second film started, Caleb leaned over and whispered to Shit, "Gollum's hands look kinda like yours, Mr. Haskell. I mean that old blue fella bites his nails almost as bad as you do."

On Shit's other side, Eric leaned over to add, "So does Frodo," wondering if Shit was picking up on the way Frodo and Gollum were supposed to be two sides of one character, as Gollum himself was a divided soul.

Looking up at the screen, Shit said, "Aw, neither of them boys knows nothin' about how to get them things right. Me or my daddy, either one of us, coulda showed them a thing or two about *real* nail bitin'," which was true. He humphed. "Haystack coulda, too."

But at least, Eric reflected, Shit seemed to have gotten himself back together after whatever had happened downstairs.

Again, Caleb whispered, "Your hands—and your feet—are almost as *big* as his. Only you're a lot better lookin' than he is."

"I should hope so," Shit said, Then, wonderingly he added, "This movie sure goes on a long time about ever'thing, don't it? Some of the music's nice, though."

Returning to Gilead that night on the ferry, when Caleb had gone to look at something at the front of the boat and Shit and Eric were alone for a couple of minutes, Eric asked him what had happened down in the john, but he wouldn't talk about it. Back on Gilead, Shit refused to go the next day. He said it was just that he couldn't take seeing the theater in that condition again—it was that, not the movie. Pretty uncomfortable about it himself, Eric stayed home with him. "I did like them fireworks," Shit confessed, "there in the beginning, in the first part, I mean. But after that, it was just a lot of people runnin' around and bangin' on everybody with swords. I got tired of that pretty fast. What was that 'pipeweed' stuff, anyway? Marijuana?" They hadn't even tried to get upstairs.

Caleb went the next day, though.

When he got back, he said he'd had fun. Really, it was a' interesting old building, he said. This time, after it was over, he'd made an effort to get upstairs—and was sorry they wouldn't let you into any of the upper balconies anymore, which apparently were no longer safe. At least that's what sign had said.

Sitting in the doorstep, half in and half out of the sun, Shit didn't say anything.

*

Not quite a year later, hours after Caleb had left the island on Ed's boat to start his trip to Tallahassee and back to graduate school, to which he'd finally applied and been accepted, Shit and Eric looked down from Gilead Bluff over the Settlement's houses—half of them built in the last six years. Shit had his arm around Eric's shoulder. "Damn—I feel like we had us our own kid, here."

"Yeah," Eric said. He glanced at Shit. Something that Eric had thought about saying a number of times over the last three years, but never had—mostly because he always had assumed Shit was thinking the same thing. "He was kinda different from Gus, there—wasn't he?"

But, this time, the expected moment of telepathy did not occur. "Gus?" Shit frowned. "What do you mean? Who's Gus?"

"You don't remember Gus—who stayed with us a little while, back in thirty-three?"

"Thirty-three—that's a long time ago."

"It ain't that long, Shit—twenty-five years."

"Man, I always thought you was good at math. That was thirty-five years ago—"

"Well, that's what I meant."

"And we had somebody livin' with us?"

"Yeah, back on the mainland—when we had the apartment, right above the projection room in the theater?"

"I don't remember no Gus." Shit's frown deepened.

"Okay," Eric said, and let his own expression become a (frustrated) smile. "Like I said, it wasn't quite the same thing. Besides, it was only for a couple of weeks—not a couple of years. We met her out here, on the island. It was right when the Three Bombs come. We took her back with us 'cause she was all upset about it. She got you off somewhere, and 'cause she was cryin' and everything about it, you got to fuckin' on her, and she said that made her feel better. So you wanted to take her home with us, when they said we could open up the Opera House again. You don't remember that?"

"Where'd this Gus sleep?"

"Right in the bed with us—so we could all fuck. Which I thought, at least for a while, you was enjoyin'. *She* seemed to be. And she didn't mind me putting my seven inches in, at least as long as we were all together. You really don't remember that?"

"I remember Big Man. But that was usually at his place. I don't remember ever havin' anybody else up there in bed with us—" Shit frowned. "A girl?"

"You don't remember how, after two weeks, you made me take her off and tell her she had to move on—'cause she didn't like you talkin' about fuckin' all the guys downstairs in the theater? She said you could do it, but she didn't want you to talk about it—at least so much. You don't remember…?"

"I remember Mex sleepin' on the floor, the night he stayed after one of your free food cookouts. And I remember gettin' up early so I could get a blowjob from him, before you got up. But that's all."

"Now I remember *that*—you just wanted to take your mornin' piss in his mouth and didn't want me to wake up and feel bad about it. So you got up instead of callin' him into bed with us—I thought you were bein' kinda silly."

"Oh…you did? Well, you always used to think I was being silly when I was tryin' to be considerate."

"No, I didn't." Eric took Shit's hand and squeezed it. "I thought it was sweet. It's one of the reasons I love you." Eric sucked his teeth. "Shit, you really don't remember how you told me I had to tell her to leave 'cause you was too chickenshit to talk to her yourself? You said you didn't know how to talk to no woman you was fuckin'—and I was surprised, 'cause I always thought you were the big stud who knew everything about sex. When I told her, she was pretty upset about it. We'd only met her about a day before the Bombs went off—and by the time you was ready to kick her out, everybody was all twisted out of shape, pretty much everywhere. She'd lost a lot of family—"

"A woman, huh? Probably the only one I ever fucked, anyway."

"What about the girl who you told me about—one of the summer people, a couple of years before I come down here?"

"I don't even remember her that well. Probably 'cause I had to think about my daddy fuckin' her, in order to get off. And if there was another one later, I probably had to think about you."

Eric frowned. "You never told me *that* before. Anyway, like I said—" with his other hand, Eric fingered behind his ear—"Gus and Caleb weren't very much alike…"

"Funny I don't remember it. In thirty-three, huh? Well, with them Bombs there, that was a funny year."

"Yeah," Eric said. "That you don't remember Gus, though—that is odd. She ended up workin' on the Produce Farm. I think she was the first woman they had out there."

"Now that's actually beginning to sound familiar. But I sure don't remember fuckin' her."

"Well, you know, you got a tendency not to remember things you don't particularly like. It's probably how you live with 'em so easily."

"Hey, don't say that about me." Shit frowned. "I can remember stuff you don't."

"Well, maybe I remember that 'cause I was kinda mad at you, too, over that one. Them Bombs had gone off. Everything was crazy, and I didn't think you was bein' very nice to her."

"Well, now, see," Shit said. "If I was mad at you, I would work on forgettin' it. Maybe I was—and that's why I can't remember it. Sometimes, you know, you wanna be *too* nice to people. And bein' nice to the point where you make yourself miserable ain't that good, either."

"Yeah," Eric said. "I know…"

Now and again, they received postcards from Caleb, from Denver and Missoula and Kansas City, and in the first three months after he left, text messages arrived regularly that Eric read out to Shit from the e-reader Caleb had left with them.

"You sure you don't want to get one of them General Screens like he had—I mean, just so you could do your marketing a little more easily?"

Eric raised an eyebrow. "You wouldn't mind?"

"I don't mind as long as you don't try to teach me how to use it. You start tryin', though, and I'll probably kill ya'. Course me and him used to watch dirty pictures on that thing—and he'd play with my dick while we watched 'em. That was fun. But you and me got along without it—*how long there…?*"

In another year, however, the postcards—then the text messages—stopped. Apparently, Caleb never did get his degree. And, no, they never got a General Screen.

Nor did Caleb visit.

* * *

[103] MOVING OUT OF the sun, gold clouds turned under themselves to become soiled bronze. West, a storm's rags slanted toward the sea, the gray of a heavily chalked blackboard, carelessly erased.

Years ago, Eric had nailed together two wooden crates to make a bench. Out on the porch, Shit had built a back to the thing, with boards. Then across the back and the seat, he'd tacked some old carpet.

One hand on his own thigh and one on the bench's arm, Eric lowered himself—*really, we need to get a comfortable porch seat*. But the fact that they'd made it themselves had extended its life fifteen years now, if not twenty.

A leaf blew along the porch edge, ticking one after another of the newels supporting the rail, till, at the opening for the steps, it swirled out over the grass with hundreds of others, blowing.

Along the road, half a dozen young people came, some laughing and skipping backwards, others running, all of them talking heatedly, their shorts and shirts glittering gold and green, metallic blue and red.

At the same time, Shit came around the bench end and sat next to Eric. He put one broad hand on Eric's thigh—and his foot over Eric's work shoe.

Eric said, "They gotta get a gate in front of the graveyard. It's one thing to walk around in it and enjoy it, but you can't have kids running and screaming and raisin' hell all over." He frowned at encroaching overcast. "They gonna get wet 'fore they get back to the Settlement. That rain can't be more than twenty minutes off."

"More like two or three," Shit said. "A graveyard is always a good place to get off to and fuck. Probably that's what they was doin'."

"All of 'em together? I don't think so."

Shit began to rub Eric's washed out denim. "That's what I would have been doin', when I was their age."

One of the girls put her fists out from her sides. In her sandals, she rose about six, eight, twelve inches off the road, and, like a levitating saint, leaning forward, began to glide along, faster and faster. A couple of boys did the same.

The first boy increased his speed—and suddenly all his clothing whipped free. He turned his invisible scooter field and started back, balancing, concentrating, grinning.

The other kids whooped.

Shit's fingers tightened on Eric's leg. "Hey, look, they've got them scooter fields!"

Another of the boys sailed over the grass toward them, then turned, and sailed away.

"You think they'd let me try that out?"

"Come on," Eric said. "Last year, Molly's nephew let you use his glide field and you fell and almost busted your hip. I am *not* lettin' you on one of those things again!"

"Aw, come on. I bet if I asked, they'd think it was funny, watchin' a seventy-five-year-old man messin' around on one of those—"

"You are *not* seventy-five! 'Cause I am seventy-nine and you are eighty-*one*! How you gonna ride it when you can't even see the goddam things—"

The gaggle of youngsters was moving forward, back toward the Settlement, circling on and off the road, some running, some soaring, half of them naked. By now, the clothing on all three with the inductance scooter fields had come to pieces, flickering in bright clouds, in glittering streamers twelve and fourteen feet off the ground, blindly trying to find their owners. Shit said, "Hey, that's...pretty!"

One of the girls halted and a cloud of bright fragments settled around her, reforming over her hips and belly, her shoulders and breasts

Eric said, "That's stupid! At least *you* gettin' on one of them field things is stupid. You say stuff like that just 'cause you wanna worry me!" He put his hand on top of Shit's. "They are pretty, though—the way their clothes come off 'em and get back on 'em, when they stop runnin' around. I'll give you that."

Shit responded by pressing harder with his foot; he chuckled. "That's right—I *do*, you know. I *like* to see you all worried about me. It's about the only excitement we got." Around them, the island rumbled, and—with the thunder—rain began to drip from the porch roof's forward edge. The youngsters released a rising wail at the rain. Then, on the invisible inductance scooters or on foot, they were gone around the bend.

Eric looked up. Here and there in the roof, drops and runnels ran down clear Plexiglas rectangles. The temperature had dropped a few breezy degrees. Eric asked, "What you think *I'd* look like, walkin' around in one of them things, that come all to pieces like that, then join up later on?"

Shit humphed. "Yeah, sure. You won't even take the sleeves off your shirt and let people see your pictures no more. You gonna put somethin' on that's gonna let people look at your butt and wave your goddam dick at 'em? Yeah, *sure* you are!" He pulled his hand loose from under Eric's, meshed it with his other, and dropped them between his knees. Then he looked where Eric was looking. "You know, you're right." He was taking up a colloquy they'd started and abandoned fifty times in the last decade. "I gotta get me up there and reconnect those solar panels we put up. It's a shame, just 'cause we disconnected them for that storm back when—was it fifty-eight? Fifty-nine?—not to have 'em workin'. With these power ups and downs, we could really use 'em today"

"Well, you ain't climbin' up there on no ladder. Neither one of us is."

Shit chuckled again. "Hey—that first kid, when his shorts come whippin' off him, he had a nice pair a' low hangers on 'im. Nice and heavy. Fun to hold—if I'd gone and asked him could I heft 'em, he might've said 'Yes.' And the worst he coulda said was 'No.' I bet you noticed 'em, too."

"Sure—some crazy old man comin' up to 'im and sayin', 'Hey, sonny, could I hold your balls there for a bit?' Yeah, they'd have you put away in about two minutes." Then, after a moment, Eric said: "But, yes, I did. And I figured that was why you was interested in goin' out and messin' with them."

"Oh, yeah. Nothin' gets by you." Again Shit laughed. "You know, if he'd let me feel 'em, I'da asked 'im to come back and let you have heft—"

"Shit…?"

"I would. I always liked to watch out for you—'cause you was always a little shy—"

"Shit…?"

"What?"

"Seriously. When's the last time you had sex with somebody who wasn't me? Was that back with Caleb?"

Shit looked out at the rain. After a while, he said, "You're serious, now?"

"Yeah. I was curious—and serious."

"Actually, it was about six weeks ago."

Eric was surprised.

Shit breathed in and sat up on the bench. "I was down town, walkin' around the Settlement. Remember that first day of Indian summer? I mean, it was one of them days when every male dog in the Settlement was runnin' around with two inches of dick stickin' out, all red and pointy, and tryin' to hump anything that would hold still, and every male from eight years old on up had a boner in his skivvies that he was pushin' around and couldn't make it go down to save hisself. I mean, you could *feel* it with the women, but you could *see* it on the men. Anyway, I was goin' by Lacy's and her girlfriend Orchid's house, and I was remembering how Anne had been tellin' us that they wanted to have a baby together, but they didn't want to do it with a sperm bank—she had a friend from school up in Michigan, who they'd invited out, to get Orchid pregnant—?"

"Yeah, I remember Anne tellin' us all that—"

"—and how Anne was sayin' she didn't think that was a good idea. But while I'm walkin' down there, I see this guy comin' out of Lacy's front door—nice lookin' feller, no shirt on him, and just this pair of loose pants, all this black curly hair on his chest, and sandals—he's a kid, thirty, thirty-five-years old maybe. And I'm thinkin', well, you know, maybe that's the new daddy. And he's pushin' at himself and pullin' and adjustin' just like me and every other guy I'd seen that day. And he comes runnin' down the steps, then looks around—he don't see me, or at least he don't look like he do—and he turns around and starts back up, then turns around *again* and comes down again, and there ain't nobody else out on the sidewalk, and like I say, he's feelin' and rubbin', and I tell you, nigger, if you said I could *smell* what he was gonna do, I wouldn't argue with you two minutes. He goes off and turns at the corner of the house to go around into the back. And so—" Shit shrugged—"I kind of followed him. Like I said, I could *smell* somethin' was goin' on! I got to the back corner and looked around where Lacy's got their hollyhocks and their irises all growin' up, and damned if that guy wasn't standing, lookin' in the corner of one of the back windows. He'd pushed his pants down and was stooped there with his ass in the sunlight, apumpin' his pecker with his fist, while he's peekin' in—so I figured, what the hell, and took my limp old dick and began pullin' on it there with 'im. I never did figure out when he actually saw me, or if he knowed I'd followed from the beginnin' and just didn't care. But once he looks over at me—and grins. I mean, just like that. I don't think he was anymore surprised than I was.

"I whispered, 'What you peekin' at...?'

"He put his finger up against his mouth in the sunlight and shushes me. Then he goes back to peekin' and pumpin'.

"So I moved about three steps closer. And he looks over again, still grinnin', and says, kinda soft, 'I just love watchin' lesbians. I swear, I could do that all day long, all fuckin' year. I just can't get enough of 'em. They're so fuckin' beautiful with each other.' I mean, he was really sweet.

"'Then you come to the right island, fella,' I told him, 'You the guy who Lacy and Orchid called in to get Orchid pregnant?'

"'You *know* about that?' he asked—ain't neither one of us missed a stroke, while he were going on. But that's the kind of day it was.

"'I thought we were all gonna do it together—this afternoon,' he explained. 'I mean, I gotta do Orchid a couple or five times. But then they got into each other, see, and asked me to go out and hang around a while and come back later.'

"So that's when I asked him, 'You want me to give you a hand, son? Or maybe a little mouth action while you watchin'?'"

"'Jesus, old man,' he said, "I was hopin' you was gonna say that.'" Shit looked at Eric and shrugged. "So I went over and squatted down—he had to help me—and I leaned back against the house. He plugged right in to my face and goes on lookin' though that crack under the window. He wasn't even that big—but, boy, was he enthusiastic! Well, damned if he didn't shoot *three* fuckin' loads down my throat—five and ten minutes apart! Then he apologizes for bein' so horny. When he was finally helpin' me get upright, he said, 'Hey, don't tell nobody about this. They're worried I'm not gonna have enough to do the deed. But, damn—I can come over that stuff all day long. And a lot.'

"'Tryin' to make sure my hip was still workin', I told him, 'Well, *I* sure ain't gonna argue with you, son.' And when I walked away, I looked back to see he's squattin' at the window again, pullin' on himself once *more*. I mean, the truth is, I was tired out! But, yes, I *did* think about tryin' to hunt you up so I could watch you get another one of his loads. But when I got home, you was out. Really. You was."

"Shit..." Eric said.

"What?"

"I am jealous of you."

Shit said, "The only reason I didn't tell you when I saw you a couple of hours later was 'cause I didn't want you to think you'd missed out on somethin'."

"And I believe you, too." Eric sighed. "I'm still jealous." He chuckled.

Before the porch, dimming the intensity of air and sea and trees, fell a glittering gray rain.

* * *

[104] "YOU BEEN COUGHIN' three days now." Beside the stained sink, Eric turned off the water. "It don't sound good."

Sitting in the chair by the table, with his knees wide, Shit leaned forward and coughed again. When he did it, he flattened his hand over the lower half of his bearded face, rather than hacking into his fist.

"And you ain't eatin' right."

"What you want me to do?" Shit asked. "See Dr. Zaya?"

"Yeah," Eric turned from the counter. "That's just what I want—"

Shit coughed again. "Pour me some coffee, will you?" He picked up his brown mug and held it out.

Eric stepped over and took it. Shit's knee knob pushed through torn pants; his size fifteen sneakers sat askew on the rag rug. (Really, the man ain't nothin' but feet and hands. And how many times have I thought that in sixty, sixty-five years?) Eric went back to the counter, to pull the carafe from under the black and chrome drip pot. Behind him, coughs came in a rasping cascade. After he poured lots of milk, he turned back, stepped over again, and handed Shit the mug.

Shit's fingers lapping over Eric's, Shit took the brown mug, brought it down, sipped, coughed once more, then sat it on the quilted green placemat. "I'm gonna lie down. I'm still pretty tired. You go call her. Ask her when she wants me to come in."

Eric put his hand on Shit's skull and rubbed, his palm going from rough hair to bald scalp. He rubbed twice, three times more.

Still holding his cup, Shit leaned his head against Eric's hip—

—then he pulled away, to stand, slowly.

Taking up his mug, with his scrawny man's lumber Shit moved toward the bedroom.

Yeah, he's sick—he ain't givin' me no argument about the doctor.

*

Eric's plan was to take the mono the quarter of a mile to the market, do some shopping for fish and vegetables (some squash, potatoes, kale), then walk up the commons and stop into Dr. Zaya's glass and wood office to ask Dona, her niece and receptionist, when would be a good time to have Shit come in.

When, with his tote bag, Eric left the mono and came down the brick ramp—their yellow gone gray over a decade-and-a-half—between the hedges and the few pines, from all the people walking about, he realized it was Saturday, not Friday.

At the far end, the Dump Produce sign's black and orange awning hung above the heads of milling people. On the other side rose the patinaed wings and—below them—the horned head of the common's bronze guardian.

Among black eggplants, green and yellow peppers, red and yellow tomatoes, green, yellow, and red apples, beige and pink peaches, Eric walked to the fish benches.

In her striped apron, with a single breast and tattooed flowers following her faint mastectomy scar, Laurel nodded to him when he strolled up. (You didn't see too many of those today.) Arna was talking with somebody down a couple of yards. While Eric looked at the fillets spread across chipped ice, at knee level the greenish pipe from the wooden wall dripped into the plastic pail. Beside him, he heard a familiar voice. "Those are nice looking bluefish."

"Dr. Zaya?" Surprised, Eric looked over. "I was about to go to your office and make an appointment. Then I realized you ain't open today."

"Mr. Jeffers." Dr. Zaya stood up, smiling. "It's good to see you. You've been under the weather?" She looked around.

Seeing the wrinkles at her eyes, Eric thought: she's older than the woman in her thirties they'd started going to twenty-five years ago. "But I must say, this is some beautiful weather to be under." In her yellow lace shawl, Dr. Zaya laughed. Through its tracery, in the sunlight, her brown shoulders looked, well, glorious. After years of shaving her head, she had started growing her hair back, rough, white, and grizzled.

"It ain't for me. It's for Shit. He's doin' poorly."

"Is he, now?"

"He's coughin' all the time—and he hardly gets out of bed or eats nothin'."

"Well, then—why don't you finish up your shopping. I did mine earlier, but I was looking around to see if I'd missed anything. I'll go back to the office, get a few things. Meet me there in twenty minutes, and I'll come on out to your cabin and take a look."

Eric raised his eyebrows. "On the weekend—and you're comin' out to make a *house* call?"

"Why not?" She chuckled. "I got my training during the thirties. As long as you don't tell too many people, I don't mind droppin' in."

He came down to the office, with broccoli, cod, fruit, collards (no kale), eggs and coffee in his bag. (Eric remembered when they used to ask him if he wanted it delivered; but he rarely said yes.) She was coming out, carrying a narrow case. They walked under the trees to the maglev station.

It came in three minutes.

Sitting beside her on the car's purple bench, Eric said, "I don't know what to say. I mean, thank you—so much."

"I've been treatin' you boys awhile," she said. "I imagine Mr. Haskell needs lookin' after or you wouldn't be asking." As it sped, the car made a musical keening.

*

Walking in off the porch, Dr. Zaya opened her case over the placemats still on the table and took out a pair of around-the-head goggles. Then she lifted out a rolled up pad.

In the bedroom, Shit was dozing.

Holding the jamb with one hand, Eric said, "You got company."

"Huh?" Blinking, stretching, Shit pushed himself up on the pillow, which was gray. "I was just thinkin' about gettin' up, there. But I been so tired..." He coughed.

"If you would just let me get this reflector pad under you, Mr. Haskell, I'll take a look."

Shit said, "You don't mind that I ain't got no clothes on—"

Dr. Zaya said, "Just means you don't have to take them off. That's all."

Shit grinned at Eric. "Gimme a hand gettin' on top of this thing."

Eric gripped his arm, then sat down and helped Shit slide over, while Dr. Zaya adjusted the goggles over her head. "*Mmmmm.*" She turned a knob on the side of the contraption near her temple. "You, my friend, have a slightly foggy spot on your lung, there—" She pointed down at his chest—"no, it's not cancer. But it looks as if you *have* picked up a touch of pneumonia."

Dr. Zaya suggested he take the air shuttle leaving in fifty minutes from the other end of the island, which would let him off at Runcible Memorial. "Mr. Jeffers can go with you. They're still honoring the Kyle Foundation Plan—"

"Nope," Shit said, from the dingy sheets and drab blankets around him.

"Pardon me...?"

"I ain't takin' no air shuttle." Shit breathed with his mouth open.

Dr. Zaya suppressed a smile. "Well, how do you intend to get to the hospital?"

"I'll take the boat, thank you for askin'—and maybe one of the Miller kids can drive me down there, Hannibal or Ed." Again, coughing brought his head forward, his hand up. He dragged in a breath. "...or maybe Holly's cousin, Lucille—what helps out Ed."

"With the shuttle—" Dr. Zaya frowned—"you can get there, go through admissions, and be in your room fifty minutes after take off. You're not going to tell me, now, you'd really rather spend four-and-a-half, five hours by boat and car—"

"I sure am—" Again, Shit began to cough.

Eric thought: Four hours was an exaggeration—once they got the ferry it would be more like two. "He can't take heights," Eric said. "And he ain't never flown."

Without sympathy, Dr. Zaya frowned. "Well, that's a little crazy. I'm not going to argue with you, but go there—and go there today. I'll call them for you and tell them you're...coming later on." She turned to Eric, pulling up her shawl. "Are you sure you can't talk some sense into him? If he's just nervous about flying, I'll give him a shot that—"

"I ain't nervous about it," Shit interrupted. "I ain't doin' it, so there ain't nothin' to be nervous about."

Dr. Zaya laughed. Her bronze ear hoops shook. "You are really my *most* eccentric patients." Lifting the reflector pad, that, under Shit's back, had let her see the shadow of Shit's lungs, she began to re-roll it. "But I do want you there—in the hospital—this evening. There's no sense in him spending another night here hacking his innards out."

In the kitchen, she closed up her case and, after refusing some warmed up coffee (in the brown mug, while Eric was rinsing it out), left.

Eric went back to the bedroom, sat on the broad bed's edge, picked up the phone from the night table, and with his thumb, pushed it into his ear.

Shit took Eric's other wrist and dragged it over his stomach to his groin. Eric looked back. "What's the matter...?"

"Grab a-hold of my dick," Shit said. "It's cold."

Eric closed his fingers around the loose inches, while he said, "Ed Miller...?" His knuckles moved in the scrotal flesh, warm, familiar, while he waited for a connecting beep.

Neither Ed nor Hannibal was answering. But Holly turned out to be on the island—and getting ready to take the boat back to the mainland, where she was going to pick up their truck in the lot and drive down to Hemmings. If they could be ready in an hour, she'd be happy to go with them and give them a lift to Memorial. "'Cause I *know* he's not going to take no air shuttle." She laughed. "I like looking at the water, too. That's why I was taking the ferry."

"Yeah…" Eric said, trying to suppress his own frustration.

Forty minutes later, Holly came by for them.

He wore a thermal-lined sweatshirt, which had spent fifteen years in a bottom drawer before—last year—it had turned up and Shit had started wearing the thirty-year-old hoody. Certainly, it looked odd. For one thing, it was gray: today people simply didn't wear that color in an outer garment.

Shit hunched between them on the maglev seat, Holly at one side (she wore a large coral necklace and a large coral comb in her graying hair), Eric at the other. He held a bag of Shit's things—dental brush, cleaning tablets, witch hazel pads and some underwear in a sealed plastic bag.

At the top of the steps down to the boat dock, Shit's grip tightened on Eric's arm. Bushes rustled beside the railing. "You're gonna have to go slow," Shit said, softly. "I feel like I'm gonna pass out."

Landing after landing, they got him down. A couple of times, Eric thought, this was the kind of thing it had been nice having Caleb around for. But Caleb was something time had excised from their lives. Once Holly said, "Mr. Haskell, you really *don't* look well. You sure you won't break down and take the next air shuttle? It would be *so* much easier—"

Shit didn't say anything, but, down the concrete steps, he kept going—step by unsteady step.

On the boat, he sat in the passenger shelter, leaning against Eric, who held his hand—sometimes tightly, sometimes loosely. (He knew the captain, but was damned if he remembered her name.) Holly said, "He really doesn't look good…"

Neither man said anything back.

* * *

          *

The gurney rolled through the green tiled halls. Shit asked hoarsely, "There ain't nobody pushin' this thing?" He held the sheet up at his neck. "Can you keep up?"

"Yeah." Eric hurried up two steps, still carrying the plastic bag. "I'm right here," though he had to walk faster than was comfortable.

Two floors up, and at the other end of the building, three orderlies waited. As they moved Shit into his room and onto his bed—and Eric hovered, trying to see but not get in the way—once and a while Shit would blow out, "Whew…!" and again fell to coughing. Soon, though, they had him comfortable. (The room was the same pale orange as the one his mother had died in, over at the Hostel—though the blinds were vertical, not horizontal. Eric wondered if Shit remembered.) The vital signs meter beeped and clicked on its stand.

A nurse said Eric should phone Dr. Zaya, just to make sure, but Shit would likely be home in three or four days.

Three small plastic cups stood on the table by the bed, and Shit was connected up to a drip bag that hung from a metal hook. "Go on home, now," Shit said. "I wanna go to sleep. You hang around here, the way everybody keeps runnin' all over this place, you gonna catch somethin' and be sick as a dog, too. Go on home, now; get some rest."

Eric said, "You're probably right. But I'm gonna sit here another five or ten minutes before I get up. Okay?"

"Yeah," Shit said. "Sure. Far as I'm concerned, you could climb in here and put your arms around me—I swear, that's gotta be the best medicine. I betcha a couple of more nights of that, and I'd be fit as a fiddle again…Not that nobody wants to hear what *I* gotta say about it—"

*

When Eric walked from under the hospital's awning, it was after three-thirty. Clouds fluffed the autumn sky. Way beyond the hedges was an orange and black sign—"Freshest Food on the Georgia Coast: DUMP PRODUCE": it was the back of the bus stop shelter out by the service road. Eric frowned. *Was* the Hemmings Mall shuttle still running? The main building at the Mall, he knew, had been shut down years before. Perhaps it had even been razed. There'd always been a hospital stop, though, since so many orderlies and nurses lived in the Dump—had *once* lived in the Dump. Himself, Eric hadn't been on it in more than fifteen…more than *twenty* years!

But if it *was* still running back through Runcible, through the Dump, to Diamond Harbor…

Getting around the hedges meant a difficult fifty yards of out-of-the-way walking. He had to cross a parking lot—but, as he neared it, he saw a bench under the shelter's plastic roof.

When he got there, Eric was surprised how tired he was.

He sat—slowly—on the metal slats…if they *were* metal. (How did just worryin' about someone take so much energy?) He ran a finger between. What was that stuff they'd used for his mother's ash canister…?

Eric saw the vehicle pulling up—which was not a flat-nosed bus but a rounded car with a more or less pointed cab. Across the top, a sign said

"Diamond Harbor," which, as Eric rose again, prompted him to think a sign must hang somewhere around the stop, surely, giving the route. He should have been looking for that to check, instead of just sitting there.

Eric got on, wondering if there would be a driver or not—someone who could tell him where they were stopping on the way to the Harbor. These days, when he came to the mainland—and so infrequently—he felt practically lost. The green observation roof curved over the aisle, above gray and maroon seats. It was rather scratched—which meant the bus was older than he'd thought from its blue and silver exterior.

There *was* a driver: a heavy brown fellow in a jacket and pants with patches of clear plastic in them. (It surprised Eric; on Gilead, service workers—drivers, caretakers, guards—were usually women.)

"Excuse me," Eric said—and surprised himself by asking, "Does this still stop at the Dump?" The notion of going to see the old place had risen, luminous, in his mind.

The man said, "It'll stop anywhere you want, as long as it's on the route."

"Oh…and the Dump is still one of the stops—on the route?"

The man nodded. The bus moved through the lot, toward the highway, more and more quickly. I sound like a tourist.

*

They stopped along the top of the bluff. "I'll have to walk down…?" Eric asked, tentatively.

"If that's where you wanna go." The driver didn't smile. (So they didn't go *through* the Dump anymore, but around it. That was a change.) "There's hardly nobody down there, now…"

Below, the hangar-like structure of Fred Hurter's was gone. So was the Gay Friendly John—the whole building was no longer there. Where both had been was a single lot—pretty uncared for, too, Eric saw, as he came closer. The Social Service building was closed up, but then, it was Saturday.

It looked liked the closing was permanent: no blinds hung in the windows. He saw no furniture inside.

The rubble to the right was where the Housing Office had been.

Many of the houses—he turned onto the gravel road—just *weren't* there.

I remember…*some* of 'em. How many years *did* I live here? (Eric walked above the Dump's remnants.) Now up the slope was a neat line of five cabins, wall to wall—none of the houses that Kyle had had Big Man Markum's dad build looked like that!

The Dump's cabins had each been different—Kyle had had a different architect (well, architectural student) design each one. But there were no repeated little post box houses, all nanobolted together. That must have been someone's attempt at a row of tourist cabins—and from their look, they *hadn't* been successful.

(*Did* people live there or were they only storage…?)

Eric walked down the path, under familiar gulls. The Potts house was gone. The path smelled dusty but not the sunny dust he remembered. If anything, it smelled like…dust from some Atlanta backstreet. Out towards the Dump's edge, where Dynamite had once lived, among the trees that seemed to have grown up, was a light…

It was bright enough—white enough—to guild the yellow grass and show up the green in the pine branches.

From up the slope, he could look down and see it was halfway between Bull's and Dynamite's, though he couldn't see its source. (It was a long walk. But there was nowhere to sit.) Around it, pine shadows fell on grass and gravel. When had all these trees gotten a chance to grow, anyway…?

Halfway down the slope, Eric thought: Damn, I could fall and twist an ankle and lie around here a week 'fore anybody found me…

Looking down the bluff, Eric frowned—and stopped.

That should be where Mama Grace's used to stand.

But, no—that cabin was gone, too. What was the name of that nice pair of guys who had taken it over…? Eric walked, again, through afternoon shadow, by weed and rock and tree.

There—that was Chef Ron's old place, though it no longer had a porch. Stands of trees, many of them, from their size, fifteen years old—or older—threw off his estimation of distances and directions.

Had it been that long since he'd visited…?

I used to lope down this thing in five or six minutes—

It took him more like twenty. As he came nearer, Eric saw people wandering around in…the yard of the house over there—which, yes, was Bull's! Though Bull and Whiteboy had quit the area long, long back.

Eric turned to look up at the old cabin…where Dynamite, Shit and Eric himself had lived…That was still there, though one corner sagged calamitously. Eric looked for the steps where, on his free day when they'd worked at the Opera, he'd come to sit, read, and re-read his *Ethica*. But Dynamite's old cabin no longer had steps going up. Had they broken away…?

As Eric approached, a lanky black woman came from the door, without a shirt, to walk to the edge and watch him.

From Gilead gossip, Eric remembered that, time and again, squatters were living in some of the Dump's collapsing cabins—though that had been news from a year, three years, four years back.

When he was ten, eight, six yards away, Eric called, "Hello, there. Afternoon, ma'am…You livin' here now?" He continued forward.

She said, "No."

"Oh," Eric said. "I'm just visiting. I *used* to live here, a million years ago. It's been a while since I seen it. It's pretty different."

The woman nodded. "Kind of a ghost town now."

"Where you from?" Eric asked.

"Chicago," she answered. (He thought: She sounded neither particularly black nor particularly local. More like someone you'd meet out on the island.) "But my mama grew up in Split Pine. Then she went up to Philadelphia. My father had family there, so that's where I ended up in school."

"My partner and me," Eric said, "I just took him to the hospital. In Runcible—Runcible Memorial. And I thought I'd come see this place, 'cause we used to live here, back in oh-nine, fifteen, eighteen…" The explanation felt unnecessary and awkward. Ten feet from the porch, Eric stopped.

"That's a long time ago." The woman smiled.

"Yeah." Eric smiled back. "I guess it is." Eric's smile was mostly at himself for having grown so old, so garrulous. "For you, anyway. But it don't seem that long to me. Name's Jeffers. We live out on the island now—me and my partner. He's gonna be back soon. They said three or four days." How in the world was he going to get back to pick up Shit? Of course, *he* could take the air shuttle. But then they'd have to return…"From the hospital."

The woman said, "That's good," as, behind her, someone else started out the door, hesitated—then came on. The second woman was almost as tall as the first and almost as dark. She, too, wore only pants and boots. Both looked remarkably buff.

The first woman glanced back, lifted an arm and put it around the second woman's shoulder as she stepped up. "This old fella says he used to live here. He lives on Gilead now. We been here a week. We took our group out to the island on the first day. It's nice out there—Oh, this is Sally. I'm Deena. Laura, Phyllis, David, Rona, and Ole are down in the house across the way. I want to go back and see more of the market. We're married—"

"—at least we're all married anywhere north of Washington D.C." After the hug, the second woman—Sally—moved a little away from the first. "We're down here to campaign for the multiple partner referendum Georgia's voting on this coming November. Hope you'll remember us, when you go in to vote."

"Are you hungry?" Deena—the first woman—stepped forward to the porch edge, then squatted. "There's some kind of dinner goin' at the house. You're welcome to stay and have some."

"That's nice of you…!" Eric said, surprised.

He watched her jump down among the loud ferns around the front of the porch. Above her, Sally squatted, too—and jumped. She landed, boots roaring in the brush.

"Did this house *ever* have steps here?" Sally asked.

Eric backed up as they walked out.

"Sure it did," Eric said. "I was kind of wonderin' myself what happened to 'em."

Sally laughed. "So were we." She extended her hand to shake; so Eric grasped it. "Glad to meet you."

"Sally's pretty much the head of the family," Deena said. "She's from California—and she's writing a book about us."

Sally said, "I think they must have had those little mechanical lifts they used to use on houses back in the forties. Those things always used to break down, anyway. They didn't replace them when people moved out. I think it was a way of discouraging itinerant homeless folks from moving in."

"Like us?" Deena laughed.

"Yeah." Sally laughed after her.

An image of the lifts with their thin rails remained in memory's corner; they'd never caught on in Gilead. Briefly, they might have been standard in the Dump, during the years when he'd never visited. Another surprise for him. "Eh…Nice to meet you," Eric said. On the Island, Californians' reputation—they had lived in Bomb country, after all—was that they had iron backbones and could survive anything. Since most of the ones Eric had known were from the herds of homeless cut loose from the coast who had ended up for days, weeks, months in the Opera, thirty years before, his personal estimation of them was aimless, easy going, and generally devoid of goals—with, perhaps, a higher percentage of outright psychotics than with other groups.

"Gilead's like a little time capsule, even from before the thirties," Sally said. "I mean with the market and everything."

Eric laughed. (Nothing about Gilead seemed to him particularly twenties.) "Oh, we ain't *that* backwards…"

"It's wonderful…nice, I mean. But it's so…odd."

What did these kids, who had been born when he was forty, fifty, or older find odd? Eric blinked. "Writin' a book? That's interestin'." But this woman seemed pretty focused. "We got some writers out on Gilead. Mostly what I know is painters and sculptors, though."

"Oh," Sally said. "Deena's a sculptor." Then she laughed. "Being family head pretty much means my job is to tell everyone we meet what everybody else in the group does. Deena went into the Navy when she was seventeen, then to Mars. She's actually fairly famous. You must have heard of the Phobos-Countersurge. Deena was in that—*and* survived!"

Eric frowned. He had not heard of it, though it was the kind of thing Shit might know something about. "Yeah, I could have. Ain't a lot of people been up there on Mars. What—about four hundred? Or is it six?"

"About seven or eight years ago, it was six hundred." Deena laughed. "Now though, it's more like six or seven thousand—but you could still say there wasn't that many. Anyway, it took coming back to Earth from all that to make me realize I only wanted to do my sculptures and have some people around who wanted to hold onto me cause I was warm and fun... instead of—" she took in a sudden breath—"'cause they were screamin' with their blood and their shit running through a couple of rips across their bellies—"

Eric grunted at the image.

"Sometimes it got pretty rough up there," Deena said. After a moment she ventured: "Jeffers...?"

Eric glanced over.

"You said your name was Jeffers? You wouldn't have anything to do with the guy who used to manage the big fuck-movie theater they used to have over in Runcible, did you? My mama told me how her dad—my grandpa—would take her over there, when they used to have these big chili picnics for all the people in the neighborhood and the guys in the—"

"Yeah. That was me—and Shit, my partner."

"That's right," Deena said, smiling at Sally. "That was his name. Jeffers...and Shit Haskell. I used to think that was *so* funny."

"Yeah—it was, I guess. But that's what everybody called him. And they still do today."

"Of course, now it doesn't seem funny at all." Deena said. (Eric wasn't sure why. But probably some rebellious youth movement had taken up obscene names just to shock—something else he'd missed.) "You guys were pretty famous down here. My mama told me how you gave her a plate of chili right out in front of the theater—off that big cooking counter with the awning and the wheels you used to keep in that place. My grandpa brought her and about three of my brothers and four of my half-sisters over there—do you remember him. Al Havers?"

Eric frowned. "You're...Al Havers granddaughter?" It struck him that Deena was well into her thirties, not her twenties, as he'd assumed.

She laughed. "I'm one of about fifty-five or sixty of 'em."

"Yeah, that sounds about right." Eric found himself chuckling. "I guess you come by your interest in group marriages honestly."

"Maybe. I...guess I do." Deena said, "I used to be really down on that stuff—'cause my mother was so set against it. I mean, you wouldn't believe the kind of arguments they would have. My dad was always defending Gramps: 'You can't say there was no surprises. He told 'em how it was gonna be from the beginnin'.' And she would say it wasn't fair, because *her* mother didn't know *what* 'how-it-was-gonna-be-from-the-beginning' would mean. I was always on her side. But then Gramps sent for us, and he really did love his kids; even if some of their moms could rub him the wrong way—actually, he was a pretty patient guy. And being the father of twenty or thirty kids, he really thought that was the greatest thing in the world. And I know he went hungry a few times, there, so they could eat. Now, a dozen years later, I'm living in the same kinda messed up life he was always in. But with two kids instead of two dozen. Only—funny—it never occurred to me, until little while ago, it *was* the same."

"Odd," Sally said. "The first time you told me about your...prolific granddad, it occurred to *me*!"

Futilely, Eric tried to remember a black girl in the hungry happy crowd around the theatre through the years. He asked, "How long ago did Al die...?"

"I came down here about seven years back, when he was going," Deena said. "A whole bunch of his kids did—and about six of our moms came, too. "He was very happy about that. He died while we were here—and then we went home. Hey, you want to see my sculpture?"

"Eh...sure," Eric said.

A sound like a wave rose in the pines. For some reason, it made Eric frown. They walked toward the light among the trees.

Sally said, "Deena makes her sculptures out of pure light. We were up there in your old house, and I was asking her questions about how she did it, so I could write about it in my book."

They stepped between more trees.

And Eric saw it—and realized he hadn't till now because he hadn't known what he was looking at.

Maybe twenty feet across, a sphere of white light, smoky, ghostly, hung about two feet off the ground. Sitting in the grass, half on a scattering of brown leaves, was some mechanism—a box about ten by ten inches, with glowing holes across its top—which Eric realized was a projector.

Centered in the white sphere was a darker, luminously blue one, maybe four feet across. Almost immediately it made Eric think of a giant... cabbage! Leaves interfolded with more leaves.

As he stood looking, one leaf pulled away and drifted off to hover in the air, and, mistily, condense and spin itself into a blue satellite some fifteen feet over his head.

Deena said, "It's not really finished. Hey, tell me. Which do you think works better? This way…the way it is now, or—" she raised her hands, so that muscles pulled to prominence across her cannon metal shoulders— "this way?" She moved her hands for the world like a conductor. At each change of direction, a color or some internal movement in the light changed, too, so that now the globe was gold with red embers burning through it. The leaves peeled off faster to shoot into the air and spin in a line of orange balls, which smoked, faded, and dissolved, making a misty diagonal through the golden sky.

Deena looked back at him.

"I…" Eric said. "I don't know. I've never seen one of these before."

Deena frowned. "Never…? You've never seen reproductions of any of the works Danely Phylum did—the great Central American sculptor? Or Klarakot? Half the people I know have miniature reproductions of the Dark Gate on a bookshelf or their desk or something."

"No." Eric shook his head. "That's…pretty, though."

"Didn't your school ever take you to the museum when you were kids?"

"But we never saw nothing like this."

Sally moved up beside her. "Deena, I think he's *really* old—seventy, seventy-five. This stuff comes out of the late twenties…and the thirties. I don't think they had this when *he* was a kid."

Eric wanted to nod. "They didn't." He felt bewildered and humbled. And annoyed—discussions of most art bothered him, even as he made himself listen to them; though it always seemed there were some aspect to it everybody understood but him—which, finally, even as Shit laughed at him for it, Eric was always putting himself in the way of.

"Oh," Deena said. "Well, I never saw *any* light sculpture down in this part of the country, anyway. Wait a minute—let me put it back the other way." She moved her hands again, one making a wiping gesture (which seemed to change the color), and one pointing here and there, which didn't do anything Eric could figure out. "You just tell me which one…you know, *feels* better. Feels righter—more *complete*." She gestured again, with both hands—Eric did not quite follow how, but again it had become a blue sphere in an envelope of white.

Another leaf peeled away and shot off, spinning.

The image of a luminous, exploding cabbage made Eric, out of nervousness, laugh.

Deena looked at him and beamed. "See…? *He* gets it! I told you. It's supposed to embody humor, as well as beauty."

"Oh…!" Eric said, surprised, losing all the access to its sense of wit, now that he knew his had been a proper response. He could laugh *at* the thing, but he was completely uncomfortable laughing with it.

"You don't have to be an art critic just to respond to a piece of art. But you really get it—I can tell. Don't you?"

A naked young man ambled into the clearing, a baby harnessed high on his belly. "They told me to come and see what was keeping you guys." He smiled at Eric. "Hello."

"Hello," Eric said.

"Hey, Ole." Deena stepped back from the sculpture. "This is Mr. Jeffers. My mom used to talk about him when I was a kid. He knew my grandfather."

"That's the grandfather you told us about who liked to fuck everything like I do." Holding his cock in one hand, Ole reached out the other to shake.

Eric shook hands with him.

"I'm sexually psychotic." The young man smiled, pumping vigorously. "See my balls jogglin' down there, under my kid? Even somethin' like that can turn me on. It makes me very polymorphous. I like fuckin' everything. Even old people, like you. I'll fuck around with you, if you'll talk to me and stuff about things. You ever fuck any animals? That's one of my favorite nasty things to talk about—especially when I'm fuckin around with guys. Not so much girls, though…"

He had not released Eric's hands, and now he tugged Eric's fist back to rub it against the red hair over his groin and the bone beneath. His abdomen seemed nervously taut.

Eric's wrist brushed the sleeping child's dangling foot. "A long time ago, yeah. A few," Eric said.

"Oh, wow. Will you tell me all about 'em? Maybe after dinner, we can go off and talk about 'em and play with each other's cocks—"

"Cut it out, Ole," Sally said.

Deena said, "Mr. Jeffers used to run a whole pornographic theater. He probably knows more about fucking than you ever dreamed of. Ole basically just likes to say things that shock people."

"Yeah?" the young man asked. "I probably won't be able to pay a lot of attention to what you tell me. That's 'cause I'm nuts. Still, it's nice to meet you. Let's go eat." He dropped Eric's hand, turned, and wandered off.

Eric said to Deena. "What do you call it?" (That's what the artists always asked each other on Gilead.) "Your sculpture."

Deena looked at Eric. "The working title is *The Valley*."

Eric was bewildered.

Sally said, "Are you gonna tell him why you named it that?"

Deena looked bemused. "No—I wasn't. Not unless he asked."

"Go on," Sally insisted. "Tell him. It's interesting."

"Doesn't it look *less* like a valley...than anything you can think of?" (Deena started walking away, and Sally—with Eric—followed.) "I mean, valleys are depressions, but my sculpture is all outside. A sphere—and things coming off a sphere. So you have to think real hard to figure out any way at all that it's like a valley—and even think about all the ways it *isn't* like a valley. Which means you have to think about a valley and what makes something a valley even more. And what about this is different."

They stepped from among the trees—

And the house that they were approaching was *not* Bull's cabin: the first thing Eric realized. For one, the front wall was entirely glass. And it was wider than Bull's house had been. Before it in the yard, a fire burned. Racks were set up over it, with pots and spits and, Eric saw now, fish cooking between the tines of the turning grills. It gave off little or no smoke, which was why he hadn't seen it from the distance. But, then, of course, he hadn't been looking.

Five or six people walked around.

Rough log benches stood at various angles to the fire.

"Hey," Eric said. "You mind if I sit?" Seven or eight others already were. (How much daily medicine did it take so that, at his age, Eric could walk comfortably for an hour-and-a-half, for two hours? He knew that Shit took a lot more.) Someone said, "Sure—" Another black woman with eight inch dreadlocks smiled at up at him and moved to make room.

As soon as he sat on the awkward bench, he realized he had to go to the bathroom. "Um..." Eric began.

Besides naked Ole, the only other man was a dark brown bear of a fellow, with a curly pad of hair over his chest, equally nappy hair on his head, and a beard. He wore pants and boots like the women. He sat a seat away, on the bench, leaning forward on his knees.

"Excuse me," Eric said. "Do you guys have a latrine area—or a working bathroom available?"

The guy looked at Eric, then laughed. "Sure. Use the one in the house."

"Oh..." Eric said.

"Just go right in and turn to the left. You'll see it in front of you."

"Thank you." Eric stood again, wondering how to get into the glass-enclosed room.

There was no porch at all.

It must have been pure accident that he was close enough to some sensor. The glass wall parted and an opening spread between gleaming panes.

Eric glanced back. The bear nodded at him, grinning.

Eric walked forward. Inside, the floor was stone. A door stood to the left, so he walked toward it. It opened automatically, and he went inside.

It was a very modern bathroom, with a dozen planters built into one wall, trailing leaves and tendrils down the tiles. Two others were bright mirrors. (The commode was also some silvery-mirrored substance, and when he unfastened his pants, dropped them down his thin thighs, and sat, he realized the silver seat was heated. He actually felt too tired to stand and urinate—he had been sitting more and more, of late.) Beside him, was a table with three different levels, each of which held a pile of magazines.

The cover illustration moved as he looked at the top one. The glimmering title said,

THE KYLE FOUNDATION
NEWSLETTER FOR
THE DUMP

The top one was dated October 2072, which was a year and a half ago. Eric picked up several. They were all old issues of the same periodical. While he sat there, Eric thought, the crazy kid with the baby just propositioned me! Actually, he's kind of cute—and I am about ninety-eight percent uninterested. Why didn't this happen to me twenty years ago?

Probably I would have enjoyed it then.

He farted—and began to urinate.

Well, at least Shit isn't here. *He* would have felt obligated to take the psychotic bastard up on it—and I would have gone along and been bored out of my skull.

Who *were* these kids? Some traveling group marriage that keeps Ole around...kind of like we used to keep Uncle Tom or Dog Dog, I guess. Well, he *is* cute. Though I wouldn't be surprised if they get tired of him, now and then. I'm going to assume the baby's safe and not worry.

The fact is, Uncle Tom got his share, but we probably kicked him out of bed more times than he wanted. And the old hound did love us.

These kids are interesting. They've been places. They done stuff—yeah, you could write about them. Stories have happened to them. They've been to Mars, they have a cause, and they are trying to make art and babies and live good lives. Again, why couldn't I have met them twenty years ago, when it would have been fun to be friends with them, to watch their progress, rather than now when I'm numb not even with worry but simply the effort of getting Shit to the hospital and back.

They have stories. (I guess other people mostly do.) I just have a life...

As he turned over pages, he kept coming on articles about some place in Oklahoma called The Fields...

I have a life—and it's mainly over. Yes, it's been a good one. But what has it allowed me to do that's worthwhile?

He looked at the newsletters beside him. With the Kyle Foundation to fight for us, we never had to fight for anything, really. Everything was arranged, from salary to security. It did a good job of taking care of us—and we all thought that was good. Did that allow us to *be* good or just... superfluous?

Eric fingered through more old issues to pull one free. Most had only the title on the cover—but this one mentioned a topic.

ROBERT KYLE THE THIRD DIES

Eric frowned. Yes, he'd known that—at age 101—Mr. Kyle had passed away. He looked at the date. He was there in the graveyard, though Shit and Eric had missed the service—if that's what you called it. FEBRUARY 2071—no, certainly that couldn't have been more than three years ago. Eric paged through the issue. "...with the death of Robert Kyle, the third, at age one hundred and one, in Columbus, Ohio, last week, some long contemplated changes in the working of the Kyle Foundation will finally be set in place..." Life spans of a hundred twenty-five were growing more common among the super rich—though ordinary folks, like Shit and Eric, lived into their eighties, their nineties—though many chose not to, since mental clarity rarely went along with it. The article said that forms would be going out to those covered by the Kyle Plan, and anyone with holdings they no longer wanted to make use of would be asked to fill them out and return the rights to land and goods to the Foundation, so that taxes could be adjusted...

Had he ever filled those things out? Really, Eric didn't remember.

Shaking his head, he put the magazine down, took some toilet tissue and wiped his ass, even though he hadn't done anything. (You know, if I had some lube, on the off chance that crazy Ole really wanted to fuck, I'd finger it in now...) Eric chuckled. Robert Kyle was another person who'd lived a life you could tell stories about—but Eric—Shit and Eric—the best we'll ever be is elements in someone else's.

Is that what good people—good Americans—were? Even ones like us, who take a hundred years to become anything else than marginal eccentricities?

Yes, help was what it was all about. But so much of it was needed, whether signaled by atrocities or just unthinking cruelties or simple annoyances, that when the vast hunger for help from *Deus sivi Natura* struck straight against the bridge of your nose, all you could do—whether you were Robert Kyle with his foundering Foundation or Eric Jeffers with his sandwiches and cookies because he no longer had energy for chili, or Deena Havers holding a wounded soldier on another world or sculpting in light on this one—was to rise and walk through the valley in tears…and think about the valley…

Eric stood up—the toilet flushed, as if it were some old fashioned public john. Eric buttoned his pants and stepped from the bathroom door.

The glass wall parted, but even before he stepped through the opening to the yard, he realized something had changed radically.

First, everyone was standing.

The fire and the fish—along with the benches—were gone.

Someone said—to *him*, Eric realized—"Come on, come on. Get out of there."

One of the women—the one with the dreads—said irritably, "Will you let the old guy finish going to the bathroom for God's sakes?"

A gaunt Asian, with a potbelly and a red and blue uniform, said, "Come on. Come on, you're not supposed to be here. Yall get the fuck out of here. Get a move on. I'm not kidding." With a billy club, he gave the glass wall a tap. Shatter lines zagged through it, though it did not crumble.

One of the youngest of the women—at least she looked very young to Eric—said, "You know, you're not doing this alone. About a hundred seventy-five people are watching us right now. Maybe more, because of the Rally. And if you do anything really violent, a minute later three thousand people will see it—and see you doing it."

The Asian turned abruptly. "That's just more of that goddam science crap. Don't you realize that stuff is weird—and unnatural?"

Eric was not even aware of recognizing the young patrolman—well, in his late fifties, early sixties. "Aim, what's a matter?" Actually, it was a second after he said the name that he realized his identification *was* right. (It *was* Aim.) Behind the lines and loose ears, enough in the face recalled the teenaged garbage helper, staggering on his injured foot, before the Bottom's edge, for recognition.

The Asian frowned at Eric—or, perhaps, Eric found himself thinking, he was frowning at the great wall of time between this and their first meeting.

Eric said, "That's you, Aim—ain't it? It's Eric Jeffers. What's the problem?"

"Mr. Jeffers—that was you in there?"

"What you givin' them a hard time for?" Eric nodded toward dark, tall Deena. "That's Al's Haver's granddaughter. Don't you remember Al, when he worked at the Bottom? He was your boss for a while. Or did he retire, just before you started drivin' there with Tad?"

"Well, that ain't nothin'. The man was the daddy or the grand daddy of three-quarters of the black kids runnin' around this county—at least for a while."

Cuddling the child strapped to his naked belly, Ole said, "I'm just twenty-eight and I got two grandkids already." He grinned through a beard that looked vaguely like Shit's at that age; though it was the color he remembered on Jay. "That's cause I'm nuts."

"Come on, Aim. This kid's just out the Navy—she been to Mars."

"Well, then what the fuck is she doin' with *these* deadbeats?" Aim turned back to them and roared, "Come on, now! Shut it the fuck down!"

It looked as though the two others walls of the house suddenly fell in. Where they hit the ground, they vanished. He could see through the glass that the roof and the stone floor were gone. Rock and leaves alone remained—the whole, Eric realized, some virtual construct.

Through trees at the far side of the clearing, light flickered from *The Valley*.

"Hey, cut it out, Aim," Eric said. "They're not messing anything up. You're doin' more damage—" he looked at the shattered pane—"than they are."

"Well, they ain't supposed to be here. It's my job to get 'em out."

"Oh, come on," Eric said. "Let 'em stay for another night. You guys are moving on tomorrow, ain't you?"

Sally said, "Yeah. We were planning to." She said it grumpily.

"They're practically locals, Aim. Why you gonna hassle them? They'll be gone tomorrow. Or, if not, a couple of days after that."

"I'm doin' my damned job. I'm supposed to be runnin' squatters off this place. They ain't nothin' but crazy science kids and…stuff. We don't like that down here. It ain't right." He stood straighter, looked around, and shook his head. "Okay, Mr. Jeffers has saved your asses tonight. But if I come back here in a couple of nights and you're still around, I'm gonna run you in. And you can say thank you to us both now."

Deena said, "Thank you."

The others began to move around again. The bear-like young man asked, "Can we put up our shelter again—and eat our dinner?"

Aim gave another grumpy look and turned away. "Hey, Jeffers."

"What?"

"You wouldn't be wantin' to make the next ferry to Gilead…?"

Eric said, "Well, actually…" When he looked back, somehow two of the house walls were again standing. Once was the glass wall, no longer broken. While he was looking at it, he heard a snapping of fire. Again the rocks and embers appeared, with their complex racks of roasting fish, their silver skins streaked black and gold.

He could even smell them.

"That is just disgusting—the way they play with reality like that." Aim shook his head. "I know you don't want to hang around with these people anymore than you have to. They have no respect—no respect at all. For what *is*. Come on. Lemme give you a lift back to the Harbor. Cookin' fish like that! That way, you can get away from these ones here—they stink like goddam Californians."

*

Two days later, Eric carried his folding table down the maglev's station's brick ramp onto the commons. His tote bag bounced from side to side on his back.

The sky had not lightened fully.

Eric turned the corner into the market, looking east where red sun came past the school's brick face and through the underpass. He squinted at the foreshortened motto—and the world was covered with the particulate rainbow of dragonfly wings, before he looked away, muttering *The gift must move*...which he had not seen but knew was what the bronze letters read because he had seen them so often before.

A few of the Tuesday morning vendors were out and already putting things on their own benches. Many more would not be getting there for another hour. The air was cool for September, with now and again a gust of warmer air, a promise of what the later day might hold.

He'd wanted to be there by seven thirty, but his table was out by six forty, and he came back from Maya with the crate from her imported pasta stand, to sit on, as well as the bag of oatmeal-raisin walnut cookies he'd baked the night before. (He'd left a third with Maya.) Ten minutes later, Dona came by with a tray in her hands—and said, "My aunt did this last night. She asked me to bring this over and give it to you, if you were here."

"That nice." When the cover came off, it was a ginger cake with coffee icing. "You take a couple of cookies." Eric said.

"I wish they weren't so good." She selected two (clearly looking for smaller ones; Eric smiled), then turned toward Dr. Zaya's office.

"You thank the doctor for me—and for comin' out to get Shit taken care of."

"Well, you know—that's just Zaya. She's *almost* as eccentric as you two."

All the details that made the market the market—the tools on the benches off to the right, the statue of the winged bronze on its pedestal up at the north end, and the fish stands among the first set up, with Laurel and Arna loading shovelfuls of ice onto their wooden trays (Laurel stopped to wave; Eric grinned and waved back), and, minutes later, the first few women from the big Office, including the one whose name he still hadn't learned yet, with all the red, matted hair, who held her large cup up in her big, grubby hand, saying, "You know this coffee is so watery, and your cookies is so good—you mind if I take two?"

"Go ahead," Eric said. "That's what they're here for."

She did. "It's a shame to waste 'em. But thank you, thank you so much." And chomping, she wandered away across the grass, with three of her friends trailing. Eric chuckled behind her.

"Mr. Jeffers! Hello…!"

He looked over.

Across the grass, two young black women were coming toward him. Both looked faintly familiar and at the same time, no names leaped into his head to go with them.

Eric called, "Hello…" trying to keep the puzzlement out of his voice.

The shorter girl had a wealth of dreads, like something out of the turn of the century. What was her name? He'd known it yesterday…

The taller one wore work pants, work shoes, and a work jacket, open over her breasts: Deena Havers, the sculptor! "Good morning." Both had knapsacks, which the taller shrugged from one shoulder to let it swing down and sit it on the grass. "Do you mind if I do some sketching? I was thinking about it the last time I saw you, on the mainland. But then you left. So I didn't get to ask you." That day, Deena's head was shaved. It hadn't been two days ago.

Eric tried to remember the dark, natural hair that had covered it. "Naw. Naw, go right on ahead." He felt a surge of pleasure, at seeing Deena and the other girl from the marriage group. "Take a cookie, if you want. Or a piece of cake." (She was the head of the group marriage. She was writing a book about them. But his mind would not give him back her name…)

"We took the early morning ferry across—when the sun was just coming up. It was…just beautiful out there on the water," Deena said. She squatted now and pulling back the canvas cover, then glanced up. "With the fog and everything."

"When we came out," the one with the dreads explained, "the sky was as red as a piece of hickory-smoked ham—and the clouds were like white fat running all through it. It was really interesting—You live out here? What do you do?"

"Well," Eric said, moving back on the crate he was using for a chair, "me and my partner, we just do handyman work—sometimes. And sometimes we sit out here and give away cookies and sandwiches to people like you who're coming through and maybe didn't have as big a breakfast as they might have liked."

The woman with the dreads—oh, come on, what was it?— laughed. "I can just...take one?"

"Sure can. They're free."

She leaned forward to pick one up, hesitated, and bit. Then she smiled. Deena was already sitting on the grass, cross-legged, and had pulled a sketchpad and a box of pastels free, and was making sweeping gestures across it he couldn't see. The pad looked twice as big as anything thing that could naturally fit into her sack—which probably meant there was something technological about it, like her sculpture, like the mainland house, which he wouldn't ever really understand, because he wasn't an artist or a scientist himself. "Right now," Eric went on, "I'm just waitin' for my partner to get back from the hospital. He's supposed to come in two days, so I'm just killin' time out here today till he gets home—I mean, it's comical." He laughed. "I'm doin' just the same thing I'd be doin' if he *was* here, but I tell you, it feels kind of empty 'cause he ain't around." There he was, running off again about what he was feeling, just 'cause it was unusual. "It's funny—I don't complain about much, but I sure wish the day after tomorrow would hurry up and get here." Shut up, he thought to himself. Come on, keep quiet. Listen to them—they're the interesting ones. (And, of course, they hadn't said thank you for his intervention with Aim back on the mainland. But that was just kids today...) "But it's kinda hard waitin' for him to come—"

Behind him, somebody said, "Day after tomorrow? That old fool is supposed to come back here from the hospital the day after *tomorrow*? You mean the one there in Runcible? Naw—I don't believe it for a minute! I don't think he's comin' then. You just put that right out of your head, Mr. Eric Jeffers—"

Frowning, Eric twisted around. Shit was standing there, with a cloth bag and his hand inside, reaching in to pull out three apples—he had the hands for it—which he set down on the table and grinned. "Hey, there, good-lookin'. You think your old fuck is gonna be home from the hospital tomorrow? I know I sure as hell don't. *I* think he's come back already!" Shit pulled out three more, set those down, then dropped his hand on Eric's shoulder and kneaded. "You talkin' to my friends here—we was laughin' and havin' a good time on the boat across from the Harbor. Wasn't we? You know who this is? This here is Al Havers granddaughter! Would you believe that? Like I told you, sweetheart, six times, on the boat comin' across, I used to look up to your granddaddy so much. I used to tease him all the time. But that's 'cause I wanted so much to be like him, when I was a kid, I didn't know what to do—only I couldn't, at least not in the daddy and the granddaddy department, 'cause—" Shit grinned wickedly—"I was a nigger cocksucker. Your granddaddy was quite a guy."

From her cross-legged position on the grass in front of the table, Deena went on sketching. "Your partner there, Mr. Haskell, is a cut-up."

Dreads shaking around her ears, the other girl laughed.

And Eric thought, the goddam *sun* has come up...!

"Hey," Shit said, "take an apple, too, with that cookie!" He turned two of the green fruits over and set them on end, so they wouldn't roll. When he'd put out four more, he started a second layer. Finishing the three-sided pyramid—the two girls (and Eric) had watched, fascinated—he said, "Hey, I'm gonna run over and ask Hap and Bulah if they got any peaches for us." Holding the empty sack by the neck, he flung it up and over his shoulder and stalked off across the grass, with the side to side sway his arthritis had given him in the last twenty or so years. "They're always good for that."

Eric had a weird expression on his face that was half frown and half grin. He was trying to think how to ask if they knew why Shit was back two days early. It would be just like Shit to get up and leave in the middle of things—though he looked healthy enough—

—when three young men came up, two of them holding hands. "Hey, you came out here, too?"

The girl with the dreads said, "You can take some fruit or some cookies, if you want. It's free." She looked back at Eric to explain soberly, "They came out here on the boat with us, too."

"Wow," one of the boys said. And did. (Eric heard the cookie breaking in his mouth.) "You know, they were right. Out here, this is like something you read about happening in the thirties." Then they walked away.

From her seat, Deena said, "All of the island here—at least this part—is like a left-over piece of the thirties. Of the good times before today. But it's nice." She went on sketching.

The girl with the dreads said, "We were talking to them last night. His brother was on the moon—but he'd never met anyone who'd been to Mars. Like Deena. We almost convinced *them* to get married. You know, you and your partner should think about it."

"Come on," Deena said. "Everything doesn't have to be politics. Besides, if you're living in the thirties, it isn't quite as important as it is today—I mean, in the rest of the country."

Two minutes later, Shit was back with a bag of peaches. "They only gimme a dozen. But that's somethin'."

Eric pushed up from the table. "Will you *please* stay still long enough for me to hug you and ask you what the fuck you're doin' back here and how you're feelin'?"

"Okay," Shit said, still grinning.

Suddenly, Eric stood up and hugged him—and Shit hugged Eric back. By his ear, Eric heard Shit say, "Excuse me, yall, but I am a tongue fucker from way back, and I ain't sucked on no part of this old bastard in three days now." And Eric had a mouth full of everything in Shit's.

The two girls laughed.

I could break down and just ask, but why can't I remember it...?

When Shit pulled his face away, Eric said, "You ain't had no coffee yet."

"Don't worry," Shit said, "I'll make some when we get home."

Finally, Eric asked, "Why are you *here?* Ain't you supposed to be in the hospital for another day? You got pneumonia!"

"Not no more, I don't. Last night," Shit said, "they told I could leave this mornin', if I wanted to. Whatever they gimme knocked that stuff out right away. They got medicines now they didn't even have when Shad come down with it—you remember Shad?"

On the ground, Deena did a last few lines on her drawing, then said, "You want to see what I'm doing?" She turned the pad around.

Shit and Eric both looked down.

So did the girl with the dreads.

It was a sketch of Shit, with his grin and his tufty beard and his caved-in cheeks and his bald spot and his incongruous hoody—seeing it drawn, and drawn so well, with folds and the ragged elbow, made it look particularly odd—bent over the table, holding his bag and setting out apples. "You can have this," she said. "This—" she gestured with the pad—"keeps a copy on store for me, if I need it later...for reference."

* * *

[105] IT WASN'T A full year later that Eric made the transition into relative sexual inactivity. He was eighty-five when he'd noticed that, along with his erections, his orgasms of every three weeks, or month or so had... well, stopped.

There'd been two and three month interruptions in them before, and for a while he'd even taken testosterone.

(*Remember you had that testosterone pump fixed in the side of your belly? You had to get it filled every month for...hell, it had to be more'n ten years. I just made mine naturally, with my balls I guess.*

(*Yeah,* Eric said. *That would be you.*)

But this seemed permanent.

Over the same time, two years older, Shit would still declare, now on one morning, now on another, "Get over here, y'ol' white bastard; this nigger's gonna fuck your cracker asshole." Fifty years before, Eric had heard Shit approach Dynamite, pretty much every second or third morning, with the same words: it made the arc of coastal life coherent, and though Eric's response to Shit's weight and rhythm was sexual in only the most general way, it rarely hurt. (Didn't I used to wonder if I would ever be able to do this? Now I can—at least if I grease myself up the night before—which probably means I could'a done it back then. Damn...) It was more pleasant than he'd remembered it when the same acts had made him come. A couple of times, looking at the pale blue KY pump on the night table (though you could get it in various sized plastic envelopes with self-sealing spouts, you couldn't find that stuff in real collapsible tubes no more), he told Shit, "You know, I understand a lot about your daddy I didn't when he was alive," not that Shit was curious about what that was.

Sometimes, panting, grinning, Shit would say, "Hey...I finished up... that time..." which made Eric realize the two out of three he didn't say it, he hadn't. Well, since Eric hadn't, either, he didn't mind. He loved his position as the object of Shit's enthusiasm. How odd that, as an eighty-five-year-old man, he could lie next to Shit, with copper sunrise coming under the window shade, and feel, now on one morning, now on another, these were the most satisfying moments in a life that, sexually speaking, had been pretty satisfying throughout.

A few times, there, Eric had said to Shit, who was still breathing hard on top of him, "Hey—don't work yourself into a heart attack. I ain't ready for your nigger ass to drop dead on me..." Then he reached up to pat the puffy hair of Shit's beard; and Shit reached down to run his fingers through Eric's.

One day, instead of making a joke about it and calling Eric a dumb nigger back, panting, Shit had said, "Don't worry. I ain't plannin' to kill myself fuckin' some damn white man to death! Even you!" For the first time, the racial slur sounded as though it had been intended to wound. Eric reached up and put his hand over Shit's, still holding his shoulder. He felt the scarred and broken pits where nails should be. (How did one learn to find such violations beautiful...?) Eric listened to the labored breath above. Shit didn't take his hand away. Well, maybe Shit was joking. Or grumpy... because he hadn't come.

But, later in the morning, Shit said, "I wanna take a nap. Come on in with me," which, as late as fifteen years before, would have been an invitation to make love.

Inside, on the unmade bed, Shit—as usual, he hadn't gotten dressed all morning—said, "Lay up here where I can feel you against me. I'm gonna pull my damn pecker for a while. I swear, if I don't get off, it's gonna fuckin' kill me!"

It began a strange and, finally, frightening spring, at the end of which, three months later (with or without Eric), rarely more than half dressed and often naked or just in an undershirt, Shit was beating off all the time... in bed, sitting at the kitchen table, out behind the house, in the bathroom, down beside the ocean, or out on the cabin's deck at night.

At first Eric would say, "You gotta stop this, Shit. You gonna get sores on yourself, now."

Shit would say, "I don't give a fuck," and keep on.

Later, Eric would say, "If somebody comes by, Ed or someone, and they see you, they gonna make me put you away. Don't you understand?"

Not stopping, Shit would grump, "I don't care. Besides, you're the one who's crazy—out there on the commons at two-thirty in the mornin', with all your clothes off, talking to a damned statue."

"Oh, come on," Eric said. "I explained that to you. Since I was naked the first time I happened to see it, at Jay's, I wanted to look at it that way again. That's all. I thought it might..."

"And you never have been able to tell me what you thought it might do. And Dr. Zaya had to bring you home with a blanket round your damned shoulders. I told you, this ain't like the damned Dump, where we could do stuff like that." Having slowed for the length of half a sentence, Shit went back to pumping.

"Shit, that was three years ago—and...well, okay. So maybe I was a little crazy that night. I told you, I thought it was late, and no one would be out. Or—okay, maybe I forgot the Settlement ain't the Dump. But that don't got nothin' to do with this. You gotta stop!"

"You're crazy already! So I'm just gonna go crazy along with you."

"Oh, don't be like that." It made him want to cry. Something was wrong with him, he knew. A couple of times Shit had tried to tell him, as had that new doctor, but it would never stick. "Stop, will you...?"

"Fuck you!"

Eating could halt it for maybe five or ten minutes, no longer.

Really, it was like a parody of that Costas fellow, back in Hugantown (odd: it was the only name he remembered from anyone in the place not in his family), who'd lived in the cabin in the lot around from Eric's grandmother—only this was without climaxes. Eric wondered if the same fate had fallen to the plumber, who'd been more than a decade his senior, anyway. Twenty-two times in a...Was Costas alive?

In June, sitting in the kitchen, naked, in one blue sock, an old man with dangling dugs and bony hips, ankles, and shoulders, fist moving in the tight white hair at his groin, Shit said, "Come here. You gotta do somethin' for me." His hand pulsed about his soft, sizable penis. Blown up to twice their former diameter with age, from what they'd been thirty years back, Shit's brown testicles moved with his fist on the chair's stained caning.

Eric put the kitchen knife on the counter, left the carrots he was cutting for the last beef stew of the year, turned, and walked across the floor. In his own jeans and bare feet, the only other thing he wore was a green T-shirt.

Shit looked up at him. "Can you get down on the floor, between my knees, here?"

"Yeah…but I may never get up." Eric began to lower himself, managing finally to sit on the rag rug that went under the kitchen table. "Now, if I asked *you* to sit down here, you'd call me a murderer—"

"'Cause with my arthritis, you would be. Hey—I'm gonna ask you to do somethin'. It's gonna be hard for you, too. I don't think you're gonna wanna do it…"

Looking up at Shit's face, Eric saw the tears in the old man's yellowing eyes, their green now mostly gray. Old man? No…as with so many older people, when he went down to the Settlement for the open air market or the groceries or sometimes went to ask Ed how the new ferry was working out and took a ride back to the Harbor, Eric saw a girl or a boy who had been oddly afflicted with one or another ailment, so that she walked slow and stiff or that he had lost most of his hair or the face was overlaid with odd folds of flesh—wrinkles. Bellies and hips were weighted with alien fat or had grown unaccountably thin. "Age" was a variety of bodily disfigurements that simply and eventually infolded the young. That's all.

Eric put his hand on Shit's thigh and looked up at the boy's eyes to which something had…happened, that had discolored them and made them tear—made them…old. The flesh underneath Shit's leg was wrinkled; what lay across the top was smooth.

Shit took a breath, and for a moment Eric was convinced Shit was going to ask Eric to castrate him. Eric's heart was not pounding…But yeah, he thought, the nigger's gone crazy. "Okay. What…?"

Shit said, "You gonna drink the piss out my dick, lick out my asshole, and eat my damned snot?"

Now Eric took a surprised breath. "Goddam it, nigger, of course I am!" The relief was disorienting. He lay his cheek against Shit's soft thigh. With his other hand, he reached forward and cradled Shit's testicles in his own old man's labor-roughened palm. Under himself, Eric moved his legs to get them more comfortable, though it was futile. Shit's goddam nuts were almost twice the size he once remembered them—not as big as Jay's had eventually gotten. (Like a goddam grapefruits!) Still, they'd been out of his damned pants for…well, weeks! "I thought you were gonna ask me to do something hard." Eric snorted. Could their bloating have had anything to do with Shit's obsessive masturbation? (He remembered how Jay's used to itch, if that wasn't just a damned excuse…) Really, as much as Shit hated it, Eric had to get them both to a doctor, for a checkup. "That's just…fun." It had been at least twelve years now that both were taking pills for blood pressure, too. Maybe that needed to be adjusted.

After a long while, Shit said, "Well, you ain't done none of it for a while…"

Was something like that really making him cry? "Well—you been so busy pounding your damned dick, how was I supposed to get your attention? What'd you want me to do? Bring you down, hog-tie you, drain your damned radiator and rape your nose?"

"Maybe you could do…a little of that." Behind the tears, Shit began to smile. "I wouldn't mind. Would you at least call me a goddam motherfuckin' piece of mule shit, so I'll know you care?" He sighed and turned to the window, as though he wondered if anyone were looking in—and his hand… stopped moving. Eric was about to do it, when Shit interrupted him:

"I remember the first time we was ridin' together in the truck with my dad, you was pickin' at yours and eatin' it, but you was too scared to give me none. So finally, about after ten minutes, when I got tired of laughin' at you to myself, I dug out a finger-full and gave it to you. Later, Dynamite told me he thought we was cute."

"Yeah, well I guess I was. Scared, I mean. Sure. I remember bein' scared to give you any with your dad there, even though I knew he wouldn't mind. But I don't remember you givin' me none."

"Well, I did. And when you took it, you looked so…grateful, there. I already knew I wanted you around. But that's when I knew I wanted you around for a long time—forever. 'Cause it was so easy to make you happy."

Eric snorted. "And I can't even remember it."

After another pause, Shit said, "'Cause I don't get hard now, I thought you didn't want to no more. Or you didn't like it now or somethin'."

"Well, I don't get hard, either—" Eric lifted his head from against Shit's leg and wondered how he was going to stand up—"no more. What you mean, I didn't want to? Nigger, you are as crazy as a damned white man— course I want to. I'd do it even if you didn't want me to. And if you do want it, that's better."

Shit looked down again. With the back of his wide, bony fingers he rubbed Eric's beard. "Your beard looks nice."

"Well, *yours* looks like an old worn out door mat…but it's still sexy as all hell…You gonna help me up from here?" Shit's hand went under Eric's arm. He tugged. "And, please," Eric said, "let's go and lie down on the bed for a while. Together. And hold each other. Please…?"

Then began three weeks where, first for an hour, then three, then five, Shit stopped—"Goddam, I'm glad I still got *your* dick to hold onto!"—till he was only doing it forty minutes or an hour each day, usually in the morning before they got out of bed, one hand pushed under Eric's shoulder.

Sometimes, with Eric, he'd even joke about that, saying he had to keep it up, in case something happened that surprised him. "We might as well, since we don't got nothin' else to do."

* * *

[106]   NOT ONLY DO Wonder Decades take their place in the past; so do perfectly ordinary years with little of interest about them save that ordinary folk like you and me and Shit and Eric survived them.

* * *

[107]   THE CYCLES OF Eric's life took in stony beaches and pine forests where you could walk in a daylight all but night dark and fields where there was no grass, only stones and moss, alongside tar and macadam measured at its edge with poles and wires and solar panels, and water, broken, flickering, so much water, as much water—salt and silver—as there was sky, enough to make you scream or laugh at such absurd vastness, swelling within until Eric became his self exploding through today toward tomorrow, water green as glass falling between rocks and wet grass, the smell of dust and docks and distances, and sometimes Shit stepped up and took Eric's rough hand in his rough hand.

Under scruffy brows, Shit's eyes watered a lot these days, so that frequently he thumbed them dry, then rubbed it away on hip or T-shirt hem.

Sometimes Shit would say, "It's nice today." And sometimes, "It's gonna rain."

Most of the time, when he said that, it did.

* * *

[108] THAT WINTER THEY hadn't gone to Anne's but rather to Hanna's. Two weeks before the solstice, while he was helping Anne pack her latest set of large pots to earn a couple of thousand, Anne herself told Eric, "Hanna wants us all—you know, the people who come to my place—to come to her studio this year, instead."

Eric pulled the tape gun over the crevice and tore off the brown strip.

Anne grasped the carton's corners and, left and right, walked it over the cement floor toward the ones by the door. "For eggnog and dinner. Yall don't mind—?"

Through the screening, the wind lifted Eric's hood from his shoulders, then dropped it, so that the fur tickled his ear. "Well, I'll tell you—since *you* ain't doin' it, we'll probably stay home and just—"

"No!" Anne insisted.

Eric pulled the sealing wand down along the next carton's overlapping flaps, covering part of a large "F." Within, foam packing held another of Anne's big pots.

"She already told me. She's gonnna come and get yall. You just gotta walk from your door to the car. She's really eager for you to meet this young woman—from the university over in Mobile."

The screen door did not quite fill the top of the kiln room's side doorframe. When the kiln was on, it could get hot in here—even in January. Anne only fired one pot at a time.

"Well—" Eric lifted the wand and turned to the last box—"I don't really got an objection. But, you know Shit—if he ain't doin' what he's always done, he gets grumpy."

"Well, you ask him," Anne said. "Tell him it would be a favor to both me and Hanna. Because of the Atlanta show, I just can't do it this year. And, besides—hell—I'm gettin' on. You know, Hanna's got heat in her big studio."

"Well, I—"

"Please." She let go of the carton corner to smile at him, under wisps of scarlet. (This month Anne's hair was scarlet.) "Tell Shit it's for me."

"Sure. I'll tell him," Eric said. "But I ain't promisin' nothin'." He smiled back. The fact was Eric was pretty sure Shit would have no objections. To his own surprise, though, Eric had become the one not too eager to try new things, new places, though he didn't like to admit it. Blaming it on Shit was one of those convenient things to say.

But then, by now all their friends knew that, too.

Finished helping Anne pack up the biggest works, he stepped outside as the truck down from the Atlanta Gallery pulled up, and, in a thermal web suit, Geraldine climbed out. "Hi, there, pretty lady. Hey, there, young man."

Eric smiled and thought: People used to say that to old fellows when I was kid. He still wondered why...?

Eric was rolling the last of them out on the red power dolly when he noticed the address on the truck bed's blue side was 4667 Montoya. "Hey, you know? Hey—Geraldine?" He worked the carton onto the tailgate, which had begun to whine and lift. "Up there in Atlanta—you fellows can't be more than half a block from where me and my daddy used to live. A big ol' private house, divided up into apartments. Guy named Condotti owned it—but I know he's long gone."

"On Montoya?" Geraldine frowned down from where she stood on the hydraulically rising platform with the carton. She had heavy, muscular arms, both of them sleeved with tattoos. It was hard to believe only that flimsy netting along with some black engineer style boots could keep you warm. For all her shoulder muscles, her tits were long and flat. (How far back had he gotten used to seeing women and men walking around in clothing that revealed pubic hair, breasts, genitals...? Drive by a road crew in winter or summer, and as the job had become safer and safer—no more hot tar, no more bits of gravel and flying lumps of macadam—it was pretty usual to see six or ten men, buck naked, at least that's what they looked like from more than fifteen feet off, in nothin' but boots and hardhats, puttin' down a road. As a young man, he remembered actually thinking it had to stop with breasts.) On her rather prominent cunt she'd attached a couple of small carved charms—two red, one gold—to the graying hair behind its length of wire with the tiny silver beads that kept in the heat.

Geraldine got the next box up. "Ain't no private houses there today. It's all business towers. Most of them went up back in the thirties." A strong woman, she had a belly and made Eric think of an only slightly less hairy Jay MacAmon—with, yeah, breasts.

"Oh...Towers?" Eric was surprised, he had the feeling he should have known that. Though he'd been to Savannah a few times, he hadn't been in Atlanta since he was a kid. Hadn't someone already told him about the changes? But when...?

Behind him Anne was saying, "Now, please, honey, when you take these off the truck, take 'em off just like you put 'em on—one at a time. If something does go wrong, there's no need to smash up two or three."

"Sweetheart," Geraldine said, "have I ever broken one of your little pottie pieces in six years of gettin' 'em back and forth?"

"No, you haven't. And this is not the time to start. Now"—Anne's hand fell on Eric's shoulder as, above them, Geraldine leaned the carton back, first to walk it into the truck bed, then to lower it on its side—"don't forget to ask Shit about coming to Hanna's. You gonna remember?"

"Oh...!" Eric said, and nodded, still trying to fix his mind to the fact that his adolescent neighborhood was really gone, the same way the untamed and uninhabited Gilead—the Holotas' Gilead, Jay and Mex's Gilead, Shit's old Gilead—from his own first years at Diamond Harbor were...gone.

As Eric walked back along the Island's winter bluff, hands swinging through dry, thigh-high grass, it occurred to him: yes, Anne knew his increasing tendency to sedentariness. But she's too nice to call me on it. Then he thought (it made him smile in the evening, as gulls swooped about): And she knows if Shit says he don't mind goin' to Hanna's, I ain't gonna put up no fuss. Well, if they're gonna bring us out there and take us back, and it's the same people, just in a different place—he sighed with the fancied difficulty of it—it should be okay.

More and more old things were going. And the new things were just uncomfortable, not because they were embarrassing or sexual or inconvenient—just new.

The great ceramic shapes Anne made, with their metallic glaze like liquid sunlight poured around them—he looked out at the copper sea— he'd always thought were beautiful when, years back, he used to see them in the pottery shop windows in Runcible or Hemmings.

But a notion that had come to him only that afternoon—that those objects, however beautiful, had displaced his Atlanta—made them seem cold, if not somehow minatory.

* * *

[109] THAT EVENING, WHEN the kitchen in their cabin was half dark and, sighing some, as Anne had requested him Eric asked, and Shit answered, "Sure. Hanna's got a nice place. I don't understand them big paintin's she does. But that ain't nothin' new. Let's go." So there was no excuse not to have their Solstice holiday at Hanna's rather than Anne's.

The young woman—who came to pick them up—was an Asian social science student named Ann Lee, doing a group dissertation on "community" at the University over in Mobile. (Group dissertations— *that* was something new since Caleb had told them about his first stay in graduate school...Or was it?) She wanted to interview both Shit and Eric about their lives in the Settlement and before.

It was one reason Hanna had been so eager that they come.

At the party in the back studio, dozens of people moved around them.

Floating beneath the beamed ceiling, glowing and glittering letters and numbers declared, "2077! HAPPY NEW YEAR! 2077!" though that was eight days off.

"Now, see," Shit said, sitting down across from him on the edge of an outdoor wooden settee, a piece of summer garden furniture brought inside Hanna's barn-like studio for the winter. Shit held a red plastic plate heaped with chicken and chopped kale cooked up with ham hocks and a helping of sliced beets and vinegar that, on one side, had already left red spots splattering his white canvas jacket. "We got us this pretty young lady who wants to take me back in the office, there, and ask me all sorts of questions about stuff—she gonna ask you, too, don't worry."

"I know that," Eric said. "This eggnog is good." In both hands, Eric held the cut glass cup. Nutmeg's scent rose from brown speckled peaks of meringue folded into whipped cream and whisky.

"You keep on puttin' it down, and you gonna be drunk as a skunk—and gassy, too. You ain't a drinker." Shit looked around. "Ask one of these kids here to bring you somethin' to eat. They'll do it. Hey—" He called one youngster who couldn't have been sixteen.

The boy turned and raised an inquiring eyebrow—iridescent blue.

"You wanna get this feller a nice plate of that ham? And some of them shrimps in gravy?"

The youngster, who was not local, frowned. He was wearing a thermal web-shirt—woven of coppery threads spaced as wide as fishnet. (Like Geraldine's…) You could turn it on or off, and it would create a blanket of warmth around you, even on really cold days. Sometimes workmen wore whole suits of the stuff, bottom and top. (Someone had even given Shit a heat-net shirt a few years back, which he'd worn exactly once, shrugging it away, finally, with, *Yeah, it's warm, but I keep thinkin' the damned thing's gonna 'lectrocute me.*) The kid's pants also had a large transparent plastic crotch panel—when *had* those come in? At least two decades before, Eric had been sure Shit would have both of them wearing them in a month. That would have been just like him. (But he'd surprised Eric by shrugging *them* off with, *There ain't no mystery left. You know exactly what you gonna get. So why bother?*) At local bars, it had taken maybe three years for men to stop joshing, "If mine was that puny, I'd be embarrassed to wear one." It didn't stop anyone from walking around in them, though. As several fashion commentators remarked, until it became a cliché, their popularity was mostly with rather small-hung straight guys—though there were occasional exceptions in the entertainment world—which, blue hair not withstanding, was what this very pleasant young fellow looked to be.

"And maybe some of that hop'n'john? You know." Shit ducked his head. "Hop'n'john? Them beans and rice? And a spoonful of them chopped-up greens. You can skip the beets. I like those, but he don't."

"Sure." The kid smiled at Eric, turned, and, between the guests, hurried toward the buffet table across the room, calling over his shoulder, "Hey, it's nice to see you guys again this year."

Eric wondered who he was, down to visit what cousin or aunt. But when your hair color (and cut) changed so radically season to season, it was hard to recognize children, given how fast they grew, anyway.

Beside Eric, solstice lights flickered in a web of red, green, and blue over a lumpy, leaning cactus. With its terracotta pot, it must have weighed almost as much as the kid.

At which point, the Asian Ann woman came up. "Mr. Haskell, if you— oh, you're still eating. Well, we can certainly wait till you're finished."

"Honey, these are my thirds. I'm just playin' with this stuff. If I eat all this mess down, good as it is, I'm gonna be fat as Ol' Daddy Christmas." Shit put the plate on the table between him and Eric. "Besides, I'm all interested in your questions there." Slowly he stood.

Eric knew it hurt his left hip and winced for him. "I wanna find out what you're gonna ask me."

"Well, if you're ready, Hanna says we can use her back office. That's where my recorder is…" and they were walking off.

Then the kid in the net shirt returned with Eric's plate. Eric took it and said, "Thank you."

The kid didn't say anything but looked very serious. Eric was about to start eating, when he realized the youngster was still staring at him.

Eric paused with his fork up and frowned inquiringly.

The kid blurted. "My name is Cum Stain. But I don't think you would call me that, would you? You're probably too old, huh?"

Eric shrugged. "Why not? My partner's name is Shit—" he nodded off in the direction Shit had vanished—"and people been callin' him that since he was younger than you."

"They have? Oh, wow!"

"Sure have, Cum Stain." Eric grinned.

The kid grinned back, then turned, and dashed away.

Even with the black plastic fork, the ham cut just as tender. It was good, too. So were the greens. He ate some more, but gas in his belly suddenly wanted to get out but wouldn't. It made him sit the plate down beside Shit's, wondering if there was any club soda.

Molly walked up, in her open orange jacket and orange slacks, gold flocking on both. "Hey, I came over to make sure somebody had taken care of you. But I see you got a plate—oh, you didn't get no sweet potatoes." (But he shook his head, and she went on.) "It's so nice of you fellows to agree to talk to Ann." She had rings in her dark, dark nipples. Her orange lipstick practically leapt from her dark, dark face. It was interesting that both men and women again were turning to make up, a resurgence from the thirties.

"Oh," Eric said, "this ain't nothin'. We're at that age where we'll talk any of you young folks ear off, if you wanna waste time listenin'. The only thing I'm worried about is Shit's stories is gonna scandalize her. Shit never did learn how to tone a tale down a little so he could tell it in a way that wouldn't make a civilized person arch an eyebrow."

Hanna laughed. Gold and orange fabric shook as did her tit rings. "Well, I don't think Ann—"

—Eric felt a mental hitch, realizing for the tenth time in three days that Ann was the university woman Ann Lee, not the potter Anne Frazier—

"—really *wants* her stories all that civilized. This is for her American Anthropology class, and she told me she needs 'em as raw as she can get 'em. Her topic, you see, is the role of sexuality in gay community development."

"Well, yeah," Eric said. "I un'erstand that. But there's raw and there's plain crude. Shit starts talkin' about sex, and he may just 'role' her out your front door on the run. We're both more than a little crude. Only sometimes I can control it. Most of the time, though, Shit don't even make the effort."

"Mr. Jeffers, I've known both you and Mr. Haskell for a long time—thirteen years, fifteen even." Molly laughed again. "You're my oldest friends in the Settlement. The fact is you are true social treasures, the both of you."

It surprised him when she said it: Eric thought of Molly as among his newest. But then, fifteen years was probably a third of the young painter's life.

"Nobody minds a little crudity, Mr. Jeffers—at least not here in the Settlement. Most of the women around this place consider themselves pretty worldly and sophisticated, but if we didn't have the two of you and the outrageous things that come out of both your mouths, we wouldn't have anything to lift our eyebrows about or to whisper with each other over or just to make us…laugh ourselves silly! I mean, that story Mr. Haskell told at Anne's, two summers ago, about the two of you in a three way with that midget, when his catheter worked loose, and started spurtin' all over everyone, has *still* got be one of the funniest things I ever heard!"

"Oh, yeah." Eric raised his chin. Shit had told that one back at Anne's summer solstice dinner and kept half her back yard in stitches twenty whole minutes. "I remember that one. That *was* pretty funny—and messy. But you know, we're all still friends." Though, as he said it, he realized they weren't: Big Man had died, at his dad's house on the mainland, maybe fifteen, twenty years ago—or more like thirty. (What he'd meant was that they'd stayed friends, despite the incident. But that's not what he'd said.) Mr. Markum was dead. For half a dozen years there, they'd gone to Christmas dinner at Big Man's in Pinewood (despite the tree and the cards, Big Man always managed to call it something else), arriving early in the day to help out, then clean up afterward, but that was...twenty-five, thirty-five years ago!

Molly was saying, "Ann said she wanted to spend about an hour and a half with Shit, then she'd be ready for you. If you don't mind sittin' here, she'll get to you. You want me to bring you some key lime pie?"

"I ain't even ate this ham and greens yet. And I ain't much for desserts. Naw, you don't have to worry about me." Eric shifted around in the chair's cushions, thought about taking up the plate of food again, but let it stay. "What I'm gonna do is sit here and take a little nap. While I'm waitin', I mean—'cause it's after eight o'clock. And after eight o'clock, that's what I usually to do."

"Well, you go ahead. I'll come get you as soon as she's finished with Mr. Haskell." Straightening up, Hanna chuckled again. "I swear—I was walking back from the commons the other evening, and I was thinkin' about that story, the way Mr. Haskell told it that night at Anne's. I started laughing out loud, right there on the path, under the trees. I couldn't stop myself. Two years after hearin' it—and I'm still laughing myself silly over the image of you lookin' all surprised and him rollin' onto his bag with that stuff just..." In the course of searching for a word, not finding it, and shaking her head, she laughed again, turned, and started away between guests.

Draperies behind the Christmas lights—whatever they called them, Christmas lights was what they were—were flowered and printed with leaves. Among their pattern, he could make out something like a face, which looked like...yes, that was his beard, and that was where his upper teeth should have been. Jay stood there, behind the colored stars, grinning. Behind him was Mike, with his denim shirt open wide over his dark, gleaming chest, because it was summer—Jay's shirt was open too, because it was winter and along the coast winter was so mild.

Like summers, sometimes...

It was funny, too—both had tails, winding, coiling, looping and unrolling, writhing behind them on the sand, pushing aside leaves, splashing down in the water, whipping up dry dirt, as they walked ahead of him over the beach. Mike's serpentine appendage was covered with what looked like coal chips—black scales, Eric realized—glistening under an aluminum sky. The scales on Jay's were hemp hued. Eric could see the bases pushing aside the frayed rip in the seat of both their work pants, allowing him to glimpse where the plated flesh joined Jay's blond-haired buttocks or his dad's, dark as gunmetal.

As the two men walked ahead, the tails overlapped and wrapped one another, so that along the writhing lengths he couldn't keep them distinct. It was like one great tail between them that, with its loopings and unloopings, as gulls flew above, ran from one of them and coiled around and around to join the other.

"Now, how're we gonna do it," Mike explained, stopping and turning and taking Eric's book from under his arm, "is that I'm gonna weld this one cover over here…weld it to the people." The volume was four-feet high—as tall, Eric thought, as one of Anne's pots. "And your friend over there—" he nodded toward Jay, who, in his big old work shoes, stood in the scurf of foam—"is gonna weld the other cover there to the sea, you see?"

Like summer, like winter…

Where he stood, Jay laughed. Out among small waves, a twenty-foot ceramic "C," chipped and ancient, stood in the slosh and slough, as though it had escaped from between the book covers.

Between, their shared tail writhed.

"Come on," Jay said. "Help us open it, now." All three took hold of the cover and pulled it up—it was heavy as a picnic table top—their hands above their heads, they worked their way under, to push it higher. Eric was shoeless and the paper slid under foot, wrinkling. The book was a lot bigger than he'd thought: more like twenty feet than four. When they got the cover vertical, it tottered a little—Mike raised both hands to catch it if it fell back, and Jay only stepped aside, staring upward.

It fell out, open, its far edge, with its leather binding down, splatting foam and seawater.

Eric took a great breath. His birthday was in less than a week…

Reaching up to tug around the orange visor (one of those old Turpens caps, like they used to sell at the truck stop four, five years ago…), Jay strode out beside it on the book's cream-colored end paper, with its intricate watermarks. In his other hand, Jay already held his welding arc in his gloved hand. Dragging behind, the red rubber hose wound back across the inside cover to become intertwined with the men's immense shared tail. "Weld it to the stars," Jay said. "And the sun—the moon. And the clouds."

"You see," Mike said, from the book's landward edge, "he got the easy job."

Jay squatted down, one knee in the water. From the arc tip, a white spark bit into the binding. Steam billowed up, hiding him.

Back where Mike stood, just on the endpaper, his boots had left footprints. Eric wondered if he should suggest his father take his shoes off.

"Yeah." Mike scratched his head. "The white man always got the easy job—You gonna help me weld this book to some of these people around here?"

The only person Eric could see was scrawny Frankie in her ragged sweater, lurking half behind a tree, one hand up on the bark. And, unlike Jay, Mike didn't even have welding tools. But, then, Mike was a senior welder. He could do the job with the black, crackling power from his bare fingers. Because he was black like Bull. "Come on, little girl—don't be scared. Nobody's gonna hurt you. We just wanna bind you here with this book—it's only philosophy..." Eric and Mike had started forward. There was Miss Louise, sitting at her table, in the dark, under the leaves. And Mr. Johnston. And, clowning around behind the fence, the guys from Dump Produce. Horm. And even Lurrie, though Eric didn't recognize him at first because he didn't have his hat.

Imploringly, Eric said to Mike, "How about Shit and Dynamite? I wanna bond with them...!"

"Well, I don't know about that." Mike sounded uncertain. "I ain't so sure if I really hold with the kind of stuff you guys been doin' out here..."

"Oh, come on. Don't be like that, Dad. Come on—"

"—Come on," Shit pushed at Eric's shoulder.

"What," Eric said. "Wha...?"

"Come on. It's your turn now."

"If he's sleeping," the Asian woman was saying, "we can do it later. You gave me a lot to think about, Mr. Haskell—"

"No," Shit said. "He'll chew my damned head off, if I don't wake him up to talk to you. He actually got some stuff to say. Me, I was just blabberin'."

"Oh..." Eric said. "Oh, I'm sorry." He moved forward in the seat. His head felt immense and hollow. Unsteadily, he pushed up, for a moment sure the floor was crooked beneath him.

"I got ya!" Shit grasped him by the shoulders. "Get your balance, now. Come on—" the floor righted—"take your time. I'm gonna get you a glass of water—or do you want some more eggnog?"

"Naw," Eric said. "Naw—just some water. With ice, if they got it. You know I ain't a drinker."

"I ain't a drinker." Shit grinned—he'd taken out his teeth again. "But sometimes I wonder about you. You put away two whole cups. That stuff's almost pure whiskey. You take 'im on back to the office. I'll bring you both a glass. Hey—make 'im show ya his tattoos. He'll do it in private, but he don't like to show 'em off in public."

"Come on, be quiet, Shit—!"

"I'm serious. I'm gettin' yall some water."

The woman said, "Water would be nice." She took Eric's arm. "You're sure you're ready for this...?"

"Oh, yes." Eric tried to exaggerate his readiness and wondered if he sounded silly. He started walking. "Of course I am. Now, which way is this office...?"

The Asian woman thought that was funny. At least she laughed. "Right back here."

But he knew this place as well as he knew Anne's. He'd helped Hanna pack her paintings the same way he helped Anne box her pots. Only he'd just woken...

As they walked through the guests, Eric took a big breath. "You know, my book—I'm sure they all told you how I'm always readin' this one book."

"Yes, that's right. Anne said something about a philosopher you were interested in."

Carefully, Eric said, "Benedict de Spinoza. *Ethics*. I was just thinkin', you know, I read that book so many times. I shoulda done somethin' with it. I always tried to do good, to help people, to feed 'em when they was hungry. But I coulda done some more—a lot more. I could have told some of the young people about him—helped them to understand what he was sayin', too. I probably coulda done it through the Library. Had a class or something, for youngsters who wanted to read it—it didn't have to be just youngsters. It could have been anyone. 'Cause it's so hard to read— especially at the start. I could have helped them all that way. But now, I think I've forgotten too much—maybe that just means it's time for me to read it once more. But I think I'm...too old."

Young Ann had walked through the door, where a desk had chairs on either side. "Hanna says you're...eighty-six?" She looked at him questioningly. "I don't see why you're too old. You could still do it."

"Maybe, but I don't think so. You see, I'm not a teacher or a writer or anything. I never was. I'm just a handyman—"

"But you're a handyman who reads Spinoza."

He thought she sounded proud of him, the way the young could sound proud of any dip-shit thing the elderly managed to do.

(*You know, I got up this morning and put my shoes on.*

(*You did? Well, I'll be!*

(I mean, it's not that they understand you almost pass out when you do it. Because you had to hold your breath when you bent over...)

"Well—" Eric smiled—"who *used* to read Spinoza. Handyman work—me and Shit—that's all we can do. And at this point, we can't do much of that. We have a perversion," he said, glancing down at the seat and readying himself to sit. "We like to eat up dried mucus. Our own, each other's. A doc told us once that it was even good for you—because it helped your immune system. Makin' it sexual—that was Nature's or God's way of keepin' you at it. It could even have been a survival trait. Lots of kids do it, but most of 'em get it shamed out of them unless they sexualize it. If we'd been into havin' babies and stuff, maybe we coulda passed it on. Maybe you don't even have to pass it on genetically, though. It could just happen socially, if we'd had 'em around us more. But we didn't do that, neither. It's too bad we wasted all that—"

He noticed now a strange look—almost distasteful—had taken over her face.

"Yes," she said, "immune system…your partner was talking about the same thing. But that sounds like science. I mean…'genetics.' I'm an academic, so I don't know much about that. We don't have time to go outside our disciplines. So I don't like to discuss it."

"Well," Eric said, "there was one time when almost all gay fellers knew somethin' about the immune system, because there were these diseases like AIDS and things that affected it so much. When I first got to the Dump, you had to have an AIDS test every few months and be ready to show it, too. But not no more."

"Please," she said. "Sit down—"

And he saw she was not looking at him.

Eric sat and frowned. "Don't you really think all this 'embarrassment of science' stuff is just more 'I don't wanna be related to no apes or no chimpanzees'? I mean—"

She looked up. "Mr. Jeffers—come on, now. No one is related to an ape. No one is related to a…chimpanzee! That's absurd. We're human beings, who can think and feel."

"But all life is related to each other…" He saw she was smiling.

So he smiled back.

And she said, "I'd like to ask you some of my own questions now. Reading Spinoza, though—now, how could something like that be wasted?"

Leaning back, Eric chuckled. "That's what Spinoza would have said—that it wouldn't have been wasted. Or even knowin' some little stuff about science. He had a great trust in knowledge for its own sake."

Again, she smiled—and sat behind the desk, under the shelf of books. "Let's not talk about things like science, all right? That's…just a little crude, even for an enlightened group of artists, out here. Like talking about your income. I want to discuss some…well, things I think are actually important. Would you mind that?"

"Thanks to the Kyle Foundation, I don't have to worry about—or talk too much—about my income. But a lotta people do—and did."

"Your partner—Mr. Haskell—was telling me that both of you, separately and together, used to spend time at the Kyle Mansion, even before it became the Settlement Library. They told me it was abandoned back then—back before the thirties."

"Naw, we used to go there when Hugh Kyle lived there—sometimes Mr. Kyle himself would come."

"Really…?" She looked seriously surprised. "Do you think you could tell me a little about that—?"

"Oh, yes. We—"

From the door, Shit leaned in. "I gotcha two nice glasses of water here—okay? With ice."

When Eric sipped his, he realized his had bubbles—soda water, like he'd have had at home. He gave Shit a quick smile. Shit smiled back toothlessly—Eric saw the shape of his teeth under the cloth of Shit's plaid shirt pocket beneath his loose white jacket—with the beet spots—and walked with his listing swagger that, Eric knew, was actually a kind of limp, back out among winter guests.

"One of the things I wanted to talk about—" Ann turned over a piece of paper, took up a pen (though it didn't seem to have an ordinary point. Some sort of stylus…?) and made a note—"is some stories that have come to us from the mainland, about how some folks used to practice Satanic magic around this area."

Eric raised an eyebrow.

"Did you know anything about that?"

"Satanic magic? Naw, I never heard nothin' about that."

She wrote something down, moved the stylus to an upper corner—and the writing disappeared, probably to be stored in some chip or bubble whose location he did not know.

She saw him peering and smiled. "I like these old fashioned devices," she explained. "In the thirties, they made these things to last. And I really don't like being bothered with new technologies, even when they're supposed to be simple. What do they say? 'If it was good enough for my dad…'" She leaned forward and wrote some more. Below where she was writing, a whole paragraph suddenly appeared on the page, which, somehow, she'd recalled—or what she had written had called up. "One of our informants tell me that when he was a child, his father took him and a bunch of other people to the island here, and they did some bizarre Satanic rites, probably sexual, which he wasn't allowed to see, of course, somewhere in the Kyle mansion and outside it. That was before any of the current residents of the Settlement had come out to—"

Eric began to laugh. "What—you been talkin' to Ed Miller? That's crazy. There wasn't no Satanic rites goin' on at the Kyle place when Mex and Jay lived there."

Ann sat back. "Now, I'm not supposed to reveal my informants names to each other, but out here, sometimes it's hard to keep them private. Still, yes, Captain Ed Miller said he knew MacAmon and his mute partner very well—and for a number of years. He said in many ways, after his own father died, Mr. MacAmon and Mr. Jalisco practically raised him. He said he always had the feeling that they were keeping something from him."

"Ed knew they was gay—life partners—like me and Shit…"

"Yes, of course. That's why we're interested in what he had to say. But he said, very explicitly, he meant something else."

"Well…" Eric had begun to frown again. "Well, I suppose they was keepin' *some* things to themselves. Ed was a straight little puppy. They wasn't out to convert him or make 'im do stuff that would turn his mind all around—though they probably wanted him to grow up comfortable with all kinds of people. And he did. But they wasn't out to rub his nose in the sex they was havin' with their friends and—hell—each other. That's all." Eric's frowned reached its strongest. "What'd you say Mex's last name was?"

"Jalisco. At least that's the name he paid his taxes under and that was on his credit union account."

"Mex Jalisco—I guess Mex had to be a nickname, too. You know, I never really thought too much about that before?" Eric eyebrows, somewhat bushy and overlong, bunched. "You know his first name?"

"Carlos." Looking down, Ann wrote some more. "A lot of people who had connections with the Dump have gone on at some length about how much respect Mr. MacAmon had for his partner. But not a one of them knew Mr. Jalisco's name, first *or* last. I confess, that seems a little odd for a respected man—"

"I think I know why that was," Eric said.

Questioningly, Ann looked up.

"Mex was here quite a while. But when he first come there was people lookin' for him from Mexico. At least, he'd run away from them, when he ended up here, with MacAmon. I think Jay was protectin' him—from the people back in Mexico what tried to cut his tongue out and made it so he couldn't talk. 'Mex' is a pretty convenient nickname for a Mexican man who don't wanna be found in a whole country full of legal and illegal immigrants. And that's what we had back then."

"Well, he was legalized, eventually—as far as we can tell, in '96 of the last century, through the efforts of Robert Kyle, the same man who started the Dump."

"So there you go." Eric sat back. "'96 was ten, eleven years before I come down here. But I bet that has *somethin'* to do with why they didn't throw around his real name. At least, whenever I thought on it, that's what I always come up with—though I confess, I did a lot of that thinkin' after they was both dead."

"There's also the fact that MacAmon kept his partner, who was deaf and dumb, I gather, pretty isolated from others like himself. I know he spoke the hand sign language fairly common back then, before they developed really efficient brain prostheses for deafness and blindness. That doesn't sound like respect to me."

"ASL," Eric said. "Naw, Jay respected him. First of all, Mex wasn't deaf. He could hear as good as we can—probably better than me today. Jay spoke that sign language, too, and they taught it to a lot of their close friends. Me and Shit both could talk that stuff back when we was young—I forgot more than half of it by now, I know. But I used to be able to say pretty much anything to Mex or Jay or anybody who knew it." Were these how stories came together or fell apart? Or is this how they did both? "And Mex went to a group of people who signed, down in Pinewood—same place as our friend Big Man lived—and Jay would drive him there pretty regular. He wasn't that isolated—Jay saw to it."

"Actually that does make me feel better about it. I surprise myself sometimes with how involved I find myself with all these dead people and how they lived their lives. My supervisor says I should just try to accept everything and not judge anything. Maybe after I've been doing this a little longer, I'll be able to." She smiled. "But it's hard not to have your own opinions."

"Sure," Eric said. "Lord knows I got enough of my own. But I can pretty well tell you, there wasn't no Satanic rites goin' on out here on Gilead, or anywhere else I know about down here. Ed Miller was just a nervous little kid—he weren't but seven or eight—maybe nine—goin' out to a funeral at the Indian Graveyard we got back there, what he didn't understand."

"Perhaps it was an Indian ceremony—which he took for something more sinister."

"No," Eric said, impatient. "It was just Jay buryin' his Uncle Shad. I was there. That's the whole point—it wasn't *no* kind of religion!" Eric suddenly found himself with a mind full of Spinoza's intentionless God, who was everything and desired nothing—neither from man nor from anything else…

"Mr. Jeffers?"

"I'm sorry there. But it…just wasn't. Some friends had come out to see him through it—that's all. And Ed was just little kid with a big imagination."

"We're also trying to run down some stories about man, a friend of Mr. MacAmon's, who lived in the Dump and who ran some kind of torture dungeon, with his partner—"

"Yeah," Eric said. "Black Bull and Whiteboy."

Ann nodded.

"They did a lot of work—mostly I think for people outside, from all over the state—and the surrounding states, I guess: they had cars comin' up to their cabin with license plates from all over. They did their work in the place, too, when somebody felt they needed it. But they must've charged pretty reasonable rates, as I understand it, 'cause it was pretty cheap livin' in the Dump with everything subsidized like it was. Yeah, they were a little strange—"

"—and the kinds of things they did don't strike you as Satanic? I've seen photographs taken in their basement, sixty and seventy years ago, that go pretty much beyond anything I could certainly imagine. We found more than seventy pictures in Kyle's personal papers on store in the library."

"Hey, I bet that was just some ordinary S&M—sadomasochism. You always gonna have some people into that wherever you got gay people. It's just one of things that goes into…what you call it? The community. Men what like to dress us like women or wear make up or just be real soft and gentle—wear their inner consciousness out where everybody can see it, even if it's a gentle one. And men who like to wear chains and leather and act like Nazis or—I don't know—they're doin' some kind of Satanic rituals. You know, I had to come all the way down here from Atlanta, before I learned that that was okay—the S&M and all the soft femininity. But that's what community is—a lot of different kinds of people. Together. It ain't the difference between. It's the difference among—the difference within, see?"

"You know, there are some people who think that sadomasochism doesn't have a place in healthy gay relations. It's a symptom that something is wrong."

Eric chuckled. "There're people who think men changin' into women—and women changin' into men—is wrong, too. But we got 'em here in the Settlement. And we should have had a lot more in the Dump—or I should've known the ones who was there better than I did. Hey, how old are you?"

Ann looked up, blinking. "Pardon me—?"

"How old are you?"

"Twenty-four," she said, "last week."

He started to say, *You too?* But that was the detritus of some dream. "And how long you been researchin'…sexuality and the gay community?"

"About three months now."

Eric laughed right out. "Oh, well…then you probably just don't…" He halted. "Naw, I ain't gonna say that. 'Cause you'd think I was one of them old guys who believe a young person can't know nothin'. And that ain't true. You young folks know as much as us old people do. But, see, all of us at different times know different things. That's all. It ain't a matter of more or less. Just different." He took his glass from the desk and sipped at his ice soda water. "Naw, Bull and Whiteboy was really nice neighbors to have— they was right across the road from our cabin. Sometimes they'd come over and have coffee. Sometimes we'd go over there and…" He stopped— for two reasons. First, because he'd been born in another century, he *wasn't* sure how far he should go in detailing what she claimed to be interested in. Second, was the surprise on her face.

She said, "You…*lived* in the Dump?"

Eric looked back with equal surprise. "That's right…"

"I didn't realize that," she said. "We've been talking to dozens of people, it seems, who *knew* people who lived in the Dump or *worked* with them or *heard* about them from parents and aunts and friends. But you're the first person—or persons, I suppose—we've talked to, or I've talked to, who actually lived there. Mr. Haskell somehow led me to believe that you first lived together upstairs in the old Opera House, when it was a pornographic movie theater."

"We did," Eric said. "Pretty much all during the thirties—till we come out here to the Settlement. But before that, we lived in the Dump, all three of us—Shit and Shit's daddy and me. I met Jay MacAmon the first day I come here. And Shit and Dynamite, too. Dynamite was what every one called Wendell Haskell, Shit's dad—though a lot of people thought he was his uncle. I guess I met Bull and Whiteboy pretty much by the end of the first week or so—though I couldn't say I was friendly with 'em till a little later. But Black Bull used to baby-sit for Shit when he was a baby."

"Baby-sit—!" Apparently the idea astonished Ann.

And Eric found himself imagining what might have been in those pictures.

"Oh…well," she reiterated. "During the time I was talking to him, Mr. Haskell didn't make that clear."

Eric put his glass down. "Truth is, Shit ain't never been too good with his dates. He'll tell you 'bout somethin' he'll say happened fifteen years back, and you go look it up and find out it was forty years ago—not that I'm too much better. But at least I know I got the tendency. Also, see, when we all lived in the Dump, that was before his daddy died—and he don't like to talk too much about that time."

"Oh, well I can understand that. Did Mr. Haskell have a particularly… difficult relationship with his father? Dr. Zucker, the supervisor of our dissertation group, told me—" and Eric had the impression that mentioning a supervisor was a great admission for her—"that many gay men—he said 'most'—have a particularly difficult relationship with their fathers."

Eric shrugged. "I had a pretty good one with mine. I don't know about most. But they were very close, Shit and Dynamite—and loved each other very much. Shit and Dynamite…Dynamite was Shit's father, like I said—were…well, best friends. That's how they described it. All three of us were…" Eric let the sentence hang, leaving her to decide wither it had ended or continued. "But when he died, it was real hard on Shit. That's why he don't like to talk about it, I guess."

"How old were you, then?"

"Thirty-seven, thirty-eight when Dynamite had his stroke. Which would make Shit thirty-nine or forty. And really, I started livin' in the Dump when I was seventeen—maybe eighteen. So that's a fair amount of time to get to know a place—not that you ever gonna know the whole thing. But enough of it."

"We had such an impossible time trying to find people who lived there." Clearly, Ann was again surprised. "There are all these mentions of it, through all this rather ephemeral gay literature from the nineteen eighties on. But when they tore it down, the people who lived there pretty much scattered to the four winds. Dr. Zucker found one man, a hundred and three, in an old-age home in Ohio who'd lived there—Ronald Jones. He used to be a cook in a couple of restaurants in this area—"

"Ron Jones?" Eric said. "Chef Ron? Yeah, we knew him. He didn't live far from us either."

"Well, he's the first person who made Dr. Zucker decide that all this would be worth researching. He died a few years back. He had a younger partner, Joe, who'd lived with him in this area, too. But Joe had some serious memory problems."

"Ron made it to a hundred and three?" Eric frowned again. "Hey, that's gettin' up there."

"So you actually lived there—and had coffee with Black Bull."

"And that ain't all I had from 'im. When he went, I was really kinda sorry. We both was." Eric laughed. "You know, Chef Ron baked me my seventeen-year-old birthday cake. At a restaurant. Chocolate…I don't like chocolate very much. Upsets my stomach—did back then, too. But he didn't know that—he was a real neighborly fella." He took his glass for another sip, then set it down again. "Real nice. Good cook too—except for birthday cakes." He chuckled. He looked because she was writing again, and in the space on the page where she was not, three paragraphs appeared and vanished in quick succession, two of them red and one of them blue.

"Hey, were you here five, maybe ten years back—it could've been longer—when that art historian was giving his talk at the Hemmings Interdenominational on Mrs. Kyle's sculpture? That's Doris Pitkin Kyle, Robert Kyle's grandmamma. I'm talkin' about the one they got out on the commons now?"

Again, she looked up. "I didn't visit Gilead for the first time till about eight, nine months ago. Ten years—or longer—back, I was fourteen—or younger. Why do you ask?"

"Well, he probably had the answers—or some of 'em—to Ed Miller's Satanic magic rumors, if you ask me. Maybe they got a copy of his talk somewhere in the library. I'd look it up, if I was you. It might be interestin'." He moved back in the chair. "You know, Shit's daddy, Dynamite Haskell—Wendell Haskell—was Robert Kyle's lover when they were kids. I mean, eight, nine, then, on through twelve and thirteen—up to fourteen, fifteen, sixteen. Then Kyle took up with Jay MacAmon—Jay and Kyle would fool around in the summer, and Jay and Dynamite would fool around in the winter, when Kyle was off at school in Europe..." He stropped, because Ann was frowning.

She said, "What do you mean—nine or ten?"

"Yeah, that was the same age I was when I used to fool around with my cousin in Texas—"

"Mr. Jeffers," she said. "I'm afraid Mr. Haskell was misinforming you. Or, at any rate, you are misremembering. Children don't have sexual relations at that age. It's a biological impossibility. Boys don't reach adolescence until thirteen or fourteen at the very least."

Eric frowned now. "Oh...?" He wondered if Harry—Hareem—were still alive.

*

After their session, Ann Lee wandered out to speak with them both and asked how they'd feel about meeting with her again.

(As they were leaving, Eric asked, "Shit, what'd you tell her about them Satanic rites she was all interested in?"

(Shit frowned. "She didn't ask me about no Satanic rites."

("Well, what did she wanna know about?"

("Sex. Lord, that woman's got a *filthy* mind!" Shit grinned. "How many and in what positions and with who and where did John put it when Jim couldn't see it—it was fun.")

Over the next month, Ann Lee recorded nine more hours of Shit, fifteen more hours of Eric, and three hours of both of them together— those didn't go too well, "'Cause we'd end up arguin' too much," Eric explained to Ed, down by the dock, laughing—though as soon as they got alone, they'd start chuckling about it and hugging each other in bed a lot, even more than usual. It wasn't exactly "fight and fuck" because fucking per se was pretty much in the past, but it was not far from it.

*

At relatively infrequent intervals, Eric would take the maglev tram and ride it around the island. Sometimes he would get off a stop early and wander up to the Old Kyle Place/New Library—he was never quite sure why.

The very first time he went, he tried to get up into the tower room but a door had been installed there, and it was locked. He managed to sit down in the downstairs office with the Library Supervisor, Arnolda Hamilton, who explained they didn't let anyone upstairs these days. No renovation had been done above the second floor. He tried to describe the orrery—he still didn't have the word. She did, however, and said she had never seen anything like that upstairs—that was the day she broke down and, in her shiny black pants and her bleached silver hair, took him up there. The shelves were empty. Nothing was on the walls. One window— broken apparently—was boarded over. It was very dusty. The floor was uncarpeted and, she told him, sections of it were actually unsafe, though, if they stayed near the stair head they should be all right. So far no one had fallen through. And it smelled funny.

Eric said thank you, smiled, they went down again, and he left—visiting the octagonal room had been like visiting a space in an entirely different building.

Once, when he returned and was walking around the ground floor, and the women who sat behind the desks would look up at him and smile and nod (Ms. Hamilton—that day in red slacks—even came through, smiled, and said hello), he saw Ann Lee coming down the central steps, from the upstairs. They said hello; she'd been here to finish up some of her research, actually.

"Well, here it is." He looked around the renovated rooms. "A thousand years later…"

"What was that?"

"Nothin'." Eric laughed. "Wasn't nothin'."

"How is Mr. Haskell?"

"He's doin' fine," Eric said. "He's just fine there." In truth, though, Shit was slowing down." And how's everything comin' with you…?"

They wandered together across the ground-floor lounge. "You know, there's a lot of history," he told her "in a place like this. But you know that. Still, the trouble is, you can't see it a lot of times. 'Cause everything gets cleaned up and rebuilt and polished over, and there it all goes." He stopped, and looked toward one of the walls, near the floor. "Over there, for example—that wall?" He wondered, did he *have* the right wall—or was he a room away? "When this was the big, downstairs livin' room, right at the door, there used to be mark—a big black dent in the molding down there, from where a sad old feller kicked a cat to death and the young feller what owned that cat and loved it lost his faith in God and, I guess, began to get his faith in humanity. You know who that was, don't you?"

"No," Ann said. "Who?"

"Jay MacAmon."

"Oh…!" Ann said, brightly. "Really? You know, he's a very important figure in our study."

"I know he is," Eric said. "You already told me that. But, see, when they made this place all modern and turned it into a library, they took that old wall out and put a new one in and tore out the molding with the dent, and put in new floorboards. So there's no way to see it no more; nobody can ask now, 'Hey, what's that mean? What must have happened, I mean, right there?'"

Ann was looking around at the ceiling, not at the floor.

"And I guess if you knew about them things, it's a little hard to see 'em go."

"With all the stories and documents and papers about MacAmon, there's almost nothing official about Jalisco, except that they lived here with Mr. Kyle."

"And before that, so did Mr. Haskell." Eric shrugged. "Havin' an alternate way of talkin' can be a pretty good thing—teaches you a lot." Eric thought: I'm fallin' in love with my own voice, tryin' to sound like a wise old man. Lemme shut up, or I'm gonna really start soundin' like an old fool.

Ann said, "I'm not even sure where Carlos Jalisco was from."

For a moment he wasn't sure who she was talking about. "Um… Mexico, I guess. But you probably mean what little town he come from."

"Have you any idea what happened to him—I mean, why exactly he couldn't speak?" Ann asked. "Was it some childhood disease?"

"The story I got from both of 'em was that some pretty nasty people had done some pretty awful stuff to him, back when he was a kid, south of the border—but he got away from 'em and run north."

They wandered slowly through the web of offices that, really, had obliterated and absorbed the mansion.

Ann said, "I wonder what they didn't want him to tell."

"Now, that's funny," Eric said. "I never thought of that."

"Shit and me was talkin' about it. Shit remembered more than I did, but then, he's lived here longer. He said there was a group of non-hearing gay men and women who used to get together in Hemmings—I told you Pinewood, but he said it was Hemmings—for about three years—on the last Thursday of the month. They met and talked with each other in ALS, and kept minutes and attendance records. They had meals together and went to movies with each other. Mex was part of that group for almost four years—"

"They have the minutes upstairs. I was reading them over last week. Most of the time they met at the house of a man named Bob Bancock, who kept the minutes. He left them to the Hemmings Library. Jay used to bring Mex over from Gilead Island, then drive him to Hemmings, and stay for the meetings. He'd practice his own ASL with Mex and the others. Bancock was very impressed with him—he made a couple paragraph long notes about how committed Jay seemed to be about him—Mex. Bancock didn't have a partner himself, and I think—oh, just from some of the things I read—that he would have liked a similar relationship. Bancock moved to Ohio in the middle of oh-three, and—like I told you—gave the minutes to the Hemmings Library, who were going to throw them out a few years ago, but they ended up here. I mean, that *is* a lot, learning a new language, bringing your friend to meetings, month after month. I understand what MacAmon did for Jalisco. I'm just wondering what Mex did for him."

...drank his piss, ate his shit, sucked his toes, fucked with any of his friends and puppies that Jay wanted him to, taught 'em to make chili, truck stop-, orgy-, and everyday-manners. Even though her study was about sexuality, maybe it would be a little crude to go into all of that, right here, right now. "I'm pretty sure they did a lot for each other," Eric said. "You can count on that. But I never knew nothin' about the deaf-folks club—that's all from Shit. Oh-three was before my time in Diamond Harbor. I didn't come till oh-seven."

*

Two weeks later, just before they came for their penultimate session together, outside Ann's door, Shit asked Eric, "We gonna have us a good argument, where we yell and cuss each other down to the devil, so we can go home and lie around and hug a lot?"

Eric chuckled. "Probably."

"Then let's make it a good one." And grinning, Shit rapped on Ann's front door under the hanging wisteria. But Ann—who was not there to see that part—seriously wondered whether these heated exchanges weren't damaging their relationship.

* * *

[110] WET SAND SWIRLED his wrists, washed under his knee, over his heels. He crawled through black sandy water slashed with light—the twentieth time, the thirtieth? Stone brushed his shoulders. He moved after the flickers before him, trying to breathe. Was Shit still ahead of him...?

Was he in some basement?

A light glimmered before Eric, and—the church cellar in Hemmings; somehow they'd gotten caught down there?—he reeled upright to stagger forward—

Sand gave under Eric's work shoes. Piled left and right, plastic sacks rose fifteen-feet here, forty-feet there. On the topmost tier of benches, half a dozen moppets, most naked, girls and boys, age nine or ten, sat with Ann. Their faces were serious, interested; many were black or Asian. Many had their hair brushed up in a small pyramid on top of their heads.

In front of the benches was a tall post. Someone had nanobolted a board to it bearing the motto:

THE GIFT MUST MOVE...

...which meant they must be in the Gilead Elementary School. Had they somehow gotten up to the first floor?

And why was the floor covered with sand...?

It didn't look like the school. It looked like a canyon among the garbage sacks making up the Bottom.

Still, the youngsters carried themselves like students.

Eric dragged in a breath: it was cool and easy to breathe—thank all the generous universe.

Shit came around the corner, wearing only a vest and work shoes—but otherwise naked. He herded some dozen more children ahead.

"Everything okay?" Eric asked. "You guys talk to Dynamite?"

Shit grinned—he wasn't wearing his upper plate. "You know, he loves them kids. They asked him all sorts of questions. They were all over him—he was great!"

From the upper benches, in her silver filigree pants, Ann Lee smiled down. Some of the students were climbing up to sit near her.

Eric felt uncomfortable. He wished he had gone with them to talk with the senior garbage man—who did love kids, but (especially if they were "all over him") so easily could have caressed one or the other in an inappropriate manner. For most of them, it wouldn't have meant anything. Still, kids had parents; and with parents, you never knew—

Shit looked about twenty-five—which meant Eric was twenty-two or twenty-three. He smiled around at them.

Above the walls, the sky glimmered opal, its pearl misted with violets, chartreuses, cerises.

Ann said, "Do you want to ask Mr. Haskell and Mr. Jeffers some of the questions you prepared? You've had a chance, now, to talk to Mr. Dynamite—Mr. Haskell's father. But he has to get back to work."

Three hands shot up—from two girls on the lower benches and one boy up near Ann. (For a moment Eric felt relief; that meant they'd be joining him soon—only that didn't feel entirely right...)

An Asian girl blurted, "That man said he fucked a pig." The children snickered, glanced at one another—and a boy put his hand down, as if that was what he'd wanted, daringly, to mention.

"Well," Ann said. "Things were different when Mr. Haskell was a little boy."

Shit pointed to a sun-darkened girl sitting just below Ann, who had her hand up. (Eric thought, Shit's mama looked like that, I bet, when she was that age...) "Yeah." Shit grinned. "Yeah, you. What you wanna know?"

"Ms. Lee says you've been together a long time, probably as long as anybody in this country. How long you lived with each other?"

"About seventy, seventy-one years." Eric looked at Shit and thought, but he's too young. We both are—unless they'd had some sort of regeneration treatment, like you were always reading about in Northern medical blogs. Eric frowned. Now wouldn't it be just like him to forget they'd done something like that?

"But you never got married...?" one of the boys asked.

"That's right," Shit said. "We didn't want to."

A girl frowned at them. "You didn't know if you were going to stay together...?"

"Both my moms are married," another girl said. "Only not to each other."

"Naw." Eric smiled. "That wasn't it."

"Hell," Shit said, "I knew I wanted him the rest of my life—" he pointed a blunt thumb at Eric—"soon as I saw the fucker—unless he turned out to be some psychotic murderer or crazy mean bastard to boot—and, hell, even if he was, I was *still* ready to give him a try. Only he turned out to be really nice. And wanted to hug and kiss on me and suck my dick and everything and we'd fuck each other any time we wanted. Then, about an hour later, when I learned he liked to read and everything, I thought maybe he wasn't gonna like me that much, after all. But it turned out, 'cause *he* could do it, he didn't really care if *I* could or not."

"It took me a little longer," Eric said. "About a week of workin' together with him and his daddy. I mean, yeah, as soon as I saw him, I thought it would be nice to have somebody like him around forever, but you never think it's gonna work out that way. At least I didn't."

One of the children on the bottom tier asked. "Why not?"

Shit looked puzzled. "Well, I guess because my daddy never married nobody, it didn't occur to me that maybe we should be doin' that kind of thing." He shrugged. "So I never thought of it."

"Besides, it's more fun." Eric chuckled. "And more interestin'—to figure out all that stuff for yourself, between you, as you go along. See, back when we got together, a lot of gay men and women didn't get married. In a lot of places, it was still illegal, like here in Georgia." A bemused whispering rose, settled among the children, and may have been the sea.

One dark skinned boy (who Eric figured must have looked a lot like young Robert Kyle, III—or a young Hugh. Could he be a relative?), said, "What you mean, figure it out for yourself?"

While he reached up to scratch his ear, Eric looked down.

Shit had moved over next to him and, in the course of it, lost his shoes. He was standing with one wide foot across Eric's scuffed orange boot toe.

"Well—" Eric looked back up and put his hand on Shit's warm shoulder—"state supported marriage comes with a whole lot of assumptions about how it's gonna be, a history of who has to obey who, when you're justified in callin' it quits, all sorts of things like that. Now, you could agree with each other to change some of those things or do 'em differently, but for thousands and thousands of years gay men and women didn't have even that—except for a few Christian monasteries here and there, where the monks were allowed to marry each other. But nobody likes to think about those. For us, decidin' to be with someone else wasn't a matter of acceptin' a ready-made set of assumptions. You had to work 'em all out from the bottom up, every time—whether you was gonna be monogamous or open; and if you was gonna be open, how was you gonna do it so that it didn't bother the other person and even helped the relationship along. Workin' all that stuff out for yourselves was half the reason you went into a relationship with somebody else. We had some friends once—back when we lived in the Dump—that was faithful for ten months out the year, but

for two months they'd go on vacation and do all their tom-cattin' around."
He realized he was making that up; but, hell, it was plausible. "Then they'd
be faithful again. But that's how they liked to do it. Then there were guys
like us that just had to make real sure that the other person was feelin' good
about things, when they did it and knew they were number one and didn't
mind. See, that's what people who get married don't have. Or don't have
in the same way."

"Damn," Shit said. "Now I never thought about that—or thought
about it *like* that. But that's probably 'cause my daddy helped us out with
so much of it, 'specially at the beginnin' of it all."

Again, Eric felt uncomfortable. Doing the stuff he'd done with
Dynamite—and Shit—had never been hard. But the prospect of having
to explain it always made him feel odd—though, when it came, Shit could
launch right into it and was no more bothered talking about it than he
was about any of their other, odder sexual practices. (Which was why Eric
left those things to Shit to talk about or not talk about more and more.
But something in the art settlement seemed to make all that more and
more normal, whatever "normal" had once meant—even if it were only
the passage or pressure of time itself. What if he'd been raised like Shit to
believe there just wasn't no normal?) If people misunderstood, so what?
But that was another thing, after all this time, Eric still envied his partner.

"Well," Ann said, from the upper benches, "I think we should all give
Mr. Jeffers and Mr. Haskell a hand…"

Politely the children applauded.

Summer lightening suddenly made Eric squint—and when it dimmed,
half the sunlight had gone with it. Wind swirled up the sand. Crying out,
the children began to climb down the benches.

"No, no…!" Ann Lee called out. "Don't run—"

Again, lightning sheeted the sky. And again. After each, it got even
darker—

Cold droplets hit Eric's face, and he rolled his head back, blinking.
Outside the room was thunder…

Beside him in the bed, someone naked was kneeling before the
window…Shit—?

Carrying Shit's familiar naked reflection before him and facing inward,
the pane slid down between the window jambs. "There—" Shit turned on
his knees in the bed, grumbling—"Jesus, I'm all fuckin' splattered, now."

"Hey, lemme get on top of the covers and hug you and get you warm."
Shit moved over the bed. "I should get a towel and—"

"Naw." Eric grabbed Shit's shoulder. The familiar flesh—and wet—
moved more loosely on the bone beneath than the flesh of Shit in the

dream. "Naw—you come here and lemme get you warm. What—it started rainin'?"

"Naw—I just nipped outside and went for swim and didn't bother to dry myself off. *Course* it's rainin'! What the fuck you *think* it's doin'?" Behind him, the window flared again and droplets sounded, splattering the glass like small stones.

Eric put his arms around Shit's hips and rubbed his face against Shit's belly and groin.

Shit went still and put his hand down on Eric's back. "Hey, your face *is* warm. That must mean I'm cold as a corpse." Shit flopped over, hunkering into the folds and dells of the blanket, while Eric moved himself further up. Eric pushed his face into Shit's neck, as Shit lifted his bearded chin. "Come on, roll on top of me."

"I'm afraid I'm gonna crush you."

"You been afraid you're gonna crush me for fifty years, and you ain't never done it yet."

"It's more like twenty-five or thirty. It's just since your arthritis—"

"Hey, you know—that's right. You used to *live* on top me, and I loved it. Come on, now. Get up on me again. I been takin' my pills. I like it. You practically lived on top of me for the first twenty years. I miss it, you know?"

"Okay." Eric rolled. "But if I hurt you, you squeak or somethin'—"

Shit grunted. "Oh, yeah—that feels good, now."

"You sure?"

"Yeah I'm sure."

Eric took in a deep breath. "Hey, Shit…?"

"What?"

"Did we go visit the school yesterday?"

It felt like Shit was half-buried in the mattress. Eric moved his head over on a pillow. "I'm doin' that so you can breathe."

"I don't wanna breathe. I wanna die under here, where I belong. The school? Yesterday? Naw—that was three days ago."

"Oh."

"We went with Ann Lee right after lunch in that social history class and the kids asked us all them questions about how long we been together and what it was like around here a hun'rd years ago and all that stuff. Smart little fuckers, too—some of 'em. And you got to talkin' about Mex and sign language and tryin' to teach them some of the letters, and I didn't think you was ever gonna shut up. I mean, that's just a kind of reading. That still makes me uncomfortable. I don't mind your doin' it. But I think sometimes you talk about it just to rile me up."

"Ah, no, Shit. No, I don't."

"Yeah, well that's what you always say."

"Hey, it's comin' back to me. In pieces. Yeah, when we went to the school. On Tuesday. I was dreamin' about that—but in the dream we were in a schoolroom. They were in a circle and we sat on the desk in the front. In the dream, they were all wearin' their hair like they did when we was young. In little pointy stacks on the top—you remember?"

"Most of the ones in the class had their heads shaved," Shit said.

"Yeah," Eric said. "Hey, did they ask us any questions about your daddy?"

"Huh?" Shit chuckled. "Naw. You know as well as I do, as far as them kids is concerned, we're too old to have no daddies—or mamas either. We just walked up out of the sea, out of the stones, the trees—all old and wrinkled like we are, like we been the same and ain't changed forever and ever."

"Yeah," Eric said. "I guess so." He rolled to the side.

"Hey, don't get off me, yet!"

"Don't worry. We can still hold each other. Come on here and get your arm around my shoulder."

That's funny, Eric thought. Dynamite gave me so much pleasure, security, learned me so much—and I'm still nervous about people finding out that Shit's father was once my fuck buddy and his fuck buddy both. Maybe that's something I'm still supposed to be workin' on. Or is that something gay guys just have to learn how to live with—I mean, always havin' someone important in your life who's a little further out than most people would be comfortable with—for whatever reason. Maybe that's how we grow—if we ever do.

Soon as he let Shit get a real breath, Eric could tell…from the change in his breathing rhythm, Shit was already back asleep.

Once more, outside the cabin window, summer lightning sizzled on the sky. The storm's rumble rose and settled over Gilead.

* * *

[111] "YOU COULD GET me a little money, if you wanted," which was about all Shit would say on finances these days, once every couple or three weeks.

"Sure," Eric said. "Hold on a second." They walked slowly along the market's edge for two, three, four steps. "Okay," Eric said. "There you go. Your chip's all filled up now. I got you your regular amount."

"Okay," Shit said. "Thank you."

Eric thought: How long ago was it that I swore before I died I was gonna teach him to do that? But finally, it got so easy—since all you had to do was think through what you wanted—I gave up and just been doin' it for 'im...how long now? And the standard way to describe it was: "Try to think at the front and top of your head, where in your mind you read at"—but that *wasn't* goin' over with Shit. Ten years? Twenty? It *doesn't* feel more than three, four months. But I know it's closer to a couple of decades.

I used to worry: what was gonna happen if I died first—and Shit was left high and dry? But now it's easier to do it for him—like it's always been.

How fast *are* we moving through this stuff called time, anyway...?

* * *

[112] EVENTUALLY, THOUGH, THERE'D been those six awful weeks, when Shit started throwing up every other day, then twice a day, then five and six times a day—and the stuff comin' out didn't look like puke no more—and Eric'd clean it up, while, drained, Shit would sit or lie down.

Toward the beginning of that, there'd been the morning, when it was still dark, that he woke to see Shit's bony back and buttocks swaying in the doorway (they still slept naked), then he was gone!

There was an immense farting, and Eric realized Shit had fallen. As he pushed from the bed himself, the smell came to him. "Dear God...What happened? You slipped?" Awkwardly, he rushed into the doorway after him, and his heel slid on something so that he almost lost his own balance. "You okay?" He hadn't realized what he'd slipped in, yet.

"No—I *ain't* okay!" Shit said, on the floor, face to the side. "I think I broke my damn hip! I got dizzy—and there was all this buzzin'. I can still hear it, some..."

He'd also lost control of his bowels.

"Here, lemme get you cleaned off...! What are you doin'? Playin' in it?"

"I'm tryin' to wipe it off!"

"Well, lemme get some rags and some paper towels—come on! Be still, will you? Keep your hands out of it."

"*You* be fuckin' still in a puddle of goddam shit!"

They managed to clean him up, get him into the bathroom, and gave him a good sponge down. The hip was not broken, just badly sprained.

It happened again that evening.

And three times the next day. You almost didn't notice the throwing up, since most of the time Shit could get that in a pail they set out for him, with some Pine-Sol in the bottom.

Then Ed and Holly both came by and said the same thing. This was serious. They said it when they came back two weeks later. And two weeks after that—

Eric was sleeping on his forearms, his head on the kitchen table.

Shit was on the kitchen floor and filthy. Had anyone compared, he probably weighed ten pounds less than Barbara had at the time of her death. "No, don't wake 'im up! Don't do it!" Shit protested from the floor near the table leg. His voice was hoarse, almost inaudible. "He ain't slept at all in four, five days! I can stay down here for another couple of hours, till he gets some sleep. I'm okay—I don't hardly feel nothin' in my legs no more." One of three puke pails to make it more convenient for Shit to get to had somehow overturned. "Hey, I'm okay! Please! Please! Leave 'im *alone*…" He was crying. "Really…come on. Leave 'im alone! *Please* let 'im get some rest. . . He been up takin' care of me for the whole week without no sleepin'…"

"Mr. Haskell, you got to get to the hospital!" Lucille (who had come this time) said. "Ed…?"

The morning Eric went along with Ed to take Shit to Runcible Memorial for what would pretty certainly be his last weeks or months or days (on the ferry, Shit didn't leave the car; so Eric only got out for two minutes—and didn't even go to the rail but looked at some gulls, then climbed back in to sit with dozing Morgan), there'd been a day's endlessly lost arguments with aides and social workers, which finally he'd stopped trying to win, about how it wasn't sensible for Eric to keep him at home.

When Ed brought him back to the cabin, Eric had a strangely lucid evening. He sat a long time at the kitchen table, listening for…the sound of Shit's puking; the sound of his hoarse breath. Finally, he heated up the leftover half-pot of coffee that, miraculously, despite illness, from a chair sitting by the counter, Shit had made that morning. Is this, he wondered, going to be the last of Shit's coffee I drink? Even heated up, his is better than mine. Or am I just used to it? Hell, it's half milk anyway. Maybe that's why neither one of us ever turned—what do they call it?—lactose intolerant? Perhaps it was the shock of being without him. Or had it just been that morning's particularly good crap? At the table, Eric thought: Suppose someone asked Shit what he'd done with his life. Would he say something like…I put apples and cookies in a pile on the table over at the market and dished out rice and chili so hungry folks could eat. I hauled garbage so people around the mainland could live decent, and I scrubbed toilets and pushed brooms so they could have a nice place to suck a dick or get their own sucked. I fixed light switches and snaked out plugged drains. And 'cause I couldn't do it all, I fucked Eric as much as I could to make him feel good enough to do what still needed doin' and pissed on him and laughed while I was doin' it—and fucked a whole lot of others besides—so people would be happier. Pissed on some of them, too.

So I would be happier.

It's so easy to remember this now—but tomorrow mornin' I ain't gonna recall a thing of it; maybe I won't even remember Shit's in the hospital.

Unless I write myself a damned note.

He looked around for paper.

Eric sat frowning over his mug. Lifting it, he took a sip, waiting for warmth to unroll down his neck and upper chest like a heated bib under his T-shit. But it was milky and cool. What Eric didn't know as he sat, imagining Shit's answer, was that, on the mainland in Runcible, some forty minutes after the hospital dinner service, which Shit had pretty much said he didn't feel like strugglin' with and left most of it in the plastic plates, a pastor from the Father Goldridge Hanover Memorial New Order of Holy Luminescence looked into the room and asked Shit if he minded his coming in and talking with him for a few minutes. The pastor was a man in his middle-thirties, with a very narrow forehead and sharp cheekbones. He wore a gray jacket and a gray shirt and held an electronic notepad in his hand. Nearing the bed, he pulled up a chair, sat, and said, "Now, you're Morgan..." He glanced down. "Haskell. That's your name?"

Shit said, "Yeah." And waited.

"My name is Brother Lucas." He smiled, but he did not reach out to shake hands. "I've been assigned to come around and speak with the older patients. I was just wondering if perhaps you could tell me some of the things you've done in your lifetime, what you remember as most interesting—maybe even most important."

This is what Shit said: "Now what kinda question is that? I ain't nobody special. Why you askin' me? See, you wanna be askin' that to somebody like Eric. He's real smart and can read and write—he reads all that philosophy stuff, and busts his ass helpin' people and tryin' to understand stuff and make it all make sense. He's a special person. They got his picture up in the Settlement Library of a big important meetin' he was at. Me, see, I ain't no different from how my daddy was. Who you really wanna be talkin' to is Eric."

"Um..." Brother Lukas asked, "...who's Eric?"

"Don't you got it down on your clipboard?" The notepad looked like a small sized clipboard. "Don't it say 'domestic partner'?"

"Oh..." Brother Lukas's eyes brightened. "You two were...married?"

Right then a nurse in blue scrubs brought in a ceramic vase that held an odd succulent. "Mr. Haskell, someone sent this. See? You got a nice present." Taking it to the windowsill and setting it on the ledge, he turned over the card. "It's from someone named—Anne. . .? She says 'Get well soon.' It's pretty." But he frowned. "The card even plays some music when you open it, and got a picture of some stars…"

Brother Lukas said, "We'll be finished in a minute—"

"No, I'm done." The nurse held up both his hands. "I'm done. Good evening to you both," and, smiling, backed halfway across the room, turned, and left.

Shit was already saying, though, "Naw—we di'n't never bother to get married."

"Was that because…your partnership did not involve…intimacy?" In the counseling workshop he'd been at last Sunday afternoon, Brother Lukas had been told about the various advantages of delicacy versus straightforwardness: frankly he'd left confused. "That is, sexual intimacy?"

Shit said, "You mean did we fuck? Goddamn, I don't even remember sometimes. But we did just about everything nasty two fellas could do— with each other and everyone else. And I mean real nasty, too." Shit laughed. "Wait a minute! What the hell am I talkin' about? Course we fucked! We fucked like damned rabbits! Each other and everything else what come by. I did most of the fuckin', but when that boy turned around and stuck his dick up my goddam ass I thought the sky had opened up and the Congress and the President of the United States had just declared Shit Haskell was the king of everything. I loved to piss in that boy's mouth— and he loved me to do it. But I got that from my daddy—Dynamite. Him, me, and Eric, we had a *lot* of fun! See, my mama was a whore—a nigger whore—and that's a real good inheritance to have if you gonna live like we did, so she probably helped a lot. And Dynamite said she was a good one—a fine colored lady. I just wished I knowed her. Hey, every night he or me wasn't fuckin' someone else, Eric and me was together. Only we did so much else…rubbin', lickin', cuddlin', suckin' out each other's assholes, eatin' each other's snot, and that boy drunk so much o' my goddam piss I'm surprised he ain't done dissolved—but I done told you that…"

Sitting up in his chair and flattening his hand over his pad, Brother Lucas said, "Mr. Haskell—?"

"I'd come home with some nigger's shit all over my dick, and he'd eat that stuff right off. And I sure ate enough shit offa his. That's how I got a taste for it, all by itself—that's what made me a real pervert—thank the Lord. God or Nature, Eric'd say. Same thing. Bein' a pervert was the only way I ever learned anything worth knowin'. I hope you do that with your partner." Shit narrowed his eyes. "You ate your partner's shit? Male or female, I don't think it matters—I used to. But not no more, since I been livin' out on Gilead."

"Huh? Uh...no, I—" Brother Lucas's eyes had gotten very wide.

"Only, see...I'm tired now. I'm real tired. If I could just hold onto him for a little, I wouldn't have to talk about it. And talkin' about that shit's just gonna get me worked up, anyway, and I ain't gonna be able to do nothin' about it." Reaching down under the covers, it was clear through the cloth, Shit had grasped his genitals. Under the sheet, clearly he was shaking them. "I still wanna—but I ain't gonna be able to. That's 'cause I'm so tired. Maybe you could excuse me...?"

"Yes!" Brother Lucas pushed back his chair, then stood. He was not exactly appalled, but he was not comfortable, either. "Yes. Of course, I—"

"Or, if it don't bother you, I'll just do it right here. Or I'll pull the sheet down so you can watch, if you want—like the guys at the Opera all used to, lookin' out the corner of their eye and pretendin' they wasn't, while me and my daddy'd sit there there and do it, till one of them got up the nerve to—"

"—understand. No. Please, no *don't*—"

"All right, then. Hey, we I had a *lot* of fun—Eric and me, we had a lot of fun together. But I'm gonna go to sleep. The only thing about fun is you always wanna little more of it..." He chuckled—but Brother Lukas had left the room. Well, that was one way to get some privacy. Shit moved his head around on the pillow. In a place like this, that smelled so sterile, Shit thought, he'd *never* get to sleep...and slept.

* * *

[113] AT FIRST ERIC remembered nothing about Shit's death.

When Ed and Lucille brought him back to the Holota cabin, he sat down on the kitchen chair and said, "Christ...I am so tired..." He put his forearm on the wooden table, on fliers, pension slips—some that still said Dump Chamber of Commerce, before they'd switched over to the Robert Kyle Foundation—advertisements (some with their pictures still changing, some with images frozen or faded, years—even decades—ago), bills...

"You're due to be tired," Ed said. "This has been a hard day, sir."

Standing inside the door, in her jeans and her plaid flannel, the woman...yes, it was the young boat woman, Lucille—had folded her arms. The light and his dimming sight made her a shadow on the screening. "Mr.

Jeffers, you could go in and lie down—I mean, if you'd like."

Ed had gone across the kitchen to look in the refrigerator. Beside the maroon enamel, the refrigerator light lit Ed's black, craggy face. "You remember—Lucille was up on your roof day before yesterday." (The cragginess still surprised him. It was odd looking at a man of seventy-five you could recall at fifteen.) "She hooked all them old solar panels you got up there to your generator wire, so you could have a little extra power, when you heat your dinner."

Eric said, "Aw, thank you, sweetheart. Shit put those up there a couple of years ago. But when we got the new generator, they disconnected them. What you lookin' in there for, Ed?"

"I'm makin' sure you got somethin' to eat." Now he looked back across his shoulder, his face sliding again into silhouette. "What's all this bubbly water in here for?"

"Shit keeps that in there for me. It settles me after meals, when I get gassy." Eric began to frown. "But I ain't even touched any since Shit's been…in the hospital." There was something he should remember.

Ed stood up and closed the refrigerator.

Eric saw Ed and Lucille glance at each other, as people did when sometime he forgot something important—like where he lived, or the name of this place. What did they call it? Yes, the Gilead Settlement. He remembered. "Shit's got to remember that stuff for me, 'cause I can't remember nothin' no more—what I'm supposed to be doin', where I put somethin' soon as I set it down. He always says I can't remember nothin' 'cause I'm busy thinkin' about too many other things—philosophy and stuff." Eric laughed. "But I think it's just because I'm a forgetful ol' fool."

Lucille said, "Those panels go back a lot further than a couple of years, Mr. Jeffers. Yall must've put them things up back in…in the thirties—lucky for you. That's when people got interested in 'em again and thought they were gonna be usin' 'em forever—built 'em to last. They look funny. But they work."

"Oh…" Eric said, bemused. "When's Shit gonna get back? Did he tell you where he was goin', Ed? I don't like it when he just runs off like that. He ain't as steady as he used to be. I don't want him to take no fall. He took a couple of falls a few years back and somebody had to…you brought him home, Ed. Remember how we thought he'd broken his hip? It like' to worried me to death! Hey, you folks want some coffee? Shit'll make you up a good pot of coffee when he gets here. He can't do nothin' else in the kitchen, but he can sure make coffee."

Lucille unfolded her arms and let out a long breath. "Mr. Jeffers? You have to understand, and I know it's hard for you. But Mr. Haskell isn't coming back anymore. You, me, and Ed, here, we all just came from buryin' him—not an hour ago."

"Now, honey—" Eric chuckled—"Mr. Haskell been dead and buried a long time, right in the graveyard over the bluff there."

Ed said, "He thinks you mean Dynamite Haskell, ol' Haskell's daddy." Ed turned toward Eric. "No, sir. That was Morgan they buried out there, right across from Jay MacAmon—" he took his computer from his shirt pocket and glanced at it for the time—"like Lucille said, not an hour back. You remember Jay, don't you? The guy before me who run the boat out here?"

Eric frowned. "That was Shit they was buryin'…? I didn't know… Did you tell me that…? That was…Morgan?…Oh, Jesus!…" It was not a curtain opening before a stage but rather falling in a heap below a window. Mostly old, mostly black, some twelve men and women stood around a grave, as four of them, three in gray jackets, one in shirt sleeves, lowered a pine box into it on canvas ribbons. Parked toward the edge of the marked out section of the graveyard was a mini-backhoe with yellow fenders, under a green throw with false grass on one side.

Only it had slid half off…

Water collected along his lower lids. "Oh, that's dreadful…that's…I didn't realize that was…Oh…That was…Shit? What am I gonna…?" They'd told him, of course—the doctor by the nurse's counter at Runcible Memorial, the people who'd come to help, Holly, Hannibal, Lucille, Ed— that it was going to happen. He'd acted resigned. But part of him had been sure they were…well, not serious. (Hadn't somebody once said something like that to him?) "What am I gonna do, now…?" Was it Ron?

Lucille said, "You sure you don't wanna go in and lie down? We'll come and check on you tomorrow."

"No," Eric said. "No, I'm gonna sit here. For a while…"

Lucille said, "Ed, this is the third time we told him since we left the cemetery. You sure he don't need somebody to stay with him?"

"Well, it can't be you," Ed said. "And it can't be me—not today. Holly's expectin' me." Stopping, he looked up at a corner of the kitchen and did something with his jaw that meant he'd activated the invisible bud deep in his ear. "Yeah, sweetheart. No, I'm on my way now."

For the hundredth time—in how many years?—Eric thought: You can't even see the phones no more, they're so small. Maybe it was time for him and Shit to break down and get some. He'd call him now, for sure.

Ed dropped his chin and said, "He'll get it, now he's in his own place." (Was he still talking to Holly—or Lucille?) "It may take him a couple of more times. Believe me, though, he'll be all right. Come on, now."

They left. Thank God, Eric thought. The young are so tiring. They thought so fast, moved so fast—always chattering with each other, no matter where they were. Watching them exhausted him. When would Shit be back? Probably he'd gone off with that boy—what was his name? Caleb? No...Within Eric, like a circling diorama, on whose stage the past replayed, time turned: and, yes, he could see it. Eric sat up and was frightened, not by the past's content, which—again—he understood, but by its suddenness.

Where in hell had Shit gone?

They should bring him back from the hospital!

Shit had wanted to die at home.

Eric had wanted him to, too—only partially because Shit had wanted it.

He said out loud, "Takin' care of that boy is the only thing I'm here for in this sea beaten world..." Or did he only think something like the last words? Or feel them? But they'd kept telling him it would be too much—that he couldn't do it. As if to care for the dying were something only women did. (Just try *that* one on some of these lesbians out here...!) Finally, though, he hadn't been up to arguing. Sending someone to help him would probably have been too...Oh, they could have done it, if they'd wanted! Still, it made him feel he'd been robbed of something as precious as a child. Who were 'they'? Ed? The doctors? He would have trusted himself with the washing, the cooking, yes. When Shit had first taken to his bed when his colon gave out (it wasn't even cancer...), he'd done that, anyway. But...

Eric stood, walked to the side of the kitchen, and with his foot pushed away the pile of newspapers that half covered the sill for the door to the porch—when's the last time they'd used it? Probably before Caleb was here. But because the road went by it now, it seemed as if going out in the front of the house was only inviting distraction and annoyance. He turned the knob—had they locked the thing? No, it still opened. It had been sitting unlocked more than a decade. That's right, someone had misplaced the key years and years back. Two decades. But now Eric wanted to see something.

He stepped outside.

In cool, low light, he didn't look at the highway's macadam but at the porch rail, then down at the warped boards flooring the thing. Each plank was a colorless gutter, running beside the newels and in front of the steps. Lord, he thought, looking at the unpainted posts. I didn't realize this needed paint so badly. I remember what those things looked like when... when I was down on the porch here, staring at those blue posts over Shit's shoulder. They were blue then. Pale blue. I remember that: how those boards felt under my arm. Oh, lord—we didn't know. We didn't...

When we lay there, holding each other, we didn't know we were going to be old. We didn't know one of us was going to be...dead—!

Hard as those boards were, we lay here, feelin' so good, because we could feel each other. Why didn't we...know?

(*You know this graveyard is really three times as big as what they got marked off with that new fence.* Who was it who said that? It was him, Eric. He said it to tourists he started talking to in the market. He'd said it to two or three people standing around the grave. But people, even someone like Anne Frazier, standing next to him under the sun shot trees, for all her quiet, compassionate smile, did not seem to understand what a great part of the world the dead actually were...)

On the road, in the afternoon sun, which glinted off a silver fender, three young folks, a young man and two women, puttered by. (Traffic like that—why we'd stopped going out here.) He looked at the old boards, at the newels, at the rail devoid of color. And that's what happens to everything, to every part of it. The young ones pass, and they don't see it, it's too washed out, they don't know people made love on it.

Maybe even the Holotas...?

Turning, he stepped back inside.

And then it was with him, clear as glass, like Shit's life, Shit's dying—Shit's death—was over. (Behind him, he closed the door.) Only going on made sense.

Shit's dead, and I am the terrified boy, who everybody knows has been doing something awful, who everybody knows has some god awful habit he'll never break. Remembering his forgetfulness (he'd been tested; not Alzheimer's, it was some nameless, still incurable dementia), he thought: Shit's dead—but he didn't die today. When? I don't remember. Two days ago? Five days? Does this mean I'm doomed to live through this, again and again? Have I gone through this every day before—only I don't remember it? That's torture—but like Dynamite's, like Barbara's, like Mike's, like Jay's, Shit's death's in the past, as, thank the heavens and the earth both, most of my life is. At least there won't be much more of it.

And...(he took a long breath) there's still nothin' to be afraid of.

Thanks to my Dump Pension and—their Health Insurance. No, they don't even call it that, no more. I can't even remember its name. The government's is okay. But it ain't never been that good. Most of the women around here don't got one half so good as Kyle's today...

Really, it's the only thing wrong with the Settlement.

At least I think so.

If I stay lucky...

Suddenly, again, he couldn't remember what Shit looked like—until, after seconds, the quarter lit face of a boy came back, in a dark truck cab, smiling over at him. But who was driving? Dynamite? Mr. Kyle? Had he ever even known anyone in Shit's family? (Hadn't Jay used to say they were related…?) What had Shit looked like last month, last year, last week…?

That's right, they weren't going to bring him back.

Rather—

They had brought him back. They had just been at the Gilead cemetery…burying him.

Then, again, mercifully, painfully, it was there…

Ed had come and told him how Shit had died. In the hospital. (Against the screening, Ed had said, *I'm afraid I'm here with the bad news, sir.* Everybody had known it was coming, everybody except him…) Only days before that, Ed had driven Eric down to Runcible Memorial—no, the old man with the tubes in his nose couldn't have been…*Shit—? Oh, you look so…*He looked wonderful! Just to see him—tubes and all. Was that years ago? The first time Shit had spent a week in the hospital? Or just days? Yes, they'd smiled at each other, and held each other's hands, and Eric had said, *I want to hug him,* and Ed had helped prop him up in the sheets that didn't fit, and Shit had said, *You're hurtin' me but it feels good.* How odd when even the good things hurt.

Shit had said, in his ear, *You know I don't sleep so well if I can't slide my hand under your shoulder, there,* something that, over the last thirty-five, forty-five years, had grown up between them. *That's the thing I miss, but you know that.* (No, he hadn't known.) Oh—and the nights, at the start of it, with one hand under Eric there, Shit had pumped at himself with the other for what seemed hours, unable to climax. (Over coffee in the morning, Shit would laugh, or sometimes grump, and say, *I wonder if I'm turnin' into one of them crazy old men what sits around pullin' on his goddam dick all day and all night and never makin' it.* And Eric would say, *Yeah, that's exactly who you turned into. But that's okay. If that's who you are, I don't mind…*Shit would say, *It's frustratin'—I'm even lookin' forward to comin' soft now. I used to hate that.* Wasn't it amazing that he would say, that he would speak, that he was…) In the hospital—Anne's bi-weekly flowers stood in the window in one of her own hand-thrown vases, next to Holly's little cactus—Shit had said, *You got to go, I know. It sure would be nice if this was a Hostel like your mama was in, where you could stay overnight sometimes.* Then he grunted: Uhn. *What would be nice is if they let a man do this dyin' thing at home in his own goddam bed!*

Eric said, *Oh, don't talk like that, Shit.*

Why not? Shit had said. *Nothin' I say is gonna make no difference. Anyway,* he sighed, *I miss you, you crazy ol' nigger.*

Eric had asked…something.

Shit had said, *Naw, I ain't really scared...I mean a whole lot. I'm just tired. Hey, I love you, you fuckin' crazy ol' piss guzzlin' cocksucker. I just wonder what you gonna do without me. 'Cause you're crazy, you know? You gonna wander around the market, askin' strange men to piss in your mouth? Or sit in the corner, playing with yourself through your pants? Or day dreamin' and pickin' your nose and eatin' your snot? They ain't gonna understand that, Eric. That you just do that 'cause you're thinkin' about important things and ways to help other people. And I ain't gonna be there to get you home where you can do all that. That's the only thing that makes me sad.* White hairs around the inner sides of his wide nostrils had grown long.

Now, don't get like that, Eric said. *Hey, I'm gonna be all right.*

The hand's grip tightened on his. *You always wanted to be black. Well, white man, as far as I'm concerned you can be as black as you want...'Cause I say so, that's why. Like you always tellin' me. Hey, nigger. I love you.*

And Eric said...

What had he said? (What had Shit said...) He couldn't remember again. Well, it couldn't have been important.

They'd smiled. (But Shit's smile looked so hesitant, so uncertain...)

Eric searched around the kitchen of the cabin they'd lived in for... (Though he remembered when they'd moved in, in their forties, he'd already figured they were getting on. Odd, how forty years wasn't that long in the second half of your life...)—till he realized once more he'd forgotten what he was looking for. Sitting at the kitchen table, out loud, he said: "But I'm not black. I'm a...a crazy old white man." How among time's neap and ebb and turnings had that come about? "I live out on Gilead Island, behind Gilead Bluff. And I'm all...all alone...and—Oh, this...this is dreadful!"

After a while, Eric got up, went in the bedroom, and lay on the bed's red and black blanket. Someone who'd been in earlier to help must have spread it up. Hannibal, surely. He rarely did himself, anymore. (Under the edge, on the rug, sat that plastic urinal thing you used three times a night, pressin' it hard up under your dick to get it flowin'—or squirtin', more accurately—so you didn't have to go all the way to the bathroom and that you cleaned with the same flat pills Shit had used to soak his dentures with...if one of you remembered. A lot of weeks there, recently, he'd let it sit and stink.) Lowering himself to lie down, he thought: This bit of stuttering light—they call it life—between black shoals...But what was the point of thinking like that? What I should do is get up and make a pot of coffee. It'll never taste like Shit's, but at least I know how to do it. He lay there, blinking at the ceiling's boards.

Maybe I can...make him come back. I mean, I'm crazy, ain't I?

That's what they all say.

Maybe I can give myself…what do they call it? An…illustration? (No. Blurred from ink migration and all but illegible, that's what covered his arms' sun-browned flesh, his blue, standing veins…) A hallucination. That was it. Maybe I can make him be lyin' here, on the bed, like we were taking a nap. He don't have to talk none—we didn't do all that much talkin', anyway. He could have his hand under…no. He don't have to have his hand under my shoulder, either. He can be asleep…that'd be okay. I could look at him, for a little. If there's a God—or a universe that does the same things—do you think, Eric thought, it could give me…that? Naw, I don't even have to look at him. My eyes could be closed. Maybe Shit could…just be here—I could believe he was here…For a hallucination, that ain't much for a crazy man—

But the dementia at whose edge Eric had lived for the last years did not give. It only took—memory, strength, sureness of movement, conviction of thought…

So little of life is direct experience, Eric pondered: Only an instant of it at a time. That's all. No more. The rest is memory. And expectation…and memory is what so much of time's failings had struck away. And what do I got left to expect? Oh, Lord, he thought. What's there to do, other than wait, to get through this awful day?

So I can start another one, without sex, companionship, or love…

One of them, Hannibal, Lucille, would come tomorrow. And if they didn't…?

Wait?

But that's pretty much all you had to do to get through any of them.

I should read my book. Mama Grace's. He hadn't done that for a long time—since…Shit had gotten sick. And tomorrow I could make something for the market—sandwiches. He hadn't done that for even longer. An aluminum tray of oatmeal cookies. Raisin. Walnut. Take 'em to the market to give away. My book? It's over there on the bureau. What's its name? Aw, no…again I can't remember its name. Come on, now—Eric Jeffers! You been reading that book, over and over, since Mama Grace gave it to you forty-five years ago. He said he'd give it to me if I promised to read it through three times. And I read it a lot more times than that by a long shot. "Concerning God"—that's the name of the first Part. Which is funny, because about the fifth or sixth time I went through it, I realized that man didn't believe in no God at all. He believed in the stars and the sea and the hills, and what grows on them and lives in them and your body and what you could figure out with your mind—and if you wanted to call that God it was all right with him. *Deus sivi Natura*. He remembered that from the

Introduction. "Of the Nature and Origin of the Mind," that was Part II. "Concerning the Origin and Nature of the Emotions" was, yes, Part III, and "Nature and Origins" are backward between them. And I can never remember what he called Part IV. But there was another big book with the same name someone had told him about—a story book about a crippled English feller who becomes a doctor, what he'd never actually read; just read about it a few times. He didn't like storybooks.

Eric thrust a middle finger up one nostril. (He wasn't no doctor. They were never his story. It was never about him. Or Shit. Or even niggers like that Caleb kid, who got off watching them do what they did.) Because he twisted his finger loose and, because he was alone, put it in his mouth. There you were, having lived most of a hundred years, half the time wantin' everyone to know and the other half tryin' to keep everyone from knowing; though the fact was, most of the time you weren't even thinking about it— but if the time you were was suddenly taken from you, you wouldn't be you anymore. That was desire.

The last Part was "Of the Power of the Intellect, or of Human Freedom." That "or" was the same or, he was certain, was the same *sivi* which had joined Nature and God. Which meant either Intellect was not exactly what most people thought it was. Or Freedom wasn't. The first time through that Part had seemed the easiest of it. The last few times it had seemed the hardest. Hurt others and you hurt a part of yourself because you hurt a part of Nature or God. Help others and you help a part of Nature or...But that's why you sit out on an old crate at the edge of the market and give away sandwiches and cookies and a wicker basket of plums, peaches, and apples to anyone who's hungry. People smile and think you're crazy—though you always feel better afterwards. No matter what. But why can't I remember the whole thing—its name?

I could get up and look.

But I'm so tired.

Tomorrow, I got to make some food and take it to the market, to give away. Because otherwise I'll die of grief.

Will I be able to get it down the bluff? Hell, even if it's just some peanut butter and jelly on whole wheat, some bologna and mayonnaise. That's what Ed should have been checking in the damned refrigerator for. See, I remember that. Thank God there's always hungry kids passing through, hanging out down there on Rockside, on Settlement Road...

Sometimes it just goes so fast...

Why can't I remember the name of my book?

Maybe he should just stop tryin'. Sitting in her green wooden lawn chair, under the willow tree that was at least twenty-five years old but had only come to the island on Ed's boat a dozen years ago, roots wrapped in burlap bound with plastic bands, Anne had said: *Honey, if you can read Spinoza, you can make sense out of anything. I know you don't like those readers. I don't blame you. Don't seem like real books to me, either. And I used them all through school.* But in the end, he hadn't read it. He worried about her willows. Sure, they were pretty. But they drank up so much water, and in twenty-five years—not to mention a hundred—if you put them too close to the house, their roots could ruin just about any cellar wall. He'd seen it in those old houses on the mainland...

—Spinoza's *Ethica!*

...there, got it! (Just put your mind on something else for a minute.) Now I got to recall that other one. It was only one word, too. A made up word. Though, he remembered, right across from Reba's restaurant used to be a dress shop with the same name, which had started out selling all black dresses and black slacks and black blouses and T-shirts and black denim jackets. Unlike Reba's, she'd only stayed in business a couple of years. (Reba had gone years ago. But the place and the name—Reba's Place—were still there.) Odd, how he could remember that and still not remember the name of that other book he'd read—not as many times as he'd read the *Ethica*, but more than six, more than seven.

I can remember—with their knapsacks, like vagabonds from a hundred years in the past, them two girls who stopped by my table, where I used to sit by the Unitarian Meetin' House. Black as coal, both—they could've been my daddy's cousins. Mike's. Such beautiful arms and breasts and faces. Both talked more proper than even Caleb. That was a few years back. Five? Seven? No—a lot longer. Fifteen. Or twenty. Even thirty—'cause we hadn't been here that long. The tall one got out her sketchbook and sat cross-legged right on the ground and began drawing. The other—her friend she was going around with—was tall. One had a shaved head, the other a wealth of dreadlocks. (Mike had really disliked dreads on pretty much anyone, not that he'd ever considered them for himself.) Eric had run into them a day before, on the mainland. They were part of some persecuted marriage group. You know, now that I think of it, the reason Shit and me never got married is probably because we didn't know any married men when we was little kids—so it never really occurred to us. Though there was half dozen in the Dump, later on, when we were older. That's what ol' Potts wanted for his boy, Lurrie. I bet he was damned surprised—when all six of them niggers took up together. Leave it to the Dump to have the first group gay marriage in the state. And we talked an hour-and-a-half, and they ate up half the cake Dr. Zaya had left with me to give out—that Dr. Zaya was a good person. And understood. And wanted to give things to people, too. Like she gave Shit pills for his hips and knees. (Damned things had made Shit horny, till he got used to them. But then, everything made that boy horny—sunsets, Bach [*Is all that diddly-doodly stuff draggin' you this way and that, up and down, back and forth practically at the same time supposed to make me wanna fuck? 'Cause it do.*], honey, and grapes…) She let me do it for her, 'cause she was working at the clinic. And when the fat one finally showed me her picture, I was so surprised because it…wasn't me!

It was a sketch of Shit, with the apple basket he'd brought, against his hip, bending over the table, putting them out on the pile with the other fruit, and grinnin' at me, with most of his teeth gone…it was the weekend so he didn't bother with his plate.

'Cause he thought I was crazy.

'Cause I'm not in the sketch.

He was the one who really thought I was nuts.

But he'd been helpin' me do it anyway, back since I started at the Opera House. (Four times a year, I did my Dynamite Memorial Free Feeds at the Opera, one each season. Solstice, equinox, solstice, equinox, just like Anne. Where it started. Yeah. And he'd look at me, shake his head, smile— and help.) He must have come by three or four times while they were sitting there with me, bringing more stuff for me to make sandwiches with. And apples. And peaches from Bulah. And clementines. And she drew… him. She give me that drawing, too, before they left. Hey, the picture's still in the bottom drawer—right on top of the picture of Dynamite and Stovepipe…I got to take it out. It's under my HUNGRY? FREE SANDWICHES, CAKE, COOKIES, & FRUIT!…sign. ('Cause the chili was too complicated and the cooker finally broke, anyway.) I'll ask one of them—Lucille, maybe—to help me. They can laminate it in some plastic and I can hang it up.

I always liked it. But now I need it…

Maybe when I'm gone, the library will come over and get all that stuff. But what'll they want with some pictures in the drawer of an old, crazy man like me. And the one of Dynamite and a pig what was dead before I was born. Sure, they already had Kyle's pictures of Black Bull and Whiteboy carryin' on in that dungeon. But then, I ain't no nigger millionaire, either… Some day I got to sit down and write who they all are on the backs, so I can remember, even if nobody else can…

Yes, I got to get that picture of Shit out, so I can find out what he looks…looked like.

I was so surprised when I saw it, too. I thought she'd been drawing me and the table the whole while. But she was drawing Shit, bent over it, with his sweatshirt, fifty years out of date, hangin' open there, smiling and puttin' out apples. For us. She got him, too—his likeness. It was just like him. His beard and his baldhead, how beautiful he was. And his smile and missin' teeth, 'cause he'd just come back from the hospital and he hadn't bothered to put his plates back in, showing how quiet and easy he was, puttin' up with his crazy life-partner, and so, though it's a picture of him, it's still a picture—of how much I…how much I love him.

Oh, others…!

Others help so much. Just looking. And seeing what they see, they help…

Which is why you have to help…

…others.

Outside the window, down the sloped grass, overlong, a breeze and the ocean that had once been the whole world mingled their whispers—which, in a way, was a blessing, because, if you let it, it could put you to sleep in minutes.

So, in minutes, Eric slept—among dreams of edging sideways through narrowing alleys, sometimes lit with green fire, sometimes underground with no light at all, while a horned and winged creature that couldn't fly in there anymore than could Eric scrabbled closer and closer, and it grew harder and harder to breathe.

—and woke, thinking, in the dark, No. I have a bit more time. He relaxed before the rumoring sea.

*
* * *
*

—November 2004–July 2011,
Philadelphia, Boulder, New York

ACKNOWLEDGMENTS

Much of the dream imagery associated with the "Bottom" in this novel comes from Mia Wolff's superb triptych of paintings, *The City of Green Fire*. My great gratitude goes to Chesya Burke for pictures and verbal descriptions of that lively neighborhood, Atlanta's Little Five Points.

My thanks as well to Joshua Lukin for steering me to the work of Rane Arroyo.

Gratitude beyond any expressable must go to Kevin Donaker-Ring for years of help—five for this book alone—readings, notes, reminders, and (without exaggeration) thousands of corrections, as generously offered for this one (without him, I could not have completed it), as for any in the past. Many writers have written many times on many, many acknowledgement pages, "without whose help this book could not have been written." Kevin's help makes me intensely aware of the myriad forms of truth that can nest in that assertion. Equally invaluable help came—repeatedly—from Ric Best, to whom I am equally grateful.

A reading by Kenneth James produced a dozen pages of incredibly helpful notes, as well as numerous marginal comments, which I have tried to address.

"The Gift Must Move"—the motto of the Gilead Elementary School—is from Lewis Hyde's luminous study, *The Gift*. My gratitude to Ron Drummond for returning it to my attention, twenty-five years after my first reading, and indeed for all Ron's active enthusiasm for life, literature, music, biblical history and science. His help as always has been tireless, wise, and invaluable. The sign in the Gilead island graveyard is, of course, a quotation from Andrew Holleran's award-winning novel, *Grief*.

Also, of course, thanks to my agent Henry Morrison and my publisher and editor, Don Weise, without whom, and against truly overwhelming odds, no one would have had a chance to read it.